PLOWED FIELDS

PLOWED FIELDS

Jim Barber

This book is a novel, and the story and events that appear herein are entirely fictional. Any resemblance of the fictional characters to a real person is unintentional and coincidental. Certain real persons are mentioned in the book for the purpose of enhancing and adding reality to the story, but obviously the fictionalized events involving either fictional characters or real persons did not occur.

Jacket and book design by Jane Hill
Jacket photo by Krivosheev Vitaly
Author photo by Brandi Williams

Morgan Bay Books
432 Princeton Way
Suite 101
Lawrenceville, GA 30044
www.plowedfields.com
www.jimbarber.me

ACKNOWLEDGMENTS

I've always loved to write, but writing a novel was never one of my big goals in life. And then, on a beautiful spring day when I was traveling between two small towns in middle Georgia as a young newspaper reporter in 1985, the idea for *Plowed Fields* came fully alive to me, and I felt compelled to write the story. I wanted to preserve a time and place that had shaped my life and positioned me to achieve my dreams. So, first, I must acknowledge my family, friends and many others whose presence influenced my growing-up years. Specifically, I credit my parents—my daddy Elmo who died in 1991 and my mama Marie who remains eternally young; my sister Caye Robinson and brother-in-law Charles Robinson, who really lived the era I wrote about; my grandmothers Flossie Lee Willis Barber and Carrie Elizabeth Weaver Baker who loved unconditionally and worked as hard as anyone I've ever known; my uncles Jake Baker and Bug Baker who managed to raise crops and earn livings—though Lord knows how—with help from a bunch of young'uns like me and my cousins, Greg, Don and Chipp Griner, and Mike and Regina Baker; my uncles Virgil Barber (a World War II hero) and LA Barber, who shared their knowledge of the old days and farming before my time; my cousin Faith Barber Noles; one of my oldest friends, Jerry Moore, with whom I shared the only real experience recorded in this book; and the best friend ever, Greg Harrell. I also must pay homage to the amazing teachers at West Berrien Elementary School and Berrien High School—particularly Wanda Vickers, Gail Danforth, Linda Davis Brooks and Calva Gill McDaniel—who gave me far more than I gave them through my efforts in the classroom. And to the late S.T. and Clarice Hamilton, who gave me my first newspaper job at *The Berrien Press*.

I populated this book with names and places near and dear to my heart, but the characters are completely fictional. The Taylor family may be villains in this story, but the real Taylors are lifelong family friends and nothing like their namesakes in this book. Not to mention some of the most amazing gospel singers God ever put on this earth!

It is no easy task to turn an idea into a book, and many people read my manuscript, offered ideas and encouragement, and helped make *Plowed Fields* a reality through their criticism, proofing and insights into the publishing industry. In alphabetical order, they were Betty Bell, Becky Blalock, Janice Daugharty, Sam Heys, Jane Hill, Maggie Johnsen, Joey Ledford, Cindy Theiler and Emelyne Williams. In addition, I would be remiss not to mention the late Jim Kilgo and Conrad Fink, two extraordinary professors at the University of Georgia who gave me confidence to believe in my talent; and the late Duane Riner, press secretary for Georgia Governor George Busbee and an *Atlanta Journal-Constitution* editor. Duane once gave me a byline above the masthead in the AJC, but more importantly, he believed in me from the beginning and proved to be an extraordinary mentor and more. Rarely a day passes when I do not recall his influence and I hope I give back a small measure of what he gave me.

No doubt, I have overlooked someone worthy of mentioning, so to all who helped make this dream a reality, I offer my sincere thanks and gratitude.

GRATEFUL ACKNOWLEDGMENT IS MADE to the publishers of the following for permission to quote from material in copyright or the public domain:

The Holy Bible
Luke 2:1-5, King James Version.
Ecclesiastes 3:1-8, King James Version.

Putting in the Seed
Frost, Robert. *Mountain Interval*. New York: Henry Holt, 1916.
1st in Poetry and Drama, December 1914.

The Thatch
Frost, Robert. *West-Running Brook*. New York: Henry Holt, 1928.
(A note in WRB dates poem: As of 1914).

Piney Woods Rooter says ...
Reprinted with permission from *The Berrien Press*, Nashville, Georgia.

The Path That Leads to Nowhere
Robinson, Corinne Roosevelt. *The Poems of Corinne Roosevelt Robinson*. New York: Charles Scribner's Sons, 1921.

The publisher has made every effort to secure the necessary permissions to reprint any quoted material and to make full acknowledgment for its use. In the event of any question arising as to the right to use any material, the publisher, while expressing regret for any inadvertent error, will be happy to make the necessary correction in any future printings, provided notification is sent to the publisher.

PRAISE FOR *PLOWED FIELDS*

"If Pat Conroy had been raised on a tobacco farm in South Georgia, this is the novel he would have written. *Plowed Fields* is a powerful story about a time in history that left more scars than we care to remember. With his rich detail of farm life, complex characters and sure sense of storytelling, Jim Barber has captured a time and place in Americana with lyrical precision and stunning beauty. Amid the darkness and evil, he has infused this story with warmth, heart and hope as promising as a newly plowed field."

– Becky Blalock, author of *Dare*

"Not since Larry McMurtry's *Lonesome Dove* have I read such a solid, unembellished, detail-rich portrayal of rural life lived out in fiction. In fact, while reading *Plowed Fields*, it seemed I was watching an intriguing TV miniseries. *Plowed Fields* is all that a family saga should be—natural, endearing, superbly written and enchanting. Add to that *fresh* and *exact*! The characters come alive under Jim Barber's control. Jim Barber is a master storyteller; so by definition, that makes *Plowed Fields* a masterpiece. Readers are in for a glad experience."

– Janice Daugharty, author of
Earl in the Yellow Shirt and *The Paw-Paw Patch*

"Set in the recent past this is the perfect novel for our time of national uncertainty, cynicism and corruption of values emanating from the very top. In nine episodes, *Plowed Fields* gives us the turbulent 1960s as lived in Georgia by the Baker family. Their haunting saga of desire and responsibility—of revolution and resolution—has a great deal to say to us today. In the words of the aphorism often attributed to Mark Twain, 'History doesn't repeat itself, but it often rhymes.'"

– Alan Axelrod, author of
The Gilded Age, 1876-1912: Overture to the American Century and
How America Won World War I

"*Plowed Fields* explores the hard choices we make, the love we give and the joy, sorrow and hope that shape our lives. It is a deeply moving story of ordinary people navigating through extraordinary times. Ultimately, *Plowed Fields* paints a portrait of faith lost and found. Joe Baker and his family will resonate with you long after the last page is read. I hope there's a sequel."

— Sam Heys, author of *The Winecoff Fire* and *Big Bets*

"Imagine a family like TV's The Waltons living and loving on a tobacco farm in South Georgia during the 1960s, and you will have a strong sense of *Plowed Fields*. The story certainly has a wholesome quality—some might even say sentimental—but it's also 'glazed with the sorrow of a devastating truth.' Jim Barber has captured a time and place with exquisite detail and superb storytelling. *Plowed Fields* will break your heart, but it's the warmth and tenderness of the people and the story that will stay with you."

— Emelyne Williams, editor of
Atlanta Women Speak

"Jim Barber's extraordinary *Plowed Fields* is reminiscent of Laura Ingalls Wilder's masterpiece series of *Little House* books. Barber's canvas is hardscrabble Cookville, Georgia, of 1960 rather than Ingalls Wilder's 1870s Minnesota. And rather than focus on a daughter, *Plowed Fields* centers on Joe Baker, the oldest of Matt and Caroline Baker's six children. The family saga tracks the Bakers over a tumultuous decade in which they weather struggles with drought, fire, a family feud, loss of faith, death and the cultural changes shaking the rural South of the civil rights era. Barber is an exciting new voice who defines family and coming of age with an engaging style."

— Joey Ledford, author of
Speed Trap and *Elkmont: The Smoky Mountain Massacre*

For Pearl, my bride

CONTENTS

PLOWED FIELDS

PART ONE

And go along with you
ere you lose sight

Of what you came for
and become like me.

Slave to a springtime
passion for the earth.

Putting in the Seed
~ Robert Frost

THE WHITE CHRISTMAS

1960

CHAPTER 1

JOE BAKER PUSHED THE throttle forward, easing the tractor to a crawl as the row-end neared. In one clumsy motion, he pulled up the machine's hydraulic lift, raising the plow from the ground, and dropped his casted leg onto the brake pedal. The back tire froze, pivoting the tractor and aligning the wheel perfectly into the furrow of the previously plowed row. Dropping the turning plow back into the dirt, he pulled the throttle down to top speed and headed the tractor up another row, leaving a wake of ripped earth, dark and moist.

Blatant self-satisfaction betrayed the boy's usual stoic approach to farm work, emerging as a smirk to the plaster mold encasing his right leg from knee to toes. Such delight was uncommon for Joe, who had negotiated more tractor turns at row-ends than he cared to count. But then again, so was the state of clumsiness that stamped the youngster's every move these days, prodding his ego on an endless effort to prove his worth, his usefulness.

Joe checked the back wheel's position against the furrow, adjusted the plow's depth and relaxed as the tractor lumbered up another row. Just a few more passes and this field, the largest of six on the Baker farm, would be plowed and settled for the winter's rest.

The boy looked across the field, which was framed against a ruby sea of late evening sunset, and surveyed his handiwork. Picture-perfect layers of earth lay end over end, concealing like a grave every trace of the fluffy white cotton that had lived in this ground a short time ago. But Joe knew instinctively that the land held no deathly quality.

The plowed field was a dazzling sight to behold, lying in wait for the springtime seed that would turn fallow land once more into a festival of life. Every year at this time—his favorite, when the air became crisp, nipped with the approaching winter chill, and the pace of the days relaxed like a sweet-flowing melody—the boy became aware of the sacred trust placed in the land. A freshly plowed field held promise and radiated beauty. Joe respected the promise, he saw the beauty; but somehow any real attachment to the land always escaped his grasp.

Nevertheless, he had volunteered—or more accurately, insisted—for the task of plowing this large field, relegating his father and grandfather to the toil of relaxing and taking care of less pressing matters. He had accomplished the job by spending the hours after school perched on the tractor, working until the evening shadows disappeared and failing daylight forced him to attend his regular chores. Now, as he surveyed the results of his labor, he permitted himself another smug glare at the cast. And, experienced a twinge of guilt over the praise the effort would reap from his family. They mistakenly saw the endeavor as another example of a good boy's dedication to the virtues of hard work, when in reality, far more than he dreaded the tedium of farm life, Joe despised any signs of uselessness in himself.

This last thought had been revealed to Joe early in a journey of self-discovery, a voyage plotted by the startling course of his sophomore year of high school. Other people had undertaken grander journeys of the mind and made more important discoveries about themselves, he felt sure. But the value of his own journey was worth more, or so thought Joe, who tended to qualify his words and thoughts as products solely of himself.

While admitting a farmer's life held no great joy for him, the overwhelming finding of this personal journey had been an acknowledgment that he needed a sense of normalcy and purpose in life. In his mind, normalcy meant daily routines, obligations and expectations that were carried out, met and fulfilled without fuss or fanfare; and a purpose was any task to accomplish, from plowing a field to doing homework.

Early in his convalescence from the broken leg, there had been too much fussing and fanfare over Joe. He had felt like an invalid, a burden to the family, which suddenly seemed to neither want nor need anything from him. Feeling weak and inadequate, he had determined to restore a semblance of normalcy to life. He tolerated the good intentions of his family for several days, then pronounced himself recuperated and set out to prove the point. Whether he had proved it to the family was a matter of debate, but the boy felt more like a man.

Still, he was not whole. While his strength had returned quickly, the splintered bone required time to heal. Until that healing occurred, Joe would seek normalcy in his own way, and he would permit himself absurd pleasures such as taking delight in the accomplishment of any task that defied the will of the broken leg.

Joe owed his handicap to the perils of high school football. He had been a member of the Cookville High School Rebels, primarily because only thirty boys attended tryouts and every available body was needed for the varsity team.

Cookville was a football doormat in South Georgia, where enthusiasm for the sport verged on religious fervor. Joe had held no illusions about his ability to elevate Cookville to unscaled heights, which a break-even season would have accomplished. Yet, in the span of two games, he had recorded one of the team's more memorable careers.

He had combined minimal talent with maximum luck to occupy a moment in the spotlight and a place in the suppertime conversations of the Cookville community. Such notoriety might have been heady stuff for some high school sophomores, but Joe was immune to fool's gold. Luck, if there was such a thing, was a two-sided coin, evidenced by the brevity of his football career.

Even before the accident, Joe had borne little resemblance to a football player. In full uniform on a full stomach, he barely weighed one hundred thirty-five pounds. Still, he carried more weight than most people realized. His grandfather described Joe as a sturdy sapling, conditioned by his environment like a tree adapted to the elements. The boy possessed strength and stamina, both physical and inner, honed on his family's farm.

His talent for the game lay in his hands. They were work-hardened, oversized paws, with long, grasping fingers and wide, bony knuckles.

Those hands had caught the eye of Coach Ben Simmons on Joe's first day of football practice during an exercise known as Milking the Cow, which was also a chore that brought Joe into intimate contact with the family milk cow virtually every day.

As an exercise, milking the cow involved stretching the arms to full length at shoulder level and repeatedly squeezing the hands open and closed. Long after the majority of his teammates tired of the exercise, arms sagging and hands cramping, Joe had stood perfectly postured, his fingers flexing at a steady pace.

Coach Simmons had approached Joe, regarded his hands with mild curiosity and asked, "Can you catch a football, son?"

"Yes, sir."

The coach had acknowledged the answer with a casual nod, but a week later, Joe was the starting tight end for Cookville.

The boy's football knowledge extended little beyond what had been learned in rough, high-spirited games on the playground of New River Elementary School. It was limited experience, but typical of rookie Rebels because Cookville was a rural community. There was no spring football practice because most team members were busy helping their families plant crops. And while fall football practice officially opened two weeks before the start of school, most of the team, including Joe, staggered in sometime during the second week.

Coach Simmons could not expect otherwise, and thus kept the game simple. The Rebels offense consisted of twenty plays, the vast majority of them designed to send the running backs into the waiting grasp of swarming defenders. There had been an element of surprise then, when—in the 1960 season opener against the Valdosta High School Wildcats—Cookville quarterback Dale Bennett took one step back after the snap and fired a quick pass over the middle on the first play from scrimmage.

Valdosta was a perennial powerhouse on the football field, four times larger than Cookville and embarrassed to have the Rebels on their schedule. Cookville was the perennial patsy, having never scored against the Wildcats in seven previous games and downright intimidated on their eighth and most likely final try.

Joe had caught the ball on a dead run, with outstretched fingers between two Valdosta linebackers, then raced seventy-seven yards for his life to the end zone for a touchdown. The Cookville bench and stands promptly erupted into frenzied exhilaration. Players rushed onto the field and hoisted Joe to their shoulders. He became an instant star. When the pandemonium calmed, Valdosta proceeded to block the extra point kick, then scored the game's last sixty-three points, chalking up the first win of a state championship season.

The 63-6 shellacking did little to dampen optimism for Cookville's second game against the Cook High School Hornets. Cookville and Cook were archrivals, but beyond their neighboring locations, name similarity and good-natured ribbing, there was little in dispute between the two schools on the football field. Cook reigned supreme. In the fourteen-year history of the rivalry, Cookville had tallied a dozen defeats and salvaged ties on the other two occasions.

The game was played under a steady drizzle. It was a head-busting, hard-hitting slugfest between two mediocre teams playing with more heart than talent. Midway through the third quarter of the scoreless game, Joe ran a sideline pattern near midfield. Dale Bennett's pass was wobbly and overthrown, forcing Joe to cut sharply back across the slippery field.

At the last second before the ball sailed over his head for an incompletion, Joe leapt into the air, snagging the leather spiral with the outstretched fingers of one hand. As he hauled in the ball with both hands, two opposing players collided in mid-air against his right leg, striking from opposite directions with bone-crushing force. One helmet rammed Joe right beneath the kneecap; the second drove through his hamstring.

In the ensuing fall from grace, when he realized the sickening snap reverberating across the field came from his body, the boy had known his football career was finished. He had banished the game to a dead place in the mind, where memories of what might have been rarely mingled with what never was.

He landed flat on his back, the ball rolling casually from his hands onto the wet grass. A mad scramble ensued around him, and a Cook player recovered the fumble, but Joe never even realized he had dropped the ball.

His knee exploded like a conflagration. He struggled to sit, fighting for consciousness. When his eyes focused on the injured knee, absorbed the splintered bone sticking through the bloodied pants leg of his uniform, Joe promptly, and smartly, gave up the fight.

He had woken sometime later on a hospital stretcher, enduring a series of X-rays before a doctor finally injected a merciful dose of morphine. The next time he woke, Joe was in a hospital bed with his leg encased in a heavy plaster cast, attached to a pulley contraption suspended from the ceiling.

From his parents, Joe had learned about the surgery necessary to set the bone back in its proper position and reattach torn ligaments and tendons. From his brothers and sisters, he heard the gorier details: how the loud crack of his leg hushed the crowd instantly; the awestruck silence inspired by the ambulance driving onto the field and off again with his limp body; the hero's standing ovation given when the sirens blared to life.

People often picked strange heroes, Joe believed, and the boy harbored not a single delusion of grandeur. At his best on the football field, he had demonstrated average talent. Lady luck had been the divining rod of his football fortunes, and he had prospered and perished with her whims—another conclusion Joe had reached on his journey of self-discovery, along with the realization that he was destined to be one of those masses of men who led a solid life of averages.

Joe could live with the averages, but the boy had made another discovery about himself on the solitary journey. It was frightening, an idea he did not fully understand but one that shared equal billing with his need for normalcy and purpose.

The boy looked out across the field once more, gazed across treetops into the sunset and acknowledged the well of restlessness running deep inside him. This restlessness scared Joe because he could not define it in exact terms, and because it provoked anxious feelings that he was destined to remain solid and would never soar as long as he was here on this place, this farm that meant so much to his family.

Joe wanted to force these thoughts from his mind, but he could not deny that his most memorable moments occurred when his actions or circumstances scraped against the grain of his character. And he could not help wondering where that grain was headed, and the scars it might sustain along the way.

The boy's thoughts ran fast these days—no doubt compensating for his legs, Joe figured—though not always so deep. In one moment, he was likely to ponder a pretty girl; the next, the approaching Christmas season; and then, this kind of brooding reflection and speculation that cluttered his head with more questions than answers, invariably leaving him confused and glum.

Confusion bothered Joe like a gnat in the dog days of summer. He preferred simplicity, which was probably why he thrived on the familiarity of routine obligations and patterns. Normalcy kept his head uncluttered, restrained him from thinking deeply and warded off confusion. When normalcy failed him, as it did now, Joe had learned to seek distractions. They were easy to find when a boy's thoughts ran as fast as his did these days. And then, without his appreciation, a distraction presented itself in the form of the last row to plow.

Joe wheeled the tractor into another perfect turn at the far end of the field and dropped the plow once more into the dirt. But instead of speeding up the last row, he idled down the engine, pausing to fish a cigarette from the pocket of his jeans.

He lit it and took a long drag, looking out across the field once more, thinking deeply about nothing in particular. Dusk had settled over the farm, leaving only a faint reddish hue over the treetops. A rustling breeze chilled him through the red flannel shirt, hinting of a hard freeze sweeping in from the Arctic hinterlands.

Joe took another drag on the cigarette, then accelerated the engine once more and headed the tractor alongside the fencerow. The boy guided the tractor with more caution on this row, ever mindful of a time long ago when he had tangled the plow in a fence and required his father's help to extract it. He passed a small meadow, where cattle grazed on light brown clumps of dried grass, and then edged his grandfather's prized blackberry bramble, now reduced to a dormant skeleton of vines woven through the fence. Finally, the tractor skirted the edge of the pecan orchard, its barren branches affording Joe the comforting sight of smoke curling away from the chimney of his home. A sudden rush of anticipation for a job well done and the hearty supper to come turned the boy's head toward the end of the row.

And waiting there was his daddy.

———

Matt Baker stood at the edge of the field with his hands shoved into the pockets of faded dungarees, searching for warmth against the evening's chill. A slight smile crossed his face as he witnessed his oldest son's smooth attempt to discard the cigarette. Joe made a quick turn to his left, leaned over the wheel shield as if checking the plow and allowed the cigarette to fall into the ground as fertilizer for next year's crop. But not before Matt, who possessed eagle eyes, saw the red glow and trail of smoke.

He'd always assumed Joe would take up smoking. But not so soon. Matt had resisted the leaf's lure until well past his nineteenth birthday, and he'd started smoking to combat the tension of war. Of course, his son had waged a war of his own these past few months, a private war carried out despite, or perhaps in spite of, the family's best efforts. The boy had endured the pain of a shattered leg and a lost dream with valor and resolve. If Joe found solace in a cigarette or two, Matt would neither begrudge him nor read the riot act over it.

No one had ever questioned Joe's perseverance and stubbornness. But equally so, the magnitude of those qualities had never rivaled the likes of that shining through in the weeks and months gone by since the boy had been carried off the football field on a stretcher. Once home from the hospital, Joe had refused their coddling, cordially but in definite terms telling the family he could take care of himself. Then he'd set out to prove his word, making a mockery of the doctors who believed the recovery process would leave him a temporary invalid.

The doctors predicted a difficult adjustment to the heavy cast; Joe was moving with athletic grace, albeit on crutches, within a week. The doctors predicted a minimum three-week absence from school; Joe was roaming the halls of Cookville High School after just eight days of lessons from the county's truant officer. The doctors predicted months of crutches; Joe was wearing a walking cast within eight weeks.

The pace of recovery was so alarming that once Matt had dreamed his son was racing down the football field, on crutches, intent on catching an overthrown ball. The dream had seemed so real that he had woken his wife with the suggestion that Joe probably should stay off the football field awhile longer.

Matt smiled in memory of that stuporous expression of concern, but was instantly sobered. In reality, Joe would never step on another football field—at least not as a player. His knee and two other bones shattered in that freak accident were now held together by steel pins, and while the boy would recover without a limp, the leg would never be the same. His son's spirit and courage, however, remained unbroken.

Matt peered across the fresh folds of earth, acutely mindful of the skill and dedication his son brought to the farm work—and achingly aware that the boy's destiny lay elsewhere.

Long ago, Matt had sensed Joe saw life differently than he did. That despite the boy's down-to-earth demeanor, he possessed vision of breadth and depth. That when Joe looked out across these fields, he saw more than treetops and a faraway horizon. A few weeks ago, though, Matt had realized with startling clarity just how differently Joe and he looked at life.

They had been butchering hogs one crisp Saturday morning. It was a messy job from the moment Matt shot the two barrows. Working in companionable silence, they had split, gutted and sliced the shoats from end to end, tapping every edible scrap of meat. The chitlins and lights had been that night's supper, the feet pickled, the head made into souse and the brains frozen for the family's traditional Christmas Eve supper.

When they were winding up the job, dumping the last washtubs of bloodied water and wiping down knives, Matt had turned to Joe and suggested, "Son, how 'bout next time we let the butcher in Cookville do this?"

Matt had expected an answer of either lighthearted agreement or a teasing scoff. Instead, without breaking stride for even a sideways glance at his father, Joe said sharply, "Beats the heck of out me why you didn't do that this time."

The quick retort struck Matt like a slap in the face. He resisted an impulse to reprimand the boy, sensing Joe was unaware of his sassy tone. In truth, Matt had intended to send the shoats to the abattoir, changing his mind only because Joe had volunteered to help with the butchering. "Wait a minute," Matt had said. "I thought you wanted to do the butcheren."

Joe looked perplexed. "What on earth gave you that idea?"

"You did," Matt answered stoutly. "The other night when I mentioned we had two hogs ready to butcher. You volunteered for the job almost before I got it out of my mouth. Hell, son, I was all for senden them to the abattoir in the first place. I didn't, only because you seemed so surefire ready to do the job yourself."

"Uh-oh," Joe groaned, rolling his eyes. "I assumed we'd be doen it at home like always. I was just offeren to help. Butcheren hogs is the last thing I wanted to do."

Matt had known then, inexplicably or perhaps from something in the way Joe uttered those words, but he had understood with certainty that father and son would never tend this farm as equals in a partnership. He had realized that Joe looked across the treetops surrounding these fields and saw a horizon beckoning with unfamiliar and infinitely interesting places, people and experiences. And Matt had understood that, like his father before him, he, too, would surrender a son to dreams different from those he dreamed.

Standing on the field's edge, Matt felt a sudden need to find out if he would be up to the task of letting go when the time came. He had an even stranger feeling that the answer would soon come to him.

As he waited for the tractor to arrive at the row-end, Matt considered anew the difficult months Joe had come through. If the boy's pace of recovery had been extraordinarily quick, then the intensity of it had been downright exhausting. In those first days home from the hospital, Joe had needed help to get from the bed to the bathroom, and his stubborn demand for no concessions on his behalf had bordered on the absurd.

Once, in particular, he'd insisted on a full-fledged bath, refusing a washbowl and cloth in favor of the tub. So Matt had carried the boy into the bathroom and left him on his own to climb into the tall claw-foot tub. There had been a loud thud and a few muffled curses from time to time, but all had gone well until Joe finished bathing and discovered he could not climb out of the tub. At that point, he'd put pride aside, calling for "a little help and cooperation."

Matt had found him stuck in the deep tub, prone on his back, with the encased leg draped over the edge, unable to right himself without wetting the plaster mold. Matt had hauled him up, offered the boy a towel and walked out without a word said between them.

Joe had suffered a few other indignities, but mostly, he was successful in compensating for the handicap. In fact, too often he overcompensated, rushing headlong to tackle any chore or task that needed doing, working like a mercenary to earn not the almighty dollar but a measure of respect. At first, Matt had tried to rein in the boy. In quick order, however, he'd turned Joe loose, allowing him to gallop a breathtaking pace on a journey for peace of mind. Whether Joe had found peace remained unclear, but certainly the harvest season had never run smoother or easier for Matt.

Apart from his regular chores, Joe had taken over the daily grind for his father and grandfather, providing the men additional daylight to work in the fields. He'd replaced Matt on the combine at times, hauled trailers back and forth between the fields and unloaded and stacked a truckload of fifty-pound bags of hog feed in the barn. Just when Matt had figured Joe to reach his limits, the boy—cast and all—had climbed into the tops of pecan trees to shake loose the nuts. Now Joe was winding up another self-appointed task, and as he brought the tractor to a stop, a rush of pride swelled Matt.

Joe cut off the engine, then swung his good leg over the steering wheel and dismounted the tractor.

"That's a fine piece of plowen, son," Matt said. "You've got the fields looken real good."

"Fields always look good this time of year, Daddy," Joe replied, smiling slyly. "I just hope they'll look good come next fall."

"Me, too," Matt agreed. "That's what I always hope for; it's why I keep doen the same thing year after year."

"Yes, sir."

"Are you glad to get a vacation from school?" Matt asked.

Joe looked quickly past his father in the direction of Cookville High School, where a few hours ago he had taken the final algebra test and history exam before the start of Christmas vacation. He enjoyed school and the separate identity it provided him from the family. The days he'd missed after breaking his leg had seemed like an eternity, leading him to believe he would never wish for another school vacation. And yet, the rigors of catching up on missed work and the spirit of the Christmas season had changed his mind, leaving him eager for the two-week vacation—just as the arrival of the new year would make him ready to return to his studies. Everything in its time, Joe thought.

"I was ready," he answered.

"I was always ready for a vacation from school," Matt said, squatting to pick up a handful of the nutrient-rich earth, sifting it through his fingers. "We only went about seven months of the year back then, but even that seemed too long to me. I always wanted to be right out here."

Joe, watching the dirt fall from his daddy's hand, said suddenly, "A boundless moment."

Matt peered up at his son, puzzled.

"*A Boundless Moment*," Joe repeated with an embarrassed shrug. "It's the name of a poem by Robert Frost. I can't think of how it goes, but you reminded me of it just now."

"Oh," Matt said, staring as if he expected a more forthcoming explanation. When none came, Matt scooped up another handful of dirt. Standing, he gestured for Joe to do the same.

Joe quickly obeyed, the black soil cool and heavy with moisture against his palm. He righted himself and faced his father.

"This dirt may not seem significant to most people, but it means an awful lot to me," Matt said evenly. "I make a liven from it. I depend on this dirt to provide for your mama and you children. I take care of it. I feed it. I understand it, and I know how to use this dirt to get what I need in life. You might even say I control it, leastways as much as a man can control a piece of earth without bowen to the will of nature."

Matt paused, measuring his words with a sweeping gaze across the field and back to Joe. "Strange as it may sound, son, you're kind of in the same position as this dirt. Right now, Joe, you're pretty much compelled to do what I tell you—whether it's plowen a field, sloppen hogs or milken a cow. But there's bound to come a day when I tell you to do somethen and what I'm really doen is asken you to do it. When that day comes—and you and I will both know when it's time—you're not gonna be compelled to do what I say anymore. And I hope very much that when you make your decision, Joe, you'll follow your heart and do what's right for you."

Matt searched the boy's eyes at length, then asked earnestly, "Do you understand, son?"

Joe wanted to tell his daddy that his heart would always urge him to do whatever Matt wanted, even if it meant lying down across a railroad track in front of a fast-coming train. He wanted to tell Matt that loyalty was the most important expression in the world, except possibly for love and making love, the latter of which he could only guess about at the moment. But instead, the boy replied simply, "Yes, sir."

Matt regarded his son carefully, concerned about the thoughts behind the boy's unreadable expression. He didn't doubt for one second that Joe understood him.

But in Matt's experience, the difference in understanding and doing was as wide as the gap between winning and losing.

Joe was a natural helper, someone who could be counted on to stick around as long as help was needed. He had a knack for making the people around him not only comfortable but also increasingly willing to accept that level of comfort. When Joe faced that moment of truth—the choice between will and obligation—Matt suspected it would take a mighty shove or supreme inspiration to push the boy toward the gateway of his heart. He hoped inspiration would rule the moment.

"Do you know the whole story about how you got your name?" Matt asked suddenly.

"After your brother, my uncle," Joe recited automatically. "He was killed at Pearl Harbor."

"That's not the whole story," Matt said coyly. "We almost named you Mark. From the day your mama found out she was expecten, she planned to name the baby Mark if it was a boy. I thought it was a fine name until a few weeks before you were born, when she finally got around to tellen me the reason she wanted to name you Mark. She was married to a Matthew, you see, and her intentions were to name our sons Mark, Luke and John. Matthew, Mark, Luke and John—your mama wanted the four gospels right in the family."

"Really?" Joe asked skeptically, with a bemused expression. "Are you pullen my leg, Daddy?"

"I swear to God it's the truth," Matt laughed, spreading his hands. "Needless to say, I put my foot down. Declared once and for all that we'd name the baby after my brother if it were a boy. I thought your mama was carryen religion a little too far."

Joe nodded tepid agreement. His father's disdain for the church warranted no comment.

"Well," Matt continued, sounding more serious. "It was a good thing we named you after your uncle, son, because you're a lot like him. Both of you born with a wanderlust."

He paused, allowing Joe to consider the thought. "As far back as I can remember, your uncle was always runnen off somewhere else."

"The prodigal son," Joe interrupted, quoting his grandmother.

"Not at all," Matt shot back. "My brother loved home, but his heart tugged him elsewhere. I'm glad he followed it and don't doubt for one minute that your grandma ain't, either. It was the right thing for him to do. In those few years with the Navy, your uncle saw more of the world than most men see in a lifetime. He truly lived the life he wanted."

Matt paused again to choose his words, then looked hard at Joe. "I'm tellen you all this, son, because I want you to know that it's okay if your heart leads you elsewhere," he said soberly. "There's no law that says a boy has to follow in his daddy's footsteps. I've got everything I need right here in Cookville, and I farm because it's the right thing for me to do. But wherever you go and whatever you do will be the right thing for you, Joe, and it'll be fine by your mama and me."

Matt allowed the dirt to trickle from his hand, watching it fall back to the ground. "But regardless, whatever you do, wherever you go," he said, returning his gaze to Joe, "remember this farm and your family will always be here for you, son. No matter what."

Joe stood dazed, stricken with disbelief, muted by the moment.

Matt smiled, slow and serious until his face dissolved into a spitfire grin. "Well, hell, I'm on a roll," he said, dusting off his hands. "I probably should tell you all about the birds and the bees, but you already know that stuff."

Joe shrugged modestly. "Did Mama mind too much about not getten a Mark in the family," he asked as Matt mounted the tractor and settled on the seat.

"Nah," Matt answered, leaning against the steering wheel. "Turned out Mark was her least favorite of the four gospels—at least name-wise. I don't rightly know how she feels about the scripture."

Joe nodded, still bewildered.

"You feed the hogs, son," Matt said a moment later, "and I'll milk the cow. Then, we'll see 'bout getten us some supper."

"Sure thing, Daddy. And thanks, for the talk."

Matt gave his son a gruff smile as the tractor roared to life. He waved a hand, then drove off along the rutted field lane running through the pecan orchard and alongside the house.

Joe stood there—transfixed as he tried to absorb the meaning of this moment with his father—until somehow his legs began moving him toward the house. Gradually, he realized his hands still held the dirt. He stopped in his tracks, unclenched his fist and allowed the black soil to fall away. Brown stains remained on his palm, and the hand suddenly felt withered and bone dry. His teeth gritted, and the same dry, lifeless feeling filled his mouth. He began moving toward the house, quickly, purposefully this time, not stopping until he reached the well, where he rinsed his hands clean in clear, cold water from the spigot. Then, he fed the hogs.

––––––––

Later, with night settled over the farm, Joe sat around the kitchen table with the family, listening to his brother deliver a lengthy, if somewhat overblown, blessing of the evening meal. Supper was waiting and everyone was hungry, but mealtime prayers took precedence over the food and the appetites. Joe's mother and grandmother did not abide religion by rote. The two women wanted prayers from the heart, believing words of simplicity and honesty far more valuable than eloquence or superficiality.

Joe was thinking about those unchanging values, the rituals of home and the ties that bound him, when he felt the heavy weight of eyes upon him. He raised his head and found his father staring back at him. They acknowledged each other with brief smiles and nods before Matt closed his eyes and bowed his head.

Joe lowered his gaze once more, but his eyes stayed open, staring at the reflection in the plate.

As a boy, he had followed his daddy's footsteps, worshipping the man who helped give him life and expecting to work the farm with Matt one day, just as Matt now did with his father. As he'd grown older, Joe had continued to worship his father but not the man's way of life. He'd tried and tried to understand where their two paths quit running parallel, why his had crossed into uncharted territory. He had brooded over the differences, the seeming inability to reconcile his own desire and ambition with loyalty and responsibility to his family.

Suddenly, the dilemma no longer mattered. His father had granted Joe a license for the future. Matt had freed him from the tightfisted chains of the farm. No longer would Joe try to smother the fire of ambition smoldering within or quench the thirst pulling him away from his family. He was free to ponder and pursue another kind of life, a different set of responsibilities.

Joe had an inkling of the future then, a sense about the way life worked—of freeing yourself from one set of chains in order to be yoked to even tighter bonds. And in a way, the boy was glad just to be sitting at the supper table, belonging to this family, with nothing more than hunger pains to satisfy.

CHAPTER 2

CAROLINE LAY SNUG IN bed, buried beneath covers with one leg draped over the warm body beside her. Even without looking at the ticking brass clock on the nightstand, she knew it was time to begin another day. Her free foot burrowed through the pile of blankets and quilts, found the bed's edge and lifted the covers. A frigid draft rushed up her flannel gown, and she dropped the covers, wanting to savor the warmth awhile longer. She snuggled closer to Matt, listening to his rhythmic breathing and feeling the steady rise and fall of his chest.

On another cold morning nineteen years ago this day, she'd woken early as well—a little fearful, yet excited over the prospect of a moment exactly like this one. She had been sixteen, driven by the impetuosity of youth and tempered by the wisdom of maturity beyond her years. Two days later, Caroline had married Matt. He had been not much older, but equally sure of his wedding vows. Even God had been certain of their union, sending a white Christmas as a blessing.

Caroline forced herself to roll away from Matt and got out of bed to face the cold morning. She dressed quickly, pulling on an everyday yellow cotton dress with long sleeves, then began her ritualistic morning inspection of the house.

In 1934, long before Caroline knew Matt, fire had destroyed the original Baker home. The family had lived in the corncrib across the road, while Matt's father, Sam Baker, hurriedly rebuilt the house. His construction skills had been marginal, but Sam had tackled the job with pride and dedication. The result was a rectangular building, with an A-frame roof and an expansive front porch pointing due east.

The front door opened into a wide hall stretching deep into the house and leading straight into the bathroom. Three bedrooms lined the left side of the hall, with the living room, dining room and kitchen on the right. A fourth bedroom—Sam and Rachel's—jutted off one side of the kitchen, with a large pantry and closed porch on the other.

The rooms were all large and spacious, with twelve-foot ceilings and long windows. Their decor was a hodgepodge collection of heavy furniture pieces destined to become antiques and flimsy articles picked up at bargain prices. Without a doubt, the front two rooms were Caroline's favorites.

The living room contained a Victorian sofa, burgundy-red velvet with brocaded black roses. Two matching chairs—one in the same shade of burgundy and another royal blue—accompanied the sofa, all sitting on a decorative rose-colored floor rug inlaid with various shades of flower patterns. The room also contained a Queen Anne sofa with worn mint green cushions, a similarly colored sturdy recliner and various tables built from cypress knots taken from a grove of the ancient trees that grew on the farm in a bog of mud and pitch-black water.

Matt and Caroline's bedroom suite was made of dark Spanish oak. A rare tiger oak mantle framed the redbrick fireplace, which stood between two closets made of pure cedar. A cedar trunk, once Caroline's hope chest, set at the foot of the bed.

A curio shelf, an upright piano, two sea captain's trunks and a mirrored dresser with a homemade curtain covering its open bottom lined the wide hallway.

Stopping at the door between the trunks, Caroline checked the girls' room, then moved on to the boys' room, which had a lopsided appearance due to a jutting corner space on the far end of the house.

Joe had claimed the corner space for himself, setting up a small desk and his ladder-backed chair with the cowhide seat. He was badgering his father to seal off the corner with a wall, so that he could have a room of his own. Caroline had resisted the idea so far. After Christmas, she intended to relent. Joe was the oldest of her six children by several years, and she agreed with Matt that the boy deserved some privacy.

The dining room contained an aging table, buffet and china cabinet, all made from black walnut. A silver coffee and tea set adorned the buffet, giving the room a sense of elegance. Unfortunately, that distinction was marred by the presence of a large chest freezer, one of two required to store the enormous amounts of vegetables and meat necessary to feed the large family.

A honey-colored oaken cupboard, along with the fireplace, dominated the comfortable kitchen, while a varnished rocking chair and church deacon's bench provided ample sitting space. The table, its side benches and two end chairs had been hewn by Matt and Sam from pine trees. Though well sanded, these homemade pieces yield the occasional splinter, interrupting meals with a howl when someone acquired one in the backside.

Her tour completed in the kitchen, Caroline built a fire, using the last piece of resin to start the blaze. She made a mental note to ask Joe to bring in more from the barrels outside, then turned her attention to preparing breakfast for the hungry brood that would soon overrun the kitchen.

Caroline appreciated these rare moments of solitude, almost as much as she enjoyed her busy days, the result of six children who, she liked to believe, required her constant attention, but were quite capable of fending for themselves.

She cracked a dozen eggs into a mixing bowl, poured in a hefty amount of canned milk and added a dash of salt and pepper. Using a wooden spoon to beat the eggs, she crossed over to the one kitchen window that afforded an unobstructed view of the horizon. Gray clouds hung heavy and low over the fields and pecan orchard, once again reminding Caroline of that December nineteen years ago.

In any other year, a snowy Christmas Eve would have been cause for celebration in Cookville, where the chance for a white Christmas was only slightly better than snow on the Fourth of July. But it had been 1941 and residents of the sleepy South Georgia community did their best to ignore the white fleece covering their flat lands. Snow nor anything else seemed special that Christmas because the community feared what they would lose in the coming years and grieved for that already lost.

As it had for so many Americans, December 7, 1941, brought tragedy to the Bakers. Among those killed when the Japanese unleashed their bombs on Pearl Harbor was Joseph Samuel Baker, the oldest of Sam and Rachel's three children. It took three days for the heartless telegram to arrive, notifying the Bakers of their son's death aboard the USS Arizona and his unaccounted burial in a watery grave.

A taxi driver brought the telegraph to Sam and Rachel and then returned to Cookville, spreading word that the backwoods county had lost its first son in the fight for freedom. There would be others, of course, but Joseph had been the first casualty and the community responded with an outpouring of respect. The county honored the fallen soldier with a memorial service in the high school auditorium two weeks after Pearl Harbor and later erected a commemorative bronze plaque on the courthouse square when it was discovered his body would remain forever lost in the sea of Honolulu.

Pearl Harbor staggered the good citizens of Cookville, but Matt's surprise wedding to Caroline three days after the memorial service socked them in the gut. Matt was just eighteen, a rakish young man with a footloose and fancy-free reputation. Caroline was a stranger, the orphaned daughter of a preacher who lived with her spinster aunt in Tifton.

There had been talk about the quick wedding, but Caroline had not minded the gossip. She and Matt had married for love and nothing else. And thanks to the war, they had proved their sudden nuptials were no shotgun arrangement.

Caroline never regretted becoming a bride at such an early age—though she figured to pitch a fit should any daughter of hers come up with a similar notion. She and Matt had been one of those blessed couples, the lucky ones for whom it was love at first sight. While she couldn't say positively that she expected to marry Matt from the moment she laid eyes on him, the idea had taken hold in short order.

Matt, of course, did claim to have decided to marry Caroline on first sight. He'd courted her shamelessly, stealing kisses and camping out on the doorstep of the home she shared with fussy Aunt Evelyn. Her aunt was mortified, but Caroline threw caution to the wind and embarked on a torrid romance. Stolen kisses quickly led to stronger feelings, and when the passion grew too ardent, they fell apart and talked.

Caroline carried conversations effortlessly, but in all her life she'd never found anyone easier to talk with than Matt. Words came naturally between them as they discovered each other. He proposed within two months of meeting her, promising the wedding could wait until she finished high school in the spring. Caroline accepted and began wishing for springtime.

Then Pearl Harbor happened. Matt proposed again, and they were married three days later—to the chagrin of the community but to the pleasure of Sam, Rachel and even Aunt Evelyn.

The Christmas Eve wedding had been a simple affair. Caroline wore a white velvet dress, and Matt donned the dark blue suit purchased a few days earlier for the memorial service honoring his brother. They had married beside the French doors between the living and dining rooms of the Baker home. It was a small service attended only by Rachel, Sam, Aunt Evelyn and Matt's best friend, Paul Berrien, along with Paul's two older sisters, April and June. Preacher Fred Cook performed the ceremony, and Caroline had promised to love, honor, cherish and obey her new husband. They honeymooned for a single night in a small guest cottage on the Berrien estate, and there Caroline had discovered the joy of unbridled passion. The next day, she had helped Rachel cook Christmas dinner, while exchanging the sly smiles of new lovers with her husband.

She had never ever once had any regrets.

———

Matt padded down the hallway, his worn socks doing little to warm his feet against the cold that had seeped into the wooden floor overnight. He did a double turn at the end of the hall—first right, then left—and caught himself in the kitchen doorway, captivated by a vision of his wife. Caroline was peering out the window, whipping a bowl of eggs with purpose, yet, undoubtedly lost in her thoughts. On countless times, Matt had come into the kitchen to find his wife gazing out the window as she handled some simple task. He never tired of this vision, the reality of his dreams.

Caroline seemed so much at home here, as well she should have been, but he was amazed, as always, at how thoroughly she had become a part of the place. Even Matt, who had expected she would adapt to his family without much fuss, never could have guessed way back when about the sense of belonging that would develop between her and his parents. But he had hoped, of course, because Caroline had come into the family at its darkest hour.

Not only had his brother Joe died in 1941, but a few weeks before Pearl Harbor, his fifteen-year-old sister, Ruth, had broken his parents' hearts by running off and eloping with a fighter pilot stationed at nearby Moody Air Field. Knowing he must soon follow his brother into the military, hurting over the twin loss suffered by his parents, Matt had broken a promise to himself and asked Caroline to marry him before she finished high school the following spring. Three days later, he'd been a married man at the age of eighteen. And he'd given his parents another child, a daughter to comfort them and take away the heartbreak of things gone terribly wrong.

Caroline had indeed become another child to Sam and Rachel, and they had become the parents she'd lost to a freak automobile accident at the age of twelve.

She had been a town girl when she came to the Baker farm, used to conveniences like electricity and indoor plumbing, luxuries like drugstore sodas and telephones. But what she lacked in farm-life know-how, Caroline made up for with a pioneer's character. She learned their ways—absorbing the knowledge that would make her a good wife to Matt when he came home from the war—and added her own special touches to the family recipe. Now, they were so akin to each other that it sometimes reminded Matt of the proverbial chicken and egg: Had he not been there from the beginning, he never would have known which came first.

Matt suspected his father came closest to the truth of explaining the special bond between Caroline and his parents. Sam maintained the Bakers were a family haunted by "the orphan spirit," which he defined as a longing for the kind of completion in life that only a family can give.

Caroline certainly had an orphan's credentials, as did Sam and Rachel to a lesser extent. Sam was comfortably estranged from his family, while Rachel's was spread far and wide across South Georgia and Florida. Caroline had been an only child, whose closest relative had been a spinster aunt when her parents died. And Aunt Evelyn herself, whom Matt had come to know and love as his wife did, had died back in 1957, leaving Caroline bereft of any family except for a smattering of cousins so far removed they hardly counted as kin.

If an orphan spirit was the culprit that linked Caroline so closely to Matt and his family, then so be it. Though his own childhood had been ideal and he could not fathom a feeling of incompleteness, Matt certainly appreciated the opportunity to fulfill that longing or any other yearning Caroline might have.

Smiling, he walked softly to his wife, put his arms around her and kissed her lightly on the neck.

The sensation brought Caroline pleasantly back to the present. "Mornen," she said.

"What's so special out there?" Matt asked by way of greeting, nuzzling her neck as he spoke.

"Most everything," Caroline replied, yielding her neck to the tender assault, the bowl of eggs temporarily forgotten.

"Such as?"

Caroline peered out the window once more, her gaze sweeping through the pecan orchard to the horizon beyond and the small outbuilding a few yards behind the house. "Oh, I see a beautiful field, newly plowed," she said respectfully. "A syrup house stocked with probably the finest cane syrup in the state and a smokehouse with a nice fat ham that will water your mouth on Christmas Day.

"And you," she added softly, turning in his arms to look at Matt, "made it all possible."

"I had a lot of help," Matt grinned, pulling her closer.

Caroline kissed him passionately, despite the bowl of eggs wedged between them.

"An almost proper way to start the day," Matt said seductively when the kiss ended. "You let that brood of young'uns eat cold cereal for breakfast and we could make it entirely proper."

Caroline cocked an eyebrow at him. "That's how we got this brood in the first place," she teased, gently breaking the embrace. "I should start the coffee," she continued, sounding suddenly practical. "Ma and Pa will be in here anytime now, and the children should be up soon."

Matt watched her purposeful stride to the stove, where she set the bowl down and turned her attention to the coffee pot. He lowered himself to the deacon's bench, retrieved a pair of work boots from beneath and began pulling them on, his gaze still fixed on Caroline.

His wife was a beautiful woman, tall and firmly built with a mane of ash brown hair and a sense of unaffected elegance. Matt loved the whole of her body, not only for the way she looked and carried herself but also in the way she fit against and meshed with him. Their bodies were the perfect blend, balanced in the right places with a few incongruities thrown in to keep the mix interesting.

Caroline nearly matched her husband in height, coming in a shade under two inches shorter than Matt, who stood exactly two inches shy of six feet in bare feet. She was the more strong-boned of the two, though both of them had medium builds. Her hair—which she pinned up during the day and spent several minutes brushing at night before coming to bed, and to Matt—was long and wavy, contrasting sharply with his straight, black crown. They both had brown eyes, but again, hers were light and shining and his dark and smoldering. Her skin tone was pure peaches and cream, tanned healthy rather than damaged by hard days of work in the sun, whereas Matt's natural swarthiness had a coppery tint baked by the sun and etched by a full-blooded Cherokee ancestor.

Caroline may not have been a classic beauty with her oval-shaped face, but her complexion was flawless, fresh and possessed of an aura that radiated generosity and caring. Her countenance adorned Caroline with the kind of beauty that Matt cherished.

If pressed to single out one bodily feature of his wife that stood out among all others, Matt would have picked her legs. Without doubt. They were long and shapely, the kind of legs that Betty Grable had used to forge a career in show business. Those legs gave Caroline an indelible stamp of grace, a sureness of movement that had been bred into their children with equal measure.

Matt considered himself a lucky man to have Caroline as a wife and the mother of his children. And from time to time he marveled as well that his love for her continued to grow day after day.

She was, of course, a different woman from the girl he had married. He remembered the girl being too thin and coltish, but she had worn her hair long almost all the time back then and Matt had made her promise never to cut it short. Somewhere along the way, probably when he was in Europe during the war, she had taken to pulling it up during the day. Matt didn't mind. His wife let her hair hang loose and long when it mattered. Giving birth to six children had changed her girlish figure, thickening the waist he once held between his fingers, but Matt preferred the womanly look of the present.

Caroline was a treasure, no doubt, deserving of more than he'd ever been able to give her, yet satisfied beyond question with the life they had carved for themselves in this piney wood community.

This last thought occurred to Matt as he spied the golden band on Caroline's left hand, wondering for the umpteenth time whether he could afford a diamond engagement ring for her. Money was already stretched too thin for Christmas, but Matt had his heart set on surprising her with a ring.

He knew buying the ring this year would amount to a foolish waste of money, dollars they didn't really have. Next year, perhaps, the farm would do better and the money would be available. Then, too, their twentieth anniversary would present a special occasion for an extravagant gift. But Matt was tired of waiting around for a special occasion to give his wife the ring she should have had before they married. He'd been doing that all his life it seemed, always managing to find some excuse to buy the ring next time. This once, he hoped to thumb his nose at fortune and do what he wanted.

Deep down, however, Matt knew more pressing matters were at hand than buying an engagement ring for the woman who had shared his life for nearly nineteen years. Like finding the money to buy Christmas gifts for six children. And on a more down-to-earth basis, feeding those children and having enough money to plant next year's crop. Still, he determined to give some serious thought to the ring on the hunting expedition planned for later this morning.

Rising, Matt crossed to the window, scanning the gray horizon for an indication of when the rain might come, wondering whether the hunting trip would be wet and cold, or just cold. Though slung low across the sky, the clouds seemed light for rain. He figured the wet stuff was still a day or two away, but the heavy overcast on this cold morning harkened him back again to the past.

"Do you remember how you felt this time nineteen years ago?" he asked suddenly, turning to look across the room at Caroline.

She glanced up at him from the table, where she was slicing pieces of streaked meat for frying. "Scared to death," she smiled coyly. "I wanted to be a good wife, to please you, and I was afraid to at the same time."

"Not me," Matt shook his head. "Guess I was too young to be scared—or too dumb. I wanted to get married and start maken babies." His brow furrowed. "Or at least practicen at it."

"You obviously were good at it," Caroline said with a wink. "You were real potent."

Matt shrugged. "You were just real fertile," he teased, finishing the private joke between them.

Matt moved in front of the fireplace, lacing his fingers behind his back to soak up warmth from the roaring blaze. "This weather reminds me of that time," he said, reminiscing while Caroline poured grits into a pot of boiling water. "The way it snowed that Christmas Eve was sure special. My whole life I'd never seen more than a few flakes and then on my wedden day, it snowed and snowed. Do you remember the drift that piled high beside the front porch?"

"By the swing," Caroline answered, taking over the story. "We sat there, swingen back and forth, draggen our feet through the snow. I remember thinken back then that the snow was God's way of blessen our marriage."

Matt shrugged his head, neither agreeing nor disagreeing with this last suggestion. Caroline brought him a cup of steaming hot coffee, black, kissed him lightly on the cheek and moved again to the window, observing the cold, leaden sky once more. "Do you think we might get another Christmas snow?" she asked hopefully.

"I doubt it," Matt said, sipping the coffee. "Temperature's supposed to climb into the fifties this afternoon, and I tend to think those clouds look a lot worse than they are. Course, the weatherman on TV last night said a cold wave is on its way south, so you never know. It might just happen."

"A big snowfall sure would bring back a lot of pleasant memories," Caroline said wistfully.

"A big snowfall might take a few minds off Santa Claus, and what he may or may not bring for Christmas," Matt said ruefully, turning the conversation to more pressing matters.

"We'll do the best we can," Caroline reassured him, returning to the stove. "Ma's made a few clothes for the children, and we can buy candy and fruit and maybe some small toys to stuff the stockens. They're smart kids, Matt. They understand Santa Claus has his good years and bad years."

"That won't make it any easier," Matt grumbled. "Hell, they're kids, honey. They don't page through that Sears catalog day after day for nothen."

"You'd be surprised," Caroline said briskly. "Sometimes the anticipation, the wishen, is better than the real thing. Besides, I don't want the gift-getten to take away from the real meanen of Christmas."

"Well, I don't think there's much chance of that happenen 'round here," Matt muttered dryly.

"Oh, hush up," she admonished, "and let me finish maken breakfast."

Matt set the empty coffee cup on the table and sauntered over, wrapping his arms around her once more. "You're some woman," he murmured, leaning around to peck her on the cheek.

Caroline gave him a sidelong glance, which meant either she knew what he said was true or wasn't in the mood for his charming. Either way, she was telling him to get lost and let her finish cooking breakfast.

"Guess I'd best get to the milken," he laughed.

"Guess so," she shrugged.

Matt released her.

"Lucas is comen over this mornen," he said, plucking a lined denim jacket off the back of the chair in his place at the head of the kitchen table and shrugging into it. "We're gonna do a little hunten after breakfast and then cut some wood. I probably won't be around for dinner."

"We're goen into Cookville this afternoon," Caroline reminded him.

"It's a date," Matt nodded, heading for the back-porch door. He stopped by the refrigerator, glancing back at her. "By the way, ask Joe if he wants to go hunten with us. He's missed most of the season so far, but he's getten around well enough on the leg that he might enjoy it."

Caroline nodded agreement, and Matt was gone to begin the day in earnest.

———

As the aroma of scrambled eggs, fried pork and perking coffee drifted through the house, Caroline heard the first stirrings of her waking brood. She finished the eggs, dishing them onto a plate and setting it on the stove to keep warm. She gave the grits a quick stir, then began setting the table. She set out the ten plates and was retrieving flatware from the cupboard when a truck needing a new muffler pulled into the yard.

Hurrying, she laid the forks and spoons on the table in a tangled pile, crossed over to the small window beside the kitchen sink and pulled back the yellow curtain in time to see Lucas Bartholomew pull up to the barn in his ancient pickup. Lucas climbed out of the truck and ambled over to the barn gate, where Matt was on the other side milking the Guernsey cow, which the children had named Brindy. Caroline let the curtain fall back in place and went to fetch a cup of coffee for him. She shared a history with Lucas, too, begun on the day she had married Matt and woven intermittently ever since.

She'd watched Lucas grow from a small, playful child to a rangy, serious young man. She recalled Sam once saying that Lucas had the backbone of two men, prophesying his willingness to take on hard work would carry the black man beyond the wrong side of the tracks in Cookville. Sam had been correct in a manner of speaking, but Lucas struggled for everything, more than most people did anyway.

His father had loved liquor too much, dying when Lucas was just fifteen and straddling the boy with a sickly mother. Two years away from a high school diploma—a rarity for colored men in these parts—Lucas had been forced to quit his formal education to care for the ailing Merrilee Bartholomew. He had gone door-to-door, doing odd jobs, working long, hard hours, most times for fair wages but sometimes not.

Lucas never complained. He just went quietly about his business, earning the reputation of a go-getter and winning the respect of the people willing to give him a fair shake in life.

His mother—a frail woman whose bedridden posture never diminished her spirit—had died a few years back, freeing Lucas from the burden of medical expenses. His response had been seemingly unpredictable and abrupt. He'd bought the pickup, packed up lock, stock and barrel and headed to nowhere in particular, intent only on seeing whether a colored man stood a better chance of improving his lot in life up North. He'd returned to Cookville in the late spring of this year, in time for the summer's work, saying simply that city life did not agree with him.

Matt had taken Lucas under his wing even before the boy's father died, offering work and steering him toward other opportunities when the Bakers had no need for an extra hand on the farm. Matt paid better than fair wages, but more than that, he instilled confidence and pride in Lucas. Actually, Matt was one of two mentors who showed Lucas the virtue of the straight and narrow. The other was Paul Berrien, and he was perhaps closer to Lucas than Matt because his mother had worked as a maid for the Berrien family many years before failing health forced her to the sick bed.

Since returning to his roots, Lucas had worked almost exclusively for Matt and Paul. He had taken up the slack on the Baker farm when Sam suffered a heart attack at the start of the tobacco season, and even now, when his service was needed little, Matt continued to find odd jobs for him. Paul also kept him busy with various projects on the Berrien estate, maintaining a vegetable garden and flowerbeds and other odds and ends. In his spare time, when neither Matt nor Paul could justify working him, Lucas hustled to keep busy.

He was no slouch and highly regarded by all but the most of hateful of their community.

Bobby Taylor belonged to this latter group.

When civil rights-minded Yankees conjured up visions of racist Southerners, Caroline felt sure someone such as Bobby Taylor sprang to mind. Bobby—the mere thought of his name brought a bad taste to her mouth—was the embodiment of everything wrong with the South's attitude toward colored folk, and then some. He was wickedness personified, guided by bonds of hatred, spite and prejudice. Bobby did not stand alone with his views in the Cookville community but he stood apart, even in the crowd.

Ironically, Caroline shared a history with Bobby that also began on her wedding day but had long since withered, except for occasional happenstance and her own strong memories.

On the morning of her wedding, shortly after arriving at the Baker house, Caroline had set out on a brisk walk to the Carter's Mercantile. The store stood at the crossroads of the unincorporated New River community where the Bakers lived, serving as a beacon for social life much like the area churches and elementary school. It was, then and now, a tidy store, stocking groceries, hardware, clothing and most any other item a body might need.

Caroline had made the long trek through the snow to fetch several cans of jellied cranberry sauce for the next day's Christmas dinner. Arriving at the mercantile, she found Lucas playing in the snow while his parents shopped. He was a thin child, with a dimpled smile and a spark of sunshine in his eyes.

Enchanted, Caroline approached the little boy and tried to strike up a conversation. Lucas promptly hid behind the red and white gas tank.

"Are you playen possum?" Caroline coaxed.

He did not answer, but instead peered from behind the tank. Caroline smiled, earning the same in response, and Lucas placed small hands across his eyes, peeking through the slits of his fingers.

"Peep-eye," Caroline said, playing the game. "Can you tell me your name?"

Lucas hesitated as the store door jingled. He seemed on the verge of answering when a black-gloved hand appeared from nowhere, shoving the little boy aside. His balance altered, Lucas tried to catch himself but stumbled and fell.

"Get out of my way, kid," a mean voice shouted.

Shocked, Caroline shifted her gaze from Lucas to the young man standing over the boy. She estimated his age about the same as hers. He was almost handsome, of average height and wiry build, with dishwater blond hair, a sculpted face and a ruddy complexion. But the face was set with a bully's sneer, and his gaze sought her approval with a lopsided, haughty smile.

"This country'd be a damn sight better off if we'd fixed his mama and castrated his daddy," Bobby Taylor declared proudly, puffing out his chest. "We oughtta send their black asses back to Africa."

Caroline found him ugly to the bone, and she faced him down with an icy glare. Bobby, who usually charmed women with his near-good looks, frowned slightly, uncertain about her attitude. So Caroline had clarified it for him.

She strode over to the cowering boy, plucked Lucas off the cold ground and cradled him in her arms. "There was no cause for that," she hissed at Bobby. "You oughtta be ashamed of yourself."

A muscle twitched in his cheek, and Bobby released a contemptuous snort. "Well ain't you high and mighty, Miss Pretty Panties," he snarled, looking her up and down. "I don't know who you are, priss, but folks 'round here don't take too kindly to nigger lovers. You'd do well to remember that before shooten off your mouth next time."

Caroline had known right then it was a useless exercise to argue with Bobby Taylor. She had leveled him with another sour glare, then stepped past him and carried Lucas into the store.

Though she found the current times confusing—fretting over the growing tension between blacks and whites, wondering whether boycotts and demonstrations proved more divisive than enlightening—Caroline despised hatemongers. Of course, when you hacked down to the meat of the issue, there was only a thin line between the blatant bias of hatemongers and the subtler prejudice of those who believed in equality for Negroes as long as it suited their own particular way of life.

People were beginning to unearth those built-in prejudices, and Caroline feared they would unleash a firestorm of wrath and unrest. She supposed her family would face the music as well, learning and struggling with the new rules of a changing society. Despite good intentions, the Bakers were virtual newcomers to the task of confronting built-in biases. It was only a short time ago, after all, that they themselves had practiced the art form of subtle discrimination.

Sighing, the waters still muddied in her mind, she slipped into Joe's denim jacket, picked up the cup of coffee and went outside to the barn.

———

"Mornen, Lucas," Caroline said, coming up behind him. The air was chilly, and her breath came out misted. "Thought you might like to warm up with some coffee," she said, offering him the steaming cup.

Lucas took the cup gingerly. "Thank you, ma'am," he nodded, smiling. "It's cold enough all right."

"We're 'bout to have breakfast," she said. "Do you want a bite to eat?"

"No'sem," Lucas shook his head. "I ate before I came out this mornen," he continued in his slow, deliberate tone of speech. "I just stopped by to see what time we was goen hunten. I'm headed over to Mr. Paul's right now. He's got a broken window pane that needs fixen."

"Okay, then," Caroline smiled as Matt stepped to the gate, carrying a pail half full of fresh cow's milk.

"I'll take that," Caroline said.

Matt handed her the bucket over the fence. "I'll be in soon."

"No rush," she said. "Everyone slept late this mornen, even Ma and Pa." Turning, she gave Lucas a quick wave. "See you later, Lucas. I hope y'all have good luck with the hunten."

"Yes'em," he answered. "So do I."

Caroline walked the short distance back to the house, leaving the two men in discussion about the best place to cut a load of wood. She picked up a lone pecan along the way, deposited it in a full bucket of nuts on the back porch and went inside, her arrival coinciding with the emergence of Rachel and Sam from their bedroom.

Sam closed the door behind his wife, smiling at Caroline above Rachel's ranting and reprimands about his heavy snoring the previous night. "Good mornen, daughter," he greeted. "I trust you slept better last night than my bride claims to have."

Rachel rolled her eyes and apologized for oversleeping. "What can I do to help?" she asked, tying a worn apron around her waist, while Sam poured them both cups of coffee.

"Everything's mostly done," Caroline replied, taking off the jacket and tossing it on the deacon's bench. "You could put the silverware out," she added, gesturing to the pile of spoons and forks on the table. "I'm gonna strain this milk. We oughtta have enough cream by tomorrow for a churn of butter."

The house came fully alive then, bolstered by the eruption of six children fighting to use one bathroom, taking out their morning grogginess on each other. One by one, they straggled into the kitchen, bringing with them different shades of brown hair and brown eyes, and personalities far more distinctive. The children had their individual routines and quirks, but there was a sameness about their morning habits that reassured Caroline.

Joe came first, as usual, kissing his mother and grandmother, questioning Sam about his state of well-being and adding wood to the fire. He then plopped down in the rocking chair by the fireplace, sipping on a cup of black coffee and contemplating the flames in silence.

Relaxing came hard for Joe, unless he was bone tired or in the mood for fishing. The boy was a mass of controlled energy, clicking from one task to the next with a metronome's precision, always aiming for a beginning rather than an end. In one way, Caroline found it odd that someone so full of vim and vigor would start the day at such an unhurried pace. It seemed a contradiction of sorts, but Joe needed a moment's peace to harness that boundless energy, to synchronize with the rhythms that would carry him through the day.

When all was said and done, Caroline had come to expect a study in contradictions from her oldest child. For such a straight arrow, the boy was remarkably flexible, able to switch gears at a moment's notice, even anticipating the dawning of such a moment. He seemed contented with whatever came his way, never complaining, utterly free of desire for material possessions, and yet, it seemed apparent that his life was destined for adventure and new experiences. And strangest of all, though Joe was the least likely of the children to be considered a dreamer, he dreamed the biggest of them all.

He was curious and inquisitive, capable of probing someone's deepest thoughts without ever once seeming like a busybody, willing to invest the time required to listen with interest. He devoured any piece of written material, from *Progressive Farmer* and the Sunday newspaper to the Bible and any other book.

He was handsome, too, though not overwhelmingly so like his father. Joe had brown hair, the color of pecan shells, dark brown eyes and clean-cut features. He was dark complexioned, turning deep brown in the summer, while needing a few more inches in height and pounds of muscle to fill out his medium-build frame.

Just days from his fifteenth birthday, Joe was beginning to feel his oats, and Caroline could not help fretting over how he might sow them.

As the firstborn child and grandchild, he occupied an extra special place in the hearts of his parents and grandparents. For such a long time, Caroline had figured her son would be an only child. She had become pregnant soon after Matt came home from the war in 1945, delivering Joe on the last day of that historic year. Almost five years passed before she gave birth again, though not for lack of trying. Then she had turned into a virtual baby factory, delivering four more children over the next six years. It made for a busy household, and somehow in the middle of tending to those babies, Caroline feared Joe had lost part of his childhood to the weight of responsibility.

Joe carried the burden of being the oldest easily, though, never seeming to let it weigh heavy. He ruled over the other children with quiet charisma, like some benevolent dictator whose subjects obeyed him loyally because they held faith in the rightness of his edicts. He did the overwhelming share of chores on the farm and set a good example in school for his brothers and sisters. Caroline and Rachel demanded that he set a good example in church as well, while Matt and Sam expected him to be a jack-of-all-trades around the house.

Joe faced heavy expectations, but he thrived under the pressure. He delivered on expectations. Failure was not part of his vocabulary, though he surely tasted it from time to time as everybody did.

Caroline fussed occasionally about the boy's diligent pursuit of achievement. She would have worried incessantly, but Joe seemed at ease and contented for the moment, so there seemed no reason to belabor a moot point.

Of course, Joe was more subdued and pensive lately, but the boy was due some privacy to recover from the recent turmoil. His shattered leg was merely a rousing finale, capping a summer of one heart-wrenching moment after another. No one could have come through such a summer unscathed or unchanged, without needing time to catch his breath and return to an even keel. Such moments were the stuff of life's turning points, and Joe had caught each hairpin curve on the rollicking ride. The turbulence was such that if Caroline had cursed—which she didn't—she would have deemed it one hell of a summer for her firstborn son.

———

It was the summer Sam had his heart attack. Technically, the attack occurred in late spring, but they were on the second sweep through the tobacco patch and the days were hot as blazes, making it seem like summer even if the calendar claimed otherwise.

They had been shorthanded that day in the effort to fill the tobacco barn. Joe and Sam had been alone at the barn around dinnertime, trying to catch up on the hanging before the leaf started sweating, which would discolor it in the curing process and result in lower prices on the auction floor.

Joe was straddled between the lower tiers of a room, hanging the heavy sticks in the barn as Sam passed them to him. Sam was having to lug the sticks off a trailer outside the barn door, haul them inside and then shove them up to Joe. The barn itself was like a hothouse, the air stagnant and stifling with the sour odor of overheated green tobacco.

They were halfway through the job when Sam pushed another stick toward Joe's waiting hands. He never completed the motion, gasping suddenly with the stick's top end just above his shoulder. His face contorted in pain, the stick fell out of his grip and Sam toppled backward, landing hard on the packed dirt floor.

Joe practically fell out of the barn in his haste to aid his grandfather.

Sam clutched his chest, making a throaty plea for help as Joe raised his head off the dirt. Then the pain became too intense. He lost consciousness, mumbling incoherently and slipping into silence as his eyes rolled back into their sockets, his full weight slumping against the ground.

Joe believed his grandpa had died. He slapped Sam across the face twice, then ran for help.

The family heard him coming from inside the house, yelling at the top of his lungs. Stark terror was etched across his face when Joe arrived, pleading for quick action.

Sam had revived when they reached the barn, and the doctors later termed the attack mild. He had recuperated slowly and surely, but the illness had shaken Joe to the core. It was the boy's first head-on collision with mortality. More would come that summer.

———

It was the summer Joe acquired the voice of a man and learned how to use it as well. The change in his voice literally occurred overnight. He went to bed with a sore throat one night and woke the next morning with a voice like deep ice. His throat got better. The voice stayed with him.

Long before the overnight change in voice, Joe had been blessed with a rich baritone, never prone to the awkward high pitches of adolescence. Even as a small child, his voice—deep, husky, spoken from the bottom of the chest—had startled friends and strangers with its heavy pitch.

The latest change in tone had been subtle maturity; Joe's discovery of the power behind the voice rang out with an ear-shattering timbre. And it had caused walls of false pretense, cloaked in a veil of self-righteousness, to come tumbling down around the Bakers.

The moment occurred on a day—rare for this particular summer—when it was raining cats and dogs. Everyone spent the morning slogging through a wet tobacco patch. At dinnertime, they returned to the house and sat down to a piping hot meal prepared by Rachel.

Paul Berrien—taking a few hours off from politicking for the sheriff's office and his regular duties as president of the Farmers and Citizens Bank of Cookville—had stopped by and was persuaded to have a bite of dinner.

Lucas, who usually ate his noontime meal under the shade of the pecan orchard or at Carter's Mercantile, was in the cab of his pickup with a bologna sandwich and his personal jar of ice water. As in Cookville, where whites and blacks used separate water fountains and bathrooms, the Baker family drank from one water jar in the fields and Lucas from another. Lucas had never set foot in the Baker house, much less used the family's bathroom.

The children were still washing their hands and changing out of wet clothes when Rachel glanced outside the side window and declared, "I feel sorry for Lucas haven to eat in his truck."

"Me, too, Ma," Matt agreed, coming to her side to peer out the window.

"I suppose we could fix a plate for him at the dinen room table," Caroline suggested hesitantly. "He never has anything but a cold sandwich. He could use a hot meal on a day like this. I imagine he'd be grateful to be inside, where he could warm up a little."

"I agree with you, daughter," Sam said. "Go tell him to come inside, Matt."

A few minutes later, Lucas was seated alone at the dining room table with a heaping plate of fried chicken, mashed potatoes with gravy, butterbeans, biscuits, a jelly glass of iced tea and a slice of pound cake, while the Bakers and Paul Berrien crowded around the kitchen table. Everyone supposed they were making a progressive statement, allowing the colored man to eat at a table in their home, and they were feeling quite proud of themselves during the blessing.

But when Sam delivered a thunderous "Amen" to the prayer, Joe piped in loudly: "Why's Lucas in the dinen room? He oughtta be in here with us."

Joe had spoken with innocent naiveté, as if it had never occurred to the boy that the mores of the times forbade Lucas from sitting down with the family at the dinner table. But silverware clattered, mouths dropped open and a few of those gathered around the kitchen table nearly fell out of their chairs as the words dishonored their token gesture to noble intentions.

"Hush up!" Rachel hissed in a whisper.

"Joe!" Caroline gasped, also whispering. "He might hear you."

Disbelief spread across Joe's face as the cause of their anxiety dawned on him. "So why is Lucas in there?" he repeated dryly.

Everyone stayed silent. Joe looked from his mother to Rachel to Sam and finally to his daddy, demanding an answer with the intensity of his gaze.

"You know why, son," Matt said finally. "White people and colored people just don't take meals together—at least not around here, not in this day and age."

"It's not proper," Rachel added softly, sounding suddenly uncertain about her admonishment.

"Why not?" Joe pressed pointedly.

Sam shrugged. Rachel frowned. Caroline dithered for an answer. "That's just the way it is," Matt said heavily.

Joe grunted softly, placing his hands flat against the table. He gazed down at his plate of food, then back to the faces around him.

"Well, *the way it is* is the wrong way," he decided aloud. "It seems to me we're the ones who oughtta have the right to choose who we want to sit at our kitchen table."

Joe pushed away from the table, picked up his plate and removed himself from the kitchen. He walked casually into the dining room, joined Lucas at the table and struck up a conversation as if nothing out the ordinary had occurred.

In the kitchen, they began to eat as well, in ponderous silence. "Chicken's good, Granny," one of the children remarked, but no one paid attention.

"Oh, good Lord!" Sam snapped finally, fed up with the weighty silence. "I think we can fit another body at this table without causen too much trouble."

Everyone looked at him, then at each other, nodding vaguely, while Joe and Lucas continued talking in the dining room, chuckling, seemingly oblivious to and unconcerned with the melodrama played out in the next room. But the following day, Caroline asked Lucas to join them for the noon meal, and he did.

It became a standard practice from then on, although Lucas announced on some mornings that he would eat a sandwich under the shade of a pecan tree or grab something at the mercantile for dinner. He was not one to take advantage of an open invitation.

———

It was the summer Pal died.

Pal was a white German shepherd given to Joe a few weeks before Summer's birth. The dog had been Matt's idea, a special gift to occupy the boy in those times when everyone else was too busy, a situation that rarely happened when Joe was an only child.

The strategy worked. Joe was smitten with the dog, and Pal with the boy. They became constant companions, living the classic story of a boy and his dog.

Pal had been a horse, allowing Joe to ride on his back. The dog had delighted in taking the boy's arm into his mouth, gently wedging it between the sharp teeth of his powerful jaws, shaking his head from side to side, never once leaving a mark on the skin. Pal had gone everywhere with Joe, tagging along on hunting trips and even sharing a rowboat in the pond while Joe pursued his favorite pastime, fishing. Joe talked to the dog, sometimes in private, often in public, and Pal seemed to understand. The boy also took excellent care of his pet, never once requiring a reminder to feed and water the dog, providing him occasional treats, teaching Pal to herd cattle and chase hogs that strayed from their pens.

As far as anyone knew, only one bone of contention ever came between boy and dog, arising shortly after Pal's first Thanksgiving with the Bakers. Even that had been a misunderstanding.

Joe came around the corner of the house one day to find Pal spread out on all fours, happily devouring the last of the holiday turkey carcass, which Caroline had given the dog. For some unaccountable reason, except maybe to a five-year-old, Joe concluded Pal had gone into the house and stolen the turkey right off the table. Enraged, he stomped the dog's tail. Pal promptly turned on the boy, sinking his teeth deep into the skin of Joe's shoulder. Joe had required four stiches and a tetanus shot, and nobody ever again questioned Pal's right to the remains of a turkey feast.

Pal took ill a few weeks after Sam's heart attack. He began coughing and wheezing, refused to eat and finally holed up in his favorite winter sleeping spot—underneath the house on the east side of the double fireplace. Joe crawled under the house hour after hour, petting the animal, coaxing him to eat, but Pal grew more listless. Finally, Matt called the veterinarian.

Dr. Byrd Hutto took one look at Pal and diagnosed a terminal case of heartworms. Joe had been crushed, but Pal was ten, the ripe old age of seventy in dog years, and had avoided heartworms longer than most farm dogs. The vet administered a painkiller and promised to check on the dog's condition the following morning. But Pal died that afternoon.

Rachel found him. Pal had crawled to his customary place at the bottom of the front porch steps, standing guard over his family one last time before giving up the ghost. Rachel covered his body with a burlap sheet, then walked down to the tobacco patch to tell Joe.

The boy had taken the news with a tired nod and returned to work. That evening he wrapped Pal in the sheet, loaded the body in the bed of the pickup and drove to the back woods. He buried the dog beneath his favorite deer stand, returning home late that evening with red eyes and going to bed without supper.

When anyone attempted to console him, Joe simply shrugged, declaring, "He was old; it was his time."

Matt acquired another German shepherd a few months later, a puppy that showed every indication of being a suitable replacement for Pal. The children even named him Pal-Two.

Joe said he was a fine dog, but only with passing interest. His little brother, Luke, however, thought Pal-Two was just swell.

———

It was also the summer Stonewall Jackson was killed.

Stonewall was related to the Confederate Army hero in name only. He was a gopher tortoise that had made his home in a burrow on the Baker place for at least nine years.

Sam, Joe and Pal had found the tortoise nibbling in a collard patch across the road one dewy spring morning. They had followed him out of the field, back across the road and down to the northern edge of the Baker property where Stonewall had his den. Joe hitched a ride on the hard shell for part of the way, and the young Pal barked continuously in furious amazement.

The tortoise took it all in stride, bravely holding his head high and plodding for home with the extra weight on his back. Sam said he had a noble look, judging from his beady eyes and erstwhile determination, and deserved a proud name. He suggested Stonewall Jackson, and the name stuck.

Stonewall became a family fixture, raiding the greens and gardens every year, giving free rides to one Baker child after another and living a peaceful existence in the same burrow. They came across the gopher countless times, wrote his name on the bottom of the shell in magic marker and considered the tortoise a family pet. Even Pal hushed his barking when it became apparent that Stonewall Jackson belonged on the place.

One Sunday in late August shortly before school resumed, the entire family had been whiling away the afternoon on the front porch, with a churn of peach ice cream. A brief shower had fallen minutes earlier, and the occasional blast of rifle shot seemed to be creeping closer to the house. But there seemed no cause for alarm.

They were well into their second bowls of ice cream when a freckle-faced, husky boy came walking up the road with a rifle slung over his shoulder.

"That's icky Wayne Taylor," Summer informed them, groaning.

Wayne had started school with Summer, but he had failed the first grade. He had passed on his second try, only to fail the second grade in the most recently completed school year, which, in Summer's opinion, meant bad news for the middle Baker daughter.

"Ooh, Carrie," she squealed. "He'll be in your class this year."

"Hush up, Summer," Caroline admonished. "I don't want to hear that kind of talk. You understand?"

"Yeah," Summer sighed dramatically.

"That's not the way you answer your mama," Matt said reproachfully.

"Yes, ma'am," Summer remarked, amending her previous answer to Caroline. She sent her mother a contrite look, then dove back into the ice cream.

Joe snickered, goosing his sister in the ribs to show Summer she was not fooling anyone with her feigned sense of regret. She stuck out her tongue at him.

Caroline, eyeing the rifle Wayne was carrying, felt a tingle of apprehension. "I know the Taylors are gun fanatics, Matt, and they may know how to use them," she said, frowning. "But it makes me a little uneasy for him to come walken up here with it so casually like that."

"There's no cause for concern," Matt soothed. "The way I hear tell it, that boy's the equal of many a man around here with a gun."

"Wayne may be good with a gun, but he sure is dumb," Summer remarked, unable to keep quiet.

"You'd be dumb, too, if you'd been struck by lightnen," Joe said.

"That's probably true, Summer," Caroline added. "Maybe Wayne can't help it. He's lucky to be alive."

Lightning had struck Wayne three summers ago during a thundershower. He had been unconscious for two days and suffered burns on his hands and arms. The doctors had detected no permanent damage, however, and the boy had emerged from the coma seemingly unchanged by the incident.

"Well, I won't argue that he's lucky to be alive," Summer agreed with her mother. "But Wayne must have been pretty dumb in the first place. The boy was swingen on a steel chain wrapped around a tree during the middle of a lightnen storm. That's not exactly the smart thing to do."

No one contradicted Summer, not even Caroline, so they waited in silence until Wayne came closer.

"Howdy, Wayne," Sam called.

"Hey," the boy replied, stepping into the yard and coming to the brick walkway. "How y'all getten along?"

"We're doen just fine," Matt answered.

"We'd offer you a bowl of ice cream, Wayne, but we've just dipped up the last of it," Rachel apologized. "We put fresh peaches in it."

"I don't like peaches," Wayne said, rubbing a hand across the stubble of sandy hair on the top of his head.

"Oh," Rachel grunted, settling back in the rocking chair and returning to her bowl of ice cream. Peach was her favorite flavor.

"How's your family, Wayne?" Sam asked with diplomacy, for Wayne was the son of Bobby Taylor, and there had been ill feelings between the two families that summer. Bobby was campaigning for the sheriff's office in a heated battle with Paul Berrien.

"Good as can be," Wayne said.

"What are you out shooten for today?" Matt asked to change the subject.

"Mainly I'm practicen," Wayne replied. His face spread into a smile. "I did shoot an old gopher back down the road a piece," he boasted, gesturing toward Stonewall Jackson's abode. "Figured I'd spare him the trouble of getten mashed on the road."

Wayne snickered. But his announcement paralyzed the Bakers momentarily, their shock giving way quickly to a horrified surmising.

"You shot what?" Joe demanded, bolting upright, spilling the last of his ice cream on the porch floor.

"Just an old gopher," Wayne replied.

"It was probably our gopher, you dumb-ass," Joe yelled.

"Joe!" Caroline admonished.

"Settle down, son," Matt warned. "We don't know that it was Stonewall."

"How many other gophers have we seen down that road?" Joe asked dryly. "I'm gonna go find out," he continued, leaping off the porch. "Where is he?" he barked to Wayne.

"Down, down there," Wayne stammered, pointing, sensing he had just worn out his welcome. "I kicked him in the ditch."

Joe headed down the road in a fast trot, with his brothers and sisters in close pursuit.

"What in the world possessed you to shoot a gopher," Caroline asked bluntly a moment later, frowning at Wayne.

Wayne frowned back, searching for a reason and coming up empty-headed. He shrugged off an answer.

"You should have known better," Matt declared. "There's no reason to kill an animal for the sake of just killen. You're supposed to be a hunter, boy. Surely you know better."

Wayne's eyes widened.

"That gopher's been liven on this place since almost before you were born," Sam said bitterly. "You had no cause comen down here to disturb him, much less kill him." He paused, then added tightly, "I think it's time for you to get on home, Wayne."

"And I'm gonna make sure you get there," Matt added. "Your daddy and I need to have a talk."

"It was just a gopher," Wayne blurted out defiantly.

A muscle twitched in Matt's cheek, and Caroline steadied him with a calm hand of reason placed against the side of her husband's leg, a gentle reminder they were dealing with a ten-year-old instead of a grown man.

"Go on and get in the truck," Matt instructed, pointing to the pickup.

"Do you want me to come along, son?" Sam asked.

"I'll handle it, Pa," Matt replied, stepping off the porch as the children came back up the road, with Joe carrying an obviously dead Stonewall Jackson.

They waited in mechanical silence as the procession marched mournfully to the porch.

"It's him," Joe confirmed bluntly a few moments later. "Shot twice through the bottom of his shell." He shifted a daggered gaze to Wayne. "What did you do, Wayne? Turn him over and watch him flop around on his back awhile before you killed him?"

The question hung in brittle silence for a short eternity.

At last, Matt motioned to Wayne. "Let's go," he said.

"Where to?" Joe snapped.

"I'm taken him home to have a talk with his daddy," Matt said.

"I'm comen, too," Joe insisted.

Matt considered the wisdom of having Joe come along, but in his moment of indecision, the boy deposited the tortoise body in the bed of the pickup and vaulted over the side, staking claim to his rights.

"Okay," Matt agreed hesitantly. "But you let me do the talken when we get there."

The order went unacknowledged for a pregnant moment.

"Are we clear on that, son?" Matt asked again, firmer this time.

"Yes, sir."

As Matt told it to Caroline later, Joe held his tongue in the ensuing confrontation. "But fire came out his eyes, Caroline," her husband exclaimed. "You know how dark they are anyway. Well, they looked like polished black marbles stuck in his head, taken note of every word, every detail. I couldn't help but think that he looked like some hangen judge who'd already made up his mind and was just waiten around to pronounce the sentence, maybe even carry it out, too. Any sane man would have wilted under that glare, and Bobby did get a little tight around the collar." He hesitated, considering. "But that might have been simply because he's afraid somethen like this could hurt his chances in the election. Folks wouldn't take too kindly to some smart-aleck kid trespassen and shooten somethen that don't belong to him."

Likewise, Bobby Taylor took issue with Matt, scowling, snarling, accusing him of exaggerating something of no consequence. In the end, however, Bobby handled the incident with more tact than Matt would have given him credit for, conceding his son had made an error in judgment and promising none of the Taylors would ever again set foot on Baker property.

"But I don't know what to make of it, Caroline," Matt said with concern. "There was some bitterness to be sure. But he almost made it sound threatenen." He shook his head thoughtfully. "I know I did the right thing by goen to Bobby."

"You did," Caroline assured him.

"I don't want anybody who doesn't have a proper respect for life comen around my family with a gun, especially some smart-assed kid," Matt continued. "But still ...." He frowned, uncertain. "We may not see eye-to-eye with the Taylors, but there's never been any bad blood between us, and I'd like to keep it that way."

Matt hesitated again, tension lines creeping onto his face. "Bobby's never struck me as the type to forgive and forget," he said heavily. "I have to say I feel a little uneasy about the whole situation, Caroline. Like maybe I was there for the beginnen of a blood feud or somethen."

He shrugged. "I just don't know what will come of it."

———

Matt's concerns had proved prophetic in a manner of speaking, except the feud developed between Bobby Taylor and Paul Berrien, two total opposites who had waged the fiercest campaign in memory for the office of county sheriff. It seemed to Caroline the Bakers had been trapped into the war between Bobby and Paul, forced to take sides, caught on the fringes of something bigger than themselves. And she agreed with Matt: It was an unsettling, uneasy situation.

Caroline shook her head, pushing the thought away to concentrate on pouring the pail of warm cow's milk into a deep pan, straining it through a clean white cloth in the process.

Her mind returned to Joe and to Matt's parting request earlier in the morning. "Joe," she said, tipping the pail upside down to drain the last of the milk. "Your daddy's goen hunten with Lucas after breakfast. He thought you might like to go."

Joe grunted, something noncommittal, his eyes still skewered to the dancing flames.

Her motherly instincts growled, her wings unfurled, on guard again for danger— to her son, to her family, both of whom seemed caught up in a rising tide of misfortune. Caroline bit the inside of her lip, eyeing Joe and glancing around the kitchen in a symbolic search for the source of her worry. But wherever she looked, the waters were receding. She supposed it was the tension of the summer making her feel this way. But that tension was fading like newsprint turns yellow with old news. And then, as if reading her thoughts, Joe turned around and smiled. "I've got somethen else to do this mornen, Mama," he informed her.

Caroline returned his smile, nodding vaguely. And though it was infuriating and did not feel right, she checked her Mother Hen instincts.

It was Christmas, after all, the season of peace, and she had her faith. Caroline turned around quickly, bowed her head and uttered a silent prayer for the gift of the season.

———

Summer followed Joe, barging into the kitchen with her usual style, smiles and a word or two for anyone who cared to listen. So they humored her, allowing their oldest girl and second child to divest herself of a night and morning's worth of silence.

Summer had turned a precocious ten over the summer and she tended to have a piece of advice for everyone these days. Her tongue was sharp, witty and a tad sarcastic on occasion, but her heart was a treasure chest for good intentions. Still, in these wonder days of discovering her place in the family, Summer had a way of upsetting people. Her steady chatter wearied the best of them, and played on frayed nerves like fingernails on a chalkboard.

Caroline had given birth to her eldest daughter on the first day of summer in 1950. Naming her after the season had been a sudden impulse.

Caroline had expected a boy, to the point that she'd given scant attention to girls' names during her pregnancy. She'd had her heart set on a John, so much so that Matt had suggested Johnetta when Summer arrived. Caroline had frowned at him, then immediately dubbed her daughter after the season of her birth.

It was a perfect match. And while Summer was not exactly perfect, she possessed an inner strength rare for someone her age. She might have chattered incessantly, but the girl was more than talk. Her character matched her beauty.

Summer shared her mother's fresh complexion, but her hair, though thick and wavy like Caroline's, was the darker brown color of her father. Like all the children, she was slight of bone and muscle, but she showed signs of developing the curves of a woman, and her face was rounder and softer than the assorted collection of leaner looks that pervaded the family.

Sixteen months separated Summer from John in age, but they were miles apart in manner and habit. The second son of Matt and Caroline had inherited a love of nature from his grandfather and a silent disposition from some unknown ancestor. John was friendly, courteous and cheerful, never one for a long face, but he filled many of his hours in solitary communion with the land. He had crisscrossed the fields and woodlands countless times, inspecting plants, observing animals, seeking beauty. Once, in the late evening shadow of a towering pine, he had watched undetected as a bobcat came down to the Old Pond for a drink of water. Another time he had come upon a turf battle between a king snake and a rattlesnake. The snakes had tussled for several minutes, but gradually the king snake coiled around its opponent. Then, suddenly, the king had flexed and straightened, snapping the rattlesnake in half.

Even Sam, who had seen his share of wondrous moments in the woods, had been impressed with John's forest fortunes.

John was also the family artist, using crayons and pencils to create pictures that reflected his love of nature. Caroline herself had always been drawn to beautiful paintings, so she figured John's talents came from her side of the family. But his inspiration was truly a gift from Sam.

John definitely favored Caroline, lean in the face with hollow cheeks, tall and thin, with a mop of straight, dark brown hair, almost always too long, falling somewhere between the nearly black color of Matt's and the lighter shade of Joe's dark brown.

Carrie was their Christmas baby, born a day after the blessed event in December 1952, arriving fourteen months after John. She was easily the most enigmatic of the bunch, an awkwardly shy little girl who hid in the shadows around strangers and sometimes among friends. True to her birthright, Carrie seemed lost in the middle of the Baker brood, the one least likely to find her voice. She seemed fragile, like a sparrow, from spirit to body, which, though painfully thin, was blessed with abundant grace. Carrie had the lightest shade of brown hair in the family, but her light brown eyes sparkled in a special way.

The hard of heart dismissed Carrie as the plainest of the six Baker children, but she was not ordinary. She radiated gentleness, a quality that shown quietly in her eyes and in the way she cared for the family. Carrie would find her wings eventually and venture from the protective nest of her family.

Eighteen months separated Luke from Carrie, and another fifteen months stood between the youngest son and Bonnie.

Luke was the most rambunctious of the children, a six-year-old sparkplug waiting to ignite and often difficult to control once sprung to life. Bonnie was four, the baby of the bunch, a bit spoiled and still young enough to get away with it. Their looks and personalities were still developing, but Luke clearly favored his father while Bonnie resembled Caroline.

Different though they all were, there were obvious patterns and linkages among the six children. Most striking to Caroline was the pattern of personalities: bold and brash for Joe and Summer, turning quiet and tender for John and Carrie, to daring and engaging for Luke and Bonnie. She had no way of knowing, but Caroline felt certain that had she given birth to two more children, this double pattern of active and passive characters would have been completed.

Caroline was also struck by the rhythm of appearances. Joe and Summer were the different ones, obviously cut from the Baker mold, yet clearly distinctive from their brothers and sisters. John and Carrie favored each other the most, while Luke and Bonnie bore the closest resemblance to their parents.

As the children gathered around the table that morning, Caroline felt a keen sense of pride. She knew the Bible warned against those who would be too prideful, but God had given her this passel of children, blessing them with good looks and noble spirits. It was moments like these that caused a wellspring of grace to bubble over in Caroline, refreshing her faith and preparing her for the battles of the day.

She took a deep breath, allowing this invigoration to wash through her, cleansed like a repentant sinner on the last day of a tent revival. And then, smiling, she took her place at the table and delivered the breakfast blessing.

BY EIGHT O'CLOCK THAT morning, breakfast was a memory except for dirty dishes, and everyone was at work. Summer was dispatched to strip the beds and put on fresh linens. Carrie and Luke were sent outside: her to gather eggs and him to feed Pal-Two and the two barnyard cats—Tom, a wiry black male with a wide face and four white paws, and Bob, a feisty female tabby that had lost her tail as a kitten. Bonnie had done her best to stay underfoot of everyone else until Rachel put an end to the shenanigans. Now the little girl was standing on a chair beside the sink, happily rinsing the dishes her grandmother washed.

Matt was somewhere on the place with Lucas, cutting wood, hunting or goofing off if the mood struck him, while Joe and John helped their grandfather bag pecans.

With everyone busy, temporarily settled, Caroline sat down at the kitchen table to plan Christmas dinner, poring through a small sampling of her cookbook collection. She loved to cook and spent many of her leisure hours reading and rereading cookbooks and magazines for recipes. Holiday meals were her favorites, although she and Rachel invariably wound up preparing a traditional feast. Still, every Thanksgiving and Christmas, Caroline pulled out one special recipe that would give a distinctive flavor to the dinner.

Now and then relatives ate a holiday dinner with the Bakers, but those occasions were seldom these days. Rachel's sister, Euna, and her family had spent the most recent Thanksgiving with them, but they lived in Ocala, Florida, and Euna's grown children, who had families of their own, obviously wanted to spend the holidays at home. Rachel also had a sister-in-law, niece and nephew from her brother Alton, who had drowned in a boating accident several summers ago. But they rarely visited with each other anymore, only a little more so than Caroline did with the few distant cousins on her side of the family.

Sam had three brothers, two of whom were dead, and Caleb, who dropped in unannounced each year in late fall, bringing with him bags of grapefruit, oranges and tangerines. This year Caleb and his fourth wife had come calling the week after Thanksgiving, unexpectedly knocking on the door one afternoon with enough citrus fruit for a small army and staying only long enough to eat supper and breakfast the next morning.

Caroline sighed, recalling Sam's frequent contention that the Bakers were afflicted with the "orphan spirit," and began flipping through a worn copy of Betty Crocker's Picture Cookbook.

Christmas dinner this year would be an affair for the immediate family, which meant Caroline would have to curb the temptation to overindulge her culinary talents. With ten mouths to feed in one house, it was a chore to cook too much food, but Caroline was equal to the task. Her holiday meals were appreciated, too, even when they were served again on the day after the holiday. On the third day of leftovers, however, everyone complained. And on the fourth day, they mutinied and demanded something different, so perhaps her late start in planning this year's dinner would prove a blessing in disguise by keeping the feast to a bare minimum.

She began her list with the turkey, a twenty-pound bird at the least, and added the ham, which was hanging in the smokehouse for the occasion. She wrote down cornbread dressing and cranberry sauce, butterbeans, creamed corn and fresh turnip greens. Dessert necessities—pecan pie and spice cake—were added to the list, along with a loaf of pumpkin bread and sweet potato pie. Something was missing, she thought, frowning, then remembered candied sweet potatoes, another necessity for a holiday meal at the Baker table.

Caroline glanced up at Rachel. "How 'bout maken some chicken and dumplens for Christmas dinner, Ma?"

Rachel turned around, drying her hands on a towel as she considered the request. "To tell you the truth, Caroline, I don't really have a hen to spare for butcheren."

Caroline considered the quandary, then beamed. "That's no problem," she said. "Matt and I are goen into town this afternoon. I have to buy a truckload of groceries as it is, so I'll just add a hen to the list."

"Good," Rachel agreed, then asked as an afterthought, "What specialty have you got planned for us this Christmas, Caroline? It's gonna be hard to top that squash casserole from Thanksgiven."

"That's my little Christmas secret," Caroline teased.

"Mama, why are you smilen so big?" Bonnie asked suddenly, scrutinizing her mother with a scrunched face.

Caroline and Rachel laughed loudly. "Because your mama loves to cook and holiday meals are her favorite," Rachel answered, hugging the girl to her chest. She looked back to Caroline. "What's on the menu this year?"

Caroline read off the list of foods, starting to write again as soon as she finished.

"Don't forget my pear tarts and fruit cake," Rachel reminded her with a touch of indignation that her Christmas staples had been overlooked.

"I'm already putten them on the list," Caroline replied swiftly. "It wouldn't seem like Christmas without your fruit cake and pear tarts, Ma."

Rachel smiled broadly, appeased by the compliment, then turned serious. "I'll need a few things from the grocery store for the fruit cake," she said, putting a finger on her chin. "Let me think."

"Candied fruit?" Caroline started.

"Yes," Rachel agreed, taking over the list of ingredients. "Some candied cherries, pineapple and orange. Lemon peel if they have it. And the nuts, too. I thought I'd try almonds and walnuts this time, so pick up a bag of those, too."

"They're already on the list," Caroline confirmed, then added, "Grandpa'll have a fit if you don't put pecans in it."

Rachel nodded agreement. "I'm plannen to," she said. "I just mentioned the almonds and walnuts because we don't have any. I also thought I'd try fig preserves in it this year. And molasses, too. I want it a little darker than usual. What do you think?"

"Good idea," Caroline remarked. "It might spice up the flavor. That reminds me: How are we set for spices?"

"Let me see," Rachel said, walking to the cupboard. She opened the cabinet and began rummaging through its bottom shelf. "All that baken at Thanksgiven cleaned us out. We're low on everything. Nutmeg, allspice, cinnamon."

"I ordered cinnamon, pepper and vanilla extract from Amelia," Caroline said, referring to Amelia Carter, the wife of mercantile owner Dan Carter, who also sold

Watkins products and Avon cosmetics. "I also ordered some butternut flavoren," Caroline continued. "Amelia showed me a butternut cake recipe in one of her catalogs, and it looks scrumptious."

"What about the liniment?" Rachel questioned. "We're completely out."

"I did," Caroline replied. "And they also had some vanilla-scented shampoo that I got for Summer. She's starten to notice her looks, and I thought it might be somethen special for Christmas."

"That's nice," Rachel agreed. "Better add ginger and baken powder to the list."

Caroline wrote on her pad, then glanced at Bonnie, who had climbed down off the chair and was stretched out on the deacon's bench. "Don't tell Summer about the shampoo, Bonnie," she urged. "I want it to be a surprise."

"Why ain't Santa Claus given it to her?" Bonnie inquired.

"He'll bring her something else," Caroline assured her young daughter. "Course, the way I hear it, Santa's elves were sickly over the winter, and Christmas is gonna be slim pickens this year, honey."

"We'll need brown sugar," Rachel interrupted to change the subject. "And eggs, too," she added regretfully. "My layers can't keep up with the holiday demand."

"A couple of dozen?" Caroline suggested.

"I'll need eight for the fruit cake alone," Rachel replied, shaking her head. "I'd make it three at least, and if we don't eat eggs for breakfast the next couple of days, we oughtta have enough to get us through."

"Three it is," Caroline concurred, again adding to her list. "I also planned on maken a couple of cakes—coconut and burnt-sugar—but that'd be too much." She hedged. "But I could make them both and then give one away," she thought aloud.

Rachel agreed, smiling at her daughter-in-law's indulgence. "We might as well have a real nice fruit salad while we're at it," she suggested, caught up in the spirit. "We got all those oranges and grapefruit from Caleb. You could pick up some apples, bananas, grapes, cherries, a can of pineapple. We've already got pears and peaches that I canned in the fall. Top it with nuts and fresh cream. I've always thought a good fruit salad was a meal in itself."

"Fruit salad it is," Caroline beamed, writing down the ingredients. "Do we need anything else?"

"I think we stopped needen back when I mentioned pear tarts and fruit cake," Rachel answered dryly. "Probably even before that."

"You promised we could make Christmas cookies," Bonnie reminded her mother in urgent tones.

Caroline smiled. "We'll do it tonight, sweetheart."

"We're set then," Rachel said.

"For a feast fit for a king," Caroline concluded triumphantly.

————

Around mid-morning, Sam tied up the last bag of pecans and Joe hoisted it onto the scales. Sam adjusted the weights until they balanced, jotted down the poundage on his note pad and scribbled through a quick set of calculations. He grunted. "The Berriens got about nine hundred pounds per acre this year," he scowled. "That's worse than our orchard. We got nine seventy-five."

"But nut for nut, their pecans are meatier than ours," John pointed out, flopping over on one of the fifty-pound bags to rest. "They oughtta bring a better price."

"True enough," Sam replied. "I'll do some figuren tonight to see what price I need to break even."

"We've still got a deal, Grandpa," Joe said questioningly, reminding Sam of his promise to allow the boy to sell the season's final load of pecans.

"I'll make you an offer in the mornen," Sam said gruffly.

They were in a one-room barn, with a porch across the front. The barn was isolated on the southeastern side of the farm, stuck in a sheltering grove of hardwoods and pines. In summer, the barn served as a storehouse for cooked tobacco. Sam ran his pecan business from it in the fall and early winter.

The business gave Sam and Rachel an income independent of the farm, which Sam had turned over completely to Matt with the exception of the pecan orchard and half the cattle operation. Sam insisted on using the pecan money to pay taxes on the farm, and he paid the children to pick up the nuts. It was about the only money they earned all year.

Though the heart attack had curtailed his business somewhat this season, Sam was making a modest profit, and he had determined to use his success to reward Joe for the boy's hard work on the farm.

Tomorrow, Sam would make a deal with his grandson. But now he needed help from Joe and John to grind sugar cane in order to carry out his promise to the children to make one last batch of syrup. He slapped John across the rump. "If we're gonna make syrup today, I'd better make hay and grind the cane," he announced. "It just so happens that I need four strong arms to haul it out of the barn and help run the stalks through the mill. Are you boys up to it?"

"All right!" shouted John.

"Sure thing," Joe agreed.

A half hour later, Sam was pushing purple cane stalks through the electric mill, which purred softly as it pulverized the sugary shafts. The juice ran down a funnel, dripped onto a grating that strained out the bulk of impurities and finally emptied into a fifty-gallon drum.

The cane mill was set up across the road from the house, beneath one of two shelters flanking either side of the corncrib. Sam and Rachel had set up house in the one-room outbuilding years ago when their home burned to the ground. It had been cramped quarters for two adults and three children, but they had managed. Now the barn floor was piled high with the recent harvest of corn.

The last of the cane crop was in one of the front corners of the crib, and Joe and John were hauling the stalks to Sam. They were playing mostly, jostling back and forth and wrestling in the bed of kernels. As could be expected, John was on the losing side of these good-natured bouts. He was covered from head to toe with a filmy white dust but smiling broadly, and the picture reminded Sam of a time years ago when his boys had done the same thing on a cold December morning.

He took a deep breath, chasing away the melancholy, helped by the timely arrival of Amelia and Tom Carter across the way. They pulled up in a red sedan, the car hardly coming to a stop before Tom bounded out and headed across the road.

Tom was twelve, fair complexioned, thinly built, with a mop of golden hair. Though they were not related by flesh and blood, Sam felt a kinship with the boy.

Tom was the son of shopkeepers and merchants, but his blood boiled for the outdoors. He spent many hours, days and nights with the Bakers, a friend to all and to
Joe in particular, despite the two-year gap in their ages.

"Hey, Grandpa!" he called to Sam.

"Howdy, Tom," Sam returned. "How are you, Amelia?" he called a little louder to
the distinguished woman with a blonde bouffant who followed her son across the
road at a leisurely pace.

"Good mornen, Sam," Amelia drawled in a voice that was pure Southern belle,
distinguished by a no-nonsense clip. "How are you feelen today?"

"Fine and dandy," Sam replied as she reached him. "Just getten ready to make
one last batch of cane syrup. I'll send along a bottle for you and Dan."

"It'd be mighty appreciated," Amelia said. "And if you have any extra, you might
consider letten the mercantile sell it for you."

Another round of greetings interrupted Sam's answer as Joe and John came
around the corner, each with an armload of cane. "Mornen, boys," Amelia said.
"How's that leg, Joe?"

Joe stood on his good foot, shook the mending leg and smiled broadly. "Almost
good as new," he told her dryly. "The best leg money can buy and steel can hold
together."

Amelia laughed at the sarcasm. "The cast is comen off soon," Joe continued more
seriously. "Hopefully next week before school starts back."

"Good," Amelia nodded, politely returning her gaze to Sam. "What about my
offer, Sam?" she pressed him.

"You're a born deal-maker, Amelia, and a dear one at that," Sam answered. "But I
don't have enough this year. We'll use all the syrup and then some around here." He
gestured to the silver ladle hanging on the edge of the barrel beneath the grinder.
"Would you like a sip of juice?"

"No, thank you," Amelia replied briskly. "I'm in a hurry this mornen—maken
deliveries so all the fine women of this community can cook up a delicious Christmas
dinner and look pretty while they're doen it." Her tone settled. "I had some stuff for
y'all that Caroline ordered, and Tom's been badgeren us all mornen about comen
over here to make the syrup."

Tom had joined the boys in the corncrib, retrieving more cane.

"Dan had him worken in the store this mornen," Amelia continued dryly. "You
can imagine how happy Tom was about that." She looked past Sam to where the
hogs were rooting beyond the fence. "I keep hopen he's gonna want to take over the
business someday, but I have a feelen he won't ever take to it."

"Everybody's gotta do what they gotta do, Amelia," Sam said gently.

She nodded, shifted her gaze to him and smiled. "I suppose they do." She shook
her thoughts. "I need to run, Sam. Just send Tom home when you're tired of him."

Tom heard this last comment as he came walking up with his arms full of cane.
"But I'm spenden the night here, Mama," he reminded her somewhat urgently.
"Remember? I'm goen with Joe to sell the pecans in Albany tomorrow."

Amelia put a hand against her forehead, feigning shock. "How could I forget?"
she drawled. "That's all you've talked about for the last week." She turned to Sam.
"Are you sure it's all right if he tags along, Sam?"

"I don't see why not," Sam replied easily. "They'll have a good time."

"Okay then," Amelia agreed. "But Tom, you'll have to come by the house later this afternoon and get clean clothes."

"Yes, ma'am," Tom promised.

Amelia smiled affectionately at them all. "Bye, now," she waved quickly, a round of farewells trailing her walk back across the road to deliver the much-anticipated order of Watkins products for Caroline and Rachel.

When she was out of earshot, Sam checked the level of juice in the barrel, weighing it against the stack of cane by the mill. "That's enough, boys," he told them. "Why don't y'all take the cover off the kettle, and we'll get this show on the road."

The massive kettle, which also served to make sour corn mash for the hogs from time to time, was kept kitchen clean by Sam. It was made of thick, black cast-iron, suspended in the middle of an enormous brick casing with a chimney running up the backside. On the side of the brick structure was an iron door, similar to a steel forge, a reminder of the old days when a wood fire had been used to cook the syrup. Sam had modernized the cooker a few years back, installing a gas burner that gave him better control of the heating process.

Joe and Tom removed the canvas cover from the kettle, while John went inside the house to inform his sisters and Luke that the syrup-making was ready to begin. Sam ran the last cane stalk through the mill, switched off the machine and with Joe's help pushed the boom-suspended grinder away from the barrel.

He picked up the ladle, dipped it into the ugly greenish-gray mixture and raised a sampling of the juice to his mouth. His nose crinkled, and Sam licked his lips as Joe and Tom waited for him to render judgment. "Sharp with a sickly sweet twang," Sam announced with connoisseuric flare. "A flavor that truly can be enjoyed only by those lucky enough to have acquired a taste for it." He hesitated dramatically. "Sad to say, I am still not one of those souls."

Joe and Tom broke into wide grins. It was a perfect batch. Sam had never acquired a taste for cane juice, but he loved the syrup it made. The boys on the other hand loved the juice almost as much as the syrup, and they quickly took turns with the ladle.

"Grandpa," Joe said cheerfully, taking his second sip of juice, "if the day ever comes when you sample cane juice and decide you like it, well then ...." He hesitated. "Well then, I think I might just have to give raisins another try."

Sam laughed, appreciating the inside humor. None of the Bakers liked raisins.

At that moment, John stepped out on the front porch of the house. "Grandpa!" he yelled across the way. "Granny says to come on in and eat dinner before you start the cooken."

Sam looked from Joe to Tom, smiling faintly. "We have our orders, boys."

Matt and Caroline left for Cookville shortly after the noon meal, promising to be home for supper, anxious for time to themselves. They were cheerful setting out, but a difficult task lay ahead of them. It had been a bad year on the farm, despite a promising start.

Spring rains had come plentiful and crops had thrived early. But then, when the crops needed rain most, the skies failed them. Corn withered in the fields, peanuts failed to mature. Decent crops of tobacco and cotton spared the Bakers a full-blown disaster, but only barely. And even the pecan crop, which Sam counted on to pay taxes and give him and Rachel spending money, had responded with its worst yield in a decade.

As usual, the Bakers were strapped for cash.

Money, money, money. It sometimes seemed the bane of their existence, and truthfully, neither Matt nor Caroline cared much for it—as long as they had enough to feed the family and keep the farm in business, meet their debts and maybe put away a few dollars for a rainy day. The problem was, they rarely did.

Sam had paid an exorbitant price for the farm's first two hundred acres way back in the 1920s. There'd been second, third and fourth mortgages along the way, and they had bought another two-hundred-forty-eight-acre parcel two decades later, again paying premium prices. Those debts were paid in full now, but the accomplishment had left their coffers empty, still struggling to get ahead of their needs.

Matt was a resourceful farmer who shunned debt whenever possible. Most of his neighbors borrowed money in the spring to plant their crops, paying off the loan later in the year with the fall receipts. But not Matt. Each fall, when receipts were totaled and debts paid, he figured out the cash amount needed to plant next year's crop and put those dollars in a separate bank account that could not be touched until the spring. They lived off what was left from the season's profit.

As resourceful as he was, however, equipment needs sometimes forced Matt to swallow his pride and call on the Farmers and Citizens Bank of Cookville for a loan. Two years ago, he had borrowed for a new pickup, replacing the worn-out Ford that had been new shortly after the war. The loan had been paid in full this year, and Matt had hoped to pad their meager savings as well.

Instead, the unexpected had occurred in the form of hospital and doctor bills— first with Sam's heart attack and then with Joe's shattered leg. There had been no insurance to cover those high bills, forcing Matt to dip into the savings, and now there were no savings to fall back on in case something else unexpected occurred.

It was the same old story—land rich and cash poor—and Matt could trace back a million times to the root of the problem. Too much of their land lay idle, not by choice but necessity. Matt was a good farmer; he worked hard and his family supported him. But the Bakers were stretched too thin for labor, despite the best efforts of Matt, Sam and Joe.

Too often in the past, they had to pay hired hands, which ate up profits like black shank wilted tobacco. But as he and Caroline drove along the newly paved black top toward Cookville, Matt saw a glimmer of hope for the future.

The children were growing up, and soon they'd be able to do the work now farmed out to hired hands. And then, too, Matt saw the possibility of clearing more land for new fields. Joe was an excellent farmer, and the boy had a few more years at home before heading off on his own. John and Luke already showed an inclination for the work, and both seemed to have considerably more interest in the job than their oldest brother. Matt suspected as well that Lucas Bartholomew would welcome a steady job from March through November.

Of course, none of that helped with the current financial dilemma. They were still poor as an Oklahoma dust bowl. But they would get by this hardship, as they had done all the others, Matt thought, just as Caroline informed in taskmaster tones:

"We have to be practical this year, Matt," she began. "Maybe we can get a doll for Bonnie because she has her heart set on one. And surely there's some little toy that'll satisfy Luke. He hasn't asked for anything in particular, anyhow. Joe, Summer and John already have a good idea that Christmas means slim pickens this year. And even Carrie realizes Santa Claus has good years and bad years."

Matt listened carefully to his wife, knowing she made sense. They had to spend their money wisely. But Matt also knew that Caroline could turn practicality into a new definition for frugality.

"We can buy them each a big bag of candy, maybe a can of mixed nuts, too," Caroline persisted, her mind churning over a whole list of practical ideas as she talked. "No, on second thought, we don't even have to do that. I can get bags of nuts in the grocery store—Brazil nuts, pistachios, almonds, English walnuts, maybe some cashews—and we can put some of each kind in the stockens. They'll have a ball cracken them. You know how hard those shells are."

His wife's plans were even grimmer than Matt had anticipated.

"Whoa, Caroline!" he said stoutly. "Now, honey, I've given this Christmas a lot of thought, and I want you to think about it, too."

It was a true statement. Matt had spent the morning considering the perfect gifts for his family while chopping wood and hunting with Lucas. He'd come home from the expedition with a load of dead wood, nary a spent shell, and a slew of ideas for Christmas presents.

"I know money's tight," he continued. "And I know the kids need clothes, shoes and all that stuff. But remember, this is Christmas, Caroline, and it's about the only time they get gifts all year long." He hesitated, then continued softly. "I think they deserve a little better than the necessities, some candy and a few nuts that are hard to crack." He paused once more, looking hopefully at his wife. "Don't you?"

Caroline reddened, embarrassed by the grim Christmas she was ready to give her family. True, she did not want them so wrapped up in the material side of the holiday that they failed to take heed of the day's real meaning. But they were good children, deserving of the kind of thoughtfulness that Matt had in mind and she had neglected.

"You're right," she sighed.

"Now take Joe, for instance," Matt continued with not a disparaging thought about her shortsightedness. "He likes to read and lately he's taken to quoten me poetry by Robert Frost. Surely, we can afford a book of poetry for him. And John likes to color and draw. Maybe we can get him a paint set. I know for a fact Luke has his heart set on a toy tractor at the John Deere dealership, and like you said, Bonnie wants her doll. And surely there's somethen special Summer and Carrie have in mind."

Leave it to Matt to check her practicality, Caroline thought, proud to be married to this man who was strong and forceful when necessary, unafraid of tenderness when the moment required a softer touch. "Summer's talked nonstop about this pale-yellow satin dress she saw at Bishop's in Tifton," Caroline said thoughtfully. "It's pretty and a tad overpriced, but she could wear it for Easter, I suppose. And Carrie wants a watch. I don't know exactly why, but I heard her tellen Summer that's what she wanted for Christmas. That's expensive, too, but I guess since her birthday falls so near Christmas, we oughtta get her the watch."

"Let's do it then," Matt said happily. "We got all year to be poor, honey, so we might as well have a little bit of fun while we're at it."

Caroline rolled her eyes, but pure joy lit her face. "Might as well," she agreed.

––––––––

After dinner, Sam repeated the cane-tasting ritual for the other children, having earlier sworn Joe and Tom to secrecy about the first sampling. Joe orchestrated the moment perfectly, even reproducing his line about raisins, drawing a chorus of gags from his brother's and sisters. Then Sam announced grandly, "Shall we pour?"

With Sam guiding, Joe, John and Tom lifting, they tipped the drum on its side and filled the iron vat to the rim with the greenish-gray juice. Sam lit the burner, played with the flame for several minutes to adjust it, and then settled back for a long wait until the cane juice came to a slow boil, which would cause the skimmings—bits of fiber, waste and trash—to rise to the top of the kettle.

Summer and John dipped several mayonnaise jars into the vat, filling the containers with juice for sipping while the syrup cooked. The children loved cooking syrup, probably as much as eating it. Syrup-cooking days were an opportunity to idle away a few hours, listening to their grandfather weave outlandish tales. Their favorites were bodacious accounts of hook-handed pirates and fire-breathing dragons, all woven to explain how Sam had come to wear the black patch that shielded his left eye and partially covered a jagged scar stretching to the bridge of his nose.

Sam stood almost six-foot-two, solidly built but carrying little excess weight, especially since suffering the heart attack. His hair was silvery white, cropped short and high on the forehead by choice. His face was long, chiseled, with a jutting chin and sharp nose, roughened by a heavy shadow of beard. He was naturally dark, pigmentation descended from a great-grandmother who was full-blooded Cherokee. He had thick, ash-gray eyebrows, and his deep brown right eye seemed proportionally small for such an imposing man. Sam was handsome, but his face was marred by the black eye patch and wicked scar. The flawed face gave him the sinister look of a pirate who pillaged without conscience. But Sam was a gentle giant of goodness to those who knew him well.

Today, he would lose the eye while dueling with an evil knight to save a fair maiden trapped in a castle tower. Sam was set to begin his yarn when Joe broke ranks.

"I'll be back in time to help you pour up the syrup," Joe informed his grandfather.

"Just what's so important that you don't have time to sit and listen to my story?" Sam demanded to know.

Joe gestured to the woods behind them, where the hogs roamed. "There's a section of fence on the backside that Daddy wants mended before the hogs push through," Joe said naturally. "I wanted to get it done this afternoon since I won't be around tomorrow."

It was an honest answer to a degree. In truth, Joe knew the real reason Sam wore the eye patch. He had seen behind the patch. And while he still enjoyed the outrageous stories spun by his grandfather, sometimes his mood preferred to forego those tales of white-knight heroes and dark-souled villains.

"The fence could wait," Sam grumbled.

"Maybe," Joe agreed. "But then again, we could spend Christmas chasen hogs all over creation."

Sam huffed.

"Do you want to come with me, Tom?" Joe asked his blond-headed friend.

Tom was stricken with a look of disbelief. He gulped, then found his voice. "To tell you the truth, Joe, I'll stay here," he said sheepishly. "I'd rather cook syrup than fix fence."

Joe nodded his understanding. "Okeydokey," he remarked cheerfully, turning away from them. "See y'all later," he called over his shoulder.

Sam frowned, wishing Joe would learn to relax, wondering what drove the boy urgently forward. But he did not dally long with such musing because he had an eager audience for a story and a kettle of syrup to cook.

The children sprawled around him, finding seats where they could under the shelter. Summer grabbed the tractor seat, and Bonnie stretched out on the machine's hood. Luke and Tom settled on opposite sides of the front wheel axle, while John and Carrie hoisted themselves into clear spaces on the workbench. Sam took his usual spot, on a fat plug of firewood tucked against the back wall of the shelter. They passed around the jars of cane juice like bottles of whiskey, everyone taking a sip at their turn, even those who had not acquired a taste for the tangy mixture.

Sam was an adroit storyteller, weaving intricate plots of love and beauty, hate and war, action and adventure, good and evil. Today, he launched into a tale of evil knights and damsels in distress. The cane juice began to bubble like a witch's caldron, the impurities rising, covering the surface with a dirty white foam, and Sam horrified his audience by allowing the hero of the story to suffer the ignominy of having hot oil poured into his face from a castle tower. The children gasped, and Sam paused to tend the syrup, skimming away the dirty foam with a white net and then turning up the heat.

His tale went fast after that, recounting the hero's tortuous recovery, the climatic jousting battle to the death between the two knights and the good knight's rescue of a fair maiden. When the tale was finished, the children were drained from the tension, so they stared hypnotically into the boiling kettle, savoring the story.

In a while, Luke broke the spell. "Grandpa," he said seriously. "Have you ever gone to merry old England really?"

"Of course, he hasn't," Summer barked. "But you went to Paris, didn't you, Grandpa?" she continued smartly, giving Luke a hopeless look. "Don't you know anything, Luke?"

Sam shushed her, then turned to Luke, who was glaring with contempt at his sister. "Summer's right," Sam admitted. "I've never gone to merry old England, but I was in France during the Great War. I saw Paris, and one day I intend on goen there again with your grandmother.

"Paris is a beautiful city," he continued, launching into another story, this tale real and mellowed in his mind over the years.

He told the children about the Eiffel Tower, the Arc de Triomphe and the Louvre, about Notre Dame, Sacré Coeur and the Latin Quarter. He told them how the Seine River cut through the city and how a grotesquely masked man haunted the Paris Opera House. He told them about French wine, French bread and French women, whom he swore could not hold a candle to Rachel. The one thing Sam did not mention was the war, the reason he'd had an opportunity to walk the streets of Paris.

"Can I go with you the next time?" John asked eventually, dazed, sighing in a voice that broke the silence of another spellbound audience. "I'd like to go someplace besides Cookville, and Paris sure sounds nice."

Sam smiled at the boy.

"You're goen to Tifton the day after tomorrow," Bonnie reminded her brother, a little testily to show her dismay over John's apparent forgetfulness about their traditional Christmas Eve trip to town.

John rolled his eyes. "Anybody can go to Tifton, Bonnie," he said dryly.

"Well I bet the people in Paris don't even know where Tifton is," Carrie interjected defensively, for Bonnie's sake.

"She's got a point, John," Summer remarked pointedly, playing referee.

John shook his head, casting a disparaging gaze upon his sisters.

Tom changed his position on the tractor wheel and drained the last drops of cane juice from one of the mayonnaise jars. He wiped his mouth with the back of a hand. "Adventures sound fun," he commented, "but if I lived on a farm, I'd never go anywhere. I'd just stay put and be happy." He looked around at his friends. "Y'all are the luckiest people in the world to live here. I wish my folks had a farm."

"Oh, shut up, Tom," Summer remarked bluntly, sending him a withering glance. "That has absolutely nothen to do with what we're talken about." She caught a breath. "Besides, you're here on this farm almost all the time as it is. And besides that, your folks have a store. A store beats a farm by a long shot."

Tom bit his lip. Sometimes he wanted to slug Summer across the face. But he reminded himself that he was a guest and had to mind his manners.

"Nope, Summer, you're wrong," he said firmly but nicely. "A farm is loads more fun than a stuffy old store." He looked at Sam for confirmation. "Don't you think so, Grandpa?"

Sam sidestepped the question. "It really depends on the person," he said diplomatically. "Personally, I prefer the outdoors, but I can see where others might find that runnen a store has its advantages."

Summer and Tom put their feud on hold, temporarily at least, though neither one seemed satisfied with the answer. Still, the children launched into another round of bantering, and it soon became obvious to Sam that his storytelling skills were no longer needed.

From their chatter, the children moved on to games of touch football, tag and dodgeball, the time flying by in a whirl of fun. They were playing hide-and-seek when Joe came silently out of the woods, emerging at the gate a few yards from where Sam watched over the syrup.

"What happened to the troops?" Joe called from the gate, surprising his grandfather.

Sam glanced behind him, watching Joe unlatch the gate and step into the yard. "They got bored with the battle," he replied. "But they'll be back for the finale."

Joe pushed the gate closed. "Is it safe around here?" he asked teasingly, his eyes shifting from side to side. "Are the dragons slain and the maidens saved?"

Sam smiled. "We battled evil knights today," he replied. "And toured Paris." He returned to the syrup, giving it a quick stir with a long stick. "I suppose you're getten too old for my stories."

"Not at all, Grandpa," Joe said sincerely, hobbling over to the shelter. He leaned against a support pole. "I just really wanted to get that fence fixed today."

Sam sighed. "I suppose I sound like my feelens are hurt because you didn't want to hear my stories?" he said questioningly. "But they're not."

"You sure?" Joe asked.

"Absolutely," Sam replied lightheartedly. He gestured to the woods and asked, "Are you finished back there?"

"I had to come back for a few more staple nails and a shovel," Joe answered. "It was pretty ragged in a few spots, and there's a washed-out place that needs some dirt thrown over it before those hogs start tryen to root their way under the fence. We probably oughtta string some barbwire across the bottom to make them think twice about goen under instead of through it. What we really need is a brand-new fence, but I don't guess there's much chance of that with money be'en the way it is around here."

"'Fraid not," Sam agreed, staring hard at Joe, then turning back to the syrup. "You better get on and finish it up," he suggested tiredly. "It's turnen awful cold out here."

Joe blew a cloud of frosty breath. "Sure is," he agreed. "I'll be back in a jiffy."

His grandson headed across the road to retrieve the needed tools, and Sam watched him, wondering when their little boy had grown so tall and so old. Joe had been a carefree child, a smiling wonder, full of wholesome anticipation, bent on a bit of merry devilment. In one way, he was still the same boy. But there was some strong force lurking within him, something guarded and intense, hell-bent on achievement and responsibility. It bothered Sam, and he made up his mind to ....

"To do what?" he asked himself, aloud.

"Sir?"

Sam shook off the cobwebs and turned to the voice behind him, finding Joe already returned with the bag of nails and shovel in hand. "That was quick," he muttered. "You goen or comen?"

"Comen." Joe stepped closer, piercing his grandfather with a concerned gaze. "Are you okay, Grandpa?" he asked worriedly.

Sam nodded quickly, reassuringly. "I was just thinken," he remarked candidly. "About you, to tell the truth."

"What?" Joe inquired.

Sam shrugged. "There's somethen I've been wanten to tell you, Joe, ever since you went off earlier to fix that fence," he said purposefully. "Now, I don't want you to think hard on what I'm goen to say because that probably would defeat the purpose. But, son, you've got a whole life ahead of you to mend fences. And if the truth be told, Joe, no matter how hard you work at it, keepen up with the patchwork is a lifelong chore. So slow down a little and enjoy, son, because those fences are gonna always be waiten. And sometimes, chasen hogs can be fun—if you know what I mean."

Joe pursed his lips in serious contemplation, then grinned. "Stop and smell the roses—is that what you're tellen me, Grandpa?"

Sam considered the inference. "To steal a phrase—yes," he said emphatically. "It's good advice."

Joe smiled again, looking away, nodding. "Grandpa, I know I've been a little intense lately," he remarked frankly. "But when you get right down to it, most everything 'round here's been pretty intense for a while now. Once this cast comes off, though, things'll get back to normal. And I promise to be my old self." Joe paused, changing his tone to lighthearted humor. "Whomever or whatever he was."

He hesitated slightly once more. "But right now, Grandpa, with all due respect to your good advice and duly noting that roses are nowhere to be seen on this brittle December day, I am taken leave of this conversation and returnen to my fence. Because as Mr. Robert Frost says: 'Good fences make good neighbors.'"

"You're missen the point of the poem," Sam replied dryly.

"Yes, sir, I probably am," Joe shot back goodheartedly. "But it's not open for argument right now because I'm cold." He affected a pout. "And I want to finish menden my fence."

Sam waved him off. "Go on then," he muttered pleasantly.

"Thank you, sir," Joe said, pushing the gate open, turning back to Sam as he closed it. "How long till you're finished here?" he asked.

Sam looked at the boiling kettle. "It's ready for the floppen," he remarked. "I'd say about thirty, maybe forty minutes at the most."

"I'll be back in time to help you pour it up," Joe offered.

Sam nodded. "I rather figured you would."

Joe saluted and disappeared into the woods, leaving Sam in a better mood.

He increased the furnace heat again, bringing the thickened mixture up to flop on—but never over—the kettle's rim. Stepping from beneath the shelter, he called across the way to the children, who were now building tunnels in the hayloft.
"It's floppen time," he hollered.

Flopping was the final stage, the children's favorite part of the syrup-making process, except possibly for Sam's stories. Sam cooked the juice another thirty minutes until the gooey mixture turned a smooth, honey-brown color, and then extinguished the flame—about the time Joe came walking up to the gate for the final time.

"We're ready to pour it up, Joe," Summer told him, motioning to her brother with a syrup bottle. "Come on and give us a hand."

Joe considered the request, then shook his head in the negative. "Y'all don't need me," he assured her, walking toward the house, muttering something incoherent about roses to smell and things to do, leaving behind a confused bunch of young'uns and a smiling grandfather.

They watched him for a while, and then funneled the syrup into an odd collection of long-necked and wide-bottomed jugs. Afterward, they cleaned the kettle, reattached its canvas cover and carried a baker's dozen of bottles to the syrup house. When Sam closed the door, wedging the wooden block in the empty space between two logs, syrup-making was finished for another year.

———

Cookville was anchored by a red brick courthouse in the middle of the town square, surrounded by neat rows of prosperous shops on all four sides. There were Top Dollar, Super Dollar and General Dollar, all dime stores; two women's dress shops, two drugstores and two restaurants; four department stores, of which Coverdale's and Moore's were considered more exclusive than Kenwin and Allied; the Majestic Theater, the Farmers and Citizens Bank of Cookville, *The Cookville Herald* offices and a pair of rival law firms. A feed-and-seed also occupied the square, along with the furniture and hardware stores. Sitting off the square, in the four corners, were a gas station, a car dealership, a combined liquor store and pool hall, and the county jail.

Two grocery stores lay behind the south end of the square, and an assortment of other small businesses flanked out in any direction. The railroad—north-south and east-west lines—intersected at a depot on the east side of town, and beyond that intersection lay the quarters, where almost all of Cookville's colored population lived. The high school and hospital were on the north side of town; the funeral home on the west side; and the Farmer's Market on the south end. There were three sprawling tobacco warehouses, numerous churches and a myriad of housing styles intertwined amid the quiet streets.

Nearly everyone knew everyone else in Cookville. Gossip and other devilishness were rampant, as were neighborliness, good deeds and general caring.

All in all, Caroline felt she lived in a progressive community. The 1960 Census showed a slight decline in population for the county, but the General Telephone Company had just last Sunday hooked up service to the north end of the county, where the Bakers lived. A man had died from a rattlesnake bite at the Holiness Church a few months earlier, suggesting a backwoods character to some, but Cookville had voted overwhelmingly in favor of a female congressman a few weeks later, electing Iris Blitch to her fourth term.

Most important to Caroline, however, was that Matt stood solidly behind his community. He believed in shopping at home. The Bakers did most of their business in Cookville, a lot at the Carter's Mercantile in their own New River community and the rest on occasional trips to Tifton or Valdosta.

On this day, Matt and Caroline did business with reckless abandon, jingling the till of store after store, cramming their packages into the cab of the pickup before assaulting the next shop, sometimes together, other times by themselves. Their last stop was the grocery store, where Caroline spent a solid hour filling her holiday shopping list, which contained the staples such as flour, sugar and tea, in addition to the items needed for Christmas dinner. They spent a small fortune there, but lady luck smiled on Caroline and her name was one of three pulled from a hat in a chamber of commerce raffle for twenty-five-dollar gift certificates.

She and Matt were in the truck, ready to go home, when her husband suggested they stop by the fish market.

"Ma's cooken up those spareribs tonight," Caroline told him.

"That's okay," Matt said. "Anything we buy tonight will still be fresh tomorrow. And besides, I got an urge for oyster stew and fish roe. Maybe even a mess of mullet to go with it."

Caroline bit her lip and conceded her point. After the extravagance of the day, a few more dollars spent at the fish store would hardly matter. "Okay," she relented. "But don't get mullet. I'd rather have perch."

Matt grinned, caressing her shoulder as they drove. "We'll get both," he decided.

"Oh, brother," Caroline muttered with feigned sarcasm. But a few minutes later, they were on their way home with two pints of oysters, a pound of roe and enough mullet and perch to feed the family and then some.

It was dark as they drove, and Caroline was tired from the shopping and addled by the amount of money they had spent. She drifted into silence, staring out the window into the darkness of the passing woods.

"Come over here and sit next to me, woman," Matt demanded playfully, startling her from the silence.

She turned to him and found her husband wearing a grin bright enough to light up the truck. "What's got into you?" she asked.

"I'm feelen feisty and wanna nibble on your ear," he teased. "So come on over," he said again, gesturing to his side.

Caroline cleared a path through the packages between them and scooted beside Matt. She put one arm around his neck and ran a finger softly down the length of a sideburn.

"Wow!" Matt moaned. "You sure weren't doen anything like that nineteen years ago tonight."

Caroline pressed her lips against his temple. "I was tryen my best to be a proper young lady," she purred, allowing her free hand to rest high on his thigh.

"You were proper all right," Matt teased. "I love you better now that you're not so proper."

Caroline smiled and laid her head against his shoulder.

"How 'bout a Christmas carol?" Matt suggested at length, sensing her concern about the shopping spree. "I'll start."

"Okay," she agreed.

He started *Jingle Bells*, his deep voice ringing true and clear in the truck cab, and Caroline joined in on the opening verse. Before long, she sang with her heart. The Christmas spirit had come.

A WHITE SEDAN WAS parked in the front yard when Matt and Caroline arrived home from the shopping expedition. The new car belonged to Paul Berrien.

The house itself looked homey and inviting. Bright lights lit one of the side bed-rooms, while the Christmas tree emanated a pale glow from the living room.

The tree was a shapely cedar, cut from the Baker timber on an outing that Sam, Luke and Bonnie had undertaken in mid-December. Sam was responsible for pro-curing the family Christmas tree each year, and he turned the effort into a memo-rable day for the children. Most years, he took the entire brood. Sometimes, like this year, he picked a select group. For the children, the anticipation of whom their grandfather would select for the outing was more fun than being picked. There were never hard feelings because everyone understood their time would come—though Caroline suspected Sam had picked Bonnie this year because her young mind might have been unable to grasp the concept of waiting until next year.

Regardless, Sam and the two youngest Baker children had set out one chilly morning after breakfast, armed with a picnic basket full of fried chicken, deviled eggs, eggnog and five seedling trees. They had traipsed across most of the farm, with Sam pointing out a variety of evergreens—cedars and Virginia pines, all planted by him over the years for just such an occasion. The cedar—nine feet of standing fra-grance with a busy spread—had been the unanimous choice. They had chopped it down, stopped for lunch; then pegged the five seedlings and came marching home with the prize and any number of scratches from the tree's prickly needles.

Matt drove the truck around to the side porch entrance and killed the engine. "I guess Paul's trained to be sheriff now," he said, referencing his friend's just-completed orientation for newly elected sheriffs. "Do you think he's up to it?"

"It's not a job I'd want," Caroline replied, "but I imagine Paul's up to the task. Why do you ask? Surely you think so, too."

"I do," Matt confirmed. "It's just that you and I talked about a lot of things duren the campaign—whether Paul could win, what a jackass Bobby Taylor was, how ugly everything turned. But you never said flat-out whether you thought Paul was qualified for the job."

Caroline considered the notion. "I admit to haven a few doubts," she said. "It's quite a jump, goen from banker to sheriff. There's probably people more qualified, but I suspect Paul will do a crackerjack job of runnen things. Nothen much ever happens around here anyway. Right?"

"Not very often, that's for sure," Matt agreed. "And for Paul's sake, let's hope for peace and quiet over the next four years."

Matt and Paul were childhood best friends, and Caroline respected the privacy of their companionship. Even now, after she and everyone else had discovered the most terrible secret of their friendship.

The two men were an odd pair: Matt, a poor farmer struggling to make ends meet and thriving amid the battle; Paul, an unmarried heir to a small fortune and living proof that money could not buy peace. Matt was the commoner, Paul the aristocrat. But their friendship cut through the distinctions of rank and privilege and forged on basic instincts like trust and faith.

It was not unusual to see them walking the streets of Cookville—Matt in dungarees and work shirt, Paul in a tailored suit—caught up in conversation, laughing and solemnizing, cajoling and counseling, supporting and cautioning. They hunted together and, many years ago, had drunk liquor together as well, until the early morning Matt had stumbled home one time too many with whiskey on his breath. Caroline had met him at the door, holding a young Joe in her arms, and told Matt to choose between booze and his family. Her husband had never required another reminder of his priorities, and she had come to tolerate that once-in-a-blue-moon pool game that lasted deep into a winter's night.

The friendship had survived despite long odds, because of bonds formed in childhood. Paul's overbearing father, Britt Berrien, had hunted with Sam, and eventually their sons had joined them on the outings. Paul was older by two months, but they had been in the same classes at school, first at New River Elementary and later at the high school in Cookville—every year but the eighth and tenth grades when Britt had shunted his son off to military academies in Atlanta and Tennessee. World War II had carried Matt to Europe and Paul to the Pacific. Returning home after the war, Matt had joined his father on the farm, and Paul had embarked on a seven-year tour of duty at the University of Georgia, pledging a fraternity and earning degrees in finance and law.

Paul had returned to Cookville, engaged, bringing home a young sophisticate from Atlanta, a woman named Paige whose beauty was matched by her flippancy. He had taken one look at his bride-to-be in the vista of Cookville and promptly sent Paige home to Atlanta, the engagement broken.

Paul had floundered a few years, working in the bank under the tutelage of his domineering father. When Britt died, Paul had assumed the presidency of the Farmers and Citizens Bank of Cookville. He ran a tight ship, increasing the bank's assets, but never seeming to enjoy the task.

And then, the county's sheriff for twenty-eight years, Marvin McClelland, announced he would not seek re-election. The citizens thought it a good idea since Marvin had been bedridden for the past year, paralyzed from a massive stroke. And Paul seemingly found a purpose.

Seven men had coveted the sheriff's job, and the voters divided sharply in the Democratic primary, with Bobby Taylor and Paul winning spots in the runoff. The runoff campaign was sharp and bitter, carried out in late August over the three hottest weeks of the year, waged on racial overtones so crass and vulgar that Caroline still blanched when she recalled the harshness of it all.

Bobby had staked his position without mincing words, vowing "to keep niggers in their place" regardless of the yellow-bellied Supreme Court of the United States, ridiculing Paul as a member of the Kennedy crowd bent on the death and destruction of this great country. Paul had taken the high road, refusing to criticize his opponent, promising only to administer justice fairly and equally. Bobby had campaigned like a bull in passion, with hell-raising stump speeches and driving determination. Paul had relied on understated charm, toying with passion, falling back on the issues.

In the end, Paul emerged victoriously, earning the sheriff's badge and a blood-sworn enemy by a margin of ninety-eight votes. In November, Kennedy had carried the county by the slightly larger margin of one hundred fifteen votes.

All this played out in Caroline's mind as she carried the Christmas purchases into the house through the back door to Sam and Rachel's room, while Matt toted in the bags of groceries through the back porch. She needed three trips to complete the task, planning to move the packages to hers and Matt's room later in the night, then stuck her head in the kitchen, greeting Paul and her in-laws, before finally cutting through the bathroom to check on the children.

She found Luke and Bonnie planted on the living room floor in front of the TV, too engrossed in a Christmas special to acknowledge her greeting. The other children were in the girls' room, with Summer leading everyone through the paces of a new dance called the Twist. Caroline stuck her head in the door, intending to quiet them, but backed away from the commotion at the last second and simply pulled the door closed behind her.

Paul was recapping his two weeks of sheriff's training when she arrived in the kitchen. He sat in the tiny rocker with his back to the fireplace, long legs stretched comfortably in front, hands wrapped easily behind the chair. He was tall and muscular, an imposing man with carefully groomed black hair, striking emerald green eyes and the face of an aristocrat. He had the swarthy look of an Italian count and spoke with a cultured Southern accent. Dressed in charcoal slacks and a white button-down shirt with a black leather bomber jacket, Paul presented a vision of irresistible manliness.

Caroline noticed all this as she hurried around the kitchen, putting away groceries and completing the supper preparations.

She often wondered why Paul had never settled down with a wife. He'd had opportunities besides Paige. Women had flung themselves at Paul with regularity for years, but he'd given them only fleeting notice. Now it seemed all the good ones were married, raising families, and Paul was still a bachelor, spending what should have been the prime of life devoted only to his aging sisters.

Caroline shook her head in dismay. It seemed like the waste of a fine man. But some situations were never as straightforward as they seemed, and she knew it was wrong to cast doubt on lives she had no reason to judge—just because they differed from her idea of fulfillment.

She put those thoughts out of mind then, stuck a pan of biscuits in the oven and began to fill glasses with ice. "Paul, have some supper with us," she suggested.

"No, thank you, Caroline," he replied, sitting up straight in the rocker. "I got in late this afternoon from Atlanta, and June and April were already in the midst of preparen a homecomen dinner for me, so I'd better get on back. I just stopped by to give you folks a personal invitation to the swearen-in ceremony."

"We're plannen to be there," Matt smiled.

"With guns blazen," Sam teased.

Paul grimaced. "Just don't shoot the sheriff," he deadpanned. "I have it on good authority that while he's a man of impeccable character, his shooten skills are suspect."

He stood, telling them, "The ceremony's scheduled for three o'clock on New Year's Eve at the courthouse. My adoren sisters have planned a little celebration back at the house afterward, and we thought it might be fun to make it a New Year's

Eve party. They're gonna grill steaks and make eggnog, and I think they've even concocted some kind of pâté made with black-eyed peas." He paused. "For luck," he added, shrugging. "Anyway, we'll just have a good old time. And make sure y'all bring the children, too, because April and June are plannen a party for the ages."

"Sounds wonderful," Caroline said. "We haven't done anything special on New Year's Eve for years."

Rachel cleared her throat. "There is church, Caroline," she reminded her daughter-in-law. "It's kind of become a tradition to see the old year out and the new year in with prayer."

Caroline put a finger to her lips. "I completely forgot about that," she frowned.

"It's no problem," Paul said. "My sisters always attend the watch service, too. They're plannen our get-together for right after the swearen-in ceremony. That way, anybody who wants can attend church. Besides, I plan to be worken at midnight. It probably wouldn't look too good for the sheriff to be whoopen it up at a party his first night on the job."

"We'll be there," Matt announced.

"Good," Paul replied, stretching a kink out of his neck. "Well then, I should get on home and let you folks eat supper."

Caroline made an impulsive decision. She should have consulted Rachel first, but there wasn't time. "Paul?" she called as he eased toward the dining room. "Since y'all are goen to treat us on New Year's Eve, we'd be honored if you, April and June would join us for dinner on Christmas Day. Ma and I are cooken enough food for a small army, and it's just goen to be the family. We'd appreciate the company, if y'all don't have anything special already planned."

Paul considered the invitation. "That's kind of you, Caroline," he replied. "I'll have to check with my sisters, but it's safe to say we'll accept." He paused, then added warmly. "It's a nice thing, folks, haven good friends like y'all."

————

The Berriens lived in a stately Georgian mansion, secluded at the end of a private lane cut through the middle of a pecan orchard. The house sat far enough off the main dirt road that even in winter when the tree branches were bare, passersby could not glimpse it. Its isolation aside, both the house and its occupants were sources of great admiration and awe, of envy and jealousy, and all other of the noble and despicable feelings that the rich and privileged inspire in those of lesser means and position.

The rank and file took for granted that the Berrien estate was a safe haven from everyday problems. Matt knew differently. He was privy to the truth concealed behind the gracious contours of that red brick facade with its brilliant black shutters. He felt the tension mixed in with the mortar and knew better than most just which closets held which skeletons and which doors were best left closed.

Berrien roots stretched deeply into the history of Cookville, beyond the town itself to the days when this part of South Georgia had been wild and pristine, untamed by civilization, ripe for exploitation by men with means and vision.

James Berrien had been such a man, possessed of only moderate means but a cunning mind fertile for opportunity. James was a distant cousin of John McPherson Berrien, the "American Cicero," who rose to leadership in the Whig Party and had a Georgia county named in his honor. He settled in South Georgia in 1817, taking advantage of the Georgia Legislature's decision to sell four-hundred-ninety-acre lots for the bargain price of eighteen dollars. Within seven years, James had acquired more than ten thousand acres of land, planting the seeds for the vast family fortune now controlled four generations later by Paul Berrien and his two sisters, April and June.

Land ownership had been merely the edge of a goldmine for a savvy prospector like James Berrien. In the 1820s, he established government-chartered ferry services across the Withlacoochee and Little rivers, using the profits to set up trading posts on the Old Coffee and Union roads, the principle routes from the heart of Georgia to either side of the Florida coast. Those businesses thrived, and James expanded his empire into cotton farming and construction. He owned about one hundred slaves before the Civil War, and convinced county leaders of the need for a new courthouse and school, acquiring the building contracts for both.

His business acumen was bounded only by the venture's limit for profit, and, ultimately, his ability to cut his losses allowed the Berrien fortune to survive the Civil War intact.

In 1858, James got himself elected to the Legislature. Sensing the coming rift between North and South, correctly concluding the South would lose, James began divesting himself of slaves and sold off some four thousand acres of land for a bargain price of four dollars and twenty-five cents an acre. The land would be worth less than three dollars an acre after the War Between the States.

On January 9, 1861, James Berrien cast a "yea" vote as Georgia declared itself a free and sovereign state. But more important was a decision he had made a few years earlier to convert the bulk of his fortune into gold and other secure investments that would hold value regardless of the war. James and his son, Alexander, buried the gold in the middle of a vast grove of young live oak trees, and then Alexander went off to war, where he was killed at Gettysburg. When the war was over, James, then seventy-five, led his grandson, twenty-one-year-old Thomas, whose arm had been shot off in the Battle of Atlanta, to the oak grove and forced the young man to dig up the gold.

It was tortured work for a one-armed man, carried out while James lectured his grandson about the virtues of hard work and the toil necessary to sustain wealth, repeating over and over, "The price of success is high, but the reward is solid gold." When an exhausted Thomas finally retrieved the cache of gold, hoarded away in a pirate's chest, James promptly buried it again and then dug it up by himself. "Loyalty to your own flesh and blood comes without cost," he told Thomas. "Beyond flesh and blood, it's wise to count."

James Berrien was ruthless and overbearing, driven by steel wheels of greed and profit. He required loyalty, he tolerated ambition, and he trampled ill-conceived dreams. Thomas Berrien learned those lessons well from his grandfather.

In those first few years of Reconstruction, James and Thomas overhauled the family empire. They planted depleted cotton fields with vast acreage of pine trees, setting the roots for another fortune to be made in sawmills and naval stores. Of more importance, however, they used the gold to open a bank in Cookville.

James Berrien had come to the South from New Jersey, and the banking venture showed his carpetbagger colors. The Berrien bank extended credit to small farmers at criminally high interest rates, placed liens on money crops and then acquired ownership of the mortgaged lands when the crops failed to bring in the cash needed to make the payments. Within a short time, the Berrien estate totaled more than twelve thousand acres of land and an untold fortune.

In 1870, Thomas Berrien fathered a son, Littleton Albrighton, whom his wife called Britt for short. A short time later, James Berrien passed away at the age of eighty.

———

All these things ran through Matt's mind a few hours after Paul Berrien had taken his leave from the Baker home. A more detailed account of the Berrien family history could be found in the leather-bound volumes of journals tucked away on solid mahogany shelves in Britt Berrien's old study in the family mansion. The journals had been penned almost daily by four generations of Berrien patriarchs.

Matt had read some of the books with Paul, he'd heard other stories from June and April and from Britt himself. He had no idea whether Paul or his sisters continued to record the family history in the journals. Matt did know the records were incomplete, however, because he himself had stripped two pages from one of the books, history that revealed a secret Matt had sworn to keep hidden.

Like his father, Britt had learned well the lessons of greed and ambition. He had learned when to cut his losses, when to count the costs; and he had humbled a family of immense wealth, power and prestige to its knees, leading them to search for treasures more lasting and rewarding.

Britt cultivated the role of a blue-blood Southern aristocrat. Armed with a degree from the University of Georgia, he assumed control of the family fortune when his father died. He mined the pine trees like panning for gold, harvesting the first yields of timber to put his sawmills in business and tapping the naval stores for tar, rosin and turpentine. He also recoined the reputation of the Berrien bank, changing its name to the Farmers and Citizens Bank of Cookville and bringing a sense of fairness to its profiteering practices.

The banking moves proved popular with the forgiving citizens of Cookville, as did his philanthropic gesture to pay for the construction of a new library in the growing town. In appreciation, county leaders voted to build new schools with Berrien timber, and voters elected Britt to the Georgia Legislature. In between, Britt hemmed his way deeper into the commerce of the community, establishing hardware and farm supply businesses that prospered like all the other Berrien ventures, until the family wealth multiplied with almost every cash exchange in the community.

By then, with his parents dead and no siblings to share the wealth, the family fortune belonged entirely to Britt. So he set out to acquire a family.

He began by building the family home, erecting a three-story mansion in the middle of the oak grove where the Berrien fortune had resided during the Civil War. He spared no expense on the house, importing the finest construction materials and hiring the best architects, builders and landscapers. The house contained six spacious bedrooms, a sitting parlor and formal living room, a library and sewing room, an eat-in dining room and formal ballroom, and an enormous kitchen with two pantries. There were Greek archways and tapestries on the walls, an expansive marble staircase swirling up three flights and elegant chandeliers hanging from the ceilings.

The grounds mirrored the magnificence of the house, which was designed to accommodate the natural beauty of the site. Sitting in the middle of a lush three-acre carpet of grass, the house was framed on its right side by a majestic live oak that anchored the grove of trees swirling away in all directions on the backside. The left side and front of the house were free to soak up the sunlight, spaciously landscaped with flower gardens and dotted sparsely with hardwoods. The guest cottage set off the left corner of the entrance lane, where the road split into a circular drive around the house.

In his thirtieth year, when the house was ready to be decorated, Britt made his annual pilgrimage to Atlanta to represent his constituents in the Legislature and, in the course of duty, plucked up one of the city's leading debutantes as his bride. Britt simply swept young Alice McMillian off her pretty feet. After a brief courtship, they married in a grand ceremony at the First Baptist Church on Peachtree Street and then whisked away to a month-long honeymoon at The Cloisters on Sea Island, followed by a two-month tour of Europe to satisfy a lifelong desire of the new bride.

When the honeymoon was officially over, Britt carried Alice back to Cookville and installed her as the lady of his grand house. Two days shy of their first anniversary, Alice gave birth to the first of two daughters. They named the child April. Two years later when their second daughter was born, she likewise was christened for the month of her birth, June.

Alice McMillian Berrien played the role of doting wife to a Southern aristocrat with skilled perfection. She opened her heart and home to the backwater community, throwing fabulous parties, organizing hunting expeditions, creating an atmosphere of dignity and respect. Invitations to these grand parties and vaunted hunts became highly sought prizes, with governors, congressmen and diplomats dancing in the elegant ballroom, sipping expensive wines and feasting on the most succulent foods.

In those first years of marriage, Britt and Alice combined deep affection for one another with a sense for style to create a state of wedded bliss. They enjoyed each other's company and found common ground in the care of their two young daughters. Then, for whatever reasons, they drifted apart as their daughters grew older. Alice tired of the constant entertaining, while Britt threw himself deeper into the pursuit of fortune. It was both shocking and pleasantly surprising when Alice Berrien became pregnant for a third time late in life.

April and June were away at college, and Britt had high hopes the new baby would restore zest to the marriage. It was not to be. The pregnancy proved torturous for Alice, and she died shortly after giving birth to Paul, the son Britt had wanted so badly.

Everyone grieved over the loss of the splendid woman, but they took solace from little Paul. There would be a man to carry on the family name.

With their mother dead, April and June abandoned their gay college life at the University of Georgia and returned home to care for their newborn brother. After a proper period of mourning, the Berriens once again opened the doors to their home and resumed the festive lifestyle that Alice had pioneered with sophisticated elegance.

April and June tried valiantly to return a halo of greatness to the Berrien mansion, but their mother's ghost doomed the effort. The luster was diminished, and the Berrien sisters simply lacked the polish necessary to restore it. Matters were not helped any by their father, who became abrasive, reclusive and more domineering than ever of his family, and increasingly ruthless in his business dealings.

Neither April nor June were beautiful like their parents, but a fair share of suitors called on both women. In turn, Britt rejected each and every one, some with calculated indifference, others more rudely. He seemed determined that his daughters would spend their youth locked inside the beautiful house, caring for the child whose life had exacted such a heavy price from the family.

April and June harbored no resentment toward Paul. They loved their brother, caring for him as if he was their own child, protecting and nourishing the little boy with tender hearts and patient skills. Mutual bonds of devotion developed between the siblings over the years as they dwelled under the heavy hand of Britt Berrien. But in her twenty-eighth year, June grew weary of the isolation.

Headstrong and smart, June stood up to her father, informing Britt that she could no longer tolerate the life of the idle rich. Against her father's wishes, she obtained a teaching position at New River Elementary School, where she met Calvin Moore. He was a robust man, six years her junior, who taught history and science to the upper grade students, and passion and romance to June. They fell in love and Calvin asked June to marry him at the end of the school term. Britt was livid when June announced her engagement. He condemned Calvin as a money-grubber in search of a quick fortune and vowed to disown his youngest daughter if she went through with the wedding.

June thumbed her nose, defying her father once more, and married the man she loved. They rented a tiny house in Cookville and lived happily off the poor salaries of schoolteachers. She and Calvin had three wonderful years together before one fall night, after working late at school, Calvin drove his car off the sharp curve below the Carter Mercantile. The car slammed into a pine tree and burst into flames. By the time a passerby came upon the wreckage, Calvin had crawled from the car. But he was burned severely and died before help could be summoned.

June was shattered by the loss of her beloved, and Britt immediately pulled his daughter back under the protective family wing. He resigned her teaching position, renewed her maiden name and sent her to an Atlanta sanitarium to recuperate from the shock. June returned home a few months later, resigned to her fate, fully devoted once more to her family, and contented with positions in social clubs and occasional stints as a substitute teacher.

April also rebelled against her father. She married on a whim to a traveling encyclopedia salesman, a man who did indeed see her as an opportunity to gain a fortune. It happened at the beginning of the Great Depression, and the marriage lasted only a few weeks before April realized her mistake. Embarrassed by her poor judgment but not enough to spend her life with the miserable man, April sought her father's help to have the union annulled. The ensuing gossip had lasted slightly longer than the marriage. Now few people remembered the man.

By the time the Great Depression took hold, gloom hung as heavy over the Berrien home as it did on Wall Street. The festivities and frivolity that once had transformed the house into a beacon for the socially prominent were retired to a bygone day and in their place, arose a prim and proper politeness. In time, the world began to think of the Berriens as reclusive and standoffish.

It was his friendship with Paul that allowed Matt into the house where others seldom went in those days.

On a muggy evening in August 1941, Matt came to the mansion in search of his friend. Unable to summon anyone to the front door, he strolled around back and came upon Britt Berrien. Britt was standing on the verandah, staring vacantly off into the darkened grove of ancient live oaks behind the house, oblivious to the visitor to his home.

The massive oaks—a few with crown spreads of more than one hundred fifty feet and trunks exceeding thirty feet in girth—provided a buffer between the house and the gentle-flowing New River. The back of the mansion—antebellum in style with six towering Greek pillars and a balcony, painted dazzling white with black shutters—contrasted sharply with the graceful lines and red brick facades on the front and sides of the house.

It was about eight o'clock when Matt arrived, and a full moon bathed the grounds. Matt noticed a half-empty bottle of Scotch on the porch railing, and ice rattled in a glass, which the old man lifted to his mouth and drank from greedily. A chill ran through Matt that not even the hot evening could warm.

It had been a brutally hot day, the kind that made dust lazy and baked the countryside to a point where even nightfall failed to bring cool relief. Crickets chirped wearily, a whippoorwill cried its lonesome tune in the distance and fire-flies darted beneath the canopy of towering oaks, streaking the evening with their reddish glow.

Matt stood perfectly still for a moment.

Ice clinked again as Britt drank deeply once more, then set the empty glass beside the Scotch bottle. The old man unbuttoned his shirt, a clumsy attempt to seek relief from the heat, and Matt realized Britt had consumed more liquor than usual. He turned away, intent on leaving, but Britt sensed the movement.

"Who's there?" he demanded to know, bracing a hand on the porch rail to steady himself. "What do you want?"

Matt detected a slur in the questioning voice, concluding with certainty that Britt was drunk. "It's just me, Mr. Berrien—Matt Baker," he answered. "I stopped by to see Paul. Didn't mean to disturb you."

"Oh," Britt mumbled. "Paul's not here, Matt. He went with April and June to prayer meeten over at the church." He paused, then exhaled a short bitter laugh. "Imagine that," he muttered with a touch of sarcasm. "Prayer meeten. I don't have much use for prayer meeten myself. Matter of fact, I don't have much use for church at all."

Britt had not always held such a low opinion of church. He and Alice had attended Benevolence Missionary Baptist Church faithfully until she died. But after her death, Britt's church appearances became increasingly rare until he finally stopped attending. Still, he insisted April and June attend Sunday services, and he made sure Paul accompanied them. Although his absence puzzled the congregation, church members consoled themselves with the gratitude that his contribution to the collection plate remained intact.

"How do you regard church?" Britt asked Matt a moment later.

"Can't say I have anything against it," Matt answered quickly, stepping to the edge of the verandah. "I try to make Sunday services. That keeps Ma happy."

"Yes, indeed," Britt replied, forcing a laugh. "Children must keep their parents happy."

He picked up the Scotch bottle, then stumbled across the porch, fell into a wicker rocking chair and motioned Matt to sit in a duplicate rocker beside him.

Matt wasn't sure whether he felt compelled to accept the invitation or just down-right curious to see where the unexpected encounter would lead. Regardless, he covered the distance across the verandah and took a place in the comfortable rocker.

"Would you like a drink?" Britt inquired, offering the bottle of Scotch. "I'm out of glasses and ice, but you're welcome to tip the bottle."

Though partial to Scotch, having sampled it with Paul on several occasions, Matt shook his head. "No, sir—none for me."

Britt frowned, then withdrew the bottle. "Well, I'm goen to have another one," he decided, pouring the tumbler half full of liquor.

Sweat glistened on the glass, and the warm liquor melted the last shivers of ice as it ran into the tumbler. Britt sipped from the glass, and some of the Scotch spilled over the rim, dripping onto his chin while watery beads from the glass trickled down his chest.

Matt turned away in disgust, frowning over his decision to stay, fixing his gaze straight ahead into the monolithic grove of oak trees. The whippoorwill was still calling its lonesome song in the distance. Somewhere closer by, an owl hooted an answer. Matt scanned the trees in search of the owl, and in that single moment, his perception of the Berriens changed forever.

"He's not really my son," Britt Berrien mumbled.

Matt shot his gaze over to the man beside him. "Sir?" he asked, certain he had misunderstood the intended message.

Britt glared back at Matt. "Paul is not my boy. I raised him, but he's not mine."

Britt looked away, dazed by his admission, once again seemingly oblivious of Matt.

"Maybe I should go, sir," Matt said after a moment, rising from the rocker. "I'd appreciate it if you'd tell Paul I stopped by to see him."

"Don't go!" Britt commanded, cutting his gaze to Matt. "I've just told you that Paul came from another man's loins. That's quite a secret to share, Matt. Give me the courtesy of hearen whatever else I might have to say about the situation."

His better judgment warned Matt to walk away from the drunken man and forget this moment. Curiosity again swayed him to stay. Matt sat down rigidly, his hands locked on the arms of the rocker. Then Britt told a story that had bound Matt to a secret only slightly less sacred than his marriage vows.

Britt explained to Matt that he had decided to marry Alice McMillian before falling in love with her. They met at a fashionable party in Atlanta, where he had gone purposefully in search of a wife. Alice had been the belle of the ball—a perky young woman schooled in the social graces, yet sarcastic enough toward her high society lifestyle to appeal to Britt's basic instincts. Britt cut in during the first dance, and they married a few months later.

"She was the genuine thing back then," Britt told Matt. "Unlike any woman I'd ever known, and quite a step up from the whores I saw. For the first time in my life, there was a person I felt at ease with, someone I didn't have to put on airs for. Hell, I couldn't even do that with my own mama and daddy."

As partners in marriage, Britt and Alice lived the high life for several years. Each grand party, every organized hunt, even the ladies' luncheons added another element to their happiness, and the birth of two adorable daughters raised the heights of marriage to yet another dimension. There should have been a fairy-tale ending to the story, but gradually, Britt and Alice became bored with the bliss. He reverted to his petulant self, she tired from the strain of trying. Within a few years, the couple had little in common beyond their children. For the sake of their daughters, Britt and Alice kept up appearances. But when first April and later June went away to college, their parents stopped pretending and retreated to their own worlds.

"We barely took meals together, much less shared a bed," Britt explained to Matt. "To say I was shocked when she told me of her pregnancy would be a gross understatement. I was positively stunned. I was fifty-three-years old, she was past forty and we slept together maybe once in a blue moon. After the shock wore off, however, I got excited about haven a new baby. I'd always wanted a son to carry on the family name, and somethen told me this baby would be my boy. I did my best to make Alice a part of my life again. But the more I tried, the colder she grew toward me. Finally, I chalked up her attitude to the pregnancy. She had a hard, hard time carryen Paul. She vomited constantly and when she wasn't thrown up her guts, she felt on the verge of it."

About a month before the baby was born, Britt returned home late one night and found his wife sprawled on the parlor floor. He first thought she was unconscious, rushing to her side only to spot an overturned bottle of bourbon beside the sofa. He smelled her breath, which reeked of alcohol, then promptly shook her awake. Groggy at first, Alice soon snapped to attention as Britt berated her.

In the midst of Britt's tirade, Alice grabbed the empty liquor bottle and hurled it at her husband. The bottle glanced off Britt's temple, then crashed and broke against a marble-topped table.

"I could have killed her at that moment," Britt told Matt in emotionless tones. "Just wrapped my hands around that delicate throat and choked the life out of her. But in a way, that knock on the head brought me back to my senses, made me realize somethen serious was wrong and Alice needed my help."

Britt forced down his anger, tried to reason with his wife and explained he was concerned for her well-being and their unborn child. "Maybe I haven't been a good husband," he told her patiently. "But I want to make you happy again, Alice. I want our baby very much. I'd like a son, but another girl would please me to no end."

His admission seemed to shock Alice back to her senses. She looked at him curiously. "This child really does matter to you?" she remarked questioningly.

"It means the world to me," Britt replied sincerely.

Alice smiled sweetly. "Well Britt," she said, speaking slowly. "I'm delighted to hear you feel such tenderness for this baby, especially when it isn't even yours. It's my fondest hope that you'll feel the same way as the child grows up under your protective care, with not even an ounce of precious Berrien blood coursen through its veins."

Britt glared at her, refusing to believe the admission. "What do you mean, Alice?" he demanded harshly.

"It's quite simple," she said flippantly. "Affairs, Britt, darlen. You didn't really think all that fun outside the marriage bed was yours exclusively, did you? I had myself one, too. A humdinger. And now I'm haven another man's child. What about you, Britt? Do you have any bastard children that I should be aware of?"

Britt slapped her then, hard across the face, the force of the blow tumbling Alice across the floor.

"I started to beat her senseless," Britt told Matt, "but I'd never been the kind of man who hit women, certainly not one who was pregnant. And too, that one slap brought Alice back to her senses. She got scared then, realized she'd made the mistake of her life. She apologized, got right down on her hands and knees and begged my forgiveness." He paused, then added in a whisper, "But I didn't forgive her. Then or now."

Britt hesitated, remembering, collecting his thoughts, then took another drink, this time straight from the bottle.

"I was never an easy man," he continued. "But I never knew just how cruel I could be until that moment." He snorted, a bitter laugh. "I had this woman on her knees, beggen me for forgiveness, sayen I could have any woman I wanted whenever I wanted, promisen she'd be good, be at my beck and call. Just to please let her live out the rest of her days in peace, and she'd do anything I asked.

"It was pitiful," Britt sneered. "Truly pitiful. A disgrace to the way she was raised. But I promised anyway to raise her bastard as my child. And I made a vow that our daughters would never take up her whorish ways or become the despised woman she had become. Then I told her to pack her bags because as soon as she had the baby, I planned to send her to a sanitarium for a long stay.

"Just the slightest mention of a sanitarium sent her over the edge," Britt recalled, now speaking in monotone. "Alice had an aunt who was sent away to some mental hospital, where she went from be'en merely loony to crazy as a bat. That the same thing might happen to her was Alice's worst fear comen true."

With his pregnant wife collapsed in a heap in the middle of the parlor floor, Britt simply walked away from Alice and retired to his room. Over the next few weeks, Alice tried to atone for her mistakes, but Britt rebuffed his wife. He continued dropping cruel hints about a sanitarium, going so far as to falsify a court order committing Alice to the state hospital in Milledgeville. He presented the document to her along with breakfast in bed one morning a few weeks before the baby was due; Alice went into labor a short time later.

The labor was tortuous, life-threatening, a sharp contrast to the ease of her first two deliveries. But Alice gave birth to a perfectly healthy son, which the doctor presented to Britt as "a chip off the old block." Sometime later that night, Alice Berrien began to hemorrhage. By morning, she was dead.

"I should have felt somethen when Alice died," Britt told Matt in a wistful tone. "But really I didn't. Unless maybe it was for the best. I don't think I would have sent her to a sanitarium, although she was surely certifiable. But it would have been almost impossible to live with her.

"Anyway, I raised Paul as my son. Promised I would, and I did. It's not his fault he's a bastard—and I'm proud of him in a way, even though he's soft just like his real father was."

Britt hesitated, then laughed contemptuously. "It's ironic, though," he commented. "Paul believes I resent him because his mother died given birth to him." He shook his head, marveling at the thought. "He truly believes I loved her that much."

Britt leaned forward in the chair and shook away this last thought. "My daughters are very much like their mother was when I first met her," he remarked proudly. "They are kind and gentle and sympathetic. Happy souls." He paused to ponder. "But they are not innocent," he continued in a sad tone. "I made them anything but innocent. Made sure the children paid for the sins of the parents."

Exhausted, Britt stood, shuffled forward to the porch edge and leaned against one of the massive white columns, staring up at the white moon hanging low over the oak grove.

Matt rose as well, crossed slowly to the end of the verandah and stopped, sensing something else must be said on this night.

"Matt, you be a good friend to Paul," Britt added quietly, still gazing up into the nighttime sky. "He needs good friends."

Matt nodded in silent agreement, but his answer went unacknowledged. He walked away from the house, carrying with him the one secret he would never share with anyone, leaving behind its teller, a man who continued to stare into the darkness for many nights to come.

———

Matt heard Caroline call his name and roused himself from the battered recliner. He crossed the living room to stand beside the space heater, soaking up the warmth, thinking of another secret involving Britt Berrien.

Matt had taken this second secret into confidence seven years ago, on the cold night that Britt stuck a pistol into his mouth and pulled the trigger.

Paul had found the body, stiff from rigor mortis, still sitting in the white wicker rocker on the verandah. He had sought out Matt a short time later, and they had calmly, carefully, taken every possible step to conceal the cause of the death. They had loaded the body into the back of Matt's pickup, scrubbed away the blood stains on the verandah and dumped the ruined rocker into the depths of New River.

Next, Paul had placed a call to an old friend, Arch Adams, the county coroner and owner of the local funeral home. Reluctant to go along with the scheme at first, Arch finally agreed to rule the death a heart attack, falling prey to Paul's persuasive argument to spare his sisters the trauma of knowing their father had committed suicide.

The three conspirators had guarded the secret closely over the years, but ultimately, they had been powerless to conceal the true nature of Britt's death. Now everyone knew. And with the knowledge came stained reputations and painful reconciliation with the past. Still, they had all survived the accusations, outlasted the innuendo and perhaps learned a lesson as well.

Of course, Matt himself carried another secret from that night, the final thoughts of Britt Berrien, which the man had entered into one of the leather-bound journals a short time before taking his own life. Matt had found the book in the grass beside the verandah. Those last two pages had contained a soulless account of the circumstances surrounding Paul's birth and Alice's death. The words made for harsh reading, and, at the time, Matt had deemed it pointless to expose his friends to anymore unnecessary pain. Uncharacteristically, he had taken it upon himself to shield his friends from the truth, ripping out the last two pages and returning the journal to Britt's study. The next morning, in the comfort of his own home, with Caroline and

Rachel preparing breakfast, while Sam sat at the table reminiscing about their dead neighbor, Matt had stood in front of the kitchen fireplace with his back to them and tossed those two pages into the roaring fire.

He and Paul had never talked about that night. And Matt had discussed it with Caroline, his parents and the children only once, back in the summer when circumstances compelled him to give them answers to the gaggle of questions that cropped up in the heat of the moment. They had listened to his explanation, believed him and put the incident in the past where it surely belonged.

From time to time, Matt questioned the wisdom of his decision to conceal Britt's last words, fretting he had overstepped the bounds of friendship with censorship of the truth. Occasionally, he even wondered whether Paul somehow knew the truth about his heritage. But when those moments occurred, Matt tried to follow the sage advice of his mother and leave the past in the past, which was what he did now as Caroline called him again to join his family in the kitchen.

He stepped away from the heater, warmed to the bone, and went into the kitchen, where the delicious smells of fresh baking assaulted his senses.

The kitchen table was covered with an assortment of merry Christmas cookies, smelling of cinnamon, oatmeal and peanut butter, shaped as wreaths, bells, stockings, Christmas trees, reindeer and Santa Clauses. There were plates of molasses cookies and gingerbread men, along with a tray of frosted, nut-filled bonbons.

Matt stood at the door, inhaling the aroma, basking in a moment of fulfillment. Summer handed him a gingerbread man, and Matt bit into the spicy brown bread, savoring every mouth-watering morsel. He rubbed his stomach to show his appreciation, then began a round of sampling. Eventually, he made his way to the side of the kitchen where Caroline was beating a bowl of cookie batter.

"I'm in my element here," she told him.

Matt nodded in agreement, wrapping his arms around her waist, kissing the nape of her neck and pressing against her. "Tonight," he whispered, as his wife pushed gently back against him.

JOE RESTED AGAINST A stack of empty burlap bags in the pecan barn, vaguely aware of the dull ache in his knee. He supposed he had overworked the leg, but the thought, like the pain, was not at the center of his mind. He watched intently as his grandfather scribbled calculations on a notepad, waiting for the deal that Sam would offer.

Outside, the rear of the pickup sagged under the weight of the pecans, sacked and bound for the trip to Levine's Pecan Warehouse in Albany. Joe, Lucas and Tom had loaded the pecans and the trio would make the journey—Lucas to drive, Joe to negotiate the sale and Tom to offer support. Once the pecans were loaded and Sam began his calculations, Lucas and Tom had retreated outside to allow the dealmakers privacy. Joe could hear them talking, though, and he knew they were eager to be on the way to Albany. So was he.

Joe saw this venture as an opportunity to prove—if not his manhood—then his capability. And while money rarely mattered to him, he needed the cash as well.

Sam cleared his throat, circling three figures on the paper. He fiddled with his eye patch and looked at Joe. "Here's the deal," he announced as Joe straightened and pushed away from the burlap stack.

"I need twenty-five cents a pound to cover my expenses and make a slight profit on the side," Sam said briskly. "These nuts ought to sell for at least twenty-eight or twenty-nine cents a pound. My offer is that we split fifty-fifty anything above twenty-five cents. Anything you sell above twenty-nine cents is all yours."

Joe ran a set of calculations in his head, deducing he should earn a minimum of forty-eight dollars from the deal if the pecans sold for twenty-nine cents a pound.

"You also pay Lucas for his time," Sam added.

"How much is that?" Joe asked.

"Your daddy pays him seven dollars a day," Sam answered, pausing to watch Joe rub his jaw and mull over the offer. "Fair enough?" he finally questioned.

Joe stuck out his hand, smiling broadly. "Deal," he answered as they shook hands. "And thanks, Grandpa."

———

It was a ninety-minute trip to Albany in the pickup, and the warehouse was packed with sellers when they arrived. "Everybody wants some Christmas jingle," observed Lucas, watching as young and old alike stood in line with various shapes of buckets, pails and sacks waiting to have their pecans weighed.

Joe, who was using the crutches to ease the pressure on his knee, took a place in line, watching as the warehousemen weighed pecans and dumped the nuts in various bins marked for improved varieties and seedlings. Other workers bagged and tied one-hundred-pound sacks of pecans, which were stacked to the rafters in piles across the warehouse floor. In a nearby corner, four machines worked methodically cracking the nuts. His attention glued to the commotion, Joe failed to hear the first summons for his pecans until, finally, the warehouseman tugged on his crutch.

"Hey, buddy, I ain't got all day, and neither do all those folks behind you."

Joe turned to find the speaker was a sandy-haired boy not much older than himself.

"So?" the boy pressed impatiently, sneering. "You got any nuts or not?"

A few feet away, Lucas and Tom snickered at the remark's snide implications. Joe shot them a withering glance, then turned to the business at hand. "Yeah," he said lazily. "I got a ton's worth. Probably more."

A quick retort appeared on the worker's lips, but he flashed a grin instead, slapped Joe on the shoulder and whistled down two co-workers to unload the pickup. "It's been a long day, buddy," he remarked to Joe. "You'll need to see Mr. Levine personally with a load like that."

"Where do I find him?"

"Over yonder," the boy said, pointing to a corner door.

A few minutes later Joe was standing with Joel Levine, a rotund man about the same age as Sam. Levine was bald, about two inches taller than Joe, with a pleasant demeanor and a booming voice. He exchanged greetings with Joe, then began inspecting the pecans, examining nuts from several bags, using a pair of massive hands to crush open the hard shells and sample the meat.

"I'll give you twenty-seven cents a pound," Levine declared.

Joe had come prepared to barter, and he quickly dismissed the offer. "Sir, I might consider twenty-seven cents if these were seedlings," he replied smoothly, "but these nuts are pure Stuart. I was expecten thirty-three cents."

"Thirty-three!"

"I'm willen to negotiate," Joe announced.

"Twenty-eight cents," Levine snapped.

"Maybe thirty-two," Joe said reluctantly. "These are quality nuts, Mr. Levine. They're heavy and they're tasty."

The pecan broker seemed to reconsider. He reached in a bag, pulled out two more nuts and cracked them against each other, producing a perfectly shaped morsel of brownish red meat from the shell. "They are tasty," he admitted. "Okay, son, I'll give you twenty-nine cents for them."

"Thirty-one and a half," Joe said firmly.

"Thirty," the pecan dealer snapped back impatiently.

"I can get thirty-one and half, probably more in Florida," Joe shot back.

"It's a long way from here to Florida, son, and you're gonna have to go down as far as Orlando or Ocala before you get much more than thirty-one cents a pound," Levine replied formally. Joe stood stiffly, afraid the portly businessman was about to call his bluff. "But I like your spunk, boy, so I'll pay your price. Come inside my office. We'll tally up and write you a check."

Joe took a deep breath. "I need part of it in cash," he said quickly.

Levine nodded. "I figured as much," he mumbled.

———

A short time later, Joe emerged from Joel Levine's cluttered office with a fat check for his grandfather and one hundred eight dollars in cold cash for himself. He whistled a jolly tune. And was frozen in his tracks by a voice, melodiously savage and dripping with animosity.

"I don't know where you come from, boy, but 'round here, niggers know their place. And we kick the asses of those that don't."

Ahead, a crowd of men gathered in a semi-circle around Lucas and Tom. The voice belonged to a barrel-chested, evil-eyed bully, a sawed-off shotgun whose life-long destiny was to prove that his tough attitude made up for his short stature. He stood a few feet from Lucas, stretched to full height and glaring at the black man. Beside him stood another paragon of brawn and menace, this one packaged head and shoulders taller than his short companion.

Joe quickly sized up the two men as the chief troublemakers, but the crowd had a lynch-mob mentality. A shattered soda bottle and its spilt contents lay on the concrete floor between Lucas and the troublemakers.

The short man edged closer to Lucas, who stood motionless, knowing any move toward a defensive posture was tantamount to throwing the first punch as well as an exercise in futility given the odds of a fight.

"Your ass is ours, boy," he spat at Lucas.

"You ever seen black turn blue," the tall one growled.

A thin sheen of sweat broke across Lucas' forehead, Tom took an unconscious step backward and Joe appeared between them like a ghost, unannounced and unexpected.

Joe stepped forward, brandishing his left crutch as a protective guard between Lucas and the two troublemakers. "If you mess with him, you'll have to go through me," he said evenly. "And him, too," he added, pointing the other crutch at the bewildered Tom, who again made another unconscious movement, this time forward.

The moment froze as the two men comprehended the turn of events. Finally, Shorty grunted. "Oh, Lord," he muttered in disbelief. "We've got us a crippled white boy full of righteous indignation." He looked at his tall companion. "Whataya make of it, Perry?"

"The boy must be a nigger lover, Bert," replied Perry. "Plain and simple."

"That true, crip?" Bert asked Joe. "Are you a nigger lover?"

"I'm a friend," Joe said firmly.

The short Bert shook his head, cursing under his breath. "Well, friend," he said sarcastically. "This ain't got nothen to do with you. We want the nigger."

Joe dropped the crutch in his left hand, the wooden brace clattering on the floor of the silent warehouse as he brandished the other crutch as a weapon. "Like I said," he replied stiffly, "if it's got somethen to do with one of us, it's got somethen to do with all of us because we're here together."

Bert stood an inch shorter than Joe, but likely could have ripped him apart with his bare hands. The shorter man cursed. "Stand aside, boy, or you're liable to get hurt," he snapped impatiently.

"Maybe so," Joe shrugged calmly. "But I'll get a lick or two in first."

A test of patience began, carried out over brittle silence. Joe and Bert glared at each other; Lucas stood with his arms by his sides, the original source of animosity now the forgotten man in this fight; and Tom stared with glazed eyes.

Bert made a slight move, a disbelieving shrug more or less, and Joe choked on his weapon. The hair on his neck straightened, his heart pounded and he came alive with animal instincts. He waited breathlessly for the next move, which came pregnant seconds later, with ear-splitting ferocity in the form of Joel Levine's booming voice.

"What in tarnation is goen on here?" the pecan broker demanded to know.

Levine moved with lightning speed despite his rotund shape. He charged between Joe and Bert like a bull picking a target. His fat neck strained against the collar of a heavily starched shirt, and his flabby jowls bristled as he came to a skidding halt in the middle of the shattered soda bottle. His hard-soled shoes crunched against the broken glass. He cast an indignant look downward, then kicked away the offending glass.

"Somebody better start talken!" he declared violently.

"Aw shucks, Joel," Perry muttered, hunching over his tall form. "Just a little friendly disagreement. Nothen for you to fret over."

"I don't fret," Levine growled, glaring at the taller of the two troublemakers. Finally, he turned his black scowl to Bert. "What kind of disagreement you got with these boys?" he asked the shorter man.

The stocky Bert pointed a fat finger at Lucas. "This nigger stepped out of line," he said contemptuously before flipping his finger to Joe. "And when we tried to put him back in place, this one got all riled up and righteous." Bert shook his head and searched for words. "Another self-righteous, nigger-loven kid," he hissed finally. "Ain't that just what the world needs."

"I couldn't care less what the world needs," Levine snorted, "but I don't tolerate these kinds of shenanigans in my warehouse." He looked from Lucas to Tom before fixing a stern gaze on Joe. "Boy," he said. "You're Sam Baker's grandson, ain't you?"

"Yes, sir," Joe answered. "How'd you know that?"

Joel Levine ignored the question and turned his fury back on Bert and Perry as Joe allowed his crutch to fall back into its rightful place.

"Listen up and listen good," Levine shouted. "This is my place of business. I treat my customers with the respect they deserve and I expect the same from them." He put a hand on his hip. "I don't know what happened here, I don't care what happened. But Bert, Perry, these people belong to one of my best suppliers. I can't imagine it's in their character to start a fuss. Even if they did, though, my warehouse ain't the place to settle it. Now, men, I want you to get your butts out of here and let these people finish their business. And if you plan on bringen an attitude back next time you come, don't bother comen. It ain't welcome here."

"Jesus, Joel," Bert grumbled.

"We're goen," Perry said contritely.

"Yeah, we're goen all right," Bert sneered. He turned slightly, then seemed to reconsider and pointed a finger once more at Joe. "Better watch your back, boy," he warned quickly. "You, too, darkie," he added, nodding at Lucas.

"Go!" bellowed Levine in a voice that shook the warehouse rafters, causing a sweet old lady to drop a pail full of nuts and sending Bert and Perry scurrying out the door without another backward glance.

"Idle threats," Levine said when the troublemakers were gone. "They're basically good old boys with short memories. They won't be botheren you anymore."

"Maybe not," Lucas mused. "But I'll feel better when we're out of this county and closer to home."

"That's where y'all oughtta be headed," Levine agreed. "It's a long drive home for you boys. Y'all best be getten to it."

He started to move away, barking orders for someone to clean up the mess of broken glass and spilt soda. "Sorry, ma'am," he said to the elderly woman, who was stooped over picking up her scattered pecans. "Vernon!" he yelled to the sandy-haired youth who had assisted Joe at the weigh-in. "Get over here and help pick up these nuts."

"Wait a second, Mr. Levine," Joe said suddenly amid the furor.

Unaccustomed to taking orders, Joel Levine stopped in his tracks, glancing back at Joe. "Y'all still here," he said reproachfully.

"How did you know who I was?" Joe asked for the second time.

Levine considered the question. "Your grandpa gave me a call this mornen and said you'd be comen my way."

"Why?" Joe asked curiously.

"He just wanted to make sure I knew who you were, so there'd be no misunderstanden between us in case we had trouble reachen a fair deal," the pecan broker answered.

Joe shook his head in disbelief. "You discussed our deal?"

"Sure we did," Levine replied. "That's a big load of nuts you were sellen. It was worth a lot of money."

Joe rubbed the back of his head, putting two and two together and coming up with betrayal at his grandfather's hands. He felt cheated of a chance at manhood. He had thought he did an outstanding job of bargaining, permitting himself a good measure of pride as the pecan dealer's secretary wrote out the check for Sam and counted out the cash for Joe. Now he felt played like a fool. "If you made a deal with my grandfather, sir," he said bitterly, "then what was the point of all that hagglen between us? Seems to me you could have saved both of us a lot of time."

"Whoa there," Levine interrupted. "I'm not gonna lie to you, son. Your grandpa and me did talk price. But you and I struck a deal fair and square."

"What if I'd accepted your first offer?" Joe asked. "Twenty-seven cents ... I believe that's what you said. I know my grandpa said not to take anything less than twenty-eight."

"I would ... I would've," the older man stammered. Finally, he inhaled uncomfortably. "Listen, son," he smiled faintly. "All I can say is that you and I struck a deal fair and square and it was a bargain different than the one I made with your grandfather. Now if that answer don't satisfy you, then I'm sorry. But you're gonna have to get Sam to fill in the particulars." He shrugged. "Now I've got business to tend to, and you've got a long drive home," he said pleasantly. "Let's both be getten to it. Okay?"

A muscle twitched in Joe's cheek, registering his displeasure, but he nodded agreement. "Sure enough," he mumbled.

———

Tom and Lucas were silent on the trip home, partly out of respect for the embarrassing discovery Joe had made about the prearranged deal between Sam and Joel Levine and partly to process the tension of the unexpected events.

Lucas kept his eyes peeled on the rearview mirror, ever mindful of the parting threat the burly Bert had heaved their way. But nothing happened: No speeding cars appeared behind them; no roadblocks sprang up before them. Gradually, he relaxed as the pickup cruised along U.S. Highway 82, passing out of Dougherty County and easing through the town of Sylvester.

"Quite a day," Tom finally remarked as the truck idled at a traffic light.

Joe shrugged and continued to stare out the side window. "I'd say that's putten it mildly," he said dryly.

The light turned green and Lucas eased across the intersection, gaining speed as the truck cleared the city limit signs and headed once more for open road.

Though still fuming over the treachery of his grandfather, Joe decided to put aside his frustration rather than spoil the journey by pouting. "What in the heck happened back there anyway?" he inquired.

"A little accident," Tom suggested.

"It was kinda my fault," Lucas contended.

Tom shook his head. "Not really, Lucas. I saw the whole thing, and he wasn't watchen where he was goen anymore than you were."

Joe waved a hand to quiet his friends. "I still don't know what happened," he said.

"We were on our way to the truck," Lucas explained. "I heard Tom call my name, turned around to see what he wanted and the next thing I knew ran slam-bang, head-on into that short white man."

"That was Bert," Tom interjected, taking over the story. "He had just bought a cold drink, and he dropped it when they ran into each other. Coke and glass every-where. Anyway, he got all huffed up and started cussen Lucas."

"Told him I was sorry, and I was," Lucas said apologetically. "But he didn't care."

"Next thing you know, the tall one, Perry, was over there tellen Lucas to buy his friend another drink, maken all kinds of threats and asken where Lucas came from," Tom continued quickly. "That got Bert all the more excited. He started toward Lucas and then ...." Tom paused. "And then you came gallopen to the rescue, Joe."

"I wouldn't say I galloped," Joe replied with a modest smile.

"You were pretty impressive," Tom said respectfully.

"Shore enough was," Lucas agreed wholeheartedly. "That was some stand you made back there, Joe-Joe." He hesitated for a second. "But you best be careful 'bout taken up for a nigger, 'cause it usually means trouble."

Joe frowned. "It never crossed my mind that I was taken up for a Negro," he replied testily. "I thought I was just helpen out a friend."

"Well, whatever," Lucas said. "Those were some fine fighten words. You proba-bly saved my butt, Joe-Joe, and I appreciate it."

Joe stared down into his lap. "Good grief, Lucas," he grumbled. "It wasn't that big a deal."

"Well, I thought it was," Tom persisted, "especially for a cripple with a crutch. There I was," he said excitedly, "scared to death and ready to pee in my pants. Then all of a sudden, here comes Joe, waven crutches every which way and tellen those overgrown apes they've got to go through him and me to get to Lucas." Tom sighed. "I do believe, Joe, that this beats all those stories about Grandpa and how he lost that eye. It's purely legendary, Joe, purely legendary."

He hesitated, glancing at Lucas. "Of course, Lucas," he added drolly, "I don't mind tellen you now that I feared for your life the whole time. Those boys were big and mean. And if they'd've taken a notion, I expect they could've wrapped those crutches around our necks."

"Nothen like a little two-edged flattery to keep me in my place," Joe commented, cocking an eyebrow at his younger friend. "Huh, Tom?"

"I'll keep that bit of information between the three of us," Tom promised. "After everybody hears about this, they'll think we're the Three Musketeers or somethen."

"Your daddy'll be proud of you, Joe," Lucas said sincerely. "Just like I was."

Joe acknowledged the compliments with a modest grin that changed almost instantly into a grimace. "Hey, boys," he said worriedly. "How 'bout we keep what happened to ourselves? Mama and Daddy find out about this, and I'm liable to be twenty-one before they let me out on my own again. Whataya say?"

Both Tom and Lucas frowned.

"I don't know Joe-Joe," Lucas fretted. "This ain't the kind of thing we should keep from your daddy and mama. They find out what happened, and they'll be plenty mad at me for keepen it from 'em."

"Come on, Lucas," Joe pleaded. "Nobody's gonna find out if we don't tell. There's no harm done. And besides, we'd just end up worryen Mama."

Lucas considered the request for several minutes. Too often these days he had to choose between responsibility and friendship when it came to Joe and Tom, and he detested such situations. He was nine years older than Joe, thirteen years younger than the boy's father, and, like his age, his loyalties belonged somewhere in the middle. He weighed the current situation, balancing Joe's request against Matt's expectations and came up with an answer. "It's against my better judgment, Joe-Joe, but I won't tell your daddy," he said reluctantly. "We should, though. I don't like keepen secrets from him."

"Thanks, Lucas," Joe replied.

Tom released a heavy sigh. "All I can say is it's the loss of a great story," he lamented, shaking his head from side to side. "Truly legendary and nobody's never gonna know it."

"Truly, Tom," Joe muttered, "it's a story the world can live without."

————

They arrived home in the shank of the afternoon to a busy household caught up in the throes of cooking, cleaning and chores. Tom and Lucas took one look at the commotion and fled to their respective homes, seeking a peaceful end to a hectic day.

Joe had no such opportunity, so he did the next best thing, volunteering for a solo performance of the evening milking and feeding-up duties he usually shared with his father. First though, the boy was obliged to tell everyone about his big day. Reluctantly, he delivered a terse description of the deal struck with Joel Levine and presented the check to his grandfather.

"That's a good deal you made, son," Matt told him when Joe had finished. "I'm proud of you."

Joe looked down at his feet, feeling foolish. "It was pretty much a sure shot, Daddy," he replied politely. He looked at his grandfather, who was standing beside the kitchen fireplace. "Actually, you could say it was a gimme, and to tell you the truth I don't feel right about taken the money. It really belongs to Grandpa."

Sam shook his head, disagreeing with his grandson. "Now why would you say that?" he asked cautiously. "We made a deal, Joe, and you kept your end of the bargain by taken care of business for me. That money in your pocket is my end of the deal."

Joe pulled the money from the pocket of his blue jeans, placing it on the kitchen table. "It's all there," he told Sam. "Except the seven dollars I paid Lucas."

"That money belongs to you, Joe," Sam persisted. "We made a deal."

"Maybe you made it too easy for me to keep my end of the deal, Grandpa," Joe hinted quietly, keenly aware of the curious eyes and ears of his family. He shrugged, disengaging himself from the conversation, put a cap on his head and laid aside the crutches. "I'm goen to feed up now," he announced, hobbling out the kitchen door.

"What was that all about?" Matt asked when the door closed behind his oldest son.

Sam bit the corner of his lip, suspecting Joe had learned about the preliminary discussions between him and Levine. "I have an idea," he replied reassuringly before finding his jacket, pocketing the money and following Joe out the door.

He found the boy in the barn. Joe was filling a tub with feed pellets and sweet hay, while uttering low throaty sounds of comfort to the cow, Brindy, who was impatient for her feeding and milking. Joe heard the approaching footsteps, glanced up to see Sam and returned to his work.

"I suppose Levine told you that I called him and said you'd be comen his way," Sam began straightforwardly.

"He did."

Sam cleared his throat. "There's no reason to be upset, Joe," he said. "I simply thought it was a good idea for him to be expecten you."

Joe laughed shortly. "Today meant a lot to me, Grandpa," he said seriously. "I believed you had the confidence in me to do a job and I wanted to prove myself."

"I do have confidence in you," Sam pointed out.

Joe shook his head. "Grandpa, everything said between me and Mr. Levine was nothing but lip service," Joe complained. "I thought I was sent to do a job for you; I thought I did a good job. Turns out I was just played for a fool." He shook his head again. "Maybe I shouldn't be upset, but the truth of the matter is I am. I'll get over it, though, so let's just drop the subject and get on with whatever's next."

Joe sat on the wooden stool and began milking the cow, refusing to look at his grandfather. Sam sighed, deciding the boy needed time to cool his temper. "Maybe I made a mistake, Joe," he admitted regretfully, "but my heart was in the right place. Regardless, this money belongs to you. I'm leaving it on the gate post, and you do whatever you want with it."

Joe listened to his grandfather's departing steps with mixed emotions and a heavy heart. Later, on his way out of the barn, he plucked the money off the gatepost and shoved it back into the pocket of his jeans.

———

Lying in bed that night in the room he shared with his two brothers, who were asleep in the double bed across from him, Joe was about to doze off when someone tapped on the door.

"It's Grandpa," a familiar voice said.

"Come on in," Joe replied quietly.

Sam entered the dark room and sat beside Joe on the edge of the bed. "Seems like we have unfinished business," he offered.

"I suppose so," Joe agreed.

"Apparently, for reasons we both thought best, neither one of us was as forthright as we should have been today," Sam said thoughtfully.

Joe sat up against the headboard, bringing blankets with him to ward off the chill. He looked questioningly at his grandfather.

"I hear you ran into some trouble at the warehouse," Sam answered.

"Oh, that," Joe replied tiredly. "Who told you?"

"Lucas mentioned it this afternoon. Said he promised not to tell your daddy and you'd be ticked at him for tellen me, but he thought somebody ought to know what happened just in case." Sam paused. "He's right, you know."

Joe sighed. "Seems like this is my day for be'en told one thing when people mean another," he said gravely. "But Grandpa, you could have told me that you already had a deal worked out with Mr. Levine. If I had known up front where I stood, I wouldn't have any reason to be disappointed. Now I truly feel like a fool and that's far worse than just feelen like a boy sent to do a man's job."

"I suppose it is," Sam agreed philosophically. "But the truth of the matter, Joe, is that you came home with two and half cents more per pound than the price Levine and I agreed on up front."

Joe sat up straight in the bed. "I did?" he said doubtfully.

"You did," Sam assured him. "I only made sure Joel understood that those pecans were worth at least twenty-nine cents a pound. You did the rest, and from what he told me, you did a good job of negotiaten. Fact is, he said if it had been me he was dealen with, he'd wouldn't have gone any higher than thirty-one cents. But he figured it was worth the extra half-penny just to see somebody cut a better deal than I do."

Joe smiled faintly in the darkness. "You're just tryen to make me feel better, Grandpa," he accused.

Sam nodded, pleading guilty. "Course, I am," he replied affably. "I wouldn't be much of a grandpa if I didn't, now would I?"

Joe smiled agreement.

"But I'm tellen you the truth when I say Levine told me you drove a hard bargain," Sam continued. "Though he was none too pleased when you threatened to drive off to Florida for a better deal."

Joe grinned. "I think that cinched it," he gloated. "Other customers were close by, and I don't think he wanted them to hear the argument."

"No, I don't reckon he did," Sam agreed carefully. "But what would you have done if he'd told you to dig off for Florida?"

Joe considered the question, a possibility he had not thought of seriously in his negotiations with Joel Levine. Finally, he grinned again. "I imagine I'd have stooped to beggen and taken his lowest offer."

Sam laughed heartily. "I tell you what, Joe," he remarked amicably. "To make amends for my lack of complete forthrightness, I'm gonna keep what happened with Lucas to myself. Mind you, I think we oughtta tell your daddy and I'm against these kinds of secrets. But you acted like a man in defenden Lucas, and you deserve to be respected accordingly. If you prefer to keep it secret, then so be it."

"Thanks, Grandpa."

"Do you really believe me?" Sam asked.

Joe stretched and cracked his knuckles. "Well," he replied with genuine cheerfulness. "Save a few tall tales about dragons and pirates and pretty maidens in distress, you've been pretty truthful with me. I don't imagine I'll lose any sleep worryen whether you'll keep your word."

Sam ruffed his head, then hugged the boy and kissed him on the cheek. "You're a good boy, Joe, and you're maken a fine man. But remember, son, it takes time and a few mistakes along the way, plus a little help every now and then. And if you follow true to form in the steps of us Baker men, you'll have plenty of each."

Sam rose from the bed, stretching and yawning. "Of course," he continued with overstated enthusiasm. "Age is the downside to becomen a man. You get old, your heart gets leaky, you get the rheumatism." He sighed. "Enjoy your youth, Joe, 'cause you really do only have it once."

Joe smiled soberly, the concern coming through in his eyes, resembling the worried watch he had kept over Sam during his recuperation from the heart attack.

"Well that's enough philosophy and ranten from an old man for one night," Sam said lightheartedly, bestowing a reassuring smile on his grandson. "I'm off to keep your grandma warm. Sleep well, Joe."

"You, too, Grandpa."

CHAPTER 6

CHRISTMAS EVE DAWNED COLD and gray. The leaden sky teased of snow, but the TV weatherman promised only rain mixed with sleet.

Caroline and Matt woke early, then lingered in bed to celebrate the dawning of their nineteenth wedding anniversary. After their lovemaking was finished, he held her as they reminisced about the past and pondered the future. When at last talk turned to the time at hand, they left the warm bed and began the new day with a sense of purpose and fulfillment.

Christmas Eve fell on Saturday that year, which in itself meant nothing unusual around the Baker household. Like any other day, it was marked with routines, meals to be made and chores to get done. But it was also a day steeped in tradition and no sooner was the last morsel of breakfast eaten than the family began adhering to their Christmas Eve rituals.

Mainly, the morning traditions focused on the kitchen, so Sam, Matt and the boys did everything possible to stay out of eyesight and earshot of the womenfolk. None succeeded completely. Sam had the misfortune of bringing in the ham from the smokehouse, an occasion for which his wife also roped him into assisting John with the task of churning butter. Matt made the mistake of mentioning he was going down the road to see Paul Berrien, and Caroline promptly shoved a coconut cake in his arms for delivery to Slaton and Florence Castleberry, the elderly couple whose farm backed up to the west side of the Baker place. Summer hunted down Joe and Luke to pass along orders from their mother to pick a mess of turnips from the field across the road.

Summer, Carrie and Bonnie were assigned the household chores, making beds, cleaning the bathroom, dusting furniture, sweeping and vacuuming.

In the kitchen, Caroline and Rachel worked like greased bakery equipment. Caroline cooked up two iron skillets of cornbread and a batch of biscuits, which she promptly set aside to dry out over the course of the day to become the substance of her cornbread dressing. Rachel put the hen on to boil and began preparing the pear tarts that consistently won high praise at church dinners.

By mid-morning, the kitchen was running in top gear at full speed and the menfolk were vanished from the place. Celery, onions and bell pepper were sliced, diced and sautéed; turnip greens and roots were minced, spiced with boiling meat and put on the stove to simmer for hours; Rachel's pear tarts joined her fruit cake in the pie safe, their place in the oven taken by pecan, pumpkin and sweet potato pies. Eggs boiled on the stove, a loaf of pumpkin bread batter waited for its turn in the oven and the aroma of Christmas cooking watered mouths.

When they felt sufficient progress had been made on Christmas dinner, Caroline and Rachel prepared the noon meal for their starving family. On this day, it was sandwiches made from a freshly boiled ham and the last of the hogshead cheese from the most recent butchering. Everyone ate their fill and complimented the cooks, but all minds were on the best part of the busy Christmas Eve day still to come—the afternoon trip to Tifton for last-minute shopping and fantasizing.

The Christmas Eve shopping trip had become a family tradition sometime between Matt's homecoming from the war and Summer's birth. Caroline thought it had arisen from a need to do some last-minute Santa Claus shopping for Joe. Matt swore it started the year he bought Caroline the two tall, fluted candlesticks that graced the sides of the French doors between the living and dining rooms. Rachel and Sam insisted the trips had begun out of necessity, to allow them to do their Christmas shopping, which probably was closest to the real reason.

For whatever reasons, Christmas Eve shopping seemed as much a part of the family's holiday rituals as the Christmas tree itself, especially to the children. None of them could ever remember a December twenty-fourth passing without the traditional trip to town, save those odd years when the day fell on Sunday and the stores were closed.

Early that afternoon, the whole family—scrubbed and bundled in their warmest clothes—packed into the big sedan and embarked on the sixteen-mile trip to Tifton, a town considerably larger than Cookville, located in the neighboring county. It was not an overstatement to say they were packed in the car like sardines in a can. Matt drove and Sam sat in the front seat holding Luke on his lap with John between them. Caroline, Rachel, Summer and Joe sat in the back, with Carrie on her mother's lap and Bonnie stretched across her grandmother and brother.

The temperature hovered near the freezing point, and a steady rain fell as they drove, but the big car's heater purred softly, bathing them with warmth.

"It's a good thing none of us is fat," Summer commented sagely as the car eased along Highway 125.

"Why's that, honey?" Matt asked, glancing at his daughter in the rearview mirror.

"We'd never fit in the car," Summer replied smartly. "We can barely squeeze in now." She hesitated, then asked, "What happens if we grow any next year?"

"Somebody'll have to stay home, I guess," Joe suggested with mock pragmatism, drawing gasps of horror from his impressionable brothers and sisters. "We'll draw straws tonight to see who stays and who goes," he teased.

"I'm not stayen home," Summer declared to uproarious approval from her younger siblings. "It wouldn't be Christmas without goen to town on Christmas Eve. You can stay home, Joe."

"Your brother's just teasen," Caroline soothed her children. "We'll find a way to get us all to town, even if we have to pack everyone in the back of the pickup."

"Mama, we'd freeze to death riden in the back of a pickup in weather like this," John remarked, pointing out a potential problem with his mother's idea. "Out in the cold with the rain and the wind, and nothing to protect us."

"I promise we won't let y'all freeze to death," Matt said quickly. "Why don't we think about next year when we get to it? We've still got this Christmas to deal with, and I'd hate to miss it because we were so concerned about next year."

"None of us will be in town on Christmas Eve next year," Joe said smugly, refusing to let the subject drop. "It falls on Sunday. All the stores will be closed."

"Then we'll go Saturday, the twenty-third," Caroline replied before anyone could voice disappointment.

"What about Santa Claus?" Luke asked suddenly from his grandfather's lap, a worried frown creasing his face. "He's gonna be out in this weather tonight. He could freeze to death riden around in an open sleigh."

"He's got that red fur suit to keep him warm," Matt reminded Luke.

"And on top of that, he's got a special heater built right into his sleigh," Sam added. "Besides, Luke, Santa Claus lives in the North Pole. They have snow and ice year-round up there, so I imagine he's used to the cold."

"Are you sure, Grandpa?" Luke asked dubiously.

"Sure as I'm sitten here," Sam answered with unmistakable confidence, quelling the boy's concern.

They sang carols from then until the merry Christmas lights of Tifton heralded their arrival in town. The children marveled at the collection of bell-shaped wreaths and Santa Claus faces attached to every streetlight, along with the glittering trees and garland suspended above each intersection.

Cars lined the avenues, making parking spaces scarce, but Matt finally found an open slot on his fourth trip down Main Street. Once out of the car, all went their own way, except Luke and Bonnie, who were too young to traipse around town without someone to watch after them. The family scattered, each with a different mission and all with at least a dollar in their pockets to spend as they wished. Sam headed for The Big Store and a brightly colored scarf he figured would be a welcomed addition to his wife's collection; Rachel set out for Western Auto and the flashlight her husband had claimed to need for the past six months.

Caroline and Matt intended to spend the day watching their children enjoy the festivities as well as helping Sam and Rachel with their shopping. But first, they had to find the few gifts still on their shopping lists, which was why Caroline took off for Bishop's department store while Matt headed for the bookstore in the opposite direction.

"I've got just two places to go," Matt told Joe, putting his oldest son in charge of Luke and Bonnie.

"But Daddy," Joe protested, "I've got things to do myself. I don't have time to baby-sit."

"Just two things, son," Matt wheedled. "I'll be finished in a snap, then I'll find you and the rest of the day is yours to do whatever."

Joe put a hand on his hip, looking from side to side while considering the difficulty of Christmas shopping with a six- and four-year-old in tow. At last, he gave a short laugh and waved his father off to his errands. "Make it quick," he admonished.

"Thanks, son," Matt grinned. "I'm sure Santa will remember what a good sport you were about this."

Joe laughed again and watched his father walk away, conscious of the loose stride and light steps that carried Matt. Joe had walked the same way once, copying the gait of his daddy. Now, however, all he did was hobble, and he momentarily felt embarrassed by his crippled condition. Quickly though, he put aside the discomfort and surveyed the Christmas festivities.

On every corner, Salvation Army soldiers stood, their bells ringing a reminder that not everyone was as fortunate this holiday as the happy shoppers who strolled along the sidewalks.

Save for the grace of God, Joe acknowledged to himself, those bells could have tolled for the Bakers this year. He knew his daddy and mama were pinched for cash worse now than at any other time he could remember. To a degree, he was older and simply more aware of the family finances than in previous years, but Joe understood implicitly that the money troubles ran deeper than usual this year. Given the poor showing of the crops, it would have been a difficult year regardless of the unexpected expenses that popped up during the year. But the medical bills alone for Joe and his grandfather probably had scuttled the likelihood of even a meager profit.

Joe pushed aside his concerns. He fully expected his parents to provide for the family. The Bakers would get by somehow, and he refused to worry over the particulars of how. Still, Joe suspected there was little money left over for frivolities like Christmas, which explained why he was determined to buy presents for everyone in the family this year.

He had managed Christmas gifts for his parents for many years and for his grandparents for several years now. But mostly they had been cheap tokens with little thought or meaning. This year, besides expanding his shopping list to include his brothers and sisters, Joe had put thought into the presents and would spare no expense. He patted the wad of money in his pants pocket and was greeted by a tug on his arm.

Joe looked down into the upturned faces of his brother and sister. "We need help," Bonnie told him expectantly.

"What's wrong?" Joe asked.

"Nothen," Luke answered swiftly. "We just want to use our dollars to buy presents for Mama and Daddy."

Joe smiled, leaning down to pull the children into an embrace. "Well now that's a swell idea," he praised, putting a finger on his chin to think. "You know," he continued thoughtfully, "I'm buyen gifts for Mama and Daddy myself. You guys could contribute a nickel or a dime each, and we could all three sign our names to it. That way you'd still have money left."

His suggestion met instant rejection from Bonnie and Luke, whose heads shook with vigorous disapproval. "No," Luke declared.

"We know what we want to get," Bonnie said quickly.

"But we need help picken it out," Luke added.

Joe nodded acceptance of their wishes. "Okay," he said patiently. "What kind of gifts do y'all have in mind?"

"Perfume for Mama," Bonnie answered.

"And aftershave lotion for Daddy," Luke finished.

Joe grinned slyly. "Do y'all have something against the way Mama and Daddy smell?"

"Noooo!" Bonnie laughed.

Luke shook his head in agreement. "I heard Mama say she was out of perfume one day," he explained to Joe. "And she's always kissen Daddy and tellen him how good he smells when he comes home from the barber shop. We figured Mama might kiss him a lot more if Daddy smelled good all the time."

Joe hugged the two children. "I can't argue with that," he smiled.

"It's a good idea, ain't it?" Bonnie asked.

"It's a great idea, honey," Joe confirmed tenderheartedly, running his fingers through the little girl's tresses.

"So where do we go to get it?" Luke inquired anxiously.

Joe stood, glancing up and down the street until his eyes settled on a pharmacy across the street beside the toy store. "I'd say the Rexall drugstore over yonder probably sells just about the best smellen perfume and aftershave in the entire town," he guaranteed them. "Whataya say we head over there to buy the presents. I bet they'll even wrap them for y'all. Then we'll check out the toy store."

He paused, then added, "We might even find Santa Claus over there."

Bonnie clapped her hands in delight. "Let's go," Luke said.

Without another word, Joe took their hands and led his brother and sister across the busy street to the drugstore, pausing only to drop a five-dollar bill in the Salvation Army's red bucket. The bell was still ringing when he steered the children into the drugstore.

———

An hour later, Bonnie and Luke proudly carried bright packages for their parents and had combed over every marvelous inch of the toy store. Besides the happiness of his brother and sister, the excursion had proven beneficial to Joe as well. He purchased a tiny porcelain carousel music box for Carrie in the drugstore and a plastic silver tea set and box of miniature cars for Bonnie and Luke, respectively, from the toy store.

Without too much difficulty, he led the children from the toy store to a jewelry store one block down the street. He window-shopped briefly, eyeing the collection of ID bracelets on display in the front window while Luke and Bonnie complained about the cold. He ignored the children until they began tugging him toward the door.

"Okay, okay," Joe relented at last.

The doorbell jangled behind him and Joe turned to find himself eyeball-to-eyeball with his father.

Matt hastily stuffed something into the pocket of his denim jacket. "What are y'all doen here?" he asked with obvious surprise.

Joe responded with a curious smile at his father. "Luke and Bonnie were cold," he answered evasively. "We were looken for a warm place." He stared pointedly at the pocket of Matt's jacket. "What about you, Daddy? What's your excuse?"

"Just browsen," Matt answered too quickly, looking from Joe to Bonnie and Luke. "You kids ready to come with me for a while?"

"Yes, sir!" Luke said.

"Let's go to the toy store," Bonnie chimed in. "We've only gone there once today."

"The toy store it is," Matt agreed. "See you later, Joe."

"Have fun," Joe told them as they walked down the sidewalk. He watched until they crossed the next street, then went inside the jewelry store to buy the ID bracelet for Summer and a cigarette lighter for his father.

His pursuit of gifts next carried Joe to Western Auto, where he bought a basketball for John and an electric blanket for his grandparents, whose room served as a protective barrier between cold northern winds and the rest of the house. Before collecting his final gift, Joe obtained the car keys from his father and deposited the neatly wrapped presents in the trunk. Although tempted to borrow the car, his good sense convinced Joe otherwise and, after returning the keys, he set out on foot to cover the half-mile journey to the Sears catalog store to pick up the present for his mother.

The goal of this trek was a package of pink drapes with white sheers. Personally,

Joe found the curtains, like most other things pink, only slightly more tolerable than nausea. The color reminded him of medicine. Nevertheless, he knew Caroline wanted those drapes in the worst way. She had spotted them in the Sears catalog and promptly declared her heart was set on them for the living room because they would match the furniture and the area rug with its brocaded burgundy and floral design. Over the course of fall as the family's financial woes worsened, Caroline had given up on the idea of the curtains. Still, her desire lingered and when Joe had come upon his mother staring at the catalog picture of the curtains like a child pining for the impossible, he had resolved to see that she got them.

Even practical women like his mother deserved moments of folly, Joe believed. For that matter, he reasoned, so did practical guys like himself.

————

Caroline hunted for last-minute bargains in Bishop's while waiting for the store clerk to wrap the yellow satin dress for Summer. She browsed through the women's winter dresses, ruled out Sunday shoes for her husband and was considering an apron for Rachel when a clerk handed her the package. Caroline thanked the clerk, admiring the dark green wrapping paper as she made her way out of the store. She was still looking at the package, running through a mental list of things to do when she collided head-on with someone who obviously had waited until the last minute to do her Christmas shopping. Both women reeled from the impact, and an assortment of boxes, sacks and packages spilled in the doorway.

"I'm so sorry," Caroline apologized immediately, bending with the woman to retrieve the parcels. "I should have been looken where I was goen." She glanced up at the stranger, smiling warmly until she recognized the sallow-faced woman staring back at her.

Martha Taylor was a gawky, thin woman with a long face and pinched features. Her straight dishwater blonde hair was pulled back in a messy braid hanging down her back, and she wore a dowdy gray dress. The reproving look Martha received from Caroline as they knelt there together on the department store floor had nothing to do with appearances, however, but rather with her relationship to Bobby Taylor.

Despite her Christian duty to forgiveness, Caroline still harbored ill will toward Bobby and the entire Taylor clan. They had brought shame, grief and heartache to the Bakers over the long summer recently passed, and Caroline's mood was short on tolerance and long on judgment.

In that long gaze between the two women, Martha undoubtedly saw the loathsome opinion Caroline held of the Taylor family. A flicker of understanding registered briefly in her dull eyes, dying like embers splashed with cold water before Martha broke the gaze. She gathered her packages without further acknowledgment of Caroline, then retreated to the rear of the store.

Caroline rose from the floor, confused by a sudden urge to reach out to the sad-faced woman and the inclination to forget this encounter. She scanned the far corners of the store for a glimpse of Martha, deciding eventually that she must appear nosy to anyone observing her actions. At last, she concluded, perhaps for all the wrong reasons, that the time was not yet right to attempt a reconciliation between the two families. Much unpleasantness had passed between them, and the memories were still too close to both sides.

In time, Caroline tried to tell herself, she could befriend Martha Taylor. But she knew such a friendship was unlikely to happen. She and Martha had been neighbors for years, and this Christmas Eve run-in amounted to the most significant moment in their relationship. Caroline accepted part of the blame due to her stubborn animosity toward Bobby Taylor. But the fact that Martha just wasn't neighborly also had to be considered. It was hard to start a friendship with someone who rarely set foot off her own property, shunning church and community activities.

This reasoning, however, did little to suppress Caroline's notion that she had missed a golden opportunity to right a wrong. Rather than offer the hand of friendship to Martha, she had responded with judgment. Caroline moved to the door, hesitating only to tighten the belt of her tweed coat before moving into the cold afternoon with a heavy heart.

She walked briskly along the sidewalk admiring the window displays of the various stores, but her thoughts stayed in Bishop's with Martha. Caroline did not know Martha well enough to understand her motives, but she'd heard enough rumor and gossip to make some educated guesses about the woman.

Although she hated to admit it, Caroline suspected Bobby had represented a single chance of happiness for Martha. And not only that, Caroline thought shamelessly, but Bobby likely had come across as some knight in shining armor to Martha. She could imagine Bobby sweeping a shy girl off her feet with false promises. While Caroline did not put much stock in appearances, Bobby was a handsome man compared with his wife. It was easy to imagine Martha bowled over by her luck at snaring a man like Bobby. But what sustained their relationship? The possibility of a shared hatred for colored people crossed her mind, but Caroline shuddered at that thought and promptly discarded the idea.

Accepting that Martha was a complete stranger for all practical purposes, Caroline forced her mind to quit its gossiping about the woman and focused instead on what she knew about the Taylor family.

She hardly considered the Taylors neighbors. They were simply people who lived down the road and kept mostly to themselves. In nineteen years of living on nearby farms, Caroline had set foot on Taylor property just once and then only out of ignorance.

Caroline had devoted the first days of her marriage to Matt and his preparations for entering the Army. He had joined up in January 1942 a few weeks after their wedding, and she had returned to Aunt Evelyn's home in Tifton to finish her final year of high school. When school ended that spring, Caroline had taken up permanent residence with the Bakers and readily set out to learn about the place she intended to call home for the rest of her life.

New River was a crossroads community located along Highway 125 beside a river and a railroad trestle. The town of Cookville lay south of the little community and Tifton to the north. Carter's Mercantile was the focal point of the crossroads, a rambling wooden structure that also served as the community post office before the government shut it down in the early 1950s. New River Elementary School lay north of the mercantile around a sharp curve, and the one-room voting precinct stood between those two structures.

Route 125 had been paved in the 1950s, but the winding path bisecting the community was a dirt road with washboard ruts and slippery ditches. The western flank of the dirt road was the more thickly populated side, with smaller farms and shorter distances between houses. The Holiness Baptist Church sat on the western flank of the road, which also eventually led to the snake-handling church where a man had died from a rattlesnake bite a few months earlier.

The Baker home lay about two miles off the main highway, on the sparsely settled eastern flank of the dirt road. Deep woods hemmed both sides of the road, broken only by the occasional field or dwelling place. Coming from the highway about a half-mile down the road, Benevolence Missionary Baptist Church and its cemetery stood on the left. On the right a short distance farther lay the Berrien pecan orchard and the private lane leading to their home. Like the church, the Baker house sat on the left side of the road, which cut a swath directly through the family's farm. A few more scattered farms and homes lay farther down the road.

As fascinated as she was with the lay of the land, Caroline was even more fond of the people who lived in her new community.

Dan and Amelia Carter were newlyweds themselves, although both several years older than Matt and Caroline. She found the Carters to be friendly shopkeepers with a willingness to lend a hand to their neighbors in times of need. They kept the mercantile in excellent shape, stocked it with all the necessities and made every effort possible to obtain any other items their customers requested.

Dan was an affable, easygoing man who more often than not deferred to the wishes of his wife, while Amelia was a strong-willed, prideful woman who spoke her mind on most occasions. Considering their personalities, Dan might have become a henpecked husband if not for two factors: He had the backbone to stand up to his wife when the situation warranted, and Amelia had the good sense to know when her husband was right. Caroline had come quickly to count the Carters among her best friends.

Her friendship with the Berriens had required more cultivation. Britt Berrien had been a stranger to Caroline, so much so that in some ways she understood the man better in death than when he had been alive. She had known and liked Paul before marrying, and the years since had deepened her respect for Matt's best friend. April and June were oddities. They had given Caroline a whirlwind tour of their stately mansion before the wedding, insisting that she and Matt use the small guest cottage for their honeymoon. But two years had lapsed before the sisters extended another invitation to their home. She saw them regularly at Sunday church services and Wednesday prayer meetings but very few times in between. She was puzzled by their reclusive behavior until Rachel had explained the strange history behind it.

The Berrien sisters had remained friendly strangers through the war and up to their father's death, which, sad as it sounded, had imbued the women with the freedom to pursue life. They still largely preferred an existence behind the facade of the Berrien estate, but they ventured out often these days, using the family money to travel extensively and lead privileged lives. And, too, they gave back a little of themselves to the community. April taught piano lessons for a minimal charge and June was spearheading a countywide effort to build a new library in Cookville.

The emergence of the sisters from the iron rule of their father compared with a graceful bird taking flight. They were two delicate creatures tapping into a rich vein of strength, and Caroline had grown to admire their courage. It was true that she found both women scatterbrained at times, but April and June exemplified the best of Southern gentility and graciousness and Caroline marveled at their fastidiousness. She counted them as true friends to her family.

Caroline was closest to the Berriens and the Carters, but she had formed lasting friendships with almost everyone else in the New River community over the years. The Taylor family was the notable exception.

Several miles down from the Baker place on the right of the dirt road was a second private lane that Caroline had traversed only once. Unlike the Berrien estate, where the vast pecan orchard and sugar maple-lined lane created a formidable aura demanding privacy, the Taylor place made a similar statement in blatant terms, with a series of "No Trespassing" signs posted on scraggly pine trees.

Caroline invaded the privacy of the Taylor place a few weeks after moving in with her in-laws in the summer of 1942 when she accompanied Sam to deliver a letter mistakenly left in the Baker mailbox. Some six months had passed since her rude introduction to Bobby Taylor, and Caroline had no idea who lived at the end of the rocky, washed-out path. Still, she'd felt a sense of foreboding as they drove past worn-out fields before arriving at a weather-beaten house almost swallowed up by a host of mature pecan trees.

The front door opened as soon as Sam stopped the truck, and Bobby Taylor stepped onto the sagging front porch. Caroline recognized him immediately as the bully who had mistreated the little colored boy on her wedding day. "Who's that?" she hissed through her teeth to Sam.

"That?" Sam repeated inquisitively. He looked at Bobby, then back to Caroline. "That is Bobby Taylor," he answered finally.

Caroline quickly eyeballed her father-in-law. "Pa," she said urgently as Bobby approached the truck, "I'd appreciate it if you spared me an introduction."

Although he had no time to acknowledge the request, Sam complied with Caroline's wishes. He passed the letter to Bobby through the truck window, inquired about the family and chatted briefly about the war and the crops before bidding goodbye to the boy.

"Now what was that all about?" he inquired of Caroline as they drove away from the Taylor house.

Caroline told him about her first encounter with Bobby on the drive home.

"Humph," Sam had snorted as she concluded the story. "Let me tell you what I know about the Taylors. Some of it is gossip, some rumor, some innuendo and some of it is fact. Very little is pleasant."

———

Robert Taylor moved his wife, Josephine, and only son, Bobby, to the Cookville community in the spring of 1939, acquiring the farm outright from the Farmers and Citizens Bank of Cookville in exchange for paying fifteen years of back property taxes. It seemed a meager price for the amount of land but it was more than any local farmer would have been willing to pay for the small farm. The locals considered it a cursed place, barren land that would never earn a decent living for a man and his family.

"I don't rightly know how the place earned its reputation," Sam had told Caroline later that evening as they ate supper with Rachel. "It's fertile land. One field is rich bottom soil right by the river. Somebody oughtta be able to make a liven out there with plenty left over to enjoy the luxuries of life. But for whatever reasons, nobody was able to make a go of the place until Robert Taylor took it over."

A young man known as Henry Anderson had owned the place before the Taylors acquired it. Henry was a tireless worker with a young wife and four children. Unfortunately, his best efforts met consistently with failure, more often than not from things beyond his control. Flood, drought and insects made it difficult for Henry to take care of his family, much less pay the bills and meet his bank note, but it was the iron fist of Britt Berrien that finally crushed the young man.

"No one could ever figure out why Britt turned against the man," Sam told Caroline. "Henry was a fine worker. When the farm left him short on cash, he went out and found whatever work he could to feed the family. He worked a lot for Britt himself, gardener and handyman stuff. Then out of the blue one day, Britt foreclosed on him. Henry and his family stole away in the middle of the night, and, to my knowledge, nobody's seen hide nor hair of 'em since."

"Henry was a handsome man, too," Rachel continued with unabashed admiration. "Dark, tall and broad-shouldered with the greenest eyes you ever saw." Rachel shook her head as if realizing how unlike herself she sounded, but she continued, unaffected by the fresh attitude. "He had that certain look," she said daringly. "Like he could have whatever he wanted, but would never take it because he was too nice. I sound like a school girl with a crush, but Henry had that kind of effect on people," Rachel concluded. "Everybody—men and women alike—were just naturally attracted to him. I can't imagine whatever happened to make a man like him just disappear into the night."

But Henry and his family had disappeared and, for fifteen years, the Anderson place lay fallow, virtually untouched by human contact. The house and barns fell into disrepair, weeds reclaimed the fields and time seemed to stop on the farm. Some locals claimed the place was still trying to reclaim those lost years, despite the best efforts of Robert Taylor and his family.

Robert was a stern man, whose penchant for hard work was overshadowed only by his desire for privacy. The Taylors made no effort to become part of the community. Rather, they shut out their neighbors, posting the land with "No Trespassing" signs and putting up a gate across the driveway to their house. Their actions effectively isolated the family, while providing fodder for the gossip mill and piquing the interest of the community.

Through the grapevine and a series of discreet inquiries, disturbing details emerged.

Robert and Josephine had once owned a farm in north Florida, selling it and relocating to the Cookville area following the death of their teenage daughter. Officially, the death was ruled suicide because the girl hung herself. Unofficially, everyone said she was driven to kill herself, and rumors sprouted like seed in spring, irrigated with innuendoes like incest and pregnancy. It was an ugly tale, lingering through the years without substantiation or repudiation.

While the past proved elusive to hang on the Taylors, the present unfolded in extremes.

Despite his curious ways, Robert earned the grudging respect of the New River community. He tamed the wretched piece of land straightaway, transforming patches of weed and bramble into thriving fields. Other farmers had better land, but none tended it more skillfully than Robert. Within a few years, his fields were the envy of the community.

"If I had half his know-how, I could turn this place into what Tara must have been before the War Between the States," Sam had admitted freely to Caroline. "Robert Taylor can get more out of nothen than anybody I know."

The first hint of trouble came during the family's third summer in Cookville. Until then, no one suspected the Taylors held colored people in such low regard.

The hubbub began on a hot day in July when Robert beat a black boy in his tobacco field. Robert claimed the boy had sassed him, asserting his refusal to tolerate back talk from a nigger. The black field workers swore out a warrant for his arrest, claiming the attack was excessive regardless of the provocation. The accused spent a night in jail before a judge dropped the charges for lack of evidence.

In a community where racism was largely passive, Robert had touched a nerve.

Colored people knew their place in Cookville in 1941. Most of them either respected white people or wisely kept contrary opinions to themselves. Likewise, whites showed a degree of respect for the colored community, reserving their acrimonious feelings for private moments. Both sides used each other, profiting from the arrangement, and only the rare extremist on either side voiced dissatisfaction with the situation.

With one angry outburst, Robert Taylor shattered the fragile peace, endangering the long-established truce between the community's black and white factions.

The white faction divided sharply over the decision to drop the assault charges against Robert. On one side were the people who felt Robert deserved punishment, considering the broken ribs suffered by his teenage victim as ample evidence of the crime. This group was lined up opposite of those who believed that white people had the authority as well as the moral obligation to enforce strict discipline over the black community as a whole and any rowdy, disrespectful teenager in particular. In between these two groups lay the majority, those apathetic souls whose opinions wavered with the wind.

Cookville's colored community had strong opinions about the incident as well and strangely enough those viewpoints were not homogenized. Nevertheless, they united on one front. While powerless against the wheels of justice, the colored folk controlled their destiny when it came to field labor and they chose not to work for Robert from that point forward.

Once he recognized their method of retaliation, Robert tried to make amends, humbling himself because he needed the blacks as a cheap source of labor. He promised higher wages, free lunches and vowed never to lay another hand on black skin. His overture met with firm rejection among the black farm workers, leaving Robert frustrated, bitter and humiliated for having stooped so low as to grovel for niggers. When the humiliation passed, he made another vow, promising no niggers would ever set foot in his fields again. Then, he went to work, doubling his efforts to make good on his claim.

No one could say for fact whether Robert Taylor's deep-seated hatred for Negroes existed prior to this incident or imbedded into his character in the aftermath of the trouble. Undoubtedly though, his bigotry became the dominating influence in the life of his only son.

"I have a theory about Bobby," Sam had told Caroline late one recent summer night when the startling events of the day naturally harkened them back to their original conversation about the Taylor family. "There's no doubt that Robert made the boy work—if you'll pardon the expression—like a field nigger. But it's also plain as the nose on his face that Bobby has a streak of laziness in him a mile wide. Well, when you put hard work and laziness together, nothen good is bound to come from it. I think that's what happened to Bobby. He's spent many a day under a blazen sun, worken his tail off and looken for somebody to blame for his predicament. Seems only natural that he would lay that blame at the feet of colored people. I'm willen to bet that once or twice the thought occurred to him that his life would be a lot easier if there were a few Negroes in the field worken with him."

Beyond their common hatred for niggers, Robert and Bobby shared little.

As much as his father preferred privacy, Bobby Taylor relished attention. Bobby was brash and crass, a combination that won over impressionable teenagers, made him several friends and charmed a few girls along the way. In high school, he became a beacon for those who shared his prejudices and a thorn in the side of those who opposed him.

From an early age, Bobby learned to pick his fights carefully, to measure the costs against the benefits and to stay away from no-win situations. It was this ability that helped him avoid service through most of World War II, plus his father's insistence to the draft board that Bobby best served the war effort by working on the farm to produce food for the country. In early 1945, however, the Army finally summoned Bobby to Fort Benning for basic training, and he went despite the pleadings of his father.

———

As she walked down the city sidewalk, pausing to glance in the window of another department store, Caroline pondered how deceitful appearances were. At first glance, the father-son bond between Robert and Bobby might have appeared unbreakable. But somehow, she knew otherwise.

Robert might have been quick to defend the cause of his son, but his call to duty had not come from love. His heart was black, and Caroline suspected his actions had been guided by a spiteful desire to control Bobby rather than to help him. Still, despite her lack of respect for Robert, she could not help wondering whether Bobby appreciated his father's role in the Taylor family's well-being. She wondered where Bobby would be without his father's guidance. And she wondered whether there was sadness in the Taylor household this Christmas or whether the feelings about Robert's death a few weeks earlier had been tossed away like slop in a bucket.

This was Caroline's last thought on the Taylor family and then she pushed them from her mind, intent on focusing on the goodwill of man and peace on earth.

CHAPTER 7

LONG AFTER CAROLINE BAKER had left Bishop's, Martha Taylor stood in the back of the department store reflecting on the woman's presumptuous nature. Martha had seen the disapproval in Caroline's eyes, knowing instantly that she had been tried and convicted by association with Bobby. Martha could live with the accusations, but she resented the sympathetic nod Caroline had bestowed on her.

Women like Caroline made Martha sick to her stomach. They presumed to understand every little detail about things they had no business worrying over in the first place, passing judgments and exercising their God-given rights to act on the wisdom of their holier-than-thou attitudes. Martha half-expected Caroline to come calling with a cake one day soon, offering the hand of friendship and asking where the coffee cups were at the same time. Well, if she did, Martha would tell the woman where to go and what to do with her cake. And under no circumstances would Caroline Baker ever know where Martha kept her coffee cups.

Martha snorted at the idea, condemning Caroline as a busybody, and then shuffled over to the shoe department, taking a seat in an empty chair. She closed her eyes, wishing for peace and quiet to take away the maddening headache. Headaches plagued her more often than not these days. It was a dull pain for the most part, but commotion brought it to a full throb. And life had brought one commotion after another for the longest time now.

Christmas was the final straw. Martha was worn out with all its trappings and cheer. She hated the shopping, she despised the crowds, she wanted to disappear. But as bad as it seemed, if she could get through one more day, Martha knew she could rest for a while. There would be no elections, no funerals, no holidays.

Just the prospect of doing the same old thing day after day, and she relished the thought. Though not fond of cooking and cleaning, Martha had gained a new appreciation for the predictability of housekeeping and the privacy it afforded her. She was more grateful than ever to have a roof over her head and food on the table every night, which had been her main motivation to marry Bobby in the first place. If she had ever desired more from marriage, even fleetingly so, Martha now knew she would willingly settle for less. She hoped the same was true of her husband's ambition, but somehow doubted it.

Indeed, Martha had a troublesome notion that the coming years might bring new commotion, or at the very least more than she had bargained for on the day Bobby Taylor swaggered into her life.

———

Bobby and Martha met at a bar in Columbus, Georgia, early on in his Army training at Fort Benning. He could not recall the exact details of their first meeting, but Bobby remembered she was easy to seduce and he was drunk the first time they slept together in a dingy motel.

When he woke the next morning to find the shy, homely girl from Opelika, Alabama, in bed with him, Bobby promptly pushed himself on her another time.

He expected Martha to disappear from his life, but she proved a strange temptation. She was putty in his hands, yielding to Bobby's every demand, doing whatever he wished, molding her desires to his needs.

Through her unwitting complaisance, Martha introduced Bobby to the heady feeling of power over other people. When he had sated his carnal desires, Bobby lay back in bed and explained the way of the world to Martha. In the process, he became a king, the master of everything in his realm, and she became his servant.

Over and over Bobby had tried to walk away from Martha. He considered her inferior, beneath his dignity. Yet, unable to find a suitable replacement for his bed or his ego, he returned to her repeatedly over the next few weeks.

She was pregnant within a month of meeting Bobby. He ordered her to get an abortion. Martha agreed without protest, readily locating someone who could perform the procedure. But when she went to Bobby to collect the money, he changed his mind, concluding fatherhood would add another dimension to his domain.

The choice was difficult to make even for Bobby, who was prone to rash decisions. In a rare moment of honest self-appraisal, Bobby admitted Martha was not the woman he wanted to marry. She was plain and dull, yet she made him feel the exact opposite about himself.

They were married in early April. Martha miscarried on V-E Day.

The loss of the baby demoralized Bobby. He was not heartbroken by any means, knowing another chance of fatherhood would come his way one day. But he felt trapped in a worthless marriage, seeing Martha as dim-witted and empty-headed, wondering how he could have deluded himself into believing she could make a fitting wife.

He inquired about a divorce. Discovering he had neither the grounds nor the money to pursue one, Bobby did the next best thing he could think of. He sent Martha to live with his parents in Cookville while he re-enlisted in the Army and spent the next few years chasing women and living the good life.

Martha complied with his decisions because she had no choice and no reason for doing anything else.

Bobby returned to Cookville in 1950, promptly impregnated his wife and later in the year became father to a son, Wayne Robert. A second son, William Robert, was born three years later, and Bobby was apt to boast about other sons he would have if Martha was not as inclined to miscarry a pregnancy as she was to carry it to full term.

Under his father's guidance, Bobby developed into a respectable farmer, paying his bills and building a small nest egg over the years. But his contributions to prosperity around the Taylor household came grudgingly because Bobby preferred the idleness of the lazy to the industriousness of the hardworking. While Robert sweated willingly for every penny, Bobby hunted for the quick and easy way to riches. In the spring of 1960, he thought he found it.

Bobby's decision to seek political office came impulsively. On the day after Sheriff Marvin McClelland announced he would not seek re-election, Bobby became the first of seven candidates to seek the job, believing a base of friends from across the county and the support of several kindred spirits would propel him to victory. He campaigned doggedly, forsaking his duty to the farm for the quest of a greater bounty. Bobby canvassed the county door-to-door, regardless of the welcome mat. His message was unwavering, and even those who opposed him admitted the candidate remained true to his beliefs, never mincing words or ideas. Good law enforcement, according to Bobby, meant strict control and discipline of the colored population, and he promised to keep them on a tight rein.

"This county needs a sheriff who will stand up for what's right, someone who won't coddle criminals, but will earn their respect and, more importantly, their fear," Bobby repeated over and over again on any and every stump. "Our way of life is fallen down around our feet, and too many of us are just standen by watchen it happen.

"Niggers are risen up, getten too big for their britches because they want c-evil rights. Don't you believe it, folks! They want to marry our women and confuse our children. They want this country to look like one big Oreo cookie, and unless someone has the guts to stand up to them and their nigger-loven, white-trash supporters, they're goen to get just what they want.

"And then where will we be?

"A bunch of Oreo cuckoos runnen 'round and 'round, biten off chicken heads, stealen, rapen, killen—all because we've elected cowards who kowtow to the niggers and everyone else who wants to see our way of life destroyed.

"Now some of y'all may think I'm talken nonsense. But, folks, if you don't believe me, then your heads are covered up in the muck and your butts are sticken up high, tall and proud for all to see. Y'all can read about it in the newspaper, you can see it on TV and I'm here to tell you it's happening—city by city, town by town, school by school.

"We're among the lucky ones here in Cookville. We have our bad seeds, to be sure, but everybody knows their place. I want to make sure it stays that way. That's why I want to be sheriff of this county. It takes a strong man to stand up to niggers in this day and age, and it's goen to take one who's even stronger tomorrow and all the days after. Folks, I am strong. And I'll stand up to what's wrong."

It was a simple message, preying on hate and fear, delivered with the venom and passion of old-fashioned politics, and it became more popular than even Bobby's most ardent supporters could have imagined from the outset of the campaign.

On a sizzling day in July, Bobby Taylor finished first in the Democratic primary, but his failure to capture a majority of the vote pushed him into a runoff with Paul Berrien. Bobby was disappointed, especially with the overwhelming rejection from voters in New River, his home precinct. Still, a victory for Bobby seemed likely, and the entire county took notice.

The runoff campaign played out over the dog days of August and early September when the air was stagnant, the sun sweltering and the ground so soaked with heat that shoes were a necessity to avoid blistered feet. So stifling were those days that it seemed the only breezes came from swarming gnats and the hot air of politicians. None stirred a hotter breeze than Bobby, and no one campaigned with more vigor or purpose.

The race seemed to come down to a matter of style over substance. Bobby and Paul offered distinct messages, and a minority of voters would cast ballots based on strong agreement or disagreement with the opposing viewpoints. But the election's outcome would be decided by the majority of voters, whose opinions waffled with the wind and who cast ballots based on the appeal of the messenger rather than the message. Unfortunately, for the voters, choosing between the styles of Bobby and Paul was a difficult choice to make because their respective strengths played perfectly into their weaknesses. On one hand, Bobby came off as a fanatic for force, the perfect foil for Paul's even-handed respect for the law. On the other hand, Paul's wooden temper came across as a lack of commitment to the cause he wanted to serve, a sharp contrast to Bobby's passion to administer the law.

"They either one could be the best of sheriffs or the worst of sheriffs," a curmudgeon was overheard to say one day among a gathering of old men on the courthouse square. "It just depends on whether you want a sheriff who reacts to a crisis by retiren to the verandah to sip a mint julep and pontificate on the matter in question, or one who shoots everybody in sight first—and I do mean everybody—and asks questions later."

————

On the last Saturday in August, ten days before the runoff election, a large crowd gathered in the cavernous confines of the Planter's Tobacco Warehouse in Cookville. Farmers from across the county, indeed, from all over South Georgia, were waiting in long lines to have their tobacco weighed and tagged for the final sale of the season.

Joe sat in the cab of the pickup, inching the vehicle forward every few minutes as the convoy of trucks passed through the warehouse to have their valuable cargo unloaded. His father, grandfather and brothers were scattered among the groups of men clustered throughout the warehouse in deep discussion. Both Paul and Bobby were there as well, but their politicking played second fiddle to even bigger news—the death of Alvah Shanks, a forty-year-old farmer, husband and father of three who had died from a rattlesnake bite at the Wednesday night prayer meeting of the Holiness Church.

Approaching one of the groups to shake hands and seek support, Paul stopped short upon a lively discussion about the good and bad of handling snakes in churches. His eavesdropping persuaded Paul to go elsewhere in search of votes and he was on his way out the door when he spotted Lucas Bartholomew emerging from the warehouse office.

Lucas had returned recently from his travels up North and was working in the warehouse. "Hello, Lucas," Paul called, genuinely pleased to see the young man.

Lucas smiled broadly. "Afternoon, Mr. Paul," he returned. "I guess you're looken for votes."

"I was," Paul admitted. "Unfortunately, everybody's more interested in Alvah Shanks than the election."

"Everybody's talken 'bout it, for sure," Lucas agreed.

Paul bit his lip. "I can see why," he said. "Elections come around like clockwork, but it's not every day somebody gets bit by a rattlesnake in church and dies."

Both men laughed soberly and drifted into conversation about job prospects for Lucas and the places and things he had seen on his trip up north. Their camaraderie did not go unnoticed.

Robert Taylor observed the easy chatter between Paul and Lucas for several minutes before the idea came to his mind. Almost immediately, he searched out the crowd, found Bobby and pulled his son apart from the group of men.

"What do you want?" Bobby demanded angrily. "I'm tryen to win an election, Pa. I don't have time for talken."

Robert scowled, shaking his head in disgust, tempted to walk away from his son. Finally, he gestured toward Paul and Lucas, who were locked deep in conversation. "There might be a vote or two to win over there," he muttered gruffly. "If you play your cards right."

The advice came in a condescending tone, but Bobby overlooked it in pursuit of a plan to turn the situation to his advantage. An idea formed quickly and Bobby soon stood in the midst of his cronies, pointing out the cozy appearance of Paul and Lucas, implying they were in cahoots on something devious and detrimental to the well-being of Cookville and the county. "Everybody knows those two are buddy-buddy," Bobby said. "Paul Berrien wins this election, then this county might just have a black deputy sheriff."

His ranting and ridicule curried rousing approval among his most ardent supporters and garnered significant interest from curious passersby, especially those inclined to distrust hobnobbing between colored folk and whites. Within minutes, with a crowd behind him, Bobby marched across the warehouse floor to Paul and Lucas, who were squatted on the floor, talking and smoking cigarettes.

Lucas noticed the advancing crowd first, and the frown creasing his forehead conveyed his concern to Paul.

Paul glanced over his shoulder, rising almost instantly to put himself between Lucas and Bobby. Until now, face-to-face encounters between the candidates had been civil affairs, but Paul sensed Bobby was ready for a direct attack. His suspicions were confirmed in quick order.

"I've heard the rumors, Paul," Bobby began contemptuously, "but deep down I didn't want to believe them. Now I don't have any other choice. I have to believe it."

Paul examined the crowd gathered behind Bobby while deciding how to respond. "What are you talken about?" he replied finally.

"You can play your little word games, Paul," Bobby hissed. "But you're courten the nigger vote and there ain't any use tryen to deny it." Bobby paused, then pointed at Lucas. "Especially not when you've been caught red-handed."

Paul glanced back at Lucas, his quick eyes expressing regret over his friend's accidental role in the confrontation. He returned his gaze to the man standing before him. "What I'm doen, Bobby," he said stiffly, "is talken with a friend. If you have a problem with that, so be it. Frankly, my business and my friends are not your concern."

Bobby stepped closer, appraising Paul with a scornful glare. "I disagree," he challenged. "You can tell a lot about a man by the company he keeps." Bobby motioned to Lucas. "My daddy always taught me that you can't trust a nigger," he continued. "But worse than that is a white man who coddles to every whim and wish of a nigger. This county don't need a sheriff who's a nigger lover."

Bobby turned slightly, shifting his gaze between Paul and the growing crowd. "From the day I got in this election, I've warned people about these kinds of things," he said boldly. "We're fighten to preserve a way of life in this county. How can voters expect you to lead that fight, Paul, when you're cozyen up to the very people who are doing their damndest to tear apart everything we stand for?"

Bobby turned his back on Paul. "This county needs a sheriff who will uphold the law and respect the traditions that go with it," he appealed to the crowd. "That's what you'll get if you vote for me." He gestured to Paul and Lucas behind him. "Vote for Paul Berrien and you'll get exactly what you see there—a man in charge of the law who's in cahoots with the very same people who are trying to overturn our laws and bury our traditions."

Several onlookers whooped in support of Bobby, who fixed another damning glare on Paul.

Tension lines gathered on Paul's face. He glanced at Lucas, then searched the crowd for a friendly face while considering a response to the attack on his character. Seeing Matt and Sam edge near the front of the crowd, Paul made up his mind. He walked over to his accuser, squaring off eye-to-eye with Bobby until the other man flinched. Satisfied, Paul shifted his gaze to the crowd.

"You people know the kind of man I am," he said slowly without apologies. "I believe everybody deserves a fair shake with the law—colored or white, rich or poor—it doesn't matter to me. You've known that about me from the very beginnen of this campaign and so has Bobby. If you're bothered because I'd treat colored criminals the same way I'd treat white criminals, then vote for my opponent. But if you're interested in justice and fairness for everyone, then vote for me. I'm a law-abiden man, and I'll be a law-abiden sheriff. It's that simple."

"No, Paul! It's not that simple."

The voice, cracked and bitter, resonated through the hushed warehouse. People looked from side to side, searching for the speaker.

Robert Taylor strode forth, parting a path through the crowd as all eyes turned toward him. He stopped a few feet from Paul and Bobby. "It's not simple at all," he repeated knowingly to Paul, who stood motionless and speechless.

"What's goen on, Pa?" Bobby asked.

Robert ignored his son, keeping his eyes trained on Paul. "You said a mouthful just then, Paul Berrien," he said mysteriously. "You sounded almost like a preacher with all that talk about upholden the law and doen what's right, and maybe you meant it. But you're no law-abiden citizen."

Paul visibly blanched.

"When it suits your needs," Robert persisted, "you're willen to bend the law. Ain't you, Paul?"

Paul shot a hollow glance toward the crowd, and Robert followed his eyes to Matt Baker. The crowd numbered about ninety men, women and children, all spellbound by the drama playing out before their eyes.

Robert waited for Paul's answer, then shrugged, turning to the crowd. "Seven years ago, Paul Berrien covered up his daddy's death," he announced bluntly. "Everyone thought Britt Berrien died of a heart attack, but the truth is someone stuck a gun in his mouth and pulled the trigger." He hesitated, allowing ample time for the enthralled audience to draw its own conclusions, daring Paul to dispute the accusation.

Everyone else waited for a response from Paul as well, some praying for a denial, others hoping for a confession. In the end, the silence convicted Paul. He stood frozen, the color drained from his lean face and his green eyes glassed over with disbelief.

The moment seemed endless, like an unwanted portion of time.

Robert drew closer to Paul. "I was at the funeral home that night," he murmured harshly. "My Josephine was a corpse, and I wanted to be with her. To tell you the truth, Paul, I never thought much about what you did till just now when you got all high and mighty and preachy about abiden by the law."

He stepped away from Paul, whirling to face the stunned crowd. "I was at the funeral home the night they brought in Berrien's body," Robert repeated loudly for the benefit of the crowd. "They said it was suicide and maybe it was. I don't know about that. But I do know Britt Berrien didn't have no heart attack." He glared across the crowd, halting his gaze on Matt. "If y'all don't believe me, just ask two more of our respected, law-abiden citizens—Matt Baker and the good coroner, Arch Adams," Robert continued. "Matt helped Paul bring the body to the funeral home, and both of 'em persuaded Arch to lie about the cause of death."

Robert paused once more, allowing the confused onlookers to mumble among themselves.

"Is he tellen the truth, Paul?" asked Virgil Parrish at last. Virgil lived in the eastern part of the county. He was the community's most prosperous farmer and people paid attention when he asked questions or spouted off opinions.

The question jolted Paul, who willed a pair of trembling knees to stand solidly. He swallowed the rising panic in his throat and squared his shoulders. "It's true," he admitted quietly.

Bobby Taylor stepped cautiously to his father's side. He glanced at Robert, then fixed his attention on Paul. "You've got a lot of nerve asken the people of this county to trust you to enforce the law, Paul Berrien," he said carefully. "Specially when breaken it came so easy to you."

Paul eyed Bobby stiffly. "I had my reasons."

"You used your reputation to break the law," Bobby countered quickly in tones both condescending and reproachful. "You lied, you cheated and you abused the people of this county with dishonesty—then and now."

"Spare me your sermon, Bobby," Paul snapped. "I neither need nor want your judgments and opinions." He swept the crowd with a challenging gaze, making eye contact with Virgil Parrish, Robert Taylor and several others before his glare settled on Bobby. "Maybe I did do wrong," he continued stoutly. "But chances are I'd do it all over again if I had to make that same decision today. Regardless, I'm more than willen to face the consequences of my actions—before the law and the people of this county. Now if y'all excuse me, I have business to tend to."

And with that, Paul Berrien marched out of the warehouse and straight to the sheriff's office, where he confessed his wrongdoing.

―――――

On Election Day, Bobby Taylor woke in a foul mood, the result of another dream about the amazing revelation regarding Paul Berrien. He lay in the sticky bed for a long time, alternately cursing the early morning heat and the gilded fortune of his opponent.

Bobby figured the election should have been handed to him by now, on a silver platter by Paul himself. It was inconceivable that his opponent had not dropped out of the election altogether, indeed, why Paul was not in jail or at the very least facing criminal charges for covering up the cause of Britt Berrien's death. So why then, Bobby wondered, did he have so many misgivings about the election outcome?

He roused himself from bed and went outside on the back porch to relieve his bladder, ignoring the morning greeting from Martha as he passed the kitchen. Bobby, his father and the boys all peed off the back porch every morning, none willing to make the long walk to the outhouse. He made a silent promise to see about indoor plumbing as soon as the election was over, then returned inside the house to the kitchen.

"Where's breakfast?" he growled, sitting down at the table.

"On the stove keepen warm," Martha answered. "I'll fix your plate."

Bobby observed his wife dish up congealed scrambled eggs and overdone bacon. Martha's movements were sluggish and heavy despite her thin build, and Bobby shook his head in dismay as she set the plate before him and turned to fetch the coffee pot. He considered complaining about the eggs but decided it would be a waste of time. Martha's cooking, like most everything else about her, left a lot to be desired.

She set the coffee cup on the table, and they made eye contact. Bobby quickly looked away, nibbling around the burnt edges of a piece of bacon. "Your daddy said to find out what time we're goen to vote," Martha told him.

Bobby dropped the partially eaten bacon back on the plate. "Sometime this afternoon," he replied. He pushed the fork through the eggs but could not work up an appetite. Finally, he picked up the coffee, pushed away from the table and went back to bed.

He sat on the edge of the bed, drinking coffee, while his thoughts wandered back to Paul Berrien and the election. If anyone ever needed proof that the rich were different and above the law, then surely this situation provided it. The whole mess bewildered Bobby. Had he conspired to cover up the cause of someone's death, tried to pass off a suicide as a heart attack, the sheriff would have slapped a pair of handcuffs on him in a heartbeat and Bobby likely would have ended up buried under the jail. No one would have given him the benefit of the doubt. Paul Berrien, however, had done wrong and walked away from it smelling like roses. Paul had gotten off scot-free as far as the law was concerned. The whole world, it seemed, was ready and willing not only to exonerate Paul but to praise his good intentions to spare his older sisters the truth about their father's decision to blow his brains out of his head. Well, April and June knew the truth now and Bobby hoped they were wallowing in every miserable ounce of it.

Bobby felt a vindictive mood coming over him. Realizing he could ill afford a short temper on this of all days, he decided to nip his anger in the bud. He forced himself from bed, determined to concentrate on something else beside the election for the remainder of the morning, deciding a walk around the farm would ease his foul mood.

It did not.

By dinnertime, his mind was off the election and Bobby was furious. The crops were withered from lack of rain, choked full of weeds from neglect, and Bobby doubted anything could be salvaged from them. He scarcely believed what he saw. Bad times had visited the farm before, but never had his father tended the fields with such dereliction. Bobby considered the possibility that his mind was playing tricks on him, that the heat had afflicted him with sunstroke and he was imagining the worst. But Bobby was sound of mind and body for the moment, and these wasted fields were laid by with reality.

In this state of disbelief and anger, Bobby sought out his father. He found Robert by the water pump outside the back door, bent over by a fit of wheezing and coughing.

"Crops look like shit, Pa," Bobby bellowed. "Just what the hell have you been doen all summer? And how do you think we are goen to get by this comen year?"

Robert coughed up a mess of phlegm, spat and wiped his mouth on his shirt-sleeve before looking at Bobby. "You get elected sheriff today, and you ought to get by fine this year and the three after it," he answered tiredly. "Besides, Bobby, you never worried much about the crops in the past. Why the sudden interest?"

"I never had reason to worry," Bobby replied impatiently, beginning to scrutinize his father. "What's been goen on around here this summer?" he demanded. "Why haven't you taken better care of the farm?"

"I did my best," Robert muttered defiantly.

For the second time that day, Bobby wondered if his eyes were deceiving him. He blinked twice, peered closer at Robert and discovered that his father, much like the fields on their farm, appeared withered and beaten. His pa was a tired old man, haggard and worn out, shriveled and used up.

He'd spent a lifetime thinking of his father as robust and impregnable, so it took a moment for Bobby to digest these appearances otherwise. He'd been hell-bent on a confrontation with Robert a moment ago, but his attitude softened with concern over his father's well-being. "You're not looken too good these days, Pa," Bobby frowned. "Are you feelen poorly?"

"I'm okay," Robert insisted.

"Maybe," Bobby agreed halfheartedly. "But maybe you ought to see the doctor."

Robert coughed again, a dry, hacking sound that made Bobby wince while his father struggled to breathe.

"I hope you win the election," Robert told his son when he had regained his composure. He fixed a stern look on Bobby. "You don't care much for hard work, and you've never impressed me as be'en none too bright."

Bobby went pale beneath the criticism.

"Of course," Robert continued, "you might not win the election, and that'll put you right back here on the farm. It's a decent farm. Bought and paid for. A man can earn a liven on it if he's willen to put forth the effort, which is about the best piece of advice I can or ever will offer you, boy."

Robert turned away and walked a few steps to the back porch, then stopped and looked back at his son. "You and me never were much alike," he said stiffly. "Except for one thing. I never cared too much about anything or anybody, and I guess you've cared even less about most everything and everybody. Don't go tryen to do me any favors, Bobby. I don't need your sympathy and I don't want it. I've seen a doctor. He says I got lung cancer and I'm dyen." Robert hesitated, glancing around the yard into the fields and back to Bobby. "It won't be no great loss," he shrugged. "Not to me, you or anybody else," he added, turning back toward the house and shuffling up the rickety porch steps.

Bobby never knew whether his father or Martha voted. He skipped dinner that day, choosing to take a long drive through the countryside. In the early afternoon, he stopped by the voting precinct to cast his ballot, then continued on to the Tip-Toe Inn, the only legitimate honky tonk in the county. He parked behind the sprawling building, spent the next two hours getting drunk on an empty stomach and finally set out for home to catch a quick nap. He woke shortly after the polls closed, with a vicious hangover and low spirits. Still, he showered and dressed neatly, piled his family into the pickup and drove to Cookville to wait on the election returns.

His home precinct of New River reported the first results, giving Paul Berrien an overwhelming majority of the vote. Bobby won six of the next nine districts reporting, but the voting margins were too small to overcome Paul's early lead. It was the closest vote in county history and Bobby came up on the short end of the count.

He watched the final tally go up on the tote board in front of *The Cookville Herald* office on the town square, shaking his head in disbelief, astonished by the thin difference in the vote, enraged by the miracle of Paul's victory.

"Bobby."

It took a moment for the sound to penetrate Bobby's consciousness. He turned around slowly, his mouth agape, to find Paul standing before him with a conciliatory smile plastered across his face.

"Bobby," Paul repeated, extending his hand. "You ran a hard campaign. The vote couldn't have been any closer." He hesitated. "I hope we can move past our differences."

Bobby, still shell-shocked by the defeat, shook his head. "You're gonna turn this county over to the niggers, Paul," he hissed loudly.

He shoved past a startled Paul, marched into the gathering crowd and stopped abruptly. "Those of you who voted for this man," Bobby exploded, gesturing to Paul. "Mark my words!" He glared out at the crowd with bloodshot eyes, venting rage and despair. "One day, you'll remember my warnen about Paul Berrien. Y'all will be sorry that you voted a lawbreaker and a rich daddy's boy into office, and you'll wish you had voted for me."

Bobby scanned the crowd, searching for enemies and the misguided, then leveled his seething gaze on Paul. "I'll be back, Paul Berrien," he sneered. "I'm gonna watch your every move like a hawk these next four years. And next time, I'll win. You can count on it."

His peace said, Bobby stormed into the darkness.

TWILIGHT WAS FADING WHEN the Bakers headed home from Tifton. Sleet fell, icing the road and forcing Matt to drive cautiously. But no one minded the slow going. The family was in a festive mood, dreaming aloud about Christmas wishes and thinking silently about preparations still to complete.

Matt was the first to realize the sleet had changed to snow. "Will you look at that?" he whistled softly.

"What's that?" Caroline asked from the backseat, where she was planning supper and making a mental list of the things she needed to do before bedtime, including baking a spice cake and wrapping gifts.

"It's snowen," Matt announced to the entire family.

The children greeted the news with shrieks and gasps. Snow fell rarely in these parts—Luke and Bonnie had never seen it—and they could hardly contain their anticipation. Faces pressed against the windows in search of the white stuff, and all six children pleaded for Matt to stop the car so that they could touch the snow. Matt considered honoring the request, but they were only a few minutes from home and he wanted to get there before the road conditions deteriorated. He continued driving, despite the disapproving groans.

The short delay merely heightened expectations and none too soon they were home. Car doors flew open and the children spilled out with yelps of happiness, crawling over parents, grandparents and each other in their eagerness to acquaint themselves with snow. They were a sight to behold, and parents and grandparents watched in wonder at their various reactions to the touch and feel of snow. Joe raised his head to the heavens, attempting to catch the tiny flakes with his mouth, while Summer and Luke ran to the front porch walkway, scraping up enough white powder to make their first snowballs. John and Carrie stood openmouthed, he staring as if afraid the white fleece would disappear with any sudden movement and she reaching tentatively out with her hands to catch a falling snowflake. Bonnie squealed in delight, shaking her head back and forth as snow landed on her hair.

The snow cast a magic spell that not even the adults were immune to. Matt gathered Caroline in a full embrace, and even Rachel permitted Sam to wrap his arms around her waist.

"Looks like we're goen to have another white Christmas," Caroline said happily.

"Twice in a lifetime," Rachel replied. "Who would have dreamed?"

They watched the frolicking children for a while longer and then, all too soon, the snow ended. It simply stopped, without warning, and a vague sense of disappointment filled the adults whose imaginations had drummed up expectations of a white Christmas similar to the one in 1941.

The children, unhampered by such expectancy, barely noticed the snow had stopped. A thin white blanket covered the frozen ground like dust and its beauty was priceless in their eyes. They had woken on many winter mornings to frost gathered more thickly on the ground, but the snow was special. They regarded it with a moment of passing reverence, then turned the yard into an ice-skating rink, slipping and sliding across the slick grass, falling down on the cold ground and soaking their clothes through and through.

Rachel opened her mouth, prepared to utter a stern warning about catching cold, flu or worse. But Caroline caught her eye beforehand. "They'll remember this night their whole lives, Ma. A cold, they'll forget. But we make them go inside now and they'll never let us live it down."

Rachel shrugged. "You're right," she agreed. "Maybe if there's a hot supper on the table and dry clothes waiten when they come inside, we can keep everybody well."

Almost an hour later, Caroline called her brood into the warm house. They straggled in one by one with red cheeks, runny noses and frozen hands, exhausted from the horseplay, soaked to the bone and glowing with high spirits. She made everyone change into dry bedclothes, then ushered them into the kitchen to a roaring fire.

Christmas Eve supper was traditional fare in the Baker household—fried pork brains, scrambled eggs, sausage, bacon, grits and biscuits sopped in cane syrup. Everyone ate a hearty meal and then focused like elves on their final preparations for Christmas Day. Stockings went up by the kitchen fireplace, presents were wrapped and put under the tree and, finally, the children were hustled into bed for the nightly devotional.

The children rarely bedded down at nighttime without a devotional and prayer. Usually, Caroline or Rachel read several verses from the Bible before prayers were said and kisses given. On this night, Caroline asked Joe to read the Christmas story.

"And it came to pass in those days, that there went out a decree from Caesar Augustus, that all the world should be taxed. (And this taxing was first made when Cyrenius was governor of Syria.) And all went to be taxed, every one into his own city. And Joseph also went up from Galilee, out of the city of Nazareth, into Judaea, unto the city of David, which is called Bethlehem; (because he was of the house and lineage of David:) To be taxed with Mary his espoused wife, being great with child ...."

Caroline stood in the doorway for a moment, listening to the wonderful story, the words ringing deep and true from Joe, and her heart beamed. Then, she made her way to the kitchen.

———

Caroline finished wrapping the presents shortly before midnight and, with Matt's help, arranged them under the Christmas tree. Next, they stuffed the stockings, filling them with oranges, grapefruit, tangerines and kumquats, almonds, walnuts, Brazil nuts and cashews, gumdrops, fudge, hard candy and chewing gum. There were trinkets and small toys, Crackerjacks and novelties—until at last the bulging stockings would hold no more.

When they were finished, Matt picked up the glass of milk and saucer of cookies left on the table by Luke and Bonnie and retired with his wife to the living room. The soft glow of Christmas lights provided the room's only illumination and they sat on the burgundy sofa, dunking cookies in milk, observing the tree and packages and relishing the peace of Christmas night.

"Are you tired?" Matt asked when Caroline laid her head on his shoulder.

"Not really," she answered softly. "Just contented."

"Me, too," Matt agreed.

He put a finger under Caroline's chin, tilted her face and kissed his wife fully on the lips, long and slow. The kiss was different from the ones they had shared nineteen years ago, absent of mystery and full of familiarity, but it kindled the same passion.

"Nineteen years is a long time," Caroline sighed, breaking the kiss. "But it's gone by so fast."

Matt nodded agreement, looked at the tree and then back to Caroline. "Sometimes, I feel like we've been married forever," he said gently, "and I can't remember a time when you weren't a part of my life."

Caroline gave him a frowning smile.

"It's a good feelen," he assured her. "A very good feelen. The time has flown, though. I remember getten married like it was yesterday. But it also seems like somethen that happened a lifetime ago. Sometimes I wonder if you married me or somebody who just happened to look like me."

"I know what you mean," Caroline admitted. "It's probably because we're different people now." She paused, gathering her thoughts. "I was just sixteen when we got married; you were eighteen. I was me and you were you. Now, I think we're us, and that makes us both different people."

She laughed. "Does that sound silly?"

Matt smiled. "Not to me." He kissed her again, then broke away with a boyish grin. "I know we decided not to give gifts this year, but I just couldn't let both our anniversary and Christmas pass without somethen to remember it by," he said cheerfully.

Caroline bowed her head, then peered up at him with guilty eyes. "We're worse than the children," she confessed. "I got you somethen, too."

Matt smiled again, mischievously. "If we give our gifts tonight, technically they count as anniversary presents," he suggested. "And if I remember right, we only agreed not to give Christmas presents."

Caroline rose from the sofa, grinning at her husband. "Yours is in the bedroom," she said, moving past him across the hall to their room. She returned shortly, carrying a tiny package wrapped in red tissue paper and sprouting a white bow bigger than the gift.

"I didn't wrap mine," Matt said hesitantly as she took her seat next to him on the sofa.

"It doesn't matter," Caroline replied, handing him the red package. "This isn't much, but I thought you'd appreciate it."

Matt tore off the bow, bringing the tissue paper with it, and found himself staring at a small cardboard box. He opened the box and pulled out a triple-bladed pocket-knife. A wide grin split his face and he looked at Caroline. "Thanks, honey," he said, genuinely pleased.

"You lost your other one this summer," Caroline explained. "I kept thinken you'd get another one, but you didn't. No man should have to go around without a pocketknife."

Matt opened the three blades. "There must have been a hundred times over the last few months when a pocketknife would have come in handy," he said, examining the knife. "I kept reachen for mine, but it wasn't there." He closed the blades. "This is good," he added, slipping the gift into the front pocket of his corduroy pants.

He kissed her quickly, then pushed away, grinning broadly and saying, "Now it's your turn."

Caroline eyed his grin with a curious frown. "What is it?"

Matt shook his head. "Close your eyes."

Caroline obeyed and Matt reached into his pocket. "Okay, open them," he said.

Caroline opened her eyes to find a delicate ring box setting on the palm of her husband's hand. "Oh, Matt!" she exclaimed softly.

She took the bone-colored box gingerly, opened it and gasped. The white gold ring lay on a velvety green cushion, its cluster of diamonds sparkling in the glow of the Christmas tree lights.

"It's beautiful," Caroline remarked finally, looking from the ring to her husband with tears of joy in her eyes.

As far as Matt was concerned, the band was too thin and the cluster of diamond chips too tiny. But the ring was the only one affordable, and he had settled for it. Now, gazing into the adoring eyes of his wife, Matt forgot what the ring lacked in splendor. He lifted the ring from the velvet bed, then slipped it carefully onto Caroline's finger.

"We didn't have much time to be engaged, but I always wanted you to have a ring," he said. "Sorry you had to wait nineteen years for it."

Caroline placed her hands on his shoulders. "I'm not," she smiled into his eyes. "Nineteen years ago, you made me the happiest woman in the world, Matt; now you've gone and done it all over again. I love you."

Her devotion and affection brought a blush to Matt's face. He glanced down at the ring on her hand, then back to Caroline. "I loved you a lot back then, honey," he said. "But I love you that much more now."

Matt kissed Caroline tenderly, then gathered her in his arms, carried her to the bedroom and made love with his wife. At last, with both of them exhausted and sated, Caroline laid her head on Matt's chest and was locked in his embrace for the night. In silence, they drifted into the familiar, comfortable and satisfying slumber of old lovers.

A stillness settled over the home that night, its quietness broken only by the occasional rustling of bed covers and the constant tick of various clocks, while outside, cascades of snow swirled silently, softly. The small flakes danced to an uncommon beat on their downward journey, settling over ground, trees and rooftops. Snow blanketed the land again and again, creating a winter wonderland and magic for a lifetime.

————

On that same night, a young black woman lay sleeplessly on a worn double mattress that had been pushed into the corner of her rented, single-room shack. Her name was Beauty Salon, and the pedigree behind it was at the top of the jumble cluttering her head and keeping the woman awake.

Beauty's mother had been born and raised in Cookville, living there until the age of nineteen when she took a notion to leave and moved to New Orleans. Some fifteen years later, Goodie Wright returned home and reintroduced herself as Goodness Salon. She brought with her a ten-year-old daughter and a sad story about her husband drowning in the Mississippi River.

Everyone accepted her story at face value, which was fortunate since every word of it was true. However, both friends and relatives scoffed at the ridiculousness of naming a child Beauty Salon. Some even accused her of lying about the girl's name, but Goodness silenced those doubters by producing authentic copies of her marriage license to Jacque Salon, his death certificate and Beauty's birth certificate. Afterward, relatives and friends decided the name was clever, and Goodness and Beauty set up permanent residence in Cookville. Goodness earned their living styling hair in the black community and Beauty, when she was older and had quit school, worked as a maid for a number of well-to-do white families in the community.

Beauty herself grew to despise the name and longed for the day when she could change it. Perhaps if she were indeed beautiful, she would have enjoyed the name. But Beauty was an average-looking woman, an inch or so taller and, perhaps, longer-limbed, smaller-breasted and leaner-hipped than most. She was moon-faced, with wide, expressive dark eyes and slender facial contours that offset her broad features. Her hair, which was jet black and tended to straighten naturally, framed her face like a picture, falling shoulder length and flipping under at the ends.

There was reason for Beauty to consider her name on this night, and it was lying beside her in the long form of Lucas Bartholomew.

Lucas had asked Beauty to marry him earlier in the evening. The proposal had shocked Beauty, who had been simply curious and mildly thrilled when Lucas showed up at her front door earlier on this Christmas Eve.

"I have somethen to ask you," he had told her when Beauty opened the door to find him standing in the frigid darkness. "Can I come in?"

She motioned Lucas inside, gesturing for him to sit in the only chair in her home, but he declined politely. "We don't know each other all that well, Beauty, but I think highly of you," he said respectfully. "I'm hopen you will marry me."

Lucas apparently interpreted her stunned silence as wariness about the proposal. "I'm a hard worker," he assured her, "and I'll make a decent liven for us. I'm not much of a drinken man, I'll go to church with you and I'll never lay a hand on you unless you want me to."

Until that moment, Beauty had considered Lucas only a passing acquaintance. He was younger than her by two years, they had never run in the same circles and most of what she knew about him came by reputation and word of mouth. No one could question his work ethic, but the Lucas she remembered also possessed a wild streak. Lucas had drunk his share of liquor and known more than a few women in Cookville before he went traipsing off across the country. To his credit, though, Lucas had been discreet about his carryings-on and his reputation was earned solely through gossip as far as Beauty was concerned.

She first took notice of Lucas one Sunday morning while singing in the choir of the Cookville African-Methodist-Episcopal Church. They were singing *I'll Fly Away* when Lucas snuck into the back pew of the church. Lucas had gone from the back pew to the altar in a few Sundays, and their first conversation had come when Beauty found the courage to welcome him into the Lord's flock.

Since then, they had spoken to each other regularly at Sunday church services and on frequent occasions in the Berrien home, where Beauty did housekeeping twice a week and Lucas often performed odd jobs.

At the age of twenty-five, Beauty had begun to think marriage was an unlikely prospect, which meant she would be stuck with her outrageous name for eternity. But it was neither her spinster status nor dislike of being called Beauty Salon that moved her to accept the marriage proposal from Lucas. It was his humbleness and sincerity.

Lucas made no pretense about loving her. He was fond of Beauty, as she was of him. Lucas wanted a companion, someone to make a home with, and the idea appealed to Beauty. There would be plenty of time for love once they were married and knew each other.

"Yes," she told him without batting an eye.

Lucas accepted her answer with equal dispassion. But it was only a moment before he flashed her a broad grin, and his obvious delight unfurled a timid smile from Beauty. They laughed quietly, like children flushed from the unexpected success of a mysterious adventure. Then unexpectedly, almost as if he had forgotten, Lucas reached inside his winter coat and produced a gift-wrapped package for Beauty.

Her smile widened, and she accepted it eagerly, tore open the wrapping and found a Bible.

"I noticed you don't have a Bible at church," Lucas said thoughtfully. "I figured you need one see'en how church is so important to you. And I thought it would be a good way of keepen track of our family."

Beauty fingered the cardboard binder, then thumbed through the pages. "I don't read very well," she murmured, embarrassed by the revelation.

"Then I'll teach you," Lucas vowed.

Beauty was a serious person, deliberate and thorough in her actions and manners. Religion and church were especially dear to her heart.

She could trace her Christian commitment to a hot summer day when she was fourteen and some lunatic had burst into the church screaming about religion, the masses and how it was a tool white people used to keep colored folk in their place. Beauty had not understood the man's ranting and likely would have forgotten him, except that had been the day she first felt the power of God.

It happened sometime after the mad man was escorted from church. They were singing strongly and the preacher called everyone to the altar. Usually, Beauty sat in the pew during altar calls but on this day, she heeded the preacher's advice to unburden herself. She never made it to the altar. Six steps from her destination, she passed out cold, sucker-punched by a power so strong that Beauty swore God had belted her so she would see the light.

Ever since, Beauty had been a devout churchgoer. She sang in the choir, a soulful alto who was particularly effective on slower hymns like *Amazing Grace*. She would have studied the Bible but her reading skills made the task difficult at best, so Beauty contented herself by trying to recall the scriptures read by the preacher each Sunday and applying the message to her life.

The offer from Lucas to teach her to read filled her heart with joy in a way that Beauty had experienced maybe once or twice before. "I'd be much obliged," she acknowledged warmly.

Lucas moved closer to Beauty, turning the pages of the Bible to the front to show where he had written her name as owner of the book, his name as its giver and the date it was given. "I took the liberty of fillen out all that information beforehand," he said apologetically. "Took it for granted you might say yes."

Beauty was plagued by an innate shyness, which often stopped her from voicing opinions or joining conversations. She was a natural listener, but with Lucas, she lost her inhibitions.

Lucas entertained her with tales about his travels around the country, visits to big cities like New York, Philadelphia and Detroit, people he had met and the things he had done. He told her about his family, a father who drank too much, a mother who endured ill health, and she told him about the feeling of always being overshadowed by her mother's gaudy style. They discovered they were both only children, although Beauty volunteered that she considered two cousins like sisters.

Beauty, who prepared a supper of boiled turnip greens, baked sweet potatoes and cornbread while talking and listening, surprised herself and Lucas by asking suddenly over the meal, "Do you believe God is a white man?"

Lucas weighed the question in his mind, at last answering, "I never thought about it much to be truthful. Why you ask?"

"I'm just curious."

"What do you think," he inquired. "Is God black or white?"

Beauty told him that she believed God was a white man, just like Santa Claus. Colored people tried to convince themselves that Jesus and Santa Claus were black men, but Beauty knew better. If Santa Claus were black, she told Lucas, then he would not pass over her house year after year without ever leaving anything.

For a long time, Lucas had simply stared at Beauty as if he thought her crazy. And then Beauty laughed mischievously, shook her head and explained she always had silly thoughts around Christmastime. She assured Lucas that she knew Santa Claus did not exist, not even for white children, but the idea was a lovely notion anyway and one she would pass on to her children one day. For as far as Beauty was concerned, if there was a Santa Claus, then he would love colored and white children equally—just as God did.

They talked late into the night, agreeing to marry as soon as possible and deciding to live in Beauty's rented shack until Lucas could arrange for more comfortable accommodations.

When Lucas finally rose from his chair, Beauty supposed he was going to leave. Instead, he walked to her and pushed a lock of hair off her face. "I can go now or I could stay the night. The choice is yours to make, Beauty."

Once again, Lucas caught her off guard with a proposal and this time Beauty's stomach leapt into her throat. She swallowed as Lucas laid the rough palm of his hand against her cheek.

"You can stay," she said nervously. "But I've never been with anyone before."

Lucas merely nodded understanding, then pulled her from the chair and led her to the mattress. He had kissed Beauty and then bedded her, gently at first to overcome her reluctance and later more frantically as her need became greater. Lucas had drifted off to sleep soon afterward, cradling Beauty in his arms for a while before falling away and turning his back to her.

Now Beauty touched his naked back, gingerly so as not to wake him. His skin was cold, so she pulled the blanket over Lucas and was stricken by the most intimate sensation of her life. She allowed her hand to linger on his back, caressing its muscled cords and bony ridges, realizing this body would share her bed and her life for all the years to come.

Joy filled her heart, and Beauty experienced profound knowledge: Earlier this night she had agreed to take Lucas as her husband; now she took him to heart. What she felt was not yet love but the beginnings of it, stirring deep inside Beauty, swelling like baker's yeast, bubbling like fine wine. She could not contain it and she could not lie still.

Ignoring the urge to rouse Lucas from his sound sleep to tell him about this revelation, Beauty eased herself off the mattress, crossing the cold floor in bare feet to the single window in her one-room shack. Beneath the window was a worn footlocker, a hand-me-down from one of the families whose homes she cleaned. Inside the cardboard trunk were Beauty's treasures, an assortment of odds and ends collected over the years through the philanthropic gestures of various employers. Pots and pans, dinnerware and flatware, candles and candlesticks, linens and coverings, a medley of miscellany no longer wanted by well-to-do white women, a hoard of household treasures for Beauty.

Working quietly, she unhitched the trunk and eased up its squeaky lid. An ivory lace doily lay on top of the neatly stacked collection. A donation from the Berrien sisters, it was delicate and dainty, one of Beauty's most prized possessions. She closed her eyes, imagining a beautiful lamp resting on top of the lace, remembering June Berrien had suggested to her sister some months ago that they should rid themselves of an old hurricane lamp stuck away in one of the empty bedrooms of their home.

Beauty blushed at the wayward thought, knowing her covetous nature violated one of the Ten Commandments. She shook away both feelings and began rummaging through the trunk, smiling to herself at the thought of using these throwaways to make a home for Lucas.

When she had examined the entirety of contents in the trunk, Beauty returned every item to its rightful place, closed the lid and reattached the locks. A combination of the late hour and personal satisfaction was waning her enthusiasm, but Beauty was not yet ready to return to bed.

She rose from the floor, reached across the trunk to pull back the curtain and discovered a miracle. It was snowing again. A few flakes had dusted the ground earlier in the evening, but this time the white stuff was falling in earnest, piling up in mounds. There would be snow on the ground in the morning, maybe all through Christmas Day. Cookville would have a white Christmas and maybe she and Lucas would have a white wedding.

Stifling a yawn, Beauty glanced one final time out the window at the falling snow. She'd always heard Christmas was the season of miracles but until tonight, she'd never understood the meaning. Now she did. Tonight, Beauty felt part of a miracle. She understood the promise of Christmas, she believed in the spirit of Santa Claus, and she felt blessed by a sign from God.

She dropped the curtain back in place, tiptoeing across the room to retrieve the Bible Lucas had given her, cradling it with reverence. Lucas had said they would fill up the blank pages with history while the printed pages guided their way.

For a while, she contemplated their behavior earlier in the night, coming together as husband and wife without the blessing of a preacher. Certainly, the Bible did not condone adultery and fornication. But had they been wrong to celebrate their commitment to each other? Did a preacher's blessing of their union matter when they already had God's blessing?

A ponderous woman might have brooded over such concerns. But Beauty was a simple woman. She had protected her virtue for twenty-five years, yielding it only to the man who would share her bed for the remainder of their lives together. Whatever doubts she had about her decision vanished in a wave of drowsy contentment.

She pattered across the room once more, to the mattress on the floor and, lying carefully down, drawing the covers around her, stretched out beside her man. Lucas, feeling her press against him, rolled over onto his side, facing Beauty, and without waking, snuggled against her. She explored his chest, found his heartbeat with her hand and closed her eyes.

It was the season of miracles, the fulfillment of promise, and she, Beauty Salon, was living a dream. That was her last waking thought, except for one: In a day or so, for better or worse, she would become Beauty Bartholomew.

———

Lamplight cast a soft glow around the elegant front room, the more formal of two parlors in the Berrien mansion. A fire crackled in the marbled fireplace, its flickering lights throwing shadows, breaking the smooth planes of muted illumination, dancing to the melodies of Christmas music playing from a stereo console. The stereo was a present to themselves from the three Berrien siblings, a purposefully self-indulgent Christmas Eve purchase of celebration.

Paul stoked the fire with another log, poked it and, laying aside the soot-stained iron rod, crossed the ivory colored floor rug with Wedgwood borders of ribbons and intertwined flower sprigs to a Queen Anne side table. On the cherry table were a crystal ice bucket holding a chilled bottle of champagne and three matching glasses.

"On an impulse I walked straight into this fancy Atlanta restaurant and told the maître d' I wanted a bottle of his most ridiculously expensive champagne in a bag to go," Paul informed his sisters, explaining how he had acquired the sparkling white wine.

"And what did the maître d' do, pray tell?" laughed June.

"He didn't bat an eye, that's for sure," Paul grinned. "He simply said, 'One moment, sir,' vanished behind closed doors and returned in a couple of minutes with the bottle, replete with a brown bag. The man assured me it was vintage quality, imported from France. I took his word for it, he charged me a small fortune and I was on my way home."

"I declare," April exclaimed as Paul plucked the champagne from the ice bucket. "Whatever would the church members say if they knew we were drinken champagne? No doubt it would be scandalous."

"I dare say, April," reasoned June, the saltier of the two sisters. "Not even the Hard Shell Baptists would begrudge us a drink or two after the year we've had. And I'm almost willen to bet the kind folks at Benevolence Missionary Baptist Church would do the honors for us were they here tonight."

"Here, here," Paul agreed, giving the bottle a final twist as the cork popped free and the bubbling foam elicited delighted gasps and clapping from his sisters.

"We haven't had champagne in ages," June reflected.

"Not since Paul graduated from law school and came home," April remembered.

"As I recall, we were celebraten my engagement," Paul reminded them drolly. "Fleeten though it was."

"Oh, yes," June frowned. "Now I remember. Paul, whatever happened to Paige?"

"She married a very respected doctor in Atlanta. They had a couple of children last time I heard, which was several years ago."

"Well, good for her," April said.

"Yes," Paul concurred, filling the three glasses with champagne. "Good for her."

He passed glasses to April and June, then picked up the remaining one for himself, bestowing a catching smile on his sisters. "To us," he toasted.

"To us," chimed in April and June as the three of them touched glasses and sipped champagne.

"Delicious," purred June. "We really should do this more often."

"We should," April agreed whimsically. "But let's not tell the Baptists if we do."

Everyone laughed lightly, using the ensuing moment of silence to collect their thoughts and savor the champagne.

It was an unusual Christmas Eve night in the Berrien home. For many years, they had given little more than passing interest to Christmas Eve, preferring to celebrate casually on Christmas Day itself. But this year, by mutual agreement, they had turned Christmas Eve night into a formal affair, dressing up in finery, dining in the ballroom and now retiring to the front parlor for quiet talk and music.

In truth, the Christmas spirit had come late this year to April and June. They had bought presents for each other and Paul as usual, decorated a small pine tree with lights only and prepared for a simple dinner on Christmas Day when, unexpectedly, the invitation to Christmas dinner with the Baker family had come and, with it, the first stirrings of the holiday's good tidings. Then, this morning, Paul had proposed they share a late Christmas Eve supper in formal attire and surroundings and suddenly April and June were ripe with Christmas cheer and full of last-minute plans. They had cajoled Paul into taking them to Cookville, where they bought additional gifts for each other, their brother, the Baker family and Beauty Salon. Finally, on impulse, all three had looked at each other with daring and carried out a longstanding threat to buy the new stereo console.

Now their eyes shone with pleasure, and their faces expressed joy.

Paul reckoned it was the happiest Christmas his sisters had seen in many years. All three of them had grown to neglect this special season over the years, losing their belief in its promise of miracles, conceding its wonders to the young, hardening their hearts to its birth of expectations. Why was it, Paul reflected to himself, when the three of them could watch over each other every day of the year with gentle love and devotion, that they could not find a warm spot in their hearts for the Christmas season?

"I think next year we might prepare a little earlier for Christmas," June suggested aloud, as if reading his thoughts, breaking the momentary silence that had enveloped them. "At least put a few more decorations on the tree, although I am partial to just the lights."

April nodded in agreement. "That's exactly what I was thinken," she said. "We've neglected Christmas far too long 'round here. June, do you remember when we used to go greenen?"

She looked at Paul by way of explanation. "It was one of Mother's traditions," she continued. "Always one Saturday shortly after Thanksgiven and before Christmas, she'd haul us out into the woods with axes and saws, and we'd come back with loads of cedar, pine, holly and mistletoe."

"Mother would put greenery in every nook and cranny of the house," June remembered, closing her eyes to inhale a faraway fragrance. "There's nothen like the aroma of winter greens fillen up a house."

"Let's go greenen next year," April said. "We'll revive a grand and glorious tradition."

"Why wait till next year?" June suggested eagerly. "Let's do it the day after Christmas. We can take Beauty with us, maybe Lucas Bartholomew, too. We'll see the new year in with a house full of fresh fragrant greens. I can hardly wait."

"Mother decorated this room, didn't she," Paul asked suddenly, provoking a startled look from his sisters.

"She did," April confirmed. "Mother had impeccable taste."

"She was partial to the Queen Anne style," June supplied, glancing around at the various chairs, sofas, and tables, all made from cherry wood, upholstered in creamy white brocaded material with Wedgwood and rosewood floral trimmings. "Everything in here is Queen Anne, except for that," she continued, gesturing to the grandfather clock in the corner near the foyer. "Daddy purchased that particular clock when they went to Europe. When Mother redecorated this room—the year before you were born, Paul—Daddy insisted she keep the clock. She did not protest as I recall."

"It's a beautiful room," April opined. "We really should use it more often."

June sipped from the champagne glass, changing the subject. "You're looken rather dashen tonight, Paul," she remarked. "Is that a new suit?"

"I treated myself in Atlanta," Paul confirmed, pulling on the sharp creases of the newly tailored black suit, fiddling with a red tie and the starched collar of his white shirt. "I probably won't have much need for it over the next four years, but I was in the mood for somethen new."

"Good for you," April saluted.

"I dare say, Paul," June asserted. "Practically every eligible woman between eight and eighty in these parts already has eyes on you. Once they see you cavorten in that handsome suit, they'll swarm like sharks to blood."

Paul laughed. "I'll be sure to wear my sheriff's uniform in public," he said. "Besides, I should say the same about you two. You're both looken especially lovely tonight."

Both women blushed from delight. April and June were pleasant looking, stylishly groomed and exquisitely mannered, but they lacked the fine qualities of beautiful people, and age was beginning to take a toll on their fair complexions.

"Thank you, darlen," said April, who was fine-boned and demure like her mother, with delicate features, faded blue eyes and long, soft white hair, which she gathered in a bun at the nape of her neck. Tonight, she had selected an ivory colored silk dress, accenting it with a red belt, red heels, pearl earrings and a cameo broach.

June, the taller and more flamboyant of the two sisters, bore a striking resemblance to April, with the exception of a prominent nose and stylishly coifed sandy red hair. She was wearing a forest green satin dress beneath a coverlet of mint green organdy, accented with emerald earrings and a matching choker.

"At our age, brother dear, any and all compliments are appreciated," she said dryly. "We are particularly fond, however, of those sincere, so I double the gratitude expressed by April."

Paul cocked his head, smiled at his sisters and poured everyone another glass of champagne. "I have somethen to tell y'all," he announced.

"Pray tell," said June, moving to warm herself by the fire.

"I hired a private detective," Paul informed them. "To track down Henry Anderson."

"We figured as much," April commented.

"Henry was your biological father, Paul," June said supportively. "You have every reason to want to find him."

"Did you?" April inquired.

Paul nodded. "But he died a few years ago. Of a heart attack." He shrugged. "It's just as well I suppose."

"Did you learn anything else about him?" April asked.

Paul nodded again. "Actually, quite a lot," he replied. "He moved his family from here to Jeff Davis County, which is where he came from originally. He and his wife had five children. Their oldest boy died in the Korean War—drove a jeep onto a mine. The others—a boy and three girls—are scattered across the state now, all of them married with families of their own. Henry gave farmen another go in Jeff Davis County, until World War II came along. Then he sold off the family place and moved to Macon. He got a job in a factory and worked there until he had the heart attack. His wife—her name is Marjorie—is still liven."

"I always wondered what happened to the Andersons," June remarked, "even before we found out what we did about Mother and Henry. I only knew them in passen, but they left under such strange circumstances. I was curious. I asked Daddy. All he said was that Henry found somethen else to do."

"What was he like?" Paul inquired.

"I was away at school, so I never got to know him," April answered.

"He was a hard worker," June recalled, stepping from the fireplace to the love seat. "But honestly, Paul, what I remember most about Henry was how handsome he was. There's a strong resemblance between the two of you. I wouldn't have recognized it without knowen what I know now. But it's there, especially in the eyes. Your eyes are his eyes, Paul."

"If Daddy saw that resemblance, then it must have been difficult for him, raisen me as his own flesh and blood," Paul concluded. "Under the circumstances, I'd say he deserves praise for the effort. I wonder if I could have been as charitable."

"Daddy was a mean and manipulative man, Paul," April said harshly. "I cried myself to sleep the night I first realized that. And when I was finished cryen, I decided to believe he had done his best—by his wife and by his children. I will go to my grave believen that."

"What you describe as charity, Paul, probably was more a matter of saven face," June continued. "Or control. Our father wanted everything in this house under his thumb, includen his children. I still can't believe I allowed him to bulldoze me into taken back my maiden name when Calvin was killed." She hesitated. "But despite his considerable faults, I loved Daddy. He did not wish one moment of sorrow in our lives. And like April, I, too, choose to believe that his overbearen manner was his misguided way of protecten us."

Paul nodded agreement. "I suppose I feel the same way," he mumbled. "I always thought he resented me because Mother died as a result of my birth." He shrugged and sipped champagne. "It's almost a relief to find out after all these years that he did not hate me or blame me for her death."

"May we deduce then that you are happy to know the truth?" June asked.

"Yes," Paul nodded. "It answers a great many troublen questions." He smiled sheepishly. "Of course, if we ever open up those journals upstairs to the public, we'd probably better invoke censorship rights."

"Yes," April agreed. "They contain quite a tale about our ancestors."

"I suggest we keep them private as long as we're all liven and breathen," June proposed. "In fact, we should continue recorden our family history. And then, after we're all dead and gone, turn over the whole shebang to the library in Cookville."

"Perhaps," April nodded.

"Maybe," Paul shrugged.

"Do you plan to tell Matt that you know about his conversation with Daddy that night?" June asked.

"No," Paul said emphatically, receiving silent agreement from his sisters. "This family has sworn Matt to silence once too often. At this point, I see no reason to burden him with more of our secrets. He—or at least his reputation—has suffered far too much already for the protection of our family name and honor."

"Paul," April said after a moment. "Known what you know now, when Daddy died all those years ago ...." She hesitated, then inquired, "Would you have done the same thing all over again?"

"Probably," Paul answered quickly. "But I would not have involved Matt. And, I would have taken greater pains to see that I didn't get caught, to make sure there was no one lurken around the funeral home late at night. Of course ...."

He hesitated, anticipating his sisters' reaction to what he was about to suggest. "Of course, what I did back then helped me to win the election."

"How so?" April frowned.

"It was my opinion that it almost cost you the election," June suggested.

"It sounds ridiculous, I know," Paul explained. "But that day at the warehouse when Robert Taylor told everybody what Matt and I had done when Daddy died, I almost crumbled. I was ready to withdraw from the race."

He grinned suddenly. "Then Bobby got all preachy, putten his virtue on a pedestal, talken down to me like I was some kind of common criminal. He wound up putten a fire in my gut. And that's when I uttered those famous words: 'Spare me your sermon, Bobby.'

"I think people heard me say that and decided maybe I had backbone after all. People like a little passion mixed with their politics. Bobby had too much of it, and I didn't seem to have any. But that day, I showed everybody my passionate side. And while I'm sure some people voted for Bobby because they thought I did wrong by coveren up the cause of Daddy's death, some people respected my intentions and probably realized I was a reasonable man. And they voted for me based on that."

"Well I declare!" April exclaimed.

"You may be right," June murmured cautiously. "It sounds plausible. But I wonder if you're overestimaten the public's tolerance for people who put themselves above the law. A lot of people did not take kindly to what you did, however noble your intentions."

Paul regarded his sisters curiously for a moment. "You raise another question, June," he said finally. "One we've all conveniently overlooked for some time. What do you two think about my intentions? Were they noble or misguided?"

"Both," June answered quickly.

"June and I talked it over," April explained. "We both agreed. We were disappointed you thought us so fragile that we needed protection from the truth, however harsh it was."

"But we also decided you did exactly what Daddy would have done under the same circumstances," June took over. "You were only tryen to protect us. And your heart was in the right place, so we can't fault you for that. In the future, however, please do not shield us from the truth simply because you fear we cannot handle it. April and I are far more resilient than you might believe."

Paul nodded agreement. "I know that now," he assured them. "Y'all have changed, though—all of us have changed since Daddy died. But when it happened back then, I saw y'all through his eyes. You were more than sisters to me. You were the ones who had indulged and disciplined me over the years, who had played nursemaid, mother and teacher to me. And, I wanted to protect you."

"See, Paul," April pointed out. "You really are a Berrien, through and through."

"Yes," Paul sighed. "I am. And glad of it."

"I might add, Paul," June said, "that you would do well to remember just how resilient your two old sisters are. You're taken on a big challenge in the next few days when you become sheriff, and you'll likely need an ear or two to bounce off your ideas and frustrations over the next four years. Please don't hesitate to use ours."

"I'll remember that," Paul smiled. "I admit to be'en a bit wary about becomen sheriff. Under the best of circumstances, the job can be difficult. My hope is that the next four years will be quiet around here, like all the decades preceden it. Bar-en that, I hope to prove my salt. I don't care about leaven a legacy from my days in the office, but I would hope to earn the public's respect. I hope I'm up to the task."

"No doubt, you are," June declared. "You are a Berrien after all, and we are a family brimmen with success."

Suddenly, the grandfather clock struck midnight, filling the room with the deep, rich timbre of Westminster chimes.

"Merry Christmas," Paul said when the last echo of the twelfth chime faded.

"Merry Christmas," chorused June and April.

"Let's open our gifts now," April asserted impulsively, with daring glances at her sister and brother.

"But we've always opened presents on Christmas mornen," June protested. "It's a tradition."

"Oh, fiddlesticks to tradition," April groaned. "If we can drink champagne without worryen what the Baptists might think of us, we can jolly well open our Christmas presents right here and now."

"And it is Christmas mornen after all, June," Paul pointed out.

June sighed. "I suppose it would be okay," she relented as April began moving toward the tree. "It's just that Christmas day—except for openen gifts and sharen dinner—has always seemed to drag on forever. But we've got a full day tomorrow, so ...."

"This one's to you from Paul," April interrupted, holding up a large box wrapped in shimmering green foil.

"Let's do it," June decided, moving eagerly to accept the gift.

She ripped away the paper, pulled open the white box and parted white tissue paper to reveal a classically designed navy silk suit. "Oh, Paul, it's just beautiful," she whispered, pulling the new clothes from the box and measuring them against herself. "Wherever did you find somethen so exquisite?"

"At Rich's in Atlanta," Paul answered. "I simply described you to the saleslady and she made a couple of suggestions. I picked that one for you."

"The color's just perfect for you, June," April admired. "What was the sales lady's other suggestion?" she asked her brother.

Paul grinned broadly, bent under the tree and came up with an identical package wrapped in red tissue paper. He presented the gift to April, who shortly discovered the box contained a suit identical to June's, except for its red wine color.

Sometime later, when all the gifts had been opened and ogled over, appreciated and admired again, the trio picked up the scattered paper, returned their presents under the tree and finally collapsed onto the furniture.

"I'm tired," admitted April, stretching out on the love seat. "But this has been the most wonderful Christmas Eve I can remember for ages. It was a good idea, Paul. The Christmas spirit is a wonderful feelen when it gets deep inside a body."

Paul smiled at her from across the room in a wing back chair.

"Indeed, it is," sighed June, who was seated in a matching chair across the room with her feet propped on an ottoman.

April bolted upright. "Let's be daren," she suggested boldly, picking up her empty glass from the coffee table. "Let's have one last glass of champagne before we retire."

"Now there's an idea," June added brightly. "And perhaps you could make a Christmas toast, Paul."

Paul rose and retrieved the nearly empty bottle from the ice bucket. He poured champagne into all three glasses, half filling them, then returned the empty bottle to the ice bucket and joined his sisters by the fire.

"A Christmas toast to us," he mused aloud, while April and June waited.

"To family ties," he finally toasted, holding forth his glass. "To our past, our present and our future. May truth guide us and love bond us through it all."

April smiled warmly, June brushed away a single tear, and both women extended their glasses to Paul. The crystal pieces touched lightly, ringing in good tidings of Christmas and, for a while longer, two spinster-like sisters and their bachelor brother sipped champagne in a circle by the firelight.

———

Joe was the first person to wake in the Baker home on Christmas morning, pulled fully alert from a dreamy sleep by the sheer force of anticipation. He cherished Christmas, with all its time-honored traditions and unexpected magic, divine inspiration and childlike innocence, holy reverence and even its overblown commercialization. While he no longer honestly gazed skyward on Christmas Eve night in search of Santa Claus and his reindeer, Joe still chanced an occasional heavenward glance. He believed fervently in Father Christmas, the power of goodness to achieve the impossible, the triumph of human kindness, the hope of the heart.

A smile plastered itself across his face as Joe lay there in the predawn cold pondering the mysteries of the most wonderful day of the year. Shortly, he eased out of bed, wrapped himself in a blanket and tiptoed through the room he shared with his brothers, down the hall to the living room. Even in the darkness, he could see the pile of presents under the tree.

Resisting an impulse to rummage through the packages, he lit the gas space heater and warmed himself before returning to the bedroom to fetch his own pile of presents from under the bed. Joe carried the packages to the living room and placed them inconspicuously among the presents already under the tree. Finally, after warming once more by the heater, he trudged down the hall again to wake his siblings.

"John, Luke," he said, tapping his brothers on the shoulder. "Wake up, guys. Santa Claus has come and gone."

Luke sprang instantly awake. "Did you see him?" he gasped.

"Not even a glimpse," Joe sighed disappointedly, ruffling his brother's head. "But the milk, cookies and candy corn are all gone."

"All of it?" Luke inquired incredulously.

"There's a few pieces of candy corn scattered on the rug," Joe replied.

"I wonder which fireplace he came down," Luke said excitedly, dropping from the bed to the floor.

"My guess is the one in the kitchen," Joe suggested.

"More likely the one in Mama and Daddy's room," John said smugly, inviting a sharp glance from Joe.

"What makes you say that, John?" Joe asked carefully.

John glanced from his older brother to Luke, who was gaping at him with wide-eyed wonder as if he expected his brother to reveal some astonishing insight. "It's just closer to the Christmas tree," he replied at last. "That's all."

"I see," Joe remarked knowingly.

Luke frowned at the reasoning. "I don't know, John," he said earnestly. "He would have made a big racket comen down the chimney with a bag of toys. It would've woken Mama and Daddy up for sure. I bet he went down the kitchen chimney."

"Does it really matter, Luker?" Joe asked tactfully, using his personal nickname for his youngest brother. "I mean, the important thing is that he came. Don't you think?"

Luke's eager face split into a grin. "Yeaaaaa!" he yelled, bounding out of bed, running from the room, down the hall, shouting, "He came! He came! Wake up everybody, wake up! Santa Claus has come and there's presents for everyone."

John started anxiously after his younger brother, but Joe caught him by the tail-end of his nightshirt. "Whoa, there," he said. "Sometime today, John, remind me to tell you about Father Christmas."

"Okay," John replied impatiently, tugging to free himself from his brother's grasp. Joe grinned. "Merry Christmas," he said, releasing him.

Laughing, already intoxicated by the joy of the day, Joe crossed the room and walked through the connecting closet between the boys' room and his sisters' room—on the unlikely chance that the girls still needed to be roused from sleep. He found Summer and Carrie already out of bed, wrapping themselves in housecoats, while Bonnie watched drowsily from beneath the covers. "Merry Christmas, girls," he greeted them, entering the room.

"Did he come, Joe?" Carrie asked anxiously.

"He sure did, honey," Joe replied, crossing the room to lie down on the bed beside Bonnie.

"Hurry, hurry," Summer urged. "Let's go see the presents." She tied the belt on her robe. "Did he leave stockens for us, Joe?"

"Why don't you find out for yourselves," Joe challenged, focusing his attention on his youngest sister. "Mornen, bright eyes," he smiled at Bonnie. "Merry Christmas."

"It's cold," Bonnie shivered. "Do you think Santa Claus brought me anything, Joe?"

"I tell you what, sweetie," Joe said. "You crawl under my blanket to keep warm, and we'll go find out whether he did."

Bonnie snuggled tightly in his arms, and Joe carried her to the living room, where their brothers and sisters, having already discovered socks bulging with goodies, were pillaging with Christmas zeal. Joe secured a spot on the rug by the Christmas tree for them and was awarded almost immediately by his little sister's sudden restlessness. Seduced by the temptation to discover treasure, Bonnie forgot the morning chill and plunged headlong into the task of emptying her stocking. Joe observed the happy scene and, then, his own resistance crumbling, reached eagerly for the stuffed sock offered to him by Summer.

In most ways, it was a typical Christmas morning at the Baker home. As always, the children rummaged through their stockings first, while waiting for their parents and grandparents to make their way to the living room. It was the one morning of the year when everyone gathered without first fully dressing for the day. They came wearing housecoats and pajamas, wrapped in blankets and quilts, and settled themselves around the Christmas tree in anticipation.

It was well after six o'clock when Sam and Rachel occupied their traditional posts on the Queen Anne sofa and Matt and Caroline took their positions on the Victorian sofa, but, in spite of their eagerness, nobody hurried.

Christmas morning was savored in the Baker home, swirled and sniffed like an exquisite nectar from God Himself, sampled for body and flavor and finally feasted upon in triumphal celebration of the season everyone had waited for all year long.

Their celebration began with a photograph of the tree itself and then more pictures of themselves gathered around the shapely cedar—until at last the moment arrived to begin the annual procession that thrilled them all.

Matt turned over the camera to Caroline, then reached under the tree to retrieve the first present, while everyone waited with clenched teeth to see who would be the recipient of the year's first gift.

Matt plucked a bright red package with a green bow from the pile, examined it, shook it and finally announced, "To Luke from Santa Claus."

A chorus of groans, ringing with happiness, excitement and good tidings, filled the room as Matt handed his youngest son the gift and stepped back to join Caroline on the sofa. Everyone opened gifts at their own pace, and no one tackled the job faster or more furiously than Luke. Seconds later, the paper lay in tatters, the green bow still intact, and Luke shrieked in delight at a blue dump truck with a hydraulic release mechanism.

In due time, Luke laid aside the truck and reached into the pile of gifts, pulling out a slender package wrapped in green foil. "To Carrie from Santa Claus," he announced, offering the present to his sister.

Carrie's style of opening gifts was methodical. She found each piece of tape and gently pried it loose until the last piece of paper revealed a white box. She lifted the lid, and her eyes widened like saucers. "A watch," she whispered with astonishment, looking first to Caroline, then to Matt and finally to Summer. "I never told anybody but you that I really wanted a watch for Christmas," she muttered wonderingly to her older sister. "How could Santa have known?"

No one answered as Carrie wrapped the band around her wrist and wound the stem, casting an inquiring gaze around the room.

"Santa Claus just knows, Carrie," Joe remarked finally. "That's the wonder of it."

Carrie admired the watch until John urged her gently, "Now come on. It's hard to be patient when you're the one waiten."

She sprang to her feet, reached into the pile of presents and emerged with a large gift wrapped clumsily in candy cane paper "To Mama from Joe," she said, carrying the gift to Caroline.

And so, the procession continued, until every present had been handed out, opened, examined, admired and appreciated by everyone. Almost two hours later, Sam delivered their Christmas prayer.

"Dear Lord," he began, filling the room with his rich baritone. "We stand humbly before you this hallowed mornen, thankful for these treasures you have sent our way, grateful for the many gifts you have given us all through the year. Father, we praise you for our prosperity, our good health, for the simple pleasure of gatheren 'round this tree this mornen to share in the birth of your Son and our Lord, Jesus Christ.

"Lord, we ask you to lead us through the comen year, to walk beside us and guide us on a path pleasen to you, to remind us daily to remember the joy and beauty and grace of the Christmas season and to keep its wonder and promise and peace in our hearts every day of the year, and to protect us from ourselves and those who would do us harm.

"Lord, we thank you for senden your Son to be born in a manger in Bethlehem all those years ago, given us a reason for the season of Christmas. We are grateful in our hearts that your Son came to Earth as a baby boy, lived and walked as a man and set a perfect example for us to follow, gave up his life willingly on the cross for our sins and finally rose from the grave, conquered death and ascended into Heaven. We pray that we will follow in his footsteps, walken and talken with you each day, dear Lord, and that you will have grace, mercy and compassion on our shortcomens.

"Dear Lord, we are most grateful for this wonderful piece of land you have entrusted to our care. We pray for your guidance in our efforts to be shepherds of the land. We give abundant thanks for the blessens of the land, and we ask your blessens on every liven creature that inhabits it.

"Lord, we are mindful, too, on this holy day of those less fortunate than ourselves, those who are sick of mind, body and heart. We pray that you touch them with your healen powers and make their lives whole again. We ask dear Lord that you would feed the starven, give shelter to the homeless and bring righteousness to the world.

"In all these things, Lord, we ask for your blessens and pray your will be done. Amen."

———

On Christmas morning, Caroline forewent her customary inspection of the house and proceeded directly to the kitchen to prepare breakfast. She buttoned her sweater upon entering the room, trying to ward off the early morning cold. The room was like ice, and she was grateful to hear the gurgling of running water from the kitchen sink. What a mess they would have found themselves in with frozen pipes and Christmas dinner to cook.

A gusting wind rattled the house, and the patter of rain sounded against the tin roof and windowpanes as Caroline made her way across the room to peer out the window. She parted the curtain and looked out across a sea of white. A hand flew up to her breast, and she blinked to see if her eyes were playing tricks.

A deep cover of snow lay undisturbed in the early morning, growing thicker with every passing moment as showers of the white fleece danced and frolicked on a whistling wind. Drifts stood several inches deep in places, icicles clung from the eaves, and snow covered everything in sight. It was a sight to behold, a vision of sheer beauty, an answer to an unspoken prayer.

"Matt! Children!" she shouted. "Grandpa, Ma! Y'all come and see how it snowed last night. We've been blessed with another white Christmas."

The children came racing to the kitchen, each clambering for a place in front of the two windows that flanked the kitchen fireplace. Only a few hours earlier they had seen snow for the first time, and the experience had proved exhilarating. With the memory of last night in mind, they were unprepared for the breathtaking beauty that lay in wait for them. Each of them had seen pictures of snowfalls in New England, blizzards in the Great Midwest. But those were faraway places, no more real than dots on a map, and their minds had neither the experience nor the imagination to ponder the possibility of a snow-covered world in their own backyard.

Yet, there it lay, the first honest-to-goodness snowfall of their young lives, piled like blankets on a bed, frosty white as far as the eye could see.

The children simply stared out the two windows, overwhelmed, marveling at the snow-crusted landscape.

"Well now," Matt said, gazing out the window over the tops of John, Carrie and Luke. "Who'd have thought we'd ever see this bunch of young'uns all quiet like this on Christmas mornen?"

"Look at it, Daddy," John instructed with pure reverence. "Did you ever see anything so beautiful?"

"Yes, son," Matt recalled. "As a matter of fact, I did. Around this time nineteen years ago on the day I married your mama."

"On Christmas Eve mornen," volunteered Caroline, who was sharing the other window with Joe, Summer and Bonnie. "I lived in Tifton with Aunt Evelyn. I woke up early and there was snow everywhere. I thought it was the most beautiful gift anyone could ever hope to have on their wedden day. I was so excited, so anxious. But then, Aunt Evelyn reminded me the roads were covered with snow. She was afraid we couldn't make the drive out here from Tifton."

Caroline looked at Matt. "I was beside myself with worry, but it kept right on snowen. There didn't seem like any way in the world we could ever get out here for the wedden, and I had no way of getten a message to your daddy."

"But I knew what she was thinken," Matt interrupted. "And I was intent on getten married that very day."

"Around eight o'clock that mornen, I was at my wits' end," Caroline continued. "It seemed like my wedden day was goen to be spoiled. And then out of the blue, there was a knock on the front door. I opened it up and who do you think was standen there?"

"Daddy!" sang a choir of voices.

"It was him all right," Caroline confirmed, smiling at her husband. "Standen there big as life with this lopsided grin on his face."

Matt took over the story: "She looked at me and said, 'Matt?'—like she was dreamen and wasn't sure whether I was real or not."

"Well, I wasn't," Caroline admitted. "At least not entirely." She laughed. "Your father seemed about as unsure as I did. We just stood there staren at each other and then finally he said, 'Roads are a mess. I figured you might need a ride out to the house.'"

"Which she did," Matt said.

"I thought it was supposed to be bad luck for the groom to see the bride before the wedden," Summer remarked with concern.

"Lucky for us," Caroline smiled, "neither your daddy nor I was superstitious."

Matt cleared his throat. "Are you kids gonna spend all day inside the house strollen down memory lane?" he asked. "Or are y'all gonna stroll outside and play in the snow?"

The children required no further encouragement. In the bat of an eye, they scattered through the house, pulling on clothes, socks, shoes and coats, and filed out the front door to the waiting snow.

It was a deep snow, suitable for romping and tumbling, snowmen and snowballs, and the children charged into it with rampant enthusiasm. They ran full speed, sliding and slipping, flying through the air and crashing to the snow-covered ground. They rolled in the snow, they tasted the white powder. But their vigor waned quickly in the face of the icy elements. The snow burned their hands, the cold froze their noses and ears and a whistling wind pelted their faces with the stinging flakes. All too soon, they retreated to the warmth of the house, where Caroline and Rachel had a hot breakfast waiting for them.

————

After breakfast, Joe put on gloves and an old aviator's cap and returned outside to feed corn to the hogs and hay to the cows. He was in a cheerful mood, calling Christmas messages to the various animals. He spent a few minutes talking with his father while Matt milked the cow, then went inside.

Entering the house through the back porch, he arrived in time to hear Rachel fretting about the late hour she and Caroline had waited to put the turkey in the oven.

"We've got plenty of time," his mother assured Rachel, glancing at Joe with a smile. "Did you get everybody fed up?" she asked him.

"Yes, ma'am," Joe said, moving past her to stand by the fireplace, listening to the melody of his mother and grandmother at work while he shrugged off his denim jacket and warmed by the fire.

"I guess we do," Rachel remarked, more to herself than anyone else. "But the dressen has to go in the oven, too, and so do the sweet potatoes. It'll be three o'clock or later before we're ready to sit down and eat."

Caroline hummed *Silent Night*.

"Course, it don't matter much when we eat today," Rachel continued. "It's Christmas Day and I don't guess none of us has anything pressen to get done."

Caroline began crooning the first verse of *What Child Is This*, her lovely alto filling the room with the peace and serenity of the day, chasing away any misgivings Rachel might have had about Christmas dinner.

Joe stood there a while longer, eavesdropping on their harmony as his mother and grandmother went busily about a task they enjoyed. His departure from the kitchen went virtually unnoticed as he ambled through the house before finally reaching his bedroom. He picked up the Robert Frost book from the fireplace mantle and settled on the floor against the bed. He flipped through the first pages to the table of contents, then to *Stopping by the Woods on a Snowy Evening* and read the first stanza before his mind wandered and his eyes drifted from the page to the room around him.

Joe was tired of sharing this room with his two brothers. He wanted the privacy of a room of his own—nothing fancy—just four walls to himself with enough space for a bed and maybe a desk. As his father said, though, privacy was a rare commodity in the Baker household. Still, Joe had broached the topic in his short conversation with Matt this morning, casually mentioning that the room he shared with John and Luke could easily be partitioned off to form a small alcove in the far corner of the house. Matt had made a noncommittal remark, but Joe read his father well enough to see he was open to the idea.

Laying aside the book, he rose and measured the panhandle space. It would make for cramped quarters, but there was room enough for Joe. He leaned against the far wall, considering the best strategy for persuading his parents to accept the idea. He was still standing there a few minutes later when John burst through the closet door with Summer on his heels.

"Tell us about Father Christmas," he demanded of Joe.

Joe regarded his brother and sister with a bemused expression, trying to determine their knowledge and feelings on the matter at hand.

"There's not really a Santa Claus," John announced smartly. "It's just Mama and Daddy putten presents under the tree. Ain't it, Joe?"

At length, Joe nodded, confirming John's suspicions. "I suppose last night that Mama and Daddy did play Santa Claus for us, John," he said slowly. "But I still believe in the spirit of Santa Claus. Maybe he's not a jolly old man who flies through the sky at night with a sled full of toys and a herd of reindeer leaden the way, but Santa Claus is just as real as you and I are."

"I knew he was made-up," John remarked, his tone changed from know-it-all to doleful.

"I had my doubts, too," Summer agreed, completely crestfallen. "For the last two years, I've had a feelen Mama and Daddy were the ones who got our Christmas presents, but I was afraid to face the truth. It was too much fun thinken about Santa Claus and Mrs. Claus, the elves and the reindeer, worken and liven happily ever after in the North Pole. It's almost as if they were real people, and now they've died."

"Y'all aren't listenen to me," Joe interrupted strongly. "There's no reason for you to quit believen in the North Pole, Summer. And, John, I'm tellen you again that Santa Claus is as real as you and me."

"You aren't maken any sense, Joe," Summer said. "Are you tellen us the truth or not?"

"And who is this Father Christmas you mentioned?" John asked.

Joe climbed into the middle of his double bed, gesturing his brother and sister to join him. When John and Summer were perched on either side, he repeated a story their grandfather had told him several years earlier."

"Let me tell you first about Saint Nicholas, the patron saint of children," Joe began. "He was a real man, flesh and blood, who lived hundreds—more than a thousand—years ago, and he devoted his life to given good things to children. Except for Jesus Christ, possibly no better man ever walked this earth than Saint Nicholas. He brought magic to people's lives. He filled their needs. He gave them the power to hope and to believe that all things are possible. Like all mortal men, though, Saint Nicholas eventually grew old and died. But his spirit lived on and flourished throughout the world. We call the spirit of Saint Nicholas, Santa Claus, and it's our custom to believe he's a jolly man who wears a red suit, flies through the sky on Christmas Eve night with his reindeer and delivers presents to all the good boys and girls."

"Now that's a wonderful story," Summer remarked when he was finished. "To think that Santa Claus was once a real man who actually gave gifts to people. I like that idea as well as Santa Claus—maybe even better. He must have had a powerful spirit to still live all these years later."

"A very powerful spirit," Joe agreed.

"How come we've never heard of this Saint Nicholas?" John inquired, still skeptical.

"I suppose because you've never needed to know about him until now," Joe replied smoothly. "I've come to think of the spirit of Saint Nicholas as Father Christmas. It is faith, hope and love, the spirit of goodness, kindness and generosity, the power of imagination, inspiration and the heart. Father Christmas is all things beautiful and magical, traditional and eternal. He can be found in the smells of walking through the woods on a winter day, of preparen for Christmas Day, in church on a December mornen, or around the Christmas tree. It's true, I suppose, that we tend to think most often of Father Christmas in December, but he's also the reason Daddy will pick a bushel of sweet corn, squash, tomatoes or some other vegetable in the dead of summer and deliver them to a neighbor down the road.

"Father Christmas is the reason I believe in Santa Claus," Joe continued. "It's the spirit—the Christmas spirit—that makes this time of year so special. And you know where we get that spirit, why we celebrate Christmas?"

"From Christ," John said.

"Because Jesus was born on Christmas Day," Summer added.

Joe nodded, then said, "The Bible defines the fruit of the spirit as love, joy, peace, patience, kindness, goodness, faithfulness, gentleness and self-control—all the essential elements of the Christmas spirit and Father Christmas. If we can believe that Christ was born almost two thousand years ago in a manger in Bethlehem—Summer, John—then surely we can find it in our hearts to believe in Santa Claus. It is our faith that makes us believe—in Christ, in Father Christmas, even in ourselves and in each other."

Joe paused, glancing at the shining faces of his oldest sister and brother, hoping he had filled a need with his Christmas story. "Let's none of us ever lose that faith," he added. "Okay?"

John nodded. "I could never not believe that story," he said a moment later, with pure worship in his voice.

"That is the most beautiful thing I've ever heard, Joe," Summer said. "I've memorized a lot of Bible verses, but I don't know that one. Where can I find it?"

"The fifth chapter of Galatians—the twenty-second and twenty-third verses," Joe answered with a guilty smile. "And it's one of the few too many verses that I have memorized, little sister."

"Faith is a wonderful thing," John surmised. "And so is Father Christmas."

"So are love and hope," Summer added. "I think I'll memorize that Bible verse today. I want somethen special to help me remember this day."

"I'll help you," Joe promised.

For a long moment, they were silent, each lost in their various thoughts of Father Christmas and this special day of the year.

"Thank you, Joe," John said abruptly, his eyes aglow with the twinkle of the Christmas spirit. "I'm gonna like this Father Christmas."

"We love you, brother of ours," Summer added with adoration. "It's neat haven someone old and wise to tell us all the answers."

Joe looked quickly at his brother and sister, then laughed joyously, hugging them both tightly in his arms.

"Y'all are too much," he said happily. "Whataya say that we get dressed in our warmest clothes and spend the rest of the day playen in the snow. Somethen tells me we're bound to feel Father Christmas outdoors on this white Christmas Day."

———

Shortly after noon, the children returned outside to play. New snow had stopped falling and the sun was trying to break through the clouds, but the temperature remained below freezing. This time they were prepared for the cold, with gloves, hats and scarves.

They had been outside only a few minutes when John noticed their Christmas visitors walking down the road. Joe put Bonnie on his shoulders and trooped down the snow-covered road with his siblings to meet the Berriens. The children were particularly fond of Paul, Miss April and Miss June, who tended to fuss over them and pay close attention to their every word.

Luke greeted the Berriens by launching a harmless snowball at Paul, who feigned surprise and swooped the boy onto his shoulders. The children filled much of the short walk home with tales of the treasures Santa Claus had left them, delighting their older audience with genuine appreciation of their Christmas gifts.

"What's in those bags y'all are carryen?" Luke asked Miss April and Miss June, boldly voicing the question on the minds of his brothers and sisters.

"I'm not for certain," April replied, "but I think Santa Claus may have accidentally left some of your presents at our house."

"I didn't think Santa Claus visited old people," Bonnie said doubtfully. "He didn't leave anything at our house for Mama or Daddy or Granny and Grandpa."

"Oh, she's just teasen," June assured Bonnie. She shook the bag in her hand. "These are from us to y'all. Just our little way of sayen how much we appreciate the opportunity to have Christmas dinner with you folks."

"You didn't get a single present?" Luke asked worriedly.

"We most assuredly did, Luke," June reassured him.

"Indeed yes," April continued. "We were paid a visit by Father Christmas himself last night." She looked from Luke to Paul and June. "We've had the most wonderful Christmas this year."

"Who is Father Christmas?" Bonnie inquired.

"He watches over those of us who are too old for Santa Claus to come and visit," April replied.

"How do you get too old for Santa Claus?" Luke inquired, perplexed by the idea.

"Y, y, you," April stammered, groping for a plausible answer.

She was rescued from further explanation by their timely arrival in the Baker yard and the appearance of Matt on the front porch. As the greetings began among the adults, Joe sent a snowball aimed in Luke's direction. The packed snow landed squarely on the boy's back and Luke's thoughts were transferred from curiosity to revenge. For another year at least, there would be no more questions about Santa Claus and Father Christmas.

In the afternoon, the children, Matt, Sam and Paul fought a war with snowballs and built matching snowmen on the two step walls flanking the front porch steps. The snow quit falling, the wind died down and the gray clouds cleared, drenching the day with cold sunshine. They played vigorously, whizzing snowballs back and forth, shouting at the tops of their lungs and running full speed. The snowmen stood guard by the house, with coal for eyes, spools of red thread for noses, crooked mouths and tree limbs for arms.

At last, everyone collapsed on the porch, feeling their first hunger pains since breakfast. They drifted quickly into silence, ready for a change of pace. As if on cue, the front door opened and Caroline appeared.

"Goodness gracious!" she exclaimed. "Y'all look plumb tuckered out."

"Some of us more than others," Sam replied wearily.

Caroline laughed. "Dinner's ready," she announced, walking down the porch steps to inspect the matching snowmen. "We're setten it on the table, so y'all come on in and wash your hands.

"Those are just the smartest-looken snowmen I've ever seen," she added a moment later before ushering everyone into the warmth of home and hearth, where Christmas dinner waited.

———

Caroline remembered every Christmas by painting pictures in her mind, slice of life details that gave the day its own special flavor. This was a Christmas Day ripe with memories, not only of the snow but also for the character of her family and friends.

More than once, Caroline caught a questioning gaze on Joe as he studied the faces around the table: the yearning in Miss April's face for something lost forever, perhaps children of her own; the joy in Miss June's eyes as one who had made peace with the will of God. Once, Caroline even glanced up to find her oldest son's gaze fixed solidly on her, and both realized with startled looks that the other was aware of what they each were doing. Caroline glanced away but quickly looked back at Joe, smiling to herself, knowing the boy possessed some part of her.

Had Caroline been a painter, she would have captured on canvas the range of emotions expressed this day. She would have painted the tired face of Bonnie, propped on the table by her elbows with a tiny thumb resting against her lips; the simple satisfaction in Matt as he savored a piece of turkey in a moment of thoughtful silence; the dazed, slightly embarrassed expression of Paul as cranberry jelly slid off his fork just before reaching his opened mouth; the unfortunate attempt by Luke to reach across the table for a pear tart and the admonishment he received from Rachel for his lack of table manners.

Caroline could not paint on canvas but she did burn these images deeply in her mind. And later, when the lazy pace of the day had meandered them through dinner and dessert, and they had gathered outside to wish Merry Christmas to each other one last time, she found a few more lasting memories. She provoked one by tossing a snowball at Sam and catching the twinkle of affection in his good eye as he cast a sidelong glance toward her. She noted the graceful movement of Summer, the gentle happiness of Carrie as the two girls chased John, who had put snow down their backs, an out-of-character action for her most mild-mannered son and yet revealing of his occasional penchant for doing the unexpected.

In the fading daylight Caroline found one final Christmas memory for the year, again of Joe, standing on the edge of the field with his back turned to her, looking toward the magnificent red and gold horizon.

The filtered hues of that deep orange setting sun spellbound Caroline, filling her with such happiness and peace that she paused a moment to bask in its radiance. This glorious horizon—like the strange white Christmas—seemed to promise a grand future for them all, and Caroline allowed her memories of family and friends to drift through her mind. She wondered what surprises the coming years would bring them, but, more than anything, Caroline clung steadfastly to the belief that better days lay ahead for her family and the farm. Finally, she prayed to God for His blessings and His will be done.

When her prayer was finished, Caroline gazed once more at the darkening sky, streaked with variegated shades of amber gold, burnt orange and gathering purple clouds. In the dusky haze of twilight, she felt anew the promise of the horizon, something impalpable and imponderable, yet commanding her attention—until at last a chilling wind sent a shiver through her, and she turned to bid her friends goodbye and hurry her family into the waiting warmth of home.

THE TRAIN

1961-1962

JOE AGREED WITH HIS father and grandfather's belief that the Cookville community offered everything a man needed. Any able-bodied man with a minimum of gumption and perseverance could make a decent life in this small farming community for himself and a family. A good life even, as demonstrated by his own father who was abler and possessed more gumption and perseverance than the ordinary man in these parts.

What bothered Joe about their viewpoint was his equally certain opinion that Cookville could never offer everything he wanted out of life. He suspected Matt and Sam would dismiss his confusion as unnecessary brooding over nothing more than semantics, but to Joe there was a big difference between needing and wanting. Whether Cookville fulfilled the wants of his father and grandfather, Joe did not know for sure. He made a mental note to clarify the issue on their next hunting trip or some other suitable occasion.

These thoughts came to Joe as he walked along a moonlit path, his destination a back field on the Bakers' rambling farm. Above him, millions of stars danced and the moon, a bright white orb, hung cold and distant, decorating the nighttime sky with ambiance, suggesting something special at hand. He dug his hands deeper into the pockets of a worn corduroy jacket for warmth and quickened his pace.

Joe should have been in bed on this, a school night, but he was preoccupied with a different obligation—a summons equally mysterious and compelling, issued a night earlier by the distant call of a train whistle. The summons had come from the Southern Railway's midnight run to Atlanta from Valdosta, weaving its way into Joe's dreams and luring him from an uneasy sleep. He had listened to the train coming closer, heard its hollow crossing of the New River trestle. And somewhere between the thunderous roar and fading echoes of steel on steel, Joe felt called to witness the next passing of the train.

Tonight, he was heeding the call only because his curiosity exceeded strong suspicions that he was being plumb silly. Nevertheless, he expected to view the train in a different light after tonight, as something other than an annoyance that woke him from a sound sleep and more important than vital transportation for the crops his family grew.

From the house, it was a brisk fifteen-minute walk to the railroad tracks, which served as the Baker farm's western border. Joe had waited until his family was sound asleep before sneaking out the window of the room he shared, reluctantly, with his two younger brothers. He covered the distance at a slower clip, still favoring his gimpy left leg two weeks into the new year. Nevertheless, unburdened of crutches, he felt a renewed sense of strength, and each step carried him closer and faster to wherever he was headed.

His thoughts were on a highfalutin course this night. In truth, they had followed the same ponderous path for months now. In the beginning, Joe had blamed their wanderlust ways on the circumstances caused by his broken leg, which left him with too much vacant time to fill. He had grown to hope this brooding preoccupation with destiny and history might simply be a phase he was going through, like puberty, which had been much easier to handle. But now, with grudging acknowledgment, he was willing to accept his fondness for deep thought.

Joe fancied himself a philosopher, yet deep down, knew he lacked the keen intellect necessary for sweeping profundity of human nature, despite the straight As on his report card. Scholars would never examine his writings for the meaning of life. Joe was unconcerned. He was far more interested in the events of life. He wanted to write the first draft of history, preserve moments in time and chronicle destinies. He wanted to be a journalist.

At times, he ached for the future. He sensed its nearness, tantalizingly close but still out of sight. Had he merely been passing time or locked into an unlimited future of weekly visits to town, Sunday newspapers and a rare trip to the State Farmers Market in Atlanta, Joe would have withered like a cornfield without water. But he was nourished, growing and mostly content to let the future arrive at its own pace.

He owed his patience to the nurturing of a wonderful family, and felt an enormous debt of gratitude for their love, care and example.

Joe had been born at home and had never strayed far from the paths of his father and grandfather or the apron strings of his mother and grandmother. These four people were giving Joe and his siblings rich lives, and material things had little to do with their treasures. Hard work and responsibility were virtues, although worthless without ample time for play and laughter. Both his parents and grandparents made sure there was plenty of everything to go around for everyone.

They were not perfect, of course. Matt avoided the church; Caroline battled pride; Sam possessed a lazy streak; and Rachel was prone to haughty stubbornness. But it was easy to overlook their faults, especially for Joe, who mistrusted perfection.

Arriving at the railroad tracks, Joe climbed over the fence and made his way across the rocky right-of-way. He stepped across the first rail to the center of a wooden tie and peered south in search of headlights from the oncoming locomotive. It was a futile gesture since he was bound to hear the train long before he saw any approaching lights. Turning south, he stared down the tracks with anticipation and was rewarded with the stillness of the night. Finally, he pulled a penny from his pocket, placed it on the rail and moved away from the tracks to claim a seat on the cold ground.

His thoughts returned to the family and the prospect of one day leaving them. Any doubts Joe had about going out into the world on his own had vanished in a single moment in another field when his father pointed Joe in a direction away from home. Matt had released Joe from family bonds. He had granted Joe impending freedom. But freedom came with a burden of responsibility, which explained why, even with his occasional impatience for the future to arrive, Joe was most happy to wait. There was time enough. It would come.

He heard the train then and rose stiffly from the ground, blowing quick puffs of frosty breath into the cold night. Retrieving a cigarette from the pack in his jeans, he lit it with a match and inhaled the smoke for warmth, then made a final check of the penny's position. Though not superstitious by nature, Joe saw no harm in having a good luck piece, especially if it served as a memento from an important moment.

The train's rumble drew closer, picking up speed, and a long whistle signaled its approach to the New River trestle. A short time later, the engine's bright headlight rounded a curve and the train was bearing down on Joe. He stepped away from the tracks and waited for the train to cover the distance. It was a short wait.

The engine roared, a long, unexpected whistle acknowledging that his dark attire had failed to conceal Joe's presence from the conductor. Joe saluted back, took a step closer to the train and was lost in the hypnotic shadows of car after car racing past him, the scrape of steel on steel drowning the noise of the night. He thought about the faraway places the cars were headed, knowing someday he would buy a ticket and ride that train across his family's land to the beckoning future.

The passing of the red caboose surprised him, coming so suddenly, leaving in its wake anxious anticipation. "It won't be long now," Joe said softly to the train's fading vibrations, watching it race away into the darkness.

When the train was gone, Joe walked over to the railroad track, collected his flattened penny and crammed the coin inside the front pocket of his blue jeans. He took one last lingering look ahead, then quickly put his mind back in the present. He snuggled deeper into the coat, stifled a yawn and began the walk home. A warm bed waited there, and Joe was eager to get to it.

———

It was one of those rare days when his patience ran thin. Along with his blood.

Winter was Joe's favorite time of year, but he had never lived through a winter like this one. And with more than half the season remaining, he wasn't entirely convinced he would make it through.

Two-thirds of January was gone, and the temperature had hovered near the freezing point since the unexpected white Christmas, rising only to melt the snow and then plunging with an icy vengeance. Joe had tired quickly of waking to frozen water pipes. He found it impossible to rid himself of the chill that grabbed him each morning when he struggled out of bed. On this, the coldest day by far, he wished for an early spring.

Spring seemed far away, however, in the midst of an ice storm and frigid cold. Rain had fallen the previous night, turning to ice in the early morning. The ice had cracked tree limbs, snapped power lines and burst water pipes. Rachel was boiling water in the fireplace for coffee, and Caroline was putting together sandwiches for a sparse supper. Everyone else huddled in the kitchen for warmth, except Matt and Joe. His father was feeding the stock and Joe was scouring the woods for a pregnant pig. It was a dismal time, made all the worse by the impending arrival of another Arctic blast.

Joe traversed a forest of bare hardwoods and an occasional green pine, aiming for a favorite rooting hole of the hogs. He was looking for Sooner, a gilt expected to deliver her first litter of pigs at any time.

He would have preferred to be somewhere else, but Sooner was the daughter of Yorkie, one of the Bakers' most prized sows for the large litters she delivered. Her smallest litter had been her first, eleven pigs, and the largest sixteen. The Yorkshire sow not only delivered large litters, she raised them, too. With eighteen teats, all capable of providing milk except for the two small buds high on her rump, Yorkie carried an ample food source for her brood.

Her merits were such that Matt and Joe tended to overlook her nasty habit of eating an offspring or two every now and then. Yorkie never ate any of the other sows' pigs. And even when she gobbled up one of her own, she still raised more pigs than any other sow on the Baker farm. Matt swore he would keep the Yorkshire mama until she started eating her neighbors.

Given her pedigree, the Bakers had great expectations of Sooner. First, though, Joe had to find the gilt and lead her to shelter. Whether she delivered one or a dozen pigs would matter little if she gave birth in these elements because the entire litter would freeze in a matter of minutes. Under the barn, newborn pigs would have a fighting chance.

As far as Joe was concerned, hogs stood at the pinnacle of the farming business. Modesty aside, he considered himself the equal of his father when it came to tending hogs. He cooked their sour mash, wormed them and tracked breeding cycles. When the time came, he castrated the young males, chose the gilts for breeding and packed off the shoats to the market. He monitored the farm markets for hog prices every week, and Matt rarely made an important decision about the stock without first consulting him.

The Bakers maintained a brood of almost two hundred pigs. Joe named a large number of them: the sows and gilts kept for breeding and the two males who serviced them. Sows carried names like Red, Sugar, Rose, Geraldine and, of course, Yorkie. Besides Sooner, there were gilts called Stripe and Friendly, while the males were named, appropriately, Big Male and Little Male.

As much as pigs could be pampered, Joe did. He treated them to overgrown vegetables like squash and sweet potatoes in the summer, turnips and other greens in the winter, which was not unusual in itself—except Joe, fed them by hand. He scratched behind their ears, petted and sweet-talked the critters. To his father and grandfather's amazement, Joe could lull a standing sow to a near stupor simply by scratching gently behind her ears and whispering sweet nothings. Some of the sows—Sugar, Rose and Geraldine, in particular—craved his attention to the point of jealousy of their swine sisters. If Joe lavished too much attention on one, then the others would push for their turn, squealing and butting in until they received a due share of notice.

"Pretty amazen," Tom Carter had acknowledged dryly one day last fall when a boastful Joe demonstrated the hogs' affection for their master. "But wouldn't you rather have a pretty girl swoonen at your feet instead of dirty old hogs?"

Joe had allowed the question to go unanswered, he recalled, as a broken limb blocked his path and he stopped to examine it. Still dangling from the tree, the limb was a casualty of the heavy ice clinging to its branches. Joe clasped the hanging piece of wood, twisted it sharply and stepped back to let the limb fall to the ground. He told himself to drag it back to the house for firewood later, then moved on toward the rooting hole.

Joe wanted girls to swoon at his feet. So far, however, Betty Beddingfield was the only girl anywhere close to swooning over Joe. Unfortunately, Betty had a heart condition, so he could never tell whether she was swooning or simply keeling over from exhaustion.

Her present infatuation with Joe excluded, Betty still occupied a prominent place in his memory.

Way back in fourth grade, Betty had been cast as Miss String Bean, a key role in the class play that required a tearful performance. In rehearsal after rehearsal, Betty failed to deliver the necessary blubbering. Everybody offered suggestions, but Betty maintained dry eyes and offered up only grunts when tears were needed.

With everyone convinced the play was doomed to failure unless Betty learned to cry, Joe took matters into his own hands. While his part in the play was minor, it cast Joe in a position behind Betty during the scene's critical moment. When the time came for Betty to shed tears during the play's final rehearsal, Joe poked her in the butt with a straight pin he had procured from Rachel's sewing box. It worked wonders.

A lusty wail erupted from Betty, both stunning and delighting her classmates and their teacher, Miss Masterson. Overcoming its initial surprise, the class quickly broke into a hardy round of applause and cheers for Betty.

"Why, Betty, dear," Miss Masterson beamed, swelling with pride for her favorite student. "That's wonderful. You sound so real."

Betty gulped for air, sniffled and launched into another round of bawling.

Until then, Joe had been clapping and cheering with his classmates. But the tone of Betty's high-pitched sobs pricked his instincts, reminding him of the Biblical passage about the wailing and gnashing of teeth. His grin disappeared as Miss Masterson started across the stage toward Betty.

"That's wonderful, Betty," Miss Masterson repeated, a smile plastered across her face, which Joe considered a perfect cross between a horse and a prune. "I just can't get over how convincen you sound." Her tone turned coaxing. "But that's enough for now, sweetie. Save some of those tears for tomorrow night."

Betty went right on sobbing, sniveling and sniffling at a torrid pace, alerting Miss Masterson that matters were amiss with the teacher's pet.

Miss Masterson rushed to Betty and wrapped the petite girl in her arms. "Betty, darlen," she consoled with soothing chirps. "What's wrong, dear?"

Betty looked up at the distressed teacher. "Somebody stuck a pin in my butt," she wailed. "And it hurts."

The class erupted into raucous laughter, but Joe hardly noticed. His attention was locked on the pair of cold, beady blue eyes glaring straight at him.

Of all his teachers, Miss Masterson was the only one Joe had ever disliked. They had bumped heads literally on the first day of the fourth grade, and that one moment of closeness had been the high point of their relationship.

Miss Masterson made no accusations, and Joe offered no defense. She grabbed him by the arm, dragged him off stage and whacked his backside with ten solid licks from a two-inch piece of oak. Worst of all, she sent him home from school with a note explaining what had happened and requiring his parents' signatures.

The paddling gave Joe newfound respect for Miss Masterson, whose waif-like appearance belied her power. The note to his parents, however, nullified any budding chance she might have had to earn his goodwill.

Caroline and Rachel were beside themselves over the incident, throwing up their hands in disbelief and reprimanding Joe repeatedly for his derelict behavior. His grandfather sat silently in the corner of the kitchen, shaking his head back and forth with downcast eyes.

"Son, what in the world made you stick a pin in the girl's rear?" Matt asked.

"I was tryen to help her cry," Joe replied hopefully, before explaining about the play and Betty's inability to perform in the crucial moment. By the time he finished the long-winded account, Joe himself was wondering what indeed he had been thinking when he plunged the pin into Betty's butt.

"Son," Matt frowned when Joe was finished. "There's not any good reason to stick a straight pin into somebody's backside." He pointed to the kitchen door and motioned Joe to it. "You and I need to talk outside for a while."

Matt had led his son to the barn, where Joe soon cried tears as real as the sobs of Betty Beddingfield. It was the last whipping Joe received from his father. There had been scant cause for another because Joe well remembered the last one.

Joe sidestepped a frozen mud puddle and thought again about Betty Beddingfield. The years since fourth grade had been unkind to her. Betty had developed the heart condition in the fourth grade and subsequently became the target of cruel jokes. Joe stood up for her, and his defense had stopped the bullying. Now Betty saw Joe as some knight in shining armor, all because he showed her a small amount of kindness. She had an obvious crush on him, batting her eyes and blushing whenever he spoke to her. Joe tolerated her silliness out of sympathy and because he knew her bad heart had already stolen Betty's first love. He remembered the way she played a piano, her hands flowing with grace and style over the piano keys, filling the New River auditorium with sweet melodies. Betty had been April Berrien's prized piano student, and Joe still recalled her passionate performance in the sixth-grade recital. It was her last performance before illness robbed Betty of music. The doctors had silenced her hands, fearing even the exertion of playing a piano would overburden her delicate heart.

Joe's arrival at the rooting hole chased away the bittersweet thoughts of Betty Beddingfield and sent his own heart racing.

Across the way, Sooner lay heavily on her side in a crude oval nest of sticks and leaves.

Joe moved slowly toward the hog, breathing easier as he came closer and saw she still possessed a rounded stomach. If he could lead her to the barn, he would. If not, he would take the pigs when they were born and feed them with a bottle at home.

Reaching the white hog, he nudged her gently with his foot. "Get up girl," he urged. "It's too cold for you to be haven babies out here."

The hog snorted loudly, grunting her displeasure, but she rose awkwardly from the nest. As Joe shooed her away, one of the hog's feet pierced a layer of ice across the top of the nest. His curiosity piqued, Joe bent to examine the nest and recoiled. A newborn pig lay frozen in the ice, its head crushed where Sooner's foot had broken through the top layer.

Joe turned away to regain his equilibrium, taking time to observe Sooner. Her belly had lost hardly any of its pre-birth roundness. Even now, she appeared pregnant. "Sorry, girl," he called. "Your time came a little too soon."

Pained by a mixture of regret and disgust, Joe returned to the nest. He pulled the dead pig from the ice and discovered three others in a half-frozen gelatinous soup of slush and birthing gook. His stomach turned unexpectedly, forcing Joe to take a deep breath of the cold air to clear the nausea.

He waited half-a-minute, then resumed the grizzly task, prying the other dead pigs from the ice and removing the congealed glob of birthing fluids. Even in a frozen state, it was a gooey mess and required a light touch as Joe carried it to the edge of the small clearing. There, he dropped to his knees, dug a shallow hole with his hands and buried the glop. He used a wad of decaying leaves to clean his hands, then returned to the birthing place and grabbed the four frozen pigs by their tails. He would bury them somewhere else, where the carcasses would stay hidden from the other hogs.

A dispirited grunt from the mother halted his departure from the rooting hole.

Sooner was standing ten yards away, eyeing Joe suspiciously with a cocked head. She was a pretty sow, with a long body and a healthy pinkish glow, and Joe expected better results from her second try at motherhood. Of course, if the hog delivered another small litter, anything less than eight pigs, then she would accompany her brood to the market when the time came. But given her potentially fragile mental state at the time, Joe opted for encouragement rather than pressure with his farewell.

"Better luck next time, old girl," he muttered en route to a nearby field.

By spring, the unfortunate critters would be fertilizer, he told himself, perhaps providing nutrients and minerals for a field of corn that would feed their mother and the other hogs come the next winter.

————

The memory of the frozen pigs lingered for several days, until one morning when a matter of more importance forced Joe to speak his mind at the breakfast table. "I need a room of my own," he announced to his family between a bite of toast and a sip of orange juice.

"You do," Sam said vaguely, leaving everyone to guess whether he was agreeing with Joe or questioning his grandson."

"I do," Joe repeated brashly.

"What about your brothers, Joe?" Caroline asked. "It's hardly fair to push them out of their room." She smiled teasingly. "And it's a little cold for anybody to be sleepen on the porch."

"John and Luke can keep the room," Joe replied quickly. "At least most of it."

Matt cleared his throat and intervened. "Joe's got a good idea," he said. "All he wants to do is wall up that panhandle in the boy's room."

"That wouldn't be much of a room," Caroline frowned, finally giving the idea serious merit. "You couldn't get much more than a bed in it. A single one at that."

"A bed, a desk and maybe a chest of drawers," Joe informed her. "I measured it all out, and there's more space than you think. Anyway, I don't need much room. Just a little privacy every now and then."

Caroline smiled with understanding and considered the request.

"It's a good idea," Matt opined. "Joe's older than the other kids, and he needs a retreating place." He observed Caroline watching him and sweetened the idea with a new proposal. "In fact," he continued, "I thought we might do some work in the bathroom, too. Maybe put up one of those shower rings around the tub and brighten it up in there a little bit."

"What about the cost?" Caroline asked, again frowning.

"Hardly anything," Matt said dismissively. "A few two-by-fours and plywood. Nails and paint. Things are slow around here right now, so Joe and I can do the work. We probably could knock out both jobs in two or three days." He hesitated, allowing his wife to consider the idea, watching the wheels of worry turn over in her head. "It's not gonna to send us to the poor house, Caroline," he told her finally.

This extra reassurance brightened Caroline. "Then I don't see why not," she agreed. "As long as it's okay with Ma and Pa."

Rachel and Sam had no objections, so Matt installed the shower ring and new plumbing the very next day. Two days later, he and Joe began work on the room. They put up the studs and braces, framed the door and dangled a light from the ceiling. Next, they added an electrical outlet, then walled in the room and hung the door. While his father painted the two rooms, Joe used the lumber scraps to build a makeshift closet.

Armed with a meager amount of money but plenty of bargaining prowess, Caroline went shopping for furnishings and struck gold at the salvage store in Tifton. She returned home with a wrought-iron single bed frame, a sturdy mattress and a ten-dollar desk. A coat of black enamel transformed the bed frame into something presentable, while a mahogany stain covered up the blemishes and added a stately quality to the desk.

On moving day, Joe transferred the furniture to his room, along with an old ladder-back chair that he had refurbished with a new cowhide seat. Rachel provided him a desk lamp, and the children arranged his clothes and other belongings in neat piles on the closet shelves.

In the shank of the evening, Joe bade the family an early goodnight and retired to the room to enjoy his newly acquired privacy. Sometime later, a nightmare woke Luke and the frightened youngster stole into his older brother's new room.

"I'm scared," Luke explained as he crawled into bed with Joe. "Can I sleep with you?"

Joe mumbled mild protest but slid over to give his little brother room. Just before drifting off, the thought occurred to him that he'd better not plan on getting too familiar with the idea of privacy.

———

It was another cold day, in the middle of February, when Sam set fire to a huge pile of wood, vines and other debris. Several other mounds of scrap dotted the newly cleared section of woods, and Matt was on the tractor harrowing a fire line around each one. They had cut the timber the previous year and now were preparing the land for its first crops.

Joe was working alongside his brothers, sisters, Lucas Bartholomew and Tom Carter, picking up roots and other obstacles that could snag a harrow or turning plow. He stretched his back for a moment and watched the fire erupt, belching gray smoke and giving off red heat, even as Sam torched a second mound in the distance.

The new field would be a welcomed addition to the farm. It was rich dirt, nurtured by years of decaying leaves, and the extra thirty acres would yield a significant boost to the farm's annual income. Come late spring, when green shoots of corn stood knee high, or early fall when the field lay brown and ripe for harvest, Joe would remember fondly these hours spent stooped over the land, tugging at entrenched roots and sweating against the cold. Right now, however, his back ached and he wanted the job finished.

He eyed the smoke a second longer, then returned to work, twisting furiously at a stubborn root and finally yanking it from the packed ground. Cursing the wood silently, he picked up another root and tossed both pieces into a nearby trailer.

"What's wrong?" his brother John inquired.

Joe glanced across the trailer, where his brother stood with a concerned frown on his face. "Nothen," he answered shortly. "Go back to work and stop yakken."

Turning away quickly, dismayed by his short temper, Joe asked himself the same question and came up with few answers. There were good days and bad days, for sure, but peace of mind was usually a consistent quality in his life. Despite his restlessness, his impatience for the future, Joe followed a familiar course of contentment, dodging obstacles with the security of knowing that each day carried him forward. As of late, however, peace of mind eluded him. Little things bothered him and stayed on his mind. He was distracted and preoccupied, all over nothing it seemed. And he needed something, yet had no idea what it might be.

This lack of focus, these bouts of moodiness and the sudden attachment to self-centeredness disturbed Joe. His inability to understand, to make sense out of the mess, irritated him. And left him with nothing else to do but take his own advice and get back to work, allowing the monotony of repetition to numb his thoughts.

In another fifteen minutes, he had cleared a stretch to the edge of the woods and was working his way back to the middle of the field when the smell of smoke penetrated the thin accumulation of cobwebs in his head.

He paused long enough to glance around the field. Smoke now rolled across the cleared land in waves, rising from the various fires that crackled ferociously with leaping flames and sizzling hisses. The first mound had been reduced to embers, but nearly a dozen others were at full blaze.

Joe was considering whether the veil of haze provided enough cover to conceal a cigarette when his sweeping gaze landed on a strange protrusion from the ground. He stared at the reddish-brown object, realizing at length that it was a rock of some kind. His curiosity aroused, Joe hurried to the rock and dropped to his knees to examine it.

The rock was imbedded in the ground, with two smaller pieces at its side. All three pieces were rough and jagged, the color of burnt ocher, scarred with streaks of carbon black and tiny porous craters.

Joe rubbed his hands across the larger piece, guessing that he had found a meteorite. He picked up the smaller rocks, examined each and estimated their weight between three and four pounds. Carefully laying them aside, he studied the larger rock and discovered a hairline fracture running down the middle of its largest outcropping. Joe braced one hand against the rock for leverage and used the other to jiggle the broken piece, enlarging the fissure. Wedging his fingers in the small cleft, he gave a swift jerk and the flat outcropping broke away from the main piece. Joe glanced quickly at the broken rock and laid it beside the two other small pieces.

He had thought perhaps the fissure would reveal a closer look at the core of the meteorite, but the fracture merely changed its shape. Joe tested the rock's sturdiness and saw it was lodged loosely in the ground. Rising to his feet, he bent over the rock, grabbed both sides at the bottom and tugged the meteorite from its landing place. It came out easily.

Joe estimated the rock weighed about twenty-five to thirty pounds. He placed the shapeless blob of space matter on the ground and studied it from all angles, flipping it from side to side, caressing the rough texture and tracing each streak of carbon black with his fingers. His senses roared with excitement over the discovery. He laughed in disbelief and gaped at the heavens with awe and appreciation.

Along with English and history, science was Joe's favorite subject, especially the study of the stars. He found the subject of astronomy as limitless as the universe itself and, now, standing here with a meteorite at his feet, he was reminded of the only cross words he'd ever had with his grandmother.

Joe was prone to speculate about the possibility of life in outer space. At the Sunday dinner table recently, he had voiced some of those conjectures. His grandmother scoffed at such ideas, believing steadfastly God had given the capability of life only to Earth and would destroy it and the rest of the universe when Jesus returned to claim his flock on Judgment Day.

"I agree, Granny," Joe had told her when Rachel objected to his speculations and voiced her beliefs. "All I'm sayen is that the universe is vast." He sent Rachel a placating smile. "It's quite possible the Almighty could have put another flock on another planet," he added a bit too blithely. "Don't you think?"

"Rubbish!" Rachel seethed. "Blasphemous rubbish."

Mealy-mouthed was an impossible description of Rachel by any stretch of the imagination. Her words were often hard-edged, but her tone rarely venomous as it suddenly had become with Joe. She slammed her fork against the table and pointed a finger at her grandson. "I will not tolerate Christian disrespect in this house, Joe," she told him in harsh tones, befitting of a fire-and-brimstone preacher. "There is one God and He made one world and one man in His own image."

"Granny!" Joe interrupted. "I wasn't questionen the creation. I was just suggesten ...."

"Enough!" Rachel shouted. "Your suggestions are not welcome at this table, young man. Or in this house. And neither are you if you intend to keep spouting off blasphemy. If you were my young'un, I'd put a belt across your backside and teach you proper respect for the good Lord and his Word. Be that as it may, I suggest you sit there and keep your mouth shut. Or leave."

Sufficiently chastised, Joe had heeded his grandmother's warning. He would keep his speculations about the cosmos to himself. But the meteorite was proof positive of the comings and goings in the vast universe, and, as far as Joe was concerned, the meteorite could be a gift from the good Lord Himself.

"The things you must have seen," Joe whistled softly to the chunk of dead matter, pondering with awe the vast gulf of space the meteor might have traveled to reach this landing point. "The places you must have been."

Shaking his head in amazement, Joe stacked the three broken pieces atop the larger portion of the meteorite and set off across the field to show the prize to his family and friends.

"What you got?" Sam called out as Joe lumbered closer with the rocks in his arms.

"A fallen star, I believe," Joe answered quietly. "Make a wish," he suggested. "I've already made mine."

CHAPTER 2

TOM CARTER MADE, IF not a wish, a request. "I become a teenager this week," he informed Joe following church services the day after the discovery of the meteorite.

"Yeah, well, congratulations," Joe muttered. "It's not all it's cracked up to be."

"Yeah, yeah," Tom shrugged. "I've heard. That's why I've got plans to celebrate the occasion. In a big way."

Joe drew a circle in the sand with his shoe. "How's that?" he asked finally, succumbing to curiosity and his friend's patience with the details.

"I thought maybe you and I would go campen by the New Pond," Tom announced. "Do a little fishen, maybe set a trot line." He paused before adding nonchalantly, "Drink a beer or two."

Joe's head flew up as he scanned the church grounds for prying ears, and Tom knew he had hooked the older boy's attention. "Whataya think?" Tom asked.

"Campen and fishen sound good," Joe replied warily. "I've tasted beer once in my life, and it wasn't that good." He hesitated. "But I'm game to give it another try … if we can get the beer. Just how do you plan to do that, hotshot? We're not exactly twenty-one."

"Bribe Lucas," Tom shot back. "A six-pack for him, a six-pack for us."

Joe glanced around the churchyard, considering the proposition. "It might work," he determined aloud. "It just might work. I've known Lucas to drink a beer or two in his time."

The two boys approached Lucas the following Friday afternoon.

Lucas and his new wife, Beauty, had moved into a one-room barn on the Baker farm shortly after the new year arrived. The barn sat far off the main road on the southeastern corner of the farm and was hidden by deep woods where the hogs roamed. It was a tightly built structure high off the ground with wooden walls, a tin roof and a porch across the front. The Bakers stored tobacco in the barn during the summer. Matt had offered the structure to Lucas as part of his payment to help on the farm when the working season arrived.

Lucas and Beauty were overjoyed with their new home. Although shy and reserved, Beauty had beamed while showing Joe the way she had fixed up the room a few days after the newlyweds settled in the barn. Dishes and food were stacked neatly in a ramshackle cupboard in a back corner, opposite a mattress on the floor that was made up pretty with a worn chintz cover. A clothes chest occupied one of the front corners, while a wood stove sat across the room. Two chairs stood in front of the stove, with a table and a hurricane oil lamp between them.

Her obvious pride had embarrassed Joe, who took conveniences such as electricity and indoor plumbing for granted, although he had been born at a time when neither existed in his own home. He was still uncomfortable about the situation, even after realizing the barn was relatively comfortable compared with the squalor of dirt floors, tarpaper walls and a leaky roof. More troublesome to him, however, was the knowledge that once summer arrived, the barn's rightful owner would reclaim it, leaving Beauty's home to play second fiddle to the Bakers' tobacco. Beauty and

Lucas, of course, were prepared to share space with the tobacco, but Joe found little peace of mind in their expectancy.

These thoughts crossed his mind as Joe approached the barn with Tom. Lucas was outside, with his head stuck under the hood of his worn-out truck, while Beauty was perched on the porch in a small rocker.

"Afternoon, Beauty," Joe called, his greeting echoed by Tom as they emerged from the concealing confines of the narrow lane that led to the main road. "You, too, Lucas. What are y'all up to?"

"Hello, Joe," Beauty returned. "Same to you, Tom."

"I'm tryen to get this heap of junk runnen again," Lucas told them by way of greeting. "The battery froze up on me last night."

He blew on the battery cable for luck, retired a screwdriver to his pants pocket and closed the hood. "I was just about to take a little drive to warm it up. Y'all wanna come with me."

Joe and Tom glanced at each other, then at Beauty and back to Lucas, conspiracy gleaming in their eyes at the perfect opening presented to them. "Sure," Joe said.

"Might as well," Tom shrugged. "We've got nothen better to do."

Beauty snorted at their false sincerity. "Those boys got somethen on their mind, Lucas," she concluded. "They're up to no good, and they're wanten you to help."

Lucas eyed them suspiciously for a long moment. "Y'all do look awful bright-eyed and bushy-tailed," he surmised. "What's on your mind?"

"Nothen," Joe lied, feigning innocence.

"Humph!" Beauty sniffed. "I smell trouble."

"You swear?" Lucas asked.

Joe rolled his eyes. "Come on, Lucas," he urged in his most believable tone, crossing his arms for emphasis. "You know I don't swear to nothen."

"What about you, Tom?" Lucas inquired.

"We were just out for a walk, passen time," Tom replied quickly, sticking his hands behind his back and crossing his fingers. "Honest, Lucas. That's all."

Lucas looked at his wife. "I don't believe either one of 'em," he announced. "But if they go along with me, then I can keep my eye on 'em. What you think?"

Beauty smiled behind a disapproving frown. "I smell trouble," she repeated emphatically. "But go ahead and go. Me, I got supper to cook. You boys make sure my husband is home on time to eat it or there'll be the devil to pay."

"I won't be late," Lucas assured her. "I'm just gonna ride around a little bit to build up the battery."

"He won't be late," Joe promised, nodding his understanding.

"We'll make sure he's home on time," vowed Tom, who was already at the door of the pickup.

The three of them waved goodbye to Beauty as the truck eased out of the yard and down the narrow lane toward the main road. "I guess you'll be glad when the weather warms up," Joe said to Lucas. "For the battery," he added by way of explanation.

Lucas gave them a long glance. "You boys are up to somethen," he decided as they approached the dirt road and Joe jumped out of the cab to open the metal gate.

"Yesterday was my birthday," Tom announced as Lucas drove the truck through the opening and they waited for Joe to shut the gate and rejoin them. "I was thirteen."

"Congratulations," Lucas replied hesitantly. "I hope you're not expecten a birthday present from me."

"Nah," Tom remarked as Joe climbed into the cab and shut the door.

"Did you tell him?" Joe asked Tom almost immediately.

"Tell me what?" Lucas demanded to know.

"About his birthday," Joe answered quickly.

"I told him," Tom said.

"Oh," Lucas mumbled with relief, at last applying his foot to the accelerator and guiding the truck away from the farm.

They rode in silence along the dirt road, past the Berrien estate and the church, until the mercantile came into view. "Mama and Daddy gave me a sleepen bag for my birthday," Tom said. "Joe and me are goen campen by the pond tomorrow night."

"Which one?" Lucas wanted to know.

"The New Pond," Joe answered. "I'll be usen blankets and quilts for a sleepen bag."

"Wouldn't it be better to wait until the weather warms up?" Lucas asked. "It's cold and damp enough to make a body shore enough sick." He paused. "I'm surprised your mamas are letten y'all go."

Lucas brought the truck to a complete stop at the highway, and the boys held their breath while he looked left and right. Finally, after lengthy consideration, he eased their minds with a right-hand turn toward the county line liquor store. Their relief was almost audible.

"We're gonna build a fire, cook out and maybe do a little fishen tomorrow night," Joe told Lucas when the mercantile was out of sight.

"Try to scare each other with ghost stories," Tom continued. "Maybe drink a little beer."

"That so," Lucas said tonelessly.

Joe leaned forward and looked directly at his older friend. "We were kind of hopen you might buy it for us," he proposed quickly. "See'en as we're not exactly twenty-one and can't do it ourselves."

"You were hopen," Lucas repeated him.

Tom continued the pleading. "We've got the money," he said, producing a rumpled five-dollar bill from his pocket. "All we want is a six-pack. And you can buy one for yourself while you're at it. Our treat!"

"No way!" Lucas exploded. "You two boys are gonna be the death of me yet, with all your cajolen and favors. We're goen straight home."

"Come on, Lucas," Joe coaxed. "A cold beer sure would taste good goen down. It might cool you off some after all that hard work you did to get the truck runnen."

"It's forty degrees outside, Joe-Joe, and the heater ain't worken in this truck," replied Lucas, unmoved by their appeals. "We're cool enough. Besides, y'all's mamas and daddies are raisen their children to be good churchgoers."

"I don't think a beer or two is gonna send us down the road to wickedness," Joe declared, sensing a chink in his friend's resistance. "You know, Lucas, there's a lot of debate in the Baptist church about whether drinken beer is sinful at all."

"Don't get highfalutin with me, Joe-Joe," Lucas barked. "I don't know and I don't care what the Baptists believe. But I do know your mama and daddy—and Mr. Dan and Mrs. Amelia—don't want their boys drinken. And that's that."

"What's the harm?" Joe persisted. "You drink it occasionally. In fact, you're the one who gave me my first taste of beer." He paused, seemingly remembering the occasion. "Frankly, I didn't like it," he continued, changing his course of persuasion. "But Tom's never tried it at all, and he needs convincen that it tastes rotten. A guy only turns thirteen once in his life, and it's supposed to be a big deal."

Joe hesitated, allowing Lucas to mull over the idea. "I tell you what, Lucas," he continued at length. "Buy one six-pack for yourself and one for us, and we'll make sure you get whatever we don't drink. How's that for a deal?"

Completely ridiculous and out of the question, Lucas thought to himself, deliberating at length over the boys' request. His head urged Lucas to turn the truck around and head for home. But a soft spot in his heart for youthful rambunctiousness kept the truck on course for the county line.

"Lordamercy!" he finally relented. "I'll do it this one time, boys. But if you ever ask me to again, I'll tell your mamas and daddies the whole story."

"We won't ask," Tom promised. "Heck, I probably won't even like the stuff."

"Fair enough," Joe agreed.

————

Saturday turned out cold and cloudless, perfect conditions for camping, even without a tent. Joe and Tom set up their sparse campsite on the east bank of the New Pond late in the day. It was quick work, spreading blankets on the grassy bank, setting out grocery bags of food and drink and gathering wood for a fire when night fell. Within minutes, they were finished and in the small rowboat paddling toward the far side of the pond to set a trotline for fishing.

The New Pond was deliberately inhospitable to humans. Accessible only from its long eastern bank and a tiny portion of its southern flank, the pond was a large body of water, carved from a mature grove of cypress, pine and water oaks. The eastern edge was clear and deep, but farther out, the pond turned swampy, with hundreds of jagged stumps and waterlogged trees breaking the surface. The pond eventually merged with a swamp known as Bear Bay on neighboring land owned by a cantankerous widow.

Matt and Sam had built the pond during the drought of 1954, the worst dry spell anyone could remember in these parts. They had financed the construction with the timber harvest necessary to clear the land, and both men claimed every ragged trunk and waterlogged tree on the premises were part of their master plan to create the perfect habitat for a fisherman's paradise. The pond was stocked with bass, bream, catfish and perch among others. Giant bullfrogs, turtles, water moccasins and at least one alligator had taken up residence on their own accord. Beavers occasionally tried to establish a colony on the banks but were promptly shot and their dams destroyed, as was the only otter ever seen on the place. Sam said beavers and otters would fish the pond clean if left unattended.

Joe shared the pond's history with Tom as he navigated the treacherous water. "We dug the pond in 1954, but it was bone-dry that year, and it took till the next spring before there was any water in it," he recalled. "We had a lot of rain in the winter of '56. That's when it filled up and we put the first fish in here. Grandpa didn't let a hook near the place for two years. Now there's some genuine monsters in here."

"What's the biggest one you've caught?" Tom asked.

"A four-pound channel cat in this pond," Joe replied. "But I nabbed a nine-pound bass from the Old Pond. That's the biggest fish I've ever caught." He gestured with an oar to the nearest field, which was hidden from view by a stretch of woods. "Grandpa says there's even bigger catfish in that little water hole in the middle of that field over yonder," he pointed out. "He's probably right. The place is so snaky that nobody ever fishes it."

"That hole makes my skin crawl," Tom said.

"Granny once sat on a moccasin there," Joe commented. "She wasn't payen attention and sat down on an old stump. Nobody noticed the snake till she got up. And there it was, all rolled up and ready to strike. I don't know how in the world she didn't get bit."

An involuntary tremor ran through Tom, who despised snakes. "She was lucky," he guessed. "Let's not talk about snakes out here."

Under normal circumstances, Joe would have honored his friend's request. But this was a special occasion, and he decided to strike with the night's first scary story.

"You'd better make sure you zip that sleepen bag real tight tonight," he advised Tom.

"I will," Tom replied. "It's getten downright chilly out here. We need our heavy jackets."

Joe shrugged agreement. "Yeah, but that's not what I'm talken about," he explained. "You know what they say about snakes and sleepen bags. I've heard stories about a rattlesnake crawlen in a sleepen bag while somebody was asleep inside it. Crawled all the way to the bottom and then bit the guy when he woke up." His tone became increasingly dramatic. "I even heard about one man who woke up with a rattlesnake curled up right beside him. Woke up and found himself face-to-face with it. Can you imagine waken up to find a rattlesnake—or a moccasin—looken you right between the eyes." He shivered his shoulders on purpose and restrained himself from a backward glance to see the horrified frown on Tom's face.

"Gee, Joe," Tom sighed. "Don't go talken that way. You know I hate snakes. I won't sleep a minute tonight from worryen."

Joe smiled to himself and picked out a stump, which would make a good tie-end for the trotline. He rowed toward it, slicing the single oar through the water with smooth strokes. At last, when he could stand it no longer, Joe pulled up the oar and turned around to face his friend. "You know what would be worse than waken up to find a snake staren you in the face?" he asked.

Tom shook his head violently. "No! And I don't want to, either."

"Waken up to find one all coiled up against your pecker," Joe told him anyway.

"Dang, Joe!"

"And if it bit you down there, imagine what big balls you'd have," Joe continued blithely, barely able to conceal his mirth as the boat bumped against a stump. "Of course, I don't guess a pair of big balls would do a guy much good if he was dead."

Tom suddenly turned a ghastly shade of white, and Joe nearly fell out of the boat with a chortle of uncontrollable glee.

"Joe!" Tom emphasized with a quiet forcefulness that failed to penetrate the older boy's rolling laughter. "Joe!" he repeated more loudly the second time."

Still shaking with smiles, Joe finally looked up, and Tom pointed past him. "Don't turn around, Joe," he ordered, "and give me the oar."

The sincerity of his tone brought Joe's laughter under control but failed to wipe away the silly grin from his face. Joe shook his head, pointedly dismissing Tom's attempt to feign attention away from his own fearful gullibility with such a feeble display of caution. "Nice try, partner," he gloated. "But I got you."

Joe made a leisurely about-face and almost fainted dead on the spot. A few feet away, two mammoth moccasins lay piled on top of each other in a stump hollow, and they were stirring, awakened from their late afternoon sunbath by the boat, which had butted against the broken tree trunk.

"J-e-s-u-s," Joe moaned unintentionally, stretching out every sound and syllable. "Let's get out of here, Tom," he whispered after what seemed like an eternity later. "Fast."

"I need the paddle," Tom said.

"Use your hands," Joe hissed. "If they get in this boat, I'm dead and you're next in line."

Tom peered cautiously over both sides of the boat, fearful his hands were about to become an inviting target for the snakes' children. Or worse, their brothers and sisters. Seeing nothing beneath the dark surface, he eased his hands into the water and began paddling. When the boat made its first slight movement, Joe slid the oar deftly across the stern and pushed hard against the stump, hurdling the small craft along with himself and Tom back several feet to safety. Seconds later, the moccasins slid off the stump into the water and slithered away from the boys.

"Dang!" Tom murmured later, when they were able to breathe freely again and the snakes had disappeared into the far reaches of the pond.

"No more snake stories from me," Joe vowed.

"Ain't beer supposed to calm your nerves?" Tom asked hopefully.

"I hope so," Joe muttered. "Let's set the trot line and find out."

Joe rowed the boat back toward the middle of the pond, and they swiftly finished the task. The line stretched forty feet between stumps, with baited hooks dangling in three-foot intervals. They planned to check the line in about three hours and put out new bait. With luck, they would catch Sunday dinner for their families.

———

The last light of day was dimming when the boys reached shore, and both felt as if a lifetime had passed on the water. Joe built a fire, while Tom fetched the beer from its hiding place.

They had wound up with both six-packs for themselves when Lucas ordered them from his truck, ranting and raving about the situations the boys put him in with their shenanigans and declaring he hoped the beer made them sick as dogs. In his agitation, Lucas had forgotten to retrieve his own six-pack. All day, Joe had expected the man to come looking for the beer, which explained why he had made himself scarce around the house as much as possible.

Joe was reposed on the blankets, smoking a Winston cigarette, when Tom returned with the beer. The brown bottles were chilled and dewy from the dampness of the night, and the boys immediately twisted off the tops and tested the brew.

"The Pilgrims drank beer," Tom remarked, primarily to assuage the trepidation he was feeling about the wrongful deed they were doing. "They called it ale," he went on seriously. "But it was nothing more than beer."

"And Jesus made wine," Joe added, amused by his friend, perhaps feeling a trifle guilty himself for partaking from the cup of sin, which was the way Preacher Cook had described drinking during a communion service in church one time. "He probably drank it, too," Joe continued. "But the Baptists are convinced it was nothen more than grape juice."

Joe tilted the bottle back and took a long swallow. "Whataya think?" he asked Tom when the amber liquid had slid down his throat and settled in his empty stomach. "Is it what you expected?"

"I'm not sure," Tom replied, matching Joe drink for drink. "But I don't think God's gonna send us to Hell for drinken a beer or two. Do you?"

"Probably not," Joe agreed.

"Of course," Tom said with uncertainty. "Now that I'm thirteen, I suppose I've reached the age of accountability. Is that right?"

"I'm not sure to tell you the truth," Joe answered. "Everybody's always talken about the age of accountability, but nobody ever tells you exactly what it is. Personally, I figure it's when you have a clear sense of what's right and what's wrong."

"But a person knows the difference between right and wrong when he's a little fellow," Tom interjected. "Surely God doesn't send a kid to Hell for breaken a few rules every now and then."

"You didn't let me finish," Joe grumbled. "Knowen right from wrong is only part of it. I think you also have to understand the consequences of doen wrong and be capable of taken full responsibility for your actions. And, too, I think people come to a point in life when they just automatically know whether they've reached the age of accountability. If you're old enough to worry about it, then I'm guessen you've reached that age."

"Wow!" Tom murmured. "I've just reached the age of accountability." He looked down at the nearly empty beer bottle in his hand. "I'm not off to a very good start at liven right, am I?"

Joe chuckled, which was easier than answering the question.

In these calming moments after their scare on the water, the boys forgot supper. They had planned to fry fish but had never gotten around to catching them. Now, neither was interested. But they were hungry, so Tom rummaged through the grocery sack and produced a bag of potato chips, while Joe added another log to the fire. They opened their second beers, put the chips between them and settled back on the blankets, contemplating the nighttime sky.

"It's pitch black," Tom remarked. "What we need is a full moon?"

"Moonlit nights are fine," Joe said, "but you can see the sky better on a night like this."

He pointed out Mars, various constellations and the Milky Way for Tom, and they speculated about the meteorite: Where it might have come from, how far it had traveled, what kind of star it might have been?

"Who knows," Tom pondered. "Maybe you actually saw it in the sky before it fell."

Joe gave a negative nod in the darkness. "Nah," he said. "From what I gather, it takes a fallen star years and years to reach Earth. If that meteorite was indeed a star at one time, then it began fallen a long time before you or I was even born."

"Still, it's kind of strange that it wound up here, and you found it," Tom suggested. "Maybe it was a sign or somethen."

"Maybe," Joe concurred. "But of what?"

There was no answer and for a while, they sat in silence, lost in their respective thoughts. Joe surveyed the heavens and contemplated the journey of the meteorite, of which one of the smaller pieces was sitting on the desk in his new room. He had given another chunk to Tom, while the larger section was displayed on the front porch of the Baker home, making for excellent conversation with anyone who happened to stop by the house.

"Joe?" Tom said sometime later when they were well into their third beer each and beginning to feel lightheaded from so much alcohol on empty stomachs.

"Yeah, Tom."

"Are you sure we're not goen to Hell for this?" Tom asked.

Joe knew there was a concerned frown on his friend's face without even looking at him. "Not for drinken beer, I don't think," he answered sincerely.

"Then I don't guess a cigarette would hurt too much, would it?" Tom supposed.

Joe snickered and offered his friend a cigarette, lighting it with the red tip of his own smoke.

"Now that we're pretty much sure we're not goen to Hell for drinken and smoken, I've got another question for you," Tom began again when he had inhaled deeply from the cigarette and chased it with a long gulp of beer. "If you died now, where would you go? Heaven? Or Hell?"

Joe sat up and crossed his legs Indian style to peer closely at his friend. "You're a bulldog tonight," he said. "What's this fixation with Heaven and Hell? Frankly, I'm plannen to stay earthbound for a long time to come. I figure—at least I hope—I have a few years to prepare for the hereafter."

"You never know," Tom said, snapping his fingers. He hesitated, then persisted, "So which is it? Heaven? Or Hell?"

Joe shifted his gaze across the blackness of the pond and mulled over the question. There was not a pat answer at hand. And since he was being pressed for a serious commitment, he wanted to give Tom a thoughtful response rather than a brush-off.

Religion baffled Joe. On the surface, it seemed easy to figure out what God expected of Christians. But scratching the surface was akin to opening a can of worms. God's expectations were complex, and while Joe considered himself a good person, he feared whether he could measure up to Christian standards. It seemed to boil down to a matter of good or good enough, and there was a thin line of distinction between the two. Of course, he knew, too, that a person must be prepared to meet his Maker as if every breath was the last. At the same time, though, he wondered whether God expected a person to remember that every move might be the last and preface it as such. Frankly, he doubted even monks could be so single-minded. And he was positive that he could not be. None of which provided him the elusive answer.

"That's a hard question," he answered at length, "and, honestly, I haven't given it much thought. But since you ask, I figure I have fairly good credentials for Heaven." He took a deep breath. "Still, when you come right down to it, I suppose I'd have to say Hell at this point in time."

An incredulous expression graced Tom. "Are you serious?" he asked gravely.

"I've felt saved a few times," Joe explained seriously. "But the Bible says you have to accept Christ publicly and be baptized, and I haven't felt called enough, or good enough, to do that. Since it's one of the key points laid out by Jesus for salvation, then I'd say my bid for Heaven is flawed right now. It all goes back to what I said earlier about right and wrong and understanden the consequences and taken responsibility. The Bible pretty much lays out the plan for salvation and if you reject it and realize you're rejecten it, then I'd say you're probably doomed to Hell."

Joe paused, then added quickly, "At least I'd say that about myself. Of course, as the Bible also says, I try not to judge others."

"We're goen to Hell," Tom murmured with the slow comprehension of a new idea.

"No, we're not," Joe assured him, laughing. "We've got time to do the right thing, Tom, and when the right time comes, we'll do it. Now let's change the subject."

There was no more talk of religion, but the conversation flowed smoothly. The more beer went into their mouths, the more nonsense flowed out of them. They were at once boisterous and boastful, crass and courageous, thoughtless and thoughtful. They discussed girls and school, girls and themselves, girls and sports, girls and sex. Both of them were virgins, lamentably so. At fifteen, Joe was particularly worried about his lack of experience, especially when other boys his age boasted of sexual conquests.

"They're lyen," Tom said.

"Probably," Joe agreed. "But town people seem to do everything faster than we do out in the country. Maybe they're more sophisticated about sex. Maybe the girls in town are more willen."

He stood and staggered over to retrieve more beers for them. "Hell, I've got all the tools for maken love," he boasted. "Plenty of it, if I say so myself. I got the prowess for it. And Lord knows, I got the interest. But I'm still a cherry, and I don't even stand a chance out here. The only girls I ever see around here are my sisters or those who come to church. And I try not to think about girls at church."

"You think you've got problems," Tom said, having heard enough. "What about me? I'm still waiten for a good bulge in my blue jeans."

"You'll get it," Joe shrugged. "I got most of mine in the last year. You just wake up one mornen and it's there, ready and willen to conquer the world. Then you spend all your time worryen it's gonna spring into action at the worst possible time and everybody's gonna see you with a hard-on."

Such was the stuff of the evening. By midnight, the pair had consumed ten bottles of beer and were staggering drunk when they reached for the last two.

"This stuff grows on you," Tom remarked, holding out the beer bottle for an examination. "It tasted horrible at first, but it gets better with each sip."

Joe belched, long and loud, and swigged down another ounce or two.

That was when they remembered the trotline, which should have been checked hours ago and plied with new bait. Falling all over themselves, they climbed into the boat and rowed a ragged course toward the trotline.

————

"This is one spooky place at night," Tom commented as the boat glided across the water, occasionally bouncing off a shadowy stump. "It's dark as sin."

"Do you remember where we set it?" Joe asked, straining to see in the darkness when he was certain they had rowed past the trotline. "I can't figure out where we are."

Tom stumbled to his feet and made a sweeping gaze around the pond, teetering on the edge before finally pointing to his right and collapsing back into the seat. The boat rocked precariously, and Tom burst into giggles.

Joe laughed, too, and shook his head. "You're drunk," he accused good-naturedly.

"Sho, nuff," Tom replied. "But I found the trot line, mister, so you must be drunker than me."

"Whatever," Joe shrugged. "But you'd better keep your butt sitten down so the boat doesn't tip over. It's too cold for swimmen."

"There ain't no way I'm goen swimmen in this snake hole," Tom shivered. "You'd either end up full of snake holes or some ornery alligator would bite off your balls for a late-night snack."

"Yours might make a snack," Joe deadpanned. "Mine would be a full-course meal."

"Either way," Tom continued. "I think I'll keep my butt sitten down."

"You do that," Joe urged. "And be quiet while you're at it."

Tom took the advice and was dozing by the time the boat reached the trotline, which was nowhere in the vicinity of the direction he had pointed. Noticing his friend slumped on his side, Joe promptly jabbed Tom in the gut with the oar. "Wake up!" he ordered. "We've got fish to haul in."

Tom sprang instantly alert. "What a night," he remarked. "Guess I picked the right place after all."

"Close enough," Joe lied.

The first four hooks netted two perch, a small bream that Tom tossed back, and a good-sized channel catfish that finned Joe and was dropped inadvertently into the water. The next two hooks were empty, which was when Tom noticed the heavy sag in the line.

"Jesus, Joe," he shouted. "We must have caught a shark or somethen. The whole line's under water at this end."

Joe was rubbing his palm and cursing his clumsiness with the catfish. "We don't have sharks," he muttered, picking up the paddle and rowing them closer to the sagging line. "Pull it up," he instructed. "Let's see what's on the other end."

"Dang, it's heavy," Tom said, tugging on the line. "I need help."

Joe dropped the oar and lifted the trotline with both hands, while Tom leaned over the edge, grabbed the hook line and began reeling in the catch. Neither one of them had an idea about what had been snagged on the line, but at that moment, their catch began fighting for its freedom. The sudden thrashing in the water caught Tom off guard, and he lost his hold on the hook line.

Joe roared with amusement, while straining to pull the main line higher out of the water. He stood on shaky legs to gain leverage. "Grab the line and pull it up, Tom," he shouted. "Whatever the thing is, it can't hurt you with a hook in the mouth."

"I ain't so sure about that," Tom yelled back before cautiously gripping the line once more. This time his grip was tight and, ignoring the thrashing water, he made steady progress in reeling the catch to the surface.

"I've got it!" he cried.

Then the water exploded.

Tom sensed rather than saw the oblong object lunge at him with powerful snapping jaws. He screamed, dropped the line and tried to scramble away as the hard-shelled monster landed in the boat.

"A snappen turtle!" Joe hollered, laughing. "Watch out!"

Tom yelled again and hurled himself away from the turtle, jumping over the snapping jaws of the long neck protruding from the wide-bodied shell.

Overweighted on one side, the boat flipped before the boys even comprehended the danger. Joe, whose balance had been in jeopardy all along while trying to stand on the bottom of the boat, pitched headlong into the water, scraping his back against a jagged edge of an underwater stump as he sank into the murky depths of the pond. It was the single most-terrifying moment of his young life, complete with a hallucination of hundreds of water moccasins, snapping turtles and hungry alligators, all lurking about their rightful abode and eager to attack any unlawful intruder.

Surrounded by total blackness, out of air, Joe decided against a watery grave. He righted himself beneath the water, kicked to the surface and received, along with a greedy gulp of air, the second, single-most terrifying moment of his life: a stillness and silence over the pond that made its black depths far more ominous than they had ever been.

Fear seized his heart, and Joe uttered a single word, softly at first and then in a long scream.

"Tom!"

———

Tom felt the boat capsizing and was all at once grateful for escaping the snapping jaws and fearful the turtle might follow him into the water. By his own reckoning, the turtle had missed Tom's flesh by a hair's breadth and he figured to have nightmares about those powerful jaws for years to come.

He landed in the water on his shoulder and went under off balance. But Tom made an immediate recovery. He turned a quick somersault, kicked up toward the surface and was promptly snagged by one of the trotline hooks.

The hook snared him by the nape of the neck, imbedding deep in the flesh. Wrought with pain, Tom involuntarily opened his mouth to yell and was choked with a gullet full of water. He floundered to the top of the pond, coughing and gasping for air, aware of someone screaming his name.

He grasped his neck, yelled for help and went under once more with another long swallow of water, most of which he inhaled.

Joe was treading water ten feet away when Tom emerged. His mind cleared instantly, and two sturdy swim strokes covered the distance in seconds flat. Joe took a deep breath, dove underwater and slammed into Tom, who was coming up a second time for air. They untangled themselves and pushed to the surface, where Joe grabbed Tom by the arm and pulled him through the water to the sturdy anchor of a waterlogged cypress stump.

"I've got a fish hook in my neck," Tom moaned, coughing up water at the same time and clinging to the ragged stump with both arms. "It's killen me," he wailed.

"You're okay," Joe said in his calmest voice. "Just keep holden on to this stump, and you'll be fine."

"Try to get it out, Joe," Tom cried. "Please."

It was impossible to see in the darkness, and Joe lacked the dexterity to keep himself afloat while performing minor surgery at the same time. Still, he examined Tom and discovered the hook was buried deep in his neck, with only a tiny portion of the straight end sticking out of the flesh. Seeing the hook was still attached to the main line, he realized the tension was adding to Tom's torment. He fished his pocketknife from his jeans and cut the line.

"Is that better?"

"Some," Tom moaned.

Joe looked around to get his bearings, trying to readjust his eyes for night vision. It was pitch black. The boat was nowhere in sight, and the oar had floated to some hidden place. He tried to remember the path they had followed in the daylight, seeming to recall they had set the line somewhere near the middle of the pond. It was a long way to shore, he realized. Whichever way it was.

———

The ice-cold water was chilling his imbibed mind to a numbing soberness, and Joe was worried.

Tom was hugging the cypress stump for dear life, moaning occasionally about his neck and shivering in violent fits.

If they stayed in the water much longer, exposure would kill them—if the snakes and alligators did not get them first.

Joe gazed heavenward for divine intervention and was rewarded with a clear nighttime sky. He sighted the North Star and the two dippers and knew immediately the pond bank lay somewhere to the right.

"I don't know about you, buddy," he told Tom, "but I don't want to be fish food or gator bait. We have to get out of here, or we're gonna freeze to death."

"I'm not sure I can make it," Tom said meekly without lifting his head from the stump. "My neck's on fire."

"You'll make it," Joe declared. "I promise. We'll swim from stump to stump and rest whenever we need to. I'll be right beside you the whole way, so there's no need to worry."

"Okay," Tom exhaled.

Joe pointed in the darkness. "The bank's that way," he said. "Are you ready?"

Tom shook his head, and they began, swimming side-by-side from stump to stump. They moved through the water in virtual silence, except for an occasional word of encouragement from Joe and a groan from Tom.

It was an agonizingly slow journey for Joe and even more so for Tom. Every stump held the potential to harbor a bed of moccasins and the worst ones were those unseen beneath the surface. His heart beat faster every time Joe touched one of the waterlogged remnants of some cypress or oak tree, and he prayed silently that it might be the last one they came across.

In a way, Tom might have been lucky to have that fishhook in his neck. His agony was all too real to dwell on anything else.

After what seemed like hours of trading one stump for another, the distance between the broken tree trunks became longer and more taxing to cover. At last, they came to a hollow stump resembling an arch, and Joe knew the pond bank lay about a hundred yards before them. They took this final opportunity to rest, each clinging to one of the thick tendrils that had once supported a massive water oak.

Joe peered closely at the pale face of Tom, who was obviously fatigued, his weakness exacerbated by the pain in his neck and the excessive alcohol in his blood.

"Are you okay?" Joe asked the younger boy for the second time that night.

"Just tired," Tom answered.

"How's the neck?"

"It hurts, but not as much," Tom said. "Maybe I'm getten used to it." He paused. "Heck, maybe I'll keep it."

Joe smiled for what seemed like the first time in ages. "The latest in fashion neckwear," he said drolly. "Who knows, Tom? You might be starten the latest, greatest fad."

Tom smiled tiredly. "We were awful stupid, weren't we?" he said.

"We were lucky," Joe agreed. "But we've still got a way to go before we're out of the woods." He hesitated. "Or should I say out of the water. Are you up to it?"

Tom looked off in the darkness. "It's a pretty long way," he surmised.

"Yeah, but you could swim it underwater if you wanted," Joe encouraged. "You go first. I'll follow, and if you get tired, I'll be right there to help. We'll make it, Tom. We've come too far not to."

"Piece of cake," Tom smiled, then suddenly surged free of the oaken anchor and began swimming strongly toward the shore.

Joe spotted him ten yards and followed at a slower pace.

Minutes later, Tom found the bottom of the pond with his feet and staggered up the bank with Joe on his heels. They collapsed face down on the grassy shore, breathing heavily and catching their breath while the tension melted in waves of weary relief.

"When's the last time you had a tetanus shot?" Joe inquired when their breathing had returned to normal.

"I don't remember," Tom answered, his words muffled against the ground.

Joe pushed himself off the grassy bed to a sitting position. "You'll need to get one, you know," he said.

"I need to see a doctor," Tom suggested, rising slowly. "I've got to get this thing out of my neck. And soon!"

"But you can't go tonight," Joe informed him with sympathy.

"No, I guess not," Tom agreed. "Everybody'd know we'd been up to no good."

"And if they found out where we got the beer, Lucas would wind up in a lot worse shape," Joe said. "We've got to keep this to ourselves, at least until we're sober and presentable."

Tom nodded in agreement. "Okay," he said, touching the back of his neck. "But we've got to get this hook out. I can't hurt like this all night."

"I can do it," Joe grimaced. "It'll hurt like the devil, though."

"I know," Tom conceded with a determined frown. "But at least there'll be some relief when you're finished. Let's go ahead and get it over with."

"Okay," Joe replied. "Let me look at it."

The hook was sunk fully into Tom's neck. Blood trickled from the ragged tear in the skin. There was only one way Joe knew to remove a fishhook, and that was to push it through the skin. Pulling the hook out would cause worse pain and rip more flesh. "I'll be back in a second," he told Tom after examining the wound.

Joe walked back to their campsite and procured a small pair of pliers with wire cutters from his tackle box, then scoured the pond bank for a stout stick. A short time later, they were ready to begin.

"Here," Joe said, offering the stick to Tom. "Put it in your mouth and bite down if the pain gets to be more than you can bear. I've heard it helps."

Tom took the stick and gazed at the pliers.

"Lie down on your stomach," Joe instructed him after a moment's hesitation. "I'm goen to sit on your back to keep you still. Try not to make any sudden movements."

"Easy for you to say," Tom muttered as he moved into a prone position on the grass. "Just make it quick. That's all I ask."

Joe kneeled beside him and studied the angle of the hook. Using his thumb and index finger, he pressed against Tom's neck to measure the depth of the imbedded angle. Tom squirmed under the pressure, and Joe withdrew his hand.

"It's deep in there," he explained. "I'll have to push it down a tiny bit and then up and through to get it out. Are you ready?"

Tom nodded.

"Remember to bite down on the stick if it hurts more than you can bear," Joe advised.

Tom nodded again and buried his face against the grass as Joe pressed against the injured area with one hand and gripped the straight end of the hook with the other. "Take a deep breath," he ordered.

Joe worked quickly and efficiently. In one sweeping motion, he pushed down on the skin and up with the hook. The curved end of the hook tore through the flesh, along with a heavy flow of blood. Using his weight to keep Tom penned to the ground, Joe used the wire cutter on the pliers to clip the end of the hook. From there, he pulled both metal ends from the wound and jumped away from Tom.

Though the whole process took less than twenty seconds, the pain was excruciating. His neck screamed for relief and Tom bounded to his feet the instant he felt Joe release his hold on him. He took three blind steps forward and promptly provided a vocal outlet for the pain. It was a yell, loud but blessedly short. A spasm of delirious laughter mixed with cries shook Tom next and then he was spent.

He collapsed and allowed Joe to wash away the blood and press a cold rag against the wound. Ten minutes later, most of the bleeding had stopped and Tom was able to drift off to sleep.

Joe built a roaring fire beside his friend and stripped out of his own wet clothes to dry them. He wrapped himself in a blanket, then gathered up the beer bottles and threw them far out into the pond rather than risk their discovery.

A thousand thoughts raced through his mind, most of them disturbing as Joe huddled by the fire waiting for his clothes to dry. He contemplated how their plans had gone awry, what might have happened to him or Tom, with each realization more chilling than the previous, leaving him colder from fright than the brisk night air.

Shortly before dawn, with his mind at last numb and his clothes dry, Joe finally dozed, secure in the knowledge that he was, at the very least, older and wiser for this perilous night.

———

The boys dragged themselves home shortly before noon and gave everyone their carefully distorted version of the previous night. To listen to them tell it, their camping trip had been unremarkable, except for a freakish boating mishap. And even the accident had been uneventful, they maintained, except, perhaps, for some minor pain to Tom.

There were a few questions to answer for their fathers and some assurances to provide their mothers, but, largely, the story won easy acceptance. Tom got his tetanus shot, which had been due anyway, and Joe caught the devil from Lucas, who was angry the boys had taken both six-packs. The entire incident might have passed without note, but for one significant milestone in its aftermath.

On the next Sunday, which was Big Meeting at church, Joe and Tom made their public professions of Christ, admitted they were sinners and asked for forgiveness and baptism. Remarkably, they insisted on baptism that very day, even though it was late February and the waters of New River were cold and running swiftly.

Preacher Adam Cook honored their request with gladness in his heart, and the boys were buried in the cleansing water of New River. A few days later, Joe came down with a miserable cold, while Tom was put to bed with a nasty case of flu.

It was worth being sick, they told each other. One never knew when a baptism might come in handy.

GERUNDS, PARTICIPLES AND INFINITIVES were the topic of the hour, and Mrs. Elizabeth Gaskins had the propensity to make them interesting. Normally, Joe would have given his undivided attention to the feisty, redheaded woman. But on this day, he spent the entire second period conjugating Spanish verbs, completing a neglected homework assignment from the previous day. He finished the task as the bell rang and reviewed his work while his classmates collected books and filed out of the room to their next class.

Stuffing the paper in his notebook, he clasped his hands behind his back and stretched. Mrs. Gaskins was staring at him when Joe looked up from his desk. He smiled easily, sobering just as quickly when he detected the piercing gaze the English teacher reserved for severe reprimands. Her eyebrows were arched, her nostrils flared and her lips pursed.

"My time is as valuable as yours, Mr. Baker," she said frostily, "and my class is not intended to serve as a study hall for someone else's homework. I do not appreciate your lack of sensitivity."

"I'm sorry, Mrs. Gaskins," Joe apologized, bestowing his most winning smile. "I forgot my Spanish homework last night, and it's due next period."

"Nevertheless, I am disappointed, Joseph."

Mrs. Gaskins was his favorite teacher and a friend as well. She taught grammar and literature with flair and panache. Once, while studying *Beowulf*, she had ordered students to bring fried chicken to class and made them ravage the food with their bare hands while reading portions of the old English epic. She viewed the grease stains on the pages of her literature books as medals of honor.

Joe worshipped the woman. Once he had dreamed about having a love affair with her in Paris or London. But she had introduced him to her husband at a basketball game one night, beginning with, "This is Joe Baker. He thinks he's my favorite student."

Her husband had smiled brightly, extended his hand and said, "I'll tell you a secret, Joe. You are her favorite student."

Joe genuinely liked the guy, so he now confined his thoughts about the teacher to friendship and her work.

As much as she brought passion to the classroom, Elizabeth Gaskins also ruled with a firm hand. She required good behavior and those who acted otherwise felt the full weight of her wrath. She also demanded excellence in everything, expected thoughtful answers and urged her students to search for meaning beyond the words. She wanted students to learn but she also asked them to think, and from her, Joe had discerned the importance of distinguishing between those two tasks.

Outside his family, Elizabeth Gaskins was the most influential person in his life and, right now, she was ticked with him.

Joe honored her with his most contrite expression, casting brown eyes downward to indicate his unworthiness. He mumbled another apology, then raised his eyes and inquired slyly, "Does this mean I'm not your favorite student anymore?"

"You're in the doghouse, buster, but I'll let it pass this time," she replied testily. "If you promise not to let it happen again."

"I promise."

Joe eased out of the desk and gathered his books, while Mrs. Gaskins shuffled papers. "Here!" she said abruptly, waving a folded set of papers to him.

"What is it?" Joe asked.

"Your last writing assignment," she answered with interest. "When I ask my students to write an essay defenden somethen unusual, I expect some strange responses. Your choice of subject was most interesten."

"Oh," Joe muttered cautiously.

"I gave it an A-plus," she continued. "It was written superbly; your logic was excellent and your examples honest. Although I suspect some college professor might make mincemeat of it, I was intrigued. Without doubt, Joe, you are the first and very likely will be my only student to write an essay defenden clichés. Frankly, I'm not sure whether to applaud your originality or worry about your psyche."

"I suppose you noticed there are no clichés in it," he boasted.

"Most certainly," the teacher assured him. "I read it twice to make sure. It's fortunate that you refrained. Just one, and I would have given you an A-minus at best, and your grade would have fallen proportionately with each cliché."

"Thank you," Joe smiled sheepishly as Mrs. Gaskins handed the paper to him. Written neatly in red and circled, the A+ appealed to his ego. Joe grinned appreciatively at his teacher. She immediately stifled his moment of glory.

"I had planned today's lesson around your paper," she said sternly. "But, of course, your attention was elsewhere." She unleashed another withering frown on Joe and added a touch of sarcasm to her voice. "And far be it for me, a mere teacher, to interfere with your busy schedule. So, I decided it better to wait until tomorrow before throwen your genius to the wolves. We have some bright students in this class, Joe, and they'll show you no mercy. I warn you in advance to come prepared to defend yourself, as well as explain why you chose to make a spirited defense of clichés of all things. Are we clear?"

"Yes, ma'am."

"Very well, then," she dismissed him. "You may go."

"Yes, ma'am."

He almost made it to the door before Elizabeth Gaskins halted him once more. "And Joe," she called as his hand grasped the doorknob. He glanced backward and found her smiling warmly. "Well done," she saluted.

"Yes, ma'am," he grinned. "Thank you."

———————

At Cookville High School, the town students set the style and the country folk did their best keep up with it. The differences between the two groups were hardly distinguishable, although some of the snootier town students cast their country counterparts in the role of bumpkins, while the rougher elements from the farms were quick to pick a fight with so-called Cookville snobs. In general, though, the two sides mixed and mingled in peace. The town students simply navigated the hallways with a little more finesse, while the country kids carried a few more calluses.

Perhaps it was the smooth way they operated that allowed the town students to dominate most high school activities. Most likely, though, it was who you were that made the difference. All qualifications aside, participation in everything from sports to the annual spring play was virtually assured if your father was a doctor or a lawyer, owned his own business or was a politician. The children of the prominent were most often the students who received the cheers at the pep rallies, on fields of play and during most every other high school assembly. And almost exclusively, they lived in town.

With a few notable exceptions, students like Joe, who passed their first eight grades in the country at New River Elementary and other outlying community schools, trolled relatively unnoticed through four years of high school. Two of Joe's elementary school classmates had found their way into the inner circle of the privileged. Their success was to be expected. Amy Shaw was too beautiful to overlook, and Greg Mathis too funny to ignore.

Joe belonged to the supporting cast, that great bulk of students who seemed to exist so that a chosen few could feel all the more privileged about their run of the place. Even among the supporting cast, there were distinctions. There were those, mostly girls, who talked too much, overdressed and tried too hard to become members of the inner circle. Then there were the ruffians, and the group that managed to remain virtually invisible through all four years of high school. And, of course, there were a very few whose ugliness, simple-mindedness or other grotesque distinction prevented them from slipping unnoticed through those hallowed, harrowing halls of high school.

Joe existed on the fringe, among those people who were liked by almost everyone and occasionally earned recognition for some minor talent, deed or happenstance. One of those occasions occurred soon after the reprimand from Mrs. Gaskins, and Joe owed his sudden notoriety to the English teacher.

As promised, she threw Joe to the wolves and made his defense of clichés a topic for discussion in her class. It generated a spirited debate. Joe defended himself admirably in his own estimation, simply stating that clichés deserved respect because they emerged from years of truth and satisfied the human need for familiarity and comfort.

"Like an old pair of slippers on tired feet," he offered.

Not everyone agreed, with the protest led most notably by Richard Golden. One of the more snobbish town students, Richard was the potential heir to a growing grocery store chain. He wrote the disjointed "School Happenings" column in *The Cookville Herald* and fancied himself a writer of unrivaled talent.

"Anyone who knows anything about language understands that clichés have no merit," Richard argued airily while sneering at Joe. "Clichés are nothen more than crutches for those who are unwillen, or unable, to think of a more suitable phrase to express themselves."

Dismissing Joe with upturned nostrils, Richard turned to the teacher for confirmation. "Isn't that right, Mrs. Gaskins?"

"In your opinion, Richard," she answered noncommittally. "And in the opinion of many others as well. But remember that we are talken strictly about opinions here. Joe is entitled to his, whether you, I or anyone else agrees with him. In this case, his opinion is no righter—or wrong—than yours."

As Richard's mouth fell open, the discussion took an unexpected twist, courtesy of Karen Baxter, another town student who occupied the desk behind Joe in the alphabetized seating arrangement required by their English teacher. "I happen to disagree with Joe," Karen announced.

Joe turned around in his seat to look her in the eye and was captivated by a pair of emerald green orbs.

"Both on the use of clichés and that dribble about familiarity and comfort," Karen continued. She smiled regretfully at Joe, then set a disparaging gaze on Richard Golden. "But regardless, Richard," she began smartly. "You'd do well to heed your own advice. I wade through that column you write every week, and it's positively rife with clichés." She paused, then added sweetly, "Perhaps, Richard, you're unwillen to express yourself more eloquently." She hesitated, then asked politely, "Or are you just unable?"

Joe detected thinly veiled sarcasm in her inquiry, recalling briefly that Karen and Richard had dated once. But it was a mindless thought, forgotten as quickly as it was dredged up from the inner recesses of his mind.

He had more important things to consider—like being struck dead center by Cupid's arrow.

———

Karen Baxter belonged to the exclusive inner circle of privileged high school students. She was a cheerleader, an honor student and prized catch for a date. In short, she was off limits to Joe, although rarely out of his thoughts during these dreary winter days of their junior year at Cookville High School.

There were prettier girls in school than Karen and one or two who made superior grades. But her aura was unmatched. She radiated innocence and fragility, bewitching and enchanting with a tilt of her head, a shift of the eyes or slender fingers combed gently through her soft chestnut brown hair. At her core, however, was cool strength, which could transform those sparkling emerald eyes into cold orbs of malevolent green, evoke a tart tongue and give rise to a guileless smile of polished steel.

Karen was a girl of winter, no doubt, and her brittle side attracted Joe. His protective instincts sharpened around her, and his hormones went haywire.

Her chestnut brown hair hung shoulder length, framing a delicate, heart-shaped face. She was petite, about five inches shorter than Joe, with a waist so tiny he felt certain his splayed fingers could clasp around it. Her figure was a perfect fit for her small frame, and her face was angelic with the dazzling emerald eyes and full, pouting lips. Her complexion was pure ivory, a sharp contrast to the swarthiness of Joe, who was consumed by this comparison when a voice interrupted his thoughts at lunch on the day of his sterling defense of clichés.

"Richard's just jealous of the way you have with words."

Joe peered up from his plate to find Karen regarding him with an amused expression. "May I join you?" she asked, setting her cafeteria tray opposite him.

"Sure," Joe said, taking a sip of milk to calm his racing thoughts, while savoring the soft lilt of her voice and ravishing her with his eyes.

Karen caught his admiring gaze, flashing a smile of pure innocence, and Joe dropped his eyes to the hamburger and French fries on his plate.

"That was quite a paper you wrote," she said. "Richard Golden would sell his mother to have an original idea like that."

Joe shrugged. "Defender of clichés," he remarked dryly. "Somehow I don't think that's gonna get me very far."

Karen laughed lightly. "Everyone has to start somewhere," she offered. "Anyway, you're farther along than most everyone else around here, especially the Richard Goldens of our class."

"Richard's not so bad," Joe suggested. "He just tries too hard."

"Richard's full of himself," Karen shot back. "He's arrogant, snobbish and thinks he's God's gift to the world. Unfortunately, he suffers from visions of grandeur when, in truth, he has neither the vision nor the talent to do but one thing in life."

"Which is?" Joe inquired with understated curiosity.

"To draw a fat paycheck from his father's grocery stores and live comfortably and safely right here in good old Cookville," she answered. "Richard will have a pleasant life."

"Interesten," Joe mused.

"Which is exactly what Richard's life will not be," Karen said sweetly.

Joe shrugged, took a bite of his hamburger and washed it down with milk. "I take it Richard's not one of your favorite people?" he inferred.

"Perceptive, aren't you?" Karen remarked with droll sarcasm.

"Y'all used to date, didn't you?" Joe pushed.

"We went out a few times," she replied, shrugging her shoulders. "He wasn't up to my standards, if you know what I mean?"

Since he had no clue, Joe allowed this last remark to pass without comment, returning to his food while Karen did the same.

"What about you?" she asked after a minute of companionable silence.

Joe glanced up, his face expressionless. "What about me?" he countered.

"Do you intend to live comfortably and safely here in Cookville?" she challenged. "Or are you looken for somethen more interesten?"

Joe matched her intense gaze while pondering his reply. "What do you think?"

"It's a mystery to me, Joe," Karen said. "You're not exactly forthcomen and open about yourself."

Joe nodded. "Actually, I think some people have everything you're talken about right here in Cookville," he replied. "Comfort, safety, interesten lives. My parents do. And my grandparents, too."

He paused, then informed her without fanfare, "I want to be a journalist. I figure I'll wind up some place besides Cookville."

"Ambitious, aren't you," Karen remarked quickly. "I should have figured. You're too smart to waste away your whole life on a backwoods farm."

Joe started to defend the farmer's way of life, but Karen cut him off with another question. "How come I know so little about you?"

"We don't exactly run in the same circles," Joe answered bluntly.

"We could," Karen suggested. "It's not a closed circle." She tilted her head, flicked her hair and unleashed an alluring smile that turned Joe's hormones inside out.

"I'm gonna keep my eye on you, Joe Baker," she purred. "And if you ever decide to venture off that farm to go someplace other than school, let me know." She smiled knowingly. "I have a feelen you and I might be ... two birds of the same feather."

––––––––

Karen drifted into the daily habit of eating lunch with Joe in the high school cafeteria.

She was a quick-witted, challenging conversationalist, who tossed out a new idea with almost every flick of her hair and every bat of her eyelids. She was coy and seductive, reserved and overwhelming, attentive and calculating. Joe was forced to stay on his toes to keep pace with her changing moods. She stimulated him as no other girl had done, both physically and mentally.

Joe considered it quite possible that he was in love, but he kept those thoughts strictly to himself, rebuffing even the curious inquiries of Tom Carter, who suspected something afoot between his best friend and this privileged girl. Had he been more certain about Karen's intentions toward him, Joe would have been more forthcoming with Tom about the status of the relationship. Of course, he reminded himself often, Karen might very well find the whole idea of a relationship between herself and Joe preposterous. It was possible that he was nothing more than her current, favorite lunching partner.

Despite her keen mind and spirited tongue, Karen suffered from flights of fancy. She thrived on inconsistency, and her appetite was fed by a carefully disguised rebellious streak. For instance, she criticized the notion of stereotypes, yet constantly categorized people under neat labels. She downplayed her popularity, while basking in the glow of the spotlight and keeping attention focused squarely on her shoulders. Her charm was ingratiating, its effect insidious.

Karen was between boyfriends, she often reminded Joe. In the fall, she had dated the quarterback of the football team, dropping him the week before the season ended. She had broken up with her latest boyfriend, the captain of the basketball team, in the middle of the season.

"He was an athlete," she explained to Joe. "Nice looken but all wrapped up in himself. And not exactly a conversationalist, either. I mean grunts and groans have their place in a relationship, but a steady diet of them is deadly dull. Don't you agree?"

"I suppose," Joe grunted.

Karen smiled. "I sound pretentious."

"Yeah," Joe nodded. "You do."

Her eyes narrowed and the smile changed instantly to a cold glare. "I have high standards," she said flatly, rising from the table and collecting her lunch tray. "And no time for those who don't, can't or won't meet my expectations."

For two days, Karen deserted him at lunch, leaving Joe to sneak quick glances her way whenever they were in class or close contact. He thought all was lost until Mrs. Gaskins came to the rescue, elevating him once again with sudden notoriety.

The vehicle was a short story assignment. Joe wrote about two brothers who discovered a secret stairway in their room. The stairway led to an underground world, and the brothers eventually abandoned their old lives for the newfound utopia.

Mrs. Gaskins flattered Joe with praise for the story, spending an entire class period analyzing it. Embarrassed by her enthusiasm, Joe nevertheless paid close attention to the teacher's theories about his intentions and nodded dutiful agreement at every request for verification of her interpretation. In actuality, her theories stunned Joe. But he did not have the heart to tell the woman he had given little thought to the story's deeper meaning, especially when it was much easier to sit back and have his ego stroked with her noble praise and dreamy gazes from Karen.

"You're brilliant, Joe," Karen told him when she returned to their table to share lunch later that day. "You've bedazzled me."

Bedazzled seemed a rather strong reaction to Joe, but he kept this thought to himself, along with many others he might have had. Just like Mrs. Gaskins, Karen maintained a constant chatter about the story, reanalyzing his intentions and spouting off her own endless theories with repeated requests for his confirmation. Joe merely nodded and gazed at length across the table.

"Do you really believe there's a world better than this one—someplace besides Heaven?" Karen asked abruptly.

Completely smitten, Joe barely heard the question, much less paid attention to it. "I do," he sighed before the significance of the admission penetrated his consciousness.

He realized his mistake almost immediately, with alarming concern, especially should word of such blasphemy ever get back to Caroline and Rachel.

"Well, no, Karen," he stammered, regaining equilibrium of his thoughts. "I most definitely believe in Heaven. And Hell, too." He hesitated, then continued in almost dreadful, yet determined, tones. "It's just a story, Karen. I wrote it for fun, and I'd rather not make more of it than it is. It's like trying to make somethen sophisticated out of plain homespun. Can we talk about somethen else?"

A pout crossed her face, and Joe feared he had made a fatal mistake. But abruptly, Karen tossed her hair and flashed him a warm smile. "Let's talk," she agreed.

Joe relaxed, then wondered what in the world he would say to her.

———

On the next Monday, Karen brought sensational news to school. She and her younger sister, Nancy, had spent the previous weekend with their grandparents, who lived on a farm in the southeastern corner of the county. At supper Saturday night, Nancy told her family of seeing a big cat pacing near the edge of the woods.

"Nancy said it looked like a female lion," Karen explained in English class. "We ignored her. Everyone figured she had seen a big bobcat. It's not unusual to see them around the farm."

A piercing scream in the middle of the night and the discovery of a cow's mutilated carcass the next morning convinced Karen and her grandparents that Nancy had seen a big cat, indeed. "It was the worst kind of scream you could imagine," Karen recalled. "My papa says it sounded like a panther, but we don't know for sure."

She shuddered, dramatically and sincerely. "Whatever it was, that poor cow was torn to pieces. I hope she died quickly."

At lunch, Joe pestered Karen for more details until she finally took her lead from her own nettling about his short story and pleaded for a new subject. Joe complied with her request, but his thoughts rarely strayed from the cat. He discussed the situation thoroughly with Tom on the bus ride to New River from Cookville, and they swapped tales of panthers prowling their community in days of yore.

In his excitement to share the story with the family, Joe covered the distance between the mercantile, where the high school bus deposited him, and home at a faster pace than usual. He barged into the kitchen telling the story, and Caroline and Rachel were beset instantly with worry. Joe left them to it, racing from the house to relay the news to his father and grandfather.

Matt and Sam were in the pecan orchard behind the syrup house and smokehouse, changing a worn tire on the tractor.

"Guess what!" Joe said eagerly as he emerged from the shelter attached to the smokehouse side of the dual-purpose outbuilding.

Sam eyed the boy closely, while Matt gave his son a sidelong glance from the hydraulic jack. "I don't know," Sam chuckled, "but you look like you're gonna burst wide open if we don't figure it out soon. Go ahead; spit it out and save us all the trouble of guessen."

"A girl in my class, Karen Baxter, says a panther killed a cow on her grandfather's farm Saturday night," Joe revealed as he approached the men.

"That so?" Matt said with interest.

"A panther, you say," Sam added with skepticism. "Are they sure? I don't think there are any panthers left in these parts."

Joe quickly relayed the details of the story. "Karen said the cow was ripped to pieces," he concluded. "And they were woke up in the middle of the night by a scream of some kind. Her little sister saw a big cat just before supper. She said it looked like a female lion, but her grandpa figured it was only a bobcat."

"Is that Phil Baxter you're talken about?" Matt asked.

"Yes, sir, I think so," Joe answered. "Karen said her grandpa wasn't certain it was a panther," he continued, to appease Sam. "He claims panthers don't usually kill somethen and leave it out in the open. He says they usually hide whatever they kill."

"Uhm," Sam mused, while Joe went to help his father raise the heavy tire to the rim of the tractor wheel. "That's true."

"You must have water in this," Joe grunted, straining to align the tire with the hub bolts.

"Yeah," Matt affirmed. "Heavy, ain't it?"

"That doesn't sound like a panther at all," Sam said, his contribution to the task at hand forgotten. "The girl must have seen a wildcat. There hasn't been a panther 'round these parts since I was a boy. And even then, it was a rare sight to see."

"You're probably right, Pa," Matt said. "But regardless, don't say anything to your mama or granny, son. They'll get scared and start worryen over nothen."

"Uh-oh," Joe gulped, tossing a rueful grin toward Matt. "Too late. I already told them." He paused, then added cheerfully, "And you're right. They're worryen."

"Way to go, Joe," Matt said dryly, a teasing frown on his face. He shook his head, picked up the tire iron and began tightening the nuts to the hub bolts on the tractor.

"Maybe Grandpa can tell them there aren't any panthers around here," Joe suggested. "At supper tonight. That should ease their minds."

"I'll give it a shot," Sam volunteered, "but I wouldn't count on it helpen much. Those women are natural born worriers and once they get somethen on their mind, it stays there."

––––––––

As soon as Rachel blessed supper that night, Joe repeated his story about the big cat and the mutilated cow, sparing none of the details. Caroline and Rachel renewed their worrying and were soon fretting over whether to allow the children outside by themselves. When the women were worked up sufficiently, Joe asked his grandfather's opinion about the potential danger of the situation.

It was an old tactic used by Joe and Sam when they had something up their sleeves, and the crafty plotting brought a smile to Matt, who himself had been suckered on a few occasions by the innocent scheming of his father and son. He attacked his supper, enjoying his father's tale, confident Sam would ease the women's worries.

"The panther is a mysterious creature," Sam began with an educator's tone. "A cousin of the African cats if I'm not mistaken. Panthers are loners. They go out of their way to avoid people and, in this day and age, it's a rare man who can honestly say he's laid eyes on one."

"Have you ever seen a panther, Grandpa?" Carrie interrupted.

Interruptions came frequently in Sam's stories, and he welcomed them. "Have I ever seen a panther?" he repeated, his lecture scuttled for an adventure. "What do you think?"

"I don't know," Carrie said.

"When I was a little boy like Luke there, plenty of panthers roamed these parts," Sam said. "How do you think I came to wear this eye patch?"

"A panther scratched out your eye?" Bonnie squealed.

"It did, indeed," Sam replied, snapping the black patch over his scarred eye. "I made the mistake of goen hunten by my lonesome in Bear Bay—one of the thickest, wickedest swamps you'll likely find anywhere. You see, children, panthers like swampy places, where it's dark and they can hide in the shadows. They prefer to ambush their prey rather than face it head-on."

"Grandpa?" Luke interrupted doubtfully. "I thought you said a dragon breathed fire on you and burnt out that eye."

"That's the trouble with you, Luke," Sam said haughtily. "You think too much, 'cept when you're in school. Then, you don't do enough of it."

"We believe you, Grandpa," John interjected, affirming shared faith in Sam. "Go ahead. Finish tellen how that panther scratched out your eye."

"Yes, please do," Rachel muttered aside. "I want to hear all about it."

His dignity salvaged by John, Sam ignored the quip from his wife. "Well, now," he continued. "As I said, I was hunten and had sighted a deer, a twelve-pointer as sure as I'm sitten here. Anyway, I was tryen to be real quiet like, so I could get a good shot. I aimed my shotgun and was just about to pull the trigger when all of a sudden, there was the most piercen, the most caterwaulen scream you can imagine." He hesitated, then added bluntly, "Sounded even worse than your grandma when she's all worked up and carryen on because things ain't gone her way."

The children came through with obligatory laughter, which they cut short out of respect for Rachel. "That scream, though," Sam continued. "It scared the daylights out of me. I froze right there in my tracks. And that's where I made my mistake. You see, a panther counts on that terrifyen scream to paralyze its prey. Then it lunges and snaps the neck of the hapless victim. A panther has some of the most powerful jaws in the world. It can kill quick as lightnen."

Sam leaned back in his chair and crossed his arms. "Fortunately, I was quicker than lightnen," he boasted. "I ducked in the nick of time. When that old cat hit me, he just did miss sinken his teeth right into my neck, which he surely would have snapped like a toothpick." His arms uncrossed, and Sam laced his fingers behind his neck. "Unfortunately," he continued, "the bugger swatted me across the face with one of his big paws. Tore my eye right out of the socket. Then the coward ran off into the shadows. I never saw hide or hair of him again."

"Is that true, Grandpa?" Bonnie questioned in a long drawl, her face mingled with excitement and fright.

"It is," Sam declared. "But don't you go fretten about it, darlen. There hasn't been a panther 'round these parts since I was about your size, and that was several years ago. Most panthers in this country live out west. They're called mountain lions. There's probably a few in Florida, too."

"Florida's only about fifty miles from here," Summer said excitedly. "Maybe one of those panthers crossed the state line without realizen it."

Sam bit back a smile. "Not likely," he assured her. "I think they mostly live in south Florida. Besides, we have too many fields and open spaces around here. Panthers prefer dark places, where they can keep to themselves and hide when necessary."

"But, Grandpa," John protested. "We got a swamp right here on the farm. The river's close by, and there's woods every which way you turn. Not to mention Bear Bay, where that old panther got hold of you. A panther could hide almost anywhere he wanted to around here."

"The simple truth is there are few panthers left, here or anywhere else," Sam proclaimed. "But people like to think otherwise because there's somethen wild and mysterious about the panther. I've heard grown men spin tales of panthers screamen in the night and big cats loiteren by streams and creak beds. But all they're doen is tellen tall tales and repeaten legends."

He paused a second, spooning mashed potatoes and gravy onto his plate. "No, sirree," he concluded. "There're no panthers around here. But ...."

The slight hesitation brought absolute stillness and silence to the table, leaving forks and spoons stranded midway between plates and mouths, glasses poised on the edge of lips and knives halted halfway through pieces of meat. "But just in case I'm wrong," Sam continued in dramatically hushed tones, "I'll tell you the one unmistakable way to know when a panther is near."

He pitched his voice lower. "If you're ever in the woods near sunset and leaves rustle like a whisper, then there's probably a panther very close by, with eyes only for you."

The children gave a collective gasp of anxiousness. "What should we do if that happens?" Luke almost whispered.

Sam was enjoying his tale, and his pleasure eased Rachel and Caroline's worries. Noticing the relaxed attitudes of the two women, Matt and Joe exchanged knowing smiles across the table.

"Well, Luke," Sam answered diplomatically after taking time to swallow a bite of his supper. "If it was me, I'd run for safety as fast as my legs would carry me. Panthers are close-up hunters, you see, and they're quick to tire in a chase. If you don't freeze in your tracks when they let go with that scream, then you might just live to see another day."

So ended the tale of the panther.

CHAPTER 4

ON A SATURDAY EVENING near the middle of February, Joe found himself with Lucas Bartholomew in the wooded acreage on the farm's southeast end. They were putting the finishing touches on a new fence, working amid a section of mature hardwoods so thick that only slivers of sunlight filtered through the stands of oak, sassafras, sycamore, poplar and the occasional pine tree. The job had brought them to an outlying corner of the farm, two hundred yards from the house where Lucas lived with Beauty, and an even greater distance from the Baker home. Usually, hogs roamed these woods, but they were penned now on the other side of the road until the new fence was in place.

The fence, which separated the Baker farm from the Berrien estate, had been mended year after year for as long as Joe could remember. It was rusted, broken, falling down in places and—in this winter of 1962, Matt at long last conceded—beyond repair. The task of replacing it fell to Joe and Lucas, and they had worked the better part of two weeks at the job. Joe thought his back would break if he dug one more hole for a fence post.

His aching back contributed to the litany of complaint that Joe was reciting for Lucas as they neared the end of the task. They had worked alongside each other in virtual silence for the better part of the two weeks, except for these moments of idle chatter when their words tended to magnify the humor of the situation. A sense of humor was necessary to spare them from the boredom of the hard work, Joe supposed, but he was disappointed by their inability to talk on a deeper level.

Joe had anticipated the fencing job as an opportunity to get inside the head of Lucas, to gain a better understanding of what made his black friend tick. But regretfully to Joe, they had failed to approach this delicate subject on even a superficial level. They would leave these woods as they had entered them, linked through a bond of friendship and separated by shackles of mutual ignorance.

It occurred to Joe that he might pursue answers to some questions in the remaining hours of the job, but the idea was discarded before the thought ran completely through his head. Instead, he continued his good-natured verbal assault on the great burden placed on him by the demands of the farm. "I've had my driver's license for almost two months now and a lot of good it's done me," he complained. "I haven't had a single date. And here I am again, spenden another Saturday night with you, planten fence posts and stringen wire. I tell you, Lucas, it's more than a body should have to stand."

Lucas laughed at the lamentations. "You sayen that spenden Saturday night out here in the woods with me ain't your idea of a good time," he chaffed. "I'm hurt, Joe-Joe, deeply hurt. I thought we were friends."

"No offense, Lucas," Joe replied dryly. "But frankly, I'd rather be in the woods with Karen Baxter. Be'en a married man and all, you should be able to understand that."

"Oh, I see," Lucas droned with exaggerated sincerity. "Now we cut to the quick of it. You're feelen frisky and ready to sew some wild oats."

Joe scratched his head. "I wouldn't exactly call it frisky," he remarked finally. "But Lord knows I'm ready and willen."

"I bet you are," Lucas said.

A million questions crossed Joe's mind and Lucas might have answered them, but the two companions lapsed once more into silence. Lucas thought about Beauty and the coming night, while Joe resolved, again, to ask Karen for a date the following Friday.

An hour later, with night falling over them, Joe hammered the last staple nail into the corner fence post and checked the wire to make sure it was secure. The line was taut and built stoutly.

Joe glanced up at Lucas. "I think it'll be here a lot longer than you and I," he predicted.

"It's a job well done," Lucas nodded. "Your daddy'll be real pleased. If he wants, we can bring those hogs back over to this side of the road on Monday."

"I think I might actually miss menden this fence from time to time," Joe remarked as he rose from his knees and dusted off his blue jeans. "It's somethen I've come to expect to do, maybe even look forward to."

Lucas shook his head in dismay. "Joe-Joe, only you'd come up with a fool idea like that. Don't fret too much, though. There's plenty more fence 'round this place that's ready to fall down. I'm sure Mr. Matt will let you fix fence till your heart's content."

"True," Joe shrugged philosophically.

"You're a strange one, Joe-Joe," Lucas smiled. "Sometimes I'm not quite sure what to make of you, but you're a good man to have around in a pinch. Now, though, I'm gonna walk this fence one last time to make sure we didn't leave any tools on the ground."

"Okeydokey," Joe grinned. "I'll get our stuff together and meet you back at the house." He pointed to an old twelve-gauge shotgun on the ground near them. "You wanna take that?" he asked.

"Nah, it's too dark," Lucas answered. "I brought it 'cause Beauty wanted me to try and get a squirrel or rabbit. I told her there wouldn't be any runnen this time of year." He rolled his eyes. "You know how womenfolk are."

Joe gave his friend an understanding nod. "Some of it," he volunteered. "But I'd like to know a whole lot more."

"You will," Lucas promised, talking over his shoulder as he started the walk along the fencerow. "But you won't ever know it all. That's what makes it exciten and keeps things cooken."

Joe smiled to himself, his eyes following Lucas' progress along the fencerow, watching him test the sturdiness of their work at regular intervals. Finally, Lucas disappeared in the dark distance, and Joe began gathering their tools and reflecting on the day.

It was an important day, one of those moments in time when there was substantial cause for reflection. While Joe and Lucas had finished their fence, the United States government had released convicted Soviet spy Rudolf Abel in exchange for Francis Gary Powers, the U-2 pilot shot down by the Russians during a reconnaissance mission nearly two years earlier. Joe had followed every twist and turn in the plight of Powers and was heartened by the man's freedom. He wondered, though, how Powers himself felt. Was he focused on his newly gained freedom or on the two years stolen from his life? Was he prepared to savor the days to come or would he dwell on the agonizing slowness of two years in captivity?

Joe himself was an astute time tracker and, depending on your state of mind, two years could seem either like a lifetime or two days.

A year ago, as he recovered from his football injury, the pace of life seemed inordinately slow to Joe. He had become impatient, aggravated, melancholy and moody, a stranger to himself and those around him. Now, the days passed in a blur. Joe was mindful of the swift, sweet passage of time and determined to preserve it with memories that he could savor on a day when he was far away from here and now, empty and longing for a taste of his past. Such a day would come, and Joe would remember affectionately his endearment to a past that had prepared him for the future he wanted so badly.

These days, more than ever, Joe felt comfortable with his burgeoning manhood. And even if the vagaries of life and women remained a mystery to him, his personal antenna was tuned on dreams and goals. He was making plans and sharing his vision with those close to him. College waited in the offing, and nobody expected Joe to lay down roots in Cookville. The plans were fluid, but his commitment was etched in stone.

He inhaled a head-cleansing breath of cold air, picked up the tools, the gun and started toward the house.

A minute or so later, he was compelled to honor nature's call. He emptied his hands, relieved his bladder and had just finished zipping his blue jeans when he sensed a presence.

Dead leaves crackled to his right and Joe froze with dreadful expectation of an eerie shriek to come. Instead, he heard a low guttural groan and saw an amber silhouette. A moment later, the big cat moved directly into his line of vision.

Man and creature glared eyeball to eyeball with stark intensity, separated by nothing more than a few yards and the dangling branches of barren trees. Their eyes flashed confusion and distrust, yet both seemed strangely unperturbed.

It was a desperate bluff on Joe's part. And yet, even in his inner panic, he admired the panther's beauty. The cat's tawny brown coat glimmered in the dying daylight, turning white as eggshells at the breast line of its stomach. Shiny brown eyes glowed in a pear-shaped face, with the white fur on its chin, lips and lower cheeks contrasting sharply with the black sides of its snout.

The panther hissed and stepped toward Joe, who took a deep breath and made up his mind to lunge for the nearby shotgun.

But abruptly, the big cat hesitated, cooed a soft purr and gazed intently into Joe's eyes. The panther took one more step forward, then turned away and slipped into the black shadows of the woods.

His legs buckled and Joe collapsed to his knees, releasing a stale breath of air, reaching for the shotgun. His hands shook violently, the gun jerking back and forth while he sought to calm the shock waves jolting his instincts. A minute passed and then another as he listened for the animal and regained his senses.

He came slowly alert but it was when his hands steadied enough to take careful aim with the shotgun that Joe remembered Lucas was walking the fencerow. And the panther had disappeared in that direction.

Joe was on his feet instantly, ready with the shotgun, stalking quickly, cautiously through the woods.

———

Merrilee Bartholomew was a proud woman who had maintained her dignity until the end of a long struggle with the consumption. Her influence on Lucas had been tremendous.

His mother had been a no-nonsense woman who instilled sound principles and laid a solid foundation for her only child. She had taught Lucas that substance mattered more than style, that honesty and responsibility were virtues, and that independence, above everything else, provided freedom.

Under her firm guidance, Lucas had matured into an unassuming, unpretentious man, who saw the value of dutiful, respectful and polite behavior. What he lacked in daring and intelligence was more than offset by his competency and reliability.

"There's nothen wrong with be'en called dependable," Merrilee had reminded her son repeatedly.

Her conviction had helped Lucas grit his teeth on more than one occasion and look the other way when one would-be master conveyed to another that third-person, bargaining-tone reference: "He's dependable."

Fortunately, Lucas had earned a reputation that afforded him the opportunity to steer his services away from the masters of the world. He treated those fools with courtesy and regard for their position. But nowadays, Lucas worked for men who understood that respect was a two-way street.

Like his mother before him, Lucas suffered no delusions about the place of colored people in a white man's world. His conscience maintained a strict awareness of black and white, the way some men carried pocket combs. But Lucas had no chip on his shoulder. Everyone had his lot in life. The burden was what a body chose to make of it, and Lucas was choosing to make the most of every opportunity.

Lucas considered himself the most capable colored man in Cookville. Others were more successful, but none extracted the amount of marrow from a bone that Lucas did. He could squeeze blood from a turnip, which was what his father had said often of his mother.

Lucas was a junior, and the name was the father's major influence on the son. The elder Lucas had died when his son was fifteen. Lucas remembered him with affection. His father was a happy-go-lucky, harmless man, whose penchant for strong drink sent him to an early grave. At one time, Lucas had resented the man's untimely demise because it denied him an opportunity to finish high school. But his forgiving nature prevented Lucas from holding a grudge, and his preoccupation with the present allowed him to forget missed opportunities.

Merrilee had adored her husband, despite his weaknesses. When he'd stagger home drunk, with half his paycheck spent on beer, booze and gambling, she'd shrug her shoulders and accept the capricious nature of her husband as inevitable.

Few ill words passed between them. Merrilee never criticized her husband, and the senior Lucas always came through with the necessities. When he died, Merrilee, sickly herself for several long years by then, had grieved deeply.

It was not until her final days that Merrilee afforded Lucas the privilege of her insight about his father. And then it was only because she saw one final opportunity to exercise influence and provide guidance for her son.

The memory of that day never strayed far from Lucas, and it was clearly on his mind as he trod along the fencerow in the gathering darkness.

The consumption, chief among many ailments, had withered Merrilee to a shell of her former self. She looked more dead than alive, shriveled and shrunken like a carcass hung out to dry. It seemed as if the decay had set in before the body was completely dead, and the buzzards were circling.

In those final weeks, Lucas had stayed with his mother day and night, keeping her parched lips moist, offering soup and playing nursemaid to her every need. Despite all its repulsive moments, her process of dying had seemed the most natural thing in the world to Lucas.

When nothing else about his mother seemed real any longer, her voice remained the one consonant of her faculties, smooth, silky and possessed with wisdom of the ages.

"Lucas, Lucas," she called, awaking from a sound sleep. "We need to talk."

"Yes, Mama. I'm right here," Lucas informed her, leaning forward in his chair beside her deathbed.

"There's somethen you need to know," she said, pulling onto her side.

"What is it, Mama?"

"It's not the most pleasant thing you'll ever hear me say, but it's probably the most important," the frail woman said. "There are exceptional people in this world, Lucas, and there are lucky people. Your daddy wasn't either one of those things, exceptional or lucky. And neither are you, son."

She searched his face for a reaction, but Lucas remained impassive, having discerned long ago that his mother had only his best interests at heart.

Merrilee Bartholomew smiled at his deferral to her judgment and settled back into a comfortable position on the bed. "Men," she continued. "Most men have the best of intentions, Lucas. But they're gullible and easily led astray by senseless things like drinken and any pretty woman who happens to shake her tail in their direction. Booze and women have been the downfall of many a man I've known in my time. It takes hold when they're young like you, and some of 'em never get over it. Your daddy was one of those who didn't. He'd have been a lost man without me by his side."

Merrilee eased onto her side again to impress her next remarks on Lucas. "Now you're a young man," she said bluntly. "You've got a thirst in your gullet for alcohol and an itch in your pants for women, and you're gonna drink your fill and chase anything that wiggles in a skirt over the next few years.

"But Lucas," she intoned sternly. "Watch out for pretty women. They'll use you, son. They'll dish it up for any man who can give more than what they've got. And to tell you the truth, despite how that tail wiggles and shakes on the outside, it's pretty much the same thing on the inside."

She fell back on the pillow and took a haggard breath. "Now, boy, I want you to have your good times," she continued. "But when you've played around and made a fool of yourself, it'll be time for settlen down. Don't make the mistake of fallen for some fancy pants, Lucas, 'cause you're never gonna have what it takes to satisfy them kind, and you'll make yourself miserable tryen.

"When you get ready to settle down, find yourself a woman who's a churchgoer and doesn't care much about getten herself a husband. A man needs a companion, boy. Someone who'll stand beside him and take care of him come hell or high water and not pass judgment while she does it. You find somebody hungry for a either a good man or no man at all, and you'll make your own luck in this world, Lucas. You fall hard for some Miss Fancy Pants, you'll spend the rest of your life wishen you'd've listened to your dyen mama."

Merrilee sat up in bed, her face full of fire and determination. "Do you understand what I'm sayen, boy?"

"Yes, ma'am."

"Will you grant your mama's dyen wish?"

"Yes, ma'am."

She glared hard and long at Lucas, memorizing this moment, impressing him with her concern, then slowly nodded her head and reached across the bed to pat his hand. "You know, Lucas," she whispered. "I believe you will."

A week later, Merrilee died quietly with Lucas at her side. His last words to her had been uttered with quiet conviction. "I promise, Mama."

Lucas was reflecting on his mother's wisdom and the promise he had made when a scream shattered the night.

———

It was a shriek, deadly shrill and bloodcurdling. Joe felt it in his veins.

The panther's scream froze him in midstride, about thirty-five yards behind Lucas. From this vantage point, Joe saw with his own eyes the incarnation of scared stiff.

Lucas froze in his tracks, paralyzed with incomprehension, stiff-necked from premonition. On his back flank was the panther, heavily muscled, slunk low to the ground and crouched for attack.

Time played out in fractions of seconds, and Joe began running forward at the same moment the big cat lunged toward Lucas.

The panther slammed into the right side of Lucas, its powerful jaws clamping down into the top of his shoulder. The force of impact was crushing, ripping an agonized scream from Lucas as man and beast crashed to the ground in a twisted, hissing heap.

Lucas landed on his back, with the big cat on top of him, its teeth tearing deeper into his shoulder. He round-housed his free arm to swat the panther in the head. Growling, the cat reared back, slapping Lucas with his paws and raking razor-sharp claws across the man's neck. Lucas landed a forearm against the panther's jaw, warding off another strike at his neck, and wedged booted feet beneath the cat's belly as the animal snapped again at his mangled shoulder. Calling on every reserve of strength, Lucas kicked hard, flinging the panther away while struggling to gain a favorable fighting position.

Momentarily surprised by his human opponent's powerful thrust, the supple cat retreated an inch, crouched and loosed another rattling growl, low-pitched this time but equally menacing.

Joe was stopped, with the gun aimed dead center before the panther sprang its attack. The shot exploded in the darkness, finding its mark in the middle of the cat's leap. Crimson spurted midway up the animal's white breast, and the panther collapsed on top of Lucas.

For a moment, the silence was deafening. Joe was frozen, with the gun still aimed, waiting to see if the danger was gone. Almost immediately, he was aware of the quiet moans of his friend. Dropping the gun, he rushed to Lucas.

"I can't breathe," Lucas gasped. "Get if off me, Joe-Joe."

Wordlessly, Joe responded. The panther was heavy, but the weight no match for Joe's adrenaline. In seconds, he dragged the dead cat away and was on his knees examining Lucas' wounds.

Blood poured from the mangled shoulder, but Joe saw no danger signs of spurting vessels among the mess of exposed muscle and raw meat. The crimson seeped at a slower pace from Lucas' neck, but the rapid loss of blood worried Joe, as did the pallor of his face and the glassy look in his eyes.

"You're gonna be okay, Lucas," Joe said firmly. "Just keep your mind on me. If you're hurten, forget it and concentrate on what I do and what I say."

Lucas lay trembling. "Easy for you to say," he mumbled, allowing his eyes to close.

"Don't do that!" Joe ordered, slapping Lucas on the cheek.

Lucas blinked and stared at Joe.

"I'm not dyen, Joe-Joe," he said. "I promise. So, I'd appreciate it if you didn't hit me in the face."

Joe examined him again, closely from head to toe. "You sure you're not dyen?"

"I'm sure."

"Well, you don't look so good," Joe remarked with dry excitement. "There's blood everywhere."

Lucas closed his eyes again and rested his head against the carpet of dead leaves. Joe stripped off his own red flannel shirt and undershirt, using the white cotton garment as a tourniquet to bandage the hurt shoulder. Lucas lay still, his breathing shallow, groaning softly as Joe tended to his wounds.

"We have to get you to a doctor," Joe said when the bandage was secured. "The house is not far from here. Can you walk?"

Lucas opened his eyes. "I think so. If you'll help me get to my feet."

"We'll take it slow and easy," Joe replied, pushing Lucas to a sitting position.

Lucas draped his good arm around Joe's neck for support, and they struggled to their feet, then rested for a moment.

"Let's go," Lucas said at last.

It was a long walk home as they stumbled through the dark woods. Conversation was rare, except for the occasional groan from Lucas and encouraging words from Joe. At last, they came to the edge of the field and the lights of the house beckoned across the way. Joe stopped their progress and lowered Lucas to the ground.

"Stay here," he ordered. "We'll bring the truck across for you."

Lucas nodded weary agreement.

"I'll be right back," Joe promised. "We'll have you to the hospital in no time."

"Send somebody after Beauty," Lucas said softly. "I want her with me."

Joe nodded and sprinted across the field toward home.

———

It was an unhurried night in the Baker house. Rachel and Caroline were finishing the supper dishes, with a plate warming in the oven for Joe. The television hummed in the living room, and the few not watching it were preoccupied with quiet pursuits. This relaxed atmosphere came to an abrupt halt the moment Joe tore open the screen door, bursting into the living room with fresh blood caked on his bare chest and matted on his face and in his hair.

Carrie screamed loudest at his sudden appearance and the room turned topsy-turvy before Joe calmed the commotion with a finger pressed to his lips. "Daddy, you've got to come quick with the truck," he said. "Lucas is hurt real bad."

"Oh, dear Lord!" Caroline cried as she stepped through the French doors into the living room. "I heard the gun go off. Is he shot?"

"No, ma'am," Joe said. "I shot a panther! It jumped Lucas. He's bleeden everywhere. We've got to get him to the hospital."

Joe pointed across the road. "He's at the edge of the woods over yonder. I told him we'd bring the truck for him."

Matt took control of the situation with quiet authority, issuing orders and directions in seconds flat. Almost instantly, he, Sam and Joe were in the truck, while Caroline gathered bandages and John raced down the road to tell Beauty what had happened.

———

Lucas was unconscious when they reached him and, for an awful moment, Matt, Sam and Joe feared he was dead. But Lucas came to when Matt pressed a finger on his throat, checking for his pulse.

"I'm okay, Matt," he said softly.

"We brought the truck," Matt informed the injured man. "We're gonna put you in the back, Lucas, and get you to the hospital."

Lucas shook his head. "I think I got some broke ribs," he said groggily. "That cat was a heavy sonofagun, and it landed hard on my chest. It hurts to breathe." He closed his eyes, then asked, "Joe, did you get word to Beauty?"

"John went to tell her," Joe answered. "She'll be waiten for us."

"Good," Lucas sighed.

They loaded Lucas gently into the bed of the pickup, with Joe using his lap as a pillow for the injured man's head. It was a bumpy ride across the field, which Lucas tolerated with clinched teeth and closed eyes. Caroline was waiting with clean rags and blankets when they arrived at the house, along with a shaking Beauty Bartholomew, who took her rightful place beside her husband. Taking the rags from Caroline, Beauty quickly dabbed at the bloodiest parts of her husband's injuries, while Caroline and Matt covered him with blankets.

Ten minutes later, the pickup arrived at the Cookville hospital.

Caroline rushed into the emergency room to seek help, and two nurses dressed in starchy white uniforms sprang into action. One called for a doctor, while the other grabbed a wheelchair and raced outside to the truck where she helped Matt and Joe seat the sluggish Lucas.

"What in the world happened?" the nurse asked as she examined the mauled arm.

"A panther got hold of him," Matt informed her. "He's lucky to be alive."

The nurse was a stout woman, whom Joe recognized but could not put a name with the face. She was blunt-spoken.

"We've gotta do somethen about all this bleeden, or his luck is fixen to run out," she said. "Follow me," she ordered Matt, who pushed the wheelchair up a concrete ramp through a swinging door with Beauty and Joe in tow.

The antiseptic odor of the hospital reassured Joe, who had grown wary of all the blood gushing from Lucas. Anything that smelled this clean had to have healing powers, he reasoned.

"You two help him up on this gurney," the nurse barked to Matt and Joe, while pulling a curtain around them to create an island of privacy in the spacious emergency room. She looked at Lucas. "I'll be back in a second," she told him. "I'm goen to get some scissors so we can cut off what's left of that shirt."

Lucas acknowledged her with a nod. "Can my wife come in here with me?" he asked.

The nurse nodded curtly. "Yes, she can," she replied, pointing a short, stubby finger at Matt and Joe. "But I want you two out of here as soon as you get him settled on that gurney," she added sternly. "Y'all can wait with your wife, Mr. Baker."

"By the way," she hesitated. "What's the patient's name?"

"Lucas Bartholomew," Matt told her.

When the nurse had gone, Matt and Joe settled Lucas on the gurney, then turned him over to the care of his nervous wife and followed their orders to wait outside with Caroline. Almost half an hour later, Dr. Ned Turner ambled through the emergency room door.

A portly man, Ned Turner was shiny bald with a droopy blond mustache and a tightly drawn round face. He wore the thick brown glasses of a scholar and carried himself with the grace and manners of an aristocrat. His regal posture, however, failed to hide the heavy paunch hanging over his dark slacks.

The doctor lived in a gabled and turreted brownstone mansion right off the square in Cookville. The house was beautiful, but Ned had a well-deserved reputation as overbearing and arrogant. He considered himself one of the privileged few and held in contempt the majority of those less fortunate.

"Good evenen, Matt," the doctor said, strolling across the polished tile floor. "Is some of your family hurt?"

"A friend of the family, doc," Matt replied, gesturing behind the curtains. "He helps me on the farm. Believe it or not, a panther got hold of him tonight." He nodded to Joe. "My boy shot it, but the cat tore up Lucas pretty bad, especially his arm and shoulder. He's bleeden a lot."

"A panther!" the doctor exclaimed. "Well I'll be damned. I'd heard they'd spotted one around here, but I figured people were just see'en ghosts." He slapped his thigh. "This I got to see," he continued, walking toward the curtain.

Dr. Turner peeled back the plastic shield, peeked inside and pulled back immediately. He dropped the curtain and glared from Matt to the young nurse who had called him to the hospital. "Matt, you should know I don't treat colored people," he bristled before venting his anger in a stream of cursing and berating aimed at the young nurse, whose name was Linda.

"I didn't know it was a Negro," Linda almost whispered. She was on her heels. "I called you back as soon as I found out, but nobody answered."

"I don't want excuses, Linda," Dr. Turner raged. "Just show some competency next time. Go call Maddox or someone else to come. I'm goen back home. And I would prefer not to be disturbed again."

The young nurse took one step backward and was on the verge of fleeing the room when Joe bounded from his chair, advancing on the doctor. "Good god!" he roared incredulously. "Are you an idiot? There's a man over there bleeden to death and you're worried about the color of his skin. Well, I got news for you, doc. That's red blood comen from his veins; it's the only color you need to concern yourself with. How 'bout getten your fat ass in there and doen what you're supposed to instead of bellyachen?"

Ned Turner scowled at Joe, turning beet red.

"Pipe down, son!" Matt ordered, stepping between Joe and the doctor.

"But Daddy!" Joe persisted before Matt eyeballed him into submission.

Dr. Turner took a single step toward Joe, then stopped and shook a pointed finger at him. "Now see here, hotshot," he lectured. "I don't have to answer to you. I have a right to treat whomever I want, and I choose not to treat coloreds. Are we clear on that?"

"No, Ned, we're not clear on it," Matt remarked abruptly, the hard edge evident in his words, despite the even tone of his voice. "We're not clear at all, but let me set you straight. My friend over there is hurt, and he needs a doctor. You're the only doctor here, and it's your responsibility to treat him. If you're offended by the color of his skin, that's tough luck. I suggest you get your ass over there and take care of the man. Or you'll have me to answer to."

Matt looked the doctor straight in the eyes. "Are we clear on that?"

Ned glared at Matt, but it was a face-saving gesture while he studied his options. There were not many in the angry face of Matt Baker. Or in the fiery eyes of his son, who stood behind Matt like a raging bull, pawing at the ground for his long-awaited chance at the matador. Even Caroline, whom the doctor looked to for sympathy, regarded him with a determined expression. But it was the stout nurse—her name, Joe now recalled, was Bobbi Jean Tucker—who pulled the final straw for the doctor.

"Dr. Turner," she called loudly, poking her head through the curtain. "I know you have principles, but you're gonna have to bend them tonight. This man is cut up bad, and he's lost a lot of blood. He needs a doctor. Now!"

Ned raised his chin and flared his nostrils. "Oh, all right," he relented. "I'll make an exception since I'm already here. But this is the first and only time. I expect everybody to understand that."

Matt visibly relaxed his jaw. "Understood," he replied, stepping aside to allow the doctor passage across the room to where Lucas and Beauty waited behind the curtain.

The first thing Dr. Turner did was order Beauty from the makeshift room. Thirty minutes later, he emerged from behind the drapes, having cleaned the wounds, stitched the deeper cuts and confirmed that Lucas suffered two cracked ribs.

"Thirty-two stitches," the doctor told them. "Six in his neck, five on his face and the rest in his arm. For his sake, he'd better be right-handed because that left arm suffered some serious damage. It'll take time to heal.

"Those cracked ribs will be sore for a while, too, but, all in all, I'd say he's lucky to have come through with nothen more serious," the doctor concluded. "A few inches deeper and that panther might have ripped open his throat. We could keep him overnight for observation. It costs money to stay in the hospital, though, and I'm not sure it's worth the expense."

"I'll take care of the bill," Matt said clearly.

"Suit yourself," Dr. Turner replied without concern. "I'd still take him home. There's nothen else that can be done for him tonight, although he should see his own doctor in a couple of days or so."

He turned to Beauty, who had followed him out of the makeshift room. "I've ordered three prescriptions," he addressed her specifically. "One is to fight infection. Another is a salve, and the third is for pain. He'll have plenty of that. I'd call Glen Adams over at the pharmacy and ask him to fill it for you tonight.

"Make sure you keep clean bandages on those wounds," he continued, "and wash your hands before applyen the salve. If that shoulder gets infected, there could be serious consequences."

"He'll be okay, though?" Beauty inquired nervously, seeking reassurance.

"Yes," the doctor sighed, glancing impatiently at his watch. "That's what I just finished tellen you."

He turned to Matt. "If it really was a panther, you ought to have it checked for rabies," he suggested. "And proceed accordingly."

"We'll do that," Matt said.

"Then I'll be on my way," Dr. Turner said. "Unless Matt," he added sanctimoniously, "you feel the urge to apologize for yours and your son's rude behavior?"

Matt smiled coldly at the doctor. "My family and I make it a policy not to apologize to pompous asses, doc," he replied without missing a beat. "So if I were you, I'd proceed accordingly."

Caroline moved quickly to her husband's side, cupping his elbow with her palm in a calming gesture. "Let's just pay the bill and leave," she urged.

Matt looked at her and smiled disarmingly. "You have the checkbook," he reminded before turning to the stout nurse. "Thanks for your help, Bobbi Jean. How much do we owe?"

Dr. Turner snorted his indignity, but was roundly ignored by everyone except Joe, who glared momentarily at the doctor, then shook his head in dismay and went to help Lucas to the truck.

No one bothered to notice as the good doctor made his grand exit, stomping from the room.

———

Sometime later that night—when the bill had been paid and Lucas ensconced in bed with instructions for Beauty to call on them if she needed help—the Baker family sat on the front porch, recounting the entire episode. Joe provided all the details about the panther and answered every question directed at him, then sat back hunched against the wall while his parents filled in the story with everything that had happened at the hospital.

"I was right proud of you both," Caroline told her husband and son when the story seemed exhausted. "You stood up for what was right."

"I lost my temper," Matt reminded his wife.

"I felt a bit ruffled myself," Caroline said. "And frankly," she laughed, "we'd still be there if you'd tried to kill the doctor with kindness."

"Some things shouldn't be tolerated," Sam declared.

"No, Pa," Matt agreed. "They shouldn't."

It was a cold night for sitting on the porch, but everyone was huddled beneath blankets and warm in their bedclothes and jackets. The night was quiet, except for the soft squeaks of rocking chairs, the glider and the porch swing.

"Joe," Matt said, "You've been quiet for a while. What's on your mind?"

"I'm a little amazed, I suppose," Joe replied. "That people think the way they do. That people who should know better don't." He rose and crossed his arms against the cold. "It's one thing to be aware of somebody's color. I'm as guilty as the next person of doen that. Even with Lucas, I tend to think of him as a black friend of mine or maybe even as the colored man who helps us on the farm. But to hate someone—or refuse to help someone in need—just because of the color of their skin ... I don't understand that."

"It's a complicated subject, no doubt," Sam remarked.

"But it shouldn't be," Joe maintained.

"No," Matt agreed. "But it is."

Joe walked across the porch to stand on the step wall and gaze into the nighttime sky. "Will things ever change?" he asked.

"Gradually, they will," Caroline answered. "But it will take patience and understanden from everybody."

"Things are bound to change," Sam agreed. "But the Ned Turners of the world will always be around to make you stop and think about what's wrong with the way things are."

"You know," Joe remarked, turning to face his family. "I've read about sit-in demonstrations, freedom marches, the Montgomery bus boycott, and I've thought all along stuff like that was the wrong way to go. Now, though, I'm beginnen to wonder if maybe those people have the right idea after all." He looked at Caroline. "Mama, I agree change will come gradually. But how patient and understanden can you expect people to be when things like what happened tonight keep happenen?"

Joe paused more out of courtesy than expectancy of an answer. "Until tonight," he continued, "I didn't really understand prejudice. Now, I have a good idea. And even though tonight had nothen to do with me personally, I felt like I had been slapped in the face by that doctor." He hesitated again before adding, "Maybe it wasn't my place to shoot off my mouth the way I did. But sometimes you can't look the other way. You can't always turn the other cheek."

He looked squarely at his father. "And to tell you the truth, Daddy, I'm glad you didn't ask me to apologize to that man, because I don't think I could have done that."

"No, son," Matt acknowledged. "I doubt you would have either. And for what it's worth, Joe, I'm glad you couldn't look the other way tonight. It makes me think that maybe you've been raised right."

"Indeed," Sam agreed. "And, Joe, you just may be right about a few other things, too. I've never set much store by all those demonstrations and shenanigans, especially when it seems like nothen more than a bunch of outsiders comen in to stir up trouble. But maybe that's what it takes. People need challenges to prod their conscience and bring out their character."

Joe treasured nights like this when his family gathered on the front porch and idled away an evening with meandering talk. But now he felt the need to bring a little levity to the moment. "Daddy?" he said to Matt. "Do you think we prodded the good doctor's conscience tonight?"

"We jarred it for sure," came the wry reply from Matt.

Laughter stirred a chilly breeze on this still night of another waning winter, and Caroline was mindful of sleepy children all around her. It was well after midnight, hours past their bedtime. She rose from the porch swing, stretched and yawned, a signal for her family to follow suit. No one objected; indeed, they were eager for an excuse to find their beds, crawl under the blankets and close their eyes.

"We'll all sleep well tonight," Rachel said as everyone crowded toward the door.

"I hope so," Caroline agreed. "Tomorrow's a church Sunday, and I'd like to carry this good feelen with us."

The brood trooped into the house until only Caroline and Joe remained. Caroline crossed over to where her son leaned against one of the porch's four brick piers that supported tapered wooden columns. "You've had quite an evenen," she suggested.

Joe shrugged. "It's been eventful. No doubt about that."

Caroline sighed. "Consideren everything that's happened tonight, Joe—and especially how proud of you I am—I hesitate to bring this up," she said softly, taking his hands. "But I'm a mother after all, and I'd be remiss to let it pass without mention."

Joe smiled at his mother, reading her thoughts. "It was the heat of the moment," he explained. "I've got my faults, Mama, but I usually keep a civil tongue about me. And I know it's best to keep the Lord's name out of arguments, unless, of course, they concern Him directly."

Caroline rolled her eyes, put a hand in his hair and embraced her son. "Like I said," she reaffirmed, "I hesitated to bring it up. But ...."

"But you're my mother," Joe interrupted, finishing the sentence for her. "And I'd have been disappointed if you had done anything else."

"You're getten too big for your britches," Caroline muttered, hugging him again, then noticing he had grown as tall as she was. She pulled away from Joe and measured the top of her head against his. "When did this happen?" she asked.

"Gradually," Joe answered. "Recently, I think."

Caroline looked him over for another moment, from head to toe and back again to his face. "Yes, I suppose you're right. But it seems sudden to me. Before long, I'll have to look up to see your face?"

Joe smiled shyly. "Probably so."

Caroline kissed him on the cheek and hugged him once more. "Are you comen in?"

"I'll be along soon," he told her. "Goodnight, Mama."

CHAPTER 5

"SO HOW DOES IT feel to be a legend in your own time?"

It was the Monday morning after Joe had shot the panther. Tales of his exploit were rampant. The story had been embellished and exaggerated by everyone but Joe. It was growing taller by the minute, and he felt compelled to lend a little perspective to the situation.

"To tell you the truth, ma'am," he said to Mrs. Gaskins in English class, "mainly, I feel lucky. Lucky that Lucas brought his gun along; lucky even that his wife wanted rabbit for supper. Otherwise, Lucas might have been supper for that panther."

"Were you scared?" the teacher asked.

"A couple of times," Joe nodded. "The first time I saw the panther, it seemed like he was comen right at me. And then, he turned and walked off into the woods. My legs turned to jelly. The second time was after I shot the cat and pulled it off Lucas. There was blood everywhere. He was hurt real bad, and I thought he might die. That scared the daylights out of me, but I tried not to let on to Lucas. I figured he had enough on his mind without known I was worried he was gonna bleed to death right out there in the woods."

"What will you remember most about all this, Joe?" Mrs. Gaskins persisted. "And did you learn anything about yourself from it?"

Joe gave her a long look. "I'm not sure I should answer that, Mrs. Gaskins," he said at last. "The answer probably would surprise you, and it might offend some people."

The teacher cast her infamous glare around the class, daring anyone to raise an objection. "Class," she challenged. "Does anyone mind be'en offended by one of their own?"

A quick glance around the room indicated no one minded. Indeed, his classmates were curious and encouraged Joe to provide them his uncensored version of the story.

"Go ahead, Joe," Mrs. Gaskins urged. "You have the floor."

He gave them a searing account of how events had transpired at the hospital. When he was finished, none of his classmates had any mistaken impressions about his opinion of Dr. Ned Turner. And, Joe had stepped across the safety line of invisibility. He had reached the perilous point of definition from which he would be judged forevermore. His passion impressed a few of his classmates, amazed others, embarrassed some and annoyed several.

"I don't see what all the fuss is about," remarked Richard Golden, who was one of those annoyed by Joe's frank indictment of the doctor. "I know Dr. Turner very well, and I don't think you're be'en fair to him with all these malicious accusations. He's a doctor, a pillar of our community. It's his prerogative to choose whether or not he wants to treat Negroes."

Joe stared coldly at the red-haired, freckle-faced boy. "Somehow, Richard, it doesn't surprise me you're the first one to defend Ned Turner. It's exactly what I'd expect from someone who makes a point week after week to remind everyone that his newspaper column is for white schools only."

"Nobody cares what's goen on in the colored schools," Richard said.

"You're wrong," Joe countered smoothly. "You may not care, Richard. For that matter, I may not care. But somebody does, and one day their caren may make a difference in the way things are."

"You sound like a nigger lover, Joe Baker," Richard accused.

"There are worse things," Joe replied calmly. "I could be like your friend, the good doctor, who doesn't have a heart. But I'm who I am, and I don't care to see one man do another man wrong. Ned Turner turned up his pompous nose at a man who needed help, simply because that man had colored skin. I can't understand that. In fact, I refuse even to try. There are differences between colored people and white people, I'm sure, but sometimes you have to look beyond the color to do what's right. The good doctor may seem like a pillar of the community to you, Richard, but as far as I'm concerned, he's nothen more than an ass. And if you share his opinions, then so are you."

Sensing trouble at hand, Mrs. Gaskins seized control of the class once more, steering the discussion to a smoother path. But the battle lines were drawn, and Joe's reputation was cast in stone. There were a few snickers heard throughout the day, and once or twice, Joe thought he detected rumblings of retribution. But Richard Golden knew better than to pick a fight he would lose, and his snobbishness had offended almost everyone at some time, so no one was eager to pick up the gauntlet for him. And then, too, people respected Joe. He might have surprised some people who simply took his and everyone else's attitudes for granted, but the majority applauded his bravery and courage, both for the deed he had done and the stand he had taken.

For Joe, the day's most memorable moment came at lunch when Karen Baxter gushed over him. Twice, she reached across the table and strummed her fingers along the length of his arm. It was a hair-raising experience and unsettled Joe until, finally, Karen looked at him, smiled, batted her eyes and announced, "I don't have a date Friday night. I wish I did."

"Would you like to go see a movie?" Joe blurted out.

Karen gave him one of her shy, coquettish smiles, glancing down and picking at the food on her plate, while Joe waited breathlessly for an answer. With his attention fixed squarely on her downturned face, Joe failed to notice Karen slide her hand across the table until it came suddenly to rest on the top of his hand. His eyes dropped to the table, then focused upward again to find Karen regarding him. She tilted her head, tossed her hair and branded Joe with the most sensual of gazes, all while raking the tips of her fingers gently down the top of his hand until they were intertwined with his splayed fingers.

Joe heated up like lightning, and they gazed intently at each other for a long moment. "Yes, Joe," Karen answered finally. "I look forward to it. You and I are goen to enjoy each other's company." She tilted her head once more. "Very much so."

––––––––

Joe reckoned it was one of the finest days life could offer, and he wanted to savor every moment, especially those with Karen. But he was stuck on the back of the school bus later that afternoon, answering one question after another from Tom Carter and the other boys who crowded around their seat.

"He was a beautiful animal, no doubt," Joe told them. "I'm sorry he had to be killed. But it was the panther or Lucas."

"My daddy says that's the one mistake you made, Joe, not letten that panther kill a nigger before you shot it."

The comment came from Wayne Taylor, who looked and sounded like a carbon copy of Bobby. "Daddy wondered if you meant to hit the spook but missed and got the panther instead," he added with a grin.

Had he listened closely, Joe would have realized the hollow tone of those remarks from Wayne. He would have grasped the question originated from the sheer curiosity of a twelve-year-old rather than from spite. But Joe was fed up with the opinions, spoken and unspoken, of those who believed he should have spared the panther and killed the nigger. In the back of his mind, too, he still held a grudge against Wayne for killing Stonewall Jackson several summers ago. Perhaps he had ill feelings for the entire Taylor clan and their gospel of hate.

These thoughts passed through his mind, and none put Joe in a forgiving mood. He planted a cruel gaze on the Taylor boy. "You tell your daddy that I hit what I aimed for," he said with contempt. "And you tell him, too, that the likes of Bobby Taylor better hope I never have to make a life-saven choice between him and anybody else. Because he'd come out the loser every time, Wayne. And so would you."

Wayne went pale.

"Can you remember to tell him that, Wayne?" Joe asked. "Every bit of it?"

The boy gulped, impaled by the ridicule, and turned away from Joe.

As for the other boys on the back of the bus, they were stunned, too. They had known Joe for most of their lives, considering him someone willing to go that extra mile to be friendly and diplomatic in unpleasant situations. Now they backed off, lapsing into such silence that everyone in the front of the bus turned around to see what had gone wrong.

Joe felt like a bully. He was on the verge of offering Wayne an apology when Tom jolted him back to reality.

"It needed to be said, Joe," his friend remarked quietly as the hum of conversation rose around them once more. "Wayne's poison, and everybody knows it."

"Maybe," Joe hesitated, staring straight ahead. "But he's just a kid. A dumb kid who's only repeaten the filth he heard his daddy say."

"Yeah, but you still did the right thing," Tom tried again to reassure him.

But Joe was not at all sure about that.

———

For a moment, Wayne thought he would cry. But he pinched the inside of his arm and turned embarrassment into anger. He had taken worse crap from his own daddy and walked away without tears. He'd be damned before he let the sorry likes of Joe Baker get the best of him.

His pride intact, Wayne raised his chin in defiance and turned his thoughts to revenge. He was uncertain how to go about it, but one day Wayne would make Joe pay for talking down to him.

"One day," he whispered to himself. "One day, you'll get yours, Joe."

———

The car windows were steamed, and Joe and Karen were wrapped around each other on the backseat. A full moon shown down on the car, casting the young lovers in a pale glow.

Karen was a vision of milky white, intertwined like lace with the swarthiness of Joe. They seemed more disheveled than undressed. Karen had discarded her blouse and bra. Her panties lay in the floorboard, and her skirt was pushed up around her waist. Joe's shirt was torn open, and he had managed to get one leg out of his pants. The other pants leg was caught on his foot but out of the way nonetheless.

Joe had wondered for years about this moment. He was too impatient to savor it. Karen was impatient, too. This was her third date with Joe and she was ready to have him. She broke a heated kiss, running her tongue down his chin and neck, pushed back his shirt and seared the top of his chest with a passion mark. It was her calling card and when she had left it, Karen lifted her eyes to Joe and demanded softly, "Now."

Breathing heavily, fumbling for a tighter embrace, they fell against the back seat.

———

On their first date, Joe had taken Karen to a movie at the Majestic Theater. It was an old Burt Lancaster flick on its first run in Cookville, but Joe barely noticed. He was too busy cuddling with Karen. After the movie, he treated her to a hamburger and a milkshake at the Dairy Queen. They ate in the car, talking like old friends. It was Karen who brought up the idea of parking when they had finished their food.

"Why don't we go somewhere quiet and talk for a while?" she suggested.

"Any place in particular?" Joe asked.

"That's your department," Karen said boldly, sliding across the car seat next to him.

Joe knew the perfect spot. It was a deserted road off the main highway between Cookville and Tifton. The road cut through the Berrien estate before coming to a dead end at an old block house that was presently unoccupied. Joe figured it was one of the most private, secluded places in the county.

Karen snuggled closer as he drove carefully along the sandy lane, which was covered by a canopy of trees. "It's dark back here," she said. "Are you gonna try to scare me with stories about men with hook arms."

Joe laughed dryly. "Hardly. I doubt even a maniac could find this place."

As they rounded a sharp curve, Joe slowed the car and turned onto a secluded field road hidden from view by a wild growth of vines, weeds and trees. He maneuvered the car a short distance down the lane, then cut the lights and switched off the engine.

"This is nice," Karen purred in the darkness, and Joe knew she was looking at his face, expecting him to make the next move. He slipped his arm around her shoulders, kissing her lightly on the lips with wonderment. But even his wildest imagination left Joe unprepared for what happened next.

Karen placed her hands on his face, drew Joe toward her and kissed him hard. The passionate assault sent shock waves through him. Her tongue pried his lips apart, wrapping around him and exploring every inch of his mouth. Joe was at first amazed, then aghast as he realized his own tongue lay dead in her mouth. He quit thinking then and kissed her back with equal fervor.

He touched her breast by accident the first time. But Karen moaned in response, pressing tighter against his hand, so Joe kept right on touching, cupping her through the clothes, then slipping his hand under her blouse and bra.

A short time later, Karen placed her delicate hand high on the inside of his thigh and Joe hardened like a rock. Karen purred in admiration, stroking lightly across his blue jeans until Joe moaned with unfulfilled pleasure. In a while, Karen broke their kiss and pulled Joe to her breast, willing him to lift her blouse and bra. He stared hungrily at her for a moment, then lowered his head and filled himself with her.

Karen groaned, opening her legs and grinding against Joe. He was ready to explode inside his jeans when Karen gasped, relaxed and fell away from him.

Joe was panting, with a hard ache in his groin, as Karen smiled lazily at him.

"I didn't expect that to happen," she murmured, lowering her eyes. "I hope you don't think I'm a bad girl," she worried. "I'm not." She paused, then leveled Joe with a pouting smile. "It's just that you make me dizzy, Joe. And you do terrible things to my self-control."

Joe figured he would have robbed a bank for her at that moment. He reached across the seat, pulled her against him and kissed her deeply. She broke away quickly, dropping her head so that his face was filled with the intoxicating scent of her hair.

"It's late, Joe, and I have to be home by eleven," Karen whispered against his throat.

"Yeah," Joe agreed reluctantly. "Do you have any plans for next Friday?"

"No," she nodded against his neck. "And none on Saturday, either."

"Is seven o'clock okay for both nights?"

Karen nodded again. "And, Joe?"

"Yeah?"

"Movies take an awful long time to see," Karen said. "We could skip it if you wanted to."

———

On their second date, they paused long enough to buy a milkshake at the Dairy Queen, then headed to the privacy of the woods. This time, they were more daring, discarding clothes and making new discoveries with their hands and mouths, but the result was the same. The night ended with Karen exhausted and fulfilled and Joe stranded just short of the brink.

Joe sat back against the front seat, taking deep breaths to calm his hormones. He glanced over at Karen and found her smiling sympathetically. "Eleven o'clock is the only thing my parents are really strict about, Joe," she apologized.

He smiled back at her. "Does this mean we're in love?"

Karen raised her eyes, almost frowning. "Not hardly," she laughed shortly. "But it's a good way to pass the time, isn't it?"

Her answer settled like lead in the pit of his stomach. Joe forced himself to look straight ahead out the front windshield and swallowed the lump in his throat.

Karen handed him his shirt, hooking her bra while Joe slipped on the pullover. "Well, isn't it?" she repeated.

"Sure," Joe answered, zipping his pants.

Karen smiled, adjusted her skirt and slipped into a silk blouse. "Besides, Joe," she said. "We've got our sights set on bigger things and better times than these. Love is the last thing we need."

Joe started to protest, but she cut him off.

"Face it, Joe," Karen argued. "You're like me. Ambition is the love of your life. You and I are destined to spend our lives cutten ties. We'd be lousy at love even if we wanted it. And I don't think either one of us could stand the thought of be'en lousy at anything. Do you?"

Joe kept his thoughts to himself for two reasons. First, he wasn't sure what to say. And furthermore, he feared Karen might have struck too close to the truth.

———

On their third date, they headed straight for the woods and, at her suggestion, moved their lovemaking to the backseat. In the darkness, Karen reminded Joe of a sheet of pure white chocolate, and he was ready to devour her when she whispered the word.

"Now."

It was a frantic coupling, fueled by groans and moans as their bodies meshed. And it finished quickly, as Joe blew like a high-pressured rocket.

Karen screamed a moment later, an anguished cry of outrage. "Damn it, Joe!" she scolded, pushing up against his chest, forcing him to withdraw long before he was ready. "It's not a race." She clinched her fist and struck him in the chest. "And you didn't use anything."

Joe sat back against the door, gaping in disbelief as hopes for a repeat performance were dashed. "What?" he asked, dismayed.

Karen punched him again, harder. "A rubber! You dumb-ass!" she yelled. "That's why I waited until tonight. So you would come prepared."

"I'm sorry," Joe mumbled.

"You will be if I wind up pregnant with your baby, hotshot," she hissed.

Joe choked visibly. "That won't happen," he suggested naively.

Karen scowled. "You'd just better hope it doesn't, big boy," she said sharply. "Because there'll be hell to pay and there's no way I'm haven a baby."

———

Karen was home well before her curfew that night. Joe made it home shortly after eleven, letting himself in through the back porch in hopes of not disturbing the family. He eased open the door, stepped into the kitchen and found the embers of a dying fire waiting for him.

Feeling chilled, he lit a cigarette and stood there smoking it, contemplating the night. Despite everything, the wrath of Karen, the fear of an unintended pregnancy, he smiled. He wasn't a cherry anymore. Few things compared, and Joe considered the possibility that perhaps Karen was right after all. Love complicated matters and the feelings that came with it obviously were not necessary for making love. It was a hollow thought, but believable.

He was lighting his second cigarette when the dining room door opened and his daddy entered the kitchen.

Matt regarded his son with a bemused expression. The match was burning down quickly, and Joe looked like a deer caught in the headlights of a car.

"You best light up, son, or you're gonna get burned," he suggested, crossing the floor to the kitchen light and flipping the switch. "The fact that you smoke is not exactly a secret, Joe, but this is the first time I've flat out caught you. I probably should give you a lecture, but experience tells me I'd be wasten my breath. So instead, I'll bum a smoke off you and we'll keep this our secret. Fair enough?"

Joe smiled stiffly as Matt came toward him.

"I was almost asleep," Matt informed him, "and remembered the fire. I thought I'd better check it."

Matt accepted the cigarette and was about to ask for a light when he noticed Joe's rumpled clothing, along with the boy's meshed hair and skittish behavior. He stepped back, making a hasty appraisal of the situation but keeping any conclusions to himself. He picked up a box of matches from the mantle and lit the cigarette.

"You're looken kind of rough, son," he remarked.

"It was a long night," Joe shrugged, easing away from the fire.

Matt took a long drag on the cigarette, allowing Joe to reach safety before looking again at the boy. "I have a feelen you and I should have a heart-to-heart talk, Joe," he said a moment later. "Man to man." He saw Joe swallow, then added quickly, "But everyone deserves privacy, and there are some things a man has to find out for himself."

He paused long enough to inhale on the cigarette once more, then tossed the unfinished portion into the embers. "I guess I'm luckier than most men, Joe," he continued at length. "I discovered what I was looken for when I was not much older than you are now, and it's made all the difference in the world to me. You think about that, son, from time to time. Will you?"

"Yes, sir," Joe promised with a cracked voice.

Matt nodded and walked past him, out of the kitchen to the room he shared with his wife.

HIS LEGENDARY STATUS FADED quickly enough. Karen sat at a different table in the high school cafeteria and ignored Joe, except to hand him a brief note in their homeroom class one morning. "You were lucky, hot shot," was all it said.

Joe read it once, crumpled the paper and dropped it in the trashcan on his way to first period.

He might have dwelled on these happenings, but work kept him too busy.

Spring rains replaced the winter cold and preparing the fields for planting took top priority. Joe woke early every day, helped with chores and went to school. In the afternoon, he returned home, ate a snack and then spent long hours on the tractor, guiding harrows, plows and planters through the fields. The hard work wore him out. He rested easy at night.

The tobacco was set and they were halfway through planting the corn when three days of heavy rain bogged the fields and halted the spring work.

Joe was grateful for the respite and made time for a late-night walk to the railroad tracks. These midnight sojourns had dwindled considerably over the past year, but the train remained a treasured symbol. In the middle of the day, when he was doubled over in some distant field with the sun beating down on his back, Joe would hear the train whistle and the work would become lighter. At night, he would wake abruptly, realizing the train had just passed, and he would take comfort knowing the wheels of his own life were turning with the same regularity, carrying him closer to his destination.

A late evening shower had brought warmth to this cool, damp spring day, shrouding the land with thick fog and hiding the heavens. As usual, upon reaching the railroad tracks, Joe searched for signs of the oncoming train, peering through the pea soup for the headlamp and straining to hear the first faint rumblings. It was a brief search, his typical exercise in futility but a harmless habit all the same on nights when Joe arrived early at the tracks.

His gaze swept down the far edge of the tracks and was coming back up the other side when a shadow snagged his eyes. His heartbeat accelerated and Joe stood still in the darkness. He looked again, his senses alert, and made out the form of a man standing thirty yards down the track.

Joe was intrigued more than unnerved by this stranger trespassing on the Baker place. He figured the fellow was an acquaintance of the family. Strangers rarely made it to Cookville without attracting attention and even less so in the New River community. Something in him wanted to leave the man to his privacy, but curiosity got the best of Joe. What kind of desperate soul would venture out on a night like this?

Picking his way along the tracks, Joe halved the distance between himself and the stranger before pausing to get his bearings and take a second look at the shadow. The dense fog continued to work against him, so he crept closer, straining his eyes in the darkness when the stranger lit a match. Blue light sprang to life, turned brownish yellow and flickered to its death, leaving behind the red glow of a cigarette tip and revealing the man's identity.

Lucas Bartholomew was no stranger. But he was a mystery to Joe.

A few centuries ago, Joe thought, Lucas might have been a loyal African tribesman, distinguished by his courage on the battlefield and quiet determination off it. Although not necessarily the first one called, he would have been a member of every great hunting expedition, leading by example and fading into the background as others stepped into to claim the glory of the kill.

It was easy to imagine, too, that slave traders would have desired his stock, while American buyers would have fought over him on the auction block. Lucas was tall and rangy, muscled and armed with the stamina for day after day of backbreaking work. His skin was smooth and colored like a milk chocolate candy bar. He wore a serious expression for almost every occasion, the wide flat features of his face seemingly cast in granite, varying only by a few degrees when he smiled or frowned. His cheekbones were prominent, and his dark brown eyes clear and alert.

As far back as Joe could remember, Lucas had been clean-shaven with a close-cropped head of hair. As of late, however, he grew a mustache from time to time and wore his hair longer and fuller, though still cropped neatly above the ears.

The change in Lucas' appearance bothered people. Amelia Carter, for one, had mentioned his longer hair to Caroline recently, and his mother had shrugged off the remark, saying people needed to change things about themselves from time to time. Joe had remained mum on the matter, concluding it best not to point out that Amelia changed the color of her hair, to some extent, nearly every other time she visited the beauty parlor.

As far as Joe was concerned, Lucas had earned the right to be taken at face value, and these veiled suspicions other people had about him were wrong. More troubling to Joe, however—though he hated to admit it—was his own curiosity about this sudden change in Lucas.

Joe regarded Lucas with great affection. Lucas had been a regular fixture around the Baker household for most of Joe's life. Some of his fondest memories were of hunting expeditions with Matt, Sam, Lucas and Paul Berrien.

Hunting relaxed Lucas, loosened his tongue and revealed a different side of him. He showed off a dry sense of humor, amusing his white companions with clever stories about the town's colored people. The stories were full of insight, regardless of whether he poked fun at someone's shenanigans or portrayed the inner strength of another's simplicity.

While Lucas was closemouthed about his personal life, his actions revealed a man who sought a fair shake in life and nothing more. He had little time or regard for those who waited on handouts. Although he might not understand the concept, Joe thought, Lucas was guided by the principles Emerson termed self-reliance. A few men such as Matt, Sam and Paul Berrien recognized the black man's able attitude. Others were slow to see it, and some would never acknowledge it.

Joe knew people had taken advantage of Lucas when he went door-to-door looking for work after his father's death. He had heard various farmers boast about the deal they worked with Lucas, the work they received for a poor man's wages. When he had been younger, Joe had asked his daddy why these men took advantage of Lucas. Matt had been at a loss for words, but Joe noticed afterward his father made the extra effort to see that Lucas worked for him or some other fair man. Now Lucas had a yeoman's reputation, which allowed him to pick his employers. That he worked primarily for Matt was a testament to his appreciation and loyalty.

Lucas was nine years older than Joe and shared more in common with Matt, Sam and Paul. But Lucas and Joe were kindred spirits and had kindled a friendship from years of working side by side. Joe confided in Lucas on occasion, the most recent being the tale of his torrid, short-lived romance with Karen Baxter, always certain what he revealed would stay between them. Lucas listened to his musings without offering advice, which suited Joe, who preferred to sort out things for himself. In fact, it was his own penchant for privacy that kept Joe from prying during those times when he wished Lucas would divulge his own thoughts and feelings.

The cigarette burned bright red as Lucas inhaled, and Joe watched in continued silence, wondering what his friend was thinking and why he was standing by the railroad tracks at this time of night. Perhaps he had an argument with Beauty, Joe considered, or was worried over something. Or like himself, Joe concluded, it was altogether possible that Lucas had ventured out to these railroad tracks this night in search of perspective.

Joe gazed up at the heavens, mindful that a world of difference separated the perspectives of a white boy and a colored man. Despite their shared experiences, proximity and genuine interest in the well-being of each other, he and Lucas were miles apart, separated by the gulf between black and white.

Joe had encountered bigotry and demonstrated his sympathy with the emerging civil rights movement. Yet, he found it difficult to reconcile the prejudice in Cookville with the ugly likes of Selma and Montgomery, Alabama. Those places seemed far away from Cookville. But were they? Joe wondered, recalling the ugly climate of the sheriff's race between Paul Berrien and Bobby Taylor two years earlier. Bobby and his cronies were exceptions in the Cookville community, where the majority of people, white and colored alike, treated each other with fairness and respect. Harmony was the trademark of relations between the races in the community, but Joe suspected it was a fragile peace.

Blacks did not complain about the separate water fountains and bathrooms in Cookville, where they had free run of the entire town, except for the churches and the schools. Brown versus the Board of Education meant nothing in Cookville. Joe had never attended school with a colored person and probably never would. This idea was so foreign that Joe rarely had given it a thought until lately. The colored students had their own school, their own football and basketball teams, and no one ever grumbled about the situation. Two years ago, the county had built a new high school and moved the Negro students into the old building. In an election year when even the few black votes mattered, community leaders nearly had broken their arms while patting themselves on the back as if to say, "Look at us. We treat our colored folk real good. We've given them a fine new school."

Joe willingly conceded that blacks seemed to have a decent life in Cookville, as good as could be expected anyway. True, most of them were poor, extremely poor. Almost all of them lived on the wrong side of the tracks in a collection of tarpaper shacks, kindling wood frame houses and block buildings with dirt floors. A few lucky ones had running water and indoor plumbing. Most used outhouses.

The poverty disturbed Joe, but he could rationalize it. Poor white people lived in the same squalid conditions, on both the wrong and the right sides of the tracks, as well as in other parts of the county, including right here in New River.

It was easy, maybe even understandable, for Joe to assume colored people might find life harsher in places other than Cookville. No one had ever challenged segregation in the community. If everyone, both black and white, was contented with the way things were, then the system must be working. Still, Joe could not help wondering what the outcome would be if someone challenged the system. But those were lofty issues to weigh, better left to someone with a vested interest. For the moment, Joe was more concerned with matters closer to home.

If he had been outraged by the shameful behavior of Dr. Turner, then how had Lucas felt? In fact, how did Lucas feel about separate bathrooms, water fountains, schools and theater seats? Could Joe understand those feelings?

Atticus Finch, a fictional hero of Joe's, seemed to think you had to walk in someone's shoes to find answers to these kinds of questions. Since that was near to impossible, Joe settled for the next best thing.

Lucas was learning to love Beauty.

His wife was like a newborn filly, finding her colt's legs and gaining confidence with each new step along the way. He was teaching her to read and write, and Beauty was an excellent student. When she set her mind to something, which she rarely did, Beauty was a bulldog, persistent and determined all the way. At the moment, her mind was set on reading the Bible for herself and bedtime stories for the children they would have one day.

With hunger pains gnawing at his stomach, Lucas hoped that one day soon Beauty would add cooking to her list of pursuits. As it was, though, his wife was more concerned with making sure the table was set properly than with the preparation of the meal itself. On some days, Lucas half expected to come home to find the table set with fine china, silverware, linens and fresh flowers, only to discover that Beauty had forgotten to cook supper. On other days, he wished that was the case.

About the best thing he could say for Beauty's cooking was that it was filling, and sometimes even that stretched a compliment. Still, Lucas refused to complain about the meals Beauty prepared and was determined to encourage her to experiment and try different things. Until then, he would try to figure out ways to wind up at the Bakers or the Berriens around mealtimes. On principle, Lucas was opposed to charity. But he was learning fast that a man could starve on principles.

Lucas smiled to himself and inhaled on his cigarette. He considered himself a lucky man, despite his wife's shortcomings at the stove. Merrilee Bartholomew would have approved his choice of a wife.

The Bible said women were made to be helpmates for their men, and Beauty was that and more to Lucas. She honored any request, supported every endeavor and treated him like a king. She was a willing lover, a trusting partner and his best friend. Beauty allowed Lucas to be the man of the house. And he wanted to make her proud.

Lucas had gone to church that Sunday two years ago for the sole purpose of finding a wife. He'd had a vague recollection of Beauty even before setting foot in the church, and was determined to wed her from the first time she approached him to offer congratulations on his acceptance into the church.

Beauty sang in the choir and, while Lucas had some qualms with organized religion, her voice was reason enough for him to attend church every Sunday. Beauty could lead a man to God with her voice. It was melodious, pitched low and soulful, and Lucas liked nothing better than coming home to a house filled to the rafters with the spiritual croonings of his wife.

Lucas stretched and yawned, glancing skyward and then lowering his gaze once more to the ground in front of him.

They were making a home, Beauty and him, and they were on the verge of something special. He had joined with Beauty to create the miracle of life. Now was the time to hurry up and wait.

Lucas was caught in this last thought when a voice in the dark startled him. His heart missed a beat; he stumbled backward, searching the fog for the intruder. He heard the voice again, calling his name this time, and he relaxed, recognizing the familiar ring.

———

"Lucas?" Joe called as he approached. "Is that you?"

Lucas groped in the darkness, trying to recognize the voice as Joe drew closer. "Lucas," he repeated. "It's me."

Joe stepped into his line of vision, and Lucas relaxed with visible relief. "Goshamighty, Joe-Joe," he grumbled. "You scared the mess out of me."

"Sorry about that," Joe laughed lightly. "I was on my way home when I saw you standen over here. What's got you out on a night like this?"

"I was doen some thinken," Lucas replied, casting a reproachful eye on Joe at the same time. "I could ask you the same thing. I bet Mr. Matt and Mrs. Caroline don't know you're out here traipsen around in the dead of night."

"Nope, they don't," Joe confirmed. "But I don't think they'd mind too much. A guy needs a place where he can think without be'en interrupted every now and then, and there aren't too many places like that in our house."

Lucas nodded understanding. "I guess not. I'm in the same boat with Beauty. Four walls can get awful close around two people."

Joe glanced off in the darkness, then deliberately changed the subject. "We had quite a night the last time we were off by ourselves," he said. "I don't suppose you brought a gun along tonight—in case some wild animal shows up and tries to make a meal of you?"

"Not this time," Lucas smiled, rotating his shoulder to show it was healing. "I don't think we oughtta worry too much about anything else like that happenen. It was one shot in a million." He paused, then added, "By the way, I never thanked you properly for saven my life, Joe-Joe, but I'm much obliged."

Joe shrugged modestly. "It was the least I could do," he grinned. "I'd call it the shot of a lifetime."

Lucas smiled again, and Joe asked him for a cigarette.

"What's on your mind?" Joe asked boldly as he lit the Camel.

Lucas dropped his own cigarette to the ground, stared briefly at the red glow and then ground it into the earth with the soul of his boot. "Well, Joe," he began hesitantly. "You might say congratulations is in store for Beauty and me. She told me tonight at supper that she's gonna have a baby." He glanced up at Joe. "I came out here tonight to think about be'en a daddy and how I can make my baby's life better than mine."

"Congratulations!" Joe exclaimed, extending his hand to Lucas and pumping the handshake vigorously as the excitement registered on his friend's poker face. "You're bloated with pride, Lucas. No doubt, you figure to get a son."

Lucas shook his head from side to side. "I don't care nary a bit. I just want a healthy, happy baby."

Joe smiled in agreement. "Give my best to Beauty," he said. "Can I tell the family?"

"Might as well," Lucas answered. "Near as we can tell, she'll be looken like she's expecten before too much longer."

"I'm proud for you, Lucas," Joe said. "You'll make a good daddy." He paused, then added with feigned indifference, "I guess every parent wants to make the world better for their children. I know Mama and Daddy do."

"They should," Lucas suggested. He hunched his shoulders, looking Joe squarely in the eye. "But don't hem and haw with me, Joe," he said with conviction. "Your mama and daddy have the world on their side. But me? I've got to try harder."

"Yeah," Joe agreed with sincerity. "I know what you mean, Lucas, and it's funny because that's been on my mind a lot lately. Fate must have meant us to meet here tonight. I have a feelen we've both had a lot of the same things on our minds lately."

"Like what it's like to be colored?" Lucas supposed.

Joe nodded. "For you in particular."

Silence ensued, and Joe worried he had stepped beyond the bounds of friendship. "Why you wanna know?" Lucas asked finally.

"Who's playen games now?" Joe shot back.

Lucas shrugged indifferently.

"You and I have known each other for as long as I can remember," Joe said, "but over the last few months especially, we've had an opportunity to get closer. I've grown to trust you, Lucas, and I hope you can say the same for me. I've got some questions on my mind—questions about you because you're my friend."

"You're worth a million in questions, Joe-Joe," Lucas said, "but you're always a dime short on answers. I still wanna know why you're so interested in wanten to know what makes a colored man tick."

"I like to know what other people think," Joe responded. "And things have happened lately that caused me to think as well. Quite honestly, Lucas, a few people have given me the feelen they'd have rather I shot you than the panther. That boggles my brain. And then there was the good Dr. Turner. He didn't want to treat you just because you're colored. That ticked me off. I've wondered how it made you feel. You've never said the first word about it."

Lucas hunched his shoulders again. "To tell you the truth, Joe, I don't remember much about that night, 'cept for the hurten. But I'm glad you were ticked off. I would have been, too, if somethen like that happened to you. As for those feelens you've been getten from other people, I'm not surprised. Some people figure the world would be a better place with one less nigger. Believe me, there's been times when I thought the world would be a whole sight better with a few less white masters.

"Does that surprise you?" Lucas asked a pregnant moment later. "Does it scare you?"

"It surprises me some," Joe answered, smiling. "But it doesn't scare me. I know you pretty well, Lucas. You're fairly mild-mannered." He hesitated, then inquired, "When you think about me, Lucas, what do you think first? Am I Joe? Or am I white?"

"First, you answer that question about me," Lucas challenged.

"Okay," Joe relented. "I think of Lucas ... my black friend. But I don't associate any of your peculiarities as having to do anything with be'en black. Actually, I think of you and me as kindred spirits to some extent. We like our privacy, you even more than me."

"Agreed," Lucas said. "When I see you, I think, 'There's Joe. He's white. He's different.'" Lucas smiled. "But eventually, I get 'round to rememberen that I'd count on you with my life."

"I can say the same for you, Lucas," Joe told him. He shifted his stance, then asked, "Is it hard to be colored?"

Lucas scratched his jaw and rubbed his nose. "Sometimes," he answered at length. "In a white man's world, it is. Most of the time, though, I don't think of myself as colored. I don't have the time to dwell on what all that means. Besides that, I figure I'm doen okay for myself. I got plenty of work to keep me busy, a place to stay and a good woman beside me all the way. Now I got a baby on the way, too. A man can't ask for much more than that, no matter whether he's a colored man or a white man."

"That sounds like my daddy and my grandpa talken," Joe commented.

"Some of it is," Lucas admitted. "I can't deny Mr. Matt and Mr. Sam have influenced my thinken more than a little. Maybe that's why I don't think of myself as colored very often. They've pretty much treated me as plain old Lucas for 'bout as long as I can remember."

Joe finished his cigarette, rubbing it out in the ground. "You ever wish you were white, Lucas?" he asked.

"When I was little, I did," Lucas confessed. "It would've made life a whole heap easier."

"And now?" Joe pushed.

Lucas crossed his arms. "There's some people who think that about me," he conceded. "I live among white people more than colored people these days. I look at your daddy and your granddaddy and Mr. Paul Berrien and what they've accomplished, and I see myself tryen to do what they've done. So on one hand, I have to admit that white men more than black men have given direction to my life. But on the other hand, my mama was a smart woman and she taught her boy well. She's the one, Joe-Joe. She's the reason I do what I do. She made me."

He unfolded his arms and rubbed his palms against his pants legs. "That's a roundabout answer to your question," he continued a moment later. "Directly speaken, though, I don't have any desire to be a white man. Not anymore. I wouldn't want to change who I am, Joe." He shook his head. "Maybe change the world, but not me."

Joe glanced at the ground, then quickly back to his friend. "I'm glad to hear that, Lucas."

Lucas nodded appreciatively, adding, "Well, I'm glad to tell you, Joe-Joe."

Joe tilted his head, sheepishly casting another curious glance at Lucas. "When did you decide you no longer wanted to be white?" he asked slyly.

"Probably when my mama was dyen," Lucas replied patiently. "But I was in Detroit when I realized it once and for all." He closed his eyes. "That's why I went North. I thought life might be easier up there. But it wasn't—least not for me."

"What about that trip?" Joe pushed again. "You've never said much about it."

"That's right. I haven't," Lucas remarked, fishing a crumpled pack of Camels and a box of matches from his shirt pocket.

Taking his last cigarette from the pack, he stuffed the empty paper into the front pocket of his worn brown trousers and struck the match. He lit the cigarette, inhaled deeply and returned the matchbox to his shirt pocket, leaving Joe to wonder once again whether he had pried beyond the boundaries of their friendship.

"I trust you, Joe," Lucas said at last, staring off into the distance. "I know what's said here tonight will stay by these railroad tracks."

"It will," Joe guaranteed him.

"When I was your age," Lucas began, "I used to lie in my bed at night and think about leaven this place and never comen back. My daddy was dead by then, and Mama and me lived in Cookville. I'd hear that train roll through town on some nights, and it was all I could do to keep from runnen after it. I wanted to hop a ride in the baddest sort of way. I didn't care where it was goen. I just wanted to leave.

"But I couldn't," he continued. "Mama was bad sick, and she needed me. Still, I started saven up for a day when there wouldn't be nothen to keep me here. Every job I worked, every heavy load I lifted, brought me one step closer to somethen better. I was sure of it. I'd find some place where I could be somethen and someone I'd never be here in Cookville."

Lucas leveled his gaze at Joe.

"Now I know better," he said, and his story began in earnest.

It was a journey of two thousand miles, traveled in a third- or fourth-hand pickup, and the first stop was Sweet Auburn Avenue in Atlanta. Lucas stayed in the city for three months. He heard Martin Luther King Jr. preach civil rights and the gospel at Ebenezer Baptist Church, and he listened to politics and protest at Paschal's Motor Inn. He respected the passions and admired the battle plans for integration. But selfish reasons kept Lucas from joining the Movement. He bid Atlanta goodbye and moved on to Raleigh, to Richmond, to Washington, D.C., picking tobacco along the way and doing any other odd job to keep cash in his pocket.

"The towns were bigger, but the life didn't seem much different from what I'd left in Cookville," Lucas told Joe. "Face it. Croppen baccer is croppen baccer, whether you do it in Cookville, Georgia, or outside Raleigh, North Carolina. I did wash dishes at a restaurant in Washington for a few weeks. That was enough time to know I needed to find somethen else to do."

Lucas spent two months in the City of Brotherly Love, Philadelphia, and landed next in New York City, where he stayed for eleven months. He found a job moving boxes at a grocery warehouse in Harlem, rented a room in a boarding house and took his meals at a nearby restaurant on 135th Street.

Food flavored his fondest memories of the city. The natives called it "soul food" in Harlem, but Lucas thought of those meals simply as good Southern cooking. He kept his belly full, feasting day after day on chicken, fish and pork chops, all deep-fried in fat; pig feet, pig tails and chitlins served with collards, turnips, mustard greens and pot liquor. There were mouth-melting corn dodgers, fatback, sweet potatoes, okra, peas and, inevitably, a delicious sweet to top off each meal.

The hardy fare filled out Lucas' rangy form, and the warehouse work hardened his muscles. It was a glorious time, and Lucas dared to believe he had found his place in life. He might have convinced himself completely if not for the grim reality of the city.

Each day, he saw dope pushers and drug addicts turn deals in back alleys, drunkards stumble from row upon row of liquor stores and bars, prostitutes turning tricks on every street corner. He stared at these people in disbelief, wondering which broken-down building the poor creatures claimed for home and thanking the Almighty for his own good fortune.

Lucas loved Harlem and he hated it at times. But in the end, when he almost died on its mean streets, Lucas was driven from it.

He discovered the party life in Harlem and took it to heart. Wine and women became the song of life, and Lucas played it like a troubadour.

His favorite nightspot was a bar on 116th Street, and one summer night there, Lucas was pointed in a direction that would lead home to Cookville. "It was on a Friday," he recalled for Joe. "The place was jam-packed. The women were easy, and I was looken for somethen sweet."

Lucas found a beauty queen, with cherry red lips and sparkling white teeth. He slid onto an empty bar stool beside the woman, ordered a beer for himself and whiskey for her. They chatted for a few minutes, then danced and Lucas figured he was on his way to getting lucky. Finishing the last of several dances, they found a table and were becoming cozy when his luck turned sour.

Lucas had just leaned close to her face when the back of his skull exploded. Although he did not realize it at the time, the woman's boyfriend had belted him with a set of brass knuckles. Struggling to remain conscious, Lucas was spun around and witnessed firsthand the driving force of another ringed fist into his face. The blow shattered his nose, and Lucas had vague memories of his laundered white shirt turning crimson as the man dragged him from the bar to one of Harlem's feared alleys.

"You pay for messing with my woman," the man told Lucas, then plunged a bowie knife into his abdomen. He was unconscious before the knife was removed from body.

When he woke, Lucas was outside an emergency clinic. He stumbled to his feet, staggered through the door and gasped for help before passing out a second time.

A young white woman was hovering over him when he next woke. Lucas was lying on a gurney, and the female doctor proclaimed him lucky to be alive.

"That knife missed your liver by a hair and a whole lot of other stuff you need as well," she told him sternly. "How did you manage to get here?"

"I don't know," Lucas answered truthfully. "One minute I was talken to a pretty woman. The next, somebody was beaten me in the head and sticken a knife in my gut."

The doctor shook her head in dismay. "I don't understand you people," she told Lucas. "You cut somebody up, then drop him off at the hospital for stitches like it's the most normal thing in the world to do. It makes no sense."

"I don't understand it, either," Lucas mused half-heartedly. "Back where I come from, people ain't so mean to each other."

"Then I suggest you go back to that place while you still can," the doctor recommended.

Instead, Lucas took off for Boston. He saw the autumn colors in New England, motored through Pittsburgh and Cleveland and spent a Christmas, New Year's and winter in the frigid cold of Chicago before moving north to Detroit.

In Detroit, Lucas attended his first honest-to-goodness civil rights demonstration. It was a peaceful rally to show support for sit-in protests at a Woolworth's lunch counter in Greensboro, North Carolina. Lucas lent his voice to the demonstration, chanting slogans for justice and equality, singing familiar freedom songs. But his heart was heavy.

Speaker after speaker condemned the poverty, inadequate education and second-class citizenship of Negroes in the South. They claimed the white man was a universal enemy in the South. They threatened to invade the region, vowing to free their Southern brothers from the final bonds of white oppression and slavery.

As they spoke, Lucas looked around and considered the plight of the people gathered around him. Perhaps many of them were better educated and wealthier than their colored counterparts in the South. But the very same problems they expounded so passionately about in the South were festering in their own backyards as well. He thought about the slums in Harlem and other cities he had seen. The white man was not the enemy in Harlem, Lucas believed. The enemy was a system that destroyed hope and swallowed up young souls into a destiny of misery and squalor.

"Colored people got more than their share of problems down here," Lucas commented, explaining his feelings to Joe. "Maybe we do need outsiders comen in to shake up people. But I don't put much store in people who set out to save the world without first taken care of their own."

At his first civil rights demonstration, Lucas decided it was time to go home. It would take him two months to get there, and he would arrive by way of St. Louis and New Orleans. But Lucas was sure of his destiny. In Cookville, his enemies were familiar and Lucas believed they would soften over time. It was slender trust, perhaps, but the first glimmer of hope that Lucas had seen in a long time.

———

"This is home," Lucas stated simply to Joe. "It's where I belong."

"But is it everything you want?" Joe asked.

"It's everything I need," Lucas replied with firm conviction. "What you want is not always what you need, Joe-Joe. But the way I figure it, if a man can get what he needs, he's bound to have enough of everything and maybe a little extra in the long run."

"You're sounden like Daddy again," Joe remarked.

"Yeah, well," Lucas arched his eyebrows. "That's not so bad, is it?"

"No," Joe agreed. "Not at all."

Lucas finished another cigarette. "Did I answer some of those questions for you?" he asked in time.

"A few. But I've got more."

"Why ain't I surprised?" Lucas laughed. "Joe-Joe, you obviously never heard that curiosity killed the cat."

"I ain't no cat," Joe declared.

"You're a tomcat for shore," Lucas teased. "I can see it in your eyes."

"What you see is cat-scratch fever," Joe countered smartly. "But seriously, Lucas, can you stand another question or two?"

Lucas made an off-handed remark about the train's tardiness, then allowed for another question.

"Do things like separate bathrooms and water fountains bother you?" Joe inquired. "Have you ever considered standen up against stuff like that?"

"Have you ever considered it?" Lucas parried.

"It's not my place to," Joe suggested.

"Who says," Lucas shot back. "I don't suspect you'd be welcome in a bathroom marked for colored people any more than I'd be in one for whites."

Joe was confused. "I hadn't thought of it that way."

"No, I didn't figure you had," Lucas said. He shrugged, then added, "I don't care about those things, Joe," he admitted. "They'll work themselves out eventually, maybe one day when somebody gets tired of keepen all those bathrooms clean. When I pick a battle to fight, it's gonna be over somethen really important, somethen that matters to me."

"Such as?"

"Opportunity," Lucas replied fiercely. "I can make a good life for myself. My needs will be met. But what's good for me won't be good enough for my children. They'll need more than I do. I want them to have opportunities that I didn't have. I want more for them than what comes with be'en grateful that a few white people are able to see beyond the color of your skin."

Lucas paused, scrutinizing Joe for reaction, finding a blank expression on his face. "I'll pick a fight one day, Joe," he continued passionately. "I'll fight to make sure my children get the same education that you're getten, to make sure they're not treated as second-class in second-rate schools. And I'll win that fight. Because the law of the land is on my side, even if it's ignored 'round here."

"Do you agree?" he asked after a slight pause. "Do you think I'll win?"

Joe glanced deliberately past Lucas, uncertain of the answer. Civil rights were a vague concept to Joe, but he understood the plainly stated goal of his black friend and appreciated the fierce determination to succeed. "I hope so," he answered finally, returning his gaze to Lucas. "I suppose we'll have to wait and see."

"Wait and see!" Lucas rolled his eyes and shook his head in exasperation. "It's always wait and see," he said angrily. "That's everybody's answer for anything unpleasant today that can be put off until tomorrow. Your daddy's said that same thing to me more times than you'd imagine. And your granddaddy was sayen the same thing to my daddy way back when."

"Well, what the heck are we supposed to say, Lucas?" Joe retorted sharply. "You're not exactly marchen off to battle yourself."

In the blink of an eye, tension came unexpectedly and thick between them. It seemed to Joe they had stepped on different sides of the same track. Lucas realized their guns were drawn as well and pulled back his attack.

"I'm talken big, Joe-Joe," he allowed. "Sounden high and mighty, too."

"It's nothen, Lucas," Joe shrugged.

"Maybe," Lucas nodded. "But I got no right asken you or anyone else to do my fighten for me, especially when I'm not ready or willen to do it myself."

"When will that be?" Joe inquired.

"When I've got a reason, too," Lucas said quickly. "When my children are ready for it."

"Why not now?" Joe asked.

"Because it's not my fight right now," Lucas answered frankly. "Because I'm self-ish. Because I'm comfortable with the way things are. There's any number of reasons. Take your pick. The way I look at it, I'll do my part when the time comes. I'll make a stand. I'll fight a battle. I'll do what I can to change things. But my first commitment is to my family, now and always. I won't sacrifice them for a cause.

"It's all about needs," he added. "I'll do what's necessary to meet the needs of my family. And if there's anything extra, then so be it."

"For what it's worth, Lucas," Joe said, "I'd fight with you."

"I don't doubt it," Lucas grinned, clapping him on the shoulder. "Joe-Joe, you'll be there with guns a-blazen."

In the distance then, they heard the train, rushing toward the trestle at the New River crossroads.

Joe glanced eagerly down the track, searching the fog for the first sign of the approaching locomotive. "I'm glad you figured out what you needed, Lucas," he said sincerely, eyes still glued to the steel tracks. "I'm glad you came home. And happy we had this talk tonight."

Joe broke his long look down the tracks and faced Lucas. "Do you realize how envious I am of you? You've done exactly what I want to do. You've gone to places I want to go. Maybe sometime you can tell me more about those places—Boston, New York, Philadelphia, Chicago, New Orleans. I'd give anything in the world to stand on top of the Empire State building or to eat crawfish and jambalaya in New Orleans."

Joe shook his head as the train reached the trestle, its whistle blasting the night, the heavy vibrations echoing through the countryside. He heeded the call instinctively, peeling his eyes once more down the track as the engine headlight loomed into view.

"Lucas, you mentioned the train earlier tonight, and I knew exactly what you were talken about," he said. "It calls out to you, and sometimes a body just has to answer. That's why I came down here tonight. One day, I'm gonna hop a ride on it, Lucas, and go far away from here. There's a whole world out there, and I think I'm gonna like it better than Cookville."

"Wait and see," Lucas suggested, smiling as Joe looked at him. "Cookville might look a whole lot better to you when you're a thousand miles away from it, especially when it seems more like you're a thousand miles from nowhere."

"Oh, I don't doubt that," Joe agreed quickly. "This place, this time—it might just be the best there is. But like you said, Lucas, it's all about needs." He smiled, almost reluctantly. "And as good as it is here, it's not enough for me."

The train was on them then, approaching fast with two long whistle blasts, and they stepped away from the steel rails in unison. As the train streaked past them, unaware that Lucas was watching him with undisguised interest, Joe reached down and grabbed a handful of the hard earth. He sifted it through his fingers, gritted his teeth and tossed the dirt at the passing cars, wondering what unknown destination awaited that little piece of earth.

Joe turned around to find Lucas regarding him with an amused expression.

"It's always too fast," Joe complained, raising his voice loud enough to be heard over the fading racket of grinding steel. "It's here one moment, then before you know it, it's passed you by again. I have to keep reminden myself that another one will come along in due time."

"Uhm," Lucas mused. "Well, I best be getten home," he said. "But Joe: Best you always remember that for every train goen away from here, another one comes back."

Joe smiled at the sage advice as the late-night companions ended their unexpected sojourn. He gazed down the tracks once more, watching the train lights disappear in the fog, closing his eyes as the last faint thunder echoed in his head.

Turning toward home, Joe thought: The train may run both ways, Lucas, but I want a one-way ticket.

PART TWO

Ordinary routines dominated their lives, yet the seemingly endless repetition remained fresh, each sunrise bringing a new twist and variation to the sameness. A bucolic cadence distinguished the days, beginning with the crowing of a single rooster, seasoned by the aroma of good Southern cooking and ending with the natural light of a fading horizon. Tranquil nights followed the eventide, spent watching the phenomenon that was television or quietly engaged in a leisurely pursuit of relaxation. It was not serene. Rarely are large households where the living is enjoyed.

There existed forty-five relationships among the ten members of the household, each an enclave of private and shared moments. Each member was the other's best cheerleader and, on occasion, an archrival as well. The best and worst of their ancestors had fused and concocted rare breeds, people remarkable in every nuance of simplicity or complexity. They understood love, responsibility and thanksgiving. They were a family in the truest sense of the word, tied by blood and the struggle of enduring.

The family's life was a blend of rituals and feats of epic proportions, a mix of precious elixir and steady servings of sustaining fortitude. Rather than simply mark time, they filled the space between the tiny and seemingly insignificant points on the ruler of life with things of lasting value. Thus, the essence of the family was found in the details. But it was random moments of forced confrontation—between soul and conscience, desire and will, want and need—that made them aware of the ruler and provided a measure of the journey.

ANGELS SING

1963

CHAPTER 1

"DAMN!"

Summer was on a warpath on this last afternoon of 1962, battling the angst of youth and forced domesticity. New Year's Eve had been uneventful thus far on the Baker place, especially for Summer, who heretofore had washed windows, ironed clothes, vacuumed floors and presently was polishing furniture in her younger brothers' room. It was unfair the twelve-year-old girl had told Joe a moment ago in his room next door to John and Luke's.

"I could just scream," Summer railed even as Joe gave her a reprieve on orders from their mother to make his bed. "The men around here never have to lift a finger in this house. Y'all are doing exactly what you want to do today, and I'm stuck cleanen up after you. I'm tellen you, it ain't right."

"Do you hear me, Joe?" she yelled a moment later when he failed to acknowledge her tirade. "It ain't right."

Glancing up from his desk where he was writing an essay—a holiday homework assignment in senior English from Mrs. Gaskins—Joe shot his sister a disinterested look. "I heard you, all right. Listen, Summer, I'm busy here, and I told you not to worry about my bed. What more do you want?"

His sister bristled, hands flying to her hips in outrage as Joe's casual dismissal of her tirade became apparent. A quick retort appeared on the edge of her tongue, then disappeared. "I could still scream," she muttered before leaving his room.

Instead of screaming, Summer apparently had decided to utter every profanity in her vocabulary. Listening to his sister's ranting, Joe smiled and sympathized with her plight. In a few years, she would learn to control these outbursts, but now the desire to vent her anger blotted out almost twelve years of training in good manners and responsibility.

"Damn!" Summer growled for the fourth time and loudly enough that Joe thought it wise to advise his sister against foolhardy conduct.

"Damn!" she said again, even as Joe leaned back in his chair and saw her admiring the shine on the fireplace mantle in John and Luke's room.

"WHAT did you say, young lady?" Rachel said unexpectedly, sternly.

The question rang with accusation and startled Summer. Gaping, she withered under the glaring eyes of their grandmother and started to apologize. Something stopped her though. It might have been indignation, but Joe figured it was more a mixture of stubbornness, frustration and plain stupidity.

"I said damn, Granny, and I meant it," Summer said, her tone sassy, her expression defiant. "It's not fair that we have to stay inside and do this durned old housework, while the men around here have a good old time doen whatever the heck they please." She crossed her arms, then declared, "I resent it."

Rachel stepped fully into the room, coming into Joe's range of observation. He approximated her temper at a slow boil as she considered an appropriate response to this willful display of temper by her granddaughter.

Like the season for which she was named, Summer was strong-willed, feisty and unrelenting on occasion. Rachel was the same way. As Joe saw it, his oldest sister and grandmother were two different patterns cut from same bolt of cloth. They shared common interests, particularly sewing and needlework, but their perspectives contrasted as sharply as the difference between a summer shower and a hurricane. Fortunately, Summer and Rachel rarely butted heads, but when they did, their sameness and differences clashed like stripes and polka dots. Joe sensed such a fashion faux pas at hand.

"Fair or not, young lady, that's the way it is," Rachel admonished her granddaughter. "And you'd better get used to it cause you're a young woman and young women are responsible for keepen a clean house." She paused, no doubt, Joe figured, to let her good advice sink into Summer's hard head. "Now you finish up your dusten. Then go copy ten Bible verses, and I won't tell your Mama what you said. But between us, you should be ashamed of yourself, Summer."

Joe smiled, thinking his sister was getting off lucky for the transgression. He made up his mind to show Summer ten of the shorter verses in the Bible as he waited expectantly for her contrite acceptance of the punishment. The girl fooled him.

"Granny, I don't think I should have to write down any old Bible verses. I've got a right to be mad. And besides, Daddy says damn all the time. If you weren't so ignorant about the ways of the world, you'd probably damn all this housework, too. There's more to life than just housework, and I'm sick and tired of all this cooken, cleanen, ironen and sewen."

Summer regretted the words as soon as they spewed from her mouth. Joe saw the remorse in her expression, as surely as he saw disappointment flash in his grandmother's eyes. For a split second, Rachel and Summer were bewildered, torn by desire to make amends and conviction in their beliefs.

Joe considered intervening to restore the peace, but the sudden appearance of his mother in the doorway doomed the prospect before it fully evolved.

"Summer!"

Caroline swept into the room on a wave of carefully controlled anger, obviously appalled by the situation. "In this house, young lady," she exhorted her daughter, "you do not talk to anyone that way, especially your elders. Tell your grandmother you're sorry this very instant; then go to the kitchen and wait there until I decide an appropriate punishment."

"I'm sorry," Summer spat, her indignation rising to another level.

"Say it and mean it, Summer," Caroline ordered.

Summer stared at her mother, then at Rachel and back to Caroline. "Mama," she replied. "That's the best I can do right now."

His sister's insolence stunned Joe. Summer always spoke her mind, but she was never deliberately spiteful. Yet, in one fell swoop, she had committed treason against her grandmother and declared open rebellion on her mother. Joe settled back and waited for her impertinence to be quashed.

More and more these days, he found himself witness to the travails of his sisters and brothers as they plodded through rough spots in the road to becoming young men and women. He deemed such observations as a due of his birthright, an act of passage that signified his coming of age and heralded a season of coming-out parties for the long line of siblings who trailed him. Joe had traversed the path of adolescence, and the road ahead—while certain to contain a few rocky places—looked relatively smooth to him. For the moment, he was intrigued more by the idea of stepping aside as his brothers and sisters took their turns as Johnny-come-lately. He considered it an obligation and a pleasure.

In some imprecise way, his salad days had passed and Joe felt as if he were between seasons. But Summer, John, Carrie, Luke and Bonnie were chomping at their bits with impatience, and Joe looked forward to watching the performance from the shadows. That was another privilege of his birthright, a position that brought huge responsibility but endowed him with the unique perspective of having been there. Joe was young enough to sympathize with the fervency of his brothers and sisters, yet old enough to understand the wisdom of his parents and grandparents.

Indeed, when he thought about it, Joe enjoyed his domain as the oldest child. It was the perfect vista, affording him the distance of deep shadows while extending leeway around the edges, providing a jumping-off place, yet allowing him to come rushing in to the rescue at a moment's notice, of his own volition or at the beck and call of someone else.

He was on the verge of plundering this last thought with more thoroughness when Caroline abruptly ended her dressing-down of Summer.

"You've disappointed me, Summer, not to mention your shabby disrespect of your grandmother," Caroline said gravely. "Nevertheless, it's your decision to be satisfied with your feeble apology and if you are, so be it. I, however, am not satisfied. Go to the kitchen."

"Yes, ma'am," Summer answered, her comedown so low that Joe leaned back once more in his chair to observe the goings-on through the doorway.

"I don't know what gets into that girl sometimes," Caroline remarked to Rachel when Summer had fled the room. This was not the first time Caroline had played mediatrix between her daughter and mother-in-law. She paused, expecting Rachel to give her version of the situation.

Instead, the older woman picked up the dust rag abandoned by Summer and used it to wipe away an invisible spot on the fireplace mantle.

"You two are so much alike that I guess there's always goen to be an occasional wrangle," Caroline prodded. "What started this one? Why was she so disrespectful?"

"Punish her for swearen, Caroline," Rachel said, looking her daughter-in-law in the eye. "But not for her insolence. It will pass, and Summer and I will work out our differences in due time."

Caroline considered the request for a moment, then nodded her agreement before casting her suspicions on Joe. "Son, did you hear your sister cursen?"

"She was haven a bad day," Joe suggested glibly.

"Well, that's no excuse!" Caroline retorted.

"No, it's not," Rachel agreed quickly. "And Joe, you should have told her so. You're a Christian, and you shouldn't condone such behavior."

Joe started to protest the rebuke, then changed his mind and smiled penitently. "You're right," he agreed. "Sorry, Mama. Sorry, Granny."

Seeing the two women sufficiently appeased, it occurred to Joe that while his sisters and brothers were coming into their own and taking center stage, he still had a few lessons to learn himself and would—of his own volition and heeding the beck and call of others—stay close in the wings as this drama unfolded. Joe shrugged his shoulders and told himself it was not a bad feeling at all to have such an important role.

CHAPTER 2

ON THE FIRST FRIDAY night of the new year, something happened that sent a wave of fear cresting through the Cookville community. Around midnight, Delia Turner, the wife of Dr. Ned Turner, was reading a book in bed when she heard someone knocking on the back door of their brownstone Victorian home located just off the main square in Cookville. Figuring the doctor had forgotten his house key—a frequent, annoying habit of her husband—Delia came downstairs wearing only a thin housecoat. Reaching the kitchen, she turned on the back-porch light and heard the screen door open as she entered the utility room.

Later, when explaining the incident to the sheriff, Delia would recall thinking that moment odd since Ned usually waited for her to open the door before he pulled back the screen. Nevertheless, she unlocked the door, cracked it open and was about to unfasten the chain lock when a man rammed his fist through the tight space and tore open her housecoat. Screaming, Delia glanced up at her assailant, then jerked free of the black man's grasp and fled through the dark house.

She heard the chain lock snap and the back door crash open as the man pushed his way into the house and chased after her. Seconds later, while she fumbled with the locks on the front door, the assailant collided with a stout coffee table. Cut down at the shins, the man howled in pain and cursed Delia as she escaped through the door. She ran into the middle of the street, screaming for help while the man recovered his senses and limped a hasty retreat back the same way he had entered the house.

Paul Berrien conducted a thorough investigation of the incident, concluding that Delia had been the victim of a drifter passing through Cookville. Ned was outraged by the outcome, accusing Paul of running a slipshod investigation and refuting the sheriff's contention that the assailant likely would never set foot again in Cookville. Ned demanded an arrest, insisting that somewhere on the other side of the tracks in Cookville, his wife's attacker was running scot-free, waiting to strike again. On the basis of Delia's description of the man and his own knowledge of the colored community, Paul refused to budge from his original position.

Ned was not someone easily put off or to be taken lightly. Despite his overbearing, snobbish ways, he wielded considerable influence in Cookville. People listened when he talked, especially when he questioned Paul's capability for enforcing the law and suggested the sheriff had a knack for "kowtowing to the niggers." Paul stayed above the fray, but the doctor's talk and accusations made the rounds through the community.

Whether to believe Paul Berrien or Ned Turner was a matter of opinion, but almost everyone agreed on one thing: It was most unsettling to have crime strike so close to home. In its aftermath, more people began to lock their doors at night; several jokesters suggested the man must have been hard up to have made a grab for Delia Turner, whose stout body and homely features defined ugliness; and one man hatched an idea.

It was a farfetched, spurious thought at first, almost inconceivable. But the man was gifted with vision, and he had a talent for making the most of every opportunity and seeing the possibilities offered up by improbable situations. Once the idea entered his head, he latched onto it with increasing clarity. To execute it would require guts, risk, foresight and luck, all things he lacked but could fake well enough when the stakes were high.

He refused to think of himself as a criminal, though he had skirted the law when the situation suited him. But his past misdeeds had been indirect associations with the main event. If his latest plans were to come to fruition, he would have to be the triggerman.

————

On a cold, damp day in early February, Rachel sat by the kitchen fireplace in her favorite rocker, humming *In the Sweet By-and-By* as her knitting needles clicked to the melody. She was knitting an afghan of royal blue, red and white for Carrie. Last winter, she had made one of forest green and black for Summer. Next winter, she would knit one for Bonnie. In addition, she was sewing special quilts for each of her grandchildren, a project started a few weeks earlier. She did her quilting at night, and her first effort, which she would present to Joe come next Christmas, was stretched across the quilting rack that hung from the ceiling over the bed she shared with Sam.

Her mind was wandering, and Rachel dropped a stitch. Chastising herself, she corrected the mistake and continued with the work.

On another winter morning more years ago than she cared to remember, Rachel had first suspected she was going to have a baby. She had been cutting a dress pattern for a neighbor when a wave of nausea rolled through her. Becoming dizzy on her feet, she had sought comfort in this same rocking chair. A few days later, the doctor had confirmed she was expecting Joseph, her firstborn, who would perish at Pearl Harbor only a few days before his twenty-first birthday.

Similar bouts of morning sickness had warned that she was pregnant on four other occasions. She had miscarried on the first occasion, in the third month, before giving birth to Matt, Ruth and Nicholas, the baby who had died of the pneumonia at six weeks. The miscarriage and the death of Nicholas had saddened Rachel, but she had attributed the losses to God's will and plunged back into a busy life filled with the shenanigans of three boisterous children.

In those days, quiet moments had been as hard to come by as money. And unless she was certain the children were asleep in their beds, Rachel had learned quickly that moments of noticeable silence and absent children usually meant mischief was afoot or in the making.

She recalled a day when Joseph had decided his little brother was too old to take a bottle and used it to feed suckling pigs. Although Rachel would have chosen another means of breaking Matt from the bottle, Joseph's tactics had done the trick. Matt, who was approaching his fourth birthday and should have been weaned years earlier, had taken one look at the pig sucking on his bottle and lost all desire for it.

Then, there had been another day years later when Joseph and Matt took it upon themselves to teach Ruth a lesson in humility. Somewhat spoiled—especially by her father, although Rachel and the boys catered to her whims as well—Ruth had taken particular fancy to matching dresses that she received for herself and her prized baby doll as Christmas presents one year. Although Rachel had sewed the dresses and was right proud of them herself, she, too, had become annoyed by Ruth's ticky behavior and vanity. Ruth would prance around in the dress, holding her doll, putting on airs and scoffing at her brothers.

Rachel laughed to herself, remembering the day she had heard Ruth's plaintiff moan when she discovered the dresses were missing. As soon as Ruth wailed, "Dolly's naked. Where's her dress; where's my dress?" Rachel realized she had a mess on her hands. She'd had to go only as far as the kitchen window, where she spotted the boys leaning against the barnyard gate, guffawing all over themselves.

Expecting the worst, Rachel had gone outside and discovered a sow and one of her shoats prancing around the lot in the prized dresses. Ruth also made the discovery for herself a few moments later. She took one look, started to cry, then changed her mind, slapped both brothers across the face and refused to speak to either of them for a whole week.

Feeling their daughter's actions were justified, Rachel and Sam had let her off without so much as a reprimand. As for Joseph and Matt, they had received a belt across their backsides. It was one of the few times Sam had whipped any of his children.

Smiling again, Rachel remembered feeling as if she were on a fast merry-go-round in those days and wondering if it would ever stop. Then, without warning, that merry-go-round went whirling like a top out of control. When it crashed, Rachel was a shell-shocked veteran of motherhood, the victim of a daughter who had eloped with a stranger, a son who had lost his life to the Japanese bombs at Pearl Harbor and another son who had answered the call of a nation at war.

At first, Rachel had been too shocked to grieve properly. Neighbors and relatives had praised her for holding up well under the strain as she carried on with the everyday business of living. But her aplomb was more a dazed response to the turmoil. She might well have been sleepwalking through those dismal winter months of 1942, but spring had awakened her senses. On some days, she thought the silence would kill her. On others, she questioned her sanity, wondering if she had imagined a life filled with children.

Even after all these years, Rachel wondered from time to time whether she would have survived the losses without her daughter-in-law.

As soon as she was finished with high school that spring, Caroline had swept into the Baker home like a breath of fresh air. She had been determined to discover everything about her chosen life with Matt, and her enthusiasm for learning had been infectious. Rachel and Sam had accommodated her every wish. Although unintentionally and perhaps unknowingly, Caroline had filled a void and helped to coax Rachel back from the edge of torment.

As Sam and she had shared the stories of a lifetime with their new daughter-in-law, Rachel had begun the grieving process over her lost children. In telling those stories, Rachel had laughed; she had cried; and she had come to understand the full extent of her loss.

On occasion, she had gone for long walks, where she could bawl her eyes out in private. At other times, she needed only to walk into the yard, where her prayer stump bided a talk with God. But gradually and true to her nature, Rachel had accepted the past and adjusted for the future. In all honesty, she could never deny wishing that things might have turned out differently in the past; but neither would she give up the present to change the past.

A tear fell on her hand as the knitting needles clicked, surprising Rachel as she realized her eyes were misty. "Pshaw," she scolded herself. "You're beginnen to think like an old woman."

The self-admonishment reminded Rachel of her approaching birthday. Come Valentine's Day, she would indeed be an old woman, at least according to the government, which would declare her a senior citizen. The notion displeased her to no end. She did not feel elderly, and she had the constitution of an ox, as her husband was prone to tell anyone should the subject arise. Sam meant it as a compliment, but bless his heart, the man's poet spirit should have come up with a more flattering form of praise.

Rachel sighed and considered again her approaching birthday. Perhaps she wasn't old by her own judgment, but she wasn't young either. Still, she'd aged well.

She was slightly built, with her thinness tending to make her appear taller than she was. Although childbearing and age had robbed her of an hourglass waist, she still weighed little more than she did when Sam had carried her over the threshold forty-three years earlier. Wearing bonnets and long sleeves over the years had protected her complexion from the elements and kept her free of age spots. Her features also had softened with age, blunting the harsh effect of her sometimes-saucy disposition. While a few wrinkles creased her forehead and the corners of her eyes, her narrow face was still smooth and her green eyes sparkled. Her hair had turned a silky light gray several years earlier, and she thought the color actually more becoming than the previous jet black. Rachel wore her hair pinned into a neat bun on the back of her head, with short bangs and several wisps covering her ears. The style had remained unchanged for as long as she or anyone else remembered.

Pushing aside these rambling thoughts, Rachel examined the precise stitches of her work and was pleased with the effort. Glancing at the hourglass clock on the fireplace mantle, she saw it was time for her morning story to begin on the television. She started to put away her knitting when an outburst of furious yelping from the dog shattered the quietness.

The racket came from Pal-Two, the white and charcoal German shepherd that watched over the Baker place with a military guard's vigilance. Like his predecessor, Pal-Two had become a member of the family. When the dog barked furiously as he was doing now, it usually meant something was amiss on the place. Setting her knitting on the table, Rachel went to the side window in the kitchen, looked out through the screened back porch and discovered the source of Pal-Two's irritation.

Several of Sugar and Geraldine's offspring had managed to break out of their pen. "Oh, good grief," Rachel groaned as one of the shoats made a beeline through Caroline's rose bed with Pal-Two nipping at its heels.

By now, the shoats probably were wishing they had stayed in the safety of the lot, Rachel thought, as the hog squealed in pain, the result of Pal-Two's incisors taking a bite out of its rump. Rachel would have preferred to let the hogs run loose until the family came home, but Pal-Two's vigilance made it impossible for her to ignore the fugitive pigs. The dog's barking and the pigs' squealing were commotion enough. But left to his own means, Pal-Two would see to it that several of the shoats were gone before their time had come. As long as the hogs and cows stayed in their place, Pal-Two ignored them. But the dog dealt severely with wayward stock.

Knowing the family could ill afford a full-course pork dinner for a dog, Rachel sighed, fetched one of Sam's jackets and headed into the cold rain to herd the pigs back into their pens while there was still an opportunity to do so.

———

"Granny's not very cheerful," observed six-year-old Bonnie at the supper table.

While Caroline privately agreed with the assessment, she was dutybound to scold her youngest daughter. She did so halfheartedly, then concentrated on her plate.

When Rachel was upset or feeling poorly, she was not a cheery person indeed. In fact, she could be downright ornery. Having spent an hour of her day chasing pigs through a cold rain, Rachel was both upset and feeling poorly on this night, and her disposition was worse.

"Y'all oughtta have a tobacco stick brought across your backside the way I belted those hogs," Rachel muttered for her husband, son and oldest grandson's benefit. "There's a right way of doen things and a wrong way, and y'all should have done better."

Rachel was convinced that either Sam, Matt or Joe was guilty of careless repairs on the hog pen, and there was no reasoning with her. She blamed the three of them for her misfortunate morning, including a nasty fall on her backside. Chasing hogs had never been one of her preferred pastimes, and Rachel wanted her family to understand the depths of her disgruntlement. By now, everyone around the table had a good taste.

When she eschewed the supper dishes and retired to her room early for the night, complaining of a tickle in her throat and fretting about a cold, everyone was frankly glad to see her go.

———

"I don't feel so good," Rachel told her husband when Sam came to their bed later that night. "I'm afraid I might be comen down with the grippe."

"You're sounden chugged up—it's a fact," Sam replied sympathetically. "Let's see what we can do to doctor you."

A while later, Rachel settled under an extra blanket and tried to sleep. Sam had rubbed her down with Vicks salve and given her a tiny dose of liniment with sugar, surefire remedies for whatever ailed her.

But rest eluded Rachel. She was miserable through the night, feeling hot one minute and chilled the next. When she dozed at last, it was a troubled slumber, lasting only a few minutes before daylight peeked into the room and woke her.

Rachel lay in bed until Matt and Caroline came into the kitchen, which was next to hers and Sam's room. Not until she heard a match strike and determined suffi-cient time had passed for a fire to warm the kitchen was she ready to face the day. Climbing slowly from bed, she eased into her brown dress, pushed Sam awake and went into the kitchen.

"Good mornen," she greeted as Matt and Caroline returned the pleasantries.

"How you feelen this mornen, Ma?" Matt asked.

"Stove up and old," Rachel answered bluntly. "I think I've got a touch of the grippe—probably from be'en out in the cold yesterday."

"Bonnie's got a nasty cold, too," Matt replied. "Caroline was up with her a couple of times last night."

"I'm keepen her home from school today," Caroline said, peering closely at Rachel. "You do look peaked, Ma," she observed. "It might do you good to go back to bed and rest. I can take care of breakfast."

Rachel shrugged off the suggestion. "I'd rather stay up and busy. I'd just toss and turn in bed, and I did enough of that last night."

In short order, Rachel helped Caroline put breakfast on the table, then ushered the older children onto the school bus and checked on Bonnie. While Caroline washed the first of several loads of dirty clothes, Rachel cleaned the breakfast dishes. She labored through a few more chores before succumbing to the tiredness that made every movement a struggle. Telling Caroline to wake her for dinner, she retreated to the comfort of her bed and buried herself beneath the covers.

While Caroline spent a busy morning taking care of the household chores, Matt and Sam idled away leisurely hours. It was their slack time of the year, and the men used the opportunity to replenish themselves for the coming spring and summer when the workload would leave little time for relaxing. They changed the oil in several vehicles and chatted with Buck Franklin while he refilled the propane gas tank. Later, they sat in the kitchen, nursing several cups of coffee while discussing the farm's need for a new tractor. Ultimately, they would put off the purchase to another time, but the discussion was progress in itself after several lean years on the farm.

Caroline kept their cups filled with hot coffee and prepared chicken soup for the noon meal.

By dinnertime, Bonnie was out of bed and well on her way to feeling better. Although she continued to suffer from the sniffles, her fever and coughing had subsided. She was restless and bored, all of which added up to an excellent prognosis for recovery according to Caroline, who sent her daughter to check on Rachel.

"Granny's asleep," Bonnie announced upon her return to the kitchen. "She's snoren."

"Well don't mention that to anybody," Caroline advised. "I've never known your granny to snore, and she wouldn't appreciate people thinken she did. Go tell your daddy and grandpa to wash up for dinner."

While Bonnie skipped away to call Matt and Sam to the kitchen, Caroline dished up a bowl of the steaming chicken broth and carried it to Rachel. As soon as she cracked open the bedroom door, she heard the sound of wheezing breaths muted by the heavy cover of blankets and quilts that Rachel had piled upon the bed. Putting the soup bowl on the dresser, Caroline sat on the edge of the bed, lifted the covers, including the electric blanket, which was turned on high, and found her mother-in-law shivering. Rachel's face was flushed and her lips parched from the burning fever. Caroline placed a palm flat against the woman's forehead and was startled by the heat.

Rachel opened her eyes at the touch. "I kept thinken I would start to feel better," she said weakly. "But I'm worse, Caroline. I haven't felt this bad in a long time."

"You're burnen up with fever," Caroline noted, "and awfully chugged up. It sounds like a bad case of the croup. We should get you to a doctor this afternoon."

Rachel nodded agreement, and Caroline's concern mounted. Over the years, her mother-in-law had shunned doctors, relying on home remedies and a resolute faith in the good Lord to keep her healthy. Her willingness to seek medical treatment was out of character, and Caroline took it as an ominous sign. She gave the sick woman a quick smile, covered her again and went to make the arrangements to see a doctor.

———————

In times like this, Caroline wished the Bakers had a family doctor.

They took Rachel to the emergency room at the Tifton hospital, where her care fell into the hands of Dr. Martin Pittman. On first glance, Dr. Pittman appeared extremely fragile, more like a shriveled old man who probably had forgotten most of what he'd ever known about doctoring than a trustworthy physician. His body was thin and brittle, almost emaciated, and his eyes literally bulged from the sockets, coming perilously close it seemed to making contact with the thick, black-rimmed glasses that rested on a crooked nose. In stark contrast to the otherwise frail features, his ears appeared remarkably sturdy. They were gigantic flappers, so much so that people were never sure whether the doctor had excellent hearing or was ready for takeoff at a moment's notice.

Despite his odd appearance, Dr. Pittman came highly recommended by the Berrien sisters, who had warned Caroline not to be fooled by the appearances of a man who had survived the brutal Bataan Death March in the Philippines during World War II. Beneath his vulnerable exterior, the doctor possessed a keen medical mind, a heart of gold and a genuine desire to ease the suffering of others.

Nevertheless, he did little to inspire confidence in the Bakers upon first introduction.

Shuffling into the room where the Bakers were waiting, Martin Pittman was overcome by a coughing spasm. The Berrien sisters had forewarned Caroline that the doctor was prone to spells of breathless coughing and she had passed the word to her family. But nothing could have prepared them for the violent nature of the coughing fit. Gasping for breath, Dr. Pittman lurched toward the edge of Rachel's hospital bed on rickety legs and motioned for someone to slide a chair underneath him. Matt snatched up a nearby stool and hurried to put it beneath the man, who collapsed upon the steel seat with such force that everyone feared he might have broken a hipbone. Such was the commotion accompanying his entrance into the room that even the ailing Rachel raised her head in a dismayed show of concern.

"Are you okay, doc?" Sam asked.

"Well, Mr. Baker," the doctor replied in a drawl that was a bit Southern but mostly tired. "I don't mind tellen you that I'm just about tuckered out for one day. But the fact is, I'm not the one who's sick here." Turning to Rachel, he asked, "Now what seems to be the problem, Mrs. Baker?"

With Rachel feeling too poorly to respond, Caroline launched into a description of the older woman's symptoms, as well as her travails with the hogs a day earlier and her own suspicions that her mother-in-law might be coming down with pneumonia. The doctor confirmed her diagnosis with a cursory examination, then informed them he was admitting Rachel to the hospital for treatment.

"I'm orderen a private room," he said. "It costs a little more, but I think she'll rest easier and we can give her better treatment."

"Whatever you think is necessary, doc," Matt agreed.

"Good then," Dr. Pittman said. "While you folks get her admitted, we'll get her situated in the room and start some medication. I'll see you soon."

A few minutes later as they watched a hospital orderly guide away the gurney with Rachel stretched on it, a chilling premonition settled over Sam, Matt and Caroline. Where minutes before they had been concerned about Rachel's well-being, they now were genuinely worried. Their worry stemmed from the doctor's change in manner while he examined Rachel. As he had listened to her congested chest, Dr. Pittman had abandoned his folksy attitude and taken on a sense of urgency in his approach.

That urgency hurried them through the admitting process and on to Rachel's hospital room, where they found her lying in bed beneath a contraption of steel poles and plastic. She had drifted into an uneasy sleep, hounded by short, gasping breaths.

"I ordered the oxygen tent to make her as comfortable as possible," Dr. Pittman explained. "Don't be too alarmed by the looks of it."

"She's goen to be all right then," Sam inferred.

Instead of answering, Dr. Pittman motioned them to follow him. "I don't want to alarm you needlessly, Mr. Baker," he said when they were in the corridor outside Rachel's room. "But I'm also not goen to beat around the bush with you. Your wife is a very sick woman. You know as well as I do how dangerous pneumonia can be. Medical science has made great strides in treating it, but pneumonia is still a touch-and-go proposition, especially for older people. In her particular case, the disease developed very quickly and it's in both of her lungs. Frankly, I would have preferred starten her on medication several hours ago. Sometimes hours can make a big difference in a case like this. Right now, however, we need to do everything possible to keep her condition from worsening, and I assure you we'll do that. I will tell you this, though: The next few hours will be critical. You can help by keepen her spirits up when she's awake. You might say a prayer, too. I'm a firm believer in the great physician up above. He can do a whole lot more for Mrs. Baker than I can."

"Amen to that," Caroline concurred, soothed by the knowledge that a God-fearing man was entrusted with Rachel's care.

"I have a few things to take care of," the doctor continued, "then I'll be back to check on her. You might think about getten somethen to eat yourselves. We could be in for a long night, and y'all need to keep your strength up to help Mrs. Baker."

The doctor took his leave, and Sam, Matt and Caroline began their vigil.

———

Joe might as well have skipped his final two classes. From the moment he was called to the school office and told to telephone his father at home, Joe had been preoccupied. Once Matt informed him that Rachel was ill enough to require a hospital's care, he lost all interest in his schoolwork. World history paled in comparison to his concern for Rachel, and twice in trigonometry, the teacher ordered him to pay attention to the problem at hand.

He mentioned to Tom that Rachel was ill on the ride to New River from Cookville, and instead of lingering to talk with his friend when they got off the bus at the mercantile, he started the two-mile walk toward home. Normally, he would have proceeded right past the Berrien place, but today's circumstances sent him on a detour down the graveled lane to the elegant home, where Bonnie had spent the afternoon with Miss April and Miss June.

On any other day, the walk would have been an occasion for his mind to turn cartwheels over thoughts about his approaching high school graduation and the following fall when he would enter college. Today, however, Joe scanned the barren pecan orchard on either side of the road and longed for spring to restore life to these acres and acres of trees. Shaking away the dreary thoughts, he focused on the tasks awaiting him at home, making a mental list of the chores that needed his attention and assigning others to his brothers and sisters.

Before realizing it, he was approaching the Berrien home. The Berrien estate was a study in splendor, with immaculately maintained grounds and the red-bricked, Georgian house rising three stories in the distance. On his left was the guest cottage where his parents had spent their honeymoon night, and Joe paused to admire the scenic beauty. Leaving the path of the road, he cut across the lush lawn and arrived at the wide staircase that led to the front door. He climbed the brick steps, rang the doorbell and was admitted a moment later by Miss April.

She greeted Joe enthusiastically, taking his hand and leading him through the Greek archways of the foyer with its tapestries, mirrored coat rack and antique wash basin, past the white marbled stairway streaked with delicate traces of ruby red and emerald green.

They arrived at the sitting parlor, which was dominated by a grand piano and a dark mahogany mantle encasing a red-bricked fireplace. Heavily carved Gothic tables of walnut and mahogany were mixed and matched with Martha Washington chairs and Renaissance sofas upholstered in creamy white and brocaded burgundy. On top of the tables and a cherry lowboy were precious lamps and many of the family's smaller treasures acquired over the years. The room had polished hardwood floors covered by two Persian rugs, each of which had a single diamond-shaped medallion and scrolled floral borders. One rug was solid red with hints of black and ivory in the scrolling; the other was a deeper red with traces of black, pale blue and dark green in the scrolling. Two chandeliers hung perfectly over the medallions in the middle of the rugs. But what Joe admired most about the parlor was the worn black leather recliner and the new television console.

The parlor reflected the tastes of the Berrien sisters and their brother. It was fancy without the slightest show of pretentiousness, a homey, cozy room where Paul, April and June spent the majority of their waking hours at home.

Bonnie was sitting on the floor beside the huge fireplace, playing with a porcelain doll and drinking hot chocolate with melted marshmallows.

"Afternoon, Miss June," Joe greeted them. "Bonnie."

He glanced at both ladies and nodded to his sister who ignored his greeting by keeping her attention glued to the doll. "If I had to guess, I'd say y'all are spoilen my little sister."

"We're doen our best," Miss June said heartily.

"I suspect she'd just as soon as stay here with y'all than go home with me," Joe told the ladies.

"And that would be perfectly fine with us," Miss April answered. "Bonnie's an adorable little girl."

"Practically an angel," Miss June said as Bonnie favored her with an angelic smile.

Joe laughed at their flattery of his baby sister. "She is sweet," he said, crossing the room to sweep Bonnie off the floor into his arms. The little girl squealed and threw her arms around Joe's neck as he kissed her on the cheek. "Hi, pumpkin," he said.

"Granny's sick," Bonnie informed him promptly. "She might have the pneumonia."

"Pneumonia?" Joe replied with a questioning glance at the two sisters.

"I'm afraid so," June confirmed. "Your daddy called here not too long ago and said they were admitten Rachel to the hospital. He wasn't sure when they'll be home tonight but said you'd know what to do around the farm. You children are welcome to have supper with us tonight if you'd like. In fact, Bonnie could just stay here with us for the night."

"Thank you, Miss June," Joe replied. "It's kind of you to offer, but I think it would be best if we waited at home. We'll be fine."

"Indeed, you will," April agreed. "It's perfectly understandable that you'd want to stay around the house. Should y'all need anything, though, don't hesitate to call on us."

"Thank you," Joe said again.

"Do let us drive y'all home, Joe," June offered. "Bonnie doesn't need to be out in this cold weather. It might freshen up her cold."

"We'd be much obliged."

————

Riding home in the backseat of the Berriens' silver Cadillac was like taking a trip with Lucy Ricardo and Ethel Mertz at the wheel, and the best thing Joe could say about the experience was that it was blessedly brief.

At home, grateful to be out of the car, he thanked the women for the ride, reassured them he and his brothers and sisters could fend for themselves and waved goodbye. He led Bonnie into the house, settled her in front of the television and returned outside to begin the afternoon chores.

His other sisters and brothers arrived home from school a short time later. Joe watched them exit the bus and head for the house. Once they were inside, he began counting to himself and walking toward the porch. At fifteen, he reached the porch steps and the front door burst open, with Summer leading the charge of curious siblings, each of them with a question.

Joe told them everything he knew about Rachel's condition, which was just enough to make them suspect he was sharing only pieces of the story. He tried to reassure them all was well, but the effort was so pitiful that even his own concern for their grandmother magnified.

"Is Granny gonna die?" Luke asked suddenly.

"No!" Joe replied testily. "There's no sense getten ourselves worked up when we don't know the situation."

"But, Joe," Carrie interrupted. "Granny must be awful sick to be in the hospital."

"That's right," chimed in Summer. "Granny doesn't put much stock in doctors and hospitals. Are you tellen us everything there is to tell?"

"I've told y'all everything I know," Joe answered patiently. "We'll have to wait until we hear from Daddy and Mama before there's anything else to tell. Until then, though, we're gonna do what we're supposed to. There's work to do, and every one of us has a job. Summer, you and Carrie are in charge of supper and taking care of Bonnie. And Bonnie, you behave yourself. Luke, you gather the eggs and feed the dog and cats. John and I will feed up and do whatever else needs to be done outside. Let's get to it."

Even Summer, who tended toward the bossy and brash side, knew when her brother meant business. With only token grumbling, she ordered her sisters to the kitchen and began planning supper. Joe barked another round of orders at his brothers, then sent them on their way.

———

Luke gathered eggs from the chicken coop and the various nests that several hens had made around the place. In deference to Rachel, he worked diligently, careful not to break any eggs, and held his tongue, even when a curse word appeared on his lips after he stepped in chicken manure. Finally, after plucking the last egg from its nest, he considered the plight of his grandmother.

He was plagued by unsettling thoughts, some of which he shared with Matilda, his grandmother's favorite Rhode Island Red layer, before he carried the egg basket into the house.

———

Joe ordered John to give Brindy a pail of sour corn mash to keep the cow still while she was milked. When the animal was eating contentedly, Joe pulled the milking stool beside her, took hold of her teats and began squeezing streams of warm milk into the waiting pail. He then directed his brother across the road to the corncrib, telling him to fill the two tubs for the hogs.

Joe detested milking nearly as much as he despised butchering hogs. In this day and age, he thought, it seemed ridiculous to milk a single cow. But whereas Matt had been willing to leave the butchering to the abattoir, he was unlikely to abandon the milking. Brindy held a sentimental spot among the family's hearts, even in Joe's. He remembered all too well the many times Brindy provided the only milk his family could afford to put on the table.

The cow gave her milk easily. When she was dry, Joe gave the old girl a friendly pat on the rear, put away the stool and carried the pail of fresh milk to the kitchen, with orders for his sisters to strain it.

On his return to the barn, he discovered that John already had carried the tubs of corn over from the crib. Picking up the first bucket, he flung the corn over the gate behind the barn, scattering the yellow kernels so that every hog could eat its share. He divided the other bucket among three special sections of the barn, which housed farrowing sows and their litters. A series of sliding gates separated the three pins, all of which contained dirt floors and water troughs carved from large tree trunks shortly after Sam and Rachel had bought the farm.

"Thanks for luggen the corn over here," Joe told his brother as John picked up the empty pails and started back across the road to the crib. "Let me water up here, and I'll be over to feed the others."

When the troughs were filled with water, Joe went across the road and tossed four more tubs of corn to the main herd of hogs, while John took care of the watering. "Luke's talken to the chickens again," John observed as they walked back across the road to the barn. "I wonder what he's tellen them."

"I wonder what they're tellen him," Joe remarked, giving the eleven-year-old boy a playful nudge on the shoulder.

With the cows growing restless, bellowing for food of their own as they grazed in the pecan orchard, John climbed the loft stairs where the sweet hay was stored.

The loft was still half full of hay that had been cut from the back pasture last fall, and the sweet-smelling, sunny aroma was ingrained in the wooden structure. John inhaled deeply, then grabbed the two nearest bales, tugged them to the edge of the porch and pushed them over the side.

Joe watched them fall to the ground, then cut apart the binding string with his pocket knife and moved on to the barn's lower crib where the scratchy peanut hay was stored. He climbed into the crib, tossed one bale out the door and returned for a second.

"Do you really think Granny will be okay?"

The question surprised Joe, who had expected his brother to be on his way down the stairs to begin feeding the clumps of hay to the bellowing cows. Instead, John was peering down at him from the loft window that overlooked the crib.

Joe gazed upwards, trying to come up with an answer that would satisfy his brother. In his contemplation, he spied a rusted nail sticking out of the wall below the loft window. Once when they had been playing in the loft, John had miscalculated a backward jump from the window, falling straight down and raking the bottom of his chin across the rusty nail. The boy carried a thin scar as a permanent reminder of the accident.

Joe pointed to his own chin. "Do you remember the time you scraped your chin on that nail there?" he asked John.

"I was shown off," John recalled.

Joe held up his left hand, pointing to a jagged scar that wrapped around the fleshy outer side to the bottom of his palm. "I was shown off, too," he said. "I jumped out of that bay tree across the road and landed smack-dab on a broken drink bottle. Needed twenty-three stitches to sew it up. I remember landen on my hand and somethen stingen like the dickens. When I looked down at my hand, there was blood everywhere. I took off runnen across the road, screamen at the top of my lungs. You'd've thought I was dyen."

"Who were you shown off for?" John asked.

"Do you remember Frieda?" Joe said. "She was Aunt Euna's granddaughter."

John shook his head negatively.

"Her family lives in Texas now and they don't come around these parts much anymore, so maybe you don't remember her," Joe continued. "Anyway, this happened before you were born. I think I was tryen to prove that I was a better tree climber than she was, and Frieda dared me to jump. Ever since then, every time I've seen her, she mentions that day and wants to see my scar."

"I guess we've all got a few memorable scars," John remarked.

On Summer's right calf was the faded reminder of the time she had fallen through a cultivator while using it as a podium to boss her younger brothers and sisters. The front of Carrie's left thigh was marked with a perfect oval from the time she had run into a hawthorn bush and one of the prickly thorns had broken off beneath the skin. Although Matt practically had performed minor surgery, the nettle had remained lodged in Carrie's leg until the sore festered several weeks later and the thorn came out by itself. Indeed, from the eye patch that covered Sam's bad eye to the gash across the bottom of Bonnie's foot, everyone in the family had suffered in one way or another, Joe reminded his brother.

"These things happen from time to time, Bud," Joe continued, invoking his personal nickname for John. "People get hurt and they get sick. I wish I knew what to tell you about Granny. I wish I could say she was goen to be fine. But I honestly don't know. All we can do is hope and pray for the best."

"You're right," John agreed, as yet another cow bellowed for food.

Joe grabbed another bale of the peanut hay and heaved it over the crib's side. He started to climb out of the crib when John stopped him with another comment about their grandmother.

"I keep thinken about that horse," he said. "The one that belonged to Granny's brother. Do you remember that story the way Granny told it?"

"It's not somethen you can forget," Joe replied.

"Would you tell it to me?" John pleaded as the cows bellowed again for their hay.

Joe was torn between honoring his brother's request and answering the cattle's call. He glanced from the cows to John, then nodded and took a seat on the crib floor, leaning against a stack of hay. "You'll have to settle for the short version," he said.

The horse tale was part of the family's folklore. Rachel repeated the story sparingly, often with a specific purpose in mind, usually as an example of the trouble that comes when people do things they shouldn't.

"When Granny's brother, Alton—the one who drowned—was nine, their daddy gave him a filly," Joe began. "It was a quarter horse, beautiful, reddish-brown with black markens on her face. Alton loved the horse. He named her Queenie and treated her like a queen. Alton taught her jumpen tricks and snuck apples, sugar and anything else he could from under his sister's nose so that Queenie could have her treats.

"Alton loved that horse probably more than anything in the world. He would have done anything for her. Unfortunately, he also had a bad habit of smoking a tobacco pipe in the barn with Queenie. Now anybody with any sense knows that it's dumb to smoke or have any kind of fire around a barn that's filled with hay. But Alton was careless. He figured nothen bad could ever happen.

"One day, when Alton should have been busy doen his chores, he disobeyed Granny. Instead of hoe'en in the garden like she had told him to do, he snuck off to the barn to smoke his pipe. For some reason, he laid his pipe down in the barn and then forgot all about it. Anyway, he went off somewhere else, and that pipe caught the hay on fire.

"Sometime that mornen before dinner, Granny glanced out the kitchen window and saw flames shooten from the roof of the barn. She knew right away that the builden was a goner, but she wanted to save Queenie. By the time she reached the barn, however, the fire had engulfed the builden. The heat was intense, and the flames were whippen toward Queenie.

"The poor horse was scared to death. She was whinnyen and kicken savagely at the walls. But she was trapped and there was nothen anyone could do to save her. Even so, Granny was determined not to let that horse suffer. She raced back to the house, jammed a shell in her daddy's shotgun and was back at the barn in seconds flat. By then, Queenie had squeezed as far away from the fire as possible, and the flames were licken at her beautiful coat. Ignoren the heat, Granny ran to the edge of the fire, took careful aim through the flames and shot that horse dead center in the head. The poor animal died instantly, and seconds later, the barn's roof caved in and turned that builden into a crematorium.

"Poor Granny was distraught. She went back to the house, told the twins, Edna and Euna, to finish cooken dinner and took to her bed for the afternoon. Later, Alton came to see her. He was torn up about Queenie, especially knowen that he had caused the fire. Granny says he never really forgave himself for starten that fire. But regardless, Alton told Granny how grateful he was that she had spared Queenie the agony of burnen to death. He told her she was brave and courageous and had done what needed to be done.

"Now Granny had always been one who believed in doen what needed to be done. But that day made her realize that life's hardships and its joys were all the same. You take things for what they are, then you put them behind you and get on with life. That afternoon was the first time Granny ever told herself, 'It's time to get on with the business of liven.' And ever since then, she's been doen just that."

Joe and John were silent for a moment.

"Sometimes I think that's the saddest story I've ever heard," John remarked at last. "But I suppose there are worse things."

"Yeah," Joe agreed.

"Anyway, I sure do hope nobody decides that Granny's so sick she needs to be put out of her misery like poor Queenie," John continued.

Joe laughed aloud at the idea. John frowned for a moment, then smiled, saying, "That was a dumb thing to say, wasn't it?"

"I just hadn't thought about it in that way," Joe replied cheerfully. "But I think everybody probably gets somethen different from that story."

John glanced across the crib, toward the house as if he were about to share a secret. "Do you wanna know somethen else about that story?" he asked.

"What's that?" Joe replied.

"A few Sundays ago, when the preacher talked about the fire and brimstone of Hell, I thought about poor Queenie and Uncle Alton and Granny," John said. "To tell you the truth, Joe, I'm not too fond of fire, and the prospect of burnen in Hell is pretty scary. Chances are that if you wind up in Hell, there's not a bullet made that's gonna spare you from the torment. And even if there was one, I feel sure Granny wouldn't be around to pull the trigger. Honestly, Joe, it made me think long and hard about repenten and getten saved."

Joe smiled again and shook his head. "Everybody has a reason for getten saved, John," he said. "I reckon yours is as good as anybody else's."

"Well, I'm just thinken about it," John admitted. "I wonder what Granny would think about my reasonen."

"She'd be pleased as punch," Joe answered quickly. "She'd say the good Lord works in mysterious ways, and she'd probably even decide He had your salvation in mind on the day when she had to shoot poor Queenie."

"Maybe I'll mention it to her when she gets home from the hospital," John remarked.

"You do that, Bud," Joe said. "And I'm glad you asked to hear that story. I think it was a good tonic for what ails us. Now come on down from there and let's feed these cows. They're hungry, and I'm beginnen to get that way, too."

———

Standing at the kitchen sink, Summer attacked the chicken fryer with the swift strokes of someone who knew how to use a cutting knife, while Carrie peeled the last of the potatoes and put them on the stove to boil.

The kitchen showed all the signs of a normal evening, with water running in the sink, pots percolating on the stove and a blaze popping in the fireplace. But the evening was far from run-of-the-mill. Without the familiar presence of Caroline and Rachel, the kitchen seemed hollow rather than homey. Carrie tried to fill the void, but Summer responded with muttered grunts and stone-faced silence. At last, Carrie abandoned attempts at making conversation and fled the room wordlessly, leaving Summer to herself.

Summer was thinking about the argument she'd had with her grandmother on New Year's Eve. After all these weeks, they still had not settled their differences. While housework and cooking were not high on Summer's list of fun things to do, she had never intended to criticize Rachel's rigid beliefs. Although her grandmother prided herself for honoring her wifely duties, she would have overlooked Summer's criticism of her devotion to household chores. But Summer had overstepped the bounds of criticism when she lashed out at one thing dear to Rachel, and that was sewing.

Sewing was a common denominator between Summer and Rachel.

Summer had inherited her grandmother's skills with a needle and thread. Under Rachel's tutelage, she had fashioned her first garment, an apron, at age six. Soon afterward, she had completed her first dress, and both her interest and skill for dressmaking seemed to increase proportionally with every stitch and hem.

This passion for sewing was unique to Summer and Rachel. Caroline had neither the talent nor the desire to try her hand at tailoring, while Carrie and Bonnie lacked the patience. Over the years, however, Summer had proven an eager apprentice and Rachel a willing mentor. The bond between them was strong, and their work had afforded ample opportunity for conversation. During these talks, Rachel had shared the stories of her life, and now as she prepared supper in her grandmother's absence, Summer reflected on that life.

As a child, Rachel had been carefree, with just enough spunk to get herself into trouble and charm to talk her way out of it. All that changed when her mother came down with rheumatic heart disease. While waiting a long year for her mother to die, Rachel had been forced to develop the discipline that now seemed such a natural part of her being. When Merry Willis finally died, Rachel had retreated to a safe, solitary place of the mind, where she could remember the good times they had shared and console herself with visions of her mother singing with angels in Heaven. Her escape had lasted until a few days after the funeral when the flock of mourners bade their final condolences, gathered up baskets of food and took their leave. When everyone was gone, Rachel was left with the reality of cooking and cleaning for her father, two small twin sisters and a baby brother.

Her childhood memories faded quickly, and her discipline rose to the challenge as Rachel became the woman of the house. She became the cook, washwoman, nursemaid and authority figure for her brother and sisters, who soon came to think of her more as their mother than a sibling. Often left alone in the house for days at a time while their father peddled the goods that provided the family its livelihood, Rachel learned early the value of a stern personality, terse words and disapproving frowns to keep the household under control. To casual acquaintances and even to her own family on occasion, she was an austere woman.

The one daydream Rachel indulged was of her mother singing with angels. She would imagine her mother's voice rolling across streets of gold, bringing Heaven to a standstill with its melodious flow and perfect resonance, and Rachel would remember her mother's love and sweet disposition. The memory kept her heart pure and nurtured her goodness.

Those qualities had attracted Sam. He had taught her to laugh again, to smile and to show affection. When the situation required, Rachel would slip back into her old, austere, stubborn ways. But she was known now for her tolerance.

Still, she retained the vestiges of her youth, including a stout belief that hard work brought rewards. When there was a job to do, whether pleasant or not, Rachel tackled it without complaint. She refused to consider work of any kind a hardship, and she never wished for a better lot in life. It was a characteristic passed along to all the Baker women, even Summer, who was proud to carry the mantle for her grandmother on this night. Someone had to prepare supper for the family tonight, and Summer was the best person for the job. As with most household chores, cooking was not her favorite duty, but she would complete the job and hope tomorrow might bring another task more to her liking.

Rachel believed people should be satisfied with today and hope for a better tomorrow. Never one to mince words, she felt obliged to share this philosophy with others when the situation warranted. For instance, her teenage years had been more tedious than festive and she tired quickly of hearing people praise "the good old days." More than once, she had rebuked Sam when he spoke fondly of simpler times when they were young. She even chided Miss April and Miss June when the Berrien sisters voiced nostalgic longings for the gay parties hosted by their parents.

"June, April, the time has come for y'all to get on with the business of liven," Rachel had informed the ladies. "The old days belong in the closet with all the old things. Or better yet, toss them out altogether. What's past is past, and the most you can get from it are good memories—not to dwell on, mind you, but to cherish and think of fondly. I've tried to enjoy every day of my life and wouldn't change a single thing even if I could. But I tell you one thing: My favorite day is tomorrow 'cause there's always that chance it will be better than today.

"So ladies," Rachel had concluded triumphantly. "If it's parties you're pinen for, then I suggest you go home and start plannen. The party you have tomorrow will bring a lot more satisfaction than the memories of years ago. And by the way, June, April, I'd be mighty pleased to be included on your guest list."

Two weeks later, Summer had heard a hint of satisfaction in her grandmother's voice when Rachel opened the mail and announced the family had been invited to a Fourth of July celebration hosted by the Berriens.

Her thoughts returned to the argument with Rachel on New Year's Eve. Summer wasn't sure why she had challenged her grandmother, but she regretted the outburst, especially her flippant criticism of sewing. She had not sewed with Rachel a single time since the argument, and she missed their friendship as well as the work itself.

Somehow, Summer told herself, she would find a way to atone for her blunder and make up for lost time with her grandmother. She refused to consider the possibility they might not have that opportunity.

———

Through the long afternoon into the evening, Martin Pittman fought for the life of Rachel Baker. He feared it was a losing battle.

The woman lapsed in and out of a coma. Her fever soared dangerously high, her lungs filled with fluid and she struggled to claim her next breath. At one point, expecting Rachel would die within the hour, Dr. Pittman decided to tell her family to brace themselves for the inevitable. He turned to motion them from the room and found himself looking into the faces of three people who expected a miracle. As much as anyone, the doctor believed faith could accomplish the impossible. Sighing to himself, he gave the Bakers a brief smile instead, asked for divine intervention, suctioned Rachel's lungs and called for more ice.

A few hours later, the fever broke; Rachel was breathing easier and resting.

"I don't mind tellen y'all—I was afraid we were goen to lose her for a while there," Dr. Pittman told Sam, Matt and Caroline. "I'm still not convinced she's out of the woods. It might be a lull, but she's definitely better for the time be'en. Mrs. Baker's a very strong woman, which is why she's alive. Now, I'm goen to get some rest, and I suggest y'all do the same. I'll check on her later."

———

With the doctor's temporary assurance, Matt heeded his wife's advice and went home to check on the children and get some needed sleep. The house seemed unnaturally quiet when he let himself in the front door shortly before ten o'clock, but otherwise, everything appeared normal. Bonnie and Luke had been put to bed, and the older children were gathered around the kitchen table doing their homework. Joe was showing Summer how to diagram complex sentences, and John was quizzing Carrie for a spelling test. The dishes were washed and drying beside the sink, and a fire crackled in the kitchen hearth. It was like a thousand other evenings at the house, but the picture was incomplete, missing a huge portion of the vitality that made this house a home.

A creaking floorboard between the dining room and kitchen betrayed his arrival home, and the quietness exploded with a dozen questions all begging for answers. Matt hushed his children, then told them Rachel was gravely ill and had come close to dying earlier in the evening. Now, however, the doctor seemed to believe she might recover.

It was a sobering answer to their questions, and the prognosis seemed only slightly less bleak. In their abstract worries, some gloomy thoughts had passed through the minds of each child. But the full scope of reality caused their hearts to flutter with fear. Afraid of what the answers might be, they ceased their questions and steered the conversation to safer ground.

"When can we see her?" Joe asked his father.

"I'm not sure," Matt answered. "We'll have to see how she's getten along tomorrow."

"You're probably hungry, Daddy," Summer commented, sliding off the bench. "There's a plate warmen in the oven for you. I'll get it."

Matt waved her back to the table. "I'll eat later," he said. "Right now, y'all finish your homework and get on to bed. We'll have to count on you for breakfast in the mornen, Summer. Maybe supper again tomorrow night."

"If y'all can stand to eat it, I can stand to cook it," Summer drawled.

Everyone chuckled quietly, as if unsure whether humor was appropriate at a time like this. One by one, they put away their homework, knowing it could be finished on the school bus tomorrow morning. At last, each of them kissed their father goodnight and went to bed, determined to honor his request to say a prayer for Rachel.

————

Sometime before midnight, Matt still sat at the kitchen table with the plate of fried chicken, mashed potatoes and gravy before him. The food was cold, and the ice in his tea glass melted. His thoughts drifted back and forth over his childhood, then settled on the single moment when he had made the largest leap to manhood.

He had been sitting with Rachel in this very room on a Sunday afternoon, listening to the radio. A brisk wind howled outside the house, echoing through the chimney. Matt was at the kitchen table reading a Superman comic book, while Rachel knitted in her rocking chair. Sam had been in Atlanta, trying to sell a truckload of vegetables at the State Farmer's Market. The trip had been a bone of contention between him and Rachel. She was staunchly opposed to commerce of any kind on Sundays, while Sam was equally determined that they needed the money.

All in all, it had been a pleasant day. Then, the news bulletin came over the radio, and their peace was shattered.

Engrossed in the end of his comic book, Matt missed the initial announcement. In fact, the whole bulletin might have escaped his attention had he not noticed a slight, uncharacteristic movement from his mother. Glancing up from his comic book, he found Rachel hunched over in the rocking chair, frowning at the radio with her knitting laying idle in her lap. Around then, his mind registered the radio announcement, especially the mention of Pearl Harbor where Joseph was stationed. He dropped his comic book, which he would never finish, and leaned forward to listen to the news.

"Pearl Harbor," Rachel said softly when the announcement had been read twice over the radio. "That's where your brother is."

"Yeah, Ma," Matt responded as if she had asked him a question.

"Oh, Lord," Rachel moaned, leaning back in the rocking chair with a dazed expression on her face. "I hope Joseph is okay."

"Don't go getten upset, Ma," Matt urged. "We don't know anything about what happened."

He'd wanted to be optimistic for his mother's sake, but actually, Matt had been struck by a gut feeling that Joseph already lay dead somewhere in Pearl Harbor. As he sat with his mother waiting for additional news and listening to the president's speech, Matt had made several decisions about his future, including marrying Caroline and joining the Army.

When dusk approached, Rachel had taken him by the hand and led Matt to the pecan orchard, where they knelt down on the ground and she delivered the most powerful prayer her son had ever heard. Rachel had intoned God to spare her son from death, but even as she prayed, Matt sensed his mother knew in her heart that Joseph was gone. The prayer, which had begun as an appeal for Joseph's life, ended as a plea for his soul and a seat at the right hand of God.

At some point in that prayer, Matt had lost his faith. He had never given up a belief in God, but he'd lost confidence in Him. It was a scary feeling, even now after all those years of being faithless, and Matt kept these thoughts to himself so that Caroline or anyone else would not see the dark spot in his heart.

Religion had been the major quarrel between Caroline and Matt throughout their marriage. From time to time, they argued over his refusal to attend church, even on special occasions like Easter and Christmas. And once Caroline had come right out and demanded to know whether Matt believed in God. The question had jarred him.

"Of course, I believe in God," he shouted angrily. "What kind of question is that?"

His forceful answer had calmed Caroline, and their arguments had ceased some-what. While he still refused to attend church, Matt forced himself to take a more active role in the Christian training of his children before they came to the perception that he did not believe in God. He read to them from the Bible, listened to their prayers and took his turn saying grace at mealtimes. And somewhere along the way, Matt realized, he had come once again to believe in the power of those prayers, which probably explained why he had exhorted his children to say a prayer for Rachel earlier in the night.

Maybe Matt had started to believe again in the power of God as he gazed on the sweet faces of his children as they asked the good Lord to bless their daddy. Or maybe he had been convinced on one of those occasions when he heard his wife and mother sharing their hopes of getting him baptized. More likely, his faith had come back to him in stages. While he still had reservations that religion could comfort him as it did Caroline and Rachel, Matt knew the time had come to put his trust in a higher authority.

Years had passed since Matt had taken the initiative to pray for anything other than thanks for food. Now, when he groped for the appropriate words, they eluded him. But Matt was persistent. He was determined to put his trust in God.

"Blind faith," he murmured, remembering an intonement from his mother years earlier.

Rachel had lived her life by blind faith in God, drawing strength from it to survive the hard times and never losing sight of it through the good times. Matt knew he must count on that blind faith to carry his mother through another ordeal and return her home.

CHAPTER 3

THE TELEPHONE JARRED THE household from deep slumber to gripping fear. Matt's eyes darted open before the first short ring ended. He lay glued to the bed, hoping that grim news might disappear if he ignored the messenger. On the third ring, he remembered the phone was ringing in the Carters' home as well. The short ring belonged to the Bakers, the long to the Carters, and this one was unmistakably short.

Matt hurried from the bed to the knotted cypress table by the front door and grabbed the phone. He took a calming breath, picked up the receiver and said hello on the fifth ring.

"Matt."

It was Caroline. Her voice whispered in his ear, and she gave him time to brace for bad news.

So much for blind faith, Matt thought.

He wondered how long he had slept. He watched Joe bound into the hall, followed by John and Luke, before his eyes caught Summer. She clung to the door-facing of the girl's room, holding on for dear life.

His heart panicked. "Yeah," he answered. "What is it?"

"She's bad off, Matt," Caroline said. "You need to get here as soon as possible."

"I'm on my way," he promised. "How's Pa taken this?"

"He's holden up well for the moment," she replied. "But he's scared."

"I'll be there soon," Matt pledged again as he hung up the phone.

"Daddy?" Joe said.

"Is Granny okay?" Luke asked.

"Your mama says she's taken a turn for the worse," Matt announced calmly. "I need to get to the hospital."

"May I go with you, Daddy?" Joe asked.

"Me, too?" Summer added.

Matt considered the request, then nodded. "Okay," he agreed. "Just get dressed as fast as you can. We need to get there."

Glancing at the brass clock on Caroline's nightstand as he jerked on jeans and a shirt, Matt noted the time was just past four. A minute later, he was standing on the front porch, giving John and Carrie a forced smile, telling them to set the alarm clock so they would not miss the school bus and urging them back to sleep. He was reconsidering the decision to leave the younger children by themselves when a set of car lights came barreling down the road.

"Who in the world is that?" Joe asked.

His answer came seconds later as Amelia Carter wheeled her blue sedan into the yard, cut the bright lights and shut off the engine. Dressed in a worn housecoat with rollers in her hair, the mercantile owner was a far sight from the pretty picture she usually presented outside the privacy of her home.

"I heard the telephone," she said by way of greeting as she came toward them. "I figured you could use some help with the children."

Matt was touched by her thoughtfulness. Few people saw this side of Amelia, because they refused to look past her faults. It was true that Amelia gossiped too much, overwhelmed the timid with her forceful personality and sometimes got grand notions about herself. But she also possessed a generous spirit, a kind heart that expressed itself through deeds more than words. When the world went awry, Amelia believed in lacing up her boot strings and setting it right—a like it or lump it attitude that prevented her from making many true friends but earned the grudging respect of many acquaintances.

Thinking of her now, Matt remembered an essay Joe had written about Amelia. Joe had described her thoughtfulness as "callused compassion," and Matt thought the description fit perfectly. Except for those times when she became Queen Amelia, she was as genuine as anyone Matt knew. Over the years, he and the rest of her friends had learned to tolerate the woman's majestic moods. And, fortunately, for everyone, especially her husband and son, Amelia's royal moods were diminishing with age.

"You've taken a load off my mind, Amelia," Matt said as she stepped onto the porch. "I was gonna leave the kids by themselves, but then started wonderen whether that was the right thing to do. I appreciate you maken the decision easy. Make yourself comfortable, and go ahead and send the kids to school in the mornen."

Amelia gave him a caring smile. "What about your mama, Matt?"

"Caroline says she's bad off," Matt replied. "That's all I know."

———

Rachel was suffocating beneath the plastic tent. She fought for a breath of air, her arms thrashing and her body contorting on the hospital bed between fits of coughing and gagging. Vaguely, she heard the doctor order Sam and Caroline from the room, then tell a nurse they were losing her. She craved a single breath of air, to fill her lungs with oxygen, but the pneumonia had a chokehold on her windpipe. The realization came to Rachel that she was fighting for her life. And losing.

She heard Dr. Pittman's cracked voice again, this time instructing the nurse to suggest that Caroline call Matt and any other close kin to the hospital at once. Although unfamiliar with the Catholic way of death, Rachel acquired a sudden understanding of last rites. But while she felt at peace with the Lord, prepared for death as Preacher Cook put it, Rachel was not ready to die. She wanted a few more years with Sam and the children. She had a quilt to finish, and she wanted to make a dress from the blue gabardine material Caroline had given her at Christmas.

Still, she supposed if God was ready for her, then she would have no choice in the matter. Everyone had an appointed time with death and if hers was at hand, then she would leave behind unfinished work. Rachel had a vague notion that she should have planned better. Then, a gagging cough sent her thoughts swirling, and she lost consciousness.

Heat as hot as the fires of Hell itself roused her sometime later. Her throat was parched, her tongue swollen. A thin line of fever blisters stretched across her bottom lip. She was drenched with sweat, and her chest felt as if it had been beaten with a sledgehammer. Her breath came in shallow gasps, and the act of breathing caused a pain worse than childbirth.

Somewhere in the room, a coffee pot percolated. Rachel tried to smell the strong aroma, but detected only the odor of anesthesia. To her horror, she realized the noise was coming from her own fluid-filled lungs. Rachel wanted to touch her heart, to make sure it still beat, but she was too weak to lift her hand. She began to wonder if each breath would be her last, and time ceased to exist as Rachel knew it.

An eternity later, the emaciated doctor stood at her bedside, sponging alcohol across her face and forehead. Two nurses packed ice around her. Her body heat dropped quickly from the boiling point to something merely lukewarm. Soon, she felt cool and then ice-cold. Chills shook Rachel, and her teeth chattered like a jack-hammer. She was too tired to think, too numb to feel, so Rachel cleared her mind and surrendered to the deep blackness.

———

Dr. Pittman sighed. "Sleep is the best medicine for her now," he told the two nurses who were with him in Rachel's room. "But how she can manage it while packed in ice is a mystery to me."

He pulled up his stethoscope and checked her lungs. Her pulse was almost steady, her blood pressure returning to normal. But the congestion in her chest was still thick.

Rachel's propensity for survival amazed the doctor. Two times now, he had been convinced she was at death's door, and twice she had been turned away. At the moment, a complete recovery seemed possible. But Dr. Pittman was determined to season his message with caution when he delivered the prognosis to her family. He saluted the nurses, then stepped outside the room where the Bakers were waiting.

He smiled thinly to ease their greatest fears, noting Matt had returned to the hospital with a young man and a girl in tow. "Your wife is a remarkable woman," he addressed Sam.

"Yes," Sam nodded. "She is at that."

"She's lucky to be alive," Dr. Pittman continued. "Honestly, I don't know how she did it. She's stabilized for the moment, but we have a long way to go before we're out of the woods. She's packed in ice now to lower her temperature. I hoped the fever would burn itself out, but it kept climben. The ice helped get a handle on it. Right now, she's sleepen. I wish I could tell you with certainty that everything will be okay. But I can't. I'm cautiously optimistic, but then again, this could be another calm before the storm. We'll have to wait and see."

Seconds later, the door to Rachel's room opened and a nurse called frantically for the doctor. "She's having trouble breathen again," the nurse announced. "You better suction her."

Dr. Pittman moved quickly inside the room, leaving Sam, Matt, Caroline, Joe and Summer to their collective fear. Caroline hugged her father-in-law in a protective embrace, as Matt slumped against the wall and Summer buried her head against Joe's chest.

They were hoping for a miracle, but all they could do was wait. And pray, Caroline decided. "Joe, you and Summer go to the chapel," she instructed her children. "Find a Bible, read John 4:16 aloud and then pray for your grandmother. God can make her better.

"Grandpa," she continued, looking Sam in the eyes. "You, Matt and I will do our prayen right here outside Ma's door. And if it's God's will, then she will get better."

"You're right, daughter," Sam sighed, taking Caroline's hands. "Prayer is our best hope."

"Will you join us, Matt?" Caroline said.

The question caught Matt by surprise. Startled, he frowned at Caroline, then saw Joe and Summer staring at him, perplexed by his indecision. Sensing their confusion, he knew at once this was not a time to create doubts of any kind. He pushed off the wall, nodded his children on their way to the chapel and went to stand beside his wife and father. They joined hands, bowed heads and offered their prayers to God. Matt did his best again to surrender to blind faith.

Rachel woke fully alert, sensing at once that she was better. She was weary from the struggle to breathe, and her chest ached with each rise and fall. But it was a dull pain, unlike the earlier crushing blows that had caved her breast. At the worst, it felt as if she had a bad case of the croup deep in her chest.

Sam was at her side, dozing stiffly in a straight-back chair that probably would crick his neck. She called weakly to him. Her voice, hoarse and strange even to Rachel, failed to rouse her husband.

She scanned the room, allowing her gaze to settle on the window blinds that shielded faded daylight. The dimness suited Rachel's mood. She felt more glum than physically sick. At a time when she should have been rejoicing over her improving health, Rachel was fretful.

For as long as she could remember, Rachel had looked to the future, hoping tomorrow or the next day would bring better times. She filled her days with hard work and sacrifice, believing those virtues would bring rewards one day—if not on this earth, then in Heaven.

Her life was dedicated to God and family, and the commitment was unwavering on both counts. Over the years, Rachel's faith in God had grown even stronger, along with her devotion to her husband, son, daughter-in-law and grandchildren. She deemed there was no price of self-sacrifice too high to serve Christ and help her family. Although Rachel believed more could always be done for the good Lord, she harbored no such compunction about her family. She had done her best, and she felt appreciated for the effort.

Still, doubts brewed in her mind.

The one thing for which Rachel had little time or patience was matters of the past. As she was prone to tell her family and friends, time tended to flavor their memories like too much sugar.

"You tell a story like my sister, Euna, sweetens tea," Rachel had scolded Sam during one of his frequent bouts of reminiscing about their early struggles on the farm. "Pour in three cups of sugar where one would have sufficed, then add six saccharine tablets for good measure. It's sweet stuff all right, but it ain't tea."

Remembering the incident, Rachel smoothed the sheets across the starchy, white hospital bed and realized she was guilty of the same thing. Except, instead of using sugar, she tended to flavor life with unsweetened chocolate or vanilla straight from the bottle. In any portion, the taste was bitter, and her conscience swallowed a double serving.

A troubling notion besieged Rachel, a sense of having traveled through a lifetime governed by her rigid philosophies rather than as master of her domain. With her expectations always put off into the future, she had managed somehow to lose sight of the business of living. She had been preoccupied with getting by and getting past, always in a hurry to get to whatever was next. In her rush to pay no mind to the past, perhaps she had forgotten dreams that could or should have been remembered.

A practical woman by choice, Rachel realized her thoughts were self-pitying. She found it odd that after so many years of refusing to subject herself to the rigors of reflection, she was now falling into the trap of second-guessing the past. It was foolish reasoning, a selfish surrender to the temptation of vanity. But nevertheless, a strong sense of emptiness plagued Rachel. She felt as if she had spent her life preparing a feast, yet forgotten to set a place for herself at the banquet table.

Without doubt, Rachel considered the family her greatest accomplishment as well as an infinite source of pride and joy. But the family was a creation of itself, and Rachel was only one of many members who were making lasting contributions to its history. As much as she felt fulfilled by those contributions, Rachel also needed to believe that she had nurtured a vital part of herself that would endure long after she was gone from this earth. And that was the crux of her melancholy: Nothing she knew validated this desire and she was beset by growing despair, the likelihood that she coveted something that did not exist.

Saddened, Rachel sought once more to wake her husband. "Sam," she called with as much energy as she could muster in that unfamiliar, throaty voice. "Sam. What time is it?"

His good eye popped open, and he flew from his chair, easing down on the bed beside her. "Rachel!" he exclaimed, relieved as he took her hand. "Thank God, you are awake at last. You've been so sick, and I've been worried sick. How do you feel?"

"Better than before," she smiled weakly. "But not very strong. What time is it?"

"About six o'clock in the evenen," Sam replied. "This is your third day in the hospital, and you've been in a coma for the last thirty-six hours or so. Until sometime early this mornen, the doctor wasn't sure whether you'd make it. Your lungs filled up with fluid, and you couldn't breathe. But you're better now, and we'll be home before you know it."

He leaned down and kissed her forehead. "You scared the daylights out of me, Rachel," he said tenderly, looking into her eyes. "I'd never before thought about you not be'en beside me." He shook his head with a fearful expression. "I need you. And I love you."

Rachel smiled softly at her husband, then pulled his big, rough hand against her cheek. She nodded, closed her eyes and drifted off to sleep.

———

She awoke an hour later to the booming voice of a stout nurse, whose cheerfulness irritated Rachel. Once her eyes adjusted to the glare of bright lights, she discovered a flock of relatives surrounding her bed.

"Good Lord!" Rachel said as her eyes lit on her sister from Ocala, Florida. "Euna, what are you doen here?" she asked seconds before she saw the preacher, Adam Cook, standing at the foot of the bed.

Chagrined by the preacher's witness of her obvious irritation, she apologized immediately for the outburst. "You'll have to excuse me, Preacher," she said. "It's not often I take the Lord's name in vain, but I'm surprised to see all these faces."

"Think nothen of it, Mrs. Baker," Adam Cook said. "We should be maken apologies for intruden on you. Perhaps, we should leave you to your rest."

"No need for that," Rachel said, returning her gaze to her sister.

Euna was tall and thin as a beanpole, a stark contrast to her twin, Edna, who had been short and stout. Edna had died years earlier during the birth of her third child, and Euna was Rachel's only living sibling.

"I must have been sick if you came up all the way from Ocala," Rachel remarked with a grudging smile.

"I wanted to make sure you were well cared for," Euna replied, giving Rachel a quick hug. "I wasn't ready to be the last of the bunch."

Rachel would have preferred solitude, but the situation called for gracious acceptance of the well wishes of her family and friends. Besides the preacher and her sister, Sam, Matt, Caroline, Joe and Summer had crowded into the room.

Soon after the nurse had taken her temperature and checked her vital signs, Dr. Pittman strolled into the room. He was seized immediately by one of his coughing spells, which caused a shock of panic among those who were unprepared for the fit.

Rushing to drag a chair under the doctor, Joe instead slammed one of his shins against the steel legs of the hospital bed. Dr. Pittman waved off the attempted help, which was just as well since Joe had crumpled into the chair himself and was already massaging his aching leg.

Had she felt better, Rachel might have laughed at the slapstick circumstances. Instead, her ire grew. She tolerated the doctor's poking and prodding, figuring he was owed as much given his role in saving her life. She was civil to her family, despite their worried smiles and stilted comments. And she was genuinely grateful when the preacher took her hand and gave thanks to the Lord for her recovering health. But when the prayer was ended and Preacher Cook took his leave, Rachel made her preferences known. Bluntly speaking, she told her family to go home where they were needed and leave her to rest.

Knowing the woman's limit, everyone left but Sam, who refused to be budged from her side. "I'm stayen right here till the doctor says you can come home with me," he declared.

"Suit yourself," Rachel replied flatly. "But that chair's gonna make a poor bed, and I'm not sharen this one."

———

Rachel slept soundly until early on her fourth day in the hospital, waking only when an orderly served breakfast. She forced down a small amount of the chicken broth, then pushed away the tray and took a short nap until Dr. Pittman arrived to check on her.

"I've already told your husband, Mrs. Baker, and now I'll tell you," he said when he had completed the examination. "You're an amazen woman. Two days ago, I thought your time had come to sing with angels. And now, you're gainen strength with every passen minute. You've surely been blessed with one of God's miracles. At this rate of recovery, you'll be goen home to your family in no time at all."

Sam clasped his hands and cracked his knuckles at the doctor's prognosis. "Do you hear that, Rachel!" he exclaimed with uncontrollable delight. "The good Lord obviously has been listenen to the singen at Benevolence, and he realizes our church needs your splendid voice more than Heaven does."

The doctor laughed, but Rachel arched her eyebrows at Sam. "He's exaggeraten, doctor," she said. "The singen is good enough at our church—with or without me."

After the doctor had gone, Rachel retreated into her private thoughts. Understanding her desire for solitude, Sam took a walk around the hospital to stretch out his stiff muscles. He spent nearly two hours chatting with acquaintances and strangers, reading an abandoned newspaper and eating an early lunch in the hospital cafeteria.

When he returned to Rachel, she greeted him with the same faraway look that had caused him to leave the room earlier and returned her gaze to the blank television screen. Although surprised by her reluctance to talk, Sam was not overly concerned by her inattentive behavior. Over the years, they had come to understand each other's various moods, always mindful of the need for privacy, yet close at hand to provide solace when it was wanted. He gave a brief description of his morning, then sat down in the chair and promptly fell asleep.

In the afternoon, a steady stream of family and friends visited Rachel. Caroline brought Euna, and Paul Berrien came with his two sisters and an arrangement of red roses. Pearl Walker, Rachel's best friend, and several members of the Ladies Aid Society from church brought her one of the quilts they kept on hand for members of the community who were gravely ill and needed cheer. Sam recognized several squares in the quilt as the handiwork of his wife, whom he suspected felt ridiculous to receive a gift of her own stitching.

Rachel treated each of her well-wishers with courtesy, but Sam could tell she was relieved when the last one left. He hoped she might be ready to talk in the hour they had before supper, but his wife continued her silent contemplation. Mildly annoyed, Sam took another walk around the hospital, counting the minutes until supper and the arrival of their nighttime visitors.

In the late evening when everyone had gone, Sam made up his mind to confront his wife. He suspected Rachel was troubled by something other than her health, and her disinclination to confide in him was both worrisome and frustrating. Not since the early days of their marriage had Rachel held her tongue when she was distressed.

He tried first to prod her into conversation with pointed questions, but Rachel evaded him with simple nods or an occasional grunt. At length, his puzzlement gave away to irritation, and Sam exploded. "Enough of this dad-blamed silence, Rachel!" he railed. "I know you feel poorly, but that's no excuse to act as if I don't exist. You cannot continue to ignore me."

When she failed to acknowledge him, Sam walked to the end of the bed, crossed his arms and continued his tirade. "This mornen, the doctor said you're menden and on the way back to good health," he said stoutly. "You should be rejoicen, Rachel, but instead, you're as gloomy as English fog. Why, I haven't even heard you give a single word of thanks to the good Lord for restoren your health."

Her eyes flashed with anger, and Sam was pleased to see the spark. He had struck a nerve.

"I'll have you know, Sam Baker, that I am thankful to be feelen better, and I have indeed told the Lord exactly that," she growled. "And furthermore, I'll have you know that my prayers are between me and the Lord. It's none of your business."

"Touché," Sam agreed. "You're absolutely right. Your prayers are your business, and I'm sorry for sticken my nose into it. But, Rachel, this silence is unlike you. Somethen's botheren you, and you're keepen it from me." He sat beside her on the bed. "I just want to help. Please tell me what's wrong. Don't shut me out."

She began to cry, so softly at first that Sam almost failed to notice. First, her eyes brimmed; then the tears spilled down her face. Sam figured he could have counted on one hand the times Rachel had cried in their years as husband and wife, and these tears disturbed him. He edged closer on the bed, grasping her by the hands and holding on until she was ready to confide in him.

"Where did the time go, Sam?" Rachel asked finally, the words coming in a hoarse whisper. "And how did we get so old so fast?"

She shifted her gaze to his face, saying, "If there's one thing I always thought we'd have plenty of, it was time. But we're getten short on even that now, aren't we? I've become an old woman, Sam, an old woman who's probably goen to die with little to show for in this life."

Her head shook tiredly, and she glanced away. "All my life, I wanted to do or make or give somethen that would last, somethen I could be proud of and leave behind when I die. But here I am now, sixty-five years old ...."

She looked again at Sam with a sad-eyed smile. "Or am I?" she asked.

Sam shrugged and rubbed the black patch over his bad eye. "I don't know the date," he confessed. "I've lost track of time these last few days."

"It doesn't matter," Rachel said. "A day late, a day early—it doesn't change the facts. It's gone way past the time to do somethen grand in life."

Sam was dumbstruck by the revelation. In his wildest imagination, he never would have expected Rachel to worry about her age. Such fears contradicted her entire nature. Rachel was the most practical woman Sam knew, and this line of worry from her sounded almost like nonsense. Yet, he sensed her fretting was sincere and he wanted to ease her mind.

"May I ask what it is you would have liked to have done?" he asked gently.

"I can't say for certain," Rachel answered with a shake of her head. "It's just a feelen, a knowen that there was somethen special I should have seen to, but I never quite got around to it when the time was right. And now, the time is gone, and I can't even figure out what it was that I should have done in the first place."

Sam considered the statement. "If it's any consolation, Rachel, I think most everything you've ever done has been somethen special. You've been a wonderful wife, a loven mother, and you've created a legacy of memories that will last a lifetime or two after you're gone."

"We all touch people's lives in some way or another," Rachel replied. "And don't get me wrong, I'm thankful to have been able to do that, and I'm proud to have been your wife and the mother of your children. Still, though, I would have liked to have left behind an inheritance, something of value."

"Rachel!" Sam said sharply. "What in tarnation do you think I'm gonna leave behind when I die? Nothen but a few acres of land," he answered, "and I wouldn't have that without all your hard work and sacrifices. If it's an inheritance you're wanten to leave, then there's no more reason to fret. You have an inheritance; it's somethen real and lasten. We poured our hearts and souls into the farm, and our spirits will roam those woods and fields for years to come."

She smiled and patted his hand. "You're right, and I am proud of the farm, maybe more than I ever thought I would be. I should count my blessens that I was able to work beside you each and every day and we were dedicated to the same goal. And I do, too. But I could have been happy anywhere as long as you were there with me. The farm was your dream, Sam, and it will be your inheritance."

She hesitated, then added, "I'm be'en selfish, but still I wish I could have been blessed with an inheritance of my own, somethen that was mine and only mine."

"I appreciate the thought, Rachel, but I'm still confused," Sam remarked. "And I think you are, too."

"Yes, I am," she replied glumly. "And rather late in life at that."

Sam toyed with his eye patch, mulling over the situation. Rachel's sentiments left him bewildered. He was unfamiliar with this notion of wanting something, yet not knowing what it was. Of course, the same was true of his wife, which explained her predicament. There had been few times of doubt in Rachel's life. She studied problems and she fixed them, all with the precision of a mathematician. Now, however, the answers eluded her, and Sam was likewise stumped.

"I wish I could help you figure it out," he offered at length.

"Pshaw!" she said, waving her hand to dismiss his concern. "I'm just acten my age," she continued gallantly. "All this carryen on does indeed make me sound like a silly old woman. You should just tell me to hush up."

"I would never do that," Sam declared. "But I do think it's best that we sleep on our thoughts. Perhaps tomorrow we'll have fresh perspective."

"No, no, no," Rachel said with forced determination. "I've ranted and thought too much nonsense as it is. It's probably just the strain of be'en sick and allowen myself to give in to self-pity. Ignore me, Sam. I'll be fine."

––––––––

Rachel's prophecy went unfulfilled. And Rachel went from the hospital bed to her bed at home.

She complained of feeling weak, refused to eat her meals and rejected plans for a late birthday celebration. For the first time in her life, she missed consecutive Sunday services at church. And yet, two weeks after he had dismissed Rachel from the hospital, Dr. Pittman pronounced her recovery complete and suggested she resume a full schedule of her normal routines.

Out of boredom, Rachel accepted his advice and returned to her daily chores. But her heart was elsewhere. In spite of her good intentions, she moped around the house, brooding in silence as the family tried to guess the cause of her malaise. Rachel felt full of self-doubt and robbed of self-worth, but she brushed off repeated attempts to bolster her spirits. As the days passed, however, this constant state of anxiety took a toll on her fragile health.

One month after coming home from the hospital, Rachel sat at the kitchen table with Sam, Matt and Caroline eating a snack for lunch. She felt a flutter above her eyelid followed by a stabbing pain in her left temple. She started to rub her head, then tried to stand. But the pain intensified, and sudden dizziness overcame her.

"Sam!" she gasped.

It was the last thing she remembered, except for the sensation of falling through air. She never felt the linoleum floor, which stopped the flight of her body, and she was unaware of being rushed to the hospital by her worried family. She regained consciousness a few hours later and was blessed to have all her faculties intact.

Dr. Pittman diagnosed the seizure as a mild stroke. He hospitalized Rachel for three days, ran a battery of tests and released her, again with an excellent prognosis for recovery.

The doctor's words of encouragement, however, fell on deaf ears. Rachel seemed resigned to ill health. It was almost as if she had given up on life. At home, she retreated to the bed, with a request for peace and quiet.

Almost overnight, the home turned into a funeral parlor, with everyone cautious of their every word, fearing they would be the one who disturbed Rachel and triggered a worsening of her illness. They were strung across a long line of caution, walking on eggshells. Caroline and Matt took out their frustrations on each other and on their children to some extent. The children battered each other with insults and occasional blows, while Sam harped like a bleating sheep on the need for family harmony.

Entombed in her room, Rachel was oblivious to the family tumult. Like a loose seam, her family was coming apart—in desperate need of a fine seamstress to mend the frayed ends.

CHAPTER 4

SUMMER FIXED HER GAZE on the blackboard, looking past Mr. Barnes, the eighth-grade history teacher who was lecturing on Georgia's rivers. For two days now, the class had heard point after point about the influence of rivers in shaping Georgia's history. As far as Summer was concerned, the discussion was pointless. She'd never so much as set eyes on any of the waterways mentioned in the history book, and she was unimpressed to learn that three nations had fought for control of the St. Mary's River or that Stephen Foster had immortalized the Suwannee River in the song, *Old Folks at Home*, without ever even laying eyes on its black waters. Furthermore, she questioned the wisdom of any history book that failed to mention the rivers close to home—New River, the Alapaha, the Willacoochee and the Withlacoochee, or Little River.

She acknowledged Mr. Barnes with an interested nod, then resumed her thoughts. At some point, she'd figure out what she needed to know about Georgia's rivers. If worse came to worst, she would humble herself and ask Joe, the family history buff, who probably knew all the pertinent facts about the 75 major rivers in Georgia and a few of the minor ones as well. But for now, Summer's mind was preoccupied with a more important matter—her grandmother's health.

In a way, it seemed as if Rachel had decided to die. Summer felt guilty for having this thought, but the truth was the truth as her grandmother had reminded her and almost everybody else on more than one occasion. And while no one at home would come right out and admit it, everyone was thinking along those lines, except perhaps Sam, who was in the process of worrying himself and everyone else to the sick bed.

For several days now, Summer had been mad at her grandmother's behavior. She considered it tacky for someone to decide to die without first consulting the ones who would suffer the consequences. And she was more than put out by the sorry state of affairs at home, all because Rachel had decided she was ready to meet her maker. Brash as these thoughts seemed, Summer knew they were nothing more than bluff and bluster. Deep down, her grandmother's illness frightened her, not so much the physical ailments but rather Rachel's apparent crisis of faith.

"A crisis of faith—not in God but rather in her own self-worth," Preacher Cook had suggested to Caroline and Sam last Sunday afternoon following one of his frequent visits to Rachel's bedside since she became ill. "Mrs. Baker is struggling with self-doubt."

Summer's instincts suggested Rachel would weather this crisis, but there was just enough doubt to keep her worried about the outcome. And it was that hint of fear driving Summer's thoughts, motivating her to search out the root of Rachel's depression.

Summer had a good idea of where the search would end. But she decided to start at the beginning anyway, hoping to discover something new or perhaps rediscover something special.

———

Rachel came from a long line of seamstresses. Her maternal grandmother had used a needle and thread to support three young children after being widowed at an early age, and her fondest memories of her own mother dwelled inevitably on times they had sewed side by side. As a young girl, even as a young woman charged with running a household in the wake of her mother's death, Rachel had dreamed of someday owning a dress shop and sewing the kind of clothes worn by women of high society. She would pore over each edition of the Sears, Roebuck catalog, identify the most exquisite dresses and then create perfect replicas for her twin sisters and herself. In time, her services were being sought by dozens of neighbor women.

Faced with the opportunity of a lifetime, Rachel had immersed herself in the work. Before too much time had passed, the majority of women in her Baptist church, as well as those of the Methodist persuasion, wore dresses made by Rachel. Eventually, her sewing attracted the attention of a downtown shop owner, who hired Rachel to do alterations and suggested she might make a handsome profit by allowing the boutique to sell some of her dresses. Excited and flabbergasted by the idea, Rachel had been ready to plunge headlong into the venture when Sam Baker made an abrupt entrance into her life. Soon afterward, Rachel was sewing her most exquisite and elegant creation of all—her wedding dress.

"If I had but one vanity, then I suppose it would be my wedden dress," Rachel had confessed on the day she first showed the garment to Summer.

She kept the dress stored away in her cedar chest and had waited deliberately until Summer was old enough to appreciate the artistry and technique required in the sewing. Fashioned from the finest broadcloth of the day, the wedding dress was a masterpiece of pure white beauty in simplicity. Long-sleeved, with a fitted bodice and a full tea-length skirt, the dress flowed with elegance and featured the richness of tiny seed pearl buttons and embroidered lace roses on the neckline and sleeves.

"It is by far the prettiest dress I've ever made," Rachel had told Summer. "I spent months on it—not so much sewen but tryen to imagine what it must look like. I thought long and hard about each cut of material and every stitch along the way. And if I do say so myself, the dress is close to perfection. I've worn it only once in my entire life, and that was on the day I married Sam. Maybe it was foolishness to put away such a beautiful dress, but I believed then and now that some things are intended for once-in-a-lifetime occasions. My wedden dress was one of them."

Rachel had lapsed into silence as she returned the dress to its protective cover, while an awestruck Summer committed details of the garment to her memory. When the dress was returned to its rightful place and the cedar chest closed, Rachel had made an admission from deep in her soul.

"I'm not one to wish for things that might have been," she told Summer. "But I would have liked the opportunity to make more dresses like that."

Finding her voice at last, Summer had asked, "Why didn't you, Granny?"

"I don't know, child," Rachel replied. "Perhaps I should have. It just seemed frivolous to me back then, an extravagance that I had neither the time nor money to indulge. First off, your grandpa and I were busy clearen fields. Then, I started haven babies. I was so busy back in those days that I could scarcely keep my head on straight, much less think about sewen beautiful dresses. At one point, we were so poor that I used flour sacks to make shirts for the boys and dresses for Ruth. Later, when times were better, I planned to make some fancy dresses—for Ruth, if no one else. Somehow, I never got around to it, though. Then Ruth was gone and I just never saw the need after that. When you're plain people liven on a farm, there's not much need for fancy dresses."

While the full significance of Rachel's answer escaped Summer, the wedding dress had captivated the girl. Long after the dress was returned to the cedar chest, Summer remained fascinated and enthralled by its beauty, the delicate embroidery, and the rich texture of the broadcloth. She felt as if she had discovered a secret door leading to a place filled with treasures of silk, lace and velvet. It was a magical feeling of knowing she possessed a key that would admit her to this realm, a sense of coming home to a place that she had always known existed for her.

Part of her discovery was the knowledge that she wanted to make many dresses, which, as Rachel put it, should be worn only once in a lifetime. But essentially, Summer made the glorious discovery of beauty, beauty in the material sense to be sure but still grace and elegance shaped from yards and yards of lovely fabrics. It was a marvelous feeling, the beginning of something special and a sense of destiny.

———

Like the arrival of daybreak, the reason for Rachel's melancholy dawned on Summer.

If she wanted to place blame, Summer supposed she could have accepted responsibility for the lately wistful ways of her grandmother. She was the one, after all, who had sown seeds of doubt in Rachel's mind about the value of dedicating her life to the needs of her husband and her family. Perhaps Rachel had never voiced her doubts, but it was easy to imagine the questions that likely claimed her attention.

Certain that Rachel had forgiven her for the angry outburst, Summer was similarly convinced her grandmother had been hurt to the core by the girl's ready rejection of sewing. At the time, Summer had lashed out with the first words that came to mind. Her denouncement of all that was dear to Rachel had come in a moment of frustration; she had rebelled against the confines of her predicament.

Regardless of the harsh words spoken, Summer would have expected her grandmother to sense the shallowness of her tirade and realize the depth of her appreciation of the beauty produced by a needle and a thread. Perhaps Rachel had, too. But hindsight told Summer that Rachel would have deemed even the slightest rejection of sewing as a personal failure, especially from the prized apprentice she had nurtured every step of the way.

Whether sewing a man's work shirt or a formal evening gown, when Rachel took a needle and thread in hand, sat down at the sewing machine or laid out a piece of material, she transformed into the young woman with big dreams. On the day she first showed her wedding dress to Summer, Rachel had glowed with the pride of accomplishment and a sense of fulfillment. Remembering the moment, Summer recalled the sense of destiny enveloping her as she had slipped into her grandmother's dreams. It was a memory tempered by the knowledge that Rachel had put aside those dreams to concentrate on more worthwhile pursuits such as loving her husband and nurturing their family.

No one should have second-guessed such a decision, and Summer didn't think for one second Rachel would make that mistake. Still, it was easy to conclude that Rachel would have felt her dreams trampled by the relentless march of time, especially when the one person with whom she had shared those dreams had made light of the legacy. If Summer had been able to tell her grandmother that she wanted to be a dressmaker on the day Rachel brought out the wedding dress from its hiding place, then the older woman's dreams would have found a refuge of safekeeping. But Summer was only twelve years old, and she had required time to figure out the future.

Rachel might have simplified the process by impressing on Summer her hopes that the granddaughter would fulfill the grandmother's dreams. But Rachel, despite all her strict, set ways, was a woman of conscience. She had shared her dreams, her skills and her talent with Summer, but she would never foist expectations on the girl. If Summer chose to become a dressmaker later in life, then she would make the decision of her own free will, without the expectations of anyone but with all the support and encouragement of everyone dear to her.

When she thought about the situation with her grandmother in those terms, Summer understood more than ever the wisdom of Rachel's decision to devote her life to God, Sam and family—even at the expense of lifelong dreams. Clothes were clothes, after all, and beautiful dresses were nothing more than that. They were lovely to behold, to touch and to wear, but it was the people who wore them that mattered most.

Having come to this conclusion, Summer supposed she could march into her grandmother's room and tell Rachel these things. But to Summer's way of thinking, actions spoke louder than words. Somehow, she had to find a way to help her grandmother remember just how important was the business of living. And somehow, she had to make Rachel realize that the dreams they shared were still within the reach of both women.

On the same day Summer decided to put purpose back into Rachel's life, the Cookville chapter of the Veterans of Foreign Wars decided to move the annual county fair to mid-April from its traditional fall dates. The reasons were unclear to Summer, who was in her homeroom class preparing for the bus ride home when the announcement was made.

Later, Summer would think how often the fortunes of fate fell her way. At the time, however, she saw only the opportunity to give new life to her grandmother's dreams.

Summer adored the fair with its carnival rides, sideshows, caramel apples and cotton candy. But she gave only fleeting thought to these thrills and instead focused attention on the various competitions that were equally important to the fair.

The Baker family had claimed their share of prizes over the years. Joe had won best of show with one of the family's prized shoats several years ago, and Summer had earned top honors in the junior dressmaking event last year. Caroline had captured blue ribbons with her pepper jelly on two occasions as well as one each for her tomato preserves and a special coconut cake.

Rachel's pear tarts had won blue ribbons several times, and she had carried home another blue ribbon three years ago for a yo-yo quilt. But the prize Rachel coveted more than any other was for specialty sewing, an event that rewarded creativity as well as technique. So far, Rachel had failed even to place in the competition, where the winning entries had ranged from a purse to a tablecloth and a formal evening gown in recent years. As she regretted every year, Rachel simply could not come up with an entry that would set her work apart from everybody else's.

With all that in mind, Summer set her sights on the competition.

As soon as the bus rolled to a stop in front of the Baker house that afternoon, Summer charged off it and headed straight for Rachel's bedroom. "Where's Granny?" she shouted as she walked down the hall.

"Hush up, Summer," Caroline admonished as her daughter entered the kitchen. "She's in her room, and you know we're not supposed to disturb her."

"I know," Summer replied. "But I've got important news, and it can't wait. We don't have much time as it is."

Dropping her books on the table, Summer marched over to Rachel's bedroom, barged through the door and announced matter-of-factly, "Granny, they're haven the annual fall fair this spring. I think we ought to team up to enter the specialty sewen. There's nothen in the rules that says teams can't enter, and I need your help. I was thinken a collection of doll clothes is just the thing that might win us first place."

Summer crossed her arms and held her ground as Caroline stormed into the room, apologizing to Rachel for the girl's behavior and ordering her daughter from the room.

"Well, Granny?" Summer insisted, ignoring her mother. "What do you think?"

"Your grandmother's not up to it this year, Summer," Caroline remarked. "Are you forgetten that she's been very sick?"

"She's not very sick at the moment," Summer diagnosed boldly. "But if you want, Granny, you can sit in bed and do your part of the sewen. The important thing is to get started as soon as possible. Will you help me? Don't you think a collection of doll clothes will do the trick for us?"

A flash of anger lit Rachel's eyes, giving way instantly to serious consideration of the proposition. She pulled herself into a sitting position against the headboard, glancing from Summer to Caroline.

Rachel frowned slightly, then said, "It's a grand idea, Summer. When do you want to get started?"

"The sooner, the better, so how 'bout right now?" Summer suggested. "I've already come up with several ideas. We can discuss designs and materials and maybe come up with a schedule to keep us on track."

"Are you sure you're up to this, Ma?" Caroline asked for the sake of caution.

Rachel shook her head affirmatively and motioned Summer to the bed. "It's time, Caroline," she nodded. "Way past time if I say so myself."

Caroline gave her mother-in-law and daughter each a hug, then left the two seamstresses to their work.

———

Later that evening, Summer invaded Joe's room for a private chat. Without knocking on his closed door, she pushed it open, marched into the tiny room and fell onto the twin bed with a heavy sigh.

"I became a woman today," she announced, slinging a forearm across her forehead and letting loose another exaggerated sigh.

Used to one or two of these interruptions a night from his brothers and sisters, Joe detected a hint of seriousness beneath Summer's dramatics. He pushed aside his research paper, leaned his chair against the wall and cupped the back of his head with his hands, more interested in her thoughts than his unstirred expression revealed.

"Should I offer congratulations or condolences?" he said, drawing a puzzled stare in response. "Are you haven cramps or anything like that?" he asked to break the silence.

"Oh, that," Summer replied, understanding his intent. "I got my period the week after Christmas, Joe—around New Year's, when I was so grumpy."

Joe cocked his eyebrows. "So why all the melodrama tonight?" he inquired. "It seems a bit late in the game for that."

Summer flipped onto her side, resting on her elbow. "Will you take me serious, Joe?"

"Sure I will," Joe answered, resting the chair on the floor and clasping hands in lap, a sure sign she had his undivided attention. "What's on your mind?"

"What I should have said," Summer began, "is that I understood today what it means to become a woman. You're a man, and you can do pretty much what you want in life. But it's different for me. I know I'll have more choices in life than Mama did when she was young or Granny, too. I might end up as a famous fashion designer or maybe nothen more than a housewife. But either way, I'll be expected to nurture my family. You on the other hand will be expected to provide for your family."

"I can nurture, too," Joe commented.

Ignoring his remark, Summer continued: "I'm not sayen there's a right way or a wrong way, but men generally go about the business of maken a liven for their family, while women run the household. But regardless, it's this idea of nurturen that fascinates me. I think I'll be good at it."

"Frankly, I've always thought of you as more bossy than anything else," Joe interrupted.

"Maybe sometimes you have to be bossy to do a good job of nurturen," Summer shot back. "And maybe you have to be tender and loven, helpful and caren, patient and understanden, too. I know I've got a lot to learn about it, but today I realized how important it is to nurture your family. Maybe it sounds dumb to you, Joe, but this is somethen I look forward to and want to be good at doen, maybe more than anything else I'll ever do in life."

Joe stared at his sister, dumbfounded by her remarks.

"Well?" Summer prompted a pregnant moment later. "Does it sound dumb or not?"

"It sounds very grown-up," he answered at last. "Exactly what I would expect a good woman to say. In fact, though I've never heard them put the thought in those exact words, it sounds very much like Mama and Granny. They're both excellent nurturers, and you'd do well to learn from them." He paused. "But it appears you've already figured that out for yourself."

Summer gloated, pleased by the compliment.

"So what brought you to this understanden about yourself, little sister?"

"In a roundabout way, it was Granny," Summer replied. "I was in my Georgia history class today—which, by the way, we need to talk about later—and she was pretty much on my mind through the whole class. I was thinken about that argument she and I had on New Year's Eve. Do you remember?"

Joe nodded his recollection of the debacle.

"Plus, I was thinken about her be'en sick and all, and then some of the things we have in common, especially our love of sewen," Summer continued. "Granny's spent her whole life taken care of other people, which is as fine a thing as anybody could ever do. But did you know she wanted to be a dressmaker when she was young?"

"I know she was worken for a dress shop when she and Grandpa got married," Joe remarked. "Guess it's not surprisen that she would have wanted to make dresses."

"You want to be a journalist, right?" Summer asked.

Again, Joe gave an affirmative nod.

"Knowen you, Joe, you'll probably be a great one," Summer admired, bringing a blushing smile to her brother's face. "But what if for some reason, you couldn't be. What if you had to choose between a career and your family?"

His smile faded, replaced by a doubtful shrug.

"Let's put it this way," Summer went on. "What if you made a choice to stay here on the farm instead of becomen a journalist because you wanted to get married more than anything and have six kids? Even if you had no real regrets about that decision, you'd probably always wonder what might have been."

"Probably," Joe agreed. "But I can't see any of this happenen, can you?"

"No," Summer replied. "But that's exactly what happened to Granny. She had a dream, but she had to give it up for somethen else more important."

"True," Joe said. "But she decided what was most important to her."

"Probably," Summer agreed. "But I've never asked her about that. Have you?"

"No, and I never will," Joe remarked with force. "That's her business."

"Agreed," Summer said. "Still, I'd like Granny to see some of her dressmaken dreams come true in one way or another."

"I smell somethen strange," Joe said suddenly. "What exactly are you cooken up, little sister?"

Summer smiled mischievously, then told her brother about the plans to enter the specialty sewing competition at the county fair, including one significant detail that she had withheld from Rachel as they discussed the project earlier in the day. When she had finished outlining the plan, she promised Joe to secrecy and predicted with confidence the Baker team would bring home the blue ribbon.

"Rowenna Rowan has won two years runnen, includen last year with the most gosh-awful purse you could ever imagine," Summer explained matter-of-factly. "The thing had feathers on it. It was ugly as sin, but it was also very different. That's what the judges seem to favor year after year—whatever's unusual. I can't ever remember anyone enteren a collection of doll clothes, and I just bet no one else will this year, except for Granny and me. We're a shoo-in to win that blue ribbon."

Joe leaned his chair back against the wall, once more relaxing his neck against his cradled hands. "You know what, Summer?" he remarked. "I don't doubt it one minute."

Summer grinned, folded her arms and sat up cross-legged in the bed. "If he heard me boasten like this, the preacher would probably tell me to read the first chapter of Ecclesiastics," she said.

"I forget that one," Joe replied.

"Vanity of vanities, saith the preacher," Summer quoted scripture. "Vanity of vanities, all is vanity."

"Vanity is not one of your faults, little sister," Joe said. "I suspect Preacher Cook would pat you on the back and ask how you managed to get Granny out of her sick bed."

"To tell you the truth," Summer admitted, lowering her voice, "Rowenna Rowan probably had more to do with it than me. She's not one of Granny's favorite people, and I'm sure she'd love to take that blue ribbon from her."

Joe laughed aloud, and Summer seized the opportunity to change the subject to something on her mind.

"So tell me, Joe," she asked, "if you had to choose between haven a family and a career, which would it be?"

"A career, hands-down," Joe answered quickly. "But since I'm a while away from having that choice, it's an easy question to answer. Ask me ten or fifteen years from now and I might have to rethink it. I've never imagined myself as a married man with children, but I think it's important."

"Do you consider yourself a man?" Summer asked, with obvious curiosity.

Joe thought a moment. "Since I can't point to an obvious rite of passage like you, I guess my best answer is that I'm worken toward it," he said. "Just from talken with Daddy and Grandpa, I get the feelen that it's a gradual process. Obviously, when I turn twenty-one, I'll be considered a man. But it's a lot more complicated than that, don't you think?"

"Yeah," she admitted. "Despite today's revelation, I've gotta long way to go to full-fledged womanhood. I suppose these things won't ever be easy, will they?"

"Probably not," Joe remarked, "but you're well on the way, Summer, and you'll be a better one tomorrow and the next day after that."

Summer grinned. "So are you, brother."

———

Using Barbie dolls as models, Summer and Rachel fashioned their collection of clothes—evening gowns of pale yellow and green satin, a suit of blue velvet and dresses of red paisley print, pink chiffon and black silk. They sewed with painstaking perfection, creating replicas of the most elegant fashions in the pattern books they collected from cloth stores.

"These are just beautiful," Summer told her grandmother one afternoon as they thumbed through the pattern books. "Maybe someday I'll design clothes that appear in these books."

The suggestion put a gleam in Rachel's eye, and her health and spirit returned in almost measurable quantities as the fair's grand opening drew nearer. She became her bustling self around the house and was once again in attendance at Benevolence Missionary Baptist Church.

In the privacy of Joe's room, Summer worked on the signature piece of the collection, a flawless replica of Rachel's wedding dress. It was a miniaturized masterpiece, faithful to every detail of the original.

At last, the day of the fair's grand opening arrived. In the living room where the family gathered shortly after breakfast for last-minute discussions of the day's activities, Summer and Rachel unveiled their collection.

Probably everyone had seen some snippet of the doll clothes over the last several weeks, but this was their first opportunity to view the collection in its entirety.

Spread across a line against a backdrop of black velvet, the tiny clothes dazzled the eye, each piece an exquisite example of design and sewing perfection. From the rich texture of materials to the elegant lines of stitching, the collection radiated an aura of excellence. In more simple terms, prizewinner was sewed all over it, even among those who did not know a backstitch from a whipstitch or basting from tacking.

"Rowenna Rowan doesn't stand a chance of winnen that blue ribbon this year," Joe declared, the first among them to find a voice of congratulations.

"Goodness gracious no," Caroline echoed him. "It's everything y'all wanted it to be and more. The technique's perfect, and the idea is not only unusual but plumb awestriken. I don't know when I've ever seen finer work."

In the midst of rounds of hearty congratulations and well-wishing, Summer cried out suddenly, "We forgot somethen, Granny."

The noise subsided instantly to dead silence as everyone looked to Summer, wondering about the missing creation.

Rachel looked over the collection piece by piece. "No, honey," she told Summer, shaking her head. "This is everything."

"What on earth else could there be, darlen," Caroline added, as everyone caught the suddenly unmistakable gleam in Summer's eye. "It's already perfect," she added, almost as a curious afterthought.

"Not quite yet," Summer replied mysteriously, looking to the hall, where Joe was walking toward them holding a brown paper bag.

Moments earlier, he had slipped away unnoticed as the family congratulated Summer and Rachel on their excellent work. Now, coming to a stop behind the Victorian couch, he handed the bag to Summer, with a wink of encouragement.

"I have somethen I'd like to show Granny before we go to the fair," Summer said coyly to her mystified family. "I know how much this meant to her, and I wanted to find some way to show how much it meant to me, too. I thought maybe we could add it to our collection."

Without further delay, Summer reached inside the bag, pulled out the tiny wedding dress and placed it on the velvet backdrop, which was draped across the coffee table.

Accustomed as they were to sharing moments, both tender and robust, none of the family was prepared to acknowledge this breathtaking tribute to their matriarch. The level of care, devotion and love resonating in the garment struck a chord of silence, even among those who were unaware the dress was a perfect copy of Rachel's wedding dress.

This time, it was Sam who first found his voice. "Your wedden dress, Rachel," he said, his words touched with the reverence of memory.

"Summer," Caroline gasped, awed as much over the obvious talent of her daughter as the sheer beauty of the dress. She wanted to thank the girl and sing her praises all at once. She settled for a crushing embrace. "It's beautiful, darlen," Caroline said before releasing her daughter. "Just beautiful."

Matt and Carrie added their voices to the swell of rave reviews, but Summer barely heard them. She was focused solely on Rachel's reaction to the dress, waiting for her grandmother's stamp of approval. Absorbed by the mastery of detail in the dress, Rachel seemed oblivious to everyone and everything around her. At last, however, she gave her blessing to the project, doing so in the crusty style of her younger years.

Almost without thinking, Sam reached for the dress only to have his hand slapped away by Rachel. "Don't you dare touch that, Sam!" she exclaimed. "Just the slightest bit of dirt on your hands, and you would stain it to ruin."

Ignoring her husband's quick sulk, Rachel took the tiny wedding dress in her own clean hands, marveling at its exactness to the garment she had created so long ago. She caressed the folds of soft broadcloth, admired the tiny seed pearl buttons and traced the delicate lace embroidery. Something happy and fulfilling deep inside brought her close to tears, but Rachel figured she had cried enough for the time being. So instead, she opted to celebrate her granddaughter.

"Land sakes, child—it is beautiful," she said with deep-felt sincerity. "It's a prize-winner on its own without any of these other dresses as garnishment." She hesitated, still trying to absorb the significance of Summer's gift. "If gamblen weren't a sin, I'd be willen to bet we do bring that blue ribbon home where it belongs," she said at last.

Still clutching the dress but careful to protect it, Rachel hugged Summer tightly, stroking her granddaughter's long brown hair as her cheek pressed against the girl's forehead. "We may have a real dressmaker in this family after all," she said at length, smiling toward Sam, watching his face narrow with puzzlement.

"We always did, Granny," Joe remarked softly, unexpectedly. "Now we have another, I think."

Rachel acknowledged her grandson, eased her embrace of Summer and looked again to Sam with a conscious smile. At once, the clouds broke on his face, replaced by a beam of full understanding.

"Yes, now we have another," he agreed with Joe. "And you have a legacy of your own, Rachel. You always have."

Giving her granddaughter a tender kiss on the cheek and a quick squeeze of the elbow, Rachel released Summer and walked into her husband's open arms. "It's a fine thing to have a legacy, Rachel, especially one as full and complete as yours," Sam said. "I hope you're proud of it."

She laid her head against Sam's shoulder and nodded.

———

In a way, the judging of the specialty-sewing event was almost anti-climactic for the family. It seemed inevitable that Summer and Rachel would walk away with the blue ribbon. Regardless, the family understood the real prize had been handed out and accepted many times over, long before the judges reached their decision. Still, everyone was on hand to applaud and congratulate the winners when the judges, after brief consideration, laid the blue ribbon across Summer and Rachel's collection of doll clothes.

With Rachel and Summer's approval, Caroline purchased an expensive glass case, framed the collection and hung it on the living room wall.

A few days later, Sam splurged on a new electric sewing machine for Rachel. Presenting it to her at suppertime, he attached two strings to the gift. "Number one is that you retire that old push-pedal machine, so I don't ever have to hear another complaint about the sorry state of the contraption," he said.

"I'll consider that," Rachel agreed.

"If you decide to get rid of the push-pedal, I'd be glad to have it for myself," Summer suggested.

Rachel regarded the girl with an affirmative nod, then cast her gaze on Sam. "What else did you have on your mind?"

"Number two," Sam said, "is that you take in enough sewen from our neighbors to pay for this high-priced gadget and earn your keep."

Rachel stiffened at the suggestion. "I shall sew whenever and for whomever I please," she said coolly. "Without any regard for your feelens on the subject. And furthermore, old man, I intend to keep every last dime I might earn off that machine. I've patched enough holes to pay for one new sewen machine in my lifetime, and I've more than earned my keep around here."

Somehow, the words were lost and their familiarity ignored by those gathered in the kitchen as the family's hum began to rise around the table—though not by everyone. Watching their grandparents exchange the briefest of smiles, Joe winked at Summer and received a wrinkled nose in return.

THE GARDEN

1963

CHAPTER 1

BONNIE DECIDED THE ENTIRE Baker family needed a strong dose of castor oil—or some such elixir that would cleanse their ill attitudes the way the medicine emptied the bowels. In these days when they should have been rejoicing over Granny's renewed health, everyone seemed to have their noses out of joint. Mealtimes had become quieter than a funeral home as everyone chose to maintain a careful silence instead of risk rebuke over the most benign of comments. The family had forgotten how to be kind.

"Good evenen, everyone."

Bonnie glanced up as Preacher Adam Cook strode up to the front-row church pew where she and other members of the primary class—mostly first- and second-grade students—were busy making sandals similar to the ones Hebrews had worn during the days of Jesus. The craft project was part of Vacation Bible School, which the preacher had initiated at Benevolence for the first time this year. One more night of the special school remained, and already Bonnie regretted that it was ending so soon. She had enjoyed the experience, even if it had taken place during spring vacation from regular school.

"Hello, preacher," Bonnie said, her voice joining the greetings of seven other classmates.

Bonnie liked the church pastor. He smiled often and always had a cheerful word to say, unless he was preaching one of his hellfire and brimstone sermons. While Preacher Cook rarely shouted in the pulpit, he had a way of putting the fear of the Lord in people. Frequently, Bonnie understood his sermons. Often, even when the sermon did not make sense to her, she still paid attention to the preacher—drawn by his kindness and sincerity as well as the knowledge that he refused to tolerate rude behavior in church. On more than one occasion, he had called talking teenagers to the floor and admonished them to hush up or leave.

Unlike some adults, Preacher Cook also seemed to enjoy children and young people. He somehow always knew what was important to them at the moment, whether it was a big football game or simply time for report cards at school. And he took time to offer encouragement and support.

Throughout the week of Vacation Bible School, the preacher had visited Bonnie's class each day, telling various stories about the crucifixion of Christ and the days that followed. This evening's story was about Doubting Thomas, the disciple who refused to believe Jesus had risen from the grave three days after He was crucified. The preacher said Thomas had demanded proof that his Lord was alive after being dead, and that Thomas had believed only after the resurrected Jesus allowed him to feel his nail-scarred hands and pierced sides. Last, but certainly not least, Preacher Cook claimed that while Thomas had been fortunate to have his faith substantiated by touching and feeling Jesus, today's Christians must believe on faith alone that Jesus had died and was resurrected so that all might have eternal life in Heaven.

Listening to the story, Bonnie decided Thomas was a lucky soul, whereas she was getting a raw deal. Believing was one thing, but honest-to-goodness proof was quite another.

Take her household. On faith alone, everyone accepted that all was well with the world. Rachel's health was restored, and their lives once again strummed along at a happy pace. Unfortunately, the proof of all this happiness was sorely lacking.

Rachel was well again, but the Bakers still suffered from her illness. It had something to do with Rachel's depression during her period of ill health. Her self-doubt had shaken the family at its very roots, replacing boundless faith with confusing uncertainty. At least, that was the way Bonnie had overheard Joe describe the family turmoil one day when Tom Carter chanced an off-handed remark about the recent unpleasantness.

"It's kind of like everybody all at once decided their life is in need of spring cleanen," Joe told Tom as they fed hogs one late afternoon, "and they're goen about it with all the energy of a female getten ready to give birth. Nobody takes anything for granted anymore, even things we've done virtually every day of our lives. And it's like taken your life in hand to tease somebody, make a simple observation or even answer a question in some cases. To tell you the truth, Tom, it's kind of like we're all at war with each other: We're all as volatile as wartime alliances and as fragile as peace treaties."

It was a highbrowed explanation—the kind her oldest brother was given to in these last days of his senior year in high school—but Bonnie understood the message. Attitudes were rotten around the house and everyone was grumpy, despite their insistence that things had returned to normal. Bonnie hoped the situation might improve, but she was reserving her opinion until she saw evidence of it.

Finishing his story about Doubting Thomas and urging the children to believe with all their heart that Jesus had died on the cross and risen from the grave for them, Preacher Cook asked if anyone had questions. Bonnie thought a quick moment, then raised her hand.

"Yes, Bonnie?" the preacher asked.

The church suddenly seemed awfully quiet. A sideways glance allowed Bonnie to see her mother and grandmother. Caroline was reading a story to the beginner's group of VBS scholars, and Rachel was helping the juniors with a craft project. Both women forgot their work temporarily, beaming with pride as they waited for Bonnie to discuss the story with the preacher.

"I enjoyed the story, Preacher, but I have a question," she said at last. "How in the world are we supposed to believe in somethen that we can't see, somethen that there's no way of knowen if it's real or not?"

"That's what Christianity is all about, Bonnie," Preacher Cook replied patiently. "Haven faith and trusten in the Lord even though we can't actually see Him as you and I see each other."

Bonnie pursed her lips in serious contemplation. "I suppose that's well and good for some folks," she said finally. "But I'm like Doubting Thomas. I prefer to see things for myself." She paused, then added loudly, "Guess this means I'll never be much of a Christian."

Her declaration resonated through the tiny church. An audible gasp greeted the assertion. Rachel snapped a child's stick house, and Caroline's book slid off her lap.

Noting all the fuss, Bonnie suddenly realized she had committed what the ladies of the church would describe as a serious breach of decorum. Her eyes widened as she glanced from Caroline to Rachel before the gaze settled on the preacher.

Preacher Cook watched her with a curious expression on his face. Then his features broadened into a big smile, and he threw back his head to release a hearty chuckle.

"Forgive me, sweetheart, but I beg to disagree," he said finally, with obvious amusement. "You have all the makens of an exemplary Christian, Bonnie, and I believe that one day you will find your faith. I may not have any proof of that at the moment, but I believe in you with all my heart."

For a long moment, the preacher regarded Bonnie with twinkling eyes. Then he patted her head and moved on to deliver another lesson in faith.

Bonnie wanted to trust his judgment. She almost believed him—but not entirely.

———

In less than a month, Joe would graduate from high school. By rights, this should have been the time to kick back and coast until graduation. Unfortunately, trigonometry, physics and a college-prep research paper—not to mention his ego—were making these last few days of high school more burdensome than pleasurable.

The classes would have been challenging in themselves, but Joe faced the added pressures of work on the farm and his own desire to finish as salutatorian of his class. From day one of high school, no one had ever doubted that Denise Culpepper would end up as valedictorian of the Cookville High School Class of Sixty-Three. The three-way race for salutatorian, however, had come as a complete surprise. Karen Baxter had been the favorite, but, undone by chemistry, geometry and home economics, of all things, her grades had faltered slightly in the tough junior year. Meanwhile, after a slow start his freshman year, Joe had begun acing every course in sight, while Deborah Faircloth had run a close third in the class academic rankings all three years.

Joe considered himself the underdog in the race for salutatorian, although not for lack of effort. He was contending with physics and trigonometry, while Deborah had only trig to worry over this year, and Karen had bypassed both courses in favor of easier credits.

While it could be debated who had the toughest classes, Joe knew that his workload at home was more demanding than anything Deborah or Karen could fathom. He was used to hard work, but the last few weeks had been brutal. Without Lucas Bartholomew around to help, the bulk of work fell upon Matt and Joe. His grandfather pitched in and so did his brothers, but one was too old and the others too young to tackle the hard work.

Joe found himself rising early to do chores, gulping down breakfast and dashing for the school bus. After school, he came straight home and usually was in the fields a good forty-five minutes before his brothers and sisters arrived, clamoring for a snack to tide them over until supper. He worked until dark, ate supper and hit the books until long after everyone else was fast asleep.

"It's nearly more than I can stand," he complained to Peggy Jo Nix as they lay in a secluded spot by the banks of New River one warm April night.

"You can take me home then," Peggy Jo replied, nibbling his ear. "I hate to take up so much of your valuable time and keep you away from the really important things."

Peggy Jo was a big-boned, buxom blonde, a high school classmate who had caught Joe's eye on the football field their freshman year. She had been a majorette in the marching band. From the moment he first saw Peggy Jo tromping across the field in a red-sequined uniform with short white boots, twirling her baton and jiggling like a bowl of firm jelly, Joe had been smitten by her generous presence.

Peggy Jo had proved to be as lighthearted as she was voluptuous, striking an instant friendship with Joe in the months following his career-ending injury on the football field. For three and a half years, they had been good friends, close like a brother and sister, with a hint of something incestuous and provocative lurking in the shadows.

Their romantic interplay had bloomed with the springtime. On a whim, Joe had asked her to go with him to the prom. The invitation had surprised and delighted Peggy Jo. Now they cavorted in the throes of a spring fling. It was a pleasant way to pass time as they waltzed through the final few weeks of school, each giving and receiving an education that couldn't be found in books.

It was all in good fun, too, a case of old-fashioned lust, from which each expected to walk away without remorse when they graduated in a few weeks. Both planned to attend college in the fall. Joe would pursue a degree in English. Peggy Jo was aiming for an M.R.S., with a specialty in P.H.D.-M.D.

Joe rolled onto his side and kissed her. "There you go again, jumpen to conclusions," he drawled. "I tell you, Peggy Jo, I got all the time in the world."

Later, when they had explored each other thoroughly and expanded their education, Peggy Jo cuddled against Joe.

"It's too bad I'm so dead set against becomen a doctor," he remarked.

"That thought crossed my mind, too," she replied. "Then I thought about it some more, and let's face it, Joe. We're really nothen more than friends when you get right down to it. I love you in a way, but we're kind of like kissen cousins. It's fun to fool around, but nothen good would come of it if we carried things too far between us."

"I suppose so," Joe agreed.

"Besides, your mama and grandma aren't too keen on me," Peggy Jo added. "They think I'm a floozy."

"They think no such thing," Joe argued. "They just happen to find you a little suggestive. That's all."

"It's my chest," she lamented. "It's not my fault I'm so well endowed."

"I don't think Mama and Granny have anything personal against your chest, Peggy Jo," he explained. "They just get a little riled up over the tight sweaters and all that cleavage. And I think the way you flirt gives them a little indigestion. They worry and maybe wonder, but they think you're a nice girl."

"And what do you think about me, Joe Baker?"

"It depends," Joe replied slyly.

"On what?" Peggy Jo inquired.

"On the moment," he said. "When you're all dressed up in red sequins marchen across the football field with your baton, I tend to think of you as a cherry tart, ripe for the picken. When we're in the cafeteria at school talken and eaten lunch, I consider you a good friend. But when you're lyen next to me—like now—I don't like to think too much, Peggy Jo."

"Want to know what I think about you?" she asked with a leer.

"What's that?"

"I think you have strong taste for cherry tarts," Peggy Jo said. "And you're very good at picken them."

Joe shrugged. "I have a very good and willen teacher," he replied.

They regarded each other for a tender moment, then dissolved into giggles and fell into a tangled mass.

————

At supper one Friday night, Sam casually mentioned that Good Friday had come and gone. "I can't remember the last time we didn't plant our garden on Good Friday," he said. "But with all the carryen-on around here, it's no wonder that we just plumb forgot."

"It's bad luck not to plant on Good Friday," John remarked. "Ain't it, Grandpa?"

"No, that's not the case," Sam replied. "It's just good luck to plant on Good Friday. It makes for the best gardens. We'll do okay, though, even if we are a few weeks late getten it into the ground."

Matt pushed back from the table and tried to rub away a headache. He was tired tonight. For weeks, he had done nothing but plant crops and fix ragged, worn-out equipment that he could not afford to replace. He had planted his fields once, before having to turn around and do it all over again after a solid week of torrential rains had washed away seed and flooded the fields.

He was working from sunup until sundown, then coming home to bickering children, nagging adults and an endless assault of bills. A garden was the last thing he wanted to think about. But if his family was going to have food on the table, a huge summer garden was a staple more valuable than sugar or flour. He leaned back in his chair, yawned and took a drink of iced tea. "We do need to get it in the ground," he commented.

"If I were you, Daddy, I wouldn't bother," Bonnie remarked absentmindedly as she picked at the last mess of the previous year's butterbeans.

"What makes you say that, honey?" Matt asked.

"It's not gonna grow, so why bother with it?" she suggested.

"Why won't it grow?" Matt responded.

"All that stuff you planted the first time around didn't," Bonnie pointed out. "And I haven't seen hide nor hair of anything you've planted this second go-round."

"It'll grow," Matt said, trying to sound patient, yet irked because everything she said was true, despite the farfetched ideas that fed her conclusions. "The seeds simply haven't been in the ground long enough to come through yet."

"I doubt it," Bonnie persisted. "I won't believe it until I see it."

Sensing his son's mounting frustration, Sam intervened in the debate. "Since you've decided to be our family's Doubting Thomas, Bonnie, I'm gonna give you a little summer experiment," he proposed.

"What kind of experiment?" Bonnie asked cautiously as supper ground to a temporary standstill.

"A garden all your own," Sam replied. "We'll fix you a little plot in the corner of the field, but you'll have to do all the planten yourself and then take care of it through the summer. I'll oversee to make sure you do everything the way it's supposed to be done, but it will be your responsibility."

"What can I plant?"

"Anything you want," Sam said. "You come along with your daddy and me tomorrow, and we'll get the seed."

Bonnie considered the suggestion. "A garden could be fun," she agreed. "I'll go along with it, Grandpa, but I still have my doubts that anything will ever come of it."

As everyone returned to their supper, Matt made a few plans in his head, hoping to accomplish the task in the quickest way possible. "Joe," he finally said. "First thing in the mornen, turn that piece across the road and get it ready for planten. Pa and I'll go into town to get the seed. Ma, Caroline, if y'all have any special requests, make out a list. I want to get through with this in one fell swoop."

His daddy's request irritated Joe, who already was ill natured because the day's work had forced him to cancel a date with Peggy Jo. Now this garden business threatened to spoil his Saturday plans.

"Can't John or Luke do it, Daddy?" he proposed. "I had somethen else planned for tomorrow."

"It'll go a lot more quickly and smoothly if you help out," Matt replied firmly to his son.

That suggestion angered Joe, who was beginning to feel put upon by the incessant demands. "We really ought to wait till Monday to worry about it," he persisted. "There's hogs in that field, and we need to move them first."

It was a feeble excuse to avoid the work, and Matt stared blankly at the boy, trying to keep his temper under control. "Well then, son," he replied with a touch of sarcasm, "I suggest you get up early and move those few shoats. Just open the gate and shoo them in with the others. It shouldn't be too much of a strain. Then you can turn the land, and we can plant a garden so you'll have something to eat this summer and next winter. That's a little bit more important than whatever you have planned."

"Yeah, yeah, yeah," Joe muttered, his tone a trifle bit more disrespectful than intended. "That's usually the way things work around here."

"Don't use that tone with me, son," Matt said sharply, "or you won't ever see the light of day."

They glared at each other with clinched jaws. Sensing the charged tempers of father and son, Sam tried to avert a crisis. Matt and Joe never exchanged cross words. Weariness was talking for them. "What's so important about tomorrow, Joe?" Sam asked.

Joe challenged Matt's gaze a second longer, then looked to Sam. "Nothen anymore. I had planned to do some fishen, maybe relax a little bit since we're almost all caught up."

"Well you can go fishen and relax on Sunday," Matt informed him. "Tomorrow, we're planten a garden."

"There'll be no fishen around here on Sunday," Caroline reminded Joe. "That's not what the Sabbath is for."

Joe rolled his eyes and shook his head. He took one last gulp of tea, rising from the table with the glass in hand.

"Don't you want dessert, Joe?" Rachel asked, trying to coax him back to good humor.

"I do not," Joe replied.

"Where are you goen?" Caroline called as he walked out of the room.

"To take a shower," he said tersely. "And then to bed unless anybody has any problem with that."

———

The thick hedge of red tips on the backside of Dr. Ned Turner's gabled and turreted brownstone mansion needed trimming, but the bushy shrubs provided excellent cover for the man to approach the house without being seen. He moved silently across the lawn, nervous and excited over the prospect of pulling off his first burglary, grateful for the moonless night. Once inside the house, he would have free run of the place because Ned and Delia Turner had left earlier in the day for a fishing trip to the Gulf Coast. But the actual act of breaking into the house scared him.

He quickly found a ground floor window leading to a spare room in the three-story house. Using the handle of his flashlight as a battering ram, he knocked out a small piece of one pane, then removed the remainder of the glass piece by piece and reached his gloved hand inside to unlock the window. To his dismay, the latch was missing. He rolled his eyes in disbelief, realizing he could have gained entry into the house simply by lifting the window. Knowing he should have checked first to see if the window was open, he attributed the blunder to inexperience.

Undaunted, the man edged the window open, unnecessarily concerned the creaking would reveal his presence. He pulled himself onto the ledge, pushed through heavy curtains and stepped onto some kind of trunk. He took a deep breath, realizing he had passed the toughest hurdle of the night.

His eyes adjusted quickly to the darkness, and he went to work. He canvassed the bottom two floors, paying particular attention to the bedrooms on the second floor, concluding the doctor and his wife slept in separate quarters.

Next, he tried to think like a thief to determine the things he would take from the house. He started with a jewelry box in one of the bedrooms, emptying the contents on the bed, picking out the most expensive pieces and dropping them into the burlap bag he carried. He took a pearl-handled, silver-plated pistol from the nightstand, then scattered the contents of a few more drawers and moved into the next room, where he found a coin collection in a bottom drawer. He put the coins in his sack, then moved to the downstairs rooms.

The dining room contained the best loot, including a silver tea set and goblets, plus what appeared to be expensive candlesticks. When the bag was filled, he considered for the first time the lucrative side of tonight's venture. He had come to the Turner house with a plan in mind. He was leaving with several valuables that could be pawned for cash. The idea pleased him.

Finally, he was ready to go. Glancing around the living room one last time, he decided the place appeared extremely neat. He considered and rejected the possibility of upending furniture and trashing drawers and cabinets. He had left his mark. There was no need to go overboard, especially when he planned to pay another visit on the good doctor and his wife.

In spite of himself, the man shook his head and laughed. He was blessed with vision, he thought, as he made his exit.

CHAPTER 2

OVERNIGHT, A SOFT RAIN fell, providing the perfect moistening for planting a garden. When the sun appeared on the horizon, it dawned on a storybook spring day, complete with a gentle breeze and stacks of fluffy white clouds.

By eight o'clock, Joe was in the field across the road, trying to drive fifteen shoats into the adjoining wooded land. He spread a pail of corn to entice the hogs near the gate. Given their piggish manners, he expected to have a relatively simple task of herding the hogs through the gate one by one. The shoats were feisty and ornery this morning, however, refusing to cooperate with his plans.

Joe argued and pleaded with the hogs, but they ignored the gate, continually running in the opposite direction every time he tried to push them through the opening. Making matters worse, the rain had turned the slop holes into slushy mud. Several times, Joe barely caught himself from stumbling into the muck. His sneakers were ruined within minutes, and he scolded himself for not having worn work boots.

After twenty minutes, he had moved only four shoats onto the other side of the fence. The others had gobbled down the corn and were drifting across the field. Joe fetched another pail of corn, spread it on the ground and opened the gate to shove through another hog.

The pig was extremely cantankerous, refusing to pass through the gate. Finally, Joe grabbed the hog by its ear, shoving and pulling the squealing animal through the gate. Instead of heeding its natural instinct to head for open space, the shoat somehow turned around and tried to slide back through the gate. Cursing the hog's pigheadedness, Joe rammed his knee against the animal, pinning its head against the wooden gatepost, intending to close the gate before the shoat gained freedom.

Seconds later, something hard slammed into his groin, knocking Joe head over heels. He went airborne before landing face down in a muddy slop hole. Before he could regain his faculties, several hogs trampled past him, stomping against his arms and back with their hoofs as they raced for their fair share of the corn.

Dazed, stricken with a sick feeling in the pit of his stomach, Joe needed a couple of minutes to come to his senses. He struggled to his knees, using a hand to steady himself against the gatepost. Finally, he pulled to a standing position and managed to close the gate before more hogs escaped into the field.

Still suffering from severe pain in his gonads, Joe took several cleansing breaths and tried to surmise the situation. In short order, he realized that Big Male, the huge Duroc hell-bent on protection of his charges, had butted him. In his preoccupation with pushing the shoat through the gate, Joe had failed to notice that the pig's high-pitched squeals had turned the other hogs into slobbering swine ready to defend their own. Big Male had led the charge.

Joe tried to rub away the pain in his groin and swallow the nausea in the pit of his stomach when he became aware of the mud clinging to him. He wiped his eyes clean, then pushed the sludge away from his forehead and mouth. His clothes were coated with mud, and his good disposition was declining.

―――――

"Mama!"

Even inside the house where she was washing dishes, Caroline heard the fury in her oldest son's voice.

Joe hollered once more, loud enough this time to attract the attention of everyone in the house. Caroline dried her hands on a towel, then pulled open the kitchen door and stepped onto the back porch. Joe stood a few feet from the porch steps, covered with mud from head to toe.

"Goodness gracious, Joe!" Caroline said as Rachel arrived to investigate the commotion and let out a short gasp.

"What in the world happened?" she whispered to Caroline.

"I don't know, but he's mad as a wet hen," Caroline answered back.

"Mama!" Joe yelled for the third time. "Tell those young'uns of yours to get on their work clothes and get their sorry tails out here with me. I need some help with those blasted hogs."

"Okay, Joe," Caroline replied calmly. "What happened, son?"

Joe gaped incredulously at his mother, a little wild-eyed, with his nostrils flared and one foot tapping furiously against the ground. "What does it look like happened?" he yelled. "The blasted things nearly killed me. I need help, Mama. Send those children out right now."

All at once, the back porch exploded with laughter as his brothers and sisters joined Caroline and Rachel. Joe simply waited for the laughter to stop, then ordered the children to help.

"They'll be out in a second, Joe," Rachel assured her grandson. "In the meantime, you might think about getten Pal-Two to help. He has a knack with wayward hogs."

Joe bit his lip, realizing his grandmother had the right idea. The German shepherd had a ruthless streak when it came it to rounding up hogs. Joe figured he could put the animal in the field with those shoats and sit back to watch the fun. Temporarily forgetting his indignation, Joe whistled for the dog, turned his back on his laughing family and headed back across the road with Pal-Two on his heels.

By the time his daddy, grandpa and little sister returned home from the seed store, the dog had chased the hogs from the field, and Joe was halfway finished plowing it.

―――――

Once the land was turned, Joe hooked the harrow to the tractor and disked the field to smooth out the plowed ground.

Across the road under the pecan orchard where the farm equipment lined the back fencerow, Matt and Sam prepared the two-row planter to lay a garden. The planter resembled a cultivator, with seven plows of varying sizes stretching across the front end to make neat rows and dig furrows for the seed. Behind the front line of triangular plows were the two planters, which created troughs in the ground, dispensed the seed and fertilizer and covered the crops with a layer of dirt, leaving orderly rows. Each planter contained two bins, with the larger ones used to dispense fertilizer and the smaller ones to apportion the seed.

In preparing the contraption to plant the garden, Matt and Sam filled the two large bins with guano fertilizer, then removed the two seed cylinders. When the planter was used to lay field crops, the cylinders were vital to dispense the seed. When planting a garden, however, Matt and Joe walked behind the planter, dropping the seed by hand through the chutes that fed into the trough. Matt had few superstitions, but he did believe in a hands-on operation when it came to planting the family garden.

By the time Joe finished harrowing the field, Matt and Sam had the planter ready. Although the two older men had been apprised of Joe's earlier misfortune with the hogs, they fell into sidesplitting laughter when they finally saw Joe.

"I've seen worse, but I don't know when," Sam commented when Joe had hitched the planter to the tractor. "You look like a dried mud cake."

Joe ignored the remark.

"Consideren everything, son," Matt said, "I think we can get by without you if you want to go fishen this afternoon. But I wouldn't get too near the water because you'll scare away the fish."

The feeble humor plunged the men into another round of choking chortles. Joe merely waited until they calmed down. "By gosh, Daddy," he said at last. "You were all-fired hot to plant a garden last night, so let's do it and be done with it."

"You heard the boy, Pa," Matt told Sam. "Let's plant a garden."

They required most of the afternoon to plant the four-acre patch with all the staples of the summer garden. Sam drove the tractor, while Matt and Joe walked behind the planter dropping the seed. When the seed had been planted, the younger children pitched in to transplant a variety of tomato, onion, eggplant and pepper plants. They worked until the patch was crammed with enough food to carry the family through another year.

When the garden was planted, Joe joined his daddy and brothers under the shade of two pecan trees in the field, watching as Sam helped Bonnie prepare her small garden. With a little coaxing, Joe provided the details about his futile efforts to move the hogs and the subsequent run-in with Big Male. He gave an embellished version of the ludicrous chain of events, sending everyone into fits of laughter. This time, Joe howled with everyone else.

"You're the only person I know who's been stampeded by hogs," Matt remarked when the laughter subsided.

Joe grinned. "Now that everyone's had a good laugh at my expense, I expect I'd better get cleaned up," he said. "Mama's not likely to let me in the house looken like this."

"That's for sure," Luke agreed.

"I think I'll go swimmen in the river," Joe said. "Who wants to join me?"

"I do!" John answered.

"Me, too," Luke added.

"What about it, Daddy?" Joe asked. "Come go with us."

Matt bunched his eyebrows. "It's warm enough today, but I bet that river water is cold as ice," he replied.

"It'll put some get-up-and-go back into you," Joe said persuasively.

Matt grinned at his sons. "Let's go!" he said.

John let out a whoop.

"Last one there's a rotten egg," Luke shouted.

―――――――

Under Sam's watchful eye, Bonnie planted corn, butterbean, cucumber, okra, pumpkin and sunflower seeds in her garden plot, along with tomato, cabbage and onion plants. Grandpa predicted the seeds would sprout within a week.

On the following Saturday, Bonnie woke with the full expectation that her garden had sprouted overnight. She was disappointed to find nothing but the same old patch of gray dirt when she went to investigate after breakfast.

"We should have planted radishes," Sam said, urging his granddaughter to be patient. "Radishes grow quickly, and they would have pushed through the ground by now."

Pushing aside her misgivings, Bonnie lugged the water hose across the road and gave the garden a good soaking. Later, she made a scarecrow out of tobacco sticks and a ragged pair of her daddy's dungarees.

In the back of her mind, the garden had become a test of faith. She was determined to believe, even without proof.

When Monday came and the garden remained barren, her faith wavered. Sam shored up her spirits, though.

"Just wait until we get a good rain," he promised. "Then you'll see nothen but peaks of green."

On Tuesday morning, the patter of rain on the tin roof woke Bonnie. Remembering her grandfather's prognostication, she hopped out of bed and went to the front door. The gentle rain quickened her heart and brought a rush of hope.

With only scant thought that she was barefooted and still in her nightgown, Bonnie opened the door and ran to her garden. Her breath caught as she came to the garden plot, where dozens of fresh green sprigs poked up from the rich earth. Gradually, she became aware of the hundreds of other shoots sprouting from the family garden.

In that moment, Bonnie felt her heart fill up with faith. She understood what Preacher Cook meant when he spoke of "things seen and unseen." And she understood that while doubts were an unavoidable part of life, faith in God was an eternal blessing.

———

On a scorching day in late summer as he carried two buckets of corn to the hogs, Joe noticed his baby sister sitting amid the remnants of her garden. Bonnie's fascination with the garden had touched the family that spring and summer. In some way, she had rekindled their passion for life and deepened their understanding of the forces shaping it.

Joe was acutely aware of all this as he watched his sister, wondering what occupied her thoughts. Bonnie had been a whir of motion throughout the summer. Now she seemed subdued, which concerned him.

He tossed the corn to the hogs, then set the buckets on the grass beside the gate and went into the field where Bonnie sat.

"Hey, there," he called. "May I join you?"

Bonnie glanced over her shoulder, then looked straight ahead again and motioned Joe to sit beside her.

"You seem deep in thought, honey," he remarked, sitting down beside the girl. "Anything you want to talk about?"

"My garden's about all played out," Bonnie said. "I'm a little sad."

"Gardens do that," Joe replied. "They come and they go."

"But this was a special garden, Joe," she explained. "It's the first one I ever took care of all by myself. I didn't want it to end. I wanted it to keep on growen."

"It was a humdinger, all right," Joe said cheerfully. "You did a great job with it. Your corn was the best I ever ate. And I know those cabbages must have been good because rabbits ate every one of them."

Bonnie smiled. "I hope they enjoyed them."

Joe pointed to two fat pumpkins still growing on the vines. "I don't think we've ever had a pumpkin quite so big on the place as those two," he pointed out. "They're spectacular. I bet Mama and Granny can make some kind of pumpkin pie out of them."

Bonnie nodded.

"Don't feel too sad about your garden, Bonnie," Joe urged. "It was your first garden, which makes it special. But you'll raise plenty more gardens if you want. Some will be bigger and better than this one, and some won't. I think part of the fun is the anticipation of it—getten the ground ready, putten in the seed, waiten for it to sprout and then watchen things grow."

"Do you know what's really on my mind?" she asked.

"I'd like to."

"When you get right down to it," Bonnie explained, "gardens are like people, Joe. They're here for a while and then they play out. No matter what, people die—always."

"But life goes on—forever," Joe said quickly. "I think that's most important to remember."

"Do you mean Heaven?" she asked.

"Just life, Bonnie. Heaven and earth and people—even you and me. It never ends, no matter what." He hesitated, then suggested, "Maybe not even your garden has to end. We could save some of your pumpkin seed and plant them next year if you want. That way, part of this garden would carry on."

"We could do that?" Bonnie asked hopefully.

"Absolutely. When you get ready to carve those pumpkins, let me know, and I'll help you with the seed."

Bonnie nodded. "I could make that one of my traditions," she said. "Do it year after year, so that it's never-ending."

"You could," Joe agreed. "It's an excellent idea."

"It's been a wonderful summer," Bonnie said in a while, a small sigh escaping her. "I hate to see it end."

"We've got fall to look forward to," Joe reminded her with cheerful optimism. "And there'll be other summers, too."

A huge smile settled on Bonnie's face. "One thing's for certain," she concluded. "There'll never be another brother like you."

Joe glanced up and bit his lip, acting puzzled. "Probably not," he grinned. "But there'll also never be another sister like you."

"Well, I suppose we should be thankful for that," Bonnie suggested.

"Among other things."

"Joe?" she asked a moment later. "Do you think we'll remember this summer when we're older?"

"I imagine we will," he said. "I certainly know we'll never forget this time."

FAITH AND GRACE
1964-1965

TOWARD THE END OF February in 1964, Florence Castleberry paid a noontime visit to the Bakers. It was a blustery day, and she knocked for a solid minute on the front door without an answer. Finally, she walked around the house to the side porch entrance and knocked on the kitchen door. Rachel answered almost immediately, inviting the neighbor woman into the warm kitchen where she was received with a round of greetings from Sam, Matt and Caroline.

"That wind cuts right through a body," Florence commented as she shook off the chill and took a seat on the table bench beside Matt and across from Caroline. "We'll have rain by nightfall."

"Probably before," Sam predicted as Rachel set a glass of iced tea before their neighbor. "These cold, damp days make my bones ache. I'll be glad for warm weather."

"It won't be long now," Florence replied, making herself at home, even though she had interrupted the family's dinner.

Florence was plumpish, grayish and in her mid-sixties. She was married to Slaton Castleberry, a struggling farmer much like Matt and Sam. The Castleberry place backed up against the western flank of the Baker place, the two farms separated by the railroad tracks. Florence and Slaton lived in a large white house that fronted Highway 125 between the mercantile and the New River school. Their three daughters and son were grown, married and living elsewhere.

The neighbors chatted for several minutes, discussing family and the upcoming revivals at Benevolence Missionary Baptist Church and the Holiness Baptist Church, where the Castleberrys attended—as well as twelve-year-old John's recent first-place prize in an art contest sponsored by *The Tifton Gazette*.

"I recognized the picture as y'all's orchard as soon as I saw it in the paper," Florence remarked. "It was a right nice picture. I didn't know John was so talented."

"He's been drawen and painten practically since he learned to pick up a color crayon," Caroline replied. "I don't know where John gets his talent, but we're proud of him."

"Florence, how's your children doen?" Rachel inquired. "Weren't they all home for the holidays?"

"They were," the woman said. "They wanted to be close to their daddy. Cheryl calls every day. It's nice haven her close by in Cookville. She's expecten again—around August. They're hopen for a girl this time."

"Do they have two or three boys?" Caroline asked.

"Two," Florence answered. "They're both pistols."

"How does Cynthia like Atlanta?" Rachel asked. "Is she adjusten to the big city?"

"She loves it," Florence said. "Her husband works for the power company, and they live in Doraville. Candace is still in Valdosta. She turns forty next month. I can't believe I got a child forty years old."

"Time sure does fly," Matt remarked. "I hit forty last year."

"My David had a ball with your Joe over the holidays," Florence said. "He's back in California now, tellen all his Air Force buddies about the deer he killed over the Christmas holidays. I think Joe and him and Tom Carter went hunten every day for a solid week."

"Joe thinks the world of David," Caroline said. "Always has ever since he was a little boy, and we swapped off help in the tobacco patch that summer. They're kindred spirits."

"Military life seems to suit David," Matt commented. "I guess he likes liven in all those faraway places, always be'en on the go. I was ready to get back home the whole time I was in the Army."

"He enjoys the lifestyle," Florence agreed. "David's gonna make a career out of the Air Force. He'll have nine years of service in June and will transfer to the Philippines this summer. I hate see'en him so far away, especially since Slaton had the heart attack."

"How is Slaton?" Sam asked. "I keep meanen to stop by and see him more often, but the winter's just slipped right past me."

"He's not doen too good," Florence confessed tiredly. "He's some better, but it's been a slow recuperation."

"We've been prayen for him at church," Rachel said.

"A lot of people have," Florence replied, "and I fully believe that's what's kept him goen these last few months. To tell you the truth, though, Slaton has a leaky heart. He's never gonna be his old self, and I guess we're finally admitten to that." She paused slightly, then added, "That's why I barged in on y'all today."

"Is there anything we can do to help, Florence?" Matt asked, setting aside his eating utensils and giving her his full attention.

"I hope so, Matt," she replied. "The truth is that Slaton's farmen days are over and done with. He'll never raise another crop."

"I was afraid of that," Sam said.

"We'll get along okay," Florence said. "We've got a little money set aside, and all our bills are paid."

"There's somethen to be said for security," Sam agreed.

"What we really need is someone to rent our land," Florence continued. "We've had several people ask about it since January. Slaton kept thinken you'd come around, Matt. When you didn't, he sent me over to see if you'd be interested. Y'all are good neighbors, and it would mean a lot to Slaton and me to have you worken our fields."

Matt crossed his arms and rubbed his chin as he considered the idea. "The only land I've ever rented is that ten-acre field behind the mercantile," he said at last. "I've always wanted to tend a little more, but it's been pretty much all Pa and I could do to keep up this place."

Florence reached into her sweater pocket, pulled out a folded sheet of paper and handed the note to Matt. "That's the price Slaton's hopen to get per acre," she explained. "We've got an even two hundred acres, Matt, plus a ten-acre allotment for tobacco. There's two tobacco barns on the place, which would be yours to use."

"That's more than a fair offer, Florence," Matt said.

"We're just looken to make ends meet," she replied. "The only other thing I'd ask is that you'd plant us a nice garden and maybe plow it once or twice to keep down the weeds."

"Honestly, Florence, I don't even know if we've got enough equipment to farm your place and ours," Matt said. "If we took on your fields, that'd almost double what I'm farmen now."

"You'd be welcome to use our equipment," she offered, "but I have to warn you, Matt: It's old and worn out, too—just like Slaton and me."

Matt smiled slightly, nodding at the woman. "You've certainly given us somethen to consider, Florence," he said. "I'm mighty tempted, but I'll need to think on it a day or two before I give you an answer."

"You do," she agreed, rising to her feet. "I just wanted to plant the seed in your mind. I know it's late in the year to be maken big decisions like this, but Slaton believes this is an arrangement that could benefit us all. You give it careful thought and let us know your answer. We hope you'll take the place, Matt, but if you decide not to, we'll understand."

––––––

Sam practically clapped his hands in anticipation the moment Florence Castleberry was ushered from the house. "It's manna from Heaven," he said to Matt, Caroline and Rachel. "We'd have more than four hundred acres of crops, plus the extra tobacco allotment. You could double your income, son."

"Or double your loss," Rachel warned.

"It's an unexpected opportunity," Matt agreed with his father. "I'm excited, but we'd have to make some adjustments. We'd definitely need a bigger and better tractor—some new equipment, too. That would mean borrowen from the bank."

"I hate to go in debt," Caroline remarked.

"I don't look forward to owen money either," Sam agreed, "but the truth is we needed a new tractor and new equipment last fall. Then we couldn't justify the loan. With two hundred extra acres to farm, we can justify the expense."

At the conclusion of the previous fall's harvest, Matt and Sam had taken stock of their equipment, and the result had been grim. They operated the farm with an aging two-row John Deere and an even older one-row Farmall. The tractors had served them well for many years but were becoming inadequate to shoulder the farm's mechanical burdens. Still, they had agreed the tractors would have to carry the load for one more year. If he tended the Castleberry place, however, Matt could justify the new tractor—a larger, stronger machine that would increase the efficiency of his operation and not break down in the middle of the growing season.

"Pa's right, Caroline," Matt said, his calm tone concealing a growing excitement. "We've got ragged equipment on this place, and, frankly, I'm not sure some of it can be fixed up to last another season."

Caroline and Rachel glanced at each other, sensing their husbands' anticipation, yet still lukewarm to the idea. "We'd be tenden ten more acres of tobacco, Matt, on top of what we already have," Caroline fretted. "We'd spend the whole summer worken in tobacco—probably six days a week."

"Since when have any of us ever been afraid of hard work?" Matt asked. "Carrie and John will be able to carry a full load this year. Lucas and Beauty will be around to help, and so will Tom Carter. We can do the work, and it'll mean extra money come fall—maybe the difference between barely getten by and getten by."

"Come fall, we'll also owe the bank a small fortune," Caroline worried still.

A silence settled around the table as Matt and Sam waited for the women to give their blessing to the proposition. Caroline and Rachel stared again at each other, then at their husbands.

Finally, Caroline sighed. "I guess my bookkeepen's gonna be a little more complicated this year," she said. "It probably is too good an opportunity to pass up, but let's think about it for a day or two before we commit ourselves."

"Fair enough," Matt agreed before grinning broadly at his family. "I have a good feelen about this. Maybe this is what we've been worken for all these years."

"Just make sure you plant a nice, big garden for Florence and Slaton," Rachel instructed her son. "And keep it plowed for them."

"I'll do that, Ma, regardless of whether we rent their land or not."

"There are some practical matters to consider before we decide for sure," Sam said. "While I can still hoe a pretty long row, the truth of the matter—which I reluctantly admit—is that you will need extra help to get those fields prepared and planted this spring, Matt. Lucas Bartholomew would be perfect for the job, but he's tied up until the first of June with his contract work. We're gonna need full-time help, son, someone strong and capable to work with you."

"Couldn't Joe do it?" Caroline suggested.

"He could, and I'm sure he would," Matt answered truthfully. "I wonder if it's fair to ask him, though. He'd have to take off from college, and that's the most important thing in the world to him. I hate to tie him down on the farm, even if it's only temporary." Matt sighed. "I suppose we had better think about everything a day or two before we give the Castleberrys an answer."

A gleam suddenly entered Caroline's eye. She glanced at Rachel, then back to Matt. "Come with us to church Sunday, and we can pray about it, Matt," she suggested, renewing a decades-old quest to entice her husband to darken the doors of Benevolence. "The Lord will lead us to an answer."

Matt grinned at his wife, knowing her suggestion had ulterior motives. "Now, honey," he replied patiently, "I got you, Ma and Pa sayen prayers for me. I think that's enough divine intervention for the time be'en."

"It's a fact, son," Sam said. "I offer up a prayer for you most every Sunday, and I'm sure the Almighty listens. Still, it might not hurt you to plead your own case occasionally. And it certainly would be beneficial to seek His guidance every now and then, especially now."

"You act just like a Catholic, Matt," Rachel remarked brusquely. "I'm not sayen that's all bad, but you seem to think that somebody else can pray you into Heaven, son. Well, it ain't so. I've read the Bible from one end to the other, and there's only one way for a body to win salvation. It's a personal matter between you and the Lord, Matt, and you need to start thinken about it."

"You're right, Ma," Matt agreed diplomatically. "It is a personal matter. And that's just how I intend to keep it."

––––––––

"Do you think about God very often?"

John's question surprised Joe. The two brothers were fishing off a rowboat in a water hole in the middle of the farm's largest field. The pond was full from winter rains, and the fishing was excellent on this first Saturday in March. The water hole's snaky reputation usually spared the fish any likelihood of winding up on the end of a hook, but the brothers had made up their minds to go after a big catch on this day. They had been rewarded with several huge channel catfish, as well as a long line of perch and bream. Twice already, a brazen snapping turtle had attacked the string of fish, making off with half a perch before Joe and John wised up to its antics and pulled the line into the bottom of the boat. On three occasions, they also had observed water moccasins gliding across the small water hole.

"Probably not often enough," Joe answered his brother as the cork on his line bobbed under the water and he hauled in another catfish.

"What does it mean to be a Missionary Baptist?" John asked when Joe had baited his hook and returned his line to the water.

Joe took a long time to answer the question.

The Bakers attended Benevolence Missionary Baptist Church, where Adam Cook presided over services on the second and fourth Sundays of each month. On the first and third Sundays of the month, Adam led services at Poplar Springs Church on the other side of the county. Prayer meeting was held the first Wednesday night of each month at Benevolence and on the second Wednesday at Poplar Springs, while Sunday school took place every week without fail. On those few five-Sunday months, the preacher got a respite from his pastoral duties, while fidgety children rejoiced over consecutive Sundays without church.

While Benevolence and Poplar Springs enjoyed their own identities, there was little theological difference in their beliefs. The Poplar Springs Baptists seemed a tad more liberal with their "Amens," but members of each persuasion felt comfortable in the other's service. They shared the services of Adam because neither church could afford a full-time preacher. During revivals, which occurred twice a year on back-to-back weeks in spring and fall, the congregations virtually became one, filling the tiny buildings to capacity to hear the exhortations of some visiting preacher.

Besides revivals, both churches were united in their desire to maintain distinct identities from the powerful Southern Baptist Convention and the hardline Primitive Baptists.

Several years earlier, Joe had asked his grandmother the same question now posed to him by John: What did it mean to be a Missionary Baptist?

"It means we're not Southern Baptists, Primitive Baptists or Methodists," Rachel had told him curtly. "And it means we're not snake handlers."

Mindful that God worked in mysterious ways, Rachel respected the path to salvation chosen by most any congregation—even the Catholics. While she believed Southern Baptists, Primitive Baptists, Methodists and snake handlers would wind up in Heaven right along with her, Rachel had preconceived notions about all four groups. The Southern Baptists and the Methodists argued too much over issues that had little to do with leading a God-fearing life; the Primitive Baptists misinterpreted the Bible's teachings on grace; and Rachel simply could not justify a place in church for rattlesnakes.

Joe agreed wholeheartedly with his grandmother on those accords, so he now told his brother: "It means we're not Southern Baptists, Primitive Baptists or Methodists. And it means we're not snake handlers."

John considered the answer for a long moment. "I can live with that."

"I wonder why people try to complicate religion so much," he added a moment later. "It's such a simple, foolproof thing if you approach it with the right attitude."

"The Lord's dealen with you," Joe commented matter of fact.

"Are you maken fun of me?" John asked quickly, skeptically.

"I am not," Joe answered strongly, smiling warmly at his brother. "It was a simple statement, John. Don't complicate it."

John considered the familiar advice, then grinned. "I see what I mean," he said. "What saved you, Joe? Why did you join the church?"

Joe lit a cigarette. "Everybody's got a different reason," he answered. "I made my public profession of faith and repented my sins, John. My reasons for doen it were between the Lord and me, and I'd prefer to keep it that way."

"I can live with that, too," John said with a sly smile. "Do you still feel saved?"

Joe took a long drag on the cigarette and checked his hook. "When you get right down to it, I guess I'm a backslider," he said at last. "I'm lusten for too many worldly things, I suppose, not prayen like I should, not readen the Bible like I used to do. But I do try to pay attention to the Sunday sermons. Adam Cook has a way of inspiren you."

"He sure does," John agreed. "He has a way of maken a person want to do good."

"I take it you are thinken about joinen the church," Joe surmised.

"Do you think I'm too young to be saved?" his brother asked.

"You're twelve," Joe began.

"Closer to thirteen," John pointed out, as he frequently did to any and every one these days.

"If the Lord's knocken on your heart, John, then you're old enough to answer," Joe suggested.

"He really is knocken," John said with wonder. "I can't rightly explain it, but I've felt so close to God lately. There's this feelen of peace and comfort and faith inside me. It's with me everywhere I go these days—walken through the woods, taken a test in school, even here today while we've been fishen. I've never felt like this, Joe, but I just know everything will be okay, no matter what happens."

Joe eyed his brother for a long moment, knowing the boy was sincere. A higher power obviously was working on John, and Joe was awestruck at the thought—as well as unsettled by the whole idea.

"I sound ridiculous, don't I?" John said suddenly.

"God is walken with you, John," Joe replied. "Follow your heart."

John searched his brother's face, found sincerity and gave Joe a shy smile. "I don't know what to make of it either, but I'll take your advice."

"I think you've hooked another one," Joe remarked suddenly, noticing the cork bobbing on his brother's line. "Let's see what you got."

A short time later, when he had caught another fish himself, Joe made a conscientious effort to lighten the serious mood of their conversation. "The decision is yours entirely, little brother, but if you do decide to join the church, I'd appreciate it if you could manage to get baptized before revival comes around," he said. "They always have foot-washen on Thursday night, and while I understand it's a beautiful gesture, I'd like to avoid a repeat of last year."

"What happened?" John asked.

"I wound up washen Mr. Millard Webb's feet," Joe said. "He had one corn after another and the longest toenails I've ever seen. Honestly, it grossed me out. I'd be more comfortable with your feet, John, and I think you could break into the routine a lot easier on my feet than on somebody like Millard Webb."

"Give me cigarette, and I'll think about it," John promised.

Against his better judgment, Joe obliged him.

———

One week later, Joe stood with his family and members of the Benevolence congregation on the banks of New River, singing *Shall We Gather at the River* as Preacher Cook led John into the cold water. It was almost like watching John the Baptist baptize Jesus Christ, and Joe chanced a skyward look, half expecting a dove to come flying toward his brother. The sky was clear, however, except for the radiant sun, which shone brightly over the occasion.

His brother's spiritual side impressed Joe. Clearly, the Lord had called John to serve a purpose. That purpose remained a mystery, however, and Joe had an uneasy feeling about it. Standing there, as John was lowered beneath the water, Joe uttered a silent prayer for his brother and turned the matter over to the Lord.

———

Benevolence Missionary Baptist Church was nestled amid a grove of mature pine trees. The church charter dated back to the turn of the century, but the current worship place had been erected in 1933 after fire destroyed the original building.

The community had always known hard times, but 1933 had been the year the Great Depression finally finagled its way into the economy of Cookville, making times harder than usual. As a result, the Benevolence congregation had taken pennywise measures when rebuilding the church. The building was constructed of sturdy pine timbers, with hardwood floors and, some people said, even harder pews. Knots and gaps in the timbers kept the church drafty and cold in winter, yet offered little relief on hot summer Sundays. The church was supposed to be painted white, but mostly it was gray due to a neglectful congregation that believed trappings were totally unnecessary to worship God.

Two long rows of rickety tables sat behind the church, where the womenfolk spread massive dinners on Big Meeting Sundays in spring and fall. The cemetery lay to the right, separated from the church by a clump of pine trees. The oldest grave dated to February 4, 1890, and a host of others appeared nearly that old.

In the fall of 1963, the congregation had decided Benevolence needed some sprucing. During the months since, they had restored the walls to a pearly white—outside and inside—installed ceiling fans and built a new altar. The crowning touch was a graceful steeple donated by the Berriens.

As the spring revival approached, the congregation looked forward to showing off and dedicating their refurbished sanctuary. Caroline had something more consequential on her mind in those days. She wanted to get her husband baptized.

The Bakers rarely missed a church service, except for Matt, who had not darkened the door to Benevolence since his first Sunday home from the war. His rigid avoidance of church was a source of great mystery and worry for Caroline and Rachel. When the mood struck them—and it frequently did—they fretted that Matt had never been baptized. Baptism was essential to salvation, and Caroline and Rachel believed staunchly that while God would overlook long absences from church, he would not forgive the lack of a public profession of faith in Christ and submergence in the pure waters of New River.

"Matt is a good man with Christian values, Caroline, but he is not a Christian," Rachel told her daughter-in-law one morning as they prepared dinner a few days before the revival was to begin at Benevolence. "We have to find a way to make him realize that."

"Every year—twice a year—it's the same old story at revival time," Caroline lamented. "I try to get him to attend just one service, but he simply refuses. Sometimes, I feel like I'm at my wits' end. Over the last few years, Matt has become as much a stickler as you and I over church matters and the children. He expects his family to be in church, makes sure we're on time and doesn't tolerate any lame excuse for missen a service. He has told me for a fact that see'en Joe and John baptized were two of the happiest occasions of his life, yet even on those days he refused to set foot inside the church. At home, however—and you know this as well as I do, Ma—he sets a Christian example. He blesses meals, he has even read our nightly devotionals. I just don't understand why he refuses to attend church with us."

"Likely, he doesn't either," Rachel replied sadly. "But we can't give up on him, Caroline."

"I'll never do that," Caroline said, reaffirming her convictions. "I want to share my happiness with Matt in Heaven one day."

Over the next few days, Caroline coaxed and prodded, blatantly asked and gently reminded her husband to attend one of the upcoming revival services, always careful never to cross that thin line where her efforts would turn into harping and sour Matt on the whole deal. In one moment of frustration, she even volunteered to turn Methodist if Matt would agree to get sprinkled.

"I appreciate the gesture, honey, but the Methodist church ain't for me," Matt replied patiently. "If I ever do decide to join up with a church, I promise it'll be the Missionary Baptists. As I hear tell, y'all has about the only choir around where I could sing out loud and not sound off key."

"Humph!" Caroline groused a minute later when his appraisal of the Benevolence choir became clear in her mind. By then, Matt was gone, having fended off another attempt to get him into church.

On the Saturday before revival services began on Sunday night, Caroline's persistence turned into nagging and Matt took offense. They quarreled loudly, fiercely, their general disagreement rapidly evolving into outright anger. The battle of wills ended with Matt cursing and stomping from the house, while Caroline wept and retreated to their bedroom.

Sam went after Matt, while Rachel tried to console Caroline. Both were told to mind their own business.

The children were disturbed. Their parents rarely shared a cross word with each other, much less yelled, cursed and cried—especially over religion. They all went to bed early, hoping the dawn would restore the peace between their parents.

Matt returned home late that night with whiskey on his breath. Caroline started to rebuke him, then changed her mind when he confessed to drinking. Instead, they apologized to each other, reached a quiet truce and quickly surrendered to complete forgiveness, making up and making love.

Matt never made it to any of the revival services.

———

The revival reached its high point on Thursday night. Day services were planned for Saturday and Sunday, with dinner to be spread both days on the church grounds, but Thursday was the pivotal night.

Instead of summoning a visiting preacher, Benevolence had opted for Adam Cook to lead the spring revival, and the result had been overwhelming. On Monday night, the preacher had delivered a stirring hellfire and brimstone message, saving Summer Baker and five other people in the process. He followed with an inspirational message on Tuesday, breathed fire again on Wednesday and delivered the promise of Jesus Christ on Thursday. Sixteen people had repented their sins over five days of preaching, and they would be baptized Sunday in New River.

Matt vowed to be by the riverside when Adam baptized Summer, but he would miss Sunday's Big Meeting service.

His daddy's refusal to attend church preoccupied Joe's thoughts as he waited to take communion, a semi-annual event at Benevolence, always offered on the Thursday night of revival week. He was seated next to John in the Baker family pew as Paul Berrien and Dan Carter passed the plates with bread and tiny cups of grape juice. He ate the bread, drank the wine and offered a hasty prayer for the Lord's Supper.

Earlier in the afternoon, Joe had almost asked Matt why he refused to attend church with the family. The question had been on the tip of his tongue as they repaired a broken chain on the tobacco transplanter. Unfortunately, Matt made an errant move with the screwdriver, the tool slipping and puncturing the fleshy part of Joe's hand between the thumb and index finger. Joe had cursed, Matt had cursed and they had both wound up laughing before sharing the last cigarette between them and finishing their work.

"It always amazes me how much we have in common," Matt had told his son. "And how that tiny bit of uncommon makes all the difference in the world between us."

Joe had felt the same way for a long while now, and the thought was firmly on his mind tonight. Despite their differences, father and son were kindred souls at heart. The notion made Joe more than a little uncomfortable as he reflected on Matt's attitude toward church, so he changed his thoughts.

On this day, he had written his final English essay and completed his second quarter of classes at Abraham Baldwin Agricultural College—commonly known as ABAC. Tomorrow, he would become a full-time farmer, embarking on a six-month mission to help his father tend their expanded operation.

When Matt had made the request for his son's assistance a few weeks earlier, Joe had volunteered without hesitation. Joe did not regret the decision to leave school temporarily to help bolster his family's fortunes. Still, he wondered what it would be like to spend six months away from classes. He expected to miss school, but he also looked forward to the hard work ahead of him. His instincts told him something special was afoot for his family, and he wanted a front-row seat to whatever it might be. Somehow, he knew, this was the year when that elusive promise of *next year* would prove fruitful for his family, and he needed to be part of the fulfillment. His future would wait awhile longer.

Instinctively, he bowed his head again, this time in silent prayer for the good Lord's blessing on the farm. When he opened his eyes a short time later, John was poking him in the ribs.

"It's time to wash feet," his brother whispered. "Let's go get a tub together. I don't wanna get stuck washen Mr. Millard Webb's feet."

Joe washed his brother first, removing John's shoes and socks, bathing each foot with water, wiping them with a soft, white cloth and finally taking the towel draped over his shoulder to dry the feet. The entire act played out in silence and when Joe finished washing his brother's feet, he glanced up and discovered John regarding him with a sincere smile.

John placed a hand on his brother's shoulder. "I dreaded this tonight," he confessed. "I thought washen somebody else's feet was a silly thing to do, but it's not. I understand it now. When you wash another person's feet, you show them how much you're willen to do for them—maybe how much you love 'em. I've always believed I could count on you for anything, Joe. You're always there, maken all the right moves, sayen all the right things. I don't know what your secret is, but I hope it rubs off on me."

Joe cocked his head, holding his brother's gaze. "I'm flattered," he admitted at length, "but what a strange thing for you to say, John. Why?"

John glanced around the sanctuary, where the women sat on one side and the men on the other as they participated in the religious act. "Because this is a special night. We could wash each other's feet and let it go at that, without ever given it another thought. But it's supposed to mean somethen. I just want us to always remember this one night."

"We will then," Joe promised. "When we're old and sitten on the porch in our rocken chairs, strollen down memory lane, we'll remember this night, John. And recall how special it really was."

They exchanged places then, Joe sitting on the church pew while John kneeled before him with the basin of water and washed his feet. When the ritual was finished, they cleaned up their space, returned to their seats and joined the congregation in singing hymns.

On a typical revival night, the service ended with an altar call as members of the congregation moved forward to kneel and pray, while others sought to confess their sins, seeking baptism and membership in the church. As was customary on the final night of the Benevolence revival, however, the congregation spread out in a crooked circle through the sanctuary, holding hands and praying aloud in a chain prayer. When Preacher Cook concluded the prayer, the singing began again with *Amazing Grace* followed by *The Old Rugged Cross* and other hymns.

Preacher Cook started the final procession, making his way from one person to the next in a parade of tearful, happy hugs and gladsome handshakes. One by one, the congregation peeled off behind the preacher, singing and acknowledging each other as brothers and sisters in Christ. It was an emotional, spiritual parade of the Christian heart, and everyone surrendered to the power of the moment.

Joe figured he must have hugged a hundred people that night—friends like the Berriens and the Carters, all of his family members, a host of neighbors, fellow Benevolence members and several strangers, even Mr. Millard Webb. He teared up right along with everyone else, thanked the Lord he had been able to humble his heart and prayed he would find the way back to the straight and narrow.

IN EARLY APRIL, ADAM Cook paid a call on the Baker farm to deliver the family's tax returns. To supplement his preacher's income, Adam and his wife ran a small accounting business in Cookville. The minister was tall and rangy, in his mid-thirties, with brown hair worn a little longer and shaggier than most men in the community. He wore blue jeans whenever possible, hunted, fished and led lost souls to the Lord.

The preacher's father had married Matt and Caroline, and his two congregations had called Adam to succeed his father six years ago when Fred Cook took ill and died.

Matt regarded the young minister with deepest respect. Adam was an easygoing, sincere man, who provided a conscience for the community without dictating the way it should be.

"I'd be pleased to have you join us for services on Sunday," Adam always told Matt when their paths crossed. Nothing else, nothing more—just a simple invitation. Matt always thanked him politely, never committing to or rejecting anything.

He was planting cotton in the field beside the house when Adam drove into the Baker yard. Adam walked into the field, carrying the tax forms and standing at the edge as he waited for Matt to reach the end of the row.

It was the busy time of the season for both men, so they greeted each other, chatted quickly and got down to business. Adam explained the tax returns, answered a couple of questions for the farmer and got Matt's signature on the forms.

"I wish all my work was as easy as your tax returns, Matt," the preacher said. "Your wife keeps excellent records. It's a pleasure doen business with y'all."

"Caroline is precise," Matt remarked. "She pretty much keeps track of every penny that comes on or goes off the place. How much do we owe you, Preacher?"

Adam started to hand the bill to Matt, then stopped suddenly and grinned. "How does one Sunday in church sound?" he asked. "I'd forgo the bill in exchange for haven you at next Sunday's service."

Matt eyed the preacher with a bewildered expression.

"Adam Cook!" he exclaimed a moment later. "I don't know much about your line of work, but blackmailen someone sure doesn't seem like the preacherly thing to do."

Adam laughed heartily. "I saw somethen like that in a movie," he confessed. "It worked well on Henry Fonda, so I thought I'd give it a try."

"Have my wife and mama been talken to you?" Matt inquired.

"They only ask me to remember you in my prayers, Matt," the preacher answered. "This isn't part of some conspiracy to get you to church. But you have been on my mind lately, probably because you were at the river when John and Summer were baptized."

"I see," Matt said.

"I wonder if you really do," Adam replied sincerely. "I don't want to belabor the point, but I'd like to say somethen to you so I can satisfy my conscience if nothen else. In a way, you and I are a lot alike, Matt. You plant your seeds in hopes of harvesten a good crop. I'm always looken for a good harvest, too, only I'm out to get a crop of souls for the Lord. I've come to realize lately that you're a crop I've neglected for one reason or another. I'm not gonna badger you, Matt, but I am goen to urge you to give some serious thought to your soul. It's not for me to judge and if that seems what I'm doen, please forgive me. But I believe you live a Christian life, Matt. Liven it is not enough, though. Christ laid a few ground rules for salvation, and I owe it to the Lord—and my conscience—to ask you to consider how those basic rules apply to your life."

"I worry about it myself, Preacher," Matt conceded. "Somethen keeps holden me back—maybe hardheadedness, maybe laziness, maybe even a little fear that I won't or can't measure up."

"The mystery of Christ is somethen to behold, Matt, but this much is clear in my mind," Adam replied. "You won't ever measure up. We are saved by the grace of Christ, but it is a matter of our faith that allows us to experience that grace."

"Faith is a difficult thing, Adam."

"Only as difficult as we choose to make it, Matt."

They were silent for a careful moment, then Adam laughed. "I'm sounden like a preacher, which is the last thing I wanted to do," he admitted. "Just give it some thought, Matt. You know your needs and the Lord knows your needs better than anyone else, including Caroline, your mama or me."

Adam offered his hand, and Matt shook it. The preacher took several steps toward his car, then turned back to the farmer.

"I've always admired you, Matt, ever since I was a kid," he said. "Your strength, your compassion, your general caren for people. Back when you did attend Benevolence, I took it for granted you were a Christian. My sermons won't save you, but I sure would like to look into the congregation on Sundays and see you looken back at me."

Matt laughed slightly. "We'll see. I'll think about it."

Adam grinned broadly. "Watch out for preachers with ulterior motives," he teased.

"You could never have an ulterior motive if you tried, Adam," Matt suggested lightly as the preacher started to walk away from him. "Keep us in your prayers, Preacher."

Adam stopped again, turned slightly sideways and glanced one last time at the farmer. "I'll do that," he vowed. "And you keep me and mine in your prayers."

The two men nodded again, then returned to their busy days.

———

"Weather's worken like a well-rehearsed play," Joe told Matt and Sam just before dinner on the day his brother and sisters ended another school year. "This might be one of those seasons, Daddy, when we have money left over come next winter. This could be the year you've been waiten for."

The three men stood on the edge of the field located directly on the south side of the house, surveying a swath of new cotton. Matt was one of the few farmers in these parts who continued to plant King Cotton.

"You may be right, son," he replied. "You may just be right about that."

Given the fickleness of the relationship between farming and profits, their expectations seemed overly optimistic. But the young season was moving along perfectly, with full cooperation from the weather. Abundant rain had ushered in the spring, followed by a dry spell that allowed ample time to plant the crops. As soon as the last seed was sown, plentiful rains had returned to nurture the young rows of cotton, peanuts, corn, tobacco and other crops that lined the family's fields.

Their hopes sprang from the knowledge that the obligations awaiting the family in the fall were larger than ever. By taking on the Castleberry place, they had nearly doubled the size of their farming operation. Matt had financed the land rent, the crop, a new tractor and equipment with an enormous loan from the Citizens and Farmers Bank in Cookville. The debt was staggering, more than the family had ever owed, and they needed a prosperous year to pay the bill. The risk came, however, with considerable opportunity for profit—certainly greater than they had ever experienced.

Without a doubt, the spring of his nineteenth year had been the most incredible time of Joe's young life. Everything within his realm filled him with exhilaration, especially these difficult days of helping his daddy accomplish twice the amount of work that previous springs had required of them. He had crisscrossed one field after another on a hard-seated tractor, lugged countless bags of seed and fertilizer into the planter and tracked once more across the same fields. He had spent long days hoeing weeds and breaking thousands of tiny suckers and flowering tops from the tobacco patch. The work had honed the boy's rangy form into a man's body. He was lean and hard, with muscles bulging in his arms and chest, while the hot sun had baked his upper body a leathery brown.

The toil of the labor exhausted Joe—for about ten minutes each night after the workday ended. Then, filled by some inexplicable and inexhaustible source of energy, he went in search of new fields, perhaps horseplay with his brothers and sisters, a quick swim in the river or a quiet moment with a book or a fishing pole. But usually, boisterous business bordered his playing fields.

"You're downright annoyen," a weary Matt told his son one night after a playful moment at the supper table.

"The world is my oyster, Daddy," Joe teased back.

"But, Joe, you don't even like oysters," eight-year-old Bonnie remarked earnestly, unknowingly, as the family dissolved into laughter around her.

Joe's enthusiasm was infectious and rampant, spreading far beyond the confines of his family and the farm.

Unable to provide his son a salary, yet wanting to reward him some way, Matt helped Joe buy a used Volkswagen Beetle. The bright red car became Joe's passport to a whole new realm.

On Friday and Saturday nights as well as some weeknights, he bounded into the car and disappeared, always careful to return home by midnight to avoid the ire of his parents. He saw movies, loitered in crowded parking lots with friends and acquired a taste for Blue Ribbon beer, preferably when a pretty waitress served it.

Often, he passed the hours in the company of Peggy Jo Nix. A year ago, they had embarked on a spring fever romance. The feelings still lingered. It was a fling between good friends, a learning experience preparing them for something more substantial in the future—with someone else, of course. They spent hours discovering each other, usually on a blanket in some secluded place.

"We're probably spoilen each other for the future," Peggy Jo told Joe one deliciously satisfying night as they shared a cigarette. "Do you think we'll ever find anyone to measure up to our standards?"

"At the worst, let's have fun tryen," Joe suggested. "And then we'll teach them everything we've learned."

"If somehow, I reach the ripe old age of thirty without ever finden a well-to-do husband, preferably a doctor, and you're still single, too, let's marry each other," she suggested.

"It's a deal," Joe promised.

As luck would have it, Tom Carter became romantically involved with Liz Barker, one of Peggy Jo's best friends. The four of them spent many evenings by the banks of New River, skinny-dipping and falling in lust, bragging and daring, pondering and reflecting, mixing pure innocence with the slightest trace of decadence to create the best of times. No one had expectations or made demands. Freedom rang, especially between Joe and Peggy Jo, and they often went their separate ways, yet always kept in close touch and made their plans accordingly.

Frequently, Joe traded Peggy Jo's company for tamer activity with his brothers and sisters or something wilder with Tom. Sometimes, the whole bunch of them crowded into the Volkswagen and disappeared for hours, leaving an empty, silent house that unsettled their parents and grandparents. On other occasions, Joe discriminated, picking a single companion or perhaps two of his siblings to frolic away the night. He ignored no one.

The spring unfolded gloriously, and the summer beckoned with an appeal all its own. Joe reckoned he was enjoying a glimmer of immortality. He lived in the moment and thrived during every minute of it.

————

After years of racial calm in Cookville, signs of unrest appeared. Aided by the National Association for the Advancement of Colored People, or NAACP, a small group of blacks petitioned the county to remove the "For Whites Only" signs on the public restrooms and water fountains at the county courthouse. The effort failed, but the group made a lasting impression, which was reinforced a few weeks later by the American Civil Liberties Union.

The ACLU provided an attorney for the trial of a Negro man accused of burglarizing the home of an influential white citizen. At the attorney's urging, the community's colored people came down out of the courthouse balcony to swamp the pews of the courtroom floor on the trial's opening day. The act enraged Judge Wilson Avera, who prided himself on courtroom decorum as much as his knowledge of the law. Judge Avera ordered Sheriff Paul Berrien and his deputies to remove the Negroes from the courthouse.

Paul had filed the charges against the burglary suspect in question and considered it an open-and-shut case. The ACLU's intervention first surprised, then angered him as the slimy lawyer sought to create distrust in the colored community by slandering Paul's sincere commitment to dish out justice fairly and impartially. Feeling betrayed by the very people he had tried to help, Paul wanted to uphold the judge's order. His conscience, however, forced him to remain true to his beliefs.

"I can't do that, sir," he told the judge when Wilson Avera ordered him to remove the colored upstarts.

"Why not?" the judge demanded to know.

"Because there's not a single law in the land, including our county ordinances, that says these people don't have a right to sit where they want to in this court-house," Paul declared. "Tradition is not the law, Judge, and I'll have no part in any scheme to railroad them out of this courtroom."

Judge Avera threatened Paul with contempt of court, but the sheriff stood his ground. Finally, the judge relented, and the trial proceeded in quick order. By the day's end, the suspect had been found guilty as Paul expected, and Judge Avera had handed down the harshest prison sentence available under the law.

Bobby Taylor maintained a close watch on the proceedings, milking the integra-tionist efforts for every political advantage possible, always careful to refrain from any direct attacks on Paul Berrien.

Bobby and Paul were in the midst of another heated election battle, and Bobby believed he could unseat the sheriff.

Bobby had campaigned for the job ever since the bitterness of his 1960 defeat vanished—or at least subsided to the point where he could deal with it. In retro-spect, Bobby had found triumph in the close outcome of the previous election. Even when all had been said and done in that bitter fight, Paul Berrien remained one of the most respected men in the county. Yet, only a few votes had kept Bobby, a rela-tive upstart, from claiming victory. Ever since coming to this realization, Bobby had waged a steady campaign to mend fences and become more respectable while still promoting his prejudiced beliefs. He already had increased his share of votes for the next election, and now, fate appeared on his side as well.

Given the tone of the last election, Bobby concluded the public was unlikely to tolerate any more slander of Paul's credibility. So instead, Bobby unleashed his attack on the NAACP and the ACLU, two organizations with motives and means that even some of the South's staunchest civil rights supporters distrusted. He deftly pointed out the current sheriff's support of these outsiders' courtroom demonstration tactics, then shrewdly reminded voters of a handful of unsolved crimes in which Negroes were the prime suspects. In particular, he cited two incidents at the home of Dr. Ned Turner, which was located right off the square in Cookville.

"People, it's time to wake up!" became the rallying cry of his campaign.

"These outsiders, carpetbaggers and scalawags, all of them, are peddlen their evil ideas all across our beloved way of life," he repeated to anyone who cared to listen. "We are under siege right here on the main square in Cookville. You need look no farther than the home of Dr. Turner to find the evidence. And while the crimes go unsolved, our sheriff spends his days in the courthouse, defenden the rights of those who spread dissension and cause turmoil in our justice system."

Paul speculated he could become the first one-term sheriff in the county's history.

He had dropped by the Baker home to visit Matt one night after prayer meeting. Politics were an unavoidable subject, and the sheriff was frank about his chances of re-election.

"The trouble is that Bobby's runnen a fairly respectable campaign this time," Paul explained. "Except for his insinuations that I'm in cahoots with the ACLU and the NAACP, everything he's done has been legitimate as far as politics goes. It is the sheriff's job to solve crimes after all. Bobby's just keepen a handful of those unsolved cases in the public eye. Pretty smart tactic if I say so myself. And effective."

"I think you're be'en too generous, Paul," Joe said. "Bobby's running a racist campaign. The only thing notable about it is that his campaign is not nearly as ugly as it could be—or may be before it's all over."

"People will see through Bobby," Matt added. "Surely, he can't pull the wool over enough eyes to win the election."

"I don't know," Paul worried. "Ned Turner is solidly in Bobby's corner this time around, and Ned supported me in the last election. The doctor wields considerable influence around Cookville, and he's been successful at getten town folk to believe they're not safe in their homes."

"The pompous Dr. Turner and the bigoted Bobby Taylor," Joe remarked scathingly. "What a partnership. It's just crazy enough to be believable, especially since the good doctor is as prejudiced as they come."

"You know the old sayen: Politicians make strange bedfellows," Paul opined. "I guess it's true."

———

On an early morning in the middle of June, Joe jumped out of bed at the first ring of his alarm clock and slipped quickly into a clean pair of ragged blue jeans, a faded red T-shirt and a comfortable pair of worn work boots. He was still feeling randy following the previous night's date with Peggy Jo.

Without bothering to tie his shoes, he pulled open the bedroom door and tapped his two sleepy brothers from happy dreams as he passed through their room. His daddy and grandpa were already in the kitchen when Joe arrived. Both men grunted inaudible greetings, which Joe returned as he poured a cup of coffee. While waiting for the sleepyheads, they drank the steaming black liquid in silence, each pondering the day's work.

A few minutes later, Sam went to milk the cow while Matt and his sons piled into the cab of a two-ton truck that needed a new muffler. The truck was used primarily to haul heavy loads and transport crops to the markets. Joe steered the vehicle down the potholed road, while his two brothers bounced around in the bed of the truck, trying to ignore the predawn chill that pimpled their arms. They were headed to the Castleberry place to unload a barn of freshly cooked tobacco.

Tobacco was the family's greatest source of income and biggest burden. Everyone pitched in to help, all of them working in the tobacco field, except for Rachel, who took care of the housework and cooked three meals a day—a filling breakfast, a huge dinner and a light supper.

With the additional ten-acre crop allotment acquired from the Castleberrys, the Bakers were growing twenty acres of tobacco this summer. Harvesting the crop would tax their sanity from the first of June until the first of September. They worked anywhere from five and a half to six full days each week during the tobacco season, gathering the crop from the fields and filling four barns, where the leaves were cooked over open flames that cured the tobacco to a tawny, golden brown color in five to seven days.

Over the years, as he acquired gumption and experience, Joe had come to understand that the law of averages did not apply to the tobacco. On a typical day in a typical year, he presumed the worst would happen, tried to prepare and still was usually surprised by whatever went wrong on any given day. Equipment malfunctioned sometimes, people got hurt occasionally and everything turned back-asswards every now and then. Yet, as difficult as the task was, Joe enjoyed working in tobacco. He figured his passion for the leaf was some form of deranged hedonism, and he believed that—if cotton was king, then tobacco was a kind of god. It was just a thought, without a single shred of sacrilege intended.

The golden leaf lured prey with seductive charms, like a spider with its web; then consumed the victim in a sensual orgy.

Tobacco was a way of life among the Bakers. Like his daddy and grandfather before him, Joe enjoyed the pleasures of smoking. Now John was leaning toward the habit, although he would be discouraged, particularly if caught by his mother or grandmother, who preferred not to see children smoking. Still, no son of Matt Baker would suffer a severe reprimand for smoking. It was a different story for his daughters, of course. While Rachel dipped snuff—as did many Southern women of her era—it simply was not proper for women to smoke.

"It looks trashy," Rachel often said with a frown—but only when the subject came up in conversation, never as a judgment.

On barn-filling days, which were every day but Sunday, the family got additional help from Lucas, Tom and either the dependable Peggy Jo Nix or the increasingly unreliable Polly Tuckerman. Peggy Jo and Polly were supposed to alternate work-days on the Baker farm, but the Tuckerman girl frequently came up with an excuse to miss her turn in the tobacco field, leaving Matt in a lurch and Peggy Jo in more demand than she wanted.

Four days a week, the men in the crew rose early to unload one of four barns—two of which were on the Baker farm and the others on the Castleberry place. On this morning, they would tackle the "chocolate barn," so named for its brown-colored shingled sides. The chocolate barn was the smaller of the two barns on the Castleberry place. The barns were tall, box-shaped buildings, containing "rooms" that were actually row upon row of wooden tiers with open walls. The tiers were horizontally spaced four feet apart and vertically separated about two feet. Three of the tobacco barns contained five rooms with eight tiers. Each tier held eighteen to twenty sticks of tobacco. The second barn on the Castleberry place was gigantic, with an extra room and nine tiers, each of which easily held twenty-one sticks of tobacco. The Baker crew needed almost two days to fill that monster.

Arriving at their destination, where Lucas and Tom were already waiting, Joe pulled the truck into place beside the barn and shut off the engine as everyone piled out of the vehicle. Except for another round of mumbled greetings, no one said a word in those first few minutes as they drifted into their accustomed places, adjusted their eyes to the dark and went to work with the first light of dawn.

While his family and friends cleared the bottom tiers in each room—taking two sticks at a time and carrying them to the truck, where Matt laid them in layers across the truck bed—Joe climbed onto the barn's lower tiers.

Joe relished a fresh-cooked barn of tobacco. He took a deep breath of the sweetly, pungent tobacco, savoring the aroma. It was an enticing, sensual fragrance, tingling his nose in the same way that Joe supposed the salty seawater of an ocean would.

Minutes later, the thrill was gone as he straddled the tiers, passing the sticks of cured tobacco down to Lucas. Joe had forgotten his cap, and the barn contained the last cropping of sand lugs, those bottom leaves on the tobacco stalk that grew on the ground and were covered with grit. Sand stung his eyes and itched his body unmercifully, especially down the nape of his neck. Joe growled, secretly suspecting the surgeon general was at the bottom of this mess.

———

They unloaded the barn in less than an hour, then transferred the tobacco to the Castleberry packhouse. The availability of the spacious Castleberry packhouse was especially satisfying to the Bartholomews who still lived in the Baker packhouse.

Lucas and Beauty now had two children. Annie was two and Danny one. Living conditions were cramped enough in the one-room shed without having to share it with a barn-full of cooked tobacco. Beauty spent her days in the Castleberry packhouse and various outbuildings on the Baker place, unstringing the tobacco and stacking the loose leaves in neat piles along the walls. In their spare time, the men-folk packed the leaves into neat circles on burlap sheets, tied the ends, loaded the tobacco onto a truck and carted it off to the huge warehouses in Cookville for sale.

When the tobacco had been stored in the Castleberry packhouse, the men returned to the Baker home where they ate a quick, filling breakfast of streaked meat, grits, eggs and toast. Before eight o'clock, they were on their way to the tobacco patch—the whole crew packed into the pickup truck, except for Joe and John who had left earlier on the new John Deere tractor.

On a typical day, the entire crew climbed aboard the double-decker harvester and was riding through the fields cropping tobacco by eight o'clock. Joe, John, Tom and Lucas sat in two rows of metal seats, picking three to five tarry, greenish yellow leaves from each stalk along their respective rows. They were the *croppers*, placing their hands of tobacco into metal clips attached to a chain that revolved around a series of fearsome cogs.

The cogs occasionally chewed up people's fingers, but such a misfortune had never befallen any member of the Baker crew. They were cautious around the cogs, always mindful of the gruesome stories they knew to be true about people who had been careless on other harvesters. The worst story was about Roy Pearson, whose finger had been chewed off by one of the cogs and circled around and around in the chain until someone made the effort to pick it off.

The chains carried the tobacco *hands*—three to five leaves—to the top floor of the two-story harvester, where Caroline, Summer, Carrie and either Peggy Jo or Polly tied them to sticks. They were the *stringers*, always careful to tape their fingers to prevent the tough twine from cutting the flesh between the joints. Each stick held anywhere from twenty-four to thirty hands of tobacco, equally spaced on either side.

Matt ramrodded the operation, taking full sticks from the stringers and hanging the heavy poles on steel tiers at the back of the harvester. Luke and Bonnie took turns driving the contraption through the fields, with the idle one expected to walk behind the harvester picking up any dropped leaves.

After making one round through the field—down fours row at a time and up another four rows—the men unloaded the full sticks from the top of the harvester and placed them on wooden pallets. Using a tractor and forklift, Sam then transported the tobacco to the barn. Twice a day—at dinnertime and the end of the day—the men hung the tobacco in the barn.

This was not a typical day, however, because Polly Tuckerman had telephoned a short time earlier with another flimsy excuse for missing work. Since they were short a stringer for the time being, John would have to spend the morning pulling weeds in the peanut patch instead of cropping tobacco.

Still, it was well before eight o'clock when the short-handed crew piled into the pickup truck and headed for the tobacco patch a few minutes after Joe and John drove away on the new John Deere tractor.

As Joe drove the tractor along the field road, he savored the first cigarette of the day and tried to figure out why he found it difficult to light up in front of his mama and grandmother. Both women knew he smoked, but they had never witnessed him in the act. And even though he smoked freely in front of his daddy and grandpa, Joe still felt uncomfortable lighting a cigarette in the house.

Caught up in his thoughts, Joe ignored John, who stood beside him on the tractor floorboard and muttered a complaint about having to pull weeds. Joe never bothered to glance his brother's way, but the complaint did alter the course of his thoughts. Instead of concerning himself over John's plight, he thought about the possibility that Peggy Jo would end up working with them today. He was determined to persuade the girl to devote her summer to working alongside him in the tobacco patch.

As he considered which arguments of persuasion to use on Peggy Joe, the radio blared some tune by the Beetles. The tractor bumped along the path, and the sun shimmered in the east, burning away the early morning coolness. It was a perfect day.

————

"Have fun by your lonesome," Joe called merrily as John jumped off the tractor.

It was a ridiculous parting sentiment, and John refused to acknowledge his brother as Joe drove away on the tractor. The fact that Joe did not have the common decency to realize he had been snubbed infuriated John even more.

At the moment, John was in full agreement with his father: Joe was indeed annoying. How else to describe someone who virtually ignored you all morning, then turned into Mr. Sunshine the moment he was rid of you. John never knew where he stood with his older brother these days. One minute, they were the best of friends; the next, like aliens from different worlds.

Daddy and Grandpa blamed Joe's condition on spring fever; Mama and Granny pinpointed a more specific cause—Miss Peggy Jo Nix. Joe was feeling his oats, and his frisky behavior made everyone else dizzy.

John released a pent-up sigh of frustration, wishing he could have some of his brother's energy. He felt weary, and the day was just beginning.

His lassitude derived from the rows of peanuts stretched before him. No one had pulled a single weed from this patch, and it seemed unlikely that he could make a dent in the problem. The chore reeked of busy work, a yoke John resented. But since resentment was a waste of time, he trudged into the field.

As he walked up and down the rows, bending to pluck offending weeds wherever they appeared, John filled the time with reflection on the family and himself. At heart, John suspected most people, including his family, perceived him as a loner. The perception was wrong. He valued companionship, especially family ties, although his friendships extended beyond the family. He had a gift for gab, a penchant for frankness and a knack for dry humor that everyone but his relatives noticed. Among the family, John had been tagged inappropriately as shy, right along with his middle sister.

Carrie was truly shy. She went out of her way to avoid unfamiliar people and strange situations. John was merely quiet. He could strike up a conversation with President Lyndon Johnson and never miss a beat if he wanted to.

As far as John knew, the only difference between his brothers and himself was the role of destiny, which had placed him in the middle. When the genes had been allotted, Joe and Luke had received the excesses while John had been doled a perfect balance.

Their excesses gave Joe and Luke a commanding presence, which came across as brash and cocksureness in Luke and boldness and quiet charisma in Joe. With his quietness and solitary ways, John often felt like a pale shadow of his brothers, even though the three of them shared far more common characteristics than differences.

Had he chosen to, John could have resented his brothers' bright stars, but he was too satisfied with his own lot to waste time on jealousy. He enjoyed privacy, which both his seventh-grade reading teacher and Joe had recognized toward the end of school. Mrs. Godwin had acknowledged the recognition first, giving John a picture of a young man standing on a rocky seacoast lashed by waves. Beneath the picture was a quote that said: "When you find me here, do not think me to be lonely—only alone."

Joe had noticed the picture lying among scattered schoolbooks on the floor of his brothers' room. A few days later, he had presented John with a sheet of notebook paper containing a handwritten quote from someone called Omar Khayyam: "The thoughtful soul to solitude retires."

"Think about it, John," Joe had said. "It's a huge common denominator between us, I believe."

Such gestures endowed John with deep respect for his brother, convincing him they would become the best of friends one day. They were pretty close as it was, especially considering the almost six-year age gap. Nevertheless, the age difference, coupled with subtle personality clashes, occasionally caused conflict.

Joe was one of those people who seemed to have been born knowing exactly what direction his life would take. He was the most purposeful person John knew, always preparing, always aiming, always achieving.

John was purposeful to a point, but he was also only twelve years old, although closer to thirteen, as he preferred to tell people these days. Sometimes, Joe lost sight of the fact that John was still a boy who had yet to grasp the full meaning of the future.

Their most recent skirmish had come over John's budding artistic talent. Already a wizard with sketching, he was now winning praise and awards for his paintings. His subject was nature, and he painted the beauty of the world—an interest fueled early by countless walks through the woods with his grandfather and later through similar solitary journeys.

Next to Sam, no other Baker family member knew the lay of the land as well as John. Together, they had stumbled across playful black bears, mating deer and other natural wonders that few people ever witnessed firsthand. From his grandfather, John had learned to identify virtually every plant and tree that grew on the Baker land. Sam had instilled in his grandson a strong reverence for the land, and the boy had cultivated an artistic touch to go with his passion.

John had begun to get an inkling of his talent during the winter when he sketched the pecan orchard behind the house. By happenstance, Joe had seen the picture and suggested John enter the drawing in an art competition sponsored by the Coastal Plains Regional Library in Tifton. John had not been interested in the contest, but Joe had badgered him into it. No one had been more surprised than John when the picture won the overall first place prize in the contest. On top of that surprise, *The Tifton Gazette* had published pictures of the contest winners, including a review written by an art professor who was one of the judges. Of John's sketch, the critic wrote:

"The stark barrenness of the pecan orchard screams with longing, which in itself makes the sketch a prize-winner. But the picture's true greatness lies in the artist's ability to convey the perception of a prideful orchard that will rise anew. This sketch is the work of twelve-year-old John Baker, and I urge you to remember that name. He has the potential to become an artist of renown."

John only half-understood what the professor meant to say, but the words had impressed his family and friends. No one had been more responsive than Joe.

"You've got real talent, John," Joe had told him again and again. "But you have to work hard and then work some more to develop it."

John harbored no grand illusions about his work. He viewed artwork as a pleasant way to fill idle hours. Instead of acting on his brother's advice to work hard, he had put away his sketching pencils and paintbrushes for several weeks, which eventually prompted Joe to yell at him about a lack of motivation and commitment.

"You're talken Greek to me, Joe," John had snapped. "I'm twelve—it's a little early for me to be motivated and committed to the future. I'm happily stuck in the present, so get off my back."

"Well ... you're closer to thirteen," Joe had shot back, the sharp edge gone from his voice.

Pausing to wipe away sweat from his forehead and freshen his cap, John smiled at the memory of his brother's clever comeback. Perhaps more than anything, Joe was disconcerted by a lack of ambition. Perhaps, too, John should heed his brother's well-intentioned advice. Talent was potential, but the true proof of success was the effort that went into the accomplishment.

He glanced upward, judging by the sun's position that precisely half an hour stood between him and dinner. There was still time to cover three more rows.

John weeded to the end of one row, then started another. The weeds were scarce in this part of the field, allowing him to cover the ground quickly. He reached the far end of the field and started back up the row.

The green peanut plants were thriving, their vines running in every direction and mingling with those on the next row. Sighting a clump of wild grass, John kneeled to pull the offensive weeds.

Frenzied burring erupted all around him. It was a rattlesnake, nearby, hissing, spitting, slithering closer.

Before John could move, something slammed against his tennis shoe with startling force, piercing the cloth, stabbing the fleshy meat between the heel and ankle of his outer foot. He heard a thud, then screamed as pain exploded in his foot and spread like wildfire up his leg.

John crashed to his hands and knees as more stings slapped his leg. The burring began again, roaring around him as John crawled toward black blotches forming in the distance.

He tried to think calmly, rationally, but dizziness overpowered his desire. His left leg throbbed, stinging currents running from the bottom of his foot to the pit of his stomach. He struggled to his feet, stumbled forward and collapsed to his knees. Dropping his hands to the ground, he struggled forward another yard on his last reserves before flopping face-first in the dirt. The warm soil felt like a featherbed, comfort to the cold creeping into his body. Darkness descended, a powerful, consuming force, claiming his last conscious thought.

AT NOON, MATT SHUT down the harvester. The women went to the house, and the men went to hang the tobacco in the chocolate barn.

The crew's hanging process varied little from day to day. Inside the barn, Joe climbed into the top tiers, while Lucas took a position beneath him on the lower poles. On the ground, Matt started the hanging process by taking the tobacco off the pallets and handing it to the first link in the human chain. Each stick eventually made its way to Tom, who handed it up to Lucas, who pushed it on up to Joe. Straddled across the higher tiers, Joe hung the bird roosts as well as the top three rows in each room. Then, he took a position on the lower tiers, and hung the bottom rows.

Usually, enough available bodies existed in the human chain to allow each man to hold a virtually stationary position as they passed the sticks onto the next person. As the position between Joe and the pallet increased or decreased, men dropped in and out of the line. No one was ever idle, using free time to pick up leaves that fell off the sticks. The leaves were placed in a pile and restrung onto sticks at the end of the day. Matt did not tolerate a messy barn floor or wasted tobacco.

On this day, because they had been shorthanded in the morning and had fewer full sticks than usual, the hanging moved quickly and they wound up with only the tops of two and a half rooms filled by dinnertime. Matt grumbled about the slow-go of progress, not wanting to fall behind and having to play catch-up as the tobacco burned in the field.

Returning home, the men found a bar of Lava soap and clean towels waiting on the back porch. They took turns washing the black tar off their hands beside the well pump, then made their way into the house, eager to dive into the feast that Rachel had prepared for dinner.

The table was set with fried chicken, mashed potatoes and gravy, creamed corn and butterbeans. Rachel was taking homemade biscuits from the oven, and the girls were setting jelly glasses of iced tea at every place.

No one noticed John's absence until they all gathered around the table and his place remained empty.

"Where's John?" Caroline asked.

"I figured he was here," Joe replied. "I drove by the peanut field to pick him up earlier but didn't see him. He's probably taken the long way home."

"You better go check again," Matt instructed his oldest son. "Your granny rounded up Peggy Jo to help us after dinner, so we're gonna need him in the baccer field."

Joe muttered something, grabbed his glass of tea and left the table before the blessing was said. He was disgusted with John for pulling this stunt and delaying their dinner as he climbed into the pickup. He drove recklessly down the lane, expecting to see his brother walking toward the house every time he rounded a corner. The way remained clear, however, and Joe's disgruntlement gradually turned to apprehension as he slid the truck to a stop near the shady water oak where he had last seen his brother early this morning.

Although John was apt to wander off in his leisure time, the boy put work before pleasure. He understood his responsibilities, and Joe began to feel uneasy.

Hopping from the truck, setting the empty tea glass on the hood, Joe moved across the edge of the field, scanning the rows. Just as he almost satisfied himself that John was elsewhere, his eyes hung on something amiss. He did a double-take and sighted the boy, collapsed near the middle of the field.

His heart stopped, then lurched into his throat. His stomach churned, and Joe sprang into action, tearing through the field in a dead run. His first fear was that his brother had suffered sunstroke. Less than twenty yards from the stricken boy, however, he saw that was not the case.

A snake had bitten John. It was obvious.

His brother's left leg was swollen grotesquely, nearly twice its normal size, constricted against the denim of his blue jeans.

Joe fell to his knees, rolling John onto his stomach and pulling the boy into his arms in one motion. He touched his neck, finding the pulse instantly. It beat like a jackhammer. His brother's face was deathly pale, suggesting Joe was too late to help. Then, instinct took over.

He wiped away the vomit dribbling from the side of John's mouth and stretched his brother on the ground. Wedging the blade of his pocketknife between the fabric and John's knee, which protruded from a hole in the jeans, he cut the tough denim. Finally, he cut a swath large enough for leverage, then ripped apart the pants leg from the knee all the way down.

The entire effort took no more than thirty seconds. Joe took one look at the leg and realized a hospital was the only hope for his brother. He picked up the thin body, hoisted the boy over his shoulder and sprinted for the pickup.

————

Sam was winding up an amusing anecdote about the life of a farmer, which he had read in the *Progressive Farmer*, and a spill of laughter drowned the first faint blasts of the truck horn. Seconds later, though, the urgent blaring pierced the racket around the dinner table, silencing the clatter with heart-stopping abruptness.

"Somethen's wrong," Caroline gasped, rising spontaneously from the bench and racing toward the kitchen door with everyone else in tow.

As soon as they rounded the corner of the house and cleared the obstruction of the smokehouse, everyone realized how right she was. The truck barreled down the field road with alarming speed, and soon, they glimpsed John slumped against his brother's shoulder.

Joe braked the truck to a sliding halt beside the house, yelling for his parents to get inside the cab.

"A snake got him," he informed them breathlessly through the window. "It's bad. We have to get him to the hospital."

His parents dashed to the other side of the truck, with Matt hollering orders for someone to call the hospital in Tifton and alert them what to expect.

Caroline had feared the worse, but she froze upon first sight of the swollen leg, which had turned such a deep shade of purple that it almost looked black.

Matt pushed her into the truck, and motherly instincts took over. With Joe's help, she pulled the boy into her lap and twisted his body so that Matt could examine the leg.

Joe floored the accelerator, and they were gone.

Matt found two sets of fang marks right away, one on his son's lower calf and the other on the backside of the knee joint. Then, while trying unsuccessfully to remove the sneaker from the swollen foot, he saw a ragged tear in the shoe and groaned with disbelief.

"Gosh, almighty," he muttered. "Near as I can tell, he's got three sets of marks on him."

The leg was a bloated mess of deep purple and distended blood vessels. Blood oozed from the two visible bites. The swelling started at the foot and extended to the hip, distorting the leg almost beyond recognition.

John convulsed twice on the way to the hospital, vomiting, choking and stiffening like a board in his parents' arms. Blotches appeared on his dark skin, his breathing turned into short gasps and more swelling began to puff his neck and eyes.

Nobody said it, but they all believed he was dying.

A stretcher, orderlies, nurses and the reassuring presence of Dr. Pittman waited for them outside the emergency room door of the Tifton hospital. The orderlies placed John onto the stretcher and rushed him inside the emergency room with everyone else following closely on their heels.

"How long ago did it happen?" Dr. Pittman asked.

"Thirty minutes at the least," Joe answered. "Beyond that, there's no way of tellen. He was by himself."

"He's got three bites, I believe," Matt added. "Two on the back of his leg—a third on his foot near the ankle. I couldn't get the shoe off."

They arrived en masse at an open door, which the orderlies pushed the stretcher through as Dr. Pittman wheeled around to face Matt, Caroline and Joe. The doctor promised to do what he could, then vanished inside the room.

Caroline insisted she needed to remain at John's side, but a nurse rejected her pleadings with a sympathetic promise to keep the family posted on John's condition.

Matt placed a calming hand on his wife's arm, led her to a nearby couch and cradled her in his arms as Caroline wept against his shoulder. Joe paced before them, chain-smoking cigarettes.

They waited and waited and waited.

"Honey," Matt said in a while. "If ever there was a time for you to have faith, this is it. I'd feel a lot better if you said a prayer instead of cryen."

The suggestion silenced Caroline's tears. She gazed into her husband's eyes, nodded agreement and hugged him fiercely for support.

"Prayer does work better than tears," she told him. "You pray, too, Matt."

He nodded, and they closed their eyes in silent pleading for a miracle.

Inside the emergency room, Dr. Pittman prayed, too, as he examined John.

Nurses attached a heart monitor to the boy, started him on oxygen and used shears to cut away the sneaker. John's foot looked like a grotesque balloon on the verge of popping.

The doctor examined the bite marks, re-examined them and shook his head in disbelief. He administered a dose of antivenin, relying on all the standard procedures for treatment. In all of his years of practice, Dr. Pittman had never come across a rattlesnake bite. He would have preferred someone else in his place, but he was in charge. He ordered a nurse to call for a surgeon, then plunged ahead with his treatment.

First, he made two parallel incisions through each set of fang marks, applying suction cups in hopes of drawing out some of the poison. It was standard procedure, but probably too late to do any good at this point. The extent of swelling and the irregular heartbeat confirmed the obvious: The poison had circulated throughout the body.

Next, the doctor made two long incisions on either side of the engorged leg, hoping to ease the pressure of the swelling and to protect the blood vessels and tissue from more damage. The venom already had destroyed large chunks of tissue near the bite marks. There was no telling what damage the surgeon would find when he opened up the leg. Perhaps muscle and nerve tissue had been destroyed as well.

Almost two hours later, the doctor concluded with certainty, and amazement, that John would survive the ordeal. The boy's vital signs were stable, the swelling had subsided and he was breathing easier.

Once, during the treatment, he had regained consciousness, moaning something inaudible and trying to sit up on the bed. The struggle had been blessedly brief, and he had slipped back into unconsciousness.

Ted Thacker, the young surgeon with a sunny disposition and an earnest desire to make sick people well, concurred with Dr. Pittman's assessment of the boy's condition. Surgery was necessary to repair the leg, but the patient first needed to recuperate from the shock.

"Do you know his family very well?" Ted asked the older man.

"Fairly well," Dr. Pittman replied. "I've been their family doctor for the last couple of years."

"Then I'll count on you to help prepare them for the surgery," Dr. Thacker said. "There's a lot of damaged tissue and blood vessels. It could mean the boy's foot, or even his leg."

———

Dr. Pittman emerged from the emergency room door with Ted Thacker at his side. Both men wore grim smiles.

"Your boy is gonna make it," the older man informed Matt and Caroline.

"Thank, God," Matt sighed as Caroline slumped against him and Joe closed his eyes in relief.

"You'll never know just how much to thank Him, Matt," Dr. Pittman said quickly. "It was a higher power that saved John. It's another miracle for your family as far as I'm concerned."

"It is," Dr. Thacker agreed. "By all rights, your boy probably should have died. No matter what else happens from here on out, you have his life to be thankful for."

Dr. Thacker's tone contained a warning, and Matt, Caroline and Joe braced for whatever it might be.

"Ted is tellen you the honest truth, folks," Dr. Pittman continued. "The venom has done tremendous damage to John's leg. Your son needs surgery. Matt, Caroline, if y'all agree, I'd like Ted to perform it."

Matt and Caroline accepted the recommendation at face value.

"How bad is it?" Joe asked.

"I want to be straightforward with y'all," Dr. Thacker replied before launching into a graphic explanation about the damage John's leg had suffered. "The leg is in extremely bad shape. You should prepare yourself for what might happen. When that boy comes out of surgery, he could be minus a foot. Or possibly part of his leg."

The surgeon's warning cut through them like a scalpel, without the benefit of anesthesia. Still, they forced themselves to remain composed, trying to focus on the blessing of John's life instead of the part he stood to lose.

Now that Matt, Caroline and Joe had been prepared for the worst, Dr. Pittman sought to encourage them. When he again reminded them that John's life was the true blessing, that anything else might be asking for the impossible, they clutched their stomachs and nodded like satisfied simpletons.

"Thank you, doc," Matt said finally when he was able to push down the lump in his throat. "We appreciate everything. We are grateful. But we have to hope for more—for John's sake."

"I would expect nothen less," Dr. Thacker replied with an honest smile.

Caroline cleared her throat and smiled at the two doctors. "Prayer gave us one miracle," she remarked. "I believe it can deliver another one."

"So do I, Caroline," Dr. Pittman confirmed.

"Please do everything you can," Joe urged. "My brother's a great kid. And he happens to love nothen better than a walk through the woods."

"I'll remember that," Dr. Thacker promised.

"We'll get John to a room shortly," Dr. Pittman said. "You can see him then."

"Okay," Matt breathed.

The doctors turned to leave, then Dr. Pittman paused. "I have to tell you this," he said. "I debated whether to, but it's not somethen I can keep to myself."

He had their attention.

"There are four sets of fang marks on John's leg," the doctor explained. "Two are similar in size, the other two considerably larger. It's probable that John stumbled upon a mama rattler and her babies. He may be more fortunate than any of us realize."

————

On the night after a female rattlesnake and her babies took four bites out of John's leg, Dr. Ned Turner was sleeping alone as usual in his Cookville house. His wife occupied the room next door.

A shuffling noise roused the doctor from a dreamless sleep.

Assuming Delia had come into the room, Ned concluded his wife was having another bout of insomnia, which was the primary reason they no longer shared the same bed. The sounds of someone fiddling with the pocket change and billfold on the dresser across the room piqued the doctor's interest. He struggled to a sitting position and reached over to switch on the bedside lamp.

A few feet away, a man dressed in solid black turned slightly askew, continued rummaging through Ned's wallet and removed two hundred-dollar bills. Dropping the wallet on the floor, the man turned fully toward the doctor, and Ned recognized him.

"What are you doen?" Ned asked. "Have you taken complete leave of your senses?"

The man regarded the doctor with detached amusement. "You've been preachen loud and clear how unsafe people are in their homes, doctor," he said, walking to stand beside the bed. "What is needed is a little proof to back up your high-and-mighty claims."

"You're crazy," Ned observed, the first hint of fear entering his pompous tone. "Get out of here! Right this instant!"

The man merely laughed, crumpled the bills and stuffed them in his pocket. When his hand reappeared, it held a pistol.

The doctor went wide-eyed with terror. And in that instant, the gun discharged a single bullet into his right temple.

———

The loud bang woke Delia Turner. She sat up in bed as footsteps shuffled past her door and headed for the stairs. The steps were light and quick, a sharp contrast to her husband's plodding movements.

Fear seized her thoughts as she tried to recreate the exact sound that had wakened her. The front door opened downstairs, then shut, and her heart hammered.

Rising from bed, Delia crossed the carpeted floor, pulled back the curtain on the front window and witnessed a single man running down the street toward nigger town.

"Ned! Ned!" she screamed, concluding their home had been violated once again.

Delia rushed from her bedroom, ran into the hall and took two steps toward her husband's room. The light coming from the Tiffany lamp in Ned's room halted her.

She told herself to return to her own room, to call for help, but genuine concern prevented her from heeding the advice. She crept toward the light, peered around the corner and saw her husband. Blood flowed from the wound in his head, already clotting in a purple shade of blue on the side of his face.

She screamed, backed away and broke into convulsive sobs as she fled down the stairs and out the front door. On the sidewalk, she shrieked again, like a wounded animal's peal for help. Car lights came toward her, coming from colored town, even as the porch lights flashed on the house next door.

Delia Turner collapsed in a sobbing heap on the sidewalk. Her neighbors reached her quickly, moments after Paul Berrien, who had happened by the house on a routine patrol.

———

Ted Thacker was a gifted surgeon, and he performed heroically during almost two hours of surgery on John's snake-bitten leg. He removed numerous layers of tissue destroyed by the venom and used skin grafts taken from the backs of the boy's thighs and buttocks to repair the damage. When John emerged from the surgery, his leg and foot were intact, but he faced a lengthy period of rehabilitation and a long haul on crutches and braces.

John was still groggy from the anesthesia when nurses placed him in a private hospital bed. As he became more alert, he had a strange feeling of omission, as if time had stood still since his face pressed against the warm soil in the peanut patch. He was confused and frightened—until the moment the door opened to his room and his parents, grandparents and Joe stood before him.

Their presence comforted him. And a surge of serenity brightened his face, emerging as a grin, so honest and unassuming that it filled his family with unwavering confidence and unshakable belief in the possibility of miracles.

Late that afternoon, when John was fully alert, Matt and Caroline informed their son about the drastic turn his life had taken. They explained about the crutches and the braces waiting for him, the painful rehabilitation in store and the likelihood that he would walk with a limp.

John accepted their warning with his usual aplomb. "Like you said, it could have been worse. When can I go home?"

Four days later, he did go home and was strong enough to carry himself into the house on crutches.

A steady stream of visitors dropped by the house all afternoon and late into the evening, welcoming John home and wishing the boy a speedy recovery. His last visitor was Paul Berrien, and Matt could not remember a time when his friend appeared so haggard.

A week's worth of black beard had collected on Paul's face, his hair needed a comb run through it and he seemed several inches shorter. His emerald green eyes, which Caroline often complimented for their vividness, were dimmed and marred by dark circles. The strain of the murder investigation had worn Paul down, a feeling with which Matt could empathize as he realized he probably appeared similarly frazzled.

Considering their friendship, it was ironic that neither man had been available as a sounding board for the other during one of the most trying weeks of their respective lives. Their sole contact had come through messages relayed by April and June, who had inquired daily about John's condition while providing only scant details about the murder.

What's the world coming to? Matt wondered as he considered how something so evil could occur right off the main square in a sleepy town like Cookville.

Paul joshed with John momentarily, then gave the boy a dozen packs of Blackjack chewing gum. His son and best friend were the only people Matt knew who enjoyed the licorice taste of Blackjack.

"Just between you and me," Paul told John, "I believe Blackjack can cure anything—even snakebites."

Eventually, the conversation turned to the murder of Dr. Ned Turner, and Joe asked, "What can you tell us about it, Paul?"

"Not very much substantial, and that's only because there's not much to go on," Paul replied. "From what we've pieced together, someone came into the house and robbed him. Ned must have woken up and surprised whoever it was. He was shot once in the head. It killed him instantly."

"There's not a suspect, then?" Matt questioned.

"Not a single one," Paul said. "The gunshot woke Ned's wife. Delia heard someone leave the house and says she saw a colored man runnen off down the street. She's still shook up and not too coherent.

"Of course," he continued a moment later, "the GBI folks are just about convinced that whoever killed the doctor is also the same person who robbed the Turners' house last year—maybe even the same man who tried to attack his wife a few years earlier. Do y'all remember that?"

"Vaguely," Sam said. "The robbery occurred while Rachel was sick with the pneumonia. We sort of lost touch with everything else back then, much like this week."

"One of the things taken in the robbery last year was a twenty-two pearl-handled, silver-plated pistol that Ned had given to his wife," Paul explained. "The GBI has determined the bullet that killed Ned came from a twenty-two. It could be nothen more than coincidence, but their feelen is that someone used that stolen gun to kill the doctor. Unless we find a murder weapon, there's no way to prove any of this. And frankly, we're not close at all, to finden a weapon or a suspect. At this point, we have nothen but a lot of speculation and fabrication."

"I guess this will make the election that much more difficult," Matt commented.

Paul nodded. "It's less than two weeks away," he surmised, "and there's a killer runnen loose on the streets of Cookville. You have to admit: It doesn't exactly inspire confidence in the local sheriff."

"Don't lose your spirit, Paul," Matt instructed.

"Or your confidence," Sam added.

Paul responded with a grim nod and tight smile.

"What's Bobby Taylor sayen about all this?" Joe inquired, trying to shift the focus off Paul. "I supposed he's pleased as punch, especially if everybody believes it was a black man who killed Ned."

"Actually, he's been fairly understated about the whole thing," Paul replied. "And why not? He probably realizes there's a noose around my neck, just waiten for me to pull the string."

The Bakers had never seen their friend so downhearted.

"You'll still win the election, Paul," Sam tried to reassure him.

Paul shook his head in obvious doubt. "I don't know," he replied. "Maybe I don't need to be sheriff anymore. And to tell you the honest truth, I'm not even sure I want to be. When you get right down to it, the election doesn't mean diddly-squat to me right now. I just want this whole business over and done with."

———

On election day, Bobby woke with a victorious feeling. He had conducted the perfect campaign, giving careful attention to every move he made and each thought he uttered. He had held his temper and never once questioned the saintly virtue of the respectable Paul Berrien.

This time around, Paul had cooked his own goose, with plenty of help from the NAACP, the ACLU and the good Dr. Ned Turner.

Bobby chuckled at his good fortune. All he had done was remain respectable and keep a solemn face as one uproarious event after another unfolded. And now, everyone had questions about Paul Berrien's ability to enforce the law.

Next to him, Martha stirred, and Bobby rolled onto his side to observe his wife. He wondered how he had managed to end up with a wretch like her as the woman in his life. Martha was such a plain Jane that Bobby was grateful for and encouraging of her reclusive behavior. He wanted as few people as possible to know she was his wife. Tonight, however, he supposed Martha would have to stand beside him as they waited for the election returns. Perhaps he could persuade her to stay home tonight. Bobby laughed obnoxiously. Of course he could.

He had never wanted to marry Martha. He had intended to screw the woman and leave. But she had proved to have an alluring quality, coming across like an anxious puppy ready to please her master. And more than anything, Bobby loved feeling masterful.

These days, Martha made a miserable mess of almost everything, but she still had that dutiful quality, especially when Bobby showed the slightest affection toward her. Though his feelings for Martha had died long ago, Bobby still felt the need to possess her. He leaned closer, with his eyes closed, and nuzzled her neck. Martha usually did whatever he said, showed whatever enthusiasm he asked of her and, as long as he closed his eyes, Bobby could imagine he was making love to anyone he wanted—but never to the homely woman who was his wife.

———

It was the closest election of any kind ever in the history of the county. So close that every single ballot was recounted to make sure there was no mistake in the outcome.

On the first balloting, Paul won by five votes, and Bobby was livid, reverting to his old self, demanding a recount. He calmed down as the votes were counted the second time, resuming the cool posturing that had been his trademark throughout the campaign. The new totals added one vote to Paul's margin of victory.

Genuine disappointment prevented Bobby from exploding in rage, dampening the animosity that simmered below the surface of his consciousness. Even with all the odds stacked in his favor, Bobby had been rejected. For the first time in his life, he was ready to put a battle behind him. Then and there, he decided to find another goal—something that would bring him more satisfaction than the responsibility of being a sheriff who had to worry about keeping the peace and solving every crime that came his way.

Bobby wanted to tell Paul Berrien that he had gotten everything he deserved with the victory. Instead, he masked the smug feeling and offered a handshake to the victor.

"You whipped me fair and square, Paul," he said, gazing intensely into the face of his conqueror. "Enjoy it."

Paul could only nod an acknowledgment, and a shiver ran up his spine. Bobby's eyes contained something unsettling, a glazed look to the future and a cold, empty disdain of the past. Beneath the complacency, those eyes presented a challenge and held a devil-may-care attitude.

As Bobby moved away toward his three sons, uncertainty overwhelmed Paul. The sheriff had a feeling of having overlooked something of vital importance. And while he believed Bobby was definitely the wrong man to have the sheriff's job, Paul could not help questioning whether he himself was the right man for it.

DURING THOSE DAYS WHEN John's life was at the mercy of God, the Bakers had fallen behind on the farm. More tobacco ripened in the field than was picked; almost overnight, other crops begged for attention; and machinery suddenly required repairs. The days seemed to have no logical end, and the weeks went on without pause, prompting Caroline to remind her husband that too many Sundays were being spent working the fields instead of honoring the Sabbath.

To make matters worse, the family work crew was short a hand in the tobacco field. John was confined to the house to convalesce under Rachel's watchful eyes. Peggy Jo Nix became a permanent fixture around the place, which pleased Joe but still left the family in need of one more hand. At Paul Berrien's suggestion, help came unexpectedly from his sisters.

April was sixty-four that summer, June sixty-two; yet they insisted they could string a stick of tobacco. Out of desperation, Matt accepted their generous offer, even though he feared the ladies' help might be more trouble than it was worth. To everyone's surprise, however, April and June caught on quickly, needing less than half a day to get the hang of tying tobacco to the stick. For the remainder of the season, the two sisters alternated their days in the tobacco field, always reliable, always bringing a freshness to their work that made the long, hot days somehow more tolerable.

Then, before anyone realized it, the work slackened, a waning so slight that it was hardly noticeable—except suddenly the days seemed shorter than usual and the weeks were long enough to get the most important work done in six days.

In addition to the long days on the farm, Joe began working nights in the Planter's Tobacco Warehouse in Cookville, hoping to earn enough money to pay for his college tuition and books when he resumed classes at ABAC in the fall. Five nights of the week, he walked out the door at a quarter till seven, returned home shortly after midnight and climbed into bed. Less than six hours later, he was up again, working alongside his family as they struggled to meet the obligations of their most pressing season ever in the tobacco field.

Finally, with one week to spare before the children returned to school, the Bakers stripped their last stalk of tobacco and paused for a brief moment of rest before the fall harvest season.

These things occupied Matt's mind as he sat at the kitchen table, alone again on another Sunday morning.

He recalled Joe's prophecy from early spring. "This might be one of those seasons, Daddy," his son had predicted. "This could be the year you've been waiten for."

And it had been. Matt reckoned he might never see another year like it—when the weather cooperated perfectly and the crops thrived as never before. His fields were bursting with a bumper crop, so beautiful that he almost hated to run a combine through them. Tobacco was bringing top price, and the leaf was heavy. He would exceed the government quota for pounds, and that was his most pressing concern. As concerns went, this one mattered little and was shrugged off without a second thought.

Matt should have been on top of the world, yet he felt oddly let down. More than anything, he was restless, torn between what he should have done on this day and why he had chosen to do otherwise.

He should have gone to church with his family, as his wife had requested. It was the first Sunday John had been able to attend services at Benevolence since the snakebite, and Caroline wanted the whole family to be with him. Even Joe, who probably was more tired than all of them, had dragged out of bed and gone to church to please his mother and support his brother. Matt had spurned the request, however, and Caroline's disappointment had been bitter. She had started to pick an argument with Matt, then stopped short as he became defensive.

"I don't see why we have to have this same old argument over and over again," he told his wife. "You see things one way on this matter, and I look at it another way. I'm not a churchgoen man, Caroline. You knew that when you married me."

"No, Matt," she replied sternly. "I did not know that when I married you. I believed the man I married counted his blessens and knew where those blessens came from. I believed we shared the same faith. I've always believed that, Matt, but I won't bother you again about it."

Caroline had not been the only one disappointed. The entire family had acted coolly toward Matt throughout the morning, almost as if they regarded him through newly opened eyes.

For the most part, Matt had been an exemplary role model for his children. He was hardworking, understanding and comforting, a man of integrity and honor, who taught his children about idealism as well as how to reconcile dreams with reality. He showed his children the virtues of compassion, caring and generosity through a never-ending series of good works and goodwill.

He had earned the respect accorded to him, but Matt was human after all and susceptible to mistakes like everyone else. In the solitude of that Sunday morning, Matt faced the consequences of his most glaring mistake—the hypocrisy of his life, the false notions given to his children by a man who taught them all the right things in life but selfishly refused to embrace the essential reason for their being.

The contradiction ran against the grain of everything Matt had been taught by his parents as well as the values Caroline and he had tried to instill in their children. Hard work, relatives, fate—a person did not have much choice in things such as those. But when the matter came down to beliefs and convictions, especially those where commitment was necessary, the decision depended entirely on choice. How many times had he told his children exactly that? And how many times had he told them about the importance of making those choices of your own free will? That commitments made when you were backed into a corner or as an easy way out of a jam often proved worthless in the long run? And that worthless commitments were the worst kind of all?

Yet, from the first moment Matt had doubted God on the day the Japanese bombed Pearl Harbor, every decision about his Christian faith had been made when he was backed into a corner or as the easy way out of a jam. There was no ready explanation for his past actions, but the time had come for an honest decision on this matter.

Either, he had faith or he did not. The decision was that simple.

If he chose to believe, however, then he had to make the commitment, too, without any suspicions and reservations as well as with the understanding that searching for the answers to the mysteries of faith was part of faith itself. And if he lacked faith, then he had to end the pretense and quit confusing his family with mixed messages.

The choice was Matt's to make—of his own free will.

On a similar Sunday well over a year ago, Matt had wrestled with this same decision. Burdened by worry over Rachel's illness and other concerns, he had been equally restless, with absolutely none of the usual desire to quell his uneasy spirit with busy chores. He had gone for a drive, taking back roads to Cookville and winding up by chance at a tiny block building on the outskirts of town. It was the African Methodist Episcopal Church where Lucas Bartholomew worshipped with his family.

Spotting Lucas' truck, Matt had stopped, intending to leave an overdue paycheck on the dashboard. Something about the preacher's voice booming from the open church doors had captured Matt's interest, however, and he had listened intently to the message based on the biblical story of Job.

It was a simple sermon of one man's blind faith, faith so strong that it had overcome the worst of trials and tribulations. Listening to the black preacher intone his flock to have the faith of Job, to believe their dedication would earn them the ultimate reward one day, Matt had felt the desire to trust a higher authority for help in dealing with life's hardships.

He had gotten back into his truck and headed toward Benevolence, determined to make his public profession of faith in Christ and repent his sins. By the time he reached the church, however, services had ended and the congregation was milling around the outside grounds. Matt had passed on by the church. Soon afterward, his mother had become her old self again, and the thoughts of repentance and forgiveness had given way to the daily rigors and joys of life.

On this day, Matt arrived at Benevolence with plenty of time to spare and with better reasons to justify his decision. He came seeking a God who would grant him inner peace for every day of life rather than provide a quick fix during the difficulties. He came as a believer in Christ, with faith restored and repentant of his sins. He needed redemption through God's saving grace, and he was humbled enough to set aside his pride.

With sweaty palms, Matt opened the front door and stepped into the church sanctuary for the first time in a long time. A lump rose in his throat as he stood there, oblivious to the few curious looks generated by his sudden appearance this late into service. For a moment, he was self-conscious, wishing he had changed into more suitable clothes than his everyday jeans and work shirt. From the altar, however, Adam Cook smiled and nodded Matt toward a seat, his actions so subtle that hardly anyone noticed the acknowledgment.

Gathering his courage and remembering his mission, Matt moved to his left and took a seat on the back row. Already, he felt the first stirrings of fellowship.

Felled by despair as never before, Caroline hardly heard Preacher Cook's sermon on *The Bounty of Living in Christ*. Her husband's stubbornness baffled Caroline, and his hard-hearted resistance worried her. For the first time, she truly doubted whether Matt would find his way to Christ.

For most of the service, she agonized, bereft of reason and hope. The sense of loss and failure was demoralizing, but something prevented her from conceding defeat in this battle for Matt's soul. Mustering up her faith, she renewed the silent, continuing prayer that her husband would see the light one day and surrender his will to a greater power.

In the middle of this prayerful contemplation, Caroline heard the doorknob turn as the church door opened. Inexplicably, her heart gladdened and filled with anticipation of the miracle for which she prayed. She risked a sideways glance, and there was Matt, completely unaware that his family occupied the pew beside him. In the happy rush of her heart, she watched her husband claim a seat on the pew opposite his family. Intuitively, she clasped Rachel's outstretched hand, bit her inside lip to keep from weeping tears of joy and stiffened to keep her body from becoming a quivering mass.

"The Lord's been worken on him hard, Caroline," Rachel whispered in a voice chockfull of emotion. "You could tell it all summer, even long before that. We knew it would happen. Sooner or later, the Lord was bound to reach him."

Caroline merely squeezed the older woman's hand one more time, unwilling to trust her own voice as the preacher concluded the sermon.

————

Adam Cook felt the Holy Spirit enter into Benevolence the moment Matt Baker walked through the church door. Sensing works of a greater power were at hand, he finished the sermon, offered up a prayer and issued the altar call as the congregation went through the ritual of finding page eighty-one in the hymnal—*Just As I Am*, a song the church members knew by heart.

As soon as April Berrien struck the song's first note on the piano, Matt rose and headed toward the preacher. An overwhelming urgency compelled him forward, building with every step, rising up from deep inside his heart and soul. Tears came of their own accord, unabashedly.

A teary-eyed Adam welcomed Matt into the body of Christ with a crushing embrace, brother to brother as they silently acknowledged the presence around them.

"I need this," Matt said. "For a long time, I've needed it."

"Unburden yourself, Matt," the preacher advised as the congregation sang.

Strength of mind and body failed Matt then. Emotion overcame him as the sense of something pitiful and wretched dominated his every thought. He was a broken man, and the congregation was humbled. People understood the cleansing taking place, especially those who had been at this low point in their own lives.

Caroline went to stand with her husband, holding Matt as he wept, then encouraging him with a gentle touch as Adam ministered with words of salvation.

In a while, something else stirred within Matt, the first feelings of comfort and encouragement, faith and hope, grace and consecration. As their tears subsided, Adam and Caroline led Matt to the altar. The three of them kneeled and prayed silently before the preacher offered another prayer on behalf of Matt, Caroline, their family and the entire congregation.

When his prayer was finished, Adam lifted his lanky frame off the floor, reclaimed a center position and urged others to unburden their souls, correctly sensing that a spirit of revival and restoration was moving through the congregation.

April heeded the call first, halting her piano playing to move to the front of the church to offer up prayers to the Lord. Others quickly followed, coming one by one and then hand in hand, as it became apparent that something extraordinary and intimate was occurring within the tiny church. Tears came in torrents, and prayers of every kind filled the sanctuary.

Sam and Rachel went to pray with Matt and Caroline, while Joe helped John to the altar to plead for his leg to be restored to full capability. Their brothers and sisters found their way to the altar as well, each on a personal mission, as did their closest friends.

On this day, everyone felt the power of the Lord and was struck by the enormous sense of awe and respect it commanded, as well as innate belief in the strength and miracles it possessed.

Eventually, the entire congregation was drained but also refreshed.

Everyone reclaimed their seats, and the day's business continued. In quick order, Adam proposed church membership for Matt. The proposal was motioned by Paul Berrien, seconded by Dan Carter and rousingly approved by the whole congregation. Then, as they sang *Amazing Grace* and *Faith of Our Fathers*, Matt stood in front of the congregation and was welcomed into the fold of Benevolence Missionary Baptist Church. A short time later, the service moved outside, where the congregation sang the standard, *Shall We Gather at the River*, and the preacher baptized Matt in the saving waters of New River.

As he did with everyone he baptized, Adam spent a private moment with Matt after he lifted the man out of the water and offered an appropriate piece of scripture.

"Fight the good fight of faith, Matt," the preacher advised. "You'll find those words in the Bible. I'm not goen to tell you exactly where, but I trust you'll come across it on your own."

Matt nodded his understanding, knowing that he had just embarked on a search for the mystery of mysteries.

Among those to whom it mattered most, everyone reckoned it was about the best Sunday dinner they had ever waited for as they finally got around to spreading food on the church grounds.

————

In bed later that night, Matt shared with Caroline the whole story about his road to salvation. When he was finished, she hugged him tightly, and they sealed the wonderful day by making love.

Finally, when they were satisfied and snuggled close to each other, drifting toward a peaceful sleep, Matt made one last observation to his wife.

"One thing surprised me more than anything else, honey," he told her. "I never once figured you and Ma for back-row Baptists."

Caroline laughed softly and started to suggest they would move up one row beginning next Sunday. Then, she changed her mind. As long as they were filling up the church, with Matt anchoring the family pew, she reckoned the good Lord would not mind where the Bakers sat.

With nothing but time on his hands, John discovered a passion for his artwork in the fall of the year. His paintings and sketches captured the season—the gathering of the harvest, the changing landscape and the people at work. His technique improved, and he experimented with different styles, shades and textures. He painted and sketched countless pieces, yet saved only a select few that appealed to his basic instincts.

His leg was healing slowly as he followed the doctor's schedule of tiring exercises and relentless physical therapy. He faced the rigorous routine with a cheerful attitude, as if it hardly mattered when he next walked without crutches, as long as he would walk again by his own power. His family regarded John as the epitome of patience. As John saw it, he simply had no other choice.

One warm day in early October as he sat on the front porch doing homework, he noticed a commotion in the field across the road where his brothers and sisters were digging sweet potatoes. Suddenly, Joe burst into a trot across the field, coming toward the house.

"It's another rattlesnake," he informed John as he approached the porch. "The place is crawlen with 'em this year."

The rattlesnake population did seem unusually large this year. Various members of the Baker family had killed eight so far—three Eastern Diamondbacks and five timber rattlers—not to mention four moccasins and a rare coral snake.

Joe went inside the house and returned quickly with his pistol in hand, loading the gun on the porch before trotting back to the sweet potato patch.

Observing from the porch, John watched his brother shoot the snake. The children then spent a few minutes poking and prodding at the dead rattler before Joe picked the snake up with a stick and brought it to the house for everyone else to inspect. It was a five-foot-long diamondback, as big around as a grown man's fist with fourteen rattles and a button.

John half-hoped it was the mother that had bitten him.

Later that night, he suffered through another nightmare about snakes. The scene was familiar. He was sitting in the glider on the front porch when he noticed the first snake slithering down the road. Others soon followed in all shapes and sizes, and John was beginning to feel the first urges of panic when the burring erupted in his dreams. Frantically, he glanced around and found the snake coiled below him ready to strike. At the precise moment the snake lunged toward him, John woke with a terrified cry, coming to a sitting position in bed, awash in a cold sweat, trembling uncontrollably as his heart pounded.

In an instant, Joe was beside him, offering words of reassurance and a protective embrace. As always, John calmed quickly, realizing his mind had played tricks on him.

"That was a bad one," he said a while later, falling back into the bed. "I thought I was a goner."

Joe crawled onto the double bed beside his brother, providing a comforting presence for John as they lay in the dark. "You know what might help," he suggested. "Try thinken of what happened as one of life's vaccinations—like for polio or smallpox. Rattlesnakes strike at very few people, much less take a bite out of them. I think the odds are on your side the rest of the way, little brother."

"That's one way of looken at it," John agreed as they began to drowse. "I've just got to find a way of convincen my dreams that it's not likely to happen again in my lifetime."

———

At school recess the next day, John sat on the walkway, soaking up the sunshine while his friends played football. The previous night's bad dream occupied his thoughts, and almost without thinking, he began doodling on a piece of notebook paper. Gradually, a form emerged on the paper, and an image of the grotesque captured John's imagination.

Over the next few days, the pencil sketch turned into a full-fledged color picture and then into a vivid painting of a coiled rattler surrounded by her babies. Every detail registered precisely and menacingly—the flat, triangular, golden head that rose hissing out of the coiled mass of brown skin and black diamonds, gleaming amber eyes with a hypnotic quality, the pinkish membranes of the split mouth, the forked tongue and raised rattles. Smaller rattlers flanked the female diamondback, each stretched to full length with angry heads rising off the ground.

"It looks as if they're about to slither off the canvas," Sam observed when John showed the painting to his family one night after supper.

"That's what I was aimen for," John replied. "The good thing is that they're stuck right where they are for the duration. There's no need to worry about them."

"It's more than a little unsettlen," Rachel suggested. "What are you goen to do with it."

"I thought I might hang it in my room," John answered.

"Then you'd better think again," Luke declared fiercely. "I don't care what you do with the ugly thing, mister hotshot painter, but it's not stayen in the room where I sleep at night."

"What's the matter, Luker?" Joe teased. "Are you afraid they're gonna getcha one night while you're sleepen?"

Everyone laughed but Luke. To keep the peace between his brothers, Joe volunteered to store the painting in his room.

Two days later, he began reconsidering the decision after a second consecutive restless night. Now, snakes were slithering through his dreams, and Joe wanted to rid himself of the painting.

Recalling an advertisement he had seen while reading the previous month's edition of *Progressive Farmer*, Joe thumbed through the magazine and located the notice. As far as he was concerned, the art contest provided a perfect opportunity to get the ghastly painting out of his room and the house as well.

Bombarded by the full extent of Joe's persuasive powers, John reluctantly agreed to enter the painting in the contest. With one day to spare before the entry deadline, the brothers wrapped the painting carefully, placed it in a large box and mailed the package to a Birmingham, Alabama, address.

———

The hunter's moon of October turned into November, and John's recovery stalled. At the suggestion of Drs. Pittman and Thacker, Matt and Caroline carried their son to Crawford Long Hospital in Atlanta. A team of specialists examined John's leg, and their prognosis was disheartening. The nerve damage had been more extensive than previously thought; John might end up as a cripple.

For the first time, the youngster felt discouraged.

His family rallied around him, however, and their faith renewed John's spirit. He put aside his artwork, preferring to spend his free time perched alongside his daddy or Joe as the men guided the combine through fields of cotton, soybeans and grain sorghum. He accompanied his grandpa to various farms and warehouses as Sam conducted the dealings of his pecan business, always learning from and amazed by the man's strength of character and perspective.

At prayer meeting one Wednesday night, the Benevolence congregation pleaded with the Lord specifically on John's behalf, praising the glory of God and asking that the boy be made whole again. John went away from the church feeling blessed beyond measure, knowing he belonged to something vast and special.

One week before Thanksgiving, John received a letter from the *Progressive Farmer*. He opened the envelope at the supper table, read the letter in silence and casually informed his family that his painting had been selected as the overall winner in the art contest. In addition to the notification letter, the envelope contained the first-place winner's check for fifty dollars, a form requesting his permission to reprint the painting in the magazine and a handwritten note from an Atlanta art patron. The man praised the quality of the painting, predicted great success for John in the future and proposed to buy this early work for an additional one hundred dollars.

No one knew quite how to take the success. Winning a contest sponsored by the local library had been surprising enough, but this latest accolade put John's artwork in another dimension.

"You're an artist, John," Joe declared as the family celebrated the accomplishment. "A real, honest-to-goodness artist who gets paid for doen what you love."

"Enjoy it, son," Sam advised. "Not everyone is so fortunate."

John nodded at the sage advice. He felt blessed, and more than a little amazed.

One Saturday in mid-December, John woke early, hauling himself and a warm blanket to the front porch. He settled in the porch swing, wrapped the blanket around him and waited for the sunrise, enjoying the wintry atmosphere. It was a chilly morning, perfect weather for snagging a deer, which Joe and Tom Carter hoped to do later in the morning.

A few minutes later, the front door opened, and his sleepy brother emerged from the house.

"What the heck are you doen up this time of day?" Joe asked, leaning his shotgun against the wall and taking a seat in the glider to wait for Tom's arrival.

"Woke up early," John explained. "I always do on days like this when the hunten's gonna be good. I bet you snag a big one today."

For several minutes, the brothers lost themselves in a discourse on hunting. They spoke about the deer that got away, the shot they missed and the one they could not fire at all. From deer hunting, their conversation rambled onto dove, rabbit and squirrels before lighting on quail.

Neither Joe nor John considered himself a good shot at quail, but both loved to eat it, especially the way their grandmother prepared the birds. Rachel stuffed the quail with pork sausage, then baked the birds brown and served them with gravy made from the pan drippings, butter, grape jelly and a touch of vinegar. Their mouths soon watered, anticipating a feast, and they made plans to set bird traps, hoping to entice a covey of quail lurking in one of the cornfields.

"We'll do it this afternoon," Joe promised, "as soon as Tom and I are finished butcheren that deer you seem so sure we're gonna get."

John smiled, then his face clouded with disappointment. "You'll have to do it without me," he said. "My crutches work well on solid ground, but they're not worth a flip in soft fields."

"I guess the goen would be tough," Joe replied. "It won't be too much longer, and you'll be walking with me."

"Do you really think so?" John asked.

"You have to keep believen, John," Joe said firmly. "Stay determined, keep your faith."

"I'm tryen," John said. "I keep tellen myself everything will be okay. I don't want to be a cripple. I don't even want to limp." He hesitated, then said, "But somethen doesn't feel right. It's not simply that my leg is weak. It's as if somethen's not connected down there—whatever it is that makes my leg cooperate with the rest of me."

He paused again, scanning the horizon across the field beside the house. "I'd give almost anything just to feel a breeze against my face from a good run," he said finally, turning back to Joe. "Lately, though, I'm beginnen to believe it's not meant to be."

"I felt that way when my leg was broken," Joe replied. "The strength will come when it's time, John, when the healen's ready for it. One day, you're gonna be overwhelmed by a knowen feelen that you're ready to walk again. You'll take that first step, and the leg will be strong enough."

"You sound entirely sure," John remarked.

"Oh, I could be wrong," Joe admitted. "You know yourself and what you're goen through better than anyone else. More than anything, I'm just urgen you to keep encouraged and not give up. Give yourself a chance and see what happens."

John nodded, returning his gaze to the dark horizon, waiting for the dawn to come.

———

John's prediction proved correct. At mid-morning, Joe and Tom returned home with a nine-point buck that had wandered into sight of Joe's shotgun. Soon, everyone was engrossed in carving up the animal for the freezer, and John used the busyness to seek a quiet moment. He planned to read a book on the front porch, but his natural instincts sent him on a different path, and the boy and his crutches followed a course that led eventually to the Old Pond.

He welcomed the solitude like a long-lost friend, soaking up the beauty of the land. A slight breeze stirred the crisp air, chapping his lips and face with a feeling of freshness that had been absent since that summer day when he almost lost his life to the rattlesnakes. The wind rippled the pond water, and an occasional fish broke the surface. Beyond the pond, cows grazed in the back pasture.

The mood was gentle and peaceful, lulling John into a deep slumber as he lay on the grassy bank, basking in the direct line of warm sunshine.

He woke sometime later with the sun directly overhead and his soul rested and refreshed. Warmed by the sunshine, he thought of the approaching winter solstice. Like his grandpa, John had keenly noted every equinox and solstice for several years now. Sam saw those days as beginnings and endings, "portending"—Grandpa's favorite word—a sense of something lost and something found, of happiness and sadness. Strictly speaking, John believed his grandfather's viewpoint gave too much weight to mere days. Nevertheless, he vowed then and there to view those seasonal markers as opportunities to take stock in what was and set his sights on what would come.

Earlier this morning, his brother had predicted the leg would heal when the timing was right. Recalling their conversation, a Bible verse came to John: "To everything there is a season, a time for every purpose under Heaven." The verse had provided the vision for John's prize-winning painting of the pecan orchard in winter. He remembered setting out to capture on canvass the beauty and quality of every season—the robust winters, promising springs, relentless summers and bountiful falls. The memory stirred a sudden anticipation about paintings still to be done, filling John with an eagerness to move forward and leave behind this dreary season of his life.

Rising to a sitting position, he experienced a keen awareness of his faith in God, a connection to all that was good and real in life. He knew then that God existed wherever people looked for Him—in the here and now, in the woods and the fields, in church and home, in hearts and minds, even in the mountains and oceans that John had never seen. He was beauty, grace and natural order. Or as the preacher put it: God was and is and will be—His hand always extended and waiting for all who sought Him.

John felt conviction and power behind these thoughts, even wished he might find a way to share the knowledge so that everyone would realize the power of God and seek His grace. It was the mystery of faith being revealed, and in that moment, John felt the beginnings of healing. One day, he might even understand the purpose for his encounter with those rattlesnakes. For now, he was content with this inner peace that his world would right itself in God's time.

A movement on the pond's far side caught his attention, and John saw his older brother emerging from the path in the woods at a trot. He pulled himself to a standing position, waving to Joe.

"Are you okay?" Joe called across the pond.

"A-Okay," John said.

"You had us worried," Joe said when he reached his brother. "You shouldn't wander off like that without tellen somebody where you're goen."

John chuckled. "Since when, big brother? Wanderen around this place is what I do best. I'm pretty good at—I think you put it—haven fun by my lonesome."

"I put what?" Joe asked, perplexed.

"The day it happened," John answered, tapping his foot with a crutch. "You dropped me off at the peanut field that mornen, and the last thing you said was, 'Have fun by your lonesome.'"

"Really? I said that?"

"I wanted to punch you," John said. "I resented like crazy haven to pick weeds by myself that day, and you were totally oblivious."

"Still feel that way? Joe asked.

"Nah. I get over things pretty quick." John glanced down at his feet, then back at Joe. "Thanks for comen to get me that day, Joe."

"Least I could do since that fun thing by your lonesome didn't work out so well," Joe shrugged. "You sure you're okay, John?"

John beamed with knowing. "I'm good. God and I just had a meeten of the minds right before you got here. It eased my mind. And you were right this mornen, too, Joe. The leg's getten better, and I'll be walken soon enough."

"You will," Joe agreed. "And runnen and wanderen and, hey, next summer, you'll even be picken weeds in the peanut field."

John grimaced. "I don't doubt it."

"Dinner's waiten for us," Joe said.

"I'm hungry," John said. "Can I ask you for a couple of favors?"

"Anything?"

"Could you set those bird traps this afternoon? I could really go for some quail," John said.

"Right after dinner," Joe confirmed. "What else?"

"How about a piggyback ride back home?" John asked. "My arms are worn out from these old crutches."

"Hop on," Joe said, dropping to a crouch.

———

The healing came slowly, sometimes grudgingly, it seemed, certainly slower than Christmas, which passed with John still in need of crutches. Indeed, all of winter came and went, and he missed most of the planting season, too. He wasn't the only one.

Facing the prospect of being drafted, Joe volunteered to join the Marines. His enlistment and departure happened so swiftly, the family never really had time to process it. One day, he was there, finishing up his winter quarter classes and helping set out tobacco; the next, he was gone to boot camp at Parris Island, South Carolina.

For a short time, his absence felt like the vacuum of a huge black hole, and then the space filled up with everyday life. Matt offered Lucas Bartholomew a full-time job on the farm to replace Joe, and everyone adjusted to the new family dynamic.

For most of spring, John felt like an empty canvas, blank and waiting to be filled. He wanted healing for his leg, but even that prospect failed to excite him. He needed something more basic, and couldn't quite wrap his thoughts around it.

Like the healing of his leg, it took time to sort through the cobwebs tangled in his head. Finally, one night in early June when a warm breeze was blowing, John observed a new moon hanging high on the horizon. Though distant and dim in the nighttime sky, the new moon beckoned with the promise of brighter times to come. The moment stirred his thoughts, the breeze blew away the cobwebs and he felt a future filled with possibilities.

The next afternoon, after a taxing therapy session, John set aside his crutches and began walking with a limp. He never again used the crutches. Still limping in July, he nevertheless worked alongside his family every day, helping to gather the tobacco and even pulling weeds from a field of peanuts without fear of rattlesnakes. At night, he relaxed by sketching and painting, each day's work an inspiration for a series of paintings that captured this season of life. By the time he started high school in September, the limp had disappeared and John was eager to see how his leg would hold up during tryouts for the basketball team.

THE FIRE
1967

CHAPTER 1

SOMETIMES LATE AT NIGHT as he either waited for Caroline to join him in bed or listened to the quiet rhythm of her sleep, Matt Baker wondered why he bothered with farming. Almost always, these doubts followed stressful, backbreaking days on the farm.

"There's got to be an easier way for a man to earn a liven," Matt would tell his wife.

"There is," Caroline would answer affectionately, "but not for men who have dirt in their veins."

On these rare nights, Matt wanted to make love to his wife, but he was usually exhausted, bone-tired to the point that no amount of red-bloodedness could will his body to carry out the wishes of his heart. Maybe the problem was old age. In his younger days, Matt reckoned he could have worked forty-eight hours straight and made love for the next twenty-four without missing a beat. At forty, however, he and Caroline would hold each other for a while and drift into a dreamless sleep that left them rested and replenished for another long day of toiling beneath a hellish sun.

On the morning after such a night, Matt sat on the front porch. The younger children had just boarded the school bus, and Joe was waving goodbye as he began a new day of college, another step in the journey that would lead him away from the farm.

As the school bus and Joe's Volkswagen disappeared down the road, Matt wondered once again why he bothered with farming. He knew the answer, of course. Farming was more than an occupation to Matt, something other than a simple job. It was a way of life, an opportunity for independence and self-reliance. Maybe dirt did course through his veins as Caroline claimed. Or maybe, as Joe once suggested, he was a slave to the earth. But pure and simple, a farmer's life was the only one Matt ever wanted.

So even though he knew the answer, Matt still liked on occasion to reflect on the reasons why he bothered with farming. If nothing else, this cogitation gave him the opportunity to consider what farming meant to him and, of more importance, to his family.

In the role of family provider, Matt began his rumination on the dollars and sense of farming, both of which were sorely lacking. The financial rewards for his sweat and toil had been scarce over the years, with Matt earning barely enough money to keep his family from being classified as poor by the government. Without gardens and livestock to feed the family, the Bakers very well might have been impoverished. As it was, they lived frugally, enjoying a few luxuries during the harvest season and praying they would have enough savings to meet their obligations in those months when there was no money coming into the farm.

Though Matt hated to admit and never resented it, the truth was that he had too many mouths to feed and care for on the income generated by one farm. When the children had been younger, Matt and Sam had labored like mules to get the job done, managing most, but not all, of the work by themselves. Year after year, they paid hired hands to help with the tobacco, and each harvest season they waited breathlessly to see if their work would earn enough money to make ends meet. Once in a great while, harvesttime arrived with money still in the bank from the previous year, seasons of satisfaction, which usually preceded the breakdown of a key piece of equipment or a cruel joke of nature. In either case, their savings, always meager at best, dwindled to near nothing. For the most part, though, Matt had managed.

Then, in 1964, fate had allowed Matt to double his operation, and the children had been able to replace the hired hands. In one year, the farm's income doubled. Another good year had followed, with the bills paid and a small nest egg laid in the bank. Prosperity beckoned as never before, and Matt acknowledged it with a spending binge, buying a new pickup truck and combine, replacing the back-pasture fence and remodeling the house. While seemingly extravagant, the invest-ment compensated for years of necessary neglect.

His reward for too much money spent in a single season came as a grim reminder that while a farmer can work tirelessly to raise his crop well, ultimately, he is a slave to things he cannot control. A year ago, the uncontrollable had been a late spring freeze, an unexplainable blight in the corn and low prices at harvest. By the time Matt tallied receipts against expenses, the family nest egg had shrunk.

Matt took nature's follies in stride. Weather was a farmer's best friend and tough-est adversary. Back in sixty-three, a spring flood had drowned the young crops, and a summer hailstorm had shredded a full-grown crop of tobacco. Two perfect years of rain had followed, and except for the spring freeze, 1966 had been a good weather year as well.

The economics of farming were an entirely different story. Matt never understood why the cost of raising a crop was almost more than it was worth to harvest. While he could count on paying more for seed, fertilizer and everything else needed to raise a crop, the job came with no guarantees that this year's corn, cotton or any-thing in his fields would command prices equal to or better than the previous year's receipts.

Last year, for instance, every bushel of corn, every bale of cotton and pound of peanuts had brought prices lower than the previous year's harvest. Apparently, prices fluctuated according to the whims of men with far more power than Matt could even fathom. Certainly, these forces were more worrisome than the weather, maybe even unfair when he compared the prices charged in grocery stores with the prices paid to farmers for their crops. Someone profited from the food business, but it wasn't the people who grew it.

If the economics of farming were not enough to drive a man crazy, then the government could finish the job. Every which way he turned, Matt found the gov-ernment staring over his shoulder. The government decided what crops could be planted, where and how much. On occasion, the powers that be even decreed the nation was producing too much food and offered incentives to leave fields empty or to plow under crops already in the ground. This notion of food aplenty irked Matt more than anything. With people hungry in America and millions starving all over the world, he found it hard to swallow the idea of producing less when more was needed.

As it was, Matt reckoned he could tolerate the whole process, but he sure couldn't make sense of it. Even so, as long as he could make ends meet for his family, the so-called experts could worry about the economics of farming. All he knew was how to raise things, and that was enough. He could tolerate the government's interference, and he could survive the market's whims. Leeway existed on both ends. Besides, Matt farmed for something more valuable than dollars and sense. Farming satisfied his basic desires.

Once, Matt had felt as if he were inheriting a life on the farm rather than choosing it. Then, he had gone away to fight the war and, while soldiering in Northern Africa and Europe, discovered the value of fields and family.

Farm work and his parents had instilled in Matt a sense of pride that showed as strength and caring, not vanity or conceit; a kind of know-how that could solve problems well beyond those found in the fields; a work ethic that allowed him independence; and the will to succeed. The farm gave general direction to life, yet preserved the freedom to choose one or many paths.

In Matt's case, his course had paralleled the direction chartered by his father, but their individual paths were marked by different approaches. While both men shared an equally strong attachment to the land, Matt wanted to conquer it, to extract life from the soil. Sam preferred to preserve the land and keep it wild. This single difference explained Matt's superiority as a farmer, a fact freely acknowledged by Sam. Under different circumstances, Sam might have become a forest ranger or a zoologist. As it was, he had taken up the farming life as the means to pursue his dreams while making an honest living for his family. Matt had chosen to farm for the same reasons, and he wanted his children to have the same values and opportunities whether they remained on the farm or followed paths leading elsewhere.

———

"You plannen to sit there all day, or are you goen out to earn this family a liven?"

Caroline's question surprised Matt, who wondered how long he had been sitting on the porch. She had come outside to empty a pan of dirty dishwater on the array of petunias lining the walkway.

"I was just thinken there must be an easier way for a man to make a liven than the one I chose," Matt said.

"Strange time of day for you to be thinken like that," Caroline remarked.

"Yeah," Matt agreed with a tempting grin. "You know what else? I'm not tired at all."

Caroline required a moment to read her husband's thoughts, the full impact of Matt's suggestive tone coming only when she observed the glint in his eyes. While the idea of making love to Matt on this morning appealed to Caroline, she concealed her desire. Summoning her most prudish posture and false airs of disinterest, she turned away from him and emptied the soapy water on the red and purple petunias. After inspecting the flowers, she marched chastely past her husband's seductive grin, setting the pan on the hall floor and allowing the door to slam close as she returned to Matt. Falling onto his lap, she nuzzled his neck and playfully bit his ear.

"This ain't helpen matters," Matt remarked as they kissed.

"It's not supposed to," Caroline said, laughing as she broke away from the embrace. "But first things first, mister: Go out there and earn us a liven."

"Work, work, work—that's all you ever think of, woman," Matt joked as she came to her feet.

"Where's Pa?" he asked a moment later.

"Ma's rubben him down with the liniment," Caroline answered. "He's all worn out and sore from yesterday. He had no business worken that hard."

"I tried to get him to take it easy, but you know how he is," Matt responded. "When he gets a notion to do somethen, it's hard to get it out of his head. I'll have to be firm with him next time."

"I heard that!"

Sam's booming voice resonated through the screen door as he stormed down the hall. Partly on the advice of Dr. Pittman and primarily to escape the nagging of Rachel, Matt and Caroline, Sam had eased his workload considerably. He was close to seventy-one this spring and enjoyed his emeritus status, offering advice, running errands and working hard until he took a notion to go fishing, pick blackberries or traipse around the farm. On occasion, however, he showed everyone he still could do an honest day's work, and, while loath to admit it, he had lifted and stacked too many hundred-pound bags of guano the previous day.

"I'll have you know that I haven't yet reached the point where my son is goen to be firm with me," he declared crossly. "I can fend for myself, and I know my limits. Now what needs doen today?"

If Matt knew anything, it was when to use caution with his father. In his present frame of mind, Sam was likely to strap a plow to his back and start marching through the fields.

"To tell you the truth, Pa, we're pretty much caught up," Matt said. "Tom's finishen up the first cultivation of the corn. There's some sprayen to be done, but I don't have the chemicals for it. Maybe you can go into Cookville this afternoon and get them. This mornen, though, I'd appreciate it if you'd take a look around the place with me. It's getten dry around here, and I'm wonderen if we might ort to get us an irrigation system."

"Dry as I've seen in many a year," Sam mused, appeased by Matt's respectful appeal. "We're short on rain, have been since last summer. I keep thinken we're gonna have a belly-washer to get us all caught up. Last time we had such a dry winter and spring was in fifty-four, and you know what kind of year that was 'round these parts."

"Don't remind me," Matt worried.

"Let me get my hat, and we'll take a look-see," Sam replied.

"Everything will work out," Caroline suggested to her husband while Sam opened the front door.

Matt nodded his agreement, kissing her on the cheek. "We'll be back around dinnertime," he called as she followed Sam into the house.

Alone again on the porch, Matt returned to the rocking chair. The dry spell was just one of the strange state of affairs. Winds of change had blown furiously across the farm, sweeping away the cast of characters who had formed the backbone of Matt's operation for many years. As a result, he now relied on a trio of more youthful, enthusiastic and inexperienced workers. Matt felt as if he understood some of what Job must have experienced when the tribulations ceased and God blessed him with a new family and greater riches. Above everything, he appreciated his newfound fortunes, yet a small part of him longed for the familiarity of the past.

Gone from his fields that spring were Joe, Lucas Bartholomew and to a great extent, Sam, who had made concessions to his age. Matt had worked closely with the three men over the years, and he knew what to expect from them. Their experience had eased the pressure of tending hundreds of acres of crops, including a burdensome twenty acres of tobacco.

Lucas had worked for Matt on and off through the years. Over the winter, however, he had cleared a section of land on the Berrien estate, agreeing to farm the acreage on shares for Paul and his sisters. Matt welcomed the opportunity for Lucas, understanding the man's yearning to work for himself. While sharecroppers often fared poorly, Lucas stood a better chance than most to succeed. The Berriens had funded the entire operation upfront and were asking only to recoup their investment when the harvest was sold. Any profit above expenses would belong entirely to Lucas. Working for Matt had given Lucas security. While that security was at risk working on his own, Lucas was poised to reap greater rewards.

Meanwhile, Joe had begun his junior year at Valdosta State College in March, following his discharge from a two-year stint as a combat correspondent for the U.S. Marines and *Stars and Stripes* newspaper. His enlistment—an alternative to being drafted—had come as a complete surprise to everyone, especially when he managed to pass the physical despite the broken leg suffered in high school. Yet, Joe had made the most of the opportunity, parlaying his high scores on the military entrance exam into the coveted correspondent's position and spending the majority of his service at bases in California and North Carolina gaining experience in his chosen profession. His discharge from active duty had come in February and he had returned home eager to resume his college education. While Matt would have preferred having Joe work side-by-side with him on the farm that spring, he never gave the idea any serious consideration. It was time for his oldest son to pursue the life he wanted in earnest, and there was no reason to keep him tied down in the fields. Matt missed his son's companionship, but he took comfort in knowing Joe would have his college degree by the end of next summer.

In Lucas and Joe's absence, Matt had not looked far to find the full-time help needed on the farm. Tom Carter had been a fixture around the place for years, cavorting with Joe, working in tobacco or listening to the tall tales that Sam spun like silk. Although he was the son of storekeepers, Tom had no intentions of succeeding Dan and Amelia in the mercantile.

Tom had graduated from high school two years earlier. Adhering to his parents' wishes, he enrolled at Abraham Baldwin Agricultural College—ABAC—aiming to obtain a degree in business. His college education lasted almost two years before he succumbed to his own desires. Just prior to the beginning of the spring quarter, Tom had informed his parents that he was dropping out of college to pursue the life of a farmer.

The news came as no surprise to Amelia and Dan. "Your daddy and I won't argue with you or try to persuade you otherwise," Amelia said when Tom broke the news. "However, we will make one request. Since you have no interest in runnen this general mercantile, we'd be much obliged if you found yourself a wife who would be."

"I promised them I'd keep that in mind when and if I ever get around to looken for a wife," Tom had relayed to Matt after they worked out the terms of his employment.

Knowing full-time help was needed on the farm, Tom had approached Matt in early winter. "I want to farm but the way I see it, there's a lot I need to learn before

I could even think about striken out on my own," he explained. "I can't think of a better place to learn the things I need to know than right here. I'd appreciate the opportunity to work with you, and I believe you know I'd work hard."

Matt never doubted Tom's word, and the young man had proved himself with hard work. He had harrowed land for ten hours a day, six days a week, then plowed that land, harrowed it again and planted it. He had repaired machinery, castrated shoats as well as steers and made one or two mistakes along the way, such as running the planter for a solid hour straight without realizing cotton seed had clogged one of the seed dispensers, leaving every other row seedless.

With Joe or Lucas, Matt took for granted they would know to do certain things that he now had to explain to Tom. But Tom was a quick learner, sufficing on one explanation and never making the same mistake twice. His enthusiasm was also appreciated as well as his dry sense of humor.

"Yeah, but did you notice how straight the rows are," he had drawled without missing a beat when Matt and Sam discovered the planter was jammed. The three of them had laughed off the mistake, and Tom had worked a long day to replant the seedless rows.

In this season of change, Matt also was learning to rely more on his two youngest sons. He had overlooked their abilities in the past by depending too much on Joe's experience and willingness. As the spring unfolded, however, he realized just how capable John and Luke were around the farm and he saw more clearly than ever the subtle similarities and differences among his three sons.

John, now fifteen, and Luke, almost thirteen, shared a strong affinity for farm work, whereas Joe tolerated it. While his youngest sons might very well tread their lives in furrows plowed by Matt, his firstborn was destined for different fields. At the same time, Joe and Luke possessed a natural talent for farming, while John approached each task with caution and planning. Faced with the same problem, Joe and Luke would solve it quickly with instinct. John would find the solution, too, but he needed extra time to study the situation.

Of all the differences and similarities among his sons, one stood out as the most obvious and unsettling to Matt. Whether working or playing, Joe and John approached life with a full degree of purpose. His two oldest sons had staying power, and they were diligent to a fault. At times, they could turn something as simple as fishing or hunting into a full-blown production. One time, when they had exasperated Sam with their preparations for fishing, their grandfather had forced them to spend a day at the pond with a fishing pole and an empty hook. On another occasion, he had made them spend the morning in a deer stand without the benefit of their guns. While unorthodox in his methods, Sam had instilled a new respect for leisurely pursuits in the boys. Over the years, his influence had tempered Joe and John's approach to the less serious side of life.

Luke, meanwhile, had yet to discover the serious side of life. He was diligent when the moment suited him, which usually was in the fields, guiding a tractor down a row, loading seed into a planter or feeding animals. Luke thrived on such work, but even then, the boy had a wild side. He bogged tractors for fun, drove recklessly and complained readily when he believed a more interesting chore required his attention than the one at hand.

Matt knew he should be stricter with the boy, but he could not always bring himself to make the extra effort. The trouble was that Luke reminded Matt of himself too much. As a child, Matt had caused his parents many headaches. Remembering his own youthful frivolity, Matt sympathized with Luke, understanding firsthand the problems faced by a free-spirited boy who raced toward adventure, often without ever looking where he was headed Frequently, Luke was blindsided in his haste.

Sympathy aside, Matt would have used the belt more if he had any inkling that Luke might not grow out of his wild ways. As it was, however, his mind was made up to tolerate a few minor inconveniences caused by bogged tractors and the like. He had noticed Luke's pranks tended to occur when there was time to spare.

Luke's one bad habit, which Matt refused to tolerate, was the boy's indifference toward school. Luke ignored homework, flunked tests frequently and was perilously close to failing the seventh grade. None of the other children—not even Matt himself—had been disdainful about schoolwork. Matt and Caroline had lectured the boy, punished him and watched over him to make sure Luke did homework. His brothers and sisters also pitched in, helping Luke study for tests and encouraging him to do better. The simple truth, however, was that Luke refused to apply himself, and his parents had reached their wit's end over the problem.

"You intent on spenden the day in that rocken chair, or are we gonna go see how dry it is around here?"

For the second time in the last few minutes, someone reminded Matt that he had more pressing business than passing time on the front porch. This time, it was Sam, who had gone inside the house to find his cap and wound up eating the last piece of breakfast toast smothered in blackberry jelly.

"I was just thinken, Pa," Matt said.

"It certainly behooves a man to do that once in a while," Sam suggested. "What's special on your mind this mornen?"

"Getten Luke through school this year," Matt answered. "Caroline got another call from his teacher last night. She says that unless Luke buckles down and shows a big improvement these last few weeks of school, he's gonna have to stay back a year."

Matt shook his head, slightly discouraged. "We've tried everything to make him do better, but he's not a bit interested."

"Luke's just sufferen from a bad case of spring fever," Sam replied. "Trouble is, he came down with it last spring and it's still runnen high in him. Face it, Matt. The boy can't tolerate be'en cooped up all day. I wouldn't worry too much about him, though. Luke's full of common sense. He'll come around soon enough and show his smarts."

"He's got to apply himself before he can show his smarts, Pa," Matt said. "If he doesn't come around soon, he's gonna spend another year in the seventh grade."

"There's a point well taken," Sam agreed. "If we can find a way to make Luke understand the seriousness of the situation, then he might just straighten up in time to get promoted. I'll put on my thinken cap and see what I can come up with. Now, though, let's decide if it's time to get into the irrigation business."

"Let's do it," Matt said.

———

Sam valued three things most in life—his family, his religion and his farm. The order of importance depended entirely on the circumstances of the moment. Religion came first when he was singing a hymn, listening to a good sermon or praying. Family mattered most when he had a rare moment alone with Rachel, Matt, Caroline or any of his grandchildren. And the land meant the world to him during those times when he was privileged to walk through the fields and woods, marveling at the beauty—fine earth that yielded a livelihood for his family, majestic forests that concealed treasures some people would never understand and hidden coves that contained mysteries still unexplored.

His most precious moments occurred when Sam experienced congruency among everything that mattered most to him. On these occasions, he saw how the family needed, used and appreciated the land, while the land sustained, unified and strengthened the family. He envisioned this trust between family and land spanning generations, decades, centuries, even millenniums. And he realized his vision fulfilled a young man's dream. At such times, Sam would thank God for giving him a small part of the world and the family with whom he shared it.

The road taken to find his dream was pocked with obstacles, sacrifices and hardships. A pioneer spirit, the companionship of a good woman and a little luck had pulled him from the deepest valleys and pushed him over the highest hills along the way.

In 1920, using his life's savings for a down payment, Sam had mortgaged his family's future for a section of prime land carved from the vast estate owned by Britt Berrien. Sam stumbled across the place by accident. Yet the very moment he turned onto the dirt road leading to his farm, Sam realized he had found tranquility, about eight miles north of Cookville in a community named New River after the tributary that meandered through it. His instincts were confirmed less than two miles down the dirt road when he came across an abandoned house obscured by weeds and run down from years of neglect. Sam had spent the entire day hiking the land, marveling at its diversity.

At the end of the day, he had approached Britt Berrien with an offer. The banker laughed, claimed he had no intentions of selling any part of his vast holdings and sent Sam on his way. Undaunted by the banker's brusque manner, Sam returned the next week with a higher offer. Once again, Britt turned him down, but Sam's persistence and genuine love for the land won the man's grudging respect. Two months after their initial meeting, Britt proposed a deal for one hundred acres—the price deliberately steep to discourage Sam.

"It's not negotiable," Britt had declared, believing Sam would reject the offer. "Take it or leave it."

"That's a ridiculous amount of money you're asken," Sam shot back, "but the land's worth every penny and more. If you trust me enough that you're willen to let your bank extend me a loan, then I'll take it."

Britt shook his head in dismay. The two men sealed the agreement with a handshake and the struggle to succeed had begun for Sam.

Sam's purchase of those first one hundred acres in 1920 coincided with a national collapse in farm prices and the ravages of the boll weevil on Georgia's cotton fields. In the early years, he had doubted his ability to keep up with the payments. On the bad days, he would curse Britt for making such an unfair offer and then berate himself for accepting the deal. But always, the appeal of his dream and Rachel's constant support would spur him forward.

In 1925, his family went an entire winter without sugar, tea, coffee and other store-bought goods because every penny was needed to make the monthly payments to the bank and still have enough money to buy the seed and fertilizer to make a crop when spring came. By the next year, Sam believed the battle had crested, and his confidence soared. He refinanced the balloon payment on his original five-year loan and bought another one hundred acres from Britt Berrien. Then the Depression hit, along with the worst drought on record in Georgia.

At first, the hard times brought on by the collapse of the nation's economy mattered little in the tiny Cookville community, which was used to being poor. Slowly, however, the poor community became Depressed. In 1933, money disappeared and commerce came to a halt. With food on their table every night, Sam and Rachel fared better than many of their neighbors. But few of the neighbors owed such a huge chunk of money to the Farmers and Citizens Bank.

A day finally arrived when Sam could not meet his obligations to Britt Berrien. Refusing to make excuses, he explained his plight to the banker. "If you want me off the property, I understand," Sam said. "All I ask is for a few days to pack my things and find a place for my family to stay."

"Let me think about it," Britt had replied.

Throughout those early years, Sam and Britt had lived as strangers, exchanging nods of acknowledgment here and there and even fewer words. Sam knew the banker had a ruthless streak. Only a few years earlier, Britt had foreclosed on a nearby piece of property owned by Henry Anderson, a hardworking man who often performed handyman jobs on the Berrien estate. Understanding Britt had been reluctant to part with the land in the first place, Sam fully expected the man to reclaim the property through foreclosure. However, Sam had underestimated the effect his hard work had on the banker. Two days later, Britt had proposed a one-year moratorium on the loan payments with an understanding that interest would accrue on the unpaid balance.

"Farm prices should improve next year, and I continue to have every confidence in your ability to repay the loan," the banker had written in a short note explaining the terms of his proposal. "As far as I'm concerned, our handshake is still good."

When all was said and done, it had taken Sam well over twenty years to pay for the first two hundred acres and Britt had profited enormously from the deal, with interest payments alone dwarfing many times over the land's original value. Yet, Sam never failed to acknowledge the financial lifeline from the banker. It was the closest gesture of friendship to pass between the two men, and Sam appreciated the opportunity. Soon afterward, the Bakers and Berriens began living in a more neighborly way. April and June began swapping recipes and gossip with Rachel, while Joseph and Matt became good friends with Paul. Britt occasionally would join Sam for hunting or fishing, but they remained mere acquaintances to his dying day.

Two decades later, when Sam sought to buy an additional two hundred forty-eight acres in 1940, Britt had readily agreed to the deal, without any persuasion required. Again, however, he had parted with his land only for an excessive price, a ready reminder that Sam and he were just acquaintances after all. As Sam once dared to observe to his wealthy companion, Britt preferred an acquaintance to a friend.

———

On county plats, the Baker place appeared as a perfect rectangle, with the long lines serving as east-west markers and the short sides showing north and south. Carved from the thousands of acres in the Berrien estate, the farm backed up against timber owned by Paul, April and June on its southern and eastern flanks. The north side bordered property owned by Ruby Davis, a cantankerous widow who possessed almost as much money and land as the Berriens, while the railroad tracks ran along the farm's western edge, separating the Baker place from the Castleberry place.

The farm contained a blend of pastures, ponds and seven cultivated fields, all stretched between woods of pine, oak, sycamore, cypress and fat lighter stumps left over from trees harvested by Britt Berrien many years earlier. Except for the small patch across the dirt road in front of the house, which was the lone piece of cultivated land on the farm's eastern flank, the fields were all vast expanses of fertile land dotted only with an occasional line of fence and trees. The largest of the fields required nearly four long days to harrow or plow, while the smallest took at least two and a half days to do the same work.

The Old Pond—so dubbed because it had been in place when Sam bought the land—was on the southwest side of the farm, its banks shaded by towering pines and majestic oaks. Primed by underground springs, the pond eventually turned into a huge bog of pitch-black water, mud and decay from some ancient swamp. Home to black bears, bobcats and rare plants among other things, the bog contained a few acres of inaccessible swampland. Having such a mysterious place plunked down in the middle of their farm had provided fodder for more than one restless night for every member of the Baker family.

Another oddity on the farm was a small water hole placed squarely in the middle of the farm's largest field. Too many large, cranky water moccasins inhabited the water hole. Twice, their poisonous bites had killed cattle. Every so often, the boys would grab their guns and spend a few minutes sighting the moccasins for target practice. By and large, however, everyone avoided the water hole or kept a close watch for snakes when they ventured near it. The beneficiaries of their reluctance to fish in the water hole were some monstrous catfish, most of which went through life never once tempted by a worm dangling on the end of a hook.

The New Pond, which had been dug in 1954 from a grove of aged, cypress trees, lay on the extreme northern side of the place, concealed within a stand of virgin pine trees and merging eventually with a swamp on neighboring land known as Bear Bay. Filled with ragged stumps and dead tree trunks, the pond simmered like an English moor on foggy mornings.

On this early May morning in 1967, however, the entire farm baked beneath a merciless sun. Wherever Matt and Sam looked, they saw crops begging for water. Tobacco had already wilted, with the hottest part of the day still to come. The slightest gust of wind sent swirls of gray dust across fields of corn, cotton, peanuts, soybeans, cantaloupes and sweet potatoes. Ponds that should have been full were far below their normal levels, lower than either man could remember in many years.

Each year, Matt depended on a tricky mix of rain, warmth and sunshine to bring life to the crops and put money in his pockets for the next year. Perfect weather was not required for a good crop, but some balance of rain and sunshine was needed. So far this year, dark storm clouds had been a rare commodity, yielding dry heaves for the most part. The short supply of rain had seemed like a blessing last fall as Matt raced to bring the harvest home, but the absence of winter rains had left the fields plenty dry when planting time arrived in early spring.

Matt counted on several days or weeks each winter and spring when the fields would be too boggy to work, meaning long days ahead later as he scrambled to prepare his land for another crop. This year, however, the weather had been dry enough that Matt had his fields harrowed and turned by the end of February. Early spring rains, while lighter than usual, had allowed the newly planted crops to take hold, but water had been sparse ever since, limited to a few afternoon showers that evaporated almost as quickly as they fell on the thirsty ground.

With his foot propped on the front fender of the pickup truck, Matt now scanned the patch of droopy tobacco, then cast his eyes skyward in a futile search for signs of an approaching rain. "Pa, these crops need water or they're gonna die," he surmised. "If we expect to make any crop at all, we'll have to irrigate, and we'll have to do it soon."

"No doubt, you're right," Sam agreed. "It's even drier than I suspected."

"Then you agree we need to invest in an irrigation system?" Matt asked.

"Did you notice how low the ponds were?" Sam replied. "Even the water hole is lower than I've ever seen it at this time of year. We probably can get two, possibly three good waterens out of them as it is now. But, son, what happens if we don't get some good rains to replenish what we take out? Then we'll have an expensive irrigation system on our hands, no water to run it, and no decent crop to help us pay for it."

"It's a gamble we have to take," Matt insisted. "Look at that tobacco. If these crops don't get water soon, they won't be worth what it cost us to plant them."

Sensing his father's continued reluctance to the idea, Matt abandoned any serious attempt to get his father's blessing. "Don't fret too much about the cost," he said. "We've got some money saved, and you know how it's always bothered us to have money in the bank."

He winked at Sam, then added with a chuckle: "Besides, Pa, I think our current situation qualifies as a rainy day. Don't you?"

"I hope we're still laughen come fall," Sam remarked.

———

"Lu-u-uke!"

The cry exploded with the pent-up fury of a launching rocket, and everyone knew Luke was in trouble again. In this last month before he became a teenager, trouble lurked around every corner for Luke. Sometimes, it blindsided him; occasionally it caught up with him. But more often than not, Luke ran smack-dab into the middle of more trouble than he could handle, frequently ignoring the warning signs pointing to an easier way.

Hearing Caroline holler for her youngest son, Sam peered down from the barn loft where he was storing the chemicals he had bought a short time ago in Cookville. His daughter-in-law was standing by the back porch, tapping her foot as she waited impatiently for Luke to answer her summons. Having long ago learned to gauge Caroline's anger by the pace of her foot-tapping, Sam judged she had reached the boiling point.

"Luke!" she shouted again. "Get out here this instant. You and I are gonna get a few things straight around here, mister."

"Poor, Luke," Sam muttered to himself as he deduced the cause of Caroline's rage. She had stopped tapping her foot and was scraping the bottom of the shoe against the porch edge, which meant one thing.

Unable to master the art of inhaling cigarettes, Luke had taken to chewing tobacco. While no one cared about his tobacco habit, everyone had tired quickly of his nasty tendency to spit used plugs anywhere the notion struck him. This was not the first time someone had stepped onto a messy clump of salivated tobacco, but it was the first such misfortunate step for Caroline.

The screen door opened, and Luke stood mystified before his mother. "Yes, ma'am?" he drawled.

Caroline pointed to her shoe, then delivered a stern lecture, managing to touch on responsibility, carelessness, cleanliness and manners in a sixty-second tirade that ended with her declaration that she would not tolerate nastiness in her backyard. When she had delivered a sufficient scolding, without any interruptions from Luke, Caroline ordered the boy to get rid of the tobacco and then wash down the back porch. Without any protest or acknowledgment, Luke obeyed her.

Luke's spiritless attitude toward Caroline annoyed his grandfather. Sam would have preferred the boy show remorse or even defiance rather than bland acceptance. While he normally would not condone disrespect to one's elders, Sam could tolerate almost anything but indifference. He abhorred people who showed neither spunk nor regret when they made a mistake, and Luke's recently acquired insipidity was particularly distasteful. The boy would fight at school, ignore homework or flunk a test, then accept his punishment without any explanation or protest. Luke needed an attitude adjustment, and Sam decided to provide it.

"Luke," he called from the loft. "I need you to help me with a little project before it gets dark."

"Can't right now, Grandpa. Mama's got me cleanen up the porch."

"Never mind with that," Sam said. "Just put that tobacco out of harm's way, and no one will be the wiser. Water's too scarce around here to waste on a porch that's clean enough. Grab a couple of hoes and the field rake, then meet me at the black-berry bramble."

"Yes, sir," Luke sighed.

———

The bramble consisted of about fifty blackberry bushes clustered along the fence between the far edge of the pecan orchard and a small meadow of sweet grass and broom sage. Each summer, the bushes yielded enough berries for jelly, cobblers and homemade ice cream. Sam had planted the blackberries over many years, and he kept the fencerow spotless to make sure no snakes took up residence in the bram-ble. He also picked most of the berries himself, contending everyone else tended to eat almost as many as they put in their baskets. When the berries ripened in early summer, Sam made a point of reminding everyone that hundreds of bushes grew wild all over the farm, the point being, of course, to stay away from the bramble.

"It's time you and I had a little talk," Sam said as Luke and he worked on either side of the fence, pulling weeds and raking away dead leaves.

"What about, Grandpa?"

"Do not play dumb with me, Luke," Sam replied testily. "You know exactly why we need to talk. It's partially about your poor work in school. But mainly, it's about your attitude, son, or I should say your lack of attitude."

Luke focused intently on his work, but Sam knew the boy was listening. One of the pleasures of being a grandparent was the knowledge that his grandchildren listened carefully to his words of wisdom. Sam would tell Luke virtually the same thing the boy had heard from his parents on countless occasions. However, because the words came from someone who rarely reprimanded or lectured, they tended to make a stronger impression coming from Sam.

"Luke, I know you're not as dumb as the grades on your report card indicate," Sam began. "But the truth of the matter is that your smarts are measured by those grades, and what's written down on your report card determines whether you pass or fail in school."

"It don't matter to me whether I pass or fail," Luke retorted. "As soon as I get sixteen, I'm quitten school."

"Maybe so; everybody's got a right to be ignorant, you included," Sam said. "But I'd think twice before tellen your mama and daddy that. In the meantime, you're only twelve right now, so you have to go to school."

Luke gave an indifferent shrug.

"You and I are alike in a lot of ways, Luke," Sam continued. "We both like worken outdoors, usen our hands. When I was a young man, I had a job in town. It was a good job, but I always felt cooped up and caged like a wild animal. It drove me crazy at times."

"That's the way I feel," Luke muttered with an understanding nod. "I can't stand it. I'd rather be home duren the day, worken around here."

"Then I suppose spenden the summer in school would be especially hard on you?" Sam suggested.

"There's no way I'd ever go to summer school," Luke said defiantly.

"Well, between you and me, I'm afraid you're gonna wind up in summer school if you don't buckle down and pass the seventh grade," Sam said. "Your mama and daddy are none too happy about it because we need you in the tobacco field, but your teacher says you're gonna fail unless she sees a vast improvement in your effort these last few weeks of school. Summer school will make up what you missed and get you promoted to the eighth grade in the fall."

Sam sometimes justified a white lie, but this suggestion of summer school was an outright deception. As far as he knew, no one had mentioned summer school. In fact, he doubted New River Elementary even offered such a thing. If he had guessed correctly, however, the mere possibility of attending summer school would light a fire under Luke and he would finish the seventh grade.

"Summer school," Luke moaned incredulously. "That'd be more than I could bear."

"I would think so," Sam replied, using Luke's sober silence to reflect on his deception.

Knowing he had broken one of the Ten Commandments bothered Sam, even though he had a good reason and had simply allowed Luke to draw his own conclusions. Of course, Rachel would disagree with his reasoning, contending there was no good lie. She would be right, too. Nevertheless, Sam would confess his sin to her anyway, just as she would say a prayer of penitence for him. His wife delivered a powerful prayer, and Sam always felt better to have her working on his side in matters with the Lord.

When they had cleared half the fencerow, Sam broached the main concern on his mind, which was Luke's lackadaisical attitude. "Now that I've got you all worried about school, Luke, let's discuss the real reason I brought you out here," Sam said. "When it comes to school, I don't have room to brag. I never graduated from high school—not that I didn't want to, mind you. Things were just different when I was younger."

Luke looked intently at his grandfather, expecting some wonderful yarn about the past. But Sam had spun enough tales for one day and figured the boy was overdue a word to the wise.

"Your attitude has changed of late, Luke," Sam said abruptly, casting a stern eye on the boy. "And I, for one, don't like it a bit. As a matter of fact, if you were my son, I'd've probably taken a belt to your hide a few times more than your daddy has these last few weeks."

Sam paused, allowing silence to emphasize the uncharacteristic harshness of his reproof. Unaccustomed to such forceful reprimand from his grandfather, Luke appeared sufficiently slack-jawed for Sam to continue his admonishment.

"Watchen you grow up is pretty much like watchen your daddy grow up all over," Sam said. "He was just as rambunctious as you are, a regular rooster. Your daddy did things and got away with stuff you've probably never dreamed of doen. And do you know why, Luke?"

The boy shook his head.

"Matt was a firecracker, but you could always count on him haven a reason for doen the things he did—even if it was a really dumb reason," Sam said. "Now reasons, even dumb reasons, don't excuse bad behavior. But, son, you don't seem to have a reason for anything you do of late. I don't know why that is, and frankly, I don't care. All I'm sayen is that a man's got to have reason in his life, a purpose for doen the things he does. I don't care if it's somethen as simple as hunten. When I hunt, Luke, I hunt because I enjoy the sport or because my family needs meat on the table. I don't go kill an animal without any reason whatsoever.

"Do you understand?" Sam asked.

"Sort of," Luke answered.

"Either you do or you don't," Sam replied firmly. "Let me put it to you this way: Next time you decide to spit out a nasty clump of tobacco right beside the back porch, think first. Ask yourself, 'Why there,' when you've got a thousand other places you could spit. Or if you miss a homework assignment, tell people why you didn't do it, even if it means admitten you were just plain lazy. Excuses won't get you far, Luke, but I'd rather hear a bad explanation from you than see that tired shrug of your shoulders and hear you say, 'I don't know.'

"The good Lord gave you a brain, son, but it's up to you to use it," Sam continued, his sharp tone softening considerably. "You may never be a scholar, and that's fine. Sometimes, I think there are too many scholars in the world as is. But there's also too many dumb and ignorant people in the world. You've always been a smart boy. Now's the time to decide if you're gonna become a smart man.

"Do you understand?" Sam asked again.

"I understand, Grandpa," Luke said.

Sam eyed the boy fiercely, wielding his pirate's face to maximum advantage, a tactic he used rarely, only when the moment was of grave importance.

Almost involuntarily, Luke nodded, again indicating he understood his grandfather, and Sam sensed half the battle had been won. With the daylight fading, they finished their weeding in silence.

CHAPTER 2

TOM FLUFFED A PILLOW cushion, yawned loudly and stretched his lanky frame across the black leather sofa in the front parlor of his home. It was a warm Saturday in the middle of May, the first time in nearly two months he had not worked a six-day week, and Tom had volunteered to mind the mercantile so that his parents could go to town. On the television, Mickey Mantle belted a home run and started his obligatory run around the bases. As the announcer started to say how many homers Mantle needed to reach the five-hundred career mark, the bell jingled on the store door, drowning out the information Tom wanted. Rolling his eyes in disgust, he pulled himself off the couch and went to wait on the customer.

It was Summer Baker, and she wanted cloth.

"Cloth?" Tom said, his mind still preoccupied with how many homers Mantle needed to reach five hundred.

Summer nodded and repeated her request. "Cloth," she said. "I'm enteren the Miss Golden Leaf beauty pageant, and I'm gonna make my own evenen gown."

"That's nice," Tom remarked absently, almost surprised to realize he knew nothing about selling material. In fact, Tom felt unusually out of place around the mercantile these days. Months had passed since he had helped his parents do any kind of work in the store, except for manning the cash register for a few transactions here and there.

As Summer babbled about the beauty pageant, Tom regarded the store, beginning with the "Carter's General Mercantile" embellished on the plate glass window beside the door. General mercantile aptly described the establishment. Dating back to the early 1920s when Tom's grandfather had set up shop in this crossroads community, the building had been razed and expanded over the years to accommodate increased traffic. The store contained a soda fountain, an over-the-counter pharmacy and the remnants of a post office. The U.S. Postal Service had discontinued the New River community postmark during the Korean War.

Children especially delighted in the store's treasures, beginning with the glass case beside the front door that prominently displayed a large selection of candy. Frequently and never with complaint, Amelia took a minute out of the day to wipe away tiny blotches left by children who had pressed their faces against the glass to obtain a better look at the candy bars, suckers and other goodies inside the case.

From the candy counter, children typically moved on to investigate the soda fountain with its ice cream box and the two drink machines. To attract adults, the store offered a cracker barrel prominently displayed in the middle of the floor—as well as a sandwich counter in the rear of the building where a refrigerated case stocked with fresh meats, vegetables and dairy products hummed. The mercantile also carried a solid line of groceries, clothing, hardware and convenience items that saved many country families a trip to Cookville or Tifton. Dan and Amelia ran a tidy, profitable store, designed to satisfy their customers.

The store's one exception to convenience and practicality was a collection of crystal, porcelain figurines and dolls, handmade quilts and other treasures that occupied a special glass counter near the soda fountain. Amelia had acquired the collection through two decades of shrewd bargaining and bartering. She set great store by the collection, regarding each piece as a prized possession, almost dreading to part with any of her precious valuables. Still, the prizes came and went, her business instincts frequently turning a hefty profit on every piece of merchandise that graced the treasure counter.

In the store's far back corner near the storage room, Tom finally spotted the cloth, realizing at the same moment that Summer had asked him a question. "Huh?" he asked.

"Do you think I can win?" Summer repeated impatiently.

"I don't know," Tom replied. "I haven't thought about it."

Whenever possible, Tom paid little attention to Summer. As children, she had bedeviled him with her quick tongue and sassy style. Over the years, he had learned to deal with Summer simply by ignoring her teasing and feigning indifference to her good-natured sarcasm. His strategy had worked for the most part. While Summer spared no one from her clever, rapier-like wit, she had developed a standoffish approach to Tom, which suited him just fine. As much as he felt a part of the Baker family, Summer had become the sister for whom he never had time, and Tom suspected she felt similarly about him.

For those reasons then, he found himself surprised for the second time in almost as many minutes. To his utter amazement, Summer Baker turned into a beautiful woman before his very eyes. She had long, thick chocolate brown hair that usually cascaded down her shoulders—but today was pulled back hastily it seemed, piled on top of her head and held in place with a rubber band. Tom resisted an impulse to push back a wayward strand as he observed her face, which managed to be round and lean at the same time, with cheeks that arched and dimpled deeply when she smiled, which Summer did frequently. Light brown eyes radiated from her face, which was clear, silky smooth and carried a healthy tan, not nearly as brownly toned as her bare shoulders, arms and legs. She was a good half-foot shorter than Tom's six-foot frame, but Summer carried herself with the regal grace that distinguishes beauty from mere prettiness.

Tom suddenly sensed without a doubt that Summer would become the next Miss Golden Leaf beauty queen.

"You're staren, Tom," she barked abruptly, obviously annoyed.

As they met face-to-face, his own midnight blue eyes clashing with Summer's sparkling brown, Tom blushed with embarrassment, feeling like a little boy who had been caught with his hand in the cookie jar just before supper. Summer giggled, and Tom felt his face flush red hot under her gaze.

"Uh, I'm sorry," he stammered. "I was just thinken."

"Well, that explains everything," Summer said with mounting sarcasm. "I realize what a strain that must be on you, but I don't have the time to wait for all that brain activity to take place." She smiled with sickening sweetness, then added quickly. "Although I'm sure that like a total eclipse of the sun, your thought would be equally spectacular, especially knowen how one comes about as often as the other." She crossed her arms. "Cloth, Tom!" she said in demanding tones. "I need to see the cloth. Are you gonna help me or not?"

He started to tell her the thought was not worth pursuing, then changed his mind, knowing she would win a battle of words, even more afraid his comment would invite further questioning. "Awe shucks, Summer," he complained. "You know I don't know nothen about cloth. You know where it is. Help yourself."

"Some storekeeper you are," Summer nagged. "If I'm gonna spend my money here, then I expect help in deciden what I want. Come on back here and help me decide."

Wordlessly, Tom followed her and unfolded one bolt of cloth after another. At a whirlwind pace, Summer sought his opinion on each piece, flustering him with a series of questions that she answered herself before Tom even had time to consider the possibilities. After ten dizzying minutes, she calmly announced, "I'll wait for your mother. She has good taste. You can put all this stuff back."

Tom shook his head in dismay, returning the cloth to the shelf while Summer inspected the refrigerated counter. This kind of whimsical behavior was infuriating, reminding him exactly why he kept his distance from Summer Baker. As he silently rebuked himself for allowing her to get the upper hand, the doorbell jingled again and he escaped to the front to wait on a real customer.

The woman and her two children obviously were passing through New River on their way to somewhere else. Tom pumped five dollars' worth of gasoline into their car, then sold a bag of potato chips, a sucker, a candy bar and three small Cokes, pleased that he remembered to collect the deposit on the bottles.

"Your wife was showen me the quilts while you gassed up the car," the woman remarked as Tom handed her change from a ten-dollar bill. "They're lovely. How much are you asken for them?"

"She's not my wife," Tom said stoutly.

"Oh, I'm sorry," she replied, smiling at Tom, then at Summer, who returned the pleasantry.

"Anything else I can help you with?" Tom asked, anxious for everyone to leave.

"The quilts?" the woman reminded him, looking quickly to Summer for assistance. "How much are they?"

Tom was slow to reply, so she continued, her tone growing more uncertain. "I've been looking for a quilt for some time now, and that wedding pattern is really beautiful."

"Oh, yeah," Tom replied at last. "Well, ma'am, my mother does the buyen and sellen from that part of the store. I really don't know the first thing about it. I'm sorry. I'd help you if I could, but I can't."

The woman's face crinkled with disappointment.

"Tom," Summer suggested. "Why don't you get her telephone number and address? That way, Amelia can get in touch with her."

"That's a splendid idea, and I'd appreciate it," the woman said, setting her drink bottle on the counter and opening her purse to retrieve a pen and paper. When she had written down the information, she handed the note to Tom and received his assurance that he would give the note to Amelia as soon as she returned home. Finally, the woman returned two of the drink bottles to the storage rack, collected her deposits and ushered her children out of the store.

"Now I know why you have no intention of taken over the store someday," Summer teased lightly when they were gone. "The place would fall apart in a matter of months, maybe even weeks or days."

"Probably so," Tom agreed with obvious disinterest. "If there's nothen else I can help you with, I'll see you later."

"Are you tryen to get rid of me?' she asked.

"The thought crossed my mind," Tom answered. "I'd like to see the end of the baseball game."

"Okay, okay," Summer conceded. "Before I leave though, you still have to answer one question for me."

"What's that?"

"Since you obviously have doubts about my ability to win the Miss Golden Leaf pageant, are you plannen to come see how I do?' she asked.

"I'll probably go—if your daddy doesn't have any work for me to do," Tom replied.

"It's at night; that shouldn't be a problem," Summer said. "Will you root for me, Tom?"

"Depends," he answered, shrugging his shoulders.

"On what?" she replied, irked by his lack of support.

"On who else is in the pageant," Tom said. "Anyway, that's more than one question. How 'bout letten me watch the game, Summer?"

"I ought to wait for your mother to get home, but I don't have time," Summer remarked. "I have to get ready to go out tonight. Oh well, when Amelia gets home, ask her to give me a call. Bye-bye now."

"Bye," Tom called as Summer opened the door to leave.

"And good riddance," he muttered when she had gone.

———

Summer enjoyed flirting. But walking home from the mercantile, she tried to reassure herself that nothing of the sort had passed between Tom and her. Her intentions had been purely innocent, nothing more than everyday conversation—until that moment Tom's eyes had pored over her like a hungry man eyeing a steak dinner. She was accustomed to approving glances, even occasional whistles from boys who found her attractive. But Tom had appraised her with the eyes of a man. And whether he meant to or not, his obvious attraction stirred new feelings in Summer.

Boys had always desired Summer. She had dated plenty of young men who wanted more than a goodnight kiss, and she had rejected every advance with ease. Now, two weeks before she graduated from high school, Summer experienced new feelings and felt the tug of old-fashioned desire.

Although subtler in her appraisal, Summer had responded to Tom's lure by looking at him in a way she had never looked at another man. She had started with his hands, which were rough, chapped and stained from his work. But they were good sturdy hands, with long fingers, huge knuckles and chewed nails. Although naturally fair complexioned as evidenced by his bare white feet, long days in the sun had darkened Tom's face and arms to a light tan. His hair was golden blond, a shaggy mass of curls because it needed a cut, and his eyes were midnight blue. A series of generous angles, with classic cheekbones and dimples, set his face, while his frame was too thin but hard and agile.

While she had never before given him more than a second glance, she was vaguely aware that girls considered him handsome. He was no Romeo, but Tom rarely lacked female companionship. Summer understood the physical attraction to Tom. The puzzling part was her sudden desire to know him as a companion. The surprise was that while she considered Tom a friend, almost a member of the family, she had lost touch with him somewhere along the way. He was Tom, a constant presence in her life, yet nothing else.

In English class earlier this year, Mrs. Gaskins had asked Summer to describe herself with a single word. Without hesitation, she had answered, "Forthright." She was bold and direct, and she tended to be drawn to similar people. Tom seemed the exact opposite, but maybe she was mistaken with her opinion.

A long time ago, Summer had categorized Tom as shy, a true country bumpkin who found pleasure in watching the wheels go round and round. Having never bothered to reconsider her views, she now realized her notions of Tom were outdated, certainly not in tune with the more recent images of a young man who bickered playfully with her brothers, joshed her sisters or charmed the family with hilariously exaggerated tales about his parents and their store. Tom still retained a certain amount of shyness, a bit of self-doubt when he ventured toward the unfamiliar and a larger portion of reluctance that often showed up through his smiles. Yet, his shyness came across as a quality, and it no longer overshadowed the confident young man he had become.

Suddenly, Summer was determined to know this man. Naturally, she began scheming.

———

Summer found Joe fishing at the New Pond. Or at least he presented a good impression of a fisherman. He was leaned against a pine tree, dozing with an open book by his side and a cigarette dangling precariously from his mouth. He had taken off his shirt to soak up the sun's warmth, and the fishing pole rested against his naval, expertly propped on the edge of his blue jeans and the tip of his sneaker.

If Tom Carter had become a mystery to Summer over the years, then Joe had become her closest friend. Their age difference had shrunk over the years, bringing them closer in spirit, and though they moved in different circles to different tunes, Summer could count on her brother for anything. She relished quiet moments like this when the opportunity allowed her to contemplate him in complete solitude. She wanted to etch these moments in her memory, so they could help fill the lonely hours ahead when the day came for Joe to leave the farm.

As much as she dreaded that day, Summer hoped it would come soon for Joe. She understood his craving for something else. Occasionally, she shared the same feelings of restlessness, but the urge was strongest in Joe. He needed new places, new people and new experiences before the desire would be satisfied. Her brother wanted to write the first draft of history, to tell people about the important stuff that shaped their world. Without a doubt, his journey would carry him far from Cookville.

Her own future seemed entirely uncertain. On some days, she imagined herself as a famous dressmaker, watching beautiful women model her designs on the runways of fashion salons in New York and Paris. The possibility dazzled her with excitement, yet Summer doubted her ability to obtain such heights and wondered whether she even wanted to try. A part of her sensed she could find contentment simply designing and making dresses for women in Cookville. Right now, Summer was glad to have time on her side. She would graduate from high school in a few weeks and begin college next fall. Long-term decisions about the future could wait until she had a better understanding of her wants and needs.

Glancing at her watch, she realized time was running short on her most pressing problem. She edged next to Joe and nudged him awake.

"Any luck?" she asked.

"Yeah, but I threw 'em back," Joe answered, rousing himself from the catnap with a loud yawn and a long stretch, the fishing pole falling to the ground between his legs. "I don't want to clean fish tonight."

"I'm glad to hear it because I have a small favor to ask if you don't have any plans for tonight," Summer said quickly, rushing her brother awake with a playful tug of the tiny hairs that lined the bottom of his stomach.

"Ouch!" Joe yelped, pushing away her hand, then casting a suspicious eye on his sister. "Small favor? Summer, you always scare me when you come asken for small favors."

"I just want you to take me to the movies in Cookville tonight," she said, frowning pretended offense at his suspicions. "*Bonnie and Clyde* is playen, and it's supposed to be really good. You can drool over Faye Dunaway, and I'll fawn over Warren Beatty. What could be more perfect?"

"That's it?" Joe asked cautiously.

"Honestly, Joe!" Summer huffed. "Let's take Carrie and John along with us. Heck, why don't you even invite Tom along?"

"Tom Carter!" Joe exclaimed, suddenly intrigued.

"Do you know any other Tom?" Summer replied casually.

"You want me to invite *Tom Carter*?" Joe puzzled aloud. "Why?"

"Don't invite him then!" Summer bristled. "It was just an idea. I was only tryen to be nice."

"Darlen sister of mine, you have never been nice to Tom," Joe replied with droll sincerity. "But that's beside the point. Tom's daten Liz Barker. I imagine he's busy tonight."

"Good grief, Joe," Summer sighed. "Even Granny knows Tom and Liz are old news. That's been over for ages."

Joe grinned, reading her mind, and a sneaky smile broke her face, her motives no longer a secret. "The truth?" he coaxed.

"Tom and I had an interesten conversation at the store a little while ago," she confessed. "I thought it might be fun to see him in a social situation."

"A social situation with Tom," Joe murmured, considering the idea. "Sounds like you have a crush on him, little sister."

"No, not yet," Summer replied. "But he might be worth a crush."

"I'm not sure if I should do this to Tom," Joe mused.

"Just call him up and see if he wants to go to the movie, Joe," Summer demanded. "But don't tell him that I'm goen with you."

"And what if I don't?" Joe asked.

Summer sighed. "Then I suppose I'll have to tell Mama and Daddy that you've been drinken beer, hangen out in shady places and the like."

"Just how did you find out about that, Mata Hari?" Joe inquired, frowning.

"You came home dead drunk a couple of weeks ago," Summer explained. "I just happened to be haven trouble sleepen that night. I heard your car, but you never came inside. Finally, I went out to check on you and found you fast asleep in your car. You smelled awful by the way, and you had red lipstick on your collar and a hickey on your neck. It was just like a scene from some tasteless movie. Of course, be'en the gracious, nonjudgmental person that I am, I helped you stumble to your bedroom."

She hesitated a moment. "You don't remember any of this, Joe?"

"I remember the night well, the mornen after painfully well," Joe groaned, recalling the hangover. "But that one little detail seems to have escaped me."

"It wasn't one of your better moments," Summer remarked.

"I won't argue with you over that," Joe agreed. "You wouldn't really tell Mama and Daddy about that, now would you?"

"Of course not, silly," she smiled. "That was entirely for your benefit—to make sure you give me the proper respect I deserve. Early or late show?"

Joe looked at his watch. "Better make it the nine o'clock show," he answered. "That should give you plenty of time to make yourself beau-ti-ful, daa-lin."

Summer kissed him on the cheek. "I really do love you, big brother of mine," she said. "Now put on your shirt and escort me home. You have a call to make, and I have to get ready."

———

Joe, Summer, John, Carrie and Tom saw *Bonnie and Clyde* at the Majestic Theater in Cookville. If Tom was surprised that Summer joined them, he gave no indication. For her part, Summer was unusually subdued, preferring to listen and watch the rapport between her siblings and Tom. In the theater, she wiggled her way between Joe and Tom, clutching both of them by the arm during the final shoot-out that left Warren Beatty and Faye Dunaway dead on the big screen.

Following the show, they went to the Dairy Queen for sodas, and Tom sat between Summer and Carrie in the crowded booth. Deciding against his better judgment to do his sister a favor, Joe gave John and Carrie money for the sodas and made an unnecessary trip to the bathroom. While he figured her infatuation with his best friend might be nothing more than a passing fancy, Joe also had decided that Summer could do far worse than pick Tom as a boyfriend.

"I thought you had a date tonight," Tom said when they were alone in the booth.

"What made you think that?" Summer asked coyly.

"You mentioned getten ready to go out, and I assumed you had a date," Tom replied. "Usually, that would be a safe assumption."

"Usually, but not tonight," Summer said. "Were you jealous, Tom?"

"What makes you think I'd be jealous?" he asked.

Summer tilted her head and smiled. "Just a hunch," she said truthfully. "Were you?"

"Nah, I wasn't jealous," Tom said at last, glancing down at the table, then flashing her a shy smile. "But I'm glad you came with us to the movie."

Moments later, Carrie and John returned to the table with a tray of chocolate sodas, and the talk turned to *Bonnie and Clyde*.

On the following Thursday, Summer volunteered to help her father, Joe and Tom set up the new irrigation system. The task seemed simple enough. Matt and Joe put the pumping engine in the New Pond, while Summer and Tom laid metal pipes through the woods, along the edge of the field and through the dry tobacco patch. But as Summer attached the last two pipes, she regretted volunteering for the job. The long metal pipes had been heavier than she anticipated, and her back already ached from several long afternoons of hoeing and thinning acres of cantaloupes.

She checked the last pipe once more, then signaled Tom to tell her father he could begin pumping water anytime and started walking from the field.

Her path followed the trail of pipe snaking through the tobacco field, and she came across two pieces that were not attached properly. Straddling the pipe, she bent over and fidgeted with the metal hinges, trying to make the connecting latches catch on the tubes.

At that precise moment, Matt cranked the irrigation pump. The engine roared to life, creating a powerful suction that snapped the loose hinges into place, snaring Summer's fingers between the metal edges.

Pain seared her breath momentarily, and then it was if someone ripped a scream from the bottom of her chest. She snatched her hands from the pipe. The flesh around her fingers ripped and, for a terrified second, she feared her fingertips had been sliced off. Closer inspection, however, showed her fingers were intact, but the pain, blood and ragged flesh frightened her. She stumbled backward, tripped over a tobacco stalk and landed on her rear in the soft dirt of the sled row.

Tom's first thought was that a snake had bitten Summer. Her scream attested to severe pain. He started to yell for Joe and Matt, realized they would not hear him above the drone of the pump and tore off down the sled row. He found Summer sitting on the ground, sobbing and rocking as she cradled her bloodied hands. By then, the irrigation system was raining torrents of pond water across the field.

"Good Lord, Summer!" he exclaimed, dropping to his knees beside her. "What in the world happened?"

As best she could between sobs and the patter of water being pumped across the field, Summer explained the situation. "I was afraid my fingers were cut off," she concluded, her sobs dwindling to sniffles.

"Let me see," Tom said gently, taking her hands and laying them crosswise on top of each other so he could examine the cuts. "It probably hurts worse than it really is," he concluded. "All eight fingers are gashed all the way around, but the cuts aren't deep. I imagine your mama or grandma can fix you up good as new without haven to see the doctor."

Summer took a moment to inspect her hands more closely, satisfying herself that Tom's diagnosis was correct. Finally, she nodded agreement with him. "It hurts like the dickens," she said, "but I guess I'll live."

"That's the spirit," Tom said with an encouraging smile as he cupped his hand beneath her elbow and helped Summer to stand. Her eyes were red-rimmed, and he surrendered to the impulse to push a wayward strand of hair off her face. He took off his T-shirt, using it to wipe away the tear stains, then wrapping it around her hands to slow the bleeding before putting his arm around her waist as they began walking toward the end of the row.

"I know this really isn't the time to ask, but I'm gonna do it anyway," he said a short time later when they were drenched and near their destination. "If your hands are okay by Saturday, would you like to see a movie or somethen?"

Summer stopped dead in her tracks, her mouth agape with disbelief. "Here I am at my absolute worst—hurten like crazy, cryen and soaked through and through on top of everything else—and you dare to ask me for a date, Tom Carter?" she huffed.

"I guess that was a pretty stupid thing to do," he remarked, clearing a spray of water from his face.

"I can't call it one of your finer moments," she replied with airs.

"Anything wrong down there?" Matt called suddenly.

"Summer's cut her hands," Tom yelled back at his boss. "We need to get her home, so someone can look after them."

Turning back to Summer, he repeated his request as Matt rushed toward them. "How 'bout it, Summer? You interested in a night out with the hired help?"

Despite herself, Summer smiled. "What time?"

"Seven," Tom suggested.

"It's a date," she agreed a few seconds before Matt reached them.

"What happened, honey?" Matt asked quickly, worried about the blood.

"Here's the long and the short of it, Daddy," she replied, her tone pouty even though she already felt better. "Somebody almost cut off my fingers when they started those irrigation pipes. My back aches, my fingers feel like they've been detached from my hands and I'm wet as a mad hen. On top of everything else, Romeo here just asked me for a date. All in all, it's been one heck of a day, but I would appreciate it if someone took me home now. This ain't no way to treat a future beauty queen."

Matt stared blankly at his daughter, then at Tom as the water cascaded down around them. Suddenly, all three of them burst into laughter. They were still laughing a minute later as they arrived at the end of the row, where Joe waited on the tractor.

At precisely seven o'clock Saturday night, Tom arrived at the Baker home. He was shaved, doused in cologne and dressed neatly in gray slacks and a white pullover. Luke answered the door.

"Hi," Tom said.

"Since when do you knock?" Luke remarked through the screen door.

"I'm here for Summer," Tom explained.

"What for?" Luke asked.

"We have a date," Tom said.

"Oh," Luke shrugged, finally opening the door. "She's still getten ready, I guess. Come on in."

Tom stepped inside the house and found himself facing the entire Baker clan, except for Summer and her mother. It was like walking into the middle of an inquisition. He mumbled greetings, trying to appear relaxed, finding it a difficult proposition, especially since he had to stand for scrutiny in front of everyone. He looked to Joe for help and received a frothy grin in return.

"If you're feelen a bit uncomfortable, we planned it that way," Sam said finally as the rest of his family yielded their silence to whelps of laughter.

"Do all of Summer's dates get such special treatment?" Tom asked when the laughter subsided.

"Not usually," Carrie answered. "With Summer, dates are like a revolven door, so you quit payen attention after a while. But this is different. She's never gone out with anyone we know as well as you."

"Is that good or bad?" Tom asked.

"We'll let you know in good time," Sam said cagily.

"Are you gonna kiss her?" Bonnie inquired. She was eleven, with an increasing penchant for asking embarrassing questions at the worst times.

"I doubt it," Tom answered, suddenly at ease among friends. Scooping Bonnie into his arms, he planted a sloppy kiss on her cheek as the girl squealed in delight. "That'll probably be the only kiss I get tonight," he teased.

"It better be," Matt growled.

Everyone laughed once more, and then John asked the question that had all of them guessing for an answer. "I want to know why you asked her out in the first place. Y'all can hardly tolerate each other."

Every eye and every ear converged on Tom, who knew they expected a truthful answer. He had no intention of being serious, though, especially since he was still trying to figure out this sudden attraction to a long-time nemesis. Taking his time, first putting Bonnie back on the floor, he finally replied, "It was like this, John. Summer was screamen, cryen and carryen on so that I didn't know what in the world to do. So, I thought of the most outrageous thing possible, which was to ask her for a date. I had no idea she'd actually say yes. But when she did, I was more or less obligated to see it through. And here I am."

"I heard that!" Summer cried as she emerged from her bedroom door with Caroline in tow. She was smartly dressed in a short-sleeved yellow blouse with a blue-green plaid skirt that fell just above her knees.

"You look very nice," Tom told her, noticing the white gauze wrapped around her hands.

"Compliments will not get you out of this, buster," Summer replied sassily. Turning to her family, she explained, "The truth of the matter is that he misunderstood my stunned reaction to his silly question. I said, 'Uh,' and he heard, 'Yeah,' so I'm stuck with him for the night. Any way you look at it, I'm the injured party in this predicament."

"Me thinks you both doth protest too much," Sam teased as the room grew suddenly suspicious about Tom and Summer's intentions toward each other.

"Y'all better get out of here while you still have a chance," Caroline urged with a cheerful smile.

"Bye, Mama," Summer said, kissing Caroline on the cheek. "Bye, Daddy."

"Home by eleven," Matt called.

"Yes, sir," Tom replied.

————

Instead of seeing the movie as planned, Summer and Tom never made it past the Shady Lane drive-in restaurant in Tifton. They sat in the cab of his pickup truck, munching hamburgers and French fries, downing vanilla milkshakes and engaging in the kind of conversation that occurs when two people are intent upon learning about each other.

They were like two old best friends, who had been separated for too long and wanted to catch up on the past. More than friendship was at work, however. The night crackled around them, sizzling like a power line on a hot summer day. They teased, tempted and tested each other, then surprised themselves with quiet moments of reflection and discovery.

Perhaps their common past put them at ease, but the entire date unfolded as naturally as the night closed around them. Summer flung the full force of her forthrightness at Tom, deciding he would like her for who she was or not like her at all. Tom discovered he liked her more than he had ever believed possible.

"So why did you ask me out?" Summer asked finally, late in the night.

Tom eyed her carefully, thinking the simple answer to her question was lust. "Truthfully?" he replied.

"The truth is always best, Tom," she said.

"I never thought of you as be'en pretty or anything like that," Tom said. "Honestly, I never thought about you much at all unless I had reason to, and then I generally was irritated with you. Last Saturday, however, I took a good look at you, Summer. And I liked what I saw."

"I'm flattered," Summer replied modestly.

"Now it's my turn," Tom said. "Why did you say yes when I asked?"

"Because I could tell that you liked what you saw when you looked me over last week," Summer answered unabashedly. "That caught my interest. Then, I realized I don't really know you very well, Tom. And I wanted to get to know you."

"Am I tolerable?" he inquired.

"A lot more so than I ever imagined," Summer replied, then added quickly, "Not that I ever imagined."

Tom deliberately cleared his throat. "We're be'en truthful," he said. "Remember."

"I never did imagine," Summer said. "I'm not tryen to burst your ego, but I've always thought of you as plain old Tom. Part of the family." She smiled slightly, then explained further: "You know those relatives that you're always tryen to ignore."

He laughed lightly.

"Besides, I should be offended," she continued. "You wanted to go out with me entirely because of my looks. That doesn't speak well of my personality."

"Honestly, Summer, I never thought you had much personality," Tom said. "Just a big mouth."

A feisty retort appeared on her lips, but Summer stopped short. "A little honesty never hurt anyone," she concluded, with uncharacteristic humility. "I hope you change your mind after tonight."

Tom shook his head. "You're the real thing," he commented, a shy smile on his face.

His words came as a casual compliment, but his blue eyes revealed the depths of the man's desire. Summer saw danger in those eyes, and her heart constricted. Shock waves coursed through her because she was not prepared or ready for such feelings, either from Tom or within herself. She tried to ease the moment with some flippant remark, stammered instead and forgot her thought in mid-sentence.

"This must be a first—Summer Baker at a loss for words," Tom teased as a warm breeze drifted through the open windows.

"Don't tell anyone," Summer said, quickly recovering her composure. "It could be damagen to my reputation."

The late hour took care of the unanswered thoughts between them. With Summer due home in twenty-five minutes, they gathered their empty food wrappers and cups, using a trip to the wastebasket to stretch their legs and cool down the sparks flying between them.

———

Many words had passed between Summer and Tom; many more remained to be said. But the ride home was dominated by silent contemplation.

"I had a great time," Tom said when they were standing on her front porch. "I hope we can do this again."

"I'd like that," Summer agreed.

For the first time that night, an uncomfortable feeling arose between them as they tried to decide how to close the night or even if they wanted to end it. "I should go," Tom said finally. "It's getten late. I'll see you at church tomorrow."

"If you're there," Summer chided. "I believe you've missed more Sundays than you've made recently. The Lord gives you seven days a week, Tom. The least you can do is give him back an hour of it."

"Maybe I should start callen you Sister Summer," Tom replied as he backed away from her.

"Aren't you goen to try to kiss me goodnight?" she asked boldly as he reached the porch steps and turned to leave.

The question stopped Tom in mid step, and he wheeled around to face her. "You wouldn't let me," he stated. "Would you?"

"Of course not, silly," she replied, "but you ort to at least make the effort. It's a man's obligation to try and a woman's prerogative to say no."

Summer had backed against the screen door, and Tom slid up close to her. He braced his hand against the doorframe over her shoulder, dipped his head to kiss her and almost fell against the screen as Summer ducked away at the last moment.

"Geez, Tom!" she said, laughing as he righted himself. "It's only our first date. If you're lucky, I might let you kiss me on the second date." She pointed to her cheek. "Right here, mister."

Tom spun toward her. "Gosh darn it, Summer!" he exclaimed a little more loudly than intended. "You shouldn't oughtta do stuff like that. I don't know what in the world to make of you."

"Shh!" Summer said, pointing to the window on the left side of the door. "Mama and Daddy sleep in that room. They might hear you and think somethen's goen on."

Tom crossed his arms, staring through her with those blue eyes. "Summer?" he said softly, his tone serious and questioning. "Somethen is goen on?"

She looked away from him, across the porch to the other side of the road where the hazy light of a full moon shone on the woods. Quickly, she nodded her agreement and reached behind her back to open the door.

"Goodnight," she whispered before escaping into the house.

———

Once in a while, the Bakers respected each other's privacy and kept their curiosity to themselves. On the morning after her date with Tom, Summer came to the breakfast table prepared to fend off a barrage of questions. Only one was asked, however, and it was nothing more than a polite inquiry from her mother as to whether she had a good time. No one bothered to ask the obligatory follow-up of whether they could expect more dates between Tom and her, and she refused to answer the unasked.

On the following Friday, Summer and Tom had their second date, an almost burdensome outing, so fraught with uneasy feelings that both of them welcomed the opportunity to sit through a bad movie. "Maybe we expected too much," Tom suggested as they stood beside her front door a good half hour before she was expected home. "How 'bout if we try again tomorrow?"

Summer offered him her cheek for a kiss.

On Saturday, they were relaxed and carefree with no plans. At Summer's suggestion, they went only as far as the New River Elementary School, stopping there to visit the playground that had been their childhood stomping grounds. Turning back the years, they played like children, balancing on the see-saw, flying down the slides and running through the warm night in a spirited game of chase that exhausted itself when they wound up at the swings. Plopping into side-by-side seats, they launched into fond reminiscing about their school days.

"This has been a wonderful evenen," Summer said sometime later. "Most people probably would think it's childish stuff, especially for someone who's just one week away from graduating high school."

"It'll be our secret," Tom promised. "Besides, I wouldn't want everyone to know how cheap I am."

"Push me for a while, and I'll tell everyone you're extremely extravagant," Summer said, giggling. "Then all the girls will want to go out with you."

Tom rose from his swing, walked behind Summer and began pushing her lightly. "Are you excited about finishen high school?" he asked.

"Mostly," she replied. "Everything seems so wide open at this point in life. It's exciten but also a little scary. Right now, I'm just looken forward to the summer and to Miss Golden Leaf."

"That pageant means a lot to you?" Tom inquired.

"I know it's vain, but I'd like to have that crown," Summer said. "If they awarded the title based on who actually worked in tobacco, I'd be a shoo-in."

"Well, if it means that much, then I hope you bring home the crown," Tom replied. "Did you pick out the material for your dress?"

"Your mama gave me good ideas," Summer answered. "Pink satin with a chiffon overlay. Sleeveless, long evenen gloves, the works. Granny's helpen me with the dress."

Tom murmured a polite reply, and they drifted into silence for several minutes. Finally, Summer asked, "What are you thinken about?"

Tom stopped the swing, walked around to face her and put his hands above hers on the chains. "You mostly," he said. "Pretty much lately, Summer, you're all I've thought about. Two weeks ago, I wasn't even sure whether I liked you. Now I'm thinken I'm in love with you, and none of it makes sense because people aren't supposed to fall in love just like that."

"Maybe it's not supposed to make sense," she replied, smiling softly. "Maybe that's what makes love so special."

In the long silence that followed, they basked in the joy of newfound love. Their relationship had moved swiftly to this important point. Now they wanted tenderness, time to savor the moment at hand and each new discovery to come. Tom stroked her hair, cupped her face and kissed her. It was a gentle, slow, uncomplicated kiss, lingering like the taste of a sweet dessert.

"I love you, Summer," he said.

"And I love you, Tom," she said.

He pulled her from the swing, and they embraced, their bodies becoming familiar and intimate, all while understanding that a certain caution was necessary. Tom buried his face in the sweet scent of her hair, and Summer pressed her cheek against the roughness of his evening beard. When they kissed again, it was passionate, ardent and forceful, and it made their hearts and bodies clamor, anticipating the day they would forgo caution.

CHAPTER 3

THE COMING OF SPRING had always meant the beginning of a new adventure for Matt. He regarded the season's arrival as the start of a pilgrimage, an expedition in which he would reap the rewards that usually beckoned to him under the pretense of next year. More often than not, the full rewards came cleverly disguised, with just enough promise to leave him hopeful for better times to come. Without some sense of sameness to serve as a guide, the journey might well have become an endless cycle of insanity.

As long as he knew what month it was, Matt could anticipate the work. In January, he limed fields, fixed fences and repaired machinery, greasing equipment, replacing and tightening bolts. In February, he planted Irish potatoes and sugar cane, while beginning to prepare the fields for the crops, harrowing, plowing and fumigating the ground. The corn and tobacco were planted in March; sweet potatoes and peanuts in April; cotton and cantaloupes in May; soybeans and grain sorghum in June after the winter wheat and oats had been harvested. When he was not planting, he mixed chemicals and sprayed, fighting the annual battle to beat down the teaweed, cockleburs, ragweed and sand spurs that choked the fields, as well as the hornworms, armyworms and boll weevils that invaded his crops. At some point, the tobacco and cantaloupes had to be hoed; the flowering tops and tiny suckers had to be broken out of the tobacco so that the stalks would grow tall and heavy; and all of the crops had to be cultivated at least twice, preferably three times.

By the time summer arrived and the children finished the school year, he was already tired from the effort. Still, the hardest work remained, with the bulk of it waiting in the tobacco field. Tobacco yielded a high profit, but the crop also exacted a heavy toll on those who grew it. In June, July and the first half of August, nothing mattered more than gathering tobacco. Unless it was critical, everything else waited or was accomplished either in the spare hours of the six-day workweek or on an occasional Sunday.

When the tobacco had been gathered and packed off to the warehouse, the family picked cantaloupes. If the summer ran smoothly, in the relative meaning of the idea, then the children got a few days of rest before returning to school in late August.

In early September, Matt picked and graded sweet potatoes, then enjoyed a temporary lull in the middle of the month before the harvest season began. Out of tradition and perhaps some superstition, he usually waited until the Harvest Moon arrived to begin combining, starting with the corn and then working his way through the peanuts, cotton, soybeans and sorghum. In his spare time, he bailed hay and harrowed the harvested fields so they could be sewn in grains and greens.

By early December, the combines had been put to rest for another year and the children were picking up the last of the pecans. At some point, Caroline and Rachel had taken care of the garden, cramming two freezers and the pantry with the vegetables that would feed the family through the coming winter. In addition, Sam had found time to gather the cane and make several kettles of syrup. Around this time, the boys often took a notion to begin plowing the empty fields, hoping to get an early start on the next year. Occasionally, they burned a field or some section of woods in the constant battle to keep the land clear of weeds and undergrowth.

Matt usually took several days to relax, hunt or fish, but his mind was never far from planning for the next year, which always began between Christmas and New Year's, when they prepared and sewed beds for the next year's tobacco plants.

Matt thought about this routine as he walked through his tobacco field, checking for hornworms and signs of disease. On this first Monday in June, dark storm clouds gathered on the horizon. If this had been any other day, he would have expected the clouds to follow their springtime precedent and yield nothing more than a dry thunderstorm. Since it was Summer's high school graduation day, however, with the ceremony scheduled for the Cookville High School football field, Matt figured rain would dampen the festivities. If his cynical forecast held, he only hoped a few drops would fall on his dry fields.

Matt was trying hard to keep a stiff upper lip about the weather. There was still time for rain to make a difference in determining whether the year would be a lean or a losing proposition. The corn already was critical, but a good rain could salvage it, while most of the other crops were still a few weeks shy of the critical time when moisture was vital for their development. Irrigation had revived the tobacco, cotton and a portion of the peanuts. But the ponds were low. In fact, the Old Pond was so low that fish were popping up dead daily. The place stank with decay, and buzzards scavenged freely, eating their fill.

The New Pond was in only slightly better condition. Matt hoped to get one more watering for the tobacco before fish began to die there as well. To avoid the waste, the boys and he planned to seine the pond before irrigating from it.

When would rain come? Would it come? When his father had posed that concern several weeks earlier, Matt had dismissed the idea as improbable, to the point that the suggestion did not even warrant worry. Now he wondered if he had been wrong.

Except for the drought of 1954, enough rain had always fallen to keep them from utter ruin. But for seven straight days now, the skies had made liars of the weather forecasters. Each afternoon, dark clouds rolled across the skies, taunting with a few drops of rain every now and then but mostly yielding dry thunderstorms. As if the unhealthy fields were not enough to cause worry, the dry clouds had added insult to injury two days ago, spawning a violent lightning storm that had zapped the well pump, which provided running water for the house and animals. Replacing the pump had taken a few more hundred dollars from their dwindling bank account.

Accustomed to praying for rain, Matt did so now as he trudged through the fields. Yet even as he sought divine intervention, doubts troubled him. He could not help wondering if nature had dealt his family a cruel sleight of hand this year.

———

As Matt predicted, the spring's only significant rain forced the high school graduation ceremony into the Cookville gymnasium. Nothing dampened their spirits, however, as the Bakers watched Summer take her place on stage with the honor graduates. She received a home economics award that came with a three-hundred-dollar scholarship, then grabbed her diploma and marched into the waiting arms of Tom Carter.

Tom had sat with the Bakers during the ceremony, and his was the congratulations Summer sought first. He responded with a tight hug and a chaste kiss on the cheek. In the initial awareness of their love, the couple intentionally had concealed their feelings about each other. Both had wanted to shout it for the world to hear, but they first needed time to acquaint themselves with the idea. Now their hesitation vanished, and the aura of new love revealed their commitment. Everyone sensed the significance of the moment.

"Next thing you know, we'll be goen to her wedden," Caroline said softly to Matt, fighting back tears that were a reflection of happiness, sadness and the emotion of the day.

Without giving her husband an opportunity to respond, she left him standing there openmouthed and went to give her oldest daughter a congratulatory hug. "If the time ever comes when you feel like talken woman to woman, I'm always available, and I'm a good listener," she whispered to Summer. "But right now, honey, I think your daddy could use a big hug from his little girl."

"Oh, Mama!" Summer said as her mother's hand touched her cheek in understanding. "Is it that obvious?"

Caroline nodded, and Summer beamed with happiness. Then she embraced her father, with tears shining in their eyes.

––––––––

In the middle of June, the air conditioner at the Carter's Mercantile rumbled loudly into a state of disrepair. A repairman confirmed the machine's demise, and Dan followed him to Cookville to look into buying a new cooling system for the store.

Alone in the mercantile, Amelia set up fans and began moving the candy bars to the drink machine from the glass case to prevent them from melting in the building's increasingly hot confines. Hearing a car pull up beside the gas tanks, she glanced at her watch, closed the cooler door and went to greet Gary James. The mercantile was the halfway point of the postman's route through the New River community, and he routinely stopped there for his morning break, always buying a Coke and a pack of peanuts.

"Good afternoon, Gary," Amelia greeted him.

"Good day to you, too, Amelia," he responded. "I trust Dan and you are well today."

"We're languishen in this gosh-awful heat just like everybody else," Amelia said. "Our air conditioner's gone kaput on us, and Dan's off in Cookville to get a replacement. The thing was old as Methuselah anyway, so we're likely better off all the way around with a new one. I just wish I could hurry things along to beat the heat."

"I'm thinken about getten me a new truck, and you can bet I'll make sure it has an air conditioner," Gary replied. "All my fan does is blow hot air. The summers are miserable."

"What you got for us today?" Amelia asked.

"A pile of it," Gary answered, handing her a stack of letters and circulars, all bundled with a rubber band.

Out of politeness, Amelia laid the mail aside while Gary fetched his drink, opened the bottle and dumped a small bag of roasted peanuts into the Coke. He took one thirst-satisfying taste, then asked, "How much do I owe you?"

"Same as yesterday," Amelia replied as the postman handed her a shiny dime and an Indian-head nickel. "You sure you don't want to keep this?" she asked, admiring the coin.

"I have one or two put away," Gary said. "Besides, I don't like to break a dollar if I don't have to."

"Dollars are harder to come by in the long run," Amelia agreed.

When the postman had gone, Amelia riffled through the mail, finding a bill from their meat supplier in Cookville and a new product announcement from the grocery wholesaler in Valdosta. But the third envelope pushed every other thought from her mind. Her most basic maternal instincts urged Amelia to shred the letter and pretend it never existed. Knowing her son would never forgive an intrusion into his privacy, however, she clutched the letter to her chest, locked up the store and headed for the Baker place.

———

Tom hated cropping the sand lugs, those bottom three or four small leaves on the tobacco stalk that grew on the ground and were covered with sandy soil. Sand coated him from head to toe, the tiny granules working their way into every open crevice in his clothes and grinding against his skin. He was scratchy and itchy, plus his back ached from having to bend his tall frame at a severe angle to reach the low leaves. The work would be easier when they were working higher on the stalk.

Despite the discomfort, Tom saw no reason to complain. With a good job to prepare himself for the future and the love of a good woman to share his life, he had everything he needed or wanted for the moment.

The mere thought of Summer aroused his passion. He felt intoxicated these days, almost giddy with fortune. Best of all was the sense of permanency, the growing belief that this good feeling would always exist even in difficult times.

Tom peered upwards, trying to get a glimpse of Summer through the cogs and chains that carried the hands of tobacco to the top story of the double-deck harvester. He was admiring the form of her slender legs in snug blue jeans when she sensed him looking. Glancing down, she smiled, a warm and glowing acknowledgment that she felt the same way, the same desire.

Then all at once, sand fell in his face, blinding Tom, stinging him senseless. He buried his face in his hands, vigorously trying to rub away the dirt that filled his eyes. As he waited for tears to cleanse them fully, he heard Summer bubble over with laughter that was loud, infectious and full of affection.

"Hey, Joe," he called to his friend in the front seat. "Keep up my row a second. I got sand in my eyes."

"If you'd keep your eyes off my sister, stuff like this wouldn't happen," Joe grumbled, straining to carry two rows by himself.

"Thanks," Tom said a long moment later when his eyes were clear enough to see.

"Yeah, yeah," Joe muttered. "You've got it bad, Tom."

"No, Joe," he disagreed. "I've got it good."

The two friends bantered back and forth as the harvester ebbed toward the end of the row, then drifted into the comfortable silence of the work and private thoughts. Finishing his row, Tom shoved the last hand of leaves into the metal clip, which conveyed the tobacco to the top floor of the harvester. He jumped off his seat, brushed off the sand and started toward the pickup truck, which contained empty sticks that needed to be handed up to the stringers. He saw his mother then.

Amelia was short but statuesque and very stylish. She was wearing a plain white dress and sandals, with a wisp of her dyed-blonde hair uncharacteristically out of place. Her slender face was pinched with concern, and the heat had blotched her makeup.

Tom first feared something was wrong with his father. As his mother walked toward him, however, he saw the letter and guessed what the envelope contained. When he had decided to leave college, he had realized the possibility of being drafted. Several of his high school classmates had received orders. One already had served in Vietnam, and another had just been shipped over there.

"This came for you," Amelia said as she reached him. "I thought it might be important."

Tom accepted the Selective Service System letter with a wan smile. He tore open the envelope, pulled out the form letter and read it twice. The Army wanted Tom to report to the National Guard Armory in Tifton for a physical examination two weeks from Saturday.

Feeling more unsettled than he appeared, Tom shrugged and handed the letter back to his mother.

"Looks like I'm gonna be a soldier, Ma," he told her. "You can read it if you want. Just put it in my room when you're finished."

Amelia resisted the urge to hug her son, instead telling him, "You'll look right handsome in uniform."

"What's that?" Summer hollered from the top of the harvester.

Both Tom and his mother looked at her, and Summer shuddered with apprehension.

"I've been drafted," Tom shouted over the roar of the engine.

The color drained from Summer's face. Tom sighed and returned to work.

Tom passed his physical and was inducted into the Army for a two-year hitch of active service. Shortly afterward, he received his orders to report to Fort Benning near Columbus, Georgia, for six weeks of basic training.

"It's not so bad," he tried to reassure Summer. "We've got six weeks between now and when I report. Fort Benning is not that far away, Summer. I'll get a few days off between boot camp and infantry school, and there's a good chance I'll be stationed at Fort Benning. Who knows? We might even be able to spend Christmas together. I'd love to spend Christmas with you, sweetheart."

His voice was steady and calm, and Summer tried to appear comforted. She kissed him. "You'd better save your money then and buy me some ridiculously expensive present," she said.

The remark was completely out of character, yet Tom responded sincerely. "I'd give you the moon and the stars if I could," he vowed.

"I know," Summer said, hugging him tightly. "And that's enough, Tom."

Lucas Bartholomew craved a drink of whiskey. Even though he was not a drinking man, he wanted to feel liquor on his lips and let it slide down his throat, stinging all the way to his belly. Drowning himself in liquor would ease the disappointment and frustration of his failed hopes for a few hours. The idea held more appeal than he wanted to admit.

Ever since Paul Berrien had agreed to let him farm a few acres on shares, Lucas had worked—like a man possessed—to succeed. He wanted to impress Paul and Matt Baker with his drive as well as his ability. He wanted to earn money working for himself instead of someone else.

Lucas had no complaints about his years working with Matt. The man had treated him well, giving Lucas a free place to stay with his family and paying wages that were more than fair. Still, he would never feel complete satisfaction working for Matt. As long as he worked for any man, Lucas would never achieve the freedom he desired.

Besides his lofty ambitions, something else gnawed at Lucas. Despite all his hard work, his best efforts, he had nothing to show for the toil. If a man came into the fields where Lucas worked, he surely would deem the black man a sorry excuse for a farmer. The man would not see the straight rows that Lucas had planted, weeded and tended like a mother watching her child. But rather, the man would see scraggly crops and believe they withered from neglect. And more than one man would view the ruined crops as confirmation that a black man should not be left to guide his own destiny.

These feelings came from a dark spot, troubled and deep in his mind. Lucas knew such thoughts never crossed the minds of Matt, Paul or a few other men who he respected and counted among his friends. Why was it then, when he had earned the unflagging respect of respectable men, that Lucas could not push aside the feelings of inadequacy, incompetence and ineptitude that preyed on him from time to time? Was he doomed to measure life by his failures instead of his accomplishments? Those fears played with his mind all too often, so much so that he was learning to answer the doubts with an even more important question. Could he rise above the nonsense that cluttered his mind, cast off his demons and meet the next challenge, which was the ultimate measure of any man?

Without a doubt, misfortune was to blame for his dying crops. Only an unreasonable man would believe otherwise and if Lucas chose to cast his lot with that line of thinking, then he deserved to wallow in misery and self-pity. Likewise, while several stiff drinks of whiskey would help him forget his troubles, the problems would still exist when he woke tomorrow morning. He would have a splitting headache and a queasy stomach, but nothing would be changed. Paul Berrien would still be out the money he had paid to buy seed and fertilizer, and Lucas would have done nothing to make a better life for his family. Besides, Lucas knew what too much liquor could do to men. Whiskey sapped a man's strength, thwarted his resolve, stole his incentive and sent him to an early grave in some cases, such as his father.

Lucas had vowed long ago never to abandon his family. So instead of whiskey, he would settle for a soda pop.

To safeguard against the possibility of an unplanned detour to the liquor store, he took Danny with him to Carter's Mercantile. Danny was four, one year younger than Annie. The boy worshipped his father, dwelling on his every deed and every word, which was fortunate since Lucas rarely treated his children in a childlike way. When he talked to his children, Lucas spoke as if they were grown-ups who understood and followed his every word. If he did nothing else for Annie and Danny, he would teach them that even though life sometimes made no sense at all, they still had to make heads or tails of the confusion and get on with it.

Lucas made one exception to this rule of thumb in raising his children. When he tried to teach them their ABCs or reading or counting, he explained the lesson with childlike simplicity. When it came to imparting knowledge in his children, Lucas had the patience of a saint. The more Annie and Danny learned as children, the easier they would find it to succeed in the confusing world of grown-ups.

As Lucas and Danny bumped along the dirt road in a beat-up pickup truck that should have been retired along with President Dwight Eisenhower, Lucas aimed a steady stream of commentary at his son. "If we could just get enough water, then the corn would form kernels and the puts would develop in their pods," he lectured. "With that river so close by, there oughtta be somethen I can do to take advantage of the situation."

Having figured out his daddy was talking about corn and water, Danny was content to listen to the rhythm of his father's voice. His round black eyes rose and fell with every change in cadence. The voice was a security blanket, and nothing else mattered. As long as he could hear his daddy's voice, regardless of the words, Danny was safe.

———

Wayne Taylor liked fast cars, fast money and fast women. Unfortunately, his experience was limited to cars, so he made the best of the situation. Wayne was a reckless driver. He knew it, and he liked it that way, especially now that he could drive with the state's permission.

Actually, the legality of his driving status or lack thereof had never troubled the oldest son of Bobby and Martha Taylor. Wayne had required three tries to pass the written portion of the test for his driver's license. He considered the exam a stupid waste of time and effort. If the government in its infinite wisdom believed niggers should vote without first demonstrating their ability to read and write, then why should respectable people have to pass a test just to get a driver's license.

Any fool could drive, Wayne thought, as his car careened past Benevolence Church, fishtailing on the sandy road as he rounded the sharp curve right before the general mercantile. The big Pontiac straightened out on the road, and Wayne gunned the engine, quickly reaching eighty miles an hour before bringing the car to a sliding halt—inches from the railroad tracks. Before crossing the highway, he waited until a fast-approaching truck passed, using the delay to light a cigarette, then catching sight of a little nigger boy playing near a beat-up truck parked beside the store's twin set of gas pumps.

"Five points if you play your cards right," Wayne told himself. "Or you could have some real fun and games."

Driving slowly, Wayne crossed the highway and parked several yards behind the truck. Cautiously checking his surroundings, he slid out of the car, threw down his cigarette and headed toward Danny Bartholomew, who stopped playing and turned to observe Wayne.

Danny watched Wayne carefully, awed by his size and the cocky way he moved.

Wayne was a burly youth, big of bone and tall, with a Marine's haircut. He carried himself with a bully's swagger, but it was his eyes that frightened Danny. They were green and burned with hatred. Instinct sent Danny scurrying behind the closest gas pump. He felt better out of sight and decided to join his father inside the store. Before he moved another step, however, Wayne's harsh voice commanded his attention.

"You come on out and show yourself, boy," Wayne ordered. "Or I just might tan your hide."

Frightened as never before, Danny peeked around the gas tank.

"Did you hear what I said, boy?" Wayne demanded, his tone menacing. "Come 'ere!"

Unable to think clearly, Danny did as told, moving slowly toward Wayne, who squatted to be face-to-face with the little boy. "You got no right to be around this place," Wayne sneered. "What's your excuse, nigger boy?"

"My daddy's getten us a soda pop," Danny answered.

"That ain't here or there," Wayne fired back. "Your kind don't belong here. You best remember that and figure out where your place is, boy, or one day you'll wind up sorry of it."

Wayne pressed a finger hard against the boy's gut, and Danny gasped, more out of fright than pain. "Are you listenen, boy?" he asked, his voice scathing. "Do you understand me?"

Now wide-eyed with fear, Danny nodded several times in rapid sequence.

"Don't you forget it, boy," Wayne hissed. "And you tell your daddy, too."

The store door opened then, the bell jingling as Lucas emerged from the mercantile followed by Tom and Summer, who were minding the business for Dan and Amelia.

Lucas moved toward Wayne like a tiger stalking prey. Lucas had fought rarely in his youth, never since marrying Beauty. In all his thirty years, however, he had never struck a white man. Now he was ready to kill one.

"He don't have to tell me nothen," Lucas said, his words clipped and threatening. "I heard it all from the goat's mouth."

Wayne rose quickly, weighing whether to stand his ground or retreat. His heart pounded, and his indecisiveness cost him any advantage. Before he realized it, Lucas was upon him.

His palm flat against the white boy's chest, Lucas shoved hard. Wayne stumbled and sprawled backward, landing on his back. Scrambling to his feet, he saw Lucas cock his fist and prepared to defend a blow. Before any punch was thrown, however, Tom grabbed Lucas from behind—momentarily restraining him and giving Wayne time to lurch backward, out of reach of the man's anger. Lucas slung away from Tom, starting once more toward Wayne. But again, Tom intervened, running in front of Lucas, placing himself as a buffer between the two men.

"Not this way, Lucas!" Tom shouted, his voice hard to command his friend's full attention. "Not this way," he repeated. "You got too much to lose to waste time on that kind of trash."

"Who you callen trash, you nigger lover?" Wayne screamed.

"Get out of here, Wayne!" Tom yelled. "Or you may just end up dead."

Wayne stood his ground, trying to decide if further action was warranted. He eyed the rage in Lucas' expression, took note of the black man's curved lip and wisely chose to back down. If they fought, Wayne suspected he would lose badly. He backed up to his car and opened the door, deciding there was sufficient distance between them to have the last word. Leaning across the car door, he sneered contemptuously at Lucas and Tom.

"You still ain't nothen but a nigger, Lucas Bartholomew," he growled. "And you ain't much better, Tom Carter."

"Go!" Tom yelled, afraid of what would happen as Lucas shrugged away from him.

Sensing the danger, Wayne dropped into the seat, slammed the door and cranked the car. Gunning the engine, he spun the car onto the highway, spewing a trail of dirt and gravel in his wake.

Neither Tom nor Lucas said anything or looked at each other until the dust settled and the doorbell jingled once more. Summer came down the steps with Danny in her arms. Fearing a fight, she had grabbed Danny the moment Lucas pushed Wayne and carried the boy inside the store. Now she put him down on the ground, and Danny ran to his father.

Not trusting his voice, Lucas lifted his son into his arms and held him tightly until the boy's shaking subsided.

"It's not right, Lucas," Tom said at last, "but be glad there was no fight."

"Sometimes, you have to fight for what's right," Lucas replied, his anger clear and determined.

"I know," Tom replied. "And you had more than enough cause. But facts are facts, Lucas, and the law don't look kindly on fights between a man and a boy—no matter what the circumstances. No matter how it seems, your fight's not with the boy. Your fight's with the man behind the boy. And as much as I hate to say it—as wrong as it is—let it go this time, friend. Just let it go."

"You can't forget things like this," Lucas said bitterly.

"Go home and take care of your son, Lucas," Tom pleaded. "It's over and done."

Lucas breathed deeply, considering the advice. "For now," he said at length, then nodded curtly at his friends and took his son home.

———

Wayne spent the afternoon on the rickety front porch of his house, trying to decide whether to tell his father about the confrontation with Lucas Bartholomew. His father would demand all the details, but it was difficult to gauge how Bobby would react. He might be angry that his son had backed away from a fight, and the last thing Wayne wanted was to appear cowardly in his father's eyes.

At supper, Wayne bided his time until the subject of "damned niggers" came up in the conversation. When his father reached the boiling point of his rage, Wayne interrupted.

"If you want to talk about uppity niggers, Pa, then let me tell you about Lucas Bartholomew," he said. "I weren't goen to mention it, but me and him had a run-in today at the store. He tried to push me around, but nothen came of it."

"That nigger came at you!" Bobby said, seeking clarification.

"He pushed me, then backed off," Wayne revealed. "There were people around us, and I guess he thought better of what he was doen. Or maybe he got scared."

"Who saw what happened?" Martha inquired.

"Tom Carter and Summer Baker," Wayne answered.

"Well, hell, son," Bobby cried. "Everybody knows those Bakers and Paul Berrien are the biggest nigger lovers in the county. They ain't likely to be on our side in this."

"I don't know much about Lucas Bartholomew, but I've always heard he's not one to go looken for trouble," Martha remarked. "Did you do anything to rile him, Wayne?"

"Hell, woman. Are you plumb crazy?" Bobby said with disgust, shaking his head in disbelief at the strange notions Martha sometimes had. "That don't matter nary one bit. You think it's okay for a nigger to come after your son?"

Martha accepted the reprimand without comment and busied herself by pushing the food on her plate from side to side. Experience had taught her when to keep her mouth shut.

"This is interesten," Bobby said to himself as he gnawed a pork chop bone. "Now tell me again what happened, Wayne. From start to finish."

———

The celebration of the Fourth of July in Cookville was a modest occasion, especially when the holiday fell on a Tuesday, as it did in 1967. With most of the county busy in the fields, only a handful of people turned out to hear a short speech by Mayor Curtis Gaddy and a rusty rendition of *The Star-Spangled Banner* played by the Cookville High School Marching Rebel Band, of which half its thirty members were absent.

A patriotic heart was the last reason Bobby Taylor came to take part in the celebration. He gathered several of his best cronies around him, then worked the men into a frenzy with an embellished tale of Wayne's run-in with Lucas. Some urged him to press charges, while others wanted Bobby himself to right the wrong. Bobby waffled back and forth on the issue, loudly weighing the merits of each option, always with a belligerent preference toward taking justice into his own hands.

More than anything, Bobby was enjoying the attention, with no intentions whatsoever of following through with either idea. As it turned out, his plans were scuttled.

"Speak of the devil," Hugh Williams said, interrupting Bobby in mid-sentence.

The interruption ticked off Bobby. "What is it, Hugh?" he asked.

"Just thought you'd like to know Mr. Lucas Bartholomew is right here in the flesh and blood," Hugh replied, pointing across the street. "Here's your chance to settle the score."

The challenge for Bobby to back up his words was clear in Hugh's voice.

"Come on, Bobby," another man urged. "We're behind you all the way."

Bobby had no choice. He had to pursue Lucas. If he backed down, his reputation would suffer irreparable harm. "Where the hell is he?" he asked, pushing forward for a clear view across the street where Lucas was walking with his wife and children.

"Well now, boys," Bobby said, "I think it's time to teach Lucas Bartholomew a thing or two about acten so uppity."

Beauty was the first to see the men coming toward her family. She tugged on her husband's shirt, alerting him to the danger.

"Take the children and get out of here," Lucas ordered quickly. "And see if you can find Paul Berrien or one of his deputies."

Beauty grabbed Annie and Danny by the hand, pulling them down the street, demanding they look straight ahead. Scared, wanting help for her husband, she made a beeline for the courthouse.

Lucas crossed his arms and waited for Bobby, willing to fight if necessary, determined not to throw the first punch.

"I got a bone to pick with you," Bobby said, halting a safe distance from Lucas. "My boy tells me you jumped on him the other day."

Lucas remained silent.

"Well?" Bobby asked loudly.

"I did what was necessary to protect my son," Lucas replied, measuring his words to ensure there was no challenge issued.

"That's not how I heard it," Bobby said, accusing. "My boy tells me you intended to beat the tar out of him and would have tried it if nobody had been around to stop you. He says you came at him for no reason."

"That's not true," Lucas claimed.

"Are you callen my son a liar?" Bobby asked, outraged by the allegation, then advancing closer to Lucas as he spied Paul Berrien emerging from the courthouse.

"If your boy said I had no cause to go after him, then he lied," Lucas replied firmly. "He's lucky someone was there to stop me. But I'll tell you this now, Bobby: If he ever messes with my child or my family again, he'll be sorry for it."

"That's a threat," Bobby said, cocking his fist, then dropping his hands as somebody warned Paul was coming toward them. He took a backward step, then hissed a parting shot. "Someday, somewhere, Bartholomew, your colored ass will rue the day you ever crossed me. You can consider that fair warnen."

"What's goen on here," Paul Berrien interrupted roughly, pushing his way between Bobby and Lucas.

Bobby sneered at his old political rival. "Lucas and me are just exchangen a few friendly threats, sheriff," he sneered. "But it's not a damn thing that's any of your business."

Paul glared at Bobby, then stared at Lucas for clarification, but the black man refused to meet his eyes. Finally, he turned back to Bobby. "If y'all don't get out of here and break it up, then I'll make it my business, Bobby," he said with authority. "And I'll make you damned miserable in the process."

Sensing Paul meant what he said, Bobby's friends abandoned him and retreated across the street. Bobby glared at his two foes, then spit on the sidewalk and spun away from them.

In a minute, Paul pressed Lucas for details about the situation. "Anything I should know about?" he asked.

"Same old stuff, Paul," Lucas answered. "And there ain't a thing you can do about it."

With that said, Lucas went to find his family.

———

Searing heat continued to scorch the land, and the sun seemed to creep closer to the earth with each passing day. When even the clouds disappeared, Matt quit looking for signs of approaching rain. Every day, he plodded across his sunbaked fields and heard the brittle crops crunch beneath his feet. He had worked himself and his family to the point of collapse and mostly their efforts had been for naught.

For a while, Matt had believed the tobacco would keep them from utter ruin. The irrigation appeared to have saved their most important crop. But then black shank attacked, and another hope was lost. In a matter of weeks, healthy stalks withered like dried grapes. Leaves turned prematurely yellow and shrunk on the stalk. Matt figured he'd be lucky to make half the poundage allotted to him annually by the government.

The drought caused other problems, too. The hot, dry air had parched his main pasture, leaving nothing but brown stubble and bare patches of dirt for the cows to graze. Matt sold half the herd to keep the other half from starving. It was money in the bank, but only a fraction of what the cattle were worth in good times. Meanwhile, the remaining cows were wasting in the heat, with ribs protruding under scruffy coats and snouts sunburned and irritated. Worst of all, they bellowed for more water in the late afternoon, a painful wail that seemed almost as sad as an injured baby's cries. Matt figured he would have to sell a few more before the situation improved.

Several of Rachel's prized laying hens also perished in the heat, but the hogs fared better. While dwindling corn supplies forced Matt to sell some of his sows and a few feeder pigs before they had reached the preferred weight, the other hogs had a shady place to spend the hot days—even if their wallows were all dried up. The boys were hauling water every day to keep them quenched, and when fall arrived, Matt would turn the hogs and the cows into the fields of corn, which would not yield sufficiently to make it worth his time to run a combine in the fall.

"When it rains, it pours," Joe quipped one day, a rare trace of bitterness in his voice, as Matt, Sam and he prepared to fire a tobacco barn.

"Don't worry so much, son," Matt replied. "We'll get by. Somehow."

"Your daddy's right, Joe," Sam added. "This, too, shall pass."

Of course, they would get through the hard times. Matt knew that. The year might be a losing proposition, but they would survive. And with a little luck, things would get better next year. They certainly could not get worse.

With the days routine, everyone began looking for ways to beat the heat. The task was not easy, but they faced it with humor and ingenuity. On a Saturday when the temperature soared past the century mark for the umpteenth day, Sam proved an egg would fry on a paved road. No one wanted to eat it, but there was no doubt that it was fried, or at least well poached, with crusted edges and a gooey yolk.

Rachel scolded her husband for wasting an egg.

Still the heat was relentless. It woke them in the morning, burned through the day and made everyone downright uncomfortable during the night.

And through it all, Tom and Summer shivered—from an entirely different kind of heat.

————

A day arrived when there was very little water in the well that fed the house. It was a particularly grimy day, when everything went wrong and tensions rose.

Long after he had hung the last heavy stick of tobacco in the barn, Joe still smelled the sickly odor of the diseased leaves. To make matters worse, his hat had disappeared mysteriously during the day, and his hair was matted with black tar. With no water for a shower, he proposed a dip in New River to his brothers and Tom.

New River was an obscure tributary with densely forested banks thick with cypress and oak trees dripping Spanish moss. The water was pure, deep and cold. And even though the river level was down sharply this summer, the water in their favorite cove remained deep enough to prevent the young men from finding the bottom.

Soon, a quick romp in the swimming hole became a daily ritual. One day, Summer, feeling wearier than usual and unnaturally subdued, asked if her sisters and she might join them.

"The more, the merrier," Joe quipped, stunning Tom and his brothers.

While waiting for the girls to change into their bathing suits, Joe explained his proposal. "We need a little fun and games to liven up things around here," he suggested as his companions guffawed over themselves.

New River meandered through the Berrien estate, about a mile away from the eastern edge of the Baker farm. To reach the swimming hole, the group trooped across the road, through the patch of sweet potatoes and across the first of two fences. Next, they cut through the woods, crossing the second fence near the spot where Joe had shot the panther. On the Berrien side of the fence, the woods became inhospitable, filled with briars and dangling tree branches. Finally, they emerged into a back-country glade of lush wild crabgrass and sandy beach beside the gurgling river.

Nature had carved the cove from a sharp bend in New River. A tangled mesh of brush and tree roots made the far side of the cove forbidding, a sharp contrast to the inviting beach area. The shaded, sandy beach turned into slippery red clay on the steep incline of the riverbank, and a huge oak tree curled high over the water. Easily accessible, the lower tree branches provided a perfect diving platform. For the more adventuresome, Joe had hung a rope swing from the higher branches and built a tree ladder that led skyward to a makeshift platform near the top of the oak.

"I'd forgotten how beautiful this place is," Summer remarked as they arrived. "It's been ages since I've been back here." Then spying the rickety boards in the top of the tree, she asked incredulously, "Do y'all jump off that thing?"

"We do," Joe answered. "It's part of our initiation into a secret society."

"That's pure crazy," Carrie said. "You could break your neck."

"Oh, we're real careful," replied Luke, who himself had yet to work up the courage to jump from the towering platform.

"And you girls be extra careful in the water," Joe added, slipping off his dirty T-shirt and snapping open the top button of his jeans. "It's deep as the dickens."

"Wait a second!" Summer objected, discerning something amiss as Tom, John and Luke tossed off their shirts. "Y'all don't have any shorts or anything. What are you gonna swim in—your underwear?"

Joe gave his sister a puzzled look. "Our underwear?" he repeated. "You're joken, right?" he continued, stripping down to his jockeys. "What do you think we swim in? Don't be offended, but we go skinny-dippen around here."

"That's disgusten," Carrie commented, her eyes growing wide with disbelief as Tom and her brothers dropped their pants in a heap.

"We're not goen swimmen without our clothes on, and neither are y'all," Summer declared loudly. "Tom! Put your pants back on."

"Gosh, Summer," Tom said sheepishly. "I just figured you knew. There's no better place in the world to get necked than a cold river on a hot day."

Joe faked a movement, suggesting he was fixing to remove his underwear. The girls screamed disapproval, turning their backs as the four young men peeled off their underwear.

"I tell you what," Joe said. "Just so y'all don't get offended, we'll keep the important stuff under water at all times. That way, there's no harm done, and we can all enjoy the river."

Summer delayed an answer, using the extra time to think. "Deal," she said finally.

"Summer!" her sisters squealed. "We can't do that."

"I'm hot, and I want to go swimmen," Summer declared. "They won't do anything. Besides, it's not like they've got somethen we've never seen before.

"Okay, Joe," she said. "Y'all go ahead and get in the water. And make sure you stay there!"

With loud whoops of laughter, the four young men turned and raced toward the river. Only when she counted four splashes did Summer turn toward the river. "It's our turn to have the fun," she whispered to her sisters. "Just follow me and act like you're fixen to take off your shorts. When we get to their clothes, grab 'em and run like the wind."

"All of them?" Carrie asked.

"Every last stitch—shoes and all," Summer replied.

Bonnie giggled as the girls advanced toward the river's edge. When they stood among the discarded clothes, Summer stopped. Placing hands on her hips, she summoned up her most haughty tone of voice and addressed her boyfriend and brothers.

"Y'all are pretty funny, but the joke's on you," she said. "When you boys get ready to come home, we'll be waiten for you on the front porch—with your clothes."

In a flash, the three girls grabbed every piece of clothing and pair of shoes, then fled with howls of protest coming from the black waters of New River.

"Dang!" Joe muttered as his sisters disappeared into the thicket.

"Double dang!" Tom added. "Joe, we should have knowed that Summer always gets the last word."

"What are we gonna do?" Luke lamented.

"Really," John chimed in. "We can't go prancen back to the house without our clothes, Joe. Granny would have a heart attack, and Mama would be fit to be tied. Even worse, Daddy and Grandpa won't ever let us live it down."

"Don't panic," Joe told them. "Even Summer wouldn't leave us out here buck-necked."

Half an hour later, Joe knew he had underestimated his sister, and they crept out of the water, embarrassed and depressed by the situation. They trekked back along the path through the woods, waging an unsuccessful battle against the briars and branches that attacked and attached against their naked skin.

"Be careful," Joe cautioned as they climbed over the first fence. "Whatever you do, don't get hung up."

"And be thankful there's no barbwire strung across the top," Tom commented with utmost sincerity.

Finally, they arrived at the edge of the sweet potato patch. Joe led his troops along the edge of the woods, and they were forced to navigate a thorny stand of hawthorn bushes to avoid open exposure to the road. At last, they reached the rear of the corncrib across the road from the house. Carefully, they peered around the corner of the building and saw their clothes bundled on the step walls of the porch, with Summer, Carrie and Bonnie rocking lazily and laughing delightedly.

Moments later, as the young men pondered their course of action, horror of horrors happened. The screen door opened, and their parents and grandparents joined the girls on the porch.

"What are those clothes doen there?" Caroline asked as she took a seat next to Matt in the swing.

"We're teachen your sons a lesson in humility," Summer replied, launching into a rip-roaring version of their escapade by the river, with her sisters providing pertinent observations along the way.

While the distance between the porch and themselves prevented the four young men from hearing the girls' version of events, the roar of laughter was loud and clear. It was equally obvious that their clothes would remain on the porch until someone retrieved them. Joe was nominated for the task.

"This was your brilliant idea in the first place," John observed dryly. "Now get us out of it. Save our faces."

"It's not my face I'm worried about," Luke muttered.

"Well I'm not about to go walken up there without any clothes," Joe said defensively. "We'll stay here till midnight before I do that."

"There's tobacco sheets in the corncrib," Tom reminded him. "You could wrap one of those around you if we can get in there."

"We can do that," Joe said, eyeing the barn's rear window, which was covered by a sturdy shutter that resembled a half-size door. Unable to scale the straight wall, Joe considered his limited options. He glanced around at his stark-naked brothers and friend and exhaled pent-up indignation.

"You can't make this stuff up," he said finally, with a disbelieving shake of his head, followed by an almost genuine laugh. "Come here, Luke."

Reluctantly, Luke stepped in front of his brother, and Joe hoisted him up to the window.

"It's locked," Luke said when the door refused to budge as he tried to push it open.

"Just knock it loose," Joe ordered testily, straining to keep his naked brother aloft. "I'll fix it back."

Using both hands for leverage, Luke hammered at the shutter, finally succeeding in breaking the inside latch. Scampering out of his brother's arms, he disappeared inside the crib window, shuffled across the remnants of the previous year's corn and reappeared moments later with one of the large burlap sheets.

"Here goes nothen," Joe said as he wrapped the course brown sheet around his body. "Lord, I hope nobody drives by and sees me like this."

Mustering up his last bit of dignity, Joe stepped from behind the crib and began walking toward the house. Summer spotted him immediately, pointing for everyone else to notice. Except for an occasional twitter, they observed his progress in silence.

"Lose somethen, did you, Joe?" Sam asked finally when his grandson stepped onto the concrete walkway.

Joe smiled thinly.

"Or have you just taken a fancy to walken around in tobacco sheets?" Matt inquired. "If that's the case, son, then you and I need to have a long talk."

"Oh, I don't know, Daddy," Summer said with relish. "I think it's rather becomen. Who knows? Your oldest son could have just stumbled onto the fashion rage of the year."

"It does give you a certain flair, Joe," Rachel remarked unexpectedly.

Joe reddened beneath his grandmother's teasing. Coming from Rachel, who was not known for poking fun at the ridiculously absurd, the comment seemed all the more astonishing—almost like license for everyone to have a good laugh at Joe's expense, which they did.

As if properly cued, their muffled giggles erupted into uncontrollable mirth. Joe chuckled, too, with as much merriment as his wounded pride would permit. Twice, he mistook temporary lulls, when everyone was catching their breath, as an end to the ordeal, only to watch his family dissolve once more into outright chortling. Finally, though, they more or less exhausted themselves, and Joe moved to retrieve his clothes. He merely provided fodder for the fire, however, while trying to keep the sheet wrapped around him with one hand and balance the clothes with the other.

"Need some help?" Bonnie asked, with absolutely no intention of providing any.

"I've got it under control," Joe said, forgetting the shirts and underwear, settling for the collection of the ragged and faded blue jeans.

Finally, he gathered the duds, nodded to his family with an embarrassed grin and headed back across the road, leaving behind an accidental exposure of his backside in the process. It was too much for his family. They fell apart with laughter; a complete recovery was a long time in coming.

———

Later that night, Caroline came to her oldest son's room and privately admonished him for allowing the prank to get out of hand. "If it had been just your brothers and you involved, Joe, I'd think it's the funniest thing I've ever seen. And it was terribly funny, regardless. But Summer and Tom are daten now, and it's improper for them to be in situations like that."

"Mama!" Joe protested. "It was purely innocent. She didn't see a thing. None of the girls did. I mean nothen like that never crossed my mind or anybody else's for that matter."

"It's the principle of the matter," Caroline said firmly.

"Yes, ma'am," Joe conceded, suddenly conscious of his mother's cause for concern. A short laugh escaped him. "I suppose things used to be a lot less complicated when we were younger," he said.

"Oh, I don't know," Caroline replied. "The concerns were different, but things pretty much stay the same, Joe."

Mother and son thought about that idea for a long moment.

"By the way," Caroline said at last, "I agree with your sisters and your grandmother, son. The tobacco sheet did give you a certain flair. And it certainly put you in a somewhat new—if still familiar—light."

Joe rolled his eyes, and they laughed, genuinely and unencumbered. Then, they began to talk, something they had not done nearly enough as of recently.

CHAPTER 4

IN LATE JULY, THE three shallow wells and an old cistern on the Baker farm ran dry. The pump well, which supplied running water, dried up first. Two days later, Rachel lowered her water bucket into the older well beside the house and brought it up filled with silt and mud.

Along with their neighbors, the Bakers discovered every conceivable way to save water. Baths became a luxury, with the daily swimming forays becoming a substitute. Instead of skinny-dipping, however, Joe, his brothers and sisters, as well as Matt and Sam, often swam with all of their clothes on, using the river in place of a washing machine and a bathtub. Even Caroline and Rachel took a dip in the cool river water, considering their predicament the ultimate humiliation. To avoid the waste of flushing the toilet, which had to be filled manually every time it was used, the men did their business in the privacy of the fields. The women coordinated their calls of nature, so that one flush might take suffice for all.

"Never thought I'd say this, but it kind of makes me long for that old outhouse we tore down," Sam remarked one day, with a rare trace of disgruntlement in his voice. Even more than electric lights, indoor plumbing shone as the ultimate modern convenience in his estimation of things.

Twice a week, Matt went to the school and drew water from a new deep well, which was tapped into one of the world's largest underground aquifers. One day, Luke and he arrived several minutes after Bobby and Wayne Taylor, who were nowhere to be seen. Failing to recognize Bobby's pickup truck, Matt pulled his water trailer near the well, unhooked it from the truck and left Luke to fill it while he drove to the mercantile to buy tobacco twine.

Luke sat down on the trailer wheel, popped a plug of tobacco in his back jaw and began contemplating the dreaded prospect of returning to school in a few weeks. He would enter the eighth grade, having passed the seventh by the skin of his teeth.

While not exactly hating school, Luke did find learning a burdensome proposition. A large part of his problem was laziness. The idea of concentrating on nouns and verbs, sums and differences as well as dates and places bored Luke, especially on warm days when he preferred to be riding a tractor through the fields or working with his father. Even so, laziness was not entirely to blame for his poor grades. Every time he mastered one idea, such as learning the names and locations of all fifty states and their capitals, the teachers thrust something new at him, like all the countries in Africa or Asia—as if it mattered.

Still, even when he buckled down and tried to learn his lessons, the task was a chore. Numbers suddenly reversed themselves in his head. Sometimes, he groped for the meaning of the simplest of words. While refusing to admit it to anyone else, Luke suspected he was just a little bit dumb, a reasonable deduction he figured since all of his brothers and sisters were fairly smart. With six children in the family, one very well could have missed out when the brains were distributed.

Luke was considering all this when Wayne Taylor rounded the nearby corner of the school. Wayne halted at the sight of Luke, giving the boy a smug stare. Luke simply leaned back against the tank and resumed his thinking. Wayne was four years older than Luke. Since they barely knew each other, the younger boy saw no reason to concern himself with Wayne's presence.

Wayne sauntered over to his water tank, checked to make sure the hose was still secure and then turned to regard Luke. With his bully instincts, Wayne could not resist this opportunity to scare the daylights out of some little ignoramus, especially when the mutt's last name was Baker.

"Hey, baby Baker boy!"

Wayne's call jolted Luke back to reality, setting off warning bells in the process. But he refused to cower.

Like Wayne, Luke carried a tough reputation, although not an ounce of bully in him. While Luke fought more often than necessary, he did so only when he felt he had been dealt with unjustly or when someone else, who could not take up for himself, had been treated cruelly.

Without batting an eye, Luke sprayed the ground with a stream of tobacco juice and allowed his eyes to wander lazily toward Wayne.

The show of disinterest annoyed Wayne. "I'm talken to you, baby Baker," he said with force.

"Am I supposed to be impressed?" Luke replied finally, feeling victorious in the initial parry.

"You will be, smart-ass, if you know what's good for you," Wayne hissed. He took a couple of steps toward Luke, then stopped and crossed his arms with a great show of superiority. "There's somethen I've been meanen to ask you Bakers for a long time. Now seems as good as any."

Luke's pride forced him to respond, ignoring his own good sense to avoid the challenge in Wayne's voice. "What's that?" he asked in his toughest tone.

"How come y'all are such nigger lovers, baby Baker?" Wayne asked. "The whole bunch of y'all coddle up to that uppity Lucas Bartholomew like worms in a rotten apple. Next thing, you know, your women probably will run off with some colored man. Maybe you already have a little nigger girlfriend, Luke."

Fueled by insults the likes of which he had never heard, anger swelled like lava in Luke. He wanted to wrap his hands around Wayne's throat, then squeeze until he crushed the windpipe, heard the last breath seep out and felt the body go limp. Luke kept his fury below the surface, however, devoid of any emotion that would reveal the soulless rage in his heart.

"I could give you an answer, Wayne," he replied finally, "but it wouldn't do a bit of good. Everybody's knows you Taylors ain't got the sense God gave a cat to get out of the rain."

Wayne bristled at the ridicule, quickly advancing to within a few feet of Luke. "You watch your mouth, baby Baker, or I'll be on you like stink on manure," he threatened.

Luke rose slowly from his seat on the trailer wheel, sniffing the air. "I thought I smelled it," he said defiantly, with a disparaging grunt.

There was no doubt Luke would lose a fight with Wayne. Luke was small for his age, while Wayne could have held his own with most grown men. Still, Luke was prepared to fight if necessary, and he intended to leave his mark, even if he was battered black and blue in the effort.

Somewhat amused by the fire in the eyes of his young foe, Wayne unwittingly stifled his first impulsive rage, opting to wage a battle of words with Luke. "Calm down, baby Baker," he urged with exaggerated mollification. "I'm just curious. Your family's about the only real-life nigger lovers I know, Luke. Just answer my questions, boy, and I'll leave you to your business with no harm done. First off, baby Baker, tell me, why your daddy cottons so much to Lucas Bartholomew."

Wayne paused, baiting the question with mocking silence, but Luke refused to take the worm.

"No answer," Wayne said a moment later. "You don't understand either, do you, Luke? There may be hope for you yet, baby Baker." He gave a disdainful snort, then continued. "I've heard all kinds of stories about you Bakers, Luke. Is it true that y'all let that nigger eat at your table? I even heard the whole bunch of you drink from the same glass in the tobacco field. Ain't you worried about catchen disease?"

Luke laughed shortly. "Wayne, that's about the stupidest, most ignorant thing I've ever heard in all my born days," he answered, the words rolling from his mouth with newfound clarity, sheer amusement and total disrespect. "First of all, son, my daddy don't cotton to nobody. Never has, never will. He just happens to respect Lucas. And so do I.

"Secondly, Lucas eats dinner with us sometimes," Luke continued. "He's even had a bite of supper on a few occasions, and breakfast, too. But you're wrong about us haven just one glass in the tobacco field, Wayne. We have two—both plastic, so they don't get broke—and we all drink from them. Every last one of us—my daddy, mama, grandpa, brothers, sisters, me, Lucas and anybody else who helps us gather tobacco and wants a drink of water. Nobody's ever gotten sick. And while we're at it, Taylor, baby, I'd a heap rather have Lucas at our dinner table or share a glass of water with him than with trash like you."

The verbal assault rendered Wayne into temporary do-nothingness.

"Now then," Luke added, pressing the upper hand. "Is your curiosity satisfied? Or did I speak too fast for you to take it all in?"

If nothing else, Wayne understood the fighting tone in Luke's impassioned defense of his family. With surprising swiftness, he rushed toward Luke with a clearly stated purpose. "I'm gonna beat the shit out of you, Luke Baker," he said. "And then I'm gonna beat some sense into you."

Luke blocked Wayne's first punch, but the bigger man grabbed his wrist, twisted it and threw Luke to the ground. In an instant, Wayne pounced on the boy, landing astride his chest, pummeling him with several quick slaps across the face.

Clearly, he held the advantage, but Wayne underestimated Luke's fighting spirit. In the very instant he slowed his attack, Luke landed a heavy punch on his right temple. The roundhouse blow stunned Wayne. In a flash, Luke wiggled free, gained his feet and exacted revenge with a flat-handed slap across his attacker's face.

"That's the price you pay," Luke declared with bared teeth.

Wayne rose slowly, more cautious now as he approached Luke for a second time.

His good sense urged Luke to turn and run. His pride made him hold his ground.

With determination and brute strength, Wayne overpowered Luke, first wrapping him in a suffocating bear hug, then jabbing his kidneys twice in quick succession. Luke gasped for air, then went limp, and Wayne hurled him backward.

Luke flew through the air in an arc, landing like dead weight against the dangerously jagged edge of the water trailer. A ghastly moan escaping him as the ragged steel gashed his back. Luke's eyelids fluttered, and he slumped to the ground in a nearly unconscious state.

"You're the one who's gonna pay," Wayne vowed, again stalking his victim.

Grabbing the boy by the hair, Wayne pulled Luke away from the trailer, flipped him onto his stomach and pinned him against the ground with the weight of his knee. The second vicious assault somewhat restored Luke's senses as Wayne grabbed him under the chin and pulled his head backward, blocking the boy's supply of oxygen. When Luke's arms flailed, Wayne momentarily released him, then repeated the chokehold a second time. Laughing scornfully, he released the hold again, then pushed Luke's face in the dirt and wrenched the boy's arm behind his back, again using his weight as leverage, applying enough twisting pressure to draw a loud groan from Luke.

———

Bobby heard the boy's first terrified cry. He witnessed firsthand the second scream. For a second, Bobby started to berate Wayne for picking on the small boy. Then, he recognized the kid and promptly changed his mind.

Instead of pulling his son off Luke, Bobby ambled over to his water trailer, pulled the hose from the overflowing tank and turned off the faucet. In his own sweet time, he finally went to see what needed to be done between the boys.

"Now here's an opportunity to teach you two boys a couple of important lessons," Bobby commented as he approached Wayne and Luke. "First off, never get in a scrap with somebody way bigger than yourself because it's almost always a losen proposition. Second, always press the advantage when you've got it, because you never know when you'll lose it." He paused, then asked casually, "Y'all understand what I'm sayen, boys?"

"Yeah, Pa," Wayne replied with enthusiasm. "I understand."

"Well then, Wayne," Bobby continued, "if you really do understand, then rub his face in the dirt a little bit and tell me what started all this."

"He called us scum, Pa," Wayne explained, grabbing Luke's hair with both hands and scrubbing his face across the rocky clay. "Said we were stupid and didn't have the sense God gave a cat to come in from the rain."

"Is that a fact?" Bobby asked with an exaggerated show of interest. "You're Matt Baker's boy," he remarked after a slight hesitation, a statement of fact rather than a question.

"He is," Wayne sneered. "I call him baby Baker boy."

"Which one are you, boy?" Bobby asked.

Luke was fully alert now, disbelieving the situation, taking note of his surroundings, praying for his daddy's quick return. "Luke," he answered.

"What makes you think we're stupid, Luke?" Bobby asked.

When no answer was immediately forthcoming, Bobby added, "A little pressure, please, Wayne. I'd really like to know why Luke here thinks we're stupid and don't have the sense God gave a cat to come in out of the rain."

Wayne wrenched the boy's arm again, and Luke screamed. "I don't know why," he wailed. "I just said it."

"It's not polite to call people names and spread lies about them, Luke," Bobby said with bad pretense of offended sensibilities. "Your parents obviously haven't taught you any manners. Maybe when Wayne's through with you, you'll think twice the next time you resort to name-callen and lies. Give him a little reminder, Wayne, about the importance of politeness."

Again, Wayne twisted the boy's arm, stretching the limb until Luke hollered and burst into tears.

"Oh, great scot," Bobby muttered, shaking his head with disgust as the boy cried. "Don't cry," he ordered. "Men aren't supposed to cry; only sissies do. And while you Bakers may be a lot of crazy things, I've never thought of any of y'all as sissies. Ease up, Wayne, and let little Luke catch his breath."

Luke willed away the tears, trying again to get his bearings. As much as it hurt, he could stand the pain. But he was scared nonetheless. The whole situation seemed unreal. Bobby Taylor and his idiot son obviously were warped beyond belief. For the first time in a long time, Luke prayed, silently pleading for his father's quick return, promising the Lord to do better in school, vowing to do all of his homework.

As Bobby resumed his interrogation, the boy's prayers vanished but not his fears.

"Luke, I know you're haven a hard time, but there's one other thing on my mind," Bobby said. "Do you like niggers, Luke?"

"He does, Pa," Wayne answered quickly. "He told me so. His whole family thinks that Lucas Bartholomew is just swell. They eat at the table with him. Drink after him, and who knows what else?"

"Is that so?" Bobby exclaimed, looking horrified by the revelation. "I've always figured your daddy was a nigger lover, Luke, and now it seems as if I was right all along. What do you say to that, boy?"

"I say let people think what they want," Luke replied, quoting an oft-used phrase by his father.

"Sounds to me that's the same thing as sayen Matt Baker is a nigger lover," Bobby said. "But just to make sure there's no doubt about it once and for all, I want you to do somethen for me, Luke. Then Wayne and I will leave, you can fill up your water tank and we'll all forget this little unpleasantness ever happened. How does that sound?"

"Good enough, I reckon," Luke answered, hopeful the ordeal would end soon.

"Atta boy," Bobby replied. "Now, Luke, what I want is to hear from the mouth of the man's very son that Matt Baker is a genuine, bona fide nigger lover. Can you do that for me?"

"My daddy does his own talken," Luke replied, heartburn rising in his throat.

"That's fine and dandy, but your daddy ain't here right now, boy," Bobby said fiercely. "It just you, me and Wayne, and we don't got all day to wait."

Taking his father's reference to him as a signal, Wayne promptly inflicted another round of pressure on Luke's arm, eliciting another howl of pain from the boy.

Bobby kneeled in front of the boy. "Come on, Luke," he urged, his expression evil and his tone wicked. "Just say the words, boy. My daddy is a nigger lover."

Luke knew he was licked. Closing his eyes, he muttered the words for Bobby.

"That wasn't so hard now, was it?" Bobby said. "A little louder this time, though, please. I couldn't hear you quite as clearly as I would have liked."

"My daddy is a nigger lover," Luke said, the words clearly audible.

"Louder, Luke," Bobby coaxed, like a crazy man. "Shout it at the top of your lungs, Luke; spread the good news. Tell the world the truth about your daddy, boy. Tell everyone what Matt Baker is."

"My daddy is a nigger lover," Luke repeated for a third time, then a fourth and a fifth as Wayne wrenched his arm.

"Thank you, Luke," Bobby said at last as if nothing extraordinary had occurred. "Let him go, Wayne."

Wayne obeyed his father, delivering one last vicious twist of the boy's arm before he released him, then scampering away as Luke lay motionless, his spirit broken.

"Oh, there's just one more thing," Bobby remarked suddenly as he started to walk away from Luke. He turned on his heels and ordered, "Look at me, Luke Baker."

Luke struggled to his back, too frightened to ignore Bobby's demand.

"I wouldn't mention this little episode to anyone," Bobby suggested. "I've heard all the talk about you, son. People already think you're none too bright. Nobody would believe your word against mine—not even your family. They'd just think you were maken up lies. And you can bet your bottom dollar, boy, that it would cause a heap of trouble for your daddy. You keep that in mind now—you hear me?"

"You hear me," Bobby repeated, this time making a statement as he turned and walked away from Luke.

———

From his vantage point as he turned the pickup into the school's parking lot, the first thing Matt saw was Luke's crumpled form lying on the ground. By the time he slid the truck to a stop, Luke had achieved a sitting position against the trailer tire and was wiping away a mixture of dust and tear stains from his face. Several yards away, Bobby Taylor was berating his oldest son, holding Wayne by the shirt collar and shaking him as he yelled at the boy.

"Son, I've told you one too many times about picken on people smaller than you," Bobby hollered as Matt exited the truck. "Don't you have any sense at all? You know the difference between right and wrong."

"But he started it, Pa," Wayne howled as Bobby twisted his ear. "He jumped on me. I was defenden myself."

"What's goen on here?" Matt asked, moving protectively toward his son as Luke managed to pick himself off the ground.

"I don't rightly know, Matt," Bobby replied. "When I got here, they were goen at each other like cats and dogs. That son of yours is a feisty one to be so small," he added, interjecting a touch of praise. "I just now got 'em broke apart."

Matt regarded Bobby with marked skepticism. Faced with the same situation, he would have given the benefit of doubt to almost any other man. With Bobby, however, he could not help wondering if the man himself had thrown a blow or two against Luke. Instead of accepting Bobby's explanation at face value, Matt turned to the one person he trusted for the truth.

"What happened, son?" he asked Luke, unaware of the full extent of the boy's pain, especially the bloody gash on his back.

Before Luke could answer, Wayne offered his version of events. "He called me and my pa, stupid," Wayne said in a disrespectful tone. "Said I was trash, too. When I told him to shut up, he came at me."

Matt recognized his youngest son had a temper like a keg of dynamite, as well as a short fuse. However, Luke tended to fight only when he had provocation. Considering who was involved, Matt figured it was more likely that Wayne had taunted Luke into a fight. Still, Matt wanted to hear what his son had to say about the situation.

"Luke? What happened, son?"

Luke stared wildly at Wayne, then at Bobby. "More or less like he said," he shrugged at last. "I wouldn't exactly call it self-defense, and he left out a few of the more important details—like how he walked over here while I was minden my own business, insulted me, you, the rest of the family. But hey, that's pretty true to character for Wayne Taylor. He's good about forgetten the really important facts. And everybody knows he's quick to pick a fight when the odds are stacked in his favor."

"You little liar," Wayne said accusingly, making a sudden move toward Luke, then stopping cold when Matt stepped in front of his son.

"Listen, Matt," Bobby said with utmost seriousness. "My boy ain't perfect. I'm willen to admit that. But Wayne's no liar. If he said Luke started it, then it must be so."

Luke laughed bitterly, clearly disrespectful of Bobby's opinion on the subject.

Matt sent him a hard look, suggesting the boy keep quiet, and Bobby picked up on the moment.

"Now that's a fine way to act," Bobby said self-righteously. "I don't let my children treat their elders like that, Matt. I've heard the talk about Luke. He's hardheaded, no doubt about it. You'd better do some disciplinen, or you're gonna have problems down the road."

"Don't tell me how to raise my son, Bobby Taylor," Matt retorted. "I don't know everything that happened here, but I know my son. He doesn't fight without cause. I'd be willen to bet your nonsense is at the bottom of all this in one way or another."

"Always have an excuse, don't you, Matt?" Bobby shot back, the tension clearly escalating between the two men. "You and your kind think you can do whatever you please because you're always right. Well, let me tell you this, Matt Baker: Sometimes you're flat out wrong. And you and your holier-than-thou attitude make me sick."

Anger flashed in Matt's eyes, but he checked his rage.

Sensing his foe's reluctance to engage in a protracted battle of wills, Bobby grabbed Wayne by the shoulder and pushed his son toward the truck. "Come on, boy," he growled, glaring one last time at Matt. "It's beginnen to stink around here too much for me."

When they were gone, Matt turned his full attention to Luke. "Are you okay, son?" he asked, inspecting the boy's skinned face and busted lip, then noticing blood on the ground. "Where'd all this blood come from?"

Recalling Bobby's earlier promise of trouble for Matt if he divulged the details of the fight with Wayne, remembering the sharp words between the two men just moments earlier and aware of the long-simmering ill will between the two families, Luke opted to conceal the worst of his injuries even though his back was soaked and sticky with blood.

"He busted my mouth," he lied. "It bled a lot, but it's okay now."

Matt accepted the explanation. Except for looking slightly ashen and skinned on the face, Luke appeared reasonably well. "Tell me what happened, son," he said. "Everything."

"Wayne started it, Daddy," Luke said. "He called us nigger lovers and stuff like that. You know all their tough talk. I said somethen back, called him stupid or somethen like that. And then he came at me."

Luke hesitated slightly, almost as if he were holding back details. "We just fought," he added, subdued. "That's all there was to it."

"What did he do to you?" Matt asked.

Ignoring the throb in his back as well as his wobbly knees, Luke gave a sanitized version of events. "Nothen too bad," he said. "Twisted my arm, slapped me around and rubbed my face in the dirt. But I'm okay, Daddy. Don't worry anymore about it."

Matt felt uneasy. "Are you sure you're not leaven anything out?" he pressed. "Is there anything else I should know?"

Again, Luke hesitated.

"No, sir," he said finally with a shake of his head. "I'd just like to forget all about it, Daddy. It's over and done with, and I'm okay. If you don't mind, let's keep this between us."

The boy sounded entirely unconvincing, and he avoided looking at Matt. In fact, the whole situation troubled Matt. Nevertheless, he grudgingly decided against pressing the issue. While he sensed this was no ordinary scuffle between boys, Matt also believed Luke had his reasons for wanting to keep quiet about the argument. He wanted to give his son the opportunity to think for himself, to begin making the decisions that would turn the boy into a man. If Luke needed guidance, Matt hoped he would seek it.

"What happened here stays between us, son," he promised. "As long as you want it to."

"Thanks, Daddy," Luke said with a relieved smile. "Come on. Let's get the water."

The fact that he lied to his father troubled Luke almost as much as the bizarre run-in with Bobby and Wayne. Matt and Caroline had instilled in their children the virtues of honesty, compassion, courage, patience and perseverance. Except for falling short where his schoolwork was concerned, Luke had lived up to their expectations.

In the aftermath of the fight, Luke's values worked against him, especially his parents' teaching to respect his elders. While he had privately questioned the motives and smarts of some grown-ups, Luke had never openly challenged the merits of anyone he considered an adult. So even though he suspected Bobby Taylor had a few loose screws in his character, Luke felt enough trepidation to withhold a full accounting of the events between the Taylors and himself.

Luke truly believed Bobby was a tad crazy, and he thought people should know. Unfortunately, his own reputation lacked credibility, forcing Luke to give serious consideration to Bobby's prophecy that people would question the boy's motives if he dared to claim harassment by a respected man whom the county had almost twice elected sheriff. Indeed, the entire episode seemed farfetched enough that even Luke wondered if perhaps he was overreacting and misjudging the situation.

In his confusion, Luke tried to forget the strange affair. First, he focused on the jagged gash in his back. Somehow, his blood-soaked clothes escaped everyone's attention. He threw away the soiled clothes and tried unsuccessfully to doctor himself before finally seeking Bonnie's assistance.

Resorting to another lie, he told Bonnie that he had fallen on a piece of farm equipment and wanted to hide the injury from their parents, fearing they might deem him too young for the job. It was the perfect excuse for his little sister, who complained constantly that she was too young for anything.

Still, Bonnie could not help Luke cope with the unease he felt regarding Bobby Taylor. He wanted to tell his father, almost did once. But then a new fear entered his mind, a suspicion that if he revealed the truth, he would succeed only in creating more problems for Matt. Luke understood the drought's devastation on his family's livelihood. He had watched the worried look in his father's eyes at the beginning of summer glaze over with despair as the rains held off. Matt continued to work doggedly in hopes of salvaging a small portion of success, even as one neighbor after another plowed up their pitiful crops, but Luke knew they were ruined. And with his father already burdened, Luke refused to trouble him further, especially with something so seemingly inconsequential.

Only it was not inconsequential, and as much as Luke wanted to forget the situation, his better judgment refused to put the matter out of mind. The pressure became more than he could handle. First, he felt as if he had betrayed his father and family. Soon, however, he began to resent Matt and everyone else for putting him into the situation in the first place. He became moody, sniping at his brothers and sisters and uncharacteristically defying his mother when she gave him a chore to do. For the disobedience, Matt whipped him, letting Luke know that he was "not too big for his britches, yet."

The punishment embittered Luke. He had taken great pains to spare his father more headaches, and Matt had rewarded his good intentions with ten hard licks with the belt, leaving welts on the boy's backside.

The stress and strain finally became more than Luke could take. After an exhausting day in the tobacco field, he became physically ill. The day had been dreary for everyone but disastrous for Luke. Beginning before dawn when he accidentally snagged a tractor on the barn, ripping the door off its hinges, everything he touched fell apart, including the harvester, which refused to crank after Luke choked it down at mid-morning.

He spent the rest of the day trudging through the field with his brothers and Tom, cropping the tobacco on foot and piling it onto sleds, which his father and grandfather pulled from the field with tractors. At noon, they ate in the field—bologna sandwiches on stale bread, seasoned with their tar-stained hands. The afternoon brought more sleds, and supper was a repeat of dinner. They worked until eleven that Friday night, hanging the last tobacco stick in the barn by the glow of a small floodlight.

Luke collapsed in bed shortly after midnight. He woke less than an hour later, vomited on clean sheets and spent the remainder of the night with his head hung over the commode, while his mother kept a close watch on his fever.

The next evening, Luke realized he had to unburden his troubles. This conclusion came as he lay in bed, recuperating from his sickness under the watchful eyes of Caroline and Rachel.

After supper, he slipped out of bed and went to see Joe. "Where you goen tonight?" he asked after entering the closed room without warning.

"Can't you knock before you barge in a room?" Joe shot back, not even bothering to look his brother's way.

Luke waited while Joe pulled on his blue jeans, tucked in his shirt and began combing his hair. "Sorry to bother you," he said finally, when Joe showed no interest in talking to him. "I was aimen to talk to you about somethen, but it can wait."

The doleful tone of Luke's voice reminded Joe of some melancholy time in his own past. He laid down the comb, giving his full attention to the boy. "Hey, little brother," he said, "I didn't mean to sound so princely. You know you don't have to knock on my door. It's always open. What's on your mind?"

"See this," Luke answered, turning his back to Joe and lifting his T-shirt to display the crooked slash on his back.

"Good Lord, Luke!" Joe exclaimed.

The wound, which had turned flaming red on the sides, oozed puss and held a lousy scab.

"What in tarnation happened?" Joe asked.

"I got in a fight," Luke replied.

"Another fight, Luke?" Joe groaned. "You should have told somebody, and you should have seen a doctor. I bet you needed stitches, and I know your back's infected."

"Daddy knows about the fight—but not about my back," Luke revealed. "We decided to keep the fight between us. Bonnie knows about my back—but not the fight. She's been doctoren me."

"Remind me to tell her not to consider nursen as a career," Joe muttered. "What in the world has she been usen to doctor you?"

"She used Merthiolate at first," Luke answered. "But that hurt worse than the cut itself. Since then, she's been putten new bandages on it for me. I was hopen it would get better by itself."

Joe rolled his eyes. "Not one of your better thoughts," he said. "Take off your shirt and lie down on my bed. I'll be back in a second."

Joe left the room, returning quickly with a bottle of peroxide, gauze, tape and a tube of salve. Using his fingers, he pressed against the inflamed sides of the wound to drain the festering puss, wiping away the yellow fluid with gauze.

"Is that gonna burn?" Luke asked as his brother prepared to pour peroxide on the wound.

"It may tickle, but it won't burn," Joe promised. "Peroxide kills the germs. It boils out the infection."

After the peroxide bubbled for several minutes, Joe wiped away the liquid, put salve on the infected area and covered the cut with a large bandage. "Well, I don't know if Dr. Pittman would approve, but that's better than nothen," he said, putting the last piece of tape in place. "We'll check it tomorrow. If it's still bad come Monday, though, you'll have to see the doctor."

"It sure beats Merthiolate," Luke muttered as he came to a standing position.

"Now I want answers," Joe said abruptly, purposefully, crossing his arms. "Why so secretive about a fight, Luke? Who did you fight? And how did that happen to your back?"

"It was with Wayne Taylor," Luke answered.

Joe grabbed his brother by the shoulders. "Wayne Taylor! He did this to you?"

"I don't think he meant to hurt my back," Luke replied. "He pushed me, and I landed against that jagged edge on the water trailer."

"Wayne Taylor is two, no, three times your size, Luke," Joe said forcefully. "Daddy knew you were in a fight with him. What did he say about all this?"

"He came up after everything was over and done with," Luke answered. "He and Bobby Taylor had words over it. There's no love lost between them. I didn't want any more trouble, so I decided to keep quiet about my back."

"This sounds awfully strange, Luke," Joe remarked. "What started it?"

Like some gossipmonger who had held his tongue too long, Luke spewed forth the details of his beating at the hands of Wayne Taylor and his father. In the middle of his confession, the boy's broken spirit crumbled, and Joe understood the despair and humiliation of his brother. Against his will, Luke cried, a stream of low, anguished sobs that built in crescendo until Joe wrapped the boy in a protective embrace and buried Luke's head against his chest. Soon, the tears dissolved to hiccupping sobs, then disappeared altogether.

When he felt Luke nod against his chest, Joe released his brother and gestured him to sit on the bed.

"Feel better?" he asked, dragging his desk chair in front of Luke and taking a backward seat in it.

Luke nodded his head. "I cried in front of Bobby and Wayne, too," he admitted. "Bobby told me to be quiet. He said only sissies cry."

"Hogwash," Joe shrugged.

"I know that," Luke replied. "Bobby also said that while he doesn't think much of Baker men in general, he doesn't think of any of us as sissies."

"Somehow, that doesn't make me feel any better about any of this," Joe said. "Finish tellen me what happened, Luke."

His fears vanished, his anxieties purged, Luke rushed through the remaining details of the assault. Joe listened with keen interest, concealing his shock, yet finding the story so freakishly truthful that none of it could be discounted to his brother's imagination. Joe had always considered Bobby a bigoted huckster who managed to disguise his ghoulish ways with clever tricks. This black-hearted side of Bobby was a new revelation. The man's obsession with the color bar had caused him to cross the wrong side of the so-called thin line between sanity and insanity.

Still, like his youngest brother, Joe had few dealings with crazy men to help him put the situation into its proper context. Despite their faults, most people were decent at the core, and Joe refused to rush his declaration of Bobby Taylor as deranged. Had there been no history of ill feelings between the Bakers and the Taylors, Joe would have gone straightaway to his father for a discussion. The past, however, persuaded him to resist his first impulse in favor of some rational thought about the problem.

"Do you ever wish that Daddy and Lucas weren't such good friends?" Luke asked suddenly, breaking Joe's train of thought.

"What?" he asked, frowning at his little brother.

"Maybe we are nigger lovers," Luke said. "The Taylors aren't the only people who think that way. I've heard other people say almost the same thing, maybe not in those words, but the meaning was there. Daddy does tend to be all high and mighty about treaten colored people fair and all."

Joe chose his response carefully, understanding Luke's confusion, yet wanting to impress upon the boy the importance of the matter. "Frankly, Luke, I've never thought of Daddy as acten high and mighty about anything," he said. "Our father is simply a good, honest man who believes in treaten everyone he meets fairly and squarely. He doesn't like to see anyone mistreated, and he'll stick up for anyone he thinks is getten a raw deal. Daddy's a true friend, Luke. I try to be just like him in my dealens with people. I've always thought you were that way, too."

Joe eyed his brother closely, receiving a nod of understanding in response. Then he continued. "I would hope that erases any doubts you have about your daddy or your family, Luke, but I'll also say one more thing. If we are nigger lovers, then we're a poor excuse for them. When you get right down to it, Lucas is the only black friend Daddy has—unless you count Beauty and the children."

"What about Choopie, Red and Miss Reba?" Luke asked. "They're always out here asken if they can fish."

"I guess you could call them friends," Joe replied. "To tell you the truth, though, they were mainly hired hands back in the days when Daddy and Grandpa needed help gatheren tobacco. Whatever, they're good people, Luke. That's what matters most. Don't begrudge them a few fish."

"I don't," Luke replied. "And I'm glad Daddy's friends with Lucas. I'm glad I'm friends with Lucas. When you get right down to it, he's almost like family. I can't remember a time when he wasn't around here in one way or another."

Joe smiled, remembering just such a time.

Luke shrugged. "Why are people prejudiced?" he asked.

"I couldn't begin to answer that one, Luker," Joe responded sincerely. "I think everybody's prejudiced in one way or another. It's human nature. Prejudice is about a lot of things, Luke—things you don't understand yet, things I don't understand, things Daddy doesn't even understand. I don't think there'll ever be a solid line between right and wrong on this subject, but the heart of the matter is whether you believe people deserve a fair shake in life."

"Not everyone gets that," Luke supposed.

"No, they don't," Joe said. "For a number of reasons—not all of them bad, I think. Some people are mistreated plain and simple. Some people lose out to circumstances. Some people just waste their opportunity."

"You're pretty smart, Joe," Luke remarked abruptly.

Joe laughed heartily. "Hardly," he replied. "Maybe I've thought about this longer than you have, but mostly, I'm maken it up as I go. Sometimes, I think that's all you can do."

"Did you ever get beat up because of what you believe?" Luke inquired.

"Not particularly," Joe answered. "But I've had a few disagreements in my time. I'll probably have a few more."

"Was it the right thing to do—not tellen Daddy everything about the fight?" Luke asked.

"I hope so, I think so," Joe said. "In his frame of mind, Daddy might just have turned that into an opportunity to get rid of his frustration. If he knew what that man did to you, Luke, Daddy would kick Bobby Taylor from here to yonder. And that's the last thing we need to happen around here."

"It's helped talken to you about it," Luke replied. "Just getten all of this out of my system makes me feel a whole heap better, although I ain't none too happy about getten the starch beat out of me."

"A little humility never hurt anyone," Joe said lightly.

"You sound like Granny," Luke commented.

"I'll take that as a compliment," Joe responded. "In any case, let's watch that back closely. I'll leave the salve and everything else in here, and we can doctor the cut some more tomorrow."

"Thanks, Joe. It's good to know you can talk to someone and know everything will stay between you and them."

"Right here in this room," Joe smiled, abruptly changing his grin to a mischievous glower. "Now get out of here. I have to finish getten ready, so I can go rescue damsels in distress. If I get lucky, one of them might relieve some of mine."

————

The Tip-Toe Inn was a genuine honky tonk. Set in the middle of nowhere on the road between Cookville and Tifton, the tavern had a notorious reputation as an abode for drunken husbands, worldly women and other lost souls.

To accommodate their varied patrons, the owners, Butch and Cassie Griffin, offered a broad mix of music, pool tables, beer and booze. Sometimes, the Tip-Toe Inn featured a live band, but the regulars preferred to pop nickels into an old jukebox. Names like Hank Williams, Patsy Cline and Skeeter Davis dominated the playlist, but some surprising selections made the cut as well. Songs like *Poor Side of Town* by Johnny Rivers, *When a Man Loves a Woman* by Percy Sledge and *House of the Rising Sun* by the Animals occupied slots in the music box because they touched the right emotions at the right time of night, when the distinction between country and rock and roll could not be made and nobody cared.

The chrome music machine was an oddity in an otherwise dreary establishment, with dark corners, pale lights and dusty wooden floors. The sprawling, ramshackle roadhouse had evolved from a one-room block building that the Griffins had built in 1960, the year the county legalized beer, wine and liquor sales.

Plunked right on the county line, the liquor store and tavern provided a profitable living for the Griffins. Over the years, Butch and Cassie had expanded the business to take advantage of the increasing trade from neighboring Tift County, which was bone dry but had some very thirsty residents who beat a steady path along Highway 125.

The couple operated their establishment with only one ironclad rule: Absolutely no fighting was allowed inside the building, and the owners had a diehard reputation for calling on the sheriff's office to enforce the rule when necessary. As for what happened outside, they cared little. The policy had served them well over the years, except on two occasions, once when a man was found stabbed to death outside the joint and another time when a drunken woman had stumbled into the path of an oncoming tractor-trailer.

Joe had begun frequenting the Tip-Toe Inn in the last few months before he turned twenty-one. On the first occasion, he had downed a few beers with friends, dropped a nickel into the jukebox to hear Patsy Cline sing and left with no intentions of ever returning. A few weeks later, however, some college buddies had persuaded him to join them for another outing, and he had fallen into the routine of dropping by on weekend nights for lighthearted fun, drinking beer, shooting pool and chasing women.

On this night, however, Joe came to the Tip-Toe Inn with rage festering in his heart, an anger that he stoked with beer and whiskey, oblivious to the evening's party atmosphere. Despite his assurances to the contrary when he advised Luke earlier in the evening, Joe believed his little brother had received an undeserved lesson in humility at the hands of Bobby Taylor and his overgrown son. He was eager to mete out the payback.

————

As usual, Bobby intended to drink a single beer, then leave. While he counted Butch and Cassie Griffin among his friends, Bobby preferred to avoid being seen at the Tip-Toe Inn. He never knew how his supporters, even the diehard tag-tails, would react to news that he frequented a bawdy roadhouse. Although he had no political aspirations or any other intentions at the moment, Bobby was never sure when a motive would arise.

With country music blaring in his ears, Bobby pushed his way through the crowd and found an empty seat at the end of the bar. "Busy night," he noted for Cassie when she brought him a beer.

"My cash registers are jinglen," she replied before moving off to slake someone else's thirst.

Bobby exchanged pleasantries with Butch, then huddled over his beer trying to keep a low profile.

————

At half after ten, Joe had glued his eyes to the tavern door, finally admitting he had come to the Tip-Toe Inn for one reason. On numerous occasions, he had observed Bobby sneak into the joint, drink a beer or two and then leave unnoticed. As soon as Bobby walked through the door, with his head down as usual, Joe spotted the man. Without bothering to watch Bobby complete his barroom routine, Joe turned away, killing the last half of his bottle of beer.

When sufficient time had passed for Bobby to feel at ease, Joe skulked his way through the throng of bodies until he stood behind the man. Squeezing against the wall, Joe gripped the man's left shoulder, while leaning down on the right side of the bar.

Bobby reacted with clockwork predictability, looking toward the hand on his shoulder, then jerking his head around to find Joe in his face. His eyes widened, panicky with instant awareness that Joe knew everything about the incident with Luke.

"Hi, Bob," Joe said caustically, his firm grip on the large tendon of Bobby's shoulder tightening into an uncomfortable hold. "Saw you drinken all by your lonesome and just couldn't stop myself from comen over to see what's new with you. How the heck are you, Bobby?"

Bobby rotated his shoulder, trying unsuccessfully to break the younger man's painful grip. "Get out of here, Joe," he advised. "You're drunk as a skunk."

"You betcha, Bob," Joe said, his face frozen with a feral grin. "For once in your miserable life, Bobby, you are right about somethen. I'm drunk—roaren drunk— and I'm ticked off, too."

He hesitated, frightening Bobby with his cold regard as well as sheer command of voice, his tone alternating between false cordiality and real menace. "Do you know why I'm ticked off, Bobby?" he asked.

"I have a pretty good idea," Bobby replied with forced casualness, "but your pa and I settled our disagreement the other day."

Joe groaned with disbelieving delight, then laughed scornfully at Bobby's feeble attempt to avoid the issue. "Maybe you did, maybe you didn't," he said, his tone again falsely cordial. "My daddy can take care of himself, and I'd never be presumptuous enough to fight his battles. That said, you'd better guess again."

"Listen, Joe," Bobby reasoned. "Maybe you think you got reason to be mad at me. Right now, though, you're drunk, and you're not thinken straight. Come see me when you sober up."

"Spare me!" Joe growled, his tone turning deadly cold. "Pretend ignorance. I know it comes naturally. But while you're at it, Bobby, I'll go ahead and tell you why I'm not thinken straight tonight.

"Somethen happened to my little brother, Bobby," he continued, leaning closer, almost eyeball to eyeball. "Seems like he ran afoul of one crazy man and his dimwitted son. They nearly broke his arm. His back has a four-inch gash in it from where somebody shoved him against a piece of jagged steel."

Joe hesitated again, narrowed his eyes, becoming even more ominous. "Bad stuff for a kid to face," he declared. "But you know what upsets me most, Bobby?" He waited, then answered: "They messed with my baby brother's mind. I'm not pleased about that. Someone is gonna pay."

"You're talken like a crazy man, Joe Baker," Bobby said defensively, his voice quivering slightly. "I don't know the first thing about any of this."

"Come outside, and I'll do a much better job explainen myself," Joe vowed.

"Leave me alone, Joe!" Bobby pleaded. "I'm just sitten here minden my own business, and I don't want no trouble. You got no cause to bother me."

"You and your son should have thought about that when you went after my brother," Joe warned. "You can either come outside, Bobby, or we can take care of business right here."

"Listen, Joe," Bobby tried again, still believing he could reason with the man.

Joe cut him off. "That's all I care to hear from you," he said.

Joe grabbed Bobby by the nape of his hair, twice pounding the man's face into the bar in quick succession. The first blow shattered Bobby's nose; the second split his lip.

Oblivious to the splatter of blood on his shirt, Joe picked Bobby off the stool, slammed him against the wall and buried his shoulder against the man's chest. The impact knocked the breath from Bobby. Joe followed with three rapid jabs in the pit of his stomach, then backhanded his victim across the face, once for good measure, then straight up for Luke.

As far as Joe was concerned, his mission was completed. Bobby was limp, dangling at the end of Joe's fingers, supported only by the firm press of his head against the wall.

Unable to read his mind, however, nearby onlookers interpreted Joe's position as a sign of more violence to come. Two men quickly grabbed Joe, pulling him from Bobby. With no one to hold him up, the unconscious man buckled at the knees and tumbled to the floor.

"My god! Why'd you go and do a thing like that," Cassie Griffin yelled at Joe.

As soon as Joe had bashed Bobby's head against the bar, Cassie had yelled for Butch to call the sheriff. She had leapt over the bar and was kneeling beside Bobby.

"Just settlen business," Joe replied.

"He's out cold," she determined, examining the battered man. "I think his nose is broken. Blood's getten all over the floor. Somebody bring me towels!"

Joe shrugged off the two men, walked over to the bar and asked a waitress to bring him a beer.

"No more beer for you!" Cassie screamed. "You'll be talken to the sheriff as soon as he gets here. I expect you'll be spenden the night in jail, mister. If there's one thing Butch and I don't tolerate, it's fighten in our establishment. You've been comen here long enough, Joe, to know that."

Cassie's disclosure about the sheriff's pending involvement brought the first tinge of regret to Joe. His remorse was short-lived, however, smothered by conviction that he had given Bobby Taylor his just rewards.

Joe believed matters had been settled between the Taylors and Luke. And he took real satisfaction in having slapped the arrogance out of Bobby. He decided to enjoy the moment while it lasted—understanding full well there would be hell to pay later.

––––––––

By the time the flashing blue lights of the law arrived at the Tip-Toe Inn, Bobby had regained consciousness and ridded himself of the grogginess. He held a bloodied towel against his broken nose, while maintaining a watchful eye on Joe and weighing his options. His contemptuousness urged Bobby to make Joe pay dearly for his actions. The smarts in him advised to pretend nothing had happened and forget the matter. His savvy suggested to wait and see before making a final decision.

Bobby watched gleefully as one of Paul Berrien's deputies handcuffed Joe behind the back, pushed him to the patrol car and shoved him into the rear seat. Joe's head smacked the car roof as the deputy pushed him, and he nearly buckled from the force of the blow. Bobby almost laughed with delight as Joe staggered into the car, clearly with the surliness knocked from him.

When Joe was locked in the car, the deputy questioned Bobby and offered him a ride to the hospital to have his nose examined. Bobby was patient with the questions and gracious in accepting Cassie's assistance to the patrol car.

The deputy was a big, beefy man named Mack, with large hands and elephant-like facial features. He was also a stickler for rules and regulations, refusing to allow Bobby to ride beside him in the front seat, insisting he sit in back with Joe.

"But he just tried to kill me!" Bobby protested.

"He can't do anything to you now because I got him handcuffed," Mack explained. "I got regulations to follow, Bobby. You either sit in the backseat or find another way to the hospital."

"I oughtta go to Tifton instead of Cookville," Bobby muttered.

"Makes no difference to me," Mack replied sourly. "But if you go with me, you gotta ride in the backseat."

"I don't think you need to worry about him anymore," Cassie assured Bobby, her soothing voice failing to conceal an impatience to return to business as usual.

Disgruntled, Bobby climbed into the backseat and found himself locked in the car with Joe. "You'll be sorry for this, Joe Baker," he vowed, pressing a fresh hand-kerchief against his bleeding nose. "You're goen to jail—maybe to prison."

"I don't think so, Bobby," Joe replied, his tone full of unsettling aloofness.

"Well you oughtta think so," Bobby challenged. "I intend to see that every charge in the books is thrown at you."

"The way I see it, Bobby," Joe interrupted, "if you press charges, then the whole ugly story will come out—every last stinken detail. And if it does, I don't think there's a person in the county who would begrudge me for one minute."

"Y'all hush up back there," the deputy ordered as he entered the car.

He pointed a long, fat finger at Joe through the rearview mirror. "You can count on facen charges," he said. "Cassie and Butch already said they want 'em filed."

Mack cast an imposing impression, despite his stiff-necked approach to the sit-uation. He wore a large brown hat, a permanent scowl and a resounding aura of authority. Joe obeyed his order, still confident he could force Bobby to persuade the Griffins to drop all charges, assuming he had an opportunity alone with his foe. The opportunity came at the hospital, where Mack needed several seconds to walk around the car and open Bobby's door.

"Bobby, you listen to me and listen good," Joe demanded, speaking quickly as soon as Mack exited the car. "You or no one else better file any charges against me. If my daddy finds out what you did to Luke, he'll beat you a whole lot worse than I did. And I wouldn't doubt there'd be a long line of other fellows right behind him—waiten for a turn of their own."

The back door opened, and the deputy ordered Bobby from the car before he responded to Joe. Still, Joe was confident of having made his point.

Bobby realized his dilemma, too. He never should have entangled himself in the skirmish between Wayne and Luke in the first place. Had he left well enough alone, Wayne would have pulverized the boy, and the matter would have been settled. But Bobby's ego had craved more than mere defeat for the Baker boy. He had wanted Luke to experience feelings of failure and worthlessness, to know the disappointed heart of a loser. In the final outcome, he had gotten what he wanted, however pain-ful the ending was. While correctly assuming Luke would keep the secret safe from Matt, Bobby had failed to consider the possibility the boy would confide in his older brother. He could not afford an even bigger mistake by risking the episode to public exposure, simply to see Joe suffer.

"Come on and get out of the car," the deputy growled, impatient with Bobby's slow exit.

Joe and Bobby glowered at one another, like two gladiators who had just fought a battle rigged for only one outcome. Bobby knew he had been licked in the arena as well as in the back room, so he accepted defeat. He would have another opportunity to play the game, and the next outcome might be predicated on terms dictated by himself. Leaving Joe with a sneer, he stepped from the patrol car.

"Deputy," he said without even glancing at the lawman. "Is there a phone around here I could use before see'en the doctor? It's important."

"No problem," Mack grunted. "They'll fix you up inside."

"By the way," Bobby added, "I won't be pressen charges."

Those were the last words Joe heard before the door slammed shut.

———

Paul Berrien ran a tidy county. The Cookville jail rarely held prisoners, excepting the occasional drunkard, wife beater and men involved in disputes similar to the one between Joe and Bobby. It was a narrow, three-story, red-brick building, with a hanging gallows on the top floor. No one had swung from the gallows since the turn of the century, but the swing door still worked. Knotted oak trees shaded the jail by day, cloaked the building in darkness at night and fanned a few nightmares among prisoners in the dreary cells.

By the time the patrol car reached the jailhouse, Joe had sobered considerably and was trying to figure out how he could return to his car. The hour was late, and he hoped to avoid entangling his family in the situation.

Deputy Mack accompanied him into the front room, ordered Joe to sit and disappeared into an official-looking office. The deputy apparently forgot the handcuffs, which were biting into Joe's wrists. Joe sat on a worn office couch, waiting for his release.

In a few minutes, an inner office door opened, and the dispatcher emerged. Joe recognized the skinny young man with thick black glasses as Donald Peavy, a lifelong resident of Cookville, who had been a year behind Joe in school. Donald Peavy personified the pompous, self-centered, overbearing ways of the small-town people who looked down on country folk like Joe. Even worse, Donald tended to be patronizing with his sentiments. While he had never condescended to Joe, Donald had once dismissed the Carter's Mercantile as a "country-bumpkin operation with an awful and gaudy glass display of what's supposed to be fine treasures."

Joe had been glad that Tom had not overheard the remark, and he had crossed Donald Peavy off a mental list of people to pity because they wanted so desperately to be popular. Joe reserved the list for people with good hearts and good intentions, who needed their confidence boosted, not their egos stroked.

"By George, it is the Joe Baker I know," Donald remarked. "It just goes to show: Once a rooster, always a rooster." He winked at Joe. "I always thought you were too smart to get yourself into this kind of trouble," he added.

Joe kept mum.

"Oh, well, don't worry too much," Donald advised. "Cassie Griffin called a few minutes ago. Said she and her husband talked it over and decided not to press charges."

"Cassie called and said what!" Mack asked as he emerged from the office with fingerprinting equipment and a small camera.

"She said to let him go with a warnen this time around—and to tell him to keep away from their place," Donald explained. "You're a lucky one, Joe. I don't ever recall the Griffins deciden not to press charges."

Mack eyed Joe suspiciously, hating to waste good paperwork. "Somethen's fishy," he declared. "Cassie was hell-bent on assault and destruction of property when I was out there."

Pausing, he followed his reasoning with a direct question to Joe. "What were you and Bobby talken about in the car? What made you so cocky about not facen charges?"

"Nothen of consequence," Joe replied. "If there are no charges against me, may I go?"

"I want to know what you were talken about," the deputy declared. "Seems strange to have that much talken between two people who were at each other's throats moments earlier."

"We were just haven words," Joe said. "It wasn't important."

Mack sighed heavily. "Peavy!" he said. "Give the sheriff a call. Tell him we have a situation and need his help to sort through it. All this sounds mighty peculiar to me."

Any leftover semblance of bravado disappeared in Joe. His heart swapped places with his stomach. He had hoped desperately to keep Paul Berrien out of the matter, dreading the embarrassment it would cause, fearing it would create a conflict of interest. To make matters worse, the deputy abruptly decided Joe should spend the next few minutes locked in a jell cell. The only worse possibility was the specter of his family discovering the events of this night.

As Donald Peavy led him to the cell, Joe had a terrible feeling of having lost control of his life. And he wondered briefly whether Luke would judge his big brother very smart if he could see him now.

––––––––

"Can you take off the handcuffs?" Joe asked when the cell door swung open.

"I don't have a key, but I'll tell Mack to come back and get them off you," Donald said, motioning his prisoner inside the steel bars. "Sorry about this, Joe," he added, sounding anything but.

Ignoring the gloat in the jailer's voice, Joe strode into the cell, trying to feign indifference as the steel door slammed behind him. He inspected the temporary arrangements wordlessly, waiting for Donald to exit, grateful that none of the other three cells were occupied. The cell had a sink and a commode, along with two stationary single beds, which contained thin rubber mattresses. He tested the mattress, then took to pacing in the tiny cage.

Joe supposed he should have used the opportunity to reflect on his motives, questioning whether he had erred in judgment. His mind was clear, however, and he had no regrets. Bobby Taylor had received everything he deserved. On second thought, the only thing he would have done differently was to have dragged Bobby to the parking lot before pounding the man.

The outer door opened again, and Donald came through it. He snapped his fingers. "I keep forgetten about those handcuffs, Joe," he said. "I'll get Mack. First, I wanted to let you know that I called your folks. I didn't want them worried about you."

"You didn't," Joe said in disbelief, gripping the cell door, pressing his face against the bars.

"Sure, I did," Donald said, grinning. "There's no tellen how long you're gonna be here. They needed to know."

Joe tightened his grip on the bars. "How considerate of you," he remarked flatly. "Thanks for your concern."

"You're welcome," Donald replied on his way out the door.

Joe checked his watch. It was well after midnight. The call would have woken up the whole house.

He plopped down on the couch, imagining the jangled nerves that would have taken flight with the late telephone call. Springing from their beds, their first fears would have been that Summer or he had been in a car wreck. Then, realizing that Summer had been home for almost two hours, they would prepare themselves for the worst—that Joe was dead or dying.

The one thing Joe could not imagine was his family's reaction to the news that he was in jail. He shook his head and waited.

———

Paul Berrien arrived at the jail a short time later. He listened to Mack explain the situation, then chastised the deputy for failing to release Joe. "When all the principles have agreed not to file charges, Mack, we don't have the right to hold somebody in jail just because you think somethen is fishy. You should have let him go. Since I'm here, though, I'll talk to him."

Paul found Joe slumped over on the cot. Joe had dozed off, sleep coming as the aftermath of too much beer and the lateness of the hour. He looked a mess, with bright bloodstains on his shirt and dark circles under his eyes. He smelled even worse, like a stale brewery.

A sympathetic pain tugged at Paul. As much as possible, Paul and his sisters doted on the Baker offspring, having realized many years earlier that the sons and daughters of Matt and Caroline were the closest they would come to caring for children of their own. In a way, Paul considered this moment an opportunity to have an important father-son talk with Joe

"Now this is a surprise," he began, opening the cell.

Joe's eyes popped open, clearly confused for a moment before focusing on Paul. He roused to an upright position on the cot, feeling the humiliation of his predicament like a balloon in the pit of his stomach, yet finding courage in the unassuming eyes of his father's best friend.

"I can't begin to tell you how embarrassed I am about all this," he replied.

"We all have moments we try to forget," Paul suggested.

"I don't think I'll ever be able to forget this one," Joe said miserably. "Your dispatcher called the house and let everyone know I was locked up down here."

Paul grimaced. "Now I really don't envy you," he said, mustering up a smile, then a frown at the handcuffs. "Sorry about the handcuffs. Mack gets carried away sometimes, but he's my best deputy. And Donald's very efficient with the office work."

He walked out of the cell to the hall door. "Mack!" he shouted. "Come back here and take off these handcuffs."

"Can't say I won't be glad to see them go," Joe muttered as Paul re-entered the cell.

Paul gave his young friend a warm smile, then pressed for details about the situation. "Joe, there's nothen in the law books that says you have to tell me what happened tonight or why you did what you did to Bobby," he began. "But I am mighty curious. This is unlike you, son. I have to figure you must've had a powerful reason to go after the man."

"Paul, I respect you enormously, and the truth is I'd like to tell you why," Joe replied. "In a way, I think it's somethen you should know, and maybe I'm maken a mistake keepen it to myself. But I have my reasons for stayen silent. My instincts tell me that's the best course for everybody concerned, at least for the time be'en."

"I can respect your reasons for wanten privacy, so I won't press you any further," the sheriff replied. "If you ever decide we need to talk, though ...."

"I won't hesitate to come see you," Joe finished the sentence for him. "In this particular case, you'd probably be the first person I'd go to, Paul. Honestly, though, I think it's a moot point at this time, so let's just leave it at that."

Paul gave the young man an obliging look of acceptance, admiring Joe's frankness. Few people had the wherewithal to be less than candid, without distorting the truth in the process. Still, he wanted to impress the seriousness of the situation.

"We'll do that," he said. "But Joe, I will say this: You need to understand that this whole mess could have blown up in your face. If somebody had pressed charges, you'd be in deep trouble. Next time you're in a similar situation, give it careful consideration before you act on an impulse."

"There was nothen impulsive about what I did, Paul," Joe replied honestly. "I did exactly what I meant to do to Bobby, and I won't apologize for that. Nevertheless, your point's well taken, and I appreciate the concern."

"You do have me curious about what inspired all this," Paul said with a smile, firmly patting Joe's shoulder to show the matter was settled as far as he was concerned.

At that moment, the hall door opened, and Mack entered the cellblock followed by Matt.

Although Matt appeared unperturbed, his calm demeanor failed to conceal the fury in his nearly black eyes. In moments of sheer anger, Matt's used his eyes to convey his feelings. He narrowed them slightly, ascertaining his position, then penetrating to the core like a drill.

As he came into the cellblock, Matt scanned the area, narrowed his focus to Joe's cell, then zeroed in on his son before casting a long glance at the handcuffs.

Unable to bear the scrutiny, Joe climbed to his feet, looking downward while the deputy removed the restraints.

No one said anything until Mack left the area and the door closed behind them. Finally, Joe forced himself to face his father, bracing for the inevitable first question by cracking his knuckles.

The popping joints infuriated Matt, who ground his teeth to keep from lashing out at his son.

"I hope you have a good excuse," Matt said finally, his voice even and straightforward. "But first, I want to know exactly what happened. Who did you fight?"

Joe hesitated, then answered, "Bobby Taylor."

"Bobby Taylor!" Matt muttered with disgust. "What on earth for?"

"Luke told me about the fight between Wayne and him," Joe explained. "I thought the odds were uneven, and I figured Bobby was the real culprit one way or another."

Matt already had revealed the details of the previous week's incident to Paul, so the revelation came as no surprise to the sheriff. He had guessed the fight triggered Joe. Still, many unanswered questions remained as to why Joe had taken it upon himself to jump into the middle of a dispute between two boys, even if one of them was the equal of a man in strength, while the other was pint-sized.

"There's got be more to it than that," Matt coaxed his son. "Tell me the rest."

"Nothen else to tell, Daddy," Joe replied. "Wayne Taylor pounded Luke pretty good, and Bobby didn't do anything to stop it. I thought he deserved to know firsthand what it's like when the fight's not fair."

"I think he got the message," Paul interjected.

Joe smiled briefly, then became serious again because his father was not amused by Paul's attempt to lighten the situation.

"I didn't mean for it to go this far, Daddy," he said, "and I'm sorry for embarrassen the family."

"Save the apologies for when you get home," Matt instructed, regarding his son with a quizzical stare.

"Yes, sir."

"Son, you didn't do any of this on my account, did you?" Matt asked.

"No, sir," Joe answered firmly. "I know you can fight your own battles."

"But you're not tellen me everything, are you?" Matt asked abruptly.

"Everything that matters," Joe said.

Matt glanced at Paul, who shrugged, suggesting the situation did not warrant further inquiry. Reluctantly, Matt agreed.

"I would have preferred the full story, Joe," he said, "but I'll trust your judgment." Turning to Paul, he asked, "Is he free to go?"

"He's a free man," the sheriff replied. "He should have been released as soon as he was brought in. I apologize for the mistake in procedure, Joe."

"I'm just sorry you got dragged out of the house for all of this, Paul," Matt said before Joe could respond. "Maybe we can all go home and get a good night's sleep."

"Sounds good to me," Paul replied as he led them from the cell. "I'll see the two of y'all tomorrow—maybe at church in the mornen."

"This one needs to be there," Matt said, gesturing to Joe, "but he may not need a sermon by the time his mama and granny get through with him."

The two older men laughed, but Joe failed to see the humor in the situation.

———

A father did not punish his adult son, and Matt never considered such a thing. He still remembered the search for good times in his own youth, drinking too much and doing things he later regretted. As a young man, Matt had been far from upright. As a soldier and later as a young father, he had strayed even farther from proper behavior.

Liquor had tested Matt in his younger days, especially after the war ended and Joe was born. Fortunately, Caroline had put her foot down, issued an ultimatum and Matt had seen the light in time to spare his family heartache. The transformation had not come overnight, of course. For a long while, he had continued to drink beer from time to time, even took a swig of whiskey on certain occasions. Long before Bonnie was born, however, Matt came to the realization that he was one of those men who should avoid alcohol.

Now, the thought crossed his mind that he should share the benefit of his experience with his oldest son on their drive home. The words failed Matt, however, as did his courage. A perfect father might have offered good advice, but Matt was the first to admit he had paternal flaws.

Besides, Matt also knew that any advice he offered would play second fiddle to Joe's own form of self-discipline. No one was harder on the boy than himself.

With other people's shortcomings, Joe showed great tolerance, responding with patience, understanding and help when and where it was needed. He gave encouragement instead of pity, offered advice instead of answers, expected progress instead of perfection. With regards to himself, however, Joe eliminated some of the key elements of his tolerance. He expected himself to do the right thing, and he set exacting standards. If he failed to measure up to his or anyone else's expectations, Joe made amends where possible, then wrote his own prescription for comeuppance and took the medicine.

Matt attributed his quirky behavior to Caroline's influence. Caroline strove for perfection and fretted when she fell short of the mark. Over the years, however, his wife had come to an important understanding with herself. Some things mattered more than others, and Caroline had drawn the fine line between perfection and pickiness. She crossed that line rarely, only when the situation warranted an extra step.

Joe was still finding his way, aided immensely by his propensity for taking the reasonable route whenever possible. Still, when his way was difficult, the distinction between high self-expectations and impossible self-demands blurred. Sometimes, Joe got hung up on his mistakes. Usually, he made all the right moves.

Matt sensed this was one of those occasions when his son would right himself, take his punishment and move on without too much hesitation.

As it was, Matt was in a forgiving and understanding mood. Bobby Taylor boiled his blood, too. Still, Matt expected complete honesty from his children. While guilty himself of resorting to them on occasion, half-truths bothered Matt. He acknowledged that the search for the truth sometimes required compromise, but Joe had failed to demonstrate a compelling need for any concessions.

Matt believed his son was withholding a critical piece of information in this business with the Taylors and Luke.

Like Joe tonight, Luke had been nearly as evasive in his description of the altercation between the Taylors and himself. Obviously, the boy had been more forthcoming with his oldest brother. What had Luke shared with Joe that he refused to tell his father? Perhaps this missing piece of information explained Luke's bratty, bumbling behavior over the past few days.

Recalling his conversation with Luke in the schoolyard, Matt remembered feeling as if he should have pressed for more details. Sensing the boy's reluctance, Matt had settled for something less than a full explanation of the incident. Maybe he should have asked the one question that had been on his mind but remained unspoken: Had Bobby Taylor hurt his son in any way?

He fleetingly considered asking that question of Joe, dismissing the idea at once. The question would be unfair to Joe, to Luke, to the values Matt and Caroline had tried to instill in their children.

As a father, though, Matt had the responsibility to protect his children. If they were in danger, he wanted, needed and expected to know the full situation when at all possible.

He lit a cigarette, then told Joe, "The day Luke and Wayne fought, I had a feelen that somethen else happened, somethen Luke felt he couldn't tell me. Now I'm thinken you know what that is, Joe. I won't ask you to tell me everything that happened, or to break any promise you made to your brother. But, son, I am goen to ask you to let me know if I have any more cause for concern—if for nothen else than to ease my mind on this matter."

It was a loaded question, and Joe delayed his answer, lighting a cigarette as he developed a response. Joe believed the matter was settled for the moment. While he had some serious doubts about Bobby's mental stability, Joe also believed Luke faced no further danger.

"It's over and done with, Daddy," he replied finally, "or at least it's finished as much as anything is ever finished with Bobby Taylor. Rest easy. Don't worry about Luke."

Matt bit his lip. "If you say so," he said at length. "I'll trust your judgment."

———

As Matt and Joe bumped along the last stretch of dirt road in the pickup, the security light in front of their house came into view. Normally, the lamp's glow shone brighter, but a full moon had stolen some of its luster tonight. Joe felt kind of like that light, although it was impossible to blame his paled image on any natural occurrence.

As Granny often said when severe mistakes had been made, he had made his bed of roses. Now he would have to lie in it. Or as Grandpa said—when his mood was sincere and there was no trace of humor in his thoughts—the time had come for Joe to face the music and march into the cannon fire.

Joe dreaded the prospect of facing his family. He could explain the fight with Bobby Taylor. He could even persuade them to see the funny side of having been thrown in jail. But nothing he might ever say or do would make Caroline and Rachel understand about the Tip-Toe Inn.

Had he merely gone out and gotten himself into trouble while drinking alcohol, his mother and grandmother would have expressed grave disappointment and reprimanded him sharply. They also would have accepted his mistake, however, and Joe would have found forgiveness in their hearts.

To Caroline and Rachel, however, the Tip-Toe Inn represented a little bit of Sodom and Gomorrah right in the midst of their community. They despised the place. If misfortune befell a person in the Tip-Toe Inn, it was tit for tat. The two women had little sympathy for people who danced in the devil's den itself. They would make no exceptions for one of their own.

The sight of his mother pacing on the front porch confirmed Joe's worst fears as the pickup rolled to a stop in the yard. He sat in the truck for a minute, trying to find either a brave face or the true courage to accept her disappointment. Finally, his father mumbled something, the truck door opened and he prepared to face the inevitable.

Exiting the truck, he followed Matt up the concrete walkway, finding some consolation in the dark windows. At the worst, he would have to explain his actions only to Caroline, at least as far as this night was concerned. A good night's sleep, he decided, would allow him to function better when he faced everyone else.

Coming to the top porch step, Joe finally looked at his mother, honoring her with his most shamed expression. Her reaction was exactly as he anticipated. If Matt unknowingly revealed anger through his eyes, Caroline betrayed her rage with her mouth and nose. Her lips pursed, and her nostrils flared. Sometimes, she also tapped one foot nervously. At the moment, she seemed like a cow ready to charge.

The only saving grace was when Caroline twirled her wedding ring, a sign that his mother would reserve final judgment until she had heard all the facts. Currently, the golden band was whirling at double-time RPMs, giving Joe one last glimmer of hope.

He decided then for an aggressive approach to the situation. He would run into the battle instead of wait for the slaughter.

The up-front, free admission from Joe that there was no excuse for his behavior doused some of the fire in Caroline. His quick confession that tonight was not the first time he had frequented the roadhouse becalmed red-hot embers. His sincere apology left only the smoldering smell of smoke.

Caroline did not expect perfection of her children. Furthermore, she believed only imbeciles would hope for such a thing. The last years between youth and adulthood were fraught with seduction. Few people managed to avoid all of the temptations. Boys were particularly susceptible to wild ways, especially the sons of Matt Baker.

Caroline figured marriage had helped her avoid flirtation with the wilder whims of youth. Matt had found the path more treacherous to negotiate, and Joe was finding some seductions hard to resist, too. Caroline was not overly worried. If Joe followed his father's footsteps, he would become a good man. Still, the time had come for a course correction.

For some months now, Caroline had known Joe drank beer and maybe even whiskey. She first suspected the drinking late one night when he fumbled with the door. On another occasion, he had tripped coming up the porch steps, cursing and burping almost simultaneously. Caroline had started to nudge Matt from a deep sleep so he could check on their son, then changed her mind. Joe had carried around a hangover the next day, which he blamed on a bad headache. Later, she had smelled beer on his clothes when washing them.

Even as the evidence of drinking mounted against Joe, Caroline had held her reprimands. She understood he had to discover the allure of the world for himself. However, she also expected some sense of morality and decency to govern his actions along the way. Judging by his tawdry behavior, Joe obviously needed a stern reminder of these expectations. Caroline was ready to give it to him.

"It goes without sayen, Joe, that I'm extremely disappointed in you," she began when her son had given a complete explanation of his behavior and answered all of her questions. "I never once suspected you were goen into a common roadhouse and doen Lord knows what.

"None of us lead perfect lives, son," she continued. "It's impossible, especially when you sow some wild oats along the way. But there's a limit on the excesses to be taken from common decency. And, Joe, you have exceeded that limit tonight and every other night you've walked out of this house, gone to that tavern and come back with beer and whiskey in you. Your daddy and I will not tolerate that kind of behavior, or embarrassment and disgrace to our family."

Here, Caroline paused to give her boy an opportunity to consider the situation. Respect showed in his eyes. She had his full attention.

"You're a grown man, son," she continued, "and a good man, too—a few nights notwithstanden. It's up to you to choose the kind of life you will lead, Joe. But your daddy and I are still raisen children in this house, and I will not have them exposed to vulgar behavior. As long as you live in this house, you are expected to live by the morals and values your daddy, your grandparents and I have set for this family. If the time ever comes when you don't feel you can do that, then pack your bags and leave."

The finality stunned Joe as well as Matt. Caroline could tell her husband especially was irked with her. Still, she wanted Joe to understand her dim view of tonight's situation and his past extremes. In Caroline's opinion, mere disapproval lasted only until the next great temptation arrived. She wanted Joe to think more than twice the next time he considered a stunt like this one.

Joe scratched his ear, looked down at his feet and waited to see what else his mother had to say.

"Do we have an understanden?" Caroline asked.

"Yes, Mama," Joe said, smiling slightly.

"Good," she replied. "Now, I'm goen to bed. It's late, and tomorrow's a church Sunday. I'll expect you to be there with us."

"Yes, ma'am."

———

Joe picked his way through his brothers' dark room, nearly tripping on a pair of jeans and sneakers that had been left on the floor. Walking between the two beds, which flanked the entrance to his own niche in the house, Joe groped for the doorknob, found it and escaped into the privacy of his room. Shutting the door, he crossed over to his desk, flipped on a lamp and discovered all of his siblings piled on the single bed.

He groaned and turned around to empty his pockets on the desk. "Good news sure does travel fast," he muttered.

"Were you really in jail?" Bonnie asked, her voice full of disbelief, yet tinged with excitement.

"I was," Joe replied.

"What the heck happened?" Summer asked.

Joe sighed, wishing they would leave, knowing he had to offer an explanation. "The short version," he said. "I went to the Tip-Toe Inn tonight and had a little run-in with somebody. We argued. I hit him, and someone called a deputy who hauled me off to Cookville and put me in jail. Fortunately, no charges were filed, so I'm a free man. Now, if you please, I'd appreciate it if you guys would get the heck off my bed and let me go to sleep. It's late, and we have church tomorrow."

"Sounds like you'd better pay close attention to the sermon," Carrie teased.

"You're right, Carrie," Joe shot back. "I'd better pay close attention. Now get out!" No one moved.

"Who'd you hit?" John asked.

Joe sat down in his chair and untied his shoes.

"Bobby Taylor," he answered at last, kicking off first one shoe, then the other.

His siblings were sufficiently shocked into silence.

"How on earth did you get mixed up with him?" Summer asked finally.

Joe saw Luke tense around the shoulders. "It was just one of those things," he said. "I'm not goen to explain it."

Everyone took him at his word.

"Were you drinken?" John asked a moment later.

"I've already covered that with Mama and Daddy," he replied.

"Well, were you?" John persisted.

"I had a few beers," Joe confessed.

"I think you've been doen too much of that lately," John observed.

Joe eyed Summer with suspicion.

"I haven't said anything to anybody," she said defensively. "Face it, Joe. You should be more careful with your wine and women."

Turning back to John, Joe said, "As I said, I've already covered that subject with Mama and Daddy." He took off his socks, then asked no one in particular, "Do Granny and Grandpa know anything about this?"

"The phone woke up everybody," Bonnie informed him.

"Granny's fit to be tied, but Grandpa told her she'd survive the scandal," Carrie explained.

"You know Grandpa with his, 'This, too, shall pass,'" Summer added.

"What did you mean by that crack about wine and women," John suddenly asked his oldest sister.

"Hey!" Joe said crossly. "This is not the time to pick apart my life."

"Has Tom ever gone with you to that place," Summer inquired, narrowing her eyes.

"Ask Tom!" Joe said, taking off the white shirt, now carrying dried bloodstains. "Get out of here, will you?"

"I *will* ask him," Summer said sharply. "Do you want me to soak that shirt in cold water for you?"

"No, I do not want you to soak it in cold water," Joe replied, exasperated by the conversation. "I'm gonna throw it away."

"Well, that's just plain ridiculous," Summer retorted. "A little cold water will take those stains right out of there. It'll be good as new."

Joe threw the shirt at his sister. "Then take it and soak it in cold water," he said slowly. "What is it with you people tonight? Can't you take a hint? I want y'all to leave. I want to go to bed."

"This is exciten stuff, Joe," Summer said. "It's not every day that a member of the family gets himself arrested and carted off to jail. We're in the middle of a full-fledged scandal, and you don't seem to have any interest in it at all. Do you realize all the gossip this will generate?"

Joe laughed, rubbing his face.

"I suppose you'll have a hangover tomorrow," Bonnie remarked.

"Of course not," Summer replied for Joe. "He'll simply have a bad headache."

Joe gave up any hopes of persuading them to abide by his wishes, half wondering whether he had stepped into the twilight zone. He slipped off his blue jeans, then unceremoniously dumped enough siblings from his bed to make room for himself. "Get off my sheet, Bonnie!" he commanded crossly.

"Do you have a thing about taken off your pants in front of everybody?" Carrie asked.

"Just in front of girls, I think," Summer said innocently, rekindling John's interest in the conversation.

"I still want to know about the women, Joe," he said. "What gives?"

"Gee whiz, John!" Summer shot back. "Can't you make those hormones of yours pipe down?"

"I'm just curious," John said.

"I know what you're curious about, little brother," Summer replied sharply. "You men are all alike."

Tired as he was, even Joe could not resist the temptation to seek further clarification on that remark. "How's that, Summer?" he asked.

Summer crossed her arms, thought a moment, then answered, "You all want to have your cake, and you want to eat it to."

"What does cake have to do with it?" John prodded with a hint of mischief in his eyes.

"Do I have to spell it out for you, brainless wonders?" Summer replied, growing testy.

"Spell it out," John challenged.

"Yeah," Joe agreed. "Please do."

"Okay!" Summer said loudly. "Men want everything—the perfect girl, sex before marriage, a virgin in their wedden bed. Half of them want to charm the pants off every girl they meet, and the other half just wants the pants off without wasten any time on the charm."

"That's disgusten, Summer!" Carrie remarked.

"I agree," Bonnie said, still with obvious wonder. Then, without realizing it, she asked, "Is Tom that way?"

"Tom is perfect," Summer replied.

"Sounds like the voice of experience speaken," John suggested.

"You wouldn't know experience if it slapped you in the face, John," Summer said.

"Enough!" Joe interrupted. "No more of this," he ordered. "If Mama and Daddy hear a single word of this, they'll think I've corrupted the whole bunch of you. I mean this now: Once and for all, get out of here."

"But you still haven't told us about the Tip-Toe Inn," John protested.

"And I'm not goen to," Joe said. "Out!"

"We're just interested because we love you, Joe," Summer remarked airily. "We're concerned about your well-be'en."

"Then you most certainly understand why my sleep is so important," Joe said, pointing to the door. "Goodnight everyone."

Grumbling, they acquiesced to his will, filing out one by one until only Luke was left. "What really happened, Joe?" he asked, obviously worried about the situation.

"Everything is fine," Joe responded, giving the boy a gruff smile and tousling his hair. "Go to sleep, little brother. Forget about Bobby Taylor and his son. They won't be messen with you anymore."

Luke nodded, rising from the bed at last. At the door, he stopped, turned and asked, "Was it much of a fight?"

"What do you think?" Joe asked with a smile.

Luke grinned. "I bet you beat him good."

Joe nodded. "I had a good incentive," he replied.

Luke returned the nod. "Sleep well, Joe."

"Goodnight, Luke."

AUGUST ARRIVED WITH NOTHING to distinguish it, except a new page on the calendar, soon stained with sweat and grime. By then, the land was burned, like a fine piece of meat cooked until nothing was left but grit. Still, for an empty stomach, that charred residue was as bitterly satisfying as it was tough—sustenance until proper nourishment was available.

For two weeks, Bobby Taylor spent the days on his rickety front porch swing, dumping the care of his useless fields on his wife and sons. Not much work was required, so Bobby had no qualms about putting undue hardship on his family. He went into a silent retreat, swilling beer, contemplating the unfairness of life, resenting the heat and plotting his revenge on anyone and everyone who had wronged him over the years. Mostly, however, he looked for new opportunities.

All his life, Bobby had fought for acceptance among the larger society. As a youngster, he had sought the admiration of other young boys. Becoming a young man, he had desired girls to think him handsome and charming. As an adult, he had wanted to lead others with his ideas. No matter which way he turned, however, Bobby found only grudging acceptance of his ways and attitudes. His best laid plans fell by the wayside, repeatedly foiled by smart alecks like Paul Berrien, Matt Baker and, now, even Joe Baker.

Some of this, Bobby had begun to realize when he lost the sheriff's election to Paul in 1964. But as he recuperated from the beating administered by the respectable Joe Baker, Bobby came to full grips with the fact that he would never win the respect he deserved—at least not from the larger elements of society. He understood at last that he would have to thrive among a smaller, more cliquish group of people.

Bobby considered himself smart, his aptitude tarnished only by a penchant for sudden, irrational decisions—primarily because he often misjudged people. Over the years, he had come across too many people who claimed to feel one way, yet failed to follow through on their promises when the moment of truth arrived. Overall, people obviously were confused as well as reluctant to declare their true allegiances and interests, which explained why Bobby continually misconstrued their feelings. If he could work within the framework of people who felt exactly as he did, Bobby reasoned he could feel the winds of success.

When he woke one morning to find his shattered nose had returned to its normal size, Bobby moved to put his plan into action.

The Ku Klux Klan had sparked fervent imagination in Bobby on numerous occasions. Yet, while he curried favor with its members, Bobby never considered joining the organization. He heard strange things about KKK members. And quite honestly, he felt uncomfortable with the Klan's ceremonial crap. The whole idea of grown men parading around in bed sheets was ludicrous.

In addition to his private misgivings about the organization, Klan membership also would have destroyed Bobby's hopes of winning full-fledged public support. Now that he had given up on the public, however, Bobby looked forward to becoming a Klansman. He envisioned himself rising quickly through the ranks of leadership, becoming a most reverend imperial grand dragon wizard and commanding the undying devotion of a whole army of hooded warriors who shared his passions and beliefs.

At seven o'clock on a Monday morning, Bobby placed a long-distance telephone call to the wizard of the closest klavern. Adjusting the story to suit his needs, Bobby wove an outlandish tale of rebellious niggers and white nigger lovers running amok in his beloved county. He began with the details of Wayne's run-in with Lucas Bartholomew, briefly mentioned his son's skirmish with Luke Baker and ended with Joe's vicious attack on himself. At times, he made vague references to Martin Luther King Jr., Mississippi, the Voting Rights Act, the NAACP, the ACLU, communists, Selma and recent race riots in New Jersey and Detroit. Bobby's knowledge of these things was sketchy, but the mere mention of them commanded Wizard Ralph Johnson's utmost attention. In a matter of minutes, the Klan leader was convinced that Cookville was primed for agitation and recruitment.

By Tuesday afternoon, Ralph Johnson had organized a parade through Cookville followed by a rally at the house of the Klan's newest recruit, Bobby. Ralph swore the event would become the focal point of the Klan's late summer activities. He predicted the state's most influential Klansman, the imperial grand wizard himself, would attend the festivities in Cookville.

"We'll burn a cross, maybe even scare a few coons," Ralph Johnson vowed. "You don't know what fun is, Bobby, until you've spent a few hours with a few good Klansmen. We're just a bunch of good-ole boys who love a good time."

When Bobby hung up the telephone, his head was swimming with anticipation.

Word of the impending KKK appearance spread quickly through the community. Bobby worked the county like a politician, drumming up support among friends, calling in all favors and putting ideas into the heads of those who stood on the edge of the fence.

Winds of success swirled, blowing a cool breeze in Bobby's direction, despite the heat of the moment.

———

Paul Berrien spent the week prior to the Saturday Klan rally trying to assuage the rising fears of the colored community. The Klan had never been active in their county, so most people had no experience to reflect upon in their consideration of the upcoming spectacle. But they were familiar with the Klan's legacy of intimidation and violence. For every true story told about the Klan, a dozen others swirled.

Exaggeration was not needed. The truth was frightening enough. The Klan lynched people, beat them beyond recognition, tarred and feathered them on occasion. Many innocent people had been whipped by the Klan, others blown apart by their bombs.

"Desperate, Dreadful, Desolate, Doleful, Dismal, Deadly and Dark," read a pamphlet circulated through the colored section of town. "Those are the seven days of the Klan Kalendar. On which day will they call for you?"

As soon as he read the pamphlet, Paul began preparing for the worst.

———

Saturday arrived, dawning hotter than usual and pushing the thermometer past the century mark shortly after the sun stood straight up in the cloudless sky. The heat came in waves, each hotter than the last. People drank gallons of iced tea, found a shady spot and attempted to keep their wits about them. The Cookville hospital treated two people for sunstroke, and an eighty-eight-year-old woman died from heat exhaustion.

"She had a fan runnen in her house, but all it did was churn hot air," Paul told his sisters when he came home for a bite to eat in the early afternoon. "The poor old lady literally cooked to death."

It was the hottest day of the year, and Paul hoped the heat would make people too lazy to care about the Klan. But he watched with keen anticipation and preparation, fearing the heat wave was an omen of an ill wind to come, which would bring out the worst in good people.

"Things could be worse," he told his best deputy, Mack, shortly before the rally was scheduled to begin. "At least we don't have a full moon to contend with tonight. Even sane people act crazy on a full moon."

"Unfortunately, we're not dealen with sane people today," Mack replied.

The rally was planned for late in the day to catch the many shoppers who filled the town on Saturday afternoons. As the final hour approached, Cookville took on a carnival atmosphere, with curious onlookers and willing participants shuffling about, anticipating the thrill of adventure or at least a welcome change from their humdrum days.

Even the black community failed to resist the temptation to see things for themselves. Ignoring the advice of Paul Berrien, who had personally visited every home, shanty and shack in the colored section of town, they swamped one corner of the town square.

Shortly after five o'clock, the distant sounds of automobile horns reached the courthouse square, and the town came to a standstill. The blaring horns grew louder, reaching a crescendo when all at once, a white pickup truck decked out in the Stars and Bars of the Confederacy rounded the northwest corner. The truck began a swift sweep through the streets, reckless, wanton and defiant. A dozen more trucks and cars joined the caravan, packed with about forty men, women and children, many wearing the Klan's official regalia, white robes and cone-shaped hats. The Klansmen waved their flags, blew their automobile horns, cheered and jeered the gathering of blacks on the northeast corner of the square.

All decked out in his new Klan costume, Bobby Taylor rode in the bed of the lead pickup truck. He smiled broadly, waving to family and friends, swelling with self-importance. On either side of him were Ralph Johnson and Larry Lester, the imperial grand wizard of the Invisible Knights of the Ku Klux Klan in Georgia. Bobby reckoned this was the most important day of his life, the beginning of a tremendous future that would lead him to glory.

The vast majority of the crowd failed to share Bobby's enthusiasm for this invasion of their town. As quickly as the first truck hurdled into their vision, most everyone's curiosity was chilled by the specter of these robed warriors coming together to share their hate. Their nearness to this fraternity of hatemongers with a mob mentality haunted some of Cookville's finest citizens. Many walked away from the freakish disgrace, berating themselves for having come in the first place. Most people, however, simply marveled at the abomination of it all, keeping their place, unable to escape the charms of their ghoulish voyeurism. Sheer boredom kept a few people there as well, while several onlookers howled approval as the cavalcade of Klansmen paraded around the square.

"Not too much rattles me in this world," Paul Berrien told his best deputy as they watched the parading Klansmen. "But this—this must have been what it was like on Calvary when they crucified Christ."

"It's disgusten, ain't it?" Mack replied. "I admit to haven my own prejudices from time to time. But these people are pathetic—the worst of the whole lot."

The procession circled three times around the square before the trucks ground to a halt beneath a sprawling live oak tree on the courthouse lawn. Klansmen leapt from the trucks and spilled out of the cars, scattering through the crowd, handing out leaflets and pumping handshakes.

In the bed of the head truck, Imperial Grand Dragon Larry Lester offered one final piece of advice to Bobby before giving him the megaphone. "Show them you care and are concerned about what's happenen in your community," he encouraged. "Tell them that's why you invited us here today. Speak clearly, but keep your voice low enough so everyone has to strain a little to hear you. People pay more attention when they have to work hard to hear what they want. And whatever you do, Klansmen Taylor, don't mention the bloody niggers. I'll handle that part of the program."

The imperial grand wizard handed Bobby the megaphone, nodded encouragement and pushed his newest recruit onto the back of a dog cage that was serving as a raised podium. For an awful moment as he faced friends and neighbors, Bobby smelled failure. His throat was dry, and he feared he was too nervous to speak.

He glanced again at Larry Lester, who only minutes ago had hailed Bobby as a "prized recruit," promising him a charter for a new klavern in the Cookville community.

"You can go far," the imperial grand wizard told Bobby. "You're a natural leader. One day, people will heed your every word, but you need the proper trainen first. Watch me, learn and you will prosper. Mark my words. Today is only the beginnen."

Bobby breathed deeply, refusing to squander his last opportunity for greatness. He gazed thoughtfully at the crowd around him, waited for the people to quiet down and began to speak.

To everyone who knew him, Bobby somehow seemed a changed man. He was unusually subdued. His voice quivered with sincerity, and his message was noteworthy for its brevity.

"Friends, neighbors," he began. "I've asked these good people here today because I'm concerned and I care about our way of life. Our rights are slowly be'en stole from us, and too many people seem to believe if they ignore all that's wrong, then the problems will simply disappear. I do not believe the problems will go away, and neither do the people who have joined us for today's rally. Folks, these men refuse to ignore the problem. They confront the issues. They are concerned, and they care about our way of life. I beg you, and I plead with you—listen to them. Thank you."

A smattering of applause rose from the crowd as Bobby returned the megaphone to the imperial grand wizard.

"Thank you, Klansman Taylor," Larry Lester said, climbing to the podium. "Thank you for inviten us here and for caren about what is happenen in your community and mine, our state and our country."

In contrast to Bobby's lack of fervor, the imperial grand wizard boomed with enthusiasm as he spoke.

"Ladies and gentleman," he said, "I will keep my remarks brief and straightforward because the day is hot and I've never trusted long-winded speakers. First, let me tell you why we are NOT here today. We are not here to start trouble with the colored community in Cookville. That is not our intentions. Now don't be confused. We haven't become fond of the Negroes. We just have other dogs to beat today."

A few people laughed, especially the robed Klansmen. Larry Lester waited for silence.

"A lot of what you've heard about the Klan is true," he continued. "We do believe Negroes are partly to blame for the bad things ailen our nation today. But they are not the only ones at fault by a long shot. In fact, the Negroes really are just enjoyen the advantages given over to them by a president, congressmen, bureaucrats and judges in Washington—people who cater to the whims and fancies of those who believe in ideas contrary to the American way. These people who we elected and appointed to high places have betrayed us. They have decreed that the majority of hard-worken Americans must give up their hard-earned money to support a small minority unwillen to do for themselves. They tell us where our children must go to school and who with—even though it's our tax dollars used to carry out their plans."

The imperial grand wizard paused for a growing round of applause, then moved toward the conclusion of his remarks.

"Day after day, our leaders in Washington impose their wills on us—wills that are dictated by smart-alecky niggers and their white liberal sympathizers," he said. "All you have to do is look around to see what's happenen. The wheels are comen off our way of life. In this county alone, I've been told that a grown black man nearly beat a young white boy to death earlier this month. Only a few weeks ago, some young white nigger lover staged an unprovoked attack on our good friend Bobby here—jumped him from behind, broke his nose and probably would have killed him if other people had not intervened."

Rumors had swirled about the altercation between Joe and Bobby, but this was the first official acknowledgment of the incident. Murmurs rippled through the crowd, and Larry Lester seized on the confusion.

"Yes, people," he bellowed. "This stuff happened right here in Cookville. And mark my word: Things will get worse before they get better. The time is just around the corner when the government and the judges come callen on Cookville, tellen y'all what you can and cannot do, demanden you run your schools their way or no way. It's happenen every day and in every place, and too many people are caught unprepared. It happened in my county. The rally cry was, 'Everyone deserves an equal education.' Now niggers and white children attend the same schools. They mix; they mingle. They become boyfriend and girlfriend. It sickens me. When your time comes, Cookville, I hope y'all will be better prepared to deal with it than we were.

"Once again, folks, you have my word that the Klan is not here to mess with anyone. Some of us might holler at them on our way out of town, remind everyone that a nigger is a nigger. Don't begrudge us a little fun. We have a reputation to uphold after all. When we leave here today, we're headen for Bobby Taylor's farm in the northwest part of the county. We're gonna do some socializen and have fun. You're welcome to join us."

The imperial grand wizard paused, glancing over the crowd. "That's all I have to say, folks, except maybe for thank you. We just wanted an opportunity to tell our side of the story, to remind you good people that the overwhelmen majority of Americans are white people, and their rights are just as important as the rights of niggers. Our government is supposed to be based on majority rule, not the whims of minorities. If you don't do anything else, take that thought with you when you leave here today. Thank you."

His speech completed, Larry Lester threw up his hands in a victory gesture and was rewarded with a hearty round of applause. About a dozen men of all ages stepped forward to claim brochures, and Klansmen milled through the crowd in search of more recruits. A few minutes later, the white-robed warriors returned to their vehicles, paraded once more around the courthouse and drove out of town.

Even as he remained on guard for problems, Paul Berrien marveled at the ease with which this first hurdle was cleared. He had expected problems, but the event had gone off without a hitch. He followed the KKK procession in his patrol car as the group headed toward Bobby's farm. Since the Klan's social gathering would be held on private property, Paul was limited in his ability to respond. He planned to monitor the function from a distance. His goal was simple—keep the peace.

———

As the Klan caravan moved down Highway 125, the day turned into early evening, with the sun setting blood red in the sky. The procession had swollen to more than two dozen vehicles as the group headed toward Bobby's farm. At the general mercantile, the caravan slowed, then made the right-hand turn onto the dusty dirt road.

Matt never planned to make any defiant gesture toward the Klan. He had spent the hot afternoon with his sons and Lucas, setting up the new irrigation system in a field of late-season soybeans on the Berrien place. Lucas had plowed up the field's original crop of withered corn and replanted in hopes of salvaging a meager profit. It was a gamble, wagered in hopes of making the Berriens amenable to the idea of allowing Lucas to tend the land again next year. When Lucas had come to Matt for advice, the white man had offered his friend free use of the irrigation equipment.

"It's not doen me a dab of good," Matt told Lucas. "There's not a drop of water on my place, but the river's a short piece from that field, Lucas. Somebody might as well get some good use out of that irrigation system. If my place was close enough to the river, I'd be maken use of it."

So it was by coincidence that Matt, his sons, his father and Lucas were standing in the front yard when the KKK procession began winding its way along the dirt road toward the Baker place. Having just spent five hours under a blazing sun to get the irrigation flowing, the men now discussed the irony of the weatherman's latest forecast. A hurricane was churning in the Gulf of Mexico, threatening to dump a downpour over drought-stricken South Georgia sometime in the next few days. Now, however, without a trace of cloud in the sky and the sting of sun blistered on their faces, everyone adopted a wait-and-see attitude to the forecast.

Luke was the first among them to spot the approaching cavalcade of cars and trucks. "Company's comen," he alerted them, his eyes full of fiery wrath.

"Uh-oh," Lucas remarked. "You want me to step around the corner, Matt?"

While Matt had ordered his family to ignore the Klan, he refused to allow his sons and Lucas to surrender their pride. "I don't see any reason why you should do that, Lucas," he replied, crossing his arms in a show of stubborn commitment to his own beliefs. "I intend to stay right here."

"Me, too," added Luke, assuming his father's position as every other Baker man quickly followed precedent.

Lucas shook out a small laugh of amazement and appreciation from deep within himself, then crossed his arms and waited with his friends.

It was more a show of solidarity, but the act enraged the Klansmen, who saw the stand as outright defiance by the enemy. The vehicles slowed to a crawl, with horns blowing incessantly and angry Klansmen hurling insults at their adversaries.

Through it all, however, Matt, his family and their friend remained impassive, staunch in their convictions and solid in their resistance to the threat. When the final truck passed, accelerating with a roar and one last insult yelled at them, the men were still standing there with crossed arms—feet firmly planted on the ground, with a whole skin and new strength in the security of their beliefs.

———

The Klansmen turned Martha Taylor's backyard into a picnic place, cavorting in the river, swilling beer and setting up portable grills to cook hamburgers and hotdogs.

Inside her home, Martha sat in a straight-backed chair, staring at the grimy mirror above the couch while trying to sort through her mixed feelings. She was furious with Bobby for bringing these intruders to their house. But she also considered the occasion a stroke of luck since no one expected her to cook and clean after them, and the children were out from underfoot as well.

Martha shared her husband's sentiments toward colored people. She had even less use, however, for the white men and women who were dressed up in bedclothes and floppy hoods, parading through her backyard. Grown people should have known better.

Unlike her husband, Martha harbored only a passive hatred for niggers. Once, when she was young and resentful of the whole world, she had shared Bobby's zeal for the fight. But the fight itself had become an insatiable quest for Bobby, and Martha had grown weary of the endless tide of losing battles. If she had her druthers, Martha would have kept her family isolated on their back-road farm. Since Martha rarely got what she wanted, she was content with simply keeping the outside world from invading her domain.

A roar from the crowd gathered outside her house provided Martha a sudden reminder of yet another failure. The world was beating on her doorsteps, and she had no place else to escape.

A long time ago, Martha had tried to convince herself that she loved Bobby Taylor. When she tugged on her heartstrings these days, however, she realized her only feelings for the man were those of undying gratitude.

Bobby had rescued her from a sordid, squalid existence in Opelika, Alabama. Coming to Cookville, Martha had felt as if she was Cinderella going to the ball, only she was leaving behind something worse than a mean stepmother and ugly stepsisters. When she escaped from Alabama, Martha was fleeing from an abusive father, who assaulted his wife and children on a whim, forcing sex on his daughters as well as his sons.

Bobby Taylor had been Martha's knight in shining armor, freeing her from a damnable life. While life with her husband had been loathsome at times, nothing bad enough had ever happened to make her regret the flight from Alabama.

Even though she had never loved Bobby, Martha still felt as if she had found her lucky star on the day he married her. The hard years since had dimmed her girlish ideas, but she still remembered the way he charmed her when they first met. While not exactly handsome, Bobby had the attitude and appearances to attract second glances from most women who passed him on the street. To a plain woman like Martha, he had seemed like a god.

Bobby had exaggerated facial features. His face was too wide, his nose too flared, his mouth too thin and his eyes too far apart. Somehow, however, his sky-blue eyes and beguiling charisma transcended his flaws, turning the man into a magnet with dirty dishwater blond hair, a sensual smile and flashy style.

Martha had been easy pickings for him when they were young, and Bobby had been trapped into marriage with her. Over the years, however, she had realized that no one woman would satisfy her husband. Early in their marriage, Bobby had covered up his indiscretions with other women. Now, however, he flaunted his affairs. Tonight, for instance, he was wooing some thirtyish-looking buxom blonde—in full view of their sons no less.

In one of her frequent trips to the kitchen window, which afforded a view of the goings-on outside the house, Martha had observed the flirting between her husband and the woman. The woman had dyed hair and wore black boots, skintight jeans and a white blouse that revealed much of her ample cleavage. Bobby had kissed the woman, and they were rubbing up against each other like dogs in heat. Martha half expected Bobby to bring the woman inside the house for a romp in the sack.

The idea saddened Martha, making her realize that she stayed married to Bobby because she had nothing else to do and nowhere else to go. As strange as it seemed, her gratitude to Bobby remained intact. Lately, however, Martha was beginning to feel she deserved better. She had borne her husband three sons, cooked and cleaned for him and done everything else he asked for nearly twenty-five years. Yet, nothing she ever did satisfied Bobby. He always insisted on something else, always demanded more.

And what Bobby wanted, Bobby got.

Nothing reminded Martha more of her husband's domineering control than the tarnished mirror hanging on the dingy living room wall. The mirror had been Bobby's Christmas present to her several years ago. The gift had come with orders to hang the mirror over the couch in their newly painted living room.

Martha hated mirrors, and the last place she wanted one was in the living room of her house, where the reflection would provide a constant reminder of her homeliness every time she passed it. She had shared none of these thoughts with Bobby. Instead, she had mustered up her most pleasant voice, informing her husband the mirror would look out of place in the living room and professing to want it hung in their bedroom.

"That way I can use it when I get dressed," she explained.

"Nope," Bobby declared firmly. He had been in a particularly happy mood, examining the various toys he had bought for the boys. "It belongs in this room. A mirror like that is too pretty to hide away in the bedroom."

Martha should have accepted his decision, but an unusual stubborn streak had caused her to press the matter. Their peaceful Christmas morning had dissolved quickly into a shouting match, ending with one of Bobby's rare beatings of his wife. Later in the day, while a battered Martha applied the finishing touches to Christmas dinner, Bobby and the boys had hung the mirror on the living room wall.

Rising from her chair, Martha walked over to the mirror and gazed into the glass. The reflection showed a woman who looked closer to fifty than forty. The oversized nose was hawkish, while the deep-set gray eyes were lifeless and spread too far apart on her face. Her ears appeared ready to fly off Martha's head at any moment, and her pencil thin mouth had a permanent downward curve from too many years of frowning. Her face was a sad oval, with the pasty skin tightly drawn like a bad face-lift.

Martha pushed a graying strand of dull hair back into place and sighed at the sad sight staring back at her. All her life, she had heard about the gaunt little girls who grew into striking women as they aged. Obviously, she was not to become one of them. Age was making Martha even uglier.

Turning from the mirror, she recrossed the living room floor to the kitchen window to inspect the curious crowd. Bobby had disappeared, and the blonde floozy was flirting with another man. Wayne was talking to a group of teenage boys, his posture suggesting a bragging mood. Near the river's edge, she spotted Billy, sitting with his back against a tree with Carl cradled between his legs.

Her youngest son was obviously asleep. Glancing at the wall clock, she saw the hour hand had sailed well past ten. The four-year-old Carl should have been in bed instead of sleeping on the ground, but Martha had allowed the time to get away from her. It was not the first time. Nor would it likely be the last because Martha often failed in her motherly duties.

She wanted to be a good mother to her sons, but somehow, the magic of raising children eluded Martha. The boys were complete mysteries to her, and she tended to think of her sons as another chore that needed tending. Occasionally, when the children did something special, Martha experienced a pain of regret because the sense of a mother's love had never filled her. The feelings were fleeting, however, always swept away by an awareness that she had never loved anyone or anything. Facts were facts, and Martha saw no reason to pretend for her own sake.

From time to time, though, Martha wished she understood her sons. While watching her stories on television, she would vow to take more time with boys. By the time a suitable opportunity arrived, however, she usually lost interest or had something better to do.

As it stood now, Martha was not even certain she liked Wayne. Her oldest son was brash like his father and dimwitted like his mother. Sometimes, the boy scared Martha. He carried around a mean streak like a belligerent rattlesnake ready to strike.

Billy was the sensitive one of the bunch. He was always helpful and considerate, running here and there trying to please everyone. Yet, even he drove Martha batty with his consuming passion for basketball. He spent hours outside, dribbling and shooting, faking and driving, counting backward from five. The basketball rarely strayed far from his side. Even in the house, he twirled the ball on his fingers and practiced whipping it back and forth between his legs. He was a whir of motion, and Martha tired of his busyness.

As for Carl, Martha had no idea what to make of him. He was the silent one.

More than anything, she was glad the boy had finally ceased wetting the bed he shared with Billy.

Prone to rash decisions, Martha suddenly made up her mind to leave Bobby. With only slightly more consideration, she decided to leave the children with him.

Abandoning her lookout at the window, she strode through the dark house to the bedroom and pulled her suitcase from the closet shelf. Bobby had bought the piece of luggage as a wedding gift for her. As she packed her things, Martha thought it odd that after all the years gone by, she could still fit her essential belongings into the suitcase.

Pushing away the thought and ignoring the new roar of noise coming from outside the house, she finished her packing.

————

A few minutes later, Imperial Grand Wizard Larry Lester, Wizard Ralph Johnson and new Klansman Bobby Taylor tossed lighted matches onto three large crosses set on the edge of New River. Already doused with kerosene, the wooden timbers burst into flames as the hooded army of hatemongers gave their final shout of the long day.

Inside the living room, Martha sat in the straight-backed chair with the suitcase by her side.

The burning crosses cast a pale shadow across the room, but she disregarded the shenanigans. She wanted these intruders to pile into their vehicles and drive away, so that she could get on with her business. Her feet tapped against the floor in anticipation.

The front door opened, and Billy entered the house with his sleeping brother draped across his shoulder. Without even glancing at his mother, Billy passed through the room and carried Carl to bed.

Martha had debated whether to leave in secret or to tell Bobby and the children about her plans. She would have preferred to leave without fanfare but decided the boys were owed an explanation.

In their room, Carl protested the covers, and Billy insisted on a top sheet. Martha smiled, grateful for the protective instinct Billy felt toward his little brother. The knowledge comforted her, made her rest easy about this decision to abandon the children.

A short time later, Billy plodded back into the living room and dropped his slight frame on the couch. Then, he saw Martha's suitcase.

"What's with the suitcase, Ma?" he asked.

"I am goen away, Billy," Martha replied boldly. "You take care of yourself and Carl, too."

Billy sat up straight on the couch, a touch of worry flying into his eyes. "What do you mean you're goen away?" he asked. "Where will you go?"

"As far away from here as I can get," Martha answered, resisting the urge to walk over and pat the boy on the head one last time. "I'll write and let you boys know where I wind up."

Billy leaned forward. "What does Pa say about this?" he asked with increasing doubt.

"I'm fixen to tell him, so we'll see," Martha explained patiently. "I doubt he'll mind too much. He can replace me with that fake blonde he was flirten with tonight."

"Ma, you're maken a big mistake," Billy pleaded, coming to his feet. "Just please put up that suitcase quick, and forget about any of this."

Hearing footsteps on the porch, Martha rose from the chair. "I've made up my mind, Billy," she said firmly. "I am leaven."

Bobby heard this last remark as he opened the screen door and entered the house. His eyes scanned the dark room, going from Billy to Martha before landing on the suitcase. Behind him, Wayne allowed the door to slam shut and flipped on the light switch.

"What's goen on?" Bobby asked at length, after everyone adjusted to the flood of light.

"I'm leaven you, Bobby," Martha announced confidently.

Bobby scratched his nose, staring first at the suitcase, then at his wife. "Why you wanna go and do a thing like that?"

"Because I can't stand it here anymore," Martha replied. "I have to get away while I can still make a life for myself. The boys are old enough to take care of themselves, and you sure don't need or want me around here."

Bobby nodded slightly as if agreeing with the suggestion. "This is some bombshell to drop on us just short of midnight, Martha," he remarked, a hint of mean amusement creeping into his voice. "But tell me, sweetheart. Where do you plan to go tonight, and how on earth are you gonna get there?"

Details had always bothered Martha, even the simplest ones. Last year, for instance, she had fretted over wrapping paper for Christmas presents. The multiple choices of brightly colored paper had befuddled her to the point that she had wound up handing out the few presents without first wrapping them. Now, her confidence wavered.

"I don't exactly know," she said to the sea of strange faces staring back at her. "I figure I'll start walken, and somebody'll pick me up along the way. Maybe I'll go to Tifton—or maybe all the way to Atlanta."

Bobby began to laugh and even Wayne chuckled at the ludicrousness of her plans. Martha looked to Billy for reassurance, but he bowed his head, unable to look her in the eyes.

"You've got it all figured out, don't you Martha?" Bobby said, the voice of controlled rage replacing his laughter. He glared at her. "I know you're crazy as a bat, but this just takes the cake. Who do you think in their right mind would pick up a wretch like you walken alongside the road? And even if you managed to find your way to Tifton or all the way to Atlanta, how would you take care of yourself, Martha? What in the world would you do?"

Her hand flew to the side of her face, tapping nervously against her neck as Martha tried to decide what to do. Every thought failed her.

"I know what a cross it is to bear—believe me, I know—but the best place for you, Martha, is right where you are," Bobby continued when it became obvious his wife was confused. "You ain't goen anywhere—not now, not ever. Get on back to the bedroom, woman. Unpack that suitcase, and we'll forget any of this ever happened."

Desperation surged through Martha. She wanted to run from the house. Instead, she dabbed away the tears streaming down her face, bent to retrieve the suitcase and carried it back to her room without further protest.

THE KLAN STARTED THE fire, unintentionally, when someone tossed a cigarette from the back of a pickup truck as the departing caravan paraded past the Baker farm sometime after midnight. The cigarette landed in a thick patch of dry grass, smoldered for a moment and finally flickered to a tiny flame. Fire quickly consumed the plot of beaten blades, then lagged along a narrow line of almost barren earth until the flame found a new source of dried turf and weeds.

Fueled by the tender clumps of brown grass, the flames flared into a bonfire, scorched the bottom of a dogwood tree and crawled through the fence. Within minutes, the blaze was licking at the parched cornfield. Now stoked and fanned by a gentle breeze, the fire roared into conflagration, incinerating stalk after stalk of the withered corn.

The flames cut a wide swath through the field, ever expanding and rolling a plume of smoke high across the nighttime sky. On the far side of the field, the fire burned through another fence, claiming its first taste of timber from a section of hardwoods on the Berrien estate. A smaller sheet of flames swept along the edge of the field closer to home, devoured a row of dogwood trees and began nipping the shingled sides of the first of the two tobacco barns.

Up to this point, the breeze had pushed the flames and smoke away from the house, which explained the failure of anyone to detect the fire. But—made prankish by the hurricane that churned in the balmy waters of the Gulf of Mexico, heading toward the Florida Panhandle and Alabama shoreline—the wind suddenly shifted, pushing flames in a new direction and wafting the first cloud of smoke toward open windows. Even before the stifling smell arrived, however, the hissing roar of the fire began to nudge awake the sleeping family.

By now, a pale yellow and orange glow lit the field, and red flames flagged from the tops of trees in the distance.

At last, the fire ate through an edge of the shingled barn side, then curled along the hot dry wood within and found the cooked tobacco hanging from the rafters. The barn became a torch within minutes, hissing and spewing red-hot embers onto the second tobacco barn.

Deep in the field, having gorged itself on dried corn and still licking at the left-overs, the blaze crossed the fencerow, found a fresh appetite for the opening bolls of stunted cotton and headed toward the towering piney wood.

The popping and cracking of barn timbers rousted Joe from sleep. Opening his eyes, he noticed the illuminated night outside his window with groggy curiosity. Immediately, however, he detected the smoky odor, coming to full sensibility as apprehension lifted him from bed and propelled him to the window. He discovered the world on fire, nearly ready to burn down around his family.

Joe yelled the initial warning, rushing to pull on clothes and shoes, even as everybody else in the house made the terrible discovery for themselves.

Everyone crowded onto the front porch to observe the raging fire, some of them hastily dressed, others still in their bedclothes or underwear. As they watched in horror, the tobacco barn farthest from the house shuddered and gave up the ghost, collapsing in a loud heap. Seconds later, flames shot through the roof of the second barn, licking at their chops, angry for having been denied too long the opportunity to feast.

Disbelief paralyzed the family. Then, the trickish wind launched a snarling wall of fire directly toward the house, and they could ill afford to stand still any longer.

"My God!" Matt exclaimed. "The whole place could go up. Go call for help, Caroline."

Even before he made the suggestion, she was headed for the telephone.

In a split second with no time to think, Matt shouted orders for his family, and everyone reacted with their instinct for survival.

Sam and Rachel rushed to the shed behind the house, grabbing shovels, rakes and anything else they figured could be used to fight a fire with scarcely a drop of water on the place. The girls, all wearing nightshirts, scattered to the corncrib, the barn and the loft in search of course tobacco sheets that could be used to beat back the flames.

Joe was ordered to cut a fire line alongside the house, an impossible task without their best tractor, which was parked in a back field along with the harrow needed for the job. He ran for the pickup, while his brothers ran to their room for clothes.

"Meet me at the orchard gate," he yelled to John, whose help was needed to hitch the harrow to the tractor.

Unless they hurried, perhaps even if they did, the flames would reach the house before there was time to cut a fire line.

———

As her husband commanded, Martha began unpacking her suitcase. When she had put away several items, she came across her nightgown and decided she was too sleepy to finish the task. She shut the suitcase, shoved it under the bed and put on the flimsy nightgown.

Turning off the light, she climbed into bed and was ready to doze off when Bobby entered the room. Over the years, she had learned to read his mind through his movements. When he wanted her body, Bobby was deliberate and watchful with his movements about the room.

Sensing his intent, Martha shut her eyes tightly while Bobby undressed. When he was naked, her husband lay beside Martha, leaned over and nuzzled her face. He reeked of stale beer and sweat. Nausea filled her throat, and Martha lay deadly still, hoping to discourage him by pretending sleep. Her shallow breaths betrayed her. When Martha was asleep, even catnapping, she snored.

"Let's do it," Bobby urged when his tender side failed to arouse his wife. "I know you ain't asleep."

Knowing it was useless to resist his advances, Martha raised her nightgown, took off her panties and allowed Bobby to mount her without a single word passing between them. She simply wanted the act finished, and if her cooperation would hasten a fast end, then she would oblige her husband.

Bobby was close to climax when their bedroom door burst open, and the

overhead light beamed on them. Wayne entered the room, claiming to have important news.

Rather than embarrassment, Martha felt relief at her son's intrusion. Her naked
husband rolled off her, cursing as he withdrew, shouting at Wayne while Martha
closed her legs and pulled a sheet over her.

"Damn it, Wayne!" Bobby hollered. "How many times do I have to tell you not to
come runnen in here when you know we're busy?"

"Sorry, Pa," Wayne lied.

Just for fun, he occasionally interrupted his parents during sex. Since Bobby
huffed, puffed and moaned loudly enough to keep anyone from sleeping through
the act, Wayne considered it a right of pleasure to disturb their copulation. Tonight,
however, Wayne had a genuine reason for barging into their bedroom.

"Turn off the light and get out of here so we can finish what we're doen," Bobby
yelled when Wayne made no move to leave the room.

"Somethen's on fire down the road," Wayne explained, flipping off the light
switch. "I think it's the Baker place, Pa, the whole place. The sky's lit up like the
Fourth of July."

"Wouldn't that be a wonder?" Bobby muttered. "Okay, okay, I'll be there in two
shakes of a stick. Get Billy out of bed for me, and y'all go wait in the truck."

Without replying, Wayne closed the door and went to wake Billy.

Bobby returned to the business at hand and finished it quickly. As he dressed, he
suggested that Martha show a little more interest the next time he approached her.
Then he opened the door and went out to see for himself what Wayne was yakking
about. In her bed, Martha heard him whoop with delight a few moments later. He
came back into the house, yelling at Billy who was grumbling about being woken
up for something that did not concern him.

"This could be a great moment for your old man, boy, and you need to be a part
of it," Bobby yelled, silencing Billy's protests. "After the day I've had, I can't think of
a better enden than watchen Matt Baker's house burn to the ground—unless maybe
if Matt and those sons of his burned right along with it."

———

Matt scanned the approaching fire once more, then decided the most pressing
demand was to save the tractor parked beneath the shelter of the still standing
tobacco barn. It was an old tractor but still in good condition, except for a faulty
starter and a sticky choke.

They needed that tractor, so Matt called for Luke's help, and the boy came
bounding out of the house, pulling on his shirt, buttoning his jeans. Side by side,
they sprinted the football field distance between the house and the burning barn.

By the time they reached the blazing building, flames were licking at the shelter
above the tractor as well as the machine's single front tire. Matt beat out the flames
on the tire, while Luke climbed onto the hot tractor seat.

While Luke pressed the starter button, Matt pumped the choke. The tractor
engine coughed, sputtered and turned over once, then fizzled. They worked frantically, trying to crank the tractor, but the engine refused to budge.

The barn's tin siding was white-hot now, throwing off blistering heat. Suddenly,
flames burned through the barn door. The heavy wood-facing fell off the hinges,

striking Matt on the back, burning the calf of his leg. He shook off the burning wood, stomped out the fire, then beat back another blaze licking at the rear tractor tire closest to the barn.

Once more, Matt fiddled with the choke, and Luke tried to crank the tractor. The engine was dead, however, and Matt realized the tractor was a goner.

"Let's get out of here!" he yelled to Luke.

As Luke climbed off the tractor, a familiar clicking came from inside the barn, where hundreds of dollars of tobacco burned out of control. Matt's face twisted with disbelief as he realized the timer on the barn cooker was signaling for an injection of gas into the furnace. Luke heard the noise, too, looking at his father for confirmation of his fear. For a flickering second, they stared blankly at one another. Then they broke into a run, their feet pounding furiously as they fled for safety.

Behind them, another ominous rumbling rattled the barn, followed by a screaming zip and a loud pop. Seconds later, the gas tank exploded, arcing a single, flaming yellow torch heavenward and peppering the sky with tiny pieces of hot steel. A second, smaller explosion followed almost instantly.

The booming blasts resonated across the countryside, shattering windows, rattling walls, piercing eardrums and jarring the entire community.

Like the trumpet of the Lord Himself, Rachel thought, and Jesus coming back to claim his flock at a most opportune time. She staggered against Sam as the force of explosion rocked them. A prized bottle fell off a shelf in the smokehouse, glancing off Sam's head before landing unharmed on the soft dirt floor. In the adjoining syrup house, a shelf collapsed, and bottles shattered.

The concussion of the exploding forces was violent, flinging Matt and Luke head over heels, airborne for several seconds before sprawling landings disoriented their faculties.

Stunned by the force, Matt needed time to pick himself off the ground after crashing. The smoke was thick around him. He shook his head, unable to get his bearings for a moment, then started on a dazed trot toward an uncertain destination.

Luke was not as fortunate. A single piece of white-hot steel landed on his shoulder, melted through his undershirt and branded him with a mark the size of a silver dime. Seared and screaming, Luke slung the steel from his body and staggered toward the house, fearful he would pass out before he could escape the burning field.

————

Caroline heard the explosion, the impact knocking the telephone receiver from her hand.

Summer saw the yellow flame streak across the sky as well as the tiny red, white and yellow pieces of shredded steel from the exploding gas tank, cascading like fireworks.

Both women had the same reaction, their protective instincts hurrying them toward the burning field in search of Matt and Luke. For one dizzying moment, Caroline wondered whether they had been blown to pieces. Summer's moment of terror arrived in the form of a single thought about her father and brother burning to death.

Their fears vanished instantly into the more important need for action, and they rushed toward the burning field, Caroline coming from the house, Summer from the corncrib across the road. They ran past each other into the rolling smoke, calling for Matt and Luke. In the distance, Luke screamed, and Summer ran toward his cry. Farther away, Caroline saw Matt trip over a bank of dirt and fall.

Moments later, the two women were leading Matt and Luke from the field to the porch.

Matt made a quick recovery with Caroline's help, resting less than a minute on the ground before his sense of duty took over, thrusting him back into the fight to save the house as well as everything else his family owned.

Luke was ravaged with burning pain. While Summer and Bonnie calmed him, Rachel applied the sap of her aloe plant to the deep burn. The natural ointment cooled the burn, enough to renew Luke's fierce determination to fight the fire. He took a deep breath, allowed Rachel to cover the burn with gauze and then ran to the field, beating at the advancing flames with a tobacco sheet.

The explosion had scattered embers across the parched field, igniting small blazes that soon burned into each other. Minutes later, a long line of flames danced furiously less than thirty yards from the house and the pecan orchard.

"If it gets into the orchard, we'll lose everything," Matt exhorted his family. "Fight it with all you've got."

Everyone answered the challenge, throwing themselves at the flames and fighting for their livelihood if not their lives. They beat at the fire with tobacco sheets, shoveled dirt on burning corn stalks and stomped at the flames with their shoes. Gradually, they lost the battle, retreating backward as the fire spread relentlessly toward the house.

At some point, Paul Berrien and Tom Carter joined the fight. Even with reinforcements, however, the sheet of fire stretched across a line too long to defend.

Blistered and exhausted, they doubled their efforts as well as hoped and prayed for a miracle. Still, the fire crept closer—until flames had pushed their backs against the fencerow no more than fifteen yards from the house.

Then, in the distance, they heard the strained whine of a tractor engine coming toward them as hard and fast as it would go.

––––––––

A short time after Bobby and Wayne left the house in high spirits with Billy grumbling in their wake, Martha heard the shotgun blast of the ages. The loud explosion rattled the windows in her house and put a notion in Martha's cluttered head.

Rolling out of bed, she kneeled on the floor and pulled her suitcase from beneath the bed. She opened it and took out her prettiest dress, a cranberry colored imitation wool frock that had never fit properly. Pushing the suitcase off the other side of the bed, she spread the dress across the rumpled sheets and ironed out the wrinkles with her hands.

Next, Martha ran a hot bath, dumping into the water the remainder of an old box of bubble bath, which had never performed as advertised.

When she finished bathing, Martha coated her body with talcum powder, combed her hair and put on the cranberry dress. As an afterthought, she rummaged through a drawer, found an old bottle of cologne and doused herself with the sweet-smelling liquid.

Now finished dressing, she went into the living room, checked herself in the mirror and saw something missing. Returning to the bedroom, she searched through a bureau drawer and found a pair of earrings that almost matched her dress. She clipped the small nuggets on her ears, then walked back into the living room for another inspection.

This time, Martha was pleased. She was still not beautiful, but she was satisfied with the way she looked. After one final self-appraisal, she crossed the room and pulled a shotgun from the heavy rack of weapons.

Martha had given the gun to Bobby as a Christmas present in the same year he had given her the mirror. There was no reason to check whether the gun was loaded because that was the only kind of gun Bobby allowed in his house. Nevertheless, she opened a heavy desk drawer near the gun rack and found the box of cartridges. She took a handful of the shells and dropped them in her pocket.

Until now, Martha had never considered suicide. But with her mind made up on the matter and no one to question her about motives and details, she wanted to get it over and done with as soon as possible.

Martha talked aloud as she carried the shotgun around the house, checking to make sure the place was clean enough to leave for Bobby and the boys. In the kitchen, she rinsed two dirty cups and set them to dry in the dish rack.

Coming to the smallest bedroom, where Carl was sleeping in the double bed he shared with Billy, she paused, considering whether to take him with her, before concluding her youngest son should be allowed to make his own decision about these things. She considered giving him a goodbye kiss, rejecting the idea with a wave of her hand.

Finally, Martha returned to the living room. She picked a hat off the floor, placed it on the television and decided everything was in order. Returning to the sofa, she lifted the shotgun to her shoulder, aimed at the wall and blew the mirror to pieces. The shot gouged a hole in the wall, and shards of glass flew everywhere.

"I could kill myself for not thinken of this earlier," she said aloud, loading a second cartridge into the gun.

Martha laughed slightly and agreed with her husband's earlier suggestion: She was crazy as a bat. Closing her eyes, she stuck the barrel of the gun into her mouth and pulled the trigger.

––––––––

The third explosion brought Carl Taylor fully awake. The night was popping like a firecracker around him, and he wondered if Pa and the boys were shooting deer outside the house. Realizing that Billy was not lying next to him, Carl decided to investigate the noise.

He eased out of bed, crossed the room and peeked out the door. The house was dark, except for the living room light, so he walked that way. Peering around the corner of the door, he saw his mother's brains and blood splattered around the room.

Carl promptly vomited, violently on the floor. When he was able, careful to keep his eyes closed, the boy turned away, pattered back to his room and returned to bed. Sleep eluded him as he wondered who would clean up the mess.

Sometime later, Bobby and his two oldest sons returned to the house and made the gruesome discovery for themselves. As it had done to Carl, the grisly scene and sickly sweet smell of perfume made Bobby and the boys violently ill.

Hearing the sounds of their retching, Carl felt certain he would not have to clean up the mess. He turned over on his stomach and went to sleep.

————

Joe resisted his brother's suggestion to turn back toward the house as the exploding gas tanks rocked the countryside. He calculated the tractor was needed more than ever to cut a fire line, especially if the streak of fire across the sky had carried flames any closer to the house. He drove the pickup as fast as he dared, treating the field lane as if it was a highway and bouncing John and himself around the cab like empty drink bottles.

Coming to the far end of the back field, Joe brought the truck to a sliding halt, both doors flying open before the truck came to a full stop. He raced for the tractor seat, while John ran toward the harrow.

The three-year-old tractor, a John Deere 1020, cranked on the first try, and Joe guided it to the harrow, backing the machine into a perfect position. With quick skill, John hooked the heavy frame of cutting disks to the tractor. He signaled Joe to go, jumped back from the harrow as his brother roared away, and ran for the truck.

Moments later, the fast-moving truck passed the tractor. By the time Joe got the tractor close enough to see how far the fire had come toward the house, his brother had parked the truck out of harm's way across the road and was beating frantically at the flames with nothing but his shirt.

The ferocity of the fire stunned Joe, who slowed the tractor only slightly to gauge the raging perimeters of the blaze. His family was stretched along the fencerow, with flames licking only a few feet from them. Matt and Sam fought desperately to keep the fire out of a large cedar tree, which was tender enough to burn in a flash and likely would toss embers onto the nearby house.

Already, the flames had scorched the roses and other flowers planted along the fencerow. Luke, Summer and Bonnie were waging a losing battle to keep flames from reaching the low branches of the pecan orchard.

Realizing the odds were against them, Joe guided the tractor through the pecan orchard, along the fence on the opposite side of the wall of flames. He felt the heat as the tractor raced past the weary firefighters, heard his daddy yelling at the top of his lungs. But Joe refused to heed Matt's frantic warning.

At the open fence gate, he braked the right wheel of the tractor and swung the equipment into the field. Revving the engine to full throttle, he lowered the harrow to the ground, shielded his face with an arm, eased off the clutch and drove straight into the cauldron.

The tractor moved through the flames as if guided by a daredevil pilot on the most important mission of his life.

Joe drove blindly along a straight line, willing himself to ignore the intense heat that singed his hair and blistered his face, arms and hands. In his wake, the harrow cut the burning stalks into the ground, turning the blaze into a faint version of its former self and making the flames manageable.

He was in the worst of the fire for no more than thirty seconds. But to his family and friends watching in terror, the ride seemed like an eternity in Hell. When the tractor burst through the far edge of the flames, Joe was coughing and sucking for air to clear the choking smoke from his lungs.

Slowing only to catch his breath, Joe continued to harrow down the edge of the field, putting a border of safety between the burning field and the larger field directly behind the house.

When he reached the stand of pine trees at the lower end of the field, Joe swung the tractor in a wide left-hand turn and cut a swath across the bottom section until another raging fire forced him to stop near the cotton patch. He halted the tractor to absorb the scope of flames, then turned around and traced over his original path, reinforcing the makeshift firebreak and cooling off lingering hot spots by harrowing the burning corn deeper into the ground.

A few minutes later, Joe reached his family as they extinguished the last of the flames closest to the house. Someone had cut a limb from one of the pecan trees to keep the fire out of the orchard, while one side of the cedar tree was charred on its lower branches. Fence poles still smoldered, and a patch of charred grass ran all the way to the side of the house.

Driving up beside his family and friends, Joe shut off the tractor and gave everyone a worried grin.

"That's one heck of a straight line you cut there, Joe," Sam praised. "I know your daddy taught you well, but I think—just this once—he would have cut you some slack had the row been a little crooked."

"It's a fact, son," Matt agreed. "You probably saved us from total ruin. The fire would have got the house, the orchard and a lot of other stuff if you hadn't plowed under those flames. I appreciate it. I'm not sure if I could have done it myself."

"Yeah, you would have, Daddy," Joe said lightly, uncomfortable with the praise.

"Face it, Matt," Caroline said, coming to her husband's side. "Among other things, we gave our children courage." She regarded Joe with a warm smile, then looked lovingly at her other children. "Joe and Summer are liven proof of that," she continued, "and so are John, Carrie, Luke and Bonnie."

Casting her gaze on Sam and Rachel, Caroline said, "You don't have to look far to see the secret of our success. Or that we've had plenty of support along the way," she added, glancing at Paul and Tom, and, finally, heavenward.

"Amen to that," Sam remarked.

"I know there's still work to do," Rachel agreed, "but I think the Lord's due a word of thanks."

No one disputed her claim, and they bowed their heads in a silent, prayerful moment of gratitude for their blessings.

When their eyes opened, everyone looked at each other, satisfaction etched on their faces along with the black soot. The moment was short-lived, however, and Joe provided the necessary closure.

"Daddy, we've got big problems back there," he said, gesturing to the flames raging in the distance. "There's fire in the cotton and in the woods closest to the bog. From what I can tell, it's burnen strong on your place, too, Paul. It's hot back there, with nothen to stop those flames without some help."

"There is the railroad," Paul remarked, an ominous warning that hundreds, perhaps even a thousand acres of timber, could burn along with everything else lost on this night.

Amid the flashing lights of heavy equipment and the blaring sirens on emergency vehicles, no one noticed the lone ambulance screaming past the Baker place on its way to answer another call for help in the community. In fact, the Bakers did not hear of Martha Taylor's suicide until morning, long after the fire had done its damage.

As Paul Berrien had warned, the rocky terrain of the railroad right of way was indeed the deciding factor in halting the fire's progress. Fortunately, the damage proved less severe than he or anyone else expected.

Flames blackened hundreds of acres on the Berrien estate, scorching the bottom trunks and exposed roots of hardwoods and pines. Few trees burned from top to bottom, however, and fewer still suffered any mortal harm because the blaze burned quickly and moved swiftly across the land.

"If you had struck the match yourself and started the fire, the results would have been pretty much the same," a young forest ranger informed Matt. "This could be a blessen in disguise for you, Sheriff Berrien. The fire thinned out a lot of scraggly oaks and underbrush that slows forest growth. It probably took care of some rattlesnakes, too."

While Paul and Tom helped the Bakers fight the fire, the Berrien sisters had joined Dan and Amelia Carter in guarding Benevolence Missionary Baptist Church from the flames. The fire curled along the edge of the church property, nipping at the cemetery and burning one of the long wooden tables where dinner was spread on Big Meeting Sundays. But the two aging sisters and the storekeepers never swerved in their dedication to keep the flames from lapping at the foundation of the little white church. Long after the real threat of danger had passed, the Berrien sisters and the Carters maintained their vigil, taking the initiative to rake and clean up the charred debris.

Arriving at the church at daybreak, on his way to offer moral support to the Bakers, Preacher Adam Cook found renewed faith in his congregants' unfaltering devotion to the church. He promptly changed the text of his upcoming sermon. Instead of dwelling on the fire and brimstone of Hell, a tactic he wielded effectively on rare occasions, the preacher would deliver a stirring sermon about unselfish service to the Lord.

One frightening consequence of the fire occurred just before daylight broke as two passersby collided in the thick smoke along a stretch of Highway 125 only moments before the State Patrol closed the road. A young woman drove her car into the smoke, which stretched a solid mile along the road, slowing the vehicle to a crawl as she attempted to navigate her way through the blinding conditions. An older man came behind her, traveling too fast for the conditions, and plowed his Volkswagen into the rear of the woman's car.

The woman cracked her head against the front window, suffering a concussion. The man broke his leg and required surgery to repair a ruptured spleen after the car's steering column crushed his chest.

Both victims were fortunate that a state trooper heard the crash as he erected a sign closing the road. Within a minute, he arrived at the crash site and rescued the woman and man from the choking smoke.

Without a doubt, the Baker place bore the brunt of damage. The fire destroyed the bulk of the front field of corn as well as the adjoining cotton patch.

Matt was unconcerned about the cotton. The dry weather had destroyed the crop long before the first flames licked it. All along, he had figured running a combine over the field would cost more than it was worth. Now the prospect of any waste whatsoever had vanished, and the field was primed for an early planting of winter grains.

While Matt also had never intended to run the combine through the corn, he had counted on the withered stalks to provide food and fodder for the hogs and cows over winter. Come fall, he had planned to graze the stock in those fields. As it stood now, he would have to sell more of his livestock. There was certainly no money to buy the feed necessary to carry the animals through the cold months— until the land could furnish enough nourishment for them.

Just as surely, he would not have to worry about the two cows that succumbed to heavy smoke. Matt needed to burn their carcasses, but he could not bring himself to start another fire. In fact, he was skittish of fire of any kind. Even the prospect of lighting a cigarette disturbed him.

Not everything about the fire was dismal, but Matt had to look hard around the blackened earth to find the bright spots. As he had explained to Paul Berrien, the forester also informed Matt that the fire would recharge his timber growth. Matt merely thanked the young man for his well-intentioned advice, refusing to point out that Sam intentionally burned the woods every few years for that very reason.

Apart from the bonus of rejuvenated timber, most of the farm had been spared the wrath of the flames. The farm's northern half, distinguished from the southern end by the dirt lane that bisected the land, escaped damage, except for one small section of corn—what else—planted in the field directly behind the house and the pecan orchard.

Fire had spread into that section of the farm when an exploding treetop rained down flaming debris on the field. Once again, Joe had come to the rescue, hemming around the fire with the harrow and containing the flames within a two-acre circle. And because his son had saved a third field from burning out of control, Matt still had crops of cantaloupes, corn, peanuts, soybeans and sweet potatoes to gather from his fields. He also had the last of the tobacco to strip from the stalks, even if there was no barn to cook it.

It seemed strange counting those crops as blessings. Of course, Matt realized some of the crops were worthless. He would not even waste the gas necessary to run the combine over the soybeans, while the cantaloupes were too thin—and the prices for them too low—to make the crop worth the picking time. Still, the cows could eat the beans, and Matt had never seen a hog—or cow either—who walked away from a cantaloupe, fresh or rotten.

Matt also knew he would not lose his shirt entirely on his peanuts, and the sweet potatoes were moneymakers despite the dry weather. And there again, his crops on the Castleberry place had fared better in the heat, benefiting from timely irrigation from the rented farm's gigantic pond.

So, yes, there were blessings to count on this early Sunday morning, which was exactly what his father tried to help Matt understand as they walked beside the rubble of their fallen tobacco barns.

"This, too, shall pass," Sam said as they surveyed the burnt timbers, which they had measured, cut and hammered with their own hands—not so long ago it seemed to both men.

"Where have I heard that before?" Matt muttered, trying to sound strong as his father offered a comforting pat on his shoulder.

In reality, Matt wanted to cry, to bury his head against his father's big shoulder and bawl like a baby. But no grown son of Sam Baker was going to act like a baby. On the contrary, he would take stock of the situation and meet the challenge as best he could. Sam understood that, even if Matt had his doubts.

"Be of good courage and play the man for your people," Sam remarked suddenly.

"Sir?" Matt replied.

"It's in the Bible," Sam explained. "That's what Joab—the commander of King David's army—told his troops one time when they fought the Syrians. Be of good courage, son. And play the man for your family."

"I'll do my best, Pa," Matt vowed, storing away that nugget of wisdom for another day when he would sorely need the inspiration.

From the rubble of ruined barns, the two men cast their gaze westward to where the bog boiled and bubbled like a witch's brew. The fire still simmered beneath that part of the earth, consuming the decayed plants and humus, which had belonged to some ancient swamp thousands of years ago and remained as a constant reminder that life rolled on without fail—in some form or another.

"I hope the black bears and bobcats and everything else in the bog fared as well as we did last night," Sam said.

Which was precisely what Sam should have said because he cared about the well-being of the animals, the plants and the trees. Suddenly, Matt realized he shared his father's concern for the living things.

"I hope so, too, Pa," he replied. "I also hope we didn't lose too many trees back there."

"Oh, we don't have to worry about the trees," Sam said. "They'll bounce back better than ever. Of course, we probably won't find much fat lighter in those woods over the next few years. But there's plenty of it elsewhere on the place. Maybe I'll go looken for some this afternoon; take John with me if he wants. Winter will be here before we know it."

It was an excuse for his father to see how the precious lay of the land had been altered by a single night of hell, which would matter as much to John as it did to Sam.

"Y'all watch out for the hot spots if you go," Matt cautioned. "There's still some out there."

"We'll be careful," Sam said, taking two steps forward, then turning to scan the distance behind Matt.

"It's a promisen sunrise we're blessed with this mornen," he observed, gesturing to where the sun rose on the horizon like a sheet of polished gold.

Matt turned and looked at the sunrise, wanting desperately to believe his father, who always watched the horizons for signs and usually saw only good things, coming and going.

Glancing again at his father, he nodded, and Sam started to leave. He took several steps westward, then whirled around to say one last thing to Matt.

"Remember one thing for me, son," Sam said with strong conviction. "There's plenty of everything we need still here on this farm—even money. We can sell timber or do whatever else we might need to get by. So rest your mind. Things'll be better next year. You wait and see."

"I know, Pa," Matt said, regarding carefully this man with the black patch over his eye, seeing from a different side how much a father loved his son.

In nearly fifty years as the principal caretaker of this place, Sam had counted virtually every tree taken from the farm. During the worst of his financial struggles to keep the farm afloat, he had sold a few acres of hardwoods near the bog. With that lone exception, every other tree harvested from the place had been cut to clear new fields or to meet some need on the farm.

Sam believed trees should grow strong and tall for as long as possible—forever, if possible. The proof towered in the distance, near the bog where he had replanted the hardwoods with the pine trees, which were recently rejuvenated by the fire but still tall and proud despite being slightly scorched.

Without giving his son an opportunity to comment on the suggestion, Sam turned away once more and moved off through the field, leaving Matt to ponder dollars and cents.

From a purely financial point of view, the fire had done the most serious harm during the first hours, with the destruction of the tobacco barns, their cookers and the tractor. The buildings and equipment would have to be replaced before Matt could raise another crop, and he would bear the full cost. Out of necessity, Matt had risked the year without insurance. He had lost that gamble, and—as surely as the summer had been dry—the cost of replacing everything lost would exceed the little bit of change Matt had in the Farmers and Citizens Bank. His family also would need money to buy the necessities of life. Even before the fire, he had worried about making ends meet over the winter, through another spring and summer, until he could harvest a decent crop next fall.

Matt supposed he would have to get another loan from the bank, but he decided to dwell on the business problems tomorrow. Just this moment, he wanted to reflect some more on his blessings. It was Sunday after all, and they had not made it to church. How long since that had happened? Matt wondered as Caroline came toward him, wearing a sleeveless, everyday summer dress that was white, worn and one of Matt's favorites.

His wife was a beautiful woman, ripe with an understanding of and a passion for Matt. Caroline came to Matt, kissed him fully on the lips, not worrying that someone on their way to church might see them standing there like that in the field. She told her husband how thankful she was that Matt and their youngest son had survived the explosion—how her heart had raced and her stomach knotted when the thunder roared and the house shook on its foundations.

It was a blessing misplaced by Matt but now remembered. Luke or he could have been dead this morning—maybe both of them killed in the blast. By the grace of God, they were alive and well, able to reflect on their blessings and ponder the future.

"I love you, Matt," Caroline said.

"I love you, too, honey," he replied.

She was gone then, to tend some other troubled spirit. Caroline knew her husband well, understood that Matt was just beginning to soak up all that had happened, trying to comprehend the meaning. The full impact would hit him hardest a few days later, and he would need his wife especially then—her courage, her understanding, her reassurance and her touch. In this way, Matt and Caroline were alike, although neither one fully realized how their respective needs played into each other's strengths. By helping Matt cope, Caroline would draw strength from his courage, his understanding, his reassurance and his touch.

Joe came next, and Matt almost dreaded to face him. How could he tell his oldest son—who had risked his life for the family's livelihood, put his dreams on hold for his father's dream and never asked for anything in return—that more sacrifices were needed?

"Listen, Daddy," Joe said at length in their discussion. "I have somethen I'd like to tell you, and I want you to hear me out before you say anything."

"Sure, son."

"I don't intend to go back to school this year—at least not right away," he announced. "I only have two quarters left before I graduate. That's hardly any time at all. I can finish college next year or whenever it's more convenient. Right now, I want to help out around here—rebuilden the tobacco barns, getten grain planted for the winter or maybe even finden a job off the farm to bring some money into the house—whatever we need most to get by until next year."

Matt shuffled his feet, looked across the blackened field and wondered when his oldest son had grown such a large, comfortable shoulder. Once again, he wanted to bury his head and cry. Instead, he forced himself to look Joe in the eye and said, "You keep gallopen to the rescue, son. Keep doen it, and you'll wind up as my right-hand man."

"I can't be your right-hand man, Daddy," Joe replied sincerely, "but I do want to be in your corner—now and always."

Matt smiled and nodded his understanding. "You're a good man to have in anybody's corner," he said. "And thank you, son. I appreciate you comen to me like this."

It was a deep appreciation, the kind that made his heart ache, and the gratitude grew in Matt as the day progressed. One by one, his family came to him—in their own way and in their own time—offering and seeking reassurances as well as anything else that was needed to make life a bit easier, a little simpler.

Their outpouring of concern was not limited to Matt by any means. They sought each other out as well—not just the odd one but everyone. Earlier in the morning when the house had been saved, they had shared an important moment as a family, a collective of themselves. Now they needed private moments, to find the right words or expressions or touch that conveyed how much they meant to each other. In various ways, they showed one another what was in their hearts, which was love.

Summer tried to persuade Joe to use her scholarship money to pay his college tuition. She had observed her brother talking earnestly to Matt earlier in the day and guessed the content of their conversation.

Joe politely rejected her offer, kissed her on the cheek and steered the conversation to Tom. "He's my best friend in the world, and you've stolen him from me, little sister," he teased. "Please be gentle with him."

Summer had a surprise herself, which was news of her impending engagement to Tom. She shared that secret with Carrie because her sister was an incurable romantic at heart and—even in the midst of these bad times—would share the feeling of elation that surged within Summer's heart.

Carrie joined John on a walk through the woods because she understood his need to see how the flames had affected the place. She knew—but never mentioned—that John had walked a similar course with Grandpa earlier in the day.

John helped Bonnie pick butterbeans in the garden on the Castleberry place, even though it was Sunday and Caroline and Rachel frowned at working on the Sabbath. John frowned over work on Sundays, too, but his sister found comfort in gardens, and he believed God would not begrudge them a few butterbeans.

Bonnie put a new bandage on Luke's branded shoulder because her brother seemed to keep getting hurt badly this summer and apparently appreciated the way his baby sister tended to his wounds.

On and on, the commiserating continued until the circle was complete, except for one tangent.

In the late evening, under another blood-red sky with the smell of smoke heavy and black drifts still rising from the burned earth, Tom Carter came to see Matt. Half-guessing what the young man had on his mind, Matt offered Tom a glass of iced tea, which Summer poured, and made the boy wait at the table while he ate fresh butterbeans.

When supper was finished, Tom walked his mentor into the pecan orchard and handed Matt a check worth three weeks of his salary.

"I realize I could have picked a better time to do this, Matt, but you know I only have one week left to work with you before I report to Fort Benning," Tom explained. "I was hopen you could keep this money for me as well as next week's check—kind of in trust until I come home in December. That way, I can be sure that I'll have enough saved to buy Summer an engagement ring.

"What do you say to that?" the young man asked.

Matt wanted to say he that he thought his daughter had found a man with a very large shoulder. Instead, he replied, "You've always been a part of this family, son. I'll be right pleased to see it become official."

He extended his handshake, then added, "I don't know of a better man for my daughter to marry than you, Tom."

Matt also started to tell Tom that while he would keep the check, he would not cash it. Then, he changed his mind. Sometimes, help came from unexpected places, and Matt did not like to kick a gift horse in the mouth—especially when the benefaction came out of respect for him and love for his daughter.

They wound up making small talk about the clouds gathering on the horizon.

CHAPTER 7

ON TUESDAY MORNING, EVERYONE overslept, fooled by an overcast sky into thinking they had time to linger in bed and just plain worn out from the strain of the last few days. No one emerged from beneath their cool sheets until Tom knocked on the door ready to begin another day of work. And Tom himself was more than an hour late, having turned off his own alarm clock, rolled over in bed and gone back to sleep on this dreary morning.

At the breakfast table with cold cereal and milk before them, the mood was sullen, dark and silent—except for the radio. As he had predicted incorrectly for two straight days now, the weatherman once again promised the first thunderstorm of the summer. With the hurricane lobbing warm moist air over South Georgia and poised to strike the Florida panhandle before noon, it was inconceivable that rain would not arrive sometime this day. He droned on, explaining why his forecasts had been wrong on Sunday and Monday, then laughed obnoxiously.

"Listen, folks," he bellowed. "If it don't rain today, we're never gonna get it."

Believing only half of what they heard, everyone marched from the house to the waiting work.

Sam, the girls and Tom spent the morning unstringing tobacco in the pack-house. Piled from floor to ceiling in stacks alongside the two long walls, the sticks of golden-brown leaf cramped the small room. With the limited floor space needed to spread out the burlap sheets on which Sam packed the tobacco in perfectly rounded mounds, Summer and Tom set up horses underneath the canopy of oak trees, which fronted the shed, while Carrie and Bonnie balanced their sticks in notches along the wall of the sagging front porch. There was a rhythm to their work as they pulled bunches of tobacco from the string that had been used to tie the leaves to the sticks.

The tobacco was in perfect *order*, which meant the leaves were not so heavy with moisture that they refused to yield the string or so dry that they crumbled at the slightest touch. Everyone worked methodically, and by dinnertime, only a few layers remained between the ceiling and the wooden floor beneath one of the two stacks.

Rachel and Caroline spent the morning in the summer garden, which just about had yielded its limit of vegetables for the year. With the pickings slim, their experienced hands flew across the bushes of beans and peas, dropping the bounty into bushel baskets without missing a beat. Their only break in routine occurred when the women wiped sweat from their brows or paused to anticipate the coming-in of the fall vegetables, which Matt had planted on the Castleberry place. The late garden had benefited from irrigation. With a little rain over the next few days, the garden would produce enough vegetables to fill the family's freezer and stock the pantry. If nothing else, Rachel and Caroline knew, their family would have food to eat during the hard winter ahead.

The task of clearing the rubble from the burned barns fell to Joe, John and Luke. They hustled through the morning. Joe lugged the charred rafters from the ruins, John stacked the smutty tin and Luke pulled melted pipes and burners from the debris. They worked in virtual silence, acknowledging one another when a particular effort demanded a helping hand, which was offered without being asked. Together, they dragged the crushed and twisted furnaces from beneath the ashes.

When dinnertime came, they were tired, streaked with black grime and satisfied with their progress. In the afternoon, they would tackle the job of removing the burned tractor.

Dinner was dismal, conspicuously noticeable for its sharp contrast to the hot meals Rachel had served virtually every day all summer long. With no apologies, Caroline and Rachel set packaged lunch meat on the table, except for one piece of leftover ham, which Luke grabbed from the refrigerator before anyone else remembered it was there.

Either Luke failed to see the envious glances cast his way, or he chose to ignore the disgusted expressions on the faces of his brothers and sisters. Regardless, he enjoyed his ham sandwich, which was more than could be said for those who slapped a piece of baloney between two slices of bread.

Only Sam and Joe dared to complain aloud about the victuals, declaring they could not stomach a baloney sandwich.

"Suit yourself," Rachel replied.

"It's a long time between now and supper," Caroline added, "and you may get more of the same."

Not intending to go hungry, Joe suited himself. He sliced a couple of mellow bananas, spread mayonnaise on four pieces of bread and offered one of the sandwiches to his grandfather.

The whole bunch of them was bored, listless and thirsty for something other than iced tea. And it was Carrie—the most silent one of them all, who could talk a blue streak when she put her mind to it, yet rarely ventured an unsought opinion—who pinpointed the cause of their malaise.

"I'd trade all the baloney in the world for just one raindrop on my face," she said.

Her declaration came as she sat hunched over the table, dreamily propped on an elbow, with a hand cupping her chin. Aimed at no one in particular, the off-handed remark startled everyone, especially Carrie. She took a long moment to comprehend the biting tone in her admission, then seemed almost embarrassed as drawn faces peered back at her with expressions of sympathy, disbelief and understanding.

"Amen to that, honey," said Matt, who had entered the house unnoticed and was standing at the kitchen door when Carrie voiced the thought on everyone's mind.

Matt had spent the morning hauling water and scouring the community for two empty barns that he could fill with the strippings of the tobacco. His appearance spared Carrie any further explanation. But her wish lingered over the table like an unfulfilled promise of dessert. And it breathed down their necks as they labored under a sweltering afternoon sun.

––––––––

The skies held an almost undeniable promise of rain early in the day. Then, something strange, yet all too familiar, happened. The gray clouds scattered and disappeared. By noon, the sun shone like every other day that summer, which explained the staleness of the family's dinner far better than the idea of eating baloney sandwiches.

Everyone was fed up and tired of having their spirits dampened by the teasing, indecisive force of nature.

Restless with waiting, they stepped up the pace of their labor in the afternoon, as if the bustle would hurry the weather. But the exertion only tired them. They took a break from the work, drank cold drinks, ate moon pies and waited with the anticipation of an audience attending the grand premiere of the season.

At long last, when the day reached its hottest point—with the air as stagnant as it had ever been—the skies made up their mind. A plain of puffy white clouds galloped onto the southwestern horizon, riding a balmy breeze blown by some hurricane whose name no one could remember. The fresh scent of a coming rain cleared the air, and heat lightning rolled lazily—far off in the distance before cresting closer on waves of darkening cumulus. When the bellies of the clouds were girdled in black and the air strangely cool, the lightning found its thunder.

The first rolling clap idled the last industrious thoughts on the farm and chased the workers to the front porch of the house, where they trained their eyes on the blackened sky in search of anything remotely wet. Time made them wait still longer—until the dark clouds tricked the outside security light into thinking it was nighttime and the wind whipped the air with angry impatience. Finally, the heavy sky relinquished the first drops from a tear in its liner. The water fell hard against the dusty ground, followed by another heave that seemed to have been sloshed from the top of a full barrel. Seconds later, the clouds ripped apart and the heavens pounded the dry earth with rain.

The storm spent its pent-up fury swiftly, then settled into a steady summer shower. It was cleansing for the soul, sweet to the touch and refreshment for the spirit.

––––––

No one made the mistake of recognizing the rain as any kind of panacea for their troubles. Especially Matt.

The smashing enormity of everything came crashing down on him as Matt watched the storm from the cab of the pickup truck. There was no way to rationalize the situation—just the cold comprehension of a hot summer filled with withered crops and dry fortunes.

Matt wanted to blank away the last few months, to remember the good feeling he had carried into the new year. But he could not push away the nagging aftermath of things unplanned and plans gone awry. He had to face the consequences.

He swallowed hard, his throat constricted as he wondered whether the promise of next year was enough to carry his family through the tough times ahead of them. So much was lost. Matt knew what it was like to take three steps forward, then fall back two. But this was the first time he had felt as if he was losing at least three steps for every two he made. Now, when there was so much that needed doing, he wondered whether his shoulders would bear the burden.

Above everything else, though, Matt ached for the sacrifices his family would have to make in the coming year. Their faith and trust in him—their willingness to do whatever was necessary—had always given Matt a sense of pride unlike any other constant in his life. Right now, however, their unabridged devotion depressed him.

Matt did not grieve alone.

Caroline had sensed the rain would bring her husband a heavy heart. She shared his sorrow. She understood her family had suffered a loss far greater than the damage done by some ordinary blight on their fields. If the next year brought little else to this family, it would give them succinct understanding of what hardship really was. But goaded by the same instincts that now burdened her husband, Caroline found courage to face the future.

Peering through the glass window of the living room, she watched Matt slump against the truck door, knowing he needed her beside him. If for nothing else, then he craved the reassurance of her presence. Without waiting for the storm to slacken, Caroline went to her husband, ignoring the curious looks and calls from the children as she stepped off the porch and ran into the driving rain.

Matt barely acknowledged her arrival, staying slouched against the door and tight-lipped. Even so, he arched his eyebrows in the thoughtful, worried look she had grown accustomed to when they faced difficult times. Her husband's concern was all the encouragement Caroline needed. She slipped close to him, resting her head on his shoulder. As the hard rain settled into a steady tap against the truck, husband and wife engaged in a quiet give-and-take that buoyed their spirits.

In a while, Caroline felt the strength surging from her husband. Then, she straightened next to him, stroked his hair and helped Matt to understand what really mattered.

"If it's true what they say about hard times maken people appreciate the good times, then we oughtta be one more appreciative family come this time next year," she said. "But, Matt, I don't necessarily believe that's a matter of fact. For the most part, this family has settled for getten by year after year. With the good Lord's help, we've done fairly well for ourselves. As for this year, well, I can appreciate it just as much as those years when we've gotten by a little better than usual. As long as we're doen it together—you and me, Ma and Pa, our children—then every ounce of sweat, every heartache and every happy moment is worthwhile. Because after all, Matt, we have so much—don't we?"

Without waiting for his answer, she added blithely, "We've faced hard times before, sweetheart. We'll get through this, too."

For a long moment, Matt stared into the summer shower. Finally, he put his arm around Caroline, and they leaned against each other.

"We will at that," he said simply.

PART THREE

Out alone in the winter rain,
Intent on giving and taking pain
But never was I far out of sight,
Of a certain upper-window light.

The Thatch
~ Robert Frost

THE WAR

1968

CHAPTER 1

JOE STARED IN WIDE-EYED disbelief at the melee playing out in real life. Beneath the Hilton Hotel sign, police and National Guardsmen clubbed antiwar demonstrators senseless, smashing heads, limbs and crotches with reckless disregard of their victims. A store window shattered somewhere, and the cops intensified their assault until blood flowed in the streets of Chicago. Paddy wagons lined the avenues, waiting to cart away those who were arrested.

"Lousy pigs," someone muttered behind Joe.

For seventeen agonizing minutes, the violence raged, with the crowd of demonstrators chanting ominously, "The whole world is watching."

Joe was part of the whole world on this last Wednesday night of August 1968. He had been camped in a folding chair in front of the television for three straight hours. His bladder urged him to find a bathroom, but Joe stayed in his seat, mesmerized by the savagery on the television screen.

He was among a crowd of college students who had piled into the tiny living room of Elliot Frankel's apartment. Elliot enjoyed the well-earned reputation as the unofficial leader of a fledgling student movement at Valdosta State College. He was a novelty among the conservative collegians, most of whom adhered to values more American than apple pie itself. Besides his authentic Brooklyn accent, which was an oddity in itself on the campus, Elliot made a conscientious effort to distinguish himself from the crowd. His jet-black hair flowed in long locks down his back. His diamond-studded earring sparkled too loudly to go unnoticed by anyone within eyeshot. He typically wore an odd assortment of rag-tag clothes, love beads and sandals unless the occasion required conservative attire. Then, he dressed in well-worn blue jeans, T-shirts and sneakers. On more than one occasion, he had inspired the question, "Is it a man or a woman?"

Despite his peculiarities and shenanigans, Elliot believed substance mattered more than style. He was no ordinary goof ball and refused treatment as such, though several professors had tried without success. He had migrated to the South Georgia college from New York University, hoping to discover firsthand the truth about race relations in the Deep South. He came across as sincere, dedicated to his convictions and resolute in his commitments. When he picked a fight with administrators, professors or fellow students, Elliot argued with passion and persuasiveness.

Joe and Elliot had become friends in the spring of 1967 during an American history class, unexpectedly brought together by their mutual praise for Martin Luther King Jr. In the face of bitter feelings among their classmates, they had defended the Nobel Peace Prize winner as a genuine American hero for his war on injustice and bigotry. Out of their battle scars, a genuine camaraderie had emerged even though they sat on opposite sides of the classroom and appeared socially at odds with each other. When the class ended, Elliot had invited Joe to join him for a bite to eat at the local Woolworth's lunch counter.

As Joe nursed a Coke and Elliot sipped coffee with the day's blue plate special—fried beef liver—the young men had spoken frankly of their misconceptions about each other. Elliot decided Joe was an unabashed square, committed to progress as long as it did not interfere too much with the way things were. Joe believed Elliot was a misguided revolutionary, whose freewheeling ways alienated the very people he hoped to change.

"You talk like McCarthy and Kennedy, but you're Buckley and Nixon in sheep's clothing," Elliot declared. "You believe change will occur simply for the sake of change, and you assume it will be change for the better. But while you're waiting and hoping for the best, very little gets accomplished, Joe. It takes men of action to bring about change. You prefer to sit back, watch and then make observations that more often than not come across as smug complicity rather than constructive feedback. Honestly, Joe, I question your commitment to change, to a great many of the things you profess to believe. With you, everything is a simple question of right and wrong. In my book, that's a selfish way to look at things. It's a set-up for a hard and fast fall. I suppose if you want to change the world—and probably you do—then you are one of those people who believe it can be done one person at a time. Assuming you're right for the sake of argument, then there's a great deal of suffering to be done while we're waiting on your piecemeal change. I'm not much for suffering, Joe."

"You act too much like a hippie for my tastes," Joe responded in equally plain tones, "and you tend to go overboard with your beliefs. Deep down, you champion essentially sound principles. No one should fault you for your commitment to civil rights, and everyone probably should pay attention to your misgivens about Vietnam. But despite your best effort, Elliot, there's no way you can make me believe that Americans should see Fidel Castro as any kind of hero. Nor does this country need a social revolution. People make mistakes—me, you, the president, Congress, everybody. But good values never go out of style, and I think most people have good values. You, on the other hand, don't always advocate good values, Elliot. You want to live in a world where anything goes: Drink this, smoke that, free love, free sex, screw anything that walks and screw the consequences. You're so danged intent on tearen everything and everybody down that you can't separate what's good from what needs to be done."

"I'll take that under consideration next time I plan a revolution," Elliot said.

"Likewise," Joe agreed. "If I ever get around to it."

Eventually, they had decided their observations about each other probably were as much accurate as flawed and as astute as they were ignorant. But they had walked away from the dime store restaurant with a grudging respect for each other's way of thinking.

Their newfound friendship had languished soon after the spring-quarter history class ended, and they had lost touch completely when Joe left college to help his father after the fire. But on the evening of April fourth earlier this year, Elliot had telephoned long-distance to inform Joe of MLK's assassination at the Lorraine Motel in Memphis, Tennessee. A few days later, against his family's wishes, Joe had accompanied Elliot to Atlanta, where they attended the fallen civil rights leader's funeral. Months later, they had repeated the ritual when Robert Kennedy was cut down by Sirhan Sirhan.

In between the tragedies, Elliot had mentioned casually that Joe might enjoy attending one of the weekly meetings he hosted for "freethinkers" like himself.

"There's nothing official about it or anything like that," Elliot explained. "It's a bunch of students and sometimes a professor or two who're feeling especially brave or oppressed. We sit around, listen to the music, drink coffee, wine, beer, booze or whatever your pleasure—maybe smoke a joint every now and then, and talk about whatever's groovy or hip."

"I probably wouldn't fit in," Joe surmised.

"You would well enough," Elliot replied. "Almost everyone who comes is more like you than me and the rest of the hard-core nuts."

"Who are the hard-core nuts?" Joe asked.

"We represent every stereotype you could want," Elliot said. "Darris Palmer is black and can't decide whether he wants to follow MLK or Malcolm X. I keep telling him they're both dead, so it doesn't matter. Cecil Bradley is light in the shoes if you catch my drift, but he can argue passionately about why the United States does not belong in Vietnam. Kevin Reid worked in Mississippi during Freedom Summer, then spent two years in 'Nam. He's generally confused about everything. Then there's Karen Baxter. She's a hodgepodge of every stereotype in our little group and then some.

"Do any of those names ring a bell?" Elliot asked.

"I went to high school with Karen," Joe answered. "She always was a freethinker, I suppose."

"Yes, indeed," Elliot sighed. "Karen has a style all her own. What she can do for peace remains to be seen. As a piece, however, the woman's not bad at all. You come to one or two of our meetings, and you're likely to learn for yourself."

"The meeten sounds interesten, but I think I'll pass on Karen and whatever she might offer," Joe said somewhat tersely.

Elliot laughed aloud, amused by the serious tone of Joe's voice. "A caustic comment that begs questioning," he teased. "But I'll be a gentleman for once and keep them to myself. Let's just say, shall we, that Karen makes sure the group's physical needs—at least those of the male persuasion—are attended to so that our minds might be at their brilliant best to satisfy her lusty liberal leanings."

"Say whatever you want about her," Joe said. "I couldn't care less."

A few days later, he had attended his first meeting. For the most part, he drank beer while everyone else analyzed a Simon and Garfunkel song. At subsequent meetings, they discussed Vietnam, the Great Society, the upcoming election and how America's youth was changing the country's way of thinking. Whether he agreed or disagreed with his new friends, Joe enjoyed the debate, as well as the companionship.

Appropriately enough, he had smoked marijuana for the first time while the group discussed the merits of legalized drugs, an idea Joe found ridiculous and flawed. But he had consumed far too much beer on that night to argue effectively against the notion, so he kept quiet and took a toke on a marijuana cigarette circulating around the room. Even in his alcoholic haze, Joe felt uneasy about smoking pot. But when the drug seemed to have no apparent effect on his behavior, he found it easier to accept the marijuana on the next occasion it was offered.

On this August night, Joe felt no remorse at all when Elliot offered him the remnants of a rolled joint. He inhaled deeply, took another drag for good measure and passed the joint to a girl waiting beside him with a roach clip. Almost instantly, his total awareness dulled as his attention zeroed in on the television screen.

As Joe saw it, the savagery in Chicago was a fitting climax to the carnage that would be remembered as 1968. He thought the violence in Chicago was hardly unexpected.

Although only a spectator to the Democratic National Convention, Joe had sensed the mounting tension and frustration that triggered this final clash between antiwar demonstrators and cops. For three days, he had watched television and read newspaper accounts of how students trashed police cars with rocks and bottles while baiting officers with taunts and threats. From the moment the cops first fired their guns into the air as a warning several days earlier, he had anticipated a frenzied climax to the madness. But even so, he watched the television in dismay. He was stunned by the show of force as the cops carried out their vicious attack. But his sympathies were tempered by the inclination that the mob of demonstrators deserved a few bruises for their own outrageous behavior.

He was wondering why both sides were not behaving more rationally when Karen Baxter interrupted his thoughts.

"This is mind-bogglen," Karen said to Joe. "It's a national disgrace and just goes to prove what we've been sayen all along. What about the right to peaceful protest?"

"I haven't seen anything peaceful about any of the whole sorry mess," Joe replied without taking his eyes off the television. "But you're right about one thing: It is a disgrace."

———

Karen backed away from Joe, biting her tongue to conceal the anger boiling within her. Once again, Joe had her on edge. She tried to decipher his remark about the bloodbath playing on television. Was there a hidden meaning in his flippant response to her observations, one she failed to understand? Had he intended to ridicule her?

Too often these days, she found herself floundering in Joe's presence. When Joe was among her circle of companions, she maintained a constant vigil on every word and thought. She felt threatened by Joe, as if he were a secret agent waiting to expose her as an intellectual and New Left fraud. The man's mere presence frayed her nerves, his smug complacency rankled her demeanor and his casual disregard preyed on her worst fears. Karen resented his intrusion into her elite group of radicals and revolutionaries. Worst of all, she despised having to hide her contempt for Joe.

Still, discretion was an annoying necessity. Karen needed every clever trick to keep these bouts of paranoia from revealing herself as a vain woman instead of the free-spirited intellectual she wanted to be.

She had orchestrated her image as a choreographer creates dance. Each step was planned with precision and flow, embracing every idea that smacked of rebellion. She maintained impeccable grades, yet flaunted her disregard for archaic institutions of learning. She denounced Vietnam, railed against prejudice, applauded Eugene McCarthy and was leading efforts to establish a chapter of Students for a Democratic Society on the VSC campus. She believed in black power, flower power, feminism and free love. She was ready to tune in, turn on and drop out. She was devoted to the ideas of rebellion and repression, revolution and resistance.

More than embracing any particular ideology, Karen adored all things extreme. On a given day, she was a devoted flower child, strolling on air as she sang *Are You*

Going to San Francisco, even while she dreamed of standing side by side with the Black Panthers and making fast and furious love with Eldridge Cleaver. She deplored violence, yet licked her lips in fascination as scores died and flames burned throughout Watts, Newark and Detroit in urban rioting. She encouraged young men to burn their draft cards and flee to Canada, yet was enthralled by the sheer numbers coming out of Vietnam: half a million American soldiers there, fifteen thousand dead, almost two million acres defoliated in a single year. She had believed passionately in Robert Kennedy and Martin Luther King Jr., but found the men's violent deaths more inspiring than their principles. Now, she supported no one in the race to succeed Lyndon Johnson unless it was Eugene McCarthy. Even so, she hoped George Wallace would run a good campaign simply for the sake of a divisive election.

Her motives had been sincere at some point. She had come to college in search of liberation and ended up with a carefully cultivated reputation as a radical. She had become the embodiment of the New Left, a radical whose reputation was surpassed only by the antics and maleness of Elliot Frankel. Earning her reputation had been pure bliss. Maintaining it was complicated. As queen of the revolution, she was expected to say all the right things, wear all the right clothes and think all the right thoughts. Often, Karen felt as if she were campaigning to become the next homecoming queen.

She owed her revolutionary status to Elliot. He was one of the few men who had seduced Karen rather than been seduced by her. From the moment she first laid eyes on the man, Karen had decided to sleep with Elliot on their second occasion together. Less than two hours later, she was underneath him, on the mattress laid across the living room floor in his tiny apartment. Men with long hair and earrings attracted Karen in the first place. Once Elliot had uttered his first words of liberal propaganda, she had become putty in his hands.

Karen had discovered the sexual revolution years before it became vogue. Sex made her heady with power and importance. She kept a running list of her sexual partners and the tab numbered more than a hundred. She had slept with schoolboys, collegians, professors, construction workers, a vacuum cleaner salesman and one black man. She advocated legalized abortion and free birth control pills for everyone. She understood the power of seduction, and she used it with great success. On a whim, she would turn a man into a sexual magnet, full of cock and swagger in his prowess. Or she might exploit every inch of vulnerability. On three occasions, she had extorted comfortable sums of money from the ignorant, telling them cash was needed to pay for an abortion. The claim had been true only once.

Karen was indeed queen of the revolution, and she enjoyed her favored status. But the mere presence of Joe Baker tarnished the luster of her crown. He evoked memories of the girl who had longed to be a hell-raiser while cast amid a sea of fuddy-duddies; a closet revolutionary who wanted to shake America at its roots while her peers thrived in their contentment; the siren who satisfied her restlessness by bringing to life the vivid fantasies of youthful lovers. Joe's presence was a direct link to the perky cheerleader, the Sunday school sweetheart, the bouffanted prom queen—all roles Karen had played at one time or another. But those were feelings that any of her high school classmates could have dredged to the surface, the cool and the popular ones, the jocks and the brains, the weirdoes and the wallflowers, even those who barely counted.

She felt ill at ease around Joe. She was jealous of his poise and unwavering self-assurance. His presence undermined her self-control, and his seeming indifference provoked her pettiness. He jeopardized her status, leaving Karen one slip of the tongue away from losing her credibility with the group.

On the first night Joe had attended one of Elliot's gatherings, Karen had picked the topic of discussion—an analysis of her favorite song, *Dangling Conversation,* by Simon and Garfunkel. The discussion had been probing, a free-spirited consideration of life's values and a welcomed relief from the endless dialectic over war, politics and violence. The lone dark spot had been Joe, who sat in his chair looking as if he deigned the entire exercise a waste of time. Irked by his silence, Karen had made a blunder. She had challenged Joe to contribute to the conversation, hoping to expose him as shallow and unable to grasp the subtle elements of the song. If she had thought first, she would have remembered Joe was a sponge, always aware of everything and willing to meet a challenge. But Karen had forgotten.

"You haven't said a word all evenen, Joe," she commented during a lull in the discussion. "Are we boren you? Or does the song have no meanen for you?"

"I like the poetry of Robert Frost," Joe answered with a shrug of his shoulders. "But I don't care much for Emily Dickinson. I don't understand her—maybe because I can't or don't want to identify with her."

When it became apparent Joe would say nothing else, Karen had pressed the issue. "You're missen the complexities of the song, Joe," she said with the slightest touch of condescension. "I don't think poetry has much to do with the message. It's about how superficial people are."

Joe considered the suggestion for a long moment. "Perhaps," he shrugged finally. "I tend to think it's up to each person to decide for themselves what is and isn't superficial. It's certainly not my place to make that decision for them."

"Right on!" said Darris Palmer, pumping his fist and winking at Joe.

"I agree," Elliot added quickly before his eyes turned lethal and his tone lecturing. "Besides Karen," he said. "Since when are we keeping score on who contributes what to the discussion?"

"I wasn't keepen score," Karen replied calmly, mustering a warm smile for Joe. "I happen to know Joe from way back when. I was hopen—maybe even expecten—somethen more profound from him."

Then, she had laughed easily. "No harm meant, Joe," she added, diffusing the tension. "You know how obsessive I get about things important to me. Didn't you once call me a bulldog?"

"I don't recall," Joe had said, shrugging off the incident as if there were no need for an apology.

From that point on, Karen had focused on making Joe feel accepted. She had smiled at him until her jaws ached and tried to draw him into conversation. But nothing she did commanded his attention. And although she had a strong inkling why he avoided her, Karen seethed over his rejection. Animosity festered within her like an infected sore, threatening to burst in an ugly spray of malice and envy.

Suddenly, a warm breath ran down her neck and across her throat. "I'd like to be inside that pretty head of yours now to see what wheels are turning," Elliot said. "What has Joe Baker done to inspire this gaze of fierce intensity?"

Karen tipped her head back and smiled through gritted teeth, allowing Elliot to muzzle her cheek with his day-old beard. "Was I staren," she asked. "I didn't realize."

"I didn't think so," Elliot laughed. "Nor do I really care." He pulled her against him. "Suppose you stick around tonight after everybody leaves," he leered. "We could stage some violence of our own, compromise each other and then make peace."

The suggestion appealed to Karen, and she knew suddenly what needed doing. She would bed a man tonight, but not Elliot Frankel.

"I don't think so, Elliot," she replied at length, slipping from his embrace. "Some other time. Tonight, I'm taken care of unfinished business."

––––––––

Willowy arms wrapped around Joe's shoulders, breaking his concentration on the televised spectacle that would go down in infamy as the 1968 Democratic National Convention in Chicago. One hand caressed his chest, while another brought a taste of hard liquor to his lips. The hardened nipples of firm breasts pressed against his spine, and moist breath whispered in his ear. Joe knew Karen Baxter was seducing him. He decided to play along with her for a while, admiring her moxie if little else.

"Vodka on ice," she said. "That is your preference, Joe?"

"It is," Joe answered as she nibbled on his ear.

Karen was oblivious to the long-lived effects of her passionate dalliance with Joe years earlier. In his twenty-two years, she was the only woman who had come remotely close to claiming his heart. Joe counted his former feelings for her as nothing more than puppy love, and he regarded the lost relationship with casual detachment. Still, Karen intrigued him. And although he knew better, Joe was still captivated by what he saw as a delicate quality to the woman. More than once recently, he had caught himself fantasizing about making love to her, wondering about the passion they could create if they took the time to appreciate each other.

These thoughts were ridiculous, he knew, a complete waste of time. His infatuation with Karen was irrational, though less now that he was older and wiser. Joe harbored few illusions about her. He knew people who piled puppies and rocks in burlap bags, then tossed the bundle off the nearest bridge, and they had more heart than Karen. Furthermore, he suspected she was the reason he approached any relationship with a woman like a skilled bank robber, making his moves only when he was certain of the getaway.

Maybe that explained why he was willing to play along with her seduction. She was skilled at the art, a mixture of coy, cunning and straightforwardness in her quest to bed him. Above all, she was relentless, charming Joe with the fickle spells of enchantment and whim that had first attracted him years earlier. On this night, he was of mind to wait and see whatever sleight of hand Karen would play.

––––––––

Hours later, Karen snuggled into the crook of his arm as Joe smoked a cigarette. She sighed contentedly, watching Joe blow smoke rings. They were sweaty, exhausted and satisfied.

"This beats the backseat of the family car, huh?" she giggled.

"Yeah," Joe said.

"Can you French-inhale?" she asked.

"I haven't done that in years," Joe answered, exhaling a straight line of smoke. "I pretty much stick to the basics."

"Do it for me," Karen said.

Joe drew on the cigarette, opened his mouth and breathed slowly, rotating the smoke in a circle between his nose and mouth. Karen giggled, pushing closer to him, resting her palm flat against his stomach.

Joe quickly exhaled the smoke and pulled away from her, pushing away the sheet as he sat up on the edge of the bed. "What time is it?" he asked, searching around the one-room apartment for a clock.

Karen rolled on her side and retrieved a clock from the floor. "It's three-thirty," she informed him. "Come back to bed. Let's sleep late and see if we can stage a repeat performance when we wake up."

"I have to get home," Joe replied. "We're diggen sweet potatoes today, and Daddy wants to get an early start. If I leave now, I can catch a little sleep before it's time to get up."

"You're leaven me?" she asked, disbelieving.

Joe stood unsteadily, found his clothes and put on his underwear and jeans. "It was fun, Karen, but I have to go," he said a moment later, his tone far more casual than his feelings about this encounter. "I guess we chalk this up as one for old time's sake."

"Beats the backseat of the family car," she said softly as Joe buttoned his shirt, stuffed socks into pants pockets and sat down beside her to tie his tennis shoes.

Joe looked at Karen for a long moment, appraising her petite figure, her milky white skin and soft brown hair. He wondered if a goodbye kiss was in order.

Karen sensed his mixed emotions. "Don't forget the protest," she reminded him. "We'll start the fall quarter off with a bang."

Joe shrugged. "I'm not sure I'll be there," he replied.

"You have to be there, Joe," she cried. "You promised."

Joe tried without success to remember the promise. "Believen the war is wrong is one thing, Karen," he said. "Protesten against it is somethen else again. I'm a veteran for gosh sake. I'm not sure I'd feel right about doen that. Those things have a way of getten blown out of proportion. A person ought to be damn sure about what—and whom—he's protesten against."

"We're sure, Joe," she argued. "We're demonstraten to stop the war in Vietnam, clear and simple."

"It's not clear and simple, Karen, and if you believe that, then you're sellen yourself a bill of goods," Joe fought back. "My best friend in the world is over there right now, right this moment. Guys you and I went to school with have been and are there now. Remember Scotty Dean. He went over there and came back without a leg, Karen. How do you think Scotty's gonna feel when he sees his friends protesten against the very thing that cost him such a high price?"

"That's why we have to protest," she pleaded. "So not one more person comes back maimed or worse. You know what we're up against, Joe. Those of us who oppose this war have to demonstrate our opposition. We have to show people the war is wrong."

"I'll think about it," Joe said. "That's the best I can do."

Karen exhaled an angry breath, sat up in bed and pulled the sheet against her. "Same old, Joe," she scoffed. "You're never able to come through when the chips are down, are you?"

"Exactly what does that mean?" Joe interrupted.

"It means you have the most half-assed convictions of anybody I've ever known," Karen said scathingly. "You start things, but you never finish them. It's one of the things that always bugged me about you."

"If it's somethen I believe in strongly enough, Karen, I'll see it through to the end," Joe said. "But I won't be pressured into doen somethen I disagree with or don't fully understand."

"What exactly do you believe in?" she asked scornfully.

Unexpectedly, surprising himself, Joe touched her face. Karen glanced up, and he saw her discontent.

"A long time ago," he said, "I believed I loved you."

She shook her head in disagreement. "Nothen but an infatuation," she replied without emotion.

"Maybe," Joe agreed, withdrawing his hand.

"Besides, Joe," she added. "I told you once: You and I aren't cut out for love."

"I'm not sure I believe that," he said. "What makes you so sure?"

"Because we're not willen to invest that much of ourselves," she snapped back. "You're just like me, Joe; you want to run away from everything that's familiar—from Cookville, from your home, from your family. We're gonna spend our whole lives runnen away and breaken ties."

Joe regarded her carefully. "That's a harsh life sentence to hang yourself with, Karen," he replied at last. "I don't buy it, at least not for myself. When and if I leave Cookville, you can be assured I'll be runnen to somethen. Maybe that's the difference between us. There's nothen or no one here that I'd ever want to run away from. It all means too much to me."

She shook her head to break the moment. "Just go, Joe," she urged softly, looking away and drawing up her knees. "Get out of here and go home."

He stood and left the room quickly, with a polite goodbye and without even looking back at her.

———

In the middle of September, Joe found himself standing on the edge of a group of students who intended to stage the first antiwar protest on the Valdosta State College campus. He was a dubious participant, reluctant to settle a battle of mind-sets that pitted his sense of loyalty against the growing notion that America had no business waging war in Vietnam. His final decision to participate was calculated, based on the facts as he saw them. His indecision arose from a belief that feelings as fierce and passionate as loyalty—whether to one's friends, family, country or brothers in arms—defied logic.

The call had been close, but Joe had gone with his head, because his heart told him the war was a mistake. No one back home knew of his decision to demonstrate against the war. Until a few minutes ago when he arrived on campus for the rally, his intentions had been declared to only one person, his best friend, who risked his life daily in the jungles of Vietnam.

In his frequent letters to Tom Carter, Joe had mentioned his concerns about the war, always careful to conceal any blatant antiwar sentiments. In writing to Tom several days earlier, Joe had chosen the words carefully to tell his friend about the upcoming protest. But he had not minced the truth about his decision to join the demonstration and his opposition to the war.

"I suppose I could keep everything a secret, Tom. I could simply attend the protest and never speak of it. But I don't want to lie to you. I'd rather lose your friendship to honesty than betray you with deception. The truth is that I think this war is a mistake.

"For years, I've watched the civil rights struggles and wanted to join in the fight. Maybe, too, I have in a small way. But I wish I could have done more to fight for something I believe in. Now I have an opportunity to make my voice heard. Although my opposition to the war in Vietnam is a murky issue compared with my belief in simple human dignity, I feel compelled this one time to join the front line of the battle rather than offer quiet support from the distance. Of course, once I get there, I might beat a hasty retreat. I wish you had that luxury.

"I have one last thing to say on the matter, and then I'll be quiet. Please don't consider my opposition to the war any reason to believe you have less than my full support for the job you're doing and the cause you're fighting for. I suppose that's an easy sentiment to lay claim to. Perhaps, too, it sounds like a coward's way out or nothing more than a feeble attempt to salve my conscience. I wouldn't blame you for feeling that way, Tom, or for feeling I've betrayed you in some way. But know this: I think about you every day over there, and I wish you were home, making babies with my sister and tending fields beside my daddy or on your own place. You belong here, Tom. Of that, I am certain."

Reflecting on the letter, Joe muttered a quick prayer for his friend and pushed aside his earlier doubts about joining the protest. His conscience was clear, and he was a willing soldier, at least for today, in this war against the War.

A group of nearly one hundred had massed beneath a grove of ancient live oak trees, draped with Spanish moss. Most were collegians, but the crowd also contained several professors and a smattering of local high school students. By far the most notable personalities gathered among the group, however, were three women whose sons had died in Vietnam. Elliot Frankel had persuaded these Gold Star mothers to share their grief, as well as their rage against the war. Their presence alone had guaranteed news coverage of the event by local newspapers, radio and television stations.

Fifteen minutes past the three o'clock starting time, the rally began officially. As Elliot stood on a flimsy wooden podium welcoming the group, Joe scouted the crowd. Several faces surprised him, belonging to people he would not have suspected to have strong sentiments against the war. About half the group carried signs and placards with antiwar messages. But generally, the protesters appeared hesitant and uncertain, almost as if they lacked the will or backbone to carry forth their cause. They shuffled their feet restlessly as Elliot outlined the itinerary and introduced the speakers, including the three bereaved mothers.

Astute as always, Elliot had asked the newest addition to the Gold Star club to deliver the first speech. The ploy seemed like shameless exploitation to Joe, who had heard Elliot predict the woman would break into tears almost at the onset.

His assumption proved correct. Speaking just two weeks after burying her son, the woman lasted less than a minute at the speaker's stand before dissolving into sobs. She was ushered to the side to regain her composure as Elliot made a public offering of condolence. Still, the deed was done. The mother's loss was fresh, and it struck a sympathetic chord with the crowd.

The next Gold Star mother's speech was equally brief and soft-spoken, but she made an impression on the protesters. "His name was Mike," she said, holding aloft an eight-by-ten photograph of a young man with blond hair. "He was my son, and he was killed last year in Vietnam. I miss him terribly. I always will. I do not believe he should have died over there. I wish there had never been a war in the first place. But most of all, I wish it would end."

People hung on those words, and the number of demonstrators was rising steadily as the third Gold Star mother took the podium. She appeared frail, but her voice was strong, and the woman delivered a resounding denouncement of the war. She tugged at heartstrings with fond reminiscing about her nineteen-year-old son and chilling details about his death. He had died on a routine mission in a village beside the Mekong River, she said. Viet Cong sympathizers had ambushed the patrol, killing three American soldiers, including her young son. The woman was crying softly as she finished her story.

"I came here today against the wishes of my husband," she concluded, taking a deep breath to control her tears. "He believes that I am betrayen the legacy of our son. But I felt it was important to add my voice to those who are callen for an end to this dreadful war." She paused, then added, "If for no other reason, then because I wish with all my heart that not one more mother would have to hear the awful news that her son has died in Vietnam."

Murmurs of sympathy rose from the crowd, which had quickly swelled to around two hundred fifty people. Soon, the hushed whispers turned to shouts of outrage as the protesters found their voice. Elliot Frankel grabbed the megaphone, chanting the first of several antiwar messages. Immediately, others joined him, their voices clamoring underneath the afternoon sun. With Elliot and the three Gold Star mothers leading the way, the crowd surged from beneath the shady canopy of moss-laden oaks, committed to their goal of occupying the college's white-stucco administration building.

Traffic halted as the throng of protesters crossed the major thoroughfare that paralleled the college grounds, picking up recruits by the dozens as they invaded the campus. They marched past the gymnasium, moving along a winding road that cut through the heart of the campus, singing *We Shall Overcome* as they neared the administration building. By now, some three hundred people were active demonstrators, with half as many standing on the sidelines. Some of the onlookers were simply curious; others derided the protesters.

"I'm glad you came," a voice whispered behind Joe as he trudged along the road.

Turning around, he found Karen Baxter beside him, holding a heavy, painted placard. She lowered the sign and pressed against him as the crowd ground to a stop near the administration building.

"What about you, Joe?" Karen asked. "Are you glad you came?"

"No, Karen," he answered, wishing the woman was somewhere else, wondering how she had managed to find him in the crowd. "I can't say I'm glad to be here, or that I'm particularly proud of it. But I believe it's the right thing to do."

"Always a rebel with a cause," Karen smiled at him. "One day, Joe, I'll probably regret giving you the big brush-off. Maybe you were right after all. We might have been good together."

"No, Karen," Joe said with a benign smile to mask his utter contempt for the woman. "I was dead wrong. Just slow to see it."

Her face was crestfallen as Joe turned away to survey the situation.

A line of police officers, sheriff's deputies and state troopers had blocked the protesters' path to the administration building. Dressed like storm troopers, armed with billy clubs, rifles and tear gas canisters, wearing hideous gas masks, the lawmen had marshaled their forces about fifteen yards in front of the demonstrators' target.

Joe was wondering what would happen next when someone pushed against his back and someone else yelled in his direction. Catching his balance before stumbling, he whipped his head around to see who was causing the commotion and found himself staring into a photographer's camera lens. He glanced away almost immediately, though not before the shutter exploded several times.

Seconds later, Elliot Frankel leapt atop the front hood of a blue Pontiac parked on the street and raised the megaphone above his head in a wordless demand for silence. The crowd quieted almost at once, with only the occasional sound of static from the police radios piercing the quietness. When he commanded the group's full attention, Elliot lifted the megaphone to speak.

"In the scheme of things," he began, "what we are doing here today may not matter much to many. But it is important. There have been bigger and better-organized peace marches, and there will be more. Thousands already have marched on our nation's capital to criticize this immoral war. Doves are on the march in cities and towns all across our country. Students are rising up on university and college campuses with reputations far exceeding that of VSC. Still, our protest is equally important. The powers-that-be cannot dismiss our actions as any less important than those who march on Washington. We are a part of the groundswell of voices against the war rising up in this nation. We are just as committed to the cause of peace as those we see on TV. We are just as committed as those who protested for peace on the bloody streets of Chicago several weeks ago. Our voices count."

A smattering of applause greeted his message, and Elliot seized the moment like a seasoned politician. "You and I," he said, before pausing until the noise died. "You and I," he declared, "are here today because we believe the American government is waging an unjust and unnecessary war on the people of Vietnam and on the people of the United States. Our government is sending thousands of young men—our friends, sons and brothers—to perpetuate unspeakable acts of violence in that little corner of Southeast Asia. The politicians tell us America is fighting in Vietnam because the Vietnamese people want us, because our presence is necessary to stop the spread of communism. They are noble intentions, perhaps. But when the very people who supposedly want them there kill our troops, I'm not convinced America is welcomed in Vietnam. And I'm not convinced the threat of communism in Vietnam or any other country in Southeast Asia merits enough concern to warrant the loss of thousands of American lives.

"I am Jewish, and I still shudder today at the atrocities committed against my people in another war not so long ago. I was not born when Hitler and the Nazis tried to exterminate Jews. But my relatives were there. Some died in those horrible gas chambers at Auschwitz. Others starved in Dachau. My parents were fortunate. They fled from Germany to the United States. They saw this country as a beacon of hope, and they believed in its greatness.

"That's one of the reasons I'm ashamed today—ashamed to see the government of the United States of America committing similar atrocities on the people of Vietnam. Maybe six million Vietnamese people have not yet died in the five years we've been fighting over there, but plenty have. Even more have suffered unimaginable pain from weapons that are every bit as vile as Hitler's gas chambers, weapons that never should have been invented, much less used on fellow human beings.

"My generation grew up fearful of the Bomb, that awesome weapon of destruction that obliterated two cities and thousands of people in a matter of seconds. The Bomb is frightening, but I wonder whether the Bomb is as gruesome as napalm.

"Do you folks know what napalm is?" Elliot asked, pausing like a teacher waiting for an answer.

"Napalm," he continued at length. "Napalm is a chemical weapon used by our military in Vietnam. Jet fighters fly over the lucky village of the hour, and they drop napalm bombs. There's no distinction between the good guys and the bad guys. Napalm sticks to the flesh of mothers, fathers and children, grandmothers, aunts and uncles. And it literally melts their flesh."

His tone, which had been thunderous at times, slowed as Elliot allowed every word to sink in deep and strike close to home among the crowd.

Without warning, he drew a cigarette lighter from the front pocket of his tie-dyed T-shirt and lit it. Everyone—protesters, police and bystanders—watched with rapt attention. With his eyes fixed solidly on the crowd, Elliot raised his arm and moved the lighter beneath one of his hairy wrists. The flame incinerated the black hairs, sending a wisp of smoke rising in the air and sparking an audible gasp of horror among the crowd.

"Napalm hurts," he said in carefully measured words. "It burns. The pain is excruciating. And children in Vietnam, and their parents, too, wish the pain would stop.

"Just like this." He snapped the lighter shut, flinching as the flame died. "But friends, if you're in Vietnam and you've been napalmed, the pain doesn't stop. It just goes on and on and on."

Elliot studied the crowd, almost as if he were searching their eyes for signs of commitment. Everyone regarded him with awe, the respectful silence broken only by the weeping of the three Gold Star mothers in the audience and occasional muffled sobs in the crowd. Joe, too, was mesmerized by the moment. His earlier reluctance to join the protest waned in the depths of Elliot's commitment to the antiwar cause. He felt as if he had witnessed history, a moment as memorable as Lincoln's address at Gettysburg or Franklin Delano Roosevelt's declaration of war in 1941.

Elliot cleared his throat at last, then raised the megaphone once more to his mouth. Speaking in measured words once again, he resumed the indictment of U.S. involvement in Vietnam. "I do not want my government committing acts of savagery in my name, and I know many of you share that point of view," he declared. "I love America. I want my country to be great. But today, I am ashamed of America.

"In ordinary times, I would not advocate defiance of authority," he continued, the tempo of his words slowly increasing. "But these are not ordinary times. It's 1968, and the world is a frightening place. For many of us, it's hard to see what's wrong, especially when we're gathered on this sun-splashed day enjoying our freedom and the right to exercise it. But ten thousand miles from here in another world—a hellish place of war—people like you and me are in pain, and they are dying. Some are Vietnamese children with napalm melting their skin. Others are American soldiers with shrapnel in their guts. Their conditions are most unordinary, and we must let our voices of protest be heard, so that the suffering does not continue."

Elliot paused to catch his breath, baiting the crowd with his silence as they willed him to continue. A long moment later, he obliged them.

"Many of us—and I've counted myself among them—can sit snugly over here and ignore the war because it's a long way from home," he said. "Some of us, too, have the luxury of student deferrals because we attend college. But the deferrals are ending my friends. I know that personally because I got a notice from the local draft board in Jamaica, New York, last week, telling me to report for a physical. They say I'm headed for boot camp; I'm not convinced."

Murmurs rippled through the crowd at this revelation, and Elliot seized the opportunity for a moment of dramatic silence before declaring, "This is not a war I intend to fight."

Again, he paused, allowing the onlookers to ponder the intent of those last words. "To end this war," he continued in quickened tones, "it will take acts of defiance and disobedience, and that is precisely what I intend to do. I need your help, too. And I would like to have your promise to act peacefully, whatever course of action you may choose. But I do hope you will heed your conscience and act."

Pausing, giving people time to wonder what he would ask of them, Elliot made a careful sweep of the crowd, seeming to make eye contact with each of the protestors. Finally, he raised the megaphone once more to speak. "When I give the signal, calmly march past these officers and try to make your way into the administration building," Elliot continued after giving the protesters a short moment to consider his request. "It will be a small act of defiance; but it will be one of the ripples of discontent spreading across this nation, sending a signal loud and clear to our leaders in Washington; a strong message that Americans will no longer tolerate a war that is immoral and unjustified."

With the crowd almost breathlessly quiet, Elliot lowered the megaphone, placed it upright on the blue car hood and reached inside his shirt pocket, pulling out his draft card, holding it aloft for everyone to see. In a surreal second, the cigarette lighter appeared almost magically from the pocket of his ragged blue jeans. A flame of brazen glory arced, and Elliot Frankel blazed his way into the annals of local folk history.

The ensuing silence was deafening, the moment reverent like a candlelight vigil, until another young man standing near the forefront of protesters incinerated his draft card, too.

For a moment, the cops seemed confused by the two men's actions. But only a moment.

In rapid-fire order, they regrouped, rushing to quell the illegal act. Someone yelled and pandemonium erupted. The crowd surged forward, then broke apart as the police officers advanced. Some swarmed toward the administration building, others engaged in hand-to-hand combat with the lawmen. Two more young men burned their draft cards in open rebellion.

In the state of confusion, the Gold Star mothers were the only people who had a clear purpose in mind. Ignored and alone in the midst of the commotion, the three women marched into the administration building and quietly occupied the office of the dean of academic affairs. Once seated in comfortable chairs, they sipped coffee served to them by the dean himself and discussed the tragedy of their sons' deaths.

———

Joe held his ground until he heard the first thud of wood crunching against bone and saw two beefy police officers tackle Elliot Frankel. The officers pummeled Elliot, cracking his skull with billy clubs, punching him and kicking him with booted feet. In a matter of seconds, Elliot lay sprawled on the ground, unconscious with blood seeping from his cracked skull. The police left him there to take aim at other protesters.

The sight of blood prodded Joe into action. He shook off his confusion over the mad turn of events, taking the first few cautious steps toward Elliot, coming suddenly face-to-face with a scrawny young man probably younger than himself. But the man wore the blue uniform of a police officer. They eyed each other quickly, testily, before the officer made a feeble attempt to lash Joe with a billy club. Joe dodged the blow, wrestled the club from the cop and hurled the man into the middle of a boisterous group of high school students. It was obvious these boys cared little about the war in Vietnam. But they loved a good fight, and Joe eyed the officer with a pang of sympathy as the roughhousers pounced on the man. The concern was short-lived, however, as Joe fixed his attention on Elliot's limp form.

Elliot lay still as death, oblivious to the surrounding turmoil he had caused. The brash New Yorker had paid a price for burning his draft card. Joe wondered whether the cost was worth it. And then he wondered whether Elliot still owed a balance due.

Joe faced a bitter decision. He fought the urge to walk away, to disavow this demonstration and Elliot. With one foolish act, Elliot had destroyed the moment. When people remembered this day, they would see Elliot perched on the car, with his draft card thrust skyward, curling under flames. Few would recall the man's stirring words or the disturbing image of burning flesh. Joe resented the theatrics. But more than that, he was offended.

He would have abandoned Elliot, except for an intruding sense that his criticism contained a self-righteous and sanctimonious tone. He had chosen his side the moment he joined the crowd of protesters, and he refused to be a fair-weather follower. And, too, Joe felt a sense of loyalty to Elliot. They had never seen eye-to-eye. They had come together as friends out of common interests. But it was their differences—or at least a healthy respect for each other and a willingness to listen to the other point of view—that had sealed their friendship. His mind made up, Joe bolted pell-mell into the jumbled mass of agitated men and women. He moved stealthily through the maze of arms and legs, finding the path to Elliot remarkably clear.

Five feet away from his fallen friend, something hard and cold struck Joe squarely in the chest. The collision reeled Joe, halting his progress. He was stunned by the unexpected more than any pain. Metal clanked against the pavement below him; muffled explosions popped all around him. Joe peered downward and caught the first whiff of tear gas.

The noxious fumes sucked away his breath. He gasped for fresh air but managed only to gulp his lungs full of the poisonous gas. His windpipe convulsed, his chest heaved and his eyes burned like fire.

Joe staggered forward, moving blindly, propelled by nothing more than disorientation. He tripped over Elliot's legs, crashed to the ground and buried his face against the pavement, searching for one breath of untainted air. Gagging, convinced the makers of this particular batch of tear gas had miscalculated the ingredients, concocting a lethal dose in the process, Joe feared he was losing consciousness.

Then, instinct took over. He cupped his hands, found a cleansing breath and took his bearings.

Pandemonium reigned around him. The tear gas had felled only a few demonstrators. Several women screamed and a few men moaned, all the victims of billy clubs. Most people were running wildly, trying to escape the expanding gas, with the cops in full pursuit.

In a moment, Joe decided what to do. Although the gas fumes were still overpowering, he pulled himself to his knees and scanned the grounds. He had a clear path to escape.

Using the chaos as cover, Joe hoisted Elliot over his shoulder and calmly stole away unnoticed by the police. Ignoring the curious eyes of passersby, he willed himself strength and strode across campus. Upon reaching his Volkswagen, he allowed himself a furtive backward glance and found the trail still clear. Assured, he opened the car door, pushed Elliot into the passenger side and drove quickly away.

CHAPTER 2

TOM HAD BEEN IN Vietnam since January. He kept the postmen busy between Southeast Asia and Cookville, offering general impressions of the country and its people. Most often, his early letters dealt with life in Saigon, where Tom was stationed for the first weeks of his tour of duty. As a country boy, he loathed the incessant honk of car horns and noxious gas fumes that permeated the city. The hordes of people made him claustrophobic, and the greed disgusted him.

"Everybody wants a dollar," he wrote to his father. "Greed has consumed these people. I don't know if it has always been this way, but everyone—and I do mean everyone from eight to eighty—is a businessman. They hawk anything you want on the street. They'll steal a blind beggar's last coin and an orphan's last meal."

In general, though, these harsh assessments were seldom made. He described the countryside as a "sea of green" and labeled the fertile Mekong Delta "a farmer's paradise." His fascination with rice paddies inspired his friends back home to consider growing the grain in the marshy areas on their farm.

For the most part, Tom's letters provided pleasant conversation for the folks on the home front. His family and friends latched onto every word, comforted by Tom's upbeat attitude. As long as he found the place tolerable, they were spared any serious consideration of the bleaker conditions that surely haunted the war-torn country and the boys fighting over there.

More than anything, these letters helped Tom bridge the lonely miles between home and Vietnam. The linkage comforted him.

He wrote to Summer every other day without fail, even if it was nothing more than a postcard with "I love you" scribbled in his endearing hen-scratch print. Often, he filled several pages of stationery with the unabashed, tender meanderings of a young man in love, recalling fond memories and regaling her with glorious visions of their future.

"There is a street here known as the Rue Catinat," he wrote to her. "Actually, its real name is Tu Do, which means freedom in Vietnamese. But most everyone calls it just Catinat, which I think is a beautiful name. Sometimes when I'm feeling blue, like today, I daydream that you and I are strolling hand-in-hand along the Rue Catinat and I feel better.

"There is also a dress here in Saigon known as an ao dais," the letter continued. "It is a long, silk dress, slit up to the waist. Vietnamese women typically wear it with white pants. Of course, they don't have your great legs. I'm going to buy you one of those in dark green silk and send it home. Maybe you will wear it on our honeymoon."

When the ao dais arrived, Summer had sworn Carrie to secrecy and enlisted her sister's help in obtaining a photograph of herself wearing the silk dress. They had feigned illness one Sunday morning, staying home from church for the privacy necessary to take the picture. In the photograph, Summer stood amid the pecan orchard with a field of young corn shining in the background, a vision of wholesomeness with a sweetly seductive side. When he received the photo, Tom promptly fired off a postcard with only two words scribbled across it: "Thank you!"

The postcard touched off an inquiry from Rachel at the supper table one night. "I picked up the mail today and couldn't help noticen Tom's postcard, Summer," she said. "I wasn't meanen to pry, but it was lyen face down in the mailbox and I saw it right off the bat. Why was he thanken you?"

"Probably not anything in particular," Summer replied, brushing off the question and seizing an opportunity to enlist her family in a letter-writing campaign to Tom. She chided them for neglecting the task, scolding all except Joe, who wrote to Tom faithfully once a week.

"Tom's halfway around the world, folks, and he's lonely," she lectured. "I know everybody's busy, but the least y'all can do is send an occasional note, just to let him know we're thinken about him. Tell him about your day, something funny or different that happened to you. Send him a postcard that says, 'I'm thinken of you.' It's not asken too much to think about him every now and then, or to let him know that you care about him."

Her ploy shamed the family into action. The women began sending care packages of cookies and candy to Tom. Matt wrote him a long letter about the crop outlook, and Sam sent a short note about fishing. Everyone did something, but the note Tom treasured most came on a postcard from Luke.

"Summer says you'd probably be interested in something I did today," Luke wrote. "Well, I flunked three tests—spelling, reading and math. I blamed it all on you. Told my teachers you needed to hear from me to keep your spirits up, so we'd win the war. Old Lady Crawford was so moved that she's giving me another crack at the reading and spelling tests. It won't matter none. I'll probably fail the second time around, too."

Tom tailored his own letters to the whims of the reader. His correspondence to his mother reflected the culture of Vietnam, with detailed descriptions of beautiful villas and tropical gardens filled with bunches of red and purple bougainvillea. He wrote to Amelia about the churches and temples where Catholics and Buddhists worshipped, the city streets where water buffaloes clomped alongside cars and the people who walked around in black pajamas. In letters to his father, Tom described the country's commerce, comparing the value of South Vietnamese piasters with the American dollar, explaining the importance of rice, rubber and bananas to the economy.

He shared the unvarnished truth about Saigon's filth and depravity with Joe. In detail, he told about the whorehouses and the prostitutes on the street, the orphans, beggars and cripples, the slums and gaudy homes of corrupt South Vietnamese officials who exploited their government positions to lead privileged lives.

He rarely talked of the war or his soldier's duties. His neglect of the war wasn't for lack of fodder. It was simply a conscious decision to restrain from spilling the grisly details. But gradually, as his tour of duty edged forward, his family and friends pieced together a chronology of his time in Vietnam.

Tom swooped into Vietnam in late January of 1968, landing at Saigon's Ton Son Nhut Airport after stopovers in Honolulu and the Philippines. Two days later, the North Vietnamese gave him a rude welcome to Southeast Asia, spoiling the promise of a spectacular celebration of the lunar new year.

"Tet—remember that word," a fellow private told Tom as his entry orders were processed.

"What's Tet?" Tom asked.

"Tet is the Vietnamese New Year," the soldier replied. "It's kind of like New Year's back home, only it's bigger and there's not any football games to watch on television. Of course, a bunch of us are planning to stage a version of the Rose Bowl. You're lucky, Carter. You've arrived at the best possible time to be in Vietnam, assuming there is such a thing. The war's taking a vacation, and it's party time."

On the soldier's assurance, Tom wrote his first letter home, telling everyone about the pending celebration and the good times expected for several days. The letter was still in a box of outgoing mail when the sound of rockets and gunfire jolted Tom from a peaceful dream on the early morning of January 31, 1968.

The Tet attack dented Tom's unwavering confidence in his ability to survive twelve months in Vietnam. He felt paralyzed as his first encounter with hostile action unfolded. He performed his soldier's duties in a daze, responding like a sluggish robot when his squad leader barked orders.

Tom was part of a detachment assigned to patrol one of the city's smaller commercial districts, which the U.S. war strategists marked as a potential target of the Viet Cong insurrectionists. For hours on end that day, through the night and into the next morning, his squad patrolled the area. When they were allowed at last to rest, Tom had come no closer to the enemy than the faraway sound of gunfire.

Day after day, he prepared to become a warrior, but nothing happened. The days assumed a routine as the skirmishes across Saigon came to a gradual halt. The U.S. troops had routed the Viet Cong guerrillas, but no one was comfortable in the city, especially Tom. He suffered through sleepless nights and tense days, dreading that first confrontation with the enemy.

A degree of his lost confidence returned to Tom as he clicked off days of guard duty. He acquainted himself with the members of his platoon, most notably a black soldier from Tupelo, Mississippi. They shared the same first name as well as a high regard for Elvis Presley. Occasionally, they showed off a flare for imitation of the King. In impromptu jam sessions, the black man did a fair impersonation of Elvis singing *All Shook Up*, while Tom Carter crooned *Are You Lonesome Tonight* with a rich baritone capable of striking all the right cords in a lonesome solider.

When the time came to swivel hips, however, Tom deferred to the man from Mississippi. Tom Welch claimed his Tupelo relatives had taught Elvis how to gyrate his pelvis and after watching him bump and grind on the dance floor, most of his fellow soldiers half-believed him.

In spare moments—and they were plenty in those days—Tom and his buddies explored Saigon. They sampled restaurants and bars, and haggled with one entrepreneur after another. Often, they bartered cigarettes on gifts for the folks back home, discovering one oddity after another in the tiny shops tucked in every nook and cranny of the city's main thoroughfares.

Two deeds earned Tom a distinction among his buddies. First, he refused to join them on forays to Saigon's many whorehouses. Second, he took to sharing his goodies from home with children in a local orphanage.

The Catholic orphanage was located in a ramshackle church amid dilapidated villas. For several weeks, Tom kept his visits a secret from his colleagues. If it were not for Welch's curiosity, his good deed might have remained a secret. On a whim one Friday afternoon, however, Welch and a fellow soldier followed Tom's winding path through a maze of streets to the orphanage.

From their hiding place behind a ginkgo tree, the two privates watched in disbelief as the courtyard sprang to life when Tom appeared. More than a dozen Vietnamese children clustered around him, transformed from listless creatures to bright-eyed urchins. Dozens of hands grabbed his arms and uniform, pulling, pushing and tugging Tom toward a wooden bench. A little girl, no more than five, claimed his lap. For fifteen minutes, Tom spoke softly to the children, telling them the nonsensical stories he had heard all his life from Sam Baker. None of the children spoke English, but they were captivated by Tom's voice and presence.

Finally, Tom pushed the girl off his lap, made some small personal gesture to each of the children and gave the package to the nun. The Vietnamese woman was in her fifties, Tom guessed, and she spoke broken English. As always, he asked the nun to distribute the cookies and candy at her discretion and to warn the children he might never return. Then, with one final wave, he walked away from the orphanage without looking back. At that point, Welch and his buddy emerged from their hiding place.

Their appearance surprised Tom, and he came to a dead stop. He expected laughter and good-natured ridicule from the men. He considered chastising them for their sneakiness. Instead, they saluted, maintaining the position until Tom reached them, then falling in step alongside him.

"There are a lot of things I'll remember about you, Tom Carter," Welch said after they had walked a few minutes in silence. "You don't want to spend a few dollars to get laid by some pretty Oriental whore, and you're about as pathetic as anyone I ever saw try to shake like Elvis. But this beats all, man, passing out candy bars to orphans. I don't know where you came from, Tom, but I'm 'bout to the point where I expect you to walk on water at any moment."

"Don't count on it," Tom replied. "But if you keep this to yourself, I just might."

Welch laughed at the suggestion, then promptly spread the good news. Later, when he described to the folks back home the ribbing he had received from his buddies, Tom explained his intentions toward the orphans.

"The last thing in the world I want to be is a do-gooder," he wrote in a letter to his mother. "But these kids have so little, Mama. When I first came across them, their eyes were empty. There wasn't even a trace of sadness or need. It was almost as if they knew they were preordained to have nothing, so they didn't even bother to want anything. I can't imagine going through life feeling that way. Now they smile sometimes, and they laugh. I can't speak for them, but I certainly feel better about the situation. Maybe something more worthwhile will come of it."

———

By April, Tom felt more like a man on vacation than a warrior. He had been in Vietnam for two months, and the war seemed as far away as home. He should have been grateful for the respite, but he was restless and eager for a new challenge. The Army obliged him in early April, packing Tom's company off to a remote encampment near Pleiku, where he discovered firsthand why he should have appreciated every minute of boredom.

On his second night of guard duty around the base's barbed-wire perimeter, snipers peppered the patrol with machine gun fire. Tom heard the hiss of bullets spray past his head. From then on, the danger was constant, the need for caution paramount.

There were more snipers and other skirmishes as Tom discovered the horrors of war. Two members of his platoon died in successive weeks, one felled by a sniper's bullet in the middle of the night, the other by a booby trap set within a half mile of the camp.

The threat of death was pervasive and wearing on the mind. But there were other dangers beside the violence. The heat became unbearable, even among the canopy of jungle. The humidity was strangling, worse than the choking gasoline fumes in Saigon. They were constantly hacking their way through dense growths of mahogany, bamboo and teak trees, always trying to avoid a maze of thick vines and rope grasses.

"There really are such things as man-eating plants," Tom wrote to Luke. "And if you stay in one place too long, they'll swallow you whole."

As difficult as the terrain was to negotiate, Tom might have viewed it as a minor inconvenience, if not for the hostile wildlife. On his first day at the base, Tom received a warning about the presence of snakes, water buffalo and tigers in the area. The idea brought a smile to his face, which, in turn, brought Tom face-to-face with a stern sergeant's gaze. A robust, ruddy man with the shoulders of an ox and an ugly scar across his chest, the result of shrapnel from an earlier conflict, he rattled off three names.

"They didn't listen either, soldier," he sneered. "And they're all dead."

Two days later, the same sergeant saved a young lieutenant's life, unleashing a round of machine gun fire to obliterate a cobra poised to strike. A witness to the encounter, Tom made a silent vow to take to heart every word of the sergeant's advice.

Despite the dangers and hardships, the location was exotic. Colorful parrots dotted tree limbs, and Tom picked clusters of bananas from the broad-leafed trees growing wild in the jungle. He wrote to Sam of his determination to grow banana trees in the sandy loam of South Georgia. Sam immediately ordered four of the trees from the local nursery, planting two on the Baker place and the others near the mercantile.

––––––

In mid-August, Tom was handpicked for a reconnaissance squad. The group embarked on its mission before dawn on a Wednesday. For three days, they hacked their way through jungle, crossing hills and ravines, slogging through muddy rivers. They humped their invisible trail for eighteen hours a day, pausing only to pick off leeches, bivouacking where their path ended. During their hours of rest, they gobbled down c-rations, shivered in cold rain and watched for phantoms of night. On their third day on the trail, they lay awake through the long night, listening to the whine of jets and the roar of exploding bombs in the distance. The fourth day brought them to an eerie stretch of defoliated jungle. Rather than risk exposure on the open plain, they skirted the edge of the jungle. The delay forced them to extend the mission for another day.

The squad eventually arrived at the hill, which had been the target of a major battle a few nights earlier. Heavy artillery had annihilated the hill, leaving a mounded skeleton, pocked with craters and jagged tree stumps. In the middle of the hill stood a single spot of green, a pine tree that had escaped the destruction. "I know there's significance to that single bit of life in the midst of all that desolation," Tom wrote to Joe. "There's either some kind of poetic justice or some awful injustice to be found there. But I'm damned to figure out which it is."

The reconnaissance detail, which Tom had mentioned briefly, was blotted out by censors.

A two-day storm, prelude to the approaching monsoons, clouded the trail back to base. The marshland, virtually impregnable before the rains fell, became a quagmire as flooding set in. Fatigue dogged the squad. They were isolated, cut off from camp by a faulty radio and stranded in the pounding rain. Their only solace came from the conjectured belief that not even the enemy would risk exposure to these elements.

Lost in the jungle, the men marched like nomads. Even when the rains subsided, progress came at torturously slow pace. They fought the muck, sinking knee deep for miles at a stretch. The jungle closed around the troops, clawing their faces with sharp-bladed grasses, choking them with darkness. Eventually, their bodies rebelled against the strain and tension.

After days of tramping in waterlogged boots and worn socks, Tom's feet were a mess of blisters. The pustules oozed yellow pus across the shriveled white skin of his feet, and every step became an exercise in pain. But he gritted his teeth and marched onward.

One day in the middle of the mission's second week, Tom was daydreaming about a dry pair of thick, white socks when he stepped into a pool of mud and sank waist-deep. It was quicksand, which he discovered when he tried to push out with his feet and sank instead to his navel. He felt the slough tugging at him, pulling him deeper.

"Come on, guys," he pleaded. "This stuff's pullen me down fast."

"Stay calm, Carter," said Captain Edward Katz, the squad commander, as the troops scouted the area for other pockets of the quicksand.

"I am calm, captain," Tom replied. "Just get me the heck out of here!"

"Take it slowly," Katz said, offering his grasp to Tom, "and give me your hand."

Tom followed the instructions, carefully withdrawing his right arm from the grainy mud and extending it to the captain. Almost immediately, the quicksand swallowed him to the neck. Panic-stricken, Tom took a deep breath and held it. His eyes shut automatically, waiting in terror to sink beneath the mire.

Suddenly, Katz grabbed his hand. "You're fine now, Tom," the captain assured him. "I have a firm hold, and you're not going any farther down. Okay?"

Tom opened his eyes, soothed by the man's calm approach to the situation. He nodded his acknowledgment.

"Now pull out your other arm and give it to Collins over here," the captain said. "Then, we'll pull you out."

Tom simply did as told, without thinking, feeling a sense of safety as soon as Collins grabbed his arm. But the suction was strong, and the quicksand reluctant to yield Tom, who went nowhere on the men's first attempt to tug him free from the murky grip. On their second try, Tom felt the muck fall away from his stomach. Seconds later, he stood on safe ground.

"I can think of better things to be remembered for than being the only person in the history of Cookville swallowed by quicksand," Tom wrote to Joe. "As a way to die, it ranks right up there with getting eaten by a tiger or bitten by a cobra. Of course, any of the three might be preferable to stumbling across a Bouncing Betty. That's a type of land mine. They detonate around waist level, and they maim more often than they kill. I watch out for them; we all do. I don't want to go through life without balls."

————

At the end of their second week in the jungle, Tom's squad ran out of c-rations and drinking water. By everyone's best guess, they were still two days from camp. They were tired, sick men, who believed their supply of luck had been exhausted along with the food and water. Grim premonitions of an early grave stalked their every move.

Like everyone else, Tom expected the worst and fared poorly. Diarrhea gnawed at his insides, forcing him, along with everyone else, to step off the trail at regular intervals to relieve the discomfort. They drank water wherever they found it, hoping luck would spare them from tetanus or worse. They ate whatever looked edible.

The fear was harder to conquer. Every step closer to the base camp also brought them nearer to enemy patrols. The men were depleted by the physical and emotional strain; their resistance was low. But their survival depended on vigilance now more than ever, so they forgot their blisters, runny bowels and hunger pains, and carried on.

It was a prudent decision, saving their lives later in the evening when they walked into an ambush. The enemy attacked as the squad crossed a small swath of open range, surrounded on all sides by dense jungle growth. Tom half expected the attack to come as they moved across the tall grass in formation. When the squad was spread out across the range, the guerrillas opened fire.

A hail of bullets came at Tom from every direction. He dropped to his stomach, crawling toward the far edge of the jungle as bullets tore up the ground around him. He heard Captain Katz shouting for the men ahead of him to take cover, then understood the order as he saw where the grass camouflage ended a few yards in the distance.

Near the edge of tall grass, Tom sized up the situation and realized he would have to risk open exposure to reach his companions. The bullets were landing too close to take a chance on staying in the grass, which was being chewed up in chunks by the artillery. He had no other option. Raising himself to a racer's starting crouch, he sprinted forward. It was the race of his life, the longest, fastest ten-yard dash he would run.

Reaching the cover of woods, he hurled himself to the ground, searching for a protective shield. His eyes adjusted quickly to the darkness, spotting his fellow soldiers crouched behind the wide trunks of nearby oaks.

"Over here, Carter," a voice called to him.

It was Collins, motioning Tom to a large tree trunk. Quickly, Tom crabbed his way to the temporary refuge.

For long hours, Tom and Collins sat back-to-back, fending off the ambush. The gunfire came sporadically from all directions. For every round fired at them, Tom and his companions fired two in return. Eventually, the gunfire died. When two hours had passed without any action, with dawn creeping onto the eastern horizon, they concluded the enemy had withdrawn under the cloak of darkness. The men raised themselves cautiously from cramped positions and discovered they were all alive and whole. Even their reserves were gone now, but the final hump remained before them, so they hobbled onward.

———

Less than half a day from the base, any leftover luck they might have had ran out on the exhausted squad. They were slogging through a familiar series of abandoned rice paddies, careless as they crossed the murky water out of formation, believing themselves safe.

Tom was thinking about blackwater fever. He was too tired to slap away the disease-carrying mosquitoes swarming in droves around him. He had concluded that malaria might be a step up from his present condition when a shattering boom blew him out of the water.

He landed in a daze, slipped under the water and was instantly revived from the concussion. He stood up in the water and found the paddy bloodied with the mine explosion's debris.

"You can't imagine what it's like to open your eyes to a tangle of arms and legs—everywhere, except where they're supposed to be," he wrote to Summer. "Men were hollering, screaming and moaning. I counted three dead right off the bat, and two more looked like goners. The only ones not hurt beside me were Leggett and Eisley. The captain had a gash in his arm, but it was nothing serious.

"I froze for a second. I wasn't sure what to do. But I finally grabbed the nearest living body I could find, and it was Collins. He was a goner, although I didn't know that at first—not until I pulled him over to the paddy's edge. The poor guy had a hole a mile wide in his chest; his guts were hanging out; and one leg was a bloody stump above the knee.

"He was screaming, too, begging for help. It's the worst sound I ever heard. But there wasn't anything to do for Collins, except shoot him up with morphine and make dying as painless as possible. I think the captain gave him an overdose to speed it up because right after the shot, Collins began to quiet down. He stopped screaming, stopped moaning and just stared at me. Then he asked me if he was dying. I didn't know what to say, Summer, so I just held his hand and recited the Lord's Prayer until he stopped breathing. I didn't have time to say the whole prayer.

"Seeing Collins die, and the others, too—I know that's bound to change me. You can't witness that violence and come away unchanged by it. I wonder what it all means; I wonder how it's changed me and when I'll understand it. I don't want to dwell on Collins and the others, but it bothers me that I forget about it so quickly. The captain says to think about it as a bad day at the office. He says dying and watching people die comes with the territory. But I'm not that callused. And I hope I never become so thick-hearted as to think of death as an occupational hazard.

"I don't know about this, Summer, but stay tuned," Tom's letter concluded.

Tom had penned the letter from a cheap hotel room in Hong Kong. The Army, which had been ready to list the ill-fated squad members as missing in action, gave the survivors a week to recuperate from the ordeal, followed by two weeks of leave.

A helicopter had ferried the survivors to Saigon, where Tom hopped a military transport to Hong Kong. He spent the first week holed up in his hotel room, fighting the flu, savoring the solitude and allowing pent-up tension to melt away during hour after hour of peaceful sleep.

By the start of the second week, he felt rejuvenated. He called home unexpectedly, giving his parents a pleasant shock. The next day, at a prearranged time, he called again, and this time Summer picked up the phone. They talked for fifteen minutes. The call would cost a fortune, but it was worth every dime he had.

Tom spent two days exploring Hong Kong, sampling the cuisine and entertainment, browsing through the shops to find gifts for Summer and his parents. He sent Amelia a dazzling cork sculpture of a pagoda encased in ebony and glass. The price was outrageous, and he paid considerable extra for premium packing and shipping insurance. For his father, Tom found an abstract collage of tiled parquetry in cool desert colors of brown, rust, eggshell and pale yellow. Summer's gift was a silk scarf, black and hand painted with two long-stemmed red roses.

With four days of leave remaining, Tom returned to Saigon. He reacquainted himself with the city, visited several buddies and spent time at the orphanage. He returned to the base camp refreshed and eager to complete his tour of duty.

Summer sat on the doorsteps of the Carter's Mercantile, chatting with Dan and Amelia about Tom's latest letter. Tom seemed in good spirits, a welcomed contrast to the tone of his more recent letters. Those letters had brought the war's dangers close to Summer. She was not naive. She was aware of what happened to men at war. But Summer had done a spectacular job convincing herself that Tom was having the time of his life in Vietnam, the great adventure he wanted before coming home to marry her. And Tom had fed her fantasy with countless love letters painting pictures of their life together—the land they would own, the house they would build, the love they would make and the children they would raise.

Summer changed to a more comfortable position on the stoop, recalling Tom's last letter to her. The words had been full of aching homesickness, loneliness and fear.

"These letters are my refuge," he had written. "They take me to the place and time I'd rather be. Maybe it's nothing but sheer schmaltz, but when I write things down on paper—about our children, our place or just being with you day in and day out—the future doesn't seem far away from here."

After that letter, Summer had quit her pretense about Tom's tour of duty. She tried to put herself in his shoes. At night, she dreamed his fears. But during the day, she shared his vision.

The drone of a combine coming closer broke her thoughts temporarily, reminding Summer that while she loafed with Dan and Amelia, John was busy picking the small field of corn behind the Carters' store.

She turned her gaze from the pair of rusting gas pumps to the man and woman who would become her in-laws when Tom returned from Vietnam. The storekeepers sat side-by-side in matching rockers. Dan read his son's letter for the third time, while Amelia skimmed over the afternoon newspaper from Tifton.

Summer looked forward to having the Carters as in-laws, especially Amelia.

Their personalities matched closely, enough so that Summer had given credence to the idea that men often marry women who remind them of their mothers. Amelia and she shared an effortless relationship, a closeness that preceded her love for Tom, and Summer believed the bond would strengthen over time.

As for Dan, Summer would need more time to build that relationship. She felt comfortable around her future father-in-law, but Dan seemed aloof to a certain extent. It was not a cold quality but rather an extreme sense of privacy. Tom was the same way, except for one major difference. In a crowd or with customers, Dan seemed at ease with the world, effusing charm and poise as easily as busybodies dished out gossip. Among family and friends, Dan shied away. Tom was the complete opposite. Crowds and unfamiliar situations made him ill at ease, but he thrived around the people closest to him.

All at once, Summer realized Amelia had asked her a question. "What was that, Amelia?" she replied, unembarrassed by her wandering attention. "I had somethen else on my mind."

"I was just sayen what a beautiful day this is," Amelia remarked, laying the newspaper in her lap. "There's a touch of fall in the air."

"Maybe we've had the last of the really hot weather," Dan mumbled, still engrossed in Tom's letter.

"Are y'all plannen on painten those gas pumps anytime soon, Dan?" Summer asked. "They're beginnen to look as if they could use a fresh coat."

"I've been putten it off because the gas company's promised a new set," Dan replied.

"They've been sayen that for six months now," Amelia interrupted. "Summer's right. Those pumps are becomen an eyesore. Next time Buck Franklin delivers, tell him we need the new pumps now or we're goen to change brands."

"Amelia," Dan said patiently. "After all these years, we're not about to change brands over the pumps. The gas company will get the new ones to us soon enough."

The sound of an approaching car ended the debate. Summer watched the white sedan turn off the highway as the Carters hurried through some last-minute bickering. In the glare of the late afternoon sun, the vehicle carried an official appearance. When the car rolled under the shadow of the store, Summer glimpsed the ramrod forms of two military men in the front seat.

An overpowering sense of foreboding lifted Summer to her feet. She gasped for breath and clutched her palpitating heart. Almost immediately, though, she calmed herself, refusing to believe these men had come with news of Tom. Still, their demeanor screamed of purpose.

Beside her, Dan and Amelia became alert, regarding Summer with concern. Seated behind the gas pumps, they had yet to see the two soldiers in the car.

"What's wrong, dear?" Amelia asked, her eyes following Summer's gaze to the white sedan.

The driver's door opened and a pair of legs swung out of the seat, clothed in the dress blue uniform of a soldier.

"Oh, dear Lord," Tom's mother sighed, falling lamely against the rocking chair. "Please don't let it be bad news."

Dan rose ever so slowly from his rocking chair, his hands shaking and the color drained from his face as he discerned the cause of worry.

The driver was a young man with slate gray eyes and rugged looks that could have translated into the perfect recruiting poster. He closed the car door, standing strongly until an older man appeared beside him. Then, the two of them walked to the edge of the concrete porch slab, regarding the Carters and Summer with somber expressions.

"Mr. and Mrs. Dan Carter?" the older man asked.

It was a voice of compassion, the standard-bearer of bad news.

Summer was crushed to the core. Already, tears spilled down her face.

"I'm Dan Carter," Tom's father answered. "This is my wife, Amelia."

"Sir, ma'am," he acknowledged formally. "I'm Captain Glen Subic, a chaplain at Moody Air Force Base. My partner is Lieutenant Mark Applegate."

The captain paused quickly, almost as if he hoped the Carters would ask him for the news of Tom. But Dan and Amelia were unable to speak, so he continued in strong and sympathetic tones. "It is my deepest regret, Mr. and Mrs. Carter, to inform you that your son has been killed in the line of duty in Vietnam."

Summer heard nothing else. She stifled a sob, clutched her stomach and fought the need to rock herself. She was empty, except for an urgency to escape this place, these people and the moment. She took two unsteady steps forward before the young lieutenant caught her. He touched her lightly on the arm, his sympathy sending a shudder through Summer.

"Please take your hand off me," she ordered. "I'm okay."

The officer withdrew his hand. "I'm sorry, miss."

Without further response, Summer began walking, her pace quickening as she crossed the highway without looking. Soon, she began running, increasing speed as her feet pounded over the beaten dirt road. She had no destination, only a sense of the inevitable, that her heart would break should she stop.

———

The two officers stared blankly at Summer until she disappeared down the road, then cast their gazes back to Dan and Amelia. Dan stared at the captain's spit-shined shoes for the longest time, shaking his head repeatedly. Amelia remained rigid against the back of the rocking chair, her face shattered with disbelief.

"How did it happen?" Dan asked finally in a faraway voice.

"Mr. Carter, I don't have all the details," Captain Subic answered forthrightly. "All I know is that it happened two days ago. Tom was on a mission with his squad, and they lost radio contact with the base. I should know more soon. I'll share any information I have with you as soon as I get it."

"What about the body," Dan asked. "They will ship it home, won't they?"

"Yes sir, Mr. Carter," the captain said. "Usually, it takes three to five days to make the necessary arrangements. But there again, I can't tell you definitely when that might be. I hope to know more tomorrow."

Dan nodded, reflecting on the captain's answer.

"Two days ago, you say?" he remarked at length. "We got a letter from Tom just today."

"Yes, sir," Captain Subic said. "The mail can move slowly between the States and overseas."

The officer gave the Carters a minute more to reflect on the news, then explained the details that would require their attention over the next few days. "Is there anything I can do for you?" he asked finally. "Is there someone you would like us to notify? Any other children or close relatives?"

"Tom's our only child," Dan replied. "But, no, thank you. My wife and I would rather be alone for the moment. We will get in touch with the necessary people."

"As you wish," Captain Subic said. "We'll take our leave then, so you can have privacy. But please understand, Mr. Carter, Mrs. Carter, you have my deepest regrets. And while it may not help ease the pain, please believe me when I say your son is a genuine American hero. He died serving his country. He was called to help, and he answered the call. I know that you've received a terrible blow today, but you should be proud, too. And these are not hollow words of condolence. I mean everything I've said from the bottom of my heart."

"Thank you," Dan said, forcing himself to look the Air Force chaplain in the eye.

Captain Subic produced a crisp business card from his coat pocket, handing it to Dan. The younger lieutenant followed suit.

"If there is anything we can do for you, anything at all, please don't hesitate to call on us, Mr. Carter," he said. "At any time of the day, I might add. Both our office and home numbers are on the cards."

Dan nodded understanding.

"Until tomorrow then," the captain remarked.

Both officers saluted the Carters, climbed into their car and drove away.

Dan watched the car disappear down the highway, then looked at Amelia for the first time since the officers had arrived at the mercantile. He reached a hand out to his wife, and Amelia accepted his assistance from the chair. Dan led her across the porch into the mercantile, pausing only to flip the "Closed" sign on the door. They walked through the store into the living room, sat side-by-side on the leather sofa and began to mourn their loss.

CHAPTER 3

SUMMER SAT BY THE river bend where Tom and her brothers had shucked their clothes and gone skinny-dipping just a little more than a year ago. She could not recall the flight that had carried her to this tranquil spot—only the need to run as far from the world as possible. Her heart broke the moment she slumped down onto the grassy knoll, sobs coming from the deepest part of her soul. The tears spewed forth, uncontrollable, a gasping, wrenching lament for the man she loved and the great love story that would remain unfinished. She cried until her body ached from the strain and her mind demanded a reprieve.

Just as Tom had found refuge in his letters, Summer sought solace in her memories. She understood the instincts that had led her to this knoll beside the river. She sank back into the grass, closed her eyes and transported herself back to that Sunday morning last year when Tom had asked her to marry him.

Romantic inclinations came to Tom at the strangest times. His marriage proposal was no different, coming on the morning after the great fire had swept over the Baker place. They were dead tired from fighting the flames, covered in black grime and smelling of smoke. They should have gone to rest, but both were wound too tightly on their last ounces of adrenaline.

At Tom's suggestion, they took a walk to the river where he kissed her softly. "You're beautiful, Summer," he said.

"If you can say that now, smoke and all, then I must be beautiful," Summer replied lightly.

Then they had kissed again, a longer, deeper union that left Summer breathless and clinging to his shoulders for strength.

"Will you miss me?" she asked him for probably the hundredth time since Tom's draft notice had arrived.

"You know I will," he answered, helping her to the ground and lying beside her on the soft grass.

They lay in silence for several minutes, the adrenaline fading as they pondered the previous night and the coming months. "Are you happy, Tom?" Summer asked eventually.

"Extremely," he answered with eyes closed, his face glistening in the sunlight.

"Will you think about this day when you're in some foreign place, and some beautiful Oriental woman is throwen herself at you?"

Tom opened his eyes, rolling onto his side to regard her. "This day, this entire summer, I'll never forget it. Not as long as I live."

"Then why are you so eager to leave?" Summer asked, voicing a question that had been on her mind for several weeks.

"That's simple," Tom answered. "The sooner I go, the sooner I come back to you."

"That's a good way to look at it," Summer commented. "But I'm not sure it's the whole truth, Tom, and I have this thing about total honesty, no hedgen the truth or leaven things out. Sometimes, I get this feelen that you're actually looken forward to be'en a soldier."

"You know me pretty well, don't you?" he asked, and Summer laughed, biting her lower lip.

"The complete truth then," Tom continued. "You're right to some extent. I am looken forward to the next few months. Maybe not so much be'en a solider but for the different kind of life I'll lead. I'll miss you, Summer. More than anything, I'll miss you. And Mama and Daddy, too, and your family and worken on the farm with them. But despite everything I'll miss, I can't help looken forward to the next few months. There's a part of me that wants to see different places and meet different people—just so I'll know I've made all the right decisions about the kind of life I've chosen to live. Does that sound corny?"

"No."

Tom sat up, propping his hands on top of his head. "All my life—at least ever since I can remember—I've wanted to be a farmer," he continued. "When the Army's through with me, I intend to come back to New River, get some land and start farmen for myself."

Pausing, he peered at Summer out of the corner of his eye. "Could you be a farmer's wife?" he asked.

"Don't change the subject," Summer replied, jabbing him in the stomach with a playful punch. "Besides, you're teasen me."

"Not really," Tom said.

His midnight blue eyes locked on her face, and Summer resisted the urge to run her fingers through his blond hair.

"The complete truth," she prompted.

"The complete truth is that besides you and be'en a farmer, there's one other thing I've always wanted," he said.

"You've always wanted me," Summer chided. "I think not."

"Now who's digressen?" Tom asked.

"I'm digressen," she confessed. "But kiss me first and then tell what else you've always wanted besides me, whom you sort of didn't even like until a few months ago, and farmen, which you've always adored."

Tom kissed her forehead. "One big adventure," he told her, stretching out again beside her. "I've always wanted one grand adventure in life. Maybe it comes from listenen to all those stories your Grandpa used to tell us. Now I'm the first to admit that fighten a war half a million miles away from home is not my first pick for life's great adventure. I'm scared to death just thinken about what could happen. It's a dangerous place, and I'll probably see things that I spend the rest of my life tryen to forget. I even worry about the whole Army thing—how they'll treat me, if I'm tough enough to make it through boot camp. What if I go 'ho' when they say 'woe?' Or what if I can't make my bed right or keep my boots polished? What if I'm such a failure that they kick me out of the Army before I finish boot camp?"

She smiled, knowing he was making a conscientious effort to ease her fears.

"For better or worse, Summer, my big adventure's gonna take place in Vietnam. I'll just have to make the best of it."

Tom gave her one of his patented shy smiles then. "Am I maken any sense at all?"

"Mostly," she smiled again.

"You know, Summer," he said wistfully. "Despite everything I've said, if there wasn't the Army, I believe getting lost in you could be my one great adventure in life."

When she looked into his dark blue eyes, seeing all his honesty and how much Tom loved her, Summer had thought she would cry. She had traced her finger along the line of blond hair running up his bare chest from the navel.

"I'm all for adventure," she said, then tried to lighten the mood. "As long as you don't decide anytime soon to take off your clothes and go skinny-dippen."

"I'd like to," Tom shot back. "I'd like to take off my clothes and your clothes and go skinny-dippen. Then, I'd like to come right back here to this spot and make love all day. What do you think about that?"

Summer moved closer to him, wrapping arms around his neck and drawing Tom to her. They had kissed until they ached with desire. When his hands began to stray, Summer had been unwilling to stop him. Tom had splayed his fingers across her chest, caressing her flat stomach, treading slowly toward her breasts. She had been on fire with desire and so was Tom. He was hard against her, and Summer had pulled him closer. Her blouse had disappeared between them then. Both had wanted more, and Tom had known he could have taken her there.

"If we keep this up," he said between kisses, "I don't think we can stop. The truth is I don't want to stop, Summer. I want to see you naked, feel you next to me, and make love to you. But this isn't the time or place. Your resistance is low, and I don't want you to have any regrets when we do make love."

"We are goen to make love, aren't we, Tom?" she remarked.

He kissed her softly once more. "If you marry me," he said.

"Are you proposen?"

Tom considered the question. "I wasn't plannen to today, but the thought's been on my mind. I love you, Summer, and I do want to marry you and spend the rest of my life with you. I don't have a ring or anything, but I'll ask the question anyway. Will you marry me?"

"Yes."

"Yes?" he smiled, almost as if he failed to believe her.

"Yes, Tom," Summer reaffirmed her answer. "I want to marry you. Just say when."

"Today," Tom blurted out. "I'd like to marry you this very minute, but we can't. Not now, Summer. Not until we're more certain about the future. It wouldn't be fair to you. Too much could happen between now and then."

"I'm willen to take that chance," Summer suggested.

"I know you are, and I love you for it," Tom replied. "But I want Vietnam behind me before we marry. It's only a year, eighteen months at the most. And then I'll come home and marry you, and we'll live happily ever after. Are you sure you want to be a farmer's wife?"

"Absolutely," Summer had answered.

A year ago, their world had beckoned with absolutes. They had found a sanctuary for dreams, seen the glimmer of security and dared to believe in eternity. They had gone away that day with a sense of destiny. But in a place ten thousand miles from this grassy knoll, a time far removed from last summer, the stroke of death had buried their dreams with one final absolute.

Summer hugged her knees and buried her swollen face against them.

She thought then about Tom as someone separate from her, and her mind conjured up the morbid questions about his death. She wanted to know the particulars about the way he had died. Had he suffered? What had been his last thoughts? In her mind, she pictured Tom clearly, tall and lean, with golden hair a little shaggy and blue eyes full of life. Summer would have deemed it impossible for anyone to take away the life in those sparkling blue eyes.

Up to this point, Summer had grieved for herself. Now she realized the consequences of dying young. Tom's dreams, of which he had spoken and written with passion, were dead now. He would never know the pleasure of farming his own land. He would miss the joy of touching his newborn child. He would never experience the unbridled passion of a woman who loved him.

The loss seemed then especially difficult to accept. Tom was a haven for goodness. He should have been in the middle of some field harvesting his crops. Instead, he was half a world away in a body bag.

She cried once more, not the painful gut-wrenching sobs that had accompanied her earlier sense of personal loss. This time Summer wept softly, an even sadder refrain for the loss of so much promise, vitality and such an earnest spirit.

The sun was still high on the horizon but already changing into evening hues when John drove the combine out of the slain cornfield. The hopper nearly overflowed with yellow kernels, and John muttered a prayer of thanks to have finished the field when he did. Even one more row would have yielded too much for the combine to hold, which would have forced John to dump the hopper before returning to the field, delaying his supper even longer.

John guided the green machine to a stop alongside a high-sided yellow trailer already filled with corn. He made an unscientific gauge of the remaining trailer capacity, measured it against the load of corn in the combine and opted to risk the possibility that the trailer was too full for the extra burden. He maneuvered the machine's controls, then watched the hydraulic lift push the hopper skyward and sideways. The bin emptied quickly, spilling bushels of corn into the trailer. A cloud of yellow dust hovered over the trailer as the corn settled dead level with the top edges.

"Cool," he said simply, returning the hopper to its normal position and switching off the combine.

His right ear ached from the combine's roar, but it was a small price to pay for an afternoon of pure pleasure. This was the first year John had run the combine by himself. He worried constantly the machine would suffer one of its notorious breakdowns, forcing him to test his inexperienced mechanicing skills in the middle of the field. Today, however, both the engine and blades had operated without a glitch.

He tried to rub away the earache, reminding himself to wear earplugs the next time he ran the combine. Closing his eyes against the dull throb, John soaked up the serenity of the quiet evening. It was a perfectly still moment, devoid of the sounds of passing cars on the highway, without even the ruffle of a breeze. The wheels of life had ground to a halt on their fast journey through time, and John basked in the brief interlude. He appreciated the purity of the moment. It was a time lag, offered by God either as a stage for dreams and reflection or as a vessel of repose.

John rested, and the lull soothed his earache. He was prepared to break the tranquil spell himself when the combine groaned with old age.

The strident creaking brought reason back to John, duly reminding him that besides supper, study for a tough test in senior English awaited his attention. He uncurled his lanky frame from the cushioned seat, scooted to the edge of the operating platform and bypassed the ladder on his way to a perfect landing six feet below on the ground. Seconds later, he was in the pickup, flipping the radio dial to his favorite station, singing along with Steppenwolf on *Born to Be Wild*.

Emerging from the field, John decided to buy a cold drink to help him study later. He skidded the pickup to a halt beside the mercantile's gas pumps, kicking up a cloud of dust and throwing open the door before the vehicle came to a full stop. The "Closed" sign showed on the screen, out early it seemed to John, but he was willing to bet the Carters would sell him a soda pop.

Slamming the truck door shut, John made a futile effort to brush off the dust from his faded jeans and white T-shirt. He stifled a whistled rendition of the song on the radio and went inside the store. "Dan, Amelia," he called as the doorbell jingled. "Any chance this tired farm boy can get a cold drink?"

John was headed toward the drink cooler when he heard Amelia's soft sobs. Stopping to look through the doorway, which separated the store from the Carters' living room, he found the couple sitting on the sofa. Amelia was slumped against Dan's shoulder with her hand on his chest. His jaw rested on the top of her head, and his arms encircled her.

John repeated their names softly, knocking on the door facing before moving deeper into the room. Their faces wore the ashen aura of despair, and John's heart sank. Even though he suspected the answer, the question begged to be asked. "What's wrong?"

"Tom is dead," Dan said. "We've just gotten the word."

A mixture of disbelief and dismay temporarily disoriented John. His legs felt shaky, so he edged closer to the couple, kneeling before them.

"I am so sorry," he said finally, not knowing what else to say or do. "Do you need anything? May I help anyway at all?"

Dan shook his head. "Not now, John," he said with a sad look. "We just need to sit here for a while longer and try to come to grips with it."

"Okay," John replied, rising to his feet, regretful to have disturbed their mournful solitude.

He walked to the doorway, then turned to them. "I wish I knew what to say or do," he said. "But I don't, unless it's to tell you that Tom's like a brother to me."

"I know," Dan soothed, smiling sadly at the boy.

John looked around the room, then thought about Summer. "I need to tell my sister."

"She knows," Dan said. "She was here when the officers came to tell us. She needed to be alone and ran off toward your house. Maybe she's there now. I don't know. We should have gone after her, but I wasn't thinken straight."

"Okay," John said. "I'll go check on her. Are you sure there's nothen I can do? Anything at all?"

Dan looked around the room. "Maybe you could turn off the front lights and pull the door shut tight," he suggested.

"Sure thing."

"One more thing," Dan added. "You might ask your mama and grandma to come over and make a few phone calls for us. I don't think I can right now. And there are people we need to tell. We need to call Mrs. Easters, Amelia's mother. Maybe we should send somebody over to Lenox to tell her in person. I don't know."

"I'll get them over here right away," John vowed. "Just sit tight, and I'll take care of everything." He paused. "I really am sorry, folks."

"Thanks, John," Dan said. "We'll see you later."

"Sure," John repeated, pulling the living room door partially closed.

His head was spinning as John located the light switches. One was in the back storeroom, another in the newer part of the store and the third behind the candy counter. He flipped off the porch light on his way out the door, pulling it shut. Once inside the pickup, he considered for the first time how Dan and Amelia would handle their son's death. And how Summer would mend a broken heart.

———

The Bakers were sitting with heads bowed at the supper table. Matt was giving an unusually long blessing for the food. His thanks were sincere gratitude for the bounty yielded by the family's fields, which had been parched by the drought and fire a year ago. The triumph of prosperity once again had gained the upper hand over disaster—for the time being.

John slipped through the front door without a sound, padding down the hall as his father's blessing resonated across the house. Crossing through the dining room, he arrived unnoticed at the kitchen doorway as Matt put the finishing touches on his blessing with a rousing "Amen."

Caroline opened her eyes and gave Matt a quick peck on the cheek. Her husband's strong blessing stirred good feelings in the woman. Four years since finding God, Matt seemed as saved today as on that day when he was baptized in New River. They smiled at each other, both amazed at the everlasting power of grace and love shared.

"That creamed corn looks good," Matt said. "Pass it over my way, please."

Caroline reached for the bowl, seeing John in the doorway at the same time. "I was wonderen when you'd show up, son," she remarked, smiling. "Come on and have your supper—creamed corn and pork chops."

"Did you finish that patch of corn, son?" Matt asked as he spooned corn onto his plate.

"Yes, sir."

"I don't suppose Summer is with you," piped in Rachel, who was upset because the iced tea was not sweet enough to her liking. "She went to the store for sugar hours ago, and we haven't seen hide nor hair of her since."

"No, ma'am, Summer's not with me," John replied, his doleful tone a clear message to everyone that something was amiss.

They looked clearly at John for the first time since his arrival home, their alarm growing as he stepped fully into the kitchen. His deeply tanned face was pallid and tear-stained.

"Is Summer all right?" Caroline asked, her voice quavered with the certainty of impending dread. She pushed back from the table to stand, gripping the edge tightly.

"What's wrong, son?" Matt implored.

"I don't know how to tell y'all this," John finally replied in a choked voice. "I've just come from the store. Dan and Amelia just found out—Tom is dead."

Everyone reacted with deathly quietness.

They stared first at John, then at each other and, finally, into their plates. Caroline was the first to react, releasing one soft whimper as she dropped back into her seat. Then Rachel dabbed at her eyes, and Sam put a comforting hand on her shoulder. Luke left the table.

"Do they know what happened?" Matt asked.

"I'm not sure," John answered. "I didn't know what to say or ask them, Daddy. But Dan asked if y'all could come over and help them make phone calls to relatives and such. He said somethen about senden somebody over to Lenox to tell Amelia's mother."

"How are they taken it?" Caroline asked.

"They were just sitten on the couch," John commented. "Amelia never said a word, never even looked my way. They could use support. They're all alone over there."

"We'll go now, Matt," Caroline said to her husband. "What about Summer?" she asked John. "Is she with them?"

"No, ma'am, she's not. But she knows. She was there when the officers came to tell the Carters. Dan said she took off runnen toward home. I was hopen she'd be here with y'all."

"Poor baby," Caroline cried, burying her face in her hands as she wondered how to console her daughter and friends. "Poor Tom."

She wept openly for several minutes, unable to control her heavy heart. Matt came to her side, kneeling to embrace her. When she was able to speak again, Caroline expressed worry for Summer. "Where do you suppose she is, Matt?" she sniffled. "She shouldn't be alone."

"She's somewhere by herself tryen to sort through all this," Matt reassured her. "She'll be along when she's ready. And we'll be here for her."

"I can't help but cry for her," Caroline said in a quivering voice. "And for Tom, and Amelia and Dan. I don't know how they can stand it. I couldn't if it was our child, one of our little boys or girls. It almost feels like it is one of our children. How will any of us ever get over this?"

"Honey, don't make yourself a mess with worry," Matt urged. "It won't help matters."

"Listen to your husband, Caroline," Sam remarked. "He is right. Let's take it one moment at a time and worry about getten through the next few hours first. Everything else will take care of itself. And believe me, Dan and Amelia *will* get through this. It'll be hard, but they'll survive. We all will. You just get through it, one day at a time, the best way you can."

"I don't mean to blather," Caroline apologized.

"You're not blatheren, Caroline," Rachel said, her voice firm with understanding. "You're thinken like a mother. I know what Sam says is right because I've been there. Three times I've given up a child, one of them to war. You know as well as I that we have to deal with what the Lord puts on us. And He doesn't put any more on us than we can stand. More than anything, you and I need to have us a good cry to get rid of some of this sorrow, but not now. Amelia and Dan need every bit of comfort we can offer. They need it more than we need to cry, so let's get on over there. Amelia's not the strongest woman in the world, and I'm worried about her. And Dan needs someone, too. We all need to be with each other at a time like this."

"You're right, Ma," Caroline replied, smiling through her tears as her resolve stiffened. "They probably could use a shoulder. Let me run a comb through my hair, and we'll get on over there."

She started to walk out of the kitchen, then offered some last-minute instructions. "Carrie, honey, fix up a couple of plates for us to carry over there," she said. "Dan and Amelia will need to keep up their strength. And call me the moment Summer gets home. Lord knows, she needs comfort as much as anyone, maybe more. She loves that boy. If she's not home soon, John, you go look for her."

"Yes, ma'am," John promised, moving aside so his mother could pass through the doorway.

"Where's Joe?" he asked a moment later as Rachel slipped into her room to change shoes.

"He'll be along soon," Matt said.

———

Amelia was stronger than Rachel believed. Or maybe she was in a state of shock. But she bore her grief well.

No one doubted the source of her strength. Her mother, Essie Easters, was a spunky woman, even as she dealt with death.

Rachel had accompanied Matt to the nearby town of Lenox to relay word of the death to Tom's grandmother. Upon hearing the news from Matt, Mrs. Easters emitted a single woeful cry of anguish and cupped her forehead. "My sweet Tom," she cried, tears sparkling in her vivid blue eyes. "He was such a good boy. And my poor Amelia: God bless her and help her bear the burden."

Mrs. Easters had packed an overnight case quickly, changed from her fashionable sleeping gown into a comfortable dress and returned with Matt and Rachel to the mercantile. The distance to the Carter home from Lenox was no more than ten miles, although half of it was via a dirt road.

Essie Easters dominated the ride with conversation, telling her companions one story after another about Tom as a little boy and his devotion to Summer. "Once he really took a good look at your lovely daughter, Matt, I think it was love at first sight," Mrs. Easters said. "He came over to my house one Sunday last spring or summer. Apparently, the night before, they had gone to a movie with your other children. All he talked about that day was Summer, though not much of it very flattern, I'm afraid. He said the girl was most difficult, impossible to get along with and extremely fickle."

"Summer can be difficult," Rachel admitted sheepishly. "She's stubborn and headstrong."

"Takes after her grandmother," Matt added.

"Stubborn and headstrong," Mrs. Easters repeated. "That's exactly how Tom described her. I saw right away he was smitten with the girl, but I didn't dare tell him that. It's best when a man recognizes those things for himself. It makes them appreciate us women more."

Her voice faltered then, tussling with melancholy before she could continue. "They will miss so much," she said finally and was quiet for the rest of the trip.

Upon her arrival at the mercantile, however, Mrs. Easters took charge of the situation. She kissed her son-in-law on the cheek, hugged her daughter fiercely and marched them both into the bedroom for a private word. No one knew what she told them, but her words did a world of good. Her whole manner suggested the world would right itself once more. Still, her charismatic approach to grief contained no foolish expectations.

Essie Easters probably should have been a counselor for the grief-stricken, Rachel thought. She supported her daughter through the hardest moments, when the pain became unbearable and the tears uncontrollable. And she gave Amelia free rein through those times when the heartbreak was sufferable. When she was not tending her daughter, Essie fluttered around Dan, nurturing him with reassuring hugs, warm milk and hot-buttered biscuits.

Of every solace Essie offered, however, none mattered as much as her unflagging effort to immortalize the spirit of her dead grandson. She simply refused to allow Tom's life force to die among the ruins of his friends and relatives who were wallowing in grief.

She satiated the mourners with slice-of-life vignettes, capturing the essence of Tom with gladdening memories of a little boy growing to manhood. She turned his short years on earth into one long jubilee. Her musing permeated the home with the strength of his presence. Her thoroughness provided a glorious litany to his existence.

The rogation brought smiles to the faces of Tom's bereft parents. But Essie hoped for more than sad smiles. She was trying to sow seeds for a good harvest in the hard days to come, when the mourners were gone, and Dan and Amelia were left to cope with the loss on their own.

———

Later that evening, Caroline phoned home to check on Summer. She was fretful over the girl's absence, feeling as if Summer had been abandoned in her most pressing hour of need. She felt anxious, unsure how to help her daughter cope with a loss of this magnitude. But one thing Caroline knew: Except for God's grace, Summer needed her family's love and support above everything else.

Carrie picked up the phone on the third ring. "Hello," she said.

"It's me, honey," Caroline replied.

"Summer still hasn't come home, Mama," Carrie said immediately. "We've all been looken for her."

"Okay," Caroline said, strangely calm even to herself. "What about Joe? Is he there yet?"

"No, ma'am, he hasn't come in," Carrie said. "How are the Carters?"

"They're taken it well for the moment," Caroline observed. "Amelia's mama is a Godsend for them. How about you and everyone else? Are you holden up okay?"

"We're fine," Carrie said. "It doesn't seem real. I'm not sure I believe it, yet. Maybe I just don't want to."

"None of us does," Caroline said.

"When Summer comes home, Mama, what do we say to her?" Carrie asked. "I'm worried we'll do all the wrong things."

"I know how you feel," Caroline said. "All we can do is love her. Maybe let Summer lead the way for us." She sighed over the phone. "When she does get home, Carrie, please call me. I'd like to be with her."

"Yes, ma'am," Carrie said. "And, Mama. Tell the Carters how sorry we all are about Tom."

———

A short time later, Matt and Rachel came home. They answered a few questions and tried to invoke the sense of uplifting bestowed upon them by Essie Easters. But the children were in no mood for consolation. They were not yet ready to accept losing one of their own.

John and Luke planted themselves on the two living room sofas, landing lethargically in prone positions. Bonnie curled up on the floor, while Carrie paced between the television and the front door, worried over her sister's absence.

"We've checked everywhere, Daddy," Carrie said. "The barns, the loft, even down at the ponds. I even went down to the packhouse. But it was empty."

"There's a hundred places she could go to be by herself," Matt said, glancing at his watch, admitting to himself he was worried, too.

All of the children had inherited Matt's need to steal away for meditation on matters with crushing consequences. But this was different.

The sound of Joe's Volkswagen coming into the yard interrupted his thoughts. Joe was standing in the doorway soon afterward, apologizing for being late, seeming pensive, almost skittish. For a moment, Matt suspected the boy had been drinking.

"Are you all right, son?" he asked.

"Yes, sir, I'm fine," Joe said quickly. "But I've got a friend in the car who needs help. He's been beaten pretty badly. He took a serious rap across the head and was knocked cold. He's groggy still. I wanted to take him to the hospital, but he's dead set against it. I brought him here, hopen Mama and Granny could take a look at him. He has a nasty gash on his head among other things and needs a bandage."

"What about you?" Rachel asked, inspecting Joe. "Are you hurt? You sound hoarse."

"No, ma'am," Joe said. "Nothen happened to me."

"What happened to the boy?" she asked. "Why won't he go to the hospital?"

"There was some trouble at school today," Joe explained. "He was right in the thick of it. Is it okay to bring him in the house?"

"Sure, it is," Matt said. "But first, we need to talk."

"Yes, sir," Joe replied, looking at his father, then at Rachel, who turned away.

Next, he scanned the room, noticing the unusual quietude about the house. No one looked at him, except for Matt, and his expression was woefully serious. "Daddy? Is everything okay?" he asked hopefully.

"No, it's not, son," Matt said. "We've had bad news. About Tom."

Joe groaned, his eyes closing. He leaned against the door facing, sick at his stomach.

"Daddy. Please tell me there's a reason to have hope," he pleaded.

"I wish I could," Matt said. "I really do. But we found out just a short while ago. Tom's gone."

Joe sagged against the wall, strength draining completely out of him. His knees trembled, and his shoulders shook with spasms. The tears came against his will, but they poured down his face nonetheless. He felt helpless, his heart cut to the quick, irreversibly changed for the worse. From here on out, Joe knew, he would live with this moment. The pain of it would subside, but he would never get over this loss entirely. He would carry the loss with him, as an empty place in his spirit—and he would wonder about it and wish it were full for the rest of his life.

These thoughts were calming to Joe, but they failed to console him or lessen the lump in his throat. Tom's death wasn't any easier to accept, and Joe felt saddened beyond sorrow.

Forcing himself, he turned to his family, leaning his back against the wall. "It's such a waste," he muttered in plaintive tones, using his shirtsleeve to wipe his face. "I wish we could know why this had to happen."

"I'm not sure there is a reason for these things, son," Matt suggested. "At least not one that's easy to get a handle on."

"There ought to be," Joe responded with conviction, looking Matt in the eye. "If it's cause enough for Tom to die, then we should know the reason for it, and it ought to be a good one."

Joe raked his hands through his hair. His despair filled the room. "Maybe I'm overreacten. If that's the case, then I'm sorry. But I don't believe there is a good enough reason that Tom should be dead, at least not this way. And I sure don't believe there's any good reason to send John over there if it comes to that. Or Luke."

"You're not overreacten, Joe," Sam assured his grandson. "You love Tom, like we all do. You have every right in the world wanten to know why he had to die. I wish we had the answers. As you say, we ought to. When your uncle was killed at Pearl Harbor, we had a pretty simple answer. That didn't make it any easier to take, didn't make it hurt any bit less. Sometimes, things go wrong, Joe, and when that happens, you carry on the best way you can."

"Maybe," Joe agreed wearily, rubbing away the beginning of a headache.

"No maybe about it," Sam said strongly. "Plain and simple, it's what you do."

"Yes, sir," Joe replied.

A moment later, he asked, "How's Summer taken this?"

"We don't know where she is," Carrie said worriedly.

"You mean she doesn't know?" Joe asked.

"She knows," Matt explained. "She was at the store when the chaplain came out from Moody to break the news. Dan said she took off toward our place, and nobody's seen her since. The kids have been out looken. Do you have any idea where she might be?"

"Did you check by the river?" Joe asked. "That was one of their special places. I think it's where Tom asked her to marry him."

Carrie sighed, closing her eyes. "I should have thought about that right off the bat," she lamented. "I bet she's there."

"Let me go to her, Daddy," Joe said, already moving toward the door.

"There's a flashlight on the dresser in our bedroom," Matt said. "Take it with you."

"What about your friend in the car?" Bonnie asked.

Joe had forgotten all about Elliot and the day's happenings. He owed his family explanations, but they would have to wait. Summer was his top priority.

"His name is Elliot Frankel," Joe said, moving toward his parents' room to retrieve the flashlight. "John, maybe you and Luke can help him into the house. Put him in my room."

"We'll look after him," Matt said. "Find your sister and bring her home."

SUMMER SAT UP ON the grass, aware for the first time of the darkness around her. She had no conception of the hours spent by the river, but her family would be worried by now. These were her first thoughts unrelated to Tom since the chaplain had brought the news of his death.

She looked to the horizon as a cloud floated off the moon, her thoughts drifting to the Christmas Eve twilight of last year. Tom was in the third day of a two-week leave. He recently had completed boot camp and eight additional weeks of specialized infantry training at Fort Benning. His blond locks were gone, replaced by a golden sheen on top of his head. The physical training had hardened his body and given him a dose of swaggering confidence. He carried about ten extra pounds, all of it muscle.

For the first time, Summer had bypassed the annual Christmas Eve trip to town with her family, telling her mother and grandmother in plain terms that she wanted to establish new traditions with Tom. Although disappointed, the older women had understood and checked their objections. Then, as soon as the family was gone, Summer had changed her mind, insisting to Tom that Christmas Eve trips to town become their first family tradition. He'd obliged her, and they had spent several hours walking the streets of Tifton with various members of the Baker family.

They'd spent the major portion of the time with Joe, helping him pick out a ridiculous ceramic rooster for Rachel. Summer had argued vehemently against the rooster, but Joe insisted it was the perfect gift for their grandmother. Tom agreed with her brother and on Christmas morning, so did Rachel. Of her gifts, none was more appreciated than that ceramic rooster, which now sat on top of the cupboard.

Tom and Summer had left Tifton long before the Baker family. He had insisted she pack a picnic basket for an outing by the river. Under protest, reminding him every step along the way that they were due for supper at his grandmother's home at precisely seven o'clock that evening, Summer had fried two pieces of chicken and baked half a dozen biscuits to go with blackberry jelly. Armed with the food basket, a mason jar of water and an old blanket, they had set off through the woods.

It was a beautiful day, leading up to one of the warm Christmases that occur some years in South Georgia. Summer had worn a white, short-sleeved sweater and a red cotton skirt. Tom wore blue jeans, with a light blue pullover.

"The last time you brought me out here, you tried to seduce me," Summer remarked as they came close to the river bend. "Are you goen to try again today?"

"As I recall, you dragged me out here, charmed me with the smell of smoky perfume and used the occasion to wrangle a marriage proposal from me," Tom replied. "But since you bring it up, I might very well try to seduce you."

"Let me warn you in advance," Summer said. "My resolve has grown stronger."

"And I warn you. My sex appeal has become invincible," Tom countered.

"I have been reminded lately by my mama that some things are better served by waiten until after marriage," Summer continued, ignoring his suggestive teasing. "I quote her: 'Maken love is God's wedden gift. Don't open it before the wedden day.'"

"Your mama is a very wise woman," Tom said. "But if she's offeren this advice to you, then I'm worried about what she thinks of me. Regardless, it's a man's obligation to try. That's quoten you from our very first date, so I will try."

"But not too hard, please," Summer pleaded. "Even good girls have their breaken points."

"I'll be gentle," Tom promised.

They had dissolved into laughter, teasing each other with kisses as they spread the blanket. Tom had set upon the picnic basket immediately, devouring the chicken and five of the biscuits smeared with jelly. Summer had watched him joyfully, feeling like a schoolgirl at first, becoming dismayed eventually by the size of his appetite.

"It's a good thing your parents own a store," she said when the picnic basket lay in ruins and Tom settled back on the blanket to relax in the sunshine. "Otherwise, they'd have never been able to feed you. Has the Army ever discharged anyone for eaten too much?"

Tom had dozed for several minutes while Summer put away the basket and strolled over to the riverbank to watch the water cascade past. He woke when she lay down beside him on the blanket, tickling his chin with a twig she had broken from a fallen oak limb. He grabbed her arms, pinned her beneath him and tickled her silly until Summer begged for mercy. He answered her plea with a long, deep kiss that stirred the dangerous feelings between them.

When the warning bells rang loudly, he rolled away and lay beside her until their breathing returned to normal. "I've got somethen for you," he said finally, sitting up and reaching into his jeans pocket to pull out an engagement ring. "I thought it was about time I marked you as mine."

The diamond glittered on a gold setting in the sunlight, and Summer thought it was the most beautiful ring in the world. For once, she had been speechless as Tom slipped the ring onto her finger. "Let's make this official because I love you very much, Summer," he told her. "Will you marry me?"

Still unable to speak, she had nodded vigorously to convey her acceptance. He had laughed, then kissed her until Summer felt lightheaded.

"I love you, too, Tom," she said at last. "Let's get married now. Or tomorrow or the next day. As soon as possible before you go overseas."

Tom had considered the suggestion for a moment. "You know how I feel about that, sweetheart," he replied at length. "Not until I get back from Vietnam. That's just a little over a year from now. It's better if we wait."

"I don't want to wait," she told him. "I want the satisfaction of be'en Mrs. Tom Carter while you're away from me. And, Tom, I want you, too."

"I do, too, Summer," he sighed. "I want it so bad it hurts. I want to feel you next to me, to hold you under me and love every inch of you. If I could touch you and hold you next to me, I think it would be enough for now.

"So do I," she responded shyly. "But could we stop ourselves, Tom?"

"I don't know," he said honestly. "You're beautiful and tempten, and I've got a lot of wanten inside me. I couldn't promise to be as strong as you."

"I'm willen to try, Tom," Summer suggested boldly. "Maybe it's wrong, but you're the only man I ever intend to be with, so I don't see how."

"I can't argue with that," Tom said, kissing her, claiming her mouth softly until the hunger of desire overwhelmed them.

The next hour had brought a tortured discovery of each other, tendered by sweet kisses and tantalizing touches, strained by an obsession to woo deeper secrets of carnal knowledge. Summer was ticklish on her feet, Tom overly sensitive on the smooth curve of neck behind his ear. Eventually, Tom had taken her hand, pulling them both to their feet where they stood on the blanket facing each other. He took the lead, shedding his shirt, and Summer followed, discarding her sweater and bra. They moved closer until they were touching, ivory against olive brown. She traced the line of golden hair on his stomach, her finger trailing from the waist of his jeans to the middle of his chest. He cupped her breasts, and they tasted each other.

When they were satisfied and staring once more at each other, Summer had removed her skirt. For whatever reason, she had been unable to make herself completely naked. Sensing the reserve, Tom had slipped out of his jeans and moved next to her once more. When they were both on fire, he pushed away her panties, stepped back and peeled off his underwear. They both had gaped in open admiration.

"You are beautiful, Summer, everything I expected," he said.

"You are beautiful, too," she replied. "And, more than I expected."

They giggled nervously, then fell against each other and began a new exploration, fettered by only the barest degree of caution. Challenging solicitude over and over again, they dipped dangerously close to the consummation of their lovemaking before falling away in the exhausted agony of restraint.

"I can't do this anymore," Tom said finally, his breathing raspy as he rolled off her. "I can't control it any longer, Summer. I'm about to blow sky high. We either stop now, or we keep goen. It's your choice."

Although she ached to continue, the desire for purity on her wedding night had conquered her longing to have him then and there. Still, the moment required fulfillment, so guided by another desire, Summer had draped herself against Tom, kissed his face and taken him into her hands. Soon, he writhed against her, panting with eyes shut tightly, legs shaking out of control. Then, his groin arched and his head rolled back with a groan.

Summer had been a little embarrassed by her ability to make Tom feel that way. Her eyes fell away from his contented face to his groin and then quickly to her own naked lap. But Tom had remained poised. He raised a hand and brought her face to him for a caring kiss. "I love you now more than I have ever loved you," he said.

She had looked into his eyes and seen it then. Tom was looking at her the way her father sometimes looked at her mother, when the obviousness of that unbreakable bond between them seemed to radiate across time and space. She glowed with her own sense of fulfillment, knowing there was a correctness to the love they had shared, grateful to have passed over the other gift until another time. At that precise moment, though, the civility of wedding vows had mattered little to Summer. Their souls had been married in a union that only God would break.

"I will make you happy, Summer," Tom said. "One day not too far away from now, I will bring you into my home, into my bed, and I will love you for an eternity and then some. The best is yet to come, honey. It really is."

Then Tom had showed her his intentions, turning her to liquid fire and taking Summer to places she never knew existed. When he was finished with her, she understood fulfillment. Unable to speak, she had nestled against the length of his body, resting her head on his chest because she wanted nothing but his warmth and presence.

Some minutes later, they had risen and dressed each other under the filtered light of a half moon.

"Can I be sentimental and maudlin for a moment?" Tom asked as she zipped and buttoned his blue jeans, kissing the underside of his chin.

"I would appreciate any mush that comes from your mouth," she told him. "But only here and now. Already, I feel certain that our families will take one look at us, all rumpled and dreamy looken, and will know instantly what we've been up to. Not that I would care. However, should we start spouten off like lovesick puppies, then I think it would be more than they could take."

Tom laughed, gently nudging her around so that he could hold her around the waist. They were still bare-chested, and she snuggled against him.

"See that moon," he observed, pointing skyward.

"It's beautiful," Summer crooned.

"Yeah, it is," Tom agreed. "I've been thinken, Summer, and maybe it's a silly idea. But I want us to have somethen in common every day while I'm away from you. I know we'll write letters and stuff like that, but I want a daily ritual, somethen that can keep us connected. What if every night, we take a minute or two and stare at the moon? If nothen else, we'll get the satisfaction of knowen we're on each other's minds."

The idea had been emotional goo, but Summer had latched onto it with fervid commitment. She had been faithful to the sentiment as well, night after night, even on those evenings when there was no moon to see. She would look skyward with her thoughts, and she would believe Tom read her mind.

The memory was sad and sweet, and it touched her on this different night, which, too, was warm and made for lovers. Summer did not want to cry, but she was lost and lonely. She gazed at the moon, which was moving toward its fullness.

"I'm still looken, Tom," she said aloud. "I'm staren at that great big moon, and you're on my mind. I'm wonderen, too, Tom. I'm wonderen if you're somewhere up there, thinken about me. Are you? I hope so."

She waited, almost as if she expected an answer. But the only sound coming back to her was the noise of nighttime and the babbling of the river.

Summer pulled up to her knees, allowing a sudden breeze to caress her face. And then she saw the light coming toward her in the distance. Her heart skipped a beat, trying to fool her with the feeling of emerging from a terrible nightmare. She waited with baited expectation, to open her eyes and find herself in bed while Carrie and Bonnie slept soundly across the room.

When Joe materialized out of the woods into the clearing a few yards from where she sat, Summer accepted the inevitable. She was not going to wake up from this nightmare anytime soon. She buried her face in her hands and wept once more.

––––––––

Joe was at her side immediately, cradling her and cooing sympathy. The gesture seemed barren, he thought, but perhaps support was all the comfort required by his sister. He allowed her to spend the tears, waiting for an invitation to talk.

"I'm glad you came," she said finally, her voice muffled against his chest. "I'm glad you're here before anyone else. It's a fitten end. You were there at the beginnen, Joe, that day when I cajoled you into inviten him to the movies. I didn't have a clue it would turn out the way it did. I was flighty about boys. Love was abstract. But it happened between Tom and me. It was pure magic. I have no regrets about loven him."

Summer lifted her eyes toward the moon, still immersed in her brother's support. "To lose him, though, to know his dreams are gone forever, that he will never get what he wanted out of life. How can we live knowen all that is gone, Joe?" She shivered in the breeze, shifting closer for protection. "I'm glad you're here to help me give him up, Joe. I need help to say goodbye."

Joe gently extracted himself from the embrace, then cupped her face in his hands. "Don't give him up completely, Summer," he said. "We shouldn't do that. There are too many good memories. One day, we will remember and recall them as sweet rather than bittersweet, and we will both be better for haven known Tom and loved him. Not just you and me but all of us—from Grandpa to Bonnie. We will know our lives are a little richer for those days we spent with Tom Carter. It's impossible to know Tom and not be touched by the goodness in him."

"Deep down, I know you're right," she said. "But that doesn't make it easier, does it?"

"Nothen will make it easier, except maybe time," he replied, "and even that may be a long time comen. Grandpa says you just get through it one day at a time, Summer, the best way you can. I'm afraid he's right."

"Starten now, I suppose?" she asked.

"Starten now," he agreed.

Summer allowed herself a wistful smile. "Let's go home," she said.

———

Caroline was waiting on the porch when Joe and Summer emerged from the darkness across the road. Summer clung tightly to his arm. Even at the distance, Caroline could distinguish her daughter's subdued form and hurt expression. She went to meet them in the yard.

Seeing Caroline, Summer dislodged herself from Joe and ran into the comfort of her mother's protective embrace and soothing condolences. She stayed there for a full minute, finding security against the winds of war raging in her mind.

"I hope I didn't worry you too much, Mama," she said at last, when her knees no longer trembled. "I had to be by myself."

"I know, darlen," Caroline agreed. "Let's get you inside and into bed. A good night's rest might help."

"I'm not sure I can sleep," Summer said dubiously.

"I'll fix hot tea or chocolate and we'll sit up for a while," Caroline replied.

Summer stepped back from her mother, gazing thoughtfully at the bright lights shining through the living room curtain. "I guess everybody's still up," she said.

"They're upset about Tom and worried for you, honey," Caroline confirmed. "If you're not up to facen them, I'll send them off to bed before you come inside the house. They'll understand."

"That's not necessary," Summer said. "They're hurten, too. We all are. It helps knowen people care about you. Maybe that's how we get through this." She hesitated, then added, "But I'll probably wind up cryen."

"Go right ahead and cry all you want," Caroline urged. "There's no shame in tears. That's one of God's ways to help us work through our grief."

Almost against her will, the tears began again, cleansing sobs that purged pain and appreciated the kindhearted concern of her family as they came to offer hugs and other acts of sympathy. When Summer had acknowledged everyone, she retreated to her bedroom followed by Caroline, who first set the household in motion with instructions for altered sleeping arrangements and quiet time.

Joe took it upon himself to make sure the other children were situated in the boys' bedroom. His efforts were unnecessary, of course. They were all teenagers now, except for Bonnie, and she was less than a year from that transforming age of thirteen. Tonight, however, Joe needed to hover over his brothers and sisters. Years ago, it seemed, he had tucked one or two of them into bed almost nightly, even wound up with one of them in his bed when the next morning came. Out of respect for the past, sensing his desire to play the part of big brother, the children allowed Joe to fuss over them.

"You guys need anything," he asked as he pulled a light blanket over Bonnie, who was lying with Carrie in the double bed usually occupied by Luke.

"We're fine," John answered from the room's second bed, which he shared with Luke tonight.

"I miss nights like these," Bonnie said as Joe kissed her on the forehead. "You used to do this all the time, Joe. I wish you still did. I'm not sure I like this business of getten older."

"Tonight, I feel pretty much the same way, Bonnie," Joe said, sitting on the bed beside her. "But time marches on. We have to roll with it and realize things don't always stay the same. It's not easy, but it's inevitable. And you know I still love you, sweetheart. Even if I never tuck you in bed ever again, I'll always love you."

Joe stood between the two beds. "For that matter, I love you all," he said. "Probably I wouldn't be sayen it if everything was fine and dandy, but it's the way I feel. It was the way I felt about Tom, too. And right now, I'd give anything to tell him that." He took three steps toward his bedroom door, then stopped. "Maybe I've embarrassed you with all this sentiment, but I won't apologize for it."

"I for one appreciate it, big brother," Luke said, surprising everyone. "It's nice to have someone fuss over you before bedtime. But in all sincerity, Joe, I will be ticked off to no end if you ask me whether I need to take a leak before I go to sleep. It's been years since I needed that reminder, and I'm in no mood to have anyone bring it up."

They all laughed softly at the throwback to days long past when Luke feared he might go through life as a bed-wetter.

"It was on the tip of my tongue to do just that," Joe teased. "But since you mentioned it first, I'll forget it."

Quietly, Joe eased open the door to his room and studied Elliot's sleeping form. Rather than risk waking him, Joe closed the door and started from the room.

"What can you tell us about your friend in there?" John asked with obvious curiosity and some expectation of an answer.

"Nothen much," Joe replied as he reached the bedroom door and flipped off the light switch. "Goodnight now."

————

The opening music of the eleven o'clock news played faintly across a small portable TV as Joe joined his father and grandparents in the kitchen for a cup of coffee. Joe busied himself at the stove until the anchorman proclaimed the day's top story as the antiwar demonstration on the Valdosta State campus. The opening picture was a lengthy shot of Elliot Frankel burning his draft card, and the station allotted almost three minutes to the story. Joe watched the montage unfold across the screen, ending with a picture of the three Gold Star mothers drinking coffee in the administration building—along with an announcement that state and local police were searching for Elliot.

"Good Lord, Joe!" Rachel exclaimed as Sam flipped off the television set. "That boy's a wanted man."

"Son, suppose you tell us the whole story about what happened today," Matt instructed quietly.

"They pretty much said it all on TV, Daddy," Joe replied. "There was a demonstration on campus, and Elliot was the leader. It got out of hand. He went too far to make his point. Way too far, and a couple of cops beat him until he was bleeden and unconscious. I decided he needed help, so I carried him to my car and drove around a while until I figured out what to do with him. I wasn't tryen to keep him from be'en arrested or anything like that, but I was worried that he was hurt. They beat on him hard with billy clubs and kicked him in the stomach and head with boots."

"He ought to see a doctor," Rachel suggested. "He may have a couple of broken ribs or even a concussion."

"You'll see that he gets to a doctor tomorrow, Joe," Matt said. "And then let the police do what they have to do with him."

"I could get him out of the house tonight, if you prefer?" Joe offered.

"There's no need for that," Sam said with a purported yawn of indifference. "Let the boy rest. Tomorrow will be here soon enough, and I think the police can wait another day for him. If I were you, however, I'd see to it that I was far away from the boy when the police do come. Your intentions may have been honorable when you dragged him away from that demonstration, but the police may not see it that way. You don't need that kind of trouble. You haven't done anything wrong as far as I can see."

Joe saw his father bristle at Sam's usurpation of the parental role. This was one of those moments when the presence of two fathers and two mothers under one roof created tension. Matt glared from his father to Joe before finally adhering to Sam's suggestion.

"Your grandpa's right," he said. "Tomorrow is soon enough."

Joe drained the cup of black coffee, then set the dish in the sink. "I'm goen to bed," he announced. "I'll see y'all in the mornen."

"Joe," Matt called to him. "Since your mama's likely to spend the night with Summer and see'en how your bed is occupied, why don't you sleep in my room. We need to talk over a few things."

Joe regarded his father with a careful look, then shrugged his shoulders in agreement and walked out of the room.

———

Matt was lying in bed by the time Joe showered and entered his parents' room. He flipped on the light, walked over to the dresser and ran Caroline's brush through his wet hair. Laying the brush aside, he crossed the room again to turn out the light, then pulled off his blue jeans and eased into the bed.

For a double bed, the Spanish Oak frame seemed small to Joe. He crunched his legs to accommodate their length against the round bar that spanned the bed's two bottom posts. A short time later, he flipped onto his stomach, wedging one foot between the mattress and the offending bar and draping his other leg over the edge of the bed. Finally, he plumped the feather pillow and tried to rest.

"Did you demonstrate today?" Matt asked.

"Yes, sir," Joe answered quickly. "At the time, it seemed like the right thing to do. I'm not so sure now."

"Because of Tom?" Matt said.

"Partly," Joe sighed, "but it's more than that, Daddy. I'm not sure demonstrations are the right way to go about getten the war stopped. Everything always gets blown out of proportion when you have somethen like that. If I had known for one minute Elliot was goen to burn his draft card, I would have stayed away. That was a stupid thing to do. It ruined the entire demonstration as far as I'm concerned."

"Did you believe in what you were demonstraten for?" Matt inquired. "Or against as the case may be?"

Joe sat up, propped his pillow against the headboard and rested against it. "I don't agree with this war, Daddy," he said plainly. "I don't see where we're doen any good over there. I don't see the sense in haven thousands of people die without ever maken any headway. If it counts for anything, I think our intentions are honorable. Maybe even noble. But somethen seems to have gone terribly wrong. We've gotten way in over our heads, and nobody's willen to jump in and save us. Maybe nobody knows how. Maybe not enough people want to. I don't know the answers, but I do know somethen needs to change. I sure don't want John or Luke sent over there. I wouldn't want to go over there myself. I would fight for my country in a heartbeat if the cause was right, but I also don't think it's asken too much to know first why you're fighten. When you went to Europe in 1942, you knew why. You were sent to stop a madman from taken over the world. I think the people be'en sent off to Vietnam today deserve an equally clear mission."

"There is a purpose, Joe," Matt maintained. "Maybe it's vague, but we are tryen to stop the spread of communism."

"If that's the case, then we should stop it and be done with it," Joe said. "As it is, we've been fighten all these years, and the communists still control North Vietnam and are maken one heck of an impression in South Vietnam, too. It took only six years to save the world two decades ago, Daddy. If you count what Kennedy did over there, then we've been in Vietnam—which I think is a pretty insignificant little portion of the world—for at least seven years. Doesn't somethen about that sound out of kilter to you?"

"Maybe," Matt agreed hesitantly. "I'm against these protesters, though, these people who burn the American flag and their draft cards. That's wrong."

"I agree; they go too far," Joe replied, "but I think there's also the possibility to consider that opposition to the war is the only way to stop it at this point—short of victory, which seems a long way off. I certainly know that if opposition to the war could have saved Tom from dyen, then I would have protested every day of my life."

Joe sank back onto the bed, deflated by the notion that he should be mourning for his friend rather than outlining his opposition to the cause that had claimed Tom's life.

Sensing his son's dejection, Matt said, "If that were the case, Joe, then I'd have stood beside you. Tom mattered more than anything in this mess."

"That's the way I see it," Joe agreed softly.

"I'm glad you and I can find common ground, Daddy," he added a moment later. "Maybe I disappoint you sometimes, but I respect what you and Mama have taught me."

"I'm proud of you, son," Matt said. "There's a lot to be said for a man who seeks to understand the whole picture before he makes up his mind. Not too many people have the patience, myself included."

"Don't think too highly of me, Daddy," Joe replied, "or give me credit where it's not due. Maybe I'm faken some of that understanden. I ignored the war for a long time. In my situation, it was easy to forget. I've been rushen to catch up this last year, and in my haste, maybe I've been influenced too much by the antiwar side of the argument."

"How's that?" Matt asked.

"Elliot and the people he hangs with are pretty strong in their opposition to the war," Joe explained. "I guess radical is a better word. They don't see the flip side at all. But I'll say one thing for Elliot: He's sincere. Right or wrong, when he burned that draft card, he knew exactly what he was doen. He believed he was maken a strong statement. And he believes enough outburst—more strong statements—will end the war."

"There's somethen to be said for passion as well as understanden," Matt replied thoughtfully. "It takes a good mix of it all to make the world interesten."

"I've enjoyed our talk, Joe," Matt continued a short moment later. "A man and his son are obliged to spend time like this every now and then. I'm just sorry for the sadness that brought us to this occasion."

"I know what you mean," Joe said woefully.

"We will miss Tom for a long, long time," Matt added.

"Probably forever," Joe suggested. "But he'll always be with us, too. Maybe when we plant the fields next spring, he'll be watchen over us. And just maybe he'll have a little say-so with the weather."

Matt considered the suggestion. "Thinken of it that way makes what happened to him easier to accept," he agreed.

Exhausted by tension, they drifted into silence. Joe fell asleep within minutes, but Matt was restless for the night. Reflecting on their conversation, he realized he was proud of Joe's thoughtful consideration of the war. But he also admitted to himself that he was let down by his son's participation in the demonstration. Reconciliation between those two distinct thoughts, he mused later, would come easier if Matt knew where he himself stood on the issue.

————

"It's goen to hurt a long time," Summer told her mother.

Summer was lying on her bed, while Caroline stretched out on the second double bed in the girls' room. They had sipped cups of hot chocolate and remained silent for the better part of an hour, listening to the house fall asleep and lost in their respective thoughts. Now Summer appeared ready to talk about Tom.

"I know, darlen," Caroline responded, fearful that her every effort of consolation would come up woefully inadequate. "But you'll get through it."

"That scares me, Mama, the idea of getten through it," Summer remarked. "It seems so cold. I keep thinken it should hurt through and through, forever and ever."

"No, no, honey," Caroline soothed. "It doesn't work that way. If it did, there would be no reason for liven. And besides, Tom wouldn't want you or anyone else to suffer like that on his account."

Summer nodded miserably in agreement. "Do you wonder what Tom's reason for liven was?" she asked abruptly a moment later. "Why does God allow someone to walk on this earth for twenty years, to have dreams and make plans for things that will never happen? It seems like such a waste of time. What's the use of it, Mama?"

"I can't answer that question, Summer; neither can you," Caroline replied. "And you'll worry yourself sick if you keep asken those questions."

Summer regarded the dire prospect, concluding that a physical illness would come as welcome relief to the current state of her sick heart. Perhaps her mother's advice was for the best, though. Caroline had faced the deaths of loved ones, including parents who had died young in similarly tragic circumstances, and she had come through stronger in the face of adversity. But Summer was unwilling to give up her thoughts about the reason for Tom's existence completely. She wanted his dreams to live awhile longer.

"It's hard to decide which hurts worse," she commented at length. "The idea that he has gone away and left me forever or just knowen that he will never grow old, that he will miss out on all that comes with life. Tom lost everything he ever wanted, Mama."

"You're forgetten somethen very important," Caroline said softly. "Tom is no longer playen by our rules. He's in God's country. Whatever he left behind on this earth has been replaced with treasures of infinite worth. Just what those treasures are, we have no way of knowen. But it is strong enough to transcend his love for you and his parents; it completes his dreams, Summer. And in God's time, you and I will understand, too."

Summer appeared doubtful, but she could not dispute the wisdom of God's time. Instead, she inquired about Amelia and Dan, apologizing for abandoning them when they needed comforting.

Caroline brushed off her daughter's apologetic tone and told Summer the Carters were bearing up admirably under the strain, adding that Essie Easters was doing a brilliant job of consoling the bereaved parents. Summer then recounted a story about a Sunday dinner she had shared with Tom and Mrs. Easters in Lenox, praising the woman's sense of humor and spirit. Finally, they lapsed into another prolonged silence, each beginning to tire from the strain of the day and lateness of the hour.

"Do they know how he died?" Summer asked sometime later, broaching the subject cautiously, uncertain whether she was ready for the grisly details of Tom's death.

"Not yet," Caroline answered. "Apparently, there's a snag in the communication process. Maybe we'll know somethen more exact tomorrow."

"I'm not sure I want to know," Summer shuddered. "What if he suffered, Mama? What if Tom knew that he was dyen? Can you imagine the loneliness, the fear that a person must feel to know that he is slippen away and there is nothen or no one to grasp onto for help?"

Then Summer told her mother about the day Tom had been in the rice paddy when the mine exploded, how he had held the hand of a man whose life ebbed away from him. She wondered aloud if Tom had died alone or whether someone had been around to hold his hand in those last seconds of life.

"Don't torment yourself with what you don't know," Caroline advised, pleading for her daughter's sake. "That is precisely why you need to know the circumstances of his death, so those awful questions can be laid to rest."

"The truth will set me free, so to speak?" Summer suggested.

"Not entirely, it won't," Caroline said. "But it may help, especially when you're troubled by those notions."

Summer eased off the bed to retrieve a brush from the vanity table across the room. When she was back in bed, sitting cross-legged while brushing her hair, she vowed to have no regrets about loving Tom, despite the heartache that had come from it.

"If I talk to you as a woman, Mama," she asked, "could you hear anything I have to say and not think less of me?"

Caroline smiled supportively, feeling a sense of camaraderie with her eighteen-year-old daughter, remembering firsthand the difficulty of being a good girl. "Honey, I can't think of anything you would do that might make me think less of you," she said quickly. "I may not always approve of everything my children do, but I would never think any less of them for it."

Summer accepted the opinion without any doubt. She dropped the hairbrush and leaned forward in the sitting position. "You've given me lots of good advice, Mama," she said, "but I particularly respect the way you feel about sex before marriage: the idea that maken love is God's wedden gift. I shared that little gem of wisdom with Tom one day."

"How did he feel about it?" Caroline asked, smiling cautiously.

"Oh, he said it sounded like good advice," Summer replied. "But there was this one moment, Mama. One moment when Tom looked into my eyes, and I knew without a shadow of doubt how much he loved me and wanted me. I've seen Daddy look at you that way, as if the rest of the world doesn't exist. Well, that's how I felt that day. Tom was looken at me from deep inside his heart, and I could tell he already thought of me as his wife. I felt the same way, too. And if he had pushed it any, he could have taken me. But he didn't. He just held me close in his arms and that was enough for the moment."

Summer glanced away, gazing at the empty fireplace, her thoughts a million miles away for a quick moment. When she turned around again, Caroline saw the regret etched on her daughter's face.

"If I had known then, Mama, that we would never have another moment like that between us, I would have wanted Tom to make love to me," Summer said plainly. "I would have wanted him to take that memory to his grave. And then I could say now with complete honesty that I did not have a single regret about haven loved and lost him."

Words failed Caroline, so she joined Summer's thoughtful gaze toward the fireplace. If she could have found the proper way to say it, though, Caroline would have told her daughter that she understood completely.

CHAPTER 5

ON THE FOLLOWING MORNING, Elliot joined the Baker family at the breakfast table. The mood was silent and somber until the morning newscast repeated the previous night's report about the demonstration on the Valdosta State College campus. Once again, the report opened with a picture of Elliot burning his draft card.

Everyone recognized Elliot immediately, their steely eyes matching the defiant young man on television with the longhaired stranger at the table. Initial disbelief turned to distrust, and the tension mounted with each revelation about the protest. The lengthy report ended with a final disclosure that the search continued for the ringleader of the protest.

A combination of good manners and dismay kept the hard-bitten questions at bay, but Caroline, who had been unaware of the protest until now, quickly changed her mind about offering Elliot a second helping of eggs. Instead, she suggested that Joe hurry with his breakfast and get his acquaintance to a doctor. Her tone was stiffly polite, but the angry undercurrents were loud and clear.

"Finish up, Elliot," Joe told his friend. "We need to be on our way."

Elliot accepted their hostility with unflinching defense of his position. "I'm sorry about what happened to your friend," he said, his eyes canvassing the table with a practiced sweep. "But what I said and did yesterday had nothing to do with him personally. This war is a mistake. Our government is dispatching thousands of men to Vietnam with the mandate to kill indiscriminately. Kill the enemy, kill the women, kill the children. They seem to believe that if we kill anything that breathes over there, then we will win the war. I disagree. America is not some knight in shining armor riding to the rescue in Vietnam. As far as I'm concerned, by the time we're finished imparting our benevolent wisdom on the people of Southeast Asia, it won't matter whether Vietnam is a communist, Fascist or democratic society. I fear there will be nothing left to govern."

"Stop it this instant!" Caroline shouted suddenly. She threw down a dishcloth on the stove, then glared at Elliot with hands squarely on her hips. "Young man, this is neither the time nor place to debate the rights and wrongs of war. I resent your cynical condemnations, and I will not tolerate your radical ideas at our breakfast table. Frankly, you could use a lesson in good manners."

Summer pushed her plate away, rose from the table bench and started to exit the room. At the doorway, she halted her flight, wheeling around to confront the intruder.

"I agree the killen is atrocious and maybe America doesn't belong in Vietnam," she said. "But we're there whether you like it or not. And you are dead wrong if you think your actions yesterday have nothen to do with Tom or any other soldier fighten over there. It has everything to do with them because—right or wrong—they have been sent to Vietnam to fight a war and lay down their lives for this country. When you protest against the war, you might as well spit in their faces or walk on their graves. It's all the same."

"I don't see it that way at all," Elliot started to explain.

"Nor do I expect you to," Summer cut him off. "But when you've gone to Vietnam, when you've felt the breeze of bullets past your head or pulled a dyen buddy out of rice paddy, then come back and tell me how grateful you are to those people who demonstrate against the war. Then I will respect your position on the war."

Elliot shook his head in disagreement. "I will not go to Vietnam," he declared. "It's not my war."

"If it's not your war, then why bother to demonstrate against it?" Summer asked sharply.

"You misunderstood," Elliot replied, but Summer cut him off again.

"Perhaps I did," she said, "but this should be simple enough for you to understand. I don't care what you think about the war or anything else. Frankly, I can't stand the sight of you, and I have no intention of sharen a table or anything else with you.

"Honestly, Joe," she continued, donning her brother with a disappointed glare, "I can't imagine what possessed you to get mixed up with the likes of him, much less bring him to our house. Be that as it may, I'd be obliged if you got rid of him."

She gave Elliot a disparaging glance, then departed the room.

Without missing a beat, Joe stood up and ordered Elliot to the car.

———

A strained quietness rode with Joe and Elliot as the Volkswagen carried them to Valdosta. Joe was preoccupied with memories of Tom, while Elliot contemplated the seriousness of his situation. After a while, however, Joe inquired whether Elliot needed to see a doctor. Elliot responded he would stop by the college infirmary later in the day, then made another effort to apologize for the trouble he had caused Joe.

"A case of bad timing," Elliot concluded, his tone a bit too blithe for Joe.

"Well, Elliot. Death rarely is convenient," Joe replied caustically.

"I'm saying all the wrong things," Elliot moaned. "All I meant was that it's unfortunate the demonstration coincided with your friend's death."

They were coming close to falling into another silent spell when Joe attempted to explain his lack of enthusiasm for the demonstration. Elliot, however, refused to listen.

"You don't owe me any explanations, Joe," he said. "It's a free country, right?"

Thick tension settled between them, as if their differing viewpoints had arrived at an impasse. Joe turned on the radio, and they continued in silence toward their destination. When they were on the outskirts of Valdosta stopped at a traffic light, Joe made another attempt to re-establish common ground.

"Maybe we disagree over tactics, Elliot, but I admired the speech you gave yesterday," Joe said. "You have a flare for words and a presence that commands the audience's attention. As far as I'm concerned, you hit a home run with your words yesterday."

"But ...," Elliot interrupted knowingly, a smile on his face.

Joe regarded him carefully.

"Spit it out," Elliot encouraged, his tone brusque. "If I've learned anything at all about you, Joe, it's that there is always a 'but' where you're concerned."

Joe shrugged his shoulders, admitting, "You crossed the wrong line, Elliot. You shouldn't have burned your draft card."

"I didn't," Elliot replied casually.

"You didn't?" Joe responded, confused.

"Of course not," Elliot said, retrieving his wallet from the back pocket of his jeans and pulling an unblemished draft card from it. "I'm not stupid, Joe."

"You didn't burn it," Joe repeated, his anger rising as he comprehended Elliot's deception.

"No way would I do that," Elliot declared as the light turned green and Joe accelerated the car. "It was just an act. I may not want to go to Vietnam, but jail has even less appeal. There are ways to avoid the war, but burning your draft card is not one of them."

"So why did you stage that little scene yesterday?" Joe inquired, making a right-hand turn.

"For the effect," Elliot replied simply. "We needed something to draw people's attention, to agitate the crowd."

"That's one helluva way to get attention," Joe said with biting condescension. "Do you realize that three guys are in jail this mornen because they followed your lead and did burn their draft cards?"

Joe paused, waiting for a response, but none was forthcoming.

"Don't you see the conflict here, Elliot?" he asked finally.

"Not really," Elliot said without remorse. "I don't intend to be a martyr, Joe. Besides, there's not much you can do to stop a war from a jail cell. In a strange way, those of us who oppose this mess in Vietnam are fighting a war, too. Unlike our enemy, we have a definite goal. We're not yet there, but the tide is turning in our favor and we will achieve a total victory in the end. Until that day arrives, however, we must do whatever is necessary to win."

"Regardless of the moral implications?" Joe asked. "Regardless of who gets hurt in the process?"

Elliot shrugged. "I know what you're driving at, Joe, and you're beginning to sound awfully self-righteous. War always has its victims on both sides. Check me if I'm wrong, but there's a vast difference between dead women and children in Vietnam and three college kids who have to spend a few days in jail for burning their draft cards."

"The end justifies the means," Joe deciphered, laughing bitterly. "You're a regular enlightened despot, Elliot. I admire your commitment."

"You're blowing this way out of proportion, Joe," Elliot said sharply. "Besides that, who are you to question my commitment? At least I have the guts to follow through on my convictions, which is more than you can say for yourself. You're about the least-committed person I've ever met."

"If deception is part of your convictions, Elliot, then your convictions are half-assed," Joe retorted evenly. "When you have to lie to make your argument valid, why even bother? As for guts, I have enough at least to admit when I'm wrong about somethen. I also have enough gumption to know the difference between right and wrong, Elliot, and I'm beginnen to see just how wrong I've been about a lot of things."

Joe skidded the car to a stop by a street curve, reaching across the seat to push open the door. "Get out!"

Elliot considered the situation, then shrugged and slid his legs onto the waiting pavement. He paused for a second, as if he had something more on his mind. But there was really nothing else to say, so he pushed out of the car and slammed the door behind him.

Joe drove away without a backward glance.

———

Tom had died September 18, on the third day of the operation to destroy enemy supply routes along the Vietnamese-Laotian border. He had been assigned to a five-man scouting team with orders to obtain visual confirmation of a major relay station used to funnel Communist equipment to the Viet Cong. The military's sophisticated reconnaissance gadgetry had detected the outpost a week earlier, but the Army wanted concrete evidence before mounting a campaign to destroy the base. Military leaders had considered similar efforts to cut off these kinds of infiltration routes successful in the past only to discover a short time later that stocks were moving once more along the trail. This time they wanted to make the operation an unparalleled success, the one by which future missions would be measured. But once again, the operation floundered and their goal was thwarted.

"It was on this third night of foraying into the valley that Tom was killed," Captain Subic said.

Just as he had promised the previous day, the Air Force chaplain and Lieutenant Mark Applegate had returned to the Carter home with the particulars about Tom's death.

Summer leaned back against the comfort of the sofa in Dan and Amelia's living room and focused on the sunlight streaming through the white curtain lace. She was sitting beside the Carters and Mrs. Easters, listening to the captain with morbid curiosity and a genuine need to know the circumstances of Tom's death. The story had been sterile to this point, but Captain Subic had promised to tell it without gloss. Now his official government voice changed abruptly to a pastoral tone, preparing them for the ugliest link in this nightmarish chain of events.

Summer closed her eyes against the glint of white lace, allowing the pitch-black darkness of Vietnamese jungle to suck her up as the chaplain finished the story.

———

It happened about five o'clock on a Wednesday morning as the surveillance squad tromped back to their makeshift camp atop a mountain cliff.

As they climbed out of the valley over rugged mountain terrain, Tom's squad marched into an ambush set up by North Vietnamese troops. Two Americans, Pettys and Boyd, died immediately, bloodied in the crossfire of the first spray of machine-gun fire. Tom also took a direct hit, a disabling salvo just below the kneecap of his left leg.

Crippled and bleeding, he dragged himself to the cover of a nearby rock, wedging his body beneath the slab for protection. On the other side of the rock, Evans, the communications expert, radioed frantically for help, relaying their position and the desperateness of their situation. While Evans pleaded for backup, Tom and Clark blasted away blindly with their rifles at anything moving in the darkness.

Outnumbered and surrounded by enemy troops, the three soldiers held off their attackers for a short eternity before the North Vietnamese soldiers overran their position. At the last moment, out of desperation, Evans and Clark grabbed Tom by the shoulders and began pulling him up the hill toward a platoon of fresh reinforcements coming toward them in a desperate rescue attempt. They never stood a chance. Mortars stopped the platoon's advance, and seconds later, all three died in a hail of bullets fired at point-blank range.

———

Maybe there was no good way to die in war. Maybe God's will would have to suffice as the only explanation for the death sentence imposed on a gentle spirit like Tom. Maybe a thousand reasons were waiting in the wings for consideration, but for Summer, none could rationalize away the sickening nausea in the pit of her stomach.

She had come home to rest for a couple of hours before the first wave of friends and neighbors began arriving at the Carters with food and sympathy. Although she drowsed, the specter of phantom North Vietnamese soldiers had tortured her sleep until Summer finally forced herself awake. She sat up in bed, hugging her pillow.

Summer had no regrets about the decision to hear the grisly details of Tom's death. True to his word, Captain Subic had given them the unabridged version of the story, and Summer had accepted the cold-blooded reality with barely a flinch. She was finding it more difficult to cope with troubling thoughts about the pain and terror Tom experienced in his final minutes of life.

Over and over, with poignant clarity, her mind played out those last few minutes as if she had been a silent witness to the chaos from the moment Tom stepped into the ambush. Summer could see him writhing in agony as shrapnel ripped open his leg, and she could feel the grip of fear as he belly-crawled toward the scant protection provided by the cover of rock. She understood the strength of character and will to live that had propelled him to fight after being wounded, and she sensed the ray of hope that would have risen when rescue appeared possible.

It was that one gleam of hope that troubled Summer more than anything else and honed her perceptions into a razor-sharp image. She pictured the backs of two faceless soldiers, each holding Tom by the shoulders and dragging him across the rugged terrain. Tom was supine against the ground, wearing the heavy flak jacket, mud-caked boots and green fatigues, with the left pants leg shredded below the knee and saturated with blood.

His face was especially vivid to Summer, who had seen Tom hurt once before when he misfired with a hammer and slammed the tool against his thumb: face scrunched, eyes squinted close, mouth open and teeth bared to withstand the pain. And his hair, which had grown thick and wavy above his ears, was a tousled mass of gold, freed of his helmet, which had been lost in the ambush.

The vision ended there, leaving only her imagination to ponder how Tom would have reacted in the final seconds of life. What kind of fears would have raced through his mind when the bombs exploded and phantom soldiers materialized into men who wanted to kill him? At what moment had he realized his fate? Had he panicked in those last few seconds or had he prepared to die with calm acceptance? Had he looked upon the faces of his killers, or perhaps spoken to them? Or had he closed his eyes and waited in silence? What had been on his mind when Tom took his last breath?

These questions would remain unanswered. No matter how well she understood

Tom, it was impossible to walk with him through the bitter end. Death was not shared easily between the living and the dead.

Summer pulled the pillow closer to her and tried to push away this vision of Tom in pain. She arched her reddened eyes across the room to gaze at a photograph of Tom on the chest of drawers, and one final question went unanswered.

Would she remember Tom in his splendor, or would she be haunted by these ghostly visions of his last minutes?

———

Amelia was pacing. Standing still, she had discovered, invited sympathy. The bidding was unintended, unwanted in fact, but nonetheless, answered promptly by swarms of well-intentioned ladies. Her friends wanted to ply Amelia with comforting hugs and words of condolence; she ached for aloneness to mourn in solitude. Since privacy was impossible, she had settled for the numbing solace of a ritual, walking back and forth between the entrance to the mercantile and the living room of her home. Her thoughts were not so easily benumbed.

Amelia felt as if she were riding a monstrous roller coaster, perched on the precipice of the initial descent. She wanted this awful ride to stop, but the head car had plunged over the top, dragging her along the treacherous ride. With the point of no return already passed, Amelia had accepted the consequences and was trying to ride out the experience. Motherhood had been her greatest treasure and proudest accomplishment in life, and she meant to meet its every challenge. She had borne the pain of her son's birth. Now she would feel the hurt that no mother should have to endure, and she would find a way to cope with it.

Her mind made up, Amelia veered off the worn course, the one in her mind as well as the path trod by her feet. She plodded through the living room into the kitchen, where she managed to fill a plastic glass with ice and pour tea in it after twice scotching the efforts of various women who wanted to ensure her every need was attended.

Turning her back on the chattering women, she acknowledged a reassuring smile from Caroline. It was the most appropriate gesture for the moment, and the smile warmed Amelia's heart. She considered and rejected an inquiry about Summer. Amelia was concerned about the girl's emotional state, but now, she simply lacked the strength to deal with someone else's feelings.

She moved past Caroline into the living room, pausing slightly as her gaze drifted through the open door into Tom's bedroom. Dan was seated on the edge of the boy's bed, no doubt lost in a swell of thoughts and emotions similar to the heavy heart Amelia carried. She wanted to enter the room, touch him tenderly and assure him everything would be okay. Only she would be lying, and Dan would know it. Oh, the world would right itself once more she guessed, because time had a way of healing the deepest wounds, even those caused by death. But the scars were bound to be lasting, and Amelia and Dan would overcome them together. With this understanding tucked comfortably into a special place in her thoughts, Amelia forced herself to move away from the doorway. She and Dan needed one another, and she wanted to reach out to him. But the need would be greater in a few days, when everyone had collected their dishes, bade them farewell and left the bereaved parents alone with memories of their dead son.

Amelia resumed her pacing, sipping the cold tea and recollecting those memories of Tom. He had been born a month shy of her thirtieth birthday and two months shy of his proud parents' tenth wedding anniversary. Her pregnancy had come unexpectedly after years of trying to have a baby. Having accepted the likelihood they would never conceive a child, Dan and Amelia had settled into a satisfied existence, their relationship grounded in deep affection for each other. Then suddenly, Amelia began to experience bouts of nausea. For a solid week, she believed the sickness was the beginnings of the flu. On the eighth day, Amelia woke from a restful sleep with the realization that she was late for her time of the month. Under ordinary circumstances, being one week late would not have garnered a second thought from Amelia. Her period was more often late than regular, and she sometimes went months on end without a normal cycle. But the nausea made her suspicious, and the idea of being pregnant promptly upset the orderly routine of the Carter household.

The first disturbance came soon after the thought of pregnancy was planted in her mind. Lost in the turmoil of thinking, Amelia burned a pan of bacon; then, in her haste to save the meat, spilled a plate of scrambled eggs. When the toast had burned, too, she gave up on breakfast and voiced the inconceivable to her husband as he entered the kitchen to check on the ruckus.

"Dan," she had told him. "I'm beginnen to think I just might be pregnant."

Her husband was dumbstruck by the suggestion, gaping at Amelia until she demanded his opinion on the subject.

"How could you be?" Dan said finally, obviously in a daze.

"Don't go dumb on me now," she scolded softly, with a seductive smile. "You know how as well as I do, and there's been plenty of times lately when it could have happened."

Unfazed by her jovial attitude, Dan replied, "But the doctor said ...."

"The doctor said it was highly unlikely I'd ever have a baby," Amelia interrupted. "He never said it was impossible."

Dan raked his fingers through his hair, obviously dismayed and groping for an appropriate response. "Gosh, Amelia," he muttered finally. "I had pretty much resigned myself to be'en childless."

"How do you think I feel?" Amelia shot back. "I'm goen toward thirty; I'm set in my ways. I'm not sure how I feel about changen diapers and boilen bottles in the middle of the night."

"I've already passed thirty by a few years," Dan remarked. "And he'll probably cry a lot. I'm not sure I could get used to that."

"It's preposterous!" Amelia concluded with a wave of dismissal that failed to conceal the uncertainty in her voice. "The whole idea of us haven a baby when we least expect it and are least ready for it."

"You're probably not pregnant at all," Dan decided. "Let's wait awhile and see what happens."

Amelia almost agreed with the idea, then suggested, "I probably should see a doctor just to make sure one way or another."

"Couldn't you wait a week or so?" Dan asked.

"If I'm pregnant, Dan, waiten's not goen to change anything," she replied.

"No," Dan agreed, "but it will give us time to get used to the idea."

Either unable or unwilling to argue with her husband's logic, Amelia had waited a week before making an appointment to see the doctor. The delay had served the couple well. By the time the doctor confirmed Amelia's suspicions, their initial misgivings had been replaced by a yearning as deep as their love for each other.

Tom had been a blessing for them. Even in this moment of deepest sorrow, Amelia clung to that thought and smiled involuntarily over the memories. She regretted nothing about the way they had raised the boy. Dan and she had nurtured Tom, given him values and then allowed him to become his own person. Perhaps they had spoiled him somewhat, but he had learned the importance of earning his way in the world. Dan and she had raised a fine son, and their boy would have become a good man in time.

Amelia's eyes misted over, and she swallowed the sadness that squeezed her throat as she grappled with the idea of what would never be. Pushing aside these thoughts, she sought refuge in the past, in the memories that would have to suffice for the future.

Long before the Army had sent Tom to Vietnam, Amelia had been aware of her vivid recall of his childhood. Sometimes, she confused the young man with the little boy who had come crying to his mother after stubbing a toe or the baby who had trusted her implicitly to meet her every need. On more than one occasion, her motherly instinct to protect her son had flared at the precise moment Tom needed to stretch his wings. Usually, this confluence of self-interests merged as easily as placid streams. But in the summer between Tom's sophomore and junior high school years, the wills of mother and son rose like flooding rivers, rushing toward a collision, creating a snarling torrent that no dam could contain.

In the summer of 1964, Tom had declared he would spend his days working in Matt Baker's tobacco fields. His announcement should not have come as particularly disturbing news to Amelia since Tom had worked in those fields every summer since age nine. Always before, however, the work had been limited to a few days each week, allowing Tom to spend time in the store with his parents. But that summer, Amelia felt as if Tom had divorced his parents. He spent six days a week on the Baker farm, eating breakfast, dinner and supper with the family and sometimes spending his nights there.

Feeling abandoned and somewhat jealous, Amelia decided to set Tom straight on her expectations. She picked a Saturday evening supper for the confrontation, the first time in a week that Tom had shared a meal with his parents. Tom had seemed petulantly silent to Amelia, speaking in monosyllables and then only when one of his parents asked him a question. Between grunts, the boy had wolfed down a grilled steak and baked potato, then blithely informed his parents that he and Joe intended to catch the late show at the Rocking Chair theater in Tifton.

Given what she considered the perfect opening for her argument, Amelia seized the opportunity, launching into a tirade against Tom, accusing him of self-indulgence and an uncaring regard for his parents. The charges were groundless. Tom knew it, and Dan did, too. Even Amelia realized she was making a mountain out of a molehill. Still, she persisted, making one blunder after another until finally pronouncing herself "hurt to the core" by Tom's abrasive attitude. On a whim, Amelia announced she was washing her hands of the whole matter and stormed from the table.

She fully expected Tom to make amends as she left the room. It didn't happen.

Tom would make no apologies for his summer of hard work. Instead, he angered his mother with an airy dismissal of her complaints to his father. And then, Dan had worsened matters with a condescending response that indicated he was in full agreement with Tom.

"Gee whiz, Daddy," Tom had complained. "Since when is worken six days a week considered self-indulgent. I thought she'd be proud of me."

"She is," Dan assured him. "Your mother's just feelen neglected. Don't be too hard on her. It'll blow over by tomorrow."

Instead, Amelia had blown hot air for the remainder of the summer. She nagged her son constantly, found fault with his every move and made impossible demands on his free time. At first, Tom tried to tolerate her whims. But his mother's over-bearing persistence soon turned his tolerance to resentment and finally to outright defiance. The situation had disintegrated into a hellish nightmare for everyone concerned, capped by an explosive argument over something as inconsequential as what clothes to wear for the first day of school.

At bedtime that night, Dan had intervened, doing what he should have done weeks earlier. "Tom's not the little boy in your baby books anymore, Amelia," he said plainly. "We've raised him right so far. Let's don't botch all that good work at this late date."

Amelia refused to respond, turning her back on Dan.

The next morning after Tom had gone to school, she had secluded herself in the bedroom, opened her cedar chest and dug out Tom's baby book and clothes. The book was filled with pictures, mementos and notes about her son's earliest years, when she and Dan had been the center of his universe. Looking at the pictures, reading the notes and touching his clothes, Amelia was hard-pressed to reconcile the young man who had bounded off to school earlier in the morning with the baby staring back at her in the pictures. Despite the similarities, they were two different people and once she realized that, Amelia decided she no longer could keep Tom under her control. His early years had passed in a blur, essentially because Tom seemed to change almost daily. But the changes were coming more slowly now, and Amelia hoped they would be easier to accept. Regardless, she and Dan had molded Tom through the formative years. Anything more, Amelia recognized, would have been manipulative.

Letting go was never easy, but Amelia believed she had done a respectable job of it. The reconciliation between mother and son had come without fanfare, one of silent understanding and appreciation for the strength of an unbreakable bond of love. Within the week, Tom once again kissed his mother goodnight, and Amelia was marveling at each new discovery about her son.

Of course, life had not become completely hunky-dory. Tom still made the occasional mistake, and Amelia harped more than once about his lack of commitment to schoolwork. But overall, the next three years had been among the most memorable for Amelia as Tom went through prom dates, high school graduation and the first day of his short-lived college career. The most special days, however, were the routine ones, and these memories were woven in Amelia's mind like a beautiful tapestry.

The hours between suppertime and bedtime had become keepsakes for Amelia. Often, their suppers were rollicking affairs, filled with entirely too much lively chatter and outrageous teasing for three people to generate. Other suppers were personal moments of quiet contemplation. The evenings were relaxed affairs, spent watching their favorite television shows, reading a book or engrossed in a personal hobby. Dan sat in his recliner, Amelia in the rocking chair and Tom on the sofa where he could use the marble-topped coffee table for homework.

Tom most often polished off his homework far too quickly for Amelia's liking. But occasionally, on nights before a test, he was diligent. Then he would shut out the sound of TV, forget the presence of his parents and, with his brow furrowed, his eyes squinted and two fingers pressed to his temples, absorb the necessary knowledge. When he decided the material was mastered, he would ask Dan or Amelia to quiz him. His father was the preferred choice because Dan supplied the answers when Tom could not. Amelia was the taskmaster, imploring her son to try harder because she believed in the importance of a good education.

"I know enough to get a B, Mama," Tom had told her countless times. "That's enough."

"But the more you learn now, Tom, the easier it will be when you go to college," Amelia advised. "College will be tougher than high school. You need to prepare for it."

Tom would simply shrug, close his books and kiss her goodnight. The boy had never wanted to attend college. A college degree was Amelia's dream for him, likely because she had completed one year of higher education herself and always wanted more.

Her son's dream had been a farmer's life. Storekeeping had bored Tom. Dan had recognized this fact early on, gradually persuading his wife to accept the inevitable, going so far as to discuss with her the extent of their ability to assist with the expensive proposition of setting Tom up for the venture when the time came. Still, her son's decision to drop out of college had been a blow for Amelia. At the very least, she had hoped he would obtain an associate degree in agriculture from the junior college in Tifton. If he accomplished that, she figured she could steer him through two more years.

On the day of his big announcement that he intended to work full time for Matt Baker, Amelia had tried to reason with her son. "Think of what you can learn about agriculture in college," she urged. "You're not ready to be a farmer, son. At best, farmer's an iffy proposition. It takes a lot more than hard work to succeed."

Tom had remained adamant about his plans, calmly explaining his thoughts. "Mama, I know as well as anybody else that I'm not ready to be a farmer," he said patiently, firmly. "I know how much I have to learn, and I know that work is about the easiest part of the job. That's why I want to work for Matt. I'll learn things from him they could never teach me in a classroom. And besides, Mama, I'm miserable sitten in a classroom day after day when I could be on the farm doen the real thing."

Grudgingly, Amelia had relented to his wishes, understanding the futility of her argument, determined to resist her urge to control the situation. Secretly, the seriousness of his commitment had pleased her. In this day and age, there was much to be said about young people committed to something real and substantial. Too many people, old and young alike, drifted through life, with little thought for the future and scant regard for stability. Tom had known where he was going—at least until the Army changed his plans and sent him off to green jungles half a world away from New River.

This last thought came without a trace of rancor toward Uncle Sam. The Indochina conflict had mystified Amelia even before Tom had gone to Vietnam and nonetheless now that he had died over there. But she believed with all her heart that the government had good reasons for sending young Americans to fight for freedom. If Tom had to die, then his death had come under the most honorable circumstances of service to his country. It was death with reason, which was more than could be said for the young people who died in drunken driving accidents or from drug overdoses.

This idea should have comforted Amelia, but not even the belief of an honorable death could buoy her sunken spirits. Her baby, her little boy, her son who had grown into a wonderful young man—was dead. He had been taken from her, his life stolen under the most heinous conditions.

Her mother's instinct—that urge to protect at all costs—seized hold of Amelia, and, for a moment, she almost prayed to God for the death of those responsible for taking Tom's life. But she forced the notion to remain nothing more than a fleeting thought. Quite possibly, the young man would die anyway and then his mother, too, would grieve and seek solace in the knowledge that he had answered his country's call to serve.

Deep down, though, Amelia realized solace did not exist at a time like this. If she searched, she likely could find a hundred reasons to take comfort, but none would perform the elusive trick. It was pain that staggered sensibilities and sucked away hope.

Amelia felt swallowed up by this desolate feeling. Her hands shook and her throat quivered with a muted sob. Despite her silent vow to experience every nuance of this overwhelming feeling of death, she really wanted the world to stop. Rather than think or function, she wanted to sit on the floor and die. Instead, she suffered through a minor breakdown, unleashing a pent-up sob that brought a flurry of ladies rushing to her rescue. She allowed them to lead her to the couch, then accepted the offer of her husband's embrace.

"What do we do, Dan?" she asked in a plaintive voice, pushing back to look at her husband. "How do we go on from here?"

Dan wanted to give her an answer. Amelia saw the desire in his eyes, but he was wasted, too. He simply took her back into his arms, cradled her tightly, giving her strength to carry on without the solace she sought.

When she was able, Amelia resumed her pacing and searching for a way to cope. She forced herself to acknowledge details about the day, surprised to discover it was well after noon. She felt as if an eternity had passed since the Air Force chaplain had notified them of Tom's death, but actually, less than twenty-four hours had elapsed.

A steady stream of visitors had begun arriving at the store at mid-morning to offer condolences, filling her kitchen with an assortment of delicious foods such as boiled ham and dumplings, fried chicken and a variety of cakes and pies. The place would be overrun with food by the evening. As storekeepers, she and Dan knew just about everyone in the community and most of those people would stop by to pay their respects.

Standing at the mercantile door, she observed the crowd mingling outside the store. The group was large, not surprising considering news travels fast and bad news even faster. Still, the number of people outside warmed a spot in her heart, especially considering the majority of these people were neighbors who needed to be at work in their fields. Amelia prized her own thoughtfulness, which made her appreciate the trait even more when others showed it.

Mostly, the gathering contained men who felt too ill at ease to extend their condolences to Amelia and Dan, preferring to keep distance between themselves and the bereaved family. They had clustered in small groups that buzzed with conversation, none of it having anything to do with Tom. Listening to their talk, Amelia heard the gamut of farm topics, from comparisons of the current summer's good weather with last year's misfortune, to discussions about the best temperature for cooking out a quality barn of tobacco.

Tom would have enjoyed the conversation, whereas Amelia found it tedious even though the subject commanded her utmost respect. She'd heard versions of this talk a thousand times before, and she knew enough about the topics to discuss them thoroughly with most anyone. A bit of agriculture know-how was a necessity for storekeepers who depended on a prosperous farm community for their livelihood.

Today, the talk soothed Amelia. Her attention drifted from one cluster to another, catching snippets of different conversations, including an occasional remark about Tom. The hum sounded almost like a lullaby to Amelia, reassuring her that the world would become bearable once more, that time would lessen the heartache. She would get through this ordeal, day-by-day or minute-by-minute.

The unmistakable whine of an approaching Volkswagen jarred Amelia from her meditation. She watched Joe wheel his car into an empty space between two pickup trucks. He listened to the engine for a moment, switched off the motor and appraised the gathering. Amelia detected his melancholy as the young man climbed from the car and trudged over to a group of men that included his father, grandfather, Paul Berrien and Lucius Foster.

Lucius was a lanky widower who farmed land nearer Cookville while trying to keep his thirty-five-year-old, thrice-divorced daughter, Louise, from making a spectacle of herself. Almost everyone agreed Lucius was fighting a losing battle on that accord, but he was still one of the most respected men in the community. He was sincere and good-humored, which said a lot about the caliber of man he was.

Lucius had seen his share of tragedy. His only son had suffered a severe head injury in a car wreck years earlier and now spent his days in a home for the mentally ill. His wife, Audrey, had succumbed to a legion of cancers that ravaged her body over a three-year period. Then shortly after Audrey had passed away, Louise had begun her shenanigans, divorcing her first husband and beginning a series of one-night stands and wild escapades that resulted in two quickly discarded marriages and rumors of an impending fourth.

Lucius had stepped in to fill the void for Louise's two daughters. He kept the girls clothed, fed and, most importantly, loved. Despite the worry and heartache Louise undoubtedly caused him, the man stood by his daughter, trying patiently to steer her back onto the right course.

Amelia admired Lucius Foster's courage and spirit. If she could survive her loss of Tom with half the dignity Lucius had shown in accepting his tragedies and dealing with the consequences, then she would emerge from this ordeal with newfound courage and a willingness to go forward in life.

Heartened by this sense of renewal, Amelia let her gaze drift from Lucius to the four men standing with him. The Bakers—Sam, Matt and Joe—as well as Paul Berrien, to a lesser extent, had wielded enormous influence on Tom's life. Sam represented the classic grandfather figure, Matt the mentor and Joe the best friend. All of them appeared stricken by a sense of loss, and Amelia realized they, too, would feel the hurt for a long time.

Somehow, this idea of grief shared among friends lightened her heavy heart. With some semblance of peace of mind, Amelia turned away and crossed the store into her home, to accept the outpouring of sympathy offered graciously with love and sorrow.

CHAPTER 6

THE SUN WAS STILL high on the horizon when Summer and the rest of the Baker family arrived at the mercantile. Rachel had spent the afternoon cooking a small feast, the bounty of which was carried into the Carter home by the four youngest Baker children. As his brothers and sisters filed past him with a pot of Irish stew, dishes of fresh butterbeans, fried chicken, sliced tomatoes, chocolate pies and two gallon jugs of tea, Joe left his father's side to open the car door for Summer.

She was pale and withdrawn, with eyes swollen and reddened by the tears that refused to stop. Even without a trace of makeup and despite her puffy face, his sister was radiantly beautiful to Joe. Her chocolate brown hair cascaded softly around her shoulders, and she was dressed in a smartly tailored wrap-around denim skirt and a simple white, short-sleeved blouse. Looking at her now, Joe saw the qualities that had attracted Tom. Now, though, Summer seemed fragile and vulnerable. Joe wanted to wrap his arms around her, to protect her from the hurt, but the dull ache in his own heart reminded him there was no easy comfort. Only time and tears would stem the pain. In the meantime, he would offer whatever support he could.

"How are you?" he asked quietly after first checking silently with his grandmother and receiving Rachel's reassuring nod.

"Miserable," Summer replied. "I dread this part of it."

"You don't have to stay," Joe suggested. "I could take you home, and you could rest awhile longer."

She rejected the idea with a quick shake of her head. "That wouldn't help matters," she responded. "I have to face everybody sooner or later, and it might as well be now. These people are my friends, and they only want what's best for me. Maybe just knowin' that will make it easier to deal with."

"You want me to walk with you?" Joe offered as Rachel moved toward the mercantile.

"I'd appreciate it," Summer said. "I'd rather not have to stop and talk to anybody until I get inside the store."

Joe nodded, then took his sister's arm and ushered Summer through the crowd, making acknowledgments for her to the polite nods and hasty words of sympathy. At the mercantile door, Summer squeezed his arm and left his side to walk by herself into the Carters' living room. Joe watched her move gracefully into the waiting crowd, with a kiss on the cheek for Dan and warm embraces for Amelia, Mrs. Easters and Caroline. With a quick smile of admiration, he rejoined his father and the others.

"How is she?" Matt asked as Joe approached.

"She'll be okay," Joe assured him. "She's strong."

Given an appropriate opening, the conversation turned to their thoughts about Tom. Everyone had a favorite story to tell, with Matt almost choking on his words as he recalled the young man's love for the land and farming. It was Lucius Foster who finally voiced the real reason for their gathering outside the mercantile on this sun-drenched afternoon.

"It's a terrible thing," Lucius opined. "Hard to imagine a young man you've known all your life dyen like that. Tom's the second boy from our county to die over there. The other one was a colored boy from Cookville. I can't recall his name."

"It was Linwood Emerson," Paul supplied. "He got killed in late sixty-six. He was just nineteen. Y'all remember him, don't you? He was a pretty good basketball player over at the colored high school."

"Well, I hope Tom and Linwood are the only two men we give up for this war," Sam remarked. "I suppose dyen in a war is an honorable way to go, but that don't make it any easier to accept. When our Joseph was killed at Pearl Harbor, I knew he was among the first of many who would die for the cause of peace. But that didn't make it any easier to give him up. You'd think mankind would be getten to a point that they can sort out differences in some other way than war."

"Mankind probably could, Sam," Paul interjected. "But the decisions about war and peace are made by professional politicians, and they're a whole different breed from the rest of us."

"There's more than a grain of truth in what you're sayen," Sam replied. "And I guess it all means that until we come up with some better way to obtain peace than fighten for it, we'll just have to justify war deaths as the honorable way to die."

It was one of those awkward moments of complete hush when everyone quiets and the next thought voiced is magnified in importance and consideration. Such a moment had occurred once before in Joe's life, when he was in the fifth grade and innocently asked Mary Grace Jackson to reveal her waist measurement. The question had not been unnatural considering the girl's stout form, and she likely would have answered it without a second thought. Except, at the very moment Joe asked, complete silence cast a pall over the lunchroom. The question rang loud and clear, reverberated like the school bell and ignited students and teachers alike in uproarious laughter. Both Joe and Mary Grace had glowed with embarrassment, and their friendship never recovered from the moment.

Now Joe found himself in virtually the same situation. "You can't justify Tom's death," he said. "I don't even want to try. It seems to me that he died for no reason at all."

It was a purely bitter, angry comment, uttered by someone trying to come to terms with the death of his best friend. His remarks were intended for the close circle of friends but broadcast loud and clear by the sudden stroke of silence. The collective gasp from the throng of mourners was sensed rather than heard. Even Joe seemed taken aback by the harsh statement. But the words scalded Amelia Carter, who had been standing at the door listening to this conversation for the last few minutes.

Amelia reeled from shock, feeling as if someone had pumped bullets from a sawed-off, double-barreled shotgun into her belly. She recovered quickly, with her mother's instinct intent on setting matters straight. She pushed open the door, allowing it to slam behind her as she stood on the two-stair stoop. The commotion commanded everyone's attention.

Amelia wrung her hands, an angry expression transforming her face as she marched toward Joe. "No, Joe, you are wrong," she scolded. "Tom was my only child. There had to be a reason for him to die: a good reason, an important reason."

She pointed her finger at him: "You should not have said that, Joe."

Seemingly on the verge of saying something else, Amelia lost her composure. Her voice cracked, and large tears spilled down her face.

Joe stood transfixed by the woman's sadness. He looked from Amelia's tear-streaked face to those gathering in the doorway behind her, including Dan, Caroline and Summer, and determined an apology was required.

"Amelia, I'm sorry you heard that," he began. "My thoughts didn't come out the way I intended."

"What did you intend?" she asked mournfully.

"I can't say for sure," he answered honestly. "But I didn't intend to cause any harm or ill feelens. I only wish Tom was here with us, right now. I wish he was alive. That's all I meant."

The truthfulness of his heart shattered Amelia's resolve. She shook with suppressed sobs, feeling almost as if her knees would collapse. Dan rushed out the door, pulling her into the security of his arms, flashing Joe a furious look.

"What's goen on, Joe?" he asked.

"He said Tom died for no reason," Amelia answered quickly. "But that's wrong, Dan. Please tell me it's wrong."

"You know it is, honey," Dan replied softly, "and I don't think Joe really meant it the way it sounded. You know that as well as I do."

His answer appeased Amelia, but other people were not as forgiving. Matt sensed open hostility directed at his son from every direction. Someone needed to diffuse this anger. Joe had taken an unpopular stance against this war, and eventually people would have to understand that position. Matt would never expect most people to agree completely with his son's position, especially in the context of what had happened to Tom. But he thought it was a position worth explaining.

"Dan, Amelia," he began, "I'm sorry about all this, and I sure don't want any hard feelens. I think Joe meant he doesn't understand why Tom had to die. And wrong or right, I see his point. I lay in bed last night thinken about this war, and I found myself lacken for answers to a lot of questions about why we're over there. Now don't get me wrong. I'm not sayen there aren't any good answers. I just don't know what they are.

"To tell you the truth, I felt ashamed of myself last night," Matt continued. "I'm a veteran of the second World War. I lost a brother at Pearl Harbor. Maybe as much as anybody I should understand what's goen on over there. But I don't. There's no excuse for that kind of ignorance and I'll be the first to admit it. I watch the news on TV night after night. I see the pictures, but it doesn't sink in. I guess I've been indifferent.

"I don't know what the outcome will be, but come what may, I don't intend to be indifferent anymore," Matt concluded. "Today, I may not know why Tom died, but I tell you this. I'm gonna make it my business to find out why. I hope the rest of you will, too, because you have sons and grandsons who could be drafted next and sent over there."

Matt had never sounded bolder than at this moment. A modest man by nature, he had risked his reputation to defend his son, and he had turned back the tide of resentment against Joe. For a moment, people considered Matt's statement. Then suddenly, from somewhere in the crowd, the gritty voice of Bobby Taylor marred the moment.

He strode out of the crowd, his hand held high, brandishing a newspaper as he put himself between Matt and Joe and the Carters. Bobby had come to pay his respects to

Dan and Amelia only after seeing splashed across the front page of *The Valdosta Daily Times* a picture of the previous day's antiwar demonstration. Taken from a side angle, the photograph captured Joe in the forefront with an intense gaze on his face.

As soon as Bobby shoved the newspaper before him, Joe felt sick to his stomach. No one would understand—much less accept—his decision to protest against the war, the very cause for which his friend and other Americans were laying down their lives. In the eyes of his neighbors and family, his actions would appear as callous disregard for the ideals of loyalty and patriotism. And as he stared at the picture of the absorbed young man in the newspaper, Joe realized he couldn't really blame people for their anger.

"Explain this, old boy," Bobby demanded before snatching the paper from Joe and thrusting it toward Matt. "How 'bout you, Matt? Maybe you can tell Dan and Amelia why your boy's taken up with the hippie-war protesters."

Bobby held the picture in front of Matt's face until he felt certain the man had a good taste of bile in his mouth. It was a sweet moment of victory, and he wanted to milk it for every bit of worth. When Matt flinched, his teeth gritting, Bobby pulled away the newspaper, spun on his heels and presented it to Dan and Amelia. With a parting glance of cold satisfaction toward Matt and Joe, he eased back into the crowd, away from the glare of curious eyes. Once enough people got a good look at that newspaper, Bobby figured he'd be the last thing on their minds. But that picture of Joe Baker fraternizing with an angry mob would linger on people's minds like stink on shit.

Bobby was the last thing on Joe's mind as his gaze darted from the steely glaze of disappointment on his father's face to the horrified reactions of the Carters. "Dan, Amelia," he said, "I'm so sorry. If I could've spared y'all any of this day, I would have. What you see there has nothen to do with the way I felt about Tom. He was like a brother to me."

"You do know how to cut to the quick, Joe," Amelia remarked, her voice edged with regret.

Joe started once more to try to justify his actions, then changed his mind, knowing there would be a better time and place to make apologies and offer regrets. Just in case he had any doubt about the wisdom of his decision, Dan settled the matter, issuing an order with uncompromising reproach.

"Joe," he said, "it would be best for everyone if you left now. We've all been upset enough for one day."

"Yes, sir," Joe agreed with a respectful nod.

Pushing past his father, Joe navigated a path through the crowd, refusing to engage in any eye contact with his neighbors and friends. These people were just as confused as Joe. They had come to mourn for a dead man and wound up as witnesses to a gossip's dream. Some allowed their eyes to follow Joe to his car. Others watched Dan usher his stricken wife into the mercantile. Almost immediately, though, this restless crowd began demanding answers, forming opinions and taking sides.

———

While the community gossip line churned at full speed, Caroline snatched up the newspaper from beside the doorstep where Dan had dropped it as he ushered Amelia inside the building. Her gaze riveted to the picture of Joe, then scanned the accompanying article for details of the demonstration. Nausea swept over her, replaced by a consuming anger toward her son. On other occasions, Joe's actions had incensed Caroline but never had a need for retribution resonated within her.

Clutching the paper in one hand, she moved close to Matt, touched his elbow and gestured for a moment of privacy. He led her around the side of the store, away from the prying eyes, to an old well that had been filled with garbage, then topped with dirt. The well now sprouted red, white and blue verbena and the fresh aroma of lemon thyme. Matt broke off a piece of the bluish green herb, sniffed its fragrance and propped his rear against the well, waiting for his wife to broach the subject of their disgrace. He seemed extraordinarily tired to Caroline, with sleepless wrinkles etched around the corners of his eyes and his mouth drawn tightly from disappointment and strain.

"What's wrong with him, Matt?" she asked. "How could a son of ours do somethen like that?"

The lingering trace of anger and disappointment Matt might have felt toward Joe transcended instantly to his wife. Her lack of faith in their son astonished him, particularly when she had only half the picture. Still, he tried to appraise the situation from her point of view, understanding the embarrassment and emotion stoking her anger. "He made a mistake, Caroline, a bad mistake," Matt said cautiously. "It's a mistake that he's gonna pay dearly for, maybe for the rest of his life. But what's done is done and can't be changed by any of us. We'll all be better off by understanden that and moven on."

Caroline peered closely at her husband, deeming his offhanded reaction as too casual. "It's not that simple, Matt. This is disgraceful behavior, far more than a matter of forgive and forget. What could he have been thinken to do somethen like that?"

"Why don't you ask him?"

"I don't want to ask him," she retorted sharply. "Frankly, I don't care why he did it. It's unacceptable behavior, to the point of indecency as far as I'm concerned. And I will not tolerate it from someone who lives under our roof. I'll expect ..."

"Stop it!" Matt shouted, pushing away from the well, his tone of voice unusually sharp with his wife. "Right now, more than anything, Joe needs our support, not our judgments. There'll be another time to get into the other stuff. For Christ's sake, Caroline! If you're haven such mean-spirited thoughts about him, imagine what everyone else will do to him. They'll crucify him."

"It might be a case of just rewards," Caroline shot back.

The malevolence of her reply shocked Caroline as much as Matt, and she started to withdraw the remark. Before she found the words, however, Matt delivered his own carefully measured barb. "That's a piss-poor attitude, honey," he declared, "but if you feel that way about the situation, then so be it." He paused, staring carefully at her. "Tell me the truth, though, Caroline," he intoned. "Are you upset with Joe for what he did? Or because of how it might reflect on you?"

A new anger roiled within Caroline, a mixture of frustration and an inkling that her husband's impressions were correct. She sensed a touch of condescension in his attitude, felt betrayed for the first time in their marriage and, therefore, slammed the door on the possibility of immediate reconciliation. "Maybe I am concerned about how this will reflect on me and my family," she answered slowly. "In fact, I may be more concerned about those things than I should. But unlike you, Matt, I don't intend to shrug it off and pretend everything is fine and dandy. As far as I'm concerned, this demonstration business is just the tip of the iceberg with Joe. He comes home at all hours of the night after doen Lord knows what, and it seems obvious that he's chosen to associate with people of low morals. I love him dearly, Matt, but he's gone too far this time."

Apprehension swept over Matt. "Exactly what are you tryen to get at, Caroline?"

"I told Joe once before what I expected from him if he was goen to live under our roof," she said. "Either he has forgotten the rules or he has chosen to ignore them and lead the kind of lifestyle that we cannot condone. We have other children, too, Matt, and they are at impressionable ages. I want him out of the house."

Matt bit his bottom lip in disgust and bafflement. For whatever reasons, grief, embarrassment or stress, his wife had gone beyond the point of reasoning, and he was tired of trying. The sense of rage that had propelled him into this argument dissipated, leaving only tired ambivalence toward his wife and son. He moved a couple of steps away, then turned on his heels to hurl one parting shot. "If you want Joe out of the house, then you kick him out," he said.

"I'll expect you to back me up," Caroline said.

Matt laughed shortly. "It will be a cold day in Hell before I'm party to that business, Caroline," he said stiffly. "But if you go through with it, remember how little we've given him in return for his lifetime of devotion, hard work and sacrifice at our every beck and whim. If he's nothen more than cheap labor with bad morals, then get rid of him by all means. You said it earlier: We have a whole passel of other children, and they work just as cheaply as Joe does."

Tears welled in her eyes, causing Matt to clip his remarks and consider apologizing. For the life of him, however, he failed to see what he was sorry for, except that Tom Carter, a boy he loved and more or less thought of as a son, was dead; and everyone seemed intent on making his death merely a footnote to all this other ridiculousness. He decided then to let Caroline and Joe work out their differences without his help. He intended to grieve for Tom.

"I have to admit," he said finally. "I'm a little bit let down by what Joe did. It was wrong and inappropriate. But before you go thrown him out of our home, why don't *you* reassess a little more closely with whom and where your loyalties lie?"

With a curt nod, he spun away from her and walked back to the front of the store.

Caroline watched him go, knowing instinctively that her own behavior was foolish, yet restrained by her indomitable pride from admitting her mistake.

And so it was, with Matt's dismissal of the whole confusing affair and Caroline's reluctance to follow her innermost convictions, that husband and wife came to, for the first time in nearly twenty-seven years of marriage, a resounding impasse of wills.

———

Joe worked beneath the radiance of a harvest moon, which clothed the half-eaten field of corn in a silvery glow, illuminating a path for the hungry combine. The green machine's giant, metallic teeth gobbled up row after row of the dried brown stalks, mined their tasseled ears for yellow meat and spit out ribbons of refuse. Tonight, the machine's appetite was insatiable only because its operator's mind desired distraction. Joe had climbed aboard the machine, not because of some compelling reason to complete the harvest, which was late this year, but to escape the persistent ache that gnawed at his soul. He wanted to erase the mistakes, blot out the sadness and forget the pain. But there was no escape, no easy way around the past.

In the beginning, an hour or so ago, he had thrown himself into the work, pursed his lips in tight concentration and focused intently on the mechanics of the giant machine. His attentiveness, though, was short-lived. He had spent too many hours in past autumns aboard the combine, absorbed in the rhythmic wonders of its workings and eventually hammered into boredom by the singsong sameness of it.

Somewhere in the middle of his third fall harvest, Joe had mastered the intricacies of the machine—but not its idiosyncrasies for they could only be tolerated or repaired—and finally felt comfortable operating it. Since then, the days spent at the combine's helm had become treasured time for meditation.

Joe always did his best thinking aboard tractors and harvesters, or even when walking behind a lawnmower. But the combines were his favorite. Perched on top of one of those mighty machines, harvesting corn, cotton or peanuts, Joe had mapped out his future and dreamed of glorious days and places that waited for him. He had puzzled over dilemmas as slight as homework, brooded over his manhood and waxed philosophically, as if he were Aristotle or Socrates. On the day John Kennedy had been assassinated in Dallas, Joe had done his grieving while combining a field of soybeans. On the night of the high school homecoming dance in his senior year, when Peggy Jo Nix, his date, had come down with an untimely case of flu, Joe had danced in a field of cotton. On this night, when he wanted to silence his thoughts, he discovered his mind was too long trained aboard this machine to avoid the voices that cluttered his head, demanding to be heard.

His thoughts were on eternity at the moment, lured there by the dazzle of the brightest moon of the year. It sparkled like a piece of china set upon a silk cloth of cobalt blue, as much an amazing tribute to perfection as a chilling reminder of fragility. It was both these qualities, fragility and perfection, that rendered Joe awestruck and left him pondering the hereafter. He was as certain of the hereafter as he was of the existence of God, and he doubted neither the impossibility nor the improbability of Him.

Religion could be simple or complicated, and Joe preferred it simple. Early on, he had decided that believing in God was a simple matter of faith and had chosen to profess it. Still, it was gratifying to have his faith reaffirmed on occasion, and nothing was more reassuring than the beauty, the goodness and the fragility of life itself.

When he pondered eternity and the hereafter, Joe mostly contemplated Heaven. Hell existed, he believed, sometimes fearful that he might end up there, despite his legacy of baptism in the saving waters of New River. But the picture of Hell, with its lake of fire and eternal damnation, left little to the imagination. Heaven, on the other hand, was another matter entirely. Depending on the point of view, it was an actual place with streets of shining gold or a state of mind with eternal happiness. Joe suspected Heaven was a little of both. Whether real or figurative, a place or a figment, he hoped Heaven would provide lasting peace of mind.

Surrounded by the beauty and serenity of this harvest moon night, Joe conceived a good idea of the kind of Heaven he wanted. It was some place exactly like this night, a solid anchor in a sea of darkness with one shining light to fix your mind on and an occasional breeze to stir your thoughts—complete tranquility, devoid of greed and grief, pain and suffering, love and hate. Joe supposed he should insert some human factor into this ethereal equation, but in this case, family and friends constituted an unknown component, like those elusive X's and Y's in algebra problems. They altered his perfect algorithm, so he ignored the human aspect, settling for a Heaven that would give peace of mind, if not utter contentment.

The end of the row brought his thoughts of Heaven and the hereafter back down to Earth and the present. He steered the combine onto a new course and reflected at long last on the past thirty-six hours.

For the first time since he had decided to attend the war demonstration, through the horrifying revelation of Tom's death, to the turmoil at the mercantile a few hours ago, everything seemed like old news. All of it, the whole sickening mess, seemed to have happened a lifetime ago, which, in a way, it had, Joe thought, stung by the truthfulness of the metaphor. The lives of virtually everyone who mattered to him had changed profoundly and irrevocably. Whatever came next, for any of them—himself included—would be couched in the heartbreaking context of these last thirty-six hours of death, delusion and disappointment.

The weight of guilt rode heavy on Joe's shoulders and his conscience. He regretted many things that had happened over the last two days. Mistake after mistake had compounded like interest on a bad loan, starting with his decision to demonstrate and his gullibility to the twisted ethics of Elliot Frankel. At another time, these errors would have been forgiven readily, chalked up to his convictions and tolerated if not understood. But on this occasion, the mistakes hovered around him, like some ghoulish apparition sent to remind the world that a covenant or bond as important as the unpardonable sin itself had been broken. The healing would be a long time in coming, if it came at all.

It was the healing that worried Joe, not so much for himself but for the people he had hurt with his sincere, yet misguided, actions. He had shamed and disgraced his family at a time when they needed strength and encouragement, and he had inflicted a deep cut on Dan and Amelia's thin grip of courage. With everyone locked in a fierce battle to overcome the sorrow of Tom's death, Joe felt as if he had dealt them a demoralizing blow.

No doubt, his family would suffer from that picture in the newspaper. Close communities such as New River and Cookville prided themselves on the ability to rally around their people in times of need. Likewise, these good people considered it an equally sacrosanct duty to condemn those who flaunted or disparaged their shared values and beliefs.

Although Joe was the culprit, all of the Bakers faced indictment by association, one of the more unfortunate byproducts of tight-knit communities. While very few of their neighbors would dare to voice their accusations and opinions directly to the Bakers, the gossip line would weave a masterful fabrication of the situation, relying on innuendo, rumor, sarcasm and one or two expedient but rarely outlandish lies. It was an ugly—though tried and true many times over—method of ostracism and punishment. And the Bakers would bear the consequences until another unfortunate soul made a similar mistake, usurping the unwanted and unwarranted attention.

Joe found needed reassurance that his family would survive the coming on-slaught in the simple knowledge that they had done so before and a strong belief in their ability to rise above the contempt. The thought brought a brief smile to his face as Joe remembered the previous July when Summer had created a minor furor in the community while carrying out her first official duty as the newly crowned Miss Golden Leaf.

In typical Summer fashion, she eschewed the traditional dress of white shorts and blouse to concoct her own rousing tribute to the golden crop of her reign, and presided over the season's first tobacco sale in a bikini made from cooked leaves. Her attire provided a sizzling beginning to a new Miss Golden Leaf tradition.

Summer had gone a long way to assuring her success by first getting approval from her parents, the beauty pageant director and the president of Planter's Ware-house before proceeding with the unusual costume. Next, she had enlisted the assis-tance of her grandmother and Amelia to design and fashion the bikini. Rachel had rolled her eyes in disbelief at first, then promptly found the broadest, most golden leaves available to use in the garment. Summer had relied on Amelia to make sure the bikini was in good taste, and the result had been a two-piece ensemble that seemed more like a mini-skirt than a bikini bottom, with a top that provided strate-gic cover and little more.

At the first sale of the season, people had been hard-pressed to decide what was more important: getting a good glimpse of Summer or watching the auctioneer sell off the prized sheets of tobacco. A few days later, however, after her picture had been splashed across the front pages of *The Tifton Gazette* and *The Cookville Herald*, people began to find fault with the costume. Women especially condemned the situation, calling the bikini improper and suggestive while criticizing Matt and Caroline for condoning such behavior. The Bakers had merely shrugged off the wagging tongues and laughed at the criticism, agreeing wholeheartedly with Tom's assessment of the matter.

"So whataya think?" Joe had asked Tom as Summer, resplendent in her tobacco-leaf bikini, stood a few feet away amid clusters of ogling admirers.

"Lord, she is beautiful," Tom replied, his gaze riveted on Summer, his face full of love and admiration.

Turning to Joe, Tom had continued, "You gotta admit it: When she makes up her mind to do somethen, she does it with style. Right or wrong, she charges onward, unafraid, flexible, determined. That's what I love best about her. I wish I had that kind of forthrightness and security, her guile and especially the guts to throw cau-tion to the wind and follow through on her convictions."

"Me, too," Joe had answered.

And still do, he now thought. "Unfortunately, I don't seem to have any idea of what my convictions are."

Hearing the words aloud startled Joe and made him realize the statement wasn't entirely true. He definitely opposed the war in Vietnam, though he conceded his opposition was Johnny-come-lately, definitely heightened by his association with Elliot Frankel.

Joe had paid close attention as the Vietnamese conflict unfolded over the years, beginning with President Kennedy's decision to send over the first wave of military advisers and volunteer American might to thwart the spread of communism. As far back as 1963, when Buddhist monks in South Vietnam began to douse their bodies with gasoline and set themselves afire, he had begun to question U.S. support for a government apparently so out of touch with its citizens that people would resort to self-immolation as a form of protest.

Despite his reservations, Joe had supported the decision to help South Vietnam remain a part of the free world. A few bombs and a small number of soldiers seemed a fair price to pay for the freedom of millions. Then almost overnight, thousands of young American men like himself were dead, with thousands more likely to meet the same fate, and Joe had begun to feel the twinges of something gone terribly wrong.

When the Army had drafted Tom, Joe had begun looking for ways to justify the war. Freedom itself seemed justification enough, except nobody seemed committed to it. The battles themselves seemed to have no purpose, with soldiers fighting for days to win a position only to abandon it, presumably back into the hands of the Viet Cong. Indeed, little about the war made sense, and no one seemed to understand the purpose of it.

With the idea stuck in his mind that the United States was floundering in its quest for a noble goal, he had met Elliot, whose all-out opposition to the war armed Joe with a new arsenal of reasons why the fighting should end. The draft was unfair to the poor, Elliot contended; the United States could not win; and Americans must protest loudly and refuse to fight to end the war. Persuaded by the degree of truth in Elliot's argument, Joe realized now, he had conveniently overlooked the other side of the situation. The draft was unfair, enormously so, but it could and would be changed; the United States could and likely would win the war; and a man always heeded his country's call to serve unless his conscience objected to killing for any reason. Even then, as history showed, it was possible to serve honorably without taking up weapons.

Ethan Connell was a perfect example of this last notion. Mr. Ethan, as everyone called him, was a lifelong resident of Cookville who had registered as a conscientious objector in World War II and wound up serving as a medic on the war-torn fields of Europe. At Normandy, he had risked his life to drag a dozen wounded American soldiers to safety, the last three after German troops had riddled his legs with machine-gun fire. The bullets had destroyed bones, muscles and blood vessels, and doctors had been forced to amputate both legs, confining the man to life in a wheelchair. But as Mr. Ethan was apt to say, he considered the misfortune a small and willing price to pay for the survival of twelve lives.

Joe regarded Mr. Ethan as a genuine American hero, a tribute to everything good about the country.

Another row-end spared Joe any further philosophical harping on the rights and wrongs of war. He guided the combine beside the waiting trailer, emptied the load of yellow kernels and switched off the engine, surveying the swath he had cut through the corn. He had made a significant dent in the field. One more day of work, perhaps half of another, and the corn would be finished for the year.

The agrarian practicality of this last thought brought a second smile to Joe's face. Tom would have made a similar appraisal.

Joe glanced upwards once more at the full moon, grudgingly allowing himself to acknowledge the smidgen of irony—and guilt, too—that he was alive and well on this night created for farmers, doing a farmer's work, while his best friend lay dead in an exotic and faraway place. But such ideas, however honest they might be, were impractical, Joe reasoned. Knowing that Tom, ever the pragmatist, would have been the first person to agree with him, he pushed those worthless thoughts from his mind.

The hour was late, close to midnight, and Joe faced a full load of classes tomorrow. He scanned the heavens once more, saw not one wisp of cloud and concluded there was no threat of rain, therefore, no need to shelter the corn trailer. He climbed off the combine, opting to walk home even though he was in the back field, hoping the distance would ease the restless edge of his thoughts.

The year's first touch of fall nipped this harvest moon night as Joe made his way toward home. Lulled by a deepening sense of loss, his thoughts settled and gave over to melancholy. Caught up in the turmoil of mistakes and accusations, he'd had little time to mourn the loss of his friend. Now he faced his grief head-on, and the impact was devastating.

Tom Carter belonged to this place. His presence was etched forever on the landscape. His memory would haunt sweetly these fields and woods, just as surely as Tom had glided across their rows and dangled fishing poles over the ponds.

Lost in his imagination, Joe almost expected to see Tom come bounding around a corner at any moment. But the image was fleeting. Too soon, Joe realized he was waiting for the impossible. On this seemingly perfect night, he would find no shooting stars to wish upon and no illusions that could alter the past. Ceding to his emotions, Joe broke down and wept in those fields of play and work and dreams.

NERVES WERE BRITTLE AND tensions taut in the Baker home. The discord between Matt and Caroline was obvious to everyone in the house. Both were furious with themselves, each other and anyone else who crossed their paths. Matt retreated to the kitchen with Sam, while Caroline barked orders to the children and Rachel rushed around trying to soothe troubled spirits.

Sam became the first casualty of the disorder when he attempted to draw Matt into a conversation about the current ruckus and was rebuffed by an air of disinterest.

"Well, you're gonna have to talk about it sooner or later," Sam declared at length, exasperated by his son's refusal to engage in plain speech.

"No, Pa! I don't have to talk about it," Matt exploded. "I've had just about enough of everyone tellen me what I do and don't have to do on this matter of Joe. I don't have to and I don't intend to do anything about it. I've said my peace, and that's all you will hear from me. Joe made the decision to take part in that protest, and he's the one who'll have to live with the stinken consequences. As for me, I don't want to hear another word about it."

The outburst reverberated through the house with shocking intensity. Moments later, the loud slam of Rachel and Sam's bedroom door hurled more vibrations through the cavernous rooms.

"I'd better go see about your grandpa," Rachel deduced, her comment aimed at no one in particular as she folded and put away clothes in the boys' room. Turning to John, she ordered him to finish the task and fled the room.

"I'll help," Carrie offered, climbing out of Luke's bed, which she was sharing with Bonnie for the second night in a row.

"I guess Joe's gone and got himself in a heap of trouble this time," Luke muttered. He was lying in John's bed with the covers pulled to his chin.

"Afraid so," replied Carrie, opening the top drawer in her youngest brother's chest to put away socks and underwear. "I'm more concerned about Summer though. I wonder how she feels about all this."

John stuffed a pair of unfolded jeans into a bottom drawer of the other chest, then kicked the empty basket aside and sat down on the edge of his bed to remove his shoes. "It's obvious consideren what she said to that draft dodger this mornen," he said. "Summer probably feels hurt because Joe took part in the demonstration, and that's understandable. But to tell you the truth, I'm not sure Joe was wrong for protesten."

"Then I would advise you to think again, young man," Caroline interrupted.

Her tone was icy and her face sheathed with anger as she stood in the doorway, glowering at John. "It was a detestable thing to do," she continued. "Joe should be ashamed of himself and so should you. Furthermore, I would suggest you keep quiet about this sorry mess. Do you understand?"

John lowered his gaze, sufficiently chastised for having improper thoughts. "Yes'em," he mumbled.

"What was that?" Caroline asked sharply.

"Yes, ma'am," John answered directly, staring straight into his mother's eyes. "I understand."

Caroline froze the room with her fury, her gaze sweeping from Carrie to Bonnie to Luke. "And the rest of you?" she demanded.

"Yes, ma'am," they answered, sounding like a choir.

Their quick response satisfied Caroline, who was somewhat embarrassed by the ferocious position she had taken with the children. Suspecting she had come across like the head of an inquisition, she considered briefly whether to explain her objections to the antiwar sentiments but rejected the impulse as too risky. Growing uncertainty clouded her thoughts on the subject. More than anything else, her feelings and actions were governed by resentment against Joe. Caroline softened her voice, bid the children goodnight and went to check on Summer.

When she had gone, Carrie climbed back into bed. John switched off the light, undressed in the dark and took his position in the bed with Luke.

"I suppose that answers my question about Joe," Luke opined.

"Yeah, Luke," John muttered. "I would say it does."

No one said anything else—not even goodnight.

———

Summer was sitting at the vanity dresser brushing her hair when Caroline came into the girls' bedroom.

"How are you, honey?" Caroline inquired in soothing tones.

"Mostly tired," Summer replied, looking at her mother through the mirror. "Maybe I'm getten used to the idea that Tom's gone. It still hurts, and I'll probably end up cryen in a few minutes. But right now, I'm just mostly tired and hopen for a good night's sleep."

"Can I get you anything?" Caroline asked. "Some hot chocolate, maybe?"

Laying down the brush, Summer turned around on the stool. "No, ma'am, not tonight," she answered, standing and crossing over to her bed. "I don't think I'll need anything to help me sleep tonight," she added, pulling back the worn white spread and top sheet and plumping her pillow.

"You could use a new bedspread," Caroline observed as Summer lay on the bed and pulled the covers to her chest.

"Not really, Mama," Summer replied. "I dug this old thing out of the closet at the beginnen of summer because it's light and cool. Soon, though, when we get cooler weather, I'll have to trade it in for a heavier one. Or put an extra blanket on the bed."

"Would you like me to sit with you until you fall asleep?"

"Yes, ma'am. That'd be nice."

Summer slipped across the bed, giving her mother room to sit on the edge. She was grateful for the comforting presence. Despite her exhaustion, she dreaded the darkness. Tomorrow night, she would insist that her sisters return to the room.

In the ensuing quietness, Summer reflected on the day. The sheer number of sympathizers and well-wishers had exhausted her. She felt as if she had performed like a robot, with polite acceptance of the condolences, courteous attention to the stories about Tom and grim endurance of the few mourners who felt an obligation to dredge up every reason why Summer should grieve. Without doubt, however, the day's low point was the revelation of Joe's participation in the war protest in Valdosta. She felt sickened by the notion that Joe had protested against the war on the very day they learned Tom had died in Vietnam.

Summer deplored the war, now more than ever, but she despised the war protesters even more. Regardless of their intentions, many of which were questionable, their actions struck ill will at the hearts of those sent to Vietnam to fight for their country and freedom. As for the draft card burners and draft dodgers, Summer regarded them as cowards without conscience, and she hoped they would lead miserable lives in Canada, Sweden or wherever else they fled.

While she had sensed Joe's growing distrust of the war, Summer had never suspected he would stoop so low as to fraternize with the instigators of the demonstrations. Deep down, she wanted to understand his motivations. Now, though, she was driven by feelings of bitter betrayal.

Without realizing, Summer allowed her drowsy eyes to close. Watching her daughter's chest rise and fall in rhythm, Caroline assumed she was asleep. Deciding to call it a night herself, she rose to leave the room, but the shifting bed caused Summer's eyes to pop open.

"How could Joe have done it, Mama?" she asked.

Caroline sat back on the bed, tracing a line across her forehead, down her face to a point beneath her chin. "I don't know," she said at last. "I just don't know. But it was a vile thing to do, and Joe will be more the sorry for it."

Summer pondered the idea, then said, "I guess that's it in a nutshell. Everything about war is vile. Even when somethen good is done in a war—like saven somebody's life or given cookies to orphans whose parents were killed by guns or bombs—you can't escape the vileness of it. There's ugliness beneath every good deed in a war." She sighed, tears streaming down her face. "Am I maken any kind of sense, Mama?"

"Perfect sense," Caroline smiled sadly, taking her daughter's hand. "Unfortunately, you're maken perfect sense."

Summer brushed away the tears and stiffened her resolve. "Why don't you go to bed, Mama?" she suggested. "I know you're tired."

Sensing the girl's uncertainty, Caroline decided Summer needed companionship. "If you want, I'll sleep in your sisters' bed tonight," she offered. "I think the company would make us both feel a little bit better and rest easier. Do you agree?"

"I'd appreciate it, Mama."

"Very well then," Caroline replied. "I'll get my nightgown and be back in a jiffy."

———

When Caroline went next door, she found the light off and Matt apparently asleep. She fetched her nightgown from a drawer, cold cream and a hairbrush from the dresser and slipped quietly from the room.

Listening to his wife move about the room, Matt almost called to her. Her brisk movements changed his mind, however, and Matt remained on his stomach, unwilling to acknowledge his wife.

In almost twenty-seven years of marriage, they had never gone to sleep with ill feelings between them, and both were aware of breaking precedent. They were also stubborn, hardheaded and unwilling to compromise. And in the next few minutes as sleep descended over the family, their sentiments settled throughout the house like a conspiracy. Practically every member of the household vowed to keep a safe distance between themselves and the discord. Like guerrilla warriors, they stole away into the night, retreating to cloistered safe havens where they could monitor the unpleasantness from afar without fear or threat of reprisal.

Unaware of their withdrawal, Joe returned home, expecting the family to pull together in this time of need, hoping to draw courage from their goodwill. To the contrary, he was ostracized, made an outcast among his family as everyone sifted through the various implications of all that had happened. Some treated Joe with polite indifference; most deliberately ignored him.

In the following days, the household took on a rancorous modality. For Summer's sake, everyone kept up appearances, swearing only under their breath. Out of necessity, most forged alliances to preserve some semblance of decorum in the midst of the turmoil. Joe, however, remained the outsider, blackballed as the instigator of everything wrong in these waning days of September. He felt an urge to put up defenses, yet no outright reason existed to support his instincts. Indeed, he was unable to rid himself of the notion that perhaps he was not entitled to any defense.

The freeze-out became a waiting game, and Joe tried to play it with patience. As the days clicked by, he hoped and prayed for the slightest crack in the icy cupola forming around him. Instead, the walls thickened, turning from a glassy sheen to a frosty white. Finally, when it seemed as if a fast-moving glacier had cornered him, Joe took action to initiate a thawing.

It was a Wednesday afternoon, more than a week after they had learned of Tom's death. Arriving home from his classes, Joe headed straight for a glass of cold milk and found his mother alone in the kitchen. Caroline sat on the deacon's bench with a bowl of colored butterbeans in her lap and a bushel basket full of the green hulls at her feet.

The new air conditioner hummed in the window. On a whim or in the midst of a tirade—no one knew for sure, not even himself—Matt had ordered the air conditioner from Sears, Roebuck in the middle of summer. The family had spent a scorching morning in the tobacco field, and they were eating one of Rachel's barn-filling-day dinners. The food was piping hot, and the steam rising into their sunburned faces stewed Matt to the boiling point. Even on high speed, the window fans were useless against the heat, and not even iced tea could douse the flames of Matt's discontent. After gagging on a bite of potatoes, Matt gave up on the meal, suggested the family would be better served with cold sandwiches and stormed from the kitchen.

Minutes later, he returned with the terse announcement that he had just telephoned the Sears catalog store in Tifton and ordered an air conditioner, which was delivered the following week. The air conditioner was a luxury, especially when they hardly had money to buy the essentials. But Matt had made the purchase on the promise of the bumper crop now being harvested from the fields. No one questioned his decision. In fact, they urged him to buy another air conditioner for the living room. Matt had promised he would as soon as they could scrounge up a few extra dollars.

Joe stood unnoticed in the doorway, his arrival drowned out by the air conditioner's low rumble. He regarded his mother for a moment, wondering whether they could find common ground on this matter of disagreement. Unlike his father, who had been willing to discuss their different ideas about the war, Caroline considered Joe's actions as a personal attack on the values she had tried to instill in her children.

Caroline despised the war as much as, or more, than anyone else, but she also carried strong opinions of what was proper, right and decent. Her personal honor code revolved around the Golden Rule and a sense of proportion. In his mother's mind, Joe understood, he not only had violated her sense of proprieties. He had assaulted it with reckless disregard and wretched excess, way out of the bounds of acceptable behavior. In her eyes, his actions constituted an abomination of the worst kind.

With anyone else, Joe would have given up on the possibility of earning a pardon. But his mother also possessed a gentle spirit and forgiving heart. More than anyone he knew, with the remarkable exception of his grandfather, Caroline believed in the virtues of reconciliation and letting bygones be bygones. Her anger faded quickly, and she willingly granted amnesty to anyone who showed either repentance or good reason for wayward ways. At many of life's crossroads, she had intoned her children never to pass judgment on another's conscience, to withhold their opinions until they had walked in the other person's shoes. These were the qualities Joe hoped to appeal to as he made the first move toward reconciliation with Caroline. And if all else failed, Joe figured he could count on the simplicity and unflinching promise of a mother's love.

"Afternoon," he said cheerily, stepping into the kitchen and depositing his books on the table.

Caroline glanced up quickly, then returned her attention to the beans while Joe retrieved a glass from the cabinet over the sink. "Hello," she said.

Joe took the milk jar from the refrigerator and poured his glass full. "We haven beans for supper?" he asked.

"Probably so," she answered without looking at him.

Joe sipped his milk and sat in the chair usually occupied by Sam at mealtimes. "You need another sheller?" he offered.

"No thanks," Caroline replied. "I'll be finished in a few minutes."

Joe abandoned the pleasantries and opted for a more direct approach. "It's kind of cold in here, Mama," he said. "It's been cold for a while now."

This time Caroline looked him squarely in the eye. "I feel fine myself," she said without a hint of expression. "If you want though, go ahead and turn off the air conditioner."

Joe stared blankly back at his mother, trying to comprehend her cold-hearted response. In all his life, Joe had never known Caroline to be vindictive, no matter how offended she was by someone else. Her sense of proportion in all things forbid such a show of malice. He tried to justify her actions in light of the circumstances only to find himself sympathizing even more with Dan and Amelia. Suddenly, he understood a little bit better the feelings of betrayal they must have felt with the revelation of his participation in the war protest. The feelings were bitter, yet Joe found a small measure of comfort in the simple knowledge that his actions were never intended to hurt the Carters. He could not say the same for his mama.

"No need for that," he responded, restraining his urge to shout some sense into the woman. He finished the milk in one long gulp, then banged the empty glass on the table, startling Caroline. "Work's waiten outside," he declared roughly. "I better get to it."

Caroline watched him go, his teeth grinding as he pushed through the door. She was ashamed of the callous way she had handled the situation, especially when Joe had tried so hard to accommodate her feelings. Stubborn pride had gotten the best of her. Again. Nothing else could explain her unwillingness to reach out a hand and listen to Joe's side of the story.

For some reason, she seemed hell-bent on revenge when understanding and forgiveness were needed. She had done wrong, and her son knew it. The good Lord knew it, too; indeed, He was accustomed to it by now. Her headstrong pride remained her greatest fault, the one sin she seemed unable to shake despite any amount of prayer.

For a moment, Caroline considered the possibility of rectifying the wrong and going a long way toward atoning for her pride simply by going after Joe, apologizing and making peace with her son. Peace was the answer, but her heart was too heavy to make the effort. So instead, Caroline closed her eyes, uttered a short prayer of repentance and decided to prepare a batch of candied sweet potatoes for supper.

———

Sam found Joe stacking hay in the loft. He was working at his usual furious, organized pace. First, he transferred five bales from the trailer to the loft porch. Next, he boosted himself onto the wooden ledge, lugged each bale inside the barn and stacked them in neat piles. Finally, he emerged from the barn, hopped back onto the trailer and started over the whole process.

As he watched his grandson work, Sam envied Joe. Or more accurately, he felt a pang of remorse for his own lost youth. As late as a few years ago, Sam would have jumped to volunteer his assistance with the chore, but those days were gone for good. He was a few weeks away from his seventy-third birthday, and his muscles and stamina no longer cooperated with his will. Still, he had little reason to complain.

Except for pitching in during the tobacco season, Sam did as he pleased. He had appropriated an acre of land in the field beside the blackberry bramble and the pecan orchard. Dubbed "Grandpa's experiment," the patch contained an assortment of fruit trees, berry vines and bushes, vegetables and herbs, things he had always wanted to grow but never had time to. He was pleased with the effort. Blueberries, strawberries and a grape arbor were flourishing, while apple, orange and peach trees were producing their first fruits. He had raised lettuce in the spring while a fall crop of Indian corn was ready for harvest. At Amelia Carter's suggestion, he had packaged his abundant herb crop in small bottles for sale at the mercantile. Since then, Sam had built a brisk trade with the Carters, selling his berries and vegetables as well. The venture had proven profitable for all concerned and while Sam would not get rich from the business, the effort was providing pocket change for Rachel and him.

For an old man, Sam figured life was treating him far better than he could have expected—and a sight better than the young men in his family.

Tears welled in his eyes as he watched Joe work. All the sadness and trouble of the last few days had thrown Sam's emotional balance out of kilter. At any time, he was apt to stagger from lightheadedness, or his voice would choke and tears would well up in his eyes. He felt like a basket case, although Sam preferred to liken the state to inner-ear trouble. Fortunately, this affliction tended to occur in private moments. Sam wanted to be a source of strength for people.

Right now, however, he felt anything but strong. He was grieving over the death and destruction. Tom's death was a heartfelt blow for everyone. Sam felt the loss acutely, almost with the same sense of despair that overwhelmed him when Joseph had been killed at Pearl Harbor. Sam had loved Tom dearly because they shared the same kind of heart and reverence for the land. Tom would have loved "Grandpa's experiment," sneaking away from more tedious chores whenever possible to lend a hand and learn a thing or two about working the land. The realization that the young man would never have such an opportunity brought a gut-wrenching hurt to Sam.

He sniffled and blew his nose, trying to shake loose the case of doldrums. The trouble was that the sadness extended beyond Tom's death, touching Sam's flesh and blood like cactus needles. Sam hurt for Dan and Amelia because he knew the pain of losing a child. He hurt for Summer's loss of love, which had been in the palm of her hand only to be snatched unmercifully away. Tom's death had rekindled sad memories for Rachel, while their grandchildren were experiencing the first of many losses to come from their own ranks. Matt and Caroline had been torn apart by the crisis and were face-to-face with fears of losing one of their children. Even closer to home, John and Luke faced the possibility of the same fate that had befallen Tom, while Joe grappled with the damage of putting his convictions on public display.

Sam wiped his eyes against the sleeve of his work shirt, regaining the upper hand in this battle with emotions. He understood the futility of dwelling on the suffering of the world. In the end, everyone would have to accept and deal with this turn of life on their own terms. Until then, Sam would sympathize with his family and friends, and he would offer guidance as best he could. Old codgers like himself had a well of wisdom to bestow, and Sam was thankful that his family remembered to draw from it in times of need.

He strolled through the pecan orchard, coming to the ragged gate beside the barn. "That's slow-goen work all by yourself, ain't it?" he asked Joe while fumbling with the rusted latch.

"Pretty slow," Joe agreed without pause as he hoisted another bale onto the loft porch. He had removed a couple of layers from the hay trailer and now was forced to heave the bales over his head to place them on the porch. "We've got another load in the field, and Daddy's afraid it's gonna rain on us before we get it baled," he explained. "I was hopen to have this load stored so that we can get started balen another load when John and Luke get home from school. The bus should be here in a half-hour or so."

"In the meantime, let me lend a hand," said Sam, who still was fiddling with the latch. "One of these days, we need to replace this gate," he decided aloud. "The wood is rotten, and the latch is useless. Come winter, the cows probably will be able to open it up themselves and march right off the place."

Joe laughed. "I don't relish the idea of chasen after cows in the cold," he said. "When I get some free time, I'll find some scrap wood and do a fixer-upper on it."

Sam climbed the stairs and began toting the hay into the loft, while Joe continued to deposit bales onto the porch. "I understand they'll be bringen Tom's body home soon," he said at length.

"Either at the end of this week or early next week," Joe replied, hoisting another bale over his head and placing it softly on the wood landing.

"I suppose they'll have the funeral as soon as possible," Sam said.

"Probably," Joe agreed, pushing back on the hay to look at Sam. "I dread the funeral. It'll just freshen up all the sadness, and we'll really have to say goodbye to him. I don't know if I can do that. I'm not even sure I should go to the funeral. Dan and Amelia might not want me there after the other day."

"They'll want you there," Sam said quickly. "That business the other day was just a matter of circumstance. Amelia and Dan know you loved Tom the same as the rest of us. That's what counts, Joe. It's what is most important, and it's why you'll be at the funeral with everyone else."

Joe nodded, and they continued working in silence for a few minutes until Sam decided to push the subject. "I always thought the politicians had a knack for the Cold War," he said, wiping sweat from his forehead. "But in the last few days, they could have learned a lesson or two from our family."

Joe regarded his grandfather, grateful for his sage mind and understanding heart. The older Sam got, the smarter and more perceptive he became. At some moments, such as the one a few minutes earlier when Sam had appeared lost in the pecan orchard, he seemed to dodder on the edge of forgetfulness. At least, Matt and Caroline believed so when they happened to observe Sam in one of those transitory states. Joe held a different view. In those moments when Sam seemed lost, Joe saw a keen mind at work, mulling over problems and coming up with solutions, contemplating or philosophizing on life, or perhaps reminiscing about the past and envisioning the future. Joe felt an urge to pay tribute to his grandfather's sagacious wit, but he held his tongue. Too much sentimentality embarrassed his grandfather.

"It's been chilly," he said finally to the relief of Sam, who was beginning to fear he had misjudged the situation by asking Joe to discuss the trouble before he was ready.

Joe had an annoying habit of withdrawing when people treaded too close to his deepest recesses. It was Rachel's fault as far as Sam was concerned, certainly her most significant hereditary contribution to the character of their grandson.

"Maybe I deserve it," Joe continued a moment later. "I should have never gotten mixed up in that demonstration."

"It wasn't all that bad," Sam said, dismissing Joe's admission with a shrug. "Besides, who's to say the protest was wrong? Unfortunately for you, the timen blew everything out of proportion. Just remember, Joe, and I've said it time and time again: This, too, shall pass."

"I don't know, Grandpa," Joe replied doubtfully. "People are angry."

"Not so much angry as hurt," Sam interrupted. "Everyone's confused right now, Joe. We're all hurten, for Tom, for ourselves, for each other. Perhaps you're bearen the brunt of all our frustrations. But you set yourself up for it, right or wrong, and you'll just have to sweat it out. Just don't ever feel sorry for yourself."

"Good advice," Joe said with a sigh of resignation. "I just wish I could do it all over. I never would have joined that protest. It was the wrong thing to do."

"Again, I ask: Who's to say it was wrong?"

"Me, Grandpa," Joe said decisively. "I'm not sayen demonstrations are wrong. In fact, they're probably needed to end this war and get us out of there. It's a slaughterhouse as far as I can tell, and I oppose it now more than ever. But protesten in the streets is not my style."

"If demonstrations are not your style and you oppose the war, then how do you propose we end it?" Sam asked curiously.

"Honestly?" Joe replied. "I don't know."

"Nor do I," Sam admitted tiredly. "But I agree that it's high time for us to find some way out of there, to stop all the killen and dyen. And I pray the day never comes when John or Luke is called to go over there."

"Amen to that," Joe said. "More than anything, Grandpa," he added a long moment later, "I wish the powers that be could have found a way out of there before we lost Tom."

"Me, too, son," Sam agreed sadly. "Me, too."

Later, Joe would come to believe that even if no one had rushed a torch to the polar cap around him, his grandfather had at least begun to blow hot air in his direction. At supper that night, Rachel made a point to include Joe in the conversation. Matt did likewise, admitting to his father that he was more upset with the world itself than with Joe. The efforts were stilted but forced a grudging recognition within everyone else that they also would have to make peace with Joe. Still, reconciliation with all remained a few days in the future. Except for John.

Joe went to bed early, tired from the day's work and nursing a throbbing headache. He was lying in bed, half asleep and grateful for the cool breeze coming through the window when John slipped into the room and eased into a sitting position on the twin bed.

"Dreamen about some pretty girl, I suppose," he said, coaxing Joe from the sand man's grip.

John watched his brother's eyes open in surprise. He had wanted to approach Joe earlier in the afternoon when they were baling hay. But the task had kept them busy, and he had felt uncomfortable raising the subject around Luke.

"Hardly," Joe muttered, blinking away the fog. "I try not to dream anymore."

John registered a disapproving expression. "Well, to steal a line from my big brother, you should."

Joe grimaced in the darkness. "Usen my own weapons against me," he complained. "That's not fair, especially when I'm half asleep."

"It occurs to me to suggest that all is fair in love and war," John replied cautiously. "But that seems so grossly close to the current situation that it's probably inappropriate."

"Highly inappropriate," Joe frowned.

John rose to make his point. "I'm here to apologize for ignoren you these past few days," he said. "It wasn't intentional, Joe. I don't blame you for anything, and I have no intentions to criticize anything you've done. Fact is, I wasn't sure what to say to you, so I said nothen, which probably was the worst thing I could have done. I know you've had some lousy days. I wish I would have been there for you."

Joe sat up against the headboard. "You've no need to apologize to me, John. We're all haven lousy days, and I did my share to make matters worse."

"That's a matter of opinion," John suggested.

Joe eyed his brother curiously, waiting for him to divulge further details. "So, how's the opinion runnen?" he asked finally, when none was forthcoming.

"Mostly indifferent about the protest," John replied. "At least Luke, Carrie and Bonnie feel that way. They're upset for Summer. As for Summer, I'm not sure. I suspect she's hurten too much over Tom to separate her feelings about him and the protest. She's taken everything personally right now; you can hardly blame her for that. She lost a lifetime on those battlefields. The rest of us only lost a close friend, and there's a world of difference." He paused, then assured his brother, "Summer will come around in time. I mean, Joe, it's not as if you committed a sin or somethen."

"No," Joe agreed, "but it sure feels like it."

John sat on the bed once more. "Between you and me, I think maybe you made the right decision to protest," he said. "I hate this war, Joe, and not just because the thought of goen over there scares the daylights out of me. If I'm drafted and pass the physical, I'll go. But the way I see it, we have a first-class screw-up on our hands and it's nothen but war for the sake of war. Every day, I hope that my snake-bitten leg will make me undesirable to the military."

"I told Grandpa earlier today that if I had the opportunity to do it over again, I would choose not to participate in the demonstration," Joe said.

"Why?" John asked.

"I can't say exactly," Joe answered. "Maybe it's nothen more than a coward's regret, but I had my doubts through the whole thing. I oppose the war, but I'll have to find some other way to show it."

John sighed. "There are no easy answers," he said, rising once more, this time to walk over to Joe's desk and lean against it. "As much as I oppose the war, I have this naggen suspicion that anything less than my wholehearted support is cowardly. What if deep down I oppose the war because I'm afraid of the fight and don't want to make the sacrifice? Does that make me a coward?"

"I can't answer that," Joe said, choosing his words carefully. "That's a suspicion you'll have to lay to rest with your conscience. Grandpa probably would tell you to just choose your guns and stick to them."

Joe paused, then continued, "For what it's worth, John, I've never thought of you as a coward in any way, shape or form. You, perhaps more than anyone I know, are guided by extremely sound instincts for what is right and wrong, and you follow those instincts very well. I trust your judgment; I wish I knew your secret."

John pushed away from the desk, straddled the ladder-backed chair backward and sat on the cowhide seat. He was obviously pleased with Joe's compliment. "Prayer," he finally said.

"Prayer?" Joe replied.

"Prayer," John repeated. "That's the secret, Joe. I fell for it hook, line and sinker. Lord knows I'm no goodie two-shoes. I've had a beer or two in my time, I swear a little and I have some decidedly unholy thoughts about girls. But I do believe in the power of prayer."

"I'd do well to remember that for myself," Joe said.

"You would, brother," John said sincerely, smiling and rising from the chair. "You really would."

John walked to the door, saying, "I've gotta go to bed. I have a geometry test in the mornen, and I'm clueless about it. I'm hopen that if I get up early enough to study, I'll absorb a C by osmosis."

"I'd suggest a prayer," Joe said slyly, "but the good Lord probably would prefer you took matters into your own hands before callen on Him in this particular regard."

"Probably He would," John agreed balefully. "But I'll try anyway to appeal to His merciful side. Goodnight, Joe."

CHAPTER 8

FOUR DAYS LATER, ON a Sunday morning when most people were in church, the Army returned Tom to Cookville. The Carters, Summer, Lieutenant Mark Applegate and Melvin Lovett, the funeral home operator, were at the railroad station when the train hove into view, the locomotive straining from the load, whistling a shrill warning and belching black smoke before it came to a screeching halt. The depot suddenly bustled with activity as workers opened three of the massive cars, one filled with a shipment of furniture for McGill's Home Furnishings, another with a load of supplies for The Feed and Seed and the third with the dull gray coffin.

The railroad required Dan's signature on several official papers, so he followed the conductor inside the depot to take care of the details. Melvin went off in another direction to secure assistance in transferring the casket from the train car to the gleaming black hearse parked outside the depot.

Though the weather had cooled noticeably overnight and dull gray clouds were gathering in the west, the fall chill was not the reason Amelia and Summer shivered. While both women had come somewhat to grips with their grief, this day reopened their wounds and carved a few new lesions as well. Fortunately, some natural tranquilizer was allowing them to cope with blessed numbness.

The previous evening, Lieutenant Applegate had visited Dan and Amelia to complete the funeral arrangements and deliver a drab olive duffel bag filled with the necessities and few luxuries that had sustained Tom in Vietnam's jungles.

Once she overcame the shock of seeing him show up at the door from time to time, Amelia had grown fond of the Air Force casualty officer. Lieutenant Applegate was a compassionate man, armed with generous supplies of kindness, dedication and honesty. As she stood near the waiting hearse, thinking the lieutenant must have a strong character to deal with these matters of life and death day after day, year after year, Amelia was curious to know more about the man.

"Tell me, Lieutenant, where are you from?" she asked.

"Stillwater, Oklahoma, Mrs. Carter," he replied. "I lived there all my life until I joined the Air Force. It's a college town—Oklahoma State University. My father pastors a church in Stillwater. I earned a degree in English at Oklahoma State and then went to the Air Force's officer training school."

"Oral Roberts runs his ministry out of Oklahoma," Amelia remarked. "Is it Tulsa?"

"No, ma'am, it's Oklahoma City," the lieutenant informed her.

Amelia nodded as if she remembered. "Personally, I prefer Billy Graham's preachen to Oral Roberts," she said. "But neither of them is as good as the pastor of our church, Adam Cook. He'll do the service tomorrow. He knew Tom all his life. I would like for you to meet him."

"I'd like to do that, too," Lieutenant Applegate said. "Perhaps this evening at your home."

"He's promised to be there when they bring Tom out," Amelia said glumly. "I suppose, Lieutenant, that you see a good many preachers in this line of business. I would think it's a difficult job to do day after day."

"It can be overwhelming at times," he admitted, "but I try to remember how important the duties are. Sometimes, it helps the family to have someone around who is a stranger, someone they can open up to and count on without worry about embarrassment. Perhaps the word I'm looking for is appearances. It's just an observation—maybe not even an astute one—but I believe some people find it easier to grieve in front of strangers."

"I know what you mean," Amelia said. "With a stranger, you don't have to worry about appearances as you put it. Strangers may remember your breakdown, but they'll disappear from your life. There's none of the lingeren embarrassment or the distress of haven been seen at your worst by the people with whom you live."

"Yes, ma'am," the lieutenant said.

Another minute passed with silence before Amelia raised another question. "Lieutenant Applegate, what is your feelen about the war?"

For the first time, the officer shuffled his feet and eased his posture. "I don't, Mrs. Carter," he answered at last. "The Air Force doesn't pay me to have feelings about this or any other war. Generally, though, I think all war is horrific, and, unfortunately, a great many of them are probably unnecessary—though please don't assume I'm implying this war is unnecessary. People should pick their wars carefully and then wage them with all their might. Fortunately, our country's wars are picked by Washington. I'm grateful for that. Once the country's leaders decide to go to war, however, I believe they should allow the military to carry it out."

"Are we to infer that you don't believe the military is be'en allowed to run this war?" Summer inquired, speaking for the first time.

The lieutenant shifted his weight and pondered an answer. "Do you want my candid opinion?" he asked.

"Please," Amelia said in a shaky voice.

"Then Mrs. Carter, Miss Baker, I must tell you that from the viewpoint of a military strategist, there have been blunders in this war, essentially because the politicians keep sticking their noses into places they have no business being."

Amelia and Summer regarded the answer for a moment as Dan emerged from the depot. Finally, Amelia asked one last question. "Tell me, Lieutenant. Was my son's death one of those blunders?"

"From what I know about Tom's mission, Mrs. Carter," the officer answered without missing a beat, "your son was performing a valid function, a very essential duty. You can take pride in knowing he served his country well on a critical matter.

"And I hope you can find comfort in that knowledge," he added after a slight pause.

Amelia smiled weakly and clutched his arm. "Thank you, Lieutenant Applegate," she said. "Thank you very much."

———

Minutes later, Melvin Lovett, the lieutenant and four railroad workers carried the casket past the Carters and Summer. The reasons for and prosecution of the war were forgotten by all as they watched the coffin being placed into the hearse.

"Could we see him?" Amelia asked after the four anonymous pallbearers had departed with murmured condolences. Her voice was choked. "I'd like to see him. I've always felt a person needed to see the body in order to accept the death." She paused, on the verge of tears, then added weakly, "I know it's ridiculous, but I keep hopen there's been a mistake and it's not Tom in that casket."

Dan put an arm around his wife for support. "Don't do this to yourself, Amelia," he urged in a shaky voice.

"I think not, Mrs. Carter," Lieutenant Applegate added gently. "I know how difficult it must be, but you have to let it go. Tom's gone. And from what you've told me about your son, the part of him you loved is gone to a better place. As the Bible instructs us, remember that our bodies are nothing more than shells for our souls. Dust and ashes. Your son is in a better place. He's with God, not here."

Tears cascaded down Amelia's face. She leaned against her husband, accepting his embrace.

"Amelia," Melvin said softly. "Trust me. I'll make sure you have no reason to doubt."

At long last, Amelia surrendered her control. Her first sobs came as an outright gasp, followed by a tormented wail and anguished cries. She sagged against Dan, who needed the assistance of Lieutenant Applegate to support her.

"My baby," she moaned. "Our baby's gone, Dan. Our boy, our son is gone, and he's never comen back." She cried, "Oh, God, I can't take it, I can't take it. I don't think I can stand it anymore. Not anymore. I've tried and tried, but I don't want it to be this way."

She was fighting exhaustion now. "Make it go away," she pleaded. "Oh, please God, make it not true. Don't take my son."

Dan regained his composure, steadied his wobbly knees and wrapped his arms around his wife, cradling her against his chest. "We can't make it go away, honey," he said through tears. "Tom is gone, and somehow, someway, we have to accept it and find a way to go on without him. Be thankful that we have each other. I want you to lean on me, and I need to lean on you, too. I need your strength, Amelia. And, honey, you've got a world of strength in you."

Amelia found solace in her husband's confidence, enough to return his embrace and stand on her own power without assistance from the lieutenant. She closed her eyes until the sobs subsided to hiccups and sniffles.

"We can make it through this," Dan said a short time later, and she felt his tears against her forehead.

She nodded and clung to him a minute longer. Hurt ran through her like a raging torrent and for the first time, Amelia understood about letting go. She had no choice; she was powerless to do anything else. A part of her felt dead, but she patted her husband's shoulder, gripped his hands and suggested they go home.

Sensing the worst of their grief was behind the Carters, Melvin Lovett took control of the moment with his polished funeral home manners. His politeness provided further distraction, preoccupying Dan and Amelia with details that required their immediate attention.

"I'll bring the casket out around six o'clock this evenen," he reminded them. "In the meantime, I have the list of pallbearers and will call everyone this afternoon to make sure they're at your house at a quarter till. Tomorrow, the Air Force will supply an honor guard to serve as pallbearers. I do have one question about the flowers. A flag will drape the coffin, so there's really no need for a blanket. Unless you want one?"

"We do," Amelia said immediately. "Yellow roses if possible. Summer? They were his favorite?"

The question jarred Summer, who had been absorbed with the consideration of variously morbid questions about Tom's remains. She, too, had wanted to comfort Amelia but was unable to tear her gaze from the coffin. Despite the lieutenant's contention that the body was nothing more than a shell, Summer wondered about Tom's condition. Her thoughts were unsettling. They knew Tom had been shot in the leg before he died. The fatal shot had been a barrage of gunfire point blank into his head, and his body had lain on the mountain for the duration of the battle, which had lasted until early the next day. She shuddered at the thoughts her mind conjured up. While Amelia's question jolted her system, it also rescued Summer from senseless worries.

"Yellow," she repeated, dabbing at her tear-stained face. "That was his favorite color."

Summer forced a tight smile for the benefit of Dan and Amelia, whose pained faces now showed concern for her welfare. Reassured, they resumed their discussion of the last-minute details with occasional sidelong glances to check on her.

Summer rubbed her arm nervously, recalling the time she had questioned Tom about his favorite color. It was early in their courtship as they discovered the trivial details about each other.

"Yellow," Tom had replied automatically when she asked the question.

"Appropriate, consideren the color of your hair," Summer responded. "Technically, though, I'd say your blond mop is more gold than yellow."

Tom had smiled sheepishly. "Well, actually," he confessed, "if we're goen to be totally honest with each other like we agreed, then I have to admit that gold is my favorite color. I'd prefer we keep that secret to ourselves."

Summer had eyed him closely. "Why the big secret?"

Tom shrugged. "I don't know. It's one of my quirks. When you think about it, gold has a lot of luxurious connotations. Given my well-noted penchant for the simple things in life, I feel weird about having such an indulgent preference for color. So when people ask me my favorite color, I always say yellow: to disguise my dark and subconscious lust for the excess."

"Tom Carter, that's about the craziest thing I've ever heard," Summer replied, deeply suspicious. "Are you maken this up just to tease me?"

"I swear it's the truth," Tom said, putting a hand over his heart. "Our secret, though?"

"It will have to be our secret," Summer said airily. "Nobody would believe me in a million years if I tried to explain somethen like that."

Tom had laughed heartily, saying, "Now it's your turn to tell me a secret about yourself."

Summer shook her head, refusing the request. "I don't have anything nearly so astonishen to tell," she said. "You'll have to be content just knowen my favorite colors, which, by the way, are red, especially in roses, and black, particularly in clothes. I'm also fond of the red and black of the Georgia Bulldogs."

Their conversation had turned to football, and Summer was trying to recall the details as Lieutenant Mark Applegate moved quietly next to her. The lieutenant worried that Summer was also on the verge of an emotional collapse. Except for one lone moment when she had questioned him about the war, Tom Carter's fiancée had seemed strangely disassociated from this moment.

Had she realized his concern, Summer would have assured the lieutenant that all was well. Her nerves were shot and her heart heavy, but all in all, she was holding up under the strain.

Aware of his presence beside her, Summer observed him with a sideways look. She judged him somewhere in his late twenties. Mark Applegate was a handsome man, with a narrow face, rugged features, dark eyes and short, straight hair somewhere between brown and black. He was tall and lean, yet moved with athletic grace and style. Summer knew with certainty that his craggy features concealed a warm heart, and she found his voice appealing. It was a rich baritone, slightly accented with a Midwestern drawl. In another time and place, Summer would have found him attractive. The realization shocked, then shamed her. How could she possibly have these thoughts with Tom lying cold in the coffin no more than a dozen feet from her?

Over the past few days, she had grappled with an inchoate idea of life after Tom. The mere thought unsettled her, almost to the point of nausea. Even the remotest of possibilities seemed unthinkable, yet somewhere, untouched in her vital center, was an awareness that with each passing day, the brilliance of Tom's memory would fade, and life would march boldly forward without him. The idea was still an abstraction, just beginning to creep out of the recesses of her mind, but it made Summer feel cheap and dirty.

She sighed, impatient and ready to leave.

"Are you okay?" Lieutenant Applegate asked. "You and I really haven't had a chance to talk. I worry I've neglected you, Miss Baker. Do you need anything?"

"Call me Summer," she said automatically. "And no thanks. I'm fine. I have this whole army of family members who are maken this as painless as possible. Dan and Amelia need you more."

"That's kindhearted of you," the lieutenant replied. "They've been worried about you, too. When we were discussing the funeral last night, Mrs. Carter said she wanted you to have the flag because Tom loved you—as she put it—more than anyone else in the world."

Summer winced, overcome by heartbreak for Tom and affection for his mother.

Seeing her blanch, the officer apologized. "The last thing I intended was to upset you."

She quieted him by laying her hand against his forearm. "You didn't upset me," she said. "I'm grateful you shared that with me. But I want Amelia to have the flag. I love her dearly, and she's sacrificed far more than I ever will. The flag should stay in Tom's home."

"Perhaps we can present the flag to you," Lieutenant Applegate suggested. "Then you could hand it over to Mrs. Carter."

"Whatever," Summer shrugged. "I'll do whatever Amelia and Dan decide. This needs to be as easy as possible for them."

Mark Applegate smiled. "I see why Tom wanted to marry you, Summer. You have a sweet nature."

She laughed aloud. "It's obvious you don't know me very well, Lieutenant. Tom would have never said somethen like that about me. One of these days, I'll tell you about that sweet nature and how Tom could barely tolerate it. I can be pretty impossible to get along with at times."

They were silent for a long moment. "Are you married, Lieutenant?" Summer asked finally.

"No, I haven't found the right woman," Mark Applegate answered. "But I keep looking and hoping. I come from a large family, and I'd like a whole passel of children of my own."

"Tom and I were goen to marry in January or February when he got back stateside," Summer replied. "Then after his hitch was up, we were comen back here to farm.

"It's funny how things work out," she continued after a slight hesitation. "I never thought of myself as a farmer's wife, but Tom changed my mind. I've known him my whole life, but we never really liked each other very much. We rather tolerated each other. Then one day out of the blue, we took a long look at each other and fell in love."

Summer hugged her arms against her stomach and shook her head in dismay. "I'll miss that farm," she said. "Does that sound silly—missen somethen you never had?"

"No, Summer," the lieutenant replied. "Not at all."

She shrugged in agreement and looked away from him. "We made a lot of plans," she said. "Now I almost wish we hadn't. Maybe then I wouldn't feel as if I'd lost a whole lifetime."

"Summer," he said, commanding her attention with the strength of his voice. "Be thankful for those plans. Speaking as someone who's been over there, who understands the loneliness, I feel certain that your plans gave Tom a great deal of satisfaction and made the experience bearable for him. It would have been far worse for him without something to plan for and look forward to."

Summer started to tell the man that it didn't seem possible for the experience to have been any worse for Tom. But she caught herself, knowing the lieutenant was correct. Besides, she told herself, anything else would have made the love she shared with Tom different and it had been perfect the way it was.

"You're right," she admitted. "And I am grateful."

Sighing, Summer gave him a smile of thanks and followed Dan and Amelia to their car.

On the drive home, halfway between Cookville and New River, Dan mentioned the duffel bag to Summer, inviting her to join Amelia and him to sort through it. Although her head ached terribly, Summer wanted to share this glimpse of Tom's things, so she accepted the offer. Otherwise, the ride home was quiet, giving each of them an opportunity to collect their thoughts and ready themselves for the last of these public periods of mourning.

None of them knew what to expect. Tom had been dead for more than two weeks. Friends and neighbors had called already to pay their respects and bring food. In those first days after they had learned the news, there had been an outpouring of sympathy, with people in and out of the mercantile almost at will. But the pace had slowed considerably, though close friends and relatives still dropped by on a daily basis to lend moral support.

"I hope people know when the funeral is," Amelia said absentmindedly.

"I'm sure they do," Summer replied, maintaining her vacant gaze out the window. "These things have a way of getten around. There was a funeral notice in yesterday's *Tifton Gazette,* too."

"That's right," Amelia remembered. "And Melvin said he put a notice in the Valdosta paper this mornen." She paused, then asked, "Y'all think a one o'clock service is okay? I thought at one time maybe eleven would be best, to go on and get it over with early in the day. Then I thought maybe later in the afternoon, about four or so. But I was afraid that might make things run late in the evenen. I wasn't sure how long everything will take."

"One o'clock is fine," Dan assured, taking her hand and smiling.

At the store, which they had kept closed since learning about Tom's death, Dan came around and opened the car doors for Amelia and Summer. "Seems musty in here," he said as they entered the mercantile. He left the door open, hoping a fresh breeze would cleanse the stale air.

Summer followed the Carters into Tom's room, where the duffel bag lay on the bed. After they had found seats, Amelia on the bed and Summer in the desk chair, Dan tried to open the bag. Someone had knotted the rope too tightly, however, so he sent Amelia to the kitchen for a butcher knife to cut the strings.

"I'm glad you're here with us," he said to Summer as they waited. "Amelia's been beside herself about includen you in the arrangements. Me, too, for that matter. When you're hurten as all of us are, it's easy to lose sight of how somethen like this affects everybody else. I sure hope we haven't left you in a lurch, Summer. As a parent, you think nobody can love your child as much as you do. But, Summer, I can honestly say that Amelia and I believe you loved Tom as much as we did."

"We're grateful for that, too, sweetheart," Amelia added, coming into the room and handing the knife to Dan. "I knew you were special a long time before Tom figured it out. I've loved you like a daughter for a long time, Summer. That will never change, no matter what."

Tears welled and flowed before Summer could help it. "I feel the same way about y'all," she said. "I keep asken myself how this could have happened, why it had to be Tom. Of all the people I've ever known, I think Tom had the most downright goodness of anybody." She paused, then went on. "When we were at the depot, the lieutenant said somethen that made me feel better. We were talken, and I told him that I wished Tom and I had not made so many plans because they remind me of what I'm goen to miss in life. The lieutenant told me to be thankful for those plans because they made Tom's life bearable over there. He's right. As much as it hurts to say this, I know that other things will come along for us. We'll make new plans and have different dreams. For Tom, though, what we gave him, the dreams we shared with him, are all he had. While it hurts knowen what we're goen to miss without Tom, I'm thankful for everything we gave him—the plans, the dreams and the love."

Dan and Amelia's eyes shone with tears of appreciation as they realized again how fortunate their son had been to love and be loved by such a remarkable young woman. Nothing else was said, and in a moment, Dan used the knife to cut the knot on the duffel bag.

A pair of mud-caked boots spilled out, followed by a watch, nail clippers, a shaving kit, a half bottle of aftershave and an unopened bottle of cologne, which had been Summer's going-way gift to Tom before he reported to boot camp. "I'll take the cologne with me," he had told her. "But I won't use a drop until I come home to you."

Summer shared the story with the Carters, and they swapped a few more memories before delving back into the duffel bag. Out came his dog tags, soiled and sweat-stained camouflage shirts and fatigues, socks, underwear and his camera, which had been a Christmas gift from his parents last year, just before Tom was sent to Vietnam. Tom had used the camera extensively in Vietnam, sending the film home to be developed and having his parents return selected pictures to him. The camera now contained a roll of exposed film, one last opportunity for Summer and his parents to see Vietnam through Tom's eyes.

As they expressed their appreciation and speculated on the undeveloped film, Amelia stood, reaching over Summer to pull two brown leather photo albums from the top shelf of the hutch over Tom's desk. "All of his pictures are in these albums," she said. "One is full. The other is about half-filled. We can go through them some-time, Summer, and you can pick out any that you might want."

"I have an album full myself at home," Summer replied. "You hang on to those."

Amelia set the albums on the desk. "Okay, but you're welcome to look at them anytime," she said. "If you want to."

Summer squeezed her hand, and they resumed their examination of the bag, which was now nearly empty, except for half a box of Snickers candy bars, two cigar boxes stuffed with letters, pictures and other incidentals as well as a Prince Albert tobacco can filled with Vietnamese coins and paper money, plus a few pieces of American money.

From the bottom of the bag, Dan pulled out a thick envelope that was unsealed and addressed to Summer. Dan fingered the letter lightly, resisting the desire to read it for himself, and handed it to her. "This is for you," he said.

Summer accepted the envelope, realizing the letter likely would have been one of the last things Tom touched, containing some of his final thoughts. She held it tightly, trying to decide whether to share it with the Carters. "I'd like to read this in private first," she said finally.

"And you should," Amelia remarked hurriedly. "Tom intended it for you. Take it home and if you decide to share it with us, we'll be pleased, honey. And if not, that's fine, too."

Summer slipped the letter into her purse, and they began examining the various coins and currency inside the tobacco can, deciding a few of the more brightly colored bills were from Hong Kong.

"Strange to think of Tom exploren a city like that," Dan commented. "I'd like to go there myself one day."

Next, they rummaged through the two cigar boxes, examining the various letters sent to Tom and sorting them into bundles depending on the author. Summer's pile was the largest by far, then Amelia's.

"I didn't realize Joe wrote so often to him," Dan remarked.

They looked at each other in the ensuing silence, unwilling to voice their feelings about Joe. At last, Amelia relented.

"Tom and Joe were the best of friends," she said. "How is Joe taken all this, Summer?"

"To be perfectly honest, I don't know," she replied. "I haven't said more than a passen word to him since the other day. I was angry with him and upset. But he was awful cut down when he found out about Tom. I know he's hurten, too."

Summer then told the Carters about running to the river after Captain Subic had broken the news, explaining that Joe had found her and recounting their conversation about Tom.

"We'll have to get this straightened out at some point," Dan said when she had finished.

"Yes, we must," Amelia agreed.

They resumed examination of the box's remaining contents, which were primarily pictures. Tom had been methodical with his record-keeping, writing names, dates, locations and an occasional note on the back of each photograph. As they looked through the pictures, they were able to place faces with the names of buddies Tom had written about in his letters. Sadly, they realized a number of these men had preceded him in death.

"Here's one of Tom and that colored boy whose name was Tom, too," Dan said, showing Amelia and Summer the photograph of the two men standing bare-chested in a rice paddy with their arms draped casually across each other's shoulders. "What was his last name?"

"It was Welch," Amelia answered. "Tom thought a lot of the boy. Said he grew up dirt poor on the Mississippi delta and joined the Army hopen to make somethen of his life. I wonder what happened to him."

"Lieutenant Applegate probably could find out for us," Summer suggested, suddenly anxious herself to know the fate of Tom Welch.

"He probably could," Amelia agreed. "Maybe an address, too. Tom told me the boy missed his mama awful bad. I'd like to write her a letter. I always thought Tom was tryen to say he missed me, too, when he wrote about that boy missen his mama."

"He missed you," Summer assured, as Amelia flushed with embarrassment over the disclosure.

"Oh, my!" Dan exclaimed with a thick drawl.

He was peering closely at a picture Summer instantly recognized as the one of her in the ao dais standing beside the pecan tree. She turned red with embarrassment. Dan laughed, motioning the picture to Amelia.

"May I?" he asked.

Summer nodded her permission. "That was a gift from Tom," Summer said as Amelia reached for the picture. "He said it was a fashionable Vietnamese dress, although I believe they wear it with pants. Tom neglected to send those. He seemed kind of down at the time and, well, I wanted to cheer him up. Carrie and I faked be'en sick one Sunday so we could stay home from church and get the picture. We used an entire role of film because I wanted it to be perfect." She hesitated, then made a request. "I'd really rather nobody saw it besides the three of us."

"Quite a morale builder, I'd say, Summer," Amelia teased lightheartedly, handing her the picture. "We'll let you take care of that one."

Summer put the picture in her purse, along with the letter. Having sorted through the bag, they now resisted the temptation to repeat the whole process.

"I wonder what happened to his wallet," Amelia remarked. "It was the leather one we gave him when he went off to boot camp. Tom seemed right proud of it."

"I really would like to know what happened to it," she added when no one volunteered an answer. "Maybe the lieutenant could find out for us."

In the next minute, the three of them regarded each other closely, breathing life into an everlasting kinship created from the joy of having shared something precious and grief over what might have been. The bond was too sacred to seal with words, so they allowed the moment to pass into their collective memory.

At last, Summer checked her watch, realizing she must get home if she expected to return to the Carters in time to witness Tom's final homecoming. "It's getten late," she announced. "I'd better scoot on home. Have you thought about what to wear this evenen and tomorrow, Amelia?"

"Not really," Amelia said truthfully.

"Can I help you pick out somethen?" Summer asked.

"No need for that," the older woman replied. "I've got plenty of black in my closet. I've never been one to rush out and buy somethen new for a funeral. My sister, Kate, tends to do that. For all I know, she's already bought me a dress for tomorrow."

"For the funeral, I thought I'd wear that black dress I made last fall," Summer said. "The plain knit one with the puffed sleeves," she added to prompt Amelia's memory. "Tom always admired it."

Amelia nodded, and Summer excused herself to use the telephone, calling home to ask someone to come pick her up. When she returned, Dan asked if she wanted any of Tom's things for herself. "Perhaps your letters," he offered.

"No thanks," she said. "I know them by heart. It would be nice to keep his stuff all in one place. I hate to think of his things be'en strung and strewed."

Amelia nodded.

"By the way, Lieutenant Applegate told me about the flag," Summer added. "I'm deeply touched, but I believe the flag belongs in Tom's home."

"Thank you, Summer," Dan said. "I'd very much like to have it here."

"Well then," Amelia suggested, "we will tell them to present the flag to you at the funeral. You can pass it on to me later. Mark, the lieutenant I mean, suggested that as one way to handle it."

"Then that's the way it will be," Summer agreed. "On second thought, Dan," she added as an afterthought, "I would like to have that bottle of cologne I gave Tom."

"One more thing before you go," Amelia said as Dan reached across the bed to retrieve the unopened box, which was buried under the clothes. "Your letters to Tom. Would it be okay if Dan and I read them sometime? I realize they were personal, and I feel like a busybody just for asken. Feel free to say no, but I would appreciate the opportunity to see Tom from your perspective."

Summer considered the request as she took the cologne from Dan and placed it in her purse. "I guess so," she said at length. "When you read them, however, please don't get the wrong impression and think bad of me. Tom and I had a knack for speaken our mind, and some of those letters ... Some of them are love letters ... And we were plannen to marry after all."

She stumbled to a conclusion, turning beet red. "I can't believe I actually said that," she said suddenly, rolling her eyes in disbelief. "Lord, you probably think I'm some awful, lecherous man-chaser," she continued, burying her face in her hands. "They're not really bad. Suggestive perhaps, although not nearly as suggestive as the ones Tom wrote me. Your son was pretty hot-blooded, you know."

Dan and Amelia were laughing, chortling with delight at her stammering explanation and embarrassment. "In my youth, I was fairly hot-blooded myself," Dan remarked through the laughter. "Amelia, too, so I guess you could say Tom came by it naturally."

This laughter, some of it mingling with tears of joy and sorrow, was pure healing magic, Summer thought. "What the heck," she decided. "Go ahead and read them all. I'll bring over the letters Tom wrote to me one day as well. But for gosh sakes, please let it stay between the three of us. Mama and Daddy would have a cow if they knew about this."

The mercantile door jingled then, signaling John's arrival for Summer. With the secret safe in good hands among friends, they went to greet him.

———

At five minutes till six that evening, Melvin Lovett brought Tom home, gliding the black hearse to a silent stop beside the mercantile door. Brisk and efficient as always in a black suit and white shirt, Melvin gathered the pallbearers, which included John, Luke, three of Tom's cousins and Doug Dillard, one of his childhood friends, and gave them instructions on the proper decorum.

The day had turned damp and dreary, with gray skies threatening a downpour. But the chill running through the large crowd on hand to witness Tom's homecoming was unrelated to the weather. Tom's friends and family were filled with dread, the sickening anticipation of knowing the hearse was making an official business call.

The entire community, it seemed, had turned out for the occasion, this time to pay respects to the deceased. Tom was one of them, and they would miss him.

Joe was among those gathered outside, lingering on the edges to avoid the slightest hint of trouble or consternation. He had considered staying away from the occasion and attending only the funeral, but his father had persuaded him otherwise earlier in the day after they had attended church. Immediately after the service, Matt had sought out his son and suggested they walk the short distance home. Their ensuing talk had been a warm elixir for Joe, who gave an unabashed accounting of his thoughts and feelings about the events of the last two weeks. In return, Matt urged him to pay his respects to Tom.

"He was your friend," Matt said simply. "You belong there with everyone else who loved him."

Now, overwhelmed by the breath-stealing sorrow that comes when death marches prominently into the midst of those gathered to pay homage to it, Joe wished he were somewhere else. Others shared his feelings. John and Luke stood like statues behind the hearse, fighting the urge to run away from the silver coffin that Melvin Lovett rolled toward them. Bonnie buried her face against Carrie, who gaped in disbelief, horrified by the reality of the moment. Matt stood stiffly beside Paul Berrien on the mercantile porch. He was choking on a lump in his throat, which forced him to take long, steady breaths to maintain his composure. Sam decided he was unable to bear this burden, so he walked away from it, strolling around the side of the store, determined to stay out of sight until the casket was safely ensconced in its overnight resting place. Tomorrow, Sam would find the courage to pay his dues like everyone else. This evening, he felt the need for self-preservation.

Inside the mercantile, the pall hung even heavier as they prepared to welcome home death. An assortment of cousins, aunts and uncles was scattered through the house, some of whom had known Tom extremely well and others, who by age or distance, were merely acquaintances. Caroline and Rachel were in the kitchen with Amelia's sister, Kate, and some of her closest friends. Torn up on the inside, they had a responsibility to maintain their composure and offer support to Tom's immediate family.

In the cramped living room, which had been rearranged to accommodate the casket, Dan and Amelia, Essie Easters and Summer stood near the windows, waiting for the casket. Ever since Melvin had announced his arrival and they had taken up watch beside the window, Summer had stared intently at the empty space usually occupied by the Carters' sofa. The sofa was a casualty of the moment, moved into Tom's bedroom. Two brass floor lamps and a portable bier covered in maroon velvet marked the place of honor.

At last, the mercantile door jingled. Summer changed the focus of her attention to the black pumps on her feet. Her eyes remained downcast as long as possible, all through the slight struggle to fit the coffin through the mercantile door, across the floor past the candy case and drink box until the procession reached the living room door. Finally, she lifted her eyes.

The flag-draped gray box filled the doorway, with John and Luke flanking it. Summer was unprepared for the moment, as was everyone else. She heard Mrs. Easters gasp, though she didn't think anyone else did. Extending her arm, she supported Tom's grandmother, giving the woman's hand a tight squeeze. Beside her, Amelia leaned against Dan.

As the pallbearers carried the casket through the door, placing it on the velvet gurney, Summer fought a wave of nausea. She pressed her hand against her mouth until the worst passed, then found herself moving forward with the others. At some point, Melvin set a brass-framed portrait of Tom in his dress grays atop the coffin, placing it squarely in the middle of the fifty stars.

Amelia was the first among them to touch the coffin, flicking a finger at some invisible speck of dust, recoiling as if she had touched a hot stove eye. Shortly, however, her hand returned, trembling, then steady as she made contact with the flag. Dan followed, his hand joining hers as they found strength. Essie Easters preoccupied herself with the picture, although she kept mum her admiration and refused to comment on his vividness.

Caught between the urge to flee and the need to stay, Summer faced a harrowing experience. Gradually, her nausea disappeared and an uneasy peace transformed her. She reached out tenderly, as if she were touching Tom himself, noted the rough texture of the flag, the cold feel of the box beneath it. As she made these observations, the advice given earlier in the day by Lieutenant Mark Applegate suddenly seemed very appropriate. This box and the body inside it had nothing to do with Tom. He was gone away from her, to somewhere far beyond this time and place where they had gathered to memorialize him. While her peace remained uneasy, Summer sensed a certain reassurance in this recognition. Tears streamed down her cheeks, and she allowed them an unfettered run. Like Tom himself, these tears would disappear soon into a place beyond her.

A while later, when Summer realized she was standing alone at the casket, the gentle hands of her mother and grandmother pried the young woman from the vigil. With a numb glow about her, Summer allowed herself to be guided from the room.

———————

There was a moment in Tom's homecoming when Melvin Lovett looked into the questioning eyes of Amelia and Dan and nodded curtly in the affirmative.

Melvin had little doubt about the identity of the corpse, although the recognition had been difficult to make. The funeral home operator had seen more than a few mangled corpses in his life, but none worse than this one. He wondered why people did these things to one another. If more people saw the savagery of war, he thought, perhaps peace would have a real chance.

———————

Alone in her room later that night, Summer grew restless. She had slept the better part of three hours, waking as fresh and relaxed as she had been since the ordeal began. Gone was the uneasy peace that she had carried from Tom's casket. An inner serenity had taken its place, a peace of mind, heart and soul more aptly described in the Bible as "peace which passeth all understanding." Unable to recall exactly where the phrase originated, she retrieved her Bible from the nightstand, peeling through the concordance to find the reference, then reading the fourth chapter of Philippians in its entirety.

When she had finished, Summer laid the Bible on her dresser and picked up the framed photograph of Tom. This was the Tom she would remember for eternity, the man with golden hair, blue eyes, a sunny fair complexion and an endearing smile.

During her nap, Tom had come to say goodbye in a dream. He had been standing alone on the edge of a beautiful garden—an image Summer knew came directly from one of the songs selected for his funeral. He had been obviously perplexed, unsure whether to enter the garden or to walk away from it. Just like Tom, he had made his decision without fanfare. He simply shrugged in that practical way of his, threw up a quick wave and disappeared into the garden, leaving one last modest grin as a remembrance. The dream seemed so real and lifelike that Summer had woken herself from it with the soft-spoken litany of "Goodbye, Tom."

Setting the picture back on the dresser, she checked the time and contemplated making a sandwich. The hour was late, and she had not eaten anything since breakfast. Hearing movement around the house as well as the drone of the eleven o'clock news on the kitchen television, she decided to forgo the sandwich and went instead to see if any of her siblings were in the next room. Entering through the connecting closet, she found the room dark and empty. The light was off in Joe's room as well, so she retraced her steps, plopping on the bed, staring vacantly at the ceiling until she remembered to lay out her clothes for the funeral.

She started for the closet, then noticed her purse setting on the fireplace mantle and remembered Tom's letter. Knowing the letter was her final personal contact with Tom, Summer was hesitant to read it. Despite her newfound peace, she feared the unknown, worried over Tom's frame of mind in those last hours before he was killed.

While mustering the courage to read his final words, she busied herself, storing away the infamous picture and unopened bottle of cologne in the bottom drawer of her nightstand. Finally, she admitted what she had known all along: As best she could, Summer wanted to trudge those last few miles with Tom. Up to this point, she had not shielded herself from any of the ugliness, listening to the horrid description of his death and allowing her imagination to supply missing details. Well, Tom's hellish nightmare was over now, and she saw no sense in speculating on the wretched details, especially when Tom had chronicled those last hours.

Retrieving the unsealed envelope from her purse, she carried the letter to her bed, sat down and anxiously unfolded three pieces of notebook paper filled with Tom's hen-scratch penmanship. Summer had teased Tom mercilessly about his handwriting, tiny markings that seemed more like scribble than print. Sometimes, she needed a decoder to decipher the words, but the style had endeared itself to her over the last few months. Smoothing out the letter, she checked its length and concluded the military censors must have missed this one, as no parts of it were redacted. She began reading.

––––––––

September 13, 1968, Friday, 8:30 p.m.

Dear Summer,

"Tai Sao?" I've learned very little Vietnamese in my nearly eight months over here, but Tai Sao, the Vietnamese expression for "why," is on my mind a lot these days.

There's a million whys I want answers to, mainly because I'm feeling down in the dumps. I've been back in the jungle four days now, and already it seems like forever. The R-and-R in Hong Kong and Saigon seems to have happened a lifetime ago. The only thing real about it was the telephone conversations with you and my parents. I'd have spent a year's pay to hear your voice.

As I write this, we're camped at the top of a mountain, with a sheer cliff at our back and a thick, sloping jungle below us. The place is beautiful, especially at sun-up, with mountains stretching as far as the eye can see in all directions. Right now, it's night, and the moon is out, beautiful, bright and white, a little over half full. Of course, I'm looking at it and thinking of you. One thing about Vietnam: The nights are as beautiful as they are scary. Even when it's pitch black, stars cover the sky like a painting. I've seen enough shooting stars over here to have more than my share of wishes for one lifetime.

Anyway, I know I've mentioned Vietnam's nights before, and no matter how splendid they are, they're not half as beautiful as you. I have a bad case of homesickness tonight, especially for you and our dreams, and Tai Sao seems an appropriate question to ask. As in, why can't I be home with you, on a farm of our own, working hard to make a living? I'd like to think we're supposed to do something worthwhile with our lives. Tonight, I don't feel that's the case with mine.

I try not to think about dying over here. But lately, I do think about it. It's not that I'm scared to die. I've always believed God predetermines when a person dies, and circumstances take care of the details. If I'm supposed to die young, I will. But if that's the case, I wish it would happen at a time when I feel some purpose to my life—not when I'm spinning wheels.

If I sound a little crazy, I probably am. This place makes you that way. In a roundabout way, I'm trying to say that I'd like an opportunity to make dreams come true—for you and me. It's like I've spent all these years growing up, preparing to be a man, getting to this point. Having come this far, I want to see what I can do with all I've learned. Anyway, in case I haven't told you—though I probably have at least a million times—chief among those dreams is growing old with you, Summer, having beautiful children, grandchildren and a blessed life. The best kind of gold, you know. Is that too much to want? I don't think so, although sometimes it seems ridiculous to want much of anything over here.

Right now, behind where we're camped, a huge battle is raging in one of the valleys below the cliff, with lots of heavy artillery, machine gunfire and jets flying constant bombing runs. The mountains shake when the jets unload their bombs, and it's like some spectacular fireworks show. But there's nothing spectacular about it. I'm amazed anybody can survive all that firepower.

Just before I started writing this letter, the North Vietnamese apparently shot down one of our planes. Some of the guys saw it crash and explode in the jungle. I only heard it. The engine started whining, louder and louder, and then there was a tremendous roar and huge explosion, like sharp thunder. Needless to say, I don't think there's much hope for the pilot, although some of those guys are like Houdini.

As I understand it, the fighting in the valley is supposed to be some kind of diversion for my company's mission. We're doing reconnaissance work, trying to pinpoint the location of enemy supply trails, so they can be knocked out. My particular squad starts work around midnight. We go down into the jungle valley below our camp and search for tunnels and other signs of routes that are being used to move supplies. The famous Ho Chi Minh trail, you know. From what everybody says, we've actually crossed into Laos. We're camped right on the border between Laos and Vietnam.

The work itself is hard and more than a little bit scary. Until tonight, it's been rainy and cloudy, and we've been traipsing around in the pitch black of jungle. Take my word: There's no darkness like jungle darkness. It's hard enough to hack your way through jungle in broad daylight, but it's sheer misery at night. Basically, you slip, stumble and fall your way through it, like a blind man. I've been slapped by every kind of limb and leaf you could imagine. Sometimes, when a particularly large, nasty sopping leaf wraps itself around my face, I feel as if I'm in the clutches of a man-eating plant. I may be at that, but so far, none has gotten the best of me. My face and hands are pretty cut up and scratched, however. It's not a pretty sight, and it hurts.

Anyway, last night in particular was one of the spookiest moments of my life. My squad was strung out along a line observing what appears to be some kind of supply station. We had been there about an hour, watching trucks and people come and go. All of a sudden, we heard voices behind us, speaking Vietnamese and coming closer in the darkness. There probably were a dozen men, although we never got a solid count because of the darkness. Since we were under orders not to fire unless absolutely necessary, we all kept crouched low to the ground and perfectly still. I don't think I even breathed until they were well past us and out of hearing range. Several of them walked between Katz and me, close enough we could have reached out and touched them. Honestly, I figured we were goners at the time, or at least in the fight of our lives. But like I said, they walked right past us. And afterward, we got out of there real fast.

To say it's scary to be going back down there tonight is an understatement. It's terrifying. I keep thinking, what if they spot us first? What happens then? Somehow, I don't think they're under orders not to shoot. I guess we'll just have to be very quiet and careful.

Maybe I'm being melodramatic, but I want this to sound real. I really am scared, more now than when I first got to Vietnam, even more than the first time I went in-country. And I'm sick to death of this war. Over and over again, I keep asking myself, "Tai Sao, why, why, why? What's the use of it?"

On the chopper coming here from Saigon, we passed over stretches of jungle, some of it scarred from bombs, other parts just barren stretches of deadness where defoliants have been sprayed. It got me to thinking how senseless all this is. The killing, the maiming, it's all horrible no matter how you look at it. But as bad as everything is, I think something worse is happening. Too many lives are being warped too much, on our side, on their side. It doesn't matter. It's not that nothing will ever be the same again after this (it never is after anything), but that nothing will ever matter as much again after this. Does that make sense?

Anyway, I have this feeling that maybe everybody who is important in this war and who should know better has lost all sense of control. Next time we have a war, the politicians should fight it—not run it, but fight it, hand-to-hand combat. Imagine a winner-take-all battle between Lyndon Johnson and Ho Chi Minh.

Maybe if I had a better military mind or understood the reasons we're over here, I could accept without question that everything being done is right. But I don't believe it.

I know we're supposed to be saving these people from the communists, but somehow, I don't think it really matters. I despise communism as much as anyone else, but these people are so poor that any kind of government they might have seems inconsequential to their well-being. It seems to me the smart thing would be to offer them the kind of help they truly need. I find it sad that people are starving over here while I'm running around in the jungle with a gun in my hand, something I'm not very good at. Instead, I should be at home, raising food for them, which is something I know a little bit about. Or better yet, if I have to be here, then I should be doing something to help them out of the Stone Age. If we had any sense, we'd stop warring and send in the Peace Corps. Trouble is, I suppose it takes two sides to stop a war, the same as it takes two to fight it. Seems obvious, too, that both sides in this war prefer to fight.

I'm probably sounding political, which Lord knows I'm not supposed to. On more than one occasion, we've been instructed to remember we're infantrymen, not politicians. Anyway, one good thing is that I'd rather be an infantryman than a politician. Take heart from that. I do.

Maybe I'm even sounding like some of the war demonstrators back home. I think maybe Joe has become friends with some of those guys. He writes me on a regular basis, and though he doesn't come right out and say it straight, I get the feeling he thinks we shouldn't be fighting this war. Well, he's right, you know. Maybe I'd never tell that to anybody but you, but this particular war, whether we win it or not, is a stupid waste of time, money and life.

Well, there's the long of it. The short of it is that none of this business about the war, the right or wrong of it, really matters. In the end, we're stuck with it. So I'll do my time and give my best, and just maybe, with a little luck, I'll come home alive and well. But if I don't, well then, we're stuck with that, too. And in that case, say a prayer for me and maybe think of me every now and again.

It's getting late now, so I'd better turn in and catch an hour or two of shuteye before we head back into the valley. Think maybe I'll keep this letter a day or two before I mail it. Regardless, when you read it, don't make too much of it. Just take what you need from it and ignore the rest. I'm not having premonitions of dying. I just needed to get a few things off my chest.

With all my love, Tom.

————

A few tears spilled down Summer's face onto the letter, smearing the ink, so she folded the papers and placed them back into the envelope. Dabbing at the tears with her blouse, she went to the closet, found the black evening purse she would carry to the funeral and stuck the letter inside it. Next, she picked out her best black shoes and laid out her dress. With puffed sleeves, a fitted waist and straight skirt, the dress was soft, accentuating her figure without being too revealing. Summer had sewed the dress last summer, eliciting praise from Tom as she modeled it during the middle of a discussion about sophistication, or the lack thereof.

"You look pretty fetchen there, lady," he had teased in the world's worst English accent. "Why don't you wear it to church on Sunday? You're sure to be the most glamorous woman there."

"Of course, I would be," she had answered with mocked disdain. "But if anything, I have a sense of style, Tom, and stylish women like myself never wear black during the summer months. It's just not sophisticated."

"Well, you are pretty stylish," he had replied, drawing her against him for a kiss. "Whenever or wherever you wear that dress, Summer, you'll be the most beautiful woman on the place. And even unsophisticated clods like me get a kick out of knowen that the prettiest girl in the room belongs to them."

Recalling the conversation, she checked the calendar and discovered tomorrow would be the last day in September. It was her first conception of time since learning Tom was dead. The last two weeks had been one long blur of indistinguishable days and nights.

At last, with her clothes laid out for the next day, including the scarf Tom had sent from Hong Kong, Summer turned off the light, climbed into bed and slept soundly for the first time in two weeks.

THE DAY OF TOM'S funeral dawned gloomily, with buckets of water falling from bruised skies. Rain pounded the tin roof of the Baker home, washing away the remnants of sleep, waking the family's subconscious rumblings about the importance of this day. Everyone was fretful.

For the grandparents and parents, the early morning anxieties provided grave reaffirmation of an easily forgotten axiom: Acknowledgment and acceptance are merely agonizing preludes in the living's treatment of death; the grand finale comes when the dead is ushered into eternity, amid all the venerable trappings of formality.

For the children, the apprehensions served as the first harsh notice about the difficulty of closing one of life's chapters, especially those not ready to be relinquished. And while a few already had figured it out, all would understand soon that the day brought a new dimension to their lives, one shaped by loss.

The day brought a jumble of all these emotions to Summer. She had waged personal warfare in acknowledging and accepting Tom's death. Having lost more than anyone else in this ordeal, she had begun the mourning process without delay. Any leftover anxieties were shaped by sympathy for Tom, who was the biggest loser in this misdeal of life and death.

Even though it was an unusual Monday in so many respects, the day began with a remarkable likeness to all the others, except for a more leisurely pace. In honor of Tom, school was canceled for the day, so there was no mad scramble for the bathroom. Everyone used the extra time for reflection or to take care of various chores that normally would have been put off until the afternoon or done by someone else altogether.

Joe milked the cow, while his father and Luke braved the rain to replace a broken chain on the combine. At the request of his grandfather, who felt poorly and was resting in bed, John took a muddy walk to the New Pond to retrieve an ax that Sam inadvertently had left there the previous day while breaking up a stump of fat lighter. Inside the house, Caroline and Carrie prepared an enormous breakfast of scrambled eggs, cheese grits, bacon, sausage and biscuits with fresh strawberry preserves, while Bonnie made beds and Rachel starched and ironed dress shirts for the menfolk.

Summer left the house early, bound for the mercantile to share Tom's letter with the Carters. Tom's misgivings about Vietnam had forced Summer to confront the divisive attitudes about the war, making her acutely aware of just how little she knew about who believed what regarding the conflict. Until now, her attention had focused solely on the war's effect on Tom and her, too much so to consider others' perceptions about it. As she told Dan and Amelia, it was unfair to make Joe the scapegoat for their frustration and anger over Tom's death, even their insecurities about the war itself. While she disagreed with Joe's decision to demonstrate against the war, Summer felt even worse about the hard feelings directed at her brother over the last few weeks.

"The worst possible thing that could come out of all this is for people to get confused and believe that someone's opinions about the war are the same as their feelens for Tom," she said. "I don't believe they are one and the same, and neither do y'all. Yet, that's what has happened. There's been a lot of anger, resentment and distrust, and Tom would have hated it. He went out of his way to avoid disagreements. He never had an unkind word to say about anybody, and he never passed judgment. It bothers me to think we might turn his death into a mockery of his life. We can't let that happen."

"No, we can't," Dan agreed. "I've been bothered about Joe ever since that day at the mercantile. Everything got out of hand. I was upset, Amelia was upset, and I just wanted to head off any more confrontation. I never meant for people to think I was taken sides against Joe, or that I wanted anyone else to."

"That demonstration business still leaves a bad taste in my mouth," Amelia remarked as she read over the letter a second time. "But I know Joe would never do anything intentionally to hurt Tom or any of us. And you are right, Summer. We can't allow people to confuse how they feel about the war with what they felt for Tom."

Summer took a deep breath. "I hoped y'all would feel that way," she said. "If you agree, I'd like the preacher to read Tom's letter at the funeral. Maybe then, everyone would realize that now is not the time for arguments among ourselves, that people should draw closer together to help each other through this rather than split apart over it."

"The letter would be most appropriate," Dan agreed quickly. "Those are Tom's feelens in that letter, the last ones he ever wrote down on paper for us. He was fighten this war, so his opinion counts a great deal. People should know how he felt before they cast stones at anyone else."

"Don't you agree, Amelia?" he asked.

"Yes," she replied emphatically. "Our son's words should count for somethen to someone. And Tom said it best about this letter: 'Take what you need and leave the rest.'"

––––––––––

When Summer returned from the Carters, she found the family seated around the kitchen table, eating the late breakfast without any of the typical mealtime chatter. Caroline was warming coffee cups and refilling milk glasses when Summer strode into the kitchen.

"Good mornen," she said, smiling distinctly at Joe.

He nodded as Summer picked up her plate and began to heap it with food, which was being kept warm on the stove.

"Did you sleep well?" Caroline asked.

"I did, and I feel all the better for it," she answered. "It's the first time I've slept soundly in the last two weeks."

Summer poured a cup of coffee, then carried the food to her customary place at the table beside Joe. "I'm glad we're all here together this mornen because there are a few things I need to get off my chest, and I think now is probably the best time for it," she said. "First, I want to thank each of you for your patience and kindness and caren. Just knowen y'all were here and willen to lend a hand or a shoulder to cry on means more to me than you will ever know. Honestly, I don't know if I could have gotten through this without your love and support, and it's wonderfully reassuren to know that you will be here this afternoon, tomorrow and all the days thereafter."

She buttered her biscuit, then asked Bonnie for the strawberry preserves. Sensing her need to purge these thoughts, everyone maintained silence while she smeared the red jam liberally over the biscuit and took a bite. "To say these last few days have been a nightmare would be putten it lightly," she continued after swallowing. "We all knew it was possible that Tom wouldn't come back alive, but I never allowed myself to truly believe anything bad could happen to him. It did though, and in those first few hours after finden out he was dead, I thought I wanted to die myself. Or maybe that the world should end. Nonsense, of course, because life doesn't work that way. We all know that, and Tom would be the first to remind us of it."

Her ravenous appetite was forgotten as Summer continued the monologue, speaking quickly with purpose. "Knowen Tom, he'd tell us that life goes on even after this—probably in those exact words. Anyway, thanks to your kindness and patience, I'm ready to jump back on the bandwagon so to speak. There'll be rough moments along the way, but there comes a time when you can't cry anymore. Don't misunderstand me. I'm not tryen to be brave or courageous. I'm still sad. Actually, sad doesn't begin to describe it. I loved Tom more than anything or anyone. I wanted to spend my life with him. To have lost that, to know I'll have a different life than the one we planned—it's not only heartbreaken, it's downright scary. But nevertheless, it's a done deal, and we have to go forward."

Summer paused, studying each face around the table. Finally, her gaze rested on Joe. "On the day we found out about Tom, Joe told me somethen that's been in the back of my mind ever since," she said, taking a deep breath to maintain her composure. "It's true that we've lost someone dear to us, but Tom left a wonderful legacy of memories. I think the way you put it, Joe, was that we've all been that much richer for haven known someone as good as Tom—and that one day, we'll be able to remember him without the sadness and the sense of loss."

Joe smiled, and Summer patted his hand, their shining eyes expressing gratitude for the solace they felt. "Well, you were one hundred percent right," she said a long moment later. She released his hand and sat back on the bench. "We are all richer for haven known Tom. He was probably the most kind-hearted person we've ever known, and I'd like to think some of his goodness rubbed off on those of us who were closest to him."

She paused once more, choosing her words carefully, wanting their full import to strike at hearts. "Long before he loved me, ever since he was a little boy, Tom loved our family," she continued. "He figured out a long time ago that we're a pretty special bunch. So, on this day when we have to attend his funeral, I hope we will go as the family Tom loved and not as one torn apart by anger and resentment because we see things differently than someone else does. After all, our differences should not affect the way we love each other."

Reaching inside her sweater, she produced Tom's letter and opened the envelope. "Yesterday, Dan, Amelia and I sorted through Tom's belongens that were in a duffel bag he used in Vietnam," she explained, taking the letter from the envelope. "This letter was inside the bag. Tom wrote it to me, but he never had a chance to mail it. I read it last night and showed it to the Carters this mornen. The preacher will read it at the funeral, but I think it's important to share with y'all. It's the things that were on Tom's mind shortly before he was killed. I believe he had somethen to say to each and every one of us."

Summer began reading the letter, starting strongly, then faltering with a choked voice when she came to the part about dreams and "the best kind of gold." Unable to continue, she handed the letter to Joe.

He was fighting a head cold, with congestion, red eyes and a sore throat, but Joe commanded everyone's attention as he finished reading the letter. When he came to the part about himself, his voice cracked. He hesitated, cleared his throat and wiped his eyes before concluding the letter.

"Well, there's the long of it," Joe read, fighting to control the emotion clutching his throat. "The short of it is that none of this business about the war, the right or wrong of it, really matters. In the end, we're stuck with it. So I'll do my time and give my best, and just maybe, with a little luck, I'll come home alive and well. But if I don't, well then, we're stuck with that, too. And in that case, say a prayer for me and maybe think of me every now and again. I'll do the same for you."

He paused, forced to wipe his nose and clear his eyes, then finished strongly, unashamed of the tears falling down his face because there was not a dry eye at the table. "It's getten late now, so I'd better turn in and catch an hour or two of shuteye before we head back into the valley. Think maybe I'll keep this letter a day or two before I mail it. Regardless, when you read it, don't make too much of it. Just take what you need from it and ignore the rest. I'm not haven premonitions of dyen. I just needed to get a few things off my chest. With all my love, Tom."

For a while, no one spoke, absorbed in their contemplation of the letter and the roles of fate, destiny and volition, which had brought them to this milestone. At the last, they focused on the memory of Tom Carter and each other, which was what they were stuck with.

"We will miss him for a long time," Joe said finally.

"True enough," Summer replied with a smile that was both somber and uplifting. "But like you said, Joe, we'll have the most important of part of Tom with us for the rest of our lives."

Joe coughed and blew his nose on a paper towel.

"You need a good rubdown with Vicks salve," Rachel suggested.

"We've got some cough syrup in the cupboard," Caroline added quickly, rising from the bench. "Let me get you a dose."

"Not now, Mama," Joe said, motioning her to sit. "There's somethen I need to get off my chest first. I'm not goen to make excuses or apologize for taken part in that demonstration. It was my decision, my business and, if I made a mistake, then I'm willen to pay for it. However, I do regret haven caused any embarrassment and hurt to the people I love. If I could, I'd do anything in the world to undo whatever harm I did. But I don't believe that any of us should have to hide the way we feel simply because we're worried how someone might perceive us. Rest assured, I do not intend to run out and join every war protest that comes along. Fact is, I probably will never take part in another one. But know also that I hope to see this war ended and ended soon. I don't ever want to sit around this table eaten breakfast on a mornen before we have to go bury John or Luke because they've been killed in Vietnam. It's not worth that kind of sacrifice—not to me."

"Not to me either," John agreed. "If I have to go, I will. But I pray I don't. It's not worth my time and especially not my life."

"I agree," Caroline remarked softly, bowing her head. "I've hated war all my life, but never more than now. Maybe I don't understand the whole truth about this war, and perhaps I should know the right and wrong about it before I make careless decisions. But one simple truth is that I don't want my sons to die over there."

She lifted her eyes, allowing her gaze to drift around the table. "My pride makes it hard for me to admit mistakes, even when I know I'm wrong," she confessed. "Never has that been truer than in the past two weeks. Pride has always been my weakness, and I've tried too often to overlook it or reason it away. But when I start letten pride come between my family and me, then I've crossed the line between right and wrong. From here on out, I'm goen to mend my ways. You'll get no more self-righteous judgments from me. Just old-fashioned honesty, even if it hurts.

"Joe, let me begin with you," she continued quickly, looking at her son. "For some reason, you have a knack for benden me out of shape. You're just too rawhided for your own good. But I don't want you to hide your feelens or ever even feel like you have to. We raised you to stand up for your beliefs, not what your father and I believe but what you believe. And if any of the rest of you is willen to put yourself on the line for somethen, then far be it for me to worry what the neighbors may think."

Turning to Matt, Caroline continued her confessional. "If someone had told me a few weeks ago that your daddy and I could be at such odds with each other, I'd have laughed in their face. Yet, here we are, hardly speaken to each other for the last two weeks, doen everything opposite of what we've done so well for almost twenty-seven years. Two weeks ago, the fault was mostly mine. I was too headstrong and stubborn to see that I was goen overboard with my ranten and raven. Since then, though, we've both done our fair share to make matters worse, which goes to show that husbands and wives have to keep worken at a marriage and should never take the important things for granted. But blame aside, I'm sorry for my hardheadedness, Matt. I know now where my loyalties lie. And I won't forget so easily the next time."

Matt smiled with forbearance. "Honey, you are headstrong and stubborn," he accused lovingly. "Unfortunately, so is your husband. And if we're all admitten to our mistakes, then I have one or two of my own to fess up, too. It's not a proud moment for a father to stand before his family and admit he abandoned them in their most pressen hour of need. But I did that. I abandoned every one of you. I can't explain it, except to say I was mad at the world. Maybe I was mad at God, too, which is a foolish way to be. Whatever, I never should have taken out my frustrations and anger over Tom's death on my family. What's done is done, though, and none of us can change what's happened. However, we still have an opportunity to salvage some good from all this—for our family and out of respect for Tom's memory. I think Summer said it best a few minutes ago: A few hours from now, when we go to his funeral, let's go as the family Tom loved, the family who leans on and supports each other through the hard times, the good times and the bad times. That may not make it any less difficult to say goodbye to Tom, but it will make liven without him a little bit easier."

———

Joe sat on the porch swing by himself, engrossed in the silent rhythm of a gentle rain and the more rambunctious grunting of the hogs across the road. The hogs were having themselves a good wallow in their mud holes. A long time ago, it seemed, he would have glanced across the road and known them by their respective names. Now, the pigs' names eluded him, though he was fairly certain the lot still contained a Yorkie, Geraldine, Sugar, Rose and Red. Good hog names never went out of style.

He shifted his gaze, closed his eyes and changed his thoughts. The old hymn, *Blessed Be the Ties That Bind,* came to mind as he recalled a touching moment with his mother a short time earlier. Caroline had come into his room, bringing cough syrup and apologizing profusely for her sometimes hostile, often indifferent behavior toward him over the past two weeks. When she was practically to the point of begging his forgiveness, Joe had hushed her.

"Mama, you don't owe me any apologies," he said. "I don't blame you for be'en angry at me, and there was never any reason for me to doubt you loved me. When it really mattered, you made candied potatoes. I knew they were for me. When you cook somethen special for someone, Mama, we all know you're talken with your heart."

Caroline had laughed, hugged her son and kissed him on the cheek. "What are you goen to do for an encore the next time you decide to get me all riled up?" she asked jokingly.

"Nothen, Mama," he vowed. "From now on, I'm gonna walk the straight and narrow."

Caroline eyed him closely. "Whatever you do, son, be your own man," she urged with sincerity. Then, she had patted his cheek and left the room.

Joe had come outside to sit on the porch, swinging and drowsing between thoughts. A deep cough roused him as the front door opened.

"May I join you?" Summer asked.

He motioned her beside him, sliding over so she could join him on the swing. She sat next to him, picking up the rhythm of the swing without a hitch.

"I've missed you most of all these last couple of weeks," she began, plunging right into the mainstream. "Everybody's been so shy about talken to me, like they thought I would fall apart if they dared to mention Tom or anything else."

"They were just concerned about you," Joe explained.

"I know," she replied. "Still, there were times when I wanted people around me, especially at night. Carrie and Bonnie have been sleepen in the boys' room ever since it happened."

"You should have asked for company," Joe suggested.

"I should have," she conceded. "As a family, we're so in tune with each other that we often take for granted that everyone else automatically knows our needs. And on those rare occasions when that doesn't happen, we're often too stubborn or maybe too blind to ask for help ourselves."

"Good point," Joe said ruefully. "I'll remember it for the future."

"Well regardless, as I said, I missed you most of all these last couple of weeks, big brother," Summer went on. "Everybody's been wonderful in their own way, Mama especially. But you have a knack for sayen the things people need to hear when they're down and out. You don't just sympathize with people; you uplift them. You're a great healer of minds and broken hearts."

Joe laughed cautiously, slightly embarrassed by the praise.

"I'm serious, Joe. I meant everything I said this mornen. That idea of us haven been touched by the goodness in Tom really has been in the back of my mind the whole way. I could have used more of that kind of thinken. It would have made what happened easier to understand and to accept."

Suddenly, she laughed bitterly. "If I hadn't been so mad at you about the protest and bringen that awful man into our house," she said, "I'd have been knocken your door down asken for some of those magic, healen words."

"I'd like to tell you about the demonstration," Joe remarked.

Summer shook off the idea. "I don't care," she said. "You had your reasons, and it doesn't matter to me anymore. Maybe someday, when we have time to kill, you can tell me. But not now. Other things are more important."

"I wish I could say the right things now to make us feel better about Tom," Joe said. "I could use some healen words myself, but the truth is, I'm fresh out of magic. I think it's just beginnen to dawn on me not only how much I'm goen to miss Tom but also the things he's goen to miss."

"That's my problem, too," Summer sighed. "I've made my peace with his death as far as what it means for me. But I can't get over what Tom has lost. He's forever stuck in time, with all these wonderful dreams never fulfilled."

Someone suddenly cleared a throat behind them, and they turned to find Sam coming around the corner. "Excuse me," he said. "I don't mean to pry, but I couldn't help overhear y'all talken."

"No harm done, Grandpa," Summer replied.

"Come out of the rain, Grandpa," Joe urged. "You'll wind up with a cold."

"Joe and I both seem to be out of perspective on this matter of Tom," Summer said.

"That's because you're young'uns," Sam explained, rounding the side of the porch. "Young'uns are never prepared for death. It ain't natural."

He climbed the porch steps, dragged the rocker near the swing and settled into it. "I understand your feelens about Tom missen out on so much in life," he said. "But y'all have to remember that Tom's no longer playen by our rules. He has a whole new set of rules, a whole new set of dreams, too."

"If we understood those rules, those dreams, maybe it would be easier to accept," Joe commented.

"Course it would," Sam replied impatiently, "but eternity is not intended to be understood by the liven. We have the promise of eternity after this life. What we make of that promise is the way we live our life on earth. Personally, I believe Tom made good on it. He's in a better place than us today, and I don't think he's worried about things beyond his control, which is exactly what y'all are tryen to do."

"God's sense again," Summer said softly.

"Indeed," Sam smiled happily. "God's sense, indeed."

"But Grandpa," Joe inquired curiously. "Don't you ever wonder what Heaven is like?"

"Sure I do," Sam answered. "A man my age would be foolish not to be a tad curious." He shrugged. "Maybe even expectant. I suspect Heaven is somethen personal for everybody."

"Not mansions and streets of gold?" Joe asked.

"If it's mansions and streets of gold you're after, then maybe that's what you'll get," Sam said. "When I think of Tom in Heaven, I picture him worken happily in some field, without a care in the world, unless it's the next row."

"Grandpa, I like your vision of Heaven better than the one I've had," Joe said at length.

"Well, I've had more time and reason to think about it than you have, son," Sam replied. "Rest assured, children. Whatever Heaven may be, it's everything we want and more, and there's no such thing as need. And, too, Tom is there."

————

Summer rode with Joe to the Carters, the two of them leaving for the mercantile about forty-five minutes prior to the one o'clock service. They were quiet on the short ride, silenced by throat-tightening nerves that had them on edge. Passing the church, they saw the doors at Benevolence already open, and mourners beginning to gather. In the cemetery, the freshly dug grave waited for Tom, covered with a green tent. Two rows of chairs were lined up beside the gleaming steel bier.

Once again, Summer felt as if she were spinning out of control. But she closed her eyes, and the moment passed with a few deep breaths.

Joe found the moment more difficult. Seeing the burial site rattled his nerves, stripping his concentration on the driving conditions. Slipping and sliding along the muddy road, the car came perilously close to running into the ditch. At the last moment, though, Joe tightened his grip on the steering wheel, navigated the car through the treacherous curve and brought them to the mercantile without further incident.

The rain had stopped momentarily, allowing a crowd of closest friends and relatives to gather outside the store while waiting for the funeral procession to get under way. Joe parked the car, then ushered Summer through the milling throng of mourners. Representing a lifetime of shared memories, these people dutifully adhered to the bereaved's wish for unspoken sympathies. They watched her closely, however, looking for cracks in the armor. But Summer was fully composed now, eager to be rid of this public period of mourning. She wanted the show on the road and over with as soon as possible.

At the mercantile, Joe halted their path and took her hands, admiring his sister's beauty and grace under pressure. Except for a slight pallor in her face, Summer was beautiful on this day. She wore a soft black dress, which highlighted her healthy complexion and firm figure. Her hair was pulled back loosely, tied into a single tress with the silk scarf Tom had sent from Hong Kong. The scarf fluttered down her back, the painted red roses dancing with every movement.

"Well, do I pass inspection?" she asked impatiently, although Joe saw the twinkle in her eyes.

"My heart tells me your beauty is beguilen on this occasion," he replied.

"Only a little, Joe," she assured him, touched by his concern. "The worst is behind me. What's yet to come may not be a bed of roses, but the worst is truly behind me."

Joe regarded her carefully, finally accepting her word. "In that case, I shall stay out here," he told her. "If you need me, though, you know I'm here."

"I know, I know," she mouthed with shining eyes. "Just please be close by when the service is over."

Joe nodded his promise and embraced his sister. Then he stepped aside and opened the door for her. Summer clasped his hand, drew a measure of strength and walked through the door.

Among those who had witnessed this heartfelt affection between Summer and Joe, the sense of reconciliation should have been complete. Yet, some people remained unwilling to forgive and forget.

When Joe turned from the door, he faced the cold glaze of suspicion and judgment. The worst of the naysayers acted as if they were appalled that he would dare to mar this somber occasion with his compromised integrity. Joe accepted their admonishment but refused to cower. Driven by conviction, not pride, he matched the callused stares, held his head high and gradually wore down all but the most hardened of hearts. When the last stern eye retreated, he waded into the club with his membership fully restored.

He was talking with a group of high school friends, including Peggy Jo Nix, when the Berriens arrived in their new Cadillac followed by his family crowded into the aging sedan and the newer pickup truck. Joe excused himself and walked over to greet the newcomers, arriving in time to hear a long story about Miss June's severe case of summer flu, which explained why she and Miss April had failed to pay their respects at an earlier date.

"I've often lamented that I never had a child," June said respectfully. "But this is one heartache I'm glad to have been spared. To have a child and then lose him. It must be maddenen."

"It's worse than that," Rachel commented bluntly. "But you get through it. With the help of your family and friends," she added quickly, more temperately since her friendship with April and June had arisen from her grief over her own son's death in World War II.

The two sisters had devoted themselves to helping Rachel cope with the loss, and her appreciation remained deep all these years later.

April and June, of course, already understood all of this and were fawning over the Baker children even before Rachel completed her thought. Joe accepted their embraces, then endured with aplomb their concern over his cold. He was grateful for friends like the Berriens, who offered fellowship without reservations and accepted others with warts and all. There was nothing pretentious about the Berrien sisters or their brother.

These thoughts occupied Joe's mind when Miss April took him by the arm, discreetly pulling him to the side. "Joe, I just wanted to tell you that I think that demonstration business was the right thing," she whispered while holding his hands. "Nothen is worse than complacency, though Lord knows I've been guilty of it most of my time. I'm an old lady, so I have a good excuse. In times of war, however, there's no excuse for complacency."

This unexpected admission doubled Joe's admiration for April Berrien, leaving him dumbfounded for a moment. Wanting to express his gratitude, he paid her the only compliment that came to mind. "Miss April," he said. "Beneath all your graciousness and gentility, I sense a very tough old broad."

April positively whooped, although she managed to cover her mouth out of respect for the moment. Nevertheless, her glee attracted the amused curiosity of those clustered nearby. She kissed Joe on the cheek, then pulled away from him with a gleam in her eyes.

"I tell you, Caroline," she remarked cagily. "If I were a few years younger—and I do mean a few—I'd snatch Joe up and marry him right out from under your nose. It's a pity he couldn't have been around all those years ago when I gave marriage a whirl, however brief it was."

Observing the bemused expressions trained on her, April took one more poke at the fettle. "June," she declared pointedly. "You and I really must find a way to eliminate those awful Misses as parts of our names. I'm divorced, you're widowed, and there hasn't been anything missy about us in several decades."

June looked haplessly at her sister. "April, I do believe you've been cooped up one minute too long taken care of me this summer," she said. "But you do have a point."

With the mood genuinely lightened for a brief moment, everyone recommenced their focus on the reason they were gathered on this early afternoon. The women-folk lumped together and slowly made their way into the mercantile, where they could tend to any last-minute emotional, spiritual or physical needs. The men stayed among themselves outside the store, talking of the weighty, the inconsequential and, on occasion, Tom Carter.

––––––

Inside the room he shared with Amelia, Dan sat on the bed. The funeral was less than thirty minutes away, but so far, he had managed only to shower and put on his boxer shorts and socks. Amelia was dressed already. In fact, Dan had never seen his wife dress more quickly or with less fuss. She had thrown on the new dress supplied by her sister, powdered her face and run a comb through her hair. Even hastily pulled together, however, Amelia was impeccable, though perhaps in need of one of those treatments that colored her hair ash blond. Years ago, her hair had been as golden as their son's. Dan tried to remember when she had taken on this new color.

A surge of emotion inexplicably overwhelmed him, and he fell back on the bed, despondent, wanting Amelia at his side, needing her strength and the comfort of her touch. Dan felt fortunate to have a wife who was his best friend as well as his lover. At times, however, he would have appreciated the close friendship of another man. He frequently loitered on the edge of such friendships, yet never found his way into the center. His insurance business and the store acquainted him with hundreds of men, but those relationships rarely strayed beyond the day-in, day-out dealings of life.

In the few months before Tom had gone away to boot camp, Dan had come as close as ever to establishing a real friendship with another man. He was grateful for those days when they had broken the last barriers between father and son to become friends, too. Dan had learned a great deal about himself and about Tom.

The effort had rewarded Dan with a newfound sense of self-worth, a gratifying realization that even bland men such as himself could leave an indelible impression on someone else. Equally important, he had discovered firsthand the kind of man his son had become, giving him pride in the job Amelia and he had done in raising Tom.

His son had trusted Dan with some very intimate revelations about love and death while explaining his reluctance to marry Summer until the Vietnam experience was behind him. Tom had been unwilling to leave behind a war widow and a fatherless child, despite an overwhelming desire to become a husband and a father, which he considered a man's greatest legacy. On their last outing together, Tom had instructed his father to halve the death benefits with Summer should he become a casualty of war.

Death benefits! What an inane label. Dan could see nothing beneficial about death, especially when it claimed a young man who was just entering the prime of life. In that moment, lying on the bed in a state of undress just minutes before his son's funeral, Dan felt the first trace of bitterness over his loss. At the very moment Tom and he had tasted the first fruits of the future, the entire banquet had been snatched from them. Dan was left with only the salty taste of tears.

Rolling onto his stomach, he wiped his eyes on the forest green chenille bedspread, leaving wet stains. Reluctantly, he sat up and reached for the white dress shirt.

As he buttoned the shirt, Dan made up his mind to take a vacation, to go somewhere exotic with Amelia as soon as they could make the arrangements, maybe as early as next week. Perhaps a vacation now would be akin to running away, but Dan didn't care. He simply wanted to get as far away as possible from everything familiar, except Amelia. Besides, he thought sarcastically, they had a death benefit to spend. Tom's government life insurance would cover the trip's cost and still leave well over half the money for Summer.

Someone knocked on the door as he pulled on his black trousers. "Come in," he said, tucking the shirt and zipping his pants.

Lieutenant Mark Applegate opened the door, then shut it as he entered the room and greeted Dan. "How are you doing, Mr. Carter?"

"Apparently, my best to be late," Dan said with resignation. "I'm usually prompt, but I don't seem to have the heart for this appointment. To tell you the truth, Lieutenant, I wish it was over and done with. Don't get me wrong. I want the service to be nice for memory's sake. I'm just ready for all this to be finished."

"It's been a long two weeks," the lieutenant apologized. "It's usually not such a drawn-out process, but the red tape got complicated."

Dan sat on the bed to put on his shoes. "Anyway, I'm sorry about be'en late," he remarked.

"Don't worry about the time, Mr. Carter," Lieutenant Applegate said. "It's no problem. We'll take ever how much time we need and do anything else to make this as painless as possible."

"Call me Dan," he urged while tying his shoes.

"And I'm Mark."

Dan finished with the shoes, then had to dig out a tie from the closet since Amelia had forgotten to lay one out with his clothes. "For some reason, Mark, I thought I'd feel differently about the funeral," he said. "Like all that pomp and circumstance would make me feel better, maybe make me prouder of Tom. But instead, I'm feelen sort of ...."

He paused, trying to find the right words.

"Anti-climactic?" Mark offered.

"Yeah, that's it," Dan agreed, dejected by the thought. "That probably sounds stupid. I mean how else would you feel. After all, a funeral is a long way from high school graduation or some such."

"It's a very natural feeling, Mr. Carter, Dan," Mark Applegate replied. "As I mentioned earlier, you've been dealing with Tom's death for two weeks now. That much time often brings a large measure of acceptance and understanding. And while I hope you take away something good from the pomp and circumstance, I empathize with your feelings about the military funeral. Your pride and love for your son are obvious. And considering those feelings, I don't see you as someone who could ever find any pride or satisfaction in Tom's death, no matter what the circumstances were. I admire you in that regard. Personally, I've never understood those people who claim to be proud of death. Certainly, you may take pride in the courage people display when they meet death. But not in the act itself."

Dan smiled. "It's good to feel understood," he said. "I won't try to explain this to you, Mark, but just your be'en here right now, willen to talk off the cuff; well, that means more to me than you'll ever know. Thanks for the patience."

"It's my pleasure. I only wish it could be under different circumstances."

"Perhaps one day, it will be," Dan responded as he straightened his tie. "I guess I'm about ready. What time is it?"

Mark glanced at his watch. "About eight minutes till."

Like Amelia, Dan had taken an instant liking to the lieutenant, whose brief interlude in their life provided a strong sense of consolation to a tragic situation. Although the time was slim, he wanted to press on with the growing camaraderie. "I believe Amelia told me your father is a minister," he recalled.

"Yes, sir. In Stillwater, Oklahoma."

"At the risk of getten too personal, are you close with him?" Dan asked.

The lieutenant shifted his position, glancing downward, obviously uncomfortable, and Dan mistook his consideration as an unwillingness to answer. "I'm sorry," he said. "I shouldn't put you on the spot like that."

"No, no, Mr. Carter," he replied without hesitation. "I'm just trying to think of how to describe the relationship. My father's a fine man, and I respect him enormously. Unfortunately, we've always run on parallel lines, never quite made an intersection. I come from a large family, smack-dab in the middle of it. When you're a minister with seven children and the Lord's flock to tend, you don't have much time on your hands. Dad's done a credible job, certainly nothing I could complain about. But to answer your question honestly, no, we are not very close."

Dan nodded understanding. "Before you came into the room, I was lyen on the bed thinken about Tom and myself. For a long time, our relationship was kind of like what you described with your father. But I'm glad to say, we made that intersection before it was too late. It meant a lot to me."

"To Tom, too, I'm sure," Mark replied.

"I think so," Dan agreed with a nod. "At a time like this, you naturally have a lot of regrets. But do you know what I regret most of all?"

The question was rhetorical, and Dan answered almost instantly. "Fishen," he said. "Tom and I never went fishen together. Heck, I don't even like to fish, but Tom sure as heck did. He was best friends with Summer's older brother, and the pair of them were crazy about fishen. They've fished together for as long as I can remember, ever since they were old enough to be trusted near the water by themselves. Even before that actually, because Summer's grandfather and father used to take them when they were little things. The Bakers live right on past the church, and they have two huge ponds on their place. Tom and Joe used to camp out, set trotlines and go paddlen around those ponds all night long. It made me nervous, but they had one heck of a time at it. One day I asked Tom what was so great about fishen, and do you know what he said? He said the fishen itself was kind of incidental. The real fun was the companionship and the straight talken."

Dan paused again, thinking wistfully of a missed opportunity. "Anyway," he shrugged. "Ever since we found out about Tom, I've wished just once I had gone fishen with my son."

Lieutenant Mark Applegate had assisted with the burials of a number of fallen warriors. Some of the families had seemed more torn up by the deaths than Dan and Amelia Carter. But Mark had never felt a stronger presence of parental love. "I understand those feelings," he said, taking a handkerchief from his pocket to wipe his face, then handing it to Dan, who was crying freely at last.

When he felt better, Dan said, "Maybe one day I'll ask Joe to take me fishen with him."

"I'm not a fisherman either, Dan," Mark responded. "But perhaps one day, I'll ask my father to do the same."

Dan stuck his hand out in friendship. "Heck, maybe one day, we'll just go ourselves," he said as they sealed this chance meeting with a handshake. "Let me rinse off my face, and we'll get on with it."

"I'll be waiting outside," Mark replied.

As the lieutenant walked out the door, both men realized they had shared something all too rare in their lives. In other circumstances, they suspected this first bond might have developed into a lasting friendship. As it was, they had composed a fitting epilogue to what might have been.

CHAPTER 10

WHILE DAN CARTER AND Mark Applegate discovered friendship inside the house, Bobby Taylor primed a wellspring of discord among those gathered outside the store. In all sincerity, Bobby felt a pang of sympathy for the Carters. While Tom Carter was nothing to shake a stick over, the boy had been their son, and Bobby figured they were hurting in an awful way. Nevertheless, whenever and wherever opportunity presented itself, Bobby felt obligated to take advantage of the situation. Indeed, since death had done more than anything to change Bobby's luck, he deemed this opportunity as a lucky sign.

As messy as it was, Martha's suicide had been a blessing in disguise. In the months since his wife had pumped a bullet through her head, Bobby had come to realize what dead weight the woman had been around his neck. Inferiority had consumed Martha like an infection, which she had passed onto Bobby. Her mere association with him had tainted Bobby with the cloying odor of failure, overpowering his sense for greatness.

Martha, however, belonged to a past that Bobby was putting behind him. Over the last few months, his reputation had soared among his fellow Klansmen, and Bobby envisioned the day when he might rule his own klavern as grand dragon. In the meantime, while he no longer toyed with the idea of trying to unseat Paul Berrien, who recently had been re-elected to a third term as sheriff, Bobby wanted to keep his fish in the frying pan. If opportunity knocked, as it often did these days, he would answer.

Bobby had laid off the booze largely, although he still enjoyed a good binge now and then. He was paying more attention to appearances as well, having knocked off twenty pounds, bought new clothes and polished his demeanor. One measure of success was the number of women he bedded. He had liked one woman well enough to move her into the house, but her housekeeping skills had paled even against Martha's low standards and Bobby had booted her out in less than a week. His proudest accomplishment was the decent profit he had turned on the ragged farm this year. Now he kept his pockets full of coins at any time. Pennies were sufficient, anything to jingle when his ego required a boost.

Currently, Bobby was engaged in an argument with the middle of his three sons. Billy was fired up over Bobby's insistence they attend Tom Carter's funeral, having the gall to suggest the Taylors were neither wanted nor needed to pay respects. When the boy finally admitted his embarrassment, Bobby put an end to his ranting.

Peering closely into the boy's face, Bobby hissed his orders. "Listen, son, either you shut up or I'm gonna shut you up for good as soon as we get home. Damn it, Billy. Sometimes you're so much like your mother that it scares the daylights out of me. Wise up, boy, and show some balls for a change."

Knowing how far he could antagonize his father, Billy hushed his protests and slunk behind the burly, imposing hulk of his older brother, Wayne. Billy was slightly built, and Bobby tended to think of him as stunted. If the boy had not been such a good basketball player, Bobby would have been hard-pressed to tolerate his wacky ways. But Billy was a wizard with the round ball, and Bobby was fond of the praises that came his way for the boy's dribbling and shooting skills. Few freshmen made the varsity team at Cookville High School, known for basketball excellence. Billy was the only one to have earned a starting position in the school's history. Heading into his sophomore season, the boy carried great expectations on his shoulders, with local sportswriters giving him a good chance to earn all-state honors, despite his slight build and lack of height.

Bobby decided there might be hope for Billy yet. He harbored no similar illusions about Wayne, who should have been a great football player in his own right but somehow missed the mark. As for Carl, the youngest of the bunch, it was too soon to tell or to care. Pleased with his fatherly inspection of the boys, Bobby returned his attention to the milling crowd, waiting for his opportunity.

Presently, his gaze fell upon Paul Berrien, Matt Baker and the latter's three sons. Bobby no longer felt obsessed with Paul or the Bakers. Still, of all the people he loathed, including communists, pantywaist politicians and limp-wristed judges, Bobby despised Paul, Matt and Joe more than anyone else. He was reserving judgment on the two youngest Baker boys, John and Luke, but he suspected none of the fruit had fallen far enough from the tree.

With age and experience, Bobby had come to understand that he would never have the upper hand in dealings with the Berriens or Bakers. He was content these days to chip away at their protective armor without trying to land a major blow. A series of small victories might inflict more damage in the long run, like the other day when he had been certain that Matt tasted the disappointment of his son.

Noticing a shift in Joe's attention, Bobby followed his gaze to the beat-up pickup truck rattling to a stop beside the highway. His own eyes lit up with anticipation as he recognized Lucas Bartholomew.

"Two birds with one stone," he said before turning to his sons. "Opportunity knocks, boys."

Returning his attention to Lucas, who was leading his wife and two children toward the mercantile, Bobby failed to notice Billy grab Carl by the arm and drag him away from their father's developing sideshow.

––––––––

Joe had broken the news about Tom to Lucas, stopping by the Bartholomew home after his blowup with Elliot Frankel. The Bartholomews were living in a snug, block house on the far side of the Berrien estate, and Lucas had come outside when he heard Joe's Volkswagen pull into the yard. Instinctively, Lucas had sensed impending tragedy, listening almost impassively to Joe's monotone recital of the sad news. Still, a sheen had come into his eyes, and a poet's passion claimed his voice when Lucas finally spoke.

"You know what was the last thing I ever talked about with Tom?" he asked rhetorically. "It was that little run-in we had at the pecan market in Albany way back when. We were discussen it when all of a sudden Tom turned real serious-like and says: 'I felt like we were the Three Musketeers that day. We didn't have much to be cavalier about. We weren't nothen but a crippled white boy with an attitude, a scared shitless colored man and a wide-eyed, white-eyed, ignorant innocent. But Lucas, I felt like we could have licked the world that day.' Tom said he was real proud to have been part of that day, to have stood with us like that."

Lucas had looked affectionately at Joe then, regret etched on his face. "Good Lord, Joe," he said. "I know it's been a long time since we were the Three Musketeers, but it shore seems like yesterday, don't it? We won't ever have another moment like that, will we?"

Unable to offer a thoughtful reply, Joe had bid Lucas farewell. They had not seen each other since—until now as the Bartholomews came toward him, dressed in their Sunday best, with Annie and Danny sandwiched hand-in-hand between Lucas and Beauty. Almost instantly, an eerie premonition pulled Joe toward them, even as the corner of his eye caught a flicker of impending trouble.

Like a bulldog in heat, Bobby Taylor burst from the crowd, trailing silently behind the Bartholomews. "Hey, nigger," he taunted quietly, his voice so low that no one heard him except Lucas and his family.

Lucas stopped abruptly, thinking perhaps his ears were playing tricks on him. But a second insult followed the first, and he deduced the situation. He stifled the urge to wrap his hands around Bobby's windpipe. Embarrassment quickly eclipsed his anger as he realized his mere presence could turn this solemn occasion into a lunatic's circus. Considering his choices, he concluded the damage was done and, after a slight hesitation, continued leading his family toward the Bakers and Paul Berrien.

"Oh, boy," Joe muttered, his disbelieving tone providing the first hint of the problem. "Daddy, Paul, I think there's fixen to be trouble," he added, taking several steps toward the Bartholomews.

At the first mention of trouble, Paul knew he had misjudged Bobby once more. He had dared to hope that Bobby would keep his bigotry on a leash this day, out of respect for the dead and the somberness of the moment. He chastised himself for the lapse in judgment.

"Damn it," he said in a rare show of temper. "For once in my life, I'd like to get through an important occasion without haven to deal with that bastard."

Paul took a deep breath to steady his nerves, then relaxed his rigid stance in order to treat this latest outrage with cool aplomb. He felt sorry for Lucas to be put in this position with his wife and children in tow. Yet, he also knew others in the crowd would agree strongly with Bobby Taylor that colored people had no business being part of a white man's funeral procession. Accordingly, if Lucas felt compelled to pay his respects in public, he should have gone early to the church and made himself as inconspicuous as possible.

Understanding his mission was to keep the peace, Paul adopted a diplomatic tone as he acknowledged Lucas and Beauty.

"Here we go again, Paul," Lucas said with genuine regret. "I should have gone straight to the church or stayed at home."

"I told you so," Beauty interjected angrily before Lucas silenced her with a harsh glance.

"The last thing I want to do is cause trouble at the funeral," Lucas explained. "I just never expected him to be here."

"I know, Lucas," Paul said. "None of us wants trouble."

Having listened to the exchange, Bobby positioned himself between Lucas and Joe. Beauty pulled her children away from their father, while the crowd of onlookers, including the honor guard assigned from Moody Air Force Base, indulged their curiosities.

"Nobody wants any trouble on today of all days," Bobby said to Paul. "Unless it's Lucas. We're here to pay our respects to one of our own, a young man who died in the service of his country. It's highly improper for this uppity nigger to intrude where he has no place be'en."

The man's mock sincerity gave Paul heartburn, which he swallowed before making his reply. "Lucas is here to pay his respects just like everybody else, Bobby," he said firmly. "You tend to your business, and let him take care of his. That's one way to make sure we don't have any trouble."

Bobby shook his head in disagreement. "This is my business, sheriff," he suggested. "It's anybody's business who don't believe it proper for niggers to stick their noses where they don't belong. It's not proper, I tell you, and I don't think Dan and Amelia will stand for it."

Perhaps it was the bewilderment in the wide-eyed gazes of Annie and Danny Bartholomew, which slowly turned to comprehension, then embarrassment. Just maybe he was destined to fight uphill battles. Or possibly, he faced a moment of truth, when values, morals and convictions are put to the test, and one's commitment must be strong and unwavering. Whatever the reasons, Joe followed his heart.

"You wouldn't know proper if it slapped you square in the face, Bobby," he said, his voice like acid. "Despite all your new window dressen, you're still walken with the same old swagger and you're still the same close-minded bigot you've always been. Not to mention just as ignorant."

He stepped closer to Bobby, leveling him with a cold gaze. "Tom and Lucas were friends," he continued forcefully. "The best kind of friends. They worked side by side, they shared lives, they cared for one another."

Joe advanced another step, almost nose to nose with Bobby, who was showing signs of discomfort. "If you knew anything at all about Tom, then you would know the color of a man's skin never mattered one hill of beans to him," Joe said emphatically. "The color of a man's heart, however, did mean a great deal to Tom. If you're truly concerned about what's proper, Bobby, then take your black heart and walk away from here with your tail tucked between your legs. Go dress up in your bed sheets and get back to your coven or your klavern or wherever it is you kluckers go to play your grown-up games. Do whatever you want, Bobby, but leave Tom's friends to their business."

For one terrifying moment, Bobby had vivid recall of the ferocity behind this anger. In Joe's cold, dark eyes, in the steel set of the man's clinched jaws, Bobby saw the controlled rage, which had been vented against him on that hot summer night just a little more than a year ago. He swallowed, almost to the point of cringing, and tried to back away on trembling knees before his enemies galloped to the rescue.

Having witnessed the browbeating and felt Joe's rage, the concern among Joe's family and friends mirrored Bobby's fearful expression. In a split second, John touched his brother's elbow, Paul stepped between Bobby and Joe, and Matt implored his son for restraint.

"He's got nothen to fear from me," Joe said frankly, taking a backward step, shrugging his shoulders. "I just thought somebody needed to get to the real point about why Bobby Taylor is here today. We all know it's got nothen to do with Tom."

Having been spared any physical harm, Bobby found a coward's courage to continue his crusade, guessing correctly he could still milk some leftover resentment toward Joe. "You're a fine one for righteous talk, Joe Baker," he said coolly. "The last we heard of you, I believe, you were be'en ordered off this place by Tom's poor parents."

Bobby paused, then asked pointedly. "By the way, Joe, what kind of demonstration do you have planned for the funeral? Any draft card burnens by chance? Or maybe a reunion of draft dodgers?"

"Here, here," a crusty voice said from the crowd.

"Maybe Lucas should stay and Joe should go," someone else suggested.

"I'll walk away this minute, if you'll come with me, Bobby," Joe said voraciously. "I'll leave even on a simple promise that you'll do nothen else to deny the respect that's due this occasion."

He glared at Bobby, waiting for an answer, which was not forthcoming. "No, I didn't think so," he said quietly for Bobby's sake. "Folks, I'll walk away in a heartbeat, because I'm not the reason you're here today," he said strongly. "And neither is Lucas nor Bobby. I'll be happy if that's what it takes to restore the peace. Just y'all please, don't allow yourselves or this occasion to be used for anything other than what it's intended."

True to his word, Joe started to walk away.

"You're not goen anywhere, son," Matt said sternly, bringing Joe to a dead stop.

A father's pride and a change of heart brought Matt to this point. On one hand, he was gratified by his son's willingness to fight his own battles. He appreciated Joe's courage. But proud as he was that Joe was willing and capable to go the distance by himself, Matt refused to stay on the sidelines. Over and over these past two weeks, he had insisted Joe had made a choice and must live with the consequences. Now Matt made a choice, too, one that had nothing to do with politics, principles or anything nebulous but was based simply on a father's love. He was more than willing to face the consequences of that.

"This should not have to be said here and now," Matt declared, moving to stand beside Joe. "As my son said earlier, it's neither the time nor the place. However, since some of you have decided for whatever reasons that you want somebody's scalp, I have this to say to you: It will not be my son's. Joe doesn't owe anybody any explanations for a blessed thing, least of all for haven beliefs and standen up for them. I fought for my country so that he could have that right—not the privilege mind you, but the right—to have those feelens and tell them to the world should he choose. My brother died for that right, and Joe himself served in the Marines for that right. And the young man we're buryen today died for the same rights. So, unless you have a quarrel with those rights, get off my boy's back. And even if you do have a quarrel, put a lid on it for this one day and act like you have some learnen."

To their credit, most of these people did not require Matt's exhortations to abide by the rules of decorum. For the most part, they were decent folk, who recognized Bobby Taylor had exploited the moment and were deeply embarrassed for everyone concerned. Still, a few remained, who sided with Bobby.

"Well, there's another long-winded speech that sounds all well and good," Bobby said with growing impatience. "But the real issue here is who the Carters want at their son's funeral. Frankly, I would have thought that settled a few days ago when they booted Joe off the place. If y'all have any question about it, why don't you ask Dan and Amelia?"

"Please do," said Dan, who had been standing behind the store door, watching with casual interest as the last few minutes of this bad melodrama unfolded. A small part of Dan wanted to vent his anger about having the farce played out only minutes before his son's funeral. But his frustration was outweighed by sullen amusement over the ludicrousness of the situation as well as general agreement with Matt and Joe. More than anything, however, Dan wanted to get the real show on road, without further fanfare.

He pushed open the door, coming down the steps in full view of everyone, taking comfort in the presence of Lieutenant Mark Applegate at his side. "It's time to stop these games," he began, determined to make no mistake about where and with whom his and Amelia's sympathies lay. "Since I myself or somethen I said seems to have been partially the cause for all this nonsense, maybe I can bring it to an end. Much has been said and done these last two weeks, some good, some bad. Despite anything you may have heard or concluded, however, Amelia and I have no bones to pick with anybody.

"I want everyone to know that my wife and I would never turn away anyone from our son's funeral," Dan continued. "If Tom meant enough to you that you feel the need to pay your respects, then we want you with us at Benevolence today. We especially want Joe there. And Lucas and his family, too. They are among the people whom Tom held in highest regards. They are some of the very best friends my boy had.

"Now, Bobby," Dan said pointedly. "If you're here to pay last respects to Tom, please join us at the church. But if you're here only to cause trouble, then leave. Because if that's the case, you're not welcome. Of all the things that were part of Tom's life, trouble and discord were not among them."

He paused for emphasis, then finished what he had to say. "Now, we're runnen a little late with the service, so let's get on with it," he said, turning to the incredulous Honor Guard members who still stood at full attention. "Boys, I think we're ready for you in there."

His peace said, Dan turned on his heels and strode back inside the store. Outside, there was some brief shuffling of feet as people digested this turn of events. By and large, they were eager to accept Dan's good advice. Bobby was willing to let it drop as well, believing he had made his points, despite the foul-up at the end. Besides, he had to spend the next few minutes figuring out how to avoid the funeral without drawing attention to his absence.

As Bobby walked away from them, Joe turned to Matt, with neither of them certain how to acknowledge this moment. They faced off first with mutual respect, then sealed the bond with a warm embrace and went their separate ways.

While Matt rejoined Paul, Joe walked away by himself to collect his thoughts. A short time later, someone tapped his shoulder. Even without looking, he knew it was Lucas. He turned slowly, again at a loss for words. Lucas was reserved, yet Joe could see the man was smiling broadly on the inside.

"You still haven't learned that it's us black folks who are supposed to have the attitude," Lucas said with feigned chagrin. "You keep this up, Joe-Joe, and you just may change the world."

Joe just shrugged.

"Oh, well," Lucas continued when no reply was forthcoming. "I've been thinken, Joe. We could still be the two musketeers."

"No, Lucas," Joe answered with certainty. "The musketeers are gone forever. They were different people than we are, I think."

"So where does that leave you and me?" Lucas inquired.

"The same as we always were," Joe said, smiling. "Just two good friends who still have each other to count on."

———

September had been dry until the last day of the month, when the weatherman apparently realized his rain total was below normal and decided to wash away the deficit in one fell swoop. A nasty drizzle began falling as the funeral procession started toward the church. Although the time was only a quarter after one, the dreary sky and failing light suggested the day was closer to an end than its midpoint. Regardless of the time, Summer believed the day would grow uglier until nightfall snuffed it out.

The thought came as she sat on the rich, burgundy leather upholstery in Melvin Lovett's Cadillac, alongside the funeral director's son, Dane, who was driving them to the service. Dan, Amelia and Mrs. Easters sat in the back, all quiet and reflective as the procession moved slowly from the mercantile. Gazing out the window, Summer decided that Amelia had made a wise decision to hold the service at one o'clock. In this wretched weather, they would have ended up burying Tom in the dark had the funeral been slated for four.

The Cadillac was the fourth vehicle in the long line of cars, some of which would be idling still near the mercantile by the time the front end of the funeral procession reached the church. A sheriff's patrol car headed the procession, followed by a military van, the black hearse and the Cadillac. Four other patrol cars blocked off the highway, forming a corridor for the procession to pass through as it departed the mercantile.

Crossing the highway, the vehicles moved slowly onto the muddy dirt road, and Summer's hands began to shake almost uncontrollably. She grasped her black clutch tightly, then dropped the single gold rose she was carrying. The rose fell onto the seat beside her, and Summer made no move to reclaim it. Instead, she pressed back against the soft seat and tried to calm her nerves.

Noticing her edginess, Dane Lovett picked up the rose, laid it across her lap and touched Summer's hand. Not surprisingly, his touch steadied Summer. Dane and she had graduated from high school together. They had even dated for about a month in their sophomore year when he had escorted her to the homecoming dance. Although Summer had broken off the romance when Dane began to have serious thoughts about her, they remained good friends. Their paths had crossed rarely since high school. Now Dane was escorting her to the most memorable occasion in her young life.

He gave her hand another gentle squeeze, then focused on his driving, leaving Summer to stare at the engagement ring on her left hand. When would she feel the desire to remove the ring? Sighing deeply, she gazed out the side window once more, staring blankly at the passing pine trees, thinking they would soon drop their cones. Would the idea of death color her every thought over the next few days and weeks? Or were these morbid thoughts simply a manifestation of the funeral's gloomy atmosphere?

Suddenly, the Cadillac lurched, sliding toward the ditch. Coming instantly alert, Summer braced herself against the dashboard to guard against the impact. For the second time this day, however, she was spared a car crash as Dane managed to halt the slide before the Cadillac slipped into the ditch. Without even a mention of the close call, they continued the silent drive to the church.

Relaxing at last, an absurd thought brought a smile to Summer's face as she tried to imagine the picture they would make trooping into the church, dripping wet with mud-caked shoes and soiled clothes.

On one important occasion before, she had graced the doors of Benevolence in soggy conditions. Years ago, one Easter Sunday when Bonnie had been only three or four, the family car had suffered a blowout on the way to church and slid into the ditch with Caroline at the wheel. With no ark handy and Caroline and Rachel determined to make the service, her mother had decided they could walk the short distance. When the rain slacked, everyone had piled out of the car and they had begun the relatively short trek, slipping and sliding with nearly every step. The three boys became bumbling clowns on the slippery hike, showing none of their endowed agility, exaggerating every pitfall along the way, responding with dewy-eyed repentance every time Caroline or Rachel admonished them. The women naturally had been mortified by the predicament, even Summer who usually adored such frivolity.

Just before they reached the church, the skies had opened once more. Running those last few steps, the bedraggled group piled underneath the covered stoop outside the front door of Benevolence. Caroline was near tears, all droopy in her new yellow dress and matching floppy hat. In fact, the entire family had been wearing new clothes, an Easter tradition, and some of the garments were never fit again for church.

At that point, Caroline and Rachel had concluded they would have to miss this Easter service. While God might not care what people wore to church, the two women had their own ideas on the subject. Unwilling to traipse back home on foot, Caroline had been on the verge of sending Joe to fetch Matt when the church door opened wide. Tom, who was making an unnecessary trip to the outhouse, simply gaped at them. Even Preacher Adam Cook had been rendered silent in the middle of *Nearer My God to Thee*. With their preacher standing openmouthed before them and rain howling through an open door on their backsides, the entire congregation turned around to investigate. The singing voices dwindled to silence, and Easter services came to a standstill. But bless their souls, no one had laughed at the family's predicament, though surely nothing in the church's history had been as funny.

"We ran into a little trouble tryen to get here this mornen, Preacher," Caroline informed him as Preacher Cook came down off the altar toward her family. "Would someone mind driven us home?"

"Nonsense," Preacher Cook declared in a booming voice. "Y'all are here and that's the important thing. Come right on in and take your seats. Otherwise, our back pew will remain empty, and I believe the good Lord wants a full church on this of all days."

To the Bakers' mortification, even among the once gleeful Joe, John and Luke, Preacher Cook led them to their usual place on the back-row pew. Meanwhile, Tom bowed his head and bolted back to his place between Dan and Amelia.

"Have you decided to stay with us after all, Tom?" the preacher asked as he returned to the altar.

Hunched between his parents, Tom turned crimson, knowing he had been caught red-handed trying to skip out on the service. He nodded his intentions to stay seated, and the service had gone on without another hitch.

Remembering the episode, Summer smiled again, recollecting Tom's remark to Joe after the service, when he thought she was out of earshot. "I felt sorry for the whole bunch of y'all, except Summer," he had said. "Frankly, she looked a sight better than normal."

"Drop dead, Tom Carter," she had replied, only to be reprimanded by her grandmother, who overheard the comment and deemed it highly inappropriate for church grounds, especially since they had been privileged to hear an uplifting sermon only minutes earlier.

Summer hoped the preacher would have an uplifting message to give everyone on this day, the thought coming to her as the procession arrived at the church.

———

For the first time since leaving the house, Amelia took notice of her surroundings, realizing she had stared at the floorboard throughout the entire journey to the church. Peculiar, how when she had vowed to commit every detail of this day to memory, she so quickly had missed the first chunk of it. She could not even recall when Dan had taken her hand, which he held tightly in his lap. She clutched his fingers and laid her head on his shoulder, aching desperately for the pain he felt, grateful to have sent Mark Applegate into their bedroom to have a private talk with her husband. Otherwise, they still might be waiting for Dan to come out the room.

Leaving the house had been difficult for everyone. When the Honor Guard had come into the living room to remove the casket, Amelia had wanted to order them from her home. Instead, she had closed her eyes, waiting until they had gone from the room before opening them. Then, they had followed the casket out the door, and someone, probably Dan, had led her to the waiting Cadillac. Amelia thought someone might have held an umbrella for them, but she could not remember with certainty.

She raised her head from Dan's shoulder as the car rolled to a stop. A throng of mourners had overrun the little country church, spilling out its doors onto the grassy lawn. Realizing the large number of people who would have to pay their respects to Tom under the slow drizzle, Amelia felt a sense of gratitude for their support, even thankfulness for the lush grass that would keep everyone out of the mud.

On either side of the car, Melvin Lovett and his son suddenly opened the car, each holding two large black umbrellas. Melvin handed one umbrella to Dan, then opened the front door for Summer while Amelia followed Dan out the car. She was vaguely aware of the people closest to her, her sister and brothers, their spouses, nieces and nephews, the Bakers and the Berriens, of car doors opening and shutting.

For a fleeting moment, she considered Lucas Bartholomew and his family, wondering whether the church had room for them. Obviously, Benevolence was already packed, but Melvin Lovett had reserved one side of the aisle for members of the funeral procession. Amelia thought of asking Dan to make sure the Bartholomews had a place in the church. But it was time to go inside, so she dismissed the idea.

At the door, after carefully climbing the steep, slick porch steps, they paused while Dan lowered the umbrella and stood it against the iron railing. Amelia was unprepared for the shocking transformation of the tiny chapel, which usually was spacious and gladsome, rarely filled to capacity, except on special occasions. Now the chapel seemed claustrophobic, with mourners jammed into every available pew on the building's left side as well as those few benches in the wings and behind the altar. Others stood, lined against the walls, while flowers filled every nook and cranny, and an American flag stood beside the altar.

The flowery fragrance permeated the church. The wreaths of carnations, chrysanthemums, mums and gladiolus, the potted begonias and ferns and the blanket of yellow roses all seemed to wave at Amelia. She reeled from dizziness, automatically glancing down, unable to bear this tribute to Tom.

"Look up and straight ahead," Melvin said suddenly, his tone formal. "It will be easier for you."

Amelia lifted her head, nodded and took a deep breath. Then, clutching tightly to Dan's arm, she walked with him to the front pew, unaware of anyone or anything else until they were seated. Amelia sat between Dan and Summer, with Essie Easters on Summer's right side and her sister, Kate, beside their mother. Feeling weak, she leaned once more against Dan for support, then, suspecting that Summer might feel shaky as well, took the girl's hand.

As she acclimated to the shock and smell of the church, Amelia became aware of the pews filling quickly behind her. The soft melody of the piano filled the chapel, and she noticed Adam Cook already seated in the pulpit. Finally, after an eternity of waiting, she heard the set-up of the portable bier and the vibrating floor boards as Melvin and Dane Lovett rolled the casket to the front of the altar, so close that Amelia could almost reach out and touch it.

When everything was in place, Tom's picture once again staring back at them from atop the flag-draped coffin, the elder Lovett gave the signal for the service to begin, and Gladys O'Steen launched the piano into the first mournful bars of the funeral dirge, *I Will Meet You in the Morning*.

The Pafford family—Riley, his wife Gloria, their daughter Marilyn, and a cousin, Patricia—performed at most of the funerals in the New River community, and this was their signature hymn. Their voices were deep and lulling, harmonizing with heavyhearted, silky precision, caressing every note with an achingly sweet melodiousness. Tears came to Amelia's blue eyes as they sang.

Through her tears, Amelia saw a vision of Tom, at the portals of Heaven, waiting for them with his smile. A sense of comfort filled her heart, a feeling she would carry with her through the remainder of this day and into the morrow.

———

Dan was slouched in his seat, hunched against Amelia as much for his sake as hers, certain he had touched the lowest point in life. He wanted the awful heartache to subside and was grateful they had asked the preacher to keep the eulogy short. In the middle of the first song, when the one thing he wanted was his son's funeral over and done with, Dan sensed a sudden surge of warmth radiating from Amelia. She laid her head on his shoulder once again, easing his sadness, almost making Dan wish time would stand still.

When the song finally ended, Adam Cook rose to deliver the eulogy, beginning with a short comforting prayer. During the prayer, Dan struggled with a nattering paradox. Tom's death was as fresh and vivid as ever, yet it belonged somewhere in the distant past, too. These contrasting ideas seemed unexplainable, so Dan put aside the thought, determined to pay attention to the sermon, hoping to glean a few words of comfort.

Adam was a model preacher, packing punch with almost every message, whether he delivered the occasional fire and brimstone, inspiration or the typical fare of daily guidance for a life with Christ. The preacher had a rare, appealing manner, a combination of poetic eloquence and homespun simplicity, passion and serenity, gravity and humor. With his style of preaching, Adam often rescued souls that seemed destined to remain lost through all eternity. Dan felt a rush of gratitude and thankfulness that the preacher's gifts had touched his son.

On occasion, more prosperous churches tried to lure Preacher Cook away from Benevolence. Congregations frequently called on him to lead revivals. Despite his popularity, the repeated opportunities to serve elsewhere, the preacher chose to remain at Benevolence and Poplar Springs. The two churches had called him to succeed his father twelve years ago. As long as his flocks wanted him to remain in the pulpit, he would minister to their needs.

Tall and thin, with hazel eyes, chiseled features and light brown hair that was in a perpetual state of slight dishevelment, Adam spoke with a rolling baritone. He was equally at home in blue jeans or the immaculate suits he wore for church services. When he wasn't preaching, counseling or tending to the needs of his flock, the minister ran a small accounting business on the side with his wife of twenty years, Catherine. Most of their work came during the tax season, although Catherine maintained the books for a few small businesses throughout the year. In addition to his pastoral duties and business, Adam was devoted to Catherine and their two children, a son and a daughter.

For someone near forty, Adam led a fulfilling life, one richly deserved as far as Dan was concerned. It was pure conjecture, but Dan believed Tom would have carved out a similarly rewarding life given the opportunity. But with no second chances available, no reason to envision a future that would never be, Dan surrendered his attention solely to the message at hand.

For his eulogy, Preacher Cook picked two faith-worthy and enduring scriptures, the twenty-third Psalm and the third chapter of Ecclesiastes. He chose the psalm because it epitomized Tom Carter, with its pastoral imagery and resounding triumph over all obstacles, even death. On too many occasions, Adam had presided over funerals where he feared for the departed souls and fretted whether he could have done more to bring God into a lost life. But not so with Tom, which is exactly what he told the mourners.

"Yes, we feel sorrow that God has taken Tom from us," he said with unembellished truthfulness and outstretched hands. "We've suffered a terrible loss. I can think of no greater grief than losen one's own flesh and blood," he continued." His gaze locked on the faces of Dan and Amelia, then tilted to Summer. "Unless, perhaps it is losen the one perfect love that is surpassed only by the love of God."

"And yet," he added, his eyes sweeping across the congregation. "As difficult as it may seem, we may also rejoice in the death of Tom." Picking up his Bible, he continued in strong tones, "Indeed, maybe we must rejoice in this loss because Tom has gone to a place of infinite goodness, a place promised to you and me. And folks ...." He paused, almost as if undecided whether to share his secret, then, smiling softly, said, "I don't believe Tom gives one iota today that we are gathered here to celebrate his life and mourn his death. Sure, as we heard in the song a few minutes ago, he'll be glad to see us when we get there. But I don't think he's goen to lose sleep waiten on us."

His tone became more serious as the eulogy continued. "I think, too," he said, "there is another message we must read into Tom's death. That message is simple, yet more important than anything else. Tom gave us an example that leads to Heaven. We should heed it and lead it, so that when our time comes, Christ will look at us and say as he already has said to Tom: 'Well done, my child. Well done."

After another slight pause, the preacher continued, weaving several anecdotes about Tom, mesmerizing his friends and family with frank reminiscing, soothing encouragement and downright heartbreaking memories, touching all with some part of Tom, death and eternity. When he had talked for fifteen minutes, Adam turned his Bible to the third chapter of Ecclesiastes, an appropriate, poignant ode to fate and God's will. Holding the Bible aloft, he read the King James language with straightforward simplicity rather than poetic license:

> "To everything there is a season, a time for every purpose under Heaven:
> "A time to be born and a time to die; a time to plant and a time to pluck
> what is planted;
> "A time to kill, and a time to heal; a time to break down and a time to build up;
> "A time to weep, and a time to laugh; a time to mourn and a time to dance;
> "A time to cast away stones, and a time to gather stones; a time to embrace,
> and a time to refrain from embracing;
> "A time to gain, and a time to lose; a time to keep and a time to throw away;
> "A time to tear, and a time to sew; and a time to keep silence and a time to
> speak;
> "A time of love, and a time to hate; a time of war, and a time of peace."

After a long pause, Preacher Cook laid the Bible on the lectern and said earnestly, "I can think of no better words of solace and comfort at a time like this. We could debate national policy over Tom's death. We could mourn a young man who had the courage and strength to make the ultimate sacrifice for his country. We could even cry because so many dreams died with Tom.

"We could do all these things and more, and probably we will ... because that's our way of copen with grief," he continued, his tone quickening. "In the final analysis, however, we are left with one indisputable fact, which is God's will be done. Some of us may question God's will today. We are only human after all, and none of us can be faulted if we fail to see any rhyme or reason in this loss of life ... to someone so young, someone standen on the threshold of a promisen future."

The preacher paused, his gaze sweeping the congregation before landing on Tom's casket. When next he spoke, his tone was full of hope and conviction. "Just maybe though, despite our questions, despite our grief, despite the sense of loss ... just maybe we can look into our hearts and find the courage in our faith to accept and understand God's will. Haven been privileged to know Tom, we certainly can understand why God would want such goodness with Him. Today, those of us gathered here at Benevolence Missionary Baptist Church are mournen with heavy hearts. But in Heaven, the angels are rejoicen.

"Personally," the preacher concluded with great respect, "I can think of no greater legacy to leave on this earth than a soul so infinite that it once touched deeply ... and will continue in memory ... touchen family and friends with purity, honesty and goodwill. And though perhaps we are still too full of grief to take comfort in what Tom brought to life, let us consider what he left to life as our good fortune ... and as a beacon to guide us along the path he already has trodden so well ... so that when the day comes and we're standen at the portals of Heaven with Tom waiten there to welcome us home, the good Lord will look lovingly upon us as he once looked upon Tom and say, 'Well done, my child. Well done.'"

The eulogy concluded, the preacher picked up his Bible and took his customary seat on the pulpit as the Pafford family began singing *Amazing Grace*.

Stirred by the power of the funeral oration and the plaintive rendition of Tom's favorite hymn, his friends and family paid one final farewell. As the song wound to its conclusion and Preacher Cook intoned one last prayer for the departed soul, everyone reflected on the short time Tom had spent among them and how much they would miss him. Many did it with teary eyes, others with a woeful fixation on the flag-draped casket and some in quiet prayer. In whatever way they chose, however, those who had known Tom best remembered him with the same honesty and homespun simplicity he had brought to their lives. As well as with bittersweet awareness that while memories are never enough, sometimes you have to make do with remembering the way things used to be and occasionally wondering what might have been.

———

As the Pafford family completed the first verse of *In the Garden*, Melvin and Dane Lovett rolled the casket down the aisle to the arched front doorway. The wheels of the portable bier squeaked across the wooden church floor, jarring Summer's thoughts from the previous night's dream in which Tom had said goodbye to her. Listening to the casket's path to the front door, Summer realized this was her first closed-casket funeral. Usually, the casket sat beside the church's front door to provide mourners one last glimpse of the deceased as they exited the building. Today, people simply would acknowledge Tom's remains. Summer favored the idea of adhering to this ritual as a means of paying one's last respects much more than having one final view of the body. For inasmuch as Tom's body had been a significant reminder of whom he was, it had nothing to do with whom he had become.

With the Paffords deep into their second reprise of the closing hymn, including a lengthy instrumental bridge between the two stanzas, Summer finally realized just how many people had crammed into the tiny church. Recognizing many of the faces, she comprehended that some of the people had come solely out of sympathy for her, and her heart fluttered with consternation. Until now, she had considered other people's sympathy for her as simply an extension of their feelings for Tom. But they grieved for her as well and considered her a victim, which was an uncomfortable notion.

At the beginning of the closing hymn's third reprise, Melvin finally gave the signal for Summer, the Carters and Mrs. Easters to leave the church, empty now except for themselves and the preacher, who came to stand beside them.

"We're almost home now," Adam reassured them.

"The service was wonderful," Amelia said, smiling through glistening eyes. "Very upliften and very truthful. It's always seemed odd to me to think of funerals in that way, but you said all the right things."

"Yes, you did," Dan agreed, shaking hands with the minister. "I feel so much better, so much more at ease. Despite everything, I'm walken away from here encouraged."

"Thank you," Preacher Cook said, hugging Dan, then Amelia, Summer and Mrs. Easters. "When you're speaken from the heart, it's easy to find the right words."

Clinging to Mrs. Easters' arm, Preacher Cook ushered her from the church. Summer took one last look around the sanctuary, observing the beautiful flowers, then followed, with the Carters and funeral home operator trailing her.

At the door, after first waiting while Tom's grandmother kissed the casket before exiting the church, Summer paused and picked up the picture of Tom. She regarded the photograph for a long moment, willing the tears to remain in her eyes as her thoughts recollected tenderly on Tom until Dan patted her on the shoulder. With a fleeting glance backward at the Carters and an understanding nod, she returned the picture frame to its resting place and allowed Lieutenant Mark Applegate to lead her down the slippery steps.

The remainder of the service passed in patches. She was vaguely aware of walking beneath an umbrella held over her by Mark Applegate as her shoe heels sank into the waterlogged ground. They walked silently through a thin stand of pine trees beside the church, coming soon to the oak-shrouded edge of the cemetery where gravediggers had prepared the final resting place for Tom. Summer noticed the gray metal vault, which would seal the casket in the tomb, as the lieutenant led her to one of the waiting chairs beneath the new green canvass tent that covered the gravesite. Shortly after she was seated, again between Amelia and Tom's grandmother, the Honor Guard arrived with the casket and set it atop the shining steel bier. Finally, with Tom's family seated in the two rows of folding chairs underneath the green canopy and dozens of friends crowding behind them as a light rain began to fall, Preacher Cook began the graveside committal service.

"Tom's parents have asked that I read a letter, which he wrote to his fiancée, Summer Baker, only a few hours before he was killed," the preacher began, removing the letter from his Bible. "Tom never had the chance to mail the letter. It was found in a bag of his personal belongens returned to Dan and Amelia a few days ago."

Summer chose not to listen to the letter this time, having already gleaned all that she needed from Tom's last words. Whatever message it might hold for everyone else was beyond her control, so she allowed her thoughts to dwell on Tom and the future. After Adam Cook had read the letter, he led the mourners in a recitation of The Lord's Prayer. Summer mouthed an occasional word or two of the prayer, but her mind was preoccupied elsewhere until the preacher at last turned over the service to the military Honor Guard.

As the military service unfolded with unique precision, grace and style, her spirits all at once plummeted to the deepest abyss, then soared above the highest reaches. A lump formed in her throat as two soldiers removed the flag from Tom's casket, folded it meticulously and handed it to Mark Applegate. The lieutenant accepted the Stars and Stripes, saluted the Honor Guard captain and turned respectfully to present the flag to Summer. For a moment, she stared long and hard at the flag, then at the man who offered it before finally accepting the token of appreciation for a job well done by Tom for his country. Despite all the grief, all the regrets the flag represented, she felt a twinge of pride, wounded though it was.

Summer took the flag carefully, with a nod and a tight-lipped smile at Mark Applegate, who offered a few final words of condolence, smiled sympathetically and moved on to console Tom's parents. She caressed invisible wrinkles for a moment, running her hands over the material, then turned to Amelia and surrendered the prize to its rightful owner, this woman who had carried herself with dignity and grace throughout the ordeal, this friend who would have been a very special mother-in-law.

The two women smiled warmly at each other, then hugged. When they were steady and consoled, Summer and Amelia released the embrace and watched the service wind its way to conclusion.

Walking crisply across the soggy ground, the Honor Guard captain lined his troops in formation and barked commands for the three-volley salute. The set of seven rifles fired three times into the failing light. As the guns fell silent, the lament of *Taps* played from a lone bugler, piercing the countryside, its lonely refrain echoing a final farewell against the soft patter of rain.

And it was over, except for a few more words of condolence from the minister, Tom's relatives and her own family, from close friends, neighbors and a few strangers. Summer sat through these expressions of heartfelt sympathy with the necessary amounts of patience and politeness as well as gratitude.

At last, when her legs felt steady and the crowd was thinning, she rose from the chair and placed upon the coffin the rose she had carried through the service. Almost without thinking, she allowed her hand to linger a moment on the cold gray box, with thoughts of her beloved swirling in her heart. Quickly, she removed her hand, then turned to bid the Carters goodbye for the day, satisfying their offer to join family and friends for an early supper back at the mercantile with a simple, "No, thank you, I'm tired right now. I'll see y'all tomorrow."

"Of course, you are," Dan agreed, giving her a quick hug. "We're all worn out."

"Go home and rest, honey," Amelia chimed in, taking Summer by the hand. "After everybody leaves tonight, we're gonna unhook the phones, turn off the lights and sleep like babies—maybe until this time tomorrow."

And that was that, which was a good thing about true friendship. Leaving the protective canopy, Summer walked into the cool rain, with fog creeping into the mid-afternoon and Joe coming to take her home. After a few steps, she turned for one last look, and everything seemed as dreary as expected. Still, she smiled half-heartedly and threw up a quick wave at the Carters before turning back to Joe.

Eager for the warmth of home, she marched onward to begin, if not exactly the life of a widow, then something akin to it. A life anyway that beckoned with the promise of a future that would turn bright once again, as surely as it would be forever shadowed by a blue-eyed boy with golden hair and the shyest smile she would ever know.

THE DREAM

1969-1970

CHAPTER 1

THE SUPREME COURT ORDERED desegregation of public schools in 1954, and fifteen years later, the U.S. Department of Justice finally got around to making the Cookville school system and a host of others in South Georgia comply with the mandate. In Cookville, the usual suspects lined up on either side of the issue, pitting a vocal minority and silent majority of those opposed to integration against the few who thought the time had come for blacks and whites to attend the same schools.

For as long as anyone could remember, the county had supported five elementary schools, a white high school and a separate school for blacks. Based on population alone, a single high school and one elementary school could have accommodated the small number of students in the county. But the elementary schools scattered throughout the county provided more than an education. These schools were the backbone of their community identities, providing a framework for socializing and fellowship as well as the revered pride that came from pulling together for a common effort. For many, the idea of integration at these sacred institutions was a fate deemed only slightly preferable to Hell itself, and certainly the beginning of a path leading to wickedness.

To have labeled integration as merely volatile would have misrepresented the issue, for the feelings it provoked were not nearly so stable. By May of 1969, it had become apparent that Cookville would stand on the frontline of the state's school desegregation battle.

Joe was mulling over all this as he waited for the monthly meeting of the school board to begin. He had been immersed in the integration issue ever since the middle of March when he graduated from Valdosta State College with a degree in English and was hired as a full-time reporter for the *Valdosta Daily Times*. For the princely salary of seventy-five dollars a week, Joe devoted his life to educational issues and the efforts to integrate public schools.

Cookville was by no means a lone gun of opposition, but it was smoking. School desegregation was occurring in counties across South Georgia, and Joe was covering it with diligence and style. Over the last two months, he had crisscrossed at least a hundred roads in pursuit of stories, writing about the good, the bad and the ugly without discrimination. He found an inordinate amount of satisfaction, plunging headlong into other people's passions and trepidations as an impartial observer, spellbound by the moment, yet able to walk away when the story was done. He also allowed himself a measure of vanity over the acknowledgment of a job well done.

After all those years of dreaming about the future, it had arrived. And, if the *Valdosta Daily Times* had never figured in his dreams, Joe reconciled its existence with understanding that he had to start somewhere and belief that his ability would carry him elsewhere in due time. Already, ability had earned him a promotion and a pay raise that would increase his salary by ten dollars a week at the beginning of June. The promotion had been to full-time reporter from part-time correspondent, a position Joe had held during his last five months of college.

His introduction to the Valdosta newspaper had been a baptism by fire, occurring a few weeks after Tom Carter had been buried. On the day Joe had approached the editor about a job, both of the newspaper's full-time reporters were at home nursing hangovers. With a major story breaking about a dead mother who had been hacked to death allegedly by her husband, the editor had acknowledged Joe's Marine correspondent credentials and offered him an opportunity. Two hours later, Joe had handed the editor a finished story, complete with a jailhouse interview with the suspect. He had been offered a full-time job on the spot, turning it down to finish college. Instead, he had begun working part-time as a correspondent for three-cents a word, with a stern warning not to pad his stories with unnecessary language just to earn a few extra dollars.

"At three cents a word, sir," Joe had replied dryly, "I don't see how anything I write will make or break either one of us."

Considering the newspaper's stinginess, Joe felt enormous satisfaction in securing a pay raise after just two months on the job. Now, however, he pushed aside these thoughts, took out his notepad and pen and turned his attention to the business at hand.

Faced with the loss of state funding unless it complied with the desegregation order, the county school board convened the May meeting to consider ways to skirt the law and keep black and white students in separate schools. In quick order, however, the five board members realized there was no alternative short of integration. So, with a pragmatic approach to a complicated problem, they unceremoniously gave tentative approval to an ordinance integrating the county's elementary schools and high school. The colored school was turned into a junior high school, with an eye toward easing crowded conditions at the town's elementary school, and the idea of busing students to achieve a racial balance in the schools was rejected.

"Damn it, we've done what we're supposed to do," board member George Mackey said when it was suggested federal officials might view the setup as selected segregation since the majority of black students would be enrolled in just two of the elementary schools, with the others having none or perhaps one or two token colored pupils walking their halls. "Every school in this county will be open to any student, regardless of his color. That's what the feds want, and that's what they'll get. But we got no business tellen people where to send their kids to school."

An added incentive to proceed with integration, duly noted by board member A.W. Hancock, was the addition of the Negro basketball players to the Cookville High School boys' basketball team, which a few months earlier had come within a game of winning the state championship. "There may be somethen good to come out of this integration business after all," Hancock told his fellow board members. "With a few of those Negroes and our good white boys playen on the same court, we're a shoo-in for a state championship next year."

Joe quoted both men in his story for the newspaper.

———

On the day after Joe's account of the meeting appeared in the newspaper, an angry mob assembled outside Superintendent Jake Perry's office to voice their disapproval of the school board's decision. Joe had figured as much and was there to monitor the confrontation for the newspaper. Jake, however, had other plans. He refused to discuss the matter with the dozens of parents and taxpayers. Serving the first year of his fifth four-year term, the sixty-seven-year-old superintendent never intended to face voters again and cared even less about the quarrel with integration.

"There's nothen I can do about it," he told the group, throwing up his hands in despair as Joe snapped a picture for the newspaper. "Bring it up at the next board meeten."

Then, Jake Perry went fishing.

His outraged constituents, however, were not put off by the superintendent's disregard of their objections. They gathered outside the red brick courthouse, organizing opposition to the integration plan and appointing Bobby Taylor to lead the effort.

Almost without realizing it, Joe found himself face-to-face with his family's longtime antagonist, forced to interview him about the group's plans. Bobby reveled in the publicity, posing for a picture and responding to every question with rambling answers that often evaded the real issues, all the while poking fun at Joe's predicament.

"This bites your ass, don't it?" he chided after Joe had snapped the photograph and asked his last question.

"Every job has its pitfalls," Joe answered flatly. "Or in this case, I should say pratfalls. Do you know the difference, Bobby?"

Bobby ignored the insult, knowing the circumstances gave him the upper hand. "You be fair now," he lectured in patronizing tones. "You know how partial I am to fairness for all parties concerned, Joe, and it's a newspaper's responsibility to be fair so that the readers get the whole truth."

"I doubt you'd recognize fairness if it slapped you in the face," Joe countered. "But I'll do my job the way I'm supposed to. No need for you to worry about that."

"Good boy," Bobby goaded him, with a wide grin that Joe wanted to smack off his face. Instead, he turned away, trudged to Cookville's lone pay telephone and dictated a story to meet the paper's morning deadline.

In the weeks that followed, Joe spent more time talking with Bobby than he wanted or needed to. Day and night, at work and at home, Bobby bombarded him with every development in his group's effort to keep the schools segregated. Joe found himself walking a thin line between reporting news and being used as a mouthpiece. There were angry school board meetings, a Fourth of July demonstration and even a lawsuit, which was given credence because it had been filed by the county's district attorney, Stan Avera Jr., the son of Judge Wilson Avera. Given the Averas' reputation as legal experts, the school board postponed final approval of the integration plan pending further review of the situation.

The delay flabbergasted Joe, especially because the school board placed so much emphasis on the opinions of a judge and district attorney who had a long history of prejudice against blacks. His dismay over the situation led to his first piece of investigative journalism. He spent three weeks examining the judge's sentencing record and his son's prosecuting record. When he had researched the piece thoroughly and offered the Averas an opportunity to defend their records, Joe wrote a blistering series of articles showing how blacks received harsher treatment than whites whenever the Averas presided over the cases. In the process, he earned two enemies.

Beauty Bartholomew sang with a poet's spirit. Hymns were her favorites, especially *Amazing Grace*, which she crooned with soulful inflection on at least one Sunday every month in church. Music made Beauty soar. To a place where she could believe the words uttered long ago by her mother on the day Beauty had asked why she had been cursed with such an awful name as Beauty Salon.

"Because child," her mother had explained patiently. "When you were born, you were the world's loveliest creation since Eve, and you already had been blessed with Goodness. Beauty was the only name fitten for one as fair as you, baby." Then her mother had laughed, with a twinkle in her eyes, and added, "Besides, your last name was Salon, and I just couldn't resist the temptation. It was meant to be, Beauty, by God Himself."

Beauty had been dubious about her mother's intentions, then and now, even all these years after cigarettes and booze had wasted the beautiful Goodness Salon to a thin waif of a woman, who had died way too young.

From an early age, Beauty had figured out she would never be beautiful. She wasn't even close to pretty. But she was virtuous, and Beauty could sing, with a voice that was powerful, husky and silky, a mixture of Billie Holiday, Martha Reeves and Goodness Salon herself. Beauty loved her church, she cherished music and, from time to time, she thanked God and the spirit of the long-departed Goodness for giving her a wonderful voice.

Beauty figured her voice was one of the reasons for the happiness ruling her life ever since Lucas Bartholomew had come into it. They had been married for nearly nine years now, a period so wonderful that Beauty sometimes pinched herself to make sure she wasn't dreaming. When it really hurt, when she was certain the pain was no fantasy, Beauty would burst into song, serenading life with every ounce of passion in her soul. Sometimes her serenade was a hymn or an old Negro spiritual; other times it was a pop song she memorized off the radio. Usually though, regardless of the song she sang, when Beauty serenaded life, her loins warmed for Lucas and she appealed to him for satisfaction later in the night.

It was not that Lucas needed wooing in bed. He had an insatiable appetite for lovemaking, and they coupled so frequently that Beauty reasoned it was only an act of God preventing them from having more than two children. A blessed act at that, she remembered often in her prayers. Beauty adored Annie and Danny, but she wanted no more children. Her two pregnancies had been exhausting nightmares, with months of nausea leading to excruciating labors. So set was her mind on this matter that if Beauty had her way, she'd pick cotton every day for nine months rather than bring another child into the world.

Considering this fear about the possibility of having another baby was just about her major worry, Beauty rarely took for granted how lucky and blessed life had been for herself and Lucas. Although the Bartholomews were poor as sin itself, always scrambling for that elusive dollar, Beauty figured poor people never had it as good as her family did. Especially poor colored people. Her family had abundant food on the table, decent clothes on their backs, a snug roof over their heads and an honest way to make a living. As far as Beauty was concerned, a person shouldn't ask for anything else. And yet, Lucas wanted more.

Granted, Lucas wanted more for the children, not for himself or Beauty. He wanted Annie and Danny to have an education.

"Not just any education, Beauty," he told her repeatedly. "A good education. The kind of education white people get in their schools, so Annie and Danny can make somethen of their lives. My children—our children, Beauty—will be more than a sharecropper and the wife of a sharecropper."

Still, despite his good intentions, Beauty could not shake the nagging worry that perhaps Lucas wanted too much. Her concern was especially strong as she sat beside her husband on the home-side bleachers of the Cookville High School gymnasium.

On this balmy August night, the gym was packed to the rafters with parents, black and white alike, and property owners, almost exclusively white, who had a vested interest in the school board's final decision on integration. The air was thick with anger and hope, the tension audible as those opposing forces set out on a collision course. There was disgruntlement and fear, regardless of which corner you stood in or what side you sat on.

Beauty felt out of place in this charged sea of bodies. She would have preferred to be inside her home, amusing Lucas and the children with some silly story or a lulling melody. Sometimes, and this was one, Beauty had an overwhelming urge to wish for the end of time, so that her family would exist forever in this pleasant moment. Deep inside her, there was fear that too many good things had happened to her family, leaving the Bartholomews with a mounting debt that would require the rest of their days to pay back.

"Well, the good Lord giveth, and the good Lord taketh," she told herself softly, trying to ease the worry.

"What?" Lucas asked suddenly from her side.

"Nothen," she replied, shaking her head. Fortunately, Lucas was too engrossed in the impending meeting to question her further and Beauty was left once again alone to her silence.

When the scriptures failed to bring comfort, Beauty fortified herself with a duty-bound sense to support her husband and his mission. There was something different about Lucas these days, a sense of purpose that prevented him from accepting the way it was and had been for so many years. In the demand for integrated schools, Lucas had found a battle worthy of the fighting. Even then, he had stumbled into the fray, taking up the cause only when the government had instigated it.

Once Lucas had become aware of the possibility of integrated schools, however, he had latched onto the idea with fevered devotion. He had studied the proposal thoroughly, pleaded with school board members to follow through on the state's recommendations and stirred up enthusiasm for integrated schools among Cookville's colored community. In the process, he had become recognized as someone who spoke up on behalf of those colored people who were scared to buck the system themselves or lacked the understanding to grasp the significance of what was happening. And, too, he had been dubbed an "agitator," the curse considered by many Southerners—no matter their views on segregation—only slightly more redeemable than the most wretched label of all, which was "outside agitator." Regardless of his reputation, any respect or animosity Lucas now commanded was due solely to his deep desire to see Annie and Danny rise above the limits society had set for them.

Though the complexities of integrated schools eluded Beauty, this much she knew: Her husband was motivated by purely selfish reasons, not some smugly compelling crusade for social change.

Once, Beauty had suspected Lucas just might give up his fight in exchange for assurances that Annie and Danny alone could attend the white schools. Her strong suspicion had even caused Beauty to voice the idea during one of her husband's many after-supper discourses on why their children must attend New River Elementary School rather than the Negro school in Cookville.

Lucas had considered the possibility with such fierce concentration that Beauty feared she might have riled him past the breaking point. Then finally, he had sighed, telling her, "I can't say I wouldn't be tempted, Beauty, but I'm no Judas. Annie and Danny are my reasons for doen most everything I do these days—I won't lie to you about that. But this business with the schools is more important than just two children, even if those two children are mine." He paused, then grinned. "Still though, I'm glad we don't have to worry about me sellen my soul just to get two colored children into a white children's school."

Then he had launched into another favorite discussion, this one an endless vision of the future in store for Annie and Danny. As seen by Lucas, the future contained the certainty of high school diplomas and even college, that sacred institution of higher education for which they scrimped and saved every extra penny. It was a grand vision, a bit high and mighty but one so glorious that Beauty wondered if it could come true, even as she dared to hope for it. For Beauty did hope that Annie and Danny would scale great heights one day, though perhaps more for her husband's sake than the children's.

Above all, Beauty wanted her children to be God-fearing, unafraid of hard work and respectful of their father's wishes. And yet, as contented with life as she was, Beauty sympathized with her husband's ache for something better for their children. On occasion, she even wished there was more of herself to give Annie and Danny. So far, it seemed her biggest contribution had been genetic, for both of them resembled Beauty with alarming similarity, frightfully thin with pointed faces and a glow like cordovan shoe polish. She hoped they might inherit her voice, prayed they would overcome her dull contribution to their smarts and marveled at their beaming dispositions.

Neither Beauty nor Lucas was overt in their relationships with others, tending to withdraw from crowds and shy away from strangers. Annie and Danny were complete opposites from their parents, embracing anyone and everyone with good-natured curiosity and unbridled enthusiasm. Beauty hoped this outgoing behavior would serve them well, especially if they wound up strangers in the middle of so many white children. Yet, there was this fear again, another one of those nagging suspicions, that Annie and Danny should use caution in their dealings with the world—certainly when their business carried them into the white man's world.

As she sat beside Lucas on the bleachers, waiting for his dream to come true, this worry was stronger than ever, troubling her mind with frightening possibilities. Beauty could not shake the notion that Annie and Danny belonged in the Negro school in Cookville rather than the New River school where they would be surrounded by a sea of white strangers, some of them unfriendly. She wanted her babies sheltered from the anger and resentment, not thrust into the midst of it to fend for themselves. Surely, Lucas saw the dangers in his dream and realized the disadvantages could swallow up the advantages. Much more seemed at stake than education and dreams and, for a trembling moment, Beauty feared she was sitting helplessly by as her children were led to the slaughter.

Right then and there, she wanted to tell Lucas to walk away from his dreams and leave things the way they were. But as Lucas had told her, this school business was bigger than two colored children, even if those young'uns were her own flesh and blood. Beauty felt trapped betwixt these two notions of right and wrong. Then finally, as she struggled to escape the steely clutches of her fear, someone gaveled the meeting to order, and the moment was gone.

———

Convened at precisely seven o'clock by Superintendent Jake Perry, the school board meeting began routinely, with a short prayer and quick approval of the minutes from the previous meeting. Those first orders of business took about three minutes, and they were the meeting's lone moments of peace. As soon as Jake issued the request for old business, a chorus of protests clamored for attention, with a hundred voices demanding to be heard.

Jake allowed them to yell awhile, until the noise dimmed by its own accord, in a state of bafflement over his continued silence. "One more outburst like that," he said finally when the gym was silent, "and I'll adjourn this meeten and send you folks home."

"You can't do that," someone yelled from the home stands. "It's illegal."

"Buster, I'm chairman of this here body, and I'll do damn well what I please," Jake said gruffly. "You can like it or lump it, but you best remember it if you want us to take care of business tonight. Do I make myself clear?"

For the moment, no one was willing to challenge his authority, so Jake proceeded. "Now then, I know there is a lot of sentiment on both sides of the issue before us tonight, but we have to be orderly about our business. Everyone will have a chance to speak their mind, but essentially, given where you stand on the issues, everyone will say the same thing. If all of you decide to give your two cents worth tonight, we'll have to count on liven as long as Methuselah to hear what y'all have to say. Taken that into consideration, I've appointed two speakers who represent both sides of the integration issue to speak first. If, when they're finished, you believe there's more to be said, then we'll hear from you. But please folks, don't get up here and talk just for the sake of be'en heard."

Once again, everyone seemed in agreement with the proposal, which pleased the aging superintendent. "This might work out easier than we thought," he muttered underneath his breath to the board member on his right.

"First up," he continued aloud, "is Bobby Taylor, who is leading the fight against integration. The floor's all yours," he added, nodding to Bobby.

With a swagger in his step and cheers of support ringing from the rafters, Bobby strolled across the varnished floor to the podium and microphone set up beneath one of the basketball goals. He waited for complete silence before speaking. "I'm here tonight out of concern for preservation of the old ways—the very principles that have served our way of life ably and honorably for so many, many years," he began with rapt sincerity.

From his position on the visiting side of the bleachers, Joe quit taking notes almost as soon as Bobby started talking. He knew this speech by heart, and he put little stock in Bobby's concern for the old ways, which nearly always manifested as the worst of Southern traditions.

As much as he despised Bobby, Joe was stupefied by the man's uncanny ability to rescue his reputation from borderline lunacy. After all the years of trying to win over the mainstream, Bobby had stumbled into acceptance and prosperity through the fringe element of society. For whatever worth, he had staked out a position in life, and he was thriving on it. In some warped way, as if simply by virtue of knowing where he stood with himself, Bobby had brought out the best qualities in himself, gained control over his destiny and won newfound respect.

The transformation disturbed Joe, who believed Bobby's success was some kind of mutated metamorphosis at best. But he could not argue with the results. Even though Bobby would lose this fight over integration, even though he lost most of the battles he waged, he would walk away from the struggle with the smug mien of a victorious warrior. Chalk one up for the bad guys, Joe figured. If there had been some tiny bit of moral justification for Bobby's ability to snatch victory from the jaws of defeat, then Joe would have found a degree of understanding in this appeal of self-righteous behavior. Instead, Joe found the man so patently deceitful that he defied logic. So he stopped trying to figure out Bobby and concentrated on the man's plea to keep segregation alive and well in the county.

"You people know me, so I won't try to pretend I'm somethen else or that I've changed my way of thinken," Bobby said, nearing the end of a ten-minute ramble over the importance of tradition, the evil of integration and the tyranny of the school board for trying to foist integration on unsuspecting parents and students. "I do not believe Negro and white students belong in the same schools. The risks are too great for our society. And while I don't know a whole lot about education, I do know that my tax dollars and your tax dollars pay for our schools and the education of our children. As taxpayers, if nothing else, we have a right to say how that money should be used, to say whether we want our children exposed to the wrong element. If we lose such a basic right, then what will we lose next? And who will take it from us?"

Bobby paused, allowing audience consideration of his questions, then concluded his statement with a pointed finger at the five school board members. "On many occasions over the last few years, my views have been on the losen side of issues important to this county," he said. "Well, that's water under the bridge as far as I'm concerned, and I respect those decisions despite my disagreement with them. This time, however, it's obvious that I represent the majority of the good people in our county. And even though you've already shown your disagreement with our position on integration, I hope you five elected leaders will reconsider your decision and show enough respect for the people who elected you—the taxpayers—to abide by the will of the people."

His speech concluded, Bobby tipped his head to the school board and walked away from the podium to deafening applause. He claimed his seat, savoring the ovation with a small smile until the clapping ended.

"Thank you, Bobby," Superintendent Perry said courteously. "I'm sure the board will give careful consideration to what you said." He cleared his throat in the microphone before introducing the next speaker. "Now to speak on behalf of those who support integrated schools is Lucas Bartholomew. Lucas is the father of two children, both of whom will be in school this fall. He lives in the New River community."

There was a gasp from the audience. No one had expected a colored man as the top choice to rally public opinion for such a touchy idea as school integration. The county was an enclave for white citizens, with blacks accounting for barely ten percent of the total population. Nearly everyone felt the undecided people would have been more easily persuaded to accept integrated schools by one of the respected white citizens who favored desegregation. Jake Perry understood this as well, but he also knew the school board had already made up its mind on the issue and would not alter its position. He deliberately had picked Lucas to make the case for integration, hoping the black man would make a compelling argument for an end to segregation and, in the process, sway a few white minds to the inequities of the current system of so-called separate but equal schools.

To most everyone's surprise, no one jeered Lucas as he took his place behind the microphone. His nervousness and lack of confidence were obvious, but he stammered into his statement, propelled by an inner courage derived from the necessity of the moment and the conviction that it was time to take the fight into his own hands.

"A few years ago," he began in quavering voice, "a great man gave a great speech in Washington, D.C. He talked about a dream. Well, I have a dream, too. It's not nearly as grand as Martin Luther King's dream, but it's just as important to me because you see, it's for my children."

With those first words uttered, confidence washed over Lucas. His voice steadied, and he spoke from the heart. "Some years ago," he continued, "I went to the black school here in Cookville. I learned to read, to write, to do arithmetic. I appreciated the opportunity, I appreciated the teachers. They did the best they could with what they had to work with; it wasn't much. There were not enough books to go around in class, much less to take home in case you needed or wanted to do extra readen or studyen. There were few supplies. Even chalk was scarce at times. But I was grateful anyway, because I knew I was accomplishen somethen important. I can read, which is somethen my daddy and mama could not do. And I can sign my name when there's a need for it. When my daddy had to sign a paper, he made a mark on it because that's all he ever learned. My daddy was proud that I could read and write and sign my own name. And I will always be grateful for having the chance to learn what I learned at the colored school in Cookville.

"I quit school when I was fifteen. Didn't want to, but had to. I don't feel sorry for myself about that, not one bit. There are a lot of people who were in the same boat as me, both white and colored. But when I quit school, I promised myself that any children I ever had would get the education I never got. I figured it was the least I could do for them, especially since my own mama and daddy did everything they could to see to it that I got the education I got.

"That's my dream, folks—that my two children can earn high school diplomas. Maybe even go to college. For that dream to come true, for my children to get the very best education this county has to offer, they need to go to the same schools that this county's white children go to. They need the best books and teachers this county has to offer. And you folks know as well as I do, they can't get that at the colored school in Cookville. They never could, and they never will be able to."

Lucas hesitated, searching the crowd for signs of acceptance. "I hope you can understand me wanten somethen better for my children than what I had," he continued. "I hope my dream gives us somethen in common. That's the main reason

I'm here tonight. I'm not a troublemaker. I don't like arguments and disagreements. But, it's my responsibility to make sure my children get the same opportunity your children have.

"Nobody should be cheated out of an education," he said almost wistfully. "Nobody should be denied the opportunity to make somethen of themselves—specially not if they got the gumption and the smarts for it. All I'm sayen is that everybody ought to have the same chance, the same opportunity to learn. Give my children that chance, and you'll not hear another complaint from me. What they make of that chance will be up to them, but the colored children in this county need the same opportunities as everyone else. I hope y'all agree with me."

An enthusiastic round of applause followed Lucas to his seat. The noise was not deafening as the cheers for Bobby had been, but it drowned out the few jeers aimed at Lucas. When he sat on the bleachers beside Beauty, Lucas felt a rush of exhilaration, brought on by the knowledge that he had spoken up for himself and the expectation of the vote to follow. There was a hand on his shoulder, and Lucas turned to find Matt smiling respectfully at him.

"Well done," said Matt, who had come to the meeting at Lucas' request. "No one could have said it better."

Beside Lucas, Beauty tugged at his arm. "You made me believe, too," she whispered proudly. "One way or another, it'll all work out for the best."

He nodded at her, then turned his attention to the floor.

"We've heard from both sides of the argument," Superintendent Perry said. "Does anybody have anything else to add?"

To everyone's astonishment, no one volunteered to make additional statements. Jake looked around in disbelief.

"Are y'all sure?" he bellowed. "Because it's speak now or forever hold your peace."

He waited and still no one volunteered. "Well, men," he said at length. "Let's put it to a vote then. The question before us is this: Will the county school system be desegregated in the manner determined by the board in May? All in favor of the plan, let it be known by saying I."

A chorus of ayes sounded in unanimous agreement.

"Any opposed?" Jake asked. "None; the motion passes. Let's move on to other business."

————

A hush fell over the gymnasium as everyone digested the sudden turn of events. In swift manner, segregation had been relegated to the history books, and integration was coming to Cookville. Then, the stands erupted in ear-splitting disbelief, a mixture of cheers and outrage. Small groups hugged and clapped each other on the shoulder. Many voices groaned their disapproval, and some hurled threats at the school board members. A semblance of decorum was restored only when Bobby Taylor leapt from the benches, his arms spread open in dismay, his loud tone rising above the cacophony to demand redress.

"What the hell was that all about, Jake?" Bobby howled at the superintendent. "It appears to me you men came to this meeten with your minds already made up on the matter."

"Our opinion on the subject wasn't any big secret, Bobby—to you or anyone else," Jake Perry replied firmly. "Tonight's meeten simply gave us the opportunity to ratify what we had already done back in May. In this particular case, how any of us feels about integration has nothen to do with our decision. Our job is to educate the children of this county, and integration is necessary if we are goen to do our job. We have no other choice. The state has a gun pointed at our head."

"Well point it back at them," Bobby snarled.

"It's not that simple, Bobby," Jake sighed. "If we don't integrate the schools, we lose the state money that pays the salaries of our teachers among other things. That means there's no school."

Bobby looked skyward for a moment, searching the ceiling for an appropriate answer as a murmur of discontent rippled through the gym. "Well then," he said finally, "if we have to open the schools, let's open them. But let's have a student strike to show we mean business and will run the schools the way we believe they oughtta be run."

The proposal quickly took hold, drawing a zealous round of approval from one half of the bleachers. "We'll have a protest of our own," Bobby suggested, seizing on the moment of discord. "Keep the children out of school until the state and feds wise up and understand we will not allow whites and niggers to go to the same schools. That'll teach those busybodies to mind their own business."

Jake rubbed his chin thoughtfully, almost as if he were considering the proposal raging around him. Actually, he was reminding himself that this brouhaha likely was the last crisis he would face in his long and undistinguished career as the county's school superintendent. He was torn between two ideas, neither of which had anything to do with school desegregation. Integration was inevitable. Jake had known that much since 1954, even before then. He was more amazed the county had staved off the unavoidable for so many years. In his private thoughts, Jake doubted whether integration would prove successful. It was a noble idea, but, in the long run, he suspected integration would hurt more people than it helped, while creating a new set of complex problems.

Perhaps somewhere in the back of his mind, Jake took note of his opinions about integration as he stroked his chin in thoughtful contemplation. Mostly, however, he tried to decide whether he wanted his career remembered as unsung or storied. He could weather this crisis with weary indifference, his calling card for more years than he cared to remember. Or he could confront it with boldness.

The foolhardy approach won out, victorious because of that egotistical need for recognition endemic in people of importance or fame, even those for whom fame is a small-time proposition at best.

"No, Bobby," Jake declared sternly. "No strikes. Classes will start on the day they're supposed to. And if you have a child under age sixteen, you'd better see to it that he or she's there or face the consequences." His tone softened suddenly. "Besides, what really is the harm in black and white children goen to school together? It's an idea whose time has come. We ought to embrace it with eager acceptance rather than fight it with pigheaded resistance."

He paused, then finished with a flourish. "Losen battles are a dime a dozen in this world, and all of us wind up fighten more than our share of 'em. In this case, folks, it's a loss we should accept with grace and be thankful for the opportunities that come with it."

If George Wallace had taken a similar stand on the steps of the University of

Alabama in 1963, the shock waves would have registered with only slightly more force than the jolt delivered by Jake Perry. In one moment, Jake had shattered long-held perceptions of himself. Never again would the community label him as an avowed segregationist, a do-nothing politician or a boorish wimp. And with his newfound notoriety, never again would Jake know the pleasant indifference and polite interest given to those men who command power but are considered harmless. The first repercussion came swiftly, seething with anger.

"You traitor!" Bobby Taylor charged with caustic disapproval.

"You're nothen but a nigger lover, old man," someone else yelled from the bleachers. "The whole damned bunch of y'all is nigger lovers."

In that moment, the aura of the meeting turned from aggravation and disgruntlement to rage and resentment. And when a black mother who'd had her fill of indignant treatment yelled back her frustration, screaming, "Go home, white boy, 'cause we done got what we want and there ain't nothen you can do about it," the inflamed feelings ignited like nitroglycerin.

Chaos ensued, in the form of insults and shoving matches, although no actual blows were exchanged. The commotion actually revolved around a few dozen people, black and white alike, scattered throughout the gym, who screamed and antagonized each other to the brink of a riot.

When the outrage threatened to engulf innocent bystanders, Paul Berrien moved in with his deputies. Just when he had thought the meeting would carry on without a hitch, the hot tempers had exploded in his face. He feared the situation would burst out of control if someone threw the first punch.

Though noted for his diplomatic approach to tempestuous situations, Paul recognized drastic action was necessary to restore the calm. He moved quickly to the microphone, took out his whistle and blew it with force. The resulting supersonic shrill—magnified, distorted and piercing in the hollow gymnasium—struck like a bomb. It was head-splitting, numbing and dazing to the crowd, and rattled windows.

Paul gave everyone a few seconds to recuperate from the shock waves, then declared the meeting adjourned and sounded an ominous warning for anyone unwilling to follow his advice. "I'm gonna say this once, and y'all had better pay attention because anyone who makes a mistake—and I do mean anyone—will face every criminal charge I can find in the book. Furthermore, I'll do my damnedest to make sure you go to prison, so think carefully before doing anything dumb because I promise it will be the mistake of your life."

He paused, allowing everyone to grasp the sincerity of his intentions. "Now then, y'all are goen to leave this gymnasium in an orderly fashion—even if it means we march out of here one person at a time and we're all here till doomsday. I don't want any talken until you're outside of the builden and even then, think twice about it. And for anybody who throws a punch or even looks cross-eyed at somebody else, remember this: There will be hell to pay.

"Now! Start moven out of here and be careful about it," he ordered.

No one dared to challenge the hard glaze of Sheriff Paul Berrien's eyes. Instead, they heeded his advice, obeyed the orders and retreated quietly.

Still, the specter of unfinished business loomed over the first day of school. And everyone knew it meant trouble.

SCHOOL OPENED ON A lovely sun-drenched day. Lucas woke before daybreak and witnessed the glorious sunrise, which was completely yellow, pale on the horizon before emerging with vivid brightness high in the sky. The sky was pure blue, full of promise; Lucas felt the hope keenly.

He made a cup of coffee and went outside to drink it, all signs of the atypical day this was.

The kitchen was Beauty's domain entirely. Lucas never did anything there, unless it was to pour himself a glass of cold water or milk from the refrigerator—and even then, only rarely, for Beauty waited on him hand and foot. As for making coffee, the act was almost without precedent in his years of marriage, and judging by the bitter taste of his brew, unlikely to be repeated anytime soon. Even his regard of the sunrise was peculiar. Although an early riser by nature, he normally paid scant attention to the sunrise unless it crossed his line of vision.

Since he was particularly observant this morning, Lucas allowed his gaze to regard the block house he rented from the Berriens. The house, which he had whitewashed in the spring, stood on the far side of the Berriens' vast estate, down a lonely dirt road that afforded the Bartholomews maximum privacy. As Joe had observed slyly, the road was so remote that anyone who stumbled across it was surely lost and in need of directions. The house itself was small, with just four rooms—a kitchen, two bedrooms and a front room. But it had electricity and running water, and Lucas considered it the finest house he'd ever lived in. It was snug, warm in the winter, shaded by ancient pine trees in the summer. Come winter, Lucas would build a bathroom and install indoor plumbing. Then, his family would have as fine a house as they would ever need.

The house was just one of the reasons Lucas considered himself a fortunate man on this morning. There were a dozen others, including his family and friends and the opportunity to earn an honest living. Chief on his mind, however, was the promise of the future.

He knew he was more excited about the first day of school than either Annie or Danny. Knew, too, he was blowing the significance of it way out of proportion for two small children. But the day's importance could not be exaggerated to Lucas.

Years ago, when he had quit school to care for his ailing mother, he had vowed to give his children the finest education possible. Now, with the fulfillment of the long-ago promise at hand, a consummate sense of satisfaction filled him. His children would not get just any education. They would get the best education, at least in these parts, and Lucas felt he had bridged the road to success for Annie and Danny.

As a boy, even as a young man, Lucas had clung desperately to the hope that some fantastic force would alter his life dramatically, or, at the very least, allow him some achievement that would foster self-pride and self-satisfaction. The life-changing moment had occurred the night Beauty informed him she was pregnant; Annie and Danny had been the fantastic force. On occasion, Lucas still wondered how his life might have turned out if he'd finished high school and gone on to college. He kept these thoughts to himself, however, partly because he could not fathom any other life and because he feared pity; but mainly because it was senseless daydreaming, which could threaten the goals he had set for himself and the children.

Today, his thoughts were grounded firmly in the present, refusing even to contemplate what lay ahead.

Annie was starting the second grade. She had excelled in her first year at the colored school in Cookville, served well by a quick mind, excellent penmanship and insatiable curiosity. But she needed a tougher challenge. Her teacher had said as much last spring, urging Lucas and Beauty to allow Annie promotion to the third grade. Although wary of pushing his daughter above her age, Lucas had agreed with the teachers. Once the door had been opened for her to attend New River Elementary School, however, he had decided she should take the second grade.

As for Danny, there was no telling how he would fare in school. He was as perceptive and quick-minded as Annie, but he lacked his sister's patience. If his son could sit still long enough, which was a dubious proposition, Lucas figured Danny could match Annie's pace. If not, then the boy would set his own pace. Already, Danny knew his ABCs and numbers, and that knowledge heartened Lucas.

When Annie and Danny were dressed—her in a blue and white dotted pinafore, him in blue jeans and a T-shirt, both wearing new sneakers—and had eaten oatmeal with milk and sugar for breakfast, Lucas sat them both on his knees, handed out lunch money and lectured them on the day's importance. It was a lengthy preachment, full of stuff about the necessity of good manners and close attention, likely perils and unlimited promise. Though some of what their father told them went right over their heads, Annie and Danny hung on his every word, out of respect for the importance Lucas attached to the day.

After rambling several minutes, Lucas finally realized there was nothing else to say, no more words of wisdom to impart on his children. In fact, he acknowledged, too much had been said. Yet, he wanted still to impress upon Annie and Danny the significance of the moment.

"You children may not understand what this day means now," he told them, peering closely at Annie, then Danny. "But when you're older, you'll recall this day as one of the most important in your lives. Try to remember everything about it, exactly as it happens, every little detail, so that when you get home, y'all can tell your mama and me all about it. And, so that one day, you can tell your own children and maybe your grandchildren all about it. Can you do that for me, Annie?"

"Yes, sir," she nodded brightly. "I'll remember everything. I'll write it down to make sure I don't forget a single thing."

Lucas smiled affectionately, then regarded his son. "Can you, Danny?"

"Yes, sir," the boy promised.

"Good enough, then," Lucas said, easing the children off his lap. "I got nothen else to say, 'cept pay attention to your teachers, do what they tell you and study hard. And when you're dealen with the other children, try and remember the Golden Rule."

"What's the Golden Rule, Danny?" Beauty inquired, looking at her son from the kitchen sink.

"Do unto others as you would have them do unto you," Danny replied automatically, earning a praising smile from his family members.

"Good boy!" Lucas exhorted with a gruff hug. "Now, let's get you two on the road, or you're gonna wind up tardy on your first day of school. I'd hate for y'all to get off on the wrong foot."

———

After all the expectation, the first day of school itself was somewhat of a comedown for Lucas, though not for Annie and Danny. It was a typical first day, devoid even of a trace of trouble Lucas had been told to expect over the prospect of integrating New River Elementary School. Children played happily, glad to be with friends they had not seen over the summer; parents reassured a handful of scared and crying first-graders; and teachers scrambled to find missing enrollment forms while accommodating anxious parents.

A secretary gave Lucas directions to the first- and second-grade classrooms, and the teachers assured him they were glad to have Annie and Danny as students and looked forward to a pleasant year for everyone. Finally, it was time to tell the children goodbye, and he did it reluctantly, almost as if the delay would provide some auspicious hallmark to commemorate the momentousness of the day. But it was an extremely normal day and when Lucas left, Danny already was engaged in the obvious beginnings of a friendship with the little boy who sat in the desk behind him.

Eventually, Lucas realized he should be grateful for the normalcy, that at first glance everyone appeared willing to accept the appearance of two colored children without any questions. As he walked down the hall, out of the building to his truck, the sense of expectation returned to him. It was only the first day after all, he told himself, and the bulk of this adventure stretched full of promise in the days, months and years to follow.

———

Integration got off to a rocky start at Cookville High School, which explained why it went smoothly at New River and the other elementary schools in the county.

By the time all of the buses arrived at the high school from the outlying communities, two fights had already erupted between white and black factions—one among students, the other between parents. Twenty robed Ku Klux Klansmen led by Bobby Taylor and dozens more of their sympathizers gathered outside the main office, shouting racial slurs at the black students getting off the buses and cursing administrators for allowing integration to proceed. About sixty black parents congregated in the opposite hall, some celebrating the moment, several mocking their white counterparts and rubbing in their success—assuming that forced integration was in their children's best interest.

The tension was unnerving at the least, downright dangerous at times.

Someone threw a rock through Carrie's senior homeroom window, striking Angie Bates in the head and sending the white girl to the hospital. The cut required three stitches in her left temple.

In another senior homeroom class, Wayne Taylor picked a fight with one of the black boys expected to help Cookville claim a state championship later in the school year. The black boy, Jerome Hill, matched him blow for blow until Wayne suddenly pulled a knife from his trousers. For one bloodcurdling moment, the day threatened to blow up in the worst possible way, but Wayne refrained from making the mistake of his life. Instead, he surrendered the knife to his shaken teacher, apologized without remorse and received a one-week suspension. It was light punishment, deemed appropriate only because of the turmoil that rocked the school.

The early part of the day produced legends of horrific proportions, yet there were many shining moments of acceptance as well, almost exclusively between the students.

One such moment cost Luke an old friendship. It occurred during fifth period, which came right after lunch, except lunch had been canceled as sheriff's deputies and several Georgia state troopers—called in by Paul Berrien as a precautionary measure—kept the angry crowd separated and at bay outside the school, while Cookville's police officers patrolled the school halls. By fifth period, however, school administrators felt a semblance of calm had been restored and allowed the students out of their homerooms for the first time all day.

Luke, who was a sophomore and star running back for the football team, was sitting at his desk, waiting for the tardy bell in geography and bemoaning to friends the fact that they had a whole week of classes to attend before Labor Day, the first holiday of the year.

"Well, it could be worse," replied Mike Harris, an offensive tackle for the Cookville High Rebels and Luke's friend since the first grade at New River. "They could have waited until the Tuesday after Labor Day to start classes. I hate it when they do that. After be'en away from school all summer, a guy needs some kind of break right after starten back. Otherwise, you go straight through till Thanksgiven."

"That's true," Luke agreed.

Then, the "Backroom Boys," as Luke's popular group was known, launched into an animated critique of nature's summer endowment to various girls. About the time the tardy bell rang, they were in an uproar over the authenticity of Patti Avera's bosoms. Luke opined that every inch was real.

"But she's a senior this year," said Donnie Polk, another friend, who came from the Jordan community. "Girls don't grow tits like that between their junior and senior year in high school. Hell, I thought they quit growen earlier than that."

"Not everything's like your dick, Donnie," Mike Harris joshed.

"Up yours, Harris," Donnie replied.

"Besides," Mike continued, "the only reason Baker says those tits are real is because he wants to find out the truth for himself. Right, Lukey?"

"Maybe it crossed my mind," replied Luke, whose hormones had kicked in furiously at the beginning of his freshman year.

"In your dreams, Baker," Donnie Polk said. "She's a senior, and you're nothen but a sophomore, who doesn't even have a driver's license yet. You don't stand a chance with Patti Avera."

At that moment, the door opened, bringing the class to attention as they expected the teacher to enter the room. Instead, it was a skinny black boy, the only Negro in the class. The boy scanned the room with wide eyes, noted the conspicuousness of his presence and fled to an available seat across from the Backroom Boys.

The black youth's presence brought a temporary silence to the room before the conversations resumed, with everyone roundly ignoring the new kid, except for Mike Harris. "Whataya say we have a little fun, boys," he suggested, motioning to the colored boy, who was staring hard at his desk top and appeared frightened to Luke.

"Leave him alone, Mike," Luke said. "Can't you see he's scared enough?"

"Now, Lukey, don't go getten all high and mighty on us," Mike replied innocently. "I'm just gonna introduce myself. It wouldn't be polite if we didn't make an effort to get to know the new kid, now would it?"

The easygoing style of the Backroom Boys disappeared at that precise moment, cracked right down the middle between the sudden conspiratorial tone of some of the friends and the cautious reservations of the others.

Egged on by friends, Mike stalked over to an empty desk in front of the black boy and plopped down backward in it, resting his elbows on the kid's desk. The colored youth kept his eyes penned on a new notebook, but trembling hands gave away his feelings.

"Don't be scared, boy," Mike urged. "We just wanna give you a friendly welcome to good old Cookville High, where we're all Rebels through and through. Now I can keep callen you boy, or you can tell me your name."

The colored youth looked up then, less cautiously as he perceived something friendly in Mike's approach. "Name's Dorsey Ryan," he said.

"Dorsey Ryan," Mike repeated curiously before his tone took a decidedly menacing turn. "Well, Dorsey Ryan, you appear to be one scared nigger child. And frankly, I don't blame you."

The kid's eyes widened with fear, then he cowed away, staring blankly at the blue notebook.

Luke should have interceded then, but following a self-given pledge earlier in the day to mind his own business and allow everyone to fend for themselves, he remained anchored in his seat. Then suddenly, Mike swept across the desk with his hand, knocking the notebook to the floor.

"Oops," he mocked. "Sorry about be'en so clumsy. But hell, Dorsey, I'm an offensive guard, and we football linemen ain't exactly known for be'en graceful. Know what I mean?" He chuckled meanly.

"Let me just pick that up for you," he continued, reaching down to grab the notebook by the loose-leaf paper, which immediately tore away from the rings.

The notebook clattered once more to the floor, followed by a few snickers through the classroom. "Damn, Dorsey," Mike said. "I dropped it again."

He reached for the notebook again, but Luke beat him to it. "Leave him alone," Luke said forcefully, setting the notebook back on top of Dorsey Ryan's desk.

Mike glared at Luke. "Hey, Lukey," he said testily. "You're rainen on my parade. Whose side are you on anyway?"

"I'm not on any side," Luke answered evenly. "Just leave him alone. He's got enough problems without be'en bullied."

"I never figured you for a nigger lover, Lukey," Mike shot back.

"Then we're equal," Luke countered. "I never figured you for an asshole."

Any hope of salvaging their friendship evaporated at that moment as both boys wondered how they had misjudged one another for so many years. Finally, Mike broke the silence.

"Just what happens if I don't leave him alone, Luke?" he asked.

"We'll see," Luke answered coldly.

"You know I could kick your ass, Baker," Mike replied with resignation.

It was a true assessment, but Luke stared him down anyway. "Come on guys," someone said at length. "Break it up before Mr. Mac comes in, and we all get in trouble."

Luke stood his ground until Mike rose from the desk and shoved past him. There was no need to push back. His point was made. No one would bother Dorsey Ryan in this classroom. Finally, Luke mustered up a brusque smile for the black boy, then returned to his seat, dumbfounded why everyone insisted on complicating the world at almost every turn.

In the end, Luke figured that Dorsey Ryan would mean nothing to him, remembered only as an asterisk. Luke despised asterisks. He always did his best to ignore them because they cluttered the essential stuff with irrelevant details. The trouble was, Luke deemed, that too many people tended to pay far too much attention to the asterisks in life, which probably explained why so many of them found a way to complicate every little thing. He shook his head in dismay.

––––––––

By the sixth and final period, the parents had been ordered off the school grounds, with two of them carted off in patrol cars to face charges for fighting.

Slumped in her desk, isolated as far as possible from everyone else in the packed home economics class, Carrie felt wearied by the frazzled beginning to her senior year. If today were any indication, her final year in high school would crackle with excitement. But if the past eleven years were a better indicator of what lay ahead—Carrie thought in these terms because she had just been told as much in her preceding history class—she judged her annual quota of excitement had been met on this first day. Then again, maybe this year would be different. She hoped so. It was the standard bearer of hope for wallflowers like herself, a tired litany used year after year.

Carrie was exaggerating the dull quality of her life, of course. There really was little to complain about, even if she did get lost in life's shuffle from time to time. Sometimes she wanted more, though, something wild, exciting or vastly different from her old-maidish expectations. Whatever it might be, whether fleeting or substantial, outlandish or solemn, private or universal, Carrie did not care. She simply wanted something to give a certain amount of distinction to her life.

The tardy bell sounded, bringing her thoughts back to home economics. It was her favorite class, though she would never admit it to anyone. It was her most embarrassing secret, and she guarded it like a family skeleton locked away in a closet. If anyone ever discovered her shame, she'd probably become a laughingstock, dismissed as hopelessly shallow, with a decided preference for washing dishes and scrubbing toilets.

From time to time, Carrie tried to imagine explaining her fondness for home economics and almost invariably the explanation sounded silly. "Oh, yes," she'd probably say with florid sincerity. "Home economics has been my salvation these last four years. Everything else—history, math, English—I've only tolerated it for an opportunity to learn about my true passion. Deep down, darlen, I have enormous talent for housewife drudgery. Give me a table to set, a casserole to bake, a spot to remove, a sock to darn, and I'll be the most satisfied woman on earth."

Yes, indeed, it was a secret to keep, especially when three Baker siblings had preceded her out the doors of Cookville High School to pursue passionate ambitions like journalism, fashion design and painting. In truth, however, Carrie suspected she kept her happy homemaker's secret because it bespoke, like a tattletale, of the certain amount of banality to her life. It almost seemed a tad unfair that an ordinary girl like herself should lean toward the most ordinary of passions. But it was to be expected, Carrie reasoned, since she rarely ever did the unexpected.

At length, she pushed aside these thoughts because a girl could get depressed if she dwelled on too many negatives. And Carrie was neither a dweller nor prone to depression.

Class had been under way about ten minutes when the door burst open, and Billy Taylor flew into the room, a little dazed by the sight of so many girls. Mortification froze him, and he flushed red with the humiliation of being in a class where he was least expected and tardy on top of everything else. The girls, including Carrie, broke into laughter, though they were tentative with their glee because it was Billy Taylor after all, the son of the man who had led the commotion surrounding their first day of school. Nevertheless, there were enough giggles to turn Billy a deeper shade of crimson.

"What are you doen here?" Mrs. Dorothea Franklin demanded. She deplored intrusions on classroom time, and so far, the day had been disastrous on that accord. She was in no mood for more shenanigans. "This is home economics," she declared with righteous indignation.

Billy shuffled his feet. "Yes'em, I know it is," he replied meekly. "Ah, I'm supposed to be here. I'm taken home-ec this year."

There were a few snickers, which Mrs. Franklin silenced with her stony glower before returning the attention to Billy.

"You are?" she asked incredulously, clearly taken aback by the prospect. "Let me see your schedule," she demanded, regaining her composure.

Billy dug the slip of paper from his pocket and handed it to her.

The teacher studied the schedule, confirming his enrollment in her class. "Very well," she said. "By all means, Mr. Taylor, welcome to home economics. Please take your seat and let's get on with it."

There was one empty space left in the classroom, a desk in the back-right corner.

––––––––

The long day finally ended. Tired students crawled onto waiting buses, glad the first day was over and hopeful for calmer times ahead of them. At supper tables everywhere that night, anxious students recounted the day for their parents.

In the Taylor home, Wayne told his father about the fight, then they discussed his suspension and mulled over ways to antagonize the black students in the days to come. In a rare display of caring, Bobby advised his oldest son to use caution with his tactics rather than risk another suspension. "You get thrown out again, son, and you'll never graduate," he told Wayne. "You're already two years past when you should have finished."

"I could quit," Wayne suggested. "They won't let me play football this year, so there's really no reason to keep goen. I could work for you."

"You need a high school diploma," Bobby instructed, before adding tiredly, "Such as it is."

As he dished up grits, fried eggs and bacon during a lull in the conversation,

Billy casually mentioned the home economics class. When no one paid attention, he quickly dropped the subject. For some reason, he felt an obligation to contribute to the mealtime conversations. So usually—except at breakfast when the talk was monosyllabic and only that when it was necessary to communicate—he brought up some unremarkable topic, waited for the perfunctory disregard and then retreated into silent oblivion, satisfied he had carried out his family duty.

The one concession Billy made to his cherished silence was for his little brother's sake. But on this evening, when he should have been bursting to tell about his first day at school, Carl merely wolfed down his food, then vanished outside to play by himself. Billy felt oddly depressed. While washing the dishes, however, he made up his mind to quiz Carl about the day later, and his mood brightened.

————

Around the same time the Taylors were eating their supper, Lucas and Beauty listened with rapt attention and pleasure as Annie and Danny recounted the day's adventures. Annie spoke endlessly about her new teacher, a young woman who had lavished praise on the girl's perfect penmanship. As she had promised, Annie remembered virtually every detail about the day, with many of them written down in a notebook, which she now expected to read to her parents. Tedious though much of it was, Lucas listened with avid interest, as well as the creeping feeling that he may have overstated the case for memorizing every detail.

Danny's recollection of the day was typically sketchier, for which both Lucas and Beauty were grateful by the time Annie concluded her dissertation. He mentioned the boy who sat in the desk behind him, telling how they had seesawed away the afternoon recess.

"What's his name?" Lucas asked.

"I think it's Carl," Danny said. "But I ain't really sure."

————

The Bakers ate their supper late that night after spending the afternoon and early evening unstringing and sheeting up the season's last barn of tobacco. They were all present at the kitchen table, except Joe, who was working late for the newspaper.

While they consumed cheese grits, fried sausage and homemade biscuits, Carrie told her family about the rock striking Angie Bates in the head during homeroom. She started to tell them Billy Taylor was sitting in front of her in home economics before changing her mind. Like Luke, she saw no need to add complications to unremarkable situations. Then, in the next instant, she prodded her youngest brother for details about the incident in his geography class.

"Did you tell anybody what happened to you to today, Luke?" she asked innocently. "Everybody was talken about it. I heard about it on the way from my history class to home-ec."

Luke shot her an annoyed glance. "It was nothen," he shrugged.

"Now, son," Matt chided. "It couldn't have been nothen if it was the talk of the school between history and home-ec. Fess up and tell us what happened."

Luke resigned himself to the inevitable. Privacy was a luxury in this household, and he always seemed short on cash when he wanted it. "I had a run-in with Mike Harris," he said.

"Mike Harris!" Caroline exclaimed. "He's one of your best friends."

"Not anymore, he ain't," Luke replied sternly.

"Well, what happened?" Summer asked.

So Luke told them, every detail and every nuance of the altercation that had cost him a friend. To his surprise, when he had recounted the dispute, what he had done for Dorsey Ryan mattered more than Luke had believed it would. He was bolstered by the pride of having done the right thing. He had stood up against something wrong, but what was more important, he had lent a hand to someone who needed help.

"It was a noble deed," Sam said when the story was finished.

"To tell you the truth, I didn't want to get involved, Grandpa," Luke replied earnestly. "And I'm sure someone else would have stepped in if I hadn't done it first. But there wasn't anything noble about it. There wasn't even time to think about what I was doen. I just acted."

With that topic exhausted, Caroline asked Bonnie—an eighth-grader and the lone Baker still at the New River school—how Annie and Danny Bartholomew had fared on their first day at school. "Pretty good, I guess," she answered. "Annie at least was excited on the bus comen home. I didn't hear of any problems at school, although they're at the far end of the hall and I never really saw them. Anyway, as far as I know, nobody never ever mentioned the first thing about integration. And I usually hear about most everything that goes on."

Bonnie's busybody reputation was well known among her family. "From what I hear," Rachel remarked, "you know more about what's goen on at that school than the principal. Just how do you manage to know so much about everybody's business?"

"I've had good teachers, Granny," Bonnie replied lightly.

Rachel frowned, then blushed at the implication.

———

Later that evening, Joe, Summer and John sat on the front porch, enjoying a pleasant breeze and discussing the day's turmoil, which Joe had covered for the newspaper.

"Seems like we graduated too soon and missed all the excitement," Summer told John. They were sitting on the green- and white-checked glider, while Joe lay on one of the wide step walls that framed the porch steps, his feet propped on the brick column.

"From the sound of things, I'm kind of glad myself," John replied. "It's nice to be too old for somethen for a change."

Soon afterward, the three lapsed into a companionable silence, lost in the contemplation of where they had been and where they were headed.

Summer and John were a few weeks from beginning fall quarter classes at ABAC in Tifton. For Summer, it was the resumption of her education, which she had delayed for a year when Tom was killed. With time on her hands, she had found a job at a boutique in Valdosta, riding back and forth to work with Joe as he had finished his college degree and gone on to full-time work with the newspaper. By mid-summer, she had been eager to return to school, which she'd never intended to abandon in the first place but was simply too restless to tolerate for the time. She'd had one year of course work under her belt before withdrawing the previous fall, so technically she was a sophomore this year. The bulk of her first-year classes had been in fashion design and electives, however, so this year, she would have to take the basics.

Since John was beginning college and Summer was taking freshman courses, they had arranged their schedules to take the same classes—English 101, College Algebra and World History. They would finish classes by eleven o'clock each day, keeping the afternoons free for work.

Joe thought their plans, while well intentioned, were a colossal mistake. "You'll get sick of each other," he predicted. "Driven to school together, goen to the same classes, comen home together, studyen for the same tests, taken the same tests. And, possibly maken different grades on those tests."

"Don't sweat it, Joe," Summer replied smartly. "I've got it all worked out. If I make better grades than John, it's because I'm older and more mature. If John somehow makes better grades than me, it will be only because I've been away from the education process such a long time and need time to readjust."

"She's absolutely right," John agreed. "Although, of course, I'll strangle her if she does too much better than I do."

In her spare time, Summer planned to take in sewing to earn spending money. She already had lined up a job to do alterations for the boutique on Saturdays and was advertising her services as a dressmaker in *The Cookville Herald*.

College had been a natural direction for John to follow, but his decision was made easier by the new draft rules and his late birthday, which kept him out of military service. Only a month away from turning nineteen, he felt as if he had already survived one of life's biggest pitfalls. Otherwise, John had a hazy view of the future. He thought he wanted to farm, but he also wanted an opportunity to discover the extent of his talent for painting. Although the basic courses would occupy his first year of college, John had found some consolation by signing up for a noncredit night class in advanced painting. He would spend his spare time working on the farm.

Of course, having two children in college at one time presented problems for the family. Money was short again this year because of late spring flooding that had forced Matt to replant several fields and drowned five acres of tobacco. Matt reckoned the tobacco crop had brought in about half of what he had expected, and he was counting on no serious financial setbacks to see the family through to the next year.

In the crunch, Joe had come through with the cash for college, using his savings to foot the tuition bills and buy books for Summer and John. His offer had met firm resistance from Matt and Caroline at the outset, but his persistence had persuaded them otherwise.

"Son, we're not so hard up that we can't scrape up the money to send them both," Matt had declared. "I know there's been many a year when we couldn't have done that, and Lord knows you've seen more than your share of the lean times. But it's not your responsibility to pay for your sister and brother's education. You've earned the right to keep whatever money you make."

"This isn't about money, Daddy," Joe had countered. "I want to do this because ..." He paused, searching. "I want to do it because it's what we do best," he said at last. "The family, I mean: Getten by the best way we can with what we've got. Well, we've got this extra money, and, as I see things, it's the best way for us to get by."

Thwarted by their own philosophy, Matt and Caroline had no other choice but to accept the offer.

FOR TWO WEEKS, CARRIE sat behind Billy Taylor in home economics without a single exchange passing between them. The avoidance was due as much to her natural instinct to shy away from strangers as any deliberate decision to ignore him. Of course, Billy was not the typical stranger. They might have known each other by name only, but Carrie and Billy were bonded by the forces of their families, by a history of mutual distrust and disrespect.

Though ordinarily nonjudgmental, particularly of strangers, Carrie prepared to assume the worst about Billy. Instead, due to their initial disregard of each other, she was simply untouched by him, except for mild flickers of curiosity aroused by his clockwork appearance in the sixth-period class. As far as she knew, he was the first boy to take home economics at Cookville High School, and that alone was enough to pique anybody's interest.

Quite by accident, John heightened her curiosity about Billy during a Labor Day outing at Cherry Lake.

A combination roller-skating rink, beach and ski area, Cherry Lake was one of the county's most popular gathering places for young people, along with the Majestic Theater and the Dairy Queen in Cookville. The swimming excursion had been a spontaneous decision proposed a day earlier by Summer as the family lazed away a hot Sunday afternoon on the front porch. On Monday morning, instead of digging sweet potatoes as they had expected, the six Baker children had rushed through a few chores, packed a picnic lunch and headed for a relaxing day in the sun.

In the middle of the afternoon, after a lengthy game of volleyball in the deep end of the swimming area, Carrie and John had stretched out on towels for a break while their siblings accepted an offer to go skiing, which none of them had done previously. John and she were chatting about the quick calm that had taken hold at Cookville High School after the ugliness of the first day. Left to their own means, black and white students had declared a truce.

"There's still a long way to go, but it's a good start," Carrie told her brother.

Then John brought up the subject of basketball, remarking that his major regret was that the Rebels had come so close to winning the state championship in his senior year. They had reached the semifinals before losing to Monticello by two points. John was the only starting player lost from the team, and he predicted Cookville was a cinch to win the title in the coming year.

The mention of basketball reminded Carrie of Billy Taylor and the rumor she had heard in the first week of school. "There was talk at school last week that Billy Taylor might not be playen on the basketball team this year," she told John.

"Why not?" he asked with obvious concern.

"I don't know for sure, but from what I gather, his daddy won't let him play because there will be colored boys on the team," Carrie explained.

"That's a shame," John replied. "Billy Taylor is a true basketball wizard. He's really somethen special on the court. There are players like me, who aren't very talented but love the game. There's players who have the talent but not the desire. And then there's somebody like Billy, who's loaded with talent and loves the game, too. He made all-state last year, and he was just a sophomore. There's no tellen how far he could go. I hope Bobby changes his mind and lets him play. Without him, Cookville might just turn out to be another good team instead of a great one."

Realizing John actually knew Billy as a person, Carrie suddenly wanted to find out more about him. "Playen ball with him, I guess you got to know Billy fairly well," she remarked casually.

John pondered her assumption thoughtfully. "Not really," he said. "We just never hit it off. We didn't dislike each other, or at least I didn't dislike him. But Billy was the one person on the team I never really got to know. There was always this wall between us, which consideren everything that's happened in the past between the Taylors and us, ain't none too surprisen. Billy was strange, though. He was the same way with the whole team. He got along well enough with everybody, and he was a great team player. But there was always a space between him and the rest of the guys. I figured maybe it was his talent that made him that way. It's as if he knew he was good but didn't want to call attention to it, so he kept to himself. Or maybe he was just shy. I don't know."

Still curious, she plied him with another question. "Was he anything like Bobby?"

"I honestly couldn't tell you," John answered. "When I say he kept to himself, I mean he kept to himself. About the only thing I ever heard him talk about was basketball. Even then, he didn't say much."

Then, as if suddenly curious himself, John asked why Carrie was interested in Billy.

"I'm not really," she answered nonchalantly. "I just thought you'd like to know what I heard about him not playen ball this season."

Her answer apparently satisfied John. He had changed the subject, and shortly afterward, they had drowsed under the broiling sun.

On Tuesday, when Billy sat in front of her in sixth period, Carrie remembered briefly the conversation with John. But when Mrs. Franklin began calling the roll, it slipped her mind. Three days later, as she sat on the bus waiting to go home, Carrie was taken aback when Billy appeared by her side, asking if he could take the empty seat next to her. She hesitated a response, long enough to regain her bearings, then motioned him to the seat and resumed staring out the window.

"I hate to bother you," Billy began apologetically. "It's just that I'm haven trouble with this sewen project in home-ec and thought maybe you could show me what I'm doen wrong."

Carrie eyed him closely, obviously skeptical, then surprised as he pulled a partially stitched man's work shirt from a paper bag and showed her two botched button holes. She finally shrugged and showed him how the holes should have been made.

"Thank you," Billy said when she had executed a perfect stitch and he had copied the instructions, earning slight praise for the finished project.

They rode in uncomfortable silence for several minutes afterward, with Carrie becoming more curious about exactly who Billy Taylor was. She had always been blessed with abundant curiosity, which was tempered by her reserved nature. Now she was overwhelmed with interest, positively nosy, like a busybody who could not be satisfied until she had ferreted out just one sliver of enlightenment.

"Why are you taken home-ec?" she asked at last, the question practically blurted at Billy.

He seemed almost relieved by the inquiry. "You're the first person who has asked me that," Billy answered happily, as if he had been waiting for an overture. He smiled disarmingly, seemingly inviting an inquisition.

"Well, you're the first and only boy I know who takes home-ec," she pressed. "My curiosity got the best of me."

He smiled again. "For some reason," he answered easily, "since my mama died, I've wound up doen most of the housework at our place. My daddy can't cook, and it's dangerous to have Wayne near a stove. Somebody has to do the cooken, cleanen and washen, so I do—although not very well. I was hopen home-ec would give me some pointers."

Carrie permitted herself a slight smile at the image of Billy puttering around the house in an apron. Knowing her own brothers' limitations for housework, she expected the Taylor home badly needed a woman's touch.

"Has it?" she prompted.

"About the closest thing I've ever done to sewen was to iron a knee-patch on my little brother's dungarees the other day," he answered. "But I'm readen ahead in the book about cooken and some of the other things I need to know. My folks have complimented me on the meals lately, so I guess I'm doen somethen right."

"Good for you," Carrie said, as if it were the most natural thing in the world for him to have done.

They fell into another silence, which lasted until the bus deposited Luke and her on the dirt road across from the mercantile, which allowed them to walk the remaining distance home rather than suffer the long ride from the New River school to the Baker house. As she squeezed by him out of the seat, Billy bade her a cheerful goodbye.

———

It was Saturday night and Carrie was alone, in the kitchen baking a pound cake that would be part of the massive dinner spread on the church grounds after tomorrow's Big Meeting service. She could have been elsewhere, alongside her brothers and sisters at the Majestic Theater in Cookville viewing a special weekend showing of *Gone with the Wind*, or with her parents and grandparents at a gospel sing in Valdosta. There had been invitations, maybe expectations, from both siblings and elders. Yet, she had chosen to stay at home by herself, the craving for privacy taking precedence over any desire for companionship.

This rare ache for privacy had been tugging at Carrie for the better part of a week. Though she could not recall the first stirrings of these occasional needs for solitude, she had come to recognize the moments as a healthy influence on her life. She used the times for what would have been labeled in sophisticated circles as self-therapy. Carrie preferred to call it introspection, and she always began the process with a thorough rumination over the state of her family. For very early on in these introspective moments, she had been struck by the link between her family to herself.

As much as she loved her family, Carrie sometimes felt swallowed by their close-knit nature, as if she owed her existence solely to a role allotted by birth. In the worst of moments, which, fortunately, were too few to count, she compared the

Bakers with some kind of blob, a sticky, gelatinous mass that absorbed anyone and everything within reach, molding any distinct qualities into its own likeness. Of course, even blobs had slight deviations in consistency, and there were members of her family who defied the norm and tainted the homogeneity of the Baker blob. Unfortunately, Carrie was not one of them.

The acknowledgment of herself tempted Carrie to skip ahead in this process of introspection, to bypass the trappings in favor of the substance. But the family came first and ignoring its dominance would cheat the therapeutic process and lessen its tonic appeal. Besides, for the most part, she accepted this powerful family bond without hesitation, even rejoiced over it. Their closeness was unique, an infatuation with each other. Only it was lasting.

She had this rudimentary conception of her family, based on the idea of old money. It wasn't easy to acquire in the first place and, once attained, even harder to come into by an outsider. This vague notion stirred intense feelings in Carrie, gratitude for the birthright that ensured her place among the family, regret for those on the outside looking in. If she had been born an outsider, Carrie believed she would have spent her whole life looking in on the family, unpossessed of the qualities that afforded entry into the privileged domain.

This idea, this view, even the comparison, was as grandiose and snobbish as the connotation of old money itself, and Carrie tempered the notion with realization that any number of families could draw a similar analogy about themselves if they were of mind to. As well as the sensibility that any comparison of her family with old money was ridiculously absurd on its face and fundamentally flawed at the heart. First of all, the Bakers never seemed to have possession of money long enough for it to become old. And second, they were among the least snobbish and openly accepting of others as any people she knew.

Still, Carrie could not rid herself of the impression of a family so absorbed with itself that the Bakers gave only passing interest to the world around them. Their attachment, their attraction and devotion to each other exceeded the normal expectations, the crux of which explained why Carrie both cherished family ties and sometimes fretted over their consuming nature. On one hand, she thought them lucky to have a source of complete satisfaction. But on the other, she worried that it limited their ability—even their need—to look at possibilities beyond the family.

Take Summer and Joe, for instance. They had emerged from Tom's funeral like two shell-shocked survivors who needed the other's companionship just to find their way in a changed world. Carrie understood the need for mutual support that Summer and Joe obviously felt in the wake of Tom's death, as well as the emotional undergirding they provided each other. In their haste to return to normalcy, however, they had lost their way, miring themselves in the mutual need to comfort and to be comforted. What should have been camaraderie between her brother and sister had come to resemble a dependency, like a drug addiction, and the intensity of it disturbed Carrie. She feared Joe and Summer's reliance on one another was robbing her brother and sister of a very important and shared trait, their resolve to get on with life, with willing respect for its dalliances and zealous anticipation of its comings.

There were qualities about every member of her family that Carrie admired: Bonnie's optimism; John's sincerity; Granny's frankness; Grandpa's cheerfulness; Daddy's steadfastness; Mama's resolve; and Luke for his incredible Lukeness, which was the only way she knew to describe her brother's penchant for turning his incorrigibilities into amazing displays of character or whimsy. Either way, Luke got away with things none of the other children would have dared to think, much less try.

In Summer and Joe, the stamp of admiration had always been one and the same: their obvious lust for life and their eagerness not only to experience but to soak up its every offering. It was understandable that Tom's death would have made them more cautious in their pursuits. After all, life had thrown its worst at them, up to this point and time, and they had been sponges for every painful nuance. Still, given the expected, acceptable amount of diminishment, it was obvious, too, that their enthusiasm had become a quality stripped of its luster. Carrie attributed this lack of sparkle in her brother and sister to their compulsive concern for one another. Summer and Joe apparently had determined that by contenting themselves with the familiar, they could avoid chance encounters with any unpleasantness.

As Carrie saw it, her brother and sister were becoming like her, on a different level, of course, but nevertheless, skittish toward life. And because timidity was one trait Carrie wanted to rid herself of, she worried over the thought of Summer and Joe shrinking away from life.

To some extent, she blamed her guarded ways on the influence of those close family ties. With such a large support system around her, she had little reason to look outside the family for friendship and adventure. And she rarely did. Her reluctance to face the unknown, however, kept Carrie locked inside a smaller world and caused her current fretfulness over the magnetic closeness of her family.

Despite her consternations, in her heart, Carrie believed that time might restore her brother and sister with the resolve to move forward, freed of worry over fear and loss, with renewed belief in possibilities and acceptance of fate.

In truth, Carrie was more certain that time would rekindle the zest for life in Summer. The sparkle of perseverance was too strong in Summer to be denied. In time, Carrie believed, her sister would no longer need a crutch to help her along the way. The pain of losing Tom would be laid to rest by her own dreams of success as a fashion designer, as well as the ardent pursuit of some male admirer. The first opportunity for Summer to resume dating had come within two months of Tom's death, and the invitations were coming with increasing frequency. So far, Summer had spurned them all, but Carrie knew it was only a matter of time until someone thawed her sister's resistance.

With Joe, the answers were not as simple. He had the same perseverance, yet the quality was strangled by a tendency to beat himself up for self-perceived transgressions.

Carrie had begun to recognize this fault in Joe during the past year, and she was beginning to suspect it ran deeper than anyone realized. At first, she had been amazed and strangely comforted by the idea of Joe having flaws because he was not an easy person to measure up to, especially for someone as self-conscious as herself. Except for rare outbursts of hotheaded temper, and then only when he was provoked, Joe always seemed benignly authoritative and unflappable, impervious to any major shortcomings that would expose a chink in his character. Now Carrie worried about his composure, and she was disturbed by his readiness to shoulder blame and burdens.

Of her own qualities, the one Carrie most admired was her watchfulness. Though sometimes slow on the uptake, once she grasped hold of a situation, no one was better at sorting out its subtle complexities. Having caught on to Joe's penchant for self-reproach, Carrie had proceeded to uncover an impostor behind that self-assured, practical mask. In his place was someone aloof, a man quietly detaching himself from others, a mass of roiling thunder behind those steely dark brown eyes.

As transparent as Joe seemed to her, Carrie wondered whether anyone else recognized the distance he was putting between himself and the family. She doubted so, because Joe hid his intentions very well. So well in fact, that Carrie doubted sometimes whether Joe even recognized what he was doing.

More than ever, he seemed devoted to the family and attentive to their needs, giving his spare time to anyone who asked, whether helping with homework, repairing machinery, feeding animals or simply lending a sympathetic ear and offering guidance. Yet, at the same time, he was putting up shields, relegating himself—his needs and his feelings—to some place of insignificance. In a strange way, it seemed Joe had decided the test of manhood depended on his ability to hide any signs of vulnerability. He neither took nor asked anything for himself (unless it was from Summer in their private moments), while giving any and everything.

If time alone would restore the lust for life in Summer, then Carrie suspected it would take time plus large doses of his own sensibility and good sense to rekindle the passion in Joe. And if she was correct on that accord, then the odds favored a complete recovery for her brother because, after all, sensibility and good sense were trademarks of the Baker family.

This last conclusion came to Carrie as she poured the cake batter into the Bundt pan, the deed gratefully rescuing her from troubled thoughts.

All of the Bakers were endowed with ample abilities to make distinctions and sound judgments. Even Luke had begun to show signs of lasting sensibility and good sense. Or more accurately, he had been forced to acknowledge their necessity.

Football had succeeded in doing for Luke what no one else could, persuading him to pay a minimum of serious attention to his schoolwork. At the start of football season last fall, when Luke had been a freshman with star potential as a running back, Matt and Caroline had issued an ultimatum to their youngest son, informing him that any grade less than a C in any class would spell the end of his football career. With their expectations non-negotiable and his love of football paramount, Luke was willing, finally, to make the sacrifice of studying, and the changes in him as well as his report card were remarkable. He might never graduate with honors, but no one worried any more whether he would bring home failing grades.

Luke was proud of his accomplishments in the classroom, as was the rest of the family. Of course, Carrie was also a tad jealous of her little brother, she admitted, pushing the cake into the oven and checking the temperature a final time.

She might as well get that single acknowledgment out of the way since it struck at the heart of her need for this moment of introspection. Here she was at the beginning of her senior year, that crowning moment of high school, and she was still the perennial wallflower, while her little brother, just out of his freshman year, was bound for glory.

Sometimes her lack of notoriety disturbed Carrie, especially when she compared her status at Cookville High School with the reputations of the three siblings who had preceded her. Actually, she excluded Joe in these comparisons since his presence in high school had been nothing more than a forgotten memory by the time

Carrie arrived for her freshmen year. And equally so, she shied away from comparisons with Summer. Few people measured up to Summer, the homecoming queen, Miss Golden Leaf, Miss Cookville High School and the senior superlative winner for friendliest girl. Popularity came easily for Summer, and deservedly, too. Carrie did not begrudge her sister.

John was the best barometer for Carrie to gauge herself against, considering their closeness in age and similarities in character. Her middle brother had carved a niche for himself in high school, as a solid if unspectacular member of a championship basketball team. He had left a mark, which was more than Carrie could say for herself. Luke, too, already had made a mark, which his handsome looks and football talent would emblazon in the coming years. And Bonnie, once she arrived with her boundless optimism and unabashed cheerfulness, no doubt would etch a place for herself in the school's hall of fame.

As for herself, Carrie feared a few yearbook pictures and dusty enrollment records would represent the lone reminders of her presence at Cookville High School. A poor legacy for four years, and the blame lay entirely with herself and her proclivity to exist unnoticed in a crowd.

At the core of this self-indictment was not a wish for attention or popularity, but rather a desire for change within herself. Perhaps she was stuck with innate shyness. Indeed, it was her badge of distinction in a large family. Still, Carrie was beginning to sense that maybe she used her shyness as a conscious buffer rather than being a genuine casualty of its constrictions. What else explained how a normal girl could have gone through high school without making any close friends and a number of dates that she could count on one hand?

There had been opportunities to form friendships, invitations to parties, occasions to join clubs, boys who showed more than passing interest. Too many times, however, Carrie had found an excuse to avoid commitments, even those of the most casual kind. That tendency to shy away from opportunities to stretch her horizons beyond the family was not contrived exactly, but it was a habit she had developed over the years.

In any case, it appeared that everything about herself was intended to keep Carrie unnoticed and indistinct.

Even her looks seemed bent on hiding Carrie from the world. This observation came as she sat on the stool in the bedroom, staring into the mirror of the dressing table while the pound cake baked. The reflection coming back showed a plain girl, with an indistinguishable shade of light brown hair and dull hazel eyes. Her face was angular, virtually nondescript, except for high cheekbones, slender lines and a perfect complexion.

No one would ever consider Carrie beautiful like Summer or captivating like Bonnie. By her own admission, Carrie was the plainest of the six Baker children. Gazing into the mirror, however, she found it difficult to believe that such a drab reflection stared back at her. Perhaps she was neither beautiful nor captivating, but certainly, she was not this plain.

Recalling the many times Caroline and Summer had intoned her to pay more attention to her looks, she began an appraisal of her features, along with a critical comparison of her appearance with those of her brothers and sisters.

Her hair bothered Carrie more than anything else, framing her face with its nameless shade, limp body and long bangs that always seemed in her eyes. For as long as she could remember, she had worn her hair straight as a board. Suddenly she was sick of it, tired of its lifeless form, fed up with the absence of luster, the kind that allowed Summer to wear her own chocolate-colored hair long and straight and still look radiant. Even the inability to identify the precise shade of brown irked her.

Carrie's hair was the lightest shade of brown in the family, except for the ash brown color of her mother. Joe had hair the color of pecan shells, Summer's was like chocolate, Bonnie's a dark mix of mahogany and darker brown, John's coffee colored and Luke's, like their father, as close to black as possible for a shade of brown. As for her own hair, Carrie finally declared it the color of a finely textured brown eggshell.

Resuming her scrutiny of the image in the mirror, she decided at length that her long, limp locks tarnished an otherwise unblemished face. Carrie had never worn makeup, primarily because her dark complexion seemed color enough for her face. Now she wondered whether a touch of blush and eyeliner would highlight the angles and slender lines of her face, while adding sparkle to those hazel eyes.

Resisting the urge to discover the effect make-up would have on her features, she rose to regard herself in the mirror. She was a good two inches taller than Summer, who like Rachel, stood at medium height, and that much shorter than Caroline. Bonnie, who already looked down at Summer and Rachel, seemed likely to land somewhere between Carrie and their mother by the time she finished growing. In sharp contrast to Summer, who was the perfect combination of voluptuousness and grace, Carrie was just plain thin, a series of straight lines with few curves. She was also the family's lone contribution to the flat-chested women of the world.

Carrie knew she would never match the physical beauty of Summer. On a deeper level, she knew, too, that she could never touch the natural grace of her older sister, whose looks explained only part of the reason Summer held all those beauty queen crowns and other honors. She gazed into the mirror again, this time beyond her reflection to Summer's chest of drawers where the Miss Golden Leaf and Homecoming Queen crowns sparkled atop a jewelry box. Inner beauty—the reason for the sparkle in her brown eyes and the smile on her face—had won those crowns for Summer.

It was a quality Carrie might develop, one Bonnie already possessed.

Of course, on a strictly physical assessment, not even Summer could match the stunning looks of their younger sister. Over the summer, Bonnie had grown a woman's figure, resembling their mother more than either Carrie or Summer, yet also generously endowed with the best features of their father. She was tall and slender, with long legs and graceful arms. With the start of her eighth-grade year, she had abandoned ponytails and pigtails in favor of freedom for her mahogany tresses, which were long and wavy like Caroline's. Sometimes, Bonnie tied a ribbon loosely in her hair and other times she swept it up into a pile, clipping it in place with a simple white barrette. When she did the latter, she looked more like a young woman than a girl, with her brown eyes, dark and vibrant, sparkling against her dark complexion. And whereas Summer's face was definitely round and Carrie's angular, Bonnie's was classic. Boys already daydreamed about Bonnie, even those much older than her. One day soon, they would deem her a breathtaking beauty.

The Baker boys were handsome as well.

Luke was a carbon copy of their father, right down to the blackish hair and classic face with thick, arching eyebrows and neatly trimmed sideburns. One contrast between Luke and his father was the boy's autumn brown eyes, which resembled a cold glaze of maple sugar. Their father's eyes were a smoldering brown, almost as dark as Joe's. The other contrast was height. Luke seemed destined to be shorter than the other men in the family, not even as tall as Caroline or Bonnie would become. Yet, there was nothing short in appearance about Luke, due to his perfect proportion of frame and the easy way he carried himself. And, while the entire family had dark complexions, none of them obtained the depth or polished quality of Luke's tan. This swarthiness gave a rakish edge to his appeal. Simply put, Luke—in the opinion of girls at school—was a heartthrob.

Neither Joe nor John was handsome like Luke and their father, but their appearances were appealing.

John was the tallest of the bunch, almost as tall as Grandpa. He also was the leanest, almost lanky, with long arms and legs, bony fingers and ankles. He wore his straight, coffee-colored hair longer than the other men, well below his collar, with thick sideburns. With his thin face, straight features and jutting chin, John seemed like a masculine version of Caroline. His eyes were unique, however, darker than those of anyone else in the family, almost black, except for the brown sparkle of his pupils.

Joe's distinction was the squareness of face, a visible cleft in his jaw and an overall economy of features. He would have been extremely handsome like Luke and their father, except for tiny flaws that marred his clean-cut looks. His eyes seemed slightly squinted, his nose somewhat crooked and his mouth simply too thin. When he smiled broadly, the flaws disappeared. Without a smile, however, his face acquired a hard edge, which sometimes came across as rugged good looks and, at other times, as cold and harsh. Joe also wore the shortest hair in the family, which typically meant he could manage it equally well with his fingers or a comb, though lately he was wearing it longer. His body was taut, not nearly as lean as John but lacking the fullness of Luke and their father, and, as with all the Baker men, his posture was firm. His eyes were the most striking feature about Joe, darkly brown and smoldering. At five-feet, eleven-inches, Joe stood an inch taller than Matt, three inches below John and Sam and five inches ahead of Luke, who still had an inch or two to grow.

As families went, they were a robust bunch, all of them, with not a hint of daintiness or fairness in the lot. Their prettiness and handsomeness contained a homespun edge, a heartiness sprung from liberal doses of hard work and clean living.

Carrie sighed as she finished this physical appraisal of herself and the family. Unfortunately, her looks seemed to have more of that homespun edge than anyone else in the family. More than ever, she felt like an oddity, a depressing sentiment unimproved upon by the subsequent observation that even her grandparents tended to outshine Carrie.

Even in old age, Sam remained a strapping man. True, he carried a heavier gut and deeper lines in his face. But there was no stoop in his shoulders or any sag in his jaw. His hair had turned hoary white and begun a slow recession up his forehead. To accommodate the high forehead, Sam simply had shorn his hair, which he always had worn thicker and longer than most men in the community. Now, his hair was extremely short all over, with long, but closely cropped, sideburns. He also retained a silvery mustache, which he had trimmed at the barbershop every time he got one of his frequent haircuts. One benefit of old age had been the fading of the jagged scar running from his eye to the bridge of his nose. Though still visible, the scar did not appear as menacing as it had been in his younger years. And the black eye patch was now such a part of his identity that Sam likely would have continued wearing it even if by some miracle, his eye had been restored.

At age seventy-one, Rachel still resembled her younger self, with only a few pounds added to her slight frame and a few wrinkles that were merely lines of distinction on her smooth face. Her hair was grayed, but it was a pretty ash color, adding a soft touch to Rachel's face. Like always, she pinned her hair in a neat bun, allowing a few strands to fall loosely behind her ears. If anything, age had softened Rachel's features and added a gentle glow to her face.

To her utter surprise, Carrie suddenly saw a strong resemblance between herself and Rachel. They both had slender bone structures and angular facial features. And Carrie was already blessed with a gentle countenance.

Since this last acknowledgment was the most positive perception of herself to come from this lengthy appraisal, she allowed a heavy sigh of relief. Of course, Rachel also had a definitive woman's figure. Then again, Carrie remembered not too many years ago when her grandmother had confided that her bosoms were the result of babies and old age.

"Maybe there's hope after all," Carrie declared aloud to the mirror as she lightly fingered her hair, trying to decide on a good style and wondering what makeup would do to her face.

With a determined set to her shoulders, Carrie picked up Summer's rarely used makeup case and some hair rollers. Then, she went into the kitchen to check on the progress of the pound cake. At last, when she was sure of her decision, she retrieved a pair of scissors from Rachel's sewing basket and headed for the bathroom to carry out her plan.

Standing in front of the mirror with the scissors poised at shoulder length on her long locks, she had second and third thoughts about both the rashness and the rationale of her decision. For a fleeting moment, she tried to change her mind with concern about the uneven ends undoubtedly to be left by an attempt to cut her own hair. But crooked ends were easy to remedy and besides, she was not doing anything drastic. When a final argument failed to change her mind, Carrie closed her eyes and made the first cut.

———

The next morning, Carrie woke early to the unusual press of curlers in her hair. She eased out of bed to avoid waking Bonnie and Summer, grabbed her toiletries and fled unnoticed to the bathroom to prepare for the unveiling.

She had styled her hair the previous night, experimented with makeup and picked out a dress from Summer's wardrobe that complimented her slender figure. Pleased with the results, she had gone to bed before anyone returned home. Now, she was eager to see the family's reaction.

Blessed with the rare fortune of no one clamoring for his or her turn in the bathroom, she spent a good half-hour putting herself together. Her hair, cut several inches off the shoulder, now flipped under to curl against her neck. Parted in the middle and pulled back behind the ears, one layer of hair framed her face, while a second layer was gathered and clipped so that it cascaded down her neck. The style was simple, yet highlighted the slender lines of her face. Once she applied makeup, primarily eyeliner, mascara and a touch of rouge, the transformation was complete.

Although church was nearly three hours away, Carrie opted to put on the dress she had selected for the occasion. The dress—a sleeveless light blue design that fit close, a couple of inches above the knee on Carrie—showed off the straight lines of her figure. Having made a conscientious effort to alter her appearance, Carrie figured she might as well present herself in the best light possible instead of her housecoat.

She took one last satisfying glance in the mirror, then went into the bedroom, where Summer and Bonnie were making the beds.

"Wow!" Summer exclaimed with a low whistle.

"Your hair!" squealed Bonnie.

Beneath their incredulous expressions, Carrie detected admiration. "Well?" she prompted. "What do you think?"

"It's fabulous," Summer answered quickly. "You look absolutely stunnen."

"To say the least," added Bonnie.

For the first time, Carrie felt truly at ease with her decision. Just as suddenly, she heard Summer mention the dress.

"I should have asked you to borrow the dress before I took it," Carrie said, "but I didn't think you'd mind."

"It's yours," Summer replied, digging through her jewelry box. "I could never do it justice now that I've seen you in it."

"Gosh you look different," Bonnie remarked, still awed as she examined the new hairstyle.

"I'll need one of you to even up the ends for me," Carrie replied. "It was hard cutten a straight line."

"Here it is!" Summer said, waving a matching light blue choker with a tiny heart pendant, inlaid with a black heart, attached to it. "This will go perfect." She hooked the choker around Carrie's neck, then stood back to admire her sister. "Keep the choker, too," she added.

"Thanks again," Carrie said, examining herself in the floor length mirror attached to the bedroom door.

"Okay!" Bonnie exclaimed with a demanding tone. "What gives, Carrie? Why all the sudden fuss?"

"Too much time on my hands last night," Carrie answered with a shrug of her shoulders as she exited the bedroom to show off the makeover to the rest of the family. "I was bored."

CHAPTER 4

ON MONDAY, MRS. FRANKLIN divided her sixth-period class into groups of two, pairing Carrie and Billy to work on a home management project.

Carrie's first instinct was to request a different partner. Any kind of partnership between Bakers and Taylors seemed doomed from the beginning, overwhelmed by the alarming dissimilarities in their backgrounds and perspectives. Too many built-in prejudices existed for them to cooperate on an important project; the lines of communication were already severed.

Carrie felt compelled to believe this reasoning given the fractious history between the two families. She even wanted to believe it. Yet, over and over, her thoughts returned to that short conversation with Billy on the bus a few days earlier. It was a pleasant memory, providing a reason to delay her approach to Mrs. Franklin.

At last, Billy, who apparently had no similar misgivings about the prospect of working with Carrie, saved her from a decision. "Wow!" he whistled softly as he turned around in his desk to regard her. "Talk about your overnight changes—over the weekend anyway."

Carrie blushed slightly at the obvious admiration. Billy was not the first person to notice her new hairstyle, but he was the first boy to voice approval. "I was tired of always haven bangs in my eyes," she explained. "It was time for somethen different."

"Well, it's different, and very pretty, too," Billy smiled. "You know, most girls do stuff like that over the summer, so they can show off the new do on the first day of school. But I like the fact that you waited until after school had started."

"It was an impulse," Carrie replied, the intensity of Billy's gaze causing her to push a few wayward strands of hair behind her ears.

"Must be nice to change overnight," Billy said at length. "Sometimes, I'd like to be able to do that."

Struck by the sincerity of his declaration, Carrie stopped the fidgeting with her hair. She stared back at him, all at once nervous that Billy might expound on this idea of overnight change. She felt cornered by the familiarity of the moment.

"You'd like to change your hair, too?" she suggested lightly.

From his hard gaze, Carrie could tell Billy was trying to decide whether she meant to mock him or was simply teasing. She immediately chalked up the nervous blunder as the final evidence to support her conclusion that a partnership between them was impossible.

"Somethen like that," Billy mumbled at last.

He glanced away to break the obvious tension and when he looked back, the moment was over and the subject changed.

"So we're gonna be partners," he said. "Pity you, but I'll try to do my part. Maybe Mrs. Franklin will have mercy on you for haven to work with me."

Once again, Carrie questioned his intentions. She stared dumbly at him, trying to figure out exactly what he meant by the remark.

Almost as if read her confusion, Billy quickly amended the suggestion. "Me be'en a guy, you know?" he prompted.

"Oh, well," she stammered, suddenly obligated to accept him as her partner and then determined to make the best of a bad situation. "I'm sure we'll do fine. But you'd better turn around now before we get in trouble for talken."

———

Billy faced the front of the classroom, unable to stop the slow smile spreading across his face. He was relieved and happy to have Carrie as a partner for the project. As soon as Mrs. Franklin had partnered them, he had begun worrying that Carrie would prefer to work with someone else. He figured she had misgivings about the arrangement. Billy did, too. But he had hoped for an opportunity that would force them to spend time together, and the home-ec project would.

For some time now, Billy had wanted to wrangle his way into the Baker family. He had hoped John might invite him to their hallowed home, going so far as to fantasize any number of situations that might bring about such an occasion and how everyone would react. During their two years together at Cookville High School, however, John and Billy had remained strangers, unable to form a friendship even within the confines of the basketball team. Part of the reason had been Billy's fault. He had felt like a star-struck fan, unable to approach his hero when the perfect opportunity presented itself.

Well, he reasoned, even all-state basketball heroes are subject to Achilles heel now and then. Of more importance, Carrie offered a second opportunity for Billy to weave his way into the Baker family. It was a small window of hope but he was willing to accept the odds.

As it stood now, he could think of nothing more improbable than a friendship with Carrie Baker. Until recently, Billy had only a vague awareness of her existence. She was a shadow caught in full sun. Now that she had been revealed, Billy saw what a lovely shadow she cast.

Billy shook away this last thought. It made even less sense than the possibility of a friendship with Carrie. Of course, he was getting used to the idea that most of his thoughts about the Baker family made little sense, especially in light of whom he was.

Though he would never admit as much to his father or anyone else, Billy admired Matt Baker, his sons and daughters, even the man's wife and parents. They represented the pentacle of success, the stuff of dreams. He sensed their closeness, their love and respect for each other, all of which explained his craving for an opportunity to experience their friendship, even if only for a moment. Perhaps just by being able to observe the Bakers up close, he might pick up some pointers on what made them tick as a family.

In his social studies class a few days ago, they had discussed the nuclear family, that ideal combination of parents and children, which some sociologists said was doomed in the coming decades. Billy could not recall the exact definition of a nuclear family, but he knew the Bakers, whether nuclear or not in the strict definition, were an ideal family. At any rate, they were far removed from the Taylor version of the nuclear family, which was a mutated one for sure.

Family was important to Billy—and a subject of mixed emotions as well. As much as he loved the concept of family, Billy thought it might be best to reject the idea of having one of his own someday. Ever since Mrs. Brogdon, his sophomore science teacher, had explained how genetics worked, Billy had questioned the wisdom of continued propagation of the twisted Taylor gene pool. He worried that should he have his own family, he might discover too late the impossibility of overcoming bad genes. But on the likelihood that he might have a family one day, Billy wanted to prepare in every way, which was one reason he had decided to take home economics and partly explained his preoccupation with the Bakers. In the meantime, he might discover some secret that would improve the lot of his current family.

Billy recognized this train of thought was ridiculous, as patently absurd as a high school junior's crush on an entire family that he barely knew. But what else could a guy do when he belonged to a family as messed up as the Taylors? Especially when he loved them all the same because, after all, they were the only loved ones he had.

Love was another strange concept to Billy. The one thing he understood about love was that it was something neither his father nor older brother did. In fact, when it came to commitment and obligations to family, Bobby and Wayne had an undeveloped sense of caring. Instead, they relied on a primitive sense of duty and responsibility to fulfill their family roles. Still, Billy figured even a primitive show of concern was better than nothing at all.

As for Carl, he was another enigma to Billy. Though only six years old, Carl lived in a shell that seemed impenetrable by either love or hate. Carl had created an ideal world where only he could tread—a place of make-believe friends, fantasy and ignorance—and it seemed a far better place than the reality of the Taylor household. Sometimes, Billy envied his little brother's ability to turn off the world. Mainly, though, he hoped Carl would stay free of the hate that consumed Bobby and Wayne, turning the Taylor household into a seething nuthouse.

The cause of all this family turmoil was hate, and the magnet for the overwhelming majority of hate was niggers.

In the Taylor house, a person could avoid trouble easily enough with judicious use of the word nigger. Ranting about niggers commanded tolerance and earned the nearest thing possible to beaming parental approval. Needless to say, Billy commanded little respect and earned few fatherly gestures. He had learned to despise the word, nigger, early in life. He spoke it rarely, only when he needed to remind his father or Wayne that he was a member of the family, too.

Billy's place in the family was easily forgotten, unless it was suppertime or the clothes were unwashed or the house became intolerably messy. On those occasions, he was the first one called, though he still could not figure out the ease with which his mother's mantle had been thrust upon him when Martha died. (Billy still said Martha had died, unable to admit she had taken her own life.)

Even more difficult to comprehend than his domestic duties was the precise moment when hate had overtaken the Taylor household and started the family on their slow breakdown.

Sometime ago, Billy had tried to convince himself the family decay actually set in when Martha died. But his argument had been short, with little or no basis of support. When you got right down to the inescapable facts, his mother's death had altered the family landscape very little. Billy had stepped in to his mother's place as the family cook and maid, and he performed the tasks as well as Martha. The cold truth was that the Taylors had prospered like never before since Martha had decided to decorate their living room walls with her brains.

This acknowledgment brought a wave of sadness over Billy. In a strange way, he hoped his mother had taken her life because she recognized the pervading atmosphere of doom around the Taylor family and felt inadequate to overcome it. He empathized with the aching desperation that had raped her soul and driven Martha to the surest escape. Once or twice, he had dared to consider such an escape for himself, but those thoughts were quickly swallowed up in an avalanche of fear and an even more crushing sense of loyalty to the family he loved and hated all the same. And then, he would begin anew the futile search for the source of all the hate within his family.

His first inclination was to place the blame on niggers. Colored people, he corrected himself, then sighed and admitted it was niggers.

Like his father, Billy resented niggers, but for different reasons. Whereas Bobby hated the whole Negro race seemingly because of their black skin, Billy despised them for the irrevocable harm they had brought to his family. It was nothing personal, but night after night of listening to his daddy ramble on and on about the loathsomeness of niggers had left Billy with a bad taste for the subject, like someone whose middling appetite for bologna sandwiches was spoiled by repeated servings of the fare. Although he acknowledged the wounds inflicted on his family by Negroes were none of their making, the understanding did little to change Billy's mind on the subject. He was way beyond the realm of reason, blaming everyone and anyone for the troubles, depending on his mood at any given moment.

In his present state of mind, Billy wanted someone to blame for the mess—or a good explanation for the sorry state of affairs at home. And so, he began a concentrated effort to find a logical explanation for the predicament.

For the sake of thoroughness, he began this search with the broad assumption that the mere existence of niggers was the source of all the Taylor family turmoil. Given that possibility, Billy supposed the blame might rest with God Himself, if one subscribed to the theory that an all-supreme, all-knowing being created the universe and everything and everyone in it. Of course, blaming God for the creation of an entire race was a preposterous notion at best—even for those who believed in God. And Billy was not at all sure on that one accord. He'd seen little evidence of God in his sixteen years, much less benefited from an Almighty's benevolence. If God existed, then Billy supposed he was shooting himself in the foot with these kinds of thoughts. But he had vowed to apply logic to this thinking and the facts of the matter were plainspoken.

Realizing he had rambled into uncharted territory, Billy reset his attention to the subject at hand. Though unsure about the existence of God, deep down, Billy knew where to lay the blame for the family discord. A great deal of it belonged to Robert Taylor, the grandfather he barely remembered and tried hard to forget—and probably to other small-soul ancestors who had steeped Robert in a pot of hatred.

As far as Billy knew or cared, his roots stretched only as far back as Robert. Vague though his memories were of the man, Billy remembered the worst about his grandfather. His earliest memory still rekindled the same nausea Billy had felt at age four when he watched his grandfather intimidate Martha into sex. It confused him as well, because bedding your son's wife seemed the ultimate fatherly sin and, as far as Billy knew, Robert had cared for only three things in life: work, his dead wife and his only son. That Robert would bed his son's wife made no sense at all, especially in light of the way he had kowtowed to Bobby's every whim and wish. But then again,

Billy had realized long ago that the oddities and complexities of the Taylor family defied logic and sense.

He also had learned early in life that Robert despised his grandsons, seeing them as nothing more than obstructions in his son's life.

Grandpa Taylor had treated Wayne and Billy with scornful disregard, meting out nothing to them unless it was his severe form of discipline. He had been savage with a belt, and his grandsons learned quickly to avoid him if possible and obey him in every instance.

Billy remembered most vividly the hard gaze of his grandfather, those cold gray eyes that bore right through a person. With a single glare, Robert challenged the very existence of his grandson and dared the boy to prove otherwise. Billy had accepted this rejection without question, as had Wayne, who closely resembled their grandfather as much in appearance as demeanor. Regardless of his own feelings about Robert, Billy considered Wayne's inability to recall a fond memory of their grandfather as the telling testament to the man's callous character.

There had been no tears shed when Robert died, not even by his beloved son. Bobby had been saddened, but it was grief that arose more from disappointment of losing an asset than a loved one. Somewhere in that hazy distinction lay the difference in character between Robert Taylor and his son, as well as the explanation for the wretched home life of Billy Taylor.

For all his shortcomings, Robert at least had the propensity to love. He had worshipped his wife and doted on their son. Of that much, Billy was certain. But on that single measure, Billy had doubts about his own father. All Bobby did was hate, and his sole passion was a towering rage against niggers.

Try as he might, Billy failed to comprehend his daddy's hatred for a whole race of people. He had truly tried to understand, even appreciate, what Bobby meant when he railed against the notion of blacks and whites fraternizing in public places and attending the same schools. To support his father's belief about blacks, Billy had noted numerous examples of local Negroes who were lazy and shiftless, mean and evil, cheaters and liars. But a similar number of white trash types also fit those same descriptions, which made a valid argument for the possibility that people were people despite the color of their skin. If he truly called a spade a spade—a phrase Bobby was particularly fond of using when he discussed blacks—Billy had to admit the actions of his own father evoked close kinship with the sordid labels he frequently used to belittle niggers.

Such thoughts scared the daylights out of Billy and were best kept locked deep inside his mind, away from any kind of consideration whatsoever. In the Taylor household, these ideas were grounds for execution, and having come to this conclusion, Billy contented himself with a more realistic and reasonable line of thought.

For as long as he could remember, his father had condemned niggers, communists and—as of late—liberal politicians for virtually every problem known to mankind. Now, however, these endless hate-filled tirades were worsening day-by-day, consuming Bobby to the point of no appeasement. Indeed, Billy believed, if his father's oft-voiced dream of having every single black American returned to the jungles of Africa came true, Bobby would remain unhappy and unsatisfied. Likely, he would follow them to the jungles with a brand-new agenda of hate.

Realizing he had strayed once again beyond the bounds of reasonable thinking,

Billy acknowledged the ludicrousness of the idea. But such was his father's obsession with niggers.

Bobby was a fanatic believer in the separation of the races. He had forced Billy to quit the basketball team rather than play on the newly integrated squad. More recently, he had gone a step further, banning his sons from watching any televised sporting event that featured black athletes.

"I don't want y'all exposed to the wrong element," he had told his sons when even Wayne the brown-noser objected to the rule.

His father had ranted and raved about niggers for as long as Billy could remember, but now his tirades seemed more like an obsession with a dangerous edge. Billy had no proof to substantiate such a claim, however, and he had realized long ago that his father had more bark than bite, especially when the odds were stacked against him.

Indeed, in the wake of the successful integration of the schools, Bobby's preoccupation seemed more ludicrous than dangerous. Night after night, he and Wayne sat at the supper table, alternating racial slurs with grandiose, yet always illogical and unthinkable, plans to cause trouble between blacks and whites. They wanted to make the idea of segregated schools seem appealing to everyone; Billy wanted to yell at them sometimes, to tell them to wise up, think straight and accept the inevitable. Yet, his father and brother continued their scheming, discussing a wide range of options from blowing up the high school (Bobby's idea) to stealing all the school's basketballs (Wayne's suggestion).

This feeble suggestion from his brother had doubled Billy over with laughter at the table a few nights earlier. Even Carl had ventured out of his shell long enough to grasp the silliness of the suggestion and roll his eyes in disbelief. Their father, of course, failed to see the humor of the situation.

"Did it ever occur to you, Wayne, that they could just go out and buy new and probably better basketballs?" Bobby had asked in his most sarcastic tone. Then, he had delivered two sharp, though harmless, flat-handed slaps to the side of Wayne's hard head. "Use that pea-sized brain, boy. We need a sure-fire plan—not stupidity."

Knowing his father and Wayne, Billy was fairly confident they would never develop a feasible plan, much less have the guts to carry it out. Whatever happened, though, he hoped the Klan would not get involved. He had come to dread the KKK activities, though many of the Klansmen seemed to think highly of his father. Nevertheless, Billy hated the attention that his father's position in the group generated and he resented the associations that naturally came his way.

While many people, maybe the majority for all he knew, opposed integration of the schools, Billy felt certain they found the idea of grown men wearing bed sheets ridiculous and even more offensive than desegregation. On the first day of school, he had overheard a group of students laughing and ridiculing the Klansmen who paraded outside the main building. When they laughed at his father, Billy had felt singled out as well. It was embarrassing, and Billy hated this idea of guilt by association. He wanted to claim immunity, but it wasn't allowed. A guy could not pick his relatives and, despite what the do-gooders preached, he was judged by his family's reputation.

Billy reeled from a sudden sense of hopelessness and frustration that dogged him like a gnat. It seemed as if someone had stuck a knife in his back and was now twisting, grinding and pushing it deeper. He reached behind his back absentmindedly to flick away this aggravation, but instead caught a warm hand in his palm. When he turned around, he found himself gazing into the depths of gentle brown eyes.

———

The room exploded in laughter around Billy. His eyes blinked as he tried to discern where he was and then realized the girls in home economics were having a good laugh at his expense. All of them, except for Carrie Baker.

"Are you okay?" she asked softly through the giggles and cackles as Billy clung to her hand.

"Yeah, sure," Billy answered, finally releasing her hand as she pulled away from him.

"Mr. Taylor!"

The booming voice of Dorothea Franklin restored Billy to his full senses and brought him face-forward in the classroom.

"Mr. Taylor," Mrs. Franklin repeated sternly. "Will you please answer the question?"

"Uh," Billy stumbled as another round of giggles erupted.

"Y'all hush," the teacher ordered in her most exasperated tone. "We're waiten, Billy."

Billy shook his head. "Sorry, ma'am. I didn't hear the question."

"In the future, young man," Mrs. Franklin lectured, "you'd be better off payen attention instead of daydreamen in my class."

The lesson continued without further interruption, but Billy's concentration was blown. As was Carrie's.

When Billy had faced her, Carrie had looked into a pair of bewildered slate blue eyes and saw a world of confusion and sadness. There had been a trace of tears as well, and she was intrigued about the powerful thoughts plaguing him. In her most melancholy moments, Carrie had never experienced the kind of lost feelings she sensed in Billy. Her interest grew as the school day moved toward completion.

By the time the bell rang, Carrie was determined to accompany Billy on the walk to the bus that would carry them to New River. Billy had other ideas. He made a fast getaway from the room, up and out of his seat before the clamor ended and rushing out the door before Carrie could gather her books. She boarded the bus a few minutes later, scanning the seats for Billy as she stepped up the entrance and taking her usual seat when a quick glance showed him absent.

Billy was still missing moments later when the driver cranked the bus and shut the door. Then, just as the vehicle made its first lumbering movement, he came bounding around a building corner running toward the bus with a composition and text book dangling in one hand. A moment later, he was standing beside Carrie, explaining to the driver his reason for being late. She observed him, realizing with surprise that he was shorter than she was by an inch.

In quick order, Billy turned from the driver, glancing down the aisle, and Carrie smiled, an invitation to the open seat beside her. He glanced past her, however, and made his way to the back of the bus. Though disappointed, she did not feel slighted. While the day had seemed to offer up the perfect setting to discuss their team project in home economics and perhaps get better acquainted, Carrie was prepared to accept the delay.

Still, her curiosity was heightened, so she maneuvered into a sideways position that afforded a direct view of Billy. He sat four rows from the back, alternately talking to the boy beside him and staring out the window. Carrie decided he was cute, modestly so, with straight ash blond hair that was parted crookedly and haphazardly combed to the side. Besides being shorter than her, he was of slight build, with fair skin and a liberal coating of freckles. His face was clean-cut and remarkably similar to her brother Joe's, right down to the distinct cleft in his chin. After a lifetime of being surrounded by brown eyes, Carrie found herself drawn to his slate blue eyes. They were soft, caring eyes—which surprised her—and, suddenly, they stared at her for the second time that day.

Carrie held the gaze purposely for a moment longer, hoping to feign a faraway look that would make her obvious interest seem more like an unintended occurrence. She never knew with certainty whether the tactic worked because Billy broke the gaze first, almost as if he was embarrassed to have been caught looking her way.

Carrie turned away and stared out her own window for the remainder of the trip. Her thoughts remained on the boy in the back of the bus, though, and the ride home seemed longer than usual.

The next week yielded little contact between Carrie and Billy. They exchanged pleasantries in class and on the bus, each always on the verge of extending the conversation, yet finding some excuse not to follow their inclination. Still, there was a mutual attraction between them, Carrie thought, or perhaps just curiosity. At last, the approaching deadline on their home management assignment forced them to give each other full attention.

"You do realize we're way behind on our project," Carrie told Billy one day as they waited for class to begin.

"We've been putten off the inevitable," Billy agreed.

"Consideren it's due Monday, we can't put it off any longer," Carrie replied. "Do you have some time this weekend when we could get together and just do the whole thing?"

"I could get away Saturday. Could we do it at your house?"

Carrie considered the suggestion, then rejected the idea. "I don't think so," she said. "You might not be comfortable around my family."

Billy forced himself to hide his disappointment. "Yeah, you're probably right," he conceded. "My daddy wouldn't be none too thrilled with that arrangement either," he continued bluntly, "but that still leaves us with the problem of getten the project done. Should we try to do the work at school?"

"I have a better idea," Carrie replied, her face brightening with a smile. "There's a place on the river near my house where we go swimmen sometimes. It's through the woods, almost straight across from our house. Think you could find that?"

"Sounds easy enough," Billy nodded. "How 'bout Saturday around noon?"

"Noon it is," Carrie smiled. "I'm looken forward to getten this over and done with. It's a big part of our grade this six weeks."

"I know," Billy grimaced. "And between you and me, I sure do need a good grade. I'd hate to be not only the first boy to take home-ec, but the first to fail it, too."

Saturday came, and Carrie rushed through her chores, then excused herself from the house, telling her mother she needed privacy to work on important homework. With books and other project materials in hand, she picked her way through the woods to the river and found Billy already waiting, sitting cross-legged on a faded blue blanket spread on the grassy bank.

"I figured this was the spot," he said in lieu of a proper greeting. "It's real pretty, and I saw the diven platform," he continued, pointing to the three boards mounted some fifty feet above the water on an oak limb. "Somebody's awfully brave," he added.

"My brothers did that a couple of years ago," Carrie explained, still standing. "In the summers, they used to go swimmen here a lot with Tom Carter, and all of them would jump off it. My little sister, Bonnie, did it, too, a few times last summer. I was too scared, though, and so was Summer."

"It's a far ways to jump," Billy observed.

Carrie nodded in agreement, then spied the silver metallic canoe tied to a tree at the river's edge. "I never thought about how you would get here without be'en noticed," she said.

"It's my fishen boat," Billy answered.

Each sensed nervous tension seeping into the moment, and pointedly looked away from the other. "I guess we'd better get down to work," Carrie remarked finally as she sat on the blanket and laid out her materials across from Billy.

"I suppose so," he added.

For nearly four hours, they worked diligently, reading instructions, making charts and preparing a five-page report. The time passed quickly, taking with it any traces of nervousness as well as their normally reserved behaviors. They treated each other like seasoned business partners, bouncing around ideas, applauding the better suggestions and laughing off the silly mistakes. When Carrie punctuated the report with a final period, they exhaled a mutual sigh of relief and shared broad smiles to celebrate a job well done.

"By George, I think we deserve an A," Billy remarked as they began picking up their books and papers.

"Nothen less," Carrie agreed. "And preferably with a plus beside it."

They finished gathering their materials, then stretched out on the blanket in a silent agreement to satisfy their curiosity about each other.

"It's always a good feelen to complete a major project," Carrie observed. "Once I'm done, I like to sit back, relax and think about what I've accomplished. Does that sound silly?"

"Nah," Billy answered, "and you're really good at this home economics stuff. I'm glad we were partners."

"Me too," Carrie smiled, "although I have to admit I wasn't too thrilled about it in the first place. I almost asked Mrs. Franklin for a new partner. I wasn't sure we were cut out to work with each other. We're a good team, though, and you're not so bad at this home economics stuff either, especially for a boy."

"One thing's for sure," Billy replied good-naturedly. "I bet nobody in class did their project under such a cloak of secrecy. Comen here today, I felt like a spy on a rendezvous."

"My fault," Carrie conceded, blushing slightly but holding a steady gaze at her partner. "I suppose we could have met at my house, but I thought you might be uncomfortable." She hesitated before confessing: "No, that's not completely true. I would have been uncomfortable and probably my family, too. You have to admit that our families haven't gotten along very well over the years."

"No," Billy agreed. "And most of the fault has come from my side," he added with candor, both surprised and relieved by the admission. "My family has a knack for stirren up trouble. I guess you could say we thrive on it."

He smiled sheepishly, then looked across the river, unable to bear the scrutiny as Carrie considered his remarks—wondering if she was looking at him in a new light.

"You're a lot different than I thought you'd be," Carrie said at last.

"What did you expect?" he replied with unexpected shortness. "That I'd come here today wearen white sheets and a hood?"

His hard gaze caused Carrie to turn away, embarrassed.

"That's not fair," Billy apologized immediately. "From past experience, you had every right to expect the worst of me. I'm just glad I didn't live up to your expectations."

Carrie faced him once more, this time with acceptance and honesty. "I shouldn't have been so judgmental in the first place," she said. "I don't know your daddy, Billy, but I admit I don't like him very much because of the things he does and what he stands for. It's contrary to everything I've been taught."

"And I agree wholeheartedly with you," Billy replied freely before Carrie had time to regret her criticism. "I do my best to stay away from that stuff, but it's easy to get tagged with labels simply by virtue of what your parents do."

"Maybe you could do somethen to let people know you're different from all that," she suggested.

"Like what?"

"I don't know," she faltered. "Make a stand for what you believe in. Tell your father you think he's wrong."

Billy laughed bitterly. "That's not allowed in my house. Maybe you're encouraged to share your opinions with the family, but in our house, my daddy makes the rules and his sons follow them. If I did what you're suggesten, I'd be kicked out of the house on my ass—literally. Course, that might not be so bad in itself, but I can't leave just now. I need to finish high school, and my little brother needs me. I'd like to go to college, but payen for it's another story. I wanted to get a basketball scholarship, but the old man's put that on hold for the time be'en."

He paused, then added, "I'm tellen you more than you need or want to know about me."

"No," Carrie said. "I wasn't tryen to pry, though. Maybe I shouldn't have started this conversation. We could change the subject."

"That's okay," Billy said resolutely. "It's good to get it off my chest, and there aren't too many people I could tell stuff like this and trust to keep it to themselves. Actually, there's no one else, so you've done me a favor. Maybe I can return it.

"Any requests, madam?" he added, suddenly rising and bowing. "Just say the word and I'm at your command."

Carrie laughed happily, infectiously, enchanting Billy with the rapturous sparkle of her hazel eyes. "I think you've been in the sun too long," she teased. "You're turnen all silly on me. Sit down."

"As you wish," he said, plopping down beside her on the blanket, closer this time. "I mean it about be'en at your command," Billy joked. "Flowers, adulations, a cape over a mud puddle. What will you have?"

"I'll take the adulations," Carrie answered. "I have to confess: I like flattery."

"Easy enough," he replied. "I bet a pretty girl like you gets lots of flattery." He paused before adding more seriously, "You should anyway."

"Thank you," she replied shyly, lowering her eyes from the closeness of his gaze, knowing without doubt that he would kiss her.

Her heart beat wildly as she waited for his overture, sensing the same abandon in Billy. She stared into her lap, achingly aware of his nearness, feeling the warmth of his breath on her neck and the touch of his hand on her shoulder as Billy urged her to give into this moment of surrender. She did, tilting her head back to accept the waiting kiss.

Billy was not the first boy that Carrie had kissed, but none of the others had stirred such wanting within her. They came together slowly, softly, with the clumsiness of inexperience. Billy pulled her against him, deepening the kiss, and Carrie responded with matched desire, wrapping her arms around him, allowing her hands to rake his hair as they fell back onto the sun-warmed blanket, exploring these new feelings with innocence and thoroughness.

It was a tender experience, right until the moment Carrie became aware of his hardness against her thigh. The romance vanished instantly, replaced by fear of something unknown and definitely unwanted. She broke the kiss, pushing Billy away and rising quickly to her feet.

"I have to go," she announced, hurriedly gathering her belongings. "See you at school Monday."

She was gone before Billy could right himself on the blanket, before he could apologize for getting too involved in the moment, before he could ask her for a date. He sat up, staring at the waiting canoe, his senses stunned from the thrill of the moment as well as the abrupt ending of it. He wanted to explain to Carrie that his bad manners had resulted from forces beyond his control, that he'd not intended to try anything wrong with her. But the situation was unexplainable probably, and Billy feared the entire episode had jeopardized the possibility of any further relationship between them.

He was fretting over his handling of the situation when he heard the soft call of his name. Slowly, he turned around, kneeling on the blanket. Carrie stood at the edge of the woods, with tousled hair and a questioning look on her flushed face.

"Except for my sisters and brothers, I've never really had a close friend," she said with genuine affection. "But you're a nice boy, Billy, and I think we could be good friends. I'd like to be your friend. You have to know, though, that friendship is all I have to offer. And it's all I'm really looken for at the moment."

She waited for his answer, and Billy smiled, nodding his acceptance of her offer. Then, she waved goodbye and vanished again into the woods.

Unable to suppress a silly grin, Billy stood and released a gleeful yell. Quietly, happily, he folded the blanket, gathered his own stuff and headed for the canoe, eager for Monday and all the days to follow.

CHAPTER 5

CARRIE AND BILLY BECAME best friends. They sat together on the daily bus rides between New River and Cookville, shared the same table at lunch and chatted away every free moment in their home economics class, where they received top marks for the team project. On Friday nights, they slipped away from the Cookville football games to talk by themselves and on Saturday nights, they had a standing date over the telephone.

It was a unique experience for them, having an outlet for new ideas and fresh insights. They put away their inhibitions and exposed their souls on any and every subject, from family relationships and expectations to private quirks and embarrassing secrets.

Carrie shared with Billy her occasional feelings of suffocation by the closeness of her family, as if she only mattered because she belonged to the Bakers. Billy told her she was bonkers for having those thoughts and suggested they swap places for a few days so that she might gain a better appreciation of her birthright. Yet, on occasion, he also spoke fondly of his family, revealing a yearning that fate might intervene with an overnight transformation of the Taylor home into a place of security and love. In one of her more brutal assertions, Carrie suggested Billy not hold his breath waiting for such a miracle.

Out of these discussions also came one of their favorite exchanges, which they repeated on numerous occasions.

"Do you think I'm normal?" Billy would ask.

"You're extremely normal," she reassured him, "for such a maladjusted young man."

On another occasion, Billy expressed regret over his absence from the basketball team. Basketball, he told her, was his one great passion, the singular talent he possessed and his possible ticket to a college education. Carrie urged him to continue practicing in hopes that Bobby might change his mind and allow Billy to rejoin the team. Then, she confessed her most embarrassing secret, the pleasures of home economics.

"Does that make me a bore?" she asked.

"Not at all," Billy replied. "You just have a fetish for cooken and cleanen. Perfectly normal."

"You make it sound so mundane."

"Well, it is," he teased.

Other conversations were more memorable, especially one in early October when they discussed their limited travels. The exchange began when Billy voiced his desire to see the ocean.

"I've gone to the ocean," Carrie said. "It was last year, a few days after Tom was buried. Daddy decided out of the blue that everyone needed a vacation, so we packed our bags and drove to Fernandina Beach, Florida. The whole family went. We missed a day of school, and Luke even missed a football game, but we had a great time. Daddy rented two motel rooms on the beach, one for him and Mama and my grandparents and one for us kids. We ate out in these great seafood restaurants—shrimp, crab, fried oysters, swordfish soup, even lobster and alligator tail."

"Alligator tail?" Billy frowned.

"Fried alligator tail," Carrie confirmed. "It sounds awful, but it was really good. It tasted like fried shrimp to me.

"It's the only vacation we've ever taken," Carrie added wistfully. "Of course, the only reason we went was because everyone was so broken up over Tom. It was still fun, though, tasten salt water, riden the waves, builden sand castles. I'll always cherish it."

"My family did somethen like that one time," Billy recalled. "It was before my Mama died. In the middle of summer, my daddy woke everyone up one mornen and said we were goen on a trip. I thought maybe he was drinken, but we got up, packed our clothes and went to Stone Mountain in Atlanta.

"We stayed for three days, and it was almost like we were a real family," he continued, mesmerized by the memory. "Daddy acted like a little kid let out to play after be'en cooped up all day. Mama probably smiled more than I ever saw her smile. And even Wayne, who is probably the unhappiest person I've ever known, was happy there. That giant piece of rock did somethen for him. He dragged me up and down it, across it and around it. He thought it was the most wonderful place in the world. Be'en way up in the sky like that, I guess Wayne probably felt like he was on top of the world for once in his life. He still talks about it every now and then. Maybe one day we can go back there. He's a pain, but I'd like to see my brother happy like that again."

"How long since you were there?" Carrie asked.

Billy bit the left side of his bottom lip, a habit he resorted to when pondering a question. "About four or five years ago," he recalled. "I remember we went about the same time your brother got bit by those snakes. And that doctor was killed in Cookville, too." He paused, then continued. "That's one time all hell broke loose, and my daddy wasn't around for it. Thank goodness for small miracles."

And so their relationship went. It was friendship, but there was more. While Carrie and Billy failed to discuss the kiss they had shared, it remained on their lips, a suggestion that they wanted more from each other than they were ready to give.

———

Most likely, someone in the Baker family would have noticed the changes in Carrie had not all of them been wrapped up in their own lives. But in the fall of 1969, the family was scattered like leaves in the wind, each in pursuit of ambitions and new horizons, enjoying newfound discoveries.

Joe worked, then worked some more, building up an impressive collection of stories for the newspaper. Summer split her time between school and work, taking in sewing from neighborhood women and doing alterations for the boutique in Valdosta. John attended school and immersed himself in night classes on painting techniques. Luke became a hero on the football field and acquired a girlfriend—a senior by the name of Patti Avera—much to the chagrin of Caroline and Rachel, who complained loudly every time the young woman blared her car horn on Saturday nights and Luke bounded out of the house. Even Bonnie became enamored with the opposite sex, choosing a steady boyfriend much more to the liking of her mother and grandmother. Ken Cook was the preacher's son, an affable eighth-grader who romanced Bonnie in school, at church and on Friday nights at the football games.

Matt found himself shorthanded as he tried to bring in a bumper harvest, working six days a week and relying on the support of his sons whenever they could pitch in. The bulk of the supporting work fell to John, although Joe spent his share of late evenings on the combine. Caroline helped as well, hauling trailers between the farm and the markets and preparing picnic lunches, which she and Matt shared nearly every day in the fields. With schoolwork, football and a buxom blonde to occupy his days and nights, Luke spent little time in the fields that fall.

Even Sam and Rachel busied themselves more than usual. Rachel took charge of the housework, with ample assistance from Carrie and Bonnie, while Sam tended his nut trees, fruit trees and exotic crops. He also made the final preparations for his last year as a pecan broker, tutoring John each step of the way in case his grandson chose to follow him in the business.

Even though the family was split apart more than ever by their respective obligations and goals in that busy fall, they still came together for common pursuits. Some came together often.

On his way home from work each day, Joe picked up Luke from football practice, giving the brothers a chance to establish a closer bond and break down the barriers of age. One day, Luke shocked his brother with an unexpected question.

"How old were you when you made it with a girl for the first time?" he asked Joe on their way home.

Uncertain whether to answer, Joe responded dumbly with a blank stare and open mouth, prompting Luke to amend his question. "I'm assumen, for your sake, that you have gone all the way at least once in twenty-three years."

This time, Joe roared with laughter. "And what makes you suddenly so interested in my sex life, or lack thereof, little brother?"

"Just looken for a comparison," Luke said slyly.

"Ah!" Joe replied knowingly. "Mama and Granny's worst fears about the buxom blonde hussy have come true."

"They think Patti's a hussy?"

"Well, they haven't come right out and said so," Joe answered, "but it's their general assumption."

"She's really a very nice girl," Luke observed.

"I'm sure she is," Joe agreed.

"Are you gonna answer my question?" Luke pressed.

"Well, Luker, if you've gone all the way at fifteen, then you've got me beat by several months," Joe replied. "But be careful, little brother. If you're playen for fun, make sure you don't wind up playen for keeps."

Luke simply nodded his head to this bit of brotherly advice.

Likewise, on the daily rides to and from Tifton for their college classes, Summer and John strengthened already close sibling ties with frank discussions about themselves and various family members. One day, they drifted into a conversation about Joe, the discussion coming in a roundabout way, initiated by John's concern for his sister's state of mind shortly after the anniversary of Tom's death.

"It's high time you put what happened to Tom behind you, Summer," John told her bluntly. "You're too beautiful and spirited to waste away your youth in mournen, especially when there's so many eligible guys who would give their right arm for a date with you."

"I'm not in mournen," Summer replied testily. "I just haven't found anyone who interests me in that way."

"You could try goen out just for fun, Summer," John replied. "I'm not suggesten you go looken for a husband, but the only men you ever spend any time with are Joe and me. You might as well be liven in a nunnery."

"Look who's talken," Summer challenged. "You're not exactly Casanova. I'd say your batten record with the girls isn't much better than mine over the past year. And furthermore, you don't have any excuses. If you're plannen on packen me off to a nunnery, brother, then find a monastery for yourself."

"Let's change the subject," John suggested.

"Fine with me."

"How's Joe these days?" he asked.

"Why not ask him yourself?" Summer answered, again testily. "Surely you have some good advice on how he should live his life, too."

"Well, I would if there was an opportunity," John said with sarcasm. "Trouble is, he's busy, and he spends his free time almost exclusively with you. And whether you've noticed it or not, Summer, y'all aren't too willen these days to invite anybody else along on your weekend parties."

"What's with you, John?" she asked. "Why are you jumpen on my case?"

"I'm just ticked because you got an A on that last English paper, and I got a C when, frankly, I thought mine was better," he responded with a contrite smile. "And maybe, too, I'm feelen a bit left out."

"Okay," Summer interrupted evenly. "Let's start this conversation over. I do plan to date again. I suspect I'll even fall in love again, marry, have two-point-five children, and life will be a dream. Now, though, I'm not ready for it. I need time."

"Fair enough," John said.

"As for Joe ...."

"Go on," John prompted.

Summer considered her reply. "He's the same old Joe," she said finally. "He's wrapped up in his job but getten itchy for somethen else. I think he's ready to fly the coup, head on to greener pastures so to speak. That shouldn't surprise you or anybody else. He's been in a horse race to leave this neck of woods for a long time. Frankly, I'm surprised he's stayed around this long."

"Now tell me somethen I don't know," John said.

"Like what?"

"Like why he's been so remote lately," John replied. "I keep getten the feelen that he's keepen stuff from us." He hesitated thoughtfully. "No, that's not it entirely. It's more like he's not sharen stuff with us anymore. He's there for us, but he's not with us?"

"Joe's always worried about looken after everyone else," John continued, "but now it's almost like he's existen for everyone but himself—like he's afraid of messen things up for the rest of us. Maybe I'm way off base, but he's not the same Joe. Do you get the same feelen?"

Summer considered the assessment. "Not exactly," she answered. "I've spent more time with Joe, and I've seen most sides of him. You have to remember that losen Tom was tough for him, too, especially with everything else that happened.

He is a little more reserved than usual, but if he seems remote, maybe that's his way of getten ready to leave the nest. I imagine that, even for someone who wants to go, leaven is easier said than done. All in all, though, Joe seems pretty normal to me. Except maybe for one thing."

"What's that," John asked.

She hesitated. "You have to swear to keep this between you and me, John?"

"Since when has trust ever been an issue?"

Summer nodded. "Joe drinks beer," she told John. "And sometimes liquor, too. Occasionally, he drinks too much. He never gets fallen down drunk or anything close to it. In fact, I'd probably never know he was drinken except for see'en him doen it. Still though, I worry about it. For his sake, I wish he'd stay away from the booze."

"You should tell him that," John suggested.

"Yeah," she agreed. "I think I will."

———

A few days later, on the first Saturday night in October, Summer followed through on John's advice. She had mulled over the decision, thinking perhaps she might be making a mountain out of a molehill with her concern for Joe's drinking habits. After all, he rarely drank more than a few beers at a time. Still, he had drifted into a pattern with his drinking, just as the two of them had fallen into the habit of spending too much of their free time with each other.

Summer could not recall exactly when she and Joe had begun spending so much time together, although she suspected it was around last Christmas when she started clerking in the boutique and they had commuted together between home and Valdosta. The drives home gradually had turned into weekend outings, a movie every now and then, eating out, even roller skating on occasion, although they made sure to include their brothers and sisters when they frequented Cherry Lake. Eventually, they had begun doing nothing more than drive around on city streets or back roads, talking and bolstering their friendship.

One night in Cookville, Joe had asked her permission to buy a beer as they drove past the Log Cabin liquor store. Without batting an eye, Summer consented. On another night, she made the suggestion, then proceeded to drink the first three beers of her life. She got tipsy, giggling and talking silly until Joe suggested she refrain from further drinking. One headache later, Summer had sworn off the stuff for life.

Yet, Joe continued to drink, often nursing three or four beers through the night. Summer had never minded until one night a few weeks earlier when Joe suggested she drive the Volkswagen because he might have had one too many beers.

The conversation with John had brought home her anxiety. So, on this particular Saturday night, as Joe slowed the car when they neared the Tip-Toe Inn, Summer made the suggestion. "You know, Joe," she said. "You really should lay off the beer."

"Why's that?" Joe said with arched eyebrows.

"No reason in particular," she answered vaguely. "I just don't think it's good for you. And I'd feel better if you passed it by tonight."

"Well, then, I'll pass right by it," Joe replied, accelerating the engine and driving past the honky tonk.

His easy acceptance of the suggestion once again made Summer question her anxiety. "I hope you're not mad at me," she said a moment later.

"Why in the world would I be mad at you, Summer?" he remarked casually. "I wish you had said somethen earlier if the beer bothered you. The last thing I want to do is make you uneasy around me."

"I'm not uneasy in the least around you, Joe," she replied, concluding her worry was unfounded. "In fact, we can go back, and you can get a whole six-pack if you want."

"Nah," Joe said. "You were right in the first place. I really oughtta lay off the beer."

She smiled and touched his shoulder. "I keep this up, and you'll think I'm turnen into a nag."

"Sooner or later, you will," Joe teased. "It's your destiny as a woman, one of the basic lessons of anatomy and physiology."

"You really are a male chauvinist pig at heart, aren't you, brother dear?" she accused lightly.

"All men are," Joe agreed with mock sincerity. "That's our destiny. And another basic lesson of anatomy and physiology."

Summer laughed. "There's probably truth to what you say," she said. "It's just that no one has yet found the right gene to prove it."

In Tifton, they pulled into the Shady Lane drive-in and ordered hamburgers, French fries and Cokes from the waitress.

"Did you know this is where Tom and I came on our first date?" Summer asked as they waited for the food.

"I seem to recall him tellen me that at one time or another," Joe answered, sensing the sadness in his sister, wishing he could make it disappear. Summer said nothing else about Tom, however, so he left her to memories, and they sat in silence until their food arrived.

"Joe," she said at length a few minutes later as they devoured the food. "Do you think we spend too much time together?"

Joe chewed on his hamburger and washed it down with Coke before replying. "To be honest, I haven't thought about it. Why do you ask?"

"Well, I hadn't thought about it either," she told him, "but apparently other people have."

"And who might that be?" Joe inquired.

"John for one," Summer answered, "although he claims it's only because he's be'en left out of—and I'm quoten—our weekend parties. Carrie, on the other hand, is a different story entirely. She says the amount of time we spend together is unhealthy and that we need to learn to depend on other people. Or somethen along those lines."

"Isn't that kind of like the kettle callen the pot black?" Joe observed. "Carrie's not exactly the most outgoen member of the family."

"I think Carrie's just had too much time on her hands to think," Summer said. "Maybe we should invite her along more often."

"And John, too," Joe added. "The more the merrier, right?"

"I suppose," Summer sighed. "But why is that things always have to change just when you get comfortable with the way they are?"

"Gee whiz, sis," Joe grumbled. "You make my company sound like nothen more than an old blanket."

"Your company has been a lifesaver, Joe," she replied affectionately. "And I don't begrudge one moment of the time we've spent together. In fact, as far as your company is concerned, the more, the merrier."

"I'm touched," Joe quipped, laying a hand over his heart.

"Can you be serious for a moment?" Summer pleaded.

"I'm the most serious person you know, Summer," he answered. "Go ahead and get whatever it is off your chest."

"Actually, I believe Granny is the most serious person I know," she replied. "But you are a close second, unless, of course, the conversation gets too close to you. Then you turn into one big tease."

"I'll accept that," Joe said. "Now to the heart of the matter, please."

"Do you think it's time I started daten again?"

"Can I assume that daten is another of Carrie's prescribed remedies for a healthier, happier you?" he asked.

Summer nodded. "John had the same suggestion. Even Mama has hinted somethen to that effect. There have been more than a few offers, you know?"

"Of course, there have," Joe teased as he pondered a more serious answer. "Truthfully, Summer," he continued a moment later. "What I think and what everybody else thinks shouldn't mean a hill of beans. It's a personal decision for you to make and nobody else's business. For what it's worth, though, if there's somebody you'd like to go out with, then you oughtta. There's no reason not to." He paused. "Is there somebody?"

"No," she replied quickly and honestly. "Not at all. And, fortunately, that's made sayen no a lot easier."

"Why do you say fortunately?" Joe asked.

Summer took a sip of Coke. "I feel a little bit guilty. I know that's stupid, silly and completely unreasonable, but I can't help myself."

"The heart's a lot more powerful than the head, Summer," Joe stated. "But there's no reason to feel guilty. Tom's gone. You're not gonna hurt him or his memory by goen out with someone else."

Summer waved away his reasoning. "It's not Tom," she said. "It's Amelia and Dan."

Joe gave her a questioning look.

"I got so close to them after Tom went overseas," Summer explained in a shaky voice. "Even before I loved Tom, Amelia and I were good friends. I have this silly notion that by daten again, I'll be cheaten them out of their last hold on Tom, out of the daughter they almost had."

Joe smiled sympathetically, sat down his drink and took his sister's hands. "You're much closer to Dan and Amelia than I am or will ever be," he told her. "But I know them well enough to realize they would never wish a single moment of unhappiness for you, Summer. They truly care about you. Tom's death did not lessen your friendship with them. It probably strengthened it because y'all suffered through the loss together. That kind of bond is irreplaceable. You will always be a daughter in spirit to the Carters—even when you have a husband and children and a life far removed from what they expected and wanted. It's possible—probable in fact—that they'll think of Tom when they see your happiness down the road. For that matter, I'd even wager to say that you will think of Tom from time to time when you consider, down the road, how your life has turned out. But Dan and Amelia will not begrudge you anything, Summer. They will not think that you are betrayen their son's memory. And neither should you."

He paused to brush away a trickle of tears from her face. "I speak the truth," he added gently.

"You do," she smiled sadly.

"It's been a tough year," Joe said, drawing her into an embrace.

"Even tougher than I expected," Summer replied.

"But things are looken up," Joe encouraged. "And in the words of our immortal grandpa, 'This, too, shall pass.'"

"I think maybe it already has," she said cheerfully, pulling away from him to drink the last of her Coke.

"Well, just you remember that advice is all I'm good for," Joe growled softly. "Don't expect me to do any matchmaken for you this time around."

"Quite the contrary," Summer said smartly. "Actually, brother, I'm thinken you could stand some romance in your life. You're almost twenty-four, Joe. It's high time you found a good woman to love."

"Nope, I've sworn off women," Joe said flatly, then amended the statement. "Or more accurately, I've sworn off romance and love. We're incompatible. Besides that, I'm a lousy judge of women, and I've decided they're probably worth more heartache than anything else. Sisters, mamas and grandmothers be'en the general exceptions."

"You just haven't found the right woman," Summer pressed.

"I also have no intentions of looken for her," Joe replied tersely to make his point. "Nor do I want anyone else looken for me."

"You're no fun," Summer pouted. "You keep this up, and I'm gonna have to find some other man to keep me company."

———

On Wednesday of the following week, Summer drove to Valdosta to return some dresses she had altered for the boutique. On the way home, she stopped by the Sears store in Brookwood Plaza to buy a white dress shirt for Joe. Personally, she would have picked a flashier shirt, or at least one with color. Joe, however, turned into a curmudgeon when anybody so much as suggested he might wear something other than a white cotton shirt to work. He occasionally wore his best blue jeans or forgot his tie, but Joe never showed up at the newspaper in anything less than a heavily starched white button-down shirt.

With this in mind, Summer passed by the rack containing a selection of light blue shirts, found a sale table filled with long-sleeved, white cotton shirts and began flicking through the packages to find the correct size. A few minutes later after finding every size other than Joe's, she began to reconsider the possibility of buying the blue shirt, despite the grouchy response it would provoke. Reminding herself that Joe would only return it—indeed, he would ask her to—she scanned the table once more, her eye at last catching the right size. Happy with her luck, she reached for the shirt, a second too late. Her hand came down over another hand, larger than hers, deeply tanned with a slight trace of black hair above the knuckles.

"Oops," she said, quickly withdrawing her hand and glancing up at a strangely familiar face.

"Summer?" the man questioned. "Summer Baker?"

As soon as she heard that flat Midwestern timbre, Summer recognized the stranger as Lieutenant Mark Applegate. She stood there dumbfounded, gaping at the last person she had expected to cross paths with on this day or at any other time since Tom's funeral.

"You look different," she remarked finally.

And he did at first, out of uniform, wearing faded blue jeans and a light blue pullover shirt. But the short dark hair and pointed features of his narrow face made the lieutenant easy to recognize as the man who had brought the news of Tom's death.

"I guess what they say about the uniform making the man is true," he commented lightly. "How are you?"

"Surprised, right now," Summer answered clearly. "No, make that shocked. You have a way of turnen up unexpectedly, Lieutenant."

"A peace offering," Mark Applegate said, offering the shirt to Summer. "I think you saw it first. I was just in closer reach."

"That's okay," she replied. "You keep it. I was only getten it for my brother. He insists on wearen nothen but white shirts, but I was thinken it's time for him to branch out to blue."

"Please, take the shirt," he urged. "I don't really need it. My closet is full of them. I'm just a sucker for a sale."

Summer regarded him with a careful eye. "In that case, I'll take it," she agreed at length, her voice hollow. "Joe really won't wear anything else to work."

"How are you really?" he asked, coming around the table to hand her the shirt.

His voice was as rich and warm as she remembered, his smile disarming and genuine. She remembered thinking once that Mark Applegate was a very handsome, reassuring man.

"Recovered, recoveren," she answered. "You learn to live with it."

He smiled encouragement.

"I guess you're still keepen busy?" she continued, then blushed at the sharp tone of her statement.

"Unfortunately," he answered.

"That probably sounded more bitter than I intended," Summer apologized. "It's just that I'm truly surprised. You're about the last person I expected to ever see again."

"Understandable," Mark replied. "Typically, I'm in and out of people's lives very quickly. Believe it or not, though, I've thought about you and the Carters often this past year. Some situations get closer to me more than others. Tom's was one of those."

He regarded her before asking, "How are the Carters?"

"They're doen okay," Summer answered. "They traveled to Hong Kong and then to Hawaii after the funeral last year. Tom had leave in Hong Kong shortly before he died, and I think it made them feel better to go where he had been alive and see and do some of the things he had seen and done."

"I'm glad to hear that," Mark said, then hesitated. "Maybe I'm being presumptuous, but would you consider having a cup of coffee with me? Perhaps a piece of pie to go with it? I would appreciate the opportunity to hear what's been going on with you and the Carters. If nothing else, you could satisfy my curiosity."

Summer glanced at her watch, which put the time at a quarter past three. "I couldn't stay long," she answered. "I have an essay to write for my English class tomorrow."

"Then I'll have to be satisfied with a few minutes," Mark smiled.

She returned the smile. "Let me pay for the shirt, and we'll go."

––––––––

They found a booth at the Woolworth's lunch counter a few doors down from Sears. Summer ordered iced tea, while Mark had black coffee with a piece of pumpkin pie.

Chatting easily as they waited for the waitress to bring their order, Summer told Mark about her current classes at ABAC and the sewing she did for extra money. To her surprise, she discovered he also had returned to school—at Valdosta State to pursue a master's degree in English.

"When I retire from the service, I'd like to teach at a small college," he said. "I'm not sure where."

"Sounds ambitious," Summer said. "How long until you retire?"

"I'll probably go out after twenty years," he said. "That leaves me with twelve to go."

"Out of curiosity, how old are you, Lieutenant?" she asked.

"Twenty-eight. And please, call me Mark."

"How long have you been stationed at Moody?" Summer inquired as the waitress set the pie and drinks on their table.

"A little over two years," he replied. "I'll probably be there another couple of years and then it'll be time to move on."

"Overseas?" she asked, visibly cringing at the prospect of a tour of duty in Vietnam.

"I served a tour in 'Nam," he told her with understanding. "I won't be goen back over there." He paused, then flashed a smooth smile. "This isn't fair," he remarked. "You're supposed to be satisfying my curiosity, and I'm doing all the talking."

"Then you ask the questions," Summer smiled.

"Tell me about yourself," Mark prompted. "So far, I know only that you're in school and have an English paper due tomorrow. What's your major?"

The man knew a great deal more than that about her, Summer thought, thinking he had been present during some of her most intensely private moments. But Mark obviously was not interested in the past. "I'm only a sophomore," she began. "I wound up taken last year off, so I got behind. I haven't decided for sure what my major will be, but somethen to do with fashion design."

She paused, then saw the interested look on his face, urging her to continue. So she did, telling him of the plans to open her own boutique one day and design many of the clothes she would sell. With total candor, she explained how the Carters had insisted she receive half of Tom's life insurance, her parents' refusal to allow her to use the money to pay for college and her own decision to finance her business with it when the time came.

"I don't know when that will be," she said. "Five years, ten years, maybe longer. Usually, I'm headstrong and plunge right in to my plans with nothen but instinct to guide me. Before goen into business for myself, however, I want to make sure I know what I'm doen. I don't want to make any silly mistakes."

"A little prudence never hurts," Mark agreed as she glanced once more at her watch and gulped down tea.

The waitress returned to refill their glasses, and Mark ate the last bite of pie so she could clear away the plate. When she left, they resumed talking, with Mark plying Summer with questions about the well-being of Amelia and Dan and the adjustments made by everyone in the wake of Tom's death. From there, the conversation turned to Mark, his roots in Oklahoma and his place squarely in the middle of a large family. He confessed to feeling overlooked on more than one occasion, although he seemed to harbor no resentment over the situation.

"It's like I told Mr. Carter," he explained to Summer. "When you've got seven children and you're a minister with a large congregation, there's just not time enough for everything and everyone. My parents did the best they could, and I happen to think their best was pretty good.

"I guess you know somethen about large families, too," he added.

Summer told him about the Bakers, how she thought none of her brothers and sisters ever went wanting for attention probably because there were four parental figures in the house, plus Joe, who filled in the gaps left by their parents and grandparents. "He's five years older than me, and ten years older than Bonnie, who's the baby, so he's always been way ahead of the rest of us in terms of goen through certain situations and dealen with them," she explained. "I think maybe the rest of us learn from his mistakes. It certainly takes off some of the pressure when somebody before you has made the same mistake."

"Sort of like having somebody run interference for you," Mark suggested.

"You must be a football fan," she observed.

"You can't grow up in Oklahoma and not be," he replied drolly. "Lately, I've even been goen to see Valdosta High School play their games on Friday nights."

"Cookville used to play Valdosta," Summer told him. "It was pretty ugly, although my brother did catch a touchdown pass against them one time. I think it's the only time in history we ever scored against them."

"Valdosta has a great team, a great program," Mark stated. "They live and breathe football. Which brother?"

"Joe."

"Was he a football star?"

"Not at all," Summer answered. "The very next game, his knee got caught between two players runnen in opposite directions. It was a mess. He wound up with a pin in his leg to keep everything in place. It ended his career and pretty much his interest in football."

"Tough luck."

"He took it in stride," Summer remarked. "Now, my younger brother, Luke, is playen, and he seems to be a true star. He's a halfback, and Mama lives in mortal fear that somethen awful's gonna happen to him."

Summer told Mark about Luke and football, about Luke and school, about Luke and his girlfriend. Once those subjects were exhausted, she told him about Joe and John, Carrie and Bonnie, too, as well as her parents and grandparents. Every time she completed one story, Mark asked another question, sending her off on tangent after tangent until the next time she glanced at her watch. It was past seven o'clock, and the waitress was closing down the lunch counter.

"Oh, my gosh!" she exclaimed. "Can you believe the time? I still have a paper to write and a long drive home to boot. They're probably worried back home. I better give them a call."

"I didn't mean to keep you so late," Mark said as they eased out of the booth, "but

I sure did enjoy the conversation. Please give my regards to the Carters next time you see them."

"I will," Summer said as the store lights blinked to signal closing time.

Mark followed her to an outside pay phone, where she made a quick call home, and then to the family car she had driven to Valdosta. She unlocked the door, opened it and tossed the shirt on the seat before turning around to say goodbye. "Well, Mark, it was most unexpected and most enjoyable."

"For me, too," he smiled as she slipped behind the wheel and rolled down the window.

The lieutenant closed the door, leaning down against the open window as they both struggled to find the appropriate farewell. "Take care, Summer," he said finally.

"You do the same," she replied before driving away, leaving him a solitary figure in the dark parking lot.

————

In her rush to complete the essay and the next day's bustle, Summer forgot the chance encounter with Mark Applegate, as well as her promise to give his regards to the Carters. Until Thursday as the Bakers ate a late supper of pork chops, creamed corn, fried okra, baked sweet potatoes and homemade biscuits. They were nearing the end of the meal, with an egg custard waiting for dessert when the telephone rang.

Carrie immediately bounced up from the table. "I'll get it," she said, making a quick exit from the kitchen.

"Is she expecten somebody," Matt asked, temporarily interrupting a conversation about the next night's football game with Fitzgerald.

"Not that I know of," Caroline answered as she brought Rachel's prized custard to the table.

Moments later, Carrie returned to the kitchen. "It's for you, Summer," she said. "Somebody named Mark."

All eyes riveted to Summer, who maintained her composure, despite the knot forming in her stomach. "You could have told him I was in the middle of supper and to call back," she said, pretending exasperation as she rose from the table.

"It sounds like long distance," Carrie remarked.

"Make sure y'all save me a piece of custard," Summer informed them sternly as she fled the curious eyes of her family.

When she had bid farewell to Mark Applegate the previous night, Summer clearly believed a chapter had closed in her life. She had detected an air of finality to their encounter, as if fate had ordained an opportunity to wrap up loose ends and put the past behind her once and for all. Obviously, her intuition had been wrong, and the error in judgment reeled her as she picked up the receiver off the cypress table.

"Hello," she said softly, conscious of sweaty palms.

"Hi, Summer. It's Mark Applegate."

He sounded almost uncertain, as if he were having second thoughts about his decision to call her.

"You really do have a way of catchen me off guard," she remarked.

"I think Carrie must have answered the phone," he replied, his tone more assured. "She seemed a bit concerned about your welfare."

"In other words, she did everything but ask about your intentions toward me," bantered Summer. "My daddy could learn a lesson from Carrie about grillen gen-tlemen callers. There's somethen about interrogation that turns her into a regular busybody."

"I'm sure she means well," Mark said.

"She does," Summer assured him. "So, why did you call?"

"Do you recall when I said you were sweet-natured, and you claimed I didn't know you very well?"

"I recall that," she replied.

"I'd really like to know you better, Summer," Mark said. "Or at least have an opportunity to."

He waited on the other end, while she considered the suggestion. "I'd like that, too," she said at length. "I could use a good friend."

"Friendship is a very good place to start," he told her.

————

Within days, Summer and Mark felt like true companions. They spoke twice on the telephone, running up huge bills and agreeing to attend the Friday night football game between Cookville and Lowndes County. Engaged in steady chatter, they saw little of the game, a notable exception being the tail end of a fifty-yard touchdown run by Luke. They missed completely his late-game, two-yard twisting plunge over the goal line that lifted the Rebels to a stunning 12-7 upset.

"Oh, well," Summer philosophized. "There'll be other football games."

Following the game, Summer introduced Mark to her parents, noting their sur-prised expressions as Matt and Caroline connected him with the past. Then, rather than fight the post-game mob at the Dairy Queen, Summer and Mark joined her par-ents for ice cream at The Dairy Bar, the smaller and less frequented of Cookville's only two late-night eateries. Over vanilla milkshakes for the men and butterscotch sundaes for the women, Mark got acquainted with Caroline and Matt, telling them about the chance meeting with their daughter and his lingering interest in the Carters.

"Time and time again, I've thought about driving up your way and paying them a visit," Mark said. "Considering the circumstances of how we met, I felt a kinship with them, especially Dan. As I recall, he and I made a tentative date to go fishing sometime. I never followed through on it."

"You should have," Caroline suggested.

"Perhaps," Mark replied. "But that's a sticky situation. I didn't want to do any-thing that would make them uncomfortable or open up painful memories." He paused to look at Summer. "I think Summer herself has a few misgivings about finding me back at her doorstep."

Matt and Caroline exchanged concerned glances, obviously puzzled by the rela-tionship between their daughter and this man.

"I did have a few," Summer commented to them, "but Mark and I are gonna be good friends, I think."

The answer apparently appeased her parents, who quickly steered the conversa-tion to more neutral grounds, quizzing Mark about his background while Summer ruminated over an emerging idea.

Even before Tom had died, Summer deemed Dan Carter as someone who need-ed more male companionship. She also suspected Mark Applegate could benefit from a fatherly figure as well. Perhaps fate had brought her and Mark together to fulfill human needs, she reasoned. These jumbled thoughts ran through her head as Summer considered how to bring Mark together with the Carters. When the perfect idea presented itself, she wasted no time putting it in motion.

"Mark, how would you like to go fishen tomorrow?" she asked, interrupting his conversation with her parents.

"I didn't mean to interrupt," she continued, "but I have this great idea for surprisen Dan. You said the two of you made a fishen date. Well, what if you just kind of showed up tomorrow and took him up on it. Knowen Dan, I think he'd get a kick out of it."

"That's a good idea," Matt agreed. "We've got two ponds on our place, and there's an old boat you can use. We've even got the poles and plenty of places to dig for worms."

The idea appealed to Mark, who looked to Caroline's judgment in the matter. She gave him an encouraging nod, and he grinned, "Why not?"

―――――

The next day, Summer arrived at the mercantile precisely at the same time Dan and Amelia opened for business. Dan greeted her at the door, his sleepy voice and droopy eyes offering strong evidence of morning grogginess.

"Come in and have a cup of coffee," he invited over an unintended yawn.

Summer planned to put her own perk in the day, so she accepted, then went on to light up the morning with the latest community and family gossip. After exhausting those topics, she brought up the real reason for her visit. "I have a surprise for you, Dan, providen Amelia can take care of the store this afternoon."

"A surprise?" Dan asked. "What kind of surprise?"

"Well, now, it wouldn't be a surprise if I told you beforehand," Summer chided. "You'll have to wait and see. But I'd appreciate if you could be ready and waiten to go around noon. And wear some old clothes."

"Good Lord, Summer!" Amelia chirped. "You've even got my interest piqued. Just what are you plannen to do with him?"

Summer smiled. "My secret, but I promise he'll return safe and sound."

"Do I need to bring anything with me?" Dan asked.

"Just yourself," Summer replied.

Mark arrived at the Baker house shortly before noon, armed with two new fishing poles and a carton of worms and dressed in cutoff fatigues, a khaki T-shirt and worn tennis shoes. "I didn't care to go digging for worms," he explained to Matt before facing a barrage of introductions and receiving an invitation to church and Sunday dinner.

He accepted, and then an impatient Summer hustled him into his car, a well-kept red Cougar convertible. "I figured you guys might get hungry," she said, putting a picnic basket on the seat between them. "There are sandwiches and a thermos of tea."

"I thought we were supposed to catch our food today," Mark commented. "Are you already doubting my fishing abilities?"

"You catch 'em, and I'll cook 'em," Summer promised, confident her culinary skills would not be needed anytime soon.

At the mercantile, Mark stayed outside while Summer went inside. "Are you ready, Dan?" she called as the doorbell jingled.

Dan and Amelia met her at the living room door, curious smiles etching their faces.

"Okay, Summer," Amelia demanded to know. "We've waited all mornen to find out what you have in mind. I'm more excited than Dan."

"Then come outside and see," Summer beckoned to them.

Followed closely by his wife, Dan strolled over to the door, opened it and immediately saw the red convertible.

"A red convertible!" Amelia gasped. "Is it yours?"

"Not quite," Summer laughed behind them.

Mark stepped from behind the gas tanks, holding two fishing poles. "Hello, Dan, Mrs. Carter," he nodded with a cautious smile, praying Summer had not made a mistake in bringing him here.

The Carters recognized him at once and his presence startled them. Their shock was temporary, however, replaced quickly with questioning smiles as they overcame their emotions.

"You're goen fishen, Dan," Summer explained.

A smile split Dan's face as he remembered his vague suggestion that Mark and he might go fishing one day. "Well I'm just bowled over," he said, stepping down onto the porch to shake the lieutenant's hand. "How are you?"

"Just fine, sir."

"I'm flabbergasted," Amelia said, looking to Summer. "Somebody's got some explainen to do."

"I'll tell you later," Summer replied as she ushered Dan and Mark toward the car. "The fish are waiten for these two. By the way, Amelia, at the risk of imposen on your hospitality, you're gonna have supper guests tonight if these two catch any fish. I've promised to cook anything they catch."

"As long as you do the cooken, honey, it's fine with me."

"Okay, you two," Summer remarked, hurrying Dan and Mark. "You've got dinner to catch."

———

To Summer's surprise, the inexperienced fishermen returned later that afternoon with a string of bream, perch and catfish, all gutted and ready to fry. "We had help with the cleaning," Mark confessed. "And your brother caught the catfish in another pond. But all in all, we had a successful day."

"Successful enough that we're gonna try it again next Saturday," Dan beamed, clapping Mark on the shoulder as he went to clean up.

What Dan and Mark left out of their fishing tales for Summer and Amelia was how they had turned over the boat while trying to launch it from the pond bank and how a turtle had stolen their first three catches. Joe supplied this information to Summer later that evening when she returned home from the Carters, as well as telling her how Dan and Mark had mistaken an inedible, bony roach fish for a bass.

"But they had a ball out there," Joe surmised. "I can't remember ever see'en Dan in such high spirits. You did a good thing, Summer, bringen those two together. I have a hunch they've got a lot in common."

"I'm a good matchmaker," Summer remarked smugly.

"Yes, you are," Joe agreed. "What other kind of matchmaken do you have in mind for the good lieutenant?"

"Nothen like what you're thinken," she snipped, shrugging off the implication.

These thoughts came to Summer as she sat on the front porch of the Baker home a day later, watching a touch football game between her brothers, sisters and Mark. She had sat out the game to help her mother wash the dinner dishes and to make everyone aware that Mark was as much their friend as hers. The ploy obviously worked, evidenced by the instant rapport he achieved with the family. Perhaps it had worked too well, Summer mused, feeling abandoned, left out of the fun and preoccupied with this portrayal of her feelings for Mark as strictly friendship.

Was she being entirely truthful?

She wanted to believe so, yet the ease with which Mark had entered her life befuddled Summer. As did the thoughts of him that came out of nowhere like now, for instance, as he glided across the lawn, matching Luke step for step as her brother ran a pass pattern.

Mark was a natural athlete, with a certain surety to every movement. She liked his confidence. Indeed, he appealed to a whole host of her senses, Summer thought, as Mark intercepted John's wobbly pass and zigzagged across the makeshift field to score a touchdown.

He spiked the ball, glancing her way and waving casually. Summer whistled approval, dished out mock insults to the defense and decided she obviously appealed to a few of Mark Applegate's senses as well.

CHAPTER 6

ONE FRIDAY AFTERNOON IN mid-October, with no scheduled football game that night to occupy his mind, Luke sat slouched in the back of the bus, drifting in and out of the various conversations around him. During debate over whether John Deere or International Harvester made the best tractor (anyone with any sense knew John Deere did), Luke daydreamed, alternating thoughts of his impending date that evening with mindless glances around the bus. On one of the latter occasions, he caught sight of Carrie seated next to Billy Taylor.

Luke bolted upright in the seat, blinking to make sure his eyes were not playing tricks even as he detected an air of smelly familiarity to this scene. As improbable as it seemed, this was not the first time Carrie had sat beside Billy on the bus. In fact, they had shared the majority of the bus rides between Cookville and New River in recent weeks—in the mornings Luke knew for sure and obviously in the afternoons, too.

Revulsion set in Luke, riveting his attention a few seats away to the burly form of Wayne Taylor. Luke still carried the jagged scar from an unfair fight with Wayne, as well as a grudge against the entire Taylor family. As far as he was concerned, every last one of them could die and go to Hell and no one would be the worse for it, save the devil himself.

As these feelings hardened Luke's heart, Wayne glanced toward the back of the bus and caught the black gaze coming his way from the youngest Baker boy. Predictably, Wayne sneered, peeling his lips just enough to reveal a set of yellowed teeth.

Luke reacted with practiced indifference, staring coldly past Wayne, refusing to acknowledge Taylor's recognition. In a while, Wayne, confused and bored, gave up his challenge, allowing Luke to resume his scrutiny of Carrie and Billy.

Their interaction left him dumbfounded, trying to equate this girl who giggled and talked a mile a minute with the Carrie he knew, and the carefree boy who flirted with and teased his sister with the image he had of Billy Taylor. Any plausible reason for their involvement escaped Luke, as did any possible justification. He determined to get to the bottom of his sister's error in judgment, or at least show Carrie the absurdity of the situation.

"Can I buy you a Coke?" Luke asked her minutes later as the bus deposited them at the mercantile.

"You sure can," Carrie gushed. "It's hot as blazes today. The weatherman needs to realize it's the middle of October."

"Accorden to grandpa's rheumatism, Joe's steel knee and John's snake-bit leg, it's just a matter of days till cooler weather comes our way," Luke said.

"Great to have such scientific forecasters available right in the home, isn't it?" Carrie joshed as they went inside the store.

A short time later, as they walked along the dusty road with books and sodas in hand, Luke brought up the sore subject. "The eye's a funny thing," he began. "You see the same thing in the same place day after day and never make the connection. Then bam! What you've seen all along jumps out and smacks you in the eye."

Carrie tensed almost immediately, her high spirits plummeting as she sensed the subject on Luke's mind.

Luke saw the strain enter her posture, yet felt dutybound to press on with the matter. "Take today," he continued. "I'm looken around the bus and notice you sitten with Billy Taylor. And it hits me like a ton of bricks that the two of you have been maken a habit of sitten with each other.

"What gives, Carrie?"

"We have a class together," she answered automatically. "He sits in front of me, and I've been helpen him with homework. What's wrong with that?"

Her tone was too defensive, her answer too faultless, so Luke changed tactics to make his point without coming off as judgmental. "I'm not sayen anything's wrong. It just surprised me, see'en you two together like that. Y'all sure didn't look like you were doen homework to me."

"We were just talken," Carrie muttered. "Billy has a good sense of humor."

"Really?" Luke puzzled. "He's always struck me as not very funny at all. He's got the personality of a wet dish rag."

Carrie looked her brother in the eye. "I bet a few of your friends would say the same about me, little brother," she lashed out. "Not everyone is Mr. and Miss Charm, Luke. That doesn't mean they have the personality of a wet dish rag."

"Touchy, aren't we," Luke said, sufficiently chastised. "Why so quick to defend him, Carrie?"

"I'm not defenden him," she retorted. "First of all, Billy strikes me as capable of doen that for himself. And second, there's nothen to defend him against. You raised the subject, Luke, and you made a snap judgment about him. I'm simply tellen you what I know about the situation."

"I've got my doubts that you've told me the whole situation between you and Billy," Luke accused.

"Listen, Luke," Carrie sighed. "You're maken a mountain out of a molehill. He's just an acquaintance and only that because we have the same class. Not that it's any of your business, but I've enjoyed getten to know him. There's nothen else to it."

"Really?" Luke pushed.

"Really," she assured him.

Luke laughed heartily, as if he had just discovered the joke of all time.

"What's so funny?" Carrie inquired.

"I thought maybe you had a crush on him or somethen," Luke explained, grinning. "Can you imagine what a riot it would cause if the two of you got involved? The house of Baker and the house of Taylor—it'd be a regular Romeo and Juliet."

Carrie forced up a throaty laugh, nodding in agreement. "Be serious, Luke. That'll never happen."

―――――――

Two days before Halloween, Billy noted the high school homecoming dance was fast approaching. It was an unusual homecoming at Cookville High School, with great expectations and reason to celebrate. The Rebels had posted their best season in history, chalking up four wins against four losses so far this season. They were heavily favored to win a fifth victory against their next opponent, a weak Atkinson

County team that had yet to score all season while giving up several hundred points. The unexpected success had turned the whole county into football fanatics, with the players getting free haircuts from the Cookville Barber Shop, half-price sales from all the stores in town and savings bonds, albeit small ones, from the Citizens and Farmers Bank. Seemingly assured of not having a losing season for the first time in history, the focal point of the season had shifted to homecoming, the final game against archrival Cook High School.

By beating Cook, the Rebels could walk away with the first winning season in the school's history. And this year, unlike all the others when the best Cookville had managed was a tie against Cook, a victory against the Hornets appeared within grasp.

The school, the players, the students and teachers, the men on the corner, the ladies in the beauty shop, police officers and doctors, virtually everyone, black and white alike, were salivating over the possibility of beating Cook on the football field.

Billy was caught up in the excitement as well, though on a more subdued level. As an athlete, he respected the team's hard work and desire to win. But he was also a trifle jealous. After all, the Cookville basketball team had gone all the way to the state championship game last year, and while fans packed the stands to watch them play, no one had offered free haircuts, savings bonds or store discounts.

Just as well, Billy thought smugly. Winning bred contentment, and content fans often took winning for granted. This year, however, the basketball team would find those wins harder to come by without Billy's leadership on the court. The notion was full of self-conceit, yet honest. The Rebels would win the majority of their games, but the absence of their star player would hurt when it mattered most.

In Billy's opinion, great basketball teams consisted of four very good players and one great player, a star. Billy had been the star for Cookville. With his deadly jump shots from beyond the perimeter and fearless drives to the goal, he had scored plenty of points for the Rebels. But his genius was dribbling wizardry and an unselfish attitude. He created opportunities for his teammates on the court—he found the open man. While he took pride in holding school records for most points scored in a game and in a season, the mark Billy cherished above all others was his record as the all-time leader in assists. No one assisted better than Billy.

The Rebel football team had a star of its own in Luke Baker, Billy thought. Although the Cookville defense was adequate, Luke was the overwhelming reason for the mediocre success of this year's team, providing punch to an otherwise sluggish offense. Luke ran with the force of a hurricane and the unpredictability of a tornado. He evaded tacklers with dazzling spins and lightning-quick changes of direction. But when the occasion required brute strength, he plowed head-on into the fray, putting his head down and slamming the full force of his body into the defense. In his spare time, Luke returned kickoffs, punts and played the free safety position for the team's stubborn defense.

Luke was a blue-chip player, and Billy respected his athletic ability. It gave them something unique in common. Billy suspected he and Luke had more in common than their athleticism but he also knew they would never discover those other similarities. Fate or history or whatever had locked them into their respective corners, but it was more than the past that kept Billy and Luke to themselves.

They treated their stardom differently. Billy ignored his reputation or was too timid to milk it for all its worth. Luke accepted the flattery and attention with relish, taking the girls and the popularity that came to him without a flinch. To his credit, though, Luke never flaunted his ability or his success. He, too, was the quintessential team player, which only deepened Billy's respect and appreciation for Luke and the football team's special season.

Out of this appreciation came the desire to make homecoming an equally special occasion for himself and Carrie, the sister of the star. Billy liked Carrie. He knew she liked him, too, and he wanted her as his date for homecoming.

All through the day, Billy rehearsed his invitation to her for the football game on Friday night and the dance on Saturday, while considering the various details that would go into making the occasion special. Carrie would not be the first girl he had asked out, but none of the others had mattered as much. He wanted everything to be perfect—from his invitation to the flowers he would give her, from his manners when meeting her parents to the dance itself.

He made his plans, rehearsed his lines and when sixth period came, Billy chickened out. His carefully prepared words failed, turning him into a stuttering idiot, who managed to flub everything he said from, "Hello." He sat hunched over his desk throughout the class, berating his cowardice and trying to figure out what had gone wrong.

This bad case of nerves hung with Billy, long after the bell rang dismissing school, well into the bus ride to New River. Carrie peppered him with questions early in the ride, then gave up in frustration when her prodding produced nothing but a series of one-word answers. They settled back against the seats, each aware of something amiss, both pondering different reasons for the wall between them.

Halfway to New River, mutual curiosity overcame them and they stole a glance at each other. Their eyes met, locked, and Billy blurted out, "Do you want go to homecomen with me?"

The question floored Carrie, coming as it did. She had wondered whether Billy would ask, perhaps even hoped he would. Well, she had her invitation, and now Billy waited for her answer.

She was on the verge of accepting when, out of the corner of her eye, she spied two girls goggling at them. They obviously had overheard Billy's question and were waiting with bated breath to hear her answer. Perhaps she imagined it, but Carrie saw disbelief in their eyes—as if, like Luke, they could not fathom the possibility of the house of Baker coming together with the house of Taylor. A regular Romeo and Juliet, she recalled Luke saying, and realized the nosy girls were ready to tell the world about the most unlikely new romance at Cookville High School.

And then she saw for herself the absurdity of a romance between the daughter of Matt Baker and the son of Bobby Taylor. She pictured her parents' amazed faces when Billy showed up at their door, the certainty of gossip and smug laughter behind their backs. It was all too much for Carrie to handle, and the odds seemed too risky even with the chance of a happy ending.

"I don't think so," she told him, glaring icicles at the two busybodies, forcing their blatant nosiness elsewhere. "You know as well as I do, Billy, that it wouldn't work out. Our family reputations are stronger than us. There'd be too much talk."

"I guess so," Billy said lamely, glancing away from her. "I just thought I would ask. Anyway, I enjoyed getten to know you."

"Can't we still be friends, keep things the way they are?" she pleaded, wanting to reach out to him, unable to make the first move. "I tried to tell you from the very beginnen that friendship was all I had to offer."

"I don't know," Billy shrugged. "Maybe friendship is just as ridiculous as anything else between us, Carrie." He looked at her again and, rising from their seat, said, "I'll see you around."

Her eyes followed him to the other side of the bus, watching until he sat down and stared out the window, before reverting the gaze out her own side of the bus.

———

Billy was vaguely aware of his brothers as the three of them sauntered down the dirt lane to their house later that afternoon. As usual, Carl daydreamed in his private world, while Wayne blabbered incessantly, this time about trouble brewing between blacks and whites at the high school. According to Wayne, the niggers were bringing knives to school and white students were arming themselves for self-defense.

"The fight's at hand, Billy Boy," Wayne remarked jovially. "I hope you're ready and willen for it."

Billy was in no mood for his brother's sudden show of good humor, even if it was welcome relief from his usual sour disposition. For all he cared, the two groups could kill each other, which was exactly what he told Wayne.

"What the hell's wrong with you?" Wayne demanded. "This is what we've been hopen and plannen for since the beginnen of this mess. We're gonna run those niggers out of school. They'll be afraid to come back after one or two of 'em get their balls cut off."

Billy shook his head in disbelief. "You're a bona fide moron, Wayne," he laughed bitterly.

"And you're an asshole," Wayne snarled. "I know what's wrong with you, Billy boy. It's that Carrie Baker. She's got your head all screwed up with her high-and-mighty ways."

Billy stopped dead in his tracks, glaring at his brother. "She has nothen to do with me, Wayne, or how I think or how I act," he said viciously. "Don't you mention her again. You hear?"

"And what if I do, Billy boy?" Wayne hissed, unimpressed by his brother's malicious tone. "Do you think I'm totally ignorant and blind to what's been goen on between you and her? I've watched y'all, flirten and carryen on like two dogs in heat. You're maken a big mistake, Billy, a big mistake by chasen after her, and you'll live to regret it."

"The only thing I regret, Wayne, is be'en born your brother," Billy replied with deadly sincerity. "Get out of my face. Go find some place nice and quiet, where you can sit and twiddle your thumbs until you have another thought in that lame brain of yours. Supper oughtta be ready by then, and I promise, I'll call you."

Wayne and Billy had always tolerated each other reasonably well. They fought as brothers close in age tend to do, with Wayne typically using his size to pound the smaller boy into submission. Overall, though, they co-existed without any major disagreements, or at least without any permanent enmity emerging from their arguments.

Wayne had never sensed such open hostility from his brother. He had always believed when the chips were down, he could count on Billy for support because they were brothers. Now, in the heat of such disgust in his brother's eyes, Wayne sensed the tide had turned in their relationship, as if Billy had lost all senses and abandoned him. Anger and disappointment, one and the same in this instance, welled up within Wayne, leaving him eager to exact revenge for Billy's hurtful words.

"You'll regret that, Billy boy," he said at last, his voice dull of emotion. "You will regret that."

For once, Billy ignored his brother's feelings. He had no desire to restore a sense of respect and tolerance between them. He was hurting himself from stinging words—and the obvious deduction that he would never be anything more than what people expected.

Carrie's rejection had shocked Billy. He was willing to concede she might be leery of considering him her boyfriend, though their lone kiss suggested otherwise. But, despite his jittery nerves about asking her, he had never doubted for one minute that she would go with him to homecoming—as friends, if nothing else. Yet, she had rejected him.

Billy knew the course of true love did not run smoothly, but he was dodging boulders at every turn. He had a sinking feeling that one of those big rocks had just flattened him like a pancake.

When he reached the house, Billy went straight to work, using his frustration to clean the house completely, rather than just straighten the mess. He washed clothes, dusted furniture, cleaned bathrooms and vacuumed. When the time came to prepare supper, his frustrations had been swept away in the cleaning frenzy. But his depression remained.

———

"Breakfast for supper again," Bobby commented later that evening as he sat down at the table with Wayne and Carl, while Billy dished up grits, eggs and sausage.

Since Billy had begun taking the home economics class, his cooking had improved considerably. Enough so that Bobby noticed the meager feeding now before him. He spooned up some of the grits, which were stiffening fast, and waited for a reply from his son about the sorry state of supper. When one was not forthcoming, he dropped the issue, figuring it wasn't worth the hassle. Everyone was entitled to a bad day now and then. Bobby had his share of those, and he'd sure eaten worse meals in his time.

Besides, Bobby felt on top of the world tonight. He'd sold the last of his peanuts earlier in the day, getting top dollar. Rather than deposit the money in the bank, he'd brought it home with him. He had never had so much cash on him at one time, and Bobby liked the aura of wealth that came with it. He smiled to himself because he owed his good spirits only partly to the six-pack of beer he had guzzled down earlier in the afternoon. Then, he smiled again, knowing he would be in better spirits in a few hours, once he partook of a second six-pack chilling in the freezer. Hell, he might even drop by the Tip-Toe Inn later in the evening to see if he could woo a woman into coming home with him. The new waitress had cozied up to him last weekend, and one glance at his bulging billfold might help her realize what a good deal Bobby could give her.

With a dismissible glance at his middle son, Bobby added salt to the rapidly congealing grits and began questioning Wayne about the state of tensions at the high school. Assuming the boy had his facts right—and he never could with Wayne—all hell was ready to break loose in the halls of Cookville High School. Bobby loved a good fight, and it seemed he might have reason to celebrate come the weekend.

———

Another night of inane conversation over supper at the Taylor table. For the better part of fifteen minutes, Billy ignored the dribble coming from his father and older brother, who talked of knives and niggers and the alleged trouble brewing at the high school. As Wayne put it so succinctly, the shit would hit the fan before the end of the week, maybe even at the ball game Friday night.

Bobby appeared to have serious questions about the extent of his son's grasp of the situation. Billy, too, doubted Wayne was right. Since the first few weeks of school, tensions had simmered down markedly once the students got to know each other. Regardless, blacks made up such a small portion of the student body that they were hardly worth counting.

Seeing how his reputation already had been defined, his life cast, Billy figured tonight might offer a good opportunity to get in a few jabs of his own about blacks. Such talk always set well with his daddy, and he needed to mend fences with Wayne, too. As much as he sometimes despised his older brother, as stupid as he considered Wayne, Billy regretted hurting his feelings earlier in the day. He had needed to vent his frustrations and Wayne had been an easy target. Besides, Wayne couldn't help being stupid, any more than Billy could ward off his birthright. They'd both had tremendous help getting where they were in life.

In the middle of these scattered thoughts, Billy became aware of something out of whack at the supper table. Carl was talking, a most strange occurrence. With animated happiness, Carl told about his friend at school, recounting the fun they had at recess and in class.

"Do you think he could come over and spend the night?" Carl asked his father.

"Who is this Danny?" Wayne said, scratching his head to come up with the kid's last name.

"Danny Bartholomew!" Carl said with exaggerated impatience, as if his family should have known whom his friend was without having to ask.

A sick feeling overcame Billy as he digested the information, and an eerie silence smothered the table. Even Carl sensed his error in judgment.

Billy risked a glance at his father, watching his blood pressure rise incrementally with the crimson rage on his ruddy face. Finally, Bobby exploded, directing the brunt of fury at his youngest son. He leaped from the table, jarring dishes and knocking over his chair as he hurled a string of profane abuse at Carl.

Billy and Wayne sat jammed against their chairs, stunned by the whirlwind turn of supper, a little nauseated, too. They had faced their father's fury, but this was Carl's first time.

Carl turned pale under the browbeating, too stunned even to draw away from his father. When his bottom lip began to quiver, Billy feared the worst. The sons of Bobby Taylor were not allowed to cry—never—not even when their mother had blown her head into a million pieces all over the living room.

"Goddamnit, Carl!" Bobby bellowed. "How can you even think of asken me if you can invite that little nigger sonofabitch into my house?"

"I oughtta beat the shit out of you right now," Bobby screamed, ripping off his belt and advancing on his son.

Carl remained glued to his chair, riveted by his father's rage. Tears streamed down his face, fear no longer an adequate reminder of Bobby's rule against crying. He had worse to fear than any stern reprimand about his tears.

Billy understood this even better than his little brother. Their father was way out of control, evidenced by the rapidly pulsing blood vessels in his temples. In this state of mind, Billy feared the man might inflict permanent physical injuries on Carl—in addition to the emotional scars already seared in the boy's mind. Someone had to intercede on his brother's behalf. He dreaded the consequences, but Billy was the only one who would step in and try to restore the peace.

"For Christ's sake!" he yelled, leaping from his chair and placing himself between Bobby and Carl. "Leave him alone. He's just a kid, a six-year-old little boy. They're just two kids, Daddy. It's not gonna cause the end of the world for them to be friends."

The intervention gave Carl a reprieve from their father's wrath. Bobby's gaze traveled from Carl to Billy. "What are you yakken about?" he asked incredulously.

"Of course, it matters," he continued, as if his whole reason for living had just been labeled unimportant and stamped irrelevant. "It matters a great deal, son. Hasn't anything I ever said sunk into that dumb-ass brain of yours?" He paused, shaking his head in disbelief. "If I've said it once, I've said it a thousand times, Billy. You obviously got that half-baked brain from your mama's side of the family."

"I'm sorry," Billy pleaded. "Just don't mess with Carl."

"Let's get one thing straight between you and me right now," Bobby replied. "Carl's my boy, and I'll do damn well what I please to him, includen beaten his ass if I so desire."

His tone of voice was subdued and stable. The anger seemed to drain from Bobby, turning his face from deep crimson to a lesser shade of red, and Billy dared to hope the worst was over. He glanced from his father to Carl to Wayne, and a premonition of the worst kind struck his heart like a cold dagger.

A smirk danced across his older brother's face, as if he had a secret that must be shared.

"Know what your problem is, Billy?" Wayne asked, as if he were initiating polite table conversation. "You've been hangen around Carrie Baker too much. That girl's fillen your head with mush."

"Carrie Baker?" Bobby asked, puzzled as he turned to Wayne for clarification. "Matt Baker's girl?"

Wayne leaned back in his chair, confirming his father's suspicion with a nod.

"Leave her out of this, Wayne," Billy implored. "I already told you—she ain't got nothen to do with anything."

"Yeah, you made everything perfectly clear, Billy boy," Wayne replied, acid dripping from every word, his eyes spitting revenge at his brother. "Well, almost everything," he added, looking once again to Bobby. "Our fair-headed Billy and Miss Carrie Baker have become a hot ticket, Daddy. You should see them together, flirten and carryen on like boyfriend and girlfriend. People are beginnen to notice. And to talk."

Billy's heart broke like a dog kicked too many times. He might as well have slapped his father in the face. Any hope of bringing reason to the table had been dashed by his brother's revelation. Fate would have dealt Billy a better hand had he spit on the grave of every Taylor who ever existed, even if he now spit into the face of his father.

"You'd better explain, boy," Bobby said at length, his tone menacing. "And you'd best do it real good with some fast and fancy talken."

The truth shall set you free, Billy thought, then cursed the unknown author of such starry-eyed philosophy. There was no way around the truth for Billy, who would have done everything in his power to avoid it had an opportunity presented itself.

"She's helped me with homework a few times," he acknowledged with repentance. "That's all there is to it, Daddy. Just homework. There's nothen else to explain."

"That's for shit," Bobby growled, advancing on Billy, grabbing the boy by the collar and pulling him eyeball-to-eyeball. "You should know somewhere in that asinine brain of yours that nobody in my family goes to Matt Baker or any of his kin for help. Do I make myself perfectly clear on that matter?"

"Yes, sir," Billy grunted, the chokehold impairing his breathing.

Bobby glared at his misguided son, his anger strangely muted. Billy closed his eyes like a condemned man prepared to accept his sentence. But nothing happened.

When the boy dared to look again, Bobby simply glowered at him, one hand falling harmlessly to his side. Billy swallowed visibly, nervous relief, daring to believe he would escape his father's wrath.

Their gazes locked, and then, coming out of nowhere, a roundhouse right struck the side of Billy's head with sledgehammer efficiency. The blow packed enough wallop to have knocked the boy clear across the room had not Bobby maintained an iron-tight grip on his shirt collar. As it was, Billy was rendered a defenseless punching bag. Bobby followed his initial attack with a brutal blow to the face, then jabbed Billy in the stomach, landed another fist against his head and drove his knee hard into the boy's groin.

The quick, savage attack dulled Billy's senses, and when Bobby released his grip, the boy balanced on teetering legs. Billy considered that perhaps his left eye was caved in beyond repair, his stomach ruptured. Pain shot through the beaten parts of his body, but Billy had little time to hurt. Bobby lashed out again, backhanding him across the other side of the head. The impact sent Billy reeling across the room. He crashed into a chair, lost consciousness and slumped to the floor.

———

Wayne woke him sometime later, tugging at his shoulders and dragging Billy into a kitchen chair. His head throbbed, his body ached and he felt torn apart at the seams.

"Stupid little faggot," Wayne admonished when he sensed Billy had regained some sense of balance. "You oughtta know by now, Billy boy, not to cross the old man."

Billy glanced up at his brother, unable to make his battered face convey the contempt he felt for Wayne. "It wouldn't have been so bad if you'd've kept your mouth shut," he said lamely. "There weren't a bit of need for this to happen."

Looking at his battered and bruised brother, Wayne realized his earlier animosity toward Billy had disappeared. Billy had paid the price for his sins. "Oh, well," he replied philosophically. "It'll teach you not to mess around with white trash like Carrie Baker. And maybe it'll teach you to have a little more respect for me, Billy boy. I'm tired of all the disrespect I get from people. It's gotta change."

Billy was too weak to respond. He sat there, staring at the floor until Wayne started to leave. At the door, Wayne hesitated.

"You're a mess," he advised over his shoulder. "I'd skip school tomorrow if I was you. You go looken like that, and there's bound to be questions. Besides, you probably ain't gonna feel much like goen."

Wayne walked out of the kitchen, leaving Billy to ponder the mess around him. No one had bothered to clean off the table. Plates of dried eggs and congealed grits stared back at Billy until his stomach roiled. He rose slowly from the chair, walked over to the sink and vomited his supper along with a small amount of blood. He was not overly alarmed. Although his stomach burned like a swamp fire, he figured the blood came from his busted lip. He rinsed out his mouth with water from the spigot, flinching as the clear liquid washed over the tender pieces of his split bottom lip. He wet a dishrag and applied it to his forehead. The coolness pushed away the leftover nausea, restoring some strength to his battered carriage.

On shaky legs, Billy waded through the kitchen into the living room where his father was stretched out on the recliner. A spent six-pack of beer lay on the floor beside the chair, and closing credits for the eleven o'clock news rolled unnoticed across the television. If he'd felt better, Billy might just have fetched one of the old man's guns and blown his brains to kingdom come. He shook away the thought, then eased into the room he shared with Carl.

He pulled on the light switch, casting the room in a bright glow, and examined his face in the dresser mirror. As Wayne had observed, he was a mess. His bottom lip had swollen grotesquely around a deep red gash, and his left eye peered back at him from a vivid purple hole. Another bruise stained the right side of his face, and an ugly blue bump marred his left temple. Billy looked freakish. He felt worse.

Undressing to his underwear, he found yet another bruise, this one on his stomach. He considered whether to put ice on his eye before deciding it was too late to do any good. And he wasn't about to put medication on the split lip. He'd endured enough pain for one day and was willing to risk infection for the night at least. He turned off the light and crawled into bed beside his sleeping brother.

As he lay there trying to drowse, Billy became aware of Carl crying softly beside him. His first thought was that Bobby had pummeled the smaller boy.

"You okay?" he worried, sitting up to inspect his brother. "Did he hurt you?"

"He didn't mess with me."

"I'm glad," Billy sighed, lying back against his pillow.

"I didn't mean to get you in trouble," Carl said with regret a short time later.

"I know," Billy assured his brother. "It's not your fault, Carl. Besides, I'm okay kiddo," he added, mustering up a sincere smile. "Now go to sleep," he urged. "You have school tomorrow."

Carl tried to muffle his cries, but the tears continued unabated, soft sobs that wrenched Billy's heart, muting any words of solace he might have shared out of fear that he, too, would weep uncontrollably if he tried to speak. In a few minutes, the first-grader's sobs turned to sniffles.

"It's not supposed to be this way, is it, Billy?" Carl asked at length. "Home, I mean?" he prompted.

"No, Carl," Billy answered, despite the lump in his throat. "It's not supposed to be this way."

"Then, why is it?"

"If I knew the answer to that, kiddo," Billy said gently, "then you and I would be sleepen like babies instead of haven this talk."

Carl considered the answer for a full minute, then spoke his mind. "Do you ever wish you could run away and live somewhere else?"

"If I did, you can bet your bottom dollar I'd take you with me," Billy assured his brother.

"Maybe someday, huh?" Carl remarked.

"Maybe someday, kiddo," Billy smiled. "Now let's get some shut-eye."

"Good night, Billy," Carl said, snuggling against his brother, a gesture he had never made until now.

Billy made up his mind then to protect his brother at all costs. If Carl needed a refuge, then he would have it. There was comfort in giving shelter to the needy, and besides, it felt good knowing that someone loved him for who he was.

———

Billy skipped school the next day, agreeing with Wayne that the black eye, swollen lip and bruises would attract too many questions. Deep inside, though, he wondered what would happen if he revealed that Bobby was responsible for the beaten state of his body.

He slept late, allowing everyone to fend for themselves at breakfast while his body and mind healed. Although the rest refreshed him, it did little to heal his body. His mouth hurt, and his head swam with every movement.

Around noon, he forced himself from bed, showered and applied medicine to his lip. The shower improved his appearance considerably, Billy admitted, noting the nasty bump on his temple had receded, leaving only a red splotch in its place. Even the bruise on the side of his face seemed to be fading, turning like mustard gone bad to an ugly shade of yellow and green.

Bobby came into the house a short time later for lunch, inquiring at once whether Billy had fixed anything to eat. Billy mumbled he had not, sending his father to the refrigerator in search of bologna and mayonnaise. Bobby ate in silence, with no mention of the previous night or Billy's swollen, bruised face.

His father's callous disregard sent shivers through Billy and made him question his decision to keep quiet about the beating. In the end, however, Billy realized he would fare worse if no one believed his story and word of his betrayal got back to Bobby. And, too, he knew Bobby was both capable and willing to administer a more severe beating, all of which explained why the boy abandoned his first impulse to give his father the cold shoulder.

"Since you've got the day off, I could use some help this afternoon," Bobby said when he had finished the sandwich and drunk a glass of iced tea. "I got some teeth to fix on the combine, and four hands can do it easier than two."

Billy stared at his feet, then chanced an answer. "Honestly," he said, finally looking at Bobby. "I don't feel up to it."

Bobby eyed him closely for a moment, then shook his head in agreement. He drained the last of the tea, rose from the chair and put on his cap. "Well, if you don't feel like worken outside, then get this place cleaned up," he ordered, walking past Billy toward the door, waving his hand at the dirty dishes. "It's filthy in here. While you're at it, fix a decent supper. I don't want grits tonight."

Billy nodded as the door slammed shut behind his father.

Throughout the same day, Carrie fretted over the wisdom of her decision to turn down the homecoming invitation from Billy. She feared she had made a mistake, jeopardizing something precious in the process. Regardless of her attraction to Billy, she valued his friendship. It was a source of joy and wonder. In the few short weeks they had come to know each other, her life had filled with a renewed sense of adventure.

It was easy to like Billy. He had a refreshing sense of humor, a cheerful disposition and an excellent sense of perception. But it was his honest and forgiving nature that most impressed Carrie and made her eager to accept his friendship.

Once they had gotten past their initial misgivings about one another, Carrie and Billy had unlocked the doors to their innermost thoughts. She had revealed secret observations that she would have told no one else—not even her brothers and sisters—admitting her own insecurities as well as pointing out the occasional flaw in the family Billy considered perfect in just about every way. Billy had done likewise, spellbinding her with the story of his mother's suicide, the events leading up to and after it, as well as his thoughts on why Martha Taylor had taken her life.

They had stepped on each other's feelings once or twice with their frank assessments. Carrie had overstepped the bounds of her right to criticize his family, prompting Billy to tell her it was really none of her business since she did not have to live in the Taylor home. Billy, on the other hand, had offended her with his smug dismissal of John's skills on the basketball court as about average or nothing spectacular. Even so, their disagreements had been minimal, certainly not worth mentioning in the whole context of what they had gained from each other.

With all this on her mind and after reflecting on the reasons she had rejected Billy's invitation, Carrie grew more miserable as the day passed. Recalling the understated bitterness of their parting the previous day, she began to wonder how she would have felt if the shoe were on the other foot. She had turned down Billy because she worried how people would react to them as a couple; and though hurting him had been the last thing on her mind, she now understood how her rejection would have done exactly that. She might as well have come right out and said to him that both of them were no more or no less than what people perceived them as, and that nothing would ever change those perceptions—not even the truth as Carrie and Billy knew it.

As this message sank in, Carrie felt more like a malefactor than a friend to Billy. She was lonely, too.

Accustomed to his company, she missed him on the morning bus ride to Cookville, at lunch by herself and in home economics class with his empty desk to occupy her mind. In fact, his absence from school heightened her anxiety, especially on the bus ride home when she discovered herself on the receiving end of a scathing glare from Wayne Taylor, who, heretofore, had never even acknowledged her existence.

As the afternoon edged toward evening under a bright sun, the pressing need for a fresh opinion overwhelmed Carrie. Finding someone to provide it proved a more difficult task. Carrie narrowed her list to her mother, grandmother and John, then picked Caroline because she wanted a woman's perspective and her mama was closer in age and more likely to understand.

When the preparations for supper were well under way, Carrie discreetly asked her mother if they could gather in the day's last load of wash from the clothesline. Despite the vexed nature of their reason for doing this day-to-day chore together, there was no hurried flow in the conversation. They chatted easily, with Caroline waiting for Carrie to bring up the matter and enjoying her daughter's perspective along the way as they unpinned and folded clothes, most of which were jeans and work shirts.

"I guess you know I brought you out here for a reason," Carrie remarked as she took the last pair of jeans off the fence line.

"I figured," Caroline smiled.

Carrie returned the smile, then turned serious. "I'd like to talk about somethen private, which maybe we could keep just between the two of us."

"You want to take a walk and discuss it or should we just sit down here?" Caroline asked.

"This is fine," Carrie replied, plopping down on the grass with her knees bent under her legs.

Caroline sat on Rachel's "prayer stump," the last vestige of a pecan tree chopped down years ago by Sam to build the barn loft. Rachel had requested he leave the stump, so that she might have a place of her own to meditate and pray.

"I'm listenen," Caroline said when they were settled under the shadow of the barn, beneath one of the many pecan trees loaded with a bumper crop of nuts this fall.

"You may find this hard to believe, Mama, but someone asked me to homecomen next week," Carrie began.

"Why should I find that hard to believe?" Caroline asked. "You've always had dates for the big dances at school."

"I turned him down," Carrie interrupted.

"You did," Caroline replied, confused. "Why?"

"Because of who he is."

"Who?" Caroline frowned.

"It was Billy Taylor who asked me, Mama," Carrie answered.

Caroline shot her daughter a questioning look. "Bobby's son?" she asked.

"Yes, ma'am, he is."

Caroline considered the situation, then made what she considered a reasonable summation. "Then, good for you, Carrie."

"No, it's not, Mama," Carrie interrupted quickly, shaking her head and stretching her long legs across the grass. "As unbelievable as it may sound, Billy and I have become friends since school started back this year—good friends actually. We have home economics together."

"Home economics," Caroline remarked. "He's taken home economics?"

"That's another story," Carrie smiled, then hurried to explain the more important one. "Anyway, he sits in front of me in class, and we just gradually became friends. I know it sounds ridiculous, and you probably think he's just like Bobby. But Mama, Billy's nothen like his daddy. He's sweet, really nice, and he's embarrassed by his daddy more than anything else. It's not his fault that Bobby does the things he does."

Caroline tried hard to keep her amazement checked, yet the situation shocked her senses. She hardly expected to have any conversation at all about boys with Carrie, much less one that began with this bombshell. How odd that when Carrie finally had serious feelings for a boy, she would have picked the son of Bobby Taylor. Of course, most often those kinds of feelings did the picking for themselves. Love or even a serious case of liking was impossible to judge, and apparently, so was Billy Taylor. Still, Caroline was not completely at ease with the idea of Carrie keeping company with the son of Bobby Taylor. She would reserve her opinion until she met the boy, however—if she met him at all, which seemed unlikely at the moment.

"No, Carrie," she agreed. "Billy should not be held accountable for his father's actions."

Carrie sighed, exhaling the tension of the past two days. "I like Billy, Mama, and I really wanted to go to the dance with him. But I was afraid it wouldn't look right. Imagine what people would say if they saw us together, and it would probably kill Daddy." She shook her head, concluding sadly, "I said no, but I feel miserable about it."

"Then tell Billy you've changed your mind and would like to go to the dance," Caroline urged, affirming her recommendation with a warm smile.

"But what about Daddy and what everyone would think?" Carrie protested. "And besides, Billy might think I'm fickle."

"A girl's permitted a certain amount of fickleness," Caroline replied. "It's part of our charm. Billy should know that." She paused. "Seriously, though, I can't tell you what Billy would think or anybody else for that matter. It would be entirely up to you and Billy to worry about what everybody and his brother conclude about your friendship, whether you decide to go to the dance or keep things the way they are." Her tone stiffened. "As for your daddy, it's not fair to use him as an excuse, Carrie. If you understand anything about your father, then you know it doesn't matter one bit to him what people think. If you believe in somethen or someone, then stand up for it. If you're willen to go out on the limb for someone, your daddy's gonna do his level best to support you."

"But what about the bad feelens between Daddy and Bobby?" Carrie asked. "Not to mention the fact that the police hauled Joe off to jail for beaten up the man."

"We're not talken about your daddy and Bobby or even Joe and Bobby," Caroline stressed. "This is about you and Billy. And you are the one who has to make the decision, Carrie."

Caroline studied her daughter as Carrie pondered that decision, worrying that her advice painted too rosy of a picture. Any kind of relationship between Carrie and Billy would raise more than a few eyebrows, several of them right in their own household. Some of their neighbors and close acquaintances would have a good laugh—at Matt's expense—to see his daughter take up with the son of a man he despised. But Caroline had learned the importance of giving her children room to grow, along with the necessary advice and guidance. Her head told her more trouble than good would come from this relationship between Carrie and Billy. But her heart believed in the girl's need to find her own way in this matter.

"I don't know what the outcome will be if you and Billy become good friends," Caroline said at last. "It probably won't be easy for either of you. I also admit that I have a few questions in my mind about Billy—about the kind of boy he is. And your daddy will, too, if it comes to that. But I can assure you that we'll give him the benefit of the doubt, and we will trust your judgment."

Carrie smiled shyly.

"I take it that you're gonna accept his invitation?" Caroline asked.

"Yes, ma'am," Carrie answered. "That is if he still wants to go with me."

"If Billy's as nice as you say he is, then I imagine he still wants you as his date for the dance," Caroline replied. "And I'd like to meet him myself," she added. "Maybe sometime soon you could invite him to church and Sunday dinner at the house."

"Thank you, Mama," Carrie said, giving her a long hug. "Right now, I just want to go to homecomen with him. I just want to be his friend for the time be'en."

"Is that all Billy wants?" Caroline inquired with a touch of seriousness. "Just friendship?"

Carrie mulled over the question. "I told him up front I was only interested in friendship," she answered. "He'll have to settle for that right now." She paused, then amended her statement with a quick smile. "We'll both have to settle for that right now."

"Good friendships are a blessen," Caroline agreed.

Carrie looked away for a moment, then her eyes clouded with a trace of doubt. "If it's okay with you, Mama, I'd still like to keep all this between you and me," she cautioned. "Billy was upset when I turned him down. He might not want to have anything else to do with me, much less take me to a dance. I'd hate for everybody to think I have a date and then wind up without one."

"I see," Caroline said. "Then we'll keep it between ourselves." She paused. "It might be wise, however, if I filled in your daddy. It might take away some of the surprise if you and Billy do make a date."

"Maybe so," Carrie agreed. "But nobody else."

"Good enough," Caroline said. "Now, have you thought about what you're gonna wear to the dance?"

CHAPTER 7

HALLOWEEN MORNING ARRIVED WITH a dreary sky and the first truly cool weather of the fall. Inside the Baker house, everyone raced to eat breakfast and dig out sweaters or light coats from the bottom of their drawers. The chilly morning was like a breath of fresh air, and they welcomed the change in season.

As had become their custom that fall, all six children gathered on the front porch shortly after breakfast. This was not an intentional ritual, but rather a habit they had fallen into for no apparent reason other than the time of day itself. The school bus arrived coincidentally at the same time Joe left for work, and Summer and John headed off to their college classes.

Standing on the porch, Joe took a deep breath of the morning fragrance and found reason to rejoice. Those people who claimed mountains or beaches as the most beautiful places in the world obviously had overlooked the hidden secrets of the coastal plains and flat lowlands of South Georgia. It was the most beautiful place on earth to Joe, never more so than on this Halloween morning.

Set out before him as far as the eye could see was a virtual virgin forest, clothed in the most glorious fall dressing Joe could remember. The colors fell short of matching the grandeur of autumn in New England, but the leaves were spectacular in their own right, decking the trees with an array of gold, russet, yellow and red, all nestled snugly amid a sea of winter green pine.

Across the road, away from the pecan and maple trees, an ancient red oak tree stood, so purely orange in color that it captured an audience among the Baker sons and daughters.

"It looks like a giant orange setten on a carpet of orange velvet," Joe observed, awed by the brilliance.

"Nope, it's a pumpkin," John contradicted. "It could only be a pumpkin at this time of the year. If it was summer, I might buy the orange theory, bro. But that's definitely a ripe pumpkin."

Joe took a second look. "A pumpkin, you're right," he admitted. "Anyway, I've never seen it more beautiful. I find it downright inspirational."

"I'm gonna paint it," John said, turning on his heels and heading back into the house.

"Not now you won't," Summer barked. "Not if you're goen to school with me. I admit the tree's beautiful, but we have an English class in thirty minutes, and that takes precedence."

"And we shall be there," John proudly informed her. "Just let me take a quick picture, and I'll paint it from that."

His source of pride was a new thirty-five-millimeter camera that John had purchased on the advice of his art teacher. "It's a good investment for a novice like me," John had explained, paraphrasing his teacher as he rationalized the expensive purchase at supper on the day he bought the camera. "Judith says it preserves a moment in those times when you don't have the luxury of sitten down to paint a liven, breathen subject."

"Judith, is it now?" Joe had teased. "Is this the same Judith who's invited you to her home for dinner on at least two occasions that I know of."

"The one and the same," Summer chimed in as John delivered the evil eye at them both. "She seems to have taken a special interest in our brother's work."

"Is that proper for a teacher and a student to have dinner like that?" Caroline worried.

"Is it proper, John?" Joe had teased, unrelenting, drawing another vicious ogle from his brother as Caroline and Rachel frowned on the tone of the conversation.

"How old is this lady?" Matt had asked finally, curiosity getting the best of him.

"I don't know," John said.

"I don't know for sure, either," Summer announced. "But it's not a day under thirty-five."

"Thirty-five!" Luke exclaimed.

"I don't like the tone of this conversation one bit," Caroline said, emphatically, putting an end to the speculation, or at least the verbalizing of it. "Eat your supper! It's getten cold."

———

"Judith says," Summer said, reading Joe's thoughts as they waited on the porch for John to retrieve the camera.

"I wonder what else Judith does," Joe said, rolling his eyes as everyone broke into laughter.

"Is she really thirty-five?" Luke asked with admiration.

"That enough, Mr. Hormones," Summer said drolly. "You guys are amazen. One hint of somethen out of the ordinary, and your dirty minds start worken overtime. I'll be glad when you get past this stage in your development, Luke."

"I don't plan on ever getten past it," Luke grinned.

"I think you insulted me, Summer, and my age," Joe remarked dryly. "But I'm with you this time. Let's drop it."

"Do y'all realize today's Halloween?" Bonnie asked suddenly.

Her question was greeted with blank stares. Perhaps because they lived in the country, Halloween had never been a special occasion in the Baker home. Their lone acknowledgment of it came every fall around this time of year when the New River school hosted its primary fund-raiser, the annual Halloween carnival. None of the children had ever gone trick-or-treating, so the day held no special relevance for them.

"I was just tryen to change the subject," Bonnie explained. "That is what y'all wanted to do, isn't it?"

"And besides," she added a moment later. "It's the perfect day for Halloween—all gray and chilly and ominous."

"Not to mention a full moon tonight," Joe observed, pointing to the previous night's pale moon still shining bright in the morning sky.

"Spooky, spooky," teased Luke. "Who's gonna keep me safe from the ghost and goblins?"

"Believe me, Luke," Summer deadpanned. "There's not a ghost or goblin gonna come within a mile of your hormones."

They were all laughing hard a moment later when John emerged from the house, followed by their father.

"Don't even ask, Daddy," Summer said, acknowledging the perplexed look on Matt's face as John snapped two pictures of the orange oak tree.

"Then I won't," Matt replied, somewhat surprised to find all his children gathered on the porch, suddenly reminded of how fast they were aging. "John, how 'bout letten me take a picture of you children all together?"

"Good grief!" Luke exclaimed. "I think Daddy's getten all sappy on us. Next thing you know, he'll be wanten to have one of those heart-to-heart talks with us."

"Just hush up and get in line, Luke," Matt ordered, oblivious to the teasing. "Oldest to youngest—y'all spread out across the steps. Your mama'll be real pleased to have a picture of the six of you."

————

The bus came at last, and Carrie ran for it, eager to leave behind the strange familiarity of the morning, wanting to see Billy. He was seated in the rear of the bus, his head buried in a book, forcing Carrie to delay telling him about her change of heart over his homecoming invitation. The delay made her anxious, and she wondered again whether Billy would welcome her acceptance.

Her morning classes dragged, and the day grew uglier by the minute as the heavens prepared a storm. All around her, the halls buzzed with talk of trouble between black and white students, the result of pent-up frustrations on both sides and, quite possibly, an edginess honed by the simple desire for a good fight. In the cafeteria, where Carrie sat alone at her usual table thinking that Billy must have skipped lunch, she overheard the details of a fight between Wayne Taylor and a black senior. Wayne had won, somebody said, delivering a knockout punch that took with it one of the boy's front teeth.

Carrie pushed the trouble out of her mind, concerned only with the approach of sixth period and an opportunity to see Billy. When the bell rang to end fifth period, she nearly ran down the halls in her haste to get to the home economics classroom. Billy arrived only seconds before the tardy bell rang.

"What happened to you?" Carrie gasped at the sight of his swollen face, cut lip and black eye.

"I made a stand of sorts at home," Billy replied bitterly.

Carrie's eyes widened into saucers. "Your father did that?"

"I got into a fight," he replied quickly, then hesitated. "With Wayne," he sighed. "It's not as bad as it looks. I'd tell you Wayne looks worse, but you'd know I was lyen, so why bother?"

"It looks awful," Carrie observed, remembering the searing glare Wayne had given her the previous day. "What caused the fight, Billy?"

"Brotherly love," he lied unconvincingly. "You know how us guys are," he continued cheerfully. "We each stake out our territory, then fight to keep it. Let's just say that my territory shrunk and leave it at that. Okay?"

Before Carrie could answer, Mrs. Franklin bellowed for them to be quiet. When Billy faced the front of the room, however, the teacher temporarily forgot home economics. "What in the world happened to you?" she demanded.

"I ran into a door," Billy said lamely.

"The truth?"

"My brother and I got into it," he shrugged. "I came out the loser."

"That appears painfully evident," the teacher surmised. "May I take it that Wayne Taylor is your brother?"

"My reputation precedes me," Billy remarked, slightly sarcastic. "Unfortunately, he is."

"Well, at the risk of insulten your kin, I think he'd be better off in a boxen ring than in this school beaten up people half his size," Mrs. Franklin observed sternly. Her voice softened and she asked with genuine concern, "Are you okay, Billy?"

Again, Billy wondered what would happen if he told the truth. He looked down at his desk, then back to the teacher. "It's not as bad as it looks, ma'am," he answered for her benefit.

"It looks worse than bad, son," she shot back. "It's too bad we're not studyen first-aid. You'd be perfect for practice. But if you're sure there's nothen I can do to help, Billy, then we'll get on with class."

Carrie felt Billy's embarrassment. She also saw it on the back of his neck, which turned red under the scrutiny of Mrs. Franklin. His injuries worried Carrie, who considered the possibility that she was the cause of them. She debated whether to bring up the subject of homecoming, wondering whether her initial inclination had been the right response. Making up her mind at last, she opened her notebook to a clean page, scribbled a message, folded the paper and nudged Billy's back, passing the note to him while Mrs. Franklin wrote on the blackboard.

She heard the paper uncurl, watched Billy decide and then heard the soft scribble of his pencil. Billy handed the note back to her. Carrie read it, smiled, dashed down her answer and returned the paper to him. She was careless with the delivery, however, and the teacher caught her passing the note.

"What's goen on back there?" Mrs. Franklin boomed suddenly, startling the entire class as Billy stole a quick look at Carrie's message. "Billy Taylor! Bring that to me this instant. If the two of you seem to think it's more important than my home economics class, then maybe you'd like to share it with the rest of us."

Oh God! Billy thought. He risked a glance at Carrie, but she smiled and shrugged, indicating he had no other choice. He rose slowly, blushed deep red and walked to the front of the room where Mrs. Franklin waited with her hand extended. Without taking her eyes from Billy, she took the paper and unfolded it. She read the note quickly, clearly surprised by the content, obligated by her own classroom policy to read it aloud. She cleared her throat, then boomed out the words in perfect monotone.

"Is that invitation to the dance still open?"

"Yes."

"I'd enjoy goen with you then."

The girls giggled, which Mrs. Franklin silenced with a glare before turning her attention again to Billy. "You've made a big impression on my class today, Mr. Taylor," she observed. "I take it that the class can assume you and Carrie are goen to the homecomen dance together."

"I guess so," Billy mumbled.

"Good!" she exaggerated with mock sincerity. "However, let me remind you that homecomen is still a few days away, so let's concentrate on home economics till then. Shall we?"

"Yes'em," Billy nodded as she pointed him back to his seat.

Billy's face was painted crimson as he returned to his desk. Carrie saw only the crooked smile tossed her way.

———

By the end of the school day, gray clouds hung precariously low in the sky, hovering barely above the tallest treetops. The air was chillingly damp, unleashing a fine mist, and, high on the western horizon, an otherwise brilliant yellow sun fought a losing battle to peek through the clouds.

Carrie noticed none of this as she sat beside Billy on the bus, telling him why she had changed her mind. "I talked it over with Mama, who reminded me of somethen I'd forgot," she explained. "We Bakers tend to stand up for what and who we believe in. For that matter, Billy, so does your daddy, even if you and I happen to disagree with him. Who knows? Maybe for once, the history of our families is on our side."

"I guess," Billy concurred cautiously. "When you get right down to it, it's not really that big a deal. After all, it's just a dance, ain't it?"

"Yes," she answered without hesitation. "And we're goen to have a swell time."

Instead of debarking the bus at the mercantile, Carrie continued on to the elementary school. She had promised to stay after school with Bonnie to help her younger sister decorate a fortune-telling booth for the next night's Halloween carnival.

"Neither one of us know the first thing about fortune-tellen," she told Billy minutes later as they stood in the school parking lot. "I don't think we have a decent idea between us on how to fix up the room, but Bonnie's got lots of bead strings, a black light and a lava lamp, so we're bound to come up with somethen. She's even got a crystal ball."

"I wouldn't sweat it," Billy said impassively. "Not many other people 'round here know what a fortune-tellen booth looks like."

Carrie was hoping Billy might ask her for a date prior to homecoming, a trial run of sorts for the big occasion. The Halloween carnival seemed like a logical opportunity to her, but Billy seemed strangely distracted. He was preoccupied with something more important, she realized, examining his battered face once more and realizing her feelings were selfish. Perhaps the reason for his indifference waited at home in the bully form of his brother. Well, she could suffer through this absent-minded mood, Carrie decided. She had, after all, the promise of his smile.

———

Wayne Taylor felt like a hero. For the first time in his life, he had masterminded and carried out the perfect plan, using lies and unfounded rumors to spread suspicion through the halls of Cookville High School. The idea had been simple: Attack one student and get the whole bunch of them in an uproar. He was amazed at the gullibility of people, especially their eagerness to embrace gossip at face value.

Wayne had gone after Eddie Wright, a tall, skinny nigger who was competing with Hal Vickers for a starting spot on the basketball team. Hal had been the perfect foil for Wayne's plan. First, he despised niggers nearly as much as Wayne did. And second, although he had started on last year's team, he lacked the skills to match up with Eddie Wright on the basketball court. Wayne simply told Hal and everyone else how Eddie was bragging about taking over the white boy's starting position. It was a partially true statement. Eddie had indeed said that he expected to earn a starting position on the team, only without any mention whatsoever of Hal Vickers.

At first, Wayne had annoyed Hal with his persistent reminders of Eddie's braggart remarks. When other friends began peppering him with questions along the same lines, however, Hal became enraged and went after Eddie. At that point, Wayne had intervened in the fracas, becoming the first to defend Hal. He had begun with tough words and ended with action, using his bulk and newfound confidence to beat the shit out of Eddie Wright.

Now, the whole school considered Wayne a hero, and currents of distrust ran deeply between the blacks and whites.

Hot damn! His daddy would be proud of him tonight once he heard the details of the day. And the truth itself, without any embellishment, would earn him respect.

Like a dog with a bone, this need for respect gnawed at Wayne. He could never get enough. Every now and then, respect came his way, providing a savory bone to bury. But soon, the hunger pains would come again, forcing him to dig up the old bone in search of fulfillment.

Wayne had gone through many bones, but none as meaty as the one thrown his way today. He'd devoured it like a hungry bulldog, demolishing Eddie Wright in a blaze of swinging fists and sheer strength. People actually had pulled him off the boy, though, fortunately, only after Eddie was flat on his back, spitting blood and missing a tooth. After years of avoiding the fight whenever possible, Wayne felt smugly confident in having been restrained. His fierceness had announced to the world that Wayne Taylor was someone to fear.

But what about his daddy? When all was said and done about today, what would Bobby Taylor think about his oldest son? Bobby expected his sons to be fierce. He was never satisfied with their accomplishments. He'd have a big laugh about today, perhaps toss a few crumbs of praise Wayne's way. But invariably, Bobby would soon ask: "What's next?"

Even as Wayne gloated, a hollow space grew in the pit of his stomach.

These thoughts came to Wayne as he sat alone in the back of the bus waiting for the New River school children to board for the ride home. The next idea came by accident when he went to scratch his chest and felt the steel bulge inside his jacket. He patted the gun, sneering at its reassurance. Suddenly, Wayne knew what had to be done—the one final act that would make him a man among men in his daddy's eyes and solve a pesky family problem as well. Then, Wayne would get the respect he craved.

He deserved respect, by god. And, if need be, he would earn it.

———

Billy tried to figure out how to escort Carrie to homecoming without his father's knowing. He fingered his lip lightly. His body could not absorb more punishment, which was exactly what Bobby would mete out if he discovered Billy messing with the daughter of Matt Baker. Even now, Billy was taking a chance. Wayne was somewhere around here and, under the right circumstances, would rat on him to their father.

He gave Carrie a brief smile, unsure what she had just told him, although certain the conversation had moved past fortune-telling.

Billy wanted desperately to ask her for a date on Saturday, maybe to the New

River Halloween carnival. But he could never pull off such a blatant violation of his daddy's order to stay away from Carrie. Too many people who knew Bobby would see them together at the carnival. On top of everything else, Bobby always made a point to show up at the carnival to play bingo and walk for cakes.

"Is that a yes or no?" Carrie asked suddenly.

He stared blankly, unable to answer because he had failed to hear the question.

"Or is it, 'I don't know?'" she queried once more.

"I'm sorry," Billy said. "My mind's wanderen today."

"It sure is," Carrie agreed. "I'm beginnen to think you're haven second thoughts about homecomen."

"No way," he smiled. "I'm all ears now. What was it you asked?"

"Would you be interested in goen to church this Sunday?" she asked. "And maybe haven dinner afterward at my house?"

Billy's mouth fell open. "Church?" he gaped.

"If you're uncomfortable about church, you could just come for dinner," Carrie said uncertainly. "Honestly, though, it would make a good impression on Mama and Daddy if you went to church, too."

Billy considered the possibility. "Nah, I'm not uncomfortable with church," he replied at last. "Heck, that'd probably be the easy part of the day. It's just that I've never gone to church before."

"Never at all?" Carrie gawked.

"Not that I can remember," Billy said, then brightened with a smile. "But I'd like to give it a try. I've heard good things about it."

There was truth to his claim, but mainly, Billy figured church offered a perfect setting to see Carrie without attracting too much attention. He was trying to figure out how to attend a church service without raising the ire of Bobby when the corner of his eye caught sight of Wayne kneeling on one knee between the school and one of the buses. He peered more closely as Wayne motioned someone to come his way.

Billy followed the length of his brother's gaze to a small black boy.

"What the heck is goen on?" he asked aloud, startling Carrie as she explained about the Sunday services at Benevolence Missionary Baptist Church.

"Huh?" she asked as Billy started walking toward the school.

———

"Come'ere, boy," Wayne coaxed sternly once he got Danny Bartholomew's attention. "Me and you need to talk, and you'd be wise to pay close attention. You hear me?"

Danny nodded, his black eyes wide and shiny as he edged near the older boy, who seemed vaguely familiar.

"Carl Taylor is my brother," Wayne told him, and Danny relaxed.

His face lit up with a smile. "I didn't know Carl had a brother," he replied, coming closer to Wayne. "Carl's my best friend. He's gonna spend the night at my house soon."

"Listen, you little sonofabitch," Wayne scowled. "You better keep your black ass away from Carl if you know what's good for you. Understand?"

Fear twisted, then froze the smile on Danny's face. He tried to draw back, but Wayne compelled him forward with the cold glare of his eyes.

"See this," Wayne continued, peeling open his jacket to reveal the gun.

Slowly, he maneuvered the gun inside his jacket until it was pointing at Danny.

Shooting the boy was the farthest thing from Wayne's mind. He simply wanted to scare him. "You quit playen with Carl and messen around where you got no business, boy," he said slowly. "Or I may just have to use this on you—or maybe on your daddy. You understand, nigger boy?"

Danny was too scared to answer, too frightened to run. He stood there, cemented to the parking lot with fear, staring down the short barrel of a pistol, oblivious of everything else.

———

Ten yards from his brother, Billy saw the gun.

His initial thought was to place himself between Wayne and the boy. Billy did not think his brother would shoot the kid. But then again, Wayne had been a ticking bomb these last few weeks, a loose cannon waiting for someone to light his fuse. Who knew what he might do?

"Wayne! Wayne!" Billy shouted, his voice pitched low. "What are you doen, man? Give me the gun.

"Now!" Billy screamed when Wayne failed to respond. "Give it to me right now."

Wayne stood up, ticked at his meddlesome brother. He aimed the gun at Billy.

Billy rushed him, nailing Wayne in the chest with his shoulder and snatching away the gun in the same motion. As Wayne made a desperate lunge to grab back the weapon, Billy whirled away and the moment exploded in hellish rage.

It took Billy a long second to comprehend the gun had discharged. He saw Danny Bartholomew falling backward, his thin arms flailing, then blood spurting through a small hole in the boy's flimsy T-shirt.

Billy stood transfixed as Carrie ran toward him, screaming as she fell beside Danny, pulling the boy onto her lap. Others came running as well, teachers, bus drivers, students, all of them gaping and pointing fingers at Billy. Dazed, bewildered by the gunfire, he glanced blankly at the gun in his hand, understanding at last that his finger had pulled the trigger.

Scared senseless, Billy grimaced in disbelief. He started to explain the situation, then told himself to get away from this place and these people. They would crucify him because he was the son of Bobby Taylor and he had shot a black child. So he fled, running as fast as his feet would carry him, running all the harder as he heard the shouts of those behind him.

———

Carrie cradled Danny in her lap with one arm and used the other to cover the hole where blood seeped from his chest. She stared into his face, willing away her tears so that sadness would not be the last thing he saw.

Danny was dying. Of that, she was certain. She refused to let him die alone, however, without anything or anyone familiar.

The whole atmosphere was freakish, casting a surreal glow on unbearable reality. Adults panicked around her, children screamed, but Carrie remained deathly calm, simply smiling in answer to the questioning look in Danny's shining eyes. She would not allow her gaze to meander from his beautiful black face. She thought Danny realized he was dying as well when his black eyes became momentarily wild and frantic, as if he grasped an understanding that he was headed for the unknown.

Carrie sympathized. She'd felt the same way once, as she was about to get on a double Ferris wheel at the county fair—the difference being that there was no turning back for Danny as there could have been for her.

She was still smiling, reassuring the little boy she had known since birth, when, moments later, Danny gasped, and the veil came down over his shining eyes.

―――――

Beauty heard the sheriff's car before she saw it. This was a game she played, based on the way a car's motor sounded and hatched from her daily isolation on the farm. With so few visitors to the house and most of them the same ones over and over again, it was easy for Beauty to match the sound of an approaching car to the visitor. The car now crunching down the drive purred heavily, which meant Paul Berrien was paying a visit.

She checked the clock, thinking Annie and Danny would be home from school soon, puzzling why the sheriff would call at this odd time of the day.

Stopping at the mirror beside the entrance to her home, Beauty patted down her hair and wiped her hands on the apron before pushing open the screen door.

Her heart started racing as soon as Beauty glimpsed Annie beside Paul in the patrol car. Once again, a feeling of premonition came over Beauty, the same fear she'd had at the school board meeting back in August when she had wanted Lucas to forget about sending Annie and Danny to school with all those white children. She craned her head forward, trying to find Danny in the car as she descended the rickety doorsteps.

Paul Berrien opened his door slowly as she came toward him. As soon as Beauty saw the grim set of his face, she knew to expect the worse.

"Mr. Paul," she greeted him hopefully. "Mr. Paul, is everything okay?"

"I'm afraid not, Beauty," Paul said gently.

Beauty looked from him to where Annie sat in the car. "Where's Danny, Mr. Paul?" she asked, not so much a question but a plea for her son's well-being.

"Beauty, there's been an accident at school," Paul said grievously. "A terrible accident."

She refused to listen any further, covering her ears with her hands, stomping her feet like an angry child as if she could make the sheriff cease to exist and bring her son home. But Paul proceeded to tell her about Danny anyway, expressing his deepest sympathy, inquiring where Lucas might be. Beauty only vaguely heard what he said. She simply fainted away, the sound of Annie's scream ringing in her ears as she collapsed on the ground.

She slept effortlessly, soundlessly, oblivious of the world, unaware of being carried to her bed by Paul Berrien. She slept peacefully until she heard the agonizing moan of her husband as Paul told Lucas the hard truth about their only son. Even then, she stayed in bed, streams of tears cascading down her face as Lucas pounded the walls with his fists, screaming an agonized litany of "Oh, God! Don't let it be true, don't let it be."

But Beauty knew the truth. In her heart and soul, she had always known it. There was no dream. It was all a nightmare, and, now, it would never—could never—end.

―――――

Carrie lay still in bed, recalling the blur of time since Danny had died. Someone—Paul Berrien, she believed—had pulled her away from Danny a few minutes before the ambulance arrived to carry away the body. There had been questions, too, a thousand inquiries from Paul and twice that many from agents with the Georgia Bureau of Investigation. She had told them the shooting was an accident, occurring as Billy tried to take the gun from Wayne, who was the real culprit in the macabre tale.

Whether they believed her was another story. There had been so many questions that sometimes Carrie seemed confused herself about the chain of events leading to the shooting. She was the sole witness to the struggle between Billy and Wayne. Everyone else avouched of having seen Billy with a gun pointed directly at Danny immediately after the pistol discharged. No one could recall seeing Wayne, and Carrie herself had no idea when he had fled. In fact, one boy swore up and down that Wayne had never left the bus, whereas everyone, including her, had seen Billy running from the scene of the crime, taking the gun with him as he escaped into the woods behind the school.

The slow opening of the door interrupted her thoughts as Rachel peeked in the bedroom to check on her.

"I'm awake, Granny," she said just as Rachel started to retreat from the door.

"How you feelen, honey?" Rachel asked sympathetically.

"I'm okay," Carrie answered, her throat hoarse from the lengthy police questioning earlier in the afternoon. "Any more news?"

"Your mama, daddy and grandpa are over at the Bartholomews right now," she said. "They've called in bloodhounds to search for those Taylor boys. Some people tried to get up a posse, but Paul put a quick end to that nonsense."

Carrie closed her eyes, imagining how frightened Billy must be as he ran through those dark, wet woods with bloodhounds chasing him and everyone convinced he had murdered a little black boy. If ever there was any truth to the notion of sons paying for the sins of their fathers, then Billy had become the ultimate sacrificial lamb. The thought sent a new wave of chills through Carrie, who snuggled deeper under the covers in a futile search for solace.

Rachel turned on a lamp in the room. "It just grieves my heart for Beauty and Lucas," she said sadly. "That poor little boy. He never even had a chance in life.

"I'm worried about you, too, honey," she added. "How awful for you to see that. Is there anything I can do for you? Are you hungry?"

"No, ma'am. I just want to sleep."

"Okay," Rachel soothed. "But you've got to get out of that dress. I'll get a gown for you."

For the first time, Carrie realized she was still wearing the black and white checked dress, now stained with the blood of Danny Bartholomew. She felt sick as she took off the garment and put on the flannel gown Rachel handed to her.

"Granny, please throw that dress away," she said meekly as Rachel left the room. "I don't ever want to see it again."

Without a word, Rachel kissed her goodnight on the forehead, picked up the dress and left the room.

Carrie drowsed again, waking around eleven o'clock when the front door opened as her parents and grandfather arrived home, along with Joe, who had covered the events for the newspaper. The muffled voices coming from the living room aroused her interest, drawing Carrie from the bed. She tiptoed across the room into better hearing range beside the door.

"Accorden to Paul, Carrie swears it was an accident, that Billy was only tryen to wrestle away the gun from his brother," Joe said. "He also says other people have told him Billy's not the kind of boy to cause trouble."

"He's a quiet one, at least what I know about him," John added. "I never figured Billy as a killer."

"I don't think he is a killer, John," Joe said sharply, not pleased with the connotative tone of judgment used by his brother.

"What else did Paul tell you, son?" Matt asked Joe.

"They got bloodhounds out looken for him," Joe replied, "but the dogs won't do much good in this rain. Paul's worried because the kid has that gun with him. He's afraid someone else is gonna get hurt."

"It's hard to tell what's goen through the boy's mind," Matt agreed. "He's probably scared and a little disoriented, too. Who knows what he might do?"

"What about Wayne?" Luke asked.

"Nobody's seen hide nor hair of him since this afternoon," Joe answered. "But Bobby's truck is missen, so chances are that either Wayne or both of them took off in it. They have lookouts posted all over the state."

"What does Bobby have to say about all this?" Caroline inquired.

Joe shook his head in disbelief. "Believe it or not, he told me Billy's been acten awful strange lately, talken back to him and causen trouble at home. Bobby says that Billy picked a fight with Wayne a few days ago, and Wayne beat the shit out of him. Excuse the language, Mama, Granny, but that's Bobby's exact words. Of course, I wouldn't put it past Bobby to have beaten the kid himself and now tell everybody Wayne did it."

"Neither would I," Luke said caustically.

Joe glanced at Luke, then back to Caroline. "To answer your question, Mama, Bobby doesn't seem too shook up over it," he told her.

"For some reason, that doesn't come as a shock to me," Sam said tiredly.

Caroline took over the conversation suddenly, ordering everyone to bed.

"How's Carrie?" Joe asked no one in particular.

"I'm fixen to check on her," Caroline answered, turning to Summer and Bonnie. "How 'bout the two of you sleepen in the boy's room tonight, so Carrie can have some privacy? She's been through a traumatic day, and I imagine she needs time to herself to sort through it all."

A few minutes later, when Caroline went into the girls' room, she found Carrie fast asleep with her face buried in the feather pillow. She tucked in the covers, stroked the girl's hair and left her to sleep.

———

Carrie felt badly about deceiving her mother, pretending to be asleep when only moments earlier she had eavesdropped on a family conversation. But she truly wanted privacy, unable to cope with the possibility of having to answer even one more question.

As the midnight hour ebbed, her fears for Billy worsened, and Carrie began trying to figure out where he might have fled. Billy was not stupid enough to go anywhere near his home, and he knew this backwoods country better than the palm of his hand. An idea began forming in her mind as she realized Billy would seek sanctuary in a place where no one would suspect to find him. And the least likely place around these parts where people would think to look for him was on the Baker place.

She knew it was a hunch, probably not a good one at that. Even if Billy had hidden somewhere on her family's farm, the chances of finding him seemed remote at best. There were hundreds of acres, with thick groves of trees and unlimited hiding places. Still, even as she tried to talk herself out of the idea, Carrie slid from bed, crept over to her chest of drawers and dug out a pair of old jeans and a sweatshirt. She slipped into the clothes, grabbed a pair of shoes and tiptoed from the room, thankful one of her brothers had sprayed penetrating oil on the squeaky door hinges a few weeks ago. She crept down the hallway, through the dining room and into the kitchen, where she paused to monitor the noise coming from Sam and Rachel's room. Assured they were sound asleep by the rhythmic snores of her grandfather, she let herself out the kitchen onto the porch and eased out the backdoor.

Lightning split the sky and thunder roared as the rain soaked Carrie to the skin before she crossed from one side of the house to the other. At the back edge of the house, she paused to get her bearings and considered where to look for Billy. She thought about the place near the river, discarding it as too close to the Taylor farm. It seemed more likely Billy would have sought refuge on the backside of the farm, perhaps near the railroad tracks or close to one of the ponds. Deciding finally to circle the farm, she set off at a fast pace, climbing over the metal gate, jumping the fence that ran beside the pecan orchard and heading across the boggy field.

———

During the years Joe had a made a habit of sneaking out of the house for his late-night walks to the railroad tracks, his sense of hearing had become finely tuned to the sounds of the family settling for the night. On this night when he was too keyed up to sleep, various little noises disturbed him as he lay in bed. Once, he thought he heard footsteps as someone slipped down the hall to the bathroom, yet there was never any evidence of a return trip. On other occasions, it sounded as if doors opened and closed slowly. Still, Joe dismissed the barely audible noises as inconsequential, products of his imagination, attributable to the rain pounding on the tin roof.

Then, he heard two sounds, distinct above the roar of the rain. The first was his parents' voices in the hallway and the second was a clanking noise on the gate just outside his bedroom window. He sat up in bed intending to peer out the window, but his attention was diverted by the sudden glow of light in the hallway. He climbed out of bed and padded into the boys' room.

"What's goen on?" he asked his brothers and sisters as he entered the hallway.

"Daddy? Mama?" he said as Matt came down the hall and Caroline opened the door to the girls' room.

"Did you hear anything strange?" Matt asked.

"I thought I heard someone in the hall earlier—doors openen and closen," Joe answered. "And just a second ago, somethen hit the gate outside my window. I thought maybe the wind had knocked a pecan limb down on it."

"Matt! Matt! She's gone!" Caroline almost shouted as she rushed from the empty room. "Carrie's not in her bed."

"Carrie?" Matt called as his other sons and daughters appeared instantly in the hall. "Where are you, honey?"

"I'll check in the kitchen," Summer commented, though the silence made it obvious Carrie was not in the house.

"Oh my God, Matt!" Caroline panicked. "Where is she? What has happened?"

"Where would she go at this time of night?" John asked, almost to himself.

"What about the front porch?" Bonnie suggested. "Maybe she's out there swingen or rocken."

Matt nearly ran to the front door, fumbling with the knob as he opened it and switching on the porch light. "She's not out here," he said disappointedly as Summer returned with Sam and Rachel in tow.

"She's not in the kitchen, either," Summer spoke the obvious.

"Billy."

All eyes turned to Caroline, who stood pale, braced against the wall.

"What about him?" Matt demanded.

"I meant to mention it earlier, but in all the commotion, I never did," Caroline wailed. "He asked Carrie to go with him to the homecomen dance next week. She turned him down, then changed her mind. She was gonna tell him today that she wanted to go, if he still wanted to go with her."

The entire family gaped at Caroline, as if she had given Carrie permission to dance with the devil himself.

"You think she went looken for him?" Matt questioned.

"I don't know," she worried. "You don't think Billy came after her, do you?"

It was a frightening suggestion, fraught with dozens of questions and some hard facts. Carrie had rejected Billy, and she had seen him fire the bullet that killed Danny Bartholomew. She claimed the shooting was an accident, but Billy had no way of knowing that. Nor did they have any way of knowing his intentions toward Carrie.

"I know what everybody's thinken, but it doesn't make sense," Joe observed.

"None of this makes sense," Matt said pensively, burying his head against a palm. "I can't believe a daughter of mine would get involved with the likes of that."

"I tried to tell her the same thing," Luke said. "But they've had a thing goen since almost the beginnen of school."

"Well, none of that is neither here nor there at the moment," Sam roared. "Matt, you've got to find her. You start looken, and I'll call the sheriff to let him know what's goen on."

"That's right," Matt agreed. "Joe, get dressed and come with me." He paused, then added. "You'd better bring your gun just in case."

"Matt?" Caroline said cautiously. "That may be taken things too far. Carrie says Billy's a real nice young man—nothen at all like his daddy."

"That may be, Caroline, but he's also killed a little boy today," Matt replied. "And regardless of whether it was an accident or not, he's probably upset and a little crazy by now. On top of everything else, he's walken around out there with a gun. There's no tellen what the boy might do. Carrie could be in danger, and I'm not taken any chances out there."

"Where will you look?" Sam asked as Joe returned dressed in jeans, a denim jacket and worn boots.

"I heard that noise at the gate," Joe volunteered as he stuffed the pistol in his jacket pocket and checked his flashlight. "My bet is somewhere on the backside of the farm. When you think about it, this is the perfect place for him to hide. Nobody would expect to find him here of all places. And who knows? He might even try to jump a train. He'd be crazy to, probably get himself killed tryen. But he'd be less likely to be seen in one of our fields than near the train crossen. The one o'clock's due by in a few minutes."

"Let's go then," Matt said as he loaded his twelve-gauge shotgun. "I'll work my way around the east side and you go up the west by the New Pond. Follow the edge of the fields to the railroad tracks and cut across the back of the place. Fire a shot if you come across anything. And be careful, son. I don't know what kind of boy Billy Taylor is, but he has a gun. And he's killed one person with it.

"John, Luke," Matt continued. "Y'all stay close by and keep your eyes open for anything strange."

"Yes, sir," the boys answered.

"I'll tell the sheriff where y'all are," Sam said as Matt and Joe headed out the door into the rain.

————

Carrie sank ankle deep in mud repeatedly as she crossed the fields, working her way around the edge of the bog to the Old Pond, across its dam and along the fencerow of a recently harvested field of cotton, its white leftovers glowing like ghosts in the pitch-black dark. Hard rain spiked her face, patches of fog settled over the fields and a howling wind stifled the few attempts she made to call for Billy. She relied on occasional flashes of lightning and instinct to guide her along the invisible path.

On the backside of the pond, she stopped to decide whether to follow the pond along its rear bank or cross the back pasture to the railroad. She chose the latter course because the walking was easier, except for an occasional gob of soppy cow manure—and an occasional cow itself, one of which she stumbled across, startling the poor beast from a cold sleep, before she came at last to the back fence. Following the fence across the pasture, she reached the woods and climbed over to the other side, deciding to walk along the Southern Railroad's rocky right-of-way rather than risk negotiating the tangled growth.

Just when she was ready to give up hope of finding Billy, the thunderclouds broke, allowing the light of a Hunter's Moon to filter down, and he materialized like a ghost, emerging from a fog bank on the other side of the railroad tracks. He took a few cautious steps across the ties, then stopped a few yards from where Carrie stood as still as a painting.

He was trembling, chilled to the marrow by the rain and his own fear. His hair was plastered to his head, clothes hung skin tight against him and two red scratches complimented the bruises on his face. Still, he appeared handsome to Carrie, as a deer is beautiful.

He began to cry, whelping tears that translated into volumes of sadness and made her want to comfort him, wrap her arms around his quaking body and tell him his tears—so agonizing and aching—were unnecessary. But sympathetic words failed her.

"Your lip's bleeden again," she finally ventured.

Her observation sailed right past him on the wind.

"I didn't mean to shoot him," Billy apologized. "I don't know how it happened. I just wanted to get the gun from Wayne. That's all I was tryen to do, and it went off."

"It was an accident, Billy," she said firmly. "I saw what happened, and I know it was an accident."

Billy looked away to consider this absolution of his guilt.

"I was wonderen if you'd come," he said in a while. "How did you know?"

"Just a hunch."

"Is Danny okay?" he asked.

Of course, he would not know, Carrie thought, thrown off balance by the suddenness of the question. She hesitated an answer, weighing whether Billy could accept the fact that he had fired the fatal shot. Although Billy seemed to realize the shooting had been accidental, she doubted whether his state of mind would allow him to make any reconciliation with his part in the killing of Danny Bartholomew.

"He'll be okay," she lied.

His shoulders literally sagged with relief, and Carrie knew she had made the right decision. Perhaps Billy would resent the deception later, but it seemed a small price to pay for a piece of his fragile sanity. And, too, he would have plenty of time to learn and live with the horrifying truth.

He smiled sadly, then spoke in a voice so soft she could barely hear him above the rain. "I prayed, Carrie. I prayed hard that if there was a God, he'd let Danny be okay. That's all I wanted was for that little boy to be okay and alive so that he could still be friends with my little brother."

Her conscience would not allow Carrie to ignore this error in faith. Too much was at stake, now and later when Billy discovered the painful truth about Danny. "It doesn't work that way with God, Billy," she told him firmly. "You can't blackmail Him. You can't hinge your belief in God on what He does for you."

He smiled again at her. "Well, you know Him better than I do, so I'll take your word on it. But whatever, I believe. All I wanted was for that little boy to be okay and alive."

Then Billy told her how Carl's friendship with Danny had precipitated the crisis at home and triggered the beating at the hands of his father. She shook her head and cried with him—for him.

Abruptly, his tears ended. "None of that matters now," he told her. "Forget I ever brought it up. My prayers have been answered. That's what matters."

Carrie decided this was not the time for a theological debate.

"The police are looken for you, Billy," she said gently. "They've got bloodhounds. You have to turn yourself into Paul Berrien. I told him it was an accident. There's nothen for you to fear."

"Not anymore, there isn't," Billy smiled. "As long as Danny's alive, it doesn't matter what happens to me."

"It matters, Billy," Carrie said.

He shrugged and bent over for a moment. When he straightened up, a frown creased his face. "I still have the gun," he announced, lifting his wet T-shirt to reveal the gun stuffed inside the waistband of his jeans. "Once or twice, I thought about doen what Mama did. But I was too scared. I guess my daddy and Wayne are right after all. I'm nothen but a coward at heart."

"You're no coward, Billy Taylor," she argued warmly. "Just good at heart and full of kindness. And when all this is over and done with, you can walk down the street and hold your head high, with nothen whatsoever to be ashamed of."

"Would you walk beside me?" he asked.

"You're my best friend, Billy," Carrie replied. "I'd hold your hand the whole way."

The forcefulness of her conviction nearly drove Billy to tears once more. He bit his lip to keep from crying and pondered her words. Maybe Carrie was right. Perhaps he had an opportunity to escape from the warped shadow of his father and make his own mark on the world. Maybe everything had happened the way it did for a reason, to give him the guts necessary to stand up to his daddy.

All at once, he felt at peace with the world and with himself—and suddenly, very tired as well, exhausted by the lack of sleep and food, the ordeal of running, the worry over Danny Bartholomew and the weight of the weapon in his hand. The gun felt heavy, and Billy had to rid himself of it.

"I don't want this anymore," he said, waving the gun in his hand.

Carrie could practically feel the burden of his exhaustion. She had no fear of weapons. Matt Baker had instilled a respect for guns in all his children and taught them how to handle weapons as well, so Carrie had no misgivings about taking the gun, except it was pointed her way, bobbing in his shaking hand.

"Be careful, Billy," she advised softly, smiling kindly. "Just give it to me, and I'll carry it for you. I'm sure the sheriff will need to see it. We can walk back to my house and call him."

Billy nodded in agreement and raised the gun to Carrie's outstretched hand.

EVERYONE SAID IT WAS another unfortunate accident, a wicked twist of fate or just old-fashioned bad luck. A few seconds either way would have made a world of difference.

Joe understood the particulars and the whims of the accident. But as far as he was concerned, the only thing that mattered was the bottom line: Someone else had died and he had pulled the trigger.

Halloween night was two days past, and Joe sat alone on the porch, rocking steadily as he stared across the road at the oak tree, which had yielded its orange leaves to the storm's lashing wind and rain. Strangely, he thought about John, who had spent a few hours after lunch on that Halloween day painting the tree and later learned the importance of preserving a moment on film when time did not lend itself to painting a living, breathing subject.

The painting was beautiful, reminding Joe of the sense of purpose and exhilaration that had filled him on Halloween morning. He had set out to conquer the world that day. Now he felt like the oak tree looked, a withered pumpkin stripped of its brilliant luster. While the oak tree still boasted a lush, velvety orange carpet around its base, Joe just felt completely bare.

He shivered in the overcast chill of late afternoon, leaning his head against the back of the rocker and allowing his eyes to close. He was wearing his best Sunday suit, navy blue with cuffed pants, a white shirt and matching tie. He had made one concession to his appearance since arriving on the porch two hours ago from Danny Bartholomew's funeral, loosening his tie shortly after he planted himself in the rocker and refused to budge from it.

With the exception of Carrie, his other brothers and sisters had barricaded themselves inside the house, giving Joe the space to dwell on the events of two nights ago. Carrie had accompanied their parents and grandparents to Billy Taylor's funeral, which was to be a simple graveside service in the cemetery at Benevolence. Joe wondered briefly whether their presence was welcomed at the funeral, then realized someone had to represent the family and it certainly couldn't be him.

Joe could not help asking himself if, given a second chance, he would have acted with more prudence—or at least more cautiously with his aim of the gun.

From his vantage point twenty yards away, Joe had witnessed Billy point a pistol at Carrie. His reaction had been instantaneous, his own weapon drawn and fired without hesitation to save the life of his sister. Joe had fired the gun seconds before Matt took aim with his shotgun. There had been no reason for Matt to discharge his weapon.

The impact of the shot had stopped Billy in his tracks. The gun fell from his hand; he stumbled backward, and collapsed on his back against the rocky terrain.

Carrie stared at him for a moment without comprehending, then slowly traced the blast of gunfire to where Joe stood with the weapon still aimed. Her anguished wail had consumed Joe like the flames of torment. He'd realized he made a dreadful mistake, even before Carrie screamed frantically, "No, no, no. He was given me the gun. He didn't want it anymore."

She ran to Billy, threw herself on the ground and pulled the body of another dead boy into her arms. She had been the first to know Billy was dead. No one who gazed into the vacant set of Billy's slate blue eyes would have believed in the possibility that a living soul still occupied his body.

Joe was beside them in seconds, dropping to his knees to examine the boy. But Carrie pushed him away, beating wildly at his chest.

"He was given me the gun," she screamed repeatedly, frantically. "He was given me the gun."

Then, her voice had softened considerably, inexplicably. "Why, Joe?" she had cried. "Why, why, why?"

The repeated questions had pierced his own heart like the cold steel of a bullet, yet Joe ignored his sister, clinging to a sliver of hope that he would find life in Billy. "Shut up!" he yelled, grabbing Carrie by the shoulders until she ceased the frantic pummeling of his chest. "Let me see him!"

Carrie relaxed her grip on Billy, allowing her brother to discover for himself what she had seen seconds earlier. And though Joe had few experiences with dead people, Billy's eyes plainly showed the truth.

Joe knew what followed was an exercise in futility, yet he searched desperately for signs of life. Finding no pulse in Billy's neck, he lifted the boy's T-shirt and leaned against his chest in another useless search for signs of breathing or a heartbeat. He came away with nothing, except a smear of blood across his face from the tiny hole in Billy's heart.

It was such a small hole, yet deadly damaging. An autopsy performed the next morning revealed that Billy had died the very instant the bullet sliced its way through his heart.

Joe had guessed as much as he kneeled beside the dead boy, whose head rested in Carrie's lap. Matt reached them moments later, and Joe conveyed the situation with a grim nod of his head.

The silence had been enormous, more powerful than the wind and rain, chaining the three of them to the very spot where Billy had died. Joe looked from his father to Billy to Carrie to the heavens, repeating the ritual time and time again as he tried to make sense of everything and keep his sanity in the process. Finally, when it became apparent that no one was prepared to seek help or the law or whoever handled matters such as these, he had risen from Billy's side and taken care of the task himself.

Joe had hoped that time, even two days, might dull the edge of reality. If anything, however, these two days had sharpened his recall of the night. His mind refused to block out the slightest of details, playing over and over again from the moment he first glimpsed Billy holding the gun to the sick expressions on the faces of his family and Paul Berrien when he staggered into the house with the terse announcement: "Billy's dead."

There had been a barrage of questions afterward, from Paul, his family and other lawmen. The details of his answers eluded Joe now, as did the questions themselves. What happened afterward was not germane. The point was, tersely said or not, that Billy Taylor was dead, probably lying at the bottom of his grave by this time. And Joe was responsible.

Joe buried his face in his hands and wondered why. Why, why, why?

His brooding was deep enough to keep Joe from hearing the approach of the family car as the second wave of funeral-goers returned home. At length, slamming doors penetrated his thoughts, and he raised his head to face them.

Sam and Rachel excused themselves almost immediately, worn out from the long day of sadness, and escaped into the house. Matt and Caroline fell into the glider across from Joe, and Carrie sat in the porch swing, as far away as possible from her brother. Still, Joe saw the tears staining her face, and grieved for his sister as well as Billy.

The true nature of the relationship between his sister and Billy Taylor remained a mystery to Joe, though he guessed there had been strong feelings between them. Why else would she have stolen out of the house on a stormy night to search for the boy? But whether they had been merely friends or more than friends was none of Joe's business. On her own terms, Billy Taylor had been someone special in Carrie's life, and she was taking his death hard in her own stoical way.

Ever since the shooting, there had been a careful silence between Joe and Carrie. They had needed the distance to separate themselves from the horror of that night by the railroad tracks. It was obvious neither one of them had been successful on that accord, and now Joe worried whether they would find their way back to each other. Apart from Billy, both of them had lost a large portion of themselves that night, too much so to lose each other as well. Perhaps, if they could come together in their pain, they could restore some of what they had lost together. Joe decided to make the first move toward reconciliation.

"Carrie," he said gently. "I'm sorry about Billy. I wish I had known about your friendship, had realized he was handen you the gun. But I didn't know. I just didn't know, and it's an awful mess. For Billy. For you. For me. For everyone involved."

"I know, Joe," she replied stolidly. "It was a crazy accident."

"It's one of those things that can't be helped and can't be explained," Caroline suggested sadly. "You're right, Joe. It is awful for everybody involved, most of all for Danny and Billy because they were so young. But it was an accident, a tragic accident, and we have to put it behind us—especially the two of you."

Carrie stood up abruptly, her heels clicking against the cracked tile as she strode across the porch to the steps. "It's probably just as well," she said softly.

"Carrie!" her mother cried. "What can you mean by that?"

Carrie wheeled around to face them. "Just what I said, Mama," she answered angrily. "I'm not tryen to be ugly, but it probably is just as well—at least for Billy's sake. His life would have been ruined anyway. Let's face it. Anytime someone bases his belief in God on a lie, there's bound to be a big letdown when he discovers the truth. And besides, Billy could have never lived with himself if he'd found out the truth about Danny. He'd have gone stark crazy. He'd probably have killed himself somewhere along the way. He told me he had already thought about it once or twice."

Joe, who was having trouble living with himself at the moment, flinched from the implications of her outburst.

An instant later, Carrie apologized. "I'm sorry," she said dully. "Maybe that's the wrong thing to say." She laughed sadly. "I'm not myself and I'm haven one crazy thought after another. I swear: That night by the railroad tracks, I even thought that I had to break this habit of holden dead boys in my lap."

She shook her head. "I don't know what to say about this. I don't even know what to think about it. Do y'all?"

None of them could even look her in the eye, much less offer a reasonable answer. "I'm goen inside to change clothes," she said at length.

In the ensuing silence that followed her departure, Matt, Caroline and Joe pondered Carrie's question, trying to come up with satisfactory answers, seeking an understanding they could live with. But they did not have long to arrange their thoughts before the last trickle of cars containing the mourners for Billy Taylor began a slow procession past them. Unexpectedly, several of the cars stopped by the side of the road.

"Get inside the house, Joe," Matt ordered as Bobby Taylor emerged from the blue sedan. "No sense in getten mixed up with him today of all days."

"Why Daddy?" Joe replied curtly. "If ever Bobby had a reason to speak his mind to me, I'd say this is it."

Joe pushed himself out of the rocker and walked near the edge of the porch as Bobby came to a halt halfway up the concrete walkway. A half-dozen other men gathered behind him, a couple of whom Joe recognized. Bobby stared madly first at Joe, then at Caroline and finally at Matt.

"I hope you Bakers are happy," he said scathingly. "I hope you finally have everything you want from me. Whatever score you thought had to be settled, I hope you're satisfied. You've killed one of my boys, sent another one runnen off to who knows where." He paused, glaring at Joe. "My other boy, Carl, is in the car over there, Joe. Got your gun handy? I can set him up right here on the front yard. Save you the trouble of traipsen all over the countryside to hunt him down."

"Bobby," Joe said contritely. "I'd give the world if I could change what happened the other night. I wish there was a way to erase everything that's ever happened between us and start over."

"Save it for some other fool, Joe," Bobby interrupted. "You've been after me for years. Well, now you've got me, right where it hurts most. And I give up. Just go ahead and take whatever else you want of my family and then leave me the hell alone. Could you do that?"

Joe bit his lip, hating himself for doubting Bobby's sincerity at a time like this, yet more determined than ever to accept the man's anger with comeuppance. After all, despite everything that had passed between the two families, Bobby had never hurt the Bakers in any way that rivaled what Joe had done to Billy.

"Again, Bobby, I apologize," he said humbly with a shake of his head. "I wish I could do more, but I can't."

"You've done quite enough," Bobby replied bitterly, turning on his heels and heading back to the blue sedan before Caroline called out to him.

"Bobby," she said. "For what it's worth, please accept our condolences. From everything I've heard, Billy was a good boy, a son you could be very proud of."

Bobby stopped without glancing back at them. "I'll rot in Hell before I accept anything from y'all," he said.

He took another step forward, then whirled around to face them one final time. "I've already said more than I intended to say to the bunch of you. But there's one more thing I'm gonna get off my chest. To my way of thinken, Matt Baker, this whole mess could have been avoided if your daughter had kept her grimy hands off my

Billy. I always told my boys to keep away from the likes of you because it meant trouble. You should've done the same thing, Matt."

Matt turned livid, his frustration emanating from Bobby's holier-than-thou chastisement. "You self-righteous …"

"Matt!" Caroline implored, catching him by the back of his suit coat as Matt started toward Bobby.

Matt scowled at his wife before venting his anger. "Did it ever occur to you Bobby that Lucas Bartholomew could say the same thing to you right now? Your boy killed his son and started this whole mess."

"Matt!" Caroline interrupted. "Let it go," she soothed. "It's time to let it go."

Matt looked perplexed. "Caroline, I'm not gonna let him come on my property and insult my daughter and my family like that."

She put her hand on his shoulder. "Not today, Matt," she urged. "Not today."

Bobby glared at them once more. "I'm leaven," he announced at last. "See'en how there's all these witnesses around here, I figure it's safe to turn my back on y'all and get the hell out of here. As far as I'm concerned, if I never lay eyes on any of you again, it won't be too soon." He paused, then added, "Unless it's in Hell."

This time when he turned away, Bobby marched straight across the yard to the waiting car, got in it and drove on down the road.

"There's more to all this than we know," Matt reflected soberly as the other cars followed suit. "Maybe more to it than we'll ever know." He looked hard from Joe to Caroline. "I'm as sorry as anyone about Billy, but y'all know as well as I do that nothen Bobby ever does or says is what it seems. There's always some ulterior motive with him."

"It doesn't matter," Caroline consoled him. "Not anymore—certainly not today."

"It does matter!" Matt exploded. "Our son has shot and killed somebody, Caroline."

The declaration stung with the authority of a jury verdict delivered to a condemned man. Matt hesitated uncomfortably, then continued more rationally. "I'm willen to bet that at the bottom of this mixed-up, crazy mess is somethen Bobby Taylor said or did. That's all I'm sayen."

"It still doesn't change things, Daddy," Joe said with resignation. "Even if Bobby had sent Billy out there with a gun and told him to point it at Carrie's head, it wouldn't make a difference in what happened. The fact is, I shot the boy. I shot a poor, scared kid who had no place to go and no one to turn to, except maybe for Carrie. I shot him down like an animal when you get right to it. It may as well have been in cold blood."

For the first time, Matt and Caroline had to confront the truth about their son's pivotal role in this nightmare. Out of convenience, they had neglected his feelings about the shooting. As parents, they had agonized for him and worried how the ordeal would affect him in virtually every way possible. But they had failed to sit him down and discuss thoroughly his reaction to the ugly turn of events. Their procrastination was understandable. It was a hard subject to raise, even more difficult to assess. Now that Joe had thrown them an opening, they seized the opportunity.

Caroline moved by her son's side, putting her arms around his waist and resting her head on his shoulder. "I think maybe it's time for us to talk, Joe."

"Way past time," Matt added. "Can we sit down, son, and discuss this?"

"I'd rather stand if it's all the same to y'all," Joe replied, pulling away from his mother and leaning against one of the porch columns.

"How are you handlen this, Joe?" Matt asked pointedly. "Are you copen with it?"

"I'm tryen. It ain't easy."

"It was an accident, Joe," Caroline reassured him. "Everybody knows that. It's why Paul said no charges would be brought against you—because it could have happened to anyone under the same circumstances."

"But it didn't happen to anyone, Mama," Joe groaned. "It was me. I did it, and Billy Taylor paid for it. He's the one to feel sorry for."

"And we do," Caroline said. "Just as we feel sorry for what happened to Danny. And for Beauty and Lucas. For Carrie and for you, too, Joe. You have to live with what happened, too."

"Son, I wouldn't have wished this on you for anything in the world," Matt added. "Ever since the other night, I've wished time and time again it could have been me who pulled the trigger instead of you. It was my fool idea that sent us out there with guns in the first place. I'm the one who should feel guilty about this—not you."

"You're still not the one who shot him down, Daddy," Joe replied. "You didn't pull the trigger. I did, and I'm the one who has to live with the mistake."

"Who's to say it was a mistake?" Matt said. "Now it seems like a mistake, but...."

"Come on, Daddy," Joe interrupted. "We have to be honest with ourselves. It was a mistake, pure and simple, then and now."

"Okay," Matt conceded. "It was a mistake. But, son, at the time you had no idea what was goen on. You saw what I saw. The boy had a gun pointed at Carrie. For the sake of argument, suppose you had done nothen and he'd shot her, even accidentally. You'd be standen here now thinken you stood by and watched while a killer gunned down your sister. Think how you would feel under those circumstances."

"Don't, Daddy," Joe shook his head. "I don't need this explained to me. I'm well aware of all the consequences of what happened and what could have happened." He paused, clenching his fists. "Mama, Daddy, if I had to live that same moment over every day for the rest of my life," he continued woefully, "I'd probably do the same thing each and every time: Shoot first and ask questions later. I know that if I had stood by and done nothen while somethen bad happened to Carrie, then I could have never forgiven myself for it. But that's all pointless. It's rationalizen away everything that happened, and I can't do that. I killed the boy, y'all. It was an accident, and I regret it, but none of that changes the fact that I killed him. It was my fault."

"Joe, listen to me," Matt argued. "You're putten too much blame on yourself. I'm the first to admit a man has to take responsibility for his actions. Some things happen beyond our willpower, though. Sometimes, the decisions get made for us, and the only thing we can do is carry them out. You did what you thought was necessary, Joe, what you thought was right. No one could have asked anything more of you in this situation—not even you, son."

"Some things are just meant to be," Caroline said tiredly.

"Oh, God, Mama," Joe grimaced. "Please don't stand here and tell me this is all part of some grand plan of life for me to have killed some kid I barely knew existed. I can take a lot of rationalizen. But I can't take that—not now, not ever."

"We're just tryen to help you sort through it, son," Matt choked. "I know it weighs heavy on your conscience. It weighs heavy on mine and, as you said, I didn't pull the trigger. Maybe we're sayen some of the wrong things and goen about it in the wrong way, but we want to help, Joe. We want to help you through it."

"That's just it, Daddy, Mama." Joe smiled ruefully. "I don't think you can. I'm not sure anyone could. It's me who has to come to grips with the situation. I have to find my own way of accepten what happened and dealen with it. And I think I have to do it by myself."

"Don't push us away, Joe," Caroline pleaded.

"I'm not pushen y'all away, Mama," he replied softly, pausing to collect his thoughts. "I appreciate what you're tryen to do. I'm also a reasonable guy, and deep down, I guess I know there's not a damn reason for me to feel guilty. Regret and sadness, yes—but not guilt. The trouble is, I can't reach that far down yet. What happened is too fresh and too real right now for me to think about anything or anyone other than Billy."

While Matt and Caroline pondered what to say next, Joe massaged his temples and the bags beneath his eyes. When he looked back at them, there was an icy hardness in his brown eyes, a sense of abandonment and withdrawal. "Maybe Carrie was right after all," he concluded vaguely. "Maybe it really is just as well. Maybe I saved Billy a lot of heartache."

He passed off an expressionless twist of face as a reassuring smile. "I'll be okay," he told them. "Don't worry about me. It's just gonna take time to digest everything. I have to do it by myself, though," he added, his rejection of their concern swift and neat. "It's just easier and simpler if I figure it all out for myself. Okay?"

His parents were too stunned to do anything other than return his wooden gaze.

Joe smiled again, this time with genuine feeling, and Matt and Caroline sensed the relief in him. "I think I'll take a walk across the road," he said. "I might even rake up under that oak tree. It's too bad the storm blew off all those orange leaves. I don't think we've ever had a prettier fall, certainly not a prettier tree in the yard at this time of year."

They had lost him then, completely, Caroline realized. Or either he had walked away, propelled by some obsession with self-preservation. But whatever, he had become a different man in those last few moments with them, someone unapproachable, who wanted an arm's length between himself and the rest of the world.

"We shouldn't leave it this way," she lamented to her husband as Joe strolled across the road and sat down on the carpet of orange leaves, resting against the oak's mighty trunk with his back turned to them.

"I don't know what else to do, Caroline," Matt said balefully. "You heard what he said. He wants to work through it for himself. If we push our advice on him, he'll just make the walls thicker. I sure don't want that to happen."

"No," she added tearfully. "You're right, but it worries me just the same. I wish there was somethen, anything we could do to make it easier for him."

"Just be there for him," Matt replied, pulling Caroline against him and wrapping her in his arms. "Support him and love him."

"But don't lean on him," Caroline finished for her husband, nodding agreement. "It used to be so simple taken care of them," she remarked nostalgically. "Merthiolate here, a Band-Aid there. Lots of hugs and kisses."

"It was never simple," Matt corrected her with a sad smile. "Certainly not this hard, but it was never simple."

"I suppose not," she replied. "Do you really think he'll be okay?" she asked a moment later.

"He's our son, ain't he? He'll bounce back better than ever," Matt assured her. "And who knows? Maybe the worst of everything is already behind him."

———

The worst was not behind Joe. An hour later, as Caroline and Matt returned from a short walk around the farm and Joe raked leaves into an enormous pile under the oak tree, Paul Berrien drove his patrol car into the front yard.

"Howdy, Paul," Caroline greeted him as the sheriff stepped out of the white car looking very official in the khaki uniform, wearing badge and gun.

"Caroline, Matt," he nodded.

The curtness of his tone alerted them to something amiss. "You look worried, Paul," Matt said. "What's wrong?"

"We've got trouble," he replied miserably, casting a glance toward Joe, who waved at him. "The DA wants to take Joe's case before the county grand jury. He thinks there's enough evidence to support an indictment of some kind."

The disclosure had opposite effects on Caroline and Matt. She blanched at the news, turning pallid white on shaky legs. He suffered through a dramatic rise in blood pressure, glowing increasingly crimson as the tension ran up from the tips of his toes to the top of his head.

"But I thought you said it was clearly an accident," Matt protested. "That under the circumstances, nothen else could have happened."

"I did," Paul assured his friends. "And I still believe that. But apparently, Stan Avera feels differently. Or either he's taken up a vendetta against Joe. Both Stan and his daddy—the judge—were upset by those stories Joe wrote in the newspaper about their judicial records."

"Can he do that against your will?" Caroline asked.

"As the district attorney, he can take up almost any matter with the grand jury," Paul explained.

"Do you think he can get an indictment?" Matt asked.

Paul mulled over the question. "I asked myself that on the drive out, Matt," he answered. "My inclination is to believe that he cannot. But then, I know Joe personally, and I have every faith in him that the shooten of Billy Taylor was an accident."

"Paul," Caroline frowned. "If you didn't know Joe, would you have brought charges against him?"

"I asked myself that, too, on the drive out," Paul replied. "Honestly, the answer is no. I also wouldn't have filed charges against Billy for shooten Danny. They were two terrible, terrible accidents."

Caroline exhaled a sigh of relief. "Thank God, somebody believes that," she said.

"What does this mean for Joe?" Matt asked worriedly. "You didn't come out here to arrest him, did you?"

"No, no," Paul assured them. "As it stands now, he's not charged with anything. But I tell you, Matt. You'd better get some advice from a good lawyer."

"What about you?" Caroline asked.

"Not me, Caroline," Paul replied. "First of all, I'm too close to Joe to do him any good. You need someone impartial. And second, should it go to trial, I couldn't represent him anyway. Besides that, I've never practiced enough law to be good at it, and this matter is a far too serious for me to start tryen now."

"Who would you recommend?" Matt asked.

"Eloise Porter," Paul said without missing a beat, bringing bewildered looks to the faces of his friends. "I know she's a character."

"Some people say she's crazy as a bat," Caroline interrupted. "And she must be eighty years old."

"She swears she's not a day over sixty-five, at least ever since I've been in office," Paul said. "Regardless of her age and eccentricities, Eloise is the best defense lawyer in the county, and she's highly respected around the courthouse. Just haven her represent him would give Joe an automatic advantage in my opinion. On top of that, she's Stan Avera's personal nemesis. She once beat him on a rape case, and you know how she did it?"

"How?" Caroline asked.

"She walked up to the witness stand and gave the victim a pencil to hold. Then she made a circle with her forefinger and thumb," Paul demonstrated, "and asked the woman to stick the pencil inside the circle. When the lady tried, Eloise jerked her hand from side to side, and, of course, the woman missed with her aim. Eloise went on to suggest that if the woman had truly wanted to have avoided haven sex with the man, she could have wiggled more."

"That's despicable," Caroline scowled. "How could she get away with somethen like that in a courtroom?"

"It was totally unreasonable," Paul agreed. "Eloise got away with it because nobody realized what she was doen until she had done it. She also won the case, which I admit, was circumspect in the first place. The point I'm tryen to make, Caroline, Matt, is that Eloise Porter is the best lawyer in the county. This case—if there turns out to be a case—is tailor-made for her. At the very least, she can give good advice on how to testify before the grand jury."

Joe came over to them then, having detected the serious tone of conversation by the grim expressions on their faces. "Evenen, Paul," he said. "How's it goen?"

"Not so good, I'm afraid, Joe," Paul replied earnestly.

The sincerity of his answer sent Joe looking to his parents for answers. Matt and Caroline were staring at the ground, however, so Joe appealed once more to Paul. "I'm afraid to ask," he said dryly. "But how so?"

"I apologize, Joe," Paul began. "You should have been in on this conversation from the beginnen since it concerns you directly. The short take is that our fair district attorney has decided to take your case before the grand jury. He thinks he can win an indictment."

"Is that so," Joe mused with iron composure. "I guess Mr. Avera has decided it's high time for equal use of the law against a few white boys.

"Well, whatever," he concluded quietly. "So what happens now?"

———

Stan Avera was a short, thickset man with a crew cut of black hair, bushy eyebrows and a constant five-o'clock shadow on his face. He was a yellow-dog Democrat, who had supported George Wallace for president in 1968, not because of the Alabama governor's one-time segregationist record but because Stan distrusted Hubert Humphrey and despised Republicans in general. Above everything else, however, the Alabama man's practicality appealed to Stan.

The fortyish district attorney was a practical man in most cases. He was also a very amiable man, a respected member of the Cookville Country Club, the First Baptist Church and several civic organizations. Unbeknownst to everyone but the editor of *The Cookville Herald*, Stan also was the secret author of a short column on the front page of the weekly newspaper. Dubbed "Piney Woods Rooter Says …," the column afforded Stan a weekly soapbox on any number of issues, and he used it to rail against, among other things, welfare, liberal politicians and the nation's spineless Congress, which he described as "the biggest collection of nitwits ever assembled under one roof."

From time to time, he also lashed out against U.S. involvement in the Vietnam War. He chafed at the absence of a declaration of war, considered the conflict unwinnable and resented the implications that anyone who opposed the war was "brainwashed, a lunatic, ill-advised and, let me add, downright unpatriotic." He deemed the government's reasons for the country's involvement in Vietnam "an outrageous bunch of lies" (how else to explain what happened in Cuba) and advocated "any way possible out of the mess over there to save American lives."

Humor rarely found its way into the column, at least not intentionally. And that explained why on this Sunday afternoon he was reviewing last week's "Piney Woods Rooter Says" before mapping out his case against Joe Baker. At church earlier that day, Stan had overheard several people discussing the piece and having a good laugh over it. It was serious business, these alarming fashion trends for young women, and he had wanted people to be worried, not amused.

"Dear Mr. Editor," he read aloud. "We note with much concern the new fashion for 1969, now being shown in Paris—and let me say before I go any further—if these fashion experts keep raising the skirt hems, there won't be any need whatsoever for a skirt.

"They can just wear a belt and Eve's fig leaf, and they will be dressed according to these fashion experts of France, who wear sideburns down to their lower jaw and hair like the Beatles. I can't for the life of me understand why any person with any pride whatsoever will blindly follow these fashion experts, regardless of how immoral their designs are in appearance.

"But I will say this—and I honestly believe it—if these fashion bugs in France were to come out and say that it would be fashionable to go nude in 1969, there would be millions of people in America who would do just that, until the law caught up with them, if the law hasn't quit catching up with people during this decade. People in this era are searching for something to satisfy their hearts and minds, but the only one who can fill that space is God Almighty. And that is just exactly what millions don't want."

Stan mused soberly over the piece, found nothing funny about it and summarily dismissed the laughter at church as work of the devil. Those people could permit their daughters to wear such scandalous attire, but he'd be damned before his little girl, Patti, decked out in nothing but a fig leaf.

The district attorney slammed down the newspaper on his desk, then turned his attention to the prosecution of Joe Baker.

It was a tough case, causing Stan to bite his fingernails in nervous consideration of all the ramifications. Getting an indictment was an iffy proposition at best. Murder in any degree was out. He would not even insult the grand jury by asking for it. But they might be won over on a manslaughter charge. He'd press for voluntary manslaughter, throw in aggravated assault with a deadly weapon and settle for involuntary manslaughter. Even if he obtained an indictment, Stan knew conviction was a virtual impossibility. A judge, his own father included, probably would not allow the jury to hear the case. The evidence was too circumstantial, the truth too evident. Billy Taylor's death was accidental. Even Stan felt sure that Joe had never intended to kill the boy.

Still, the truth counted for only so much in a courtroom. The illusion of truth was a far better weapon for a lawyer. With the leeway afforded him before a grand jury, Stan figured he could create quite an illusion surrounding Joe's guilt or innocence. Even if he failed to win an indictment, the man's reputation would be tarnished, which was all Stan really wanted in the first place. If he won the indictment, well, so much the better. After all, it was Joe himself who seemed to believe white boys got off easy in the Cookville court system. He'd soon learn otherwise. Nobody carried a grudge as zealously as Stan did. And no one insulted Stan or made a mockery of his father's courtroom experience and got away scot-free with it.

Joe's newspaper series about the Averas' zealous pursuit of colored offenders still rankled Stan, especially since the State Press Association had recently awarded the reporter a first-place prize for investigative journalism. Although the articles were flawlessly accurate, they appeared biased against the Averas, making both father and son appear as throwbacks to the days of hanging judges, one-man juries and lynch mobs. Perhaps, if he had defended his actions to Joe, the articles would have seemed more balanced. However, his defense was difficult to describe. How could he explain that colored criminals deserved harsher treatment in the court system? The same ones kept coming back on new charges, progressively worse, from drinking and fighting to stealing and killing. If he was harsher with first-time black offenders than whites, it was only because he hoped they would reconsider a life of crime after serving a stiff prison sentence. As far as Stan was concerned, his strategy was perfect. Yet he could not explain it rationally, so he had not even tried when Joe sought a response from him before the articles were published.

For a moment, Stan experienced a pang of guilt for carrying his grudge against Joe into the courtroom. Stan tried to avoid vengeful behavior on the job because a district attorney bent on revenge made a bad prosecutor. He needed every ounce of levelheadedness to perform well in the courtroom. This case had special circumstances, however, and he was unwilling to back down from it. Stan reasoned away the fleeting moment of guilt, telling himself he would have sought an indictment against Billy Taylor, too, had the young man stuck around long enough to face the repercussions of his role in Danny Bartholomew's death. And Danny was a colored boy, which in itself should prove the Cookville district attorney did not discriminate against black or white. If he was zealous about anything, Stan concluded, then it was using the full extent of the law to put wrongdoers behind bars.

It was a reassuring conclusion for the district attorney, and he should have turned his attention to laying out his case for the grand jury. Yet, Stan could not shake the nagging concern that this case would blow up in his face. That the grand jury would not only ignore the request for an indictment but see through it and question his judgment and effectiveness. Cookville was a small community and Stan could ill afford to lose the trust and confidence the citizens placed in him. On top of everything else, the Baker family was held in good esteem by many people in the county and Matt's close ties with the sheriff carried extra clout in the eyes of many. Paul Berrien was adamantly opposed to bringing charges against Joe, and while more than a few people might view the sheriff's position as favoritism for a close friend, the majority would agree with him.

In the midst of this consternation, the doorbell rang and Stan's wife ushered the sheriff and Arch Adams, the country coroner, into his home office. After exchanging perfunctory greetings, Stan's wife exited the office, closing the door behind her, and the district attorney addressed his two elected colleagues bluntly: "Why are y'all here?"

"We need to discuss this business with Joe Baker," Paul said.

"What's to discuss?" Stan replied. "It's grand jury business now. Nothen for you to worry about, Paul."

"I disagree," Paul said. "You know as well as I do, Stan: This was an accident, pure and simple."

"I know no such thing," Stan said strongly. "And I'm willen to bet, Sheriff, if this was anybody else but the son of your good friend, you wouldn't be here meddlen in this business."

Paul's jaws clinched, and Stan knew he had scored a direct hit. Then the sheriff took a deep breath and surprised Stan. "You may be right; I'll give you that," Paul said, "but I have a couple of questions for you. In all the years you've worked with me, Stan, have you ever had reason to question my judgment or my impartiality? And if this was anybody but Joe Baker, would you be so bound and determined to take the case before the grand jury?"

The second question raised Stan's hackles and he bristled at the implication. "Funny you should ask," the district attorney said smugly. "I was asken myself that very question when you two showed up. And the answer is emphatically, 'Yes.' On top of that, if young Mr. Billy Taylor, bless his soul, were still with us, I'd be asken the grand jury to indict him, too."

"Really?" Arch asked, finally inserting himself into the conversation. "Because, Stan, it's my duty to rule on the cause of death, and I can't for the life of me see how either of these cases are the result of anything more than accidental shootings."

Stan started to protest, then fell momentarily quiet. "It's a damn mess anyway you look at it," he finally conceded hotly. "But I will not turn my head and sweep this under the rug. I'm not convinced it was an accident—there's a long history and damn hard feelens between the Bakers and the Taylors, and between you and Bobby Taylor, Paul. I have a responsibility to find the truth."

"I agree," Arch told the district attorney. "This is a damn hard mess, and it's a no-win situation for you and for Paul, too. If you're not careful, Paul's goen to come out of this looken like he plays favorites, and you're gonna come off as petty and vengeful for all the wrong reasons."

Stan muttered a profanity.

"I have a solution," Arch continued. "It's unusual, but I want to convene a coroner's jury to rule on the cause of death in the Taylor boy's killen. We don't use it often, but an inquest is a great way to handle a tragic situation like this."

Stan considered the idea and immediately saw the merit of it. An inquest, with a verdict rendered by a jury, would provide an effective tool for analyzing the case against Joe in the shooting death. While the jury—after weighing the evidence—could classify the death as accidental or unlawful, the proceeding was not a criminal trial and, even better, as a prosecutor, his hands would not be tied by the jury's decision. Even if the coroner's jury ruled the death was accidental, Stan would have the flexibility to proceed with criminal charges if he believed they were warranted. It was definitely a workable solution, but the district attorney still had reservations.

"It could work," he said cautiously, "but it would depend on how the evidence is presented to the jury. I respect you, Arch, but let's face it: You have a history with Matt and Paul, too. You falsified Britt Berrien's cause of death at Paul's request. It could be argued you would swing the evidence in Joe's favor."

Arch resisted an impulse to punch the district attorney in the face and responded stoically. "You're right again, Stan. I can't argue with you, and I'll go one step further. I think the shooten was justifiable homicide based on the evidence I've seen."

"Then it's already a rigged outcome," Stan interrupted.

"Hear me out," Arch said. "It may be unusual, but there's nothen to preclude you from presenten witnesses and leaden the examination. It's my responsibility to lead the inquest, but you can participate in any way you see fit. It'll be just like taken your case to the grand jury, without the weight of consequence."

"You know, regardless of how the jury rules, I'm not bound by their decision," Stan pointed out. "I can still take it to the grand jury."

"You could, but why would you, Stan?" Paul interjected. "There's nothen to be gained from doen that and a lot to lose. I'm danged sure I'm not showen favoritism to Joe by refusen to press charges. And I'm choosen to believe you don't have any ulterior motives here either. If this coroner's jury clears Joe of any wrongdoen, then you oughtta accept the verdict and let it go."

Stan smiled at the suggestion, knowing Paul was looking for the easy way out for his friend. "Can't promise that," he said, "but I will agree to the inquest. It's not my first preference, but it may be the best way to handle the case in the long run. You never know: That jury may just see it the way I see it, and if that's the case, I'll have Mr. Joe Baker indicted before you can say shucks."

———

On the first Wednesday in November, five days before the coroner's jury convened, Joe met Eloise Porter for the first time. Wrinkled beyond age, she was a feisty woman, standing a shade over five feet, with a hunched back, a crooked face and the raspiest voice Joe had ever heard. She also had a shock of thinning red hair. Or was it orange?

Joe's uncertainty led to their introduction.

"You're staren at my hair, aren't you?" she asked him seconds after a secretary ushered Joe into her office, a dark-paneled, immaculately decorated, yet cluttered room.

"No, ma'am," Joe stammered. "I was just ...."

"Don't lie, boy," she ordered. "I expect my clients to be honest with me. Makes the job easier if I know the truth of the matter."

She sat down behind an enormous oaken desk, pushing aside a stack of files. "You're still staren at my hair, am I right?"

"Yes, ma'am," Joe confessed.

"Well, don't get used to it," the attorney snapped back. "It's been this way about a month now, and I'm getten the hankeren to be a brunette. Don't be surprised if that's what I am come Monday, unless I decide to wear a wig. My hair's thin, you know. Can't do a damned thing with it."

Eloise motioned Joe to an overstuffed, black leather chair, while shuffling through papers. He took the seat and made a slow appraisal of the dark room.

"I get splotches," she announced, pointing to the rich, green damask drapes that stretched across a picture window.

"Ma'am?"

"The sun," she explained. "It makes my face break out in splotches, and liver's not my best color. That's why I keep the drapes pulled shut. Now is there anything else personal you'd like to know about me before we get started."

"How old are you?" Joe asked quickly, hoping to catch her off guard.

A grin split her face. "I can tell you're a reporter," she boomed. "There aren't too many people bodacious enough to ask my age. But since you had the guts to come right out and ask, and since you're a reporter, can we go off the record?"

Joe leaned forward. "It won't go any further than this room," he promised.

"I'm a few days past my sixty-fifth birthday, son," she lied brightly. "But I'm not ready to be put out to pasture yet, so let's get cracken on this little problem of yours."

The attorney scanned over her notes, then checked her watch, which Joe knew would read a few minutes after their two o'clock appointment. "I need a little pick-me-up before we get started," Eloise announced, rising from her chair and crossing the room to a dark mahogany wall cabinet that housed an impressive collection of liquor, crystal decanters, shot glasses and a polished silver ice bucket.

"I prefer bourbon this time of day," she told him, using ornately sculptured silver tongs to drop three small ice cubes in a glass, then splashing the liquor over it. "Can I get you anything?"

"Vodka on ice," Joe answered without hesitation, deciding a stiff drink might make this whole process a little less painless.

"Now, we're ready to begin," Eloise announced a few moments later after handing Joe the drink and reclaiming her own leather chair. "As you know, I've already spoken with your father and sister. Carrie's a lovely girl, a bit brittle around the edges, but full of spunk nonetheless."

"She's special," Joe agreed.

"Yes, well," Eloise Porter continued. "Unless you tell me somethen different from what I've already heard, Joe, I'd say that you are a victim of your own success."

She paused to observe him, then, pleased with his understanding, continued her analysis of the case. "Basically, you have to go through this rigamarole with the coroner's jury because our good district attorney is still ticked at you for those articles you wrote in the newspaper about him and daddy dearest.

"It was a fine piece of investigative work by the way and some very good writen," she added. "I had never noticed there were so many discrepancies in the judge's sentencen records. But then, I'm long removed from pro bono cases and only represent coloreds once in a blue moon."

"Thank you, ma'am," Joe said.

"Listen, Joe," she said abruptly. "Quit commenten every time I toss out a plaudit. I appreciate your good manners, but save it for the jury. And it bugs me to be interrupted. You let me talk for now, and you talk only when I ask you a question."

Joe sat perfectly still in his chair, not even nodding to show he understood.

"Good!" she exclaimed, showering him with a smile. "Essentially, Stan Avera doesn't have a pot to pee in. It's your word against a dead boy whose reputation is not exactly white as snow. Plus, you have the testimony of your daddy and your sister to support you."

Joe flinched involuntarily at the attorney's summation, causing Eloise to halt her analysis. "Before we go any further," she said, "I do need to ask one pertinent question." She paused. "I assume the shooten was an accident," she continued. "You did shoot the boy because he had a gun pointed at your sister's head and not for any other reason?"

"Yes, ma'am," Joe answered. "Only I'm not certain the gun was pointed at Carrie's head."

"A lawyer's semantics," she replied. "And there was no malice on your mind when you pulled the trigger?"

"None whatsoever," Joe answered sincerely. "I swear it."

"Good," the lawyer drawled. "Now you have to convince the coroner's jury. Normally, I would not put a client like you on the stand, but I think there's more to be gained from be'en forthcomen than invoken your right to remain silent. It shows you have nothen to hide, and the jurors will respond positively to that. I understand your dealens with this boy's family have not been pleasant in the past, and I suspect the DA will build his case around that. When you go before the jurors, don't dance around the fact that you've never gotten on well with the Taylor family. Be truthful to a fault. And be flawless in your presentation of the truth, Joe. Mistakes create doubt in the minds of jurors. They can overlook what happened to the boy. They can overlook the bad blood between you and the Taylors. But if you make mistakes before them, they're more likely to make connections based on feelens rather than facts, which is the one thing that could get you in trouble. Understand?"

Joe nodded.

"Now, in the unlikelihood the jury rules this was an unjustified homicide or that you bear liability in some form or fashion, don't fall apart," Eloise Porter continued. "I don't think there's a judge in the judicial circuit, including Judge Wilson Avera himself, who would allow the case to go to trial. Even if it did go to trial—assumen you still wanted me to represent you—I'd make mincemeat of little Stan in the courtroom. The only cases he's ever won against me are the ones I've plea-bargained because my clients didn't have a pot to pee in. And even in those cases, I got 'em off with less time than they probably deserved."

"You sound certain I don't have anything to worry about," Joe said.

"Not in the courtroom, you don't," Eloise said knowingly. "How you handle all this beyond the courtroom is another matter entirely, Joe, and way beyond my realm of expertise.

"But, son," she added, "I wish you Godspeed with that struggle."

Joe smiled slowly at this ageless woman, amazed by her insight, unaware of just how extensively she had picked the brains of his father and Carrie before meeting with him. The lawyer returned the smile, offered him a toast and gulped down the last of her bourbon. Joe did likewise with the vodka.

She refreshed their drinks, and they spent the next four hours rehearsing Joe's appearance at the coroner's inquest.

CHAPTER 9

THE WEATHER TURNED STEAMY hot on the day Coroner Arch Adams convened a special session to hear evidence in the killing of Billy Taylor. Inside the courtroom, it was even stuffier because some imbecile had left the heat running over the weekend, none of which helped to improve the district attorney's frame of mind.

Stan Avera was in a foul mood, having discovered over the weekend the identity of his daughter's latest boyfriend as well as scandalous gossip about her relationship with Luke Baker. He had grounded Patti, although his action came too late to have scuttled her plans to attend the homecoming dance with the star football player for the Cookville Rebels. It was allegedly what happened after the dance and possibly before it as well that riled the DA's temper and established the basis for the gossip going around town about his daughter.

His stomach burned from an ulcer on this morning, so Stan downed a dose of milk of magnesia before entering the courtroom.

Set in the middle of the town square, the courthouse was a two-story red brick structure, with graceful Georgian lines. Grecian columns and double turrets marked entrances on all four sides; larger turrets capped the four corners; and an impressive silver dome with a working clock tower sat atop four additional columns. Built in the decade after the War Between the States, the courthouse rested amid stately live oak trees. Historical markers on the surrounding lawn pointed out the occurrence of Indian fights in the area as well as the town's one-time noted trading route. The courthouse lawn also contained a granite statue of an American soldier commemorating the two sons of Cookville who had died in World War I on the north side and—on the south side—the names of Joseph Baker and others who had lost their lives in World War II.

Unfortunately, the inside of the courthouse fell short of the outside's architectural elegance. The offices were cramped, the polished concrete floors needed a good scrubbing and the whole place ached for a paint job. The courtroom itself was a little more appealing, spacious enough to accommodate a jury, the judge's bench and witness stand, court officials, attorneys and defendants, and several rows of visitors—not to mention the balcony where colored folk had been relegated until Paul Berrien defied Judge Wilson Avera and allowed them to sit on the main floor if they so chose. The flags of Georgia and the United States perched proudly on opposite corners behind the judge's bench, a utilitarian piece of oak furniture that dominated the room.

No judge presided over the coroner's inquest. Instead, Arch Adams, with the willing and able assistance of the district attorney, set the agenda and presented the case and witnesses to the jury, composed of six of the county's hardworking men and women. On this Monday morning, it did not take these fine men and women long to realize what direction the district attorney was taking with his presentation of the case against Joe Baker.

Stan Avera wanted them to believe the death of Billy Taylor was the result of a longstanding feud between the boy's family and the Bakers, of malicious intent on the part of Joe, who had perceived an opportunity to settle old scores and promptly taken advantage of it. Stan declared a murder indictment judicially unfeasible, although in his opinion, certainly warranted given the cold-blooded circumstances of the slaying. The DA told the grand jurors he would be satisfied with nothing less than an indictment for voluntary manslaughter. Arch calmly interrupted to remind jurors that their task was to determine the cause of death, whether the shooting was accidental, justified or unjustified, aptly reminding that an indictment of any kind was not for them to decide.

The first witness was the sheriff, who outlined the facts of the case as he knew them. Shortly after Halloween midnight, Sam Baker summoned the sheriff to the Baker home under the pretense of fear following Carrie's disappearance from the house. Paul testified how Joe had appeared at the house a few minutes after his arrival, with the shocking news that Billy Taylor lay dead beside the railroad tracks on the southwest side of the Baker farm. He described the details of his investigation, explained the coroner's report about the cause of death and, finally, discussed the past animosity between the two families, including Joe's arrest for beating Bobby Taylor at the Tip-Toe Inn.

"We really didn't arrest him," Paul explained. "A deputy picked him up and brought him to the jail for questionen. No charges were ever filed against Joe. Bobby didn't want that."

"Sheriff Berrien?"

The summons came from Jack Parker, a farmer in the south section of the county who had attended high school with the late Joseph Baker in the 1930s.

"Yeah, Jack."

"Why didn't you bring charges against Joe in this latest incident?" the farmer asked.

"I don't think they're called for," Paul replied. "As far as I'm concerned, it's a worst-case scenario. Everything that could have gone wrong did go wrong. And the result is an awful tragedy for everyone involved."

"So you don't think the suspect wanted to kill Billy Taylor?" someone else asked.

"Not in a million years," Paul replied.

"One question, sheriff," the district attorney interrupted. "Could your opinion in this case be jeopardized by your close relationship to the suspect and his family?"

"It could be, and I'm sure it is to some degree," Paul answered quickly. "But I pride myself on be'en a fair man and an impartial enforcer of the law, Stan. *That* is the reason I chose not to bring charges against Joe. I do not believe they are warranted."

Stan fought to conceal a grimace at the sharp tone of Paul's answer, knowing he had made his first serious blunder of the day. Paul had earned his reputation for fairness and was highly respected by the vast majority of the jurors, even if his own past showed he was not above operating on the edge of the law. No doubt, some of the jurors disapproved of the district attorney's effort to impugn the sheriff's integrity and would side in favor of Joe for that reason if nothing more.

He hurried Paul off the witness stand, then distributed a few pieces of material evidence, including the weapon used in the killing and pictures of the body, in its bruised and battered condition. The two women jurors gasped at the extent of Billy's facial injuries, but remarkably, nobody questioned the cause of them. Unwilling to provide any information not sought, Stan chalked up a point in his favor and called Bobby Taylor to testify.

Bobby's testimony was brief, recounting several of the disagreements between himself and the Bakers and focused on his reasons for not bringing charges against Joe two years earlier. "I just didn't see the sense of it," Bobby explained mildly. "Joe was drunk out of his gourd when he attacked me, and bringen charges would not have helped heal my broken nose. I thought it'd be more trouble than it was worth. And I didn't want to get the boy in trouble, either." He paused, then grinned. "I've never been one who believed in carten somebody off to jail for fussen and fighten."

Stan ignored the comment. "What about the present situation?" he asked Bobby. "You could have had charges filed against Joe yourself, even if the sheriff chose not to. Why didn't you?"

"Didn't figure it would do any good," Bobby replied quickly. "I've been on the losen end of every battle I ever fought in this county, and there's no reason to think it would be any different in a case like this. The way I see it, the law has a way of looken over the sins of some people."

Stan gave the jurors several seconds to consider the answer, hoping it would generate sympathy for the grieving father. "Now, Bobby," he continued, "I know this may be difficult to answer and I respect your bereavement, but I do have to ask you some questions about Billy."

"Sure, go ahead and ask."

"If Billy were alive today, he could be facen serious charges himself for the death of Danny Bartholomew," Stan commented. "Everybody seems to be in agreement that Billy shot Danny by accident. However, one of the key issues in this case is whether your boy was pointen a gun at Carrie Baker when Joe shot Billy. And while we have to stick to the facts, opinions are relative in this case because it boils down to whom this grand jury decides is tellen the truth and whether the suspect had good cause to shoot your son."

"I don't think he had good cause," Bobby remarked angrily.

"That may be, but it's not for you to determine," Stan replied with deliberate callousness. "What I need to know from you, Bobby, is whether you think Billy was capable of pointen a gun at Carrie and firen it."

"Honestly, Stan, I don't know what to think anymore," Bobby sighed. "I was under the impression the girl was sweet on Billy, and maybe he was on her, too. She was chasen after him from what I knew. I can't imagine Billy shooten anyone, not even that other little boy. My son was a good, quiet kid."

"Okay, Bobby," Stan said. "That'll be all. Thank you."

"Mr. Taylor?" one of the female jurors called as Bobby stood. "Do you know how your son got those bruises on his face?"

"He'd been in a fight with his older brother a few days earlier," Bobby answered. "About the worst scrap they ever had. It had somethen to do with the Baker girl, but I never got the whole story." He hesitated, before adding, "Guess I never will."

Bobby ambled from the witness stand to the audience benches, and Stan licked his lips in acknowledgment of another point in his favor. Then, he called Matt Baker to the witness stand.

Once again, Stan rushed through the early part of Matt's testimony, re-establishing what Paul Berrien had said earlier. Near the end, however, he began backtracking.

"Okay, Matt," he said. "We can all appreciate your concern for your daughter's well-be'en. I know I certainly do. But I'm still a little confused. What made you think Billy might harm Carrie? We've been led to believe quite the opposite here today, that Carrie was sweet on Billy and him on her."

"I didn't know about their friendship until after Carrie disappeared from the house," Matt said tensely. "My wife told me once we realized Carrie was gone. Apparently, he had asked her for a date, and she turned him down. There'd been all that other trouble with Billy earlier in the day, and I figured if he was upset, there was no tellen what he might do."

"Your daughter told authorities that Billy shot Danny accidentally, as he tried to get the gun away from someone else," Stan commented. "Right?"

Matt shook his head. "That's right."

"Didn't you believe her?" Stan asked. "Couldn't you have assumed from her opinion that Billy was not a dangerous killer?"

"I did," Matt replied. "But the boy had gone through a lot that day. He was bound to be upset. He had a gun. I was scared out of my mind what might happen. Everything was set up, just waiten for somethen awful to happen ...."

Matt stopped abruptly.

"You're right about that," Stan said sharply, glancing at his watch to let the moment settle over the courtroom. "Okay," he continued. "Let's move on to when you arrived by the railroad tracks and found Carrie with Billy. What exactly did you see?"

"He had a gun in his hand," Matt answered. "It was pointed at Carrie."

"Pointed where at her?" the district attorney pressed. "Her head? Her chest? Her foot? Exactly where was it pointed, Matt?"

"In her general direction," Matt replied. "I can't say exactly where. Her chest, I guess."

"Upper chest? Lower chest?"

"I can't say for sure," Matt answered.

"So, you saw Billy, with a gun, presumably pointed at your daughter," Stan continued. "Then what happened?"

"I thought he was gonna shoot her," Matt said. "I took aim at him."

"You aimed your gun at Billy—the twelve-gauge," Stan clarified. "Did you say anything to him? Maybe yell to get his attention?"

"I did not," Matt said. "There wasn't time to."

"Why not?"

Matt hesitated.

"Why not, Matt?" the prosecutor repeated again, quickly.

"Because that's when he was shot," Matt answered balefully.

Score another point for the prosecution, Stan thought, then counted it as a double victory when none of the jurors questioned Matt. He broke the session early for lunch, intent on bringing Carrie Baker to the stand when the proceedings resumed.

———

The district attorney's line of inquiry caught Carrie by surprise. She had been unprepared for such an intimate probe of her relationship with Billy, and she was uncomfortable answering the questions in front of the jury and the courtroom audience. She had been ill at ease ever since the bailiff escorted her through the heavy double doors, down the center aisle past two dozen or so people clustered on either side of the gallery, courtroom officials and jurors, and, finally, into the massive witness stand. Her initial distress had quickly dissolved into sheer mortification when she fumbled the oath and had to have the instructions repeated. Nothing had occurred since to bolster her composure.

Answering the first questions had been easy enough. The district attorney had wanted a brief understanding of why she went looking for Billy and what made her suspect he might be hiding on the Baker farm; and Carrie promptly revealed that all her actions had been based on worry and hunches, nothing else. Apparently satisfied, the prosecutor had moved onto another line of questions, establishing the scene of her discovery of the trembling Billy beside the railroad tracks, their conversation, his fragile state of mind, the decision to give her the gun, and her reaction when Joe fired the fatal shot. Then, the questions took a different tone, suggestive it seemed, as Stan Avera did an about-face in the progress of his inquiry and sought a closer look at details they already had covered.

"Okay, Carrie," he said gently, then with heavy emphasis. "I want to remind you that you're under oath, sworn to tell the truth before this panel. Do you understand?"

"Yes, sir."

"Now, Carrie, you've told us you and Billy were friends and you were worried about him consideren everything that had happened earlier in the day and his predicament," Stan continued. "That's certainly understandable, even commendable. Personally, though, I have a hard time believen you acted completely on a hunch when you went looken for him. I take it, young lady, that you do not make a habit of sneaken out of your home late at night to go looken for just any boy."

Carrie stared blankly at him, muted by the salacious pitch of the statement.

"We're waiten for your answer, Carrie," he pressed.

"No, sir," she choked.

"So we can infer then that this was a special case with Billy?" Stan asked.

"Yes, sir."

"Then tell me, Carrie," he zeroed in on his point. "Had you ever snuck away from your house on any other occasion to have a secret rendezvous with Billy?"

Carrie blinked back tears, then looked out at the sea of tantalized faces in the courtroom.

"Carrie?"

"Yes, sir," she answered.

"Do you mind explainen for us?" Stan asked.

"We had a class together and were partners on a homework assignment," she replied meekly. "We got together one Saturday afternoon."

"Where did this meeten take place?"

"By the river close to my home," Carrie answered.

Stan considered the answer, then decided he had exploited that particular aspect of questioning as far as good manners would permit. "Another thing, Carrie," he said, shifting gears. "Why so secretive about your friendship with Billy?"

"I don't know," she answered.

"You're under oath," the DA reminded her. "We need an answer."

"I was afraid of what people might think," she said.

"What people?"

"Anybody who knew both of us, who knew his family and my family and their differences in opinion," Carrie explained. "Billy felt the same way."

"And you and Billy were nothen more than friends?" Stan followed quickly. "I don't understand such secrecy about mere friendship. Did you think just be'en friends with Billy would cause trouble for your family? Or was there more to your relationship with Billy than friendship?"

"We were just friends, Mr. Avera," Carrie replied defensively, upset by his smear of reputation, sensing the ideas of indecent behavior planted in the minds of those in the courtroom. "Just friends," she repeated.

"Essentially then, you feared what your family would do if they discovered the existence of your friendship with Billy?" Stan pressed on. "They must not have thought very much of him for you to have concealed somethen so harmless as friendship."

"They didn't even know Billy," she interrupted. "I just didn't want to cause problems."

Stan waved away her explanation before Carrie could provide further details, including her mother's encouragement to attend the homecoming dance with Billy. She resented the impression of her family created by the prosecutor.

"Let's move on," he said.

"Can I finish what I had to say?" she interrupted.

"You didn't want to cause any problems between your family and the Taylors," Stan commented. "What else is there to say?"

Jack Parker suddenly stood up in the jury box. These details seemed irrelevant to the case, and he privately wondered whether the district attorney could be censured for unethical behavior. His mind was made up on the question before them, but he wanted his grand jury colleagues to have the complete picture before they made any decisions. "I want to hear what else she has to say, Stan," he commented sharply. "So far, what we've heard today seems to indicate you think there was some conspiracy on the part of the Baker family to get the Taylor family. If that's correct, then I think what Carrie has to say about the matter is entirely relevant."

Carrie smiled in relief at the farmer. "Thanks," she told him. "Maybe I shouldn't have hidden my friendship with Billy from my family," she continued. "I guess I blew it all out of proportion, worryen about how they would react. But they would have accepted Billy. In fact, my mama had already told me she saw no reason why I shouldn't accept Billy's invitation to the homecomen dance at school, and she had suggested I invite him to church and Sunday dinner at the house. No one in my family would have intended Billy any ill-will just because he and I were friends."

It was her strongest moment on the stand, and Carrie turned her gaze from Jack Parker to the district attorney. "Do you understand, Mr. Avera?" she asked firmly.

"Fine," the prosecutor replied, mentally clicking off a point for the other side and deciding to stick more closely to the facts through the remainder of her testimony. "Now you've told us what happened when your brother shot Billy. But we need to clarify a few things.

"Did Billy point the gun at you?" he asked.

This was one of the tricky questions Eloise Porter had warned Carrie to expect. "He was handen it to me," she replied.

"But was it pointed at you?" Stan asked again.

"I suppose it was," Carrie answered, recalling the pointed way Eloise had asked whether she believed Joe had shot Billy to save her life or with vengeance first and foremost on his mind. Carrie knew without doubt that Joe had her well-being at heart when he pulled the trigger, but the knowledge did not make it any easier to accept what had been done.

"You suppose it was, but you can't say for certain whether the gun was pointed at you," Stan said, summing up her answer. "Well then, Carrie, were you scared for your life at any time? Did you think Billy intended to shoot you?"

"No, sir," she replied, choking back a sob, suddenly overwhelmed by the fallout of so many good intentions gone wrong.

Stan saw the sag in her shoulders and sensed an opportunity. "And your brother, Joe, he never tried to ascertain what was transpiren between you and Billy? He never called out or alerted you to his presence?"

"No, sir," Carrie replied, no longer able to stop the tears.

"In other words, your brother simply stumbled out of the darkness, came across the two of you and shot Billy. Is that the way it happened?"

Carrie could not answer him. She had gone past the breaking point. She stared blankly at her lap, weeping softly, until the coroner dismissed her and the bailiff escorted her from the courtroom.

In contrast to his sister, Joe was tough as nails in the delivery of his testimony. His rigid control of emotions frustrated Stan Avera time after time as the district attorney angled for a chink in the story, the smallest opening that might cast doubt on the witness. In time, the prosecutor realized that this apparent lack of feeling in Joe could not be exploited as cold-heartedness. Indeed, rather than projecting the slightest trace of emotionlessness or even vulnerability, Joe came across as intensely concerned with the seriousness of the situation and entirely truthful in his recollection of the incident.

Frustrated though he was, Stan had not earned his hard-nosed courtroom reputation without the presence of a killer instinct. Of more importance, he also possessed the legal skills necessary to support his bulldoggish pursuit of a witness. With Joe, he belabored the minute points early in the process before moving into the meat of the testimony. He spent the first thirty minutes putting Joe through the paces, belaboring the issue of his past confrontations with Bobby and Wayne and his opinion of the entire Taylor family in general.

The DA thought he succeeded on a small scale when Joe admitted that revenge had been foremost on his mind when he attacked Bobby in their barroom brawl. Even when Joe promptly revealed the motive for his vengeful state of mind—the unfair fight between Wayne and Luke and Bobby's full sanction of the beating—Stan hoped the jurors would remember the suspect was not above seeking retribution.

"On what other occasions did you seek revenge against the Taylors?" Stan pressed.

"None."

"What about the other night?" the DA asked. "Can you say with absolute truthfulness that revenge never crossed your mind before you shot Billy?"

"I didn't even know him," Joe replied.

"Apparently, my question wasn't clear," the prosecutor continued. "Did it occur to you that shooten Billy might exact a measure of revenge for all the past trouble that you believed Bobby and Wayne Taylor had caused you and your family?"

"It did not," Joe reaffirmed.

"Fair enough, Joe," Stan conceded once more. "Now, you've said you didn't know

Billy. I find that hard to believe consideren the two of you are—I mean were—practically next-door neighbors. Are you sure you never even said hello or acknowledged each other in some other way?"

"We did not."

"Did you know anything about him?" Stan asked. "What kind of person he was?"

"He played basketball with my brother in high school," Joe recalled. "He was a very good player."

"And that was the extent of your knowledge about him?" Stan commented. "That he was a very good basketball player, as well as the son of Bobby Taylor?"

"Yes, sir."

"Tell me then, Joe," the prosecutor said coldly. "Why in the world would you shoot some kid whom you knew only as a very good basketball player and the son of the man you despise most in life."

"He had a gun pointed at my sister," Joe answered decisively. "I thought her life was in danger."

"But your sister says Billy was merely handen her the gun," Stan pressed. "There's a big difference between handen someone a weapon and pointen that weapon at them. Couldn't you make the distinction?"

"The barrel was pointed at my sister, and he was holden the gun," Joe replied coolly. "I thought he was goen to shoot her."

"How long did you actually take to assess the situation before you fired your own weapon, Joe?" Stan asked.

"Not long," Joe answered truthfully. "A matter of seconds, I suppose."

"One, two, three," the DA counted. "How many seconds, Joe?" he asked before exaggerating a sigh.

"Okay, Joe," Stan continued. "Help me reconstruct exactly what happened from the time you came across Carrie and Billy talken to each other beside the railroad tracks. In your own words, tell us what you saw and what you did."

"It was a miserable night, with hard rain and thick fog," Joe recalled. "There was a full moon out, but the clouds covered it. It was difficult to see. I came to a clearen in the fog, and Carrie and Billy were in front of me—a little to my right. Almost immediately, as soon as I saw them, Billy raised the gun and pointed it at my sister. My first thought was he's gonna shoot her. And then I fired my gun."

"Many things happened immediately, didn't they, Joe?" the DA stated. "But I'm gonna give you the benefit of the doubt and suggest that within a matter of ten seconds—probably somewhere between five and ten—you made the decision to take another person's life. Is that a fair judgment?"

Joe wavered for the first time. "I don't think it was a conscious decision," he said at length. "I just reacted to the situation."

Stan ignored the answer. "Ten seconds seem like a very short time to deliberate over the fate of someone else's life," he mused. "Did it never occur to you to announce your presence or do anything to create a diversion?"

"No, sir," Joe answered. "I was just concerned about Carrie. I thought it was a life-or-death situation."

"It was," the prosecutor replied acidly, "especially for Billy Taylor." He paused, again to allow the moment to settle over the courtroom, then asked unexpectedly, "When you shot Billy, were you thinken that he was Bobby Taylor's son?"

"No, sir."

"When you started out hunten for him and your sister earlier in the night, did you think of Billy as Bobby Taylor's son then?"

"Probably, I did," Joe sighed.

"And did you have a bad image of Billy simply because he was the son of a man you dislike?" Stan asked.

"Possibly," Joe answered. "But I did not go out there thinken he was a killer, Mr. Avera, or that he was out to hurt my sister. I figured he was probably mixed up after what had happened with Danny Bartholomew. I believed then and still do that it was an accident that Billy shot Danny."

"But it wasn't an accident when you shot Billy, was it, Joe?" the prosecutor said.

"No, you couldn't call it an accident," Joe conceded. "It was a mistake."

"That's putten it mildly," Stan remarked sarcastically, "but you're entitled to your opinion. If you had to do this all over again, Joe, would you do things differently?"

"Knowen what I know now, of course I would."

"But not knowen what you know now," the DA pressed. "Would you do the same thing all over again?"

Again, Joe wavered ever so slightly, his head doing a quick downturn before he looked again at his inquisitor. "Unfortunately, I probably would," Joe said blankly. "I'm not sayen it would be the right decision, but it's probably the one I would make. My only concern that night was for my sister. I love her. I'd do everything in my power to keep anything bad from happenen to her."

"Includen killen, I presume," Stan commented.

Joe maintained his silence.

"Given your willingness to shoot Billy without any qualms," the prosecutor moved on, "do you think your judgment is sound, Joe?"

The question rattled Joe, who had continually questioned his judgment in the days since Billy's death. "It was a bad decision, rashly made. Okay?" Joe said heatedly. "I won't deny that. But under the circumstances, it was the decision I made, and I have to stand by it and live with the consequences. Everything I did that night was completely reactionary. I did not shoot to kill Billy. I simply aimed and fired without thinken because I believed my sister's life was in danger. I cannot explain it any better or any differently than that. I wish I could, but I can't. For the life of me, I just can't."

"Then answer this for me, Joe," the DA replied. "Should people be punished for their poor judgment?"

"They usually are, sir," Joe answered without missing a beat. "In one way or another."

Stan Avera regarded the witness with quiet detachment for a moment. "A very neat and tidy explanation, Joe," he said coldly. "One final question: Are you remorseful at all about any of this?"

Joe took a deep breath to steady his nerves, then soothed the creases of his dress pants with his palms. He wanted to tell them his life would never be the same. He wanted to ask them how he could learn to live with the gut-wrenching, soul-searing reality of having taken an innocent life. He needed someone to explain the meaning of it all, to tell him what possible place his role in the death of Billy Taylor meant in the scheme of life. But those were worries and questions better left for another time.

"Mr. Avera," he said, "I regret it more than you could ever know."

CHAPTER 10

THE CORONER'S JURY RETURNED its decision about six o'clock, rejecting the prosecutor's plea to make Joe pay for his bad judgment by ruling the death of Billy Taylor to be a case of unjustified homicide. Their deliberations lasted less than an hour and only that long because the six jurors debated whether to label Billy's killing as an "accidental death" or a "justifiable homicide." They settled uneasily on the former. When the decision was announced, there was no backslapping, joyous celebration by anyone, but instead, sober sentiment and sympathy for all involved, along with a few tears of joy shed by Caroline and Rachel and prayers of thanks uttered by everyone.

Joe permitted himself a small measure of relief over the decision, expressed gratitude to Eloise Porter for her assistance and then excused himself from his family. He was determined to get dead-drunk on this night. He figured it was one sure way to block out the torment tearing him apart, to fill the hollow place inside him, to escape the personal limbo that remained with him—despite this declaration of his innocence. Joe knew it was the wrong way to deal with the problem. But for this one time, he chose not to care and drank himself into oblivion.

With every sip taken straight from two pints of vodka, Joe asked himself many of the same questions the district attorney had posed before the coroner's jury. This time, however, he allowed every emotion and susceptibility to shade his answers.

Had there been some subconscious, malicious intent on his part to exact revenge against Bobby and Wayne when he fired the weapon at Billy? Joe did not think so, but the question nagged him nevertheless, as did a hundred others. Had the gun been pointed at Carrie or was it held harmlessly in Billy's hand? In a situation of lesser consequences, he might have shrugged off these doubts. But for a man who demanded exactness, who liked his answers straight up without the blur of distractions, the doubts gnawed at him like a raw nerve.

Even in those rare moments of absolute trust in his motives, Joe could not ignore the gravity of the deed, or the poor judgment that had twisted his actions into a misdeed. In the span of ten seconds, probably closer to five, he had made a deadly miscalculation, a mistake in judgment that could have been prevented with even fewer seconds of foresight. He could have shouted a warning, could have been more cautious in his assessment of the situation, could have done any number of things that would have changed the outcome of that fateful night. But a litany of "could have been" was a poor excuse to Joe and of little consequence to Billy Taylor. He was still left with the cold, hard facts: Joe had killed the boy, and he would live forever with Billy's blood on his hands. And, despite what everyone said about mistakes happening, despite the jury's decision, despite even his own convictions about his motives, Joe simply did not know if he could bear to live with the truth. He might not be guilty of taking a life; but neither was he innocent.

Sometime after consuming the first pint of vodka, Joe broke down and cried, stricken by the combination of liquor, the strain of the court proceedings and plain sadness over the unfair way life had unfolded for so many decent people.

When his tears were finished, Joe opened the second bottle of vodka and sought the comfort of an old friend. He had not seen Lucas since the day of Danny's funeral. Nor had they spoken since the day of Danny's death when Joe had offered his condolences.

Driving drunkenly along the back roads, Joe arrived at the Bartholomew home shortly before eleven o'clock. Leaving the liquor in the car, he walked stiffly to the front door and knocked. In a minute, the door cracked open and Beauty greeted him cautiously. There was no small talk between them. Joe asked to see Lucas.

"He's asleep," Beauty said shortly. "It's late, Joe. You should go home."

"Yeah, I should," Joe agreed, his voice slurred by the liquor. "I don't think I should be driven, though. Could I borrow your couch for the night?"

Beauty regarded him with distrusting eyes. "You shouldn't have come here, Joe," she said at last. "Get on home to your own kind."

"Come on, Beauty," Joe pleaded. "I don't want to go home like this. Lucas would let me stay."

"Probably would," Beauty agreed, "but you're not dealen with Lucas. I got one drunk man in my house tonight, Joe. I don't need or want another. I hope you can respect that."

Joe looked off into the darkness. "I do," he told her at length. "And you're right, Beauty. I shouldn't have come here. My apologies to you."

He backed down the stairs, stumbled but caught himself before falling.

Beauty regarded him carefully, and Joe could tell she was rethinking her decision.

"Take care, Beauty," he said before she changed her mind.

"Be careful, Joe-Joe," she called as he climbed into the Volkswagen. She was still standing in the doorway seconds later when he drove out of the yard.

———

In his nearly twenty-four years at home, Joe had never stayed away from the house overnight without telling the family not to expect him. He had crawled home in the wee hours of the morning on occasion but when the house came alive at the crack of dawn, he had always risen from the comfort of his own bed to join his family at the breakfast table.

So it was that shortly after sunup on the morning after the court proceedings, his first thought was that the family would miss him at breakfast. It was only a passing thought as he awoke in his car, which was parked near the river a mile or so from the Bartholomew home. Unsure whether he was still drunk or suffering from the worst hangover of his life, Joe staggered from the Volkswagen and straightway vomited on the riverbank. His head throbbed, his stomach churned and his legs wobbled. All in all, though, he expected to recover, which stopped him short of swearing off another drinking binge.

Hoping to clear his head, Joe stripped off his clothes, plunged headlong into the river and tried to swim his way to sobriety. He emerged from the water a few minutes later, chilled to the bone, reconditioned for the drive home and temporarily numbed by the mayhem of his recent days. The carnage, the waste and the improbability of this trouble defied the normal rules of thought, assaulted his sense of fairness and shattered his faith. It was madness best avoided until another time, so he dressed and drove home, arriving a few minutes after the family sat down to breakfast.

Still obviously drunk, even to himself, Joe tripped his way into the house and stumbled down the hall to his room. Once there, he stripped again, collapsed on the bed and passed out promptly.

His slipshod entrance was heard by everyone in the kitchen and brought breakfast to a standstill. A knowing, uncomfortable silence settled around the table. Everyone was embarrassed and worried, and no one said a word for a full minute.

"At least he's home," Sam muttered finally, and Rachel patted his hand.

"Should we check on him?" Caroline asked her husband. "You think he's okay?"

"He'll be fine, honey," Matt assured her. "He had a lot to think about last night. Maybe the best thing we can do right now is to leave the man alone and let him rest. And maybe, too, we could forget this mornen happened. I don't see any need in bringen it up again, especially to Joe. He knows right and wrong as well as anyone around this table. Don't you think?"

Caroline nodded in agreement and began picking at her breakfast.

A few minutes later, Summer, John, Luke and Bonnie checked on their oldest brother and found him lying across the bed. John and Luke righted Joe on the mattress and Summer pulled the covers over him.

"What do y'all think?" John inquired. "Will he be fine?"

"Yes," Summer replied quickly. "Maybe not today, tomorrow or the next day, but he'll come around in his own time."

Summer pulled the blankets over Joe's chest and patted his head. "His hair's damp," she remarked. "Why don't you close that window, Bonnie? There's a chill in the air this mornen, and we don't want him to catch a cold."

"No," Luke said, his tone so sarcastic that it rang with truth. "Especially not when he's already caught so much hell."

————

Joe woke later that afternoon with his sobriety fully restored and a severe hangover. He lay in bed to get his bearings straight, then eased into a sitting position and opened the window, allowing a fresh breeze to clear away the cobwebs in his aching head. In a while, he threw off the covers, eased out of bed and pulled on a pair of cut-off jeans that had been lying on the floor for several days. When his legs were steady, Joe went to the bathroom and made a futile effort to make himself presentable, splashing water on his face, which did nothing for his bloodshot eyes, and running fingers through his hair in place of a comb.

Emerging from the bathroom, he followed the melodic contralto of his mother's hymn to the kitchen where she was ironing clothes. "Afternoon," he greeted her when Caroline looked up to see him enter the room.

"Good afternoon to you, too," she replied, unexpectedly cheerful Joe thought as he made his way to the refrigerator, opened it and took a long gulp straight from the water bottle to moisten his cotton-mouth. "How are you feelen, Joe?"

"Like I deserve to," he answered truthfully. "I'm sorry about last night, Mama. It won't happen again."

Caroline smiled at him. "No, I don't imagine it will," she said. "And I hope not, too, son. That's not the answer you're looken for."

"No, ma'am, it's not," Joe agreed, then grinned contritely. "And no one knows that better than me at the moment. I know you'd probably like to wring my neck right now, and with good cause. But I appreciate you for be'en so agreeable. I probably deserve a stern lecture, but your good company means more."

Caroline set down the iron, walked over to Joe and ruffled his hair. "You're absolutely right," she commented lightly. "I'd like to wring your neck. But instead, I'm goen to fix you a sandwich. How long since you had anything solid in your stomach?"

Joe thought a moment. "Not since breakfast yesterday."

"Sit down," Caroline ordered, pushing him into a chair. "We've got some leftover ham. A sandwich and a glass of iced tea ought to perk you up. And from the looks of you, son, you could use some perken up."

For a short while, Caroline believed a state of normalcy had returned to their everyday life and Joe had made peace with himself. She was right to a point.

November marched swiftly past with its busy days, the children always rushing off to their various pursuits of happiness and Matt working from sunup to sundown to harvest cotton and soybeans. She felt pulled in four different directions trying to support everyone. Before she realized it, Thanksgiving had come and gone, and December was only a few days away on the calendar.

It was then that Caroline realized all was not normal, especially not Joe. Maybe she had wanted so much for her son to find peace with himself that she had fooled herself into believing he had. There had seemed reason to believe. She had seen it with her own eyes, heard with her own ears as she and Joe sat in the kitchen, talking over ham sandwiches on that day after the coroner's inquest. There had been flashes of his old self in Joe that afternoon—the easygoing manner, the dry humor, unbridled anticipation of days to come. She had even allowed herself to laugh as he cracked jokes about the previous night's drinking binge.

Even in the days that followed, nothing appeared out of the ordinary. Perhaps he was more reserved than usual, but Caroline had attributed her son's persistent lassitude and desire for privacy to the long days Joe was putting in at the newspaper. He certainly honored his promise to refrain from drinking. Joe had not touched a drop of alcohol, which Caroline knew because she had questioned him about it one night out of the blue and his answer had been sincere.

Her realization of something amiss came suddenly one night at the kitchen table as Bonnie returned thanks for supper. For some reason, Caroline opened her eyes during the prayer and found Joe staring vacantly off into space. Joe never noticed her. He simply waited for the blessing's end, then ate, with mumbled answers to the rare question tossed his way and lackluster regard of the people around him. It hit her then, this difference in her boy, and Caroline's mind raced back to the day of Danny and Billy's funerals, when she had sensed the barriers come up around Joe. She remembered fearing that her son had become a different person on that day. Now, she knew without doubt that he had metamorphosed into a stranger.

Joe had always been closemouthed about himself, although he rarely kept secrets. If someone cared to pry into his business or private thoughts—and they usually did in this family—Joe gave them straightforward answers. He was defined best, however, by his willingness to avail himself to others. He carried a genuine interest in people, listened willingly to their stories and problems and was always eager to do whatever necessary to help anyone, especially his family members.

Yet that was no longer an accurate description of her firstborn. Joe had isolated himself from the family over the past few weeks. He was putting in an occasional appearance but never showing up for the main event.

She should have seen it earlier, Caroline thought, as she discerned a spate of recent peculiarities in Joe's behavior. Joe never missed church, yet, he had not attended a single service since the two funerals. Then, on Thanksgiving, his favorite holiday, he had left the house shortly after dinner with a broken promise to eat dessert later. His excuse had been work, a deadline to meet with no time to spare.

Caroline had been unable to argue with his excuse, especially when everyone understood the high priority Joe placed on honoring commitments and loyalties. In fact, she couldn't fault any aspect of his behavior. Perhaps Joe had changed, but his transformation had harmed no one—unless it was himself. He was missing out on a slice of life that had sustained and nurtured him for all his years. Still, Joe had made his wishes clear. He wanted to find peace his way, on his time. And, as his own man, he had the inalienable right to do exactly that—without any interference.

Her head told Caroline all this. Her heart suggested otherwise. Maybe if Joe seemed more himself, she would have trusted his instincts to find light in the darkness. But she feared the changed man lacked the confidence to trust his instincts. Caroline was torn by a mother's love and her duty, and the decision on which to follow was not easy. In the end, though, she put her faith in God and left Joe to make his own decisions.

———

The one positive constant for Joe in those desolate days after he shot Billy Taylor was the abiding self-assurance that he had acted out of fear for Carrie's life. He loved his sister, which made their recent estrangement all the more difficult to accept. They had always been the best of friends, but now they hardly could stay in the same room with one another, much less look each other in the eye and deal with this turning point in their lives.

If he'd ever had hopes of joining forces with his sister to reclaim what they had lost by the railroad tracks on Halloween night, Carrie quickly quashed them. She rebuffed Joe, effortlessly and never with malice, but completely. The breaking point came on Thanksgiving morning when Joe climbed into the loft to fetch a bale of hay and found his sister weeping.

"Carrie?" he called.

She looked up, and Joe glimpsed in her eyes the despair he had felt in his soul over the last few weeks. She was shattered, too, trying to cope with feelings too complex to understand, about events too unreal to accept.

"Could we talk, Carrie?" Joe pleaded.

"No!" she answered with an emphatic shake of her head, glancing away from him. "I can't, Joe. I can't, and I don't want to. Just please go away and leave me alone."

Joe wanted to press her, to demand a clearer truth about her feelings. But Carrie hated confrontations and would freeze him out completely if he followed that instinct. She also had a right to privacy, to pick up the pieces of her shattered soul the best way she could.

No one should understand that better than he should, Joe thought. It was, after all, rather pompous of himself to believe he could right every wrong, save every soul and fix everything, especially when he could not even come to grips with his own feelings. Perhaps, if he sat back and watched the world for a while rather than tried to run interference for it, life would be easier for everyone. It would have been easier for Billy Taylor and Carrie and for himself, too, he thought. Regardless of what Joe did or how Carrie felt, life would roll right along and carry them with it, if necessary.

Joe backed away from his sister, moving in virtual silence out the door and down the loft stairs, already planning his next move. He understood Carrie's refusal to discuss the experience with him. He felt the same way every time someone tried to console him about Billy, every time he found himself on the receiving end of a sympathetic gaze. The compassion was too much to bear, especially when he could not shake the feeling that it was misplaced.

––––––––

Once he made up his mind, Joe moved with lightning quickness and confidence to carry out his plans. The quickness arose from the oppressive need to escape, as well as the sense of restlessness that had plagued him long before the recent troubles. His confidence came from ability and success at his job. He was a good reporter, and he knew it. Other people also recognized his talent.

The Atlanta Constitution had hired Joe as a part-time correspondent once it became evident that controversy would mar the integration of schools in Cookville. His coverage of the issue had earned him numerous bylined stories in the newspaper, boosting his income considerably and winning high praise from the assistant editor who had sought his help. Ray Fields had promised to put in a good word for Joe with the Atlanta paper's editors when he was ready to leave Valdosta. In the first week of December, Joe took him up on the offer.

"Well, make my day, boy—it's about time you dragged your sorry self up to the big city," Ray boomed when Joe revealed his intentions during a telephone call. "Let me make a couple of inquiries, and I'll get back to you."

Two days passed before Joe heard from the editor. It was a chilly Saturday afternoon, and he was in the top of a pecan tree shaking the limbs. His brothers and sisters, along with Mark Applegate, were picking up the nuts, and they were having an uproarious time, caught up entirely in the moment without a single fleeting thought of the past. Mark had parked his red convertible beside the orchard gate, rolled down the top and turned up the car stereo, all of which conspired to make for more play than work. Everyone was racketing, dancing to Credence Clearwater's *Proud Mary* when Rachel showed up suddenly on the other side of the orchard fence.

"Joe," she yelled above the commotion. "You've got a phone call."

He heard his name but nothing else from his perch in the top of the tree. "Ma'am?" he called back to her.

"You've got a phone call," Rachel repeated, frustrated by the noise, frowning her disapproval at the silliness of her grandchildren.

"Tell 'em to call back," Joe said. "I'm busy right now."

"I did tell him that," Rachel groused. "He said it was a matter of life and death, and he had to speak to you as soon as possible."

"Did he say who he was, Granny?" Joe asked.

"Ray somebody," Rachel muttered. "You comen or not?"

Joe obviously was coming to take the call. He slid down the tree with little regard for safety, jumping the last eight feet and hitting the ground at a dead run, barely wincing at the sharp pain in his knee. "Thank you, Granny," he said, dropping a kiss on her cheek as he ran past Rachel. "I've been waiten for his call."

"Did you think I'd forgot you?" Ray Fields asked after they exchanged greetings.

"I figured sooner or later I'd hear somethen," Joe responded. "What's the news?"

"Good and bad," Ray replied mysteriously. "Which first?"

"In keepen with the times, I think the bad," Joe muttered, unwilling to believe he might not have the job he coveted.

"The bad news is I never got around to bringen up your name to the people who hire and fire at the *Constitution*," Ray said.

"Well, at least, I haven't been rejected outright," Joe exhaled deeply.

"On the contrary," Ray said. "I have no doubt they'd hire you in an instant. But I have a better proposal. Are you interested?"

"How 'bout curious for right now," Joe suggested.

The Atlanta Constitution and *Journal* were the kingpins of journalism in the city, but a third newspaper, *The Atlanta Herald*, had a solid reputation as well. Backed by recent gains in circulation, the *Herald* had decided to expand its staff, and one of the first hires had been Ray Fields as news editor. Ray wanted Joe to work with him.

"It's not the biggest newspaper in the city, it's not even the best," Ray explained candidly. "But opportunity is there, especially for someone like you, Joe. It's easy to get lost in the shuffle at a big newspaper like the *Constitution*. Over here at the *Herald*, we're leaner. We don't have the luxury of picken and choosen who we want to cover a story. If you're half the hotshot I think you are, you'll be worken the big stories in no time at all. And, Joe, you'll kick the big boys in the ass. In a few months' time, I'm willen to bet both the *Journal* and *Constitution* will come courten you. And when they do, I promise I'll send you to the best offer, along with my blessings.

"How does that sound?" he asked.

"Why did you go over there?" Joe asked cautiously.

"For the same reasons," Ray answered. "I'm thirty-five years old, and I'm tired of waiting in the wings. It's my opportunity to put my stamp on a big-city newspaper. If I do a good job, I go up, up and up. If not ... Well, that doesn't matter because I'm a hotshot in my own right." He paused, then asked, "What do you say, Joe?"

"I'll take it."

———

Joe shared the news with the family and Mark Applegate at supper later that night. His excitement was masked by concern over how everyone would react, so he explained in detail about the opportunity to cover the really big stories, the hefty pay raise and even the medical and insurance benefits. But it was soon obvious that everyone was happy for him, showing no small amount of pride in his success and offering hearty congratulations along with tender sentiments of regret to see him leave.

"We knew it would come eventually, son," Matt philosophized. "I'm just glad we kept you around here as long as we did."

"Now that you're gonna be a hotshot, city slicker," John asked, "does this mean you'll forget about us common folk down here on the farm?"

"Not hardly," Joe said dryly, then added with affection. "We're a lot of things, John, but common's not one of the adjectives I'd use to describe us."

"I guess not," John agreed. "Anyway, Atlanta's not all that far away. I'm sure we'll see plenty of you."

Joe smiled, but his absence of reply was noted silently around the table.

He gave a two-week notice at the Valdosta newspaper, then started planning for the move.

Moving, or at least preparing to move, proved more difficult than Joe had expected. On the advice of Ray Fields, he planned to rent a furnished apartment, which eliminated the worry of moving furniture. Joe made a list of things to take with him, essentially his personal belongings such as clothes, books and a toothbrush, and decided the whole of it could be packed in a single suitcase and a couple of cardboard boxes. Then, he made his first mistake by asking Summer to buy him a suitcase. It was not an unusual request, Joe thought. Summer usually did his shopping, but this time she was irritated with him.

"I know you think shoppen for anything other than Christmas gifts is a curse among curses, Joe," she told him sharply. "But honestly, who's gonna do your shoppen when you're in Atlanta?"

He stared blankly at her.

"I suppose I could send a few white shirts through the mail," Summer continued glibly. "But what about groceries, Joe? How do you think a steak will taste after three or four days in the mail between Cookville and Atlanta?"

Joe had not thought about such questions before, but they started coming to him in bunches shortly after he sweet-talked his sister into picking up several new white shirts along with the suitcase. He checked his list once more, realizing it lacked many of the basic necessities as well as the comforts for life—things he had always taken for granted such as sheets and blankets, pots and pans, plates, glasses and tableware. He sought advice from Caroline and Rachel.

During the next few days, it became painfully apparent to Joe how ill-equipped he was to live by himself. He had never realized he took for granted the many things his mother, grandmother and sisters did to make their house a comfortable home. His work around the house had been confined exclusively to outside chores. He'd never even had to make his own bed, much less run a vacuum cleaner or iron clothes. His culinary skills consisted virtually of the ability to fill a whistling teakettle with water and set it on the stove to boil—unless being able to turn on a stovetop burner was a skill in itself.

"I'll starve," he lamented only somewhat facetiously a few days before Christmas as his mother and grandmother tried to teach him the basics of cooking.

"You might at that," Rachel agreed somewhat worriedly. "Honest to goodness, Joe, I've never seen anyone with less aptitude for cooken."

"Maybe Santa Claus had better bring you a cookbook for Christmas, son," Caroline remarked.

"He better bring it before Christmas," Rachel suggested. "Joe's leaven the day after, and that doesn't leave us much time to work with him."

Washing clothes proved equally challenging for Joe. "Why can't you just throw everything together?" he asked sincerely on the day Caroline and Bonnie explained the washing machine to him.

"Because you'll wind up with pink underwear and pink shirts," Bonnie replied sarcastically. "You're hopeless, Joe. Find a woman and marry her immediately. You can learn to love her after the wedden, and she can keep you functionen in the meantime."

Joe ignored his sister. "You know what, Mama?" he said to Caroline.

"What, son?"

"It occurs to me that maybe you should have started teachen all this washen and cooken stuff to me a little earlier," he said. "What if they don't have washen machines or clotheslines where I live?"

"I'm sure they'll have a Laundromat nearby," Caroline said.

"Isn't there somebody you could pay to wash clothes for you?" Joe inquired. "What about the cleaners? Don't they wash people's clothes?"

"Good question," Caroline mused. "I've always thought of the cleaners as taken care of just really nice clothes, like suits and formal dresses. But they might do regular washen as well. It's worth checken into."

"If you don't want pink underwear," Bonnie said, "then definitely check into it."

Two days before Christmas, Caroline took Joe shopping to complete the preparations for his move. She bought a multitude of groceries, including everything from canned foods to dry goods, from toilet paper to toothpaste. She also bought kitchen essentials, including a boiling pot, frying pan and teakettle, as well as bathroom necessities like towels and wash clothes. Unsure whether his apartment would have a full or twin bed, she explained the difference and promised to send some of her old sets once he was settled.

At last, Joe was ready. He could scramble eggs, make lumpy grits and scorch rice, which, fortunately, he liked cooked that way. His most impressive accomplishment was iced tea, steeped with a pinch of baking soda and sweetened exactly like any pitcher made by his mother and grandmother. Everyone assured him that the rest of the cooking and household duties would come naturally, but none of them truly believed it.

On Christmas afternoon, Joe packed his belongings into the Volkswagen. To his dismay, the contents included considerably more than the suitcase and two cardboard boxes he had originally thought suitable. In fact, there wasn't a suitcase at all. Summer had purchased a footlocker instead, deciding it was more practical. Despite the clutter in the car, Caroline and Rachel assured him that he was taking only the bare essentials, which was true. Among other things, he packed within the limited confines of the Volkswagen were two cookbooks, one for beginners; detailed, handwritten instructions for washing clothes; enough paper plates to feed half of the city's population; a brand new portable colored television, which was a Christmas gift from his parents; and his favorite possession, another Christmas gift, John's painting of the oak tree in its orange brilliance on Halloween morning.

"The way I see it, you and that tree have a lot in common," John told him privately. "Neither one of you have been the same since that night. But when you look at the painten, Joe, try to remember how you both were that mornen—alive, majestic and ready to face the world with your best foot forward. Because that, brother, is what I miss most about you when you're not here."

Joe knew better than to suggest that John seemed to think he was already gone. So instead, he hugged him tightly. "Who died and made you Mr. Sensitive," he said gruffly before pushing back to look his brother squarely in the eye. "No one could have given me a more thoughtful gift, John. I'll treasure the painten always, and it will have a place of honor in my home—wherever that may be."

Early the next morning after a breakfast feast of pancakes, bacon, sausage and scrambled eggs, Joe loaded the last item into the car: a cooler filled with a week's supply of home-cooked meals, which he only had to heat before eating. Then, he returned to the front porch, where everyone was gathered to bid him farewell. He was trying to figure out how to handle the occasion when both his mother and grandmother began to cry.

"I don't think your mama and granny are ready to see their first chicken fly the coop," Sam told Joe. "And if the truth be known, neither am I."

Joe walked over to his grandpa and hugged him fiercely. "I've got a few dragons of my own to slay, Grandpa," he said earnestly. "Maybe a few ships to plunder, too."

"Well, then," Sam smiled. "From one pirate to another, I wish you Godspeed on the journey, son."

Joe hugged the rest of them, deliberately bringing a light touch to the moment, offering various wisecracks about this hallowed treatment of his departure. The tactic worked, bringing back to him jibes about his cooking and housekeeping abilities.

"As soon as the food runs out," Luke predicted as Joe gave his teary-eyed mama one final hug, "he'll come runnen back, beggen us to let him come home and stay forever."

"He won't have to beg," Matt declared weightily. "As long as any of us is here, the rest of us have a home."

Luke shook his head wearily. "You really are getten mushy sentimental in your old age, Daddy," he observed.

"Shut up, Luke," his siblings all groaned in unison.

Luke insisted on the last word in this matter. "Y'all didn't hear me out," he accused airily. "I was gonna say it's nice to hear that kind of stuff from time to time."

"Be good, Joe," Caroline intoned one last time.

Joe grinned. "I'll try, Mama."

Finally, there was nothing to keep him there, no more goodbyes to say, no final piece of advice to impart. He understood all too well the time had come to leave.

Joe backed off the porch, waved and went to the Volkswagen. He took a quick glance around the place, then was on his way, waving to the family one final time as everyone followed the car onto the road. They were still waving to him a moment later when he risked one last glance in the rearview mirror at the best home a boy could have wanted.

One more distinction touched his departure, almost as if it had been preordained by a wish upon a shooting star. Indeed, maybe it had been, Joe reasoned, as he waited in the idling car for the morning train to pass over the rail crossing at the crossroads.

He should have felt elated at this culmination of dreams, positively giddy about the journey that lay beyond the moving train. On one level, he was—eager for the future. Yet, strangely, the big moment fell short of his expectations, as if the decision to leave had been made for him rather than by him. At last, however, the red caboose sailed past, leaving the road ahead clear. Joe gunned the engine and started on his way.

The time had come to make good on a promise made by a boy of boundless optimism, in a simpler time one night by a railroad track.

ON THE SURFACE, ATLANTA was a mover and shaker among Southern cities by 1970, well on its way to becoming one of the nation's more progressive urban communities. It was a financial, manufacturing, industrial and communications center, possessed of a world-class airport and a Midas touch to its every whim and resolve. Beneath the surface, the wheels of progress rolled even faster, and Joe quickly became absorbed in the eclectic vibrancy.

He rented a sparsely furnished, four-room apartment on a dead-end street off Piedmont Avenue, near the heart of the city. The gray-stone flat had a series of street-level alcoves that granted entry to clusters of separate dwellings and an open basement that doubled as a parking garage and storage space for the tenants. Joe padlocked his cellar door after discovering that a bum considered home to be one of the worn-out sofas stashed below his own apartment. The old man seemed harmless enough, spending the majority of his time huddled under a rag pile with a cheap bottle of booze, but Joe felt uneasy with the situation.

Despite the bum, Joe loved his apartment. It had high ceilings like home, large spacious rooms that gave him a sense of freedom after years of having his possessions housed in cramped confines, and worn hardwood floors requiring a minimum of upkeep. The front door opened into a living room, with an opening off the right that led to a fully equipped compact kitchen with a pass-through bar. To the left was a door that led to the double-closeted bedroom and a large, stone-floored bathroom with a massive, claw-footed porcelain tub complete with a shower attachment. The furnishings consisted of two relatively new tallboy chairs for the bar; an aging brown vinyl recliner in the living room; a comfortable double bed; and a small chest of drawers in the bedroom. In addition, Joe bought a small desk for his typewriter, a new radio to replace the one he had left at home for his brothers, a mirror to hang over the bedroom chest and a couple of throw rugs for the cold bathroom floor. He set the television against a wall on the living room floor beneath the apartment's lone, tiny window, hung John's painting on an empty wall and got down to the business of living.

For a piney wood farm boy, life moved at a dizzying pace.

His job far surpassed the expectations laid out by Ray Fields when he had offered the position to Joe. He hardly believed his good fortune every week when payday rolled around and he deposited his check in the bank. The money seemed almost sinful. The *Herald* had nearly doubled his previous salary, his expenses were minimal and Joe's savings account grew quickly. But the money, while sensibly appreciated, was secondary to the job satisfaction, which was unrivaled even by his boyhood dreams of a reporter's life.

Joe was assigned to cover the Fulton County courts. In his spare time, he also worked on a variety of feature articles, writing about the changing face of the city, bringing the fresh perspective of a newcomer to the subject. Right away, he impressed his editor with a flair for capturing the dynamic elements of a story, turning in impressive efforts on the city's small hippie population and rising drug culture in the Virginia Highlands area, the seedy roots taking hold in the Underground Atlanta entertainment complex, and a sense of despair and growing acceptance of a dependent way of life in the ghettos. The gritty realism of the lives he wrote about shocked even Joe, giving him a different kind of education and an appreciation of the somewhat sheltered lifestyle in Cookville.

As good as his features on the city were, Joe proved even more impressive reporting on his assigned beat. He covered the courts like a hawk circling over an open coup of biddies. Whenever possible, he went beyond the courtroom testimony to tell the stories. On one occasion, his enterprise reporting paid off handsomely.

The idea came to Joe during his first week on the job as he waited in the courtroom for an arraignment on a murder case. He was intrigued more by the prior arraignment of a young woman on prostitution charges. Jotting down the thin brunette's name in his notepad, he covered the murder arraignment, then looked up the prostitute in the Fulton County jail.

Her name was Alycia May, and she willingly discussed her experiences. It was a sordid tale. She had fled a wretched home life in a small Alabama town to the streets of Atlanta where prostitution became her daily meal ticket. On good nights, Alycia told Joe she turned five or six tricks. Her prices were set in stone, and she demanded payment up front. Some customers had stolen her services on occasion, and she had wound up battered and bruised by at least three customers. It seemed like a pathetic existence to Joe, but excepting her current predicament, Alycia expressed few regrets about her chosen profession, vowing to return to the streets as soon as she paid her bail.

"It's a liven," she told Joe with a sexy leer, "and sometimes the work can be fun. If you're interested, you could sample the merchandise. And since I like you, Mr. Reporter, I'd break my rules and give you a discount."

Joe declined, politely. "What I'd really like to do is maybe observe you on the job one night."

Alycia May pretended to pout, then rolled her eyes mirthfully. "You like to watch, huh?" she asked.

"No," Joe said. "I'd hang out in the background and watch you work the streets. Your business would stay private."

She agreed, and Joe followed discreetly as Alycia worked the streets one night, starting at seven in the evening and ending at five the next morning. It was a slow night, and they were discussing hazards of the trade over coffee when she pointed out two colleagues in the restaurant.

"They have a man who takes care of them," she explained. "Both of them have been picked up by the cops at least three times, but they're in and out of jail within a few hours at the most. Their man always makes sure they go before the same judge; he gets them off on a technicality or something. Still, I don't want a pimp watching over me. I take care of myself."

Her comments intrigued his reporter's instinct, and Joe began watching Judge Jerrell Monroe's treatment of prostitution cases while reviewing records of previous cases. An uneven pattern of disposition emerged quickly, and Joe realized something was amiss. In a testament to his lucky stars, he uncovered the truth within two weeks, revealing that the respected judge was accepting bribes from two known pimps in exchange for the court's protection of their whores.

It was an unbelievable, improbable stroke of fortune to come across such a story in his first months on the job, much less work through it with relative ease. But such was Joe's luck in those first few weeks in Atlanta. Of course, the Judge Monroe story represented the extreme side of the newspaper business. The bulk of Joe's court coverage was routine, but he strove to make it interesting for the everyday reader. He also found that one good story led to another, so the best stories just seemed to fall in his lap.

In mid-February, *The Atlanta Journal* offered him a job. A few days later, *The Atlanta Constitution* did likewise.

Ray Fields was elated by the news—and ecstatic when Joe declined both offers. The cagey editor reconfirmed his promise to submit the Judge Monroe story for the Pulitzer Prize and came up with a small pay raise as well. Of more importance to Joe, however, Ray packed him off to Chicago to cover the waning days of the turbulent twenty-one-week federal trial of the Chicago Seven.

"You've made your mark in Atlanta," Ray said. "Let's see how you handle the national scene."

Joe handled it superbly with a gripping account of the jury's acquittal of the seven defendants on charges of conspiring to incite riots during the 1968 Democratic National Convention, as well as guilty verdicts against five for crossing state lines with intent to incite riots. His story went beyond the trial, however, to capture the reaction to the verdicts of the Chicago cops who had battled the unruly demonstrators and protesters themselves who had felt the sting of billy clubs on their backs.

Away from work, Joe moved with less certainty and smaller helpings of fascination. Still, he garnered enormous satisfaction from his place in the city whose official seal was the phoenix, the fabled bird that rose from the ashes to begin a new life.

He enjoyed his role as a stranger in a strange place. City life fitted him, drawing Joe to a realm of experiences unavailable in Cookville, and he sampled as much of the lifestyle as time permitted. He made friends with his colleagues at the *Herald* and with people he met through the newspaper. A steady stream of invitations to parties from people who ran in the fast lane came his way, and Joe often went along for the ride, taking advantage of the fringe benefits, including women who viewed a night of passion as a good time and nothing more. More than ever, Joe remained determined to keep his new life uncluttered.

Between work and leisure, Joe moved at a demanding pace, but he never lacked energy or resilience. He kept his comings and goings balanced almost every minute of the day, and on the rare occasion when they overlapped, he compensated without missing a beat.

He was aided somewhat by occasional urges to be a homebody. After years of living amid so many people, he basked in the freedom of privacy. If he wanted to walk around his apartment naked, he did. If he wanted to pass flatus aloud, he did without worry of embarrassing himself or anyone else.

His culinary skills remained unremarkable, essentially limited to tossing TV dinners or potpies in the oven and boiling water for tea or instant coffee. He ate cold cereal for breakfast every morning and skipped lunch except on Mondays and Thursdays when he joined Ray Fields for the finest in Southern food fare at Mary Mac's Tea Room. His major accomplishment in the kitchen was broiled steaks and baked potatoes, which he ate on those nights when the cardboard fare was unappealing. On some evenings and weekends, he enjoyed nothing better than to sit at home, watching television or reading a good book, while savoring a steak and baked potato sopped in butter with several vodka martinis or screwdrivers on the side.

Overall, though, as much as he preferred living by himself, any aptitude for household chores eluded Joe. He kept a reasonably clean apartment, due primarily to his economy of possessions, and maintained a spotless kitchen, helped by his fear of attracting roaches and the result of eating most meals from the same box in which they were cooked. Usually, such subtleties as the dirt ring in the bathtub and shaving clippings in the sink escaped Joe. Then, out of the blue, he would cringe at the filth, dig out the pine cleaner and Comet and scrub down the entire bathroom until it sparkled. By far, though, he considered his biggest household accomplishment to be the discovery of a cleaner who washed clothes. Joe considered the pricey rate money well spent, an investment in a steady supply of crisply starched shirts and pants, clean underwear and fresh socks.

Every two weeks like clockwork at eight on Sunday evenings, he called home to catch up on the latest news from his family. Almost always, these calls lasted approximately half an hour and included conversations with his parents, one grandparent and two siblings, excluding Carrie who always had something else to do when he called. Invariably, each phone call ended with someone asking when Joe was coming home.

"Maybe soon," he replied each time. "I'm so busy these days. I hardly know whether I'm comen or goen. But maybe soon, I'll be comen your way."

Joe saved the bulk of news about himself for the two letters he wrote home on a weekly basis. One letter generally contained information of interest to everyone and was earmarked for Matt or Caroline. The other was more personable and sent randomly until he had covered all nine bases, at which point he would begin another round of correspondence. On occasion, he also found time to write letters to Paul Berrien and his sisters, as well as to Lucas and the Carters. Hardly a week passed without Joe receiving at least one letter from home as well. His mother and grandmother were far and away the most diligent correspondents, but everyone else returned his letters, except for Sam, who expressed his apologies but plainly stated that he preferred the telephone to writing, and, Carrie, who continued to avoid him.

It was a comfortable, busy, fulfilling life he had carved out for himself, Joe thought one Sunday night in early March after telling Matt goodbye and hanging up the telephone. The future appeared bright, the present seemed exceptional and he was coping with the past. Yet, the past was never far from his mind, popping up repeatedly like a childhood bully who disappeared for a while only to return with a more menacing smirk.

Joe tried to shake away the troubled thoughts, the nagging suspicion that he was getting more from life than he deserved. The idea stayed with him, however, and almost without thinking, he walked into the kitchen, took a glass from the cabinet, poured a healthy dose of vodka and drank it in one long gulp. The liquor burned down his throat to his stomach and then Joe went to bed early, praying for a dreamless sleep, which was a sure anesthetic for what ailed him.

———

On the first Saturday in March, Joe went grocery shopping to replenish his supply of

TV dinners for the next two weeks. He also bought several steaks, baking potatoes and staples such as sugar, tea, milk and cereal. Next, he stopped by a neighborhood liquor store to stock up on beer, vodka and cigarettes. Shopping remained a miserable task to Joe and it was even more so on this day as he hurried to get home before the day's promised spectacular of a total eclipse of the sun.

His fascination with the heavens continued unabated from his boyhood days. One of his earliest explorations of the city had carried Joe to the Fernbank Science Center planetarium for a close-up look at the nighttime sky. One of the things Joe missed most about home was the clear nights and wide-open spaces that displayed the heavens in full panoply. If he had not chosen a career in journalism, Joe figured he would have considered astronomy.

He was thinking all of this as he carried the first two bags of groceries up the stoop of his apartment building, opened the heavy steel door and found himself staring at the lovely backside of a woman bent over on the alcove floor. He stood immobilized by the shapely sight of tight cutoff jeans and firmly toned light brown legs.

"Are you always so obvious when you ogle a lady, sugar, or am I a special case?"

The question rolled toward Joe on the husky wave of a sultry Southern lilt, with a power all its own to capture his imagination. He waited almost unconsciously for the woman to rise to her knees, then shifted his gaze to the face of that seductive voice. There was no feature wasted or lacking on her face, which was creamy tan and wholesomely fresh. Her hair was the color of honey and molasses, about shoulder length, full bodied and casually pulled back and tied loosely with a ribbon. She was wearing a sleeveless white blouse that showed off her figure and provided the perfect backdrop for slender, tawny brown arms. Joe was struck most by her eyes, clear and full of sparkle, as lightly brown as his own were dark.

"Listen, sugar," she said. "I'm willen to admit that frank admiration from a relatively good-looken man in snug-fitten jeans is appreciated. If you want, I could stand up and twirl around for you. But if you're really interested in maken an impression, then how about some help picken up this stuff?"

Realizing how rude his uncharacteristic behavior must appear to the woman, Joe practically dropped the grocery bags in his haste to help her pick up the dozens of record albums scattered in front of the door directly across from his apartment. "My name's Joe Baker," he said, extending his hand to her. "I think we're neighbors."

She accepted his handshake, smiled appreciatively and conducted a quick appraisal of her own. "Neighbors we are," she said. "You're a reporter for the *Herald*, right?"

Joe nodded. "How did you know that?"

"Well, sugar, I'd love to bolster your male ego and say I was so captivated by all those wonderful articles you've written that I made it a point to remember your name should our paths ever cross. But lies of any kind are not one of my strong suits, so I confess that our elderly neighbors over there, Mr. and Mrs. Marshall, told me who you were and where you work."

Joe had spoken briefly with Mr. Marshall, a frail, white-haired man, on several occasions when they met in the entry alcove. "I see," he said.

"I have read one or two of your articles," she continued. "I'd wager you're very good at what you do."

"Thank you," Joe replied. "My male ego is sufficiently bolstered. But this is unfair because you know at least two things about me, and I don't even know your name. Do I get an introduction?"

"Annemarie Morgan," she smiled.

"Very pleased to meet you, Annemarie Morgan," Joe said. "May I offer you a hand with this stuff?"

"Now that really would be appreciated," she replied cheerily. "I dropped them while tryen to dig the key out of my pocket."

Joe glanced over the scattered albums, which included stuff by Elvis and the Beatles, classical music and practically everything ever released by Patsy Cline. "This is quite a collection," he observed, picking up a greatest hits album from the late country music queen. "I'm a big fan of Patsy Cline, too."

"She was the best," Annemarie lamented.

They piled the albums in a stack, which Joe picked up and held while Annemarie unlocked the door to her apartment. She cracked the door open, then took the records from him. "It was nice meeten you, Joe," she smiled. "Let's not be strangers."

Joe nodded, grinning like an idiot as he sensed neither of them wanted this first meeting to end so soon. "I was plannen to walk over to the park in a few minutes to watch the eclipse," he remarked sheepishly. "Would you care to come along with me?"

Annemarie regarded him curiously. "I suppose you probably have one of those little paper contraptions rigged up to protect your eyes?" she said.

"Well, yes," Joe replied. "I'm fond of my eyes."

"So am I, sugar," she drawled. "I'd love to watch the eclipse with you. And believe it or not, I have my own paper contraption. I'm fond of my eyes, too."

"Me, too," he grinned again. "Let me put away my groceries, and I'll be ready to go."

Annemarie glanced down into the bags, which were brimming with a variety of chicken and turkey potpies, Salisbury steak and other TV dinners. Her face twisted in a grimace. "Icky, icky," she groaned. "Do you really eat that cardboard stuff?"

Joe shrugged off the good-natured criticism. "It's easy, and I'm not much of a cook."

She appraised him closely once more. "No, sugar, I doubt you are," she agreed. "Go put up your groceries, Joe, and let's see that eclipse."

———

Annemarie Morgan had a sound understanding of astronomy, almost as good as Joe's. Still, he was able to provide one or two pertinent details about the eclipse, either impressing her with his knowledge or boring the woman to a stupor. Fortunately, the topic exhausted itself as they plundered mutually for details about each other as the sky darkened and then became bright once more.

She was twenty-three, with a dual degree in history and education obtained three years earlier from the University of Georgia in Athens. Her resume included one year as a history teacher at nearby Grady High School, but her working days were spent presently in the sky, aboard a jetliner as a stewardess for Delta Air Lines. Coming out of college, she'd had a burning desire to bring the world to unfortunate kids stuck in some inner-city high school. The desire still burned, Annemarie Morgan maintained, but she wanted to see more of the world for herself before trying to share it with others. Her current work was exciting, once she got past the notion that stewardesses were really nothing more than waitresses and maids who tended to their customers in unusual circumstances. And, she emphasized, the hassles were more than offset by the fringe benefits of working with the airline. In the short span of eight months, New York, Philadelphia and Washington had become homes away from home for Annemarie. She planned to spend her approaching vacation in Paris.

Joe provided a highly condensed version of his recent arrival in Atlanta and the happenings of the last two months. He was more interested in learning about Annemarie than talking about himself.

"Okay, Annemarie," he said. "I know where you've been and where you're goen. Tell me where you're from?"

"Boston," she replied promptly.

"Almost a Floridian," Joe mused.

"Very good, sugar," she replied. "You'd be surprised at the number of people who assume I'm of the Massachusetts variety."

"With that voice?" Joe laughed.

"I'll take that as a compliment, since it's so very obvious that your roots also can be traced to somewhere in South Georgia," Annemarie responded smugly.

"And where might that be?" she prompted when Joe failed to reply.

"A little town called Cookville," he answered. "Not too many people know about it, even those who live in South Georgia."

"Heard about it and seen it on the map, but I've never been there," Annemarie replied. "If I remember correctly, it's stuck somewhere between Nashville, Lenox and Adel."

"It's off the beaten path even for our neck of the woods," Joe said. "You haven't missed much if you've never been there."

"I'm not sure about that," she grinned. "They have marvelous basketball teams up your way."

"They do," he agreed. "My brother played on the high school team. They made it all the way to the state semifinals last year, then lost by a few points in double overtime when practically the whole team fouled out. How come you know so much about basketball?"

"I was a regular jock in my high school days," she replied with a stretch. "Four years of cheerleaden for the football team. Four years on the basketball team, the last three as a starten guard. And four years on the tennis team. I was active, and I like sports."

"Impressive," Joe said with a dry tease in his voice. "Should I assume you were homecomen queen and class valedictorian as well?"

"Football queen and salutatorian," Annemarie shot back. "We had this nitwit male who studied day and night, even in the summer. He wound up at Harvard on a scholarship. He's probably a millionaire by now. But enough about my past success, sugar. I'm much more interested in how you know the whereabouts of Boston, Georgia." She swept her arms in a wide arc. "Cookville's practically a megalopolis next to Boston."

"I'm a geography buff," Joe explained. "When I was a kid, I wiled away hours at a time looken at maps. I know practically every town and county in the state."

"Well now, there's somethen we have in common," she said. "But just so I know you're tellen the truth, what's the seat of Wilkes County?"

"Washington," Joe answered without missing a beat. "Jasper County?"

"Monticello."

"So we're both experts on Georgia geography," Joe said. "What else do we have in common?"

"Is your expertise limited to Georgia?" she asked.

"Not hardly," he answered. "I know the U.S. capitals and most world capitals. You'd be hard-pressed to stump me, I think."

"Washington state?" Annemarie said suddenly.

"Olympia," Joe supplied. "New Hampshire?"

"Not even west of the Mississippi," she teased. "It's Concord. Now one last test for you. Mongolia?"

"Not even close to difficult," Joe bragged. "Ulan Bator." He clasped his hands. "Now I get one last chance to stump you."

"Fair is fair," Annemarie agreed. "Give it your best shot."

"The Republic of Guinea?"

She started to answer, then clamped her mouth tightly. "Georgetown?" she offered finally.

Joe smiled. "Wrong continent," he corrected. "Georgetown is the capital of Guyana in South America. Guinea is in Africa, and the capital's called Conakry."

"I'm deeply insulted," she pouted. "And vaguely impressed."

"I guess it's not very useful to take up all that brain space with useless information," Joe shrugged. "But faraway places have always fascinated me."

"Ah, then," Annemarie brightened. "We're kindred souls, you and I, Joe Baker," she said mysteriously. "Both of us born with a wanderlust."

His mouth fell open and he gaped at the woman—incredulous at her observation.

"Did I say somethen wrong?" she asked finally.

"Oh, no," he answered, blinking away a memory. "It's just …." He stammered. "Well, no one's ever coined that exact phrase to describe me, except for my daddy one time. And that was a long time ago."

"Well, sugar," Annemarie responded. "Since I've done most of the talken, about myself at that, you owe me at least this one story about yourself—especially since you've just taken flagrant liberties with my geographical pride."

So Joe told her the story, beginning with his late uncle's desire to leave Cookville, leading to the day Matt had drawn comparisons between his son and the uncle Joe had never known. He spared no detail in the story, right down to the moment Matt had forced him to pick up a fistful of dirt, to the overwhelming urge to wash his hands and the knowing smile his father had given him during the blessing at supper later in the evening. He was animated and spellbinding as he wove the tale, which was exactly what Annemarie told him when he finished the story.

Joe blushed at the praise, amazed to find full daylight around them once more. "We missed most of the eclipse," he told her.

"We saw enough of it," she replied. "There'll be another one in twenty years or so. We can watch it from start to finish."

He nodded agreement. "Since I insulted your geographical pride, how 'bout given me the chance to make a peace offeren. Supper tonight at my place—I'll do the cooken."

Annemarie cringed. "Talk about adden injury to insult," she remarked.

"I promise you won't even see a TV dinner," Joe pressed. "Actually, I broil a pretty good steak with baked potato."

She considered the proposal. "I have another idea," she said finally. "Let me cook for you. A real home-cooked meal. Think about it, Joe. You look like you could use one."

"Now who's insulten who," Joe teased. "What's wrong with the way I look?"

"Nothen at all," she answered sweetly. "You're just a little hollow around the edges. But it's nothen a woman's touch wouldn't cure."

"Then by all means," Joe encouraged. "Touch away."

––––––––

He had been cautious in their first meeting, until that moment near the end of the conversation when she had touched off the story about his father and uncle. Then, Annemarie had seen a different side of Joe, a very friendly and caring man, in sharp contrast to the aloof image painted by their neighbors.

"He's nice enough, I suppose," Mr. Marshall had told her one day when she casually inquired about their new neighbor. "But he's also cool enough to freeze over Hell itself, if you know what I mean."

At supper that night, over roast beef and Yorkshire pudding, which Annemarie confessed had been in the oven before his dinner invitation, Joe became cautious once more about himself. Still, their conversation flowed like tap water, scalding hot at times, with undercurrents of an undeniable attraction between them.

After their walk home from the park, Joe had gone inside his apartment, showered, shaved and returned two hours later dressed casually in gray chinos, a light blue polo shirt and tan and navy oxford shoes. Annemarie showered as well, then threw on her sandals and a sleeveless white sundress that hugged her tightly at the waist and flared at the skirt. At the last minute, she dabbed on a generous amount of her favorite perfume and arranged her hair in its usual style, flipped under, pulled back behind the ear on one side and swept down the side of her face on the other. Then, she had hurried with the final preparations of the meal, intent on giving him food fare to write home about to the folks in Cookville. If the frequency of comments coming her way about the delicious food were any indication, she had succeeded on that account.

Annemarie had a knack for getting her way, and she wanted Joe's life story. After supper, with apologies for the lack of dessert, she led the man into her soft, lamp-lit living room, sat him on the sofa, plied him with sweet tea and went to work. Every time she steered the conversation toward Joe, however, he sidestepped the issue and manipulated it back to her. The problem was, she reflected later in the evening when she realized what was happening, that Annemarie simply enjoyed talking too much to resist an invitation. So finally, she relented to the impulse, gave up on Joe and told him her life history.

Their stories were similar, with a few cast changes and different plot lines. She was the daughter of Thad and Frances Morgan. "But mostly just Frances," Annemarie explained to Joe.

A pulpwooder by trade, her father apparently preferred booze and good times to family obligations. Or so Annemarie had been told by practically everyone who ever knew Thad Morgan—a claim she could not make herself. Under the circumstances, she tended to agree with people's assessment of her father, who had celebrated her birth with a few drinks and then wrapped his truck around a pine tree. Even his ill-fated celebration of her birth had come a day after the auspicious event itself because Thad Morgan had been out carousing with the boys on the night his daughter was born.

"It must have been difficult growen up without a father," Joe suggested. "Did you miss him?"

"Good ole Daddy Dearest?" she reflected somewhat sarcastically. "No, not really. My mother had five brothers, so I was never lacken for a male influence in my life. And I refuse to feel remorse over somethen I never had in the first place. There's too much sorrow in our lives as it is to worry about things beyond our control."

Joe hummed over that suggestion, and Annemarie wasn't sure whether he believed her, but she continued the story.

She was the second child of Frances and Thad. She'd had a brother, Jerry, seven years older than she, who had been shot out of a helicopter somewhere over Laos in 1966 and presumably lay dead in the mountain jungle. "Technically, he's missen in action," she explained. "But essentially, the Army told us not to expect him home anytime soon. Likely, we'll never know for sure, but I feel without a doubt that he's dead and gone."

"Were you close to him?" Joe inquired.

Annemarie shrugged. "I'd like to say we were," she answered, "but the truth is, sugar, that he and I were as different as night and day, separated by light years more than seven years. He was a carbon copy of my father; I'm the more demure type like my mama."

Joe smiled at her self-assessment. There was very little of any demure quality about this woman.

"Still, it must have been tough to lose him?" he pressed.

"Oh, don't get me wrong," she replied quickly. "I loved Jerry, because he was family after all. It was sad to lose him under those circumstances. But the truth is, Joe, my brother was one of those people destined to crash and burn early in life. He was truly a rebel without a cause. The reason he wound up in the Army and subsequently the war was that he robbed a liquor store one night when he was drunk out of his gourd."

"Really?" Joe remarked, clearly surprised.

"Really," she confirmed. "It was the last straw in a long list of run-ins with the law. My Uncle Charles—he's the DA down there—cut a deal to save Jerry's hide. He could join the Army and avoid prosecution on robbery charges. At the time, in 1964, it seemed like a good idea. Frankly, I still think it was. But my uncle suffered the most when Jerry was killed. He feels guilty over it, like he's the one who sent Jerry to his death. That's a ridiculous notion to my way of thinken."

"Why so?" he asked.

"I'm a firm believer in God's way of doen things, Joe," she replied easily. "And deep down, I believe my brother got a better deal than he would have back home. At least this way, he died for somethen. That beats the heck out of rotten away your life in prison."

"Is religion important to you," Joe asked, changing the subject.

"I'm a Baptist, sugar," she answered huskily. "A Missionary Baptist. Don't confuse us with the Southern Baptists, although I do believe my church back home pays dues to the Southern Baptist Convention."

Joe doubled over with laughter. "Do you know the difference between a Missionary Baptist and a Southern Baptist?" he inquired.

Annemarie eyed him closely, trying to decide if he was toying with her beliefs or sincere with the question. "Are you about to tell me a dirty joke?" she asked cautiously.

"No, no," Joe said, recovering his composure. "It's a serious question—sort of."

"I'm not totally clear on the particulars," she answered at length. "It has somethen to do with the way the churches support missions and missionaries— who chooses which missions to support and who manages the money given to them. But generally speaking, I think Missionary Baptist is a generic term, which means all Southern Baptists are really Missionary Baptists, but not necessarily vice versa. My brand of Missionary Baptists has our own association of churches. Of course, you also have your Holiness Baptists, your Free Will Baptists, Full Gospel Baptists, Primitive Baptists and a slew of others. I'm not sure how they all fit into the puzzle, but any way you look at it, that's a lot of Baptists, so there must be somethen to it."

Joe stared in disbelief.

"Sugar, you have to quit given me these openmouthed looks," she pouted. "They make you look dumb and me feel even dumber."

"I can't help it," Joe remarked, regaining his composure. "You've actually answered a question that I thought didn't have an answer."

"There's always an answer, Joe," Annemarie suggested.

Joe ignored her philosophy, then recalled how Rachel—as God-fearing a woman as he knew, except possibly for his mother—had little use for Southern Baptists and knew little history about Missionary Baptists. "One time I asked Granny what it meant to be a Missionary Baptist," Joe recalled. "Her answer was somewhere along the lines of, 'It means we're not Southern Baptists, Methodists or snake handlers.' Maybe not those exact words but close enough. She's not fond of Southern Baptists—thinks they meddle too much."

"She sounds feisty," Annemarie observed with admiration. "I'd like to meet her."

"I'm tempted to call home and share your explanation with her," Joe replied.

"Exactly, what does your brand of Missionary Baptists believe," Annemarie asked.

"Probably the same as yours," Joe answered. "They don't give a hoot for denominations, though. They're even charitable toward Catholics. Benevolence is a fairly simple church. You read the Bible, you do what it says and you go to Heaven when you die. You don't, you go to Hell."

"Tell me, Joe," Annemarie queried. "How do you measure up to those simple rules?"

He ignored her again, this time with a slight smirk. "We're getten off track," he said. "I believe we were discussen you, sugar."

"I've been talken practically all night," she shot back. "It's time you told me somethen about yourself."

"I'd put you to sleep," Joe argued. "My life's been deadly dull compared with yours."

Annemarie arched her eyebrows at him. "Somehow, sugar, I don't think there's too much dull about you," she drawled. "But you win this time. I'll spill the rest of my guts. Where were we?"

"You lost your brother in Vietnam, and your uncle feels guilty about senden him over there," Joe reminded her.

"Ah, yes," she replied. "I think we've pretty much covered that subject." She paused to look at him at the other end of the sofa, then slipped off her sandals and drew up her feet on the couch. "I guess my life sounds awfully bleak so far," she continued. "Well, I have to warn you, Joe: It gets worse before it gets better. Are you sure you can stand it?"

Joe smiled an open invitation. "I'd really like to hear the rest of it."

So she told him about Frances, who had succumbed to cancer when Annemarie was just fifteen. "Now that was truly hard to bear—losen Mama," she said sadly. "She was sick for such a long time, yet I always held out hope for a miracle to make her well again. I don't think I ever really expected her to die. There were times when I prayed for God to take her, to do anything to make the pain go away because she suffered so much. But even on the day she died, I never really expected it. It seemed so shocken. Before and since then, I've heard people say death is easier to accept when you know it's the best thing for the person dyen. Don't believe it, Joe. It's never easy to take. To this day, I'd do anything to have my mama back—even sick and sufferen. It's selfish, but I can't help it."

Joe felt a protective urge toward her. "My mama was an orphan," he said. "Her parents were killed in a car wreck when she was twelve. She's never really talked much about them, though. It's funny, but I've always thought of my grandparents as her parents, too. In a way, they are. Mama's lived in the same house with Granny and Grandpa longer than she lived with her own parents. She was only sixteen when she and Daddy married, and that was twenty-eight years ago."

Annemarie crossed her arms stubbornly. "That does it," she announced. "I'm not gonna say another word about myself until you give me every single detail about the courtship and marriage of your parents."

This time, Joe did not hesitate, spinning the complete story from Matt and Caroline's chance meeting on a city sidewalk in Tifton to their one-night honeymoon in the Berriens' guest cottage. Annemarie was struck most by the unlikely snowfall and Caroline's interpretation of it as God's blessing of the marriage, so Joe told her about the white Christmas nineteen years later when Matt surprised his wife with an engagement ring.

"Both of them say it was love at first sight," he concluded. "I don't know about that, but whatever it was between them, it's still some kind of powerful."

"Cool," she said simply. "I think I'm envious. No, I know I'm envious. That's storybook stuff."

"You've just heard a few chapters of it," Joe interrupted lightly. "Now it's your turn to tell me about the good parts of your life."

Annemarie mulled over the question. "There are so many good parts," she confirmed finally. "It's hard to know where to begin."

So, she started at the beginning, amusing Joe with stories about her mother's five brothers, their wives and hordes of cousins all older than herself. She told him about her late grandmother, who had died two years earlier, summers spent working in her uncles' tobacco fields and pranks that had skirted her close to trouble in school. Then, she told him about her love of travel, music (an upright piano dominated her living room), books and cooking, about her junior and senior years at the University of Georgia and her freshman and sophomore years at Valdosta State College, Joe's alma mater. Annemarie talked until words failed her.

"You probably know more about the life of Annemarie Morgan than I do," she concluded. "I'm apt to forget half this stuff, half the time. I feel as if I've talked my whole life right out of my memory."

Joe smiled back at her, amused.

"I'm not kidden," she rambled on. "I hope you have a good memory, Joe, so you can refresh mine from time to time."

"It's tolerable," he admitted.

Annemarie stretched the kinks out of her back and shoulders, eliciting considerable interest from the other end of the sofa. "What's next, sugar?" she purred.

"Patsy Cline," Joe offered.

"A very good suggestion," she agreed. "I don't know why we didn't think of it earlier. Music's always good for the soul."

Annemarie rose from the sofa, glided over to the stereo stand and set up the player with the album of greatest hits from the late queen of country music. Joe followed her off the sofa, walking over to examine the polished black piano and the sheet music scattered across it. Her mix of musical taste astonished him, ranging from the haunting melody of Simon and Garfunkel's *Bridge Over Troubled Water* to the classical sounds of Chopin and the country blues of Ray Charles.

"I bet you're good at this," he suggested a moment later when she came over beside him.

"The piano is one of my passions," she confessed. "Playen it refreshes the soul, corny though that may sound."

Joe had never been excessively forward with women, although his recent string of one-night stands had made him bolder. But it was not confidence that guided his next move as he looked straight into her beautiful eyes. Neither of them spoke until he stroked her silky-smooth face and she pressed her cheek against the roughness of his palm.

"Would you like to dance?" he inquired as the stirring refrain of *I Fall to Pieces* settled around them.

"That would be nice," she replied softly.

Joe pulled her close, folded the woman in his arms and buried his face in the softness of her hair as Annemarie responded to his touch. She rested her head against the hollow of his throat, and her arms encircled his neck. He tensed as her slender fingers raked seductively through his hair, and she arched against him as the heat of his breath whispered against her forehead. They moved in a slow circle, oblivious to the beat of the music, unwilling to part in the quiet interlude between *I Fall to Pieces* and *Sweet Dreams*.

In all his experiences, no woman had ever drawn Joe as irresistibly as this one; none had ever melded against him in an exact fit. They both wanted more than to share a dance, so he lifted his head, tilted her face to him and kissed Annemarie deeply. The kiss was tender and urgent, and she melted in his arms. Her head fell away from him, and Joe covered the slender neck with the gentle caress of his mouth until her breath came in deep gasps. His hands slid down the length of her figure, cupping the rounded bottom and pressing her to the fire in his groin. She clung to him to stay on her feet, and his own breath came raggedly until they broke apart their faces to judge how far this moment might go.

"I want you," he stated simply.

"I can tell," Annemarie replied breathlessly, following his eyes to the bedroom door across the room. "This is crazy, Joe, and I don't mean the song."

Crazy wafted seductively around them. "It's not crazy," Joe replied. "It's really simple because you want me, too."

"I never figured you for an assumen man," she responded coyly.

"I'm not," he countered.

"This ain't exactly coffee, tea or me, sugar," she said uncertainly. "Maybe I do want you, and maybe you've turned me into a mass of quiveren jelly."

Joe smiled. "Then, let's finish what we've started," he suggested.

"No, Joe," she decided firmly, pulling away slightly from him. "It's tempten, very tempten. But I just met you a few hours ago, and unlike a bitch in heat, I don't give into any urge that strikes my fancy."

"What if it strikes again?" he hinted, smiling again, persuasively so. "Real soon."

The remark came in the voice of resignation and teasing acceptance of her decision. Yet, Annemarie sensed the temptation could strike again with the fury of lightning. He should know where she intended to draw the line, so Annemarie backed away completely from their embrace.

"Listen, Joe," she said, with a tinge of regret thrown in for good measure. "Maybe I'm brash and too forward for my own good. But I also have some very old-fashioned notions, particularly in regards to marriage and sex. I warn you: Be very careful about the conclusions you draw from what happened between us tonight. Plain and simple, the man who takes me to bed is either goen to be my husband or well on his way to becomen it. Make no mistake about that."

"You get top marks for maken your intentions clear, Miss Morgan," Joe said with a grin.

"Intentions have nothen to do with it," she shot back. "I was merely maken note of my values."

"Oh," Joe said.

"Now, sugar," she suggested sweetly. "Why don't you straighten out your pants, go home and take a cold shower. You could use one, and I could, too."

———

Later that night as he lay in bed smoking the day's last cigarette, Joe concluded he had never met a woman like Annemarie Morgan. Brash and forward seemed an apt description of her, not to mention seductive and teasing. She was unforgettable.

Just as she'd suggested, he had come home and taken a cold shower. But even now, with his urges settled, he could not vanish her from his thoughts.

Annemarie was not someone who could be labeled neatly and stuck on a shelf for future reference. Her plate was heaped high with a mass of contradictions and complexities that should have scared the living daylights out of Joe, who preferred straightforward and simple women. And yet, she came across as refreshing and engaging, sure of what she wanted and honest about her intentions. She captivated

Joe; she made him nervous. No woman had ever gushed so openly to him about sexual tension, or explained as honestly the implications of making love to her.

Making love to her appealed to Joe. No man in his right man could turn away such a beautiful woman, especially when she fit against him as Annemarie did with Joe—as if they were made for each other. Even without the physical attraction, Joe would have been hard-pressed to forget Annemarie. She appealed to his senses in every way, as no other woman had ever done.

Joe may have sworn off permanent attachments, but Annemarie could make a man reconsider his past motives and declarations.

The woman had substance. She had faced more than a few hardships and come away from her troubles remarkably adjusted and accepting of God's will—as she had put it to Joe. Her headstrong attitude and vivacious spirit made Joe wonder whether she ever just had a bad day. Somehow, he imagined, even if she did have a bad day, Annemarie would find a way to gloss over it and maintain her cheery disposition. Obviously, she had worked through some of life's darker moments without losing touch with her soul. No one who had witnessed the eradication of her entire family and was left alone in the world could come away unscathed from the loss. Yet, despite the sense of isolation she must have felt, Annemarie found the silver lining in those dark clouds and focused on the giving nature of life rather than its taking.

Joe admired her perseverance.

He also admired her spunkiness and tenderness. She was full of grit, yet radiated an innate softness. Whether teaching young students or serving people twenty-five thousand feet above the ground, he suspected Annemarie brought the same caring nature to her work. She seemed like someone who could smile despite her frustrations. Few people probably felt her wrath. With her forgiving nature, she probably tolerated the bad manners and rude behavior of others much better than the average person.

She also went beyond the call of duty to make people comfortable in her home. Perhaps he was too far removed from the savory pleasures of home cooking to make a sound judgment, but Joe could not remember pot roast ever tasting as good as the one he had eaten tonight. She had browned it to perfection—just the way he liked it, dark and tough on the outside, juicy and tender on the inside. And while he had no culinary equivalent to compare with the Yorkshire pudding, Joe figured the dish deserved a place among the world's great recipes. On top of everything else, she even sweetened tea just right, with enough sugar to take away the bitterness and enhance the flavor.

He considered briefly how to wrangle another dinner invitation, then thought about the inviting, homey atmosphere of Annemarie's apartment.

Her home offered a stark contrast to his own abode. As contented as he was with his apartment, Joe had to concede that Annemarie's contained the niceties of home. Instead of eating her meals at the kitchen bar as Joe did, she had a small table for two, which had been covered with an emerald green tablecloth and set with her mother's china and sensible jelly glasses. There had been candlesticks on the table, lighted at that.

The living room seemed like a creation of Norman Rockwell. It was neat and comfortable in contrasting shades of light blue and navy, with a sofa, a recliner, tables, lamps, two bookshelves and a walnut cabinet for the television and stereo.

Whatnots and family pictures graced the tables and walls, and a vase of red carnations centered the coffee table. The piano was the most impressive feature of the room, however, even more so because of the sheet music scattered around it. He had only glimpsed the bedroom on his way to the bathroom, but it contained stoutly built, darkly stained oak furnishings, including an impressive canopy bed with a feather mattress and surprisingly simple coverings. There was nothing femininely frilly about the room, which made Joe think a man could take up residence there without feeling trapped.

He tried to push this last thought from his mind because it scared him. Try as he might, however, Joe could not escape the notion that Annemarie Morgan would make a very good home for some lucky soul. Then it dawned on him what set her apart from other women he had found attractive in the past. She possessed a wholesomeness, distinctive and deeply imbedded with beauty, grace and seasoning.

Joe finally fell asleep, regretting the boundaries Annemarie had set in her relationships with men, thankful for the safeguards that would cool the fire between them.

————

Annemarie was as practical as she was virtuous. She did not believe in love at first sight, but Joe Baker set her heart aflutter and her loins afire. She had wanted more from him than she was willing to accept, and the desire continued to send tremors through her insides long after he had gone.

She was due at the airport in less than four hours. She had an early flight to Toledo, and all Annemarie could think about was the smoky taste of his kiss, the fire in those darkly brown eyes and the primal passion he aroused in her. Men more handsome had desired her, but none measured up to this one. No one had ever crumbled her resistance so quickly, or made her question whether to save her virginity for one man. Indeed, no man had come closer to storming the castle as this one had done. And several had mounted serious assaults.

Joe was a most appealing man in every way, from thickly textured hair the color of pecan shells and the hollow places in his strong-boned body, to the swarthy complexion and deep baritone voice. But the response he elicited from Annemarie was deeper than the physical attraction, and therein lay the secret to the man's magnetism.

Along with the urge to make wild, passionate love with him, came a desire to nurture the man—as well as the nagging intuition that Joe was not someone who easily accepted the caring of others. It was this last impression that made Annemarie wary of getting involved in a relationship with the man, and finally, reluctantly, cooled the raging hot embers deep inside her.

A nice enough man but cool enough to freeze over Hell, she recalled, thinking for the second time that her neighbor's description of Joe seemed overly harsh. Still, she could understand why the elderly man had made the statement, especially if his contact with Joe had been only in passing. Annemarie had glimpsed the man's caring side, yet she also had come away with the distinct impression that demons rattled around inside Joe's soul. She had never crossed paths with a man who became pricklier than Joe when a conversation moved close to him. He clammed up like a smart oyster at a fish fry.

Annemarie prided herself on the ability to roll with the punches. She could tolerate a mercurial man. But womanly intuition convinced her that Joe was not a man given to sudden mood swings or flights of fancy. His actions were deliberate, perhaps too much so, and Annemarie refused to trust a man who controlled feelings on such a short leash. On that acknowledgment alone, she should have put thoughts of him out of her mind. But there were other warning flags to bolster an argument against a serious relationship with him. Something disturbed her about Joe, not the least of which was the inner-turmoil emanating from him.

She admired a small amount of caution in a man because it conveyed a refreshingly quiet strength. Joe, however, was more than just cautious about himself. He was downright edgy, the kind of edginess that suggested dark secrets waited to rip the man apart, leaving those closest to him to pick up the pieces. That was the clinching argument, the main reason to steer clear of Joe. Perhaps her assessment was melodramatic, but Annemarie had picked up the pieces after more than her share of lost lives. She had seen enough of the people closest to her crash and burn, and she opposed the idea of setting herself up for another fall.

But still … Joe Baker might be worth the risk.

The man had mettle, a sense of endurance and raw vitality that suggested he could overcome any odds. Something powerful and hearty had sustained him thus far against whatever demons stalked his soul. Annemarie suspected someone from a lesser background would have already caved under the persistent pressure. But Joe, despite his ragged edges, bore up well under the strain. She thought maybe it had something to do with the glow that lit his eyes when he regaled her with those stories about his family. She suspected, too, that glow explained her willingness to risk her heart on the man.

For regalement really was the only way Annemarie knew to describe her response to the heartfelt stories Joe had spun about his family. He had filled her mind with a picture of the Baker home, the warm people who lived there and the strong family bonds that sustained them. She wondered whether the man himself realized the depth of love and caring that shone in his eyes when he wove tales about those people closest to him, or the extent of his own self he revealed in those stories.

His family occupied a powerful place in Joe's heart, and the force of it mesmerized Annemarie. She had come away with a deeper understanding of the real Joe than was intended, even if he tried to exclude his role in those reflections on his family. Joe obviously relished close ties and understood the importance of virtues like love and understanding, patience and tenderness, caring and nurturing. They were precious qualities to Annemarie, too, and she wanted very much to find someone to share a lifetime filled with these basic elements.

Annemarie had no doubt whatsoever of Joe's ability to give such goodness, but whether he could accept it was an entirely different, even worrisome, proposition. Still, a seed of hope was planted deeply within her. Because deep down, despite her life's many blessings, an empty place dwelled within her, a hole unfilled by her vast collection of cousins, aunts and uncles.

She drifted off in the last hours before dawn, dreaming of a man who could fill that empty place.

SOMEONE POUNDING ON HIS door woke Joe, though failed to bring him completely to his senses. He staggered from bed, found his underwear on the floor and dressed on the way to the door.

"I'm comen," he yelled irately to whomever had ruined the end of his good night's sleep.

Joe woke like clockwork shortly after six on weekday mornings but lingered in bed until eight on weekends. Judging by the darkness, the current hour was well before his weekday wake-up call. This interruption on his effort to catch up on his sleep was unappreciated, and he meant to convey his annoyance to the untimely caller.

Grumbling all the way, he stumbled to the door, yanked off the chain and unbolted the dead lock. "Whataya want?" he growled, jerking open the heavy door.

Annemarie stood before him, beautiful in her dark blue airline uniform, although not exactly fresh looking. Her eyes seemed slightly puffed from lack of sleep, and her hair just missed the mark of a well-styled coiffure. Joe kept these impressions to himself.

"Charmen," she mused. "I figured you for a mornen person, sugar, but I could have been wrong. Are you always this grumpy in the mornen?"

"Only when it's such an ungoodly hour of the mornen," Joe replied dryly. "May I assume there's reason for you to pound on my door at this early hour?" He smiled seductively. "Or did you just miss my charm?"

Once again, Annemarie was aware of her physical attraction to the man as Joe stood there in nothing but his jockey shorts, drowsy and irritated, with a thin line of hair snaking out of his shorts up his chest. She pasted a smile on her face to keep her mind occupied.

"Don't flatter yourself," she told him. "I just wanted to tell you I had trouble sleepen last night."

"Yeah," Joe grinned. "Why was that?"

Annemarie gave him a serious look. "I thought maybe our really nice day ended on a sour note," she said with regret. "I didn't want you to walk away with a bad taste in your mouth."

"Believe me, I didn't," Joe smiled. "As a matter of fact, your cooken was one of the last things on my mind before I fell asleep last night." He paused, then grinned again. "Dessert was good, too, even if I didn't get enough."

She blushed at the obvious teasing behind his effrontery. "Flattery will get you nowhere," she huffed.

"Rest assured, Miss Morgan," he said seriously. "Your effort to make everything clear was much appreciated and respected. I came home and took a cold shower as you suggested. You'll have no other reason to worry about my intentions."

"Things moved a little too fast for me last night, Joe," she replied. "I'm not usually so forward, so familiar. I gave you the wrong impression, and I apologize."

"Things did move too fast," Joe agreed. "I was presumptuous, and I apologize for that. Like I said, it won't happen again. I'll be a gentleman to a fault."

Annemarie faked another smile. "You think it's possible to be just friends?" she asked, uncertain that was all she wanted from him.

Joe considered the possibility. "To tell you the truth," he replied at length, "I haven't had much practice just be'en friends with women."

"Just what kind of practice have you had with them?" she asked shamelessly.

He ignored the question. "But yeah, I think it's very possible that you and I were meant to be friends," he remarked. "I'd like that very much. You're a fetchen woman, Annemarie Morgan. And you're one heck of a cook, too."

She eyed him suspiciously. "You have a habit of ignoren the tough questions," she deduced. "But I know now what's on your mind. You just want me for my cooken."

"I confess," Joe said sheepishly. "The thought crossed my mind. I don't suppose you brought along any of that leftover pot roast this mornen."

"Sorry, sugar. It completely slipped my mind."

"Some friend you're turnen out to be," he groused. "But now that we have everything settled between us and have decided to be the best of friends, may I go back to my bed?"

Annemarie considered the request, almost as if she had something else to say about the matter. "I'm not sure whether we've settled anything or merely opened a can of worms," she remarked. Then, she smiled, reached into her purse and pulled out a single gold key. "Help yourself to the pot roast, Joe," she said, offering him the key.

Joe blinked and accepted the key. "I don't suppose I could keep this?" he suggested.

"Not on your life," Annemarie answered, smiling as she kissed him lightly on the cheek and waved goodbye.

"Have a good day," Joe told her as she went out the alcove door.

He followed her to the door and watched until she disappeared down the street, then padded back to his bed and fell into a contented slumber.

————

"Joe! There's nothen but TV dinners in here," Annemarie wailed as she peered into the icebox of his refrigerator. "How can you eat this stuff?"

"There is, too, more than TV dinners," Joe said. "I also have pot pies—beef, chicken and turkey. They're really good."

"I'm sure they are," she said sarcastically, giving the freezer door a solid shove close and pulling open the bottom door. "This isn't any better," she lamented.

Though he had gone grocery shopping earlier in the day, she could hardly tell it from the contents. "Are you sure that's real food you're cooken?"

It was the middle of May and Joe was just getting around to returning the favor of several suppers at Annemarie's apartment. He was broiling steaks to go with baked potatoes and tossed salad.

"I'm sure," he answered, taking a long gulp from his can of beer. He turned the steaks, then crossed over to the refrigerator. "Excuse me, but I need to get somethen from there."

Annemarie moved away from the refrigerator. "There's nothen in here to get," she chided with a shake of her head.

Joe ignored the barb, then pulled out a bottle of salad dressing, Worcestershire sauce and another cold beer for the meal. "Can I refill your tea?" he asked.

"Would you, sugar?" Annemarie called over her shoulder as she examined the sparse contents of his kitchen cabinets.

Joe shook his head, baffled by her preoccupation with his kitchen, occasionally irritated by her well-intended criticism, regardless of whether it was justified. Her nosiness was one of two habits that irked Joe about Annemarie. The other was her steady stream of well-intentioned advice. Annemarie nagged with the skill of a woman far more advanced in years than her own age. Most of the time, Joe shrugged off her prodding as one of the frailties of women—some inborn sense that made them women, an assessment of their condition that Annemarie accepted. Sometimes, however, he told her politely what to do with her advice, as he had done a few moments ago when she suggested plain oil and vinegar with a dash of garlic made a better salad dressing than the bottled stuff. She was right, of course, and, in fact, Joe was accustomed to homemade dressings when his family ate salad at home. But pouring the stuff straight from a bottle was easier than mixing it from scratch. And furthermore, a person could detect only the barest of differences in taste.

He gave both the Worcestershire and salad dressing bottles vicious shakes, banged them down on the bar and popped the top on another beer before refilling her tea glass.

Despite hectic schedules that had him coming and her going, or vice versa, Joe and Annemarie had become fast friends over the past few weeks. Their relationship remained platonic, excepting a few torrid kisses here and there, but Joe often felt as if they were fighting the irresistible forces of nature to maintain mere friendship. Joe wondered if a good romp in the sack would cool the flames between them, but mostly, he suspected making love would only fan the fires. Regardless, making love was not an option. Annemarie had laid the ground rules on that accord, and Joe had no intention of accepting the responsibility for breaking them.

Still, Joe knew he was working overtime not to fall in love with the woman, a difficult order considering that Annemarie gave him every natural reason in the world to fall head over heels. They shared a host of common interests from books to *Get Smart* on Friday nights, along with enough interest in their differences to enjoy each other's private pleasures. Annemarie had fostered a deep respect for classical music in Joe, especially the expressiveness of the Polish composer, Chopin, and the poetic touch of German Richard Strauss. On successive Sundays in early April after she had returned from church, they had whiled away entire afternoons, first playing a selection of Chopin's work on the piano and then listening to a recording of Strauss' *Death and Transfiguration*.

Her musical appreciation ran the gamut. She wowed Joe with a perfect rendition of Jerry Lee Lewis' *Great Balls of Fire*, taught him to pick out notes on the guitar and even coaxed him into harmonizing with her on the vocals of certain songs. The breath of her musical talent also impressed Joe. Besides the piano and guitar, she played the banjo, an accordion and a dulcimer with equal skill. Her voice was pure silk, equally at home on hymns and rocking blues.

"You should do this professionally," Joe had encouraged her one day. "I bet you could be the next queen of country music."

"I don't have the hair for it," she joked.

"I'm serious, Annie," Joe persisted. "With your voice and your talent, you could make the big time."

"I'm serious, too," she replied. "I don't have the hair for it." She paused, then continued, "I admit I'm somewhat talented musically. But that's my problem, Joe. I'm somewhat talented at a lot of things, but I lack the guts to make a full-time commitment to any one thing."

Add honesty to the growing list of things he appreciated about Annemarie, Joe told himself.

As uplifting as her music was, however, Joe's most appreciated gift from Annemarie was an introduction to tennis. It was a sport Joe had never given any attention, yet he took right to it. They played together whenever possible on the courts at Piedmont Park, and Joe often wandered over to the courts himself to find someone looking for a match. The game came naturally to him, providing an opportunity for exercise and an outlet for venting tension. When he stepped on the tennis court, his mind eliminated all distractions and focused solely on the game and its strategy.

Joe was less certain about the impact of his passions on Annemarie, perhaps because they were vaguely defined interests even to him. The sole exception was the poetry of Robert Frost, which she loved for Joe to read aloud from the book he had received as a Christmas present years earlier. Inevitably, when she asked him to read poetry, she tacked on a separate request for details about the white Christmas or the day when Joe had quoted Frost to his father in the fields. Joe willingly obliged all requests. The poetry breathed life into a few of the dead places in his soul, while the reminiscing cured the occasional pangs of homesickness that struck his heart.

Her favorite poem was *Stopping by the Woods on a Snowy Evening,* Frost's tribute to a late-night wayfarer, which Joe had read one recent Friday night after slaking yet another of her requests for details about the white Christmas. When he had read the poem, he bedazzled Annemarie with his interpretation of it as Santa Claus, stopped to rest his reindeer on Christmas Eve night while reflecting on the spirit of the most wonderful night of the year. Her wonder-struck reaction made Joe uncomfortable, and he tried to bluff his way through a sentimental moment.

"I'm no poet," he claimed staunchly. "Just strictly prose and mostly prosaic at that." He paused, then added cautiously, "I suppose, though, that Frost moves the poetic side of me, maybe because he wrote about things I can understand and relate to."

Until then, Annemarie had sat on the floor with her chin resting on her knees as Joe talked. Suddenly, she rose to her knees, pulled Joe from his resting position on the sofa and kissed him tenderly on the mouth. "I think you're very much a poet, Joe Baker," she said softly. "You may not always rhyme or work in iambic pentameter, but you speak volumes of poetry."

He'd allowed the remark to pass without seeking a clearer explanation, partly because their sudden closeness sent powerful surges through him. Mainly, however, he figured her comments had something to do with all those stories he had told her about his home and family, tales she never tired of hearing. Some of those stories, Joe realized, Annemarie now knew as well as he did.

"Sugar, I hate to interrupt such serious thoughts," she now said. "But I'm wonderen if the secret of these allegedly famous broiled steaks of yours is burnen them to a crisp."

Her comments brought Joe back to the present and sent him scurrying to the smoking oven just in time to save supper.

"Close call," he grinned a few minutes later as they sat on the bar stools with the slightly charred meat on their plates. "Would you believe me if I told you this is the first time I ever came close to burnen dinner?"

Annemarie laughed. "You're lucky I like my steaks well done," she remarked.

"I mean it," he persisted. "They were a little too rare a couple of times early on when I was tryen to figure out what to do, but they've never been this done."

She changed the subject without missing a beat as they attacked the meal. "It's good to see you, sugar. I've missed you."

Joe had missed her, too. Their schedules had been a complete mishmash in recent weeks. First, the *Herald* had packed Joe off to New York to cover the explosion of a four-story townhouse that served as a bomb factory for the violent Weather Underground. Then, Annemarie had left town for a two-week vacation in Paris and London, the latter city added to her plans as a last-minute decision. Upon her return, the newspaper had sent Joe to Ohio to cover the fatal shootings of four students by National Guardsmen at Kent State University.

"Has it occurred to you that for two kids from the sticks of South Georgia, we're liven in the fast lane?" Joe asked.

"Kind of glamorous, huh, sugar?"

Joe considered the suggestion between bites of steak. "It's far beyond my expectations when I came here," he answered. "Sometimes, I think it's too good to be true, like maybe everything's gonna come crashen down one day."

Her face twisted in a grimace. "Please, sugar," Annemarie advised. "I'm not overly superstitious or even uncomfortably predisposed to the power of suggestion. But in my line of work, phrases like 'come crashen down,' don't go over well at all."

"Oops!" he uttered with remorse. "My apologies for the bad choice of words. No harm intended."

"None taken," Annemarie replied.

Their conversations flowed like wind on an open plain, so effortlessly that it never ceased to amaze Joe. It was a constant reminder of the creeping closeness between them and the compelling need to stem the incoming tide before it swept him away in a flood of unwanted emotions. He resolved to have a date for the following Friday night, with someone else.

On this night, however, he was compelled to watch *Get Smart*, which they did after clearing the dirty dishes. When the world had been saved from KAOS once again, Annemarie excused herself to retrieve something from her own apartment. She returned a minute later with a package wrapped in the Sunday comics and handed it to Joe.

"I found this in London," she explained. "It's not Robert Frost, but I think you'll like it."

Joe tore off the paper and discovered two battered books by Dylan Thomas, the Welsh writer whose works were unfamiliar to him. One book was *How Green Was My Valley*, which Joe recalled had been made into a movie. The other was a collection of poems.

"I really appreciate this, Annie," he thanked her. "I've heard good things about his stuff, and it's probably time I branched out past Robert Frost."

"It doesn't get any better than Frost, sugar," she said. "But I came across these while browsen in an old bookstore in London and thought you might like them. I studied Dylan Thomas in an English Lit class in high school, or rather we studied one of his poems. Anyway, as soon as I saw the book, I thought about you and what your voice could do with that particular poem. I bought it, which means you now have to read it to me."

They spent the rest of the evening stretched out on the floor, with Joe reading *Do Not Go Gently Into the Night*, while Annemarie lay with her head in his lap.

————

His talent on the tennis court annoyed Annemarie, who considered herself a good player. In the few short months since Joe first stepped onto a court, he had developed a clearly superior game. He played aggressively, stepping into the court to smack the ball hard and deep into the corners, then rushing the net to swat away weak returns. His serve had zip and accuracy, and he had mastered the delicate touch and spin shots as well. Even worse, he covered the court with the grace of a natural, his movements compact, economical, unbetrayed even by his weak knee or the slightest hint of clumsiness.

Her competitiveness had always been Annemarie's best asset as an athlete, more than compensating for any deficiency in skills. At tennis or basketball, she battled to win and concentrated flawlessly. Yet, what irked her most about Joe was his unrelenting ruthlessness on the tennis court. It was bad enough to accept the fact that his skill on the court had quickly surpassed hers but positively disheartening to realize that his will to win exceeded hers.

Setting aside her envious thoughts, Annemarie acknowledged that his prowess for the game had a good side as well, especially when they paired up for doubles matches as they had done earlier this late May afternoon. Under a broiling sun, they had ripped apart another couple in quick fashion, losing only four games in two sets. Now they were sharing a Coke, side by side under the shade of a massive oak tree in the sprawling park.

"You know, sugar," Annemarie commented as her thoughts changed abruptly, while observing his arms. "You'd be a hit among the nursen crowd. They'd probably drool in anticipation if they ever got a look at those pipes in your arms. Are you sure they're not artificial?"

Joe set the soda can on the grass, then stretched out his arms to inspect the blood vessels that ran up and down between his knuckles and elbows. The collection of arteries and veins was bulging. When his hands were relaxed as they were now, it was difficult to distinguish between the blood vessels and tendons. He closed his palm for a closer inspection, and Annemarie began to trace slowly up the length of particularly large vessel. Her index finger connected where the vessel emerged from his knuckles, then followed the blue trail along the side of his wrist, across the top of his forearm to the underside and finally to the crook of his elbow, where the vessel disappeared under muscled biceps.

She nudged the blood vessel at its widest convex, then shook her head in dismay at the tremendous chain reaction up and down the length of the pulpy trail. "I don't think this is normal, Joe," she emphasized, turning his arm over for a closer inspection of the even more pronounced blue stitching on its underside. "Not normal at all," she concluded worriedly.

"Well, who's asken you?" Joe shot back, jerking his arm away from further scrutiny.

"It's just an observation," she said lightly, trying to mollify him. "I just happen to have never seen such big blood vessels. You'll probably never have a problem with poor circulation."

Joe gaped in disbelief at her. "Do these observations about my various body parts come naturally to you?" he asked sincerely. "Or do you sit around and try to figure out some new way to shock me?"

"You don't have to be huffy," Annemarie pouted. "I'm just extremely observant. As a newspaper reporter, you should appreciate that."

"Well, in the last few weeks, you've observed just about everything negative about my body that there could possibly be," he replied with sarcasm. "And frankly, sugar, I've heard all I care to hear about bony ankles, bony hands and fingers, hollow places and bulgen blood vessels."

"Tell me then," she said, unperturbed by his outburst, touching his right knee. "How did you get such a long scar on this graceful knee of yours?"

Joe rolled his eyes and surrendered to this latest round of interrogation.

Annemarie had found recently that good-natured needling was a successful tactic in her quest to understand this man, who fought desperately not to be understood. Though she never tired of hearing the stories about Joe's family, she had grown restless with his wholehearted effort to keep so much of himself hidden from her. Since she was certain she loved him, Annemarie owed it to herself to understand him. Unfortunately, the more she understood Joe, the more warning bells clanged in her head. The signals warned against a serious relationship with him. She feared he would break her heart—not necessarily intentionally—but as an effect of the fallout sure to come when his tightly constructed barriers came crashing down around him.

More than ever, Joe seemed like someone else in her life who was destined to crash and burn. He was on the edge of Hell and ready to fall into the fire. And more than ever, Annemarie was determined to save him, or to cushion the fall enough to salvage him.

Piece by piece, she was unraveling his demons. Any psychiatrist with the slightest inclination to sort through a truly complex mind probably would have paid Joe to spend time on a couch, just for the research possibilities. But Joe would never submit to analysis. He was far too independent and self-willed, which was the root of his demons. He refused to reach out for help and, when it was offered, refused to accept it.

His demons manifested in a variety of ways—from the quirky compulsiveness to wear nothing but heavily starched white shirts to work—to the meticulous arrangement of his closet, with a place for everything and everything in its place. Annemarie could not help being amused by the contradiction provided by his closet arrangement. Joe was one of the least domestic people she had ever known, yet he refused to tolerate the slightest hint of disarray in his closet. Similarly, he loathed disorder in the kitchen, which he kept spotless and squeaky clean. If he used a dish—a rare occasion since he ate most meals from cardboard boxes or right out of cans—he cleaned it immediately, bringing to mind the image of a fuss-budget who picked up an unfinished cup of coffee the second it was set down. Of course, these were his lesser demons, the ones that hardly counted, except they represented building blocks for a slew of far more complex anxieties.

One of his more significant demons was the solid steel rigidity that governed Joe's life—from his everyday way of doing things to the emotions he kept sealed in a hardened shell. He demanded perfection of himself. Anything less reeked of failure to him and provoked a personal browbeating behind that unruffled facade of coolness. Annemarie surely had never met a person whose emotions were more contained than Joe's, or who was more bent on self-protection. He positively flinched when she got too close to his secrets, then quickly wrapped himself in some recessive guise. His revelations of those carefully guarded secrets came with crystallized dispassion, as if he refused to be affected by their place in his life and was impervious to the open wounds they left on his soul.

His impassiveness was downright scary. And yet, it was confined solely to himself.

Far from being cold, the man had deep feelings for people in general, but especially those closest to him. He was, Annemarie suspected, capable of even deeper feelings once he learned the value of accepting compassion as well as giving it. For that reason alone, she continued to ignore the danger signals coming from Joe. If that singular reason needed support, then she could rely on the reassurance that Joe was slowly allowing her to pry his secrets from their hiding places. Maybe she was grasping at straws, but this one act of concession seemed like a solid foundation. Annemarie was eager to build on it, but first, she had to uncover his darkest demon, the secret that brought on the dark moods.

Joe could hardly be described as carefree, but he was typically easygoing, tolerant and interested in the current order of the day. He carried around a small amount of orneriness, which, fortunately, came through as a dry sense of humor in most instances, and only as its true self when he was riled. Overall, however, Annemarie had never come across a man who possessed the number of appealing qualities as Joe. He had an amazing capacity to cancel out the nonstop serious side of his personality with an outlandish sense of mirthful devilment.

Out of nowhere, though, dark moods transformed the man into a brooding silhouette, someone glazed with the sorrow of a devastating truth, frozen in its torment. Usually, Joe shrank away when these moments struck, paid lip service to Annemarie when necessary and escaped her presence as quickly as possible. Too many times, she had allowed him to leave. The next time it happened, she would refuse his flight.

All of this and more crossed her mind as Annemarie sat beside Joe beneath the shade of the oak tree.

Her mind was made up on this matter, but she would have to move cautiously to break down the walls around Joe or risk a battle with steel beams. However warped his sense of self-protection was, Joe had fought long and hard to build up his barriers. He would not throw up the white flag simply because the woman in his life wanted to dismantle the last wall between them.

Annemarie finally smiled at this last thought, imagining herself as the woman in Joe's life. She loved him enough to want to make love to him, and she sensed he felt the same way. They were far removed from the point of mere friendship in their relationship. Their mutual attraction was too strong to deny, even if they did for the time being.

"You're grinnen like a Cheshire cat," Joe remarked suddenly, interrupting her thoughts. "What's on your mind?"

"Have you ever seen a Cheshire cat?" she countered easily.

"Well, no," he admitted, taken aback.

"Then please spare me the cat references," she said. "I can't stand the little fur balls."

"Not even a good mouser that stays outside?" Joe asked.

She mulled over the possibility. "I suppose I could stand that."

"So why are you grinnen, Annie?" Joe asked again, undeterred by her ploy to change the subject.

Annemarie looked him straight in the eye. "We make a good team," she observed. "On the tennis court," she clarified. "Don't you think so?"

Joe glanced away, though not before he left a crooked smile for her. "It's my serve," he suggested.

Still noncommittal, Annemarie thought, laughing heartily. "Yes, sugar," she agreed. "It is your serve.

"By the way, Joe," she added intently. "I think you should go to church with me tomorrow."

———

Joe refused to accompany Annemarie to church the next day, but they shared supper in his apartment and spent a quiet evening in front of the television. He watched the movie ensconced in his recliner, leaving her to a more uncomfortable spot on the floor with a pillow. As the movie's closing credits rolled across the screen, she suggested her apartment would provide more comfortable seating arrangements for them in the future and pushed herself off the floor to turn down the volume. They both had early mornings awaiting them, and Annemarie figured Joe was ready for sleep just as she was. She made a comment about the movie and turned to tell him goodnight.

Except for the glow of the television screen, the room was dark and she thought he was asleep in the chair. But he wasn't, she realized, on closer inspection. She followed his eyes to the painting on the wall. It was the oak tree in the yard of his family's home. She recalled Joe telling her that it had been a Christmas gift from his brother John, the painter in the family.

Annemarie recognized the moment as one of the dark moods then. Joe sat motionless in the recliner, completely unfocused, even though his eyes were glued on the painting. She would have judged him catatonic, if not for the twitching muscles in his jaw, the narrow set of his eyes and his pursed lips. The man was trapped in a moment, absorbed by the memory of something so profound that it had altered his life radically. There was a devastating truth to be told, and Annemarie sensed Joe would reveal it on this night.

"Tell me about the painten, Joe," she called softly from across the room.

He blinked, shifting his gaze to her. "Huh?"

"The painten?" she repeated, crossing the room, pushing the recliner to an upright position and kneeling before him with her hands on his knees. "Why is it so special?"

"It was a Christmas gift," he replied pensively. "From my brother."

"What was so special about that particular tree?" she pressed.

Joe glanced at the painting. "Last fall was unusual," he shrugged. "We'd never had such a colorful fall around our place. The oak tree was brilliant orange. John wanted to preserve it, I suppose."

"But why did he give it to you?" Annemarie asked quickly. "I feel there's somethen very important about that tree. Please tell me what it is."

He tensed under the pressure. "If I told you I'd rather not discuss it, Annie, would you be disappointed?"

She stared at his lap, then back to his face. "Joe," she replied finally. "I realize this is none of my business, and you have every right to your privacy. I also feel very strongly about our friendship—if that's what you want to call it. Over the last few months, I've bared my soul to you, shared my life story and dragged yours out in bits and pieces. But you're holden somethen back from me, Joe. I figure it must be somethen awful because it causes you to freeze up and frown and disappear inside yourself every now and then, like just now. I'd like to think we mean enough to each other that you could share it with me. Getten it off your chest might help."

For a space of time, Annemarie feared he would reject her. But finally, his brow dipped slightly and a sigh escaped him.

"It's terrible," he suggested, withdrawing involuntarily against the chair, unable to look at her face. "When I tell you this, Annie, you'll never think of me in the same way."

She ran her palms up his thighs, gently reassuring him.

Joe brought his gaze slowly to her. "My brother painted that picture last Halloween," he began. "Later that night, it stormed; the wind and rain ripped off the leaves." He hesitated, then confessed in a whisper, "On that same night, Annemarie, I shot a sixteen-year-old boy. And killed him."

For a quick moment, her conscious thought went black. Then Annemarie felt ghastly, horrified and shaken to the core. She wasn't sure what she had expected Joe to reveal, but it was nothing as gruesome as this. She willed herself expressionless, instinct telling her Joe needed her trust, not any kind of judgment.

He cocked his head, searching her face for a reaction to his revelation, expecting shock, finding only an unshakable belief in his motives.

"An accident," she assumed without any hint of question.

Joe sighed again and swallowed the desire to keep secret the voyeuristic specifics of the deadly night. "The kid's name was Billy Taylor," he said in a cold monotone, tensing hard as steel as he explained the story from start to finish. "I never even really knew who he was—except that he was the son of a man who I loathe, even to this day. A hatemonger, a racist, the worst excuse for a human be'en you could ever imagine. To make a long story short, there's a considerable history of differences between the Bakers and the Taylors."

Joe explained that history in detail.

"Stonewall Jackson?" Annemarie interrupted when he told about Wayne Taylor shooting the family gopher.

"The one and the same," Joe confirmed, moving the tale forward to Halloween day and the circumstances surrounding Billy's accidental shooting of Danny Bartholomew. He then told her about Lucas and their longtime friendship, the dream Lucas expressed years earlier about a good education for his children, the rage he had felt—but never expressed—when the dream had been killed.

Eventually, Joe worked the story back to Danny's shooting, which had been witnessed by Carrie, and later still he told everything he knew about his sister's friendship with Billy Taylor, which was not much—even now, after everything that had happened. He explained Carrie's decision to search for Billy and the family's subsequent discovery that she was missing from the house.

"Everyone presumed the worst when she turned up missen," Joe recalled. "No one ever came right out and said what they were thinken, but you could feel the tension. It was like a silent conspiracy against Billy Taylor, almost as if the kid had stolen into our home, kidnapped Carrie from her bed and was plannen to do somethen awful to her."

Joe led Annemarie step by step through his pursuit of Billy, skirting along the edge of the woods, bogging in the muddied fields, coming finally to the railroad tracks on the far edge of his family's property, where he crossed the fence and made a westward turn, following the railroad's right-of-way. The rain slapped their faces, the fog came in waves and the fear of tragedy waiting to happen built with every step. And then, when it seemed nothing was likely to happen, that he was on a wild goose chase, the fog lifted, a full moon shone down from a break in the clouds and Joe came upon his sister and Billy beside the railroad tracks. Billy was pointing a gun at Carrie; he was going to shoot her. But Joe had fired first, drawing instinctively, bracing his trigger hand with his free hand, aiming at the body. His every move was reactive. One, two, three, four, maybe five seconds—the decision was made ... the act carried out ... the result irreversible.

Time did not stand still. In even less time, Joe had known things were not as they seemed. Billy was flat on his back, and Carrie was screaming.

"The thing was," Joe explained quietly, "the kid never pointed the gun at Carrie at all. She had asked him for it, and he was handen it to her because he couldn't bear to hold it a second longer. He was just a scared, frightened kid, who only wanted his own nightmare to be over and done with. And it was."

When Joe told her that, Annemarie swallowed, a bout of nausea, a wave of sympathy that went down under his intense gaze. She felt pale.

"The bullet struck his heart," Joe told her. "Killed him instantly."

She thought he was finished, maybe hoped that he was. But the horrid details continued.

Joe told her about his desperate search for signs of life in Billy, of unanswered prayers and faith lost; about a pair of clear, slate blue eyes, staring back at him, only not seeing; of forcing those eyes closed because their vacant gaze penetrated his soul; about his sister's anguished cries and frantic fists.

"Why, Joe?" Carrie had asked her brother, her fists pounding into his chest. "Why, why, why?"

Joe had not answered his sister then; he could not answer her now. But he was an innocent man: The sheriff, his father's best friend, believed in Joe's innocence, and a coroner's jury agreed, ruling the death was "accidental."

His voice faltered, then drifted away, and they stared at separate walls for several minutes.

"I see," Annemarie muttered when she could find her voice and look at him.

Joe regarded her carefully, then shook his head. "No, not yet, you don't," he replied at length. "You've heard half the story, Annie. Can you stand the rest of it?"

An involuntary shudder ran through her, and she withdrew her hands from his thighs to a prayerful gesture beneath her chin. At last, she nodded for him to continue.

Joe told her about the dreams that had haunted his sleep for months afterward. Of visions of Billy Taylor running scared and frightened through the woods, chased by bloodhounds and men with revenge on their minds; scratched by briars, chilled by the wind and rain, with nothing but a flimsy T-shirt to ward off the weather. Of reliving his key role in the boy's death night after night, hunting the kid down and shooting Billy time and time again. Of how dreams twisted real life, turning an accident into cold-blooded murder, and then blurred with his waking hours until Joe had begun to question his motives and wonder if he was indeed a killer in sheep's clothing.

The dreams had been unbearable, Joe said, but he had learned to live and function with a minimum of sleep until, finally, the dreams diminished. At some point, he had slept all night without dreaming of Billy Taylor. But when he woke the next morning, he was physically ill, nauseous, wondering what monstrous part of his soul could ever forget the deed or accept it as a done deal. Eventually, even that was gone.

Joe was freed of the guilt, resigned to the will of God, but the memories remained close to him. On occasion, he said, a pair of slate blue eyes stared back at him from a battered face and Joe would wonder who put the bruises there. It was beyond his control, he realized, but he could not help believing Billy Taylor's last days had been one nightmare after another, and that bothered him to no end.

"Now you know the whole story, Annie," he said lamely, his voice hoarse with exhaustion and emotion.

Annemarie was crying silently, her face streaked with tears, and she hated herself for not being strong for him. It struck her that Joe had been a pillar of strength through the whole sad state of affairs. She suspected he could use a strong shoulder to lean on during the hard times.

"I wish I could think of just one thing profound to say about all this," she told him.

He laughed bleakly. "But you can't," he said for her. "It was all so senseless," he groaned with resignation. "So damn senseless. If I could just understand the why of it, then maybe I could get past it."

"I don't think somethen like this is ever understood, Joe," she said. "You just have to accept it."

"I have, but that doesn't make it any easier to ...." He stopped short of finishing the thought.

"To live with," Annemarie finished for him.

Joe eyed her closely. "That sounds like a plea for pity, and I hate pity," he said emphatically.

She nodded agreement. "I know you do," she responded softly. "I'm just tryen to help, Joe. I'd like to help."

"You can't," he declared bluntly. "I know your intentions are good, but this is my problem and I'll handle it my way. Understand that."

"Is your way worken?" Annemarie interrupted him.

"Well enough," Joe replied with quiet authority. "It's my way, Annie, and if it drags me down, then so be it. I can deal with that, too. But I refuse to allow my problems to drag down the people I care about."

She started to argue with him but decided enough had been said for one night. Whatever else she had to tell him was better left to another time.

Quickly, she stood and brushed her lips lightly across his mouth, ignoring the tensing of his posture. "Thank you for tellen me, Joe," she smiled. "Sleep well tonight."

"You, too," he said, relieved that she was leaving.

———

Annemarie stood in the alcove—leaning against the wall beside his door, listening as Joe bolted it for the night—and she made a vow to heal the man. If she could break down the walls around him, she could heal him. And when the time came for action, she planned to use a sledgehammer against those walls, regardless of his will.

His wounds were deep and still raw below the protective scars. Joe was right, too. There had been no sense in what had happened to Billy Taylor. To have such blood on your hands and heart would leave scars on any reasonable person, whatever the reason behind the killing. Someone prone to rash and impulsive decisions, someone who could forgive and forget easily, even someone who needed little justification, would have lasting regrets.

For a split second, Annemarie thought about her dead brother. Jerry and she had never been close. Too much difference in age and temperament doomed any allegiance beyond blood. But Jerry had written a letter to her shortly before he disappeared over Laos, sharing some thoughts on his feelings about the fighting.

"I know those people want to kill me, and it's easy to shoot at them when they're shooting at me," he wrote. "But after it's all over, sometimes I think about what I've done. Taking someone's life is serious business. And living with what you've done can be downright difficult, even when you know you did the right thing."

The letter had made it doubly hard for Annemarie to accept her brother's death. Now, it underscored her thoughts on Joe. Jerry Morgan had been one of those people who acted rashly and impulsively, then forgave and forgot. Yet, he obviously had lost more than his share of sleep over killing people.

For someone like Joe—who was deliberate and precise, who never forgot and rarely forgave himself, who demanded a reason for almost every action—the taking of an innocent life had the power to drive him stark crazy. Long after he recognized that Billy's death had been a horrible accident—as Annemarie believed Joe had done—he was still trying vainly to make sense of a senseless situation. In Joe's way of thinking, there had to be a cause, a reason in the grand scheme of life, to explain why he had fired the bullet that took life from Billy Taylor. Annemarie imagined him trying to make the connection, over and over again, until the effort itself became a meaningless blur, and Joe no longer trusted his instincts or had faith in his ability to make the right choices.

Killing Billy had demolished something vital in Joe's soul. Trying to understand it was destroying the whole man, forcing him to put up his walls of resistance. Isolation was the motive behind his fierce independence. As he'd suggested himself, if Joe went down, he wanted to go by himself, the captain of his own ship.

Annemarie thought now she understood at last why he always found excuses to avoid a weekend trip home to visit his family, why he refused to allow anyone to get close to him. If he did go down, Joe wanted the people close to him as far away as possible in order to spare them as much heartache as possible. It was a noble sentiment, Annemarie supposed, but downright stupid at heart. Because if the people closest to Joe were anything like those he described when telling her about his family, then they could not be spared—just as he would not be spared if the situation were reversed.

Fortunately, Joe was not a stupid person. He merely needed someone to straighten him out, someone to help him see the virtue of having people in his life who cared about him through good times and bad times, someone who could penetrate those hard walls of isolation. If he could be convinced or cajoled or even forced to rely on his instincts and feelings once again, Joe would slay the demons of doubt that undermined his ability to trust himself.

The man needed an outlet. And Annemarie was ready and willing to accept him.

———

Her overly optimistic approach aside in the campaign to rescue Joe from his walls of self-doubt—despite the forbearance she carried into battle—Annemarie was unprepared for the man's stubborn resistance.

Plenty of factors worked against her effort, all of them attributable to Joe's resolve to face his enemies as a solitary warrior. None of them, however, proved a more formidable opponent than the one powerful demon Annemarie had failed to consider, the one intolerable specter whose presence turned her radar completely awry and allowed her to overlook her own past, which was littered with the memory of wandering souls consumed by evil spirits.

She hadn't reckoned on the demon alcohol, with a power all its own to ruin her fight for Joe's soul. Once she did, however, Annemarie was worried and frightened—worried that she could not win against liquor and frightened that booze would alter Joe into someone not worth the fight.

This sobering truth assailed her one night in the early dog days of late July as she observed Joe passed out on the recliner in his living room. He had broiled steaks for them earlier in the evening, guzzling down the majority of a six-pack of beer while cooking and eating the meal, then switching to icy vodka as they settled down to a listless game of gin rummy. Bored with the cards, they had drifted into another one of their discovery conversations, started when she casually asked Joe to explain the appeal of beer and liquor.

"If you ever tasted a cold beer on a hot night like this, you'd understand the appeal," Joe said. "It's refreshment for a parched throat."

Annemarie had made her mistake there, allowing him to get away with the pat answer. She had compounded the error a moment later when Joe inquired whether she wanted to try beer.

"No, and I never have," she assured him quickly. "The smell of it's bad enough, sugar. Heaven forbid if it touched my lips." She hesitated. "I have always harbored a secret desire to try one certain drink."

"What's that?" he asked, intrigued.

Annemarie shamelessly confessed to the longtime wish for a mint julep. "I like to consider myself the core of Southern femininity," she teased, exaggerating the drawl of her sultry voice. "It's purely scandalous that a paragon of Southern virtue such as myself has never tasted the most gracious drink of our fabled culture. Sugar, do you realize I could be kicked out of the Daughters of the Confederacy if my secret were ever revealed."

Joe pretended to be aghast. "Then let's remedy the situation right now and avert a scandal," he proposed gleefully. "One mint julep comen up for the core of Southern femininity."

He jumped off his bar stool and strolled into the kitchen, then suddenly pivoted her way as he rounded the corner of the bar. "Uh-oh," he said with a furrowed brow. "We've got a small problem, sugar. I have no idea how to make a mint julep."

"Don't look at me," she laughed. "I don't even know what a julep is."

"This is truly scandalous," Joe suggested as devilment crossed his smoldering eyes. "Two hearty Southerners such as ourselves, so ignorant of our culture. I propose we rectify the situation, immediately."

"How so, kind sir?"

"Come with me you paragon of Southern virtue," he teased, grabbing her hand and ushering Annemarie to the door. "I'm taken you out for mint juleps."

Although it went against the grain of her nature, Annemarie had accepted the proposal, caught up in the lightness of the moment. "My strict Baptist upbringen warns me against this, and I certainly don't think the Daughters of the Confederacy would approve," she told him as they walked onto the street. "But what the hay. Let's go for it."

Joe had taken her to a bar somewhere between Tenth and Fourteenth Streets—one of the hipper, wilder sections of the city crowded with vagrants, hippies, flower children and thousands of young people like themselves, along with gawkers and curiosity seekers. He candidly admitted to frequenting the bars along this strip on many of the evenings they spent apart. Annemarie had gone there several times as well, as a curiosity seeker, and although she enjoyed the area's diversity and energy, a feeling of comfort always eluded her. Tonight had been no exception.

"Vastly overrated," she grimaced to Joe an hour later with most of the bourbon concoction still in her glass. "I'll settle for be'en scandalized and ignorant."

Joe smiled drunkenly at her, the result of two powerful mixed drinks on top of the alcohol he had consumed earlier in the evening. "May I try it?" he asked.

"Don't you think you've had enough?" she suggested.

"Probably," he agreed. "But who's counten?"

He laughed humorlessly before downing the remainder of the minty drink in one swallow.

"Let's go, Joe," Annemarie pleaded.

He'd complied reluctantly with her request, and she had hoped the walk home would sober him. Instead, the liquor had settled in, slurring his speech and turning his movements awkward. As soon as she opened the door to his apartment, Joe had headed straight for the recliner, collapsed in it and maintained consciousness barely long enough to jerk the chair into its repose. He had been in the same position for the past half hour, with his head cocked to one side as his chest rose and fell to the rhythm of a heavy sleep.

Annemarie wanted to kick herself for either missing or ignoring all the warning signs of someone with a drinking problem. She'd heard stories all her life about her father's addiction to the bottle, lived with its consequences since the day of her birth and witnessed firsthand liquor's contribution to her brother's downfall. Countless times, her mother had warned Annemarie to avoid—at all costs—men contaminated by the demon alcohol.

"They'll drag you down right along with them," Frances Morgan had told her daughter a few weeks before she died. "When I married your father, I was sure I could change him, make him love me more than the bottle. But I was wrong, Annemarie. I couldn't change him because he didn't want to be changed. The demon alcohol's grip was too strong for me to beat."

Her mother's warning came rushing back as Annemarie gazed sadly at Joe and realized her predicament. As much as she loved Joe, she was frightened by the dreadful prospect of making the same mistake her mother had made, committing to a man who had brought her heartache and misery more than anything else. She recalled many times having heard the theory of children doomed to repeat the mistakes of their parents and the sad stories of those who put that theory into practice. She wondered whether her life, brimming over with good things, had spoiled her with success, leaving her unprepared, perhaps even unwilling, to make the hard choices in crucial decisions.

Annemarie wanted to believe otherwise, yet her recent track record suggested she was willing to fool herself. Liquor had never appealed to her in any form, fashion or shape—not even in mint juleps. Although the idea of mint juleps rolled graciously across Southern culture, with its vision of women in long, white dresses, wearing wide straw hats and sitting on stately verandahs, Annemarie had never bought into that image. She simply had been carried away by the teasing nature of their conversation earlier in the night when she voiced the desire to sample a mint julep. She should have told Joe she abhorred alcohol when he offered to take her out for a drink. Yet, Annemarie had backed down from her teetotaler beliefs, as she had done ever since meeting Joe. Maybe there had been some subconsciously absurd assumption that her tolerance of his drinking represented a cosmopolitan, sophisticated outlook on life. But there was nothing glamorous to be found in that flawed assumption now as she stared at the drunken man in the chair. She felt only disgust with herself and Joe—along with the still sobering truth that she loved the man and wanted him.

Annemarie rolled her eyes in disbelief at the exceptions she remained willing to make for Joe, this unswerving notion that he could be transformed into the whole man of her dreams. She still wanted to fight for him, for his soul, his sanity. And admittedly, she wanted the fight for herself, too.

She thought again of the warning about the demon alcohol uttered in the dying days of Frances Morgan. It was sage advice. Nevertheless, Annemarie found a glimmer of hope in her mother's warning, a small flicker of light in the dark tunnel. Perhaps her father had not wanted to change his ways. From all accounts, Thad Morgan had been a foolhardy man who enjoyed a jug of moonshine, a rousing good time, and damned the consequences.

But Joe was not that kind of man. Annemarie refused to believe he wanted to be chained to liquor. And she refused to believe that he could love a bottle more than he loved her.

JOE FELT LIKE A first-class heel. Two weeks had elapsed since he turned an enjoyable evening with Annemarie into a personal drinking binge, and not a word had passed between them. She probably despised him, which might be just as well he thought, but Joe wanted to make amends nonetheless.

He had not avoided her intentionally. In fact, Joe had missed her more than he thought possible. He had even laid off the booze these past two weeks, knowing the gesture would please her, unwilling to share it with her.

As much as he had missed her, Joe figured the time apart had done them a world of good. They needed to put some distance between them. Their relationship had reached its limit, given the boundaries set by Annemarie. He could have extended those boundaries, and Joe was willing to admit the idea of marriage had crossed his mind once or twice. But he wasn't husband material. Joe knew that now, and Annemarie probably realized it as well.

He thought about the marriages of his parents and grandparents, perhaps even envied their companionship and shared experiences. Then, he forced his mood to brighten, thinking of another wedding apparently in the offing, even if the intended bride had yet to receive the proposal.

This idea of Summer married to the man who had orchestrated the funeral of her first fiancé seemed downright improbable to Joe. Still, it was uplifting to see a measure of happiness emerging from the sorrow of Tom's death. If a wedding between Summer and Mark Applegate came to pass, Joe thought, Tom probably would come down from Heaven to give his personal blessing. It was easy to imagine Tom chuckling in that quiet way of his over the bodaciousness of Summer to fall in love again under such uncanny circumstances—perhaps even suggesting she tie on a tobacco bikini for the walk down the aisle.

Such thoughts had been with Joe all day—of Tom and Summer, Summer and Mark, of his family and friends back home. He was fighting homesickness, brought on by a visit from Mark Applegate, who had stayed overnight in Joe's apartment before catching an early flight to Oklahoma this Saturday morning. They had talked late into the night, then overslept this morning, leaving themselves with a race to the airport so that Mark could catch his flight.

Joe genuinely liked Mark. The lieutenant was affable, honest and disarming, with a good measure of humor. Summer was fortunate to have someone like Mark, a sentiment he suspected ran both ways. Mark had seemed cocksure of himself when he announced casually that he expected to marry Summer, even while admitting she was still warming up to the idea of him as the man in her life.

"She went out with a few other guys earlier this year," Mark said easily. "Mainly because I think she needed space between Tom and me. But she's coming around to the idea that we're meant for each other."

Joe had let out a low whistle. "I have to admit, Mark: I find it strange how things are worken out between the two of you," he remarked. "Especially consideren your point of origin. This ain't exactly the typical romance."

"You're telling me," Mark replied with a sigh. "How would you like to compete with a ghost for the woman you love?"

The question had endless implications for Joe, but he confined his speculation to his sister and Mark. "Summer has never struck me as someone who would compare Tom with other men," he said, a bit defensively. "If you're under the impression that she's tryen to determine how you stack up to Tom, then I'm willen to bet you're wrong. I know my sister better than that."

"No, no, you misunderstand me," Mark explained. "I don't think Summer is comparing the two of us at all, but she is still getting used to the idea that life goes on after Tom. Your sister is not someone who feels things lightly. In fact, I've yet to run across anyone in your family who does that. I've gotten to know them well this last year, and they're as fine a bunch of people as I've ever met."

He paused, then continued. "Summer will never forget Tom, and I don't expect her to. She understands there's a life still ahead of her, but reaching out to embrace it fully is something else. She's taking her time to do that, but I'm a patient man. And your sister is about ready to reach out to me."

Surprisingly, at Mark's request, they had also spoken extensively about Tom, bringing back a host of good memories to Joe as he reminisced about the good times between himself and his late best friend.

"Why are you interested in Tom?" he asked finally.

Mark mulled over his answer. "I guess for Dan and Amelia's sake," he answered at length. "Now you may think this is truly strange, but they've become like second parents to me. Tom was the focal point of their lives. They're brave folks, but they feel his loss keenly. I care for them, Joe, and maybe I'm looking for information that will help me better understand their feelings. That might sound cornball, but I can't help it."

"It's not cornball at all," Joe assured him. "You're doen somethen for Dan and Amelia that I wish I could have done after Tom was killed. I had good intentions, but instead, I retreated from them."

"Because of that demonstration business?" Mark suggested.

"Partly," Joe conceded. "But more because I never figured out how to approach them. Tom always had more rapport with my family than I did with Dan and Amelia. I don't know," he sighed. "Maybe I was so uncomfortable with what went down around the time Tom died that I was too embarrassed to approach them and offer my support. Or maybe I was just too scared. To this day, I don't know why I never went up to them and told them what a great guy their son was and how much I would miss him."

"They know how you felt about Tom," Mark said soothingly. "They've told me a few stories about the two of you."

"What do you think about Vietnam?" Joe asked abruptly.

"I prefer not to, although in my line of work, it's hard not to," Mark answered. "Who knows what to think? It's a bad situation, getting worse. Maybe one day soon, it'll be finished. I feel sorry for the guys sent over there, the ones who come back in body bags, the ones who come back strung out and the ones who come home to find nobody cares anymore."

"That's sort of how I feel about it these days," Joe mused. "I used to think this war was the worst thing ever to happen to this country, but the country will recover one day. I feel sorry for the guys, though, maybe even a little guilty that I'm over here nice and comfortable while they're sloggen it out over there."

Mark frowned. "Joe, you served two years in the Marines. You did your time."

"Yea, but it's not the same," Joe replied. "It was a cushy gig—writing stories and never leaving the states. You can't compare that with those guys serven in Vietnam."

"You're not Super Man, Joe, and you can't save the world," Mark said. "You did what you were asked to do; you even volunteered when your bad knee offered a legitimate way out. That's a lot more than all these guys who never had any excuse. Just plenty of daddy's money, influence and maybe even smarts on their side."

Joe pondered the thought, and Mark closed the subject once and for all: "It's like I said before, Joe. Who knows what to think about all this?"

"Who knows?" Joe repeated.

"When are you coming home?" Mark had asked as they drifted toward sleep. "I'm supposed to ask. Your family really misses you."

"Soon, I hope," Joe had replied. "Pretty soon."

That was when the homesickness had begun to creep inside Joe, and it had been with him ever since.

He missed talking with Summer and John and seeing Luke and Bonnie discover whole new dimensions about themselves. He missed the nurturing love between his parents, their private kisses and the way they communicated with their eyes and expressions. He missed his grandparents' feisty rapport, and he missed Carrie simply because he had no idea what was going on in her life. His sister had placed herself off limits from him, and no one else had divulged any details about her.

Joe came close to telephoning the family right then and there to tell them he was coming home the next weekend. Something held him back, however, perhaps an awareness that he had not been completely separated from them during the last eight months. In addition to Mark Applegate's overnight stay, he had received periodic visits from both family and friends. Paul Berrien and his sisters had visited his apartment on a weekend shopping trip to Atlanta. Even Dan and Amelia Carter had spent an hour with Joe one Sunday afternoon before returning home from a small business convention in the city. His father had visited Joe's apartment twice, once when he accompanied Paul on sheriff's business shortly after Joe came to Atlanta and again less than two months ago when he and Caroline had stayed overnight after selling a load of produce at the Farmer's Market. Another trip to the Farmer's Market had rewarded Joe with an overnight visit from his brothers, who skipped a day of school to deliver a truckload of collards to Atlanta.

Remembering the rowdy visit with his brothers, Joe thought again of Annemarie. She had wanted to meet John and Luke, just as she had wanted to meet the Berriens, the Carters and his parents, too. But Annie had been working when the Carters dropped by and his parents made their visit, and Joe had nixed the idea of acquainting her with the Berriens and his brothers, simply by withholding an invitation when Annemarie hinted for one. Joe knew she had been eager to put faces with names, yet he concluded her presence might give the wrong impression about their relationship. She had been disappointed with him then, as she probably was now.

He would try to make it up to her.

———

"Hi, stranger."

The greeting came from Joe as Annemarie eased open her apartment door. His shoulder rested against the doorway, and his dark eyes regarded her with an intense show of repentance. She stifled a laugh before it developed, seeing right through the beguiling surface to the glint of mischief in those eyes. The man obviously knew the way to her heart.

"Hi yourself," she said, wedging her face between the cracked door.

Impulsively, he leaned forward and kissed the tip of her nose, sealing the apology. "Thought I'd better come over and beg forgiveness for my latest bad show," he repented. "I've missed you these last two weeks."

Annemarie had missed him as well, although she had put their time apart to good use. She had worked overtime to make extra money, and she had done considerable thinking about herself and Joe.

"And to think, sugar, all this time, I thought you were ignoren me," she told him.

"Not on your life," Joe said. "I've been busy with work. My erstwhile editor has had me on the road most of the last two weeks." A gag registered his distaste for the assignment. "Coveren politics of all things," he explained.

"Oh," she replied knowingly.

Joe had earned his reporter's reputation by covering real people, whose lives were touched by events and circumstances. Politics seemed removed from the rigors of real life, except for those occasions when the business affected the people up close and personal. And politicians, wearying with their constant bickering and posturing, rarely related to real people as far as Joe could tell.

"Did you to complain to Ray Fields about such shabby treatment of his star reporter?" Annemarie asked teasingly.

"I did," Joe confirmed. "But only mildly."

"And Ray was unmoved by the mildness of your objection, I take it," she surmised.

"Mildly unmoved," Joe replied with a grin. "He suggested that if I had any ideas of becomen a prima donna—a few adjectives notwithstanden—then I could get my heart set on a career as a political reporter. So, of course, I told him I'd be very happy to traipse after the peanut farmer from Plains who wants to be the next governor of the great state of Georgia. I made Ray a very happy man."

"And what did it do for you, sugar?" Annemarie asked, a teasing smile on her face.

"It sent me traipsen all across the state after the man," Joe frowned. "Seven days on the road, and I've seen every nook and cranny, every curve and every bump this state has to offer, from Ringgold to Valdosta and from Savannah to Columbus. It also earned me a boxed story on tomorrow's front page, with a full-page spread on the inside. It's a dazzlen piece of work, if I say so myself."

"Did Ray think so?" she inquired.

"Do you really have to ask?" Joe boasted, deliberately out of character. "He realizes the priority that prima donnas like myself place on open admiration of our talents." He paused, then a grin split his face. "Of more importance though, the effort has earned me a reprieve from any more politicians, temporarily at least," he explained, pausing thoughtfully before concluding, "though this particular one was not bad. He seems sincerer than most, which, of course, means he's doomed to failure in the world of politics."

Amusement turned to curiosity as Annemarie listened to the story. "Did any of these highways and byways take you to Cookville?" she asked.

"Only as close as Valdosta," he answered blithely. "Cookville's too far off the beaten path even for aspiren peanut farmers."

"But it's only thirty-five miles or so from Valdosta," she pointed out. "You could have stopped by for a quick visit with your family."

"We were on a tight schedule," Joe explained, fending off the accusation in her voice. "I called them just before we left town. They got a kick out of knowen I was so close."

Annemarie frowned. "They would have gotten a bigger kick had their firstborn paid a visit home," she suggested.

"Next time," Joe replied with an uninterested shrug, then changed the subject. "What did you do while I was gallivanten across the state?"

She allowed this sore spot between them to drop. "I haven't been around much either," she explained. "I had a couple of layovers in New York and then filled in on some flights to Boston on my days off."

Joe smiled again as he imagined Annemarie rushing madly about New York in her haste to see as much of the city as possible in a few short hours, which she did every time the opportunity presented itself. He also resisted the urge to kiss her once more, this time on the slightly puckered, pouting lips as she told him about visiting the Metropolitan Museum of Art and attending the Boston Symphony.

"I guess Boston to the north has a little more to offer than Boston to the south," he remarked when she was finished.

"Not of the really important things," she shot back, fixing a reproachful glare on him. "I would have traded the symphony for a visit home, especially if I had been a mere thirty-five miles from either of the two."

Joe rolled his eyes. "Okay, Annemarie!" he relented. "You've made your point, and I get it. But honestly, Annie, I didn't have the time to make it home. We were on a tight schedule, rushen from here to there."

He appealed to her forgiving nature with such penitence in his eyes that Annemarie scolded herself for her busybody ways. "I'm sorry," she apologized. "You probably think I'm tryen to pick a fight."

Joe gave her a crooked smile. "Nah," he shrugged. "You're just tryen to run my life."

Another pout crossed her face. "I am not tryen to run your life, either," she replied, then added smugly, "I'm just tryen to put it in perspective."

Joe gave an exasperated laugh. "Would you settle for supper at my place tonight?" he asked.

Annemarie mocked serious consideration of the offer, then finally consented. "I could settle for that. What time?"

————

An hour later, Annemarie let herself into Joe's apartment with the key he had given her a few months earlier. A mouth-watering aroma of seasoned cooking assaulted her nostrils, blowing away expectations of the broiled steaks and baked potatoes that Joe usually served. She closed the door, leaned against it and savored the peppery aroma wafting through the apartment.

Moments like this carried her thoughts back home to Boston—and then forward to another place, where the delicious aromas were her makings and they would be appreciated by Joe. Yet, as much as she craved the tradition of home and hearth, Annemarie would willingly settle for an alternative, as long as Joe was part of the mix. Over the last two weeks, she had come to understand the meaning of "Home is where the heart is." The idea had particular relevance for Joe and her, two people born with a wanderlust. With so many things to do and places to see, neither Joe nor Annemarie was ready to be tied to home and hearth. Just maybe, however, they were ready to begin making their own home for the day somewhere down the road when the urge to work and travel would give way to the desire for children and the same hearth to lie down beside each night.

She checked her imagination, long after it had been carried away with presumption. Marriage to Joe might make for an unusual mix in the beginning, but the main ingredients would be there for the duration. Of course, the big assumption in her plans for happily ever after was that Joe felt the same way. The major flaw was assuming that even if Joe wanted to marry her, he would find the peace and faith within himself necessary to bring them together as husband and wife.

Perhaps later tonight, she would discover the accuracy of her assumptions. Joe would think she was meddling in his life again, but it was her business that Annemarie was looking out for as well. Their lives had intertwined, and her future hinged on Joe. She needed to know whether her heart was free to love or wrapped up in a strangling wisteria bush. If she had to lose Joe, better it be now than later when her heart was beyond saving.

Whatever the outcome, the time had come for push to shove. In the last two weeks, more than anything, Annemarie had discovered how hard it was to live without Joe. The sense of loss had been aching. But the uncertainty about where they stood with each other overrode any sense of loss, compelling her to fight for answers. A risky proposition, perhaps, but things of worth often came with risks. And besides, Annemarie had a history of good things on her side. If life went her way, then it was meant to be. If not, then she would pick up and move on to whatever else waited for her.

She forced herself to think optimistically, taking a deep breath to calm her nerves. In doing so, she glanced down at the key in her hand and blushed at the reason she carried it in her possession.

Annemarie had volunteered to wash his clothes, sure signs of a desperate woman and a lame excuse if ever there was one to win over a man's heart. Joe had condemned her suggestion as ridiculous at the outset, telling her that maid service was not a requirement of their friendship. In the end, she had gotten her way, with some preposterous explanation about always needing extra clothes to round out the load in the washing machine, an idea only someone as completely ill-suited to household chores as Joe could have believed. Even at that, he had been circumspect, until Annemarie assured him the offer would not have been forthcoming if it would cause her the least inconvenience. He had agreed reluctantly, but only to the basics of his wardrobe, socks, underwear, jeans and such. His white dress shirts and trousers continued to go to the cleaners once a week, which was fine with Annemarie. Even she had limits: She would not slave over an ironing board to finagle her way into any man's heart.

A smile lit up her face as she suddenly called to Joe and crossed the room to knock on his closed bedroom door.

"Be out in a second," he shouted. "I grabbed a quick shower."

"You've had company from home," she accused, stopping at the closed door. "I can smell the evidence."

"What makes you think I haven't turned into a veritable chef over the last two weeks?" he teased through the door.

"Sugar, not even the great chefs of France could turn you into a cook of any means, even if they had two years to try," Annemarie joked back. "Broiled steaks aside," she amended because Joe did very well indeed with that one meal. "Who came this time?" she asked with a sigh. "And why was I once again denied the courtesy of an invitation to join you?"

The door opened suddenly, and Joe stood a foot from her, bare-chested and barefooted in blue jeans, with tousled damp hair, smelling soapy clean. Pure sexual attraction made Annemarie want to swoon in his arms. Or drag the man into the nearby bed.

"Do me a favor," he said as she tried to decide which of the two options held more appeal. "The food's warmen in the oven. Please go check on it while I brush my teeth. And then, I promise I'll answer every one of your questions and throw in the kitchen sink as well."

Involuntarily, she licked her lips. Or maybe it was willfully. Regardless of her motive, the effect transformed the teasing glint in Joe's eyes to smoking desire. Boldly, Annemarie leaned forward and kissed him lightly on the lips.

"I've missed you, too," she said softly, her breath spilling warm across his face.

Joe caught her swiftly, crushed her warm body against him and smothered the woman with the desire of a kiss too long denied by both of them. His hands explored her through the clothes, and her own fingers raked slowly down his chest, coming to rest just inside the band of his jeans, pressing slightly against his bare stomach. He groaned, deepened the kiss, and she responded with equal passion, aching with desire.

Joe pulled her inside the bedroom, closed the door and leaned her against the wall, pressing closer, breaking the kiss only to nibble at her ear and neck. She kissed him in the hollow of his neck and pulled his lips back to her mouth, fully surrendered to their passion. When their kiss ended, she slumped weakly against his chest, the rubbery pliancy of her body matched by the tremble in his knees. His arousal expanded and throbbed against her shorts, coming with a rapid upheaval in his breathing, and the whole effect melted her insides. Annemarie wanted him badly as he pulled her closer, resting his jaw atop her head. Her own breath came in short bursts, with her head buried against his chest.

"This isn't supposed to happen between friends," he said raggedly.

"It didn't," she managed to say.

Joe backed slightly away at the implication, then brought her against him once more. It was hard to read his thoughts, but she knew instinctively that he was beyond a point of no return, where she could ask him to make love to her and not even his sense of honor would stop him. Annemarie was there herself, but she wanted a commitment first, so she forced herself from him, pulling away with an intake of breath to override her raging desire.

"I should go check on the food," she commented vaguely, grasping for the door-knob.

Joe found it for her, opening the door, and Annemarie stumbled from the room, unwilling to look him in the eye because she knew they would not walk away from another moment of intimacy.

Joe was several long minutes in following her to the kitchen.

———

"I thought we could make sandwiches," he suggested upon joining her in the kitchen.

Propped against the refrigerator door, she nodded agreement. Joe had taken another cold shower, which apparently had calmed the coursing blood of his passion, but there was no relief for Annemarie, except the steady assault of chatter aimed her way as he explained the reason for this unexpected feast of fried cubed steak, creamed corn, fresh butterbeans and ripe tomatoes.

Little by little, the tension seeped out of her, though not the desire. It was impossible to stay keyed up as Joe showed off the bounty of his visit from Mark Applegate. He was like a little boy with a secret treasure to share, showing off one container after another of the food sent to him by his mother and grandmother. There was fried chicken and dressing, ham and dumplings, fresh vegetables and potato salad—enough food to last him for a week, all ready to eat once it was warmed on the stove. Caroline also had packed along a butternut cake. "And," he finally concluded with a flourish as he opened a large plastic container for her inspection, "Summer baked me four dozen molasses cookies."

"They're my favorite, you know," he added a moment later, suddenly embarrassed by his giddiness.

"I know," she smiled. "Are you sure you want to share this stuff, Joe? I'd understand if you wanted to save it all for yourself. Every little morsel I eat brings you that much closer to another TV dinner. And, sugar, you know what an appetite I have."

"I know," he laughed. "And I'm sure."

The food was delicious. They spread steak sauce over bread, slapped on hunks of tender fried meat and gorged themselves. Joe provided the pertinent details of his visit with Mark as they ate, and Annemarie expounded on the earlier account of her overnight stays in New York and Boston.

"Oh, one more thing," Joe said abruptly as they lingered over second helpings of cake and coffee. "I can't believe I almost forget, but I think my sister's gonna get married."

"Do tell," Annemarie drawled.

Joe tried to remember the way Mark had explained the nuptials allegedly to come. "Well, apparently, Summer's not fully aware of it just yet," he said. "But Mark assures me it's just a matter of time. From the way he described things between them, I'm inclined to agree with the lieutenant."

"She's gonna marry the guy who presided over her first fiancé's funeral," Annemarie remarked more to herself than Joe.

"I know it sounds weird," Joe nodded. "I found it bizarre myself at first," he continued, shrugging off the first impression. "But later, when I really thought about it, the whole situation struck me as entirely appropriate for someone unpredictable like Summer.

"And more importantly," he continued somberly, "I think Mark Applegate is a good man. He'll do well by Summer, and that's the main thing to consider. She can't live her entire life in the shadow of memories. What good would that do?"

Annemarie stared skeptically at Joe, slow to accept that he had given her the perfect opportunity to bring up the subject of the evening. "Do you really believe that, Joe?"

"Sure, I do," he confirmed. "Tom Carter was a great guy, the best I've ever known. But as awful as it is, even now, he's dead and gone. I would hate to see my sister stay bound to a past that cannot be changed."

The unshackled sincerity of Joe's thoughtfulness and love for his sister unleashed a powerful yearning within Annemarie, as well as deepened her belief that the two of them could fulfill any longing in each other. She smiled her thoughts, even as a more sobering idea clouded her face. As impossible as it seemed in light of his recipe for Summer's happiness, Joe completely missed the relevance of that philosophy to his own life. The man was clueless when it came to realizing that not only his happiness but his entire well-being depended on his ability to apply those truths to his own situation.

"Well said, Joe," she told him gently, demanding his full attention with the softness of her voice. "I wonder whether you can see the wisdom of your own advice."

He stiffened immediately into uncomfortable posture. "What are you driven at?" he shrugged.

Annemarie stiffened her backbone, drew guns and fired the first volley at the hard walls around Joe. "It's simple," she replied evenly. "I want to know, Joe—I need to know—if you intend to stay bound to a past that cannot be changed. Are you goen to live in the shadow of your memories?"

His eyes turned darkly cold, piercing with their fury, but Annemarie held her ground, matching his glare with a determined expression.

"Well?" she asked a moment later. "Do I get my answer?"

"Leave it alone, Annie," Joe told her, his voice low and hesitant as he reached across the bar for a pack of cigarettes and his lighter.

Annemarie nodded, understanding his will, but she refused to accept his wishes. "We have to talk about it, Joe," she countered as he tapped a cigarette from the package, stuck it between his lips and lit the tip.

"For my peace of mind if nothen else," she added softly.

"I've said everything there is to say," he said gruffly. "Anything else on the subject is none of your business and shouldn't mean a hill of beans to your peace of mind."

Annemarie refused to take offense at his highhanded tone. "Your business has everything to do with my peace of mind," she said patiently. "You know as well as I do, Joe, that there's somethen between us. But your past is standen in the way. It's not letten happen what should happen between us."

Joe inhaled deeply on the cigarette, then dismounted the stool and walked into the kitchen, putting the bar between them. "What do you want from me, Annie?" he asked bluntly. "Why do you keep senden all these mixed signals?"

"I'm not the only one senden them," she interrupted, sounding defensive even to herself. "They're comen my way, too."

"From day one," Joe continued, his tone lethally composed, his eyes boring right through her, "*you* set the boundaries in our relationship, and I've done my part to honor them. If you want a roll in the hay, I'm more than willen to go along for the ride. But if you're looken for somethen more substantial from me, then you're barken up the wrong tree and wasten your time."

"Charmen, Joe," she spat back instinctively, without the bat of an eye. "Is this a new tactic from the man of steel?" she asked, turning on the sarcasm. "A new way to keep the world at arm's length? Do hurt unto others before they do it unto you— before they get too close and threaten your precious self-control."

Her breath came harshly, and his calculated indifference impaled her heart. Annemarie succumbed to the hurt feelings, dabbing at an eye to wipe away the beginning of tears.

"Oh, gosh, Annie," Joe apologized immediately, stepping toward her and dropping his cigarette into the ashtray. "I'm sorry."

She waved him off, finding renewed strength in her shame. "No need to feel sorry for me," she said frankly. "If I mean nothen more to you than a potential roll in the hay, then I'm of far too little consequence for you to have feelens of any kind."

Joe reached across the bar and placed his hand on her wrist, compelling Annemarie to look at him. "That was uncalled for and downright mean of me," he said sincerely. "You know how much you mean to me."

"No, I don't, Joe," she replied. "But a little clarity on the matter would be appreciated."

"You're my friend," he tried. "My best friend."

Annemarie shook her head, rejecting the answer. "People who are just friends don't have these kinds of feelens between them," she determined, pulling away her hand from him. "They don't fall into each other's arms without warning. They don't have tension between them that's thick enough to cut with a knife because they're holden back on their feelens. Admit it, Joe. We're more than friends, more than best friends. There are deep feelens between us."

Joe reached for his cigarette only to find the fire dead. He lit another one, took a long drag and exhaled.

"Maybe so," he conceded at last. "But Annie ...." His voice drifted off to a whisper. "I don't want those kinds of emotions in my life right now. I don't have room for them. I can't deal with them."

"Why not?" she asked, rising from her seat to join him in the kitchen.

Joe stared blankly at her, then shrugged off the answer. "I just can't," he replied flatly, massaging his temples.

Give the man credit for his honesty, Annemarie thought sadly. His feelings were so bottled up inside him that she doubted whether Joe could recognize them, much less express them. Still, one way or another, she intended to reach inside his heart and head, and drag out all that clutter.

"I can accept that," she relented, then moved decisively forward with her effort as Joe retrieved a beer from the refrigerator.

"But I can't accept that," she complained as he popped the top.

"Huh?"

"You said I was your friend, Joe, your best friend," she charged ahead, taking the can from his hand and setting it on the counter top. "So let's talk strictly as one friend to another for a minute."

Annemarie took a deep breath, swallowed any lingering misgivings about the appropriateness of her comments and informed Joe that he drank too much. "Way,

way too much," she emphasized. "I say that not because of what happened two weeks ago, but because of what I've seen with you from almost the very day we met. You guzzle down beer, and you're hitten the hard stuff heavy. Have you considered the possibility that you're drinken to forget the past, Joe?"

His eyes narrowed, angered by the meddlesome flow of the conversation. "Do you always get your way?" he asked with another humorless laugh.

"I hate it when you laugh that way," she replied, "and this is not about getten my way. It's about asken my friend to wise up and take a good look at where he's headed. I've told you before, and I really like to think that I can give a fresh perspective to your way of looken at things."

"Come off it, Annie!" Joe shouted. "What gives you the right to come in here with all your advice on how I should run my life? You may be my friend, but I'm tired of your interference if the truth be known."

He reached around her defiantly, picking up the beer and then moving toward the doorway. "With you, Annemarie, it's always, 'Do this, Joe. Do that, Joe. Come to church, Joe.' Well, Annemarie, I don't need your advice and I don't want you to run my life. I'm doen fine on my own, thank you."

He punctuated his tirade by draining half of the beer can in one long drink, and Annemarie laughed at his close-minded view of himself.

"Oh, you're doen fine all right," she quipped. "If you can't summon up the will-power to forget the past, then you can always escape into the liquor."

"Shut up, Annie!" Joe growled, advancing toward her. "Shut up and go home."

"Too close to the truth, aren't I?" she pressed, folding arms against her stomach. "Well, have another drink, Joe, and maybe it won't seem like I came so close. One more drink after that, and maybe you'll forget how close I came to the truth alto-gether. And then, if you still remember, you can have another drink to forget. Do you get the picture, Joe? Is that what you want out of life? Is that what you're redu-cen yourself, too?"

"Just go home," he mumbled, half-listening.

"Just walk away, right, Joe? That's what you're doen," Annemarie pushed on. "Makes it so much easier to shut me out, shut out your family, shut out the whole world and wallow in your guilt."

He walked away from her then, out of the kitchen into the living room.

"That's what it all comes down to, Joe," she observed, trailing him at a distance. "You can't accept what happened, and you can't bear to let anyone think you're less than perfect behind those steely expressions. You can't live with yourself, and, therefore, you don't see any reason why anybody else should have to put up with you. You'll probably never forgive me for suggesten this, but I don't believe for one minute that you're as cucumber cool on the inside as the icy exterior suggests. In fact, I get the distinct impression that all this guilt is eaten away your precious self-control. Or could it be that your self-control is eroden your guilt, and you can't bear the thought of forgetten what happened?"

Annemarie hated herself for laying into him like this, for dredging up his care-fully hidden insecurities and poking holes in them. But they needed exposing. If Joe was unwilling or unable to lay them on the line himself, then she would force the man to take a hard look inside his heart and soul, to separate the truth from the lies, the substance from the whole, the certainty from the doubts.

"Are you completely opposed to the idea of people sympathizen with each other when things go wrong in their lives," she asked him, a hard edge in her voice. "Or do you see some point of honor in neither asken for nor wanten sympathy? I realize how important your composure is to you, Joe. But what if I told you that your precious composure is turnen slowly into mush? Or that keepen everything inside you and then drinken to forget eventually will turn you into a nervous wreck that no amount of willpower can control? What if I told you that the one quality you seem to value most about yourself—be'en a man of steel emotions—is the one you can least afford at this point in life?"

Her voice softened considerably. "Is it really so hard to let someone care about you, Joe? Or to share the rough and tough spots in life? Don't you want somebody, anybody, to share those feelens with you?

"Can't somebody get close to you, Joe, close enough to touch who you really are?" she concluded, reaching her hand to caress the bony jut of collarbone and massage the strained tendons in his neck. "Will you let me get close?"

Joe tensed impossibly tighter beneath the touch, shrugging off her hand and lengthening the distance between them.

"What happened that night, Joe," she said gently, encouragingly. "It was terrible and horrible and regrettable in the worst way. But it's in a past that cannot be changed and is getten farther and farther from you every day. Life really does go on, Joe. Don't leave yourself behind it, especially when so many people are reachen out to pull you along the way. Please don't give up on yourself."

He faced her, raking a hand through his hair. "What else can I tell you, Annie?" he asked beseechingly. "Life does go on, and I'm tryen to get on with my life the best way I can."

"You dwell on it," Annemarie observed. "It's eaten you alive, Joe, from the inside out. You've lost faith in yourself, and you're afraid of hurten other people."

Joe shook his head tiredly. "Is this the point where I'm supposed to break down and confess all my self-doubts?" he asked evenly. "Offer up all my insecurities and seek reassurance that any misgivens I have about myself are completely misplaced?"

"It might help," she suggested hopefully.

"Well, it's not goen to happen," he snapped.

"Billy's death was an accident," Annemarie said.

"Yes, it was," Joe agreed bluntly. "I made a judgment call, and it was the wrong one. Now, I'm liven with the consequences. If I have trouble dealen with those consequences, then it's my problem, Annie. Not yours or anybody else's. I don't want your help, I don't want your sympathy, I don't want your pity. I don't need any of that. Why is it so hard for you to grasp?"

His bullheadedness infuriated Annemarie, and his rejection stung.

"You deserve my pity!" she scowled, turning away and taking a few uncertain steps toward the door before whirling around to face him once again. "For someone who keeps everything inside, you sure do have an empty life, Joe," she told him dolefully. "And if you're really determined to go through life that way, then you might as well have put that gun to your head and pulled the trigger that night by the railroad tracks."

"I'm no coward."

Though uttered slowly, the words seethed across his lips.

"I may not measure up in many ways, Annemarie, but I intend to survive," he vowed smoothly. "And I would never take the easy way out and leave everybody else holden the bag for my mistakes and problems."

The vehement passion behind his declaration renewed Annemarie's faith in healing powers and gave her strength to try once more.

"Good Lord!" she gasped, taking several cautious steps toward Joe, sensing his walls were ready to crumble with a bit more prodding. "Such emotion from the man of steel," she told him, gloating. "Do you realize, sugar, that's the first time you've ever taken a decidedly offensive tone with me?

"And frankly, I'm glad to see it, Joe," she continued. "It's good to see you can get worked up about real feelens. Good to know you can express somethen you feel within yourself—other than the animosity generated by hopeless busybodies like me who want to ferret out all of your carefully guarded secrets and emotions. I think maybe I've just been given a glimpse inside those brick walls around you, Joe. There may be windows, after all, that you forgot to cover up."

Annemarie moved directly in front of him. "Please let me inside all the way, Joe," she pleaded softly, placing her hand on the side of his face, smiling tenderly. "Dramatics aside, sugar, I will give you a reason to trust yourself. And together, we can slay the dragons."

Joe stiffened once more against the touch, then looked into her eyes and declared calmly, "I'm a lone ranger, Annie. I prefer to slay my own dragons."

Her hand fell away abruptly, a shimmer of tears came into her eyes and Annemarie stumbled back from him. For someone used to getting her way, this loss of what she wanted most in life should have been a bitter pill to swallow. But there was not a selfish feeling in her heart, and bitterness was the last thing on her mind. She had embarked on a quest for truths this night. She had sought answers to troubling questions, and she had wanted an end to the uncertainty about her future with Joe. Her mission was accomplished now and although the results had failed her hopes, far from being bitter, she was humbled instead by the magnitude of Joe's loss on this night.

"There's just no give in you, is there, Joe?" she told him, choking over the words.

"Too much gristle, huh?" he agreed glumly, to her amazement, his tone suggesting that final farewells demanded complete candor.

"Survivors need gristle," she said sharply. "Too many of them don't have much else."

Joe probably would survive, she realized then, despite the heavy cost extorted from his soul. In fact, maybe the man was destined to become one of the world's great survivors. He was too boneheaded to see the alternatives and possessed too much vanity to fail miserably.

Annemarie recalled a conversation with him about beaches and seashells, particularly Joe's fascination with the vastness of the ocean's beauty. The man was like a seashell, not the garden variety but one spiraled and twisted, beautiful and complicated in formation, hollow on the inside, except for the roar of something wonderful. And like a seashell, Joe probably would flounder in vast oceans, carried and rolled on uncontrollable tides, washing up on occasional shores. Only time would tell whether the currents and rocks would chip away his formations until nothing special remained. Or perhaps someone with something more substantial to offer than

Annemarie would pluck up the man and save him from the ravages. For his sake, she prayed time would bestow on Joe the peace of mind he desperately needed.

Annemarie bit her lip to fight back the tears, and the edge came off her voice. "I guess it's better to know where I stand with you now than down the road," she told him, trying valiantly to suppress the most stubborn of her lingering misgivings, wishing Joe would spare a small portion of his ample composure, knowing even that would take more than he could give.

She tried to collect herself. For the sake of friendship, if nothing else, she wanted a dignified end. The need for candor, however, demanded precedence over dignity. Too much had gone between them to part ways without simple honesty, too much had been gained and lost to leave any doubts—all for the sake of something as imprecise as dignity. Just in case Joe had any misunderstandings about her intentions toward him, Annemarie wanted to make sure the man knew what he was sacrificing to preserve his self-control.

"You've made everything clear for me, Joe," she said shakily, her face crestfallen. "You've said your peace, and Lord knows I've said probably more than I had any right to and certainly more than you cared to hear from me. But just so you know why I tried tonight, Joe, and where you've stood with me over the last few months ...

"Well," she admitted freely. "You could've taken me to bed with a snap of your fingers. I wanted you to do that." A plaintive silence followed her admission and then she found the courage to return her gaze to him "And, Joe, you know what that would have been worth to the both of us."

His response was true to character. Joe continued to glare above her at the door as Annemarie backed away until she could no longer contain the short, humorless laugh of her own that volunteered itself as she finally reached the door and turned the knob. His eyes betrayed how much her words meant to him. But there was no trust of his emotions, no willingness to follow through on his gut feelings. He watched quietly as Annemarie cried, the tears rolling silently down her face as she stifled the urge to try one last time to make him see the light.

"There's a lot of years ahead of you, Joe," she said at last, "and at the risk of leaven you with a bad line from a dime-store novel, I hope they're not lonely. I hope you find your own way of fillen them with good things."

Annemarie was offering him so much—more than survival, more than a beautiful woman in his bed, more than he could imagine. But Joe let her walk right out the door. He let her go gently, as well as heartbroken, into the night.

———

It was the hardest thing Joe had ever done. He watched over the closed door for a long while, knowing full well he was allowing the best part of life to slip away from him. Not quite true, he corrected himself. Actually, he had ushered Annemarie from his life, without even the common decency to hold open the door for her. She had laid open heart and soul for him, and he'd shut her out completely. She'd offered him a future full of miracles, and he had clobbered her with a past full of sins.

His frustrations magnified in a heavy sigh.

Something warm trickled across his palm, weaving through his fingers, down the underside of his arm, and when Joe finally looked from the door to his hand, he found the beer can slightly crushed. He guzzled down the last of the warm amber liquid, then went into the kitchen to fetch a cold one from the refrigerator. This one went down smoothly and fast, replaced immediately by another full can.

Annemarie was right: He drank too much, he drank to forget the past. And right now, he wanted generous amounts of drinking and forgetting.

Wearily, Joe crossed over to the bar, fished out his last cigarette and crumpled the package, letting it fall from his hand to the countertop before he lit the smoke. Then, he took both beer and cigarette into the living room, plopped into the recliner and wondered why so much of life seemed damned senseless.

Joe knew a great many of the answers would not come. Like why some men died in wars and others broke bones on football fields; why good intentions so often turned into serious mistakes; why white people hated black people and black people hated white people; why people in general dwelled on the bad when there was so much good in the world; why the masses insisted on complications over simplicity; why melodrama trampled over the true grit of ordinary life.

Such questions defied sense, but Joe thought about them anyway because they kept his mind off more troublesome questions. Like why Billy Taylor had died and why Joe had played the pivotal role in his death; why a simple friendship between Carrie and Billy had spawned such deadly consequences; why fate or God or whatever had set in motion such violent conspiracies and why one wrong turn after another had played perfectly off each other—either ruining good lives or scarring them beyond recognition.

Finally, Joe wondered how all this applied to him, why he dwelled on the wrong turns he took rather than the right ones; why he allowed the little bit of bad in life to overwhelm the mostly good things; why he questioned the will of the past rather than accepted its experience; why he feared being vulnerable more than he wanted understanding; why he wanted to give so much happiness and feared being on the receiving end of it; and why, when he set great store by simplicity and honesty, he insisted on complicating such a simple thing as love and denied the truth of his feelings for Annemarie.

For one enlightening moment, Joe considered running next door and declaring the truth of his feelings to her. She had made her feelings obvious and if he did the same, perhaps, as Annie had suggested, they could slay dragons and make something lasting, beautiful and magical. He thought about the happiness of his parents and grandparents, the love they shared, the pleasures derived from it.

Joe and his siblings had grown up with several unspoken maxims in their home, but none more vividly expressed than the need for a good man or a good woman in their life. Having someone to share your life laid the groundwork for good things to follow and made the whole of it worthwhile.

His thoughts harkened back to Annemarie's parting words: "And, Joe, you know what that would have been worth to the both of us."

Joe knew all right. It was so simple. Somewhere deep inside, though, rising up to haunt him, came another message, one equally true and understood implicitly by Joe. Things were rarely as simple as they seemed. Joe carried the scars of too many complications, and he feared fresh wounds.

He was also not so gullible as to believe in fairy tales and happy endings. There were too many chances for good things to go helplessly wrong, a theory to which his own life bore striking testament. Joe had no intentions of ever feeling helpless again—at least not of his own making. He might not could control what life threw at him, but he could avoid obvious dangers with a little foresight and caution. True enough, he might lose something in the process, like the love of a good woman. But he'd already lost huge chunks of his heart and soul, and, at the detestable risk of feeling sorry for himself, Joe could not afford to lose another measure and still survive.

For survival really was the ultimate issue here. Despite Annemarie's belief that survivors had little in their lives beside gristle, Joe disagreed. He'd always had more than his share of good things in life. And still did. Not everybody his age could boast of so many dreams fulfilled. As a boy, he'd conceived the kind of life he wanted to lead. As a young man, he had charted the course, following it haphazardly perhaps but never losing sight of where he was headed. Now that he had arrived, the reality exceeded his expectations. Few dreams boasted such successful endings in real life. Joe figured he had everything he wanted not only to survive but also to prosper. Now was the time to preserve what he'd attained and perhaps set his options for the future.

In the meantime, he would do whatever necessary to forget the one thing he did not have—the love of a good woman. He'd drink, too much if necessary, because he could handle it. He also would prove Annemarie had been wrong with all her well-intentioned advice on how Joe should run his life. Indeed, wasn't her litany of "do this, do that" proof positive of good intentions gone wrong? She had tried to force her will on him, and they'd both lost a valued friendship, along with the chance for anything more substantial to develop between them.

He might be alone in the world, but alone did not translate into the loneliness and emptiness Annemarie had predicted for Joe. But if life turned out that way, Joe would handle it, too. He would do whatever necessary to forget her, even if he had to lie to himself to do it. And he intended to start this very minute. Joe finished his beer and headed for the door.

———

By the time Joe arrived in the basement of the old building, the party was in full swing. A stereo blared, psychedelic lights flickered and thick cigarette smoke, mingled with the sickly sweet smell of pot, hovered over too many bodies pressed too close together.

He was somewhere among a cluster of shadier establishments between Tenth and Fourteenth Streets, businesses that catered to the whims and desires of the younger generation. The strip contained something for everyone, ranging from the cerebral atmosphere of coffee houses to the incense in head shops serving the city's rising drug culture. The particular bar chosen by Joe on this night had a reputation as the meat market of choice for anyone interested in meaningless encounters. On this night, half of Atlanta seemed in the mood.

The room pulsed with the beat of hard-driving music and the frenzied pace of sexual cruising. Desire mattered most in this scene, scruples counted the least. Past experience suggested Joe only had to bide his time before crossing paths with someone of a similar mindset, a woman willing to share the night and walk away tomorrow morning.

For a flickering moment, the memory of Annemarie Morgan tested his scruples.

He remembered the desire in her hazel eyes when they had fallen into each other's arms earlier in the evening, the press of her body against him and the honest feelings sparking their kiss. They could have made love then, and angels would have sung praises. What Joe had in mind now, however, defied his moral sense of right and wrong. He was not opposed to sex for the simple sake of pleasure, since his previous experiences had been confined to that particular vein. But there was something unnatural about seeking meaningless sex to replace real feelings, something wrong about using the body of one woman to forget the love of another.

Joe hushed the natter of moral debate by focusing on his vow to do whatever necessary to forget Annemarie. He had promised to lie to himself if necessary and he would. At least no one would be hurt this way. Just maybe, though, when the time came to leave with someone on this night, there would be no lies. If desire really did matter most of all, then he figured he would have no trouble acting on it. He was full of pent-up lust from the restraints of the last few months, and Joe was ready and willing to release it.

He straddled up to the bar, ordered a double vodka on the rocks and drank it down quickly before calling for another. He nursed the second drink, while talking to a couple he had met here several months earlier and sharing a marijuana cigarette with them.

Joe realized he was running out of control, even if no one else did. He had tried marijuana on a few occasions, and he hated it. The stuff dulled his senses so completely that he would walk around days after the high with a listless feeling that nothing mattered. Despite his initial misgivings, however, the drug's intoxicating effect was too powerful to fight, and Joe began to enjoy the sense of abandon. He was high but played it cool, forgoing an offer to share a second joint with the couple and excusing himself to prowl around the bar.

He ordered another drink, bought a pack of cigarettes from a vending machine and began casing for women.

His path crossed first with a pretty brunette who had been one of the first women Joe had slept with after moving to Atlanta. Her name eluded Joe. They chatted briefly, sized each other up and decided in mutual silence to seek their respective pleasures elsewhere on this night. Joe wanted something completely strange, without the slightest hint of familiarity.

Straining to hear the Beatles sing about a long and winding road, Joe strolled right into the path of meaningless pleasure. He practically walked over the woman as she grabbed his shirt to keep from being trampled. The collision brought him to a stop and sent his eyes on a downward spiral, way down for she stood barely five feet. She had pearly blonde hair that hung straight down her back, coming close to her rounded bottom. On first glance, she seemed fragile, with a tiny build and fair complexion. But, diminutive though she was, Joe could not overlook the curvaceous touches and swell of breasts on her slight frame. Her glassy blue eyes conducted a similar appraisal of Joe. Apparently, he passed muster because her face broke into a come-hither smile.

"Oops," Joe smiled back at her. "I should pay more attention to where I'm goen."

The woman laughed, a husky, throaty sound that conveyed the distinct impression she was glad he had done otherwise. "If you had been looking where you were going, we might have missed each other," she remarked, confirming his assumption in a soft, savvy voice. "But since you didn't, I have a feeling this is our lucky night."

"I'm getten the same feelen," Joe agreed.

Her name was Sylvia and she dragged him onto the dance floor, where they rocked to Credence and then swayed to a couple of soulful ballads, leaving no mistake about their intentions toward one another. She kissed him, tantalizing with the stroke of her fingers and pressing erotically against Joe, who needed no seductive encouragement to want her. The combination of recent abstinence, liberal amounts of liquor and the dope of marijuana already had him primed for what she had in mind—conquering his moral doubts as well, if not entirely vanishing the memory of Annemarie Morgan.

"Dancing's fine," Sylvia suggested when the stereo launched into another fast song. "Unless you're more interested in a private party for two."

The swiftness of her come-on surprised Joe. He was accustomed to women making passes, but typically, some kind of pursuit followed the introductions, even if the chase was routine. "I thought it was us guys who moved fast," he told her.

"Why waste time when my interest is piqued," Sylvia retorted, daring him with a smile. "But if you prefer, we can wait."

Joe accepted the dare without another thought. "Let's go," he said, grabbing her hand and leading them through the throng of bodies, out the door and onto the street.

They walked several blocks to his apartment, allowing their faces and eyes to carry the conversation, generating the heat of desire with their impatience to satisfy simple urges and explore one another. The nearer they came to his apartment, the more Joe wanted to experience her lithe and tiny body. He had never made love to such a diminutive woman, which became his substitute for the missed thrill of the pursuit.

Sylvia had substitutes and motives as well. Once inside the apartment, she gave Joe time enough to turn on the radio, then beckoned him to her. She repeated her seductive routine, this time with more abandon until Joe ached for release. Then she delayed the inevitable, teasing him with dirty talk and requests for her own pleasure. For the longest time, at her request, they sought each other through their clothes. But finally, when breath went ragged and bodies shook with anticipation, they stripped off their clothes and came together frantically on the floor.

It was not love they made, which had never been the point for either of them. Instead, they labored for pure sexual gratification, performing an act that might as well have been masturbation since each of them was aware of the other only as the means to reach an end. When it was over, they moved into the bedroom and repeated a slower version of the same act. Then, they showered and Joe extended the perfunctory courtesy of asking whether she preferred to stay the night or to be driven home.

The question caught Sylvia off guard. She looked curiously at Joe as they stood naked in the bathroom. "I'm not ready to do either just yet," she said. "The night is young. And like I told you earlier, this is your lucky night."

Joe saluted her with a lopsided grin. "I'd say I've had more than my share of luck tonight. But I'm willen and ready to press it."

"I bet you are," she teased. "Now that we have the mood set, are you ready for me to make your dreams come true?"

"What if I don't like dreams?" Joe suggested.

"Be assured, lover, you'll like the dreams I make for you," Sylvia promised as she led him into the bedroom. "Go stretch out on the bed; I'll be back in a flash."

"Do you have any liquor in the house?" she asked as Joe sprawled on the bed.

"Beer's in the refrigerator," he answered. "There's vodka in the cabinet under the sink."

A minute later, she returned with her purse, their clothes and a full fifth of vodka procured from the kitchen. She dropped the clothes on the floor and brought the purse and bottle to bed, opening both as she sat cross-legged beside him. Sylvia took a small sip from the bottle, then handed it to Joe, who swilled down considerably more of the clear liquor as she fished in her purse and produced two tiny pink pills.

"What's that?" Joe asked hesitantly, his cautious nature bringing him to a sitting position.

Beyond marijuana, he knew little about the drug culture. Pills had never appealed to him. Even as a child, he had required considerable persuasion from his parents to take an aspirin tablet to cool a fever and, to this day, the pain of a headache had to be excruciating before he submitted to drugs.

"Dream makers," she told him with an auspicious lilt to her answer.

"Acid?" Joe guessed.

"You've never done LSD?" she remarked.

He shook his head.

"Then take your first trip with me," Sylvia suggested, popping one of the pills into her mouth and washing it down with vodka. "Your turn," she smiled, offering him the pill with one hand and extending the bottle back to him.

His reluctance to accept the pill brought more encouragement. "It's like nothing you've ever tried in your entire life," Sylvia gushed. "Acid makes everything clear for you. It expands the mind and allows you to discover and understand all those things hidden so deep inside that they can't get out and be understood any other way."

The decision at hand sobered Joe. His nature rebelled against the very idea of ingesting anything in his body that would alter his mind. Somewhere inside him, though, a voice of doubt clamored for freedom. And from somewhere else, there came a solemn reminder of his vow to do whatever necessary to forget the past. But what finally made the decision was the powerful urge to cede control of himself, to allow something other than his own willpower to dictate his thoughts and actions for a short while.

Joe swallowed his misgivings, pushing aside the feeling that he was stepping onto a runaway train, then took the pill and swallowed it with another liberal gulp of vodka. Immediately afterward, he wanted to have sex again, but Sylvia refused his advances.

"Later," she promised, smiling. "But right now, lie back, relax and allow magic into your life. Every fantasy you've ever had is about to come true."

He took her word, stretched back on the bed and waited for magic. They did not talk, but every so often, Sylvia propped up on an elbow and encouraged him with a smile, her blonde hair spilling across his body. For the longest time, nothing happened. And then the woman took on a dreamy quality.

Slowly, as she had promised, vast new horizons of his mind did begin to open, but only into an even larger arena of nothingness. Neither reasons nor answers, doubts nor questions existed here, all of which Joe understood with picture-perfect clarity. The room expanded beyond him, and the pace of time slowed like a bad New York traffic jam.

Joe forgot Sylvia until she rolled over and began kissing his mouth and face, rubbing her hands across his body until he ached with desire. She coveted his entire body, tasting every inch of him until he writhed and moaned beneath her. They made love in slow motion, each thrust a deliberate and new experience, taking Joe deeper than he had ever gone. The woman virtually absorbed him until convulsions shook his body, and he exploded in a final release.

When it was over and Joe lay spent, Sylvia kissed him lightly on the forehead. She crawled over him off the bed, picked up her rumpled clothes and dressed as Joe watched.

"This is where I get off," he heard her say. "Enjoy the rest of your trip."

Joe wanted to say something as she disappeared through the door, but he was unable to, failed by either the lack of voice or the inability to form a thought. He was unsure, so he lay perfectly still and savored the passing of blank time as the safe feeling of sleep settled over his fully alert self.

Much later, he became aware of something out of kilter, then discovered he could not move. He fought for the freedom of movement only to find himself paralyzed completely, glued to sheets that reeked the sweaty scent of exhausted sex. His mouth dried up, sealing shut, and his head throbbed. He gasped for breath, wondered whether he was dying and consciously considered the possibility that the LSD had been laced with poison.

Later still, the room turned into his very own casket.

He was lying deadly still, on a satin pillow surrounded by white upholstery. One by one, the people most important in his life came to peer down at him, shaking their heads sadly. Lucas and Beauty were there, with Annie and Danny somewhere near them. Billy Taylor came to the coffin by himself, still blessedly unaware that his own hands carried the bloodstains of Danny Bartholomew. The Carters appeared along with Tom, followed by Paul Berrien and his elderly sisters. John, Luke and Bonnie were there together, Mark Applegate stood by Summer's side and, eventually, his parents and grandparents came to peer despondently into the casket.

"I'm alive," Joe screamed as each face hovered over the open casket. However, he had no voice, so no one heard his plea for recognition.

At long last, Carrie came. Rather than look at Joe, she prepared to close the casket, even as a lone voice cried out to be heard. Joe recognized the voice of Annemarie Morgan, nearby, yet restrained by a pair of invisible arms.

"I can save him," she screamed. "I can save him."

"No," droned another voice, familiar and overpowering. "He'd only take you down, too. He'd drag us all down to the bottom. It's best this way."

Joe knew then that his life no longer mattered. He shut his eyes and allowed Carrie to close the casket top without further protest. After trying so hard for so long to see the light, the dark of pitch-blackness came as welcome relief.

CHAPTER 14

IT WAS A DREAM.

Sunday morning had dawned, and he had hallucinated. And no matter how real the vision seemed, despite its looming occupation of his waking thoughts, the dream had no bearing on reality. It was simply a creature of deception, a demon manufactured by the Devil himself to steal his soul. It had to have been a dream because the collective torment of everything gone wrong in real life could never match the hopeless desolation of the nightmare.

His life mattered.

Joe opened his eyes at last, to a light, a pale glow seeping through the door from the small living room window. That his brain assimilated even this tiny bit of information, without fragmented thought, was proof enough that his mind retained some working order—and a reason in itself to thank God for his sanity before he tested his physical well-being.

Joe uttered a short, silent prayer, then began a cautious inspection of his body, noting first the soaked sheets plastered beneath his back and legs. The clammy, cold feeling on his exposed front side suggested he had sweated through the night. Remembering the earlier paralysis, he swallowed a lump in his throat and embarked on a slow discovery of movement, first in his fingers and then extending to his arms, feet and legs. Another silent prayer later, he eased into a sitting position in the middle of the bed and pulled the crumpled top sheet against his wearied body to ward off chills.

Eventually, Joe grasped full understanding that some sort of normalcy had reclaimed his life. He forced himself from bed, showered, dressed and made a pot of coffee.

In time and without question, he came to accept that some of life's tragedies defied explanation and sense—and that what really mattered in the aftermath was not some fruitless search for vague answers to things that no longer existed, but rather finding a way to cope with the strait of those that did.

Having come to these conclusions, he should have been encouraged because coping had always been one of his strengths. But instead, the keen sense of a loss undefined, yet very real, burdened him, and Joe dreaded the relentless effort of coping anymore. He had a raw notion of a vital force gone wrong in his being, an element that had nothing to do with circumstances and was beyond the power of his control. He had been stripped of the basic substance that provided life's connection and adhesion, which was necessary not only to go on, but made the effort worthwhile as well. And with no idea of what it was or where he might have lost it, Joe had no way of getting back to it.

Sometime that afternoon, Joe fetched the bottle of vodka from the bedroom. He carried it to the kitchen, filled a jelly glass with ice and poured the liquor until it sloshed over the rim. Despite a few qualms, he took the first sip without hesitation and continued drinking until he passed out into a dreamless stupor.

On Monday morning, his body's internal alarm clock woke him at the usual time. He pushed himself out of the recliner, suffering the effects of a severe hangover. His head pounded, and he was sick to his stomach. On unsteady legs, he made it to the bathroom just in time to hang his head in the toilet and vomit.

A cold shower improved his condition slightly, and after getting dressed, Joe went into the kitchen and made another pot of steaming coffee. He forced down two cups of the black liquid to settle his queasy stomach, then rushed off to work.

Somehow, he endured the long day on the job, despite the sense of dread and foreboding that he was bound to mess up his work, the one thing he'd always been able to count on when everything else went wrong.

On his way home from work that evening, Joe stopped by the liquor store and replenished his supply of vodka. Once inside his apartment, he skipped supper, choosing to drink himself into another dreamless stupor. The next morning, he did it all over again.

In that way, his life settled into a numbing routine—mornings filled with steaming black coffee, days of dread and nights consumed with vodka.

———————

A whole year exactly had gone by since her quiet, comfortable world turned upside down and sent Carrie tumbling head over heels on a tidal wave of despair.

In spite of herself, Carrie smiled at the thought, remembering that she'd told Billy about visiting the ocean, riding waves, tasting salt water and eating alligator tail. She no longer thought about Billy Taylor every single day. Getting to that point had not been easy, but she had done it with the help of her family. They had literally smothered her with love, compassion and companionship in those long, painful days as she fell apart in the aftermath of that stormy Halloween night.

A year ago, she would have suffocated under their endless efforts to rescue her from the depths of sorrow. Then again, a year ago she had not yet needed their help. Now, with the worst of the breakdown in the past, she found nothing suffocating about her family's concern and caring, rejoicing instead at their insistence on holding her aloft as wave after wave of despondency had threatened to overwhelm the shallow tread of sanity that kept her afloat during those dark days.

Carrie suspected she had suffered a nervous breakdown in the months after Billy died, or at least come very close to the experience. No doctor had ever told her as much, but everything had changed after that night. There had been no homecoming dance for Carrie, no senior prom and almost no high school graduation. Always a respectable student, her grades had declined drastically as she spent days and nights engrossed in the horrors of Halloween, unable to concentrate on schoolbooks and homework assignments. She'd passed senior year by the skin of her teeth and, quite possibly, the compassion of teachers who had decided to cut her some slack. Carrie had wanted to skip graduation ceremonies as well, but Matt and Caroline had required her to attend both the baccalaureate and commencement services. In hindsight, she was grateful for their intervention. She needed a good memory or two to weigh against the missed opportunities in her crowning year of high school achievement.

Unable to function at even the basics, she had given up the prospect of extracurricular activities. Not only had she abdicated as president of the Future Homemakers Club of America, Carrie had quit the club as well, thus losing her chance to make a mark on the state level competitions. Carrie regretted the decision now, thinking about the plans she had made for the club, knowing someone else had carried them out while she struggled to get through the very basics of life. She shrugged off the regret quickly, however. It was impossible to plan cake sales and driver safety programs when your mind was muddled by the memory of cradling one boy in his dying moment and standing by idly as the life was snuffed from another boy.

Those were the kinds of thoughts that Carrie no longer managed on a daily basis. The bad memories still played on her mind with some frequency—perhaps they always would—but she had relegated them to the past where they surely belonged. Constant dwelling on their sad consequences made her miserable and accomplished nothing.

Today, however, was different. It was an anniversary of sorts, a cruel reminder of an even crueler time, but nevertheless a time for reflection and possibly looking ahead.

It was a Saturday, and she had come outside to retrieve the mail and take a short break from the afternoon's work. In the distance, a tractor engine droned under the effort of pulling the peanut combine through the field beside the house. John had the duty of running the machine today, while Sam and Matt relaxed with fishing polls in hand and the company of Paul Berrien and Dan Carter. Carrie had no idea whether they were trying their luck at the Old Pond or the New Pond.

Closer home, Luke and Mark Applegate went cheerfully about the business of stacking hay in the loft, bantering back and forth with the rhythm of two people tossing a football on a lazy afternoon. Inside the house, Rachel was putting the backing on her latest quilt, while Summer was working at the boutique in Valdosta—the same one where Caroline and Bonnie had gone to buy a formal dress. Bonnie needed the dress for the following Friday night when she would stroll across the football field as a freshman representative on the Cookville High School homecoming court.

Temporarily forgetting the mail, Carrie soaked up the sounds and ambiance. Over the last year, she had learned to appreciate these moments as rare gifts.

A year ago, she had stood on this porch, with the skies preparing a storm and a day of horror unknowingly at hand. Today, however, was the perfect showcase for fall. There was a slight chill in the air, enhanced by a stiff breeze and preceding days of balmy weather that had ushered out October with a summer-like feel until this, its very last day. The sky was azure blue and the clouds fluffy white.

Across the road, goldenrod dappled brilliant and burnished yellow under the shadows of sun and woods, and the sprawling oak, which had been bright orange last year, donned its more familiar fall coat of dull brown. On the whole, the fall colors seemed duller this year, mostly brown and mustard, except for sparse patches of lusterless red, gold, russet and orange. Last year, of course, had been the anomaly. This was the kind of understated fall expected in South Georgia, where the lack of seasonal color in hardwoods was more than compensated by the velvety texture of winter green pines.

So much the same and yet so different since her world had turned upside down, Carrie thought again. The world had spun quietly, quickly back into its orbit after the horrors of that day, and Carrie had recovered as well, though slowly with several sputters along the way.

She had been too gentle, too unsuspecting of tragedy to cope with the unmuzzled terror of unspeakable acts. Nothing in life had prepared her for the violence, especially under such innocent circumstances. It was the innocence behind the trag-edy that made it so hard to accept. So many people striving to do good but missing the mark and dealing out life and death in the process.

Although Carrie had put that night behind her, the details still seemed as real as ever when she put her mind to remembering certain images: The wildness in Dan-ny's eyes as life ebbed out of him, the dead set of Billy's gaze when he no longer saw. Such memories could sap a person's sanity if they went unchecked, and she'd almost allowed them free rein to ruin her life. Almost, but not quite. Now she took comfort in whatever way possible—in this case, the knowledge that both Danny and Billy had gone into the hereafter with her smile of encouragement stamped in their eyes.

The horrors of that night had been the catalyst for her breakdown, but the after-math of the tragedy had played a significant role, too. Carrie had come away from the innuendo-laced coroner's inquest feeling the dirty and whorish implications that the district attorney had tried to foster in the minds of the investigative panel. She knew her relationship with Billy had been entirely innocent, but Stan Avera had made it seem tawdry. Carrie had been unable to resist the notion that other people concluded she shared more than friendship with Billy. It might have been unspoken gossip, but more than one person suspected that star-crossed lovers lay at the heart of the violence.

Although she never heard one word to support her runaway thoughts, Carrie had felt cheapened by her own imagination. For a while, even attending church had been an ordeal because every time she walked through the doors, Carrie felt brand-ed with a scarlet letter on her chest.

In time, the goodwill of the Benevolence congregation had quieted those feel-ings. No one had stood in line to pass judgment. Instead, they had offered her sym-pathy and prayers, both of which had gone a long way toward restoring her faith in healing powers.

Unfortunately, the student body at Cookville High School had not been as un-derstanding. In those first few days after she returned to school, fellow students had stared openly at Carrie, gawking over the freakish appeal of her newfound celebrity and trying to make associations between her outward shyness and some secret life. Perhaps if she'd had a true friend on campus, Carrie could have dealt with the scru-tiny. But she didn't and since her one real friend had died from his association with her, she had faltered under the intense glare of the spotlight. No one had stepped forward to help pick her up off the floor—no one that is except Luke, who had proved that blood counts between sisters and brothers. Her little brother had stayed by Carrie's side throughout the year, putting his own reputation at risk and sacrific-ing his rising star in the process. For that, she was eternally grateful to Luke.

Carrie could not point to a single moment when she had conquered the break-down. It had been a gradual process, starting perhaps in the last week of school when she forced herself to buckle down and study hard for finals. Or maybe it had been at the graduation ceremony itself when she marched across the football field to collect her diploma, with her head held high and pride in the accomplishment. Likely, though, the healing had taken place over the summer of hard work alongside her family.

What a strange spring and summer it had been, Carrie thought. First, the weath-er had cooperated with the crops and then it had ravaged them. There had been ample rain for spring plantings—and then more rain followed by more rain until the summer seemed as wet as the one in 1967 had been dry. Not quite, though. The crops had been salvageable this year, with corn, soybeans and peanuts prospering in the unusually wet conditions.

Tobacco had been a disaster, however. Black shank had gotten into the leaf early, wilting it on the stalk and reducing the crop to a smelly, sickly yellow color long before it should have ripened. The heavy rains had soaked the fields, turning them into a soggy mess, making them impassable for the harvester. As a last resort, the Bakers had abandoned machines and gathered the crop on foot, the decision made for them after the double-deck harvester had toppled over onto its side twice in the span of a few minutes. Matt had been at the helm on the first turnover, with Caroline, Summer, Bonnie and a hired hand alongside him on the top floor. Carrie, who had been relegated to the role of cropper that summer, had watched in sheer terror as the huge machine tried to make a turn in the boggy field and toppled into the mire. Everyone on the top floor had grabbed hold of the nearest stable piece of metal and hung on for dear life as the harvester fell onto its side. Miraculously, no one had been hurt, although they were plenty scared.

Using the tractor, the men had stood the harvester upright and then, with Luke at the wheel this time, Matt had tried to pull the machine out of the bog, only to send it lumbering once more onto its side. In contrast to the fright of the first episode, the second turnover was almost a jolly occasion, with Luke, the only one aboard the harvester this time, bellowing a Tarzan yell as the machine listed onto its side. Afterward, however, Matt had decided to use sleds to gather the tobacco, and Carrie had wound up slogging through the fields day after day, bent over at the back alongside her brothers as they picked the leaves and lugged them onto the sleds, which were hauled to the barn, where another crew strung the leaf onto sticks and hung them for curing.

Such work came naturally to Luke and John, who could walk through the fields snatching leaves and carrying on a conversation at the same time without breaking stride. Carrie, on the other hand, required every ounce of concentration and effort just to stay in sight of them and even then, the brothers usually helped to keep the progress of her row even with the theirs and that of Ken Cook, the preacher's son who was hired help in the Baker fields that summer. Despite her shortcomings in comparison with John and Luke, the hard fieldwork had satisfied Carrie and removed her thoughts from the past. When the principle fieldwork had ended, her slender body had been toned and her mind healed.

Of course, hard work alone had not been the salvation of her sanity. The value of her family remained inestimable. Working so close with John and Luke had been one rousing revelation after another into the minds of men, all of which Carrie had shared fondly during girl talk with Summer and Bonnie. And unlike any other time in her life, she'd had a mystical affair with the summer itself. It had been a season of liberation, from the plaint of the recent past to the self-imposed constraints of a more distant time. Keenly aware of her surroundings, Carrie had become more plainspoken and less timid—not just around the family but with neighbors and acquaintances, those close and those passing. Maybe no one noticed the transformation as much as she experienced it, but Carrie felt the change, and it altered her perspective.

The final link in her rescue from the breakdown had been John's unwavering companionship.

A year ago, Carrie had fretted over the close attachment between Summer and Joe as they sought solace from each other in the wake of Tom Carter's death. Now she understood better how they had bolstered each other's spirits with unconditional friendship. John had been a stalwart companion in trying times, and Carrie believed she had given him something in return. The bond between them always had been a little extra special, as it was between Summer and Joe and Luke and Bonnie. But she and John had gravitated more than usual toward each other's companionship at the start of the year, as Summer drifted into her friendship with Mark Applegate, Luke asserted newfound freedom through his driver's license and Bonnie blossomed in the throes of self-discovery and a significant relationship with the preacher's son.

It was John who best understood Carrie's moods and gave his candid reaction. He allowed Carrie to express sorrows and doubts without feeling sorry for herself, while providing a testing ground for her burgeoning self-esteem. In turn, she gave her brother a sounding board for his budding artistic and business sense, the latter of which had churned out possibilities for her own future as well.

Forgetting why she had come outside in the first place, Carrie began strolling through the orchard as she reflected on John's decision to follow his grandfather into the pecan business. Under Sam's tutelage, John had learned the ropes of orchard management, buying and selling pecans. But whereas Sam had gone here and there buying pecans from local growers and then selling them at higher prices to local wholesalers, John envisioned a much broader business. He wanted to become one of the wholesalers, selling to the manufacturers of pecan products.

In spare moments over the summer, John had conceived the idea and founded The Baker Pecan Company. It was an ambitious project for a nineteen-year-old, but his enthusiasm alone convinced Carrie the venture would become successful over the long haul.

Zeal aside, however, John already had a proven track record with successful commercial enterprises.

Over the winter, he had gone into the beekeeping business, setting up three dozen white boxes of hives in a clearing of woods a short distance from Sam's experimental trees and vegetables. The amount of honey produced by the bees had been extraordinary, and Carrie had pitched in with the processing and bottling effort. John had sold hundreds of bottles of fresh honey, recouping the cost of his investment and halving the leftover profit with Carrie despite her protest.

If the beekeeping venture in itself was not enough proof of his business savvy, then surely the garden enterprise—raising pumpkins, ornamental gourds and Indian corn for commercial markets—completed the picture. John had entered that venture on an experimental basis to determine the feasibility of growing the crops without the risk of heavy losses. The payoff had proven substantial compared with the investment, thanks to an eager supply of buyers at farmer's markets in Cookville, Tifton and Valdosta. Already, he had plans to expand production next year, assuming he could find the time between his regular duties on the farm, beekeeping and the pursuit of an art degree from Valdosta State College.

Currently, The Baker Pecan Company was his top priority, and Carrie was assisting as the plans took shape, keeping track of all the details as they poured forth from John. When the time had come to consider financing for the project, they had approached their parents and grandparents with a detailed, feasible plan to create the company and make it prosper. Their proposal had won praise, and Matt had agreed to cosign a loan when the time came to secure financial backing for the venture.

With that blessing, John and Carrie had gone to Paul Berrien in late summer and laid out their plans with an eye toward a fall startup date, assuming his family's bank would loan them the necessary money to cover startup costs, rent warehouse space and purchase equipment. Paul had listened, offered advice and then sent them to Philip Perkins, the chief loan officer at The Citizen's and Farmer's Bank. Perkins had been equally impressed, concluding The Baker Pecan Company had potential to become a good investment. However, the loan officer also had come up with some suggestions and requirements before the bank would provide financial backing.

Perkins had suggested John slow down his plans, insisting he spend this fall doing exactly what Sam had done for so many years in order to strengthen his grasp of the pecan business and learn the art of precise record-keeping, which Sam had never needed. If John showed a healthy profit, then the loan was guaranteed for the next year. Upon hearing all this, Paul Berrien gave John a management contract to handle his already vast orchard and decided to add new trees. And, Matt had agreed to clear three acres of timber to expand the Bakers' orchard, too.

Despite the delay in their plans, there was still plenty to be excited about as they continued planning. Then, in late August, John had come up with a caveat to his plan, literally picking up Carrie off the floor as he entered the kitchen one day, extolling the virtues of candy making and outlining a venture to complement the pecan business. Though the idea had never crossed Carrie's mind, the suggestion made sense. Cooking was her favorite pastime, and she certainly had no qualms about making a career of it.

As John showed her dozens of brochures and catalogs distributed by other small confectioneries, the idea had taken a firm hold in Carrie. Ever since the end of the summer's hard work, she had floundered in uncertainty over the future. She had no desire to attend college, no wish to clerk in a dime store and no designs on snaring a husband. But she needed a purpose in life and she wanted dreams and goals for her future.

In the space of one week, she had absorbed every bit of candy making knowledge within the purview of the Cookville library, the county home economics agent and the dozens of cookbooks within the Baker home. Next, she developed a limited line of products, turning the family kitchen into a mini-factory as she roasted pecans and dipped them in various chocolates. She settled on seven products: dark- and white-chocolate covered pecans, dark- and white-chocolate pecan bark, pecan brittle, pralines and fluffy white divinity.

In the process, she had depleted the family's store of pecans and was forced to resort to the grocery store for new supplies. She also had invested a portion of her beekeeping money in various tins, boxes and homemade labels for packaging the products, then placed a couple of small advertisements in magazines to promote the venture. Finally, she had plied the Carters and several other local stores to sell her candies, set up a display booth at the county fair and donated a slew of goodies for tonight's Halloween carnival at the New River school.

So far, she was close to breaking even on the venture, and several factors pointed toward eventual success. In a few weeks, she would have an unlimited supply of cheap pecans. In addition, the candies had sold quickly in the stores around home and there had been requests for additional orders as the holiday season approached, while the magazine ads could lure customers from more established companies. Carrie had priced her confectioneries deliberately lower than the gourmet costs quoted in the various brochures and mail-order catalogs, whose distributors appeared to rake in enormous profits. Carrie was not working to become rich. She would deem the business a tremendous success if receipts equaled expenditures.

As her thoughts about business came to an end, so did Carrie's stroll through the pecan orchard. It was a testament to her complete recovery from the breakdown that her thoughts once again could change with such swiftness. A few months ago, the sorrowful memories of Billy and Danny would have stayed on her mind until she became physically ill and overcome by sadness. Now, she could summon up those memories and release them when the time came. She even had a handle on the painful feelings that came with the memories.

So much the same this season and yet so different from fall a year ago. The refrain echoed once more through her mind and this time she focused on the family.

Despite the rapid pace of change taking place among the sons and daughters, her parents and grandparents remained refreshingly steadfast in their approach to life. They accommodated the changes and provided a sage reminder of values that never went out of style. As for Summer, she obviously loved Mark Applegate. Marriage seemed very probable between them, so much so that Carrie expected their engagement by Christmas. Luke continued to impress the fans and the sportswriters with his speed and fleetness on the football field. Last night, he had scored the game-winning touchdown against long-time nemesis Irwin County, securing the first region football championship in the history of Cookville High School. Bonnie was becoming a woman right before their very eyes. She was beautiful in every way, had smarts aplenty and was caught up in a romance with the preacher's son.

And then there was Joe, on his own in the big city, with a life completely alien to the rest of the family. When he had moved to Atlanta, Joe had called home regularly and been a faithful letter writer as well. Now, the calls came sporadically and the letters didn't come at all. Like a sow disassociating from her brood, Joe had weaned the family slowly and now appeared ready to sever the ties completely.

Everyone chalked up a busy lifestyle as the reason for his recent failure to keep in closer contact with the family. Carrie suspected otherwise—although she had no rights whatsoever to make assumptions about his life, given her behavior toward Joe over the past year. She had not meant to push him away every time he tried to approach her. But his very presence had hurt Carrie in those first trying days after Billy's death and the coroner's inquest. First, Joe had been a painful reminder of something she wanted to forget; later, he had become a target of resentment for having taken away someone special from her life. Maybe now it was time to accept without reservation that Joe had acted out of love for her when he shot Billy. And maybe now, Carrie had the strength to do that.

As difficult as it had been for Carrie to come to grips with her witness to that most awful day in their lives, she couldn't begin to imagine coping with the grief alone—without the love and support of her family. She wondered how Joe had managed it; she wondered if he had. Carrie had overheard similar puzzlement in private family talks, but the general assumption seemed to be that Joe would come to terms with his remorse over shooting Billy in his own time. In Carrie's studied opinion, however, Joe rarely came to grips with his personal feelings. Instead, he shuddered them away and pretended they no longer mattered. But killing Billy had tormented Joe, probably more than anybody realized. He had agonized over that night by the railroad tracks. Despite his closemouthed reactions, anybody who had been near him in the weeks after Billy died would have had to be completely blind and deaf not to have noticed the constant state of anxiety and flux in which Joe existed. Even Carrie had noticed, and she had consciously avoided Joe.

Carrie recalled the Thanksgiving morning last year when Joe had found her in the barn loft, pleading softly for nothing more than a chance to talk. At the time, she had pushed him away to protect herself from bad memories. Thinking back on it now, however, she realized Joe would have felt rejected by her rebuff. Perhaps her brother had needed some love and support after all, or just the company of someone who had shared the experience. Seeking out comfort did not come easily to Joe. If that had been his intentions when he called out to Carrie, then he'd gone away empty-handed.

And sought his comfort elsewhere. But had he found it?

Another memory came back vividly to Carrie, this one on the afternoon of Billy's funeral when Joe had offered a heartfelt apology. She remembered the anger welling up inside her as she grappled for understanding. Her feelings had been honest at the time, even when she suggested Billy's death had spared him the rigors of coming to grips with the killing of Danny Bartholomew. Joe had not been spared that task, however, and he'd probably gone half-crazy in the process of trying to sort through it for himself. Not so anyone would notice, of course, because no one hid their emotions better than Joe.

Maybe Joe had reached out to her for help in understanding those conflicting emotions about Billy's death. And maybe she had overlooked his extended hand. Well, to be fair, in her state of mind back then, Joe had not been her top priority. But now, with her sanity preserved, Carrie thought perhaps the time had come to reach back to her brother. He might not want her help anymore. He might not have wanted it in the first place. But maybe, her knowledge about what happened this day a year ago could help him in the search for his own understanding.

Smiling, Carrie went to collect the mail.

————

On Halloween night in 1970, a lone man sat unnoticed in an idling car, gazing out the windshield at the glow of television light coming through the tiny window in Joe's apartment.

Wayne Taylor had been here before, many times over the last few weeks as he plotted revenge against the man who had killed his brother and blackened the family reputation.

He had discovered Joe's presence in the city by accident one day while thumbing through *The Atlanta Herald*, searching for a story about a bank robbery in the metropolitan area. Wishful thinking had led him to scan the front-page headlines for the story, and his eyes had sighted something familiar as he searched. He did a double take, discovering the byline of one Joe Baker and knowing beyond a shadow of doubt who had written the story.

Forgetting the original purpose of his search through the newspaper, Wayne had read the article in its entirety, learning more than he wanted to know how niggers would play a key role in electing Georgia's next governor. Anyone with any sense at all knew the best man for the job was J.B. Stoner, the Marietta lawyer who knew where niggers belonged and was committed to keeping them in their place.

Wayne scowled as he concluded the article, certain then it had been authored by the Joe Baker he knew from back home. Who else but a nigger lover like Joe would have written such hogwash?

Unable to quell the bad memories associated with Joe, Wayne completed his task, finding an article about the bank robbery buried in the middle of the newspaper's metropolitan section. It was the third bank Wayne had robbed and, so far, no one suspected that one perpetrator was responsible for all three crimes. Nor should they. He had gone to great lengths to strike banks with no approximation to each other. Bank jobs scared Wayne, although the lucrative payoffs made life considerably easier.

Since turning to a life of crime after fleeing from the law in Cookville, Wayne had concentrated on burglarizing households and robbing various out-of-the-way businesses like small grocery stores and gas stations. He donned a stocking over his head for each robbery and avoided an area once he struck. There was no pattern to his crimes, thus no way for the cops to make any connection with him. As long as he played it safe, Wayne figured he could earn a decent living off burglaries and robberies until something better came his way.

As he sat outside Joe's apartment, Wayne realized he needed to strike somewhere soon. The rent was due, and Rhonda was griping for spending money.

Wayne lived with Rhonda and her little boy in a one-bedroom apartment in the Atlanta suburb of Stone Mountain. Rhonda wasn't much to look at, but she set a decent supper on the table almost every night and made up for her lack of looks with considerable eagerness in the bedroom. She was the first woman Wayne had bedded, and he truly liked her. Her kid wasn't bad either. He rarely cried, seemed happy most of the time and stayed away from Wayne for the most part. All in all, it wasn't a bad life, much better anyway than the one he had left behind in Cookville.

Indeed, as soon as he settled an old score, Wayne figured life would be damn good.

The idea brought not a smile to Wayne's face but a scowl. He hated Joe with a passion. He'd always hated the man and his family, for almost as long as he could remember.

Sometimes, it seemed Wayne was born to hate people like Joe and his precious family, who thought they were so much better than everybody else and acted as if the rest of the world was just scum. Now, though, Wayne's feelings toward Joe crystallized beyond hate—to something he could not put into words but brought thoughts of murder into his heart. Wayne wanted Joe dead—just like Billy was dead.

Ever since learning that Joe shot his brother down in cold blood, Wayne had wanted to seek his revenge. How to get it had been his dilemma. He had been unwilling to risk a return anywhere near Cookville because not even revenge, as sweet as it would be, was worth rotting in prison. Accordingly, the idea of gaining his revenge had dimmed quickly in Wayne as he concentrated on learning the business of his chosen profession. But his motives for revenge had only strengthened with time.

As dumb as the kid was, Billy had been a good brother to Wayne. Billy had treated Wayne with more kindness than anyone else back home. He had not deserved such a big screw in the end. Over and over, Wayne asked himself why Billy had gotten involved with Carrie Baker in the first place. He had tried to tell Billy that nothing good would come from messing with that girl. And Wayne had been right, too. Still, Billy had suffered punishment too severe for the crime, and Joe was the man responsible.

Now, Wayne intended to make Joe pay the same price.

Ever since confirming that the Joe Baker in the newspaper was indeed the same Joe from back home, Wayne had been making his plans and following his enemy's every movement. He'd even neglected his criminal pursuits to map out every step on his road to revenge—to learn every detail of Joe's comings and goings.

Of the two orders, the former had been the most difficult. Wayne had given weeks to consideration of the perfect murder, weighing how best to make Joe suffer the most for killing Billy. Ideas had come to him like a kid in a candy store, all delicious and his for the choosing. Once he'd made up his mind, Wayne had detailed his plans, then practiced them step-by-step so there would be no opportunity for mistakes. Nothing in his life had ever been more important than making Joe suffer, and Wayne had never put forth such a studious effort to ensure his plans went off without a hitch.

In contrast to making plans for his revenge, learning about Joe's lifestyle had been a piece of cake for Wayne, mainly because the man had no life beyond work and home. Almost like clockwork, Joe departed the apartment at the same time every morning and drove to the newspaper office. He put in his day at work, then returned home for the night. Once every two weeks, he stopped by the cleaners to leave his dirty laundry, always picking it up the next day. On a couple of occasions in the last month or so, he had gone to a grocery store as well, coming out with a single bag once and two sacks the next time, causing Wayne to wonder what the man put in his stomach besides enormous amounts of vodka.

The one place Joe visited regularly was a neighborhood liquor store on his way home from work. He stopped there at least twice during the work week, never missing a Friday. Wayne was so intrigued by Joe's taste for liquor that he had taken his greatest risk in tailing Joe by planting himself in the liquor store one Friday afternoon and waiting for Joe to show up there, which he had done precisely on schedule. The man had brought three fifths of vodka and four cartons of cigarettes. Then, on the following Monday, he had made yet another stop at the liquor store, emerging with another sack full of booze and cigarettes.

This last thought brought a genuine smile to Wayne.

Despite the Bakers' highfalutin ways and all his high-and-mighty talk over the years, Joe was nothing but a sot. Wayne's smile broadened as he concluded such a fate could not have befallen a more deserving person than Joe. He hoped the drunkard puked up his guts every morning before going to work. He hoped every last one of the Bakers and all their self-righteous, nigger-loving friends knew the kind of life Joe was leading. Not that anyone should be surprised by the outcome, Wayne told himself. After all, Joe had been raging drunk on the night he attacked Bobby in the Tip-Toe Inn, and Wayne himself had seen the man's Volkswagen passing through the drive-in windows of more than one liquor store in Cookville.

One thing for certain, the liquor obviously seemed to be getting to Joe. His appearance had gone downhill considerably in the weeks Wayne had followed him. From a distance, Joe appeared sallow, lethargic and thin, far different from the healthy, robust person Wayne remembered from back home. Over the last month, Joe also had grown a mustache and full beard, which gave him a gaunt appearance. Wayne just hoped the man had the physical capability to withstand the fun and games he had in store for Joe before his life came to a merciful and dead end.

The scowl returned to Wayne's face as his gaze broke from Joe's apartment window and drifted into the clear nighttime sky. He had hoped with all his heart that this Halloween night would brew up a storm similar to the one last year. Because when he killed the bastard, Wayne wanted every detail exactly as it had been when Joe had shot down Billy. He wanted Joe tired and exhausted, he wanted him cold and wet and he wanted him scared shitless when the end came.

For all that, Wayne was willing to sacrifice the idea of getting his revenge on the anniversary of Billy's death. Time would come soon enough when Mother Nature made the conditions perfect for revenge, and Wayne would be ready and waiting for the moment.

His scowl changed into a sneer as Wayne revved the engine and backed away from the apartment, spinning the car tires as he tore down the street.

Inside the apartment, Joe failed to hear the squealing tires or even the soft sound of the television. Laid out in his recliner, he had passed out several minutes earlier after downing the last swallow of his last bottle of vodka. His last waking thoughts had been a reminder to stop by the liquor store on the way home from work tomorrow, as well as to remember to shave the next morning.

CHAPTER 15

JOE BEGGED OFF AN after-hours meeting with Ray Fields on the first Wednesday in November, lying to his mentor about a more pressing engagement. Or maybe it was half a lie, Joe tried to convince himself as he pulled the Volkswagen into the parking lot of the liquor store. After all, he had made prior plans to stop by the liquor store this afternoon and he needed a new supply of vodka.

A few minutes later, he emerged from the store with enough liquor and cigarettes to carry him through the coming weekend and headed for the apartment.

Ray had become a friend as well as a mentor to Joe, who respected his editor's sense of fair play and craftsmanship with language. Under his tutelage, Joe had honed his journalistic skills and perfected the art of good reporting. Once they went their separate ways, Joe doubted he would ever again have the fortune of working with another man who he trusted and liked half as much as Ray, both as a boss and friend.

He also knew he had put off the man for as long as possible because Ray very much wanted straight talk from Joe, as an employee and as a friend. Tomorrow, they would sit down to talk and Joe would promise to do a better job. Right now, however, he wanted to get home and have a drink.

Joe parked the car inside the basement garage, giving passing notice to an unfamiliar blue sedan parked backward with its trunk open as he stepped from the Volkswagen. He had started parking beneath the building after the owners evicted the basement dweller, sending the old man in search of a new residence by threatening to have the police arrest him for trespassing. Joe felt sorry for the man, but rainy days like this one made him grateful for a covered parking space.

He locked the car, then carried the two bags of liquor and cigarettes up the flight of stairs and let himself into the apartment. Joe no longer kept the door padlocked, relying instead on the single door lock. He kept meaning to get a dead bolt, too, but somehow always managed to forget. Apparently, this morning, he had forgotten to push in the lock on his way out the door.

He walked across the kitchen, setting the bulky bags on the counter by the sink. Resisting the urge to first have a drink, he followed through on an earlier promise to check his mail, a task he had overlooked for several days. He walked through the living room, unlocked the front door and stepped into the alcove, risking a quick glance at the door to Annemarie's apartment before retrieving his mail from the glass box with his name on it. He scanned quickly through the letters outside the door, noting the electric bill and bank statement as he flipped past them, taking time to open the unmarked envelope with an overdue rent notice inside and discarding several pieces of junk mail in a nearby trash can before coming to the bottom of the stack.

His heart stopped momentarily as he recognized the handwriting on the last envelope. A letter from Carrie and Joe was eager to read it. He walked back inside the apartment, dropping the bills on the floor as he closed the door and plopping down in the recliner as he ripped open the envelope and pulled out several handwritten pages from his sister.

Joe read only as far as the greeting before sensing an eerie presence. In a flash, his mind recalled himself checking the cellar door on his way out of the apartment earlier this morning, making sure it was locked. At the same moment, he glanced sideways toward the open bedroom door on his left, seeing only a silver streak and a large, gloved hand as something steel cracked against his skull. He slumped unconscious before there was time to wonder what had happened.

————

Piece of cake!

Wayne smiled as he closed the trunk lid on his car after depositing Joe's bound and gagged body inside it, pausing only to bend the unconscious man's legs so that the cramped space would accommodate the length of his frame.

The actual abduction had been the part of his plan Wayne feared most, the one component in which the details were vague and sketchy. In fact, Wayne had not decided how best to proceed until that very morning after he followed Joe to work. He had watched Joe enter the newspaper building on Commerce Street, then driven quickly back to the apartment, knowing the dark basement garage provided the best opportunity to carry out the deed unnoticed by prying eyes.

Picking the lock on Joe's door had been easy. Once inside, he had nosed around the place, taking particular interest in the trash can full of empty liquor bottles and the scarcity of food in the cabinets and refrigerator. The rest of the apartment had been sparse as well, leading Wayne to conclude that Joe certainly lived uncluttered of possessions. The place was spotless, except for a full ashtray beside the recliner, an unmade bed and a smelly towel on the bathroom floor. If anything else, Joe appeared to be a good housekeeper to Wayne, who figured Rhonda could learn a lesson or two from the man since cleaning was not one of her strong suits.

After making the decision to conceal himself in Joe's bedroom, Wayne had left the apartment and returned to his own home. He napped for several hours, then woke and ate a hearty mid-afternoon lunch that Rhonda cooked specially at his request. Finally, he showered, dressed warmly and left with a warning that she should not expect him home until late, if at all.

Fortunately, Rhonda never questioned Wayne about his whereabouts or his work, as long as he kept food on the table and money in her pocketbook. Since Wayne had pulled off his fifth bank robbery a week earlier, netting enough cash to carry them easily into the new year, she had no gripes at all with him.

He'd arrived at Joe's apartment about a half hour before the unsuspecting man was due home, backed his car into the garage and opened the trunk before going inside the building to wait. Panic had set in Wayne only once as the clock ticked past Joe's usual arrival time at home. A few minutes later, however, he'd heard Joe come into the apartment, deducing immediately from the clink of bottles that an unexpected trip to the liquor store was the reason for his lateness.

Wayne had waited patiently for Joe to come into the bedroom, but when the man had sat down in the recliner instead, it had been simple enough to reach through the door and club him in the head. A bruise had already formed on Joe's temple as Wayne shoved him in the trunk. It was the first of many more to come on this evening, Wayne told the unconscious man, as he drove the car from beneath the garage onto the rain-slick road.

He followed the gravel lane leading from the basement, turned right onto the side street and crossed over Piedmont before making a left onto Juniper Street. Driving along Juniper, which turned into Courtland Avenue, he went past the front of the gold-domed state Capitol, turning left at the corner of Mitchell Street and passing between the Capitol and several officious-looking marble buildings. Another right at Capitol Avenue and a quick left carried the car onto Memorial Drive.

Wayne drove slowly along the street, past housing projects and historic Oakland Cemetery as he headed the car toward Stone Mountain Park. The hour was still early to begin what he had in mind, although daylight was fading fast beneath thick gray skies and building fog.

Knowing the whack on the head would keep Joe subdued for a while longer and groggy still once he woke, Wayne used the leisurely drive to review once more every detail of the coming night. There was no room for mistakes, and Wayne did not intend to make one.

———

Joe struggled to open his eyes, then realized they already were, only peering into deep blackness. His head ached, making the struggle to orient himself with the present all the more difficult. Gradually, he remembered that someone had clubbed him in the head, probably with a handgun. Joe considered that perhaps he had come home to a burglar, discarding the notion quickly on doubts that a common thief would have kidnapped him.

Someone had abducted him, Joe realized with sheer disbelief as he deduced his location in the trunk of a slow-moving car. His mouth was taped shut, his arms and legs bound.

His mind raced through the possibilities of why anyone would want to kidnap him, but no motive sprang to mind. He considered the possibility of a realistic dream, but his senses were too alert for sleep. He remembered opening the letter from Carrie, reading the greeting and sensing someone nearby before the weapon thudded against his skull. And then, as if he needed more proof of reality, a cramp caught in the calf of his oddly bent leg.

Joe twisted and turned, trying to stretch out the cramp, skinning his back on what felt like a tire jack. Finally, he managed to ease the cramp, then laid back to consider his predicament.

It was not until the car slowed considerably and turned onto a gravel road that the first trace of fear crept into Joe. As the car bounced along a rutted gravel lane, he concluded serious trouble awaited him when the vehicle came to a halt. Once more, he tried to figure out who would want to kidnap him. Again, he came up without an answer. He quit trying and settled back against the trunk floor, conserving his thoughts, waiting for the mystery to solve itself.

He did not have long to wait.

———

Despite his pledge to remain completely serious throughout the evening, Wayne permitted himself a snide smile at the utter shock registered on Joe's face as the trunk lid opened. He stood about three yards behind the car with a pistol aimed straight at Joe.

"Long time, no see, huh, Joe?" he said blankly.

Wayne allowed the disbelief to sink further into his captive, then produced a hunting knife from a sheath on his belt and cut loose the rope around Joe's legs. "Get out," he barked, his first order of the evening.

Joe struggled upright in the trunk, trying to balance himself, despite the awkward position of his arms tied behind his back. He threw his legs over the trunk and rocked himself into a standing position on the wet ground. Wayne approached Joe cautiously, cut the ropes around his arms and ripped the silver tape from his mouth.

It felt as if half his beard was torn away with the adhesive, but Joe blinked back the pain with only the slightest grunt betraying his anguish.

"Put that rope and tape in the trunk, and close it," Wayne ordered.

Joe obeyed the command in silence, closing the lid softly as he turned to face Wayne. He straightened his cramped body to its full height and massaged the bump on his temple, wondering what Wayne had in mind. Again, he did not wait long for an answer.

"You probably thought you'd seen the last of me, didn't you?" Wayne said, almost glibly as his mean green eyes ran up and down the length of the man before him.

When he spoke again, the facetious tone was gone, changed into a menacing clip that clarified his intentions. "Time's come to settle unfinished business between me and you, Joe," Wayne said maliciously. "Between the Bakers and the Taylors."

Joe froze under the penetrating gaze of spite and hatred leveled on him.

"You took somethen from my family, Joe Baker," Wayne hissed. "Now I aim to take it back. I think you Bible thumpers call it an eye for an eye and a tooth for a tooth."

Joe made no reply, staring openly as he appraised his abductor and assessed their whereabouts. Wayne had brought him to a remote hillside picnic area amid towering pine and oak trees. Considering the current state of fine mist and the failing light of day on this rain-washed afternoon, it seemed unlikely that anyone would happen by with the intent of using the grounds for picnicking. A paved road ran beside the picnic area, which was concealed by the thick stand of trees and gnarled undergrowth. Joe listened for the sound of a passing car but heard nothing. He was on his own.

"Go ahead and holler for help if you want," Wayne mocked, guessing the other man's thoughts. "But there's nobody around to hear you—'cept me."

Joe returned his gaze to Wayne and the gun pointed toward his chest, fighting heart and head to keep the pervading fear and desperation off his face. He steadied his nerves with closer scrutiny of his old neighbor, noting immediately the remarkable changes in Wayne's demeanor.

Joe had long considered Wayne burly, but doughy beneath the shell. The man before him now, however, was strapping and brawny. His brash cockiness, once a mixture of cowardice and bully, had callused into a bold edge with a heavy dose of cunning. And while Wayne always had swaggered with every move, a truer confidence now governed his actions, suggesting he had found something substantial to forge his life.

His prisoner's lasting silence offended Wayne, who abruptly waved him away from the car, pointing with the gun to a path down the graveled lane. "Let's go," he barked. "I warn you, Joe. Don't try anything dumb, or I'll shoot you dead in your tracks."

With Wayne in the rear, giving directions with the pistol, they moved down the hillside path, crossed the deserted paved road and entered another thickly wooded area. Pushing through dense and dying foliage, the two men emerged soon on a rough animal trail, following its faint markings in complete silence for the next three quarters of an hour. They came at last to a swollen creek, which Wayne forced his prisoner to wade across at waist level while he avoided the water and remained dry by using a nearby path of rock.

Stepping onto the creek bank, Joe came to a sudden halt. The feeling of dread that had been with him for most of his waking hours over the last two months momentarily overwhelmed his senses. He stood there alone, awed by the immensity of circumstances and his own frailty. The image Wayne presented only reinforced the budding terror—and made the possibility of dying on this damp November evening seem very real.

Joe stared first at Wayne, very robust and dressed appropriately in comfortable jeans, a thermal T-shirt, black flannel top shirt, hiking boots and a jacket vest. He glanced down at his own attire—chinos soaked to the thigh, a white cotton shirt and tie with thin-soled shoes—and came up with the ridiculous desire to be at home with a bottle of vodka and a cigarette. He felt almost farcical, crushed by a combination of fear and his own mental and physical collapse.

Only the husky voice of his captor saved Joe's courage from failing completely.

"Do you plan on playen dumb all night, Joe?" Wayne asked suddenly, breaking the long stretch of silence. "Aren't you a little curious about what's goen on?"

The insulting tone of inquiry restored Joe's dignity before it failed him. "It's crossed my mind a time or two," he said dryly, refusing to cower under his own shortcomings.

"So, you wanna be smug to the very end," Wayne replied. "Go ahead and have it your way, Joe. We'll see how smug you are a few hours from now when I have the last word between us."

Wayne advanced closer, holding out the pistol until its barrel touched the other man's forehead. "You and I are gonna play a little game this evenen," he told Joe dispassionately. "You can call it high stakes hide-and-seek, pin the tail on the donkey, one-potato, two-potato, or my personal favorite: Eeny, Meeny, Miny, Moe, catch a nigger lover by his toe. I don't give a damn what we call it, Joe, because regardless, I'm gonna win this game. I'm gonna stalk you across this whole damned mountainside, Joe. I'm gonna hunt you down just like you hunted Billy down that night, and I'm gonna see your ass dead before the night is done."

He paused, then clicked off an empty chamber in the pistol.

Joe's legs dissolved beneath him in sheer terror, and no amount of willpower could lessen the choke inside his throat.

"How does that grab you, old friend," Wayne threatened, pushing the weapon slightly against Joe's sweating forehead, which dropped him to his knees.

Wayne stepped back as Joe slumped against the wet ground, and the ominous tone disappeared instantly as he issued yet another order. "On your feet, Joe. Let's get moven."

Joe rose to his knees, wiped away the dead leaves matted to his forehead and stood upright. The trembles disappeared from his legs as quickly as they had come, and he moved laconically to obey the order, again following the direction pointed out by the gun.

They walked another ten minutes along the animal trail before the wooded path ended at a stretch of railroad track laid on a rocky bed. As soon as they emerged into open space at the base of the giant rock, Joe deduced their location.

They were on the world's largest piece of exposed granite. More commonly known as Stone Mountain, it was an oasis of rock, now operated as a state park in the developing, yet still heavily wooded eastern suburbs of Atlanta. Joe had come to the park once before, a few months earlier on assignment for the *Herald* to cover dedication ceremonies for a gargantuan sculpture of Confederate heroes Robert E. Lee, Jefferson Davis and Stonewall Jackson, which was carved on the side of the mountain.

His knowledge of the mountain ended there. The vast area of rocky terrain remained a mystery, even though Joe sensed he was about to make its acquaintance. Crossing the steel tracks onto the base of the mountain, Joe paused to stare up at the massive spread of rock. Shrouded in cloud and fog, the granite towered like a majestic stone fortress, unwilling to be conquered. He wondered how the rock supported the vast groves of trees that dotted its surface.

Wayne did not allow him much time for such considerations, however, poking a gun in his back to push Joe forward.

They walked up several yards on an incline, then veered sharply to the right. As they moved across the stony expanse, Wayne perversely recounted the days of stalking and preparation that had gone into this moment, concluding with the Halloween night four days earlier when he had waited and watched unobserved outside Joe's apartment.

Joe was too amazed to be disturbed by the scaremongering of having been stalked. What had gone before mattered little in light of his current predicament.

"I really wanted to do this on Halloween night," Wayne regretted as Joe tried to assimilate the details. "It would have been a more fitten payback for Billy. But tonight will do. Do you know why, Joe?"

Joe shook his head, having decided earlier, while lying face down in the muck, that it was unwise to provoke Wayne any further.

"Because I want you to know what Billy went through on that night you killed him," Wayne explained bitterly. "I want you cold and wet, scared out of your freaken mind, dead tired and on the run. Then, I'm gonna hunt you down like an animal and kill you in cold blood."

Strangely, hearing Wayne pronounce his fate did not panic Joe, who took the death sentence with calm acceptance and some disbelief. But his lack of reaction irritated the man who wanted him dead. Wayne shoved him violently, sending Joe sprawling on the stone, and aimed the gun once more directly at his head.

"Do you ever think about what you did to my brother, Joe?" he snarled. "Was it easy to forget you killed an innocent kid? Well, I didn't forget. And unlike the other fine people of Cookville, I'll never forgive you for it—not even after you're dead and the buzzards are fighten over your filthy, stinken carcass."

All of the sudden, Wayne kicked him savagely in the ribs. Joe gasped and attempted to roll away, only to be caught in the kidney with another kick. He curled on the ground, hoping to give Wayne a smaller target, but the viciousness was finished for the moment.

"Get up," Wayne commanded with sudden calm.

Joe uncoiled and came to a sitting position on the rock, touching his ribs gingerly. Discerning no serious damage, he stood before Wayne and looked him straight in the eyes. "Maybe it doesn't matter now, Wayne," he said impassively, "but I do regret things turned out the way they did. I'm sorry for what happened to Billy."

"Save it for the pearly gates, Joe," Wayne interrupted coldly. "The last thing I want from you is an apology, especially when revenge is gonna be so much sweeter."

The fine mist turned into a steady drizzle, and Joe nodded, understanding, if not accepting, the other man's will.

"Start runnen, Joe," Wayne commanded a moment later, directing the way with his gun.

"What?"

"Run! That way," Wayne explained, pointing straight across the mountainside. "As hard and fast as you can, and who knows, Joe? If you're quick on your feet, you just might get away from me."

Joe stared uncertainly, questioning the sincerity of the instructions and his ability to keep his footing on the terrain. His doubting nature lasted only momentarily, though, as Wayne leveled the gun at him once more. Then, Joe spun on his heels and took off across the rock at a quick pace. Behind him, Wayne let out a gleeful whoop and started his pursuit.

Joe covered the ground fast and hard, running on a slant across algae so old that it looked black instead of green. He tried for caution, but the slippery souls of his soft shoes made the going difficult. His run lasted no more than half a minute before his feet slipped on the treacherously smooth rock. His feet flew out behind him, pitching Joe forward into the air. He landed hard on his side, the full pressure of his weight coming down on his left wrist. Pain shot up and down his arm as he rolled onto his back, grasping the sprained wrist in a futile effort to ease it.

Wayne arrived a moment later, screaming at Joe, "Get up! Get up!"

Fearing another kick in the ribs, Joe jumped to his feet, letting the injured wrist fall to his side.

Wayne glared at him, then dissolved into a fit of laughter. "This is gonna be fun," he drawled exuberantly. "Hell, it's gonna be even more fun than I thought in the first place."

They began a sidelong ascent of the mountain, stepping over and on every size and shape of rock possible. Strewn across the base of the granite formation, the broken rocks gave the appearance that the entire mountain was crumbling. Joe touched his wrist, and corrected his impression: The granite surface was unyielding.

As they skirted the edge of a thick grove of trees, Joe noted in failing light the outline of the railroad tracks at the base of the mountain, a football field's length below them. It was the only sign of civilization. Beyond those tracks stretched acres and acres of green lushness and fall colors. The rise of the mountain lay first on the left and then directly ahead as Wayne steered them on a straight-up course.

In itself, the fast pace of their climb became increasingly difficult for Joe, but Wayne magnified the conditions—forcing Joe to scamper over any bolder in their path. The higher they climbed, the more ragged Joe's breathing became.

"You're in pitiful shape," Wayne observed as Joe gasped for air. "I could let you rest, but a good hunter never eases up on the chase. You understand that, Joe."

Joe forced himself to keep moving and was rewarded a moment later as the terrain leveled off. Without stopping, he risked a backward glance to get his bearings.

"Keep looken ahead, Joe," Wayne demanded. "There's nothen back there for you." A few steps later, he added, "But just so you know, the city's directly over your right shoulder. The clouds are too thick, though, to see the lights. And like I told you earlier, there's no one around for miles to hear you holler for help. Nobody hardly ever comes on this side of the mountain on the best of days, Joe, leastways on a rainy night like this."

Without doubt, Wayne spoke the truth.

———

After crossing a plateau and pushing up the steepest incline yet, Wayne pointed Joe in the opposite direction. As they covered essentially the same ground as before, on a downward trek this time, Wayne spewed forth random observations about his long days of spying on Joe. He spoke at length about the lack of activity in Joe's life, briefly mentioned biweekly trips to the cleaners and visits to the grocery store that not even the prisoner could recall. He praised the uncluttered look of Joe's apartment in one breath, then divulged the details of personal letters he had read while inside waiting for Joe to come home. Finally, Wayne confessed to rifling through drawers, cabinets and closets just to be nosy.

Though rattled by the thoroughness with which the man had combed over every detail of his life, Joe maintained silence throughout the ordeal, staring straight ahead until Wayne suggested, "You never did like me, Joe. From as far back as I can remember, you hated my guts. Why was that?"

Joe stopped in his tracks, regarding the man for signs of mockery. Wayne seemed sincere, however, so he shrugged and replied somberly, "You never gave me much of a chance to like you."

"Why does it always have to be my fault?" Wayne sneered. "You're not exactly blameless."

Joe resumed his careful walk down the mountain. "You killed our gopher for no reason, Wayne," he explained patiently over his shoulder. "You beat up my kid brother for no reason. Things like that, when they happen over and over again, don't exactly make for friendly feelens between people."

"Well, you insulted me," Wayne replied hotly. "Tellen everybody you'd save the life of a damn nigger over me or my daddy. That really pissed me off, Joe. That's the first time I ever swore to get your ass one day."

Joe recalled the incident on the school bus shortly after he had shot the panther and saved the life of Lucas Bartholomew. He'd felt a tinge of regret for the harsh words spoken back then to Wayne, but Joe kept mum about those thoughts and allowed the other man to purge his mind.

Wayne continued to ramble on as they came to the bottom of the mountain and started another march up its slope. Joe grunted an occasional response when pressed, but the exertion of climbing left him too weary to listen closely to the one-sided conversation. When Wayne suddenly began to talk about Billy, however, Joe gave his undivided attention.

Although repulsed by his own perverse curiosity, Joe had carried a burning desire for insight on Billy. Over the past year, he'd wondered countless times about the dreams and goals snuffed out with the bullet fired by his own hands. In his own crude and obnoxious way, Wayne supplied some of the details about his brother.

He told Joe that Billy had been a mother hen, keeping the house clean and food on the table once Martha Taylor had wallpapered the living room with her brains. Billy had protected their younger brother, Carl, from the abusive hands of their father, and he had considered school an opportunity rather than the prison it was to Wayne. Basketball had been the one true love of his life, and Billy had cried alone in his room when their father barred him from playing on the integrated Cookville squad. According to Wayne, Billy was a mixed-up kid, who tended to have tender-hearted feelings, sensitivities that had no place in the Taylor family.

"If he hadn't been my brother, I'd've sworn he was a little faggot," Wayne declared. "But we both know Billy liked to sniff a little leg, don't we, Joe?" he added with a leer. "Specially those long legs on your sister."

Visibly worn and dragging on his third trip up the rock, Joe was too tired to defend Carrie's honor.

Wayne spared him the opportunity, declaring abruptly, "That's enough talk about Billy. I'd rather hear about you. What happened, Baker? When did you become a full-fledged drunk?"

The observation rang too true for Joe, who continued to crave a good drink of vodka, even in the midst of such desperate straits as these. He purposely stiffened his shoulders and quickened the pace, hoping to lead Wayne away from the subject.

"What! No answer," Wayne drawled condescendingly. "You mean the high-and-mighty Joe Baker has lost his voice of righteousness. Or did you think all that vodka you've been drinken was just your little secret?"

He laughed jeeringly, then swore. "I'll say this for you, Joe: You must have the constitution of a jackass to handle all that liquor. How many fifths do you go through in a week's time?

"Come on, Joe," Wayne pleaded in mocking tones. "Tell me what it's like to be a lousy drunk."

Coming from Wayne, only minutes after the revelations about Billy, the ridicule deepened Joe's self-deprecating mood. A while earlier, the idea of confronting his own mortality had been met with calm acceptance and outright disbelief. But not so now as the possibility of dying on this dark, rainy evening suddenly loomed very real. Joe wanted to fight for his life. But his life seemed worthless and he felt too weak for the battle. In this frame of mind, disbelief settled into a lonely vigil for the arrival of divine punishment; and his willing acceptance of the odds became genuine regret over the way he had loused up his life.

Joe withdrew inside himself to await the unavoidable outcome and mull over the life that would soon end. Not even Wayne's constant needling penetrated his thoughts as they trudged up and down the dark and slippery mountainside. But gradually, the changing terrain forced Joe's thoughts back to the present as he negotiated the treacherous granite. Even Wayne became temporarily closemouthed.

Joe lost count of how many times they went up and down the piece of granite, but he felt like a mule at the end of a long day's work, having been led up and down the rows of an endless field. If anything less than his life had been at stake, he would have been bored by the repetition. It seemed like hours ago when they had first approached the mountain, now cloaked in the double darkness of a new moon and black clouds. A heavy fog turned visibility into a game of chance, and the soft-soled shoes continued to play havoc with his footing.

They were negotiating another extremely steep downward trek when his shoes lost their hold on the slippery surface. Despite his cautious navigation, Joe slipped without warning, landing on his bottom and bouncing. He hurdled several long feet through the air, then bumped once more against the slick stone. The sheerness of the incline, coupled with his rate of speed, left Joe helpless to stop the free fall. He bounced up again, somersaulted through the air and landed in a roll on the vertical grade, his descent unabated for a good forty yards until he slammed headlong into a growth of trees and underbrush at the bottom of the mountain.

Joe lay dazed in the scratchy bushes, grateful to have survived the fall, amazed to have done so without any serious damage to his bones. He staggered to his feet a short time later, just as Wayne completed a safer journey down the incline, laughing hard as he jabbered about Joe's ungainly descent. Joe stumbled out of the undergrowth and examined the dangerous slope with its severe incline, unable to believe Wayne had managed to come down it without a similar fall.

"Pretty steep, huh?" Wayne sneered. "But don't worry none, Joe. It's easier goen up than comen down."

He waved the gun once more, pointing him up the wall of rock, and Joe complied without protest, finding that Wayne was right. Going up the incline was easier than coming down it. Joe climbed on all fours, curling his toes through the soft shoes to gain traction against the slippery surface and bloodying his hands with the strength of his grip. Twice more, they came down this portion of the mountain, and twice more Joe's descent ended in a heap at the bottom.

On their third ascent up the dangerous slope, the two men finally veered away from the incline and crossed relatively flat ground to a natural tree-filled canyon, which they followed back down at a safe distance from its ragged edge. As they walked in the pitch darkness across broken rock, they passed chisels still stuck in the granite from long ago, and Wayne began a lengthy discourse on the history of the mountain, telling about the Creek Indians who had occupied the area during Colonial times and the mining activity that had taken place where they were walking before the Venable family sold the mountain to the state in 1958.

Wayne's knowledge of the mountain's history and topography was extensive, with revelations about unusual clams and fairy shrimp that lived in eroded depressions on the mountain during the rainy seasons, as well as unique plants that grew on the stone surface, including the extremely rare Confederate Yellow Daisies that splashed bright color across the gray granite in early fall. Under different circumstances, Joe would have been impressed with the completeness of the man's knowledge about the mountain, just as he would have admired Wayne's physical conditioning. Now, however, the history lesson fell on uncaring ears as Joe clung to tree limbs and grabbed rock outcroppings as they climbed down into the canyon.

They came at last into one of the old granite quarries, where an excavating machine had removed elongated slabs of the precisely chiseled rock. Rusted steel cables lay twisted along the strewn boulders, and the long, smooth sides of the quarry still bore the mechanically notched scars of the mining work. Joe stepped off one boulder onto a smaller one and suddenly found himself careening several feet down a slight incline, spinning like a carnival ride before the loose rock struck a stable counterpart. The impact sprawled Joe on his back.

As usual, Wayne found the situation deliriously funny.

Ignoring the derisive laughter, Joe lifted himself to his feet once more and followed the motion of Wayne's gun. They moved across the quarry floor back to the edge of the woods, pushing through brushy undergrowth and saplings to a twenty-foot wall of rock, its smooth sides marred only by tiny ledges, thin crevices and small jagged points.

"Climb it," Wayne demanded harshly.

"You've got to be kidden," Joe replied hotly. "There's no way."

"I've done it time after time," Wayne pointed out impatiently. "You just have to be careful. Of course, one slip and it's a long way down—not to mention these rocks. I imagine they're pretty unforgiven on ankles and legs, so I'd watch my step if I were you, Joe. Keep in mind, too, just how slippery and wet it is tonight."

Joe knew he had no choice. He sized up the wall, unable to see the top through the darkness, and began his ascent. Using every nook and cranny within grasp and toehold, he shinnied up to the first narrow outcropping and eased along its slippery edge until the next ledge was at eye-level. From the ground, this portion of the climb had not seemed anymore difficult than the rest. But as Joe scanned the wall for leverage, this next ledge seemed insurmountable. He glared down haplessly at Wayne, who bellowed for him to continue climbing.

Ignoring the sweat and rainwater streaming in his eyes, Joe measured the distance between the outcroppings once more and contemplated the challenge. There was nothing solid to balance his weight against, no substantial grip to hang onto and pull himself up to the narrow ledge. In fact, his sole motivation was the ceaseless demands from Wayne several feet below him, compelling him to take a chance.

Joe slid a hand along the wall once more, locating a slight depression in the rock, and then fearfully clawed an impossible grip, hefted his legs and used the brace of his elbow to power up onto the slither of outcropping. Once his legs and bottom rested against the rock, it was easy to scramble to his feet. He pressed his body against the wall and stood there trembling from the success of his gamble, grateful to have been spared a hard fall that could have broken his back or worse. A moment later, his nerves calmed and Joe completed the rise.

Wayne was waiting at the top.

"There's a natural walk-up over there," Wayne explained, pointing out an easy climb over several large boulders some thirty feet to their right. "I figured you'd be too worried about your own skin to consider how I made it up."

The top of the rock wall flattened into an earthen dam, carrying them along the edge of quarry pit filled with brackish water. Joe walked quickly along the straw-covered path until Wayne ordered him to stop. Brandishing the gun, he walked in front of Joe and intentionally panned his eyes to the murky pit.

"Care to take a little swim?" he asked.

Joe maintained his silence.

Wayne smiled uglily. "Drownen might not be such a bad way to die," he suggested as Joe's skin began to crawl with suspicion.

"There's no tellen what's just below the surface of that water," Wayne continued. "Pieces of rock and trash. If you dove in headfirst, you might get lucky and break your neck, Joe, which would make the dying quick and painless," he added optimistically before his tone turned suddenly doleful. "But if you jumped in feet first, you just might break a leg or two. I don't know, but I expect it's hard to stay afloat with a broken leg. Whataya think, Joe?"

Joe stared at the water, undisturbed by the threat. He expected Wayne to shoot him, and the implication that his life would end in a pool of smelly water did nothing to convince him otherwise.

"Supposen you do get in the water without injury," Wayne went on cagily, "then I guess I'd just have to wait around until you got dog-tired from swimmen and drowned the old-fashioned way. Because you know, Joe, I'd never let you out once you were in there."

Wayne stared back and forth between Joe and the water for a full minute, as if undecided about his plans. Then, he spewed out a geyser of hideously insane laughter.

Joe regarded his captor with careful concern, and the idea of surviving this night seized its first thin hold on his fragile psyche.

"Come on, Joe," Wayne bellowed, motioning the gun. "I've got somethen else in mind for you tonight, somethen much better than drownen."

They circled the edge of the pit back toward the mining area, where Wayne forced his prisoner to scale a treacherously smooth curl on the quarry wall. Following perilously close along the edge of the gaping hole, they began another ascent of the mountain, finally veering away from the forty-foot drop and heading straight up another steep slope. Although they were moving away from the quarry, Joe had little opportunity to feel relieved. The incline was sharp and Joe knew that one wrong move could send him into an irreversible slide over the quarry edge to a certain death.

At last, when Wayne altered their course into a sidelong ascent, Joe breathed easier, grateful that his fate would not be decided by an accident of his own cause. By then, however, he was so worn out from the exertion and his own poor shape that every breath came hard and ragged.

———

The two men were scaling another near-vertical slope, guided by a natural trough eroded in the granite through years of runoff from lashing rains like the one now drenching them. Propelled by a howling wind, the rain came down in sheets across the barren mountainside, impeding the progress of their climb with its ferocity and turning the walking channel into an ankle-deep rivulet.

Dizzied by the rushing current below him, Joe stared straight up into the black night, trying to summon up the reserves of guts and courage needed to survive. He found the cupboard not bare but strained dangerously low. He was exhausted physically, worn out mentally and running on the fumes of empty reserves. His thighs and calves burned, rebelling against the taxing nature of the current climb. The steel pin holding his left knee together seemed to be poking against skin and bone, gouging harder and deeper with every upward step until Joe could go no farther.

He came to a halt in the relative security of a tiny pool that afforded the most stable footing possible on the steep incline. Winded and sweating profusely in the chill of wind and rain, he faced Wayne. "I can't go on," he shouted hoarsely above the roar of nature. "I have to rest for a second."

Wayne, who had grown deadly quiet over the course of this latest ascent, regarded Joe's request with cold indifference. "You gotta keep moven, Joe," he replied with malevolence. "If you want to live awhile longer."

Joe's fatigue erupted into angry despair. "What the use then?" he asked. "I don't stand a chance anyway."

"Probably not," Wayne admitted, unruffled. "But you stand more of a chance with me than Billy ever did with you. At least you know someone's comen after you, Joe, which is more than can be said for my brother."

A distraught gaze came into Joe's eyes as he comprehended his inability to change the situation. He turned jerky, one hand shaking as it combed through his hair and raked his bearded face. Fear and fatigue reduced him to the point of willing surrender, a readiness to end the ordeal on his own accord.

The rebellion must have showed in his eyes or perhaps Wayne simply grew restless with the stall in their progress up the mountain. Either way, he pointed the gun once more at Joe and issued his most chilling threat of the night. "Don't be a fool, Joe," he commanded, lowering the gun's aim on the leg of his prisoner. "Move out now, or I'll shoot you just to make sure you're hurt enough to see the wisdom of doen exactly what I tell you when I tell you."

Joe stared into the cold-blooded conviction of wicked eyes and saw Wayne was not making an idle threat. The man was hell-bent on revenge, determined to see Joe suffer and die on this night.

Given the slow burn of his own guilt over Billy and the sorry state of affairs he had managed into his life, Joe could have crumbled in the face of this evil ambition. He could have felt vanquished and accepted Wayne's will as long-delayed punishment for his own bad turn. He could have felt overwhelmed by the moment and concluded his life had no value. He could have caved in to fatigue and given up on himself. But instead, Joe remembered that needless suffering bothered him. He smelled the first sweet fumes of courage renewed and tasted the tart sweat of blood-and-guts survival.

Without wasting another breath in protest, he turned on his heels and assaulted the incline with newfound resolve to gain freedom or die in the effort. His tired body continued to rebel against the strain, but the man inside churned with relentless determination. Every step brought a new reason to live and replenished the empty reserves of his best qualities: perseverance, endurance and instinct. His insides smelted and fused into iron will, his heart pumped boldly and his mind focused with photographic precision.

By no means did his doubts and fears vanish entirely, though. Over and over again, they congealed in a tight lump at the bottom of his throat. Each time the nausea gathered in his gullet, however, Joe swallowed back the bile of foreboding and converted it to food for an anorectic soul. If he died on this hellish night, it would not be for lack of heart or the will to live but rather a power beyond his control. Still again, as he and Wayne moved higher up the granite mountainside, Joe bided his dwindling time, waiting for an opportunity.

————

The rain slackened as the two men left the natural path of the sluice and began a diagonal trek across the mountain. Clouds lifted and the fog broke in patches, but the wind continued to whip around them and thunder rolled in the distance as another storm approached.

Skirting the edge of another small grove of trees, they rounded the corner and stepped onto yet another cliffside. Wayne weighed the merit of ending Joe's life right here against the desire to carry out the remainder of his plan. They were near the climax he had in mind for the night, and Joe was dead-tired. But Wayne was, too, although he still had enough reserves to reach the top of the mountain. Deciding to rely on the natural impulse of the moment, he guided Joe to a long chasm in the cliff.

"It's about a foot wide," Wayne explained ominously as Joe stared into the black depths of a natural tomb. "And who knows how deep."

Joe lifted his gaze to Wayne. "What am I supposed to do?" he asked audaciously. "Jump in and die a slow death?"

"Maybe," Wayne replied slowly, caught off guard by the defiant tone.

He scrutinized Joe more closely, trying to determine the state of mind behind the worn-out face. "But probably not," he suggested at length, backing away from Joe and motioning him toward the cliff's edge.

Joe approached the rim cautiously, stopping a good foot from the edge.

"Closer," Wayne ordered, and Joe eased out farther, this time halting only when the tips of his shoes evened with edge of the rock.

"Look down!" Wayne demanded.

Joe peered nervously over his shoe tops, seemingly ready to topple over on his own accord. Wayne moved behind him and stuck the gun in his back.

"A person could slip real easy off such a slippery ledge," he whispered to Joe. "Specially on a wet night like this. It's a good thirty- to forty-foot fall, with nothing but hard rock for a landen. A fall like that would hurt a man bad, Joe, likely do permanent damage. Probably kill him, don't you think?"

Joe swayed against the gun as his knees buckled slightly. Wayne heard the man swallow, he savored the fear in Joe, and decided then to see his plan all the way through. He pressed the gun slightly between Joe's shoulder blades.

"It would be a long way to fall from here, Joe, but it's a helluva longer way on the other side of the mountain. A person falls from there and he's bound to die—just as the people who find him are bound to figure he jumped on purpose."

Wayne gave another slight push against Joe's back and eased away from him. "Assumen you come away safely from this ledge, Joe, that's where you and me are headed," he continued coldly. "To the other side of the mountain, where I have a nice suicide all planned for you. And then, just so you'll know what it feels like to lose a member of your family—how I felt when I heard what you'd done to Billy—I'm gonna tell you all the plans I have in store for that sister of yours. Miss Carrie Baker and I are gonna get acquainted, and we're gonna have ourselves one rip-roaren time."

Joe seemed paralyzed on the edge of the precipice, except for shaking knees, and, for a moment, Wayne thought the man might topple over the side. Slowly, however, his right foot inched back a step, followed by the left one and suddenly Joe was a safe distance from the rim, regarding Wayne with cool reserve.

"You will regret ever tellen me that," Joe said with firm conviction.

"I doubt it," Wayne replied cockily. Then he barked out directions that back-tracked across the rocky terrain and brought them to yet another set of boulders leading into a thick stand of pine trees.

Joe hoisted himself easily over the craggy rocks, found a set of natural steps in the stones and scampered to the top, momentarily disappearing in the trees before Wayne caught up with him.

"Slow down, you bastard," Wayne hissed. "And don't even think about maken a run for it because I'll shoot you in the back without a second thought."

Joe slowed his pace, and as they wound through the trees, the strongest storm of the night arrived on the mountain. At last, they came to a chain link fence that was designed to keep people off the very part of the mountain they had traversed through the night. Wayne watched Joe climb over the low fence, then ordered him a safe distance away to make his own crossing. Once on the other side, his waning confidence returned.

"It's not very long now, Joe," he teased, unable to suppress his budding excitement. "Up and over and then we'll both go down the other side." He laughed again, feeling deliriously insane. "You'll just get to the bottom a lot faster than I do."

Once more, they started up the mountain, this time on the final leg of their ascent. The rain beat their faces, the wind roared and banks of black cloud darted past them. Visibility virtually disappeared beyond arm's length, forcing Wayne to follow close on the heels of his prisoner to keep Joe in sight. Wayne was pondering whether Joe would go over the side of the mountain without resistance or require prodding from the gun when the mountainside exploded like a megaton bomb.

Always squeamish around lightning, Wayne threw up his hands in a protective shield and pierced the cannonade of thunder with his own shriek of terror. He collapsed on the rock, anticipating with dread the shock to come.

CHAPTER 16

THE AIR SNAPPED LIKE a whip, and the night erupted like flashbulb photography, sheeting the mountain in brilliant incandescence. Thunder roared, and electricity slithered all across the granite slope. In the midst of the lightning strike, Joe barely flinched.

He glanced over his shoulder, saw Wayne cowered on the ground and broke into a hard run, giving only slight credence to the possibility of running straight into the hissing current as he charged up the slope. He ran doggedly, his feet pumping and clinging voluntarily to the slippery surface, oblivious to his tired body. A powerful surge of adrenaline carried him to the top of the mountain, and through the fog, the white glow of a tower light and the faint outline of a building complex beckoned to him.

Approaching from the front side of the building, he paused at the corner to catch his breath for two seconds, then resumed his flight, expecting Wayne was in close pursuit. A short walkway led him to a set of double doors, which he rattled and determined locked. Rejecting the hidden destinations of several side walkways—possible escape routes but also potential traps—Joe raced along the major catwalk of the building, passing four more sets of locked plate glass doors before coming to the corner of the L-shaped structure. He halted once more, this time to get his bearings and consider his next move.

Almost immediately, his instincts detected an eerie sense of déjà vu. He searched forward, then backward—in time to see Wayne emerge from the shadows of an opening some twenty yards away. Gunfire rang out, and Joe dove behind the ramp's low wall as the bullet whined behind him. The slug slammed against the building's stone wall, then ricocheted past Joe, who crabbed ten yards to the end of the catwalk, coming to an exit ramp from the building. Risking exposure, he stood straight up, lunging several steps forward before another pistol shot whistled near him. Unwilling to risk his luck any further, he changed course and vaulted over the ramp's wall.

It was a long free fall to the uneven rock surface below, with a jarring landing on his feet. The impact jetted up through his legs, settling hard between his shoulders, and his weak leg buckled under the shock. Somehow, he held his balance, even as footsteps echoed on the suspended concrete above him, a reminder that Wayne was in hot pursuit. Shrugging off the trauma, Joe fled into the sanctuary of thick fog and heavy black clouds without another wasted second.

Wayne stood at the end of the catwalk, contemplating the blackness where Joe had disappeared moments earlier. He sniffed the damp air like an animal searching for the scent of prey and was rewarded with a nostril full of rainwater. He blew out the spray with a snort, then chewed over the situation with his hunter's mind.

Any normal prey would make a beeline for safety, putting distance between itself and the hunter. If it had been a deer he had lost track of on this night, Wayne would have given up the chase and gone home. But Joe wasn't normal prey, and the territory limited his escape routes. Clearly, the tangibles in this hunt lay with Wayne. He knew the terrain and the various vistas off the mountain with the precision of a topographer, whereas Joe was relying solely on the whims of fate to guide him. Based simply on the advantages in his favor, Wayne expected to recapture his quarry.

It was the intangibles, however, that boded well for his success and bolstered his confidence. Just as fear of the intangibles gave cautious guidance to his successful criminal pursuits, so, too, a basic understanding of them made Wayne believe that very soon his path would cross again with Joe. The night, circumstances, even history, demanded a resolution.

Wayne chuckled dryly, a low growl of determination to come out the victor on all counts. True, Joe had escaped him, evening the odds in this high stake's game that had begun weighted heavily toward Wayne. But Wayne was a master hunter. He never returned empty-handed from an expedition unless it was by choice, and he was not of mind to fail now when the hunt offered the opportunity to bag the single-most important trophy of his life.

He sniffed the air once more, then set off at a brisk pace, charting a course across the heart of the mountain.

A wet pine limb slapped Joe across the face as he ran into an imposing formation of giant boulders, trees and brush. Without pause, he wiped away the scratch with a wet sleeve and scrambled through the bushes, across rocks to the edge of a small chasm. There, he paused for a brief rest and to get his bearings.

Even in the darkness, Joe could tell the formation figured prominently on the mountainside; he judged the rocky cluster set near the middle of the giant granite rock. Somewhere below lay the remainder of his escape off the mountain.

His flight from the mountaintop had ambled first directly away from the stone building on top, then veered back across the wide expanse in search of a trail. Hampered by flaring pain in the injured knee and fog so thick he could barely see his feet, Joe had advanced down the slick surface more slowly than he would have liked. Still, he figured the head start had helped him outdistance Wayne to this point.

Joe crouched on the slab of rock, bracing his knee with thumbs and index fingers in a vain attempt to massage away the throbbing. His confidence was growing with each step off this mountain, and his instincts were razor-sharp. In the last half-hour, his brain had done more work than in the whole of the preceding two months of stupor.

He stood up to plot his next move. The storm still raged but showed signs of slackening. He lifted his face up to the sky, opening his thirsty mouth to catch a few drops of refreshment, and, in that moment, his instincts again detected danger and took charge.

Whipping his head around, he found Wayne standing less than ten yards away on another boulder, with the pistol already aimed. Fire spewed from the weapon as the first shot rang out through the wailing wind, headed straight for Joe and followed instantly by a second discharge.

Joe dove headfirst, arms flailing, into the chasm below him, quick enough to avoid a bullet through the chest but not before the slug ripped into his left shoulder. His breath caught for a fraction of a second before he crashed face first into the granite bottom of the chasm, his bad knee impaling against the pointed outcropping of a lone rock.

By rights, Joe expected he should have been rendered unconscious either by the fall itself or the acutely sharp crack of a shattered nose and damaged knee. Even in a dazed state, though, his mind focused on the danger at hand. His instincts acted on the warning, sending him crawling across the chasm bottom. He passed through a small patch of sopping dead grass to the protective cover of an overhang as two more slugs glanced harmlessly off a rock several feet to his left.

Concluding Wayne was firing at phantoms, Joe crawled to the end of the overhang, then assumed a crouching position and peered out from under its edge. His current refuge seemed temporary at best, so Joe took a chance and made another dash for safety, fleeing once again into the black darkness.

Joe half-ran, half-hobbled across the steeply slanted slope, straining to keep his balance. He resisted the urge for a backward glance to see if Wayne pursued him, even though his back felt hair-raising exposure on the open plain. The chill of fear stayed with him until he stumbled straightway into the parallel side of the chain link fence Wayne had forced him to cross earlier in the evening.

His fugitive course halted, Joe stepped back from the fence and examined his whereabouts under a brief parting of clear sky. He checked behind him and saw no signs of Wayne. Next, he looked beyond the fence, realizing the barrier had spared him from the fate Wayne had in mind on this night. Without the fence to halt his advance, Joe would have plunged over the mountain's steepest side, a fall that would have ended some thousand feet later on the ground below the famous memorial carving of Confederate leaders.

A slow smile spread across his bruised face as Joe stood there pondering this night.

Blood streamed from his cracked nose, trickling into his mouth at the corners. More blood oozed warmly from the gunshot wound in his shoulder, staining the sleeve of his soaked shirt. His left leg felt useless, and the sprained wrist smarted for its share of attention. He was tired and hurting, yet Joe felt jubilant and light on his feet.

He was touched with gold and Godspeed in every way.

Whether this night turned his wayward life around or whether he carried this good faith off the mountain mattered little to Joe. Just having his confidence rekindled for this one moment was satisfaction enough. He would get off this cursed piece of rock without any more suffering. He would live to see another day.

Finding bloodstains in the bottom of the chasm where Joe had vanished moments earlier restored Wayne's confidence. At least one of his bullets had found a fleshy target. Joe was wounded and running.

Wayne followed the path beneath the overhang, coming to the open slope and considering his options. He stared into the darkness, listening, trying to gauge the direction Joe would have taken. It was a useless exercise. He would be stupid to attempt to track Joe in these conditions. His best bet was to ambush the man at the bottom of the mountain.

As he started down the path, Wayne was more sullen than disappointed about the missed opportunities to end this night. In his fanaticism to make Joe suffer, Wayne had dragged out the matter too long. It had been a tactical mistake, but he still expected to see Joe dead before the night was finished.

His sulking made him careless, though, and as he moved down the slope, Wayne lost his footing, landing hard on his rear, then sliding fifteen feet before level ground stopped his fall. He cursed, picked himself off the ground and continued his downward course toward the wide-open base of the giant rock formation. From there, he would have the best position to monitor almost any attempt Joe made to exit the mountain.

Wayne moved at a fast clip, increasing speed as the rock surface flattened out closer to the bottom of the mountain. He was nearing his destination, mulling over the best place to stand guard, when a clumsy step trapped his right foot between two misshapen slabs of granite and a gnarled tree root intertwined within them.

Wayne tried to twist his foot free, but his forward momentum cost him balance. His foot remained wedged in nature's version of a steel trap, while Wayne tumbled face down against the granite surface. Using his hands as a brace, he cushioned the fall somewhat but was helpless to protect his ankle. The tender joint rolled over, bending at a vicious angle, tearing ligaments and stretching tendons to the breaking point.

Wayne crashed to the ground, his loud groans evolving into violent curses as he struggled to free the trapped foot. His body writhed, contorted, then finally stilled as he realized fighting only aggravated the pain. Gritting his teeth, he sucked in air, rose to a sitting position and extracted the foot from the tangle of root and rock.

The pain brought tears to his eyes, launching Wayne into another round of wailing and gnashing of teeth. He thrashed around the ground in false hope that the frantic motion might somehow alleviate the pain, yet fiery embers continued to run unabated up and down his leg. Finally, Wayne came to his senses. He forced himself to calm down with more violent curses, his anger gradually subsiding to the point that he was able to examine the twisted ankle.

He was in serious trouble. The ankle was already puffy, ballooning tight against the confines of his boot. His brow broke out in a cold sweat as he tried to unlace the shoes, fighting excruciating pain all the way. When the laces finally were removed, he clenched his teeth once more, sucked air again and tugged off the boot.

His white sock came off more easily, but the sight of his foot sickened Wayne. The ankle was blown up twice its normal size, with the swelling extending from the arch to just below the calf muscle. Broken blood vessels had turned the ankle into a highway road map in varying shades of blue and purple that were turning black before his eyes.

"Damn!" he muttered repeatedly, trying to figure out how he could complete the short walk off the mountain, much less make it back to his car on a gimpy leg. Then, another thought took precedence:

Joe was still alive, possibly nearby and coming closer every second.

Wayne glanced around and found some consolation in his predicament. There was shelter in the hollow crook of the nearby tree, the same one whose protruding roots had crippled him. The tree would provide the perfect hiding place to lie in wait for an ambush should Joe happen along the trail. If Joe did not come by, then the dark corner would allow him to rest and recuperate before he tried to reach his car.

Careful of his foot, Wayne started sliding toward the tree only to realize he had dropped the gun during the fall. It had to be close by, he told himself, as every thought turned to finding the weapon.

———

Joe limped down the mountain in a hurried but cautious gait, fearful of running into Wayne as he followed a marked path. He was tuned on a constant state of awareness, his eyes scanning back and forth in surveillance and his ears straining to catch any sound above the soft patter of rainfall. Every low-slung rock and broken tree stump off the beaten path had the potential to materialize into Wayne. Joe fully expected the man to pop out from a curtain of darkness at any second, ready to finish what he had started hours, days, months, maybe even years earlier.

The fog broke completely as he emerged from a cover of trees onto an open plateau that led to another grove along the path. The ground was flattening out now, suggesting the bottom of the mountain was near, and even as he made the assumption, Joe heard uncontrolled cursing somewhere in the distance before him.

He slowed to a stealthy step, scanning ahead as the path carried him under the dark cover of trees, then came to a sudden stop as the back of Wayne Taylor blocked his passage some ten yards in the distance. Joe conducted a careful appraisal of the situation, deducing from the empty boot, the moaning and the groaning that his adversary had suffered a bad sprain.

Preoccupied with his suffering, Wayne was oblivious to the shadow advancing on his rear flank. Aided by the cover of an increasing tap of rain and a strong breeze, Joe moved silently closer, spying the abandoned gun and claiming possession in one motion. He arrived unnoticed, close enough to whisper in Wayne's ear had he chosen to do so.

Settled by a complete calm, he waited in perfect stillness to be discovered as Wayne cast around in a frantic search for something. Probably the gun, Joe realized, even as the change of fortune struck him as too easy to be possible.

A little over an hour ago, Joe had been at Wayne's mercy. Now the tables were turned. Any number of explanations might have conveyed why, but Joe needed none. He was more than willing to accept the will of fate on this occasion.

In the moment Wayne reached back for the pistol, Joe's shoe pinned his hand to the ground and the gun pressed hard into the fleshy base of his skull.

Fear froze Wayne.

A murderous rage surged through Joe.

Conditioned by years of experience, Wayne regarded his latest failure as a fact of life and thus accepted the consequences without protest. He went completely numb, indifferent even to the sense of helplessness and loathing that gnawed at his soul.

Joe repressed his own vindictive inclinations, not through indifference but with the unquestionable will of his heart. There had been too much killing and too much suffering; he was worn out by the bloody business. Those were his only thoughts on the matter; too much business remained at hand for further distractions, and Joe was in a foul mood to get on with it.

"Call it whatever you want, Wayne," he growled, pressing the gun barrel deeper into his prisoner's skull. "But I win."

Joe took two quick steps back, freeing the man's smashed hand. "On your feet," he ordered Wayne.

"I can't walk," Wayne replied sullenly, rubbing the circulation back into his shocked fingers. "My ankle's hurt real bad."

Joe laughed bitterly. "You're missen the point," he snapped, "and you're maken the mistake that I care about your ankle. I don't care how much it hurts, Wayne. We are walken off this mountain now, and we're gonna keep walken until I find someone who can take your sorry self off my hands." He paused, then added coldly, "Now, Wayne. On your feet."

Wayne wasn't bluffing. He doubted whether he could walk on the injured ankle. But the set tone of Joe's order also convinced him that it was in his best interest to give it his best shot. He grabbed his boot, pushed up with hands to a standing position and tested the lame foot. He winced and lost his breath. Then, he locked his jaws and did as told.

The Stone Mountain police were thorough with their questioning of Joe and Wayne and, initially, maybe a little dubious about the real culprit in the farfetched story. Their skepticism died, however, as soon as they verified that Wayne was a wanted man, under indictment in Cookville for attempted murder. From then on, they treated Joe with utmost respect, even giving him a light coat to ward off the chill of shakes and chattering teeth.

Joe could hardly blame the officers for their first impressions of him, especially if his appearance came across to them as it did to himself.

He had come into the bathroom of the village police station to splash cold water across his face. Raising his head to the mirror, Joe found a stranger staring back at him.

His face was sallow and sunken beneath the heavy beard, despite the color of bruises and blood. Bedraggled as he was, with hair plastered to his head, wearing clothes torn and soaked, Joe cut a gaunt figure on this night. On first impression, he seemed either creepy or sick. Joe took another quick glance at the man in the mirror and decided not even second impressions would help his case.

Oh well! He thought jovially. The hour was late, well after midnight, and he had not spent the previous evening engaged in leisurely pursuits. Now his spirit was waning, despite its earlier revival, and the night's toll was pealing fresh on his body.

Joe sat down on the toilet for a brief rest and leaned his head against the sink. Against his will, his mind reconstructed the harrowing night, from disbelief to despair to determination.

He felt much like the park ranger had looked when Wayne had come limping up to the entrance gate with Joe hobbling behind him in close guard. The poor bespectacled woman had peered up from her perch and gone instantly aghast and agape at the sight of them. She had remained confounded until Joe finally asked for help. When he repeated his request, she had made a game attempt to spring into action and perform her official duties. But she'd bungled everything, from her call to the city police to intentional refusal to budge from her chair.

"Is this a joke?" she asked Joe, repeating the question three more times before the police had arrived.

"It's for real," Joe had told her several times.

It was for real, and it was over. Almost anyway.

He still had a couple of telephone calls to make. Languorously, he got to his feet and returned to the main office of the police station, where detectives were completing their paperwork on the case. Wayne had been led away in handcuffs a few minutes earlier, and Joe was relieved to see him gone.

He served himself a Styrofoam cup of black coffee, then asked the idle dispatcher where he might have the privacy for a phone call. The man led him to a corner desk with a single phone on it, telling Joe, "This is about as private as it gets around here."

"It'll do just fine," Joe replied.

He waited until the dispatcher walked away, then dialed the home number of Ray Fields. The *Herald* editor picked up the phone on its fifth ring, answering with a groggy, "Hello."

"It's Joe."

"Baker?" his mentor inquired, coming instantly alert on the line.

"Yeah."

"What's up, Joe?" Ray asked anxiously. "Is everything okay?"

"I got a story for you, Ray," Joe informed him.

Silence filled the line momentarily. "Well, Joe," the editor said at last, "I've been wondering when you'd turn up another big one. It must be one heck of a story to wake me at this time of night."

"It is," Joe confirmed. "It's the story of a lifetime, Ray, but the thing is, I can't write this one for you. I'm gonna give it to you over the phone, all the details, and you can do whatever you want with it. Okay?"

"What's going on?" Ray interrupted.

"There's two conditions that I want your word on before I talk," Joe continued. "You cannot quote me, and somebody else will have to fill in whatever holes there are in the story. Agreed?"

"Agreed," the editor answered, trusting his reporter.

A half hour later, Ray knew all the details about the ordeal Joe had gone through on this night, as well as the whole truth behind the recent decline in his star reporter's work. He whistled low and long, and Joe overheard him tell his wife, Rose, that everything was okay.

"Gee whiz, Joe," Ray said at last. "When you come up with a story, you come up with a humdinger. I'm gonna play it big on the front page, hotshot, so get ready for a repeat of your previous infamous notoriety. It's sensational stuff, Joe, on its own, regardless of the past."

"It wouldn't be a story if there wasn't a past," Joe said.

"I'm glad you're okay," Ray said quietly. Then he exploded. "But damn it, Joe! You should have come to me when you realized you were in trouble."

———

Ordinarily, the ringing telephone would have woken Paul Berrien and his sisters at such a late hour. On this rain-soaked night, however, Paul had just returned home from a bad wreck on the most notorious curve of Highway 125.

Years ago, the same curve had claimed the beloved husband of June Berrien. Tonight's victim had been more fortunate, coming away from the accident with only a broken leg and concussion. Still, the accident stirred memories in the Berrien household, and Paul, April and June reminisced over hot chocolate in the cozy parlor of their elegant home. They were on the verge of returning to bed when the phone rang.

Paul set down his empty cup on the lamp table, bolted upright in his recliner and picked up the receiver on its third ring. Expecting to hear the voice of the night dispatcher in the sheriff's office, he instead received an official greeting from a police detective in Stone Mountain.

"Sheriff Berrien," the detective began after they had exchanged names. "We've had quite a night up our way, and your dispatcher tells me you've been busy, too."

"We had a bad car wreck," Paul confirmed, puzzled by the call. "The state patrol worked it, but we had to help them cut the boy out of the car. Kid wrapped it around a pine tree."

"Kids do the darndest things," the detective said with a dry laugh. "Sheriff, the reason I'm calling is because we've had an incident tonight involving a couple of men from your neck of the woods. One's a suspect down there from what I gather."

Paul instinct's peaked, then fell in a sickening wave of fear as the detective continued. "Sheriff Berrien?" he asked. "Do you know a fellow by the name of Joe Baker?"

"Yes," Paul replied in a tight voice. "I know Joe. Has somethen happened to him?"

"He's bruised and battered right now, but all in all he's okay," the detective answered quickly. "Says he needs to talk to you, but first I wanted to give you the official version of what happened up here tonight."

In rapid succession, the detective reeled off the details as he knew them, leaving Paul dumbfounded as his sisters looked on with consternation. Joe Baker was the only Joe that June and April could place with the limited information they had picked up in the one-sided conversation, and their brother's occasional mumbles and worried expression doubled their anxiety over the fate of their young friend. The sisters were prepared to assume the worst until their brother's expression changed abruptly to relief and he greeted Joe warmly on the phone.

"Hard to believe, huh?" Joe said by way of a greeting.

"Are you okay?" Paul asked immediately to assuage his foremost concern.

"A little tired," Joe replied vaguely. "But nothen so serious that a good night's sleep won't cure me."

"The detective made it sound a little worse than that," Paul commented, fishing for more details.

"I'm fine, Paul," Joe assured him.

"Your mama and daddy'll be glad to hear that," Paul sighed, accepting Joe's word. "Have you spoken with them yet?"

"Not yet," Joe hesitated. "I was wonderen, Paul, if you wouldn't mind tellen them for me. I've told the same story about three times tonight, and I'd prefer not to have to go through it again."

"I can do that," Paul agreed. "I'll run right over after we hang up."

"There's no need for that," Joe suggested. "Everything's over and done with now, Paul, and I'm fine. Let everybody, includen yourself, get a good night's sleep and tell them in the mornen. That will be soon enough"

Paul hesitated before agreeing with the request. "First thing in the mornen then," he said finally. "But I want all the details, Joe, and I want to know exactly where and how you're hurt."

Joe gave his friend an unabridged version of the ghastly ordeal, beginning with the letter from Carrie and ending with, "That's everything, Paul. After we hang up, I'm gonna get checked out by a doctor and then it's home to my apartment for some sleep. You can tell Mama and Daddy that I'll call them sometime tomorrow—or later today, I mean. Just whenever I wake up. Okay?"

"I'll tell them," Paul promised. "Is there anything else?"

The silence lasted several seconds.

"Yeah, there is, Paul," Joe said at last. "I didn't mention this to the police up here, and it's just a hunch. I could be way off base."

"About what?" Paul pressed, his lawman's instincts flaring with curiosity.

"The gun Wayne was carryen," Joe explained slowly. "It was a silver-plated twenty-two. And, Paul—it has a pearl handle."

Paul's eyes narrowed before his sisters. His mind churned in the silence, a state not lost to Joe despite the many miles between them. Although the community largely had forgotten the murder of Ned Turner, the unsolved case still hounded Paul. It was the reason he wanted out of law enforcement, as well as why he stayed in it.

"The good doctor's gun?" he stated laconically.

"Unexpected news, huh?" Joe replied.

"I should be surprised," Paul answered stoically. "But somehow I'm not. It almost makes perfect sense when you think about it."

———

A short time later, Joe hung up the telephone and pushed out of the chair. He rose too quickly, however, and his head began spinning. He wobbled two steps forward on his last ounce of adrenaline, then collapsed on the floor in front of the startled police officers. He revived soon afterward, just long enough to inform the faces hovering over him of one last thing.

"I forgot to mention it, but he shot me. In the shoulder, I think. It's probably nothen serious."

He was unconscious a moment later.

———

Paul arrived at the Baker house shortly before seven o'clock the next morning, eschewing the front door for a more direct route to the kitchen through the back porch. On his way around the side of the house, he met Matt, who was carrying a gleaming silver pail of warm milk freshly delivered a few minutes earlier from the udders of an aging Guernsey.

"There's a milk truck that runs out this way twice a week; a store up the road that sells the stuff by the gallon," Paul chided his friend. "And you still insist on milken that cow."

"As long as Brindy is willen to give, I feel obliged to take," Matt defended deftly. "There was a time not too many years ago when I'd've been hard-pressed to keep milk on the table without the old gal."

Paul exhaled an exaggerated sigh. "A faithful friend to the end," he said glibly. "But between you and me, Matt," he accused with mock seriousness, "I think you get a thrill squeezen the old milk bag?"

Matt arched an eyebrow toward the barn, where the brindled bovine stared placidly out of the pin, chewing on her cud. "She's got a lot of tit," he agreed with deep respect.

The two friends looked earnestly, first at the milky brown cow, then at each other before short laughs and shaking heads ended the moment.

"Care for some breakfast?" Matt asked as Paul followed him onto the back porch.

"Not this mornen," Paul replied. "I need to get to the office early. First off, though, I needed to stop by here. I have some news for you and Caroline."

Matt pushed open the kitchen door, then turned toward Paul. "You make it sound almost like an official call," he suggested.

Paul glanced at his feet, then back to his friend. "In a way, Matt, it is."

"Come on inside then," Matt urged.

The aroma of fried sausage and eggs, grits and fresh biscuits caused Paul's mouth to water and his stomach to growl as he entered the kitchen.

"Mornen, Paul," Caroline smiled from the stove.

"Howdy, Paul," Rachel piped in as she pulled forks and knives from the cupboard.

"The same to y'all, Caroline, Mrs. Baker," Paul replied.

Matt set the milk pail on the counter beside the sink and washed his hands while the women inquired about the well-being of the Berrien sisters. He dried his hands, then turned around and leaned patiently against the counter as Paul provided quick answers to several neighborly questions.

"Do you want some breakfast?" Caroline asked Paul a moment later.

"A cup of coffee?" Rachel added.

"Coffee would be fine," Paul answered. "I don't have time for anything else this mornen."

"Caroline, Ma," Matt interrupted. "Paul's here on some kind of official business this mornen, and I for one am interested in what he has to say."

A grave look came into the sheriff's eyes as he peered among his friends. "To tell you the truth, Matt," he suggested, "I don't want to alarm you, but it probably would be best if you got the whole family together, so everyone could hear at the same time."

"This sounds serious, Paul," Caroline frowned, spooning out a fried egg and turning off the electric stove eye as she concluded breakfast could wait a few minutes longer.

"It is," the sheriff said as Matt called the family to the kitchen. "But it's over and done with now, and everything is fine. There's no reason to worry."

Less than a minute later, when the children and Sam had filed into the kitchen, Paul told them what had happened the previous night. "I got a call from the Stone Mountain police department last night," he began slowly. "They have Wayne Taylor in custody up there."

"That's good news," Sam said warily as the faces around him demanded further explanation.

"How'd they catch him?" Matt inquired.

"They didn't," Paul sighed. "That's why I'm here so early this mornen. It appears that Joe's the one who caught him—in a roundabout way, that is."

Nine different versions of the same question were hurled at Paul, all of them preceded by "What!"

"First, let me assure you right off the bat that Joe is okay," Paul said quickly. Then, he told them the whole story exactly as Joe had relayed it to him.

Their faces ran the full gamut of emotions, from disbelief to horror, as the story unfolded with one shocking detail after another. When Paul was finished, Caroline fell into Matt's chair, leaned her head against the table and uttered a silent prayer. A shudder ran down her spine.

"Are you sure he's all right," she asked before a muffled sob escaped from her throat.

Matt moved quickly beside his wife, kneeling down on the floor to wrap her in a protective embrace. "I wish you'd have told us last night, Paul," he said shakily. "We had a right to know."

"I'm truly sorry, Matt, Caroline," Paul replied. "I wanted to come over here right away, but Joe insisted that it wait until the mornen. He didn't want y'all to worry unnecessarily. He was exhausted and wanted a good night's sleep first and foremost. He promised to call home as soon as he wakes up."

"Wayne tried to kill him," Summer remarked incredulously.

"The boy wanted Joe dead," Rachel fretted. "That's too awful to believe."

"I don't want to believe it," Caroline said. "I don't even want to think about it."

"Then don't," Sam commanded with an air of finality. "The worst is over now, and nobody's any worse for the wear. Joe is okay, Wayne's in jail where he belongs and everything is fine. We ought to be thankful for all that's right instead of dwellen on useless fears about what could have happened. I say we sit down here at the table, offer up a prayer to the Almighty and have ourselves a good breakfast to celebrate good news."

"You're right, Pa," Matt agreed somberly, rising and tugging Caroline to her feet. "We should be counten our blessens instead of worryen about what's over and done with."

"Come on and join us, Paul," Sam urged their friend. "Whatever pressen sheriffen business you have this mornen can wait a few more minutes until you've had yourself a hot breakfast."

Paul considered the offer and the advice, then concluded Sam was right. He'd waited more than six years for a break in the biggest case of his life. And, if the pearl-handled gun was the weapon that had killed Ned Turner, then fifteen minutes more of waiting would not matter. He'd soon have his suspect.

———

Against his will, Joe spent the rest of the night in a hospital bed. He wanted treatment followed by recuperation at home. But the emergency room physician, one Bill Conaway, insisted on treatment followed by observation at the hospital. The doctor's opinion carried more clout.

Joe slept in starts and stops, with both his waking and sleeping minutes preoccupied with harrowing details of the previous night. In the morning, he was stiff and sore, with every muscle and tendon in his body rebelling from overexertion.

His right arm rested in a sling. The bullet had passed through the fleshy part of his outside shoulder, nicking a muscle on its way out the other side, but Dr. Conaway predicted a complete recovery.

A large bruise blemished his abdomen, marking the place where Wayne had kicked him savagely in the ribs, and another nasty contusion covered his right temple where the pistol had bashed his skull. His nose was swollen, a black and purple mess of ruptured membranes and broken cartilage, scraped raw across the tip.

"It looks and likely feels worse than it really is," Dr. Conaway assured Joe. "A week or so from now, and it'll be good as new. Maybe a tad crooked, but not noticeably."

The sprained wrist was a minor injury, which would heal with a few days of rest. His left knee was a different story. It was in shock, strained beyond its ability and in need of recuperation. The kneecap had a hairline fracture, while a deep gash below it required six stitches. And although X-rays determined the steel pin remained secure in his leg, Joe second-guessed the opinion every time his knee throbbed. It felt almost as if the steel was rubbing against the bone.

"The best thing for you is rest and relaxation," Dr. Conaway said. "I'll give you a prescription for a mild sedative. It will help you rest easier."

"Thanks," Joe said.

The doctor pursed his lips, as if he were debating whether to say anything else. Bill Conaway was young, fresh out of his internship. He was affable and easygoing, a straight-talker who dispensed advice without preaching, and Joe respected him.

"Is there anything else?" he asked, sensing the doctor's dilemma.

"There is," the doctor said. "You need to get some food inside you and take better care of yourself, Joe. Last night was hard on your body, but you weren't in good shape to begin. You need good nourishment to build yourself back up and put some weight on those bones." He hesitated only slightly before adding, "We did bloodwork last night, and your body chemistry is shot to hell right now. Frankly speaking, you have about as much alcohol in your bloodstream as the stuff that's supposed to be there. In a roundabout way, I'm tellen you to lay off the booze. I don't know how much you drink, but keep in mind that liquor can make a young man old before his time."

Joe nodded sheepishly. "Good advice, doc," he said. "Can I go now?"

"You can go," Dr. Conaway saluted. "Home to bed. You've got a friend outside waiten for you."

"I do?"

"You do," the doctor said. "I'll send him in. A nurse will be along in a minute with the discharge papers, so you can go ahead and get dressed. I'll leave the prescription with her, as well as instructions on how to take care of that bullet wound. Your regular doctor needs to look at it in a couple of days to make sure it's healing properly."

"You're the closest thing I've had to a regular doctor since I moved here," Joe replied. "Do you keep office hours?"

Bill Conaway laughed. "I'll take patients any way I can get them," he said. "I'll leave my office number with the nurse. You can call for an appointment."

"Thanks again, doc."

"My pleasure, Joe," he said. "And by the way, I'm glad you came through last night. It must have been some ordeal."

Joe shook his head.

The doctor let the door close behind him, and Joe eased out of the bed. He was wearing a flimsy hospital gown that left him exposed on the backside. A check of the closet and drawers turned up no sign of his clothes, so he sat down on the side of the bed and tried to remember when he had undressed.

He recalled feeling faint in the police department and remembered waking up on a gurney in the hospital emergency room. Somewhere in between, someone had stripped off his soggy clothes and shoes. The idea of getting back into them, all wet and stiff, had as much appeal as staying in the hospital gown, which at least was dry.

Joe was pondering his predicament when the door burst open and Ray Fields strode into the room with a cheerful greeting and a paper sack full of clean clothes and shoes. Having discovered Joe's whereabouts while putting the finishing touches on the *Herald*'s front-page story about the kidnapping of its star reporter, Ray had ramrodded his way into his employee's apartment, found dry clothes and come to drive him home.

"I'm in your debt," Joe told him as he finished dressing.

"Yes, you are," Ray agreed bluntly. "And the payback starts as soon as we get back to your apartment."

Less than an hour later, Joe was resting in his recliner, while his boss paced back and forth across the living room in deep thought. "Your work's been lousy," Ray began bluntly.

Joe concurred with a nod. "Are you firen me?" he asked.

Ray scratched his head. "If it were anybody else, I'd fire them on the spot," he continued. "The truth is, though, your lousy work is better than the best of most others. You've also done too much good work for me—for the newspaper—to toss you out on your butt. You've been loyal beyond the call of duty, and that counts a great deal with me. Above everything else, you're not just any employee, Joe. You're a good friend, and I respect you. On top of that, my wife and daughters adore you. They'd never forgive me if I fired you."

Joe smiled. "You're not firen me," he sighed, visibly relieved.

Ray exhaled a deep breath of his own. "Of course not," he answered. "But I am giving you an unpaid sabbatical, a leave of absence if you will, until the new year. I don't know what's been goen on with you the last few months, Joe, but you need time to recharge your batteries and get your head back on straight."

Joe cringed at the thought of six weeks without work, but he accepted the order without protest. "I'll be fine again, Ray," he said.

"Yes, you will," Ray agreed. "Otherwise, I'll have no choice but to fire you."

"Now what would Rose and the girls say about that?" Joe suggested meekly, trying to lighten the mood.

"I'd tell them you quit," Ray deadpanned, still serious. "Now let's talk, Joe. Friend to friend. I expect you to spill your guts, and then I'm gonna give you some friendly advice."

"I've been drinken too much, I suppose," Joe said.

"Now tell me somethen I don't know," Ray challenged. "Are you taken drugs?"

"Just once," Joe confessed. "It was a bad experience. I think it caused me to start drinken more than I should." He hesitated, then looked at Ray. "I swear it won't happen again, Ray. Drugs are bad business."

"So is booze," Ray replied tersely. "I know. I've been there, too."

Joe nodded distantly.

"I mean it, Joe," Ray continued. "I was twenty-nine and drinken like there was no tomorrow—beer for breakfast, double-martini lunches, afternoon pick-me-ups, liquid suppers and brandy for a nightcap. I was the quintessential newspaper stereotype. It was crazy, and I was going nowhere fast. Finally, I was lying in bed one night with a bottle of gin, and it hit me that I'd much rather have a woman with me. Right then, I made up my mind to become respectable. I tossed the booze, cleaned up my act and the rest, as they say, is history."

"You make it all sound so simple," Joe remarked.

"It is, Joe," Ray shot back. "Forgive me if I'm preachen, but you can have a life or you can be a drunk. There's no compromise. You should have already figured it out, Joe, but booze is a lonely companion. It messes up everything."

"Yeah," Joe agreed vaguely." You're right."

———

Annemarie weaved her way through the crowded terminal of Hartsfield airport, wanting to escape the throng of travelers arriving and departing on afternoon flights. Her return flight to Atlanta from New York had landed more than an hour ago. It had been a rare experience, the kind of flight that made her question the wisdom of waiting hand and foot on obnoxious people just to earn a living and free travel privileges.

Annemarie was not overly concerned about her current depression. By tomorrow morning, her enthusiasm would return and she would wear a genuine smile when she greeted Delta travelers at the jetliner's door. But for now, she wanted to go home and enjoy a relaxing bath. She intended to splurge on the luxury of a taxi rather than endure the long bus ride to the city.

Passing an airport newsstand, she stopped automatically to buy the afternoon edition of the *Herald*. Annemarie purchased the newspaper daily, a habit left over from her relationship with Joe.

In those first days of getting to know him, she had begun cutting out his bylined articles from the newspaper and pasting them in a special scrapbook. She had maintained the practice until a few weeks after their breakup when she condemned it as silly and useless. Now she simply read his stories. They were her only link to the man who continued to dominate her thoughts.

Annemarie regretted the loss. She missed Joe's friendship. She missed his companionship, playing tennis with him, reading poetry, sharing meals. Despite herself, she longed for his touch, the rich, graveled tone of his voice, the piercing gaze of his dark eyes. She missed his devilment. And on occasion, even thoughts of his hardheaded stubbornness kindled warmly in her heart.

Joe was not easily forgotten, but Annemarie had tried her best to. She had dated several men, polite encounters that left her empty and hungrier for Joe. One of the men, Wesley Young, was a member of her church and seemed eager for a serious relationship. She had gone out with him on five separate occasions, not counting their meetings at church, and another date was set for Saturday. It would be their last. Wesley was a nice man, a banker who would earn respectable amounts of money one day while providing a stylish life for his wife and children. Annemarie wished him well, but she wasn't interested.

As for herself, Annemarie knew she was wishing for the impossible. It was a foolish waste of time. She harbored no illusions about fairy tales coming true, but the idea persisted like the haunting melody of an unfinished song. She suspected her thoughts would cling to Joe until another man stole her heart, or perhaps until time dimmed her memory.

Thoughts about Joe came suddenly and lingered sadly these days. Today, however, Annemarie was too tired to dwell on the ramifications. She picked up a copy of the Herald, tossed a dime on the counter and started toward the terminal exit. She glanced idly down at the newspaper clutched in her hand and was struck first by the bold size of the headline spread across the front page. Premonition urged her to read it closely.

Herald reporter fends off murder attempt;
Kidnapped, beaten and shot before escaping

The airport buzzed around her, but Annemarie was aware only of the thumping of her heart. She felt limp and lightheaded. Her throat swelled around her windpipe. She clutched the newspaper tighter, closed her eyes against the airport ceiling, then calmed her overwrought nerves by scanning the terminal for a nearby bench. Spying one twenty yards away, she walked quickly to it and sat down without bothering to remove the blue flight bag from her shoulder. She read the lengthy article completely, then reread the part about Joe being in stable condition.

Maybe it was true. Maybe Joe was fine, despite a bullet wound. But Annemarie wanted to see for herself. She needed to see Joe. And she prayed he would welcome her.

––––––––

It was late afternoon or early evening. Dark shadows fell across the room and the silence weighed on Joe. He sat upright in the recliner, watching a cigarette burn in the ashtray. He'd slept soundly in the chair for five hours straight after Ray Fields had returned to work earlier in the day. Upon waking, he had gone into the kitchen without thinking, filled a tumbler with ice and vodka and returned to the chair to spend the evening. Now the ice was melted, and the glass remained half-full. Joe felt the same way.

Over the past few months, his core had melted. Now the vital juices were beginning to reconstitute, shaping Joe into someone different from the person he had been. The basic elements remained inside him, but leaching and infusion had changed Joe in ways not easily defined—perhaps not even known.

And the process remained incomplete. The reconstituted Joe was still far from solid.

Out of habit, Joe picked up the glass and took a small sip of vodka. The liquor burned all the way down his throat into an empty stomach. A few days ago, he would have welcomed the sensation and tipped the glass for another drink. Now he wondered.

Joe rested the glass against the recliner arm and closed his eyes. He recalled fondly a time many years ago when he had recognized a need for normalcy in his life, along with a decided preference for simplicity. Somewhere along the way, he had allowed complications to clutter his thoughts. He had violated his own cardinal rules, trying to change situations beyond his control, while accepting or ignoring things he should have controlled.

He opened his eyes, stared distantly into the semi-darkness of the room and wondered how to catch a falling star.

Annemarie found him this way a short time later when she let herself into the apartment with the key Joe had given her months earlier. She opened the door quietly, peered into the dark room and saw Joe silhouetted in the red glow of a cigarette. He seemed unsurprised by her sudden appearance, casting a sideways glance toward Annemarie as she slipped into the room and leaned against the door as it closed behind her. She stood there uncertain, with her blue flight bag hanging off her shoulder, wishing she had changed out of her uniform.

"I should have knocked," she said at last, her voice soft. "I would have come sooner, but I just now read the paper."

Annemarie hesitated, searching the darkness for his eyes and any sign of whether she was wanted or needed.

The silence engulfed her. "I'll leave if you want me to," she offered.

"Please don't, Annie," he said at last. "I'd appreciate the company."

She nodded, then crossed the room and set the flight bag on the kitchen bar. "May I turn on the kitchen light?" she asked.

"Sure."

She flipped the switch, illuminating the living room with a pale white glow that allowed her to see Joe clearly. Annemarie was hard-pressed to recognize him. His face was heavily bearded above sunken cheeks and he needed a haircut. He was haggard, pale, torpid, and appeared to have lost a minimum of twenty pounds since she'd last laid eyes on him. But his eyes still captivated and his voice still drew her. She was still in love with him.

Annemarie crossed the room toward Joe, smiling softly. She wanted to support him, to soothe and care for him.

The closer she came, however, the more her strength wilted. Her eyes regarded him carefully, taking in the arm sling, the bruised face, the cracked nose and the half-empty glass of vodka in his hand, and fear overcame her resolve. She collapsed on her knees in front of him, laid her head in his lap and sobbed.

Joe caressed her hair and pleaded for an end to the tears.

"I'm sorry," she said in a quivering voice a few minutes later, "but I read that story in the paper, and it completely unnerved me, Joe. I was so scared."

"I'm fine," Joe reassured her.

Sniffling, she stood, appraised Joe once more and declared, "You sure don't look fine."

"I've missed you," Joe chuckled. "And to tell you the truth, I don't feel fine. In a week or two, though, I'll be as good as new accorden to the doctor who treated me in the emergency room last night."

Impulsively, Annemarie combed her fingers through his hair and traced his beard. "When did you sprout this?" she asked.

"Over the last two months," he answered. "What do you think of it?"

She nodded vaguely. "It's okay."

Joe smiled knowingly at her. "I don't like it much myself," he said. "I was thinken of getten rid of it."

Annemarie returned the smile. "I'd be happy to shave it off for you."

Joe nodded. "I think maybe I'd like that."

She went into the kitchen and filled a dishpan with hot water, then procured a razor, shaving cream, aftershave lotion and towels from the bathroom. From her flight bag, she produced a pair of scissors.

When all of the materials were laid out on the floor beside Joe, he leaned back in the recliner and Annemarie set to the task with a surgeon's skill. She wrapped a towel around his neck, then used the scissors to cut away most of the thick beard. Next, she bathed his face with a warm washrag and lathered it with a thick froth of menthol shaving cream. She stroked the razor first along his jaws, then scraped away his sideburns and cleared his chin.

Annemarie worked in silence, and Joe closed his eyes, lulled into a drowsy state by the rough scrape of the razor against his skin, basking beneath her touch. She nicked him once, on the curve of his chin, but Joe barely noticed as he dozed. Soon afterward, she woke him with the soft sting of aftershave lotion against his clean face.

Joe opened his eyes to the gaze of a woman in love.

His chest constricted, his throat tightened, his fingers floated up to touch the side of her face. And Joe realized that he loved her, too. Had loved her for a long time, and he digested the implications as Annemarie leaned down and brushed her lips lightly against his.

She pulled back gently, penetrating him with a featureless gaze. "I'm a fast-moven train," she declared. "Too brash and too forward for my own good at times. Maybe this is one of those times. Maybe I'm chasen after somethen I can't have and maken a fool of myself. So be it. I'm willen to take that chance because I love you, Joe."

Her admission rolled through Joe like a warm spring breeze. His heart soared with wonder, then hammered with uncertainty.

"You may want to reconsider once you find out how badly I've messed things up over the last two months," he suggested.

"I've already tried to talk myself out of loven you, Joe," Annemarie stated plainly. "I couldn't do it, so don't you bother tryen. And don't push me away this time. I love you—plain and simple."

"You need to know the whole truth about me, Annie," he said urgently. "I've been a regular fruitcake these last two months. I've loused up everything, soused up my life."

She took his hand and nodded.

"I mean it, Annie," he emphasized. "A lousy drunk—that's what I've been. I can't guarantee I'm the same person you knew two months ago. I can't say for sure everything's gonna turn out okay. I've made a mess of my life, Annie. I don't want to do the same thing to yours."

Annemarie smiled warmly, undaunted by his confession.

"We're not exactly starry-eyed youngsters, Joe," she proclaimed. "We're not old and wise by any stretch of the imagination, either. But my life, with all its goodness and blessens, has been grounded by some pretty sober messages. Yours, too. I trust you, Joe. I have faith in your instincts and yourself. You will not make a mess of my life."

His cautious nature was hard to convince, and Joe responded grudgingly, vulnerably, with insecurities and intensity. "Whatever happens between us, we should take it slowly," he explained in a broken voice. "Maybe you're a fast-moven train, Annie, but I like to build bridges."

Annemarie tossed her head back and gave a throaty laugh. "Sugar!" she crooned, leaning close to his face. "I told you the first day we met that I have some very old-fashioned values. One of those, I assure you, is that a girl oughtta wait for the man to make the marriage proposal."

Joe nodded self-consciously as closeness enveloped them, sating the yearnings of two ready souls. It was love, coming softly, tenderly and timidly. Annemarie embraced it and, at last, Joe, too, was ready and willing to listen to his heart.

"I love you, Annemarie," he admitted, a throaty, salutary confession. "I have for a long time now."

She lifted his hand and pressed the palm flat against her face. He cupped her neck, pulled the woman into his lap and sealed the moment with a tender kiss. It was sweet, with the promise of passion and more, something very real and lasting.

For a long time, they sat and gazed at one another, exchanging an occasional kiss and basking in the newness of their love. At last, Annemarie smiled at Joe, touched his throat and transformed back into her vibrant, headstrong self.

Like a mother hen, she fussed and fretted over him. She conducted a thorough examination of his battered body, tracing and pressing the outline of every bruise with the light touch of her hands, changing the dressing on the bullet wound in his shoulder and massaging the bruised ribs and strained knee with ample amounts of liniment.

At Joe's suggestion, she took the glass of vodka and poured it down the kitchen sink. Finding his cabinets bereft of food, she ran next door to her own apartment and whipped up a supper of melted cheese sandwiches on toasted bread with hot chocolate. She carried it back to his place on a pie plate and served him in the recliner. It was not fancy, but Joe ate half a sandwich and downed the whole cup of hot chocolate.

"It's a start," Annemarie beamed and declared her intentions to put the meat back on his bones.

When they were finished with supper, Annemarie turned off the lights, nestled against Joe in the recliner and listened intently as he volunteered the details of his ordeal the previous night. He presented her the unvarnished version of events, and several shudders ran through her as the violent, insane behavior of Wayne Taylor became apparent. Once or twice, Joe trembled at a bad memory, and Annemarie soothed his jangled nerves with comforting touches and reassuring words. When he was finished with the story, they sat in companionable silence and contemplated the blessings of life.

"I never read Carrie's letter," Joe remembered at length. "I could hardly wait to read it, and now I'm not even sure where it is."

"Let me look for it," Annemarie offered, slipping out of the crook of his arm and over the side of the chair.

Her search was rewarded instantly as she spied the opened letter on the floor between the recliner and the wall. She retrieved the handwritten pages and offered them to Joe.

He reached for them, then changed his mind and withdrew his hand. "Would you read it to me?" he asked.

Her heart lurched, touched by his obvious attempt to share something very personal. "Are you sure? It's private, and I know things have been strained between the two of you."

"I'm sure," Joe nodded.

Annemarie crossed the room, switched on the overhead light, then returned to Joe's side, sat on the floor and read the letter aloud:

"Dear Joe,

"I can hardly believe a whole year has passed since that awful night. Thankfully, time is indeed the great healer. At least it has been for me, and I hope for you, too. That night remains vivid in my mind and still haunts my thoughts and dreams from time to time. But lately, I don't dwell on it anymore. I've learned to accept what happened, and that, more than anything else, has eased my mind.

"The idea for this letter came to me on Halloween afternoon as I took a walk through the pecan orchard. I waited a couple of days, however, before sitting down to write. I needed the time to think about exactly what it was I wanted to say to you.

"First of all, I want to tell you what Billy Taylor meant to me. We were friends, very good friends, perhaps on our way to falling in love with each other. Maybe we were in love and simply afraid to admit it. Outside the family, I've never had a friend like Billy. I trusted him, I enjoyed his company. He was a good person—nothing at all like his father or Wayne.

"It's hard to explain what his friendship meant to me, but it was very important. It was something I earned, and Billy was a part of me that was separate from the family. Maybe that sounds silly and hard to comprehend, but it was important to me at the time. And it hurt to lose him, Joe. I can't begin to tell you how much it hurt to lose Billy as a friend and companion. I still miss him.

"As much as it pains me to write this, I have to tell you, Joe, that I resented you after Billy died. It was wrong of me, and I realize that now. At the time, however, I was angry and horrified and half out of my mind. As I saw it, you caused my grief, so I wanted nothing to do with you. Understand, too, Joe, that I avoided you because your presence was a constant reminder of what happened. That whole day was all too much for me to handle. First, Danny was shot and died in my arms—then Billy, too. Nothing in my life prepared me for such senseless violence, Joe. To this day, it still seems senseless, and I've asked myself a million times why it happened.

"Knowing you, Joe, I'm sure you've asked yourself the same question, probably a few dozen times more than I have at that. If you're like me, you've discovered there are no easy answers. What happened defied sense then and still does now. It probably always will. I've learned to accept that, and I'm trying to move past the question of why.

"If there was a reason, though, then it was God's reason. We've heard all our lives that God works in mysterious ways. Well, what happened to Danny, to Billy, to you and me, certainly qualifies as mysterious. Of course, I don't believe God planned the awful things that happened that day, but maybe He made the best of a bad situation. One of the last things Billy said to me that night was that he believed in God. His belief was based on a lie, and that bothered me to no end for the longest time. But maybe, Joe, everything happening as it did saved his soul before he died. Farfetched thinking perhaps, but it's helped me come to grips with what happened. Whatever the reasons were, I don't think God created a set of circumstances such as they were just to ruin perfectly good lives.

"That's enough philosophy from me. Now let me tell you about myself and what's happened since you left home.

"Probably no one mentioned it to you, but I had a breakdown, Joe. I completely lost my way in trying to come to grips with what happened. I can't explain it precisely, but every day was miserable for a while. I barely graduated from high school. I became a complete and total social misfit. Hard to imagine, huh, considering the social butterfly I've always been? The good news is I made it through the bad days. And the days since have been better and better.

"I still have regrets. Maybe regrets are an inevitable part of life. But you can't dwell on them, Joe. One of my regrets is that I lost a whole year of your friendship and brotherly advice. I hope this letter begins to bridge the gap between us.

"Recently, I've thought a lot about the various relationships between the respective members of our family. They're a complex lot, especially those between us brothers and sisters. We're all so much alike and yet so different at the same time. The way we mix and mingle is indescribable. And yet, I've noticed there are a number of recognizable patterns. I've concluded you and I are really the most alike of all us children. We're both extremely private people. We'll stick our noses in everybody else's business, but when it comes to ourselves, we keep everything inside.

"Lately, I've learned the value of loosening up. It helps not to hold everything inside, especially when there are so many people who want to accept and help you without any kind of judgments. Love is pretty powerful in all its forms. And never was there more proof of that than when you shot Billy. I understand now, Joe—you shot Billy because you loved me. Knowing that doesn't make the way things turned out any less awful. But any understanding out of something so senseless is worthwhile.

"I hope this letter finds you well and close to a visit home. Everyone misses you. Even Lucas stopped by the other day to ask about you, although I think in a roundabout way, he was interested in the opening of deer season. Anyway, take care and come home soon, brother. If you don't, Luke might carry out his threat to take over your room. And, you might miss Summer's last days as a single woman—though you never heard it from me.

"Love from your sister, Carrie."

Annemarie gave the closing her full attention for a solid minute before looking up from the letter. Joe was staring at his brother's painting on the wall, miles away from her. Or so she thought.

He felt her gaze, glanced down and smiled plaintively. "Love is pretty powerful in all its forms," he quoted Carrie.

Annemarie let the remark pass without comment. Vagueness suited this moment.

"I should call home," Joe said at length. "I told Paul to tell everyone that I would. They're probably worried sick."

She concurred with a nod and went to fetch the telephone for him. Upon handing the receiver to Joe, she dialed the number, then left him to privacy, with a promise to return after a quick visit to her apartment.

"I've got to dig up a recipe for molasses cookies," she quipped as the door closed behind her.

Caroline picked up the kitchen phone midway through its first ring. "Hello!"

"Mama?" Joe said hesitantly. "That was quick."

Caroline exhaled a breath that she had carried around for what seemed like most of the day. "I was hopen it was you," she told her son. "If it wasn't, I planned to get in the car and drive to Atlanta to see you for myself."

Joe laughed slightly.

"Let me get your daddy on the other extension and then you can tell us how you are," Caroline continued.

"When did you get a second extension?" Joe inquired as his mother called loudly for Matt to pick up the living room phone.

"About a month ago," she replied. "In the kitchen. For the sake of convenience."

Another receiver picked up on the line. "Son?"

"Hi, Daddy," Joe replied.

His parents made simultaneous inquiries.

"How are you, son?" Matt asked.

"Are you okay?" Caroline wailed.

Joe laughed again, this time more freely, at their urgency. "I'm fine, folks," he assured them. "A little banged up and bruised. But nothen that won't heal soon."

Caroline dissolved into tears, and Matt and Joe spent the next minute trying to calm her. "We could come up and take care of you," she finally suggested, through sniffles. "Or bring you home until you're recuperated."

Home!

Joe closed his eyes and savored the memories. He wanted to accept the offer, but he couldn't bring himself to do it. His battered body aside, if the family saw him in his current condition, they would worry more than ever. Joe was not up to explaining the weight loss, the gauntness and baggy eyes, the shaking hands caused by his excessive binge on vodka. He was a wreck, physically and emotionally. The emotional healing had begun, but Joe wanted the physical recovery well under way before any reunion with his family.

"By the time y'all got up here or I got down there," he teased, "I'd already be recuperated. Don't worry, Mama. I'm okay, and I'll be home soon for a long visit."

Caroline listened carefully as her son spoke. He sounded normal—just like Joe. "I'd rather take care of you myself," she apprised him, then acquiesced. "But if you promise you're okay and to come home soon, then I'll let it pass."

"I promise," Joe agreed.

"Can you tell us what happened?" Matt asked. "Paul gave us the major details, but we'd like to hear it from you, son—if you don't mind talken about it."

Joe gave them a tepid account of the ghastly night. He told them how Wayne had stalked him for months after seeing his byline in the *Herald*; how he had been bashed in the head, then bound, gagged and stuffed in the trunk of the car; how Wayne had forced him up and down the mountain time after time; how lightning aided his escape; and how Wayne's twisted ankle made the difference. He gave them a few other details, admitted to fearing for his life at times and revealed that he had suffered the gunshot wound.

Even without the most chilling moments of the ordeal to prey on their fears, his parents were haunted to the core. Maybe one day, when the terror was a distant memory and no longer real in his mind, Joe would tell them the whole story, the one he had shared with Annemarie.

"I wonder what will happen to Wayne," Caroline said at length.

"They ought to put him away for a long time to come," Matt suggested. "I suspect they will."

"I'm just glad it's over," Joe remarked wearily, "although I'll probably have to testify if there's a trial. Maybe he'll plead guilty."

"Enough of it," Caroline said. "The law will take care of Wayne Taylor, but I'm still worried about you, Joe. Is there somebody there who can lend a hand if you need it?"

"Yes, ma'am," Joe answered. "My boss, Ray Fields, brought me home from the hospital, and I'm sure he and his wife will keep close tabs on me. I have a good neighbor, too, who made supper for me tonight and is very good at taken care of people. What I need most over the next few days is peace and quiet. I'm sore in places I never knew existed. And I'm tired—exhausted's more like it. I figure I could sleep away the next day or two. I'm off to bed as soon as we hang up."

"Do you have time to talk to the rest of the family?" Matt asked. "They're real anxious about you."

"Honestly, Daddy, I don't feel up to it tonight," Joe confessed. "I'm really beat—in every sense of the word. Give everyone my love, and I'll talk to them soon."

"We'll do that," Matt agreed.

"Can we call you tomorrow?" Caroline asked.

"I'll expect it," Joe replied heartily, suddenly changing his mind about talking to anyone else. "Come to think of it, I will say a word or two to Carrie if she's close by."

"Good enough," Matt said. "I'll get her on the line. And, Joe, I'm thankful that you're all right, son."

"We love you, Joe," Caroline said.

"We do, son," Matt added.

"I love y'all, too," Joe said. "Goodbye now."

They bade him farewell, and Carrie came on the line a moment later with an anxious tone. "Joe?"

"Hi, Carrie. How are you?"

"Terribly worried about you at the moment," she said. "Are you really okay?"

Her voice sounded strong and clear, and Joe smiled as he imagined her on the phone. "I'm a tough guy," he teased.

"Definitely one of the good guys, too," she lauded him without missing a beat.

Joe blushed in spite of the distance between them. "You'll never guess what I had just sat down to read when an old friend bashed me in the head," he said.

"Have you read it?" Carrie asked.

"Only a few minutes ago," Joe replied. "I wanted to tell you how much I appreciated what you had to say, Carrie. Your honesty means a great deal to me. My only wish is that I could have been there for you this past year."

"Thanks, but it's probably best you weren't," she stated simply. "Things worked out well enough for me, Joe. I hope they have for you, too."

"I'm getten there," Joe said.

"Well, hopefully, after everything that happened last night, we can close the book on that part of our lives," Carrie suggested. "We've all grieved and suffered enough. Don't you think?"

She went straight to the heart of the matter, Joe thought. He swallowed a lump in his throat and answered, "I think so, Carrie. I think so."

––––––

Annemarie returned to the apartment a few minutes after Joe hung up the telephone, bringing with her two cookie sheets covered with drops of brown dough, an overnight satchel and a box of Epsom salts. She popped the cookie sheets into the oven, dropped the bag on the kitchen bar and carried the Epsom salts into the bathroom, where she ran a tub of steaming water laced with the medicine.

Returning to the living room, she sent Joe to a half-hour soak in the hot water, telling him, "The salts will soothe your sore muscles and make you sleep better tonight."

"Are you gonna wash my back?" Joe asked, teasingly, wishfully.

"Not this time," she replied primly. "But I'll have a batch of your favorite cookies ready and waiten when you get out of the tub."

Joe smiled, then went into the bathroom and closed the door.

The water was excruciatingly hot, and he needed several tries before submerging his whole body. Once he was settled in the tub, he found the slightest movement burned his skin as the water repositioned around him. So he remained motionless, closed his eyes and promptly dozed. He slept for a half-hour until Annemarie knocked on the door.

Exiting the tub, he unplugged the drain, then dried himself clumsily with one hand, wrapped the towel around his waist and went into the bedroom.

Annemarie was waiting for him. She had turned down the bed covers and placed a plate of warm molasses cookies and a glass of cold milk on the nightstand.

Joe grinned. She smiled softly.

He sat down on the bed and positioned the sling around his arm and neck. Then, he tried the cookies. They were warm and oozing with the slightly sweet taste of molasses. "Yum," he complimented her. "Very tasty."

Although he had no appetite, Joe ate two cookies and washed them down with half a glass of milk before proclaiming his stomach full.

Annemarie moved closer and handed him two of the sleeping pills prescribed by Dr. Conaway. "They're exactly what you need tonight," she said, sensing his reluctance to take the pills.

He mumbled an agreement, then took the pills and stretched out on the bed while she rubbed the fronts and backs of his legs with liniment. When she was finished, he climbed under the covers, tossed away the towel and allowed her to rub his chest and back. He fell asleep on his stomach, lulled by her firm kneading of his tautly stretched back muscles and the bony ride of his shoulders.

When Joe was asleep, Annemarie put on her nightshirt, locked the doors and turned out the lights. Then, she crawled into the double bed beside him and went to sleep. She was still there when Joe woke the next morning.

HORN OF PLENTY

1970

The cornucopia came out of hiding from beneath Rachel and Sam's bed every year on the first day of November, to grace the dining room buffet until New Year's Eve when it quietly disappeared to await the summons of another fall harvest. It was a sturdy horn, wove from grapevine, reed, honeysuckle and sweet grass.

Sam had presented the horn to Rachel as a belated wedding gift several days after their marriage on the twenty-fourth day of October 1919. Along with the gift came a promise that one day the empty basket would overflow with good things. The horn's place of honor in their home had become the first family tradition established by the newlyweds; the promise had evolved into the centerpiece of the Baker heritage. Now, both the horn and the promise stood as family treasures, commanding respect and radiating pride.

On Thanksgiving Day in 1970, the cornucopia was indeed a horn of plenty, overflowing with the bounty of the fall's harvest and surrounded by a feast to celebrate the holiday.

A fat turkey, roasted golden brown, centered the dining room table on an ivory lace tablecloth, flanked by a deep dish of piping-hot cornbread dressing, a tureen of steaming oyster stew and a boat of giblet gravy. Smoked ham, turnips, cranberry sauce, fruit salad, candied sweet potatoes, butterbeans, baked squash, roasted corn, sliced tomatoes, peppers and stuffed celery filled the assortment of bowls, platters and trays that covered the matching walnut buffet and smaller sideboard. Two cauldrons of dumplings—one simmered in chicken broth, the other in ham juice—sat on a white tablecloth atop the freezer, beside a washtub of iced tea, jugs of apple cider, bottles of honey, cane syrup and hot pepper sauce, and a crock of fresh butter, churned earlier in the day especially for Rachel's biscuits. Pecan, pumpkin and sweet potato pies, pear tarts and a spice cake were tucked in the pantry pie safe, while a pot of coffee percolated on the stove for dessert. The table was resplendent, set with Caroline's blue willow china, worn flatware and practical jelly glasses.

Sixteen people, all of them family and friends, would partake of the feast, squeezed around a table crafted to seat a dozen in comfort. Despite the chaotic seating arrangements and beckoning mounds of food, something was missing. And the absence loomed above everything else.

THE SECOND WEEK OF November 1970 proved hectic and eventful for nearly everyone in Cookville, but even more so for several families in the New River community.

The chaos began Monday when Paul Berrien arrested Bobby Taylor for the murder of Ned Turner way back in 1964, as well as for an earlier burglary of the doctor's home. Ballistics tests matched the bullet found in Turner's head with the pearl-handled pistol once owned by the doctor's wife and more lately in the possession of Wayne Taylor. The most damaging evidence against Bobby came from Wayne himself, who crumbled under the pressure of intensive questioning and the prospect of spending life in prison.

Bobby's oldest son admitted to having accompanied his father to Cookville late one night, ostensibly so that Bobby could confer with a potential business associate. Wayne had been left to mind the car, which had been parked out of sight near the Turner's brownstone home in Cookville. Wayne confessed to having suspected all along his father played a role in Ned Turner's death and reported Bobby had given him the pearl-handled gun a few months later as a birthday present.

Bobby went kicking and screaming to jail, claiming his son was telling an outrageous pack of lies to save his own hide. Cookville's district attorney, Stan Avera, concluded ample evidence existed to convict Bobby and vowed there would be no plea-bargaining in exchange for Wayne's critical testimony.

On Tuesday, Carl Taylor went about business as usual, oblivious to the predicament of his father and older brother. His father's absence from home the previous night aroused only passing interest from the seven-year-old boy, who had been forced, for the most part, to fend for himself since Billy had gone away to the place where he could not take Carl with him.

Carl caught the school bus early in the morning and paid close attention to his second-grade teacher. During lunch, however, the teacher inquired where Carl had spent the previous night and discovered the child's welfare had been overlooked in the confusion surrounding Bobby's arrest. The sheriff was summoned to the school and, before the day was out, Paul Berrien had persuaded the county's juvenile court judge to award him temporary custody of Carl. Tongues immediately began wagging about the propriety of the custody hearing.

On Wednesday, shortly after learning he would transfer overseas the following spring, Mark Applegate gave Summer an engagement ring and asked her to come with him to Germany. She accepted wholeheartedly, and the beaming couple shared their happy news first with Dan and Amelia Carter before informing the Bakers. Wedding plans commenced immediately, even before the rounds of hugs and backslapping finished.

Thursday belonged to Bonnie and Ken Cook. In the morning, they were named freshman class favorites at Cookville High School, an accolade owed equally to their striking appearances, outgoing personalities and romantic involvement. In the afternoon, they picked up pecans in the Baker orchard and pondered aloud whether their relationship could endure the ups and downs of high school romance. In the dusk of that brisk day, the young couple concluded they belonged among those rare childhood sweethearts who were destined to grow old together.

Bonnie and Ken sealed their perfect day with a kiss under those stately pecan trees. They wrapped themselves in a passionate embrace, a tangled mass of arms and legs, dark and golden hair, which was the way Matt found them sometime later. He stifled a father's urge to strangle this son of a preacher, remembering the potency of young love, then broke the moment by clearing his throat, twice. Bonnie and Ken stumbled apart, too dreamy to feel chagrin at being caught, too much in love to care.

On Friday night, Luke turned in a stellar performance on the gridiron, scoring four touchdowns and rushing for three hundred yards—a school record—as the Rebels routed archrival Cook High School to claim Cookville's first appearance in the state football playoffs. Afterward, a scout from the University of Georgia looked up Luke in the locker room and promised the Bulldogs would keep a keen eye on him during his senior year.

Between all these happenings, John worked night and day to meet the obligations of his fledgling pecan business and keep up with his college classes; Carrie spent every waking hour in the kitchen to fill a deluge of orders for her confectioneries; and Matt and Caroline teamed to harvest a bumper crop of soybeans.

On Saturday night, everyone stayed home and rested. Summer and Mark sat on the front porch swing, making wedding plans; Carrie and Bonnie swapped girl talk in their room while trying on different clothes; John and Luke discussed the approaching hunting season and watched television; and Matt and Caroline enjoyed a quiet time behind the closed door of their bedroom.

Sam and Rachel used the occasion to telephone Joe. The conversation was cheerful: full of talk about the weather, old times and recent events, carefully steered away from the exacting details of Joe's harrowing ordeal with Wayne Taylor, except to say that their grandson was fine and recovering from the various injuries. When the goodbyes were said, Sam laid down in the bed to ruminate over his grandson's hollow tone of spirit, while Rachel read her Bible and dozed.

Sam was not one to meddle in the private feelings of other people. But neither was he reluctant to point out an astute observation or two when the state of affairs warranted sage advice. As he saw it, Joe required guidance at this juncture in life. The boy had been too far away from his roots, for too long. He needed a tactful reminder of who he was and where his heart belonged.

"Rachel!" Sam announced, startling his wife from sleep. "We are goen to Atlanta to see our grandson."

"Fine with me," she replied curtly. "Just tell me when we're leaven and how long we're gonna stay."

Having expected his wife to put up initial resistance to the idea, Sam changed the persuasive course of his thoughts and took a long minute to consider the particulars of the trip. "We'll leave Friday," he declared finally. "Maybe stop in at the State Farmer's Market, look around Atlanta some and get to Joe's place sometime in the middle of the afternoon. How does that sound?"

"Don't you think we should mention all this to Joe before we make our plans?" Rachel suggested.

"I'll take care of that first thing in the mornen," he replied.

"It will be good to see him," Rachel remarked a while later, glancing up from her reading as Sam drifted toward sleep. "It's been such a long time. People like us shouldn't go so long without see'en our close kin, Sam. We all need to touch each other every now and then just to keep in mind what's most important in our lives."

Without opening his eyes, Sam reached out to claim his wife's hand. "And to satisfy that empty feelen in our souls," he agreed solemnly. "It's the orphan's spirit in us, Rachel. Takes more than a generation or two to breed out that fear of not haven nothen or no one. Of course, in the end, maybe it's best that we always have a little bit of orphan in us. Makes us appreciate each other more—and makes us less likely to take for granted what's most important in life."

Rachel squeezed his hand, then turned out the bedside lamp. They fell asleep holding hands and dreamed of good things—past, present and future.

————

Joe almost dreaded the visit from his grandparents. It was a case of wanting to see Sam and Rachel without having to be seen by them. His wraithlike appearance provided a dead giveaway to the debauchery that had ruled his life until recently. Sam and Rachel would recognize the injuries sustained at the hands of Wayne Taylor as window dressing for the troubles that really ailed their grandson, and Joe was shamed for them to know just how far he had fallen into disgrace from his upbringing.

Joe was sitting with Annemarie on the front stoop. She had been invited to this reunion for three important reasons. First, she had worked tirelessly to give Joe's apartment a homey touch for his grandparents' visit. They had moved her sofa and rocking chair into his living room, and she had stocked the kitchen with edibles and elixirs. Second, Annemarie was the most important person in Joe's life, and he figured it was time for the other people close to him to get acquainted with her. And third, she vowed to strangle Joe if he so much as hinted there might come a better time down the road for a first meeting between herself and members of his family.

Annemarie's eagerness to meet his grandparents delighted Joe, as well as provided support to overcome his own misgivings about the reunion. Still, his apprehension lasted until the moment their car came rolling down the street toward the apartment building, with Sam and Rachel sitting tall in the seat. Then, his humbled pride vanished in a rush of love. He rose and went to meet them as Sam eased the car into a parking place.

————

"Good Lord!" Rachel gasped to Sam as their grandson walked toward them. "Is that our Joe?"

"Appears to be," Sam muttered, trying to concentrate on his driving while smiling at Joe and appraising his haggard appearance.

Besides being emaciated, pale and hollow-eyed, Joe still sported a slightly swollen nose and discolored bruises on his face. His arm rested in a sling to protect the wounded shoulder, and he walked with a definite limp.

"He must be sick as the devil," Rachel fretted, pasting a smile on her face for Joe's benefit. "A body don't start looken that way in a day or two, Sam. What do you suppose is wrong with him?"

"Nothen that a good visit from us won't cure," Sam decided, in assuring tones for his wife's sake. "Try not to act too much like you're worried about him, Rachel. And, for goodness' sake, don't go tellen him he looks like somethen the dog dragged in out of the woods ... even if he does."

The car rolled to a stop beside the sidewalk, and Sam switched off the engine as Joe opened Rachel's door.

In the background, Annemarie marveled at Joe's transformation as he gave hearty greetings and hugs to his grandparents. Their mere presence gave him strength. His face, which had seemed permanently pinched and prematurely aged over the last few days, opened wide with sheer joy. Annemarie smiled solemnly. She had an idea this visit with his grandparents would push Joe a long way back toward his destiny.

"Did you have any trouble finden the place?" Joe asked Sam.

"Not a bit," Sam lied.

Rachel sent her husband a stern look. "Let's put it like this," she corrected. "We took the long way around to get here. And likely, we'd still be goen around in circles if your grandpa hadn't accidentally gotten the car onto Piedmont Avenue while we were looken for the Capitol, which, incidentally, we had already circled at least half a dozen times."

"I just wanted us to see a little bit of the city," Sam protested.

"And that's what we saw," Rachel contended. "A little bit of it, over and over again."

Joe laughed at the good-natured bickering between his grandparents. He had missed their unique way of loving each other.

"Well, then, Granny," he told Rachel. "I promise to make sure y'all see the rest of the city this weekend."

"When did you grow this?" Sam asked, running a finger across Joe's mustache.

"Over the last few weeks," Joe said. "I had a beard, too, but shaved it off. I plan to get rid of the mustache, too, as soon as my nose shrinks down to its normal size and the soreness goes away."

"I like it," Sam announced. "I've never liked be'en the only man in the family with a mustache. You should keep it."

"Sorry, Grandpa, but it's gonna go," Joe replied, glancing toward Annemarie and motioning his grandparents to follow him. "Y'all come on over here. There's someone I'd like you to meet."

Annemarie stepped forward as Joe led the elderly couple toward the stoop. There was nothing subtle in the way Sam and Rachel appraised her. They looked her up and down, from the tips of her shoes to the crown of her head. Their eyes noted every detail of appearance, lingered over the blue Delta Air Lines uniform, then settled on her face, which was lit with a radiant smile. So frank was their assessment that Annemarie felt like a heifer up for auction. Her fresh smile began to feel like plastic, and, for a distressing moment while Joe made the introductions, she feared the bidding would pass by her.

Sam returned her smile first, with a broad grin, and Rachel followed suit, with a slower, careful spread of face. Both reactions put Annemarie in mind of Joe, his devilment and his caution. If she had appreciated Joe's grandparents before meeting them, Annemarie adored Sam and Rachel on this first impression. She recognized instantly the important role they played in shaping the man of her dreams and respected them all the more for it.

"I've heard so much about y'all that I feel as if we're already old friends," Annemarie said.

"That's strange, ain't it, Rachel?" Sam replied with an offended glance at his grandson. "We haven't heard the first thing about Miss Morgan, have we?"

Rachel gave Annemarie a brusque smile. "I guess you know then that I'm married to a rascal," she remarked.

"But a very handsome rascal, nonetheless," Annemarie replied, with a wry smile of her own.

Sam preened like a peacock. "Your friend's one very smart woman, Joe," he noted. "You'd be wise not to let someone like her too far out of your sight."

Joe grinned at his grandfather, then bravely volunteered, "I'm getten to be a right smart man, Grandpa."

"You're also getten downright wormy looken," Rachel intervened abruptly. "I've never seen you looken so puny, Joe. What are you eaten, son? Or should I ask if you're eaten?"

Joe rubbed his bony ribs through his shirt. "I've missed a few meals lately," he replied, "but I'm fixen to pick back up."

"Starten tonight," Rachel declared. "I've got a cooler of food in the trunk, and I'm gonna spend the weekend cooken and maken sure you eat. By Sunday afternoon, Joe, I want to see some meat on your bones."

"No, ma'am, you are doen no such thing," Joe replied, overruling his grandmother. "Y'all are on vacation, and I intend to see you enjoy every minute of it. You're not gonna lift a finger in the kitchen, Granny. We're goen to eat at fancy restaurants and be as lazy as we can, starting tonight."

"But I brought all that food," Rachel protested.

"And I'll eat every bit of it," Joe promised. "Next week, after y'all have gone home."

"He means what he says," Annemarie told Rachel. "I'd take him up on the offer, ma'am."

"Will you be joinen us, Miss Morgan?" Sam asked.

"Unfortunately, I have other plans," Annemarie replied. "I'm worken tonight and tomorrow."

"Anne's a stewardess for Delta," Joe explained.

Annemarie shrugged her shoulders. "I have flights back and forth to Miami on both nights," she said.

"But she's graciously volunteered to cook Sunday dinner for us at my place," Joe piped in. "It'll be worth the wait."

Sam and Rachel exchanged glances. "Oh!" they both remarked.

"I do look forward to spenden time with y'all," Annemarie said. "Joe has told me so many wonderful stories about his family. I'm grateful for the opportunity to meet some of his inspiration."

"Good gracious!" Sam groaned. "I hope we can live up to our reputations."

Annemarie regarded Joe for a tender moment. "Well, sugar," she replied, turning back to Sam, "I honestly believe you and Mrs. Baker must be very special people to have produced such a fine grandson. It's been a pleasure and an experience getten to know him."

Joe and Rachel blushed, while Sam beamed. "If you say so," he said. "But tell me: Is he still as hardheaded and stubborn as ever?"

Annemarie arched her eyes at Joe. "Hardheaded and stubborn, I can take," she answered sincerely. "He just needs to ease up on himself a bit."

Joe rolled his eyes. "I believe these kinds of analytical conversations are supposed to go on when the subject is out of earshot," he teased. "Would the two of you prefer I go inside and give you privacy?"

"I don't have the time, sugar," Annemarie replied, touching his elbow. "I'm gonna be late as it is. Besides, it will be much better if you have this conversation with your grandparents.

"I really am pleased to have met the two of you," she continued, turning back to Sam and Rachel. "I'm looken forward to spenden more time with y'all on Sunday."

"The same here," Rachel said, smiling warmly.

"Most certainly," Sam agreed, clasping Annemarie's hand. "She really is quite a girl," he commented a short time later after Annemarie had taken her leave."

"That's putten it mildly, Grandpa," Joe observed, his eyes trained on Annemarie's back as she disappeared around the corner of the building. "She comes on like a tornado, she's kind of a busybody and she likes to have the last word more often than not."

"But is she special to you?" Rachel interrupted bluntly.

Joe smiled mysteriously. "Pretty special," he confirmed.

"And she can cook, I assume," Sam said.

"Boy, can she cook," Joe said. "You'll see on Sunday, Grandpa."

"So how come you look like a sack of bones?" Rachel inquired, again bluntly to the point.

"That's a long story, Granny," Joe replied, putting off his grandmother, who, fortunately, was not offended by the offhanded tactic. "Why don't we get y'all settled inside, then I'll tell you all about the weekend I have planned for us. We're goen to have a wonderful time."

––––––––

Joe spent the rest of the afternoon getting reacquainted with his grandparents and catching up on the news from home. In the evening, he took Sam and Rachel to the blue dome-shaped revolving restaurant on top of the Hyatt Regency, where they dined on thick steaks and topped off the meal with a Baked Alaska.

Saturday brought a whirlwind tour of the city, beginning with the *Herald* offices, the gold-domed state Capitol, Fulton County Stadium, Peachtree Street, the city's first skyscraper and "The Dump," the ramshackle apartment building where Margaret Mitchell had written *Gone with the Wind*. They shopped at Rich's, the city's premier department store, where Rachel treated herself to a new dress and Sam splurged on a hat, then lunched at The Abbey, where waiters dressed as monks served them roast beef sandwiches and iced tea.

In the afternoon, Joe took his grandparents to Grant Park, where they visited the zoo and viewed the Cyclorama, a magnificent, lifelike mural depicting the Battle of Atlanta fought during the Civil War. Finally, as the sun set like an orange fireball, they strolled through Piedmont Park to work up an appetite for supper.

When night fell, they changed clothes and went to Underground Atlanta, a series of shops, restaurants and nightclubs located below street level near the old Atlanta railroad depot. They browsed in several boutiques before strolling over to Cain

Street to eat supper at Miss Pitty Pat's Porch, a former funeral parlor that had been converted into a restaurant named for Scarlett Ohara's prissy aunt in *Gone with the Wind*. Sam and Rachel feasted on the restaurant's antebellum atmosphere; the food proved far less satisfying. When they returned to Joe's apartment, he broke out a batch of molasses cookies that Summer had sent along with Sam and Rachel and made coffee. The three of them sprawled out across the living room and ate with considerably more enthusiasm.

Sam settled back in the recliner and let loose a soft whistle. "This vacation business can leave a body plumb tuckered out," he announced. "I'd say we've seen about everything there is to see in Atlanta."

"The highlights at least," agreed Joe, who had stretched out on the floor with a throw pillow.

"I'll sleep easy tonight," Sam commented.

"Which means he'll snore to beat the band," Rachel expounded for Joe. "I hope the walls are thick, or he'll wake up the neighbors."

"Thick enough, they are," Joe said.

Rachel had kicked off her heels and was sitting on the couch with her feet tucked under her legs. She took a bite of cookie, sipped the coffee and smiled at her grandson. "We brought along Sunday clothes in case you planned to go to church tomorrow," she said. "Should I lay them out tonight?"

Joe sat up, crossing his legs Indian style, ignoring the pain in his knee. "I'm ashamed to say, Granny, but the truth is I haven't been very good about goen to church since I moved up here. Annie goes, though. She never misses a Sunday unless she's worken. I'm sure y'all could go along with her if you wanted."

"No, no," Rachel replied. "I just mentioned it in case you were plannen to go." A teasing smile crept across her face. "I don't think the good Lord will begrudge us missen a Sunday service so we can visit with our grandson."

Joe had expected admonishment for his slacker's attitude toward church. But the casualness of Rachel's response served as a far more effective reminder that he was long past the age of accountability. "There was a time, Granny, when you would have jacked me up for overlooken church," he said wistfully. "I think I miss that."

"There also comes a time when you can't force church on a person, Joe," Rachel replied. "You can encourage them, but they have to be led by a higher power and desire in their heart. Naturally, though, I would encourage you to get back to Sunday services. Church does a body good if you go looken for somethen good."

"And from the looks of you, son, you could use somethen good," Sam added, pushing the recliner into the upright position. "I know you're not one to wear your heart on the sleeve, Joe, but do you care to tell us what's gone wrong?"

From anyone else, the suggestion would have come across as prying. Joe recognized it as an invitation for honesty.

Of all the people in Joe's life, his grandparents were the least judgmental. Sam and Rachel were sharply opinionated and full of advice when the situation warranted, yet also tolerant and understanding of differences and shortcomings. While most people measured the character of others against inflexible—and often unattained—personal standards, Sam and Rachel used an unmarked ruler for their every comparison. The grandparents also bestowed compassion without coddling, and they preferred redemption to damnation.

Joe decided he could benefit from a dose of their solicitude.

"Do y'all remember when I found out that Mama and Daddy and Santa Claus were one and the same?" he asked.

"You were six," Rachel recalled.

"And you were crushed that such a wonderful person didn't really exist," Sam said.

"You walked around for days with the weight of the world on your little shoulders," Rachel continued.

"As if you alone knew the most terrible of all dreaded secrets," Sam added. "None of us knew why for days and days."

"Until I finally told the two of you what was on my mind," Joe interrupted. "And then, Grandpa, you told me that wonderful story about the real Saint Nicholas."

"The patron saint of children," Sam mused.

"Someone who loved deeply and abidingly and was kind and generous: a repository for all good things," Joe continued reverently. "That story, Grandpa, was the most wonderful thing you ever told me. It even allowed me to continue believen—or at least wish—that a fat, jolly man who lived in the hinterlands of the North Pole could indeed dress up in a red suit and fly across the sky on a sled driven by reindeer on the most special night of the year. Most of all, though, that story made me aware of the Christmas spirit for the first time. And every Christmas since, I've always managed to get that feelen of lasten faith and infinite beauty and eternal goodness."

Rachel wiped away an invisible tear from her eye, and Sam smiled slyly.

"The thing is, Grandpa, Granny," Joe continued gravely. "Y'all had an answer back then for what troubled me deeply. I wonder if you might have a little more wisdom to impart about what bothers me now."

"Billy Taylor's still weighen heavy on your mind," Sam guessed.

"Like a steel ball and noose around my neck," Joe groaned. "I've always thought I could work my way through the worst of anything. Always believed if I approached a problem calmly and rationally, then I could deal with it. But this time, everything I've tried has begot one miserable failure after another. I can't forget it."

"You won't ever forget what happened, Joe," Sam said firmly. "Your soul wouldn't be worth much if you did."

"But I have to find a way to live with it, Grandpa."

"You do," Sam agreed readily.

"I keep thinken there ought to be some explanation, some reason why things happened the way they did," Joe mused ruefully.

"That's part of the problem," Sam suggested abruptly. "You tend to see life as some mathematics problem where there's always an answer to be found." He turned to Rachel, pointed a long finger and leveled an accusation against his wife. "It's your fault he's that way."

"Part of your genetics, I'm afraid," he added, looking back to Joe.

Rachel stiffened her shoulders and raised her chin in defiance of her husband. But only for a moment. "It's true, Joe," she conceded with a shrug. "All my life, I've sought answers that were as simple as the difference between black and white. And, I've had a hard time dealen with the complicated questions. Unlike you, though, I tend to ignore the really messy ones—whenever possible anyway."

"Very little in life is as simple as black and white," Sam asserted. "We deal almost exclusively in shades of gray. Fortunately, for us, the distinctions usually are easy to make when we're faced with a critical choice. Sometimes, though, one shade looks just as right as the one beside it—or every shade seems just as wrong as the next one. Even so, you have to make your choice and then live with it. Harsh though it sounds, Joe, you made a choice. The repercussions were damnable for all concerned. But you're still stuck with the consequences, and you have to live with it. There is no escape, no way to ignore it or to forget it."

Joe pondered those unsettling ideas for a long while. "Deep down, I know now that I can live with myself," he said at last, "but there's somethen awful about admitten to that. It almost seems as if I'm getten away with somethen—somethen I should have suffered for or paid a price. I just wish there was some way to figure out why it happened—why things turned out like they did. I guess I'll always wonder what it was that it was all about."

"At this point, Joe," Sam suggested sincerely, "it's all about forgiveness."

"Sir?"

"Forgiveness," Sam repeated with emphasis. "About forgiven yourself for killen Billy Taylor."

"But how?" Joe wanted to know.

"I can't answer that for you," Sam declared. "Speaken for myself, though, I've made my share of mistakes, but I like to think I've always tried my best to do the right thing. And when I've missed the mark on that accord and not given my best, then I'd like to believe the honesty of my intentions counted for somethen."

"And if they didn't?" Joe asked pointedly.

"Maybe I've been foolen myself, but it always has so far," Sam replied. "Enough leastways to keep faith in myself. That's me, though. You still have to come up with your own way of forgiveness. It's a very personal thing."

Joe nodded, then stared vacantly at the floor, his mind still troubled.

"I don't think our collective wisdom has been very beneficial," Sam remarked to his wife.

Joe glanced up at them.

"Go ahead, Joe, and get everything off your chest," Rachel urged.

Joe swallowed hard. "Y'all might be disappointed when you hear the rest of it," he warned.

"More likely, we're apt to be worried and concerned," Sam intervened. "You're not carryen around a big secret, Joe. It doesn't take a genius to figure out you must have been hitten the bottle hard and heavy."

Joe smiled weakly. "It's got me scared," he confessed. "I don't know what happened. I took complete leave of my senses. The last two months have been wretched. I fell apart—messed everything up. I don't ever want to get in this shape again. This is not me. It's not what I want for my life." He shuddered, then added: "In a way, Wayne Taylor may have saved my life. He made me stop and be somebody different—maybe who I used to be."

"Then maybe you've learned your lesson," Rachel said.

"I never drank myself," Sam announced. "But Joe, you've got a whole bunch of history worken against you. There's a long list of men in our family who drank way too much. My pa did, and he was a mean drunk. And though I should not be the one to tell you this, so did your daddy at one time."

"Daddy?"

"When he got back from the war, Matt took a nip every now and then," Rachel took over. "He would get pretty happy at times, but nothen too bad at first. Gradually, though, it got worse, maybe out of hand. He started carousen around with Paul Berrien. He'd leave the house after supper, stay out late and come home drunk. Not all the time, mind you, but too much."

"He did that for about two years," Sam continued. "And then, one day your mama had enough of it. She laid down the law to Matt and to Paul."

"Told Matt not to ever come home drunk again," Rachel explained. "Told Paul he was not welcome in our home as long as he took Matt away from his family so that the two of them could carry on and get drunk."

"As you well know, Joe," Sam said sagaciously, "when your mama puts her foot down, she makes a big impression."

"After that," Rachel continued, "the nights of carousen ended for both your daddy and Paul."

"They still took a snort every now and then—over a game of pool or while they were hunten," Sam concluded. "But after a while, even that stopped. As far as I know, your daddy hasn't touched a drop of alcohol in many a year."

Joe stared dumbly at his grandparents, stunned by their revelations.

"We're tellen you this for your sake, Joe," Sam resumed. "I don't know what made your daddy drink. I don't know what made my pa drink. But I do know that nothen good ever came of it—not from even one drink as far as I'm concerned."

Sam paused, directing a hard gaze at his grandson. "To put it bluntly, Joe, liquor's taken down far better men than you."

It was well-intentioned advice his grandfather offered. Nothing more, nothing less. "How did y'all get so wise?" Joe asked a long moment later.

"Son, all we have on you is age," Sam claimed. "We've gone a little farther down the road than you have, and we've seen more of the ups and downs."

"Somethen else, Joe," Rachel offered. "You can't dwell on the past, son, always worryen that it's gonna catch up with you. I know I've said this so many times that you're probably sick of hearen it. But I tell it because the message is true: You've got to get on with the business of liven."

"And you still have plenty of liven ahead of you, Joe," Sam said. "I don't want to sound preachy, but the best thing I've learned in my seventy-five years is the importance of haven someone who can share all the joys and heartaches with you. Family and friends are the most important part of life, and you got a gracious plenty of them willen and wanten to share with you."

A gleam came in his eyes, and Sam looked at Rachel. "Maybe you even have that one special person above everyone else who makes life complete," he told Joe. "Don't run away from all that. Don't throw it all away. Because if you do, you'll lose the best part of yourself. Embrace the people in your life, Joe, be a little possessive with them; allow them to do the same to you. In the process, I think you'll find what makes this business of liven, which your granny keeps talken about, such a worthwhile pursuit."

Rather than muddle with wisdom, they offered the moment to quiet abeyance. A while later, Rachel declared she was tired. Sam yawned loudly, and Joe suggested it was bedtime.

Annemarie found Joe sitting on the floor of the dimly lit alcove. His back rested against the apartment door. One leg stretched to full length, while the other was drawn against his chest to provide a prop for his arm. He was smoking a cigarette and greeted her with a slow-burning smile.

"This is a nice surprise," she told him in a weary voice.

"I wanted to see you," he replied.

Annemarie set the blue flight bag on the floor, then lowered herself to a sitting position beside Joe, snuggling close to him as he draped an arm around her shoulders. They kissed, softly at first, then deeper, before mouths closed and their lips touched lightly.

"You should have on a jacket," she observed, noting the chill on his bare arms. "This is perfect weather for catchen cold."

Joe arched his eyebrows. "You can keep me warm," he suggested.

Annemarie kissed him quickly once more, then laid her head on his shoulder and began a slow massage of his lame knee. "Was there any special reason you wanted to see me?" she asked.

"Just because."

"Because?"

He took a drag off the cigarette, slowly exhaling a thin line of smoke. "No special reason," he explained. "I had a very good day, and wanted to end it with you."

A glow burned deep within Annemarie. "Well, sugar, I had a miserable flight down and back," she sighed. "But I can think of no better way to salvage the day than be'en here with you."

Joe ground out the cigarette against the floor and tightened his grip on her. "I love you, Annemarie."

She kissed the underside of his jaw. "I love you, too, Joe."

He held her several minutes while they basked in the warmth of fresh feelings.

"I take it you've had a good visit with your grandparents?" Annemarie asked at last.

"The very best," Joe replied. Then he told her every detail about the visit, right down to the moment earlier in the night when he had been lying on the couch and was overcome with desire to see Annemarie. "My grandparents are remarkable people," he concluded.

"What's most impressive about them?" she asked impulsively.

"The way they complement each other," Joe answered quickly. "And their compatibility."

"How's that?" Annemarie asked.

"Granny has one set of strengths and weaknesses, and Grandpa has another," Joe explained. "Their various strong points offset each other's faults. They make each other complete. They're great lovers, too, but I've always had a feelen that love was a bonus for them. That they got together because they wanted the same thing very badly: somethen they never had in the first place or maybe somethen they had lost early on."

"And what was it they both wanted so badly," Annemarie inquired.

"A lot of different things, I guess, but it all boils down to fulfillment," Joe replied.

"We're all looken for that, Joe," she said.

He put an index finger under Annemarie's chin, tilted her face up and nodded in agreement. "Maybe you and I have found it."

She nodded back, then changed positions against him and slowly rubbed his left hand until their fingers were intertwined. At length, she looked up to meet his gaze. The man's dark eyes shone like polished marbles—clear at last and full of her.

"You have a strong jaw," Annemarie told him, running a finger across the stubble of black beard that glazed the sturdy framing bones of his face. "And, Joe," she added a moment later, pausing to reclaim his gaze. "You and I are gonna be great lovers from the very beginnen."

"Yeah," he agreed with certainty.

———

Joe considered Saturday a wonderful day, but Sunday proved perfect in every way. Despite its inauspicious beginnings.

He woke stiff and aching with a raw throat, to the morning sounds of his grandparents as Sam and Rachel shuffled between the bedroom and the bathroom. He heard mumbled voices, water running, bedclothes snapping—and dreamed briefly of sharing a similar morning with Annemarie.

Throwing off his covers, Joe forced himself off the sofa, then slipped into yesterday's blue jeans. By the time Sam and Rachel emerged from the bedroom, he had water boiling for instant coffee, thick pieces of salty, streaked meat frying and was whipping eggs to scramble.

Joe wanted to show off the few kitchen skills he had acquired in the last year. He performed an admirable job, too, until he tried to butter the bread for toast, and the meat started cooking too fast as Sam asked for a coffee cup. In one fell swoop, he forgot the bread to save the bacon, turned down the stove eye and tried to reach up into the cabinet to fetch a cup for his grandfather. That was when hot grease popped and spattered in tiny drops across his bare chest.

Joe howled over the tiny burns, and his vision of a homey breakfast went up in smoke.

Rachel calmly stepped in, taking over the kitchen chores with superior skill. "Let me handle breakfast, honey," she suggested to Joe. "You just butter that bread and have yourself a hot cup of coffee. We'll be eaten in no time at all."

A chuckle escaped Joe, despite the ignominy of being relegated to the role of helper in his own kitchen. "Believe it or not, Granny, I really can cook a decent breakfast."

"I'm sure you can," Rachel agreed as she laid fresh pieces of meat in the hot pan. "But if I were you, I'd stay away from hot grease when you're bare-chested. Come to think of it, honey, you sound awfully hoarse this mornen. You got any Vicks salve?"

"There's a bottle around here somewhere," Joe answered.

"Better go rub yourself down with it then and get a shirt on, too," she ordered. "You oughtta put on an undershirt, too. It's mighty easy for a person to get chilled and catch a cold on a cool mornen like this. And colds can turn into the pneumonia before you now it."

"Yes, ma'am," Joe replied.

By the time Joe returned to the kitchen, smelling of the menthol and camphor vaporizing medicine, Rachel was setting a hot breakfast on the kitchen bar.

Annemarie arrived at his apartment shortly after breakfast, bringing a generous rump roast and all the fixings for Sunday dinner. Her kitchen skills spoke for themselves, without any need of intervention to keep the preparations running smoothly. Still, she invited Rachel to join her, and they struck an instant friendship while keeping watch over the slow-cooking dinner.

Despite its stark furnishings, the apartment filled with good smells and homey touches.

Joe had seen similarly special days played out countless times, but none matched the splendor of this Sunday with Annemarie and his grandparents. Between reminiscing and prophesying with Sam, his mind plundered the future, conjuring up other days that would unfold in an equally wonderful fashion. The idea of sharing his home and hearth beckoned to Joe. The thought both scared and exhilarated him.

And then there was Annemarie herself, soaring above everything else. She glided through the morning, cooking and talking with Rachel, laughing and joking with Sam. Once, she even kissed Joe. He went into the kitchen to refill a glass of tea, and she waylaid him. Her hands were dusty with flour, so she draped her arms over his shoulders and planted two chaste pecks on his face. The first landed on the tip of his nose, the second full on the lips.

Joe blushed and gulped at the show of intimacy, while Rachel fidgeted and busied herself with an unnecessary task. Sam smiled approvingly, and Annemarie simply returned to her work as if nothing out of the ordinary had occurred.

She cooked the roast in an iron pot on top of the stove, until it was brown and tender, with chunks of potatoes, carrots and onions. She baked a casserole with green beans and cottage cheese, made homemade yeast rolls and tossed a salad with oil, vinegar, garlic and freshly ground pepper. Dessert was a magnificent flaming peach jubilee—two layers of spice cake iced with sweetened whipped cream and topped with peach halves, each centered with a sugar lump soaked in lemon extract.

She served the concoction with the sugar lumps aflame and boldly confessed, "I'm showboaten, no doubt about it, Mr. and Mrs. Baker. I'm tryen to make a good impression on you folks. And all modesty aside, I only hope this thing tastes as good as it looks."

It was superb.

"I can't tell you when I've had a finer meal," Sam told Annemarie when the dishes were washed and the four of them sat in the living room. "When Joe suggested you were merely a good cook, he served you a great injustice."

"Now, now, sugar," Annemarie teased. "I'd be spare with the compliments if I were you. I don't know too many wives who care to hear their husbands gush over another woman's cooken."

"She's got a point," Rachel said, miffed.

The bristling tone left Annemarie agape at the mouth. She stuttered for a contrite response, then saw the corners of Rachel's mouth turn out in an abashed grin and realized the older woman had duped her with uncharacteristic teasing.

Joe and Sam burst out laughing.

"Honey, it was an excellent meal," Rachel lauded. "I was most impressed with everything you did in the kitchen. When a woman can cook like that, there ain't much need for modesty or resentment."

They drifted into conversation, and the grandparents put Annemarie through a round of third-degree questioning about her background. She exuded patience and sincerity, with every answer deepening the admiration and respect the elderly couple felt for her. That Sam and Rachel liked Annemarie pleased Joe in great measure—and set him to wondering how Caroline, Matt and the rest of the family would take to her.

When his mind drifted back to the present, the flow of conversation had changed, and his grandparents were telling their story. Sam talked about the farm and its rich land, while Rachel spoke of the children and the travails of raising them.

"How did you two first meet?" Annemarie asked eventually.

Rachel scowled. "He ran slapdab right over me on Ashley Street in Valdosta," she announced indignantly.

"I worked at the Feed and Seed store and was late comen back from lunch one day," Sam explained. "Rachel did some sewen work for a nearby store, and she came out of it with a load of packages at the same time I was walken by the door. It was an unavoidable run-in. She scolded me like a wet hen, as if I had walked into her on purpose."

"When I'm scared, I tend to talk loud," Rachel confessed. "And Sam caught me completely off guard."

"But I apologized profusely," Sam interjected, "and helped her pick up the packages."

"It's true," Rachel told Annemarie. "He did do that."

"Rachel was a mite sterner back then," Sam said tenderly. "She tended to frown a lot, but I saw right away that she had poise. She was wearen the most beautiful frock, an indigo summer dress." He turned to Rachel. "Whatever happened to that dress?"

"It wore out," she answered with a shrug.

"Oh, well," Sam continued, turning back to Annemarie. "I knew right off the bat from the way she wore that dress and carried herself that Rachel was someone who appreciated beauty in all its forms and was capable of given and accepten tenderness. I made a few inquiries, found out who she was and what she did."

"And that's how Sam came to know the Lord," Rachel beamed.

Annemarie smiled at the woman, then looked again at Sam. "Sounds promisen," she said.

"Oh, it is," Sam agreed. "Once I found out that Rachel was a God-fearen woman, I decided to become a Christian. I hardly knew the first thing about church and God. But I started goen to her church and really liked it. About a month later, they had a church social, and I invited Rachel. She agreed to go, eventually complimented me on my singen voice and urged me to get baptized."

"Which he did the very next week," Rachel said.

"So I could begin courten her proper," Sam explained.

"We were married three months later," Rachel concluded.

"And eventually I did become a Christian," Sam added.

"You always had a Christian heart, Sam," Rachel said kindly before telling Annemarie, "His family was not much for church."

"What about your family, Mr. Baker?" Annemarie asked, having previously quizzed Rachel about her early days. "What were they like?"

A grimace twisted Sam's face. "They did their best," he said at last. "We farmed a small piece of land in Lowndes County. My pa never cared much for farmen, though. He drank too much and preferred the rowdiness of roadhouses to the comforts of home. That was mostly fine with Mother. She never seemed to want much from life. I always felt she gave up on life way too early. When I was twenty, she died, and my pa sold the farm. He gave me twenty-five dollars and went off to live in Plant City, Florida, where my three older brothers had moved several years earlier. After that, he settled down some from what I gather. I never saw him again. He died a few years later."

"What about your brothers?" Annemarie inquired. "Did you keep in touch with them?"

"Off and on," Sam answered. "They're all dead now. I was the youngest. My last brother, Caleb, died a couple of years ago. Caleb was good about visiten us at least once a year. I was sorry when he passed on. Rachel and I went to the funeral in Florida; we got to see where my pa was buried."

Turning to Rachel, Annemarie asked what had attracted her to Sam.

"What attracted me to him?" Rachel reflected for a long moment. "Sam knew what he wanted out of life: a perfect piece of land, a good wife, a fine family. He spelled it all out for me from the very beginnen, and I knew right away we would be compatible. He also seemed like a stable sort of man, and that was important to me because my pa walked in a drifter's shoes. And, too, Sam was a dreamer, which I wasn't."

Rachel looked thoughtfully at her husband, then back to Annemarie. "He brought a new kind of happiness and contentment to my life. He still does."

"And he was handsome to boot," Annemarie teased.

Rachel frowned slightly. "Actually, he was more fierce than handsome," she confided. "Kind of sinister-looken, to tell you the truth. He was so tall and dark, with almost jet-black hair, which he wore a little longer than he should have. He wore that black eye patch, and the scar on his face was jagged and stood out more prominently back then than it does now."

"What did happen to your eye, sugar?" Annemarie inquired of Sam. "If you don't mind me asken."

"Oh, brother," Joe groaned.

"Oh, boy," Rachel sighed.

"Fighten dragons this time?" Joe suggested to his grandmother.

"Probably pirates," Rachel proposed.

For a rare occasion, however, Sam told the true story about losing his eye. It was a story Rachel knew by heart, one Joe had pieced together in bits and pieces.

"I lost it in the Great War fighten Germans in a place called Belleau Wood," Sam recollected as the memory transported him back in time. "I was in the Marines, and we were sent to take Belleau Wood from the Germans. It was a little piece of land east of Paris, where the Germans had established a stronghold during their Spring Offensive. We were a green outfit, and the brass wanted to give us some experience in a real fight. So, in June of 1918, we spent two weeks getten indoctrinated into the rigors of fighten. It was bad business. One day, when we were close to winnen the battle, a German bomb exploded a few yards away from my bunker. The force hurled me face-first into a stand of barbwire, wire that I had helped put in place myself. It hurt somethen awful—blinded my left eye immediately."

Sam looked at Annemarie, then Joe, and shrugged off the misfortune. "But I was lucky," he contended. "My best buddy got a piece of shrapnel buried in his chest. He died instantly."

He glanced once more at his grandson. "In a roundabout way, Joe, my buddy had a tremendous influence on your life. He was from Parkersburg, West Virginia, and his name was Joseph Owen Cooper."

"One of the first things Sam told me—even before we married—was that he intended on namen his firstborn son, Joseph, after his friend," Rachel said. "And we did."

"And Joe was named after his uncle—for an entirely different reason," Annemarie remarked. "Wow! What a piece of history." She turned to Joe, who had remained speechless throughout his grandfather's story. "Why didn't you tell me all this?" she demanded.

"It's news to me," Joe replied hoarsely.

"I don't usually care to talk much about what happened back then," Sam explained. "It was all too ugly, too painful. But I'm glad you know the whole story of how you got your name, Joe. It's part of your heritage, and you need to know as much of that as possible. I've been negligent for keepen some things to myself."

Sam looked at Annemarie specifically. "I'm a big believer in preserven family history," he continued. "Unfortunately, our family is starved for it. There's not much to reach back for—past Rachel and me. I guess that's why it was always so important for me to have a place like our home. I wanted somewhere where Rachel and I could set down roots and let them grow deep over the years ... develop family traditions and legends that'll be around long after we're gone ... handed down from one generation to the next. Maybe that's a lofty ambition for poor people like us, but every man worth his salt should want to leave a legacy of good things for his family to build upon."

A tear formed in Annemarie's eyes. "You're doen just that, sugar," she told Sam, reaching out to clasp his hand. She patted him, then stared at Joe and cocked her head in a gesture toward Sam. "Is he another reluctant poet?"

"Not at all," Joe answered. "Grandpa can quote Whitman, Tennyson and just about every major poet of the last two centuries. I marvel at his memory."

"I love poetry, too," Annemarie sighed.

So Sam and she discussed poetry, which led to music and, finally, to Paris, France, where Sam had spent several weeks in a military hospital recovering from his wounds at Belleau Wood.

"I had three days to see Paris before they shipped me home," he said in another transported voice. "That was not nearly enough time for such a magnificent city. One day, I intend to go back there with Rachel. We will walk along the Champs-Élysées and see all those wonderful sites again: the Eiffel Tower, the Arc de Triomphe, the Louvre, the Paris Opera House. Not that I like opera, but the name has a certain ring to it. Like Sacré-Coeur—what a beautiful church that was. And two places I did not see but very much hope to are Notre Dame and Versailles." Sam sighed. "There wasn't enough time when I was there back in 1918. Since then, there hasn't been enough money. But maybe one day still, Rachel and I will wend our way to Paris."

Sam was lost in a dream, one he had vowed to make come true for as long as his wife and grandson could remember. Everyone allowed a quiet moment for his memory to meander through the streets of Paris and soak up the city's many treasures.

Joe finally broke the spell by clearing his scratchy throat. "You've hijacked my grandparents," he accused Annemarie. But it was a trumped-up charge, brought with a glad smile and a mellow heart.

———

They were later leaving than Sam would have preferred, but still he figured to reach home before dark. It was a good visit Rachel and he had with their grandson and Annemarie. The four of them were reluctant to bid farewell. At last, though—after Rachel urged Joe to eat proper meals and take care of his sore throat, Annemarie pledged to see that he did and Joe promised to come home for Christmas—Sam eased the car away from the apartment building, tossed one last wave over his shoulder and headed for home.

It was a beautiful day for driving, clear and mild with little traffic to clutter the interstate. The trip sped by, an endless series of exit ramps, billboards and tourist traps, moving too fast. Sam thought he could have driven forever with Rachel beside him, even though they traveled in contemplative silence for most of the journey.

Another feeling warmed him as well, a sense of accomplishment and pride.

Success had been a stranger to Sam for most of his life. The pursuit of happiness had lured him away from the rigors necessary to achieve prosperity. On too many occasions, the honesty of his intentions to do the right thing had shored up his failure to follow through on his plans. Sam had settled for getting by as best he could. He had little to show for his life, but he had accomplished everything he set out to do as a young man. He had his farm, a good woman and a fine family. He had planted roots, nurtured and established them. In time, those roots would grow deep and flourish. In some small way, so would Sam.

And so would Rachel.

Looking at his constant companion of fifty-odd years, Sam still saw the beauty that had first attracted him. The passing years had softened the harsh countenance of her youth, but Rachel remained a stubbornly proud woman. Her overabundance of pragmatism balanced his excess of dreamer's deeds. His poet's heart gave voice to her stark beauty. Her tendency to worry got lost in his habit of making the right moves. And his shiftless streak found a home in her settled existence. Sam had thought they would complement each other when he married Rachel, but they were blended in ways unimagined even by him all those years ago.

"Did you love me when we got married, Rachel?" Sam asked.

"Not the way I love you now," she answered swiftly, truthfully. "I had great affection for you, Sam—the beginnen of love—but not love the way it is today."

"I fell in love with you the first time I laid eyes on you," Sam said.

"You are a romantic, Sam," she replied.

"It's one of the few endowments of my loner's heritage that I can be right proud of," Sam stated.

There was a story behind his statement. A legend, the rare piece of family lore strong enough to survive generations of neglectful caretakers.

In the 1830s, Sam's great-grandfather, William, eighteen at the time, had fallen in love with Holly Spiceland, a sixteen-year-old Cherokee squaw. The young lovers kept their affair secret, preferring the perils of clandestine meetings and stolen trysts in the glens and hills of the North Carolina mountains to the risk of wrath and scorn from their white and Indian cultures. In 1838, however, William and Holly encountered a greater obstacle than even their families. That was the year the government forced the relocation of the Cherokee Nation to Oklahoma, and thousands of Indian men, women and children embarked on the Trail of Tears. Her family was among those who left their home in North Carolina, but Holly stayed behind with William.

Defying social customs as well as the wishes of his family, William took the Indian woman as his wife. They married themselves when no preacher would perform the ceremony. When William's family disowned him, he moved his Indian wife to South Georgia and declared they would spend the rest of their lives on those wide-open, coastal plains.

William and Holly settled virgin territory on the Georgia-Florida border in Lowndes County. She gave birth to four children, but only two outlived their parents. William was never a prosperous man, but he kept his family nourished. He hunted and fished for food and traded animal hides for a meager living, while Holly raised a small garden virtually year-round. The couple lived a simple, happy existence until a late September day in 1884 when Holly died. On the same date a year later, William passed away.

The story of William and Holly Baker had been told to Sam by his grandmother Flossie. She had married Patrick Baker, the only son of the half-breed couple. Patrick was a man who always meant well but rarely delivered on his plans. He became a farmer, survived the Battle of Atlanta and still died a young man when a mule kicked him in the head a few years after the Civil War ended.

Flossie was left to raise their only child, Daniel, who was four when his father died. She remarried a year later, to a neighboring farmer, a widower who was steady, dependable and moderately successful—all the things Patrick Baker had aspired to but failed to achieve. Flossie's second marriage was a good union, but Daniel never accepted the man or the passel of half-brothers and sisters.

As a child, Daniel was a mischief-maker with a mind of his own. In his grown years, he was shiftless and never satisfied, always in a state of flux between duty and desire. His happiest days came after his wife died and his sons were grown, leaving Daniel unattached and free to follow his wandering ways.

Sam had never understood his father's selfishness. He never would.

"It's not a loner's heritage anymore, Sam," Rachel observed, sensing her husband's melancholy. "And it won't ever be again."

Sam smiled brightly at his wife "What kind of lovers are we compared with my great-grandparents?" he asked.

Rachel shook her head. "There's no comparison," she said airily. "They were the greatest of lovers in their time. And so are we in our time."

Sam reached out to take her hand, and Rachel slid across the seat close to him, resting her head against his shoulder. They rode in companionable silence for nearly half an hour, until the car left the interstate and they were traveling the familiar route of Highway 125.

"I guess you know by now that we'll never get to Paris," Sam commented with regret.

"I never wanted to go to Paris," Rachel informed him. "That was your dream, Sam. I'm sure it's a grand city, but I'd have been too ready to get back home to enjoy it properly."

"Oh."

"Besides, you've done such a good job describen it over the years that the real Paris probably would be a let-down," Rachel concluded.

"Is there any place you would like to go?" he inquired.

She considered the question. "If we could scrape up the money, I would like to go to Washington and see the place where Ruth is buried. I still miss her from time to time, even after all these years."

This memory of Ruth brought a sad smile to both Rachel and Sam's faces. Their beautiful daughter gone all these years, becoming a wife when she was still a girl, whisked across the country to live on a dairy farm and then killed in a tractor accident before she was twenty. Indeed, Ruth had been dead and buried for a month when the short note arrived from her husband, Karl Stoll, informing Rachel and Sam of what had transpired on his family's dairy farm in Snohomish, Washington.

"We'll do it," Sam vowed heartily, refusing to let melancholy claim this moment. "Do you remember the time when Joseph decided Ruth was sickly and he made her drink that bottle of special elixir."

"It was special alright," Rachel declared, still in disbelief and embarrassed almost forty years after the fact. "One-hundred-percent-proof alcohol. Poor Ruth never knew what hit her."

"But you have to admit," Sam said. "It did the trick. She was pretty much healthy from then on."

They both laughed as this mention of their daughter touched off a rollicking trip down memory lane, a happy voyage, which carried them over the last miles of their journey home.

———

On their arrival home, Sam and Rachel found Matt and Caroline on the front porch, where the concerned parents had waited for the better part of two hours to hear firsthand details about their oldest son. Matt sat in the rocker, Caroline on the glider, and both beat a steady motion through the afternoon. They barely restrained themselves when the car pulled under the carport, rushing through the welcomes and enduring another wait while Sam and Rachel each sojourned in the bathroom. At length, the four of them were ensconced on the porch, and the grandparents relayed a full account of their visit with Joe.

Sam and Rachel trod a fine line between the truth and the trust Joe had put in them. They withheld nothing about the injuries Joe had suffered in the grueling encounter with Wayne Taylor. They sought to allay Matt and Caroline's worries about Joe's increasing remoteness without revealing the full extent of his troubled mind. And they tried to present an accurate portrait of his weakened physical condition without revealing the cause of his decline. Most of all, however, they assured Matt and Caroline that their son was on the road to recovery from whatever ailed him.

"He's lost some weight, gotten kind of run down," Rachel told them. "But it's nothen that some proper meals won't fix."

"I'd wager there's more to tell than what we've heard," Matt interrupted.

"He's become so distant, so far away from us," Caroline fretted.

"Joe has done a lot of soul-searchen this year, which shouldn't come as a surprise to any of us," Sam said firmly. "He's learned some of life's harder lessons, the hard way. You might even say he's gone to Hell and back. But the important thing is that he's begun to heal. And he'll be a stronger, wiser man for it."

"I guess we'll have to take your word for it, Pa," Matt said gruffly. "Did he say when he might come home?"

"Christmas," Rachel answered. "He'll be home for Christmas."

"Isn't there anything else you can tell us?" Caroline pleaded.

Sam glanced at Rachel, and they smiled broadly. "Well," Rachel said, "there is one thing."

"What?" Matt and Caroline demanded in unison.

"He has a girl," Rachel confessed.

A different kind of concern overtook Caroline and Matt as they absorbed the idea of Joe with a woman in his life. "Well, that's good news, I suppose," Matt remarked.

"She's not just *a* girl," Sam noted. "She's *the* girl."

"He's that serious?" Matt asked.

"I don't think he knows how serious he is," Sam said cheerfully. "But the boy's smitten, and the girl is head over heels in love. In my book, it all adds up to y'all losen a son."

Caroline smiled for the first time in what seemed like several weeks. "Now, Pa," she admonished. "Y'all didn't lose Matt when he and I got married. You just gained me."

"And we got the best bargain of our lives in that deal," Sam boasted. "But that was another time, Caroline. Things are different now, especially for young people starten out married. The way we live—all of us under one roof—it's out of step with the times. Families are scatteren out, moven away, and ours is no different."

Caroline nodded, understanding, regretting and accepting the idea. "I would be happy for Joe to get married and be settled," she said at length. "Honestly, it seems like we've already lost him. This girl might even bring him back to us in some way."

"Oh, I think she will indeed do that," Sam agreed. "Of most importance, though, I believe she will help bring Joe back to himself."

"What's her name," Matt asked.

"Annemarie Morgan," Sam replied. "She's from a little town south of here called Boston. She's an airline stewardess—and an orphan, too."

"What kind of girl is she?" Caroline asked Rachel, getting down to the nitty-gritty, which required a woman's point of view.

"She's different," Rachel admitted, groping for an explanation of the young woman. "Joe told us she comes on like a tornado, and that's a pretty apt description. But Annemarie's a good girl, Caroline, a Christian girl. I liked her."

Rachel paused, then added: "Come to think of it, I must have liked her a whole bunch because she kept callen my husband, 'sugar,' and I never once gave it a second thought."

CHAPTER 2

ILLNESS HAD AVOIDED JOE for most of his life. He could virtually count the times he had been sick on two hands. There were several sore throats, one bout with tonsillitis, a few overnight bugs—but nothing serious. Even the usual childhood diseases had treated him kindly. He had escaped the measles and mumps every time they made the rounds through school, even when they erupted within his home. He had contracted the chicken pox, but suffered only a mild fever and minor rash.

When serious illness finally attacked, it came with a vengeance, catching Joe with his resistance low.

His throat tightened and grew raw overnight. He woke Monday morning with white splotches across his tonsils and a chest cold. All day, he fought a soaring fever, a battle that eventually sent him out into the chillingly damp air to buy aspirin and a bottle of orange juice. When evening came, he felt better, well enough to eat Annemarie's hearty supper of fried ravioli seasoned with parmesan cheese.

A dull ache settled in his head after supper, spreading throughout his body as the evening wore on. Around ten o'clock, he glumly announced he was coming down with something and thought it best to turn in for the night.

Annemarie kissed him on the forehead, sent him to bed and returned to her apartment for a good night's sleep to prepare for the next day's flight to Miami.

As Joe lay in bed that night, a dull throb hammered his head. He grew queasy, and a feverish ache settled in his muscles. He drifted into a conscious state of sleep, which proved more disturbing than restful. In fact, Joe thought his eyes were merely closed until he woke abruptly in the pitch-black darkness of his bedroom.

Never had he experienced such ghastly sickness. His swollen stomach rolled and lurched; his throbbing head expanded and contracted with every labored breath. Chills sent small convulsions through his clammy body, bringing the entire contents of his stomach to the top of his throat. Joe willed himself to swallow the nausea, accomplishing the task with several deliberate breaths.

He sat up carefully in bed, allowing his feet to fall against the floor and standing on shaky legs. He covered half the distance to the bathroom before his energy gave out. Swaying, almost falling, he caught himself, and lowered his body to the floor, lying on the cold hardwood to regain his strength.

When the nausea rose once more, he crawled into the bathroom, hung his head over the commode and vomited supper.

Annemarie found him fast asleep on the bathroom floor the next morning and felt sick herself for a moment. She stared a long minute, aghast at his forlorn form, fearful he was passed out from too much alcohol. Finally, she gulped, deciding to trust him—and to walk away without ever looking back if he was indeed drunk.

A battle raged within her as Annemarie approached Joe. Was he drunk? Had his claim to never want another drink of liquor been false sincerity?

He was prone against the floor, freckled with chill bumps across his naked back and legs. The odor of vomit permeated the bathroom, originating from the toilet bowl, which contained the disgorged contents of his stomach.

Annemarie had seen and smelled worse. She flushed the toilet, then knelt beside Joe and touched his forehead. He was burning up with fever and shivered at her touch.

"Joe," she called softly. "Wake up, hon."

He stirred, rolling onto his back to peer at her through unfocused eyes. "Oh, hi," he said as if the situation was perfectly normal. "When did you get here?"

"Just now," Annemarie smiled, supporting his head.

"I think I'm sick," Joe informed her.

She smiled again, both relieved and sympathetic to his announcement. "Bad, is it?" she asked.

He gave her a wan grin, then sat up slowly against the wall and asked Annemarie to leave the room.

"Why, sugar?" she replied.

"Because I'm gonna be sick again," he answered, gagging on the last words, falling toward the commode.

Joe threw up again, retching hard as his stomach emptied completely and green bile came up. Annemarie stood over him, bracing his forehead, supporting his back. The convulsions kept coming, long after there was nothing left to escape his body. When the spasms finally subsided, Annemarie wet a washcloth with cold water and held it against his head.

Joe tripped the toilet handle, then rested his head against the bowl until his quivering insides seemed manageable. He sat back against the wall once more, breathing evenly with his eyes closed.

In a minute, he opened them to peer up at Annemarie, reassuring her that the worst had passed. For the effort, he was rewarded with a severe stomach cramp that doubled him over against the floor. He waited until the pain was bearable, then told her he wanted to take a shower and suggested she leave him alone for the moment.

She honored the request after first turning on the shower and laying out a fresh towel for him.

It was the first shower Joe had ever taken lying down in the tub. Lacking strength to stand, he lay in a huddle, allowing the scalding spray to soothe his aching muscles and temporarily chase away the chills. He stayed there until the water began to lose its warmth, then pulled himself out of the tub, dried off, stumbled to bed and slipped quickly into sleep.

———

Annemarie decided Joe was too ill to leave alone, so she called in sick and missed her scheduled flight to Miami.

For most of the day and late into the night, Joe slept. During his waking hours, she tried to get liquids down him, but Joe threw everything back up. Annemarie feared he would become dehydrated and suggested with persistence that they visit the emergency room at nearby Crawford Long Hospital.

But Joe was typically stubborn, hardheaded and hell-bent to suffer and recover on his own. "I've put a lot of poison in my body over the last few months," he explained during one of his rare moments of coherence that long day. "I think maybe this is my body's way of ridden me of all that mess—purgen the poison, so to speak."

All through the night, his body continued to purge the poison. When nothing but bile came up from his stomach, diarrhea set in, turning his intestines into a cramping mass. Joe rode it out through the long hours, like the captain of a crippled ship. If he was embarrassed by the rebellious nature of his body, he refused to show it. Each time he emerged from the bathroom, he closed the door behind him, smiled weakly and lurched toward the bed.

Annemarie dozed on and off until tiredness overcame her in the early morning hours, and she sank into a deep slumber at Joe's side. He woke her several rested hours later, padding into the bedroom with a small glass of Coke in hand.

"I would have got that for you," she greeted him. "You should have woken me."

"You needed the sleep," he replied, coming to sit beside her on the bed, his hair damp and tousled from another shower. "Besides, I'm feelen better."

Annemarie sat up, touching his forehead and neck. "You still have some temperature," she fretted. "But you aren't quite as peaked as last night."

Joe pulled her against his chest, rubbing her back. "It's amazen what a little tender loven care can do for a guy," he remarked, his voice hoarse and low. "I felt awful bad last night and yesterday. Haven you here with me, though, made it not as bad as it could have been."

He pushed her back slightly, bracing their foreheads together so they could gaze into each other's eyes. "When this is over, Annie," he vowed, "I'm gonna start taken care of you."

She knew he meant her welfare, but the promise melted her insides like liquid fire. Maybe it was his tone. Or the fact that he was wearing only jockey shorts, and they were pressed close together on the bed.

"Kiss me," Annemarie urged.

Joe cocked his head, unsure. "And risk maken you sick?" he cautioned.

"I don't care about that, Joe," she replied, her fingers trailing lightly down the thin line of hair in the middle of his bare chest.

Joe required no further encouragement. He threw caution to the wind and kissed her thoroughly.

It was a powerful kiss but no panacea for the sickness ailing Joe.

Annemarie made her next-scheduled flight, and Joe suffered a relapse. He remained deathly ill for two more days, sleeping soundly for hours at a time, still unable to keep food and liquids on his upset stomach.

On Friday night, however, he pronounced himself better and consumed a can of chicken soup without bringing it back up for a second look. Later, he listened to Annemarie's plans to spend Thanksgiving with her family in Boston and brushed off her efforts to send him home to Cookville.

"You shouldn't spend Thanksgiven alone when you've got that wonderful family back home, waiten and wanten to see you," she told him. "Go home, Joe. I know that's what you want to do."

Joe shrugged off her persuasive tactics with a grin. "I'd scare the daylights out of everybody if I turned up looken like this," he teased. "Besides, I won't be alone, honey. Ray and his family have invited me to eat dinner with them."

"It won't be the same as be'en with your family," Annemarie remarked.

"Maybe not, but Ray's brood is almost like a second family," he said. "Truthfully, Annie, I'd like nothen better than to go home for Thanksgiven. But I want to perk up a little first. Call it vanity, call it pride—I don't care. I simply prefer to look a little less like a scarecrow when I go marchen home for the first time in a year."

She understood his point of view, but Annemarie also believed his family would prefer a scarecrow to nothing at all.

Reluctantly, she gave up on the quest to get Joe home and finalized her plans. After Saturday's flight, she had five days off, including Thanksgiving. She would drive down to Boston on Sunday in Joe's Volkswagen and return late Thursday in time to rest up for the next day's layover flight to New York.

"You could come home with me," she suggested impulsively to Joe as she prepared to return to her apartment late that night.

"I don't think so," Joe said. "I'd hate for your folks to get the wrong impression and think you have poor taste when it comes to picken men."

Annemarie gave him a disgruntled shrug. "Well, then, Mr. Hardheaded, I guess you'll have to settle for cold turkey and leftover trimmings. But I promise to bring you back a plate anyway."

"No oyster dressen," Joe reminded her.

Oyster dressing was a holiday tradition in Annemarie's family. Like Joe, however, she was not fond of oysters and never ate it.

"No oyster dressen," she agreed primly. "Though you probably deserve it for not goen home to be with your family."

"How about a piece of pumpkin pie?" he asked.

Annemarie softened. "I'll make one especially for you, sugar."

———

On the kind of day that Yankees call Indian Summer, Sam went fishing at the Old Pond. He left after Saturday dinner and was gone all afternoon. When the day's shadow grew long and suppertime drew near, Rachel dispatched Luke to usher her tardy husband home.

Luke found his grandfather propped against his favorite oak tree, with his head bent down and the fishing pole lying unattended beside him. The old man might have been asleep, but he seemed much too still.

Instinctively, Luke sensed his grandpa was dead.

His first thought was that Sam had gone fishing for the last time. Almost without thinking, Luke started toward the water's edge to examine his grandfather's catch, then stopped in mid-stride—stunned and mournful.

Turning back, he ran a hand through his hair, mulling over what needed to be done. Luke approached the body, touching Sam lightly on the neck and discovering he had been dead for several hours on this warm afternoon.

Holding his tears, he began the slow walk home. He saw no reason to hurry. There was plenty of time ahead for all the sadness sure to follow.

At the house, watching over the simmering supper, Rachel wondered as well about the fish Sam had caught. Hers were troubling thoughts, causing her mind to wander from supper and carrying Rachel back and forth between the stove and the kitchen window that looked out over the fields and the pecan orchard. She kept hoping to see Sam coming toward home, bringing a big line of perch, bream and maybe a catfish or two.

On her umpteenth trip to peer out the window, Rachel spotted Luke—her grandson walking home by himself—and she sensed the moment she dreaded worst in life had come to pass. Rachel had always assumed she would know the exact moment when Sam died—that she would feel his life ebb away because of the life-sharing bond between them—that she would be there with him when the time came.

Those were foolish thoughts. Death came unexpectedly, as surely as Judgment Day would.

She sat down heavily in the small kitchen rocker to begin pondering the idea of life without Sam. She sensed the void, already beginning to feel some of the sadness and loneliness. The matter was too close to her heart to deal with for the moment, so Rachel sat still in the rocking chair, fiddling with the worn band of gold around her left ring finger.

––––––––

The smell of cornbread beginning to burn drew Caroline to the kitchen from the dining room where she had been putting away the last packages of meat from the slaughtered shoat. She placed the hog head on top of everything else, intent on making a batch of souse early next week, then went to check out the offending odor.

Burned food of any kind was a rarity in the Baker house, with the lone exception of rice. When Caroline and Rachel cooked rice, they always scorched it slightly on the bottom, intentionally, because several of the children preferred it that way.

Rachel took a great deal of care and pride with hoecakes, however, and her daughter-in-law could not remember a time when one had burned—especially with Rachel in the kitchen.

"Your cornbread's burnen, Ma," Caroline commented as she came into the kitchen and discovered Rachel sitting idly in the rocker. She fetched a spatula from the cupboard, then flipped the hoecake and examined the damage. It was highly brown, but they could scrape off the worst and make do for tonight's supper.

"That's not like you to let the cornbread burn," Caroline continued, turning toward Rachel with a smile.

Rachel appeared not to have heard her, and Caroline became concerned. "Ma? Are you alright?"

The kitchen door squeaked open then, and a stricken Rachel looked up. Caroline followed the path of her eyes to the doorway, where Luke stood motionless, gaping back at his grandmother with the same dazed expression on his face.

In that instant, Caroline grasped the meaning of their torpor. A sharp pain pierced her breast, but it was more important to be at Rachel's side. And Caroline was there at once, with a comforting, consoling embrace to catch the first trickle of a new widow's grief on her dress and to wet an older, wiser face with tears of her own.

Luke was beside his grandmother, too, seconds later, sharing the grief with tight, hiccupping sobs. No one spoke for the longest while until Caroline found a shaky voice: "Luke, go tell your daddy to come here."

––––––––

Joe was on an errand to the grocery store when the call came from his mother, and Annemarie was preparing fish for the broiler. She dried her hands on the way to the bedroom, picking up the receiver on the fourth ring. "Hello," she said cheerfully.

"Hello?" The return greeting sounded uncertain, almost beseeching. "I'm looken for Joe Baker. Is this the right number?"

"Yes, ma'am, it is," Annemarie replied. "Joe's not here at the moment, but he should be back any minute."

"I see." The woman hesitated.

"May I take a message," Annemarie prompted. "I'm a friend."

"Are you Annemarie?"

She sensed then it was Joe's mother on the other end of the line. "Yes, ma'am. Annemarie Morgan."

"I'm his mother—Caroline Baker," she confirmed. "I really need to speak with Joe." She paused, thinking over the phone. "Perhaps, though, it would be better for him to hear my news from you."

Apprehension formed a knot in Annemarie's stomach. "Is everything okay, ma'am?" she asked instinctively.

"Unfortunately, no," Caroline sighed. "Joe's grandpa passed away this afternoon."

"Oh, ma'am!" Annemarie mourned, fighting the urge to cry. "I'm so terribly sorry. How is Mrs. Baker?"

"As good as can be expected," Caroline replied. "She's hurten, but she's a strong woman. Thank you for asken." She paused, then asked, "Would you mind breaken the news to Joe when he gets home? I understand the two of you are good friends. It might make it easier for him to hear about this in person instead of over the telephone."

Annemarie considered the suggestion. "I'll do whatever you prefer, ma'am, but perhaps Joe should hear from you," she replied. "He's bound to be upset, but if he hears your strength, maybe he'll feel stronger for it."

A long moment of silence followed, then Caroline told her, "I don't feel very strong at the moment, but that's kind of you to say. Maybe I should be the one to tell Joe. Please ask him to call home as soon as possible."

"I'll do that," Annemarie assured. "And, ma'am, please accept my condolences and extend my deepest sympathies to Mrs. Baker. I had the good fortune to spend time with the two of them last weekend, and they were lovely people. I know she'll miss him deeply. You all will."

"Thank you, Annemarie," Caroline replied sincerely.

The front door opened then. "One moment, Mrs. Baker," Annemarie said. "I believe Joe just came in. I'll get him to the phone."

She laid the receiver on the nightstand, walked over to the bedroom door and called Joe to the phone.

"Who is it?" he asked, coming toward her.

"Your mother," Annemarie answered with downcast eyes.

Joe stopped beside her, lifting her chin with a finger. "Annie?" He peered closely at her face. "Honey, you have tears in your eyes. Is somethen wrong?"

Annemarie motioned him to the phone, and Joe dashed across the room. "Mama?" he greeted Caroline.

Seconds later, Joe sat down on the edge of the bed. "I can't believe it," he mumbled, with a blank expression on his face.

Annemarie went to sit beside him, putting her arm around his shoulders as Caroline completed the grim task of providing the pertinent details, and Joe inquired over the state of his grandmother and father. In a couple of minutes, he promised, "I'll be home soon." His voice was choked. "Tell Daddy and Granny that I love them," he said. "And Mama, I love you, too."

He hung up the phone slowly, then clutched his stomach and sat stiffly. Annemarie rubbed his cheek, then embraced him. Almost instantly, he buried his head against her chest and wept softly until the grief seemed bearable. In short order, she cleaned up the kitchen while Joe packed his clothes. Then, after gathering her own things, she drove with him home to Cookville.

———

They arrived at the house shortly before eleven o'clock that night—to a solemn gathering of friends and family. In true fashion, the community had responded quickly as news of Sam's death spread. Sam was admired and respected by almost everyone who knew him. This first group of sympathizers was thinning in the late hours, but they would return in multiples in the coming days.

Joe parked the car across the road and took a minute to absorb the familiar surroundings. "The place looks exactly as it did when I left last year," he observed distantly. "Nothen seems to have changed." He hesitated, then lamented, "But everything has changed."

Annemarie squeezed his hand. "Things will be okay, Joe," she tried to reassure him.

"In time," he agreed, smiling sadly, kissing her lightly on the forehead.

Joe peered out the car window and saw Bonnie emerge from the crowd, coming toward the Volkswagen. "That's my youngest sister," he remarked, opening the car door and stepping out to meet her.

The commiseration began the moment Bonnie walked into her big brother's arms and never let up over the next two hours. Annemarie stayed near Joe's side throughout this consolatory passage of time. When it was over, she understood the man a little better—and loved him more for the understanding.

For the people he loved, Joe was a source of strength—a lamb for sacrifice, an outlet for troubles, a maker of miracles. But it was not a one-sided deal by any means. For every ounce given of himself, Joe received back a double measure. He nourished and thrived among his family.

Amid all the sadness, despite the grief over Sam, Annemarie exalted in this affirmation of her faith. From the very beginning, her heart had trusted Joe, believing he possessed the stuff of dreams as well as the character needed for real life. For whatever reasons, Joe had sunk into despair, but he was climbing out of it. She knew now that he had achieved a lasting victory—and realized she, too, had come home at long last.

With a joyful heart, Annemarie left his side to seek a private moment with Rachel. "I wish I'd have had a lifetime to know your husband," she told the older woman as they embraced. "But I'm grateful for the moment we did have. He was a special person and so are you. Just be'en here this short time, I've seen for myself that y'all's roots are well established, and they've already begun to produce that legacy of good things he talked about." She hesitated, then confessed, "I've seen firsthand what a wonderful legacy it really is, ma'am. And between you and me, I feel as if I owe you a debt of gratitude."

Rachel smiled. "I can't tell you how many times this past week that Sam and I mentioned last weekend, especially sharen that Sunday with Joe and you," she said. "Sam thought you were a special person, honey, and so do I."

Later, as she prepared to leave, Annemarie sought out Caroline. "I'm glad to have met you, Mrs. Baker, but so sorry it was under these circumstances."

"Pa and Ma speak highly of you, Annemarie," Caroline replied with an honest smile. "I have to confess that I'm glad to see that they didn't exaggerate any."

Annemarie laughed slightly. "We had a wonderful time last Sunday," she remarked. "I'll always treasure it."

Glancing at her wristwatch, Caroline frowned. "It's awfully late to be on the road," she said. "You're welcome to stay the night here."

"That's kind of you to offer, ma'am, but Boston's only an hour or so away," Annemarie replied. "I'd like to be there in the mornen. I feel a need to be in church tomorrow."

"I can certainly understand that feelen," Caroline admitted, "and respect you all the more for it. I wish we had time to talk, but this isn't the best time."

"There'll be another time," Annemarie said. "Before I go, though, I do think you should know that Joe has been sick as a dog this week with the flu."

Her tone was worried. "He's some better, but he's hardly had anything to eat all week. He simply couldn't keep anything down—even threw up once on the trip down here. You might keep an eye on him in case he suffers a relapse and needs to see a doctor. And if he really starts vomiten badly like he did a few days ago, it helps just to hold his head."

She paused suddenly, embarrassed by the forward tone of her fretting. "I guess you already know that."

As Annemarie spoke, her eyes sought the end of the hall where Joe stood talking with Mark Applegate. The concern reflected in the young woman's hazel eyes reminded Caroline of times gone by when she had worried over Matt, Joe or one of the younger children. Her husband rarely took ill but when he did, Matt usually wound up in bed for a day. No one in the family had been sick less often than Joe. His constitution had been remarkable, warding off most ailments before they established a firm hold on him. And when he had been sick, Joe, like his father, had simply secluded himself for a long nap and woken up some hours later on the road to recovery.

Caroline felt a stab of jealousy that Annemarie Morgan should have made a discovery about Joe, which had eluded his own mother over all these years. But the feeling passed quickly. It appeared very likely this woman was destined to make a hundred other private discoveries about Joe in the coming years. As far as Caroline was concerned, the knowledge that someone would make those discoveries about her son outweighed any regret over her own missed opportunities.

"Actually," she replied, "I didn't know that about Joe. He was hardly ever sick, even as a baby. I'll keep what you said in mind, although I have my doubts that Joe would be inclined to want his mother's hand on his head at this juncture in life."

Annemarie peered intently at Caroline, then nodded in agreement. "Joe's hard-headed, no doubt," she confirmed. "He didn't want my hand there either. I just muscled my way in and put it there. Now he's used to it. And I do believe he even appreciates it."

———

Nature provided another beautiful Indian summer day for the funeral, and Benevolence overflowed with mourners wishing to pay their last respects to Sam. Rachel insisted the occasion celebrate life, and Preacher Adam Cook delivered a eulogy crammed with every appropriate scripture and personal anecdotes.

The Bakers walked away from the church uplifted and encouraged.

They buried Sam on the land he loved so well, under a cluster of towering pines and stately oaks nestled between the Old Pond and the Back Pasture.

The benediction was a poem that Sam had remarked upon to Rachel one summer day when the urge to go fishing had overwhelmed the need to work. They had been young then, still discovering each other. But Rachel had remembered the poem all these years, and she deemed it an appropriate epitaph for her beloved husband.

So it was, that on a clear afternoon dappled with sunshine, warmth and simplicity, Preacher Cook read from a yellowed sheet of magazine paper, which had been tucked away in Rachel's Bible for many years—and sent poetry rolling through those fields and woods:

> In a meadow that I know,
> Where an inland river rises
> And the stream is still and slow;
> There it wanders under willows
> And beneath the silver green
> Of the birches' silent shadows
> Where the early violets lean.
>
> Other pathways lead to Somewhere,
> But the one I love so well
> Has no end and no beginning
> Just the beauty of the dell,
> Just the wildflowers and the lilies
> Yellow striped as adder's tongue,
> Seem to satisfy my pathway
> As it winds their streets among.
>
> There I go to meet the Springtime,
> When the meadow is aglow,
> Marigolds amid the marshes,
> And the stream is still and slow;
> There I find my fair oasis,
> And with carefree feet I tread
> For the pathway leads to Nowhere,
> And the blue is overhead.
>
> All the ways that lead to Somewhere
> Echo with the hurrying feet
> Of the Struggling and the Striving,
> But the way I find so sweet
> Bids me dream and bids me linger
> Joy and beauty are its goal;
> On the path that leads to Nowhere
> I have sometimes found my soul.

THANKSGIVING CAME THREE DAYS after the funeral, and someone suggested the Bakers might find it easier to forgo their usual holiday celebration.

"Why would we do that?" Rachel bristled.

The someone was one of Rachel's nieces—Euna's daughter, Chloe—and her good intentions rated a dressing down from her feisty aunt. "Thanksgiven is not a day for pinen over what you don't have," Rachel declared, reprimanding her middle-aged niece. "It's a special time of the year set aside for people to look back and count their blessens for all the good things in this life. As far as I'm concerned, our family has more than ever to be thankful for this year. If there's a single one of us who doesn't feel that way, then we've lost somethen more important than Sam."

No one disagreed with Rachel, and the holiday preparations began in earnest on the day after Sam was buried.

Most of the meal came from the toil of their labor; the rest from the grocery store in Cookville and the Carter's Mercantile. Caroline did the shopping, procuring the turkey, oysters and other staples for the dinner; the ham came from a shoat delivered by one of the farm's prized sows, Yorkie; Rachel butchered a hen; Summer and Carrie picked the turnips, sweet potatoes and other vegetables; and Bonnie collected pecans and cleaned the house.

They divvied up the cooking as well. Rachel stewed the hen, made the dressing, dumplings and pear tarts; Caroline roasted the turkey, made the giblet gravy, oyster stew and candied sweet potatoes and baked the spice cake; Summer boiled the turnips, with corn dodgers, and the butterbeans; Carrie made the fruit salad and baked the pies; and Bonnie did everything else.

Now, the Thanksgiving feast awaited them.

Matt and Rachel sat at opposite ends of the table, flanked by Caroline, Amelia, Dan, Mark, Summer, Joe and June on one side—and Paul, Carl, Bonnie, John, Carrie, April and Luke on the other.

There was a holiday custom in the Baker house that the oldest man at the dinner table give grace over the meal, and the honor fell this year to Dan. This was the first time the Carters had shared Thanksgiving with the Bakers, and Dan was taken aback when Rachel asked him to return thanks. He was the last person to bow his head, taking the extra moment to study the faces around the table.

When he closed his eyes and began to pray, the words came with humbleness and thoughtfulness. It was not a lengthy blessing, but the prayer made its point. And when grace was given, everyone felt a little sad for what they had lost—but a bit more grateful for all they still had.

Soon, the dinner table hummed with its normal melody.

———

Caroline listened to the sounds around her with mixed messages from a heavy heart. She was thankful on this day, grateful for the many blessings bestowed on her family and pleased that everyone seemed ready to get on with the business of living as Rachel put it. Sam would have wanted it this way. But even so, she was grieving.

Losing Sam was like losing her own parents all over again. Maybe worse. Caroline could not explain the pain entirely, although she suspected it had to do with her constant effort to be strong for Rachel, Matt and the children over the last few days. Perhaps she had not grieved enough. After all, Sam had been a father to her for more years than she had lived with her own parents. Caroline had loved him deeply, and she already missed him terribly.

Her eyes drifted to his customary place at the end of the long table. She tried to picture Sam sitting there, tall, proud and full of life. But Rachel had taken her husband's place, and Caroline could not conjure up the vision she wanted. In a while, the thought occurred that she was looking for the wrong picture, so she abandoned the effort. Rising from the table, she took a minute to refill empty tea glasses and urge everyone to eat seconds.

Back in her seat, she made small talk with Amelia and Dan, then slipped once more into contemplative silence as the Carters, Matt and Paul plunged into a discussion over the government's recent decision to ban cigarette commercials from television.

———

"Peanuts!" Rachel declared.

"Pecans," June Berrien retorted.

Luke glanced from his grandmother to June, then turned to April Berrien sitting beside him. "What do you think, Miss April?" he inquired. "Which makes the best syrup candy?"

"When you've got false teeth, it don't matter one iota," April complained. "Pecans, peanuts—I can't eat either, so they're all the same to me. Besides, I never was fond of syrup candy, even when I had all my teeth."

Caroline was intrigued by the conversation at the other end of the table, where Rachel and June debated the merits of using pecans or peanuts to make syrup candy, and Luke moderated the friendly disagreement. The subject abruptly changed to false teeth, however, particularly April's tendency to misplace her bottom plate, and Caroline lost her appetite for the discussion.

Closer to her, Matt and Paul launched into a discourse on their plans to turn the Berrien estate into a working plantation. Against his better judgment—in Caroline's opinion—Matt was about to take on another four hundred acres of rented cropland, which would require the purchase of another tractor. Already this year, they had borrowed heavily from the bank to buy the Castleberry place, which Slaton Castleberry's widow, Florence, had sold them contingent upon her being allowed to live in the house until she died.

Being in debt up to their ears worried Caroline, despite three consecutive years of unmatched prosperity on the farm. But her concern extended beyond the money matters. She fretted over the tremendous workload they would inherit. They were stretched in too many directions as it was, trying to do everything that needed doing, and she wondered how her husband would deal with the extra burden. At the moment, Matt seemed too caught up in the expectations of success to consider the hard work it would require.

Perhaps she was being overly cautious, but Caroline missed the simpler times on the farm—when the money had been short but adequate, and the workdays long but tolerable. John and Luke would do all they could to help with the additional work in their spare time, of course, but Matt still would need an extra hand to meet his new obligations. Caroline wondered where he might find it.

"Granny, Miss June, I have a suggestion," Luke declared all at once, drawing Caroline back toward the other end of the table. "We're obviously at an impasse on this important matter of whether pecans or peanuts make the best syrup candy. I suggest you both make your best batches and let me be the judge. And y'all should do it tomorrow because syrup candy is one of my favorites, and I haven't had any in ages."

"Excuse me, Luke," Mark Applegate said, wiping his mouth with a cloth napkin. "In the spirit of compromise, I suggest the ladies make a single batch using both pecans and peanuts. That way, you get the best of both worlds."

Luke considered the proposal in quick order. "That would work, too," he told Rachel and June.

The good-natured finagling by her youngest son to get a batch of his favorite treat brought a smile to Caroline—and gave her the first lasting memory of this special day. There was spirit and spunk in the conversation that not even death could throttle, and the determination to persevere was etched across those old and young faces. It was a quality that Caroline wished could be captured on a painter's canvas and preserved for the tough times to come.

This idea of painting came almost as a surprise to Caroline, who noted the possibility of asking John to teach her or perhaps taking an art class on her own. More than anything, however, the thought of a paint canvas reminded Caroline of the white Christmas a decade ago and the images she had stored in memory.

She could still see the faces and expressions of her family and friends on that special day—eternally young and happy and innocent. So innocent. Too innocent to escape the turbulent times that had left them and their community with deep scars.

She remembered her high expectations of ten years ago and wondered why the decade had treated them so harshly when they had tried to achieve only good things. Maybe there were no sanctuaries from the violence and ugliness of life. But certainly, they had suffered more than their share of troubles. Maybe, too, they were ready again for some permanent sense of normalcy in their lives. Sam's death seemed to suggest as much.

Caroline understood there was a certain appropriateness to the sadness at the table. Losing Sam hurt all of them, and they would miss him dearly. But at least, there was nothing unnatural about his death. As much as Sam loved to be among the living, he would have agreed with Caroline on this idea. The old and the affirmed should have a monopoly on death—instead of the likes of Tom Carter, Danny Bartholomew and Billy Taylor.

Caroline wanted to reach out to the future, but a feeling lying somewhere between homesickness and nostalgia kept her yearning for the past. A decade ago, on a similar occasion, her family and friends had seemed poised on the brink of a grand experience, having endured the hardships of another age and facing a future that beckoned with the promise of better days ahead. Now that time had passed, too.

In a sense, they were on the brink again, but before she allowed them to move ahead, Caroline needed images to preserve her family's experience of the era, which had begun on that unusual Christmas and was ending with this Thanksgiving celebration.

She began her mental picture-taking with Matt. Her husband had aged over the decade. His brow was furrowed, thin lines creased his cheeks and white flecks gave a silvery glow to his hair. But sitting at the head of the table, with elbows propped on the edge and hands clasped beneath his strong jaw, Matt appeared ready and able to assume fully the role of family patriarch.

Caroline chose to remember Sam and Rachel on the day of their return home after visiting Joe in Atlanta—sitting tall and proud in the front seat of the car. Of all the years she had known her in-laws, Caroline had never seen them pressed side by side in a car unless they were crowded together by necessity. A sight almost as rare was the intimate gesture, the way Rachel had rested her head against Sam's shoulder. It was a vision of loveliness and love.

The invisible camera clicked again, this time on Summer and Mark sharing a private moment through their eyes, bound by heart and soul as they prepared to embark on the most special journey of their young lives; on John who was silently making his own careful observations of the dinner table, no doubt planning to immortalize a portion of the holiday meal on canvas; on Carrie, still the fragile beauty but growing stronger day by day as she found her place in life; on Luke and Bonnie, a young man and woman on the crest of trading glorious childhoods for promising futures.

Every now and then, Caroline stole glances at Carl Taylor, as well as Dan and Amelia. Carl was out of place at the table, but Caroline wanted him to feel comfortable in his strange surroundings. The child was a refugee of sorts, and he would need strength to survive the coming years. Paul Berrien would make a good teacher for the boy, as would the Carters, who knew more than their share about picking up the pieces of shattered lives.

Caroline had a good store of memories to mark the occasion, yet one piece was missing from her collection: How to remember Joe on this day?

She refused to recollect her oldest child as the haggard young man who sat staring at the plateful of food, seemingly oblivious to the mellow commotion surrounding him. This Joe—with dark lines beneath his eyes and a slight tremble in his hands—seemed dislocated. He obviously had traveled a treacherous path to get to this low point in life. Likely, Matt and she would never know how difficult the road had been for Joe. And surprisingly, she felt no compelling need to know the whole story.

Joe had survived the turmoil; he was beginning to heal. Grandpa had said as much, and Caroline trusted his judgment. Asking for anything more would be like borrowing trouble.

Still, her son needed a few home-cooked meals to put the meat back on his bones. Caroline suspected Miss Annemarie Morgan would prepare most of those meals in the coming years. Perhaps Joe had yet to realize it, but he had met his match in that young woman. It was a good one as far as Caroline was concerned. Until the match was made complete, however, someone still needed to provide Joe assistance with basic necessities—like cooking—and Caroline was happily obliged to do the honors.

"I declare, Joe! We've got to put some meat on those bones of yours."

His mama's remark coaxed Joe from his meditation. He looked up to find Caroline hovering over him with a bowl in hand.

"Care for more candied potatoes?" she offered.

Joe glanced down at his plate and discovered the sweet potatoes were the one portion of this Thanksgiving meal he had eaten. Otherwise, he had simply picked at his food. "Please," he said, holding up his plate.

The dish trembled in his hands, and Caroline noticed. She would have allowed the unsteady movement to pass, but Joe saw the worry in her eyes.

"They used to be dead still," he observed quietly, giving her a hesitant smile and getting one in return.

"Nerves?" she suggested.

"Among other things," Joe said. His smile broadened with reassurance. "You should have seen them two weeks ago—they were regular vibrators. Another week or so, Mama, and they'll be steady again."

Caroline spooned an extra helping of the syrupy potatoes on the upheld plate. She wanted to impart some philosophical advice to her son, but an appropriate message eluded her. "It doesn't matter," she told him at last. "As long as you're still you, son, everything will work out."

Joe glanced down again, embarrassed by his fallen star. Then asked himself why, and nodded agreement with his mother. He was her son, which was all that ever really mattered to his mama in the first place. She left him with a sincere smile, moving on to refill tea glasses and dish up seconds and thirds on the empty plates.

It was not lack of appetite keeping Joe from eating—but rather neglect as he pondered life. Pushing aside his thoughts for the moment, he attacked the full plate with ravenous hunger and devoured the food in short order before requesting a second serving of turkey and dressing and a third helping of the sweet potatoes.

"Are you gonna stay around for a few days?" John inquired as he dished up the food.

"Maybe a few weeks," Joe replied, raising several eyebrows around the table. "I have vacation time comen," he explained.

"It'll be good to have you home," John said. "If you don't have any plans, I could use some company haulen a load of pecans to Florida next week. I even thought about swingen by the beach on the way back—just for a look-see if nothen else."

"Sounds good," Joe accepted.

"Don't make too many plans, son," Matt interrupted. "There's a couple of fields on Paul's place that need to be turned, and they've got your name on 'em."

Joe nodded. "I guess it's time for me to do some real work again."

"I don't know, Daddy," Luke observed. "Joe's been gone so long he might not remember what a plow looks like, much less what to do with it."

"I remember," Joe grinned. "And unless you've improved drastically, I'd put my plowen up against yours any day, Mr. Football Star."

Luke brushed off the derogatory remark. "Actually, Joe, you came home just in time. I was just about ready to take over your room."

"He needs the extra space for his big head," Bonnie observed dryly. "You know how conceited big football stars are."

She paused, looking closely at her oldest brother. "Still, don't give him another chance, Joe. And next time, don't stay away so long. We miss you."

"Don't worry, little sister," Summer chimed in. "If he ever pulls another stunt like this, stayen gone for virtually a whole year, we'll just go up to Atlanta and kidnap him."

"Look who's talken!" Joe remarked with pretended offense. "You're about to run off to Germany. Who knows when you'll be comen home again!"

"Don't change the subject," Summer commanded. "We're talken about you, not me. And anyway, I have the best excuse of all for leaven." She smiled at Mark, then focused a determined look on Joe. "Since you brought up the subject, big brother," she said sweetly. "Just who is Annemarie Morgan? And why haven't we heard about her before now?"

Everyone looked at Joe, waiting for his answer. "She's just a good friend," he replied vaguely, shrugging his shoulders.

Summer rolled her eyes and snorted. "And I suppose you also think the pope's just a good Catholic. Let me be a little more direct, Joe. Are you plannen to marry this girl or what?"

Joe nearly choked on the piece of turkey in his mouth. "Good Lord, Summer!" he sputtered. Peering around his sister, he glared at her fiancé. "I hope you know what you're getten yourself into, Mark," he warned. "She can be pretty impossible to live with at times."

"I have a fairly good idea," Mark replied.

"Well?" Summer demanded.

"Well, what?" Joe parried.

"Are you getten married or not?" she insisted.

"You're amazen, Summer," Joe said, exasperated. "You hardly know the girl. What on earth would make you think we have wedden plans?"

"Probably the way y'all look at each other," Carrie answered unexpectedly. "Or maybe I should say *into* each other. It's intense, Joe."

Joe shook his head. "Mama, Daddy," he said. "I'd appreciate some help right now—maybe a little admonishment of your busybody children."

"Frankly, Joe, I was wonderen the same thing," Matt said.

Joe shot his daddy a disgruntled look. "I appreciate all this concern," he said at last, his tone light. "Annemarie is special, I'll admit. But I have no wedden plans at this time."

"Well, you ought to," Summer replied gruffly. "It's obvious you need someone to take care of you. You look just awful, Joe, downright wormy looken."

Joe roared with laughter. "Ah, dear sister of mine," he said affectionately. "That's one of the many things I love about you, Summer. You speak your mind, and you don't mince words."

Summer leaned over to whisper in his ear: "Especially not with big brothers who I care so much about and love."

Joe patted her leg, then glanced around the table, grinning as the conversation drifted quickly, easily away from him.

His mind drifted back to the afternoon after Sam's funeral when he had bid farewell to Annemarie. She had driven up for the service, and Joe had tried his best to persuade her to stay over and spend Thanksgiving with the Bakers. But Annemarie had firmly refused him.

"You need this time with your family," she said as they stood between the two towering pine trees across the road, a flaming sea of goldenrod waving behind them. "And your family needs you, too, Joe, without any distractions."

Joe had mulled over her reasoning for a long minute. "I guess you're right," he agreed reluctantly.

"I am," Annemarie assured him. Then, after a slight hesitation, she had added a caveat to the suggestion. "But, Joe, if the invitation is still open come Christmas, then I'd love to accept."

"On one condition," he replied.

"What's that?"

Joe had taken her by the hands. "That you promise to spend next Thanksgiven with me, too—no matter whether I'm here with my family or wherever else I may be."

Annemarie cocked her head, regarding him with a mock expression of curiosity. "Does this deal include the next Christmas as well?" she inquired.

Joe had cradled her face in his hands then, oblivious to the curious faces staring at them from across the way. "How do all my Thanksgivens and Christmases sound to you?" he replied.

"Suspiciously like a proposal," she guessed, holding him around the waist.

"Under the circumstances, it's the best I can do," he responded. "But I'll make it a proper one someday soon."

She had placed her hands on his shoulders and kissed him lightly on the lips. "I don't care about proper, Joe. Just you and us."

They had gazed at each other for a few dreamy minutes, then at the goldenrod, each wishing they could wade into the flowery field of gold and lose themselves in making love. Finally, Joe had led her to the waiting car, leaning down to kiss her goodbye through the open window.

"I love you," Annemarie said.

"And I love you, Annie."

She had left him with a joyous smile, driving away in the car as Joe watched with his hands stuffed in the front pockets of his dress trousers.

And ever since Annemarie had gone away, Joe had indulged in a process of reflection and rediscovery. He had lived a loner's life among his family these past two days, taking long walks through the woods and fields, fishing and picking up pecans. Once, he stood amid the remnants of a cotton field with his eyes closed, simply allowing a warm breeze to clear his head. On the same day, he went skinny-dipping in New River, then stretched out on the grassy bank and fell asleep while his body dried in the sunshine. Finally, yesterday, he had returned to that spot by the railroad tracks where Billy Taylor had died. The horror of that awful night had come back in ghastly detail, but Joe had outlasted the memories. He had gone away from there with remorse and regret as well as forgiveness in his heart.

The solitary days of aimlessness had restored something vital in Joe, bringing him like a wayward son back to the nurturing bosom of his family.

Their table was filled with sustenance, which had little to do with the gobs and gobs of food. It replenished Joe, made him whole. He knew the meaning of thanksgiving. And he was thankful.

"Carl, may I get you anything else?" Caroline asked, noting the child's empty plate.

The boy looked at Caroline, then glanced at the sweet potatoes and up to Paul beside him.

"How about some more candied potatoes?" Paul asked him. "They sure are good, and nobody makes them as well as Caroline."

Smiling at them both, Caroline passed the bowl of syrupy potatoes to Paul.

Carl had always been a quiet child. Ever since his father's arrest for the murder of Ned Turner, however, the boy had not spoken. The doctors assured Paul and his sisters that the condition was temporary, a form of shock or perhaps a way of coping with too much tragedy.

When he had come to live with the Berriens, Carl had been a sad sight, virtually immured in a closed world. His face was a blank expression, as if he had been lobotomized to steal away his emotions.

In the short time Carl had been with the Berrien family, however, his condition had improved substantially. He remained mute, but the boy now smiled and his eyes lit up with enthusiasm and inquisitiveness. He obviously had taken a shine to Paul and his doting sisters, and the Berriens were doing their best to make the boy feel the magic of childhood.

"Is anybody ready for dessert?" Caroline asked a long moment later.

"Personally, I need to let everything settle a little before tacklen dessert," Dan replied, leaning back in the chair and patting his stomach. "Ladies, that was without doubt the best Thanksgiven dinner I've ever had the pleasure of enjoyen, which I can say because my wife has never cooked a Thanksgiven dinner in her entire life."

Amelia grimaced. "We usually eat at Mama's," she explained. "She just up and decided this year to spend Thanksgiven with my brother, Hilton, in Birmingham, and the rest of the family kind of scattered in all directions. Dan and I appreciated the invitation to spend the day with y'all."

"Yes, indeed," April agreed. "Over the years, we've shared some very fine holiday meals with you folks. But Caroline, Rachel: This feast sets a new standard for excellence."

"It surely does," June continued. "I came here today determined to ask y'all to eat Christmas dinner with us this year. Now, though, I fear anything my sister and I could serve up would pale in comparison."

"It was a mighty fine dinner," Rachel agreed. "But the real pleasure was the company. I was dreaden today more than I wanted to admit. There's nothen better, though, than family and friends to make a lonesome spot in a body's heart a little less so. I know I feel a little less lonely today than I did yesterday. And that's because of all of y'all and your kindness."

Her sincerity brought an awkward moment to the table, but Rachel refused to allow gloom to intrude on this day. "Now I know there must be some football game or somethen on the TV that you men want to see," she continued, rising from the table. "Why don't y'all move into the liven room. We women will wash up the dishes and get out the coffee and dessert for a little later."

"Sounds like a good idea to me, Ma," Matt said as everyone pushed back from the table, filling the room with the scraping of chairs across the floor.

Another holiday ritual received its due. The men retired to the living room presumably to watch television. Mostly, however, they talked, smoked cigarettes and sank into blissful slumbers. The women set about clearing the table, washing dishes and putting the final touches on dessert. In between, they shared secrets, swapped recipes and began making plans for Christmas.

It was a distinct verse of their familiar Thanksgiving melody.

———

That afternoon, Lucas Bartholomew came back to the life he knew best, returning home for the second time in his thirty-three years. His first departure had been a flight of fancy, a young man's search for a better life and good times. The second parting had been an escape, a wiser man's way of fleeing the pain of lost dreams and a sense of betrayal at the hands of those who dared him to dream in the first place. Like the young man, the wiser man had discovered he belonged among the familiar faces of old friends and the beaten paths of worn roads.

"What brings you out this way?" Matt asked when Lucas came calling between Thanksgiving dinner and dessert.

Lucas stood on the front walkway, feeling embarrassed and shy, while Matt, Joe and Paul took positions on the porch. He had put in an appearance a few days earlier to pay his respects to Rachel and Matt when Sam lay a corpse. That visit had been brief and pointed. This one seemed awkward and uncertain.

"Suppose I was feelen restless," he answered finally. "We were haven dinner with one of Beauty's cousins, and I got tired of all the lollygaggen. Decided to take me a ride."

"Well, we're mighty glad you rode out this way," Matt replied.

Lucas shifted positions and asked, "How's Mrs. Rachel?"

"She's comen along," Matt replied. "It takes time, you know. It's a big adjustment to make, for all of us but especially for Ma."

Lucas nodded agreement, and the door opened behind Matt.

"Why hello, Lucas!" Caroline greeted him. "I haven't seen you in ages. How are you?"

"Fine, ma'am," he said. "Just fine."

"And Beauty and Annie?" Caroline inquired. "I saw Annie's name in the paper a few weeks back for maken the honor roll at school. I know you're proud of her."

"Yes, ma'am, she's doen real good at the school in town," Lucas said. He smiled shyly, looking at his friends. "Beauty's doen real good, too. She's gonna have another baby."

"Well, congratulations!" Paul exclaimed.

"That's wonderful news," Caroline added. "When is she expecten?"

"Sometime this summer, nearest we can figure," Lucas said. "We're both happy about it."

"I don't doubt it," Caroline said. "You give Beauty my congratulations now. And let us know if there's anything we can do to help."

"I'll do that," Lucas vowed. "And thank you, ma'am."

Caroline smiled. "We're getten ready to have dessert, Lucas," she informed him. "Care to join us?"

Lucas took a deep breath and shook his head. "I already had two pieces of mincemeat pie," he explained. "I couldn't eat another bite."

"I understand," Caroline replied. "There'll be plenty left over tomorrow, so you come on back if you want. And bring Beauty and Annie with you. We'd love to see them. We've missed y'all, Lucas."

Lucas shuffled his feet, glancing down at the concrete walkway. "I'll keep that in mind," he promised, realizing the invitation was genuine and open-ended.

He rubbed his ear, then grinned at the men. "I need to get goen soon," he remarked, "but first, I thought I'd see if y'all had any plans to do any hunten anytime soon."

"None in particular," Matt answered, "but I don't think you'd have to twist our arm."

"No, sirree," Paul agreed. "Is Saturday soon enough?"

"That's good for me," Matt said.

Lucas nodded. "I'll be here," he promised. "Same time as usual."

He looked at Joe closely for the first time. More than a year had passed since they had spoken to each other. "What about it, Joe-Joe? Think you might like to join us?"

Joe scratched his neck, considering the request. "I'll pass this time," he said finally. No one questioned his decision.

"How's the carpet mill treaten you, Lucas?" Paul asked quickly.

"Gives me a steady paycheck every two weeks, so I can't complain," Lucas responded.

"Well, come spring and you get tired of a steady paycheck, just remember I could use a good man worken with me in the fields," Matt said. "The pay's lousy, the schedule's unpredictable, but I can promise you a lot of hard work."

"I'll keep that in mind," Lucas replied with a broad smile as the front door opened again.

Carl Taylor walked out the door, coming to a stop beside Paul, with his eyes focused sharply on Lucas. "You're Danny's daddy, ain't you?" Carl asked.

It was the first words Carl had spoken in several weeks, and everyone regarded the boy for a long moment. Finally, Lucas nodded an answer.

"Yeah, Danny was my boy."

"I thought so," Carl said. "Listen, mister. I'm sorry the way things turned out. I'd've never been friends with Danny if I'd knowed everything would turn out the way it did. You can blame it all on me if you want, but please don't hold anything against my brother Billy. I always wanted you to know that Billy wouldn't have hurt Danny on purpose. What happened—every bit of it—had to be nothen but a bad mistake."

Lucas had expected to see Carl at some point, having been informed earlier that Paul was now the boy's guardian. He honestly wanted to feel bitter about the situation, to rail about the injustice of his son's death, to criticize his friends for sheltering the son of Bobby Taylor. He almost wanted to blame his son's death on the unlikely friendship between Carl and Danny. Instead of animosity, however, the only feelings he could dredge up were sympathy. And maybe hope.

"You're right, Carl," he said at last, smiling at the boy. "It was all a bad mistake, except for one thing. I'm glad you and Danny were friends, son. Him and you be'en friends had nothen to do with the way things turned out. You don't have anything to feel sorry about. Remember that, okay?"

Carl nodded, then glanced up at Paul. "Can I get a piece of pumpkin pie now?" he asked.

"You sure can," Paul said, tousling the boy's hair. "I'll join you."

Caroline extended the offer of dessert to Lucas once more and received another polite decline. A round of farewells followed, and the men reaffirmed their hunting plans before everyone went inside the house, except for Joe and Lucas. They watched the door close, then looked at one another with the natural curiosity of old friends who had lost touch with each other.

"You're looken puny, Joe-Joe," Lucas remarked at length. "I heard about what happened with the Taylor man. Sounds like he worked you over awful bad."

"Somethen like that," Joe replied, coming down the porch steps to stand beside Lucas. "That was a fine thing you did for that little boy," he ventured. "I believe it's the first time he's spoken since his daddy was arrested."

"I meant it," Lucas said, starting toward his truck. "The kid's gone through enough without haven to carry around a load of guilt. I wish him the best, and Paul will be a good influence on him. He was on me."

"Yeah," Joe agreed. "So how have you been, Lucas?"

Lucas stopped, staring across the road into the patch of goldenrod and glancing at the field beside the house before his gaze landed on Joe. "It's been a hard year, Joe-Joe," he admitted. "I miss my son. Miss him as much now as I did this time last year. I'll start to go somewhere, and have to think twice about not callen Danny to come with me." He shrugged. "A person can't stop liven, though. You can't run away from who you are, though the good Lord knows I've tried to this last year."

"I tried to do that myself," Joe remarked. "It didn't get me very far."

"I don't expect it did," Lucas replied. "I wound up wanderen in the dark myself."

"Remember that night we met beside the railroad tracks?" Joe asked.

Lucas nodded.

"I keep wanten to think that we've both come a long way since that night," Joe continued. "But the truth is, Lucas, we've both still got a far piece to go."

"We do," Lucas agreed. "And I'll tell you somethen else. I miss worken out here, and Beauty misses liven out here. It was home."

He paused, glancing around the place once more, inhaling the fragrance of the farm. "Come springtime," he continued, "I just might take your daddy up on that offer of his. I think I belong out here instead of in some factory rollen carpet."

Joe smiled at his friend and patted his shoulder. "You always have belonged here, Lucas," he agreed. "It's a good feelen, ain't it?"

Lucas simply shook his head, got into his truck and drove back to Cookville to spend the remainder of the day with his family.

———

The day was winding down to darkness. They had put a huge dent in the desserts, washing down pie, tarts and cake with hot coffee and cold milk. The dishes were washed, the leftovers put away for the moment. And still Caroline was trying to find that elusive picture to immortalize Joe on this day.

She felt certain her son was on the way back to his old self. She saw the spark in his eyes. Joe had always spoken volumes of happiness with his eyes, the one emotion he could not contain. When he had returned inside the house after the brief visit with Lucas, his eyes had been full of spirit. He had downed pieces of pumpkin and pecan pie, along with a slab of spice cake and two glasses of milk. In that short time, Joe had been the son she remembered, talkative, interested and assertive.